Toll
the Hounds

Also by Steven Erikson

Gardens of the Moon
Deadhouse Gates
Memories of Ice
House of Chains
Midnight Tides
The Bonehunters
Reaper's Gale

STEVEN ERIKSON

Toll the Hounds

Book Eight of
The Malazan
Book of the Fallen

TOR®

A TOM DOHERTY ASSOCIATES BOOK
NEW YORK

TOLL THE HOUNDS: BOOK EIGHT OF THE MALAZAN BOOK OF THE FALLEN

Copyright © 2008 by Steven Erikson

Originally published in Great Britain in 2008 by Bantam Press, a division of Transworld Publishers.

Maps by Neil Gower

A Tor Book
Published by Tom Doherty Associates, LLC
175 Fifth Avenue
New York, NY 10010

www.tor-forge.com

Tor® is a registered trademark of Tom Doherty Associates, LLC.

Library of Congress Cataloging-in-Publication Data

Erikson, Steven.
  Toll the hounds / Steven Erikson.—1st U.S. ed.
     p. cm.—(The Malazan book of the fallen; bk. 8)
  "A Tom Doherty Associates book."
  ISBN-13: 978-0-7653-1008-8 (hardcover)
  ISBN-10: 0-7653-1008-2 (hardcover)
  ISBN-13: 978-0-7653-1654-7 (trade paperback)
  ISBN-10: 0-7653-1654-4 (trade paperback)
  I. Title.
  PR9199.4.E745 T65 2008
  813'.6—dc22   2008029872

Printed in the United States of America

0 9 8 7 6 5 4 3 2

This novel is dedicated
to the memory of my father,
R. S. Lundin, 1931–2007.
You are missed.

Contents

Acknowledgements

Gratitude as always goes to my advance readers: Bowen, Rick, Mark and Chris, with special thanks to Bill and Hazel for their kind words and support over the course of what proved to be a difficult year. Appreciation also goes to the staff of the Black Stilt Café and the Pacific Union Café for their generous loan of office space.

Love to Clare and Bowen, for everything.

Darujhistan

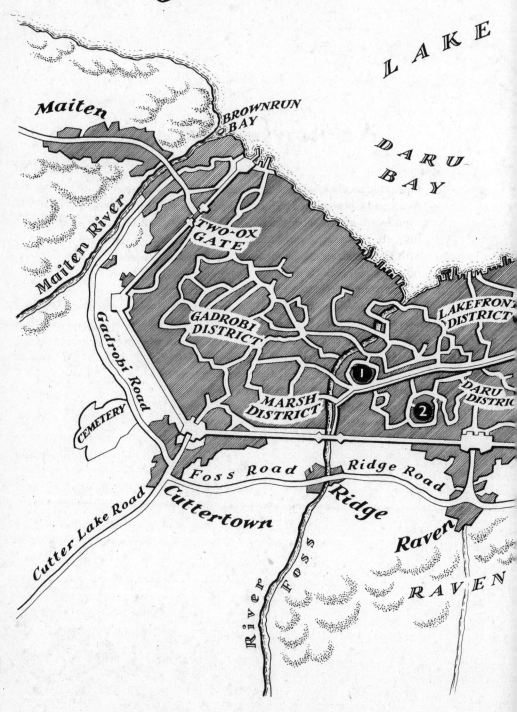

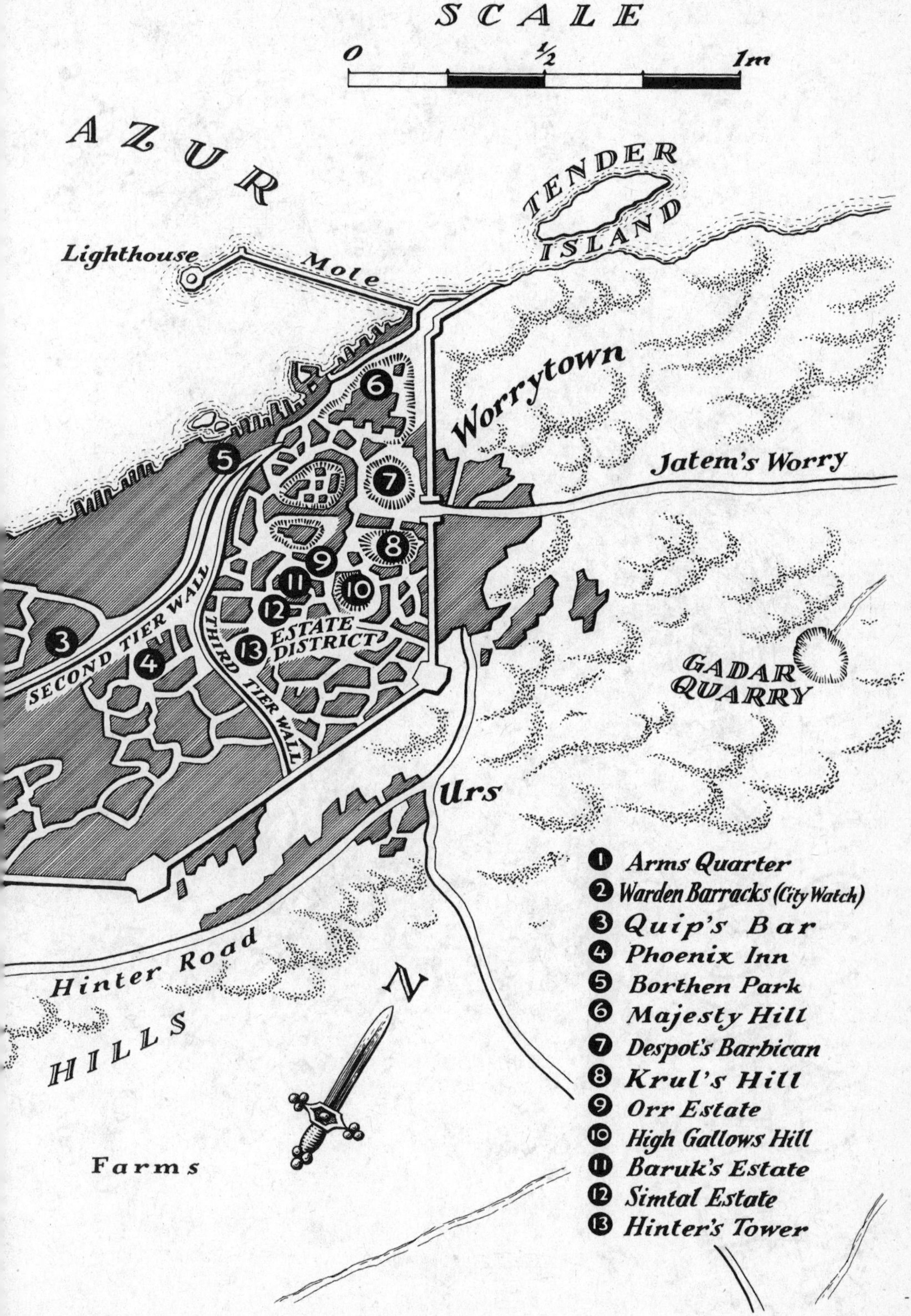

SCALE

0   ½   1m

AZUR

Lighthouse   Mole

TENDER
ISLAND

Worrytown

Jatem's Worry

①   Borthen Park

⑥
⑦
⑧
⑨
⑪ ⑩
⑫
⑬   ESTATE
DISTRICT

Second Tier Wall

Third Tier Wall

③

④

GADAR
QUARRY

Urs

Hinter Road

N

HILLS

Farms

❶ Arms Quarter
❷ Warden Barracks (City Watch)
❸ Quip's Bar
❹ Phoenix Inn
❺ Borthen Park
❻ Majesty Hill
❼ Despot's Barbican
❽ Krul's Hill
❾ Orr Estate
❿ High Gallows Hill
⓫ Baruk's Estate
⓬ Simtal Estate
⓭ Hinter's Tower

BLACK CORAL & ENVIRONS

N

Great Barrow

Pilgrims' Track

Road

Outer Wall

Barrows

Pilgrim Camp

BLACK CORAL

Ruins

Catfolk Cut

Harbour

Royal Forest

New Palace

Old Palace

TRENCH RISES

FOREST

CORAL BAY

Dramatis Personae

Cutter, an assassin
Scillara, his companion
Iskaral Pust, High Priest of Shadow, the Magi, God of the Bhokarala
Sister Spite, a Soletaken
Mogora, Iskaral's occasional wife
Barathol Mekhar, a tourist
Chaur, a gentle man
Mappo Runt, a Trell

Picker, a retired Bridgeburner and partner in K'rul's Bar
Blend, a retired Bridgeburner and partner in K'rul's Bar
Antsy, a retired Bridgeburner and partner in K'rul's Bar
Mallet, a retired Bridgeburner and healer
Bluepearl, a retired Bridgeburner
Fisher, a bard, a regular at K'rul's Bar
Duiker, once the Malazan Empire's Imperial Historian

Bellam Nom, a young man
Rallick Nom, an awakened assassin
Torvald Nom, a cousin of Rallick's
Tiserra, Torvald's wife
Coll, a Council Member in Darujhistan

Estraysian D'Arle, a Council Member in Darujhistan
Hanut Orr, a Council Member in Darujhistan, nephew of the late Turban Orr
Shardan Lim, a Council Member in Darujhistan
Murillio, a consort
Kruppe, a round little man
Meese, proprietor of the Phoenix Inn
Irilta, a regular at the Phoenix Inn
Scurve, barkeep at the Phoenix Inn
Sulty, server at the Phoenix Inn
Challice, wife of Vidikas, daughter of Estraysian D'Arle
Gorlas Vidikas, newest Council Member in Darujhistan, past Hero of the Fete
Krute of Talient, an agent of the Assassins' Guild
Gaz, a killer
Thordy, Gaz's wife

Master Quell, Trygalle Trade Guild navigator and sorcerer
Faint, a shareholder
Reccanto Ilk, a shareholder
Sweetest Sufferance, a shareholder

Glanno Tarp, a shareholder

Amby Bole, a retired Mott Irregular and newfound shareholder

Jula Bole, a retired Mott Irregular and newfound shareholder

Precious Thimble, a retired Mott Irregular and newfound shareholder

Gruntle, a caravan guard on extended leave

Stonny Menackis, a caravan guard

Harllo, a child

Bedek, Harllo's 'uncle'

Myrla, Harllo's 'aunt'

Snell, a child

Bainisk

Venaz

Scorch, a newly hired bodyguard

Leff, a newly hired bodyguard

Madrun, a newly hired compound guard

Lazan Door, a newly hired compound guard

Studlock (or Studious Lock), a castellan

Humble Measure, a mysterious presence in Darujhistan's criminal underworld

Chillbais, a demon

Baruk, a member of the T'orrud Cabal

Vorcan, Mistress of the Assassins' Guild

Seba Krafar, Master of the Assassins' Guild

Apsal'ara

Kadaspala

Derudan, a witch of Tennes

K'rul, an Elder God

Draconus, one of the Slain within Dragnipur

Korlat, a Tiste Andii Soletaken

Orfantal, a Tiste Andii Soletaken, Korlat's brother

Kallor, a challenger

Lady Envy, a bystander

Anomander Rake, Son of Darkness, Knight of Darkness, Ruler of Black Coral

Spinnock Durav, a Tiste Andii

Endest Silann, a Tiste Andii wizard

Caladan Brood, a Warlord

Hood, the God of Death

Ditch

Samar Dev, a witch

Karsa Orlong, a Teblor Toblakai warrior

Traveller, a stranger

Shadowthrone, the God of Shadow

Cotillion, The Rope, Patron God of Assassins

Prophet Seech, the High Priest of the Fallen One, once a middling artist named Munug

Silanah, an Eleint

Crone, a Great Raven

Raest, a Jaghut Tyrant (retired)

Clip, Mortal Sword of Darkness

Nimander Golit, a Tiste Andii

Skintick

Nenanda

Aranatha

Kedeviss

Desra

Sordiko Qualm, a High Priestess

Salind, a High Priestess

Seerdomin

Gradithan

Monkrat

Baran, a Hound of Shadow

Gear, a Hound of Shadow

Blind, a Hound of Shadow

Rood, a Hound of Shadow

Shan, a Hound of Shadow

Pallid, a new Hound of Shadow

Lock, a new Hound of Shadow

Edgewalker, a wanderer

Dog walkers, two witnesses

Toll
the Hounds

Prologue

Speak truth, grow still, until the water is clear between us.

MEDITATIONS OF THE TISTE ANDII

I have no name for this town,' the ragged man said, hands plucking at the frayed hems of what had once been an opulent cloak. Coiled and tucked into his braided belt was a length of leather leash, rotting and tattered. 'It needs a name, I think,' he continued, voice raised to be heard above the vicious fighting of the dogs, 'yet I find a certain failing of imagination, and no one seems much interested.'

The woman standing now at his side, to whom he companionably addressed these remarks, had but newly arrived. Of her life in the time before, very little remained. She had not owned a dog, yet she had found herself staggering down the high street of this decrepit, strange town clutching a leash against which a foul-tempered brute tugged and lunged at every passer-by. The rotted leather had finally parted, freeing the beast to bolt forward, launching an attack upon this man's own dog.

The two animals were now trying to kill each other in the middle of the street, their audience none but their presumed owners. Dust had given way to blood and tufts of hide.

'There was a garrison, once, three soldiers who didn't know each other,' the man said. 'But one by one they left.'

'I never owned a dog before,' she replied, and it was with a start that she realized that these were the first words she had uttered since . . . well, since the time before.

'Nor I,' admitted the man. 'And until now, mine was the only dog in town. Oddly enough, I never grew fond of the wretched beast.'

'How long have you . . . er, been here?'

'I have no idea, but it seems like for ever.'

She looked round, then nodded. 'Me too.'

'Alas, I believe your pet has died.'

'Oh! So it has.' She frowned down at the broken leash in her hand. 'I suppose I won't be needing a new one, then.'

'Don't be too certain of that,' the man said. 'We seem to repeat things here. Day after day. But listen, you can have mine – I never use it, as you can see.'

She accepted the coiled leash. 'Thank you.' She took it out to where her dead dog was lying, more or less torn to pieces. The victor was crawling back towards its master leaving a trail of blood.

Everything seemed knocked strangely askew, including, she realized, her own impulses. She crouched down and gently lifted her dead dog's mangled head, working the loop over until it encircled the torn neck. Then she lowered the bloody, spit-lathered head back to the ground and straightened, holding the leash loose in her right hand.

The man joined her. 'Aye, it's all rather confusing, isn't it?'

'Yes.'

'And we thought life was confusing.'

She shot him a glance. 'So we *are* dead, are we?'

'I think so.'

'Then I don't understand. I was to have been interred in a crypt. A fine, solid crypt – I saw it myself. Richly appointed and proof against thieves, with casks of wine and seasoned meats and fruit for the journey—' She gestured down at the rags she was wearing. 'I was to be dressed in my finest clothes, wearing all my jewellery.'

He was watching her. 'Wealthy, then.'

'Yes.' She looked back down at the dead dog on the end of the leash.

'Not any more.'

She glared across at him, then realized that such anger was, well, pointless. 'I have never seen this town before. It looks to be falling apart.'

'Aye, it's all falling apart. You have that right.'

'I don't know where I live – oh, that sounds odd, doesn't it?' She looked round again. 'It's all dust and rot, and is that a storm coming?' She pointed down the main street towards the horizon, where heavy, strangely luminous clouds now gathered above denuded hills.

They stared at them for a time. The clouds seemed to be raining tears of jade.

'I was once a priest,' the man said, as his dog edged up against his feet and lay there, gasping, with blood dripping from its mouth. 'Every time we saw a storm coming, we closed our eyes and sang all the louder.'

She regarded him in some surprise. 'You were a priest? Then . . . why are you not with your god?'

The man shrugged. 'If I knew the answer to that, the delusion I once possessed of enlightenment – would in truth be mine.' He suddenly straightened. 'Oh, we have a visitor.'

Approaching with a hitched gait was a tall figure, so desiccated that its limbs seemed little more than tree roots, its face naught but rotted, weathered skin stretched over bone. Long grey hair drifted out unbound from a pallid, peeling scalp.

'I suppose,' the woman muttered, 'I need to get used to such sights.'

Her companion said nothing, and they both watched as the gaunt, limping creature staggered past, and as they turned to follow its progress they saw another stranger, cloaked in frayed dark grey, hooded, of a height to match the other.

Neither seemed to take note of their audience as the hooded one said, 'Edge-walker.'

'You have called me here,' said the one named Edgewalker, 'to . . . mitigate.'

'I have.'

'This has been a long time in coming.'

'You might think that way, Edgewalker.'

The grey-haired man – who was clearly long dead – cocked his head and asked, 'Why now?'

The hooded figure turned slightly, and the woman thought he might be look-ing down on the dead dog. 'Disgust,' he replied.

A soft rasping laugh from Edgewalker.

'What ghastly place is this?' hissed a new voice, and the woman saw a shape – no more than a smeared blur of shadows – whisper out from an alley in flowing si-lence, though he seemed to be hobbling on a cane, and all at once there were huge beasts, two, four, five, padding out around the newcomer.

A grunt from the priest beside the woman. 'Hounds of Shadow. Could my god but witness this!'

'Perhaps it does, through your eyes.'

'Oh, I doubt that.'

Edgewalker and his hooded companion watched the shadowy form approach. Short; wavering, then growing more solid. Black-stick cane thumping on the dirt street, raising puffs of dust. The Hounds wandered away, heads lowered as they sniffed the ground. None approached the carcass of the woman's dog, nor the gasping beast at the feet of her newfound friend.

The hooded one said, 'Ghastly? I suppose it is. A necropolis of sorts, Shadow-throne. A village of the discarded. Both timeless and, yes, useless. Such places,' he continued, 'are ubiquitous.'

'Speak for yourself,' said Shadowthrone. 'Look at us, waiting. *Waiting.* Oh, if I were one for decorum and propriety!' A sudden giggle. 'If any of us were!'

All at once the Hounds returned, hackles raised, gazes keen on something far up the main street.

'One more,' whispered the priest. 'One more and the last, yes.'

'Will all this happen again?' the woman asked him, as sudden fear ripped through her. *Someone is coming. Oh, gods, someone is coming.* 'Tomorrow? Tell me!'

'I would imagine not,' the priest said after a moment. He swung his gaze to the dog carcass lying in the dust. 'No,' he said again, 'I imagine not.'

From the hills, thunder and jade rain slashing down like the arrows from ten thousand battles. From down the street, the sudden rumble of carriage wheels.

She turned at that latter sound and smiled. 'Oh,' she said in relief, 'here comes my ride.'

He had once been a wizard of Pale, driven by desperation into betrayal. But Anomander Rake had not been interested in desperation, or any other excuse

Ditch and his comrades might have proffered. Betrayers of the Son of Darkness kissed the sword Dragnipur, and somewhere among this legion toiling in the perpetual gloom there were faces he would recognize, eyes that could meet his own. And what would he see in them?

Only what he gave back. Desperation was not enough.

These were rare thoughts, no more or less unwelcome than any others, mocking him as in their freedom they drifted in and out; and when nowhere close, why, they perhaps floated through alien skies, riding warm winds soft as laughter. What could not escape was Ditch himself and that which he could see on all sides. This oily mud and its sharp black stones that cut through the rotted soles of his boots; the deathly damp air that layered a grimy film upon the skin, as if the world itself was fevered and slick with sweat. The faint cries – strangely ever distant to Ditch's ears – and, much nearer, the groan and crunch of the massive engine of wood and bronze, the muted squeal of chains.

Onward, onward, even as the storm behind them drew closer, cloud piling on cloud, silver and roiling and shot through with twisting spears of iron. Ash had begun to rain down on them, unceasing now, each flake cold as snow, yet this was a sludge that did not melt, instead churning into the mud until it seemed they walked through a field of slag and tailings.

Although a wizard, Ditch was neither small nor frail. There was a roughness to him that had made others think of thugs and alley-pouncers, back in the life that had been before. His features were heavy, angular and, indeed, brutish. He had been a strong man, but this was no reward, not here, not chained to the Burden. Not within the dark soul of Dragnipur.

The strain was unbearable, yet bear it he did. The way ahead was infinite, screaming of madness, yet he held on to his own sanity as a drowning man might cling to a frayed rope, and he dragged himself onward, step by step. Iron shackles made his limbs weep blood, with no hope of surcease. Figures caked in mud plodded to either side, and beyond them, vague in the gloom, countless others.

Was there comfort in shared fate? The question alone invited hysterical laughter, a plunge into insanity's precious oblivion. No, surely there was no such comfort, beyond the mutual recognition of folly, ill luck and obstinate stupidity, and these traits could not serve camaraderie. Besides, one's companions to either side were in the habit of changing at a moment's notice, one hapless fool replacing another in a grainy, blurred swirl.

Heaving on the chains, to keep the Burden in motion, this nightmarish flight left no energy, no time, for conversation. And so Ditch ignored the hand buffeting his shoulder the first time, the second time. The third time, however, was hard enough to send the wizard staggering to one side. Swearing, he twisted round to glare at the one now walking at his side.

Once, long ago, he might have flinched back upon seeing such an apparition. His heart would have lurched in terror.

The demon was huge, hulking. Its once royal blood availed it no privilege here in Dragnipur. Ditch saw that the creature was carrying the fallen, the failed, gathering to itself a score or more bodies and the chains attached to them. Muscles strained, bunched and twisted as the demon pulled itself forward. Scrawny bodies, hanging limp, crowded like cordwood under each arm. One, still conscious though her head lolled, rode its broad back like a newborn ape, glazed eyes sliding across the wizard's face.

'You fool,' Ditch snarled. 'Throw 'em into the bed!'

'No room,' piped the demon in a high, childish voice.

But the wizard had used up his sympathy. For the demon's sake, it should have left the fallen behind, but then, of course, they would all feel the added weight, the pathetic drag on the chains. Still, what if this one fell? What if that extraordinary strength and will gave way? 'Curse the fool!' Ditch growled. 'Why doesn't he kill a few more dragons, damn him!'

'We fail,' said the demon.

Ditch wanted to howl at that. Was it not obvious to them all? But that quavering voice was both bemused and forlorn, and it struck through to his heart. 'I know, friend. Not long now.'

'And then?'

Ditch shook his head. 'I don't know.'

'Who does?'

Again the wizard had no answer.

The demon persisted. 'We must find one who does. I am going now. But I will return. Do not pity me, please.'

A sudden swirl, grey and black, and now some bear-like beast was beside him, too weary, too mindless, to even lunge at him – as some creatures still did.

'You've been here too long, friend,' Ditch said to it.

Who does?

An interesting question. Did anyone know what would happen when the chaos caught them? Anyone here in Dragnipur?

In his first moments following his kissing the sword, in between his frenzied attempts at escape, his shrieks of despair, he had flung questions at everyone – why, he'd even sought to accost a Hound, but it had been too busy lunging at its own chains, froth fizzing from its massive jaws, and had very nearly trampled him, and he'd never seen it again.

But someone had replied, someone had spoken to him. About something . . . oh, he could not recall much more than a name. A single name.

Draconus.

She had witnessed many things in this interminable interlude in her career, but none more frustrating than the escape of two Hounds of Shadow. It was not for one such as Apsal'ara, Lady of Thieves, to besmirch her existence with the laborious indignity of tugging on a chain for all eternity. Shackles were to be escaped, burdens deftly avoided.

From the moment of her first stumbling arrival, she had set upon herself the task of breaking the chains binding her in this dread realm, but this task was virtually impossible if one were cursed to ever pull the damned wagon. And she had no desire to witness again the horrible train at the very end of the chains, the abraded lumps of still living meat dragging across the gouged muddy ground, the flash of an open eye, a flopping nub of a limb straining towards her, a terrible army of the failed, the ones who surrendered and the ones whose strength gave out.

No, Apsal'ara had worked her way closer to the enormous wagon, eventually finding herself trudging beside one of the huge wooden wheels. Then she had lagged in her pace until just behind that wheel. From there, she moved inward, slipping beneath the creaking bed with its incessant rain of brown water, blood and the wastes that came of rotting but still living flesh. Dragging the chain behind her she had worked her way on to a shelf of the undercarriage, just above the front axle, wedging herself in tight, legs drawn up, her back against slimy wood.

Fire had been the gift, the stolen gift, but there could be no flame in this sodden underworld. Failing that, there was . . . friction. She had begun working one length of chain across another.

How many years had it been? She had no idea. There was no hunger, no thirst. The chain sawed back and forth. There was a hint of heat, climbing link by link and into her hands. Had the iron softened? Was the metal worn with new, silvery grooves? She had long since stopped checking. The effort was enough. For so long, it had been enough.

Until those damned Hounds.

That, and the inescapable truth that the wagon had slowed, that now there were as many lying on its bed as there were still out in the gloom beyond, heaving desperate on their chains. She could hear the piteous groans, seeping down from the bed directly above her, of those trapped beneath the weight of countless others.

The Hounds had thundered against the sides of the wagon. The Hounds had plunged into the maw of darkness at the very centre.

There had been a stranger, an unchained stranger. Taunting the Hounds – *the Hounds!* She remembered his face, oh yes, his face. Even after he had vanished . . .

In the wake of all that, Apsal'ara had attempted to follow the beasts, only to be driven back by the immense cold of that portal – cold so fierce it destroyed flesh, colder even than Omtose Phellack. The cold of *negation. Denial.*

No greater curse than hope. A lesser creature would have wept then, would have surrendered, throwing herself beneath one of the wheels to be left dragging in the wagon's wake, nothing more than one more piece of wreckage, of crushed bone and mangled flesh, scraping and tumbling in the stony mud. Instead, she had returned to her private perch, resumed working the chains.

She had stolen the moon once.

She had stolen fire.

She had padded the silent arching halls of the city within Moon's Spawn.

She was the Lady of Thieves.

And a sword had stolen her life.

This will not do. This will not do.

Lying in its usual place on the flat rock beside the stream, the mangy dog lifted its head, the motion stirring insects into buzzing flight. A moment later, the beast rose. Scars covered its back, some deep enough to twist the muscles beneath. The dog lived in the village but was not of it. Nor was the animal one among the village's pack. It did not sleep outside the entrance to any hut; it allowed no one to come close. Even the tribe's horses would not draw near it.

There was, it was agreed, a deep bitterness in its eyes, and an even deeper sorrow. God-touched, the Uryd elders said, and this claim ensured that the dog would never starve and would never be driven away. It would be tolerated, in the manner of all things god-touched.

Surprisingly lithe despite its mangled hip, the dog now trotted through the village, down the length of the main avenue. When it came to the south end, it kept on going, downslope, wending through the moss-backed boulders and the bone-piles that marked the refuse of the Uryd.

Its departure was noted by two girls still a year or more from their nights of passage into adulthood. There was a similarity to their features, and in their ages they were a close match, the times of their births mere days apart. Neither could be said to be loquacious. They shared the silent language common among twins, although they were not twins, and it seemed that, for them, this language was enough. And so, upon seeing the three-legged dog leave the village, they exchanged a glance, set about gathering what supplies and weapons were near at hand, and then set out, on the dog's trail.

Their departure was noted, but that was all.

South, down from the great mountains of home, where condors wheeled between the peaks and wolves howled when the winter winds came.

South, towards the lands of the hated children of the Nathii, where dwelt the bringers of war and pestilence, the slayers and enslavers of the Teblor. Where the Nathii bred like lemmings until it seemed there would be no place left in the world for anyone or anything but them.

Like the dog, the two girls were fearless and resolute. Though they did not know it, such traits came from their father, whom they had never met.

The dog did not look back, and when the girls caught up to it the beast maintained its indifference. It was, as the elders had said, god-touched.

Back in the village, a mother and daughter were told of the flight of their children. The daughter wept. The mother did not. Instead, there was heat in a low place of her body, and, for a time, she was lost in remembrances.

'Oh frail city, where strangers arrive . . .'

An empty plain beneath an empty night sky. A lone fire, so weak as to be nearly swallowed by the blackened, cracked stones encircling it. Seated on one of the two flat stones close to the hearth, a short, round man with sparse, greasy hair. Faded red waistcoat, over a linen shirt with stained once-white blousy cuffs erupting around the pudgy hands. The round face was flushed, reflecting the flickering flames. From the small knuckled chin dangled long black hairs – not enough to braid, alas – a new affectation he had taken to twirling and stroking when deep in thought, or even shallowly so. Indeed, when not thinking at all, but wishing to convey an impression of serious cogitation, should anyone regard him thoughtfully.

He stroked and twirled now as he frowned down into the fire before him.

What had that grey-haired bard sung? There on the modest stage in K'rul's Bar earlier in the night, when he had watched on, content with his place in the glorious city he had saved more than once?

'Oh frail city, where strangers arrive . . .'

'I need to tell you something, Kruppe.'

The round man glanced up to find a shrouded figure seated on the other flat stone, reaching thin pale hands out to the flames. Kruppe cleared his throat, then said, 'It has been a long time since Kruppe last found himself perched as you see him now. Accordingly, Kruppe had long since concluded that you wished to tell him something of such vast import that none but Kruppe is worthy to hear.'

A faint glitter from the darkness within the hood. 'I am not in this war.'

Kruppe stroked the rat-tails of his beard, delighting himself by saying nothing.

'This surprises you?' the Elder God asked.

'Kruppe ever expects the unexpected, old friend. Why, could you ever expect otherwise? Kruppe is shocked. Yet, a thought arrives, launched brainward by a tug on this handsome beard. K'rul states he is not in the war. Yet, Kruppe suspects, he is nevertheless its prize.'

'Only you understand this, my friend,' the Elder God said, sighing. Then cocked its head. 'I had not noticed before, but you seem sad.'

'Sadness has many flavours, and it seems Kruppe has tasted them all.'

'Will you speak now of such matters? I am, I believe, a good listener.'

'Kruppe sees that you are sorely beset. Perhaps now is not the time.'

'That is no matter.'

'It is to Kruppe.'

K'rul glanced to one side, and saw a figure approaching, grey-haired, gaunt.

Kruppe sang, ' "Oh frail city, where strangers arrive" . . . and the rest?'

The newcomer answered in a deep voice, ' ". . . pushing into cracks, there to abide." '

And the Elder God sighed.

'Join us, friend,' said Kruppe. 'Sit here by this fire: this scene paints the history of our kind, as you well know. A night, a hearth, and a tale to spin. Dear K'rul, dearest friend of Kruppe, hast thou ever seen Kruppe dance?'

The stranger sat. A wan face, an expression of sorrow and pain.

'No,' said K'rul. 'I think not. Not by limb, not by word.'

Kruppe's smile was muted, and something glistened in his eyes. 'Then, my friends, settle yourselves for this night. And *witness*.'

Book One

Vow to the Sun

This creature of words cuts
To the quick and gasp, dart away
The spray of red rain
Beneath a clear blue sky
Shock at all that is revealed
What use now this armour
When words so easy slant between?

This god of promises laughs
At the wrong things, wrongly timed
Unmaking all these sacrifices
In deliberate malice
Recoil like a soldier routed
Even as retreat is denied
Before corpses heaped high in walls

You knew this would come
At last and feign nothing, no surprise
To find this cup filled
With someone else's pain
It's never as bad as it seems
The taste sweeter than expected
When you squat in a fool's dream

So take this belligerence
Where you will, the dogged cur
Is the charge of my soul
To the centre of the street
Spinning round all fangs bared
Snapping at thirsty spears
Thrust cold and purged of your hands

Hunting Words
Brathos of Black Coral

Chapter One

Oh frail city!
Where strangers arrive
Pushing into cracks
There to abide

Oh blue city!
Old friends gather sighs
At the foot of docks
After the tide

Uncrowned city!
Where sparrows alight
In spider tracks
On sills well high

Doomed city!
Closing comes the night
History awakens
Here to abide

FRAIL AGE
FISHER KEL TATH

Surrounded in a city of blue fire, she stood alone on the balcony. The sky's darkness was pushed away, an unwelcome guest on this the first night of the Gedderone Fete. Throngs filled the streets of Darujhistan, happily riotous, good-natured in the calamity of one year's ending and another's beginning. The night air was humid and pungent with countless scents.

There had been banquets. There had been unveilings of eligible young men and maidens. Tables laden with exotic foods, ladies wrapped in silks, men and women in preposterous uniforms all glittering gilt – a city with no standing army bred a plethora of private militias and a chaotic proliferation of high ranks held, more or less exclusively, by the nobility.

Among the celebrations she had attended this evening, on the arm of her husband, she had not once seen a real officer of Darujhistan's City Watch, not one genuine soldier with a dusty cloak-hem, with polished boots bearing scars, with a sword-grip of plain leather and a pommel gouged and burnished by wear. Yet she had seen, bound high on soft, well-fed arms, torcs in the manner of decorated soldiers among the Malazan army – soldiers from an empire that had, not so long ago, provided for Darujhistan mothers chilling threats to belligerent children. *'Malazans, child! Skulking in the night to steal foolish children! To make you slaves for their terrible Empress – yes! Here in this very city!'*

But the torcs she had seen this night were not the plain bronze or faintly etched silver of genuine Malazan decorations and signifiers of rank, such as appeared like relics from some long-dead cult in the city's market stalls. No, these had been gold, studded with gems, the blue of sapphire being the commonest hue even among the coloured glass, blue like the blue fire for which the city was famous, blue to proclaim some great and brave service to Darujhistan itself.

Her fingers had pressed upon one such torc, there on her husband's arm, although there was real muscle beneath it, a hardness to match the contemptuous look in his eyes as he surveyed the clusters of nobility in the vast humming hall, with the proprietary air he had acquired since attaining the Council. The contempt had been there long before and if anything had grown since his latest and most triumphant victory.

Daru gestures of congratulation and respect had swirled round them in their stately passage through the crowds, and with each acknowledgement her husband's face had grown yet harder, the arm beneath her fingers drawing ever tauter, the knuckles of his hands whitening above his sword-belt where the thumbs were tucked into braided loops in the latest fashion among duellists. Oh, he revelled in being among them now; indeed, in being above many of them. But for Gorlas Vidikas, this did not mean he had to like any of them. The more they fawned, the deeper his contempt, and that he would have been offended without their obsequy was a contradiction, she suspected, that a man like her husband was not wont to entertain.

The nobles had eaten and drunk, and stood and posed and wandered and paraded and danced themselves into swift exhaustion, and now the banquet halls and staterooms echoed with naught but the desultory ministrations of servants. Beyond the high walls of the estates, however, the common folk rollicked still in the streets. Masked and half naked, they danced on the cobbles – the riotous whirling steps of the Flaying of Fander – as if dawn would never come, as if the hazy moon itself would stand motionless in the abyss in astonished witness to their revelry. City Watch patrols simply stood back and observed, drawing dusty cloaks about their bodies, gauntlets rustling as they rested hands on truncheons and swords.

On the balcony where she stood, the fountain of the unlit garden directly below chirped and gurgled to itself, buffered by the estate's high, solid walls from the raucous festivities they had witnessed during the tortured carriage ride back home. Smeared moonlight struggled in the softly swirling pool surrounding the fountain.

The blue fire was too strong this night, too strong even for the mournful moon. Darujhistan itself was a sapphire, blazing in the torc of the world.

And yet its beauty, and all its delighted pride and its multitudinous voice, could not reach her tonight.

This night, Lady Vidikas had seen her future. Each and every year of it. There on her husband's hard arm. And the moon, well, it looked like a thing of the past, a memory dimmed by time, yet it had taken her back.

To a balcony much like this one in a time that now seemed very long ago.

Lady Vidikas, who had once been Challice Estraysian, had just seen her future. And was discovering, here in this night and standing against this rail, that the past was a better place to be.

Talk about the worst night yet to run out of Rhivi flatbread. Swearing under her breath, Picker pushed her way through the crowds of the Lakefront market, the mobs of ferociously hungry, drunk revellers, using her elbows when she needed to and glowering at every delirious smile swung her way, and came out eventually at the mouth of a dingy alley heaped ankle-deep in rubbish. Somewhere just to the south of Borthen Park. Not quite the route back to the bar she would have preferred, but the fete was in full frenzy.

Wrapped package of flatbread tucked under her left arm, she paused to tug loose the tangles of her heavy cloak, scowled on seeing a fresh stain from a careless passer-by – some grotesque Gadrobi sweetcake – tried wiping it off which only made it worse, then, her mood even fouler, set out through the detritus.

With the Lady's pull, Bluepearl and Antsy had fared better in finding Saltoan wine and were even now back at K'rul's. And here she was, twelve streets and two wall passages away with twenty or thirty thousand mad fools in between. Would her companions wait for her? Not a chance. Damn Blend and her addiction to Rhivi flatbread! That and her sprained ankle had conspired to force Picker out here on the first night of the fete – if that ankle truly *was* sprained, and she had her doubts since Mallet had just squinted down at the offending appendage, then shrugged.

Mind you, that was about as much as anyone had come to expect from Mallet. He'd been miserable since the retirement, and the chance of the sun's rising any time in the healer's future was about as likely as Hood's forgetting to tally the count. And it wasn't as if he was alone in his misery, was it?

But where was the value in feeding her ill temper with all these well-chewed thoughts?

Well, it made her feel better, that's what.

Dester Thrin, wrapped tight in black cloak and hood, watched the big-arsed woman kicking her way through the rubbish at the other end of the alley. He'd picked her up coming out of the back door of K'rul's Bar, the culmination of four nights positioned in the carefully chosen, darkness-shrouded vantage point from which he could observe that narrow postern.

His clan-master had warned that the targets were all ex-soldiers, but Dester

Thrin had seen little to suggest that any of them had kept fit and trim. They were old, sagging, rarely sober, and this one, well, she wore that huge, thick woollen cloak because she was getting heavy and it clearly made her self-conscious.

Following her through the crowds had been relatively easy – she was a head taller than the average Gadrobi, and the route she took to this decrepit Rhivi market in Lakefront seemed to deliberately avoid the Daru streets, some strange affectation that would, in a very short time, prove fatal.

Dester's own Daru blood had permitted him a clear view of his target, pushing purposefully through the heaving press of celebrants.

He set out to traverse the alley once his target exited at the far end. Swiftly padding at a hunter's pace, he reached the alley mouth and edged out, in time to see the woman move into the passageway through Second Tier Wall, with the tunnel through Third just beyond.

The Guild's succession wars, following the disappearance of Vorcan, had finally been settled, with only a minimum amount of spilled blood. And Dester was more or less pleased with the new Grand Master, who was both vicious and clever where most of the other aspirants had been simply vicious. At last, an assassin of the Guild did not have to be a fool to feel some optimism regarding the future.

This contract was a case in point. Straightforward, yet one sure to earn Dester and the others of his clan considerable prestige upon its summary completion.

He brushed his gloved hands across the pommels of his daggers, the weapons slung on baldrics beneath his arms. Ever reassuring, those twin blades of Daru steel with their ferules filled with the thick, pasty poison of Moranth tralb.

Poison was now the preferred insurance for a majority of the Guild's street killers, and indeed for more than a few who scuttled Thieves' Road across the rooftops. There'd been an assassin, close to Vorcan herself, who had, on a night of betrayal against his own clan, demonstrated the deadliness of fighting without magic. Using poison, the assassin had proved the superiority of such mundane substances in a single, now legendary night of blood.

Dester had heard that some initiates in some clans had raised hidden shrines to honour Rallick Nom, creating a kind of cult whose adherents employed secret gestures of mutual recognition within the Guild. Of course, Seba Krafar, the new Grand Master, had in one of his very first pronouncements outlawed the cult, and there had been a cull of sorts, with five suspected cult leaders greeting the dawn with smiling throats.

Still, Dester had since heard enough hints to suggest that the cult was far from dead. It had just burrowed deeper.

In truth, no one knew which poisons Rallick Nom had used, but Dester believed it was Moranth tralb, since even the smallest amount in the bloodstream brought unconsciousness, then a deeper coma that usually led to death. Larger quantities simply speeded up the process and were a sure path through Hood's Gate.

The big-arsed woman lumbered on.

Four streets from K'rul's Bar – if she was taking the route he believed she was taking – there'd be a long, narrow alley to walk up, the inside face of Third Tier Wall Armoury on the left, and on the right the high wall of the bath-house thick and solid with but a few scattered, small windows on upper floors, making the unlit passage dark.

He would kill her there.

Perched on a corner post's finial at one end of the high wall, Chillbais stared with stony eyes on the tattered wilds beyond. Behind him was an overgrown garden with a shallow pond recently rebuilt but already unkempt, and toppled columns scattered about, bearded in moss. Before him, twisted trees and straggly branches with crumpled dark leaves dangling like insect carcasses, the ground beneath rumpled and matted with greasy grasses; a snaking path of tilted pavestones leading up to a squat, brooding house bearing no architectural similarity to any other edifice in all of Darujhistan.

Light was rare from the cracks between those knotted shutters, and when it did show it was dull, desultory. The door never opened.

Among his kin, Chillbais was a giant. Heavy as a badger, with sculpted muscles beneath the prickly hide. His folded wings were very nearly too small to lift him skyward, and each sweep of those leathery fans forced a grunt from the demon's throat.

This time would be worse than most. It had been months since he'd last moved, hidden as he was from prying eyes in the gloom of an overhanging branch from the ash tree in the estate garden at his back. But when he saw that flash of movement before him, that whispering flow of motion, out from the gnarled, black house and across the path, even as earth erupted in its wake to open a succession of hungry pits, even as roots writhed out seeking to ensnare this fugitive, Chillbais knew his vigil was at an end.

The shadow slid out to crouch against the low wall of the Azath House, seemed to watch those roots snaking closer for a long moment, then rose and, flowing like liquid night over the stone wall, was gone.

Grunting, Chillbais spread his creaking wings, shook the creases loose from the sheets of membrane between the rib-like fingers, then leapt forward, out from beneath the branch, catching what air he could, then flapping frenziedly – his grunts growing savage – until he slammed hard into the mulched ground.

Spitting twigs and leaves, the demon scrambled back for the estate wall, hearing how those roots spun round, lashing out for him. Claws digging into mortar, Chillbais scrabbled back on to his original perch. Of course, there had been no real reason to fear. The roots never reached beyond the Azath's own wall, and a glance back assured him—

Squealing, Chillbais launched back into the air, this time out over the estate garden.

Oh, no one ever liked demons!

Cool air above the overgrown fountain, then, wings thudding hard, heaving upward, up into the night.

A word, yes, for his master. A most extraordinary word. So unexpected, so incendiary, so fraught!

Chillbais thumped his wings as hard as he could, an obese demon in the darkness above the blue, blue city.

Zechan Throw and Giddyn the Quick had found the perfect place for the ambush. Twenty paces down a narrow street two recessed doorways faced each other. Four drunks had staggered past a few moments earlier, and none had seen the assassins standing motionless in the inky darkness. And now that they were past and the way was clear . . . a simple step forward and blood would flow.

The two targets approached. Both carried clay jugs and were weaving slightly. They seemed to be arguing, but not in a language Zechan understood. Malazan, likely. A quick glance to the left. The four drunks were just leaving the far end, plunging into a motley crowd of revellers.

Zechan and Giddyn had followed the two out from K'rul's Bar, watching on as they found a wine merchant, haggled over what the woman demanded for the jugs of wine, settled on a price, then set out on their return leg of the journey.

Somewhere along the way they must have pulled the stoppers on the jugs, for now they were loud in their argument, the slightly taller one, who walked pigeon-toed and was blue-skinned – Zechan could just make him out from where he stood – pausing to lean against a wall as if moments from losing his supper.

He soon righted himself, and it seemed the argument was suddenly over. Straightening, the taller one joined the other and, from the sounds of their boots in the rubbish, set out by his side.

Simply perfect.

Nothing messy, nothing at all messy. Zechan lived for nights like this.

Dester moved quickly, his moccasins noiseless on the cobbles, rushing for the woman striding oblivious ahead of him. Twelve paces, eight, four—

She spun, cloak whirling out.

A blurred sliver of blued steel, flickering a slashing arc. Dester skidded, seeking to pull back from the path of that weapon – a longsword, Beru fend! – and something clipped his throat. He twisted and ducked down to his left, both daggers thrust out to damn her should she seek to close.

A longsword!

Heat was spilling down his neck, down his chest beneath his deerhide shirt. The alley seemed to waver before his eyes, darkness curling in. Dester Thrin staggered, flailing with his daggers. A boot or mailed fist slammed into the side of his head and there was more splashing on to the cobbles. He could no longer grip the daggers. He heard them skitter on stone.

Blind, stunned, lying on the hard ground. It was cold.

A strange lassitude filled his thoughts, spreading out, rising up, taking him away.

Picker stood over the corpse. The red smear on the tip of her sword glistened, drawing her gaze, and she was reminded, oddly enough, of poppies after a rain. She grunted. The bastard had been quick, almost quick enough to evade her slash. Had he done so, she might have had some work to do. Still, unless the fool was skilled in throwing those puny daggers, she would have cut him down eventually.

Pushing through Gadrobi crowds risked little more than cutpurses. As a people they were singularly gentle. In any case, it made such things as picking up someone trailing her that much easier – when that someone wasn't Gadrobi, of course.

The man dead at her feet was Daru. Might as well have worn a lantern on his hooded head, the way it bobbed above the crowd in her wake.

Even so . . . she frowned down at him. *You wasn't no thug. Not with daggers like those.*

Hound's Breath.

Sheathing her sword and pulling her cloak about her once more, ensuring that it well hid the scabbarded weapon which, if discovered by a Watch, would see her in a cell with a damned huge fine to pay, Picker pushed the wrapped stack of flatbread tighter under her left arm, then set out once more.

Blend, she decided, was in a lot of trouble.

Zechan and Giddyn, in perfect unison, launched themselves out from the alcoves, daggers raised then thrusting down.

A yelp from the taller one as Giddyn's blades plunged deep. The Malazan's knees buckled and vomit sprayed from his mouth as he sank down, the jug crashing to a rush of wine.

Zechan's own weapons punched through leather, edges grating along ribs. One for each lung. Tearing the daggers loose, the assassin stepped back to watch the red-haired one fall.

A short sword plunged into the side of Zechan's neck.

He was dead before he hit the cobbles.

Giddyn, looming over the kneeling Malazan, looked up.

Two hands closed round his head. One clamped tight over his mouth, and all at once his lungs were full of water. He was drowning. The hand tightened, fingers pinching his nostrils shut. Darkness rose within him, and the world slowly went away.

Antsy snorted as he tugged his weapon free, then added a kick to the assassin's face to punctuate its frozen expression of surprise.

Bluepearl grinned across at him. 'See the way I made the puke spray out? If that ain't genius I don't know what—'

'Shut up,' Antsy snapped. 'These weren't muggers looking for a free drink, in case you hadn't noticed.'

Frowning, Bluepearl looked down at the body before him with the water leaking from its mouth and nose. The Napan ran a hand over his shaved pate. 'Aye. But they was amateurs anyway. Hood, we saw those breath plumes from halfway down the street. Which stopped when those drunks crossed, telling us they wasn't the target. Meaning—'

'We were. Aye, and that's my point.'

'Let's get back,' Bluepearl said, suddenly nervous.

Antsy tugged at his moustache, then nodded. 'Work up that illusion again, Bluepearl. Us ten paces ahead.'

'Easy, Sergeant—'

'I ain't no sergeant no more.'

'Yeah? Then why you still barking orders?'

By the time Picker arrived within sight of the front entrance to K'rul's Bar, her rage was incandescent. She paused, scanned the area. Spotted someone leaning in shadows across from the bar's door. Hood drawn up, hands hidden.

Picker set off towards the figure.

She was noticed with ten paces between them, and she saw the man straighten, saw the growing unease betrayed by a shift of those covered arms, the cloak rippling. A half-dozen celebrants careened between them, and as they passed, Picker took the last stride needed to reach the man.

Whatever he had been expecting – perhaps her accosting him with some loud accusation – it was clear that he was unprepared for the savage kick she delivered between his legs. As he was going down she stepped closer and slapped her right hand against the back of his head, adding momentum to the man's collapse. When his forehead cracked against the cobbles there was a sickly crunch. The body began to spasm where it lay.

A passer-by paused, peered down at the twitching body.

'You!' Picker snarled. 'What's your damned problem?'

Surprise, then a shrug. 'Nothing, sweetie. Served 'im right, standin' there like that. Say, would you marry me?'

'Go away.'

As the stranger ambled on, bemoaning his failure at love, Picker looked around, waiting to see if there was someone else . . . bolting from some hidden place nearby. If it had already happened, then she had missed it. More likely, the unseen eyes watching all of this were peering down from a rooftop somewhere.

The man on the ground had stopped twitching.

Spinning round, she headed for the entrance to K'rul's Bar.

'Pick!'

Two strides from the battered door, she turned, and saw Antsy and Bluepearl – lugging jugs of Saltoan wine – hurrying up to join her. Antsy's expression was fierce. Bluepearl lagged half a step behind, eyes on the motionless body on the other side of the street, where a Gadrobi urchin was now busy stealing whatever she could find.

'Get over here,' Picker snapped, 'both of you! Keep your eyes open.'

'Shopping's gettin' murderous,' Antsy said. 'Bluepearl had us illusioned most of the way back, after we sniffed out an ambush—'

With one last glare back out on to the street, Picker took them both by their arms and pulled them unceremoniously towards the door. 'Inside, idiots.'

Unbelievable, a night like this, making me so foul of temper I went and turned down the first decent marriage proposal I've had in twenty years.

Blend was sitting in the place she sat in whenever she smelled trouble. A small table in shadows right beside the door, doing her blending thing, except this time her legs were stretched out, just enough to force a stumble from anyone coming inside.

Stepping through the doorway, Picker gave those black boots a solid kick.

'Ow, my ankle!'

Picker dropped the stack of flatbread on to Blend's lap.

'Oof!'

Antsy and Bluepearl pushed past. The ex-sergeant snorted. 'Now there's our scary minder at the door. "Ow, oof!" she says.'

But Blend had already recovered and was unwrapping the flatbread.

'You know, Blend,' Picker said as she settled at the bar, 'the old Rhivi hags who make those spit on the pan before they slap down the dough. Some ancient spirit blessing—'

'It's not that,' Blend cut in, folding back the flaps of the wrapper. 'The sizzle tells them the pan's hot enough.'

'Ain't it just,' Bluepearl muttered.

Picker scowled, then nodded. 'Aye. Let's all head to our office, all of us – Blend, go find Mallet, too.'

'Bad timing,' Blend observed.

'What?'

'Spindle taking that pilgrimage.'

'Lucky for him.'

Blend slowly rose and said round a mouthful of flatbread, 'Duiker?'

Picker hesitated, then said, 'Ask him. If he wants, aye.'

Blend slowly blinked. 'You kill somebody tonight, Pick?'

No answer was a good enough answer. Picker peered suspiciously at the small crowd in the bar, those too drunk to have reeled out into the street at the twelfth bell, as was the custom. Regulars one and all. *That'll do.* Waving for the others to follow, Picker set out for the stairs.

At the far end of the main room, that damned bard was bleating on with one of the more obscure verses of *Anomandaris*, but nobody was listening.

The three of them saw themselves as the new breed on Darujhistan's Council. Shardan Lim was the thinnest and tallest, with a parched face and washed-out blue eyes. Hook-nosed, a lipless slash of a mouth perpetually turned down as if he could not restrain his contempt for the world. The muscles of his left wrist were twice the size of those of the right, criss-crossed with proudly displayed scars. He met Challice's eyes like a man about to ask her husband if his own turn with her was imminent, and she felt that regard like the cold hand of possession round her throat. A moment later his bleached eyes slid away and there was the flicker of a half-smile as he reached for his goblet where it rested on the mantel.

Standing opposite Shardan Lim, on the other side of the nearly dead fire, with long fingers caressing the ancient ground hammerstones mortared into the fireplace, was Hanut Orr. Plaything to half the noble women in the city, so long as they were married or otherwise divested of maidenhood, he did indeed present that most enticing combination of dangerous charm and dominating arrogance – traits that seduced otherwise intelligent women – and it was well known how he delighted in seeing his lovers crawl on their knees towards him, begging a morsel of his attention.

Challice's husband was sprawled in his favourite chair to Hanut Orr's left, legs stretched out, looking thoughtfully into his goblet, the wine with its hue of blue blood slowly swirling as he tilted his hand in lazy circles.

'Dear wife,' he now said in his usual drawl, 'has the balcony air revived you?'

'Wine?' asked Shardan Lim, brows lifting as if serving her was his life's calling.

Should a husband take umbrage with such barely constrained leering from his so-called friends? Gorlas seemed indifferent.

'No thank you, Councillor Lim. I have just come to wish you all a good night. Gorlas, will you be much longer here?'

He did not look up from his wine, though his mouth moved as if he was tasting his last sip all over again, finding the remnants faintly sour on his palate. 'There is no need to wait for me, wife.'

An involuntary glance over at Shardan revealed both amusement and the clear statement that *he* would not be so dismissive of her.

And, with sudden, dark perverseness, she found herself meeting his eyes and smiling in answer.

If it could be said, without uncertainty, that Gorlas Vidikas did not witness this exchange, Hanut Orr did, although his amusement was of the more savage, contemptuous kind.

Feeling sullied, Challice turned away.

Her handmaid trailed her out and up the broad flight of stairs, the only witness to the stiffness of her back as she made her way to the bedroom.

Once the door was closed she threw off her half-cloak. 'Lay out my jewellery,' she said.

'Mistress?'

She spun to the old woman. 'I wish to see my jewellery!'

Ducking, the woman hurried off to do her bidding.

'The old pieces,' Challice called after her. From the time before all this. When she had been little more than a child, marvelling over the gifts of suitors, all the bribes for her affection still clammy from sweaty hands. Oh, there had been so many possibilities then.

Her eyes narrowed as she stood before her vanity.

Well, perhaps not only then. Did it mean anything? Did it even matter any more?

Her husband had what he wanted now. Three duellists, three hard men with hard voices in the Council. One of the three now, yes, all he wanted.

Well, what about what *she* wanted?

But . . . what is it that I want?

She didn't know.

'Mistress.'

Challice turned.

Laid out on the vanity's worn surface, the treasure of her maidenhood looked . . . cheap. Gaudy. The very sight of those baubles made her sick in the pit of her stomach. 'Put them in a box,' she said to her servant. 'Tomorrow we sell them.'

He should never have lingered in the garden. His amorous host, the widow Sepharla, had fallen into a drunken slumber on the marble bench, one hand still holding her goblet as, head tilted back and mouth hanging open, loud snores groaned out into the sultry night air. The failed enterprise had amused Murillio, and he had stood for a time, sipping at his own wine and smelling the fragrant scents of the blossoms, until a sound alerted him to someone's quiet arrival.

Turning, he found himself looking upon the widow's daughter.

He should never have done that, either.

Half his age, but that delineation no longer distinguished unseemly from otherwise. She was past her rite of passage by three, perhaps four years, just nearing that age among young women when it was impossible for a man to tell whether she was twenty or thirty. And by that point, all such judgement was born of wilful self-delusion and hardly mattered anyway.

He'd had, perhaps, too much wine. Enough to weaken a certain resolve, the one having to do with recognizing his own maturity, that host of years behind him of which he was constantly reminded by the dwindling number of covetous glances flung his way. True, one might call it experience, settling for those women who knew enough to appreciate such traits. But a man's mind was quick to flit from how things were to how he wanted them to be, or, even worse, to how they used to be. As the saying went, when it came to the truth, every man was a duellist sheathed in the blood of ten thousand cuts.

None of this passed through Murillio's mind in the moment his eyes locked gazes with Delish, the unwed daughter of widow Sepharla. The wine, he would later conclude. The heat and steam of the fete, the sweet blossom scents on the moist, warm air. The fact that she was virtually naked, wearing but a shift of thin silk. Her light brown hair was cut incredibly short in the latest fashion among maidens. Face pale as cream, with full lips and the faintest slope to her nose. Liquid brown eyes big as a waif's, but there was no cracked bowl begging alms in her hands. This urchin's need belonged elsewhere.

Reassured by the snoring from the marble bench – and horrified by own relief – Murillio bowed low before her. 'Well timed, my dear,' he said, straightening. 'I was considering how best to assist your mother to her bed. Suggestions?'

A shake of that perfectly shaped head. 'She sleeps there most nights. Just like that.'

The voice was young yet neither nasal nor high-pitched as seemed the style among so many maidens these days, and so it failed in reminding him of that vast chasm of years between them.

Oh, in retrospect, so many regrets this night!

'She never thought you'd accept her invitation,' Delish went on, glancing down to where she had kicked off one of her sandals and was now prodding it with a delicate toe. 'Desirable as you are. In demand, I mean, on this night especially.'

Too clever by far, this stroking of his vaguely creped and nearly flaccid ego. 'But dear, why are you here? Your list of suitors must be legion, and among them—'

'Among them, not a single one worth calling a man.'

Did a thousand hormone-soaked hearts break with that dismissive utterance? Did beds lurch in the night, feet kicking clear of sweaty sheets? He could almost believe it.

'And that includes Prelick.'

'Excuse me, who?'

'The drunk, useless fool now passed out in the foyer. Tripping over his sword all night. It was execrable.'

Execrable. Yes, now I see.

'The young are prone to excessive enthusiasm,' Murillio observed. 'I have no doubt poor Prelick has been anticipating this night for weeks, if not months. Naturally, he succumbed to nervous agitation, brought on by proximity to your lovely self. Pity such young men, Delish; they deserve that much at least.'

'I'm not interested in pity, Murillio.'

She should never have said his name in just that way. He should never have listened to her say anything at all.

'Delish, can you stomach advice on this night, from one such as myself?'

Her expression was one of barely maintained forbearance, but she nodded.

'Seek out the quiet ones. Not the ones who preen, or display undue arrogance. The quiet ones, Delish, prone to watchfulness.'

'You describe no one I know.'

'Oh, they are there. It just takes a second glance to notice them.'

She had both sandals off now, and she dismissed his words with a wave of one pale hand that somehow brought her a step closer. Looking up as if suddenly shy, yet holding his gaze too long for there to be any real temerity. 'Not quiet ones. Not ones to pity. No . . . children! Not tonight, Murillio. Not under this moon.'

And he found her in his arms, a soft body all too eager with naught but filmy silk covering it and she seemed to be sliding all over him, a sylph, and he thought: *Under this moon?*

Her last gesture at the poetic, alas, since she was already tearing at his clothes, her mouth with those full lips wet and parted and a tongue flickering as she bit at his own lips. And here he was with one hand on one of her breasts, his other hand slipping round to her behind, hitching her up as she spread her legs and climbed to anchor herself on his hips, and he heard his belt buckle clack on the pavestone between his boots.

She was not a large woman. Not at all heavy, but surprisingly athletic, and she rode him with such violence that he felt his lower spine creak with every frenzied plunge. He sank into his usual detachment at this point, the kind that assured impressive endurance, and took a moment to confirm that the snoring continued behind him. All at once that sonorous sound struck him with a sense of prophetic dissolution, surrender to the years of struggle that was life's own chorus – *and so we shall all end our days* – a momentary pang that, had he permitted it to linger, would have unmanned him utterly. Delish, meanwhile, was wearing herself out, her gasps harsher, quicker, as shudders rose through her, and so he surrendered – not a moment too soon – to sensation. And joined her in one final, helpless gasp.

She held on to him and he could feel her pounding heart as he slowly lowered her back on to her feet, gently pulling away.

It was, all things considered, the worst moment to witness the blur of an iron blade flashing before his eyes. Burning agony as the sword thrust into his chest, the point pushing entirely through, making the drunken fool wielding it stumble forward, almost into the arms of Murillio.

Who was then falling back, the sword sliding out with a reluctant sob.

Delish screamed, and the look on Prelick's face was triumphant.

'Hah! The rapist dies!'

More footsteps, then, rushing out from the house. Voices clamouring. Bemused, Murillio picked himself back up, tugging at his pantaloons, cinching tight his belt. His lime green silk shirt was turning purple in blotches. There was blood on his chin, frothing up in soft, rattling coughs. Hands pulled at him and he pushed them all away, staggering for the gate.

Regrets, yes, jostling with the oblivious crowds on the street. Moments of lucidity, unknown periods of dim, red haze, standing with one hand on a stone wall, spitting down streams of blood. Oh, plenty of regrets.

Fortunately, he did not think they would hound him for much longer.

Was it habit or some peculiar twist in family traits that gave Scorch his expression of perpetual surprise? There was no telling, since every word the man uttered was delivered in tones of bewildered disbelief, as if Scorch could never be sure of what his senses told him of the outside world, and was even less certain of whatever thoughts clamoured in his head. He stared now at Leff, eyes wide and mouth gaping in between nervous licks of his lips, while Leff in turn squinted at Scorch as if chronically suspicious of his friend's apparent idiocy.

'All them ain't gonna wait for ever, Leff! We should never have signed on to this. I say we hitch on the next trader shippin' out. Down to Dhavran, maybe all the way t'the coast! Ain't you got a cousin in Mengal?'

Leff slowly blinked. 'Aye, Scorch. They let 'im furnish his cell himself, he's in there so much. You want us go up there and take on his mess too? Besides, then *we'd* end up on the list.'

Astonishment and dread filled Scorch's face. He looked away, whispered, 'It's the list that's done us in. The list . . .'

'We knew it wouldn't be easy,' Leff said in a possible attempt at mollification. 'Things like that never are.'

'But we ain't gotten nowhere!'

'It's only been a week, Scorch.'

The time had come for a modest clearing of the throat, a dab of the silk handkerchief on oily brow, a musing tug on the mouse-tail beard. 'Gentlemen!' Ah, now he had their attention. 'Witness the Skirmishers on the field and yon Mercenary's Coin, glinting ever as golden lures are wont to glint . . . everywhere. But here especially, and the knuckles still reside in the sweaty hand of surprised Scorch, too long clutched and uncast. Interminable has this game grown, with Kruppe patient as he perches on very edge of glorious victory!'

Leff scowled. 'You ain't winning nothing, Kruppe! You're losing, and bad, Coin or no Coin! And what use is it anyway – I don't see no mercenary anywhere on the field, so who's it paying for? Nobody!'

Smiling, Kruppe leaned back.

The crowd was noisome this night at the Phoenix Inn, as more and more drunks stumbled back in after their pleasing foray in the dusty, grimy streets. Kruppe, of course, felt magnanimous towards them all, as suited his naturally magnanimous nature.

Scorch cast the knuckles, then stared at the half-dozen etched bones as if they spelled out his doom.

And so they had. Kruppe leaned forward once again. 'Ho, the Straight Road reveals itself, and see how these six Mercenaries march on to the field! Slaying left and right! One cast of the knuckles, and the universe changes! Behold this grim lesson, dear companions of Kruppe. When the Coin is revealed, how long before a hand reaches for it?'

Virtually no cast in the Riposte Round could save the two hapless Kings and their equally hapless players, Scorch and Leff. Snarling, Leff swept an arm through the field, scattering pieces everywhere. As he did so he palmed the Coin and would have slipped it into his waistband if not for a wag of Kruppe's head and the pudgy hand reaching out palm up.

Cursing under his breath, Leff dropped the Coin into that hand.

'To the spoiler, the victory,' Kruppe said, smiling. 'Alas for poor Scorch and Leff, this single coin is but a fraction of riches now belonging to triumphant Kruppe. Two councils each, yes?'

'That's a week's wages for a week that ain't come yet,' Leff said. 'We'll have to owe you, friend.'

'Egregious precedent! Kruppe, however, understands how such reversals can catch one unawares, which makes perfect sense, since they are reversals. Accordingly, given the necessity for a week's noble labour, Kruppe is happy to extend deadline for said payment to one week from today.'

Groaning, Scorch sat back. 'The list, Leff. We're back to that damned list.'

'Many are the defaulters,' Kruppe said, sighing. 'And eager those demanding recompense, so much so that they assemble a dread list, and upon diminishment of names therein remit handsomely to those who would enforce collection, yes?'

The two men stared. Scorch's expression suggested that he had just taken a sharp blow to the head and was yet to find his wits. Leff simply scowled. 'Aye, that list, Kruppe. We took the job on since we didn't have nothing else to do since Boc's sudden . . . demise. And now it looks like our names might end up on it!'

'Nonsense! Or, rather, Kruppe elaborates, not if such a threat looms as a result of some future defaultment on monies owed Kruppe. Lists of that nature are indeed pernicious and probably counterproductive and Kruppe finds their very existence reprehensible. Wise advice is to relax somewhat on that matter. Unless, of course, one finds the deadline fast approaching with naught but lint in one's pouch. Further advice, achieve a victory on the list, receive due reward, repair immediately to Kruppe and clear the modest debt. The alternative, alas, is that we proceed with an entirely different solution.'

Leff licked his lips. 'What solution would that be?'

'Why, Kruppe's modest assistance regarding said list, of course. For a minuscule percentage.'

'For a cut you'd help us hunt down them that's on the list?'

'To do so would be in Kruppe's best interests, given this debt between him and you two.'

'What's the percentage?'

'Why, thirty-three, of course.'

'And you call that modest?'

'No, I called it minuscule. Dearest partners, have you found *any* of the people on that list?'

Miserable silence answered him, although Scorch was still looking rather confused.

'There is,' Kruppe said with an expansive swell of his chest that threatened the two stalwart buttons of his vest, 'no one in Darujhistan that Kruppe cannot find.' He settled back, and the brave buttons gleamed with victory.

Shouting, a commotion at the door, then Meese crying out Kruppe's name.

Startled, Kruppe rose, but could not see over the heads of all these peculiarly tall patrons – how annoying – and so he edged round his table and pushed his grunting, gasping way through to the bar, where Irilta was half dragging a blood-drenched Murillio on to the counter, knocking aside tankards and goblets.

Oh my. Kruppe met Meese's eyes, noted the fear and alarm. 'Meese, go to Coll at once.'

Pale, she nodded.

The crowd parted before her. Because, as the Gadrobi are wont to say, even a drunk knows a fool, and, drunk or not, no one was fool enough to get in that woman's way.

Picker's sword lay on the table, its tip smeared in drying blood. Antsy had added his short sword, its blade far messier. Together, mute testaments to this impromptu meeting's agenda.

Bluepearl sat at one end of the long table, nursing his headache with a tankard of ale; Blend was by the door, arms folded as she leaned against the frame. Mallet sat in a chair to Bluepearl's left, with all his nerves pushed into one jumpy leg, the thigh and knee jittering, while his face remained closed as he refused to meet anyone's eyes. Near the ratty tapestry dating back from the time when this place was still a temple stood Duiker, once Imperial Historian, now a broken old man.

In fact, Picker was mildly surprised that he'd accepted the invitation to join them. Perhaps some remnant of curiosity flickered still in the ashes of Duiker's soul, although he seemed more interested in the faded scene on the tapestry with its aerial flotilla of dragons approaching a temple much like the one they were in.

Nobody seemed ready to start talking. Typical. The task always fell at her feet, like some wounded dove. 'Assassins' Guild's taken on a contract,' she said, deliberately harsh. 'Target? At the very least, me, Antsy and Bluepearl. More likely, all us partners.' She paused, waiting to hear some objection. Nothing. 'Antsy, we turn down any offers on this place?'

'Picker,' the Falari said in an identical tone, 'ain't nobody's ever made an offer on this place.'

'Fine,' she replied. 'So, anyone catch a rumour that the old K'rul cult has been resurrected? Some High Priest somewhere in the city wanting the old temple back?'

Bluepearl snorted.

'What's that supposed to tell us?' Picker demanded, glaring at him.

'Nothing,' the Napan mage muttered. 'I ain't heard nothing like that, Pick. Now if Ganoes Paran ever comes back from wherever he's gone, we could get ourselves a sure answer. Still, I don't think there's any cult trying to move back in.'

'How do you know?' Antsy demanded. 'Can you smell 'em or something?'

'Oh, not now,' Bluepearl complained. 'No more questions tonight. That Mockra's chewed everything in my skull to pulp. I hate Mockra.'

'It's the ghosts,' said Mallet in that odd, gentle voice of his. He glanced across at Bluepearl. 'Right? They're not whispering anything they haven't been whispering since we moved in. Just the usual moans and begging for blood.' His gaze shifted to the swords on the table before him. 'Blood spilled here, that is. Stuff brought in from outside doesn't count. Luckily.'

Blend said, 'So try not cutting yourself shaving, Antsy.'

'There's been the odd scrap downstairs,' Picker said, frowning at Mallet. 'Are you saying that's been feeding the damned ghosts?'

The healer shrugged. 'Never enough to make a difference.'

'We need us a necromancer,' Bluepearl announced.

'We're getting off track,' Picker said. 'It's the damned contract we got to worry about. We need to find out who's behind it. We find out who, we throw a cusser through his bedroom window and that's that. So,' she continued, looking at the others, 'we need to come up with a plan of attack. Information to start. Let's hear some ideas on that.'

More silence.

Blend stepped away from the door. 'Someone's coming,' she said.

Now they could all hear the boots thumping up the stairs, hissed protestations in their wake.

Antsy collected his sword and Bluepearl slowly rose and Picker could smell the sudden awakening of sorcery. She held up a hand. 'Wait, for Hood's sake.'

The door was flung open.

In strode a large, well-dressed man, out of breath, his light blue eyes scanning faces until they alighted on Mallet, who rose.

'Councillor Coll. What is wrong?'

'I need your help,' the Daru noble said, and Picker could hear the distress in the man's voice. 'High Denul. I need you, now.'

Before Mallet could reply, Picker stepped forward. 'Councillor Coll, did you come here alone?'

The man frowned. Then a vague gesture behind him. 'A modest escort. Two guards.' Only then did he note the sword on the table. 'What is happening here?'

'Picker,' said Mallet, 'I'll take Bluepearl.'

'I don't like—'

But the healer cut her off. 'We need information, don't we? Coll can help us. Besides, they wouldn't have set more than one clan on us to start and you took care of that one. The Guild needs to recover, reassess – we've got a day at least.'

Picker looked across at the councillor, who, if he didn't quite grasp what was going on, now had enough for a fair guess. Sighing, she said to him, 'Seems there's someone wants us dead. You might not want to get involved with us right now—'

But he shook his head, fixed his gaze once more on Mallet. 'Healer, please.'

Mallet nodded to a scowling Bluepearl. 'Lead on, Councillor. We're with ya.'

'. . . *came upon Osserick, stalwart ally, broken and with blood on his face, struck into unconsciousness. And Anomander fell to his knees and called upon the Thousand Gods who looked down upon Osserick and saw the blood on his face. With mercy they struck him awakened and so he stood.*

'*And so stood Anomander and they faced one another, Light upon Dark, Dark upon Light.*

'*Now there was rage in Anomander. "Where is Draconnus?" he demanded of his stalwart ally. For when Anomander had departed, the evil tyrant Draconnus, Slayer of Eleint, had been by Anomander's own hand struck into unconsciousness and there was blood on his face. Osserick, who had taken the charge of guarding Draconnus, fell to his knees and called upon the Thousand Gods, seeking their mercy before Anomander's fury.*' '*I was bested!*' cried Osserick in answer. '*Caught* by Sister Spite unawares! Oh, the Thousand Gods were turned away, and so was I struck into unconsciousness and see there is blood on my face!'

' "One day," vowed Anomander, and he was then the darkness of a terrible storm, and Osserick quailed like a sun behind a cloud, "this alliance of ours shall end. Our enmity shall be renewed, O Son of Light, Child of Light. We shall contest every span of ground, every reach of sky, every spring of sweet water. We shall battle a thousand times and there shall be no mercy between us. I shall send misery upon your kin, your daughters. I shall blight their minds with Unknowing Dark. I shall scatter them confused on realms unknown and there shall be no mercy in their hearts, for between them and the Thousand Gods there shall ever be a cloud of darkness."

'Such was Anomander's fury, and though he stood alone, Dark upon Light, there was sweetness lingering in the palm of one hand, from the deceiving touch of Lady Envy. Light upon Dark, Dark upon Light, two men, wielded as weapons by two sisters, children of Draconnus. Who stood unseen by any and were pleased by what they saw and all that they heard.

'It was decided then that Anomander would set out once more, to hunt down the evil tyrant. To destroy him and his cursed sword which is an abomination in the eyes of the Thousand Gods and all who kneel to them. Osserick, it was decided, would set out to hunt Spite and exact righteous vengeance.

'Of the vow spoken by Anomander, Osserick knew the rage from which it was spawned, and in silence he made vow to answer it in his own time. To spar, to duel, to contest every span of ground, every reach of sky, and every spring of sweet water. But such matters must needs lie upon calm earth, a seed awaiting life.

'This issue with Draconnus remained before them, after all, and now Spite as well. Did not the Children of Tiam demand punishment? There was blood on the faces of too many Eleint, and so Anomander and so Osserick had taken on themselves this fated hunt.

'Could the Eleint have known all that would come of this, they would have withdrawn their storm-breath, from both Anomander and Osserick. But these fates were not to be known then, and this is why the Thousand Gods wept . . .'

Rubbing his eyes, High Alchemist Baruk leaned back. The original version of this, he suspected, was not the mannered shambles he had just read through. Those quaint but overused phrases belonged to an interim age when the style among historians sought to resurrect some oral legacy in an effort to reinforce the veracity of eyewitnesses to the events described. The result had given him a headache.

He had never heard of the Thousand Gods, and this pantheon could not be found in any other compendium but Dillat's *Dark and Light*. Baruk suspected Dillat had simply made them up, which prompted the question: how much else did she invent?

Leaning forward once more, he adjusted the lantern's wick, then leafed through the brittle sheets until another section caught his interest.

'In this day there was war among the dragons. The First Born had all but one bowed necks to K'rul's bargain. Their children, bereft of all that they would have inherited, burst skyward from the towers in great flurry yet even these were not united beyond rejecting the First Born. Factions arose and red rain descended upon all the Realms. Jaws fastened upon necks. Talons opened bellies. The breath of chaos melted flesh from bones.

'Anomander, Osserick and others had already tasted the blood of Tiam, and now there came more with raging thirst and many a demonic abomination was spawned of this crimson nectar. So long as the Gates of Starvald Demelain remained open, unguarded and held by none, the war would not end, and so the red rain descended upon all the Realms.

'Kurald Liosan was the first Realm to seal the portal between itself and Starvald Demelain, and the tale that follows recounts the slaughter committed by Osserick in cleansing his world of all the pretenders and rivals, the Soletaken and feral purebloods, even unto driving the very first D'ivers from his land.

'This begins at the time when Osserick fought Anomander for the sixteenth time and both had blood on their faces before Kilmandaros, she who speaks with her fists, took upon herself the task of driving them apart. . . .'

Baruk looked up, then twisted in his chair to regard his guest, who was busy preening herself on his map-table. 'Crone, the inconsistencies in this text are infuriating.'

The Great Raven cocked her head, beak gaping for a moment in laughter, then said, 'So what? Show me a written history that makes sense, and I will show you true fiction. If that is all you want, then look elsewhere! My master concluded that Dillat's nonsense would make a fine gift for your collection. If you are truly displeased, there are plenty of other idiocies in his library, those that he bothered to extract from Moon's Spawn, that is. He left whole rooms crammed with the rubbish, you know.'

Baruk blinked slowly, struggling to keep his horror from his voice as he said, 'No, I did not know that.'

Undeceived, Crone cackled. Then she said, 'My master was most amused at the notion of falling to his knees and crying out to the Hundred Gods—'

'Thousand. The Thousand Gods.'

'Whatever.' A duck of the head and the wings half spread. 'Or even making a vow to battle Osserc. Their alliance fell apart because of a growing mutual dislike. The disaster with Draconus probably delivered the death-blow. Imagine, falling for a woman's wiles – and a daughter of Draconus at that! Was Osserc not even remotely suspicious of her motives? Hah! The males among every species in existence are so . . . predictable!'

Baruk smiled. 'If I recall Fisher's *Anomandaris*, Lady Envy managed pretty much the same with your master, Crone.'

'Nothing he was unaware of at the time,' the Great Raven said with a strange clucking sound to punctuate the statement. 'My master has always understood the necessity of certain sacrifices.' She fluffed up her onyx feathers. 'Consider the outcome, after all!'

Baruk grimaced.

'I'm hungry!' Crone announced.

'I didn't finish my supper,' Baruk said. 'On that plate—'

'I know, I know! What do you think made me hungry in the first place? Sit in wonder at my patience, High Alchemist! Even as you read on interminably!'

'Eat now and quickly, old friend,' Baruk said, 'lest you die of malnutrition.'

'You were never such a careless host before,' the Great Raven observed, hopping over to the plate and spearing a sliver of meat. 'You are troubled, High Alchemist.'

'By many things, yes. The Rhivi claim that the White Face Barghast have disappeared. Utterly.'

'Indeed,' Crone replied. 'Almost immediately after the fall of Coral and the Tiste Andii investiture.'

'Crone, you are a Great Raven. Your children ride the winds and see all.'

'Perhaps.'

'Why then will you not tell me where they went?'

'Well, the Grey Swords as you know marched south, down to Elingarth,' Crone said, circling the plate in short hops. 'And there they purchased ships.' A pause and cock of the head. 'Could they see the wake before them? Did they know to follow? Or is there perhaps a great hole in the world's ocean, drawing every ship into its deadly maw?'

'The White Face took to the seas? Extraordinary. And the Grey Swords *followed* them.'

'None of this is relevant, High Alchemist.'

'Relevant to what?'

'Your unease, of course. You fling queries at your poor bedraggled guest in order to distract yourself.'

It had been months since Crone's previous visit, and Baruk had come to believe, with some regret, that his cordial relations with the Son of Darkness were drawing to a close, not out of any dispute, simply the chronic ennui of the Tiste Andii. It was said the permanent gloom that was Black Coral well suited the city's denizens, both Andii and human.

'Crone, please extend to your master my sincerest thanks for this gift. It was most unexpected and generous. But I would ask him, if it is not too forward of me, if he is reconsidering the Council's official request to open diplomatic relations between our two cities. Delegates but await your master's invitation, and a suitable site has been set aside for the construction of an embassy – not far from here, in fact.'

'The estate crushed by a Soletaken demon's inglorious descent,' Crone said, pausing to laugh before spearing another chunk of food. 'Aagh, this is vegetable! Disgusting!'

'Indeed, Crone, the very same estate. As I said, not far from here.'

'Master is considering said request, and will continue considering it, I suspect.'

'For how much longer?'

'I have no idea.'

'Does he have concerns?'

The Great Raven, leaning over the plate, tilted her head and regarded Baruk for a long moment.

Baruk felt vaguely sickened and he looked away. 'So, I have reason to be . . . troubled.'

'Master asks: when will it begin?'

The High Alchemist eyed the stack of loosely bound parchment that was Anomander's gift, and nodded. But he did not answer.

'Master asks: do you wish for assistance?'

Baruk winced.

'Master asks,' Crone went on, relentless, 'would said assistance better serve you if it was covert, rather than official?'

Gods below.

'Master asks: should sweet Crone stay the night as Baruk's guest, awaiting answers to these queries?'

Clattering at the window. Baruk swiftly rose and approached it.

'A demon!' cried Crone, half spreading her enormous wings.

'One of mine,' said Baruk, unlatching the iron frame and then stepping back as Chillbais clambered awkwardly into view, grunting as he squeezed through. 'Master Baruk!' he squealed. 'Out! Out! Out!'

Baruk had felt ill a moment earlier. Now he was suddenly chilled in his very bones. He slowly shut the window, then faced the Great Raven. 'Crone, it has begun.'

The demon saw her and bared needle fangs as he hissed, 'Grotesque monstrosity!'

Crone made stabbing motions with her beak. 'Bloated toad!'

'Be quiet, both of you!' Baruk snapped. 'Crone, you will indeed stay the night as my guest. Chillbais, find somewhere to be. I have more work for you and I will collect you when it's time.'

Flickering a forked tongue out at Crone, the squat demon waddled towards the fireplace. It clambered on to the glowing coals, then disappeared up the chimney. Black clouds of soot rained down, billowing out from the hearth.

Crone coughed. 'Ill-mannered servants you have, High Alchemist.'

But Baruk was not listening. *Out.*

Out!

That lone word rang through his mind, loud as a temple bell, drowning out everything else, although he caught a fast-fading echo . . .

'. . . *stalwart ally, broken and with blood on his face* . . .'

Chapter Two

Anomander would tell no lie, nor live one,
and would that deafness could
bless him in the days and nights
beyond the black rains of Black Coral.
Alas, this was not to be.
. . .
And so we choose to hear nothing
Of the dreaded creak, the slip and snap
Of wooden wheels, the shudder on stone
And the chiding rattle of chains, as if
Upon some other world is where darkness
Beats out from a cursedly ethereal forge
And no sun rises above horizon's rippled
Cant – some other world not ours indeed –
Yes bless us so, Anomander, with this
Sanctimony, this lie and soft comfort,
And the slaves are not us, this weight
But an illusion, these shackles could break
With a thought, and all these cries and
Moans are less than the murmurs
Of a quiescent heart – it's all but a tale,
My friends, this tall denier of worship
And the sword he carries holds nothing,
No memory at all, and if there be a place
In the cosy scheme for lost souls
Pulling onward an uprooted temple
It but resides in an imagination flawed
And unaligned with sober intricacy –
Nothing is as messy as that messy world
And that comfort leaves us abiding
Deaf and blind and senseless in peace
Within our imagined place, this precious order . . .

ANOMANDARIS, BOOK IV SOLILOQUY
FISHER KEL TATH

Dragon Tower stood like a torch above Black Coral. The spire, rising from the northwest corner of the New Andiian Palace, was solid black basalt, dressed in fractured, faceted obsidian that glistened in the eternal gloom enshrouding the city. Atop its flat roof crouched a crimson-scaled dragon, wings folded, its wedge head hanging over one side so that it seemed to stare down on the crazed shadowy patchwork of buildings, alleys and streets far below.

There were citizens still in Black Coral – among the humans – who believed that the ferocious sentinel was the stone creation of some master artisan among the ruling Tiste Andii, and this notion left Endest Silann sourly amused. True, he understood how wilful such ignorance could be. The thought of a real, live dragon casting its baleful regard down on the city and its multitude of scurrying lives was to most truly terrifying, and indeed, had they been close enough to see the gleaming hunger in Silannah's multifaceted eyes, they would have long fled Black Coral in blind panic.

For the Eleint to remain so, virtually motionless, day and night, weeks into months and now very nearly an entire year, was not unusual. And Endest Silann knew this better than most.

The Tiste Andii, once a formidable, if aged, sorcerer in Moon's Spawn, now a barely competent castellan to the New Andiian Palace, slowly walked Sword Street as it bent south of the treeless park known as Grey Hill. He had left the fiercely lit district of Fish, where the Outwater Market so crowded every avenue and lane that those who brought two-wheeled carts in which to load purchases were forced to leave them in a square just north of Grey Hill. The endless streams of porters for hire – who gathered every dawn near the Cart Square – always added to the chaos between the stalls, pushing through with wrapped bundles towards the carts and slipping, dodging and sliding like eels back into the press. Although the Outwater Market acquired its name because the preponderance of fish sold there came from the seas beyond Night – the perpetual darkness cloaking the city and the surrounding area for almost a third of a league – there could also be found the pale, gem-eyed creatures of Coral Bay's Nightwater.

Endest Silann had arranged the next week's order of cadaver eels from a new supplier, since the last one's trawler had been pulled down by something too big for its net, with the loss of all hands. Nightwater was not simply an unlit span of sea in the bay, unfortunately. It was Kurald Galain, a true manifestation of the warren, quite possibly depthless, and on occasion untoward beasts loomed into the waters of Coral Bay. Something was down there now, forcing the fishers to use hooks and lines rather than nets, a method possible only because the eels foamed just beneath the surface in the tens of thousands, driven there by terror. Most of the eels pulled aboard were snags.

South of Grey Hill, the street lanterns grew scarcer as Endest Silann made his way into the Andiian district. Typically, there were few Tiste Andii on the streets. Nowhere could be seen figures seated on tenement steps, or in stalls leaning on countertops to call out their wares or simply watch passers-by. Instead, the rare figures crossing Endest's path were one and all on their way somewhere, probably the home of some friend or relation, there to participate in the few remaining rituals of society. Or returning home from such ordeals, as tenuous as smoke from a dying fire.

No fellow Tiste Andii met Endest Silann's eyes as they slipped ghostly past. This, of course, was more than the usual indifference, but he had grown used to it. An old man must need a thick skin, and was he not the oldest by far? Excepting Anomander Dragnipurake.

Yet Endest could recall his youth, a vision of himself vaguely blurred by time, setting foot upon this world on a wild night with storms ravaging the sky. *Oh, the storms of that night, the cold water on the face . . . that moment, I see it still.*

They stood facing a new world. His lord's rage ebbing, but slowly, trickling down like the rain. Blood leaked from a sword wound in Anomander's left shoulder. And there had been a look in his eyes . . .

Endest sighed as he worked his way up the street's slope, but it was an uneven, harsh sigh. Off to his left was the heaped rubble of the old palace. A few jagged walls rose here and there, and crews had carved paths into the mass of wreckage, salvaging stone and the occasional timber that had not burned. The deafening collapse of that edifice still shivered in Endest's bones, and he slowed in his climb, one hand reaching out to lean against a wall. The pressure was returning, making his jaw creak as he clenched his teeth, and pain shot through his skull.

Not again, please.

No, this would not do. That time was done, over with. He had survived. He had done as his lord had commanded and he had not failed. No, this would not do at all.

Endest Silann stood, sweat now on his face, with his eyes squeezed shut.

No one ever met his gaze, and this was why. This . . . weakness.

Anomander Dragnipurake had led his score of surviving followers on to the strand of a new world. Behind the flaring rage in his eyes there had been triumph.

This, Endest Silann told himself, was worth remembering. Was worth holding on to.

We assume the burden as we must. We win through. And life goes on.

A more recent memory, heaving into his mind. The unbearable pressure of the deep, the water pushing in on all sides. *'You are my last High Mage, Endest Silann. Can you do this for me?'*

The sea, my lord? *Beneath the sea?*

'Can you do this, old friend?'

My lord, I shall try.

But the sea had wanted Moon's Spawn, oh, yes, wanted it with savage, relentless hunger. It had railed against the stone, it had besieged the sky keep with its crushing embrace, and in the end there was no throwing back its dark swirling legions.

Oh, Endest Silann had kept them alive for just long enough, but the walls were collapsing even as his lord had summoned the sky keep's last reserves of power, to raise it up from the depths, raise it up, yes, back into the sky.

So heavy, the weight, so vast—

Injured beyond recovery, Moon's Spawn was already dead, as dead as Endest Silann's own power. *We both drowned that day. We both died.*

Raging falls of black water thundering down, a rain of tears from stone, oh, how Moon's Spawn wept. Cracks widening, the internal thunder of beauty's collapse . . .

I should have gone with Moon's Spawn when at last he sent it drifting away, yes, I should have. Squatting among the interred dead. My lord honours me for my sacrifice, but his every word is like ashes drifting down on my face. Abyss below, I felt the sundering of every room! The fissures bursting through were sword slashes in my soul, and how we bled, how we groaned, how we fell inward with our mortal wounds!

The pressure would not relent. It was within him now. The sea sought vengeance, and now could assail him no matter where he stood. Hubris had delivered a curse, searing a brand on his soul. A brand that had grown septic. He was too broken to fight it off any more.

I am Moon's Spawn, now. Crushed in the deep, unable to reach the surface. I descend, and the pressure builds. How it builds!

No, this would not do. Breath hissing, he pushed himself from the wall, staggered onward. He was a High Mage no longer. He was nothing. A mere castellan, fretting over kitchen supplies and foodstuffs, watch schedules and cords of wood for the hearths. Wax for the yellow-eyed candlemakers. Squid ink for the stained scribes . . .

Now, when he stood before his lord, he spoke of paltry things, and this was his legacy, all that remained.

Yet did I not stand with him on that strand? Am I not the last one left to share with my lord that memory?

The pressure slowly eased. And once again, he had survived the embrace. And the next time? There was no telling, but he did not believe he could last much longer. The pain clutching his chest, the thunder in his skull.

We have found a new supply of cadaver eels. That is what I will tell him. And he will smile and nod, and perhaps settle one hand on my shoulder. A gentle, cautious squeeze, light enough to ensure that nothing breaks. He will speak his gratitude.

For the eels.

It was a measure of his courage and fortitude that the man had never once denied that he had been a Seerdomin of the Pannion Domin; that, indeed, he had served the mad tyrant in the very keep now reduced to rubble barely a stone's throw behind the Scour Tavern. That he held on to the title was not evidence of some misplaced sense of manic loyalty. The man with the expressive eyes understood irony, and if on occasion some fellow human in the city took umbrage upon hearing him identify himself thus, well, the Seerdomin could take care of himself and that was one legacy that was no cause for shame.

This much and little more was what Spinnock Durav knew of the man, beyond his impressive talent in the game they now played: an ancient game of the Tiste Andii, known as Kef Tanar, that had spread throughout the population of Black Coral and indeed, so he had heard, to cities far beyond – even Darujhistan itself.

As many kings or queens as there were players. A field of battle that expanded with each round and was never twice the same. Soldiers and mercenaries and mages, assassins, spies. Spinnock Durav knew that the original inspiration for Kef Tanar could be found in the succession wars among the First Children of Mother Dark, and indeed one of the king figures bore a slash of silver paint on its mane, whilst another was of bleached bonewood. There was a queen of white fire, opal-crowned; and others Spinnock could, if he bothered, have named, assuming anyone was remotely interested, which he suspected they were not.

Most held that the white mane was a recent affectation, like some mocking salute to Black Coral's remote ruler. The tiles of the field themselves were all flavoured in aspects of Dark, Light and Shadow. The Grand City and Keep tiles were seen as corresponding to Black Coral, although Spinnock Durav knew that the field's ever-expanding Grand City (there were over fifty tiles for the City alone and a player could make more, if desired) was in fact Kharkanas, the First City of Dark.

But no matter. It was the game that counted.

The lone Tiste Andii in all of the Scour, Spinnock Durav sat with four other players, with a crowd now gathered round to watch this titanic battle which had gone on for five bells. Smoke hung in wreaths just overhead, obscuring the low rafters of the tavern's main room, blunting the light of the torches and candles. Rough pillars here and there held up the ceiling, constructed from fragments of the old palace and Moon's Spawn itself, all inexpertly fitted together, some leaning ominously and displaying cracks in the mortar. Spilled ale puddled the uneven flagstones of the floor, where hard-backed salamanders slithered about, drunkenly attempting to mate with people's feet and needing to be kicked off again and again.

The Seerdomin sat across the table from Spinnock. Two of the other players had succumbed to vassal roles, both now subject to Seerdomin's opal-crowned queen. The third player's forces had been backed into one corner of the field, and he was contemplating throwing in his lot with either Seerdomin or Spinnock Durav.

If the former, then Spinnock was in trouble, although by no means finished. He was, after all, a veteran player whose experience spanned nearly twenty thousand years.

Spinnock was large for a Tiste Andii, wide-shouldered and strangely bearish. There was a faint reddish tinge to his long, unbound hair. His eyes were set wide apart on a broad, somewhat flat face, the cheekbones prominent and flaring. The slash that was his mouth was fixed in a grin, an expression that rarely wavered.

'Seerdomin,' he now said, whilst the cornered player prevaricated, besieged by advice from friends crowded behind his chair, 'you have a singular talent for Kef Tanar.'

The man simply smiled.

In the previous round a cast of the knuckles had delivered a Mercenary's Coin into the Seerdomin's royal vaults. Spinnock was expecting a flanking foray with the four remaining mercenary figures, either to bring pressure on the third king if he elected to remain independent or threw in his lot with Spinnock, or to drive them deep into Spinnock's own territory. However, with but a handful of field tiles remaining and the Gate not yet selected, Seerdomin would be wiser to hold back.

Breaths were held as the third king reached into the pouch to collect a field tile. He drew out his hand closed in a fist, then met Spinnock's eyes.

Nerves and avarice. 'Three coins, Tiste, and I'm your vassal.'

Spinnock's grin hardened, and he shook his head. 'I don't buy vassals, Garsten.'

'Then you will lose.'

'I doubt Seerdomin will buy your allegiance either.'

'Come to me now,' Seerdomin said to the man, 'and do so on your hands and knees.'

Garsten's eyes flicked back and forth, gauging which viper was likely to carry the least painful bite. After a moment he snarled under his breath and revealed the tile.

'Gate!'

'Delighted to find you sitting on my right,' Spinnock said.

'I retreat through!'

Cowardly, but predictable. This was the only path left to Garsten that allowed him to hold on to the coins in his vault. Spinnock and Seerdomin watched as Garsten marched his pieces from the field.

And then it was Spinnock's turn. With the Gate in play he could summon the five dragons he had amassed. They sailed high over Seerdomin's elaborate ground defences, weathering them with but the loss of one from the frantic sorcery of the two High Mages atop the towers of Seerdomin's High Keep.

The assault struck down two-thirds of Seerdomin's Inner Court, virtually isolating his queen.

With the ground defences in sudden disarray on the collapse of command, Spinnock advanced a spearhead of his own mercenaries as well as his regiment of Elite Cavalry, neatly bisecting the enemy forces. Both vassals subsequently broke in uprising, each remaining on the field long enough to further savage Seerdomin's beleaguered forces before retreating through the Gate. By the time the game's round reached him, Seerdomin had no choice but to reach out one hand and topple his queen.

Voices rose on all sides, as wagers were settled.

Spinnock Durav leaned forward to collect his winnings. 'Resto! A pitcher of ale for the table here!'

'You are ever generous with my money,' Seerdomin said in sour amusement.

'The secret of generosity, friend.'

'I appreciate the salve.'

'I know.'

As was customary, the other three players, having retreated, could not partake of any gesture of celebration by the game's victor. Accordingly, Spinnock and Seerdomin were free to share the pitcher of ale between them, and this seemed a most satisfying conclusion to such a skilfully waged campaign. The crowd had moved off, fragmenting on all sides, and the servers were suddenly busy once more.

'The problem with us night owls,' said Seerdomin, hunching down over his flagon. When it seemed he would say no more he added, 'Not once does a glance to yon smudged pane over there reveal the poppy-kiss of dawn.'

'Dawn? Ah, to announce night's closure,' Spinnock said, nodding. 'It is a constant source of surprise among us Tiste Andii that so many humans have remained. Such unrelieved darkness is a weight upon your souls, or so I have heard.'

'If there is no escape, aye, it can twist a mind into madness. But a short ride beyond the north gate, out to the Barrow, and bright day beckons. Same for the fishers sailing Outwater. Without such options, Spinnock, you Andii would indeed be alone in Black Coral. Moon's Spawn casts a shadow long after its death, or so the poets sing. But I tell you this,' Seerdomin leaned forward to refill his flagon, 'I welcome this eternal darkness.'

Spinnock knew as much, for the man seated opposite him carried a sorrow heavier than any shadow, and far darker; and in this he was perhaps more Tiste Andii than human, but for one thing, and it was this one thing that made it easy for Spinnock Durav to call the man friend. Seerdomin, for all his grief, was somehow holding despair back, defying the siege that had long ago defeated the Tiste Andii. A human trait, to be sure. More than a trait, a quality profound in its resilience, a virtue that, although Spinnock could not find it within himself – nor, it was true, among any fellow Tiste Andii – he could draw a kind of sustenance from none the less. At times, he felt like a parasite, so vital had this vicarious feeding become, and he sometimes feared that it was the only thing keeping him alive.

Seerdomin had enough burdens, and Spinnock was determined that his friend should never comprehend the necessity he had become – these games, these nights among the eternal Night, this squalid tavern and the pitchers of cheap, gassy ale.

'This one has worn me out,' the man now said, setting down his empty flagon. 'I thought I had you – aye, I knew the Gate tile was still unplayed. Two tiles to get past you, though, and everything would have been mine.'

There wasn't much to say to that. Both understood how that single gamble had decided the game. What was unusual was Seerdomin's uncharacteristic need to explain himself. 'Get some sleep,' Spinnock said.

Seerdomin's smile was wry. He hesitated, as if undecided whether or not to say something, or simply follow Spinnock's advice and stumble off to his home.

Speak not to me of weakness. Please.

'I have acquired the habit,' the man said, squinting as he followed some minor ruckus near the bar, 'of ascending the ruins. To look out over the Nightwater.

Remembering the old cat-men and their families – aye, it seems they are breeding anew, but of course it will not be the same, not at all the same.' He fell silent for a moment, then shot Spinnock a quick, uneasy glance. 'I see your lord.'

The Tiste Andii's brows lifted. 'Anomander Rake?'

A nod. 'First time was a couple of weeks ago. And now . . . every time, at about the twelfth bell. He stands on the wall of the new keep. And, like me, he stares out to sea.'

'He favours . . . solitude,' Spinnock said.

'I am always suspicious of that statement,' Seerdomin said.

Yes, I can see how you might be. 'It is what comes from lordship, from rule. Most of his original court is gone. Korlat, Orfantal, Sorrit, Pra'iran. Vanished or dead. That doesn't make it any easier. Still, there are some who remain. Endest Silann, for one.'

'When I see him, standing alone like that . . .' Seerdomin looked away. 'It unnerves me.'

'It is my understanding,' observed Spinnock, 'that we all manage to do that, for you humans. The way we seem to haunt this city.'

'Sentinels with nothing to guard.'

Spinnock thought about that, then asked, 'And so too the Son of Darkness? Do you people chafe under his indifferent rule?'

Seerdomin grimaced. 'Would that all rulers were as indifferent. No, "indifferent" is not quite the right word. He is there where it matters. The administration and the authority – neither can be challenged, nor is there any reason to do so. The Son of Darkness is . . . benign.'

Spinnock thought of the sword strapped to his lord's back, adding the tart flavour of inadvertent irony to his friend's words. And then he thought of the dead cities to the north. Maurik, Setta, Lest. 'It's not as if any neighbouring kingdoms are eyeing the prize that is Black Coral. They're either dead or, as in the south, in complete disarray. Thus, the threat of war is absent. Accordingly, what's left for a ruler? As you say, administration and authority.'

'You do not convince me, friend,' Seerdomin said, his eyes narrowing. 'The Son of Darkness, now that is a title for a bureaucrat? Hardly. Knight of Darkness to keep the thugs off the streets?'

'It is the curse of a long life,' Spinnock said, 'that in eminence one both rises and falls, again and again. Before this, there was a vast and costly war against the Pannion Domin. Before that, an even deadlier and far longer feud with the Malazan Empire. Before that, Jacuruku. Seerdomin, Anomander Rake has earned his rest. This peace.'

'Then perhaps he is the one who chafes. Staring out upon the harsh waters of the Cut, the twelfth bell tolling like a dirge in the gloom.'

'Poetic,' Spinnock said, smiling, but there was something cold in his heart, as if the image conjured by his friend's words was somehow *too* poignant. The notion sobered him. 'I do not know if my lord chafes. I have never been that important; little more than one warrior among thousands. I do not think we have spoken in centuries.'

Seerdomin's look was incredulous. 'But that is absurd!'

'Is it? See me, Seerdomin, I am too capricious. It is my eternal curse. I was never one for command, not even a squad. I got lost in Mott Wood, five days stumbling through briar and brush.' Spinnock laughed, waved one hand. 'A hopeless cause long ago, friend.'

'It's commonly held, Spinnock, that all you remaining Tiste Andii – survivors from all those wars – are perforce the elite, the most formidable of all.'

'You were a soldier, so you know better than that. Oh, there are heroes aplenty among the Andii ranks. But just as many of us who were simply lucky. It's the way of things. We lost many great heroes in our battles against the Malazans.'

'A hopeless cause, you claim to be.' Seerdomin grimaced. 'Yet a master campaigner in Kef Tanar.'

'With soldiers of carved wood, I am most formidable. Living ones are another matter entirely.'

The man grunted, and seemed content to leave that one alone.

They sat in companionable silence for a time, as Resto delivered another pitcher of ale, and Spinnock was relieved, as the ale flowed from pitcher to flagon to mouth, that no more talk of past deeds in distant fields of battle arose that might unhinge the half-truths and outright lies he had just uttered.

And when the moment came when dawn unfurled its poppy blush upon the far eastern horizon, a moment unseen by any within the city of Black Coral, Spinnock Durav nodded, but mostly to himself. Eternal darkness or not, a Tiste Andii knew when light arrived. Another irony, then, that only the humans within Night were oblivious of the day's beginning, of the passage of the unseen sun beyond the gloom, of its endless journey across the sky.

Before they both got too drunk, they agreed upon the time for a new game. And when Seerdomin finally rose unsteadily to his feet, flinging a careless wave in Spinnock's direction before weaving out through the tavern door, Spinnock found himself wishing the man a safe journey home.

A most generous send-off, then, even if delivered in silence.

Anomander Rake would be setting out for the throne room by now, where he would steel himself to face the brutal demands of the day, the allocation of stipends, the merchant grievances to be adjudicated, reports on the status of supplies, one or two emissaries from distant free cities seeking trade agreements and mutual protection pacts (yes, plenty of those).

Oh, the Knight of Darkness fought all manner of beasts and demons, did he not?

Darkness surrendered. But then, it always did. There was no telling how long the journey took in that time within Kurald Galain, nor the vast distances covered, stride by stride by stride. All was in discord, all was unrelieved and unrelieving. Again and again, Nimander Golit seemed to startle awake, realizing with a shiver that he had been walking, an automaton in the midst of his comrades, all of whom glowed dully and appeared to float in an ethereal void, with the one named

Clip a few paces ahead, striding with a purpose none of them could emulate. Nimander would then comprehend that, once more, he had lost himself.

Rediscovering where he was elicited no satisfaction. Rediscovering who he was proved even worse. The young man named Nimander Golit was little more than an accretion of memories, numbed by a concatenation of remembered sensations – a beautiful woman dying in his arms. Another woman dying beneath his hands, her face turning dark, like a storm cloud that could not burst, her eyes bulging, and still his hands squeezed. A flailing body flung through the air, crashing through a window, vanishing into the rain.

Chains could spin for eternity, rings glittering with some kind of life. Worn boots could swing forward, one after another like the blades of a pair of shears. Promises could be uttered, acquiescence forced like a swollen hand pushing into a tight glove. All could stand wearing their certainty. Or feeling it drive them forward like a wind that knew where it was going. All could wish for warmth within that embrace.

But these were empty things, bobbing before his eyes like puppets on tangled strings. As soon as he reached out, seeking to untangle those strings, to make sense out of it all, they would swing away, for ever beyond his reach.

Skintick, who seemed ready with a smile for everything, walked at his side yet half a step ahead. Nimander could not see enough of his cousin's face to know how Skintick had greeted the darkness that had stretched ever before them, but as that impenetrable abyss faded, and from the way ahead emerged the boles of pine trees, his cousin turned with a smile decidedly wry.

'That wasn't so bad,' he murmured, making every word a lie and clearly delighting in his own mockery.

Damp air swirled round them now, cool in its caress, and Clip's steps had slowed. When he turned they could see the extent of his exhaustion. The rings spun once round on the chain in his hand, then snapped taut. 'We will camp here,' he said in a hoarse voice.

Some previous battle had left Clip's armour and clothes in tatters, with old bloodstains on the dark leather. So many wounds that, if delivered all at once, they should probably have killed him. Little of this had been visible that night on the street in Second Maiden Fort, when he had first summoned them.

Nimander and Skintick watched their kin settle down on the soft loam of the forest floor wherever they happened to be standing, blank-eyed and looking lost. Yes, *'explanations are ephemeral. They are the sword and shield of the attack, and behind them hides motivation. Explanations strive to find weakness, and from the exploitation of weakness comes compliance and the potential of absolute surrender.'* So Andarist had written, long ago, in a treatise entitled *Combat and Negotiation*.

Skintick, his long jester's face faintly pinched with weariness, plucked at Nimander's sleeve, gestured with a nod of his head then set out to one side, threading between trees. After a moment, Nimander followed.

His cousin halted some thirty paces from the makeshift camp, where he settled on to his haunches.

Across from him, Nimander did the same.

The sun was beginning to rise, bleeding light into the gloom of this forest. With it came the faint smell of the sea.

'Herald of Mother Dark,' Skintick said quietly, as if measuring the worth of the words. 'Mortal Sword. Bold titles, Nimander. Why, I've thought of one for each of us too – not much else to occupy my time on that endless walk. Skintick, the Blind Jester of House Dark. Do you like it?'

'You're not blind.'

'I'm not?'

'What is it you wished to talk about?' Nimander asked. 'Not silly titles, I should think.'

'That depends. This Clip proudly asserts his own, after all.'

'You do not believe him?'

A half-smile. 'Cousin, there is very little I truly believe. Beyond the oxymoronic fact that supposedly intelligent people seem to revel in being stupid. For this, I blame the chaotic tumult of emotions that devour reason as water devours snow.'

' "Emotions are the spawn of true motivations, whether those motivations be conscious or otherwise," ' said Nimander.

'The man remembers what he reads. Making him decidedly dangerous, not to mention occasionally tedious.'

'What are we to discuss?' Nimander asked, in some exasperation. 'He can claim any title he wishes – we can do nothing about it, can we?'

'Well, we can choose to follow, or not follow.'

'Even that is too late. We have followed. Into Kurald Galain, and now here. And in the time ahead, to the journey's very end.'

'To stand before Anomander Rake, yes.' Skintick gestured at the surrounding forest. 'Or we could just walk away. Leave Clip to his dramatic accounting with the Son of Darkness.'

'Where would we go, then, Skintick? We don't even know where we are. What realm is this? What world lies beyond this forest? Cousin, we have nowhere else to go.'

'Nowhere, and anywhere. In the circumstances, Nimander, the former leads to the latter, like reaching a door everyone believes barred, locked tight, and lo, it opens wide at the touch. Nowhere and anywhere are states of mind. See this forest around us? Is it a barrier, or ten thousand paths leading into mystery and wonder? Whichever you decide, the forest itself remains unchanged. It does not transform to suit your decision.'

'And where is the joke in that, cousin?'

'Laugh or cry, simple states of mind.'

'And?'

Skintick glanced away, back towards the camp. 'I find Clip . . . amusing.'

'Why does that not surprise me?'

'He has created a vast, portentous moment, the moment when he finally stands face to face with the Son of Darkness. He hears martial music, the thunder of drums, or the howl of horns sweeping round the high, swaying tower where this fated meeting no doubt will occur. He sees fear in Anomander Rake's eyes, in answer to his own fury.'

'Then he is a fool.'

'Us young folk commonly are. We should tell him.'

'Tell him what? That he is a fool?'

Skintick's smile broadened briefly, then he met Nimander's eyes once more. 'Something more subtle, I should think.'

'Such as?'

'The forest does not change.'

Now it was Nimander's turn to glance away, to squint into the greyness of dawn, the misty wreaths shrouding the ankles of the trees. *She died in my arms. Then Andarist died, bleeding out on to the cobbles. And Phaed was pulled from my hands. Thrown through a window, down to her death. I met the eyes of her killer, and saw that he had killed her . . . for me.*

The forest does not change.

'There are,' Skintick said in a low voice, 'things worth considering, Nimander. We are seven Tiste Andii, and Clip. So, eight. Wherever we now are, it is not our world. Yet, I am certain, it is the same world we have come to know, to even think of, as our own. The world of Drift Avalii, our first island prison. The world of the Malazan Empire, Adjunct Tavore, and the Isle that was our second prison. The *same* world. Perhaps this here is the very land where waits Anomander Rake – why would Clip take us through Kurald Galain to some place far from the Son of Darkness? We might find him another league onward through this forest.'

'Why not to his front door?'

Skintick grinned his pleased grin. 'Indeed, why not? In any case, Anomander Rake will not be alone. There will be other Tiste Andii with him. A community. Nimander, we have earned such a gift, haven't we?'

To that, Nimander wanted to weep. *I have earned nothing. Beyond remonstration. Condemnation. The contempt of every one of them. Of Anomander Rake himself. For all my failures, the community will judge me, and that will be that.* Self-pity tugged at him yet further, but he shook it off. For these who followed him, for Skintick and Desra and Nenanda, Kedeviss and Aranatha, yes, he could give them this last gift.

Which was not even his to give, but Clip's. *Clip, my usurper.*

'And so,' he finally said, 'we come back to the beginning. We will follow Clip, until he takes us to our people.'

'I suppose you are right,' Skintick said, as if satisfied with the circular nature of their conversation, as if something had indeed been achieved by the effort – though Nimander could not imagine what that might be.

Birdsong to awaken the sky to light, a musty warmth hinted at in the soft breaths rising from the humus. The air smelled impossibly clean. Nimander rubbed at his face, then saw Skintick's almond-shaped eyes shift their gaze to over his shoulder, and so he turned, even as a fallen branch crackled underfoot to announce someone's arrival.

Skintick raised his voice, 'Join us, cousin.'

Aranatha moved like a lost child, ever tremulous, ever diffident. Eyes widening – as they always did whenever she awakened to the outside world – she edged forward. 'I couldn't sleep,' she said. 'Nenanda was asking Clip about all sorts of things, until Desra told him to go away.'

Skintick's brows lifted. 'Desra? Stalking Clip now, is she? Well, my only surprise is that it's taken this long – not that there was much chance within Kurald Galain.'

Nimander asked her, 'Did Nenanda manage to get an explanation from Clip about where we are? And how far we still have to go?'

She continued creeping forward. The muted dawn light made her seem a thing of obsidian and silver, her long black hair glistening, her black skin faintly dusted, her silver eyes hinting of iron that never appeared. *Like some Goddess of Hope. But one whose only strength lay in an optimism immune to defeat. Immune to all reality, in fact.* 'We have emerged somewhere south of where we were supposed to. There are, Clip explained, "layers of resistance".' She shrugged. 'I don't understand what that means, but those were his words.'

Nimander briefly met Skintick's eyes, then smiled up at Aranatha. 'Did Clip say how much farther?'

'Farther than he'd hoped. Tell me, do either of you smell the sea?'

'Yes,' Nimander replied. 'Can't be far, either. East, I think.'

'We should go there – perhaps there will be villages.'

'You possess impressive reserves, Aranatha,' said Skintick.

'If it's not far . . .'

With a wry smile, Skintick straightened.

Nimander did the same.

It was simple enough to walk in the direction of the rising sun, clambering over tree-falls and skirting sinkholes. The only trails they crossed were those left by game – nothing taller than deer and so branches hung low over them – and none led to the sea. The air grew warmer, then, all at once, cooler, and ahead was the sound of wind singing through branches and leaves, and then the crashing of surf. Slanting bedrock pushed up between trees, forcing them to climb, scrambling up a sharply rising cant.

They emerged to find themselves atop a cliff of wind-scoured rock and stunted, twisted trees. The sea was before them, glittering fierce in the sun. Enormous swells rolled in, pounding the jagged, unforgiving shoreline far below. The coast to the north and the south was virtually identical as far as could be seen. Well out from shore, explosions of spume betrayed the presence of submerged reefs and shallows.

'Won't find any villages here,' Skintick said. 'I doubt we'd find much of anything, and as for skirting this coast, well, that looks to be virtually impossible. Unless, of course,' he added with a smile, 'our glorious leader can kick rock to rubble to make us a beach. Or summon winged demons to carry us over all this. Failing that, I suggest we return to our camp, burrow down into the pine needles, and go to sleep.'

No one objected, so they turned about to retrace their route.

Seeing the rage ever bridling and boiling beneath the surface of the young warrior named Nenanda was a constant comfort to Clip. This one he could work with. This one he could shape. His confidence in Nimander, on the other hand, was virtually nonexistent. The man had been thrust into a leader's role and it clearly did not suit him. Too sensitive by far, Nimander was of the type that the world and all its brutal realities usually destroyed, and it was something of a miracle that it had not yet done so. Clip had seen such pathetic creatures before; perhaps indeed it was a trait among the Tiste Andii. Centuries of life became a travail, an impossible burden. Such creatures burned out fast.

No, Nimander was not worth his time. And Nimander's closest companion, Skintick, was no better. Clip admitted he saw something of himself in Skintick – that wry mockery, the quick sarcasm – yes, other traits common among the Andii. What Skintick lacked, however, was the hard vicious core that he himself possessed in abundance.

Necessities existed. Necessities had to be recognized, and in that recognition so too must be understood all the tasks required to achieve precisely what was necessary. Hard choices were the only choices that could be deemed virtuous. Clip was well familiar with hard choices, and with the acceptable burden that was virtue. He was prepared to carry such a burden for the rest of what he anticipated would be a very, very long life.

Nenanda might well be worthy to stand at his side, through all that was to come.

Among the young women in this entourage, only Desra seemed potentially useful. Ambitious and no doubt ruthless, she could be the knife in his hidden scabbard. Besides, an attractive woman's attentions delivered their own reward, did they not? Kedeviss was too frail, broken inside just like Nimander, and Clip could already see death in her shadow. Aranatha was still a child behind those startled eyes, and perhaps always would be. No, of this entire group he had recruited from the Isle, only Nenanda and Desra were of any use to him.

He had hoped for better. After all, these were the survivors of Drift Avalii. They had stood at the side of Andarist himself, crossing blades with Tiste Edur warriors. With demons. They had tasted their share of blood, of triumph and grief. They should now be hardened veterans.

Well, he had managed with worse.

Alone for the moment, with Aranatha wandering off and probably already lost; with Nenanda, Desra and Kedeviss finally asleep; and with Nimander and Skintick somewhere in the woods – no doubt discussing portentous decisions on things relevant only to them – Clip loosened once again the chain and rings wrapped about his hand. There was a soft clink as the gleaming rings met at the ends of the dangling chain, each now spinning slowly, one counter to the other as proof of the power they held. Miniature portals appearing and disappearing, then reappearing once more, all bounded in cold metal.

The fashioning of these items had devoured most of the powers of the Andii dwelling in the subterranean fastness that was – or had been – the Andara. Leaving his kin, as it turned out, fatally vulnerable to their Letherii hunters. The cacophony of souls residing within these rings was now all that remained of those people, his pathetic family of misfits. And his to control.

Sometimes, it seemed, even when things didn't go as planned, Clip found himself reaping rewards.

Proof, yes, that I am chosen.

The chain swung, rings lifting up and out. Spun into a whine like the cries of a thousand trapped souls, and Clip smiled.

The journey from the Scour Tavern back to the New Palace skirted the ruins of the great fortress, the collapse of which had brought to an end the Pannion Domin. Unlit and now perpetually shrouded in gloom, the heaped rubble of black stone still smelled of fire and death. The ragged edge of this shattered monument was on Spinnock Durav's left as he walked the street now called Fringe Stagger. Ahead and slightly to the right rose Dragon Tower, and he could feel Silanah's crimson eyes on him from atop its great height. The regard of an Eleint was never welcome, no matter how familiar Silanah's presence among Rake's Tiste Andii.

Spinnock could well recall the last few times he had been witness to the dragon unleashed. Flames ripping through the forest that was Mott Wood, crashing down in a deluge, with a deafening concussion that drowned out every deathcry as countless unseen creatures died. Among them, perhaps a handful of Crimson Guard, a dozen or so Mott Irregulars. *Like using an axe to kill ants.*

Then, from the very heart of that fiery maelstrom, virulent sorcery lashed out, striking Silanah in a coruscating wave. Thunder hammering the air, the dragon's scream of pain. The enormous beast writhing, slashing her way free, then, trailing ropes of blood, flying back towards Moon's Spawn.

He recalled Anomander Rake's rage, and how he could hold it in his eyes like a demon chained to his will, even as he stood motionless, even as he spoke in a calm, almost bored tone. A single word, a name.

Cowl.

And with that name, oh, how the rage flared in those Draconean eyes.

There had begun, then, a hunt. The kind only a fool would choose to join. Rake, seeking out the deadliest wizard among the Crimson Guard. At one point, Spinnock remembered standing on the high ledge on the face of Moon's Spawn, watching the mage-storms fill half the northern night sky. Flashes, the knight charge of thunder through a smoke-wreathed sky. He had wondered, then, if the world was on the very edge of being torn apart, and from the depths of his soul had risen a twisted, malignant thought. *Again . . .*

When great powers strode on to the field of battle, things had a way of getting out of hand.

Had it been Cowl who first blinked? Bowing out, yielding ground, fleeing?

Or had it been the Son of Darkness?

Spinnock doubted he would ever find out. Such questions were not asked of Anomander Rake. Some time later, it was discovered by the Tiste Andii, Cowl had resurfaced, this time in Darujhistan. Causing more trouble. His stay there had been blessedly brief.

Another vision of Silanah, laying the trap for the Jaghut Tyrant in the Gadrobi Hills. More wounds, more ferocious magic. Wheeling over the ravaged plain. Five Soletaken Tiste Andii whirling round her like crows escorting an eagle.

Perhaps he was alone, Spinnock reflected, in his unease with the alliance between the Tiste Andii and the Eleint. There had been a time, after all, when Anomander Rake had warred against the pureblood dragons. When such creatures broke loose from their long-standing servitude to K'rul; when they had sought to grasp power for themselves. The motivation for Rake's opposition to them was, typically, obscure. Silanah's arrival – much later – was yet another event shrouded in mystery.

No, Spinnock Durav was far from thrilled by Silanah's bloodless regard.

He approached the arched entrance to the New Palace, ascending the flagstone ramp. There were no guards standing outside. There never were. Pushing open one of the twin doors, he strode inside. Before him, a buttressed corridor that humans would find unnaturally narrow. Twenty paces in, another archway, opening out into a spacious domed chamber with a floor of polished blackwood inset with the twenty-eight spiralling *terondai* of Mother Dark, all in black silver. The inside of the dome overhead was a mirror image. This homage to the goddess who had turned away was, to Spinnock's mind, extraordinary; appallingly out of place.

Oh, sages might well debate who had done the turning away back then, but none would dismiss the terrible vastness of the schism. Was this some belated effort at healing the ancient wound? Spinnock found that notion unfathomable. And yet, Anomander Rake himself had commissioned the *terondai*, the Invisible Sun and its whirling, wild rays of onyx flame.

If Kurald Galain had a heart in this realm's manifestation of the warren, it was here, in this chamber. Yet he felt no presence, no ghostly breath of power, as he made his way across the floor to the curling bone-white staircase. Just beyond the turn above wavered a pool of lantern light.

Two human servants were scrubbing the alabaster steps. At his arrival they ducked away.

'Mind the wet,' one muttered.

'I'm surprised,' Spinnock said as he edged past, 'there's need to clean these at all. There are all of fifteen people living in this palace.'

'You've that, sir,' the man replied, nodding.

The Tiste Andii paused and glanced back. 'Then why are you bothering? I can hardly believe the castellan set you upon this task.'

'No sir, he never did. We was just, er, bored.'

After a bemused moment, Spinnock resumed his ascent. These short-lived creatures baffled him.

The journey to the chambers where dwelt the Son of Darkness was a lengthy traverse made in solitude. Echoing corridors, unlocked, unguarded doors. The castellan's modest collection of scribes and sundry bureaucrats worked in offices on the main floor; kitchen staff, clothes-scrubbers and wringers, hearth-keepers and taper-lighters, all lived and worked in the lower levels. Here, on the higher floors, darkness ruled a realm virtually unoccupied.

Reaching the elongated room that faced the Nightwater, Spinnock Durav found his lord.

Facing the crystal window that ran the entire length of the Nightwater wall, his long silver-white hair faintly luminous in the muted, refracted light cast into the room by the faceted quartz. The sword Dragnipur was nowhere in sight.

Three steps into the chamber and Spinnock halted.

Without turning, Anomander Rake said, 'The game, Spinnock?'

'You won again, Lord. But it was close.'

'The Gate?'

Spinnock smiled wryly. 'When all else seems lost . . .'

Perhaps Anomander Rake nodded at that, or his gaze, fixed somewhere out on the waves of Nightwater, shifted downward to something closer by. A fisher boat, or the crest of some leviathan rising momentarily from the abyss. Either way, the sigh that followed was audible. 'Spinnock, old friend, it is good that you have returned.'

'Thank you, Lord. I, too, am pleased to see an end to my wandering.'

'Wandering? Yes, I imagine you might have seen it that way.'

'You sent me to a continent, Lord. Discovering the myriad truths upon it necessitated . . . fair wandering.'

'I have thought long on the details of your tale, Spinnock Durav.' Still Rake did not turn round. 'Yielding a single question. Must I journey there?'

Spinnock frowned. 'Assail? Lord, the situation there . . .'

'Yes, I understand.' At last, the Son of Darkness slowly swung about, and it seemed his eyes had stolen something from the crystal window, flaring then dimming like a memory. 'Soon, then.'

'Lord, on my last day, a league from the sea . . .'

'Yes?'

'I lost count of those I killed to reach that desolate strand. Lord, by the time I waded into the deep, enough to vanish beneath the waves, the very bay was crimson. That I lived at all in the face of that is—'

'Unsurprising,' Anomander Rake cut in with a faint smile, 'as far as your Lord is concerned.' The smile faded. 'Ah, but I have sorely abused your skills, friend.'

Spinnock could not help but cock his head and say, 'And so, I am given leave to wield soldiers of wood and stone on a wine-stained table? Day after day, my muscles growing soft, the ambition draining away.'

'Is this what you call a well-earned rest?'

'Some nights are worse than others, Lord.'

'To hear you speak of ambition, Spinnock, recalls to my mind another place, long, long ago. You and I . . .'

'Where I learned, at last,' Spinnock said, with no bitterness at all, 'my destiny.'

'Unseen by anyone. Deeds unwitnessed. Heroic efforts earning naught but one man's gratitude.'

'A weapon must be used, Lord, lest it rust.'

'A weapon overused, Spinnock, grows blunt, notched.'

To that, the burly Tiste Andii bowed. 'Perhaps, then, Lord, such a weapon must be put away. A new one found.'

'That time is yet to arrive, Spinnock Durav.'

Spinnock bowed again. 'There is, in my opinion, Lord, no time in the foreseeable future when you must journey to Assail. The madness there seems quite . . . self-contained.'

Anomander Rake studied Spinnock's face for a time, then nodded. 'Play on, my friend. See the king through. Until . . .' and he turned once more back to the crystal window.

There was no need to voice the completion of that sentence, Spinnock well knew. He bowed a third time, then walked from the chamber, closing the door behind him.

Endest Silann was slowly hobbling up the corridor. At Spinnock's appearance the old castellan glanced up. 'Ah,' he said, 'is our Lord within?'

'He is.'

The elder Tiste Andii's answering smile was no gift to Spinnock, so strained was it, a thing of sorrow and shame. And while perhaps Endest had earned the right to the first sentiment – a once powerful mage now broken – he had not to the second. Yet what could Spinnock say that might ease that burden? Nothing that would not sound trite. Perhaps something more . . . acerbic, something to challenge that self-pity—

'I must speak to him,' Endest said, reaching for the door.

'He will welcome that,' Spinnock managed.

Again the smile. 'I am sure.' A pause, a glance up into Spinnock's eyes. 'I have great news.'

'Yes?'

Endest Silann lifted the latch. 'Yes. I have found a new supplier of cadaver eels.'

'Lord of this, Son of that, it's no matter, izzit?' The man peeled the last of the rind from the fruit with his thumb-knife, then flung it out on to the cobbles. 'Point is,' he continued to his companions, 'he ain't even human, is he? Just another of 'em hoary black-skinned demons, as dead-eyed as all the rest.'

'Big on husking the world, aren't ya?' the second man at the table said, winking across at the third man, who'd yet to say a thing.

'Big on lotsa things, you better believe it,' the first man muttered, now cutting slices of the fruit and lifting each one to his mouth balanced on the blade.

The waiter drew close at that moment to edge up the wick in the lantern on the table, then vanished into the gloom once more.

The three were seated at one of the new street-side restaurants, although 'restaurant' was perhaps too noble a word for this rough line of tables and un-matched wooden chairs. The kitchen was little more than a converted cart and a stretch of canvas roof beneath which a family laboured round a grill that had once been a horse trough.

Of the four tables, three were occupied. All humans – the Tiste Andii were not wont to take meals in public, much less engage in idle chatter over steaming mugs of Bastion kelyk, a pungent brew growing in popularity in Black Coral.

'You like to talk,' the second man prodded, reaching for his cup. 'But words never dug a ditch.'

'I ain't alone in being in the right about this,' the first man retorted. 'Ain't alone at all. It's plain that if the Lord Son was dead and gone, all this damned darkness would go away, an' we'd be back to normal wi' day 'n' night again.'

'No guarantees of that,' the third man said, his tone that of someone half asleep.

'It's plain, I said. Plain, an' if you can't see that, it's your problem, not ours.'

'Ours?'

'Aye, just that.'

'Plan on sticking that rind-snicker through his heart, then?'

The second man grunted a laugh.

'They may live long,' the first man said in a low grumble, 'but they bleed like anybody else.'

'Don't tell me,' the third man said, fighting a yawn, 'you're the mastermind behind what you're talking about, Bucch.'

'Not me,' the first man, Bucch, allowed, 'but I was among the first t'give my word an' swear on it.'

'So who is?'

'Can't say. Don't know. That's how they organize these things.'

The second man was now scratching the stubble on his jaw. 'Y'know,' he ven-tured, 'it's not like there's a million of 'em, is it? Why, half the adults among us was soldiers in the Domin, or even before. And nobody took our weapons or ar-mour, did they?'

'Bigger fools them,' Bucch said, nodding. 'Arrogance like that, they should pay for, I say.'

'When's the next meeting?' the second man asked.

The third man stirred from his slouch on his chair. 'We were just off for that, Harak. You want to come along?'

As the three men rose and walked off, Seerdomin finished the last of his kelyk, waited another half-dozen heartbeats, and then rose, drawing his cloak round him, even as he reached beneath it and loosened the sword in its scabbard.

He paused, then, and formally faced north. Closing his eyes, he spoke a soft prayer.

Toll the Hounds   67

Then, walking with a careless stride, he set off, more or less in the direction the three men were taking.

High on the tower, a red-scaled dragon's eyes looked down upon all, facets reflecting scenes from every street, every alley, the flurry of activity in the markets, the women and children appearing on flat rooftops to hang laundry, figures wandering here and there between buildings. In those eyes, the city seethed.

Somewhere, beyond Night, the sun unleashed a morning of brazen, heady heat. It gave form to the smoke of hearth fires in the makeshift camps alongside the beaten tracks wending down from the north, until the pilgrims emerged to form an unbroken line on the trails, and then it lit into bright gold a serpent of dust that rode the winds all the way to the Great Barrow.

The destitute among them carried shiny shells collected from shoreline and tidal pools, or polished stones or nuggets of raw copper. The better off carried jewellery, gem-studded scabbards, strips of rare silk, Delantine linen, Daru councils of silver and gold, loot collected from corpses on battlefields, locks of hair from revered relatives and imagined heroes, or any of countless other items of value. Now within a day's march of the Great Barrow, the threat of bandits and thieves had vanished, and the pilgrims sang as they walked towards the vast, descended cloud of darkness to the south.

Beneath that enormous barrow of treasure, they all knew, lay the mortal remains of the Redeemer.

Protected for ever more by Night and its grim, silent sentinels.

The serpent of dust journeyed, then, to a place of salvation.

Among the Rhivi of North Genabackis, there was a saying. *A man who stirs awake the serpent is a man without fear. A man without fear has forgotten the rules of life.*

Silanah heard their songs and prayers.

And she watched.

Sometimes mortals did indeed forget. Sometimes, mortals needed . . . reminding.

Chapter Three

And he knew to stand there
Would be a task unforgiving
Relentless as sacrifices made
And blood vows given
He knew enough to wait alone
Before the charge of fury's heat
The chants of vengeance
Where swords will meet
And where once were mortals
Still remain dreams of home
If but one gilded door
Could be pried open.
Did he waste breath in bargain
Or turn aside on the moment
Did he smile in pleasure
Seeking chastisement?

(See him still, he stands there
While you remain, unforgiving
The poet damns you
The artist cries out
The one who weeps
Turns his face away
Your mind is crowded
By the inconsequential
Listing the details
Of the minuscule
And every measure
Of what means nothing
To anyone

He takes from you every rage
Every crime . . .
Whether you like it
Or you do not . . .
Sacrifices made
Vows given
He stands alone

Because none of you dare
Stand with him)

FISHER'S CHALLENGE TO HIS LISTENERS,
BREAKING THE TELLING OF
THE MANE OF CHAOS

On this morning, so fair and fresh with the warm breeze coming down off the lake, there were arrivals. Was a city a living thing? Did it possess eyes? Could its senses be lit awake by the touch of footsteps? Did Darujhistan, on that fine morning, look in turn upon those who set their gazes upon it? Arrivals, grand and modest, footsteps less than a whisper, whilst others trembled to the very bones of the Sleeping Goddess. Were such things the beat of the city's heart?

But no, cities did not possess eyes, or any other senses. Cut stone and hardened plaster, wood beams and corniced façades, walled gardens and quiescent pools beneath trickling fountains, all was insensate to the weathering traffic of its denizens. A city could know no hunger, could not rise from sleep, nor even twist uneasy in its grave.

Leave such things, then, to a short rotund man, seated at a table at the back of the Phoenix Inn, in the midst of an expansive breakfast, to pause with a mouth crammed full of pastry and spiced apple, to suddenly choke. Eyes bulging, face flushing scarlet, then launching a spray of pie across the table, into the face of a regretfully hungover Meese, who, now wearing the very pie she had baked the day before, simply lifted her bleary gaze and settled a basilisk regard upon the hacking, wheezing man opposite her.

If words were necessary, then, she would have used them.

The man coughed on, tears streaming from his eyes.

Sulty arrived with a cloth and began wiping, gently, the mess from a motionless, almost statuesque Meese.

On the narrow, sloped street to the right of the entrance to Quip's Bar, the detritus of last night's revelry skirled into the air on a rush of wild wind. Where a moment before there had been no traffic of any sort on the cobbled track, now there were screaming, froth-streaked horses, hoofs cracking like iron mallets on the uneven stone. Horses – two, four, six – and behind them, in a half-sideways rattling skid, an enormous carriage, its back end crashing into the face of a building in a shattering explosion of plaster, awning and window casement. Figures flew from the careering monstrosity as it tilted, almost tipping, then righted itself with the sound of a house falling over. Bodies were thumping on to the street, rolling desperately to avoid the man-high wheels.

The horses plunged on, dragging the contraption some further distance down the slope, trailing broken pieces, plaster fragments and other more unsightly things, before the animals managed to slow, then halt, the momentum, aided in no small part by a sudden clenching of wooden brakes upon all six wheels.

Perched atop the carriage, the driver was thrown forward, sailing through the air well above the tossing heads of the horses, landing in a rubbish cart almost buried in the fete's leavings. This refuse probably saved his life, although, as all grew still once more, only the soles of his boots were visible, temporarily motionless as befitted an unconscious man.

Strewn in the carriage's wake, amidst mundane detritus, were human remains in various stages of decay; some plump with rotting flesh, others mere skin stretched over bone. A few of these still twitched or groped aimlessly on the cobbles, like the plucked limbs of insects. Jammed into the partly crushed wall of the shop the conveyance's rear right-side corner had clipped was a corpse's head, driven so deep as to leave visible but one eye, a cheek and one side of the jaw. The eye rolled ponderously. The mouth twitched, as if words were struggling to escape, then curled in an odd smile.

Those more complete figures, who had been thrown in all directions, were now slowly picking themselves up, or, in the case of two of them, not moving at all – and by the twist of limbs and neck it was clear that never again would their unfortunate owners move of their own accord, not even to draw breath.

From a window on the second level of a tenement, an old woman leaned out for a brief glance down on the carnage below, then retreated, hands snapping closed the wooden shutters.

Clattering sounds came from within the partly ruined shop, then a muted shriek that was not repeated within the range of human hearing, although in the next street over a dog began howling.

The carriage door squealed open, swung once on its hinges, then fell off, landing with a rattle on the cobbles.

On her hands and knees fifteen paces away, Shareholder Faint lifted her aching head and gingerly turned it towards the carriage, in time to see Master Quell lunge into view, tumbling like a Rhivi doll on to the street. Smoke drifted out in his wake.

Closer to hand, Reccanto Ilk stood, reeling, blinking stupidly around before his eyes lit on the battered sign above the door to Quip's Bar. He staggered in that direction.

Faint pushed herself upright, brushed dust from her meat-spattered clothes, and scowled as scales of armour clinked down like coins on to the stones. From one such breach in her hauberk she prised loose a taloned finger, which she peered at for a moment, then tossed aside as she set out after Reccanto.

Before she reached the door she was joined by Sweetest Sufferance, the short, plump woman waddling but determined none the less as both her small hands reached out for the taproom's door.

From the rubbish cart, Glanno Tarp was digging himself free.

Master Quell, on his hands and knees, looked up, then said, 'This isn't our street.'

Ducking into the gloom of Quip's Bar, Faint paused briefly until she heard a commotion at the far end, where Reccanto had collapsed into a chair, one arm sweeping someone's leavings from the table. Sweetest Sufferance dragged up another chair and thumped down on it.

The three drunks who were the other customers watched Faint walk across the room, each of them earning a scowl from her.

Quip Younger – whose father had opened this place in a fit of ambition and optimism that had lasted about a week – was shambling over from the bar the same way his old man used to, and reached the table the same time as Faint.

No one spoke.

The keep frowned, then turned round and made his way back to the bar.

Master Quell arrived, along with Glanno Tarp, still stinking of refuse.

Moments later, the four shareholders and one High Mage navigator of the Trygalle Trade Guild sat round the table. No exchange of glances. No words.

Quip Younger – who had once loved Faint, long before anyone ever heard of the Trygalle Trade Guild and long before she hooked up with this mad lot – delivered five tankards and the first pitcher of ale.

Five trembling hands reached for those tankards, gripping them tight.

Quip hesitated; then, rolling his eyes, he lifted the pitcher and began pouring out the sour, cheap brew.

Kruppe took a mouthful of the dark magenta wine – a council a bottle, no less – and swirled it in his mouth until all the various bits of pie were dislodged from the innumerable crevasses between his teeth, whereupon he leaned to one side and spat on to the floor. 'Ah.' He smiled across at Meese. 'Much better, yes?'

'I'll take payment for that bottle right now,' she said. 'That way I can leave before I have to witness one more abuse of such an exquisite vintage.'

'Why, has Kruppe's credit so swiftly vanished? Decided entirely upon an untoward breaking of fast this particular morning?'

'It's the insults, you fat pig, piled one on another until it feels I'm drowning in offal.' She bared her teeth. 'Offal in a red waistcoat.'

'Aaii, vicious jab. Kruppe is struck to the heart . . . and,' he added, reaching once more for the dusty bottle, 'has no choice but to loosen said constricture of the soul with yet another tender mouthful.'

Meese leaned forward. 'If you spit that one out, Kruppe, I will wring your neck.'

He hastily swallowed, then gasped. 'Kruppe very nearly choked once more. Such a morning! Portents and pastry, wails and wine!'

Heavy steps descending from the upper floor.

'Ah, here comes yon Malazan saviour. Mallet, dear friend of Kruppe, will Murillio – sweet Prince of Disenchantment – recover to his fullest self? Come, join me in this passing ferment. Meese, sweet lass, will you not find Mallet a goblet?'

Her eyes narrowed into thin slits. 'How about one for yourself, Kruppe?'

'Delightful suggestion.' Kruppe wiped at the bottle's mouth with one grimy sleeve, then beamed across at her.

She rose, stalked off.

The Malazan healer sat down with a heavy sigh, closed his eyes and rubbed vigorously at his round, pallid face, then looked round the bar. 'Where is everyone?'

'Your companion of the night just past Kruppe has sent home, with the assurance that your self is safe from all harm. 'Tis dawn, friend, or rather morning's fresh stumping on dawn's gilt heels. Ships draw in alongside berths, gangplanks clatter and thump to form momentous bridges from one world to the next. Roads take sudden turns and out trundle macabre mechanisms scattering bits of flesh like dark seeds of doom! Hooded eyes scan strangers, shrikes cry out above the lake's steaming flats, dogs scratch vigorously behind the ears – ah, Meese has brought us her finest goblets! A moment, whilst Kruppe sweeps out cobwebs, insect husks and other assorted proofs of said goblets' treasured value – there, now, let us sit back and watch, with pleased eyes, as Meese fills our cups to brimming glory. Why—'

'For Hood's sake,' Mallet cut in, 'it's too early for your company, Kruppe. Let me drink this wine and then escape with my sanity, I beg you.'

'Why, friend Mallet, we await your assessment of Murillio's physical state.'

'He'll live. But no dancing for a week or two.' He hesitated, frowning down into his goblet, as if surprised to find it suddenly empty once more. 'Assuming he comes out of his funk, that is. A mired mind can slow the body's recovery. Can reverse it, in fact.'

'Fret not over Murillio's small but precise mind, friend,' Kruppe said. 'Such matters ever find solution through Kruppe's wise ministrations. Does Coll remain at bedside?'

Mallet nodded, set the goblet down and rose. 'I'm going home.' He glowered across at Kruppe. 'And with Oponn's pull, I might even get there.'

'Nefarious nuisances thrive best in night's noisome chaos, dear healer. Kruppe confidently assures you a most uneventful return to your atypical abode.'

Mallet grunted, then said, 'And how do you plan on assuring that?'

'Why, with worthy escort, of course!' He poured himself the last of the wine and smiled up at the Malazan. 'See yon door and illimitable Irilta positioned before it? Dastardly contracts seeking your sad deaths cannot indeed be permitted. Kruppe extends his formidable resources to guarantee your lives!'

The healer continued staring down at him. 'Kruppe, do you know who offered this contract?'

'Ringing revelations are imminent, treasured friend. Kruppe promises.'

Another grunt, then Mallet wheeled and walked towards the door and his escort, who stood smiling with brawny arms crossed.

Kruppe watched them leave and weren't they just quite the pair.

Meese slouched down in the chair Mallet had vacated. 'Guild contract,' she muttered. 'Could simply be some imperial cleaning up, you know. New embassy's now up and running after all. Could be somebody in it caught word of Malazan deserters running a damned bar. Desertion's a death sentence, ain't it?'

'Too great a risk, sweet Meese,' Kruppe replied, drawing out his silk handkerchief and blotting at his brow. 'The Malazan Empire, alas, has its own assassins,
of which two are present in said embassy. Yet, by all accounts, 'twas a Hand of
Krafar's Guild that made the attempt last night.' He raised a pudgy finger. 'A mystery, this one who so seeks the death of inoffensive Malazan deserters, but not a
mystery for long, oh no! Kruppe will discover all that needs discovering!'

'Fine,' Meese said, 'now discover that council, Kruppe, for the bottle.'

Sighing, Kruppe reached into the small purse strapped to his belt, probed
within the leather pouch, then, brows lifted in sudden dismay: 'Dearest Meese,
yet another discovery . . .'

Grainy-eyed, Scorch scowled at the teeming quayside. 'It's the morning fisher
boats,' he said, 'comin' in right now. Ain't no point in hangin' round, Leff.'

'People on the run will be coming here early,' Leff pointed out, scooping out
with his knife the freshwater conch he had purchased a moment ago. He slithered
down a mouthful of white, gleaming meat. 'T'be waitin' for the first ships in from
Gredfallan. Midmorning, right? The new locks at Dhavran have made it all regular,
predictable, I mean. A day through with a final scoot to Gredfallan, overnight there,
then on with the dawn to here. Desperate folk line up first, Scorch, cause they're
desperate.'

'I hate sitting anywhere my feet have to dangle,' Scorch complained, shifting
uncomfortably on the stack of crates.

'Decent line of sight,' Leff said. 'I'll join ya up there anon.'

'Don't know how you can eat that. Meat should have blood in it. Any meat
without blood in it ain't meat.'

'Aye, it's conch.'

'It's a thing with eyes on the ends of its tentacles, watching as you cut its body
apart – see how the stalks swivel, following up to your mouth, tracking every
swallow? It's watching you eat it!'

'So what?'

Seagulls shrieked in swarming clouds over the low jetties where the fishers
were heaving baskets of sliverfish on to the slimy stone, children scurrying about
in the hopes of being hired to slip the wriggling fish on to monger-strings in time
for the morning market. Grey-backed Gadrobi cats, feral now for a thousand generations, leapt out in ambush to kill gulls. Frenzied battles ensued, feathers skirling, tufts of cat hair drifting on the breeze like thistle heads.

Below the inside docks old women wandered in the gloom between pylons, using long, thin, barbed pokers to collect up the small, hand's-length sliverfish that
managed to slip through the baskets and fall in gleaming rain as the catch was
carried ashore. When the harvest was small, the old hags were wont to use those
toothed pokers on each other.

Scorch could see them from where he was perched, muffled forms moving this
way and that, pokers darting in the perpetual shadows. 'I swore to never again eat
anything this lake gave up,' he muttered. 'Gran above,' he added in a hoarse whisper,

'y'see I remember them cuts an' holes in your scrawny arms. I remember 'em, Gran, an' so I swore.'

'What's that?' Leff asked from below.

'Nothing, only we're wasting our time—'

'Patience, Scorch. We got us a list. We got us trouble. Didn't we hear that Brokul might be making a run?'

'The place is a damned mob, Leff.'

'We just need to concentrate on the lines forming up.'

'Ain't no lines, Leff.'

Leff tossed the shell over the end of the lake wall, where it clattered down below on to ten thousand others. 'Not yet,' he said. 'Soon.'

Just past the fork at Urs, the battered remnants of the caravan headed up towards South Worrytown. Herders and quarry workers on their way out to the Ravens edged to the sides of the road, then stopped and stared at the four charred and smoke-streaked trader-wagons rocking past. A single horse struggled in a makeshift yoke before each wain.

Of the usual assortment of guards that might be expected, even for a caravan as small as this one seemed to be, only one was visible, slouched down in a Gadrobi saddle and almost entirely hidden beneath a dusty, hooded cloak. From seamed slits in the faded brown cape, just above the man's shoulder blades, jutted the worn grips and pommels of twin cutlasses. The leather gauntlets covering his hands where they rested on the high saddle horn were stained and mostly in shreds, revealing to those close enough to see skin tattooed to very nearly solid black.

From the shadow of the hood, strangely feline eyes held fixed on the road ahead. The first decrepit shanties of South Worrytown emerged from the morning mist like the dishevelled nests of some oversized carrion bird, lining the dirt track to either side. From cracks and holes in the leaning walls, liquid eyes peered out as the guard led his clattering train past.

Before long, they were well and truly within the maze and its crowds of life's refugees, rising like ghosts from the shadows, raising faint voices to beg for coin and food. Few caravans coming up from the south chose this route into Darujhistan, since the track through the city's shabby outskirts was both narrow and twisting. And those that proved insufficiently defended could become victims of the raw, desperate need drawing ever closer on all sides.

A hundred paces still south of the main road known as Jatem's Worry, it seemed that such a fate would befall this hapless caravan and its guardian of one.

As grasping, grimy hands reached out to close round spokes in wagon wheels, and others snatched at the traces of the horses, the hooded man glanced back at the growing boldness and reined in. As he did so he seemed to suddenly fill out as he straightened in his saddle.

Eyes fixed on him, furtive and wary and with fading diffidence. One rag-clad man swung up beside the first wagon's driver who, like the guard, was hooded and wrapped in a leather cape. As the Worrier clutched the driver's shoulder and yanked him round, the hood fell back.

Revealing a dead man's withered face. The mostly hairless head turned, hollow sockets settling on the man crouched on the bench.

Even as the Worrier shrieked, twisting to fling himself from the wagon, the lone caravan guard drew his cutlasses, revealing broad iron blades stained in a pattern of flaring barbs of black and pale orange. The hood dropped back to unveil a broad face tattooed in an identical fashion, the mouth opening to reveal long canines as the guard smiled. There was no humour in that smile, just the promise of mayhem.

That was enough for the crowd. Screaming, flinching back, they fled.

Moments later, the four wagons and their lone guard resumed their journey.

On to Jatem's Worry, edging into the traffic slowly working towards the city gate, where the lone, tattooed guard resheathed his weapons.

The unhooded corpse guiding the lead wagon seemed disinclined to readjust its head covering, and before too long the lifeless driver acquired a flapping, squawking escort of three crows, each fighting to find purchase on the grey, tattered pate. By the time the caravan reached the gate, the driver sported one crow on its head and one on each shoulder, all busy tearing strips of desiccated meat from its face.

A gate-watcher stepped out to squint up at the barbed, bestial guard as he drew rein beneath the arch.

'Gruntle, ain't it? You been in a fight, man. Is this Sirik's caravan – gods below!' This last cry announced the watcher's discovery of the first wagon driver.

'Best just let us past,' Gruntle said in a low, rasping voice. 'I'm in no mood for more than one conversation, and that one belongs to Sirik. I take it he's done his move into his new estate?'

The man nodded, his face pale and his eyes a little wild. Stepping back, he waved Gruntle on.

The journey to Sirik's estate was blessedly brief. Past Despot's Barbican, then left, skirting High Gallows Hill before reaching the freshly plastered wall and broad, high-arched gate leading into the merchant's compound.

Word must have gone in advance for Sirik himself stood waiting, shaded from the morning sun by a servant with a parasol. A half-dozen armoured men from his private bodyguard were clustered round him. The merchant's expression descended in swift collapse upon seeing a mere four wagons roll into the compound. Curses rode the dusty air from the guards when they spied the first driver, whose centre crow at that moment decided to half spread its wings to regain balance as the withered hands twitched the traces, halting the wagon.

Gruntle reined in and slowly dismounted.

Sirik waved his hands in a helpless gesture. 'But – but—'

Drawing off his cloak revealed the damage on Gruntle's chain hauberk, the slashes through the black iron links, the gouges and punctures, the crusted blood. 'Dwell raiders,' he said in a rumble, grinning once more.

'But—'

'We gave good account,' Gruntle resumed, squinting at the guards behind the merchant. 'And if you'd let loose a few more of your precious preeners there, we might ha'done better still. The raiding party was a big one, a hundred shrieking savages. The fools torched the other wagons even as they looted 'em.'

One of the bodyguard, Sirik's scar-faced captain, stepped forward, scowling at the wagons. 'A hundred, was it? Against what, eight guards under your command, Gruntle? Do you take us for idiots? A hundred Dwell and you'd not be here.'

'No, Kest, you're not an idiot,' Gruntle allowed. 'Thick-skulled and a bully, but not an idiot.'

As the captain and his men bridled, Sirik held up a trembling hand. 'Gruntle, Gisp sits that wagon but he's dead.'

'He is. So are the other three.'

'But – but how?'

Gruntle's shrug was an ominous roll of his massive shoulders. 'Not sure,' he admitted, 'but they took my orders anyway – granted, I was desperate and yelling things I normally wouldn't, but by then I was the last one left, and with four surviving wagons and as many horses . . .' He shrugged again, then said, 'I'll take my pay now, Sirik. You've got half the Bastion kelyk you wanted and that's better than none.'

'And what am I to do with four undead drivers!' Sirik shrieked.

Gruntle turned, glared up at Gisp. 'Go to Hood, you four. Now.'

The drivers promptly slumped, sliding or tottering from their perches. The three crows picking at Gisp's shredded face set up an indignant squall, then flapped down to resume their meal once the body settled on the dust of the compound.

Sirik had recovered enough to show irritation. 'As for payment—'

'In full,' Gruntle cut in. 'I warned you we didn't have enough. Kest may not be an idiot, but you are, Sirik. And sixteen people died for it, not to mention a hundred Dwell. I'm about to visit the Guild, as required. I get my pay in full and I'll keep my opinions to myself. Otherwise . . .' Gruntle shook his head, 'you won't be hiring any more caravan guards. Ever again.'

Sirik's sweat-sheathed face worked for a time, until his eyes found a look of resignation. 'Captain Kist, pay the man.'

A short time later, Gruntle stepped out on to the street. Pausing, he glanced up at the morning sky, then set out for home. Despite the heat, he donned his cloak and drew up the hood once more. The damned markings on his skin rose flush with battle, and took weeks to fade back into a ghostly tint. In the meantime, the less conspicuous he could make himself the better. He suspected that the hovel he called home was already barricaded by a murder of acolytes awaiting his return. The tiger-skinned woman who proclaimed herself High Priestess of the local temple would have heard the fierce battle cry of Trake's Mortal Sword, even at a distance of thirty or so leagues out on the Dwelling Plain. And she would be in a frenzy . . . again, desperate as ever for his attention.

But Gruntle didn't give a damn about her and the mangy losers she'd gathered to her temple. Killing those raiders had not been a task he had welcomed. No pleasure in spilling blood, no delight in his own savage rage. He'd lost friends that day, including the last pair who had been with him ever since Capustan. Such wounds were far deeper than those his flesh still carried, and they would take much longer to heal.

Mood foul despite the bulging purse of councils at his belt, he was disinclined to suffer the normal jostling necessary to navigate the city's major avenues and streets – one push or snarl too many and he'd be likely to draw blades and set about carving a path through the crowds, and then he'd have no choice but to flee Darujhistan or risk dangling from High Gallows Hill – and so once through the Estates Gate just south of Borthen Park, and down the ramp into Lakefront District, Gruntle took a roundabout route, along narrow, twisting alleys and rubbish-filled wends between buildings.

The few figures he met as he walked were quick to edge aside, as if struck meek by some instinct of self-preservation.

He turned on to one slightly wider track only to find it blocked by a tall carriage that looked as if it had been through a riot – reminding Gruntle that the fete was still on – although, as he drew closer and found himself stepping over withered, dismembered limbs and streaks of slowly drying blood, and when he saw the gaping hole in the carriage where a door should have been, with the dark interior still and grey with motionless haze, and the horses standing with hides crusted in dried sweat and froth – the entire mess unattended and seemingly immune to looting – he recognized that this was one of those damned Trygalle Guild carriages, well and truly infamous for sudden, inexplicable and invariably violent arrivals.

Just as irritating, the Trygalle was a clear rival to the city's own Caravanserai Guild, with its unprecedented shareholding system. Something the Caravanserai should have thought of long ago, although if what Gruntle had heard was anywhere near the truth, then the attrition rate among the Trygalle's shareholders was appallingly high – higher than any sane guard would accept.

Then again, he reconsidered, here he was, the lone survivor of Sirik's caravan, and despite the councils he now carried his financial return was virtually nothing compared to the profits Sirik would harvest from the kelyk, especially now that he didn't have to pay his drivers. Of course, he'd need to purchase new wagons and repair the ones Gruntle had delivered, but there was insurance to offset some of that.

As he edged round the carriage in the street, he was afforded a closer look, concluding, sourly, that the Trygalle built the bastards to weather just about anything. Scorched, gouged as if by the talons of plains bears, bitten and chopped at, gaudy paint peeled away as if splashed with acid. As battered as a war wagon.

He walked past the horses. Then, five strides onward, Gruntle turned about in surprise. That close and the beasts should have panicked – they *always* panicked. Even ones he had broken to his scent shivered uncontrollably beneath him until sheer nervous exhaustion dulled their fright. But here . . . he scowled, meeting the eyes of one of the leaders and seeing naught but jaded disinterest.

Shaking his head, Gruntle resumed his journey.

Damned curious. Then again, he could do with a horse like one of those.

Better yet, how about a dead one? Dead as Gisp?

The thought brought him back to certain unpleasantries he didn't much want to think about at the moment. *Like my being able to command the dead.*

He was, he considered, too old to be discovering new talents.

The walrus-skin coracle bobbed perilously in the chop between two trader barges, at risk of being crushed between them before a frantic scull by the lone occupant squirted the craft through, to draw up moments later alongside a mud-smeared landing crowded with crayfish traps. The man who clambered up from the coracle was soaked from the hips down, and the knapsack he slung on to one shoulder sloshed, then began to drain incontinently as he worked his way up the dock to the worn stone steps that climbed to the quayside.

He was unkempt, his beard two or three days old, and the leathers he wore seemed a strange mix of those normally worn beneath armour and those a Nathii fisher might wear in a squall. The floppy sealskin hat covering his head was misshapen, sun-faded and salt-rimed. In addition to his knapsack he carried an odd-looking scimitar in a split scabbard bound together by frayed strips of leather. The serpent-head pommel revealed empty sockets where gems had once resided for eyes, fangs and collar. Tall, wiry, he moved with a vaguely furtive haste once he reached the quay, cutting through the crowds towards one of the feeder alleys on the other side of Front Street.

From the landing down on the water, someone was yelling, demanding to know who had left a half-awash coracle beside his cages.

Reaching the alley mouth, the man walked in a few paces, then paused in the shadow between the high-walled warehouses. He drew off his floppy hat and wiped the grime from his brow. His black hair, while thinning from the front, hung in a long ponytail that had been tucked up beneath the hat but now fell to the small of his back. His forehead and face were seamed in scars, and most of his left ear was missing, slashed away some time past. Scratching a moment at his beard, he settled the hat back on, and headed off down the alley.

He was set upon less than ten paces later, as two figures closed on him from alcoves, one to either side. The one on his left jammed the point of a dagger against his ribs, while the other waved a short sword in front of his eyes, using it to direct the man against a grimy wall.

Mute, the man complied. In the gloom he squinted at the one with the sword, then scowled. 'Leff.'

A stained grin. 'Hey, old partner, fancy you showing up.'

The one with the knife snorted. 'Thought we'd never spy you out wi' that stupid hat, did you?'

'Scorch! Why, I can't tell you how glad I am to see you both. Gods below, I would've thought you two would have met grisly ends long ago. But this is a great discovery, friends! Had I any coin – any at all – why, I'd buy you both a drink—'

'Enough of that,' Leff said in a growl, still waving the sword in front of the man's face. 'You're on our list, Torvald Nom. Aye, way down on it since most people figured you were long gone and almost as long dead. But you ran out on a debt – a big one and bigger now, aye – not to mention running out on me and Scorch—'

'Hardly! I seem to recall we formally absolved our partnership, after that night when—'

Scorch hissed, 'Quiet, damn you! Nobody knows nothing about none of that!'

'My point was,' Torvald hastily explained, 'I never ran out on you two.'

'Don't matter,' Leff said, 'since that ain't why you're on the list now, is it?'

'You two must be desperate, to take on one of those—'

'Maybe we are,' said Scorch, 'and maybe we ain't. Now, you saying you're broke is bad news, Torvald. For you more'n us, since we now got to deliver you. And my, won't Lender Gareb be pleased.'

'Wait! I can get that money – I can clear that debt. But I need time—'

'No time to give ya,' Leff said, shaking his head. 'Sorry, old friend.'

'One night, that's all I'm asking.'

'One night, for you to run as far as you can.'

'No, I swear it. Gods, I've just returned! Here to honour all my debts!'

'Really, and how are you planning to do that?'

'Best leave the details to me, Scorch, just to keep you and Leff innocent. Now, I'm way down on that list – I'd have to be, since it's been years. That means nobody's expecting you to come up with me, right? Give me a night, just one, that's all I'm asking. We can meet again right here, this time tomorrow. I won't run out on you two, I promise.'

'You must think we're idiots,' Leff said.

'Listen, once I've cleared Gareb's debt, I can help you. With that list. Who's better than me at that kind of stuff?'

Scorch's disbelieving expression stretched his face until it seemed his eyes would fall out of their sockets. He licked his lips, shot Leff a glance.

Torvald Nom saw all this and nodded. 'Aye, you two are in trouble, all right. Those lists chew up whoever takes 'em on. I must tell you, I'm amazed and, well, deeply disappointed to find that you two have sunk that far since I left. Gods, if I'd known, well, I might've considered staying—'

Leff snorted. 'Now that's a damned lie.'

'All right, perhaps an exaggeration. So what is Gareb saying I'm owing him now?'

'A thousand silver councils.'

Torvald Nom gaped, the colour leaving his face. 'For Hood's sake, he just bought me a supper and a pitcher or two! And even then, I figured he was simply being generous. Wanted me to do some work for him or something. I was insulted when he sent me a bill for that night—'

'Interest, Torvald,' said Leff. 'You know how it is.'

'Besides,' added Scorch, 'you just up and ran. Where ya been all this time?'

'You'd never believe me.'

'Is that shackle scars on your wrists?'

'Aye, and worse. Nathii slave pens. Malazan slavers – all the way to Seven Cities. Beru fend, my friends, none of it was pretty. And as for the long journey back, why, if I was a bard I'd make a fortune spinning that tale!'

The sword hovering in front of his face had wavered, dipped, and now finally fell away, while the knife point jabbing his ribs eased back. Torvald looked quickly into both faces before him, and said, 'One night, old friends, and all this will be cleared up. And I can start helping you with that list.'

'We already got us help,' Leff said, although he didn't seem pleased by that admission.

'Oh? Who?'

'Kruppe. Remember him?'

'That oily, fat fence always hanging out at the Phoenix Inn? Are you two mad?'

Scorch said, 'It's our new taproom, Torvald, ever since Bormen threw us out for—'

'Don't tell him stuff like that, Scorch!'

'One night,' Torvald said, nodding. 'Agreed? Good, you won't regret it.'

Stepping back, Leff sheathed his short sword. 'I already do. Listen, Torvald. You run and we'll chase you, no matter where you go. You can jump straight back into the Nathii slave pens and we'll be there right beside you. You understanding me?'

Torvald frowned at the man for a moment, then nodded. 'That I do, Leff. But I'm back, now, and I'm not going anywhere, not ever again.'

'One night.'

'Aye. Now, you two better head back to watching the quay – who knows who might be readying to flee on the next outbound ship.'

Both men suddenly looked nervous. Leff gave Torvald a push as he worked past, Scorch on his heels. Torvald watched them scurry to the alley mouth, then plunge into the crowd on Front Street.

'How is it,' he asked under his breath, of no one, 'that complete idiots just live on, and on? And on?'

He adjusted his Moranth raincape, making certain that none of the items secreted in the underside pockets had been jostled loose or, gods forbid, broken. Nothing dripping. No burning sensations, no slithering presence of . . . whatever. *Good.* Tugging down his floppy hat, he set off once more.

This thing with Gareb was damned irritating. Well, he'd just have to do something about it, wouldn't he? *One night. Fine. So be it. The rest can wait.*

I hope.

Born in the city of One Eye Cat twenty-seven years ago, Humble Measure was of mixed blood. A Rhivi woman, sold to a local merchant in exchange for a dozen bars of quenched iron, gave birth to a bastard son a year later. Adopted into his father's household eight years on, the boy was apprenticed in the profession of iron-mongery and would have inherited the enterprise if not for one terrible night when his sheltered, stable world ended.

A foreign army had arrived, investing the city in a siege. Days and nights of high excitement for the young man, then, with the streets aflame with rumours of the glory promised by the city's membership in the great, rich Malazan Empire – if only the fools in the palace would capitulate. His father's eyes had glowed with that imagined promise, and no doubt it was on the rising tide of such visions that the elderly trader conspired with agents of the Empire to open the city gates one night – an attempt that ended in catastrophic failure, with the merchant suffering arrest and then execution, and his estate invaded by city garrison soldiers with swords drawn.

That assault had left nightmare memories that would never leave Humble Measure. Witnessing his mother's rape and murder, and that of his half-sisters. Screams, smoke and blood, everywhere blood, like the bitter gift of some dark god – oh, he would remember that blood. Beaten and in chains, he had been dragged into the street and would have suffered the same fate as the others if not for the presence of a mercenary company allied with the city. Its commander, a tall, fierce warrior named Jorrick Sharplance, had taken command of the handful of surviving prisoners.

That company was subsequently driven from One Eye Cat by the city's paranoid rulers, sailing out on ships across Old King Lake, shortly before yet another act of treachery proved more successful than the first attempt. Another night of slaughter, this time at the bloodied hands of Claw assassins, and One Eye Cat fell to the Malazan Empire.

Jorrick Sharplance had taken his prisoners with him, setting them free on the wild south shore of the lake, at the very feet of One Eye Range, with sufficient supplies to take them through the mountain passes on to the Old King Plateau. From there, Humble Measure had led his household's survivors, slaves and free citizens alike, down the trader tracks to the city of Bear. A brief stay there, then southward to Patch and on to the Rhivi Trail.

A short stay in Pale, until, fleeing yet another Malazan siege, down to Darujhistan in the midst of a decrepit column of refugees.

Whereupon Humble Measure had settled in the last surviving office of his father's business, there to begin a long, careful rebuilding process that honed his tactical skills and, indeed, his fortitude.

Such a long, fraught journey had ensured the loyalty of his staff. The slaves were rewarded with emancipation, and not one refused his offer of employment. His trade in iron burgeoned. For a time, it seemed that the curse that was the Malazan Empire might well track him down once more, but there had been a gift, a gift of blood that he well understood now, and the city's life had been spared.

For how long? Humble Measure was well acquainted with how the Empire got things done. Infiltration, clever acts of destabilization, assassinations, the fomenting of panic and the dissolution of order. That they now had an embassy in the city was no more than a means of bringing their deadly agents into Darujhistan. Well, he was done running.

His father's ancestors had traded in iron for twelve generations. Here in the office in the Gadrobi District of Darujhistan, in the vaults far below street level, he had found written records reaching back almost six hundred years. And among the most ancient of those vellum scrolls, Humble Measure had made a discovery.

Darujhistan would not fall to the Malazan Empire – he had found the means to ensure that. To ensure, indeed, that no foreign power could ever again threaten the city he now called home, ever again endanger his family, his loved ones.

To achieve this, Humble Measure well understood that he would need all his acumen in bringing complicated plans to fruition. He would need vast sums of coin, which he now had at his disposal. And, alas, he would need to be ruthless.

Unpleasant, yes, but a necessary sacrifice.

The central office of Eldra Iron Mongers was a sprawling collection of buildings, warehouses and work yards just north of Two-Ox Gate. The entire complex was walled and virtually self-contained. Three sets of forges fronted an elongated, single-storey foundry resting against the west wall. Beneath it ran a subterranean stream that provided outflow into the Maiten River, the effluent and wastes issuing from that stream giving the bay beyond its name of Brownrun, and most days the stain spread out far on to Lake Azure, an unfortunate consequence of working iron, as he said often to city officials when the complaints of the Gadrobi fishers grew too strident to ignore. Offers of recompense usually sufficed to silence such objections, and as for the faintly bitter irony Humble Measure felt when paying out these sums – an irony founded on the cold fact that iron was needed by all, the demand unending, from fishhooks to gaffs to armour and swords – well, he wisely kept that to himself.

The administration building rose against the south wall of the compound, both office and residence. Staff quarters dominated the wing nearest the south end of the foundry. The central block housed the records and clerical chambers. The final wing was the oldest part of the structure, its foundations dating back to an age when bronze was the primary metal, and civilization was still a raw promise. Far beneath the ground level of this wing, ancient stairs wound down through layers of limestone, opening out on to a succession of rough-hewn vaults that had been used as storage rooms for generations. Long before such mundane usage, Humble Measure suspected, these crypts had held a darker purpose.

He had recently converted one such chamber into a secret office, wherein he could work alone, protected by a skein of long-dormant wards, and here he would remain for most of each night, strangely tireless, as if the very nobility of his cause blessed him with inhuman reserves – further proof to his mind that his efforts had begun to yield gifts, a recognition of sorts, from powers few even suspected still existed.

His thoughts were on such matters even during the day, and this day in particular, when his most loyal servant – the only man who knew of the secret crypts and, indeed, of Humble Measure's master plan – entered his office and placed a small wax book on his desk, then departed.

A sudden quickening of anticipation, quickly crushed once he opened the book and read the message scribed into the wax.

Most unfortunate. Four assassins, all failing. The Guild assured him that such failure would not be repeated.

So, the targets had proved themselves to be truly as dangerous as Humble Measure had suspected. Sour consolation, alas. He set the book down and reached for the roller on its heated plate. Carefully melted away the message.

The Guild would have to do better. Lest he lose faith and seek . . . other means.

In the yards beyond, bars of iron clanged as they were rolled from pallets on to the rail-beds leading to the warehouse, like the sudden clash of armies on a field of battle. The sound made Humble Measure wince.

Whatever was necessary. *Whatever was necessary.*

In a very short time the foreign ship edging ever closer to the Lowstone Pier captured the attention of the crowds on the quayside, sufficient to dampen the constant roar of the hawkers, stevedores, fortune-tellers, prostitutes, carters, and fisherfolk. Eyes widened. Conversations died as lungs snatched air and held it taut in numbed shock. A sudden laugh yelped, swiftly followed by others.

Standing at the bow of the low-slung ship, one pale, perfect hand resting on the carved neck of the horse-head prow, was a woman. If not for her stunning, ethereal beauty, her poise was so regal, so haughty, that it would have verged on caricature. She was swathed in a diaphanous blouse of emerald green that flowed like water in a glacial stream. She wore a broad black leather belt in which were thrust three naked-bladed daggers, and beneath that, tight-fitting, tanned leather breeches down to rawhide leggings. Behind her, on the deck and in the rigging, swarmed a score of bhokarala, while three more fought over the steering oar.

All harbours the world over possessed tales of outrageously strange arrivals, but none matched this, or so it would be claimed by the witnesses in homes and bars for years to come. As the ship glided closer to the pier, disaster seemed imminent. Bhokarala were mere apes, after all, perhaps as smart as the average dog. Crewing a ship? Ridiculous. Drawing into berth with deft precision? Impossible. Yet, at the last moment, the three creatures struggling for control of the steering oar miraculously heeled the ship over. The straw bumpers barely squeezed between hull and stone as the craft nudged the pier. Lines sailed out in chaotic profusion, only a few within reach of the dockside handlers – but enough to make the ship fast. High on the main mast, the topsail luffed and snapped, then the yard loosened and the canvas folded as it dropped down, temporarily trapping a bhokaral within it, where the creature squawked and struggled mightily to free itself.

Down on the main deck, bhokarala rushed from all directions to fight over the gangplank, and all on the quayside watched as the grey, warped board jutted and jerked on its way down to clatter on the pier's stones, a task that resulted in three or four of the black, winged beasts falling into the water with piteous squeals.

A dozen paces away stood a clerk of the harbour master's office, hesitating overlong on his approach to demand moorage fees. The dunked bhokarala clambered back on to the deck, one with a large fish in its mouth, enticing others to rush in to fight over the prize.

The woman had stepped back from her perch alongside the prow, but instead of crossing the main deck to disembark, she instead vanished down through the cabin hatch.

The clerk edged forward then quickly retreated as a half-dozen bhokarala crowding the rail near the gangplank bared their fangs at him.

Common among all crowds, fascination at novelty was short-lived, and before too long, as nothing else of note occurred beyond the futile attempts by the clerk to extract moorage fees from a score of winged apes that did little more than snarl and make faces at him – one going so far as to pelt him with a fresh fish-head – fixed regard wavered and drifted away, back to whatever tasks and whatever demands had required attention before the ship's appearance. Word of the glorious woman and her absurd crew raced outward to infest the city, swift as starlings swirling from street to street, as the afternoon stretched on.

In the captain's cabin aboard the ship, Scillara watched as Sister Spite, a faint smile on her full lips, poured out goblets of wine and set them down before her guests seated round the map-table. That smile collapsed into a sad frown – only slightly exaggerated – when Cutter twisted in his chair, too frustrated to accept the peaceable gesture.

'Oh, really,' Spite said, 'some maturity from you would be a relief right now. Our journey has been long, yes, but I do reiterate that delaying our disembarkation until dusk remains the wisest course.'

'I have no enemies here,' Cutter said in a belligerent growl. 'Only friends.'

'Perhaps that is true,' Spite conceded, 'but I assure you, young assassin, Darujhistan is not the city you left behind years past. Fraught, poised on the very edge of great danger—'

'I know that! I feel it – I felt it before I ever came aboard your cursed ship! Why do you think just sitting here, doing nothing, strikes me as the worst decision possible? I need to see people, I need to warn—'

'Oh dear,' Spite cut in, 'do you truly believe that you alone are aware of the danger? That all hangs in the balance right there at your fingertips? The arrogance of youth!'

Scillara filled her pipe with rustleaf and spent a moment sparking it alight. Heavy, brooding emotions filled the cabin. Nothing new in that, of course. This entire journey had been chaotic and contrary from the moment she, Cutter, Barathol and Chaur had been fished from the seas even as the sky flung giant gobbets of fire down on all sides. Worshipful bhokarala, a miserable mule, an old hag who collapsed into a heap of spiders if one so much as looked askance in her direction. A scrawny, entirely mad High Priest of Shadow, and a brokenhearted Trell. And while Spite comported herself with all the airs of a coddled princess, she was in truth a Soletaken sorceress, dreadfully powerful and as dangerously fey as some Elder Goddess. No, a more motley shipload of passengers and crew Scillara could not imagine.

And now here we are. Poor Darujhistan! 'Won't be long now,' she said to Cutter. 'We're better off trying to stay as far beneath notice as possible.'

Iskaral Pust, seated on his chair with his legs drawn up so that his toadlike face was between his knees, seemed to choke on that comment; then, reddening and eyes bulging, he scowled at the table. 'We have a crew of mad apes!' His head tilted and he stared agog at Scillara. 'We could smoke dried fish with her – just hang 'em in her hair! Of course, the fish'd end up poisoning us all, which might be her plan all along! Keep her away from food and drink – oh yes, I have figured her out. No High Priest of Shadow can be fooled so easily! Oh, no. Now, where was I?' His brows knitted, then suddenly rose threateningly as he glared at her. 'Beneath notice! Why not just sneak out in that cloud of yours, woman?'

She blew him a smoky kiss.

Spite set her goblet down. 'The dispositions facing us now are probably worth discussing, don't you think?'

This question, addressed to everyone, yielded only blank stares.

Spite sighed. 'Mappo Runt, the one you seek is not on this continent. Even so, I would advise you cross overland here, perhaps as far as Lamatath, where you should be able to procure passage to the fell empire of Lether.'

The Trell studied her from beneath his heavy brows. 'Then I shall not linger.'

'Oh, he mustn't linger,' Iskaral Pust whispered. 'No no no. Too much rage, too much grief. The giant oaf cannot linger, or worse *malinger*. Malingering would be terrible, and probably against the law anyway. Yes, perhaps I could get him arrested. Locked up, forgotten in some nefarious dungeon. Oh, I must cogitate on this possibility, all the while smiling benignly!' And he smiled.

Mogora snorted. 'Husband,' she said sweetly, 'I have divined your fate. In Darujhistan you shall find your nemesis, a catastrophic clash. Devastation, misery for all, the unleashing of horrible curses and ferocious powers. Ruin, such ruin that I dream each night of blessed peace, assured that the universe is in balance once more.'

'I can hardly imagine,' Spite said, 'Shadow imposing balance of any sort. This husband of yours serves a diabolical god, a most unpleasant god. As for your divination, Mogora, I happen to know that you possess no such talents—'

'But I can hope, can't I?'

'This is not the world for wishful thinking, dear.'

'Don't you "dear" me! You're the worst kind of witch, a good-looking one! Proof that charm is naught but a glamour—'

'Oh, wife,' Iskaral Pust crooned, 'would that you could glamour yourself. Why, an end to my nausea—'

With a snarl Mogora veered into a seething mass of spiders, spilling down over the chair and on to the plank floor, then scattering in all directions.

Iskaral Pust snickered at the others. 'That's why I sit like this, you fools. She'll bite you all, at every chance!' He jabbed a gnarled finger at Scillara. 'Except you, of course, because you make her sick!'

'Good,' she replied, then glanced across at Barathol. The huge black-skinned man was half smiling as he observed the others. Behind him stood Chaur, his foolish grin unwavering even as he tried stamping on spiders. 'And what of you, blacksmith? Eager to explore this grand city of blue fire?'

Barathol shrugged. 'I believe I am, although it has been some time since I last found myself among crowds. I imagine I might even enjoy the anonymity.' He seemed to take note of his hands where they rested on the table before him, and saw something in their skein of scars that made him frown, then slowly withdraw them from view. His dark eyes shifted from hers, almost shyly.

Not one for grand confessions, Scillara well knew. A single regret could crush a thousand proud deeds, and Barathol Mekhar had more regrets than most mortals could stomach. Nor was he young enough to brazen his way through them, assuming, of course, that youth was indeed a time of bold fearlessness, that precious disregard for the future that permitted, well, almost anything, so long as it served an immediate need.

'I admit,' said Spite, 'to a certain melancholy when visiting vibrant cities, as is this Darujhistan. A long life teaches one just how ephemeral is such thriving glory. Why, I have come again upon cities I knew well in the age of their greatness, only to find crumbled walls, dust and desolation.'

Cutter bared his teeth and said, 'Darujhistan has stood for two thousand years and it will stand for another two thousand – even longer.'

Spite nodded. 'Precisely.'

'Well, we hardly have the leisure of living for millennia, Spite—'

'You clearly weren't listening,' she cut in. 'Leisure is not a relevant notion. Consider the weariness that often afflicts your kind, late in their lives. Then multiply that countless times. This is the burden of being long-lived.'

'A moment, then, while I weep for you,' Cutter said.

'Such ingratitude! Very well, young man, please do leave us now, and if this be the last I see of you then I will indeed know the reward of leisurely comportment!'

Cutter rubbed at his face and seemed but moments from pulling at his own hair. He drew a deep breath, slowly released it. 'I'll wait,' he muttered.

'Really?' Spite's thin, perfect brows rose. 'Then perhaps an apology is forthcoming?'

'Sorry,' Cutter said in a mumble. 'It's just that, with what I fear is about to happen to my city, then wasting time – any time at all – well, it's not easy.' He shrugged.

'Apologies with caveats are worthless, you know,' Spite said, rising. 'Is it dusk yet? Can't you all crawl off to your bunks for a time? Or wander the hold or something? For all that rude Cutter frets over things he cannot control, I myself sense the presence of . . . personages, residing in Darujhistan, of a nature to alarm even me. Accordingly, I must think for a time . . . preferably alone.'

Scillara rose. 'Let's go, Cutter,' she said, taking his arm.

Trailed by Chaur, Barathol followed the Trell warrior down into the hold. There were no berths aboard large enough to accommodate Mappo, so he had fashioned an abode of sorts amidst bales of supplies. Barathol saw that the Trell had already packed his kit, hammock, armour and weapons all stuffed into a lone sack knotted at the mouth by a rawhide cord, and now he sat on a crate, glancing up to regard the blacksmith.

'You wish to speak of something, Barathol?'

'Spite tells me that the Trell were driven from this continent long ago.'

'My people have been assailed for thousands of years.' He shrugged his massive shoulders. 'Perhaps we are so ugly to others that our very existence is unacceptable.'

'You have a long journey ahead,' Barathol said. 'My thought is—'

But Mappo raised a hand. 'No, my friend. I must do this alone.'

'To cross an entire continent, in the face of hostility – possibly on all sides – Mappo, someone must guard your back.'

The Trell's dark, deep-set eyes studied him for a half-dozen heartbeats. 'Barathol Mekhar, we have come to know each other well on this journey. I could not imagine anyone better to guard my back than you.' He shook his head. 'I do not intend to cross the continent. There are . . . other paths. Perhaps indeed more perilous, but I assure you I am not easy to kill. The failure was mine and to make it right, well, the responsibility is mine and mine alone. I will not – I *cannot* – accept that others risk their lives on my behalf. Not you, friend. Not blessed Chaur. Please, leave me to this.'

Barathol sighed. 'You force upon me an even more terrible choice, then.'

'Oh?'

A wry grin. 'Aye. What to do with my life.'

Mappo grunted a laugh. 'I would not call that terrible, at least from my own point of view.'

'I understand what it is to be driven,' Barathol said. 'I think that is *all* that I understand. Back in Seven Cities, well, I'd almost convinced myself that what I'd found was all I needed, but I was lying to myself. Some people, I now believe, cannot just . . . retire. It feels too much like surrender.'

'You were a blacksmith—'

'By default. I was a soldier, Mappo. A Red Blade.'

'Even so, to work iron is a worthy profession. Perhaps you were a soldier, once, but to set down your weapons and find another profession is not surrender. Yet if it feels so to you, well, this city is no doubt crowded with estates, many of which would welcome a guard of your experience. And there will be merchants, operating caravans. Indeed, the city must have its own garrison – no warrior ever fears unemployment, for their skills are ever in demand.'

'A sad admission, Mappo.'

The Trell shrugged again. 'I would think, now, Barathol, that if anyone needs his back guarded, it is Cutter.'

Barathol sighed in frustration. 'He says little of what he plans to do. In any case, this is his city. He will find those who know enough to protect him. Besides, I must admit, having seen Cutter practise with those knives of his, well, perhaps it is Darujhistan that must fear his return.'

'He is too precipitous.'

'I trust Scillara to rein him in.'

'Barathol, let us now make our farewells. I intend to depart soon.'

'And had I not followed you down here?'

'I do poorly saying goodbye.' His gaze shied away.

'Then I will convey such to the others, on your behalf. Cutter will be . . . up-set. For he has known you the longest among us all.'

'I know, and I am sorry – in so many ways I am a coward.'

But Barathol well understood. This was not cowardice. It was some sort of shame, twisted past any possible reason, any conceivable justification. The loss of Icarium was a wound so raw, so irreconcilable, that its spreading stain swept all from its path. Friends, loyalties, lives and histories. And Mappo could not fight against that onrushing tide and the fate he sought at its very end. There would be grief at that conclusion, Barathol suspected, of incalculable measure.

If Icarium Lifestealer was not yet unleashed, he would be soon. Mappo would be too late to prevent that. It was difficult, then, to leave the Trell to all that awaited him, to simply turn away, yet what else could he do, when Mappo's own desires were so clear? 'I will leave you to your . . . paths, then, Mappo. And I wish you the best: a peaceful journey, its satisfactory conclusion.'

'Thank you, my friend. I hope you will find Darujhistan a worthy home.' He rose to clasp the blacksmith's hand, then moved past to embrace Chaur, who laughed in delight and tried to begin a dance with the Trell. Grimacing, Mappo stepped back. 'Goodbye, Chaur. Take care of Barathol here.'

When Chaur finally understood that he would not see Mappo again, there would be tears. There was a simple beauty to such open, child-like responses. Perhaps, Barathol considered, Chaur alone walked the truest path in life.

Settling a hand on Chaur's muscled shoulder, he smiled at Mappo. 'He is a gift I do not deserve.'

The Trell nodded. 'A gift this world does not deserve. Now, I would be alone, in these final moments.'

Barathol bowed, then guided Chaur back to the ladder leading up to the hatch.

Iskaral Pust clambered on to his bunk, the middle of three stacked against the curving hull. He scraped his head against the underside of the top one and cursed under his breath, then cursed some more as he had to fish out a handful of disgusting offerings left beneath his pillow by the bhokarala. Rotting fish-heads, clumps of scaly faeces, baubles stolen from Spite and a cracked kaolin pipe filched from Scillara. Flung off, they clumped and clattered on the two-plank-wide walkway at the very hoofs of his mule, which had taken to standing beside his berth at random intervals – each one proving succinctly inconvenient, as be-fitted a thoroughly brainless but quaintly loyal animal.

From the bunk above came a rattling snort. 'The hatch is too small, you know,' said Mogora. 'You make it too obvious, husband.'

'Maybe obvious is my middle name, did you think that? No, of course not. She never thinks at all. She has ten thousand eyes and not one of them can see past her nose-hairs. Listen well, woman. Everyone knows mules are superior to horses in every way. Including the navigation of hatches. Why, my blessed servant here prefers using outhouses over just plopping any which where along the roadside. She possesses decorum, which can hardly be said for you now, can it?'

'Shouldn't you be picking your nose or something? Your worshippers are praying for a sign, you know.'

'At least I have worshippers. You just scare 'em. You scare everybody.'

'Even you?'

'Of course not. Gods below, she terrifies me! Better not let her know, though. That would be bad. I need to do something soon. Twist off her legs, maybe! Yes, that would do it. Leave her lying on her back scratching at the air and making pathetic mewling sounds. Oh, the imagination is a wonderful thing, is it not?'

'When it's all you have.'

'When what's all I have? What idiocy are you blabbering about now? That was uncanny. Almost as if she can read my mind. Good thing she can't, though.'

'Hold on,' hissed Mogora. 'That mule was male! I'd swear it!'

'Checking him out, were you?'

'One more step on that track, husband, and I will kill you with my own hands.'

'Hee hee. What a terrible, disgusting mind you have, wife.'

'No, you won't distract me this time. Your mule has just changed sex and knowing you I might be looking at a rival, but you know what? She can have you. With my blessing she can, oh yes!'

'Popularity is a curse,' Iskaral said, stretching out with his hands behind his head and staring up at the taut ropes of the mattress above him. 'Not that she'd know anything about that. I'd better visit the local temple, assert my tyrannical dominance over all the local acolytes and fakir priests and priestesses. Priestesses! Might be a pretty one or two. As High Priest, I could have my pick as is my right. Make offerings in the shadow between her legs, yes—'

'I'd know, Iskaral Pust,' Mogora snapped, moving about on the bed above. 'I'd just know, and then I'd take my knife, one night when you're sleeping, and I'd *snick snick* and you'd be singing like a child and squatting t'piss and what woman or mule would want you then?'

'Get out of my head, woman!'

'It's not hard to know what you're thinking.'

'That's what you think! She's getting more dangerous, we need a divorce. But isn't it why most mates break up? When the woman gets too dangerous? Must be. I'm sure of it. Well, I'd be free then, wouldn't I? Free!'

The mule brayed.

Mogora laughed so hard she wet herself, if the rank dribbles from above were any indication.

———————

Scillara and Cutter had taken the berths closest to the stern in an effort to achieve some sort of privacy, and had rigged a section of spare canvas across the walkway. Despite this, Mogora's half-mad laughter reached through, triggering yet another scowl from Cutter.

'If those two just realized how perfect they are for each other, we'd finally get some peace.'

Scillara smiled. 'I'm sure they do. Most marriages involve mutual thoughts of murder on occasion.'

He glanced over at her. 'You've some strange ideas, Scillara. About all sorts of things.'

'I was wondering, when you head out tonight, will you want my company? Or would you rather go on your own?'

He could not hold her gaze and made a show of stretching his back before reclining on his bunk. 'Of course not,' he said. 'You'll like the Phoenix Inn. Meese, Irilta, Murillio, Coll and Kruppe. Well, maybe not Kruppe, who rubs some people the wrong way, but he's harmless enough . . . I suppose.' He rummaged in the pouch at his belt for a moment, then drew out a single coin. A Blue Moranth silver sceptre, which he began deftly working through his fingers. 'Won't they be surprised to see me.'

She managed a smile. 'Cutter's belated return.'

'Well, "Cutter" isn't the name they know me by. I was Crokus Younghand back then.'

'And where is he now? This Crokus Younghand.'

He spent a moment squinting at the coin before replying, 'Dead. Long dead.'

'And what will your friends make of that?'

He sat up, suddenly restless and still unwilling to meet her eyes. 'I don't know. They won't be happy.'

'I think I will leave you to it, Cutter,' Scillara said. 'I'll join Barathol and Chaur wandering the night markets and such – there's a fete going on, yes? That sounds inviting. As for my meeting your friends, best it wait a day or two.'

He glanced at her. 'Are you sure? You don't—'

'I'm sure,' she cut in. 'You need this night to yourself. You'll have enough questions to answer without my presence confusing things even more.'

'All right,' and despite his efforts his relief was palpable. 'But come tomorrow – everyone knows where the Phoenix is, so all you need do is ask.'

'Of course,' she replied, rising from where she sat on the edge of her own berth. 'I'd best hunt Barathol down, so he doesn't leave without me.'

'Must be nearing dusk.'

'So it is, Cutter. Lady's pull on you this night.'

'Thanks.' But it was a distracted response.

As she made her way forward, forced to shoving the damned mule to one side, Scillara told herself that the hurt she was feeling was unwarranted. He'd found comfort in her arms, because there was no one else. No love was involved. Not once mentioned, not even whispered nor murmured in the thick, sleepy moments after lovemaking. Little more than mutual satisfaction, comfort and convenience.

And now, well, that time had passed. Reunion with friends beckoned Cutter – that old world in which he had known his place. Difficult enough that he might no longer fit – explaining the overweight, pipe-sucking ex-whore at his side would only embarrass him.

He had changed her, she realized, pausing just inside the hatch. As if she'd absorbed some essence of his uncertainty, his lack of confidence. She no longer felt her usual brazen, bridling self. No longer ready with a sneer, no longer armoured against the vagaries of this damned world. Here, a dozen strides from the largest city she had ever seen, was neither the time nor the place for such weakness.

Well, Barathol's solid presence could answer her need. For a time, anyway.

Emerging on to the main deck, she found herself in the midst of a growing storm. The bhokarala crowded the dockside rail and scampered back and forth along its length, while at the other end of the gangplank stood an agent of the harbour master along with a half-dozen city guards even now drawing their batons, readying to assault the ship.

Barathol and Chaur had just climbed up from the hold and the blacksmith began pushing his way through the screeching, spitting apes.

She well understood his desire to prevent an escalation of the situation. Spite was not the most evenly tempered woman Scillara had known. An argument gone awry could well result in an enraged dragon's devastating the quayside and half the city beyond. All for a misunderstanding on moorage fees.

So much for a quiet arrival.

Scillara hurried forward, kicking aside bhokarala and pulling loose her coinpouch.

A blow to the side of his head and he rolled, suddenly awake, both knives coming into his hands and blades scraping across the gritty flagstoned floor beneath him. His shoulder struck a wall and he blinked in the gloom.

A tall figure stood over him, black leather and banded iron in tatters, the dull gleam of snapped ribs showing through torn, green skin. A face in shadows, pitted eye-sockets, a broad slash of mouth hinting at up-thrust tusks.

Rallick Nom studied the apparition, the knives feeling useless in his gloved hands. The side of his head still rang. His gaze dropped to the stiffened leather toes of the demon's half-rotted moccasins. 'You kicked me.'

'Yes,' came the rasping reply.

'Why?'

The demon hesitated, then said, 'It seemed the thing to do.'

They were in a narrow corridor. A solid door of black wood and bronze fittings was to Rallick's left. To his right, just beyond the demon, there was a T-intersection and double doors facing on to the conjunction. The light cast by the lantern the creature held in one withered, long-fingered hand seemed both pale and cold, casting diffused, indifferent shadows against the stone walls. Overhead, the ceiling was roughly arched, the stones thinner and smaller towards the peak, seemingly fitted without mortar. The air smelled of dust and decay, lifeless and dry.

'It seems . . . I remember nothing,' Rallick said.

'In time.'

Every joint was stiff; even sitting up with his back against the wall left Rallick's muscles trembling. His head ached with more than just the echoes of that damned kick. 'I'm thirsty – if you're not going to beat me to death, demon, then find me something to drink.'

'I am not a demon.'

'Such things are never easy to tell,' Rallick replied in a growl.

'I am Jaghut. Raest, once a tyrant, now a prisoner. "He who rises shall fall. He who falls shall be forgotten." So said Gothos, although, alas, it seems we must all wait for ever before his name fades into oblivion.'

Some strength was returning to his limbs. 'I recall something . . . a night of blood, the Gedderone Fete. Malazans in the city . . .'

'Portentous events as bereft of meaning now as they were then. You have slept, assassin, for some time. Even the poison on your weapons has lost all potency. Although the otataral within your veins courses unabated by time – few would have done as you did, which is, I suppose, just as well.'

Rallick sheathed his knives and slowly pushed himself upright. The scene spun sickeningly and he closed his eyes until the vertigo passed.

Raest continued, 'I wander in this house . . . rarely. Perhaps some time had passed before I realized that she was missing.'

Rallick squinted at the tall, hunched Jaghut. 'She? Who?'

'A demon in truth. Vorcan is her name now, I believe. You lay beside her, immune to the passage of time. But now she has awakened. She has, indeed, escaped. One might consider this . . . perturbing. If one cared, that is.'

Vorcan, Mistress of the Assassins' Guild, yes, now he remembered. She was wounded, dying, and he struggled to carry her, not knowing why, not knowing what he sought. To the house, the house that had grown from the very earth. The house the Malazans called an *Azath*. Born of the tyrant's Finnest – Rallick frowned at Raest. 'The house,' he said, 'it is your prison, too.'

A desiccated shrug that made bones squeak. 'The stresses of owning property.'

'So you have been here since then. Alone, not even wandering about. With two near-corpses cluttering your hallway. How long, Raest?'

'I am not the one to ask. Does the sun lift into the sky outside then collapse once more? Do bells sound to proclaim a control where none truly exists? Do mortal fools still measure the increments leading to their deaths, wagering pleasures against costs, persisting in the delusion that deeds have value, that the world and all the gods sit in judgement over every decision made or not made? Do—'

'Enough,' interrupted Rallick, straightening with only one hand against the wall. 'I asked "how long?" not "why?" or "what point?" If you don't know the answer just say so.'

'I don't know the answer. But I should correct one of your assumptions. I did not dwell in here alone, although I do so now, excepting you, of course, but your company I do not expect to last. That legion of headlong fools you call your people no doubt pine for your return. Blood awaits your daggers, your pouch thirsts for the coins that will fill it with every life you steal. And so on.'

'If you weren't alone before, Raest . . .'

'Ah, yes, I distracted myself with notions of human futility. The Master of the Deck of Dragons was, in the common language, a squatter here in the house, for a time.'

'And then?'

'He left.'

'Not a prisoner, then, this Master.'

'No. Like you, indifferent to my miserable fate. Will you now exploit your privilege, assassin?'

'What do you mean?'

'Will you now leave, never to return? Abandoning me to eternal solitude, with naught but cobwebs in my bed and bare cupboards in the kitchen, with mocking draughts and the occasional faint clatter of dead branches against shutters? And the odd scream or two as something unpleasant is devoured by earth and root in the yard. Will you simply leave me to this world, assassin?'

Rallick Nom stared at the Jaghut. 'I had no idea my unconscious presence so eased your loneliness, Raest.'

'Such insensitivity on your part should not surprise me.'

'My answer is yes, I will indeed leave you to your world.'

'You lack gratitude.'

Rallick drew his cloak round his shoulders and checked his gear. There was old blood but it simply flaked off like black snow. 'Forgive me. Thank you, Raest, for the kick in the head.'

'You are welcome. Now leave – I grow bored.'

The door opened with a loud, groaning creak. Beyond was night, yet darkness was driven back, pushed skyward, by the defiant blue fires of Darujhistan. Somewhere out of sight from where he stood at the landing, streets seethed and churned with drunken revelry. Another fete, another half-mindless celebration of survival.

The thought stirred some anticipation in Rallick Nom's soul, blowing aside the last dust of what he suspected had been a long, long sleep. Before the door behind him was closed he turned about and could just make out Raest's elongated form, still standing in the corridor. 'Why did you wake me?' he asked.

In answer, the Jaghut stepped forward and shut the door with a thunderous slam that woke birds to panic and sent them bolting into the night.

Rallick turned back to the path, saw roots writhing like serpents in the mulch to either side.

Checking his knives once more, he drew yet tighter his cloak, then set out to rediscover his city.

And so the denizens of Darujhistan grew raucous, enough to give the city itself a kind of life. Headlong indeed, with nary a thought for the future, be that the next moment or a year hence. Gas hissed into blue flame, acrobats and mummers whirled through crowds, a hundred thousand musical instruments waged war on the plains of song, and if it was said by some scholars that sound itself was undying, that it rode unending currents that struck no fatal shore, neither in space nor through time, then life itself could be measured by its cry. In the times of free, blue clarity, and in the times of gathering clouds, in the chorus of pronouncements that sang out . . . arrivals, worlds lived on, as immortal as a dream.

On the rooftop of a bastion tower, on this night, there stood a woman all in black. Eyes cold as a raptor's looked down upon the sprawl of rooftops, spark-lit chimneys in the distant slums of the Gadrobi District, and, drifting silent over all, this woman thought long and thought hard of the future.

On a street close to Coll's estate, a cloaked man paused, stood rooted like a stone whilst the fete swirled round him, and even as he concluded that a public return, such as had first occurred to him, might prove unwise, so walked another man – younger but with the same look in his hardened eyes – on his way to the Phoenix Inn.

Far in this one's wake, down at the quayside, a blacksmith, his halfwit servant, and a woman whose generous curves drew admiring glances from all sides, ambled their way towards the night markets of the Gadrobi, seeing all with the wonder and pleasure only foreigners could achieve when coming for the first time upon one of the greatest cities in the world.

Closer to the ship from which they had disembarked, a High Priest of Shadow scurried for the nearest shadows, pursued mostly unseen by spiders drifting on the lake breeze, and on the trail of both scampered a score of bhokarala – many burdened with new offerings and whatever baubles they claimed as rightful possessions – a fang-bearing squall that flowed through crowds accompanied by shouts of surprise, terror and curses (as their collection of possessions burgeoned with every pouch, purse and jewel within reach of their clawed hands).

Aboard the ship itself, the captain remained. Now she was wearing loose, flowing robes of black and crimson silks, her face white as moonlight as she frowned at the city before her. A scent on the air, some lingering perfume redolent with memories . . . oh, of all places, but was this truly an accident? Spite did not believe in accidents.

And so she hesitated, knowing what her first step on to solid stone would reveal – perhaps, she decided, it would do to wait for a time.

Not long.

Just long enough

In another part of Darujhistan, a merchant of iron dispatched yet another message to the Master of the Assassins' Guild, then retired to his secret library to pore once more over ancient, fraught literature. Whilst not too far away sat a merchant guard with fading barbed tattoos, frowning down at a cup of spiced, hot wine in his huge, scarred hands; and from the next room came a child's laughter, and this sound made him wince.

Down among the new estates of certain once-criminal moneylenders who had since purchased respectability, a destitute Torvald Nom stealthily approached the high, spike-topped wall of one such estate. Debts, was it? Well, fine, easily solved. Had he lost any of his skills? Of course not. If anything, such talents had been honed by the rigours of a legendary journey across half the damned world. His glorious return to Darujhistan still awaited him. Come the morning, aye, come the morning . . .

At this moment, in a small chamber above the taproom of the Phoenix Inn, a man was lying on his back on a bed, still weak from blood loss, and in his thoughts he walked the cemetery of his past, fingers brushing the tops of weathered tombstones and grave markers, seeing the knots of tangled grass climbing the sides of dusty urns, while stretching away in his wake was the shadow of his youth – fainter, longer, fraying now at the very edges. He would not lift his hand yet to feel his own face, to feel the wrinkles and creases that wrote out in tired glyphs his age, his waning life.

Oh, flesh could be healed, yes . . .

Below, amidst a mob of bellowing, reeling drunks and screeching whores of both sexes, a small round man, seated as ever at his private table, paused with his mouth stuffed full of honeyed bread, and, upon hearing the tenth bell sound through the city, cocked his head and settled his tiny, beady eyes upon the door to Phoenix Inn.

Arrivals.

Glory and portent, delightful reunion and terrible imminence, winged this and winged that and escapes and releases and pending clashes and nefarious demands for recompense over a single mouthful of spat wine, such a night!

Such a night!

Chapter Four

We were drowning amidst petals and leaves
On the Plain of Sethangar
Where dreams jostled like armies on the flatland
And to sing of the beauty of all these blossoms
Was to forget the blood that fed every root
On the Plain of Sethangar
We cried out for shelter from this fecund storm
The thrust and heave of life on the scouring winds
Was dry as a priest's voice in fiery torment
On the Plain of Sethangar
And no wise words could be heard in the roar
Of the laughing flowers reaching out to the horizon
As the pungent breath left us drunk and stagger'd
On the Plain of Sethangar
Must we ever die in the riches of our profligacy
Succumbing to the earth cold and dark each time
Only to burst free wide-eyed in innocent birth
On the Plain of Sethangar?
Which god strides this field scythe in hand
To sever the grandiose mime with edged judgement
Taking from our souls all will in bundled sheaves
On the Plain of Sethangar
To feed as befits all burdensome beasts?

Flowers will worship the tree's fickle blessing of light
Forests reach into the sweetness of a sky beyond touch
Even as streams make pilgrimage to the sea
And the rain seeks union with all flesh and blood
Hills will hold fast over every plain, even Sethangar
And so we dream of inequity's end
As if it lay within our power
There in the plainness of our regard
So poorly blinded to beauty . . .

DECLAMATION (FRAGMENT)
(?) KENEVISS BROT
FIRST CENTURY BURN'S SLEEP

Groaning like a beast in its death throes, the ship seemed to clamber up on to the black rocks before the keel snapped and the hull split with a splintering cry. Cut and bloodless corpses rolled and slid from the deck, spilling into the thrashing foam where pale limbs flopped and waved in the tumult before the riptide dragged them tumbling over the broken sea floor, out and down into the depths. The lone living figure, who had tied himself to the tiller, was now tangled in frayed ropes at the stern, scrabbling to reach his knife before the next huge wave exploded over the wreck. A salt-bleached hand – the skin of the palm hanging in blighted strips – tugged the broad-bladed weapon free. He slashed at the ropes binding him to the up-thrust tiller as the hull thundered to the impact of another wave and white spume cascaded over him.

As the last strand parted he fell on to his side and slid to the crushed rail, the collision driving the air from his lungs as he pitched across the encrusted rock, then sagged, limp as any corpse, into the churning water.

Another wave descended on to the wreck like an enormous fist, crushing the deck beneath its senseless power, then dragging the entire hull back into the deeper water, leaving a wave of splintered wood, lines and tattered sail.

Where the man had vanished, the inrushing seas swirled round the black rock, and nothing emerged from that thrashing current.

In the sky overhead dark clouds clashed, spun sickly arms into a mutual embrace, and though on this coast no trees rose from the ravaged ground, and naught but wind-stripped grasses emerged from pockets here and there among the rock and gravel and sand, from the wounded sky dried, autumnal leaves skirled down like rain.

Closer to the shore heaved a stretch of water, mostly sheltered from the raging seas beyond the reef. Its bottom was a sweep of coral sand, agitated enough to cloud the shallows.

The man rose into view, water streaming. He rolled his shoulders, spat out a mouthful thick with grit and blood, then waded on to the strand. He no longer carried his knife, but in his left hand was a sword in a scabbard. Made from two long strips of pale wood reinforced with blackened iron, the scabbard revealed that it was riven through with cracks, as water drained out from a score of fissures.

Leaves raining on all sides, he walked up beyond the tide line, crunched down on to a heap of broken shells and sat, forearms on his knees, head hung down. The bizarre deluge thickened into flurries of rotting vegetation, like black sleet.

The massive beast that slammed into him would have been thrice his weight if it was not starved. Nor would it have attacked at all, ever shy of humans, but it had become lost in a dust storm, and was then driven from the grasslands leagues inland on to this barren, lifeless coast. Had any of the corpses from the ship reached the beach, the plains bear would have elected to scavenge its meal. Alas, its plague of misfortunes was unending.

Enormous jaws snapped close round the back of the man's head, canines tearing through scalp and gouging into skull, yet the man was already ducking, twisting, his sodden hair and the sudden welter of blood proving slick enough to enable him to wrest free of the bear's bite.

The sword was lying, still in its cracked scabbard, two paces away, and even as he lunged towards it the bear's enormous weight crashed down on to him. Claws raked against his chain hauberk, rings snapping away like torn scales. He half twisted round, hammering his right elbow into the side of the bear's head, hard enough to foul its second attempt to bite into the back of his neck. The blow sprayed blood from the beast's torn lip along the side of its jaw.

The man drove his elbow again, this time into the bear's right eye. A bleat of pain and the animal lunged to the left. Continuing his twist, the man drew up both legs, then drove them heels first into its ribs. Bones snapped.

Another cry of agony. Frothing blood sprayed out from its mouth.

Kicking himself away, the man reached his sword. His motions a blur of speed, he drew the weapon, alighted on his feet in a crouch, and slashed the sword into the side of the bear's neck. The ancient watermarked blade slid through thick muscle, then bit into bone, and through, bursting free on the opposite side. Blood and bile gushed as the bear's severed head thumped on to the sand. The body sat down on its haunches, still spewing liquid, then toppled to one side, legs twitching.

Blazing heat seethed at the back of the man's head, his ears filled with a strange buzzing sound, and the braids of his black, kinked hair dripped thick threads of bloody saliva as he staggered upright.

On the sword's blade, blood boiled, turned black, then shed in flakes.

Still the sky rained dead leaves.

He staggered back down to the sea, fell on to his knees in the shallows and plunged his head into the vaguely warm water.

Numbness flowed out along the back of his skull. When he straightened once more, he saw the bloom of blood in the water, a smear stretching into some draw of current – an appalling amount. He could feel more, streaming down his back now.

He quickly tugged off the chain hauberk, then the filthy, salt-rimed shirt beneath. He tore loose the shirt's left sleeve, folded it into a broad bandanna and bound it tight round his head, as much against the torn skin and flesh as he could manage by feel.

The buzzing sound was fading. A dreadful ache filled the muscles of his neck and shoulders, and in his head there now pounded a drum, each beat pulsating until the bones of his skull seemed to reverberate. He attempted to spit again, but his parched throat yielded nothing – almost three days now without water. A juddering effect assailed his vision, as if he stood in the midst of an earthquake. Stumbling, he made his way back up the beach, collecting his sword on the way.

On to his knees once more, this time at the headless carcass. Using his sword to carve into the torso, then reaching in to grasp the bear's warm heart. He tore and cut it loose, raised it in one hand and held it over his mouth, then squeezed it as if it was a sponge. From the largest of the arteries blood gushed into his mouth.

He drank deep, finally closing his lips round the artery and sucking the last drop of blood from the organ.

When that was done he bit into the muscle and began to eat it.

Slowly, his vision steadied, and he noticed for the first time the raining leaves, the torrent only now diminishing, as the heavy, warring clouds edged away, out over the sea.

Finished eating the heart, he licked his fingers. Rose once more and retrieved the scabbard, sheathing the sword. The drumbeat was fading, although pain still tormented his neck, shoulders and back – muscles and tendons that had only begun their complaint at the savage abuse they had suffered. He washed the one-sleeved shirt then wrung it – tenderly, since it was threadbare and liable to fall apart under too rigorous a ministration. Slipping it on, he then rinsed out the chain hauberk before rolling it up and settling it down over one shoulder.

Then he set out, inland.

Above the crest of the shoreline, he found before him a wasteland. Rock, scrub, drifts of ash and, in the distance, ravines and outcrops of broken bedrock, a rumpling of the landscape into chaotic folds that lifted into raw, jagged hills.

Far to his left – northward – a grainy, diffuse haze marred the sky above or beyond more hills.

He squinted, studied that haze for thirty heartbeats.

Patches of dusty blue above him now, as the storm rolled westward over the sea, its downpour of leaves trailing like claw marks in the air, staining the whitecaps beyond the reef. The wind lost some of its chill bite as the sun finally broke through, promising its own assault on mortal flesh.

The man's skin was dark, for he had been born on a savannah. His was a warrior's build, the muscles lean and sharply defined on his frame. His height was average, though something in his posture made him seem taller. His even features were ravaged by depredation, but already the rich meat of the bear's heart had begun to fill that expression with stolid, indomitable strength.

Still, the wounds blazed with ferocious heat. And he knew, then, that fever was not far off. He could see nothing nearby in which to take shelter, to hole up out of the sun. Among the ravines, perhaps, the chance of caves, overhangs. Yet . . . fifteen hundred paces away, if not more.

Could he make it that far?

He would have to.

Dying was unthinkable, and that was no exaggeration. When a man has forsaken Hood, the final gate is closed. Oblivion or the torment of a journey without end – there was no telling what fate awaited such a man.

In any case, Traveller was in no hurry to discover an answer. No, he would invite Hood to find it himself.

It was the least he could do.

Slinging the scabbard's rope belt over his left shoulder, checking that the sword named Vengeance was snug within it, its plain grip within easy reach, he set out across the barren plain.

In his wake, stripped branches spun and twisted down from the heaving clouds, plunging into the waves, as if torn from the moon itself.

The clearing bore the unmistakable furrows of ploughs beneath the waist-high marsh grasses, each ribbon catching at their feet as they pushed through the thick stalks. The wreckage of a grain shed rose from brush at the far end, its roof collapsed with a sapling rising from the floor, as exuberant as any conqueror. Yet such signs were, thus far, all that remained of whatever tribe had once dwelt in this forest. Fragments of deliberate will gouged into the wilderness, but the will had failed. In another hundred years, Nimander knew, all evidence would be entirely erased. Was the ephemeral visage of civilization reason for fear? Or, perhaps, relief? That all victories were ultimately transitory in the face of patient nature might well be cause for optimism. No wound was too deep to heal. No outrage too horrendous to one day be irrelevant.

Nimander wondered if he had discovered the face of the one true god. Naught else but *time*, this ever changing and yet changeless tyrant against whom no creature could win. Before whom even trees, stone and air must one day bow. There would be a last dawn, a last sunset, each kneeling in final surrender. Yes, time was indeed god, playing the same games with lowly insects as it did with mountains and the fools who would carve fastnesses into them. At peace with every scale, pleased by the rapid patter of a rat's heart and the slow sighing of devouring wind against stone. Content with a star's burgeoning light and the swift death of a raindrop on a desert floor.

'What has earned the smile, cousin?'

He glanced over at Skintick. 'Blessed with revelation, I think.'

'A miracle, then. I think that I too am converted.'

'You might want to change your mind – I do not believe my newfound god cares for worship, or answers any prayers no matter how fervent.'

'What's so unique about that?'

Nimander grunted. 'Perhaps I deserved that.'

'Oh, you are too quick to jump into the path of what might wound – even when wounding was never the intention. I am still open to tossing in with your worship of your newfound god, Nimander. Why not?'

Behind them, Desra snorted. 'I will tell you two what to worship. Power. When it is of such magnitude as to leave you free to do as you will.'

'Such freedom is ever a delusion, sister,' Skintick said.

'It is the only freedom that is *not* a delusion, fool.'

Grimacing, Nimander said, 'I don't recall Andarist being very free.'

'Because his brother was more powerful, Nimander. Anomander was free to *leave* us, was he not? Which life would you choose?'

'How about neither?' Skintick said.

Although she walked behind them, Nimander could see in his mind's eye his sister's face, and the contempt in it as she no doubt sneered at Skintick.

Clip walked somewhere ahead, visible only occasionally; whenever they strode into another half-overgrown clearing, they would see him waiting at the far end, as if impatient with lagging, wayward children.

Behind Nimander, Skintick and Desra walked the others, Nenanda electing to guard the rear as if this was some sort of raid into enemy territory. Surrounded by suspicious songbirds, nervous rodents, irritated insects, Nenanda padded along with one hand resting on the pommel of his sword, a glower for every shadow. He would be like that all day, Nimander knew, storing up his disgust and anger for when they all sat by the fire at night, a fire Nenanda deemed careless and dangerous and would only tolerate because Clip said nothing, Clip with his half-smile and spinning rings who fed Nenanda morsels of approval until the young warrior was consumed by an addict's need, desperate for the next paltry feeding.

Without it, he might crumble, collapse inward like a deflated bladder. Or lash out, yes, at every one of his kin. At Desra, who had been his lover. At Kediviss and Aranatha who were useless. At Skintick who mocked to hide his cowardice. And at Nimander, who was to blame for – well, no need to go into that, was there?

'Do not fret, beloved. I wait for you. For ever. Be strong and know this: you are stronger than you know. Think—'

And all at once another voice sounded in his mind, harder, sour with venom, 'She knows nothing. She lies to you.'

Phaed.

'Yes, you cannot be rid of me, brother. Not when your hands still burn. Still feel the heat of my throat. Not when my bulging eyes stay fixed on you, like nails, yes? The iron tips slowly pushing into your own eyes, so cold, such pain, and you cannot pull loose, can never escape.'

Do I deny my guilt? Do I even flinch from such truths?

'That is not courage, brother. That is despair. Pathetic surrender. Remember Withal? How he took upon himself what needed doing? He picked me up like a rag doll – impressive strength, yes! The memory heats me, Nimander! Would you lick my lips?' and she laughed. 'Withal, yes, he knew what to do, because you left him no choice. Because you failed. So weak you could not murder your sister. I saw as much in your eyes; at that last moment, I saw it!'

Some sound must have risen from Nimander, for Skintick turned with brows raised.

'What is wrong?'

Nimander shook his head.

They walked round pale-barked trees, on soft loam between splayed roots. Dappled sunlight and the chattering alarm of a flying squirrel on a bony branch overhead. Leaves making voices – yes, that was all it was, whispering leaves and his overwrought imagination—

Phaed snorted. ' "Sometimes being bad feels good. Sometimes dark lust burns like parched wood. Sometimes, my love, you awaken desire in someone else's pain." Recall that poet, Nimander? That woman of Kharkanas? Andarist was reluctant to speak of her, but I found in the Old Scrolls all her writings. "And with the tips of your fingers, all this you can train." Hah! She knew! And they all *feared her, and now they will not speak her name, a name forbidden, but I know it – shall I—'*

No!

And Nimander's hands clutched, as if once more crushing Phaed's throat. And he saw her eyes, yes, round and swollen huge and ready to burst. In his mind, yes, once more he choked the life from her.

And from the leaves came the whisper of dark pleasure.

Suddenly cold, suddenly terrified, he heard Phaed's knowing laugh.

'You look ill,' Skintick said. 'Should we halt for a rest?'

Nimander shook his head. 'No, let Clip's impatience drag us ever onward, Skintick. The sooner we are done . . .' But he could not go on, would not finish that thought.

'See ahead,' Desra said. 'Clip has reached the forest edge, and not a moment too soon.'

There was no cause for her impatience, merely a distorted, murky reflection of Clip's own. This was how she seduced men, by giving back to them versions of themselves, promising her protean self like a precious gift to feed their narcissistic pleasures. She seemed able to steal hearts almost without effort, but Nimander suspected that Clip's self-obsession would prove too powerful, too well armoured against any incursions. He would not let her into his places of weakness. No, he would simply use her, as she had so often used men, and from this would be born a most deadly venom.

Nimander had no thought to warn Clip. Leave them their games, and all the wounds to come.

'Yes, leave them to it, brother. We have our own, after all.'

Must I choke you silent once more, Phaed?

'If it pleases you.'

The clearing ahead stretched out, rolling downward towards a distant river or stream. The fields on the opposite bank had been planted with rows of some strange, purplish, broad-leafed crop. Scarecrows hung from crosses in such profusion that it seemed they stood like a cohort of soldiers in ranks. Motionless, rag-bound figures in each row, only a few paces apart. The effect was chilling.

Clip's eyes thinned as he studied the distant field and its tattered sentinels. Chain snapped out, rings spun in a gleaming blur.

'There's a track, I think,' Skintick said, 'up and over the far side.'

'What plants are those?' Aranatha asked.

No one had an answer.

'Why are there so many scarecrows?'

Again, no suggestions were forthcoming.

Clip once more in the lead, they set out.

The water of the stream was dark green, almost black, so sickly in appearance that none stopped for a drink, and each found stones to step on rather than simply splash across the shallow span. They ascended towards the field where clouds of insects hovered round the centre stalk of each plant, swarming the pale green flowers before rising in a gust to plunge down on to the next.

As they drew closer, their steps slowed. Even Clip finally halted.

The scarecrows had once been living people. The rags were bound tightly, covering the entire bodies; arms, legs, necks, faces, all swathed in rough cloth that seemed to drip black fluids, soaking the earth. As the wrapped heads were forward slung, threads of the thick dark substance stretched down from the gauze covering the victims' noses.

'Feeding the plants, I think,' Skintick said quietly.

'Blood?' Nimander asked.

'Doesn't look like blood, although there may be blood in it.'

'Then they're still alive.'

Yet that seemed unlikely. None of the forms moved, none lifted a bound head at the sound of their voices. The air itself stank of death.

'They are not still alive,' Clip said. He had stopped spinning the chain.

'Then what leaks from them?'

Clip moved on to the narrow track running up through the field. Nimander forced himself to follow, and heard the others fall in behind him. Once they were in the field, surrounded by the corpses and the man-high plants, the pungent air was suddenly thick with the tiny, wrinkle-winged insects, slithering wet and cool against their faces.

They hurried forward, gagging, coughing.

The furrows were sodden underfoot, black mud clinging to their moccasins, a growing weight that made them stumble and slip as they scrambled upslope. Reaching the ridge at last, out from the rows, down into a ditch and then on to a road. Beyond it, more fields to either side of a track, and, rising from them like an army, more corpses. A thousand hung heads, a ceaseless flow of black tears.

'Mother bless us,' Kedeviss whispered, 'who could do such a thing?'

'"All possible cruelties are inevitable,"' Nimander said, '"every conceivable crime has been committed."' Quoting Andarist yet again.

'Try thinking your own thoughts on occasion,' Desra said drily.

'He saw truly—'

'Andarist surrendered his soul and thought it earned him wisdom,' Clip cut in, punctuating his statement with a snap of rings. 'In this case, though, he probably struck true. Even so, this has the flavour of . . . necessity.'

Skintick snorted. 'Necessity, now there's a word to feed every outrage on decency.'

Beyond the ghastly army and the ghoulish purple-leaved plants squatted a town, quaint and idyllic against a backdrop of low, forested hills. Smoke rose above thatched roofs. A few figures were visible on the high street.

'I think we should avoid meeting anyone,' Nimander said. 'I do not relish the notion of ending up staked above a plant.'

'That will not occur,' said Clip. 'We need supplies and we can pay for them. In any case, we have already been seen. Come, with luck there will be a hostel or inn.'

A man in a burgundy robe was approaching up the track that met the raised road. Below the tattered hem of the robe his legs were bare and pale, but his feet were stained black. Long grey hair floated out from his head, unkempt and tangled. His hands were almost comically oversized, and these too were dyed black.

The face was lined, the pale blue eyes wide as they took in the Tiste Andii on the road. Hands waving, he began shouting, in a language Nimander had never heard before. After a moment, he clearly cursed, then said in broken Andii, 'Traders of Black Coral ever welcome! Morsko town happy of guests and kin of Son of Darkness! Come!'

Clip gestured for his troupe to follow.

The robed man, still smiling like a crazed fool, whirled and hurried back down the track.

Townsfolk were gathering on the high street, watching in silence as they drew nearer. The score or so parted when they reached the edge of the town. Nimander saw in their faces a bleak lifelessness, in their eyes the wastelands of scorched souls, so exposed, so unguarded, that he had to look away.

Hands and feet were stained, and on more than a few the blackness rimmed their gaping mouths, making the hole in their faces too large, too seemingly empty and far too depthless.

The robed man was talking. 'A new age, traders. Wealth! Bastion. Heath. Even Outlook rises from ash and bones. Saemankelyk, glory of the Dying God. Many the sacrifices. Of the willing, oh yes, the willing. And such thirst!'

They came to a broad square with a bricked well on a centre platform of water-worn limestone slabs. On all sides stood racks from which harvested plants hung drying upside down, their skull-sized rootballs lined like rows of children's heads, faces deformed by the sun. Old women were at the well, drawing water in a chain that wended between racks to a low, squat temple, empty buckets returning.

The robed man pointed at the temple – probably the only stone building in the town – and said, 'Once sanctified in name of Pannion. No more! The Dying God now, whose body, yes, lies in Bastion. I have looked upon it. Into its eyes. Will you taste the Dying God's tears, my friends? Such demand!'

'What horrid nightmare rules here?' Skintick asked in a whisper.

Nimander shook his head.

'Tell me, do we look like traders?'

'How should I know?'

'Black Coral, Nimander. Son of Darkness – our kinfolk have become merchants!'

'Yes, but merchants of what?'

The robed man – a priest of some sort – now led them to an inn to the left of the temple that looked half dilapidated. 'Few traders this far east, you see. But roof is sound. I will send for maids, cook. There is tavern. Opens of midnight.'

The ground floor of the inn was layered in dust, the planks underfoot creaking and strewn with pellets of mouse droppings. The priest stood beside the front door, large hands entwined, head bobbing as he held his smile.

Clip faced the man. 'This will do,' he said. 'No need for maids, but find a cook.'

'Yes, a cook. Come midnight to tavern!'

'Very well.'

The priest left.

Nenanda began pacing, kicking detritus away from his path. 'I do not like this, Herald. There aren't enough people for this town – you must have seen that.'

'Enough,' muttered Skintick as he set his pack down on a dusty tabletop, 'for planting and harvesting.'

'Saemankelyk,' said Nimander. 'Is that the name of this dying god?'

'I would like to see it,' Clip said, chain spinning once more as he looked out through the smeared lead-paned window. 'This dying god.'

'Is this place called Bastion on the way to Black Coral?'

Clip glanced across at Nimander, disdain heavy in his eyes. 'I said I wish to see this dying god. That is enough.'

'I thought—' began Nenanda, but Clip turned on him sharply.

'That is your mistake, warrior. Thinking. There is time. There is always time.'

Nimander glanced across at Skintick. His cousin shrugged; then, eyes narrowing, he suddenly smiled.

'Your god, Nimander?'

'Yes.'

'Not likely to die any time soon, then.'

'No, never that.'

'What are you two talking about?' Clip demanded, then, dismissing any possible reply, he faced the window once more. 'A dying god needs to die sometime.'

'Notions of mercy, Great One?' Skintick asked.

'Not where you are concerned.'

'Just as well, since I could never suffer the gratitude.'

Nimander watched as Desra glided up to stand beside Clip. They stood looking out through the pane, like husband and wife, like allies against the world. Her left arm almost touching him, up near her elbow, but she would not draw any closer. The spinning rings prevented that, whirling a metal barrier.

'Tonight,' Clip said loudly, 'no one drinks.'

Nimander thought back to those black-stained mouths and the ravaged eyes above them, and he shivered.

Mist drifted down from the parklike forest north of the Great Barrow, merging with the smoke of cookfires from the pilgrims encamped like an army around the enormous, circular mound. Dawn was paling the sky, seeming to push against the unnatural darkness to the south, but this was a war the sun could not win.

From the city gate the cobbled road ran between lesser barrows where hundreds of corpses had been interred following the conquest. Malazans, Grey Swords, Rhivi, Tiste Andii and K'Chain Che'Malle. Farther to the west rose longer barrows, final home to the fallen citizens and soldiers of the city.

Seerdomin walked the road through the gloom. A path through ghosts – too many to even comprehend – but he thought he could hear the echoes of their death-cries, their voices of pain, their desperate pleas for mothers and loved ones. Once he was past this place, who was there to hear those echoes? No one, and it was this truth that struck him the hardest. They would entwine with naught but themselves, falling unheeded to the dew-flattened grass.

He emerged into morning light, like passing through a curtain, suddenly brushed with warmth, and made his way up the slope towards the sprawled encampment. For this, he wore his old uniform, a kind of penance, a kind of self-flagellation. There was need, in his mind, to bear his guilt openly, brazenly, to leave himself undefended and indefensible. This was how he saw his daily pilgrimage to the Great Barrow, although he well knew that some things could never be purged, and that redemption was a dream of the deluded.

Eyes fixed on him from the camps to either side as he continued on towards that massive heap of treasure – wealth of such measure that it could only belong to a dead man, who could not cast covetous eyes upon his hoard, who would not feel its immense weight night and day, who would not suffer beneath its terrible curse. He was tracked, then, by no doubt hardening eyes, the fixation of hatred, contempt, perhaps even the desire of murder. No matter. He understood such sentiments, the purity of such desires.

Armour clanking, chain rustling across the fronts of his thighs as he drew ever closer.

The greater vastness of wealth now lay buried beneath more mundane trinkets, yet it was these meagre offerings that seemed most potent in their significance to Seerdomin. Their comparative value was so much greater, after all. Sacrifice must be weighed by the pain of what is surrendered, and this alone was the true measure of a virtue's worth.

He saw now the glitter of sunlight in the dew clinging to copper coins, the slick glimmer on sea-polished stones in an array of muted colours and patterns. The fragments of glazed ceramics from some past golden age of high culture. Feathers now bedraggled, knotted strips of leather from which dangled fetishes, gourd rattles to bless newborn babes and sick children. And now, here and there, the picked-clean skulls of the recent dead – a subcult, he had learned, centred on the T'lan Imass, who knelt before the Redeemer and so made themselves his immortal servants. Seerdomin knew that the truth was more profound than that, more breathtaking, and that servitude was not a vow T'lan Imass could make, not to anyone but the woman known as Silverfox. No, they had knelt in *gratitude*.

That notion could still leave him chilled, wonder awakened in his heart like a gust of surprised breath.

Still, these staring skulls seemed almost profane.

He stepped into the slightly rutted avenue and drew closer. Other pilgrims were placing their offerings ahead, then turning about and making their way back, edging round him with furtive glances. Seerdomin heard more in his wake, a susurration of whispered prayers and low chanting that seemed like a gentle wave carrying him forward.

Reaching the barrow's ragged, cluttered edge, he moved to one side, off the main approach, then settled down into a kneeling position before the shrine, lowering his head and closing his eyes.

He heard someone move up alongside him, heard the soft breathing but nothing else.

Seerdomin prayed in silence. The same prayer, every day, every time, always the same.

Redeemer. I do not seek your blessing. Redemption will never be mine, nor should it, not by your touch, nor that of anyone else. Redeemer, I bring no gift to set upon your barrow. I bring to you naught but myself. Worshippers and pilgrims will hear nothing of your loneliness. They armour you against all that is human, for that is how they make you into a god. But you were once a mortal soul. And so I come, my only gift my company. It is paltry, I know, but it is all I have and all I would offer.

Redeemer, bless these pilgrims around me.

Bless them with peace in their need.

He opened his eyes, then slowly climbed to his feet.

Beside him spoke a woman. 'Benighted.'

He started, but did not face her. 'I have no such title,' he said.

There was faint amusement in her reply, 'Seerdomin, then. We speak of you often, at night, from fire to fire.'

'I do not flee your venom, and should it one day take my life, so it will be.'

All humour vanished from her voice as she seemed to draw a gasp, then said, 'We speak of you, yes, but not with venom. Redeemer bless us, not that.'

Bemused, he finally glanced her way. Was surprised to see a young, unlined face – the voice had seemed older, deep of timbre, almost husky – framed in glistening black hair, chopped short and angled downward to her shoulders. Her large eyes were of darkest brown, the outer corners creased in lines that did not belong to one of her few years. She wore a woollen robe of russet in which green strands threaded down, but the robe hung open, unbelted, revealing a pale green linen blouse cut short enough to expose a faintly bulging belly. From her undersized breasts he judged that she was not with child, simply not yet past the rounded softness of adolescence.

She met his eyes in a shy manner that once again startled him. 'We call you the Benighted, out of respect. And all who arrive are told of you, and by this means we ensure that there is no theft, no rape, no crime at all. The Redeemer has chosen you to guard his children.'

'That is untrue.'

'Perhaps.'

'I had heard that no harm befell the pilgrims this close to the Great Barrow.'

'Now you know why.'

Seerdomin was dumbfounded. He could think of nothing to say to such a notion. It was madness. It was, yes, *unfair.*

'Is it not the Redeemer who shows us,' said the woman, 'that burdens are the lot of us all? That we must embrace such demands upon our souls, yet stand fearless, open and welcoming?'

'I do not know what the Redeemer shows – to anyone.' His tone was harsher than he'd intended. 'I have enough burdens of my own. I will not accept yours – I

will not be responsible for your safety, or that of any other pilgrim. This – this . . .'
This is not why I am here! Yet, much as he wanted to shout that out loud, instead
he turned away, marched back to the avenue.

Pilgrims flinched from his path, deepening his anger.

Through the camp, eyes set on the darkness ahead, wanting to be once more
within its chill embrace, and the city, too. The damp grey walls, the gritty cobbles of the streets, the musty cave of a tavern with its surround of pale, miserable
faces – yes, back to his own world. Where nothing was asked of him, nothing demanded, not a single expectation beyond that of sitting at a table with the game
arrayed before him, the twist and dance of a pointless contest.

On to the road, into the swirl of lost voices from countless useless ghosts, his
boots ringing on the stones.

Damned fools!

Down at the causeway spanning the Citadel's moat, blood leaked out from bodies
sprawled along its length, and in the north sky something terrible was happening.
Lurid slashes like a rainbow gone mad, spreading in waves that devoured darkness. Was it pain that strangled the very air? Was it something else burgeoning to
life, shattering the universe itself?

Endest Silann, a simple acolyte in the Temple of Mother Dark, wove drunkenly round the bodies towards the Outer Gate, skidding on pools of gore. Through
the gate's peaked arch he could see the city, the roofs like the gears of countless
mechanisms, gears that could lock with the sky itself, with all creation. Such was
Kharkanas, First Born of all cities. But the sky had changed. The perfect machine
of existence was broken – *see the sky!*

The city trembled, the roofs now ragged-edged. A wind had begun to howl, the
voice of the multihued light-storm as it lashed out, flared with thunderous fire.

Forsaken. We are forsaken!

He reached the gate, fell against one pillar and clawed at the tears streaming
from his eyes. The High Priestess, cruel poet, was shrieking in the nave of the
Temple, shrieking like a woman being raped. Others – women all – were writhing
on the marble floor, convulsing in unison, a prostrate dance of macabre sensual-
ity. The priests and male acolytes had sought to still the thrashing limbs, to ease
the ravaged cries erupting from tortured throats with empty assurances, but then,
one by one, they began to recoil as the tiles grew slick beneath the women, the
so-called Nectar of Ecstasy – and no, no man could now pretend otherwise, could
not but see this the way it was, the truth of it.

They fled. Crazed with horror, yes, but driven away by something else, and
was it not *envy*?

Civil war had ignited, deadly as that storm in the sky. Families were being torn
asunder, from the Citadel itself down to the meanest homes of the commonry.
Andii blood painted Kharkanas and there was nowhere to run.

Through the gate, and then, even as despair choked all life from Endest Silann,
he saw *him* approaching. From the city below. His forearms sheathed in black

glistening scales, his bared chest made a thing of natural armour. The blood of Tiam ran riot through him, fired to life by the conflation of chaotic sorcery, and his eyes glowed with ferocious will.

Endest fell to his knees in Anomander's path. 'Lord! The world falls!'

'Rise, priest,' he replied. 'The world does not fall. It but *changes*. I need you. Come.'

And so he walked past, and Endest found himself on his feet, as Lord Anomander's will closed about his heart like an iron gauntlet, pulling him round and into the great warrior's wake.

He wiped at his eyes. 'Lord, where are we going?'

'The Temple.'

'We cannot! They have gone mad – the women! They are—'

'I know what assails them, priest.'

'The High Priestess—'

'Is of no interest to me.' Anomander paused, glanced back at him. 'Tell me your name.'

'Endest Silann, Third Level Acolyte. Lord, please—'

But the warrior continued on, silencing Endest with a gesture from one scaled, taloned hand. 'The crime of this day, Endest Silann, rests with Mother Dark herself.'

And then, at that precise moment, the young acolyte understood what the Lord intended. And yes, Anomander would indeed need him. His very soul – *Mother forgive me* – to open the way, to lead the Lord on to the Unseen Road.

And he will stand before her, yes. Tall, unyielding, a son who is not afraid. Not of her. Not of his own anger. The storm, oh, the storm is just beginning.

Endest Silann sat alone in his room, the bare stone walls as solid and cold as those of a tomb. A small oil lamp sat on the lone table, testament to his failing eyes, to the stain of Light upon his soul, a stain so old now, so deeply embedded in the scar tissue of his heart, that it felt like tough leather within him.

Being old, it was his privilege to relive ancient memories, to resurrect in his flesh and his bones the recollection of youth – the time before the aches seeped into joints, before brittle truths weakened his frame to leave him bent and tottering.

'*Hold the way open, Endest Silann. She will rage against you. She will seek to drive me away, to close herself to me. Hold. Do not relent.*'

'*But Lord, I have sworn my life to her.*'

'*What value is that if she will not be held to account for her deeds?*'

'*She is the creator of us all, Lord!*'

'*Yes, and she will answer for it.*'

Youth was a time for harsh judgement. Such fires ebbed with age. Certainty itself withered. Dreams of salvation died on the vine and who could challenge that blighted truth? They had walked through a citadel peopled by the dead, the broken open, the spilled out. Like the violent opening of bodies, the tensions, rivalries and feuds could no longer be contained. Chaos delivered in a raw and bloody birth, and now the child squatted amidst its mangled playthings, with eyes that burned.

The fool fell into line. The fool always did. The fool followed the first who called. The fool gave away – with cowardly relief – all rights to think, to choose, .to find his own path. And so Endest Silann walked the crimson corridors, the stench-filled hallways, there but two strides behind Anomander.

'Will you do as I ask, Endest Silann?'

'Yes, Lord.'

'Will you hold?'

'I shall hold.'

'Will you await me the day?'

'Which day, Lord?'

'The day at the very end, Endest Silann. Will you await me on that day?'

'I said I would hold, Lord, and so I shall.'

'Hold, old friend, until then. Until then. Until the moment when you must betray me. No – no protestations, Endest. You will know the time, you will know it and know it well.'

It was what kept him alive, he suspected. This fraught waiting, so long all was encrusted, stiff and made almost shapeless by the accretion of centuries.

'Tell me, Endest, what stirs in the Great Barrow?'

'Lord?'

'Is it Itkovian? Do we witness in truth the birth of a new god?'

'I do not know, Lord. I am closed to such things.' As I have been since that day in the Temple.

'Ah, yes, I have forgotten. I apologize, old friend. Mayhap I will speak to Spin-nock, then. Certain quiet enquiries, perhaps.'

'He will serve you as always, Lord.'

'Yes, one of my burdens.'

'Lord, you bear them well.'

'Endest, you lie poorly.'

'Yes, Lord.'

'Spinnock it shall be, then. When you leave, please send for him – not with haste, when he has the time.'

'Lord, expect him at once.'

And so Anomander sighed, because no other response was possible, was it? And I, too, am your burden, Lord. But we best not speak of that.

See me, Lord, see how I still wait.

Incandescent light was spilling from the half-open doors of the temple, rolling in waves out over the concourse like the wash of a flood, sufficient in strength to shift corpses about, milky eyes staring as the heads pitched and lolled.

As they set out across the expanse, that light flowed up round their shins, star-tlingly cold. Endest Silann recognized the nearest dead Andii. Priests who had lin-gered too long, caught in the conflagration that Endest had felt but not seen as he rushed through the Citadel's corridors. Among them, followers from various factions. Silchas Ruin's. Andarist's, and Anomander's own. Drethdenan's, Hish Tulla's, Vanut Degalla's – oh, there had been waves of fighting on this concourse, these sanctified flagstones.

In birth there shall be blood. In death there shall be light. Yes, this was the day for both birth and death, for both blood and light.

They drew closer to the doors of the temple, slowed to observe the waves of light tumbling down the broad steps. Their hue had deepened, as if smeared with old blood, but the power was waning. Yet Endest Silann sensed a presence within, something contained, someone waiting.

For us.

The High Priestess? No. Of her, the acolyte sensed nothing.

Anomander took his first step on to the stone stairs.

And was held there, as *her* voice filled them.

No. Be warned, Anomander, dear son, from Andii blood is born a new world. Understand me. You and your kin are no longer alone, no longer free to play your vicious games. There are now . . . others.

Anomander spoke. 'Mother, did you imagine I would be surprised? Horrified? It could never be enough, to be naught but a mother, to create with hands closed upon no one. To yield so much of yourself, only to find us your only reward – us slayers, us betrayers.'

There is new blood within you.

'Yes.'

My son, what have you done?

'Like you, Mother, I have chosen to embrace change. Yes, there are others now. I sense them. There will be wars between us, and so I shall unite the Andii. Resistance is ending. Andarist, Drethdenan, Vanut Degalla. Silchas is fleeing, and so too Hish Tulla and Manalle. Civil strife is now over, Mother.'

You have killed Tiam. My son, do you realize what you have begun? Silchas flees, yes, and where do you think he goes? And the newborn, the others, what scent will draw them now, what taste of chaotic power? Anomander, in murder you seek peace, and now the blood flows and there shall be no peace, not ever again.

I forsake you, Anomander Blood of Tiam, Dragnipurake. I deny my first children all. You shall wander the realms, bereft of purpose. Your deeds shall avail you nothing. Your lives shall spawn death unending. The Dark – my heart – is closed to you, to you all.

And, as Anomander stood unmoving, Endest Silann cried out behind him, falling to his knees in bruising collapse. A hand of power reached into him, tore something loose, then was gone – something, yes, that he would one day call by its name: *Hope.*

He sat staring at the flickering flame of the lamp. Wondering what it was, that loyalty should so simply take the place of despair, as if to set such despair upon another, a chosen leader, was to absolve oneself of all that might cause pain. Loyalty, aye, the exchange that was surrender in both directions. From one, all will, from the other, all freedom.

From one, all will.

From the other . . .

The sword, an arm's length of copper-hued iron, had been forged in Darkness, in Kharkanas itself. Sole heirloom of House Durav, the weapon had known three wielders since the day of quenching at the Hust Forge, but of those kin who held the weapon before Spinnock Durav, nothing remained – no ill-fitting, worn ridges in the horn grip, no added twists of wire at the neck of the pommel adjusting weight or balance; no quirk of honing on the edges. The sword seemed to have been made, by a master weaponsmith, specifically for Spinnock, for his every habit, his every peculiarity of style and preference.

So in his kin, therefore, he saw versions of himself, and like the weapon he was but one in a continuum, unchanging, even as he knew that he would be the last. And that one day, perhaps not far off, some stranger would bend down and tug the sword from senseless fingers, would lift it for a closer examination. The water-etched blade, the almost-crimson edges with the back-edge sharply angled and the down-edge more tapering. Would squint, then, and see the faint glyphs nested in the ferrule along the entire blade's length. And might wonder at the foreign marks. Or not.

The weapon would be kept, as a trophy, as booty to sell in some smoky market, or it would rest once more in a scabbard at the hip or slung from a baldric, resuming its purpose which was to take life, to spill blood, to tear the breath from mortal souls. And generations of wielders might curse the ill-fitting horn grip, the strange ridges of wear and the once-perfect honing that no local smith could match.

Inconceivable, for Spinnock, was the image of the sword lying lost, woven out of sight by grasses, the iron's sheath of oil fading and dull with dust, and then the rust blotting the blade like open sores; until, like the nearby mouldering, rotting bones of its last wielder, the sword sank into the ground, crumbling, decaying into a black, encrusted and shapeless mass.

Seated on his bed with the weapon across his thighs, Spinnock Durav rubbed the last of the oil into the iron, watched the glyphs glisten as if alive, as ancient, minor sorcery awakened, armouring the blade against corrosion. Old magic, slowly losing its efficacy. *Just like me.* Smiling, he rose and slid the sword into the scabbard, then hung the leather baldric on a hook by the door.

'Clothes do you no justice, Spin.'

He turned, eyed the sleek woman sprawled atop the blanket, her arms out to the sides, her legs still spread wide. 'You're back.'

She grunted. 'Such arrogance. My temporary . . . absence had nothing to do with you, as you well know.'

'Nothing?'

'Well, little, then. You know I walk in Darkness, and when it takes me, I travel far indeed.'

He eyed her for a half-dozen heartbeats. 'More often of late,' he said.

'Yes.' The High Priestess sat up, wincing at some pain in her lower back and rubbing at the spot. 'Do you remember, Spin, how all of this was so easy, once? Our young bodies seemed made for just that one thing, beauty woven round a knot of need. How we displayed our readiness, how we preened, like the flowers of carnivorous plants? How it made each of us, to ourselves, the most important thing in the world, such was the seduction of that knot of need, seducing first ourselves and then others, so many others—'

'Speak for yourself,' Spinnock said, laughing, even as her words prodded something deep inside him, a hint of pain there was no point paying attention to, or so he told himself, still holding his easy smile as he drew closer to the bed. 'Those journeys into Kurald Galain were denied you for so long, until the rituals of opening seemed devoid of purpose. Beyond the raw pleasure of sex.'

She studied him a moment from beneath heavy lids. 'Yes.'

'Has she forgiven us, then?'

Her laugh was bitter. 'You ask it so plain, as if enquiring after a miffed relative! How can you do such things, Spin? It should have taken you half the night to broach that question.'

'Perhaps age has made me impatient.'

'After the torture you just put me through? You have the patience of lichen.'

'But rather more interesting, I hope.'

She moved to the edge of the bed, set her bare feet on the floor and hissed at the stone's chill. 'Where are my clothes?'

'They burned to ash in the heat of your desire.'

'There – bring them over, if you please.'

'Now who is impatient?' But he collected up her priestly robes.

'The visions are growing more . . . fraught.'

Nodding, he held out her robe.

She rose, turned round and slipped her arms into the sleeves, then settled back into his embrace. 'Thank you, Spinnock Durav, for acceding to my . . . need.'

'The ritual cannot be denied,' he replied, stroking her cut-short, midnight-black hair. 'Besides, did you think I would refuse such a request from you?'

'I grow tired of the priests. Their ennui is such that most of them must imbibe foul herbs to awaken them to life. More often, of late, we have them simply service us, while they lie there, limp as rotting bananas.'

He laughed, stepping away to find his own clothes. 'Bananas, yes, a most wondrous fruit to reward us in this strange world. That and kelyk. In any case, the image you describe is unfairly unappetizing.'

'I agree, and so, thank you again, Spinnock Durav.'

'No more gratitude, please. Unless you would have me voice my own and so overwhelm you with the pathos of my plight.'

To that, she but smiled. 'Stay naked, Spin, until I leave.'

'Another part of the ritual?' he asked.

'Would I have so humbly asked if it was?'

When she was gone, Spinnock Durav drew on his clothing once more, thinking back to his own ritual, servicing his sword with a lover's touch, as if to remind the weapon that the woman he had just made love to was but a diversion, a temporary distraction, and that there was place for but one love in his heart, as befitted a warrior.

True, an absurd ritual, a conceit that was indeed pathetic. But with so little to hold on to, well, Tiste Andii clung tight and fierce to anything with meaning, no matter how dubious or ultimately nonsensical.

Dressed once more, he set out.

The game awaited him. The haunted gaze of Seerdomin, there across from him, with artfully carved but essentially inert lumps of wood, antler and bone on the table between them. Ghostly, irrelevant players to each side.

And when it was done, when victory and defeat had been played out, they would sit for a time, drinking from the pitcher, and Seerdomin might again speak of something without quite saying what it was, might slide round what bothered him with every word, with every ambiguous comment and observation. And all Spinnock would glean was that it had something to do with the Great Barrow north of Black Coral. With his recent refusal to journey out there, ending his own pilgrimage, leaving Spinnock to wonder at the man's crisis of faith, to dread the arrival of true despair, when all that Spinnock needed from his friend might wither, even die.

And where then would he find hope?

He walked the gloomy streets, closing in on the tavern, and wondered if there was something he could do for Seerdomin. The thought slowed his steps and made him alter his course. Down an alley, out on to another street, this one the side of a modest hill, with the buildings stepping down level by level on each side, a cascade of once brightly painted doors – but who bothered with such things now in this eternal Night?

He came to one door on his left, its flaked surface gouged with a rough sigil, the outline of the Great Barrow in profile, beneath it the ragged imprint of an open hand.

Where worship was born, priests and priestesses appeared with the spontaneity of mould on bread.

Spinnock pounded on the door.

After a moment it opened a crack and he looked down to see a single eye peering up at him.

'I would speak to her,' he said.

The door creaked back. A young girl in a threadbare tunic stood in the narrow hallway, now curtseying repeatedly. 'L-lord,' she stammered, 'she is up the stairs – it is late—'

'Is it? And I am not a "lord." Is she awake?'

A hesitant nod.

'I will not take much of her time. Tell her it is the Tiste Andii warrior she once met in the ruins. She was collecting wood. I was . . . doing very little. Go, I will wait.'

Up the stairs the girl raced, two steps at a time, the dirty soles of her feet flashing with each upward leap.

He heard a door open, close, then open again, and the girl reappeared at the top of the stairs. 'Come!' she hissed.

The wood creaked beneath him as he climbed to the next level.

The priestess – ancient, immensely obese – had positioned herself on a once plush chair before an altar of heaped trinkets. Braziers bled orange light to either side, shedding tendrils of smoke that hung thick and acrid beneath the ceiling. The old woman's eyes reflected that muted glow, murky with cataracts.

As soon as Spinnock entered the small room, the girl left, closing the door behind her.

'You do not come,' said the priestess, 'to embrace the new faith, Spinnock Durav.'

'I don't recall ever giving you my name, Priestess.'

'We all know the one who alone among all the Tiste Andii consorts with us lowly humans. Beyond the old one who bargains for goods in the markets and you are not Endest Silann, who would have struggled on the stairs, and bowed each one near to breaking with his weight.'

'Notoriety makes me uneasy.'

'Of course it does. What do you want with me, warrior?'

'I would ask you something. Is there a crisis among the faithful?'

'Ah. You speak of Seerdomin, who now denies us in our need.'

'He does? How? What need?'

'It is not your concern. Not that of the Tiste Andii, nor the Son of Darkness.'

'Anomander Rake rules Black Coral, Priestess, and we Tiste Andii serve him.'

'The Great Barrow lies outside Night. The Redeemer does not kneel before the Son of Darkness.'

'I am worried for my friend, Priestess. That is all.'

'You cannot help him. Nor, it is now clear, can he help us.'

'Why do you need help?'

'We await the Redeemer, to end that which afflicts his followers.'

'And how will the Redeemer achieve such a thing, except through chosen mortals?'

She cocked her head, as if startled by his question, then she smiled. 'Ask that question of your friend, Spinnock Durav. When the game is done and your Lord is victorious yet again, and you call out for beer, and the two of you – so much more alike than you might imagine – drink and take ease in each other's company.'

'Your knowledge dismays me.'

'The Redeemer is not afraid of the Dark.'

Spinnock started, his eyes widening. 'Embracing the grief of the T'lan Imass is

one thing, Priestess. That of the Tiste Andii – no, there may be no fear in the Redeemer, but his soul had best awaken to wisdom. Priestess, make this plain in
your prayers. The Tiste Andii are not for the Redeemer. God or no, such an embrace will destroy him. Utterly.' *And, by Mother's own breath, it would destroy
us as well.*

'Seerdomin awaits you,' she said, 'and wonders, since you are ever punctual.'

Spinnock Durav hesitated, then nodded. Hoping that this woman's god had
more wisdom than she did; hoping, too, that the power of prayer could not bend
the Redeemer into ill-conceived desires to reach too far, to seek what could only
destroy him, all in that fervent fever of gushing generosity so common to new believers.

'Priestess, your claim that the Great Barrow lies beyond my Lord's responsibilities is in error. If the pilgrims are in need, the Son of Darkness will give answer—'

'And so lay claim to what is not his.'

'You do not know Anomander Rake.'

'We need nothing from your Lord.'

'Then perhaps I can help.'

'No. Leave now, Tiste Andii.'

Well, he had tried, hadn't he? Nor did he expect to gain more ground with
Seerdomin. Perhaps something more extreme was required. *No, Seerdomin is a
private man. Let him be. Remain watchful, yes, as any friend would. And wait.*

If he had walked from the nearest coast, the lone figure crossing the grasslands of
north Lamatath had travelled a hundred leagues of unsettled prairie. Nowhere to
find food beyond hunting the sparse game, all of it notoriously fleet of foot and
hoof. He was gaunt, but then, he had always been gaunt. His thin, grey hair was
unkempt, drifting out long in his wake. His beard was matted, knotted with filth.
His eyes, icy blue, were as feral as any beast of the plain.

A long coat of chain rustled, swinging clear of his shins with each stride. The
shadow he cast was narrow as a sword.

In the cloudless sky wheeled vultures or ravens, or both, so high as to be nothing but specks, yet they tracked the solitary figure far below. Or perhaps they but
skirled in the blue emptiness scanning the wastes for some dying, weakening
creature.

But this man was neither dying nor weak. He walked with the stiff purpose
characteristic of the mad, the deranged. Madness, he would have noted, does not
belong to the soul engaged with the world, with every hummock and tuft of grass,
with the old beach ridges with their cobbles of limestone pushing through the
thin, patched skin of lichen and brittle moss. With the mocking stab of shadow
that slowly wheeled as the sun dragged itself across the sky. With the sounds of
his own breath that were proof that he remained alive, that the world had yet to
take him, pull him down, steal the warmth from his ancient flesh. Madness
stalked only an inner torment, and Kallor, the High King, supreme emperor of a
dozen terrible empires, was, in his heart, a man at peace.

For the moment. But what mattered beyond just that? This single moment, pitching headlong into the next one, over and over again, as firm and true as each step he took, the hard ground reverberating up through the worn heels of his boots. The tactile affirmed reality, and nothing else mattered and never would.

A man of peace, yes indeed. And that he had once ruled the lives of hundreds of thousands, ruled over their useless, petty existences; that he had once, with a single gesture, condemned a surrendered army of fifteen thousand to their deaths; that he had sat a throne of gold, silver and onyx, like a glutton stuffed to overflowing with such material wealth that it had lost all meaning, all value . . . ah well, all that remained of such times, such glory, was the man himself, his sword, his armour, and a handful of antiquated coins in his pouch. Endless betrayals, a sea of faces made blurry and vague by centuries, with naught but the avaricious, envious glitter of their eyes remaining sharp in his mind; the sweep of smoke and fire and faint screams as empires toppled, one after another; the chaos of brutal nights fleeing a palace in flames, fleeing such a tide of vengeful fools that even Kallor could not kill them all – much as he wanted to, oh, yes – none of these things awakened bitter ire in his soul. Here in this wasteland that no one wanted, he was a man at peace.

Such truth could not be challenged, and were someone to rise up from the very earth now and stand in such challenge, why, he would cut him to pieces. Smiling all the while to evince his calm repose.

Too much weight was given to history, as far as Kallor was concerned. One's own history; that of peoples, cultures, landscapes. What value peering at past errors in judgement, at mischance and carelessness, when the only reward after all that effort was regret? Bah! Regret was the refuge of fools, and Kallor was no fool. He had lived out his every ambition, after all, lived each one out until all colour was drained away, leaving a bleached, wan knowledge that there wasn't much in life truly worth the effort to achieve it. That the rewards proved ephemeral; nay, worthless.

Every emperor in every realm, through all of time itself, soon found that the lofty title and all its power was an existence devoid of humour. Even excess and indulgences palled, eventually. And the faces of the dying, the tortured, well, they were all the same, and not one of those twisted expressions vouchsafed a glimmer of revelation, the discovery of some profound, last-breath secret that answered all the great questions. No, every face simply pulled into itself, shrank and recoiled even as agony tugged and stretched, and whatever the bulging eyes saw at the last moment was, Kallor now understood, something utterly . . . banal.

Now there was an enemy – banality. The demesne of the witless, the proud tower of the stupid. One did not need to be an emperor to witness it – scan the faces of people encircling an overturned carriage, the gleam of their eyes as they strain and stretch to catch a glimpse of blood, of broken limbs, relishing some pointless tragedy that tops up their murky inkwells of life. Watch, yes, those vultures of grief, and then speak of noble humanity, so wise and so virtuous.

Unseen by the ravens or condors, Kallor had now bared his teeth in a bleak smile, as if seeking to emulate the face of that tragically fallen idiot, pinned there beneath the carriage-wheel, seeing the last thing he would see, and finding it in the faces of the gawkers, and thinking, *Oh, look at you all. So banal. So . . . banal.*

He startled a hare from some scrub, twenty paces away, and his left hand flashed out, underhand, and a knife sped in a blur, catching the hare in mid-leap, flipping it round in the air before it fell.

A slight tack, and he halted to stand over the small, motionless body, looking down at the tiny droplets of spilled blood. The knife sunk to the hilt, driven right through just in front of the hips – the gut, then, not good. Sloppy.

He crouched, pulled loose the knife then quickly sliced open the belly and tugged and tore out the hare's warm intestines. He held the glistening ropes up in one hand, studied them and whispered, *'Banal.'*

An eye of the hare stared up sightlessly, everything behind it closed up, gone away.

But he'd seen all that before. More times than he could count. Hares, people, all the same. In that last moment, yes, there was nothing to see, so what else to do but go away?

He flung the guts to one side, picked up the carcass by its elongated hind limbs and resumed his journey. The hare was coming with him. Not that it cared. Later, they'd sit down for dinner.

High in the sky overhead, the black specks began a descent. Their equally empty eyes had spied the entrails, spread in lumpy grey ropes on the yellow grasses, now in the lone man's wake. Empty eyes, but a different kind of emptiness. Not that of death's banality, no, but that of life's banality.

The same kind of eyes as Kallor's own.

And this was the mercy in the hare's swift death, for unlike countless hundreds of thousands of humans, the creature's last glimpse was not of Kallor's profoundly empty eyes – a sight that brought terror into the faces of every victim.

The world, someone once said, gives back what is given. In abundance. But then, as Kallor would point out, someone was always saying something. Until he got fed up and had them executed.

Chapter Five

Pray, do not speak to me of weather
Not sun, not cloud, not of the places
Where storms are born
I would not know of wind shivering the heather
Nor sleet, nor rain, nor of ancient traces
On stone grey and worn

Pray, do not regale the troubles of ill health
Not self, not kin, not of the old woman
At the road's end
I will spare no time nor in mercy yield wealth
Nor thought, nor feeling, nor shrouds woven
To tempt luck's end

Pray, tell me of deep chasms crossed
Not left, not turned, not of the betrayals
Breeding like worms
I would you cry out your rage 'gainst what is lost
Now strong, now to weep, now to make fist and rail
On earth so firm

Pray, sing loud the wretched glories of love
Now pain, now drunken, now torn from all reason
In laughter and tears
I would you bargain with the fey gods above
Nor care, nor cost, nor turn of season
To wintry fears

Sing to me this and I will face you unflinching
Now knowing, now seeing, now in the face
Of the howling storm
Sing your life as if a life without ending
And your love, sun's bright fire, on its celestial pace
To where truth is born

PRAY, AN END TO INCONSEQUENTIAL THINGS
BAEDISK OF NATHILOG

Darujhistan. Glories unending! Who could call a single deed inconsequential? This scurrying youth with his arms full of vegetables, the shouts from the stall in his wake, the gauging eye of a guard thirty paces away, assessing the poor likelihood of catching the urchin. Insignificant? Nonsense! Hungry mouths fed, glowing pride, some fewer coins for the hawker, perhaps, but it seemed all profit did was fill a drunken husband's tankard anyway so the bastard could die of thirst for all she cared! A guard's congenitally flawed heart beat on, not yet pushed to bursting by hard pursuit through the crowded market, and so he lives a few weeks longer, enough to complete his full twenty years' service and so guarantee his wife and children a pension. And of course the one last kiss was yet to come, the kiss that whispered volumes of devotion and all the rest.

The pot-thrower in the hut behind the shop, hands and forearms slick with clay, dreaming, yes, of the years in which a life took shape, when each press of a fingertip sent a deep track across a once smooth surface, changing the future, re-shaping the past, and was this not as much chance as design? For all that intent could score a path, that the ripples sent up and down and outward could be surmised by decades of experience, was the outcome ever truly predictable?

Oh, of course she wasn't thinking any such thing. An ache in her left wrist obliterated all thoughts beyond the persistent ache itself, and what it might portend and what herbs she would need to brew to ease her discomfort – and how could such concerns be inconsequential?

What of the child sitting staring into the doleful eye of a yoked ox outside Corb's Womanly Charms where her mother was inside and had been for near a bell now, though of course Mother had Uncle-Doruth-who-was-a-secret for company which was better than an ox that did nothing but moan? The giant, soft, dark-so-dark brown eye stared back and to think in both directions was obvious but what was the ox thinking except that the yoke was heavy and the cart even heavier and it'd be nice to lie down and what could the child be thinking about but beef stew and so no little philosopher was born, although in years to come, why, she'd have her own uncle-who-was-a-secret and thus like her mother enjoy all the fruits of marriage with few of the niggling pits.

And what of the sun high overhead, bursting with joyous light to bathe the wondrous city like a benediction of all things consequential? Great is the need, so sudden, so pressing, to reach up, close fingers about the fiery orb, to drag it back – and back! – into night and its sprawled darkness, where all manner of things of import have trembled the heavens and the very roots of the earth, or nearly so.

Back, then, the short round man demands, for this is his telling, his knowing, his cry of *Witness!* echoing still, and still. The night of arrivals, the deeds of the arrived, even as night arrives! Let nothing of consequence be forgot. Let nothing of inconsequence be deemed so and who now could even imagine such things to exist, recalling with wise nod the urchin thief, the hawker, the guard. The thrower of pots and the child and the ox and Uncle Doruth with his face between the legs of another man's wife, all to come (excuse!) in the day ahead.

Mark, too, this teller of the tale, with his sage wink. We are in the midst!

Night, shadows overlapping, a most indifferent blur that would attract no one's notice, barring that nuisance of a cat on the sill of the estate, amber eyes tracking now as one shadow moves out from its place of temporary concealment. Out goes this errant shadow, across the courtyard, into deeper shadows against the estate's wall.

Crouching, Torvald Nom looked up to see the cat's head and those damned eyes, peering down at him. A moment later the head withdrew, taking its wide gaze with it. He made his stealthy way to the back corner, paused once more. He could hear the gate guards, a pair of them, arguing over something, tones of suspicion leading to accusation answered by protestations of denial but *Damn you, Doruth, I just don't trust you—*

—No reason not to, Milok. I ever give you one? No—
—To Hood you ain't. My first wife—
—Wouldn't leave me alone, I swear! She stalked me like a cat a rat—
—A rat! Aye, that's about right—
—I swear, Milok, she very nearly raped me—
—The first time! I know, she told me all about it, with eyes so bright!—
—Heard it made you horny as Hood's black sceptre—
—That ain't any of your business, Doruth—

And something soft brushed against Torvald's leg. The cat, purring like soft gravel, back bowed, tail writhing. He lifted his foot, held it hovering over the creature. Hesitated, then settled it back down. By Apsalar's sweet kiss, the kit's eyes and ears might be a boon, come to think of it. Assuming it had the nerve to follow him.

Torvald eyed the wall, the cornices, the scrollwork metopes, the braided false columns. He wiped sweat from his hands, dusted them with the grit at the wall's base, then reached up for handholds, and began to climb.

He gained the sill of the window on the upper floor, pulled himself on to it, balanced on his knees. True, never wise, but the fall wouldn't kill him, wouldn't even sprain an ankle, would it? Drawing a dagger he slipped the blade in between the shutters, carefully felt for the latch.

The cat, alighting beside him, nearly pitched him from the sill, but he managed to recover, swearing softly under his breath as he resumed working the lock.

—She still loves you, you know—
—What—
—She does. She just likes some variety. I tell you, Milok, this last one of yours was no easy conquest—

—You swore!—

—You're my bestest, oldest friend. No more secrets between us! And when I swear to that, as I'm doing now, I mean it true. She's got an appetite so sharing shouldn't be a problem. I ain't better than you, just different, that's all. Different.—

—How many times a week, Duroth? Tell me true!—

—Oh, every second day or so—

—But I'm every second day, too!—

—Odd, even, I guess. Like I said, an appetite.—

—I'll say.—

—After shift, let's go get drunk—

—Aye, we can compare and contrast—

—I love it. Just that, hah! . . . Hey, Milok . . . —

—Aye?—

—How old's your daughter?—

The latch clicked, springing free the shutters just as a sword hissed from a scabbard and, amidst wild shouting, a fight was underway at the gate.

—A joke! Honest! Just a joke, Milok!—

Voices now from the front of the house, as Torvald slid his dagger blade between the lead windows and lifted the inside latch. He quickly edged into the dark room, as boots rapped on the compound and more shouting erupted at the front gate. A lantern crashed and someone's sword went flying to skitter away on the cobbles.

Torvald quickly closed the shutters, then the window.

The infernal purring was beside him, a soft jaw rubbing against a knee. He reached for the cat, fingers twitching, hesitated, then withdrew his hand. Pay attention to the damned thing, right, so when it hears what can't be heard and when it sees what can't be seen, yes . . .

Pivoting in his crouch, he scanned the room. Some sort of study, though most of the shelves were bare. Overreaching ambition, this room, a sudden lurch towards culture and sophistication, but of course it was doomed to failure. Money wasn't enough. Intelligence helped. Taste, an inquisitive mind, an interest in other stuff – stuff out of immediate sight, stuff having nothing to do with whatever. Wasn't enough to simply send some servant to scour some scrollmonger's shop and say 'I'll take that shelf's worth, and that one, too.' Master's not too discriminating, yes. Master probably can't even read so what difference does it make?

He crept over to the one shelf on which were heaped a score or so scrolls, along with one leather-bound book. Each scroll was rolled tight, tied with some seller's label – just as he had suspected. Torvald began reading through them.

Treatise on Drainage Grooves in Stone Gutters of Gadrobi District, Nineteenth Report in the Year of the Shrew, Extraordinary Subjects, Guild of Quarry Engineering. Author: Member 322.

Tales of Pamby Doughty and the World Inside the Trunk (with illustrations by some dead man).

The Lost Verses of Anomandaris, with annotation. Torvald's brows rose, since this one might actually be worth something. He quickly slipped the string off and unfurled the scroll. The vellum was blank, barring a short annotation at the bottom that read: *No scholarly erudition is possible at the moment.* And a publisher's mark denoting this scroll as part of a series of Lost Works, published by the Vellum Makers' Guild of Pale.

He rolled the useless thing back up, plucked out one more.

An Illustrated Guide to Headgear of Cobblers of Genabaris in the fourth century, Burn's Sleep, by Cracktooth Filcher, self-avowed serial collector and scourge of cobblers, imprisoned for life. A publication of Prisoner's Pit Library, Nathilog.

He had no doubt the illustrations were lavish and meticulous, detailed to excess, but somehow his curiosity was not up to the challenge of perusal.

By now the commotion at the gate had been settled. Various members of the guard had returned from the fracas, with much muttering and cursing that fell away abruptly as soon as they entered the main house on their way to their rooms, telling Torvald that the master was indeed home and probably asleep. Which was something of a problem, given just how paranoid the bastard was and the likely hiding place of his trove was somewhere in his damned bedroom. Well, the world presented its challenges, and without challenges life was worthless and pointless and, most crucially, devoid of interest.

He moved to the door leading to the hallway, pausing to wrap a cloth about his face, leaving only his eyes free. The cat watched intently. Lifting the latch he tugged the door open and peered out into the corridor. Left, the outer, back wall not three paces away. Right, the aisle reaching all the way through the house. Doors and a central landing for the staircase. And a guard, seated facing that landing. Black hair, red, bulbous nose, protruding lower lip, and enough muscles slabbed on to a gigantic frame to fill out two or three Torvald Noms. The fool was knitting, his mouth moving and brow knotting as he counted stitches.

And there was the horrid cat, padding straight for him.

Torvald quietly closed the door.

He should have strangled the thing.

From the corridor he heard a grunting curse, then boots thumping down the stairs.

Opening the door once more he looked out. The guard was gone, the knitting lying on the floor with one strand leading off down the stairs.

Hah! Brilliant cat! Why, if he met it again he'd kiss it – but nowhere near where it licked itself because there were limits, after all, and anywhere a cat could lick itself was nowhere he'd kiss.

Torvald quickly closed the door behind him and tiptoed up the corridor. A cautious glance down the wide, central staircase. Wherever the cat had run off with the ball of wool, it was out of sight, and so too the guard. He faced the ornate double doors directly behind the vacated wooden chair.

Locked?

Yes.

He drew his dagger and slid the thin blade between the doors.

Ornate decoration was often accompanied by neglect of the necessary mechanisms, and this lock followed the rule, as he felt the latch lift away. Boots sounded downstairs. He tugged open the door and quickly slipped inside, crouching once more. A front room, an office of sorts, with a single lantern on a short wick casting faint light across the desk and its strewn heap of papyrus sheets. A second door, smaller, narrow, behind the desk's high-backed plush chair.

Torvald Nom tiptoed towards it.

Pausing at the desk to douse the lantern, waiting for his eyes to adjust to the darkness, crouching yet lower to squint at the crack beneath the bedroom door, pleased to find no thread of light. Drawing up against the panelled wood with its gold-leaf insets now dull in the gloom. No lock this time. Hinges feeling well oiled. He slowly worked the door open.

Inside, quietly shutting the door behind him.

Soft breathing from the huge four-poster bed. Then a sigh. 'Sweet sliverfishy, is that you?'

A woman's husky, whispering voice, and now stirring sounds from the bed.

'The night stalker this time? Ooh, that one's fun – I'll keep my eyes closed and whimper lots when you threaten me to stay quiet. Hurry, I'm lying here, petrified. *Someone's in my room!*'

Torvald Nom hesitated, truly torn between necessity and . . . well, necessity.

He untied his rope belt. And, in a hissing voice, demanded, 'First, the treasure. Where is it, woman?'

She gasped. 'That's a good voice! A new one! The treasure, ah! You know where it is, you horrible creature! Right here between my legs!'

Torvald rolled his eyes. 'Not that one. The other one.'

'If I don't tell you?'

'Then I will have my way with you.'

'Oh! I say nothing! Please!'

Damn, he sure messed that one up. There was no way she'd not know he wasn't who he was pretending to be, even when that someone was pretending to be someone else. How to solve this?

'Get on your stomach. Now, on your hands and knees. Yes, like that.'

'You're worse than an animal!'

Torvald paused at the foot of the bed. Worse than an animal? What did that mean? Shaking his head, he climbed on to the bed. *Well, here goes nothing.*

A short time later: 'Sliverfishy! The new elixir? Gods, it's spectacular! Why, I can't call you sliverfishy any more, can I? More like . . . a salmon! Charging upstream! Oh!'

'The treasure, or I'll use this knife.' And he pressed the cold blade of the dagger against the outside of her right thigh.

She gasped again. 'Under the bed! Don't hurt me! Keep pushing, damn you! Harder! This one's going to make a baby – I know it! This time, a baby!'

Well, he did his part anyway, feeding his coins into the temple's cup and all that, and may her prayers guide her true into motherhood's blissful heaven. She collapsed on to the bed, groaning, while he backed off, knelt on the cold wooden floor and reached under the bed, knuckles skinning against a large, low longbox. Groping, he found one handle and dragged it out.

She moaned. 'Oh, don't start counting again, darling. Please. You ruin everything when you do that!'

'Not counting, woman. Stealing. Stay where you are. Eyes closed. Don't move.'

'It just sounds silly now, you know that.'

'Shut up, or I'll do you again.'

'Ah! What was that elixir again?'

He prised open the lock with the tip of the dagger. Inside, conveniently stored in burlap sacks tagged with precise amounts, a fortune of gems, jewels and high councils. He quickly collected the loot.

'You *are* counting!'

'I warned you.' He climbed back on to the bed. Looked down and saw that promises weren't quite enough. *Gods below, if you only were.* 'Listen,' he said, 'I need more elixir. In the office. Don't move.'

'I won't. I promise.'

He hurried out, crept across the outer room and paused at the doors to the corridor to press his ear against the panel.

Softly, the slither-click of bamboo knitting needles.

Torvald slid the dagger into its scabbard, reversed grip, opened the door, looked down at the top of the guard's hairy head, and swung hard. The pommel crunched. The man sagged in his chair, then folded into a heap at the foot of the chair.

The cat was waiting by the library door.

Uncle One, Uncle Two, Father None. Aunt One, Aunt Two, Mother None.

Present and on duty, Uncle One, Aunt One and Cousins One, Two, Three. Cousin One edging closer, almost close enough for another hard, sharp jab with an elbow as One made to collect another onion from the heap on the table. But he knew One's games, had a year's list of bruises to prove it, and so, just as accidentally, he took a half-step away, keeping on his face a beaming smile as Aunt One cooed her delight at this sudden bounty, and Uncle One sat opposite, ready to deliver his wink as soon as he glanced over – which he wouldn't do yet because timing, as Uncle Two always told him, was everything. Besides, he needed to be aware of Cousin One especially now that the first plan had been thwarted.

One, whose name was Snell, would have to work harder in his head, work that cunning which seemed to come from nowhere and wasn't part of the dull stupidity that was One's actual brain, so maybe it was demons after all, clattering and chittering all their cruel ideas. Snell wouldn't let this rest, he knew. No, he'd remember and start planning. And the hurt would be all the worse for that.

But right now he didn't care, not about Cousin One, not about anything that might come later tonight or tomorrow. He'd brought food home, after all, an armload of food, delivering his treasure to joyous cries of relief.

And the man whose name he'd been given, the man long dead who was neither Uncle One nor Uncle Two but had been Uncle Three and not, of course, Father One, well, that man would be proud that the boy with his name was doing what was needed to keep the family together.

Collecting his own onion, the child named Harllo made his way to a safe corner of the single room, and, moments before taking a bite, glanced up to meet Uncle One's eyes, to catch the wink and then nod in answer.

Just like Uncle Two always said, timing was how a man measured the world, and his place in it. Timing wasn't a maybe world, it was a world of yes and no, this, not that. Now, not later. Timing belonged to all the beasts of nature that hunted other creatures. It belonged to the tiger and its fixed, watching eyes. It belonged, too, to the prey, when the hunter became hunted, like with Cousin One, each moment a contest, a battle, a duel. But Harllo was learning the tiger's way, thanks to Uncle Two, whose very skin could change into that of a tiger, when anger awakened cold and deadly. Who had a tiger's eyes and was the bravest, wisest man in all of Darujhistan.

And the only one, apart from young Harllo himself, who knew the truth of Aunt Two, who wasn't Aunt Two at all, but Mother One. Even if she wouldn't admit it, wouldn't ever say it, and wouldn't have hardly nothing to do with her only child, her *son of Rape*. Once, Harllo had thought that Rape was his father's name, but now he knew it was a thing people did to other people, as mean as an elbow in the ribs, maybe meaner. And that was why Mother One stayed Aunt Two, and why on those rare occasions she visited she wouldn't meet Harllo's eyes no matter how he tried, and why she wouldn't say anything about nothing except with a voice that was all anger.

'Aunt Stonny hates words, Harllo,' Gruntle had explained, 'but only when those words creep too close to her, to where she hides, you see?'

Yes, he saw. He saw plenty.

Snell caught his eye and made a wicked face, mouthing vicious promises. His little sister, Cousin Two, whose name was Mew, was watching from where she held on to the table edge, seeing but not understanding because how could she, being only three years old; while Cousin Three, another girl but this one named Hinty, was all swathed in the cradle and safe in there, safe from everything, which was how it should be for the littlest ones.

Harllo was five, maybe close to six, but already tall – *stretched*, laughed Gruntle, *stretched and scrawny because that's how boys grow*.

Aunt Myrla had the rest of the vegetables in a steaming pot over the hearth, and Harllo saw her flick a knowing look at her husband, who nodded, not pausing in massaging the stumps below his knees, where most people had shins and ankles and then feet, but Uncle Bedek had had an accident – which was something like Rape only not on purpose – and so he couldn't walk any more which made life hard for them all, and meant Harllo had to do what was needed since Snell didn't seem interested in doing anything. Except torment Harllo, of course.

The air in the cramped room was smelling earthy and sweet now, as Myrla fed more dung on to the small hearth beneath the pot. Harllo knew he'd have to go out and collect more come the morrow and that might mean right out of the city, up along the West Shore of the lake, which was an adventure.

Snell finished his onion and crept closer to Harllo, hands tightening into fists.

But Harllo had already heard the boots in the alley outside, crackling on the dead fronds from the collapsed roof opposite, and a moment later Uncle Two swept the hanging aside and leaned into the room, the barbs of his face looking freshly painted, so stark were they, and his eyes glowed like candle flames. His smile revealed fangs.

Bedek waved. 'Gruntle! Do come in, old friend! See how Myrla readies a feast!'

'Well timed, then,' the huge man replied, entering the room, 'for I have brought smoked horse.' Seeing Harllo, he waved the boy over. 'Need to put some muscle on this one.'

'Oh,' said Myrla, 'he never sits still, that's his problem. Not for a moment!'

Snell was scowling, scuttling in retreat and looking upon Gruntle with hatred and fear.

Gruntle picked up Harllo, then held him squirming under one arm as he took the two steps to the hearth to hand Myrla a burlap-wrapped package.

Bedek was eyeing Gruntle. 'Glad you made it back,' he said in a low voice. 'Heard about you at the gate and that moment in Worrytown – damn, but I wish I wasn't so . . . useless.'

Setting Harllo down, Gruntle sighed. 'Maybe your days of riding with caravans are done, but that doesn't make you useless. You're raising a fine family, Bedek, a fine family.'

'I ain't raising nothing,' Bedek muttered, and Harllo knew that tone, knew it all too well, and it might be days, maybe even a week, before Uncle One climbed back up from the dark, deep hole he was now in. The problem was, Bedek liked that place, liked the way Myrla closed round him, all caresses and embraces and soft murmurings, and it'd go on like that until the night came when they made noises in their bed, and come the next morning, why, Bedek would be smiling.

When Myrla was like that, though, when she was all for her husband and nothing else, it fell to Harllo to tend to the girls and do everything that was needed, and worst of all, it meant no one was holding back Snell. The beatings would get bad, then.

Myrla couldn't work much, not since the last baby, when she'd hurt something in her belly and now she got tired too easy, and even this glorious supper she was creating would leave her exhausted and weak with a headache. When able, she'd mend clothes, but that wasn't happening much of late, which made Harllo's raiding the local markets all the more important.

He stayed close to Gruntle, who now sat opposite Uncle Bedek and had produced a jar of wine, and this kept Snell away for now, which of course only made things worse later but that was all right. You couldn't choose your family, after all, not your cousins, not anyone. They were there and that was that.

Besides, he could leave early tomorrow morning, so early Snell wouldn't even be awake, and he'd make his way out of the city, out along the lake shore where the world stretched away, where beyond the shanties there were hills with nothing but goats and shepherds and beyond even them there was nothing but empty land. That such a thing could exist whispered to Harllo of possibilities, ones that he couldn't hope to name or put into words, but were all out in the future life that seemed blurry, ghostly, but a promise even so. As bright as Gruntle's eyes, that promise, and it was that promise that Harllo held on to, when Snell's fists were coming down.

Bedek and Gruntle talked about the old days, when they'd both worked the same caravans, and it seemed to Harllo that the past – a world he'd never seen because it was before the Rape – was a place of great deeds, a place thick with life where the sun was brighter, the sunsets were deeper, the stars blazed in a black sky and the moon was free of mists, and men stood taller and prouder and nobody had to talk about the past back then, because it was happening right now.

Maybe that was how he would find the future, a new time in which to stand tall. A time he could stretch into.

Across from Harllo, Snell crouched in a gloomy corner, his eyes filled with their own promise as he grinned at Harllo.

Myrla brought them plates heaped with food.

The papyrus sheets, torn into shreds, lit quickly, sending black flakes upward in the chimney's draught, and Duiker watched them go, seeing crows, thousands of crows. Thieves of memory, stealing everything else he might have thought about, might have resurrected to ease the uselessness of his present life. All the struggles to recall faces had been surrendered, and his every effort to write down this dread history had failed. Words flat and lifeless, scenes described in the voice of the dead.

Who were those comrades at his side back then? Who were those Wickans and Malazans, those warlocks and warriors, those soldiers and sacrificial victims who perched above the road, like sentinels of futility, staring down at their own marching shadows?

Bult. Lull. Sormo Enath.

Coltaine.

Names, then, but no faces. The chaos and terror of fighting, of reeling in exhaustion, of wounds slashed open and bleeding, of dust and the reek of spilled wastes – no, he could not write of that, could not relate the truth of it, any of it.

Memory fails. For ever doomed as we seek to fashion scenes, framed, each act described, reasoned and reasonable, irrational and mad, but somewhere beneath there must be the thick, solid sludge of motivation, of significance, of meaning – there must be. The alternative is . . . unacceptable.

But this was where his attempts delivered him, again and again. The unacceptable truths, the ones no sane person could ever face, could ever meet eye to eye. That nothing was worth revering, not even the simple fact of survival, and certainly not that endless cascade of failures, of deaths beyond counting.

Even here, in this city of peace, he watched the citizens in all their daily dances, and with each moment that passed, his disdain deepened. He disliked the way his thoughts grew ever more uncharitable, ever more baffled by the endless scenes of seemingly mindless, pointless existence, but there seemed no way out of that progression as his observations unveiled the pettiness of life, the battles silent and otherwise with wives, husbands, friends, children, parents; with the very crush on a crowded street, each life closed round itself, righteous and uncaring of strangers – people fully inside their own lives. Yet should he not revel in such things? In their profound freedom, in their extraordinary luxury of imagining themselves in control of their own lives?

Of course, they weren't. In freedom, such as each might possess, they raised their own barriers, carried shackles fashioned by their own hands. Rattling the chains of emotions, of fears and worries, of need and spite, of the belligerence that railed against the essential anonymity that gripped a person. Aye, a most unacceptable truth.

Was this the driving force behind the quest for power? To tear away anonymity, to raise fame and infamy up like a blazing shield and shining sword? To voice a cry that would be heard beyond the gates of one's own life?

But oh, Duiker had heard enough such cries. He had stood, cowering, in the midst of howls of defiance and triumph, all turning sour with despair, with senseless rage. The echoes of power were uniform, yes, in their essential emptiness. Any historian worthy of the title could see that.

No, there was no value in writing. No more effect than a babe's fists battering at the silence that ignored every cry. History meant nothing, because the only continuity was human stupidity. Oh, there were moments of greatness, of bright deeds, but how long did the light of such glory last? From one breath to the next, aye, and no more than that. No more than that. *As for the rest, kick through the bones and wreckage for they are what remain, what lasts until all turns to dust.*

'You are looking thoughtful,' Mallet observed, leaning forward with a grunt to top up Duiker's tankard. 'Which, I suppose, should not come as a surprise, since you just burned the efforts of most of a year, not to mention a high council's worth of papyrus.'

'I will reimburse you the cost,' Duiker said.

'Don't be ridiculous,' the healer said, leaning back. 'I only said you looked thoughtful.'

'Appearances deceive, Mallet. I am not interested in thinking any more. About anything.'

'Good, then this is a true meeting of minds.'

Duiker continued studying the fire, continued watching the black crows wing up the chimney. 'For you, unwise,' he said. 'You have assassins to consider.'

Mallet snorted. 'Assassins. Antsy's already talking about digging up a dozen cussers. Blend's out hunting down the Guild's headquarters, while Picker and

Bluepearl work with Councillor Coll to sniff out the source of the contract. Give it all a week and the problem will cease being a problem. Permanently.'

Duiker half smiled. 'Don't mess with Malazan marines, retired or otherwise.'

'You'd think people would know by now, wouldn't you?'

'People are stupid, Mallet.'

The healer winced. 'Not all of us.'

'True. But Hood waits for everyone, stupid, smart, witty, witless. Waits with the same knowing smile.'

'No wonder you burned your book, Duiker.'

'Yes.'

'So, since you're no longer writing history, what will you do?'

'Do? Why, nothing.'

'Now that's something I know all about – oh, don't even try to object. Aye, I heal someone every now and then, but I was a soldier, once. And now I'm not. Now I sit around getting fat, and it's fat poisoned through and through with some kind of cynical bile. I lost all my friends, Duiker. No different from you. Lost 'em all, and for what? Damned if I know, damned and damned again, but no, I don't know the why of it, the why of anything.'

'A meeting of minds, indeed,' Duiker said. 'Then again, Mallet, it seems you are at war once more. Against the usual implacable, deadly enemy.'

'The Guild? I suppose you're right. But it won't last long, will it? I don't like being retired. It's like announcing an end to your worth, whatever that worth was, and the longer you go on, the more you realize that that worth wasn't worth anything like you once thought it was, and that just makes it worse.'

Duiker set down his tankard and rose. 'The High Alchemist has invited me to lunch on the morrow. I'd best go to bed and get some sleep. Watch your back, healer. Sometimes the lad pushes and the lady's nowhere in sight.'

Mallet simply nodded, having assumed the burden of staring at the fire now that Duiker was leaving.

The historian walked away from the warmth, passing through draughts and layers of chill air on his way to his room. Colder and colder, with every step.

Somewhere above this foul temple, crows danced with sparks above the mouth of a chimney, virtually unseen in the darkness. Each one carried a word, but the sparks were deaf. Too busy with the ecstasy of their own bright, blinding fire. At least, until they went out.

Gaz stormed out early, as soon as he realized he wasn't going to get enough coin from the day's take to buy a worthwhile night of drinking. Thordy watched her husband go, that pathetic forward tilt of the man's walk which always came when he was enraged, the jerky strides as he marched out into the night. Where he went she had no idea, nor, truth be told, did she even care.

Twice now in the past week that skinny mite of an urchin had raided her vegetable stand. Gods, what were parents up to these days? The runt was probably five years old, no older that's for sure, and already fast as an eel in the shallows – and why wasn't he leashed as a child should be? Especially at that age when there were plenty of people who'd snatch him, use him or sell him quick as can be. And if they used him in that bad way, then they'd wring his neck afterwards, which Thordy might not mind so much except that it was a cruel thought and a cruel picture and more like something her husband would think than her. Though he'd only be thinking in terms of how much money she might make without the thieving going on. And maybe what he might do if he ever got his hands on the runt.

She shivered at that thought, then was distracted by Nou the watchdog in the garden next to hers, an unusual eruption of barking – but then she remembered her husband and his walk and how Nou hated Gaz especially when he walked like that. When Gaz stumbled back home, drunk and useless, the mangy dog never made a sound, ignored Gaz straight out, in fact.

Dogs, she knew, could smell bad intentions. Other animals too, but especially dogs.

Gaz never touched Thordy, not even a shove or a slap, because without her and the garden she tended he was in trouble, and he knew that well enough. He'd been tempted, many times, oh, yes, but there'd be, all of a sudden, a glint in his eyes, a surprise, flickering alight. And he'd smile and turn away, saving that fist and all that was behind it for someone else. Gaz liked a good fight, in some alley behind a tavern. Liked kicking faces in, so long as the victim was smaller than he was, and more drunk. And without any friends who might step in or come up from behind. It was how he dealt with the misery of his life, or so he said often enough.

Thordy wasn't sure what all that misery was about, though she had some ideas. Her, for one. The pathetic patch of ground she had for her vegetables. Her barren womb. The way age and hard work was wearing her down, stealing the glow she'd once had. Oh, there was plenty about her that made him miserable. And, all things considered, she'd been lucky to have him for so long, especially when he'd worked the nets on that fisher boat, the nets that, alas, had taken all his fingers that night when something big had waited down below, motionless and so unnoticed as the crew hauled the net aboard. Then it exploded in savage power, making for the river like a battering ram. Gaz's fingers, all entwined, sprang like topped carrots, and now he had thumbs and rows of knuckles and nothing else.

Fists made for fighting, he'd say with an unconscious baring of his teeth. *That and nothing more.*

And that was true enough and good reason, she supposed, for getting drunk every chance he could.

Lately, however, she'd been feeling a little less generous – no, she'd been feeling not much of anything at all. Even pity had dwindled, whispered away like a dry leaf on the autumn wind. And it was as if he had changed, right in front of her eyes, though she now understood that what had changed was behind her eyes – not the one looked at, but the one doing the looking. She no longer recoiled in the face of his fury. No longer shied from that marching tilt and all its useless anger, and would now study it, seeing its futility, seeing the self-pity in that wounded pitch.

She was empty, then, and she had first thought she would remain so, probably for the rest of her life. Instead, something had begun to fill the void. At first, it arrived with a start, a twinge of guilt, but not any more. Now, when thoughts of murder filled her head, it was like immersing herself in a scented bath.

Gaz was miserable. He said so. He'd be happier if he were dead.

And, truth be told, so would she.

All this love, all this desperate need, and he was useless. She should have driven him out of her life long ago, and he knew it. Holding on to him the way she was doing was torture. He'd told her he only fought weaklings. Fools and worse. He told her he did it to keep his arms strong, to harden his knuckles, to hold on to (hah, that was a good one) some kind of reason for staying alive. A man needs a skill, aye, and no matter if it was good or bad, no matter at all. But the truth was, he chose the meanest, biggest bastards he could find. Proving he could, proving those knuckles and their killing ways.

Killing, aye. Four so far, that he was sure of.

Sooner or later, Gaz knew, the coin would flip, and it would be his cold corpse lying face down in some alley. Well enough. When you pay out more than you're worth, again and again, eventually somebody comes to collect.

She'd not mourn him, he knew. A man in love could see when the one he loved stopped loving him back. He did not blame her, and did not love her any less; no, his need just got worse.

The Blue Ball Tavern occupied one corner of a massive, decrepit heap of tenements that stank of urine and rotting rubbish. In the midst of the fete, the nightly anarchy on these back streets up from the docks reached new heights, and Gaz was not alone in hunting the alleys for trouble.

It occurred to him that maybe he wasn't as unusual as he might have once believed. That maybe he was just one among thousands of useless thugs in this city, all of them hating themselves and out sniffing trails like so many mangy dogs. Those who knew him gave him space, slinking back from his path as he stalked towards his chosen fighting grounds, behind the Blue Ball. That brief thought – about other people, about the shadowed faces he saw around him – was short-lived, flitting away with the first smell of blood in the damp, sultry air.

Someone had beaten him to it, and might even now be swaggering out the opposite end of the alley. Well, maybe the fool might circle back, and he could deliver to the bastard what he'd done to somebody else – and there was the body, the huddled, motionless shape. Walking up, Gaz nudged it with one boot. Heard a blood-frothed wheeze. Slammed his heel down on the ribcage, just to hear the snap and crunch. A cough, spraying blood, a low groan, then a final exhalation.

Done, easy as that.

'Are you pleased, Gaz?'

He spun round at the soft, deep voice, forearms lifting into a guard he expected to fail – but the fist he thought was coming never arrived, and, swearing, he stepped back until his shoulders thudded against the wall, glared in growing fear at the tall, shrouded figure standing before him. 'I ain't afraid,' he said in a belligerent growl.

Amusement washed up against him like a wave. 'Open yourself, Gaz. Your soul. Welcome your god.'

Gaz could feel the air on his teeth, could feel his lips stretching until cracks split to ooze blood. His heart hammered at his chest. 'I ain't got no god. I'm nothing but curses, and I don't know you. Not at all.'

'Of course you do, Gaz. You have made sacrifice to me, six times now. And counting.'

Gaz could not see the face within the hood, but the air between them was suddenly thick with some pungent, cloying scent. Like cold mud, the kind that ran in turgid streams behind slaughterhouses. He thought he heard the buzz of flies, but the sound was coming from somewhere inside his own head. 'I don't kill for you,' he said, his voice thin and weak.

'You don't have to. I do not demand sacrifices. There is . . . no need. You mortals consecrate any ground you choose, even this alley. You drain a life on to it. Nothing more is required. Not intent, not prayer, nor invocation. I am summoned, without end.'

'What do you want from me?'

'For now, only that you continue harvesting souls. When the time comes for more than that, Gaz of the Gadrobi, you will be shown what must be done.'

'And if I don't want—'

'Your wants are not relevant.'

He couldn't get that infernal buzzing out of his skull. He shook his head, squeezed shut his eyes for a moment. When he opened them again the god was gone.

The flies. The flies are in my head. Gods, get out!

Someone had wandered into the alley, weaving, mumbling, one hand held out to fend off any obstacles.

I can get them out. Yes! And, all at once, he knew the truth of that, knew that killing would silence those cursed flies. Swinging round, he pitched forward, hands lifting, and fast-marched towards the drunken fool.

Who looked up at the last moment, in time to meet those terrible knuckles.

Krute of Talient slowed as he approached the recessed entrance to the tenement where he now lived. Someone was standing in the shadows, blocking the door. He halted ten paces away. 'That was good work,' he said. 'You was behind me most of the way, making me think you wasn't good at all, but now here you are.'

'Hello, Krute.'

At that voice Krute started, then leaned forward, trying to pierce the gloom. Nothing but a shape, but it was, he concluded, the right shape. 'Gods below, I never thought you'd come back. Do you have any idea what's happened since you vanished?'

'No. Why don't you tell me?'

Krute grinned. 'I can do that, but not out here.'

'You once lived in a better neighbourhood, Krute.'

He watched Rallick Nom step out from the alcove and his grin broadened. 'You ain't changed at all. And yes, I've known better times – and I hate to say it, but you're to blame, Rallick.'

The tall, gaunt assassin turned to study the tenement building. 'You live here? And it's my fault?'

'Come on,' Krute said, 'let's get inside. Top floor, of course, an alley corner – easy to the roof, dark as Hood's armpit. You'll love it.'

A short time later they sat in the larger of the two rooms, a scarred table between them on which sat a stubby candle with a badly smoking wick, and a clay jug of sour ale. The two assassins held tin cups, both of which leaked.

Since pouring the ale, Krute had said nothing, but now he grunted in amused surprise. 'I just thought of something. You showing up, alive and hale, has just done what Krafar couldn't do. We had a cult, Rallick Nom, worshipping the memory of you. Krafar outlawed it in the Guild, then tried to eradicate it – forced us deeper. Not deep enough for me – I'm under suspicion and they've gone and isolated me, like I was already dead. Old contacts . . . look right through me, Rallick. It's been damned hard.'

'Krafar?'

'Seba, Talo's brood. In the squabble over who was gonna take over after Vorcan, he's the one got through unscathed – still breathing, I mean. The Guild's decimated, Rallick. Infighting, lots of good killers getting disgusted and just up and leaving. Down to Elingarth, mostly, with a few to Black Coral, if you can believe that. Even heard rumours that some went to Pale, to join the Malazan Claws.'

Rallick held up a red-stained hand. 'A moment, damn you. What idiot decided on a cult?'

Krute shrugged. 'Just sort of happened, Rallick. Not really worship – that was the wrong word. It's more like a . . . a philosophy. A philosophy of assassination. No magic, for one. Poisons, lots of poisons. And otataral dust if we can get it. But Seba Krafar wants to take us back to all that magic, even though you made it obvious which way was the better one, the surer one. The man's stubborn – it's in the blood with them, eh?' Krute slapped the table, momentarily knocking over the candle, which he hastened to right before the paltry flame went out. 'Can't wait to see Krafar's face when you walk in—'

'You will have to,' Rallick replied. 'Something else, friend. You don't say a word, to anyone.'

Krute smiled knowingly. 'You plan on an ambush, don't you? You, stepping over Krafar's body, to take mastery of the Guild. And you need to make plans – and I can help you there, tell you the ones sure to be loyal to you, sure to back you—'

'Be quiet,' Rallick said. 'There's something you need to know.'

'What?'

'The night I disappeared, recall it?'

'Of course.'

'Someone else vanished that night too.'

Krute blinked. 'Well, yes—'

'And now I am back.'

'You are.'

Rallick drank down a mouthful of ale. Then another.

Krute stared, then swore. 'Her, too?'

'Yes.'

Draining his cup, Krute quickly refilled it, then leaned back. 'Gods below. Poor Krafar. You working with her on this, Rallick?'

'No.'

'Not that she'd need help—'

'I don't know where she is, Krute. I don't know what she's planning. If anything. I don't know, and can't guess, and neither can you.'

'So, what do we do, Rallick?'

'You change nothing, stay with your routine.'

Krute snorted. 'What routine? Slow starvation?'

'I have coin, enough for both of us. Hidden here and there.' Rallick rose. 'I assume the rooftops are quiet these nights.'

'Except for thieves, coming out like mice with not an owl to be seen – like I said, the Guild's on its knees.'

'All right. I will return before dawn. For now, Krute, we do nothing.'

'I'm good at that.'

Rallick grimaced, but said nothing as he turned to the window and unlocked the shutters.

He didn't need to say anything, as far as Krute was concerned. True enough, Krute was good at doing nothing. But Rallick Nom wasn't. He wasn't good at that at all. *Oh, this is going to be fun, isn't it?*

The murmurings chased him down the alley, guttural noises issuing from a score of fanged mouths, tongues wiggling, black lips lifting clear. The glimmer and flash of rolling eyes in the gloom. Looking back over one shoulder, Iskaral Pust, Magus and High Priest of Shadow, bhokaral god, made faces at his worshippers. He cursed them in twitters. He waggled his tongue. He bared his teeth and bulged his eyes.

And did this frighten them off? Why, no! The very opposite, if such madness could be believed. They scrabbled ever closer, still clutching their loot from hapless victims in the markets, their faces writhing in constipated anguish or something equally dire. Infuriating!

'Never mind, never mind *them*. I have tasks, missions, deeds of great import. I have stuff to do.'

And so he hurried on, kicking through rubbish, listening to the creatures behind him kicking through the same rubbish. He paused at each alley mouth, shot quick glances up and down the streets, then darted across to the next opening. In his wake, the bhokarala gathered in a clump at the alley mouths, looked one way, looked the other, and then tore off in pursuit.

A short time later he skidded to a halt, the sound of his heels echoed a moment later by countless claws gouging cobblestones. Iskaral Pust pulled at his hair and whirled. The crouching bhokarala all had their knobby fists up to either side of their tiny skulls.

'*Leave me be!*' he hissed.

They hissed back at him.

He spat.

And was sprayed with gobs of foul saliva.

He beat at his head.

They pounded their own heads with fistfuls of jewellery and globes of fruit.

Eyes narrowing (eyes narrowing), Iskaral Pust slowly stood on one leg. Watched the bhokarala stand tottering on single legs.

'Gods below,' he muttered, 'they've all gone entirely insane.'

Spinning round once more, he glared across at the squat, octagonal temple fifty paces down the street to his right. Its walls were a chaotic collection of niches and misshapen angles, a veritable plethora of shadows. Iskaral Pust sighed. 'My new abode. A modest hovel, but it suits my needs. I plan to do it up, of course, when there's time. Oh, you like the gold place settings and silk napkins? Just something I threw together, mind, but it pleases me well enough. Spiders? No, no spiders round here, oh, no. Simply not allowed. Ghastly creatures, yes, disgusting. Never bathe, don't you know. Ghastly.'

Wordless singsong at his back.

'Oh, don't mind them. My ex-wife's relations – if I'd have known, well of course I'd never have taken the leap, if you know what I mean. But that's how it is – get married and you end up saddled with the whole family menagerie. And even though she's gone now, nothing but a dried-out husk with her legs sticking up in the air, well, I admit to feeling responsible for her hapless kin. No, no, she looked nothing like them. Worse, actually. I confess to a momentary insanity. The curse of being young, I suppose. When did we get married? Why, four, five years ago now, yes. Only seems like a lifetime and I'm glad, so glad, to be done with it now. More wine, sweetness?'

Smiling, Iskaral Pust set out for the temple.

Shadowed steps, leading to a shadowed landing beneath a pitted lintel stone; oh, this was all very well done. The twin doors were huge, very nearly gates, panelled in polished bronze moulded into an enormous image of charging Hounds. Delicious touch! Lovingly rendered, all that snarling terror.

'Yes, the doors were my idea, by my own hand in fact – I dabble. Sculpture, tapestry, portraiture, caricature, potterature – pottery, I mean, I was simply using the technical term. See this funerary urn, exquisite, yes. She's inside. Yes, my beloved departed, my belovedly departed, my blessedly departed, hee hee – oh, folding up her limbs was no easy task, let me tell you, quite a tight fit. I know, hard to believe she's in there, in an urn barely larger than a jar of wine. I have many skills, yes, as befits the most glorious mortal servant of High House Shadow. But I'll tell you this, she fought hard all the way in!'

He crouched in front of the bronze doors, glowering into the gaping jaws of the Hounds. Reached up one knuckled hand, and rapped Baran's nose.

A faint, hollow reverberation.

'I knew it,' he said, nodding.

The bhokarala fidgeted on the steps, knocking each other on their snouts, then sagely nodding.

The door to the left opened a crack. A hood-shrouded head poked out at about chest height, the face peering up vague and blurry. 'We don't want any,' said a thin, whispery woman's voice.

'You don't want any what?'

'They'll soil the furniture.'

Iskaral Pust scowled. 'She's insane. Why is everyone I meet insane? Listen, wretched acolyte, step aside. Scrape your pimply forehead on the tiles and kiss my precious feet. I am none other than Iskaral Pust.'

'Who?'

'Iskaral Pust! High Priest of Shadow. Magus of the High House. Our god's most trusted, favoured, valued servant! Now, move aside, let me in! I claim this temple by right of seniority, by right of rightful hierarchy, by right of natural superiority! I will speak with the High Priestess immediately! Wake her up, clean her up, prop her up – whatever you need to do to get her ready for me.'

The door creaked back and all at once the acolyte straightened, revealing herself to be ridiculously tall. She swept her hood back to display an exquisitely moulded face surrounded by long, straight, rust-red hair. In a deep, melodic voice she said, 'I am High Priestess Sordiko Qualm of the Darujhistan Temple of Shadow.'

'Ah, a master of disguise. Just like me.'

'Yes, I can see that.'

'You can?'

'Yes.'

'Oh, isn't that funny.' He tilted his head. 'Not funny at all.' Then smiled winningly up at her. 'And what do you think I am, dear?'

'Some sort of sunburned toad, I believe.'

'Just what I want you to think. Now, invite me in, before I lose my temperature.'

'Temper, you mean.'

'No, temperature. It's getting chilly.'

Her amber eyes shifted to the steps behind him. 'What of your offspring?'

'Ha ha. Offspring they are not. Never mind them. They can weep, they can whimper, they can grovel, they can—'

'Right now they are all waving their hands about in perfect mimicry of you, Iskaral Pust. Why would they do that?'

'Forget them, I said.'

Shrugging, she stepped back.

Iskaral Pust scrambled inside.

Sordiko Qualm shut the door and locked it. 'Now, you claim to be a High Priest. From where?'

'Seven Cities, the secret monastery.'

'What monastery?'

'The one that's a secret, of course. You don't need to know and I don't need to tell you. Show me to my chambers, I'm tired. And hungry. I want a seven-course supper, plenty of expensive, suitably delicate wine, and nubile female servants eager to appease my delighted whim.'

'I cannot, alas, think of a single servant here who would touch your whim, as you so quaintly call it. As for the rest, let it not be said I am remiss in according fellow seneschals every courtesy as befits a guest of my temple.'

'Your temple, is it?' Iskaral Pust sniggered. 'Not for long, but say nothing at the moment. Leave her such pathetic delusions. Smile, yes, and nod – and how in the Abyss did *they* get inside?'

The bhokarala were now crowding behind the High Priestess, heads bobbing.

She swung about. 'I don't know. There are wards . . . should be impossible. Most disturbing indeed.'

'Never mind,' Iskaral Pust said. 'Lead on, underling.'

One fine eyebrow lifted. 'You claim to be the Magus of High House Shadow – that is quite an assertion. Have you proof?'

'Proof? I am what I am and that is that. Pray, pray. Pray, I mean, do pray and perchance all manner of revelation will afflict you, humble you, reduce you to wondering adoration. Oh,' he added, 'wait until she does just that! Oh, the song will change then, won't it just! Never mind servants servicing my whim, it will be this glorious woman!'

She stared at him a moment longer, then, in a whirl of robes, swung about and gestured that he follow. The grace she no doubt sought was fouled almost immediately as she had to kick and stumble her way through the squall of bhokaral, each of which bared teeth in rollicking but silent laughter. She shot a glance back at Iskaral Pust, but not, he was certain, in time to see his noiseless laugh.

Into the sanctum they went.

'Not long,' Iskaral Pust whispered. 'Those doors need paint, yes. Not long now at all . . .'

'Gods below,' the guard gasped, 'you're bigger than a Barghast!'

Mappo Runt ducked his head, embarrassed that he had so shocked this passing watchman. The guard had staggered back, clutching momentarily at his chest – yes, he was past his prime, but it seemed that the gesture had been just that, a gesture, and the Trell's sudden dread that he had inadvertently sent the first citizen he met stumbling through Hood's Gate slowly gave way to shame. 'I am sorry, sir,' he now said. 'I thought to ask you a question – nothing more.'

The guard lifted his lantern higher between them. 'Are you a demon, then?'

'You regularly encounter demons on your patrols? A truly extraordinary city.'

'Of course not. I mean, it's rare.'

'Ah. I am a Trell, from the plains and hills east of Nemil, which lies west of
the Jhag Odhan in Seven Cities.'

'What, then, was your question?'

'I seek the Temple of Burn, sir.'

'I think it best that I escort you there, Trell. You have been keeping to the alleys this night, haven't you?'

'I thought it best.'

'Rightly so. And you and I shall do the same. In any case, you are in the
Gadrobi Distirct, while the temple you want is in the Daru District. We have
some way to go.'

'You are very generous with your time, sir.'

The guard smiled. 'Trell, you plunging into any crowded street is likely to
cause a riot. By taking charge of you, I hope to prevent that. Thus, not generous.
Simply doing my duty.'

Mappo bowed again. 'I thank you even so.'

'A moment, while I douse this light, then follow me – closely, please.'

The fete's celebrants in this quarter seemed to be concentrated in the main
streets, bathed in the blue glow of the gas lamps. It was not difficult to avoid such
places with the watchman guiding him down narrow, twisting and turning alleys
and lanes. And those few figures they encountered quickly slunk away upon seeing the guard's uniform (and, perhaps, Mappo's massive bulk).

Until, behind a decrepit tavern of some sort, they came upon two corpses.
Swearing under his breath, the guard crouched down beside one, fumbling to re-
light his lantern. 'This is becoming a problem,' he muttered, as he cranked the
wick high and a golden glow filled the area, revealing filth-smeared cobblestones
and the gleam of pooled blood. Mappo watched as he rolled over the first body.
'This one's a plain beating. Fists and boots – I knew him, poor man. Losing a
battle with spirits . . . well, the battle's over now, Beru bless his soul.' He moved
on to the next one. 'Ah, yes. Hood take the one that did this – four others just the
same. That we know of. We still cannot fathom the weapon he uses . . . perhaps a
shovel handle. Gods, but it's brutal.'

'Sir,' ventured Mappo, 'it seems you have more pressing tasks this night. Directions—'

'No, I will take you, Trell. Both have been dead for a couple of bells now – a little
longer won't matter. I think it's time,' he added, straightening, 'for a mage or a
priest to be brought into this.'

'I wish you success,' Mappo said.

'I can never figure it,' the guard said as he led the Trell onward. 'It's as if peace
is not good enough – someone needs to crawl out of the pit with blood dripping
from his hands. Delivering strife. Misery.' He shook his head. 'Could I but shake
reason into such abominations. There's no need. No one wants them and no one
wants what they do. What's needed? That's what I wish I knew. For them, I mean.
What do they need, what do they want? Is it just that sweet sip of power? Domi-
nation? The sense of control over who lives and who dies? Gods, I wish I knew
what fills their brains.'

'No, sir,' said Mappo, 'be glad you do not. Even the beasts succumb to such aggression. Killers among your kind, among my kind, are just that – the savagery of beasts mated with intelligence, or what passes for intelligence. They dwell in a murky world, sir, confused and fearful, stained dark with envy and malice. And in the end, they die as they lived. Frightened and alone, with every memory of power revealed as illusion, as farce.'

The guard had halted, had turned to regard the Trell as he spoke. Just beyond the alley's mouth was a wall and, to the left, the unlit cave of a tunnel or a gate. After a moment the man grunted, then led Mappo on, into the reeking passageway through the wall, where the Trell warrior was forced to duck.

'You must be a formidable tribe back in your homeland,' the guard observed, 'if your kin are as big and broad as you are.'

'Alas, we are, generally, not killers, sir. If we had been, perhaps we would have fared better. As it is, the glory of my people has waned.' Mappo then halted and looked back at the gate they had just passed through. He could see that the wall was but a fragment, a stretch no more than fifty paces in length. At both ends leaning buildings thrust into the spaces where it should have continued on.

The guard laughed. 'Aye, not much left of the Gadrobi Wall. Just this one gate, and it's used mostly by thieves and the like. Come, not much further.'

The Temple of Burn had seen better days. Graffiti covered the plain limestone walls, some the blockish list of prayers, others elliptical sigils and obscure local symbols. A few raw curses, or so Mappo suspected from the efforts made to deface the messages. Rubbish clogged the gutter surrounding the foundations, through which rats ambled.

The guard led him along the wall and to the right, where they came out on to a slightly wider thoroughfare. The temple's formal entrance was a descending set of stairs, down to a landing that looked ankle deep in rainwater. Mappo regarded it in some dismay.

The guard seemed to notice. 'Yes, the cult is fading. She had slept too long, I suppose. I know I have no business asking, but what do you seek here?'

'I am not sure,' Mappo admitted.

'Ah. Well, Burn's blessings on you, then.'

'Thank you, sir.'

The guard set out to retrace his route, no doubt returning to the alley with the corpses. The memory of them remained with Mappo, leaving him with a gnawing disquiet. He had glimpsed something of the mysterious wounds on the second body. Brutal indeed. Would there could be an end to such things, yes. A true blessing of peace.

He made his way down the steps. Splashed through the pool to the doors.

They opened before he could knock.

A gaunt, sad-faced man stood before him. 'You had to know, Mappo Runt of the Trell, that it could not last. You stand before me like a severed limb, and all that you bleed stains the ether, a flow seeming without end.'

'There will be an end,' Mappo replied. 'When I have found him once more.'

'He is not here.'

'I know.'

'Would you walk the veins of the earth, Mappo Runt? Is that why you have come to this temple?'

'Yes.'

'You choose a most perilous path. There is poison. There is bitter cold. Ice, stained with foreign blood. There is fire that blinds those who wield it. There is wind that cries out an eternal death cry. There is darkness and it is crowded. There is grief, more than even you can withstand. There is yielding and that which will not yield. Pressures too vast even for one such as you. Will you still walk Burn's Path, Mappo Runt?'

'I must.'

The sad face looked even sadder. 'I thought as much. I could have made my list of warnings even longer, you know. We could have stood in our places for the rest of the night, you in that sodden pool, me standing here uttering dire details. And still, at long last, you would say "I must" and we would have wasted all that time. Me hoarse and you asleep on your feet.'

'You sound almost regretful, Priest.'

'Perhaps I am at that. It was a most poetic list.'

'Then by all means record it in full when you write your log of this fell night.'

'I like that notion. Thank you. Now, come inside, and wipe your feet. But hurry – we have been preparing the ritual since your ship docked.'

'The breadth of your knowledge is impressive,' Mappo said as, ducking, he stepped inside.

'Yes, it is. Now, follow me.'

A short corridor, ceiling dripping, into a broader transept, across a dingy mosaic floor, down a second corridor, this one lined with niches, each home to a holy object – misshapen chunks of raw ore, crystals of white, rose and purple quartz and amethyst, starstones, amber, copper, flint and petrified wood and bones. At the end of this passage the corridor opened out into a wider colonnaded main chamber, and here, arrayed in two rows, waited acolytes, each wearing brown robes and holding aloft a torch.

The acolytes chanted in some arcane tongue as the High Priest led Mappo down between the rows.

Where an altar should have been, at the far end, there was instead a crevasse in the floor, as if the very earth had opened up beneath the altar, swallowing it and the dais it stood on. From the fissure rose bitter, hot smoke.

The sad-faced High Priest walked up to its very edge then turned to face Mappo. 'Burn's Gate awaits you, Trell.'

Mappo approached and looked down.

To see molten rock twenty spans below, a seething river sweeping past.

'Of course,' the High Priest said, 'what you see is not in this realm. Were it so, Darujhistan would now be a ball of fire bright as a newborn sun. The caverns of gas and all that.'

'If I jump down there,' Mappo said, 'I will be roasted to a crisp.'

'Yes. I know what you must be thinking.'

'Oh?'

'Some gate.'

'Ah, yes. Accurate enough.'

'You must be armoured against such forces. This is the ritual I mentioned earlier. Are you ready, Mappo Runt?'

'You wish to cast some sort of protective spell on me?'

'No,' he replied, with an expression near to weeping, 'we wish to bathe you in blood.'

Barathol Mekhar could see the pain in Scillara's eyes, when they turned inward in a private moment, and he saw how Chaur held himself close to her, protective in some instinctive fashion as might be a dog with a wounded master. When she caught Barathol studying her, she was quick with a broad smile, and each time he felt as if something struck his heart, like a fist against a closed door. She was indeed a most beautiful woman, the kind of beauty that emerged after a second look, or even a third, unfolding like a dark flower in jungle shadows. The pain in those eyes only deepened his anguish.

Cutter was a damned fool. Yes, there had been another woman – his first love, most likely – but she was gone. Time had come to cut the anchor chain. No one could drown for ever. This was what came of being so young, and deftness with knives was a poor replacement for the skill of surviving everything the world could throw in the way. Longing for what could never be found was pointless, a waste of time.

Barathol had left his longing behind, somewhere in the sands of Seven Cities. A sprawl of motionless bodies, mocking laughter disguised as unceasing wind, a lizard perched like a gift on a senseless black-crusted hand. Moments of madness – oh, long before the madness of the T'lan Imass in Aren – when he had railed at remorseless time, at how *too late* was something that could not be changed – not with blood spilled at the foot of a god, not with a knife poised to carve out his own heart. *Too late* simply grinned at him, lifeless, too poignant for sanity.

Those two words had begun a chant, then stride by stride a gleeful echo, and they had lifted to a roar in the raiders' camp, amidst screams and the clash of iron; lifted, yes, into a deafening maelstrom that crashed inside Barathol's skull, a surging tide with nowhere to go. *Too late* cannot be escaped. It crooned with every failed parry, every failed dodge from a scything weapon. It exploded in eyes as death hammered home, exploded along with blood and fluids. It lunged in the wake of toppling bodies. It scrawled messages (ever the same message) in the sands dying men crawled across.

He could have chanted for ever, but he had left no one alive. Oh, a dozen horses that he gave away to a caravan some days later, a gift for taking in the half-dead warrior, for treating his raging fever, for cleaning his wounds and burning out infection. They would accept no payment for their efforts – they could do nothing for the bleak anguish in his soul, they explained, and so to ask for anything would be dishonourable. Now a gift, well, that was different.

In the desert nothing disguised time's cruel face. Its skin was stretched to the bone. Its lone eye burned the sky and its gaping mouth was cold and airless as a mountain peak. The traders understood this. They were as much a tribe of the desert as anyone, after all. They gave him bladders of water – enough to take him to the nearest garrison outpost – *'Aye, give the Mezla that – they know how to build waystations and equip them well. They turn no one away, friend.'*

They gave him the strongest of the raiders' horses, a fine saddle, jerked meat and dried fruit. They gave him feed for the mount to last four days and, finally, they showed him the track he would take, the path that cheated death and yes, it was the only one.

Death stalked him, they said. Waited, for now, out beyond the glare of the dung-fires, but when Barathol finally rode out the reaper with the long legs would set out after him, singing of time, singing of the hunger that never ended, never slowed, never did anything but devour all in its path.

'When longing comes to you, friend, step not into its snare, for longing is the fatal bait – find yourself in its snare and you will be dragged, dragged through all the time allotted you, Barathol Mekhar, and nothing you grasp will remain, all torn from your fingers. All that you see will race past in a blur. All that you taste will be less than a droplet, quickly stripped away. Longing will drag you into the stalker's bony arms, and you will have but a single, last look back, on to your life – a moment of clarity that can only be some unknown god's most bitter gift – and you will understand, all at once, all that you have wasted, all that you let escape, all that you might have had.

'Now ride, friend. And 'ware the traps of your mind.'

Too late. Those two words haunted him, would perhaps for ever haunt him. The cruel chant had filled his head when he'd looked down upon Chaur's drowned face. *Too late!*

But he'd spat into that gleeful cry. That time, yes, he had. He had said *no* and he had won.

Such victories were without measure.

Enough to hold a man up for a while longer. Enough to give him the courage to meet a woman's eyes, to meet unflinching what he saw there . . .

In cavorting, clashing light, faces smeared past as they walked through the crowd. Rollicking songs in the local tongue, jars and flasks thrust at them in drunken generosity. Shouted greetings, strangers in clutches by walls, hands groping beneath disordered clothing. The smell of sex everywhere – Barathol slowed and half turned.

Scillara was laughing. 'You lead us into most unusual places, Barathol. This street called out to you, did it?'

Chaur was staring at the nearest pair, mouth hanging open as his head unconsciously began bobbing in time with their rhythmic thrusts.

'Gods below,' Barathol muttered. 'I wasn't paying much attention.'

'So you say. Of course, you were on that boat for a long time, pretty much alone, I'd wager – unless Spite decided—'

'No,' he cut in firmly. 'Spite decided nothing of the sort.'

'Well then, the city beckons with all its carnal delights! This very street, in fact—'

'Enough of that, please.'

'You can't think I'll ease up on you, Barathol?'

Grimacing, he squinted at Chaur. 'This is disturbing him—'

'It is not! It's exciting him, and why wouldn't it?'

'Scillara, he may have a man's body, but his is a child's mind.'

Her smile went away and she nodded thoughtfully. 'I know. Awkward.'

'Best we leave this,' Barathol said.

'Right. Let us find somewhere to eat supper – we can make plans there. But the issue won't go away, I suspect – he's caught the scent, after all.'

Moving to either side of Chaur, they turned him about and began guiding him away. He resisted briefly, but then fell in step, joining in a nearby chorus of singers with loud, wordless sounds not quite matching their somewhat better efforts.

'We really are the lost ones, aren't we?' Scillara said. 'We need to find ourselves a purpose . . . in life. Aye, let's grasp our biggest, most glaring flaw, shall we? Never mind what to do tomorrow or the day after. What to do with the rest of our lives, now there's a worthy question.'

He groaned.

'Seriously. If you could have anything, anything at all, Barathol, what would it be?'

A second chance. 'There's no point in that question, Scillara. I'll settle for a smithy and a good day's work, each and every day. I'll settle for an honest life.'

'Then that's where we'll start. A list of necessary tasks. Equipment, location, Guild fees and all that.'

She was trying hard, he could see. Trying hard to keep her own feelings away from this moment, and each moment to come, for as long as she could.

I accept no payment, Scillara, but I will take your gift. And give you one in turn. 'Very well. I can certainly use your help in all that.'

'Good. Look, there's a crowded courtyard with tables and I see food and people eating. We can stand over a table until the poor fool sitting at it leaves. Shouldn't take long.'

Blend withdrew her bared foot from Picker's crotch and slowly sat straight. 'Be subtle,' she murmured, 'but take a look at the trio that just showed up.'

Picker scowled. 'Do you always have to make me uncomfortable in public, Blend?'

'Don't be silly. You're positively glowing—'

'With embarrassment, yes! And look at Antsy – his face is like a sun-baked crabshell.'

'It's always like that,' Blend said.

'I don't mind,' Antsy said, licking his lips. 'I don't mind at all what you two get up to, in public or in that favourite room you use, the one with the thin walls and creaking floor and ill-fitting door—'

'A door you were supposed to fix,' snapped Picker, only now half turning to take in the newcomers. She flinched, then huddled down over the table. 'Gods below. Now, don't that grizzled one look familiar.'

'I been trying to fix it, honest. I work on it all the time—'

'You work all right, with one eye pressed to the crack,' Blend said. 'You think we don't know you're there, sweating and grunting as you—'

'Be quiet!' Picker hissed. 'Didn't you two hear me? I said—'

'He looks just like Kalam Mekhar, aye,' Antsy said, poking with his knife at the chicken carcass on the platter in the centre of the table. 'But he's not Kalam, is he? Too tall, too big, too friendly-looking.' He frowned and tugged at his moustache. 'Who was it said we should eat here tonight?'

'That bard,' said Picker.

'Our bard?'

'For the rest of the week, aye.'

'He recommended it?'

'He said we should eat here tonight, is what he said. Is that a recommendation? Might be. But maybe not. He's an odd one. Anyway, he said it would be open till dawn.'

'The chicken was too scrawny. And I don't know who they got to pluck the damned thing, but I'm still chewing on feathers.'

'You were supposed to avoid the feet, Antsy. They didn't even wash those.'

'Of course they did!' Antsy protested. 'That was sauce—'

'The sauce was red. The stuff on the feet was dark brown. Want something to get embarrassed about, Picker, just drag Antsy along to supper.'

'The feet was the best part,' the Falari said.

'He's Seven Cities for sure,' Picker noted. 'All three of them, I'd wager.'

'The fat one likes her rustleaf.'

'If she's fat, Antsy, then so am I.'

Antsy looked away.

Picker cuffed him on the side of the head.

'Ow, what was that for?'

'I wear armour and quilted underpadding, remember?'

'Well, she's not, is she?'

'She's delicious,' Blend observed. 'And I bet she don't get embarrassed by anything much.'

Picker offered her a sweet smile. 'Why not go stick your foot in and see?'

'Ooh, jealous.'

Antsy sat up, suddenly excited. 'If your legs was long enough, Blend, you could do both! And I could—'

Two knives slammed point first into the table in front of the ex-sergeant. His bushy brows shot upward, eyes bulging. 'Just an idea,' he muttered. 'No reason to get all uppity, you two.'

'Could be he's another Kalam,' Picker said. 'A Claw.'

Antsy choked on something, coughed, hacked, then managed a breath. He leaned forward until he was very nearly lying on the table from the chest up. He chewed on his moustache for a moment, eyes darting between Picker and Blend. 'Listen, if he is, then we should kill him.'

'Why?'

'Could be he's hunting us, Picker. Could be he's come to finish off the Bridge-burners once and for all.'

'Why would any of them care?' Picker asked.

'Maybe the bard set us up, did you think of that?'

Blend sighed and rose. 'How about I just go up and ask him?'

'You want to take a grab at a tit,' Picker said, smiling again. 'So, go ahead, Blend. Go on. See if she blows you a kiss.'

Shrugging, Blend set out to where the three newcomers had just acquired a table.

Antsy choked again, plucked at Picker's sleeve and gasped, 'She's heading straight over!'

Picker licked her lips. 'I didn't really mean—'

'She's almost there – they seen her – don't turn round!'

Barathol saw the Malazan threading her way to where they now sat. By hue of skin, by cast of features, by any obvious measure one might find, there was nothing that differentiated the woman from any local Daru or Genabarii; yet he knew, instantly. A Malazan, and a veteran. A damned *marine*.

Scillara noted his attention and half turned in her chair. 'Good taste, Barathol – and it seems she likes—'

'Quiet,' Barathol muttered.

The slim woman came up, soft brown eyes fixed on Barathol. And in Malazan, she said, 'I knew Kalam.'

He snorted. 'Yes, he's a popular man.'

'Cousin?'

He shrugged. 'That will do. Are you with the embassy?'

'No. Are you?'

Barathol's eyes narrowed. Then he shook his head. 'We arrived today. I never directly served in your empire.'

She seemed to think about that. Then she nodded. 'We're retired. Causing no trouble to anyone.'

'Sounds retired indeed.'

'We run a bar. K'rul's, in the Estates District, near Worry Gate.'

'And how does it fare?'

'Slow to start, but we're settled in now. Getting by.'

'That's good.'

'Come by, I'll set you the first round.'

'We just might.'

She glanced down at Scillara then, and winked. Then turned away and walked back to her table.

'What just happened?' Scillara asked after a moment.

Barathol smiled. 'Do you mean the wink or all the rest?'

'I figured out the wink, thank you. The rest.'

'They're deserters, I'd wager. Worried that we might be imperial. That I might be a Claw, come to deliver a message from the Empress – the usual message to deserters. They knew Kalam Mekhar, a relation of mine, who was once a Claw, and then a Bridgeburner.'

'A Bridgeburner. I've heard about them. The nastiest company ever. Started in Seven Cities and then left with Dujek.'

'The same.'

'So they thought you were here to kill them.'

'Yes.'

'So one of them just decided to walk up and talk to you. That seems either incredibly brave or profoundly stupid.'

'The former,' said Barathol. 'About what you'd expect from a Bridgeburner, deserter or otherwise.'

Scillara twisted round, quite deliberately, to study the two women and the red-bearded man at the table on the other side of the plaza. And did not flinch from the steady regard they then fixed on her.

Amused, Barathol waited until Scillara slowly swung back and reached for her jar of wine, before saying, 'Speaking of brave . . .'

'Oh, I just don't go for that kowtowing stuff.'

'I know.'

'So do they, now.'

'Right. Shall we join them, then?'

Scillara suddenly grinned. 'Tell you what, let's buy them a pitcher, then watch and see if they drink from it.'

'Gods, woman, you play sharp games.'

'Nah, it's just flirting.'

'With what?'

Her smile broadened, and she gestured over a nearby server.

'Now what?' Antsy demanded.

'Guess they're thirsty,' Picker said.

'It's that quiet one who worries me,' Antsy continued. 'He's got that blank look, like the worst kinda killer.'

'He's a simpleton, Antsy,' said Blend.

'Worst kinda killer there is.'

'Oh, really. He's addled, a child's brain – look how he looks round at everything. Look at that silly grin.'

'It's probably an act, Blend. Tell her, Pick, it's an act. That's your Claw, right there, the one that's gonna kill us starting with me, since I ain't never had no luck, except the pushin' kind. My skin's all clammy already, like I was practising being a corpse. It's no fun, being a corpse – take it from me.'

'That explains the fingernails,' Blend said.

Antsy frowned at her.

The server who had just been at the other table now arrived, delivering a large clay jar. 'Wine,' she said. 'Compliments of them three o'er there.'

Picker snorted. 'Oh, that's cute. And now they want to see if we drink from it. Get that wench back here, Blend. Buy them a bottle of white apricot nectar. Returning the favour, like.'

Blend rolled her eyes. 'This could get expensive,' she said as she rose.

'I ain't drinkin' from nothing I didn't buy myself,' Antsy said. 'We shoulda brought Bluepearl, he could've sniffed out whatever. Or Mallet. They got poisons so secret here there's no taste, no smell, the one drop that kills ya don't even feel wet. Why, all you need to do is *look* in its direction!'

'What in Hood's name are you going on about, Antsy?'

'You heard me, Pick—'

'Pour me some of this wine, then. Let's see if they got good taste.'

'I ain't touching that jar, could be powdered with something—'

'Only if the wench was in on it. If she wasn't and there was, she'd be dead, right?'

'She don't look too healthy to me.'

'You'd look pretty rough too with all the cysts she's got on her head and neck.'

'Some Daru poisons show up as knobby lumps—'

'Gods below, Antsy!' Picker reached across and collected the jar, filled her goblet. Drank down a mouthful of the amber liquid. 'There. Not half bad. We got better in our cellar, I'm pleased to say.'

Antsy was studying her with slightly bulging eyes.

Blend returned, sank into a slouch in her chair. 'On its way,' she said. 'How was the wine, Pick?'

'Passing. Wants some?'

'All this trudging back and forth has worked up a fierce thirst, so fill it up, darling.'

'You're both suicidal,' Antsy said.

'We're not the ones feeling clammy, are we?'

'There are some poisons,' Picker said, 'that kill the person next to the one who took it.'

The ex-sergeant lurched back in his chair. 'Damn you – I heard of those – you killed me!'

'Calm down,' Blend interjected. 'She was teasing you, Antsy. Honest. Right, Picker?'

'Well . . .'

'If you don't want his knife in your throat, Pick, tell him quick.'

'Aye, a jibe. A jest. Teasing, nothing more. Besides, if you're naturally clammy, you're immune.'

'You must think me an idiot, Pick. Both of you!' When neither objected to that assertion the Falari snarled and took the jar from Blend, raised it defiantly to his mouth and downed the rest of the contents in a cascade of gulps, his oversized Adam's apple bobbing as if he was trying to swallow a cork.

'A fearless idiot,' Blend said, shaking her head.

Antsy sucked on his moustache ends for a moment, then thumped the empty jar on to the tabletop. He belched.

They watched as the wench delivered the bottle of white apricot nectar. A brief conversation with the woman ensued, whereupon she flounced off with a toss of her knobby head. The pleasantly plump woman and the Mekhar both poured a healthy measure of the liquor. With a bold toast in the Malazans' direction, they sipped.

'Look at that,' Blend said, smiling, 'such handsome shades of green.'

And the woman was on her feet, was marching over.

Antsy set a hand on the grip of his short sword.

In Malazan tainted with the accent of Seven Cities, the woman – with a hard frown – said, 'You trying to kill us or something? That was awful!'

'It gets better,' Blend said with an innocent blink.

'Really? And when would that be?'

'Well, embalmers swear by it.'

The woman snorted. 'Damned Mezla. This is war, you know.' And she spun about and walked, a little unsteadily, back to her table.

The server was simply waiting in the wings, it turned out, as she arrived at the table moments after the Seven Cities woman sank down into her chair. More conversation. Another toss of the head, and off she trundled.

The bottle she showed up with was of exquisite multihued glass, shaped like some giant insect.

'This is for you!' the server snapped. 'And I ain't playing no more no matter how much you tip me. Think I can't work this out? Two women and a man here, one woman and two men o'er there! You are all disgusting and when I tell the manager, well, banning the likes of you won't hurt us none, will it?' A whirl, nose in the air, and a most impressive stalk to the restaurant's nether regions or wherever it was managers squatted in the nervous gloom common to their kind.

The three Malazans said nothing for a long time, each with eyes fixed upon that misshapen bottle.

Then Picker, licking dry lips, asked, 'Male or female?'

'Female,' Antsy said in a thin, grating voice, as if being squeezed from below. 'Should smell . . . sweet.'

Clearing her throat, Blend said, 'They just won the war, didn't they?'

Picker looked at her. 'A damned slaughter, too.'

Antsy moaned. 'We got to drink it, don't we?'

The two women nodded.

'Well,' he said, 'I once plunged straight into a squad of Crimson Guard—'

'You fell out of the tree—'

'—and made it out alive. And I once stood down a charging wild boar—'

'Wasn't wild, Antsy. It was Trotts's pet, and you made a grunt that sounded just like a sow.'

'—and at the last moment I jumped right over it—'

'It threw you into a wall.'

'—so if anyone here's got the guts to start, it's me.' And with that he reached for the bottle of Quorl Milk. Paused to study the sigil on the stopper. 'Green Moranth. The cheap brand. Figures.'

The normal dosage was a thimbleful. Sold exclusively to women who wanted to get pregnant. Maybe it worked, maybe it didn't. Maybe all it did was shock the body into pregnancy – anything to avoid another taste of *that* stuff.

Picker drew out a pale handkerchief and waved it over her head. They'd have to offer them rooms now, at least a week's stay, she judged. *Us Mezla just got trounced. Gods, it's about time we met folk worth meeting.*

Makes it almost worth drinking Quorl Milk.

Antsy drank down a mouthful then set the bottle down. And promptly passed out. Crumpling like a man without bones, except for his head which crunched audibly on the cobbles.

Almost worth it. Sighing, she reached for the bottle. To Blend she said, 'Good thing your foot's been neutered, love.'

'Don't you mean sterile?'

'I ain't that delusional,' Picker replied. 'Be sure they promise to hire us all a carriage, before you drink, Blend.'

'I will. See you tomorrow, sweetie.'

'Aye.'

Crone circled the edge, fixing one eye then the other on the strange apparition swirling above the enchanted dais. The power of the High Alchemist's sorcery was as sweet and intoxicating as the pollen of d'bayang poppies, but that which came from the demon was foul, alien – yet, the Great Raven knew, not quite as alien as it should be. Not to her and her kind, that is.

'You are bold,' she said to Baruk, who stood facing the dais with hands folded. 'And the reach of your power, and will, is most impressive.'

'Thank you,' replied the High Alchemist, squinting at the demon he had conjured and then trapped. 'Our conversations have been . . . most enlightening. Of course, what we see here is not a true physical manifestation. A soul, I believe, disconnected from its corporeal self.'

'With eyes of jade,' Crone noted, beak opening in silent laughter. She hesitated, then asked, 'What has it told you?'

Baruk smiled.

From the mantel above the fireplace Chillbais wheezed derisively and made insulting gestures with its stubby hands.

'You should spike that thing to a wall,' Crone hissed. 'At the very least send it back up the chimney and thus out of my sight.'

Baruk spoke as if he had not heard Crone's complaining: 'Its flesh is very far away indeed. I was granted an image of the flesh – a human, as far as I could tell, which is in itself rather extraordinary. I was able to capture the soul due to its heightened meditative state, one in which the detachment is very nearly absolute.

I doubt the original body draws breath ten times a bell. A most spiritual individual, Crone.'

The Great Raven returned her attention to the apparition. Studied its jade eyes, its jagged traceries of crackling filaments, pulsing like a slowed heart. 'And you know, then,' she said.

'Yes. The demon is from the realm of the Fallen One. His birthplace.'

'Meditating, you say. Seeking its god?'

'That seems likely,' Baruk murmured. 'Reaching, touching . . . recoiling.'

'From the agony, from the ferocious fires of pain.'

'I will send it home, soon.'

Crone half spread her wings and hopped down on to the tiles. Cocking her head, she fixed an eye upon the High Alchemist. 'This is not simple curiosity.'

Baruk blinked, then turned away. 'I had a guest, not so long ago.'

'In truth?'

The High Alchemist paused, then shook his head. 'Half-truth.'

'Did he sit in a chair?'

'Well now, that would hardly be appropriate, Crone.'

She laughed. 'Shadowthrone.'

'Please, do not act surprised,' Baruk said. 'Your master is well aware of such matters. Tell me, where are the rest of them?'

'Them?'

'The gods and goddesses. The ones cringing every time the Crippled God clears his throat. So eager for this war, as long as someone else does the fighting. None of this should be set at your Lord's feet. I don't know what Shadowthrone has offered Anomander Rake, but you would do well to warn your master, Crone. With Shadow, nothing is as it seems. *Nothing.*'

The Great Raven cackled, then said, 'So true, so true.' And now it was his turn, she noted, to regard her with growing suspicion. 'Oh, Baruk, people raise standing stones, one after another, only to topple them down one by one. Is it not always the way? They dig holes only to fill them in again. As for us Great Ravens, why, we build nests only to tear them apart next season, all because the mad lizard in our skulls demands it. See your demon on the dais. It pays nothing to be spiritual, when it is the flesh that ever clamours for attention. So send him back, yes, that he can begin to repair all the severed tendons – whilst his comrades witness the distance of his gaze, and wonder, and yearn to find the same otherworldliness for themselves, fools that they all are.

'Have you exhorted him to pray all the harder, Baruk? I thought as much, but it's no use, I tell you, and who better to make such judgement? And consider this: my master is not blind. He has never been blind. He stands before a towering stone, yes, and would see it toppled. So, old friend, be sure to stay a safe distance.'

'How can I?' the High Alchemist retorted.

'Send the soul home,' Crone said again. 'Look to the threat that even now creeps closer in the night, that is but moments from plucking the strands of your highest wards – to announce her arrival, yes, to evince her . . . desperation.' She hopped towards the nearest window sill. 'For myself, I must now depart, yes, winging away most quickly.'

'A moment. You have lingered, Crone, in search of something. And it seems you have found it.'

'I have,' she replied, cackling again.

'Well?'

'Only confirmation, to ease my master's mind.'

'Confirmation? Ah, that Shadowthrone spoke true.'

A third cackle from the sill – as threes were ever preferable to pairs, not that Crone was superstitious of course – but if but two, then a third would sound somewhere, and might that one not be at her own expense? Not to be, oh no, not to be! 'Farewell, Baruk!'

Moments after he closed the window in the wake of that oily black-tarred hen, Chillbais lifted his head and cried out: 'She comes! She comes!'

'Yes,' Baruk sighed.

'Deadly woman!'

'Not this time, little one. Fly to Derudan, and quickly. Tell her, from me, that the one who once hunted us has returned. To discuss matters. Further, Chillbais, invite Derudan to join us as soon as she is able. She will understand, I am sure, the need.'

Chillbais flapped (well, mostly fell) to the floor in front of the fireplace, then scrambled into the embers and vanished up the chimney.

Baruk frowned at the conjured demon spinning above the dais; then, with a single gesture, he released the spirit, watching as the swirling energy dwindled, then winked out. *Go home, lost one. With my blessing.*

And then he stood, facing the wall she would come through.

Stood, awaiting Vorcan.

No longer afraid of her.

No, the terror he was feeling belonged instead to her reason for coming. As for the Mistress of Assassins herself, damn but he had harsh words awaiting her.

You killed the others, woman. All but myself and Derudan. Yes, only the three of us left. Only three.

To stop, if we can, the return of the Tyrant.

Oh, Vorcan, you toppled far too many stones that night.

Should he have asked Anomander Rake for help? Gods below, it had been as close to offered him as it could have been, if he understood Crone and he was sure that he did – at least in that matter. And if he chose to accept that offer, should he tell Derudan and Vorcan? How could he not?

Neither would be pleased, he was sure. Especially Vorcan. And their fragile (and yes, it would be most fragile) alliance might die in the very moments of its birth.

Oh, Baruk, be open, be honest with them both. Ask them. Simple as that.

Yet, even as he saw the wall before him blurring, seeming to melt, a figure slowly, cautiously stepping through, he knew he would not. Could not.

There were but three of them left, now. Not enough to stop the Tyrant's return. Even with Rake's help . . . not enough.

Which means one of us will choose to betray the others. Currying favour for when He returns. Favour, well. Bargaining to stay alive would be more accurate.

One of us will betray the others.

Maybe Derudan. Maybe this one here.

Gods, maybe me.

He stood thirty paces up the street. Beneath the hood his eyes held unwavering on the ill-lit entrance to the Phoenix Inn. On the old steps, on the tattered sign still hanging misaligned above the inset door. For a hundred heartbeats he had watched, as figures entered, others left – no one as yet familiar to him, as if in his absence all that he had known had vanished, melted away, and now strangers sat where he had once sat. Held tankards he had once held. Smiled at the servers and flung out over-familiar suggestions as they swayed past.

Cutter imagined himself inside, imagined the resentment there on his face as he looked upon a score or more intruders, invaders into his own memories, each one crowding him, trying to push him out. And on, to whatever new life he had found, which was not in the Phoenix Inn. Not even in Darujhistan.

There was no returning. He had known that all along, at least intellectually, but only now, as he stood here, did the full realization descend upon him, a burden of such emotion that he felt crushed by it. And was it not equally true that the man behind the eyes was not the same man from those years past? How could he not see it differently, with all that he had been through, with all that he had seen and felt?

His heart thundered in his chest. Each drumming thud, he now understood, was, once done, never to return. Even the repetition was in truth nothing but an illusion, a sleight of similitude. It might be a comfort to pretend that the machinery never changed, that each pulse and swirl was identical, that a man could leap back and then forward in his mind and no matter where he ended up all that he saw would remain the same. Fixed like certainty.

The rough stones of the dank walls. The quality of the yellow light bleeding from the pitted glass window. Even the susurration of sound, the voices, the clank of pewter and fired clay, the very laughter spilling out as the door was opened, spilling out sour as bile as far as Cutter was concerned.

Who was left in there that he might recognize? The faces tugged a little older, shoulders a fraction more hunched, eyes framed in the wrinkled map of the weary. Would they light upon seeing him? Would they even know him? And even then, after the slapped backs and embraces, would he see something gauging come into their eyes, painting colourless their words, a certain distance widening with every drawn-out moment that followed?

The faintest scrape of a boot two paces behind him. Spinning round, ducking low as he did so, daggers flashing in both hands. Left blade half raised, point downward, into a guard position. Right blade darting out in a stop-thrust—

—and the figure leaned back with a soft grunt of surprise, tjaluk knife snapping out from beneath a cloak to block the dagger—

Cutter twisted his wrist to fold into that parry, flicking his blade's edge into a deep slice across the base of the attacker's gloved palm, even as he lunged forward – staying low – and slashed his left-hand dagger for the indent beneath his foe's right kneecap.

Avoiding that attack very nearly toppled the man straight into Cutter's arms, but Cutter had already slipped past, slicing both blades for thigh, then hip, as he darted by on the man's left.

Amazingly, that heavy tjaluk caught every slash – and another of the over-sized, hooked knives now appeared in the man's other hand, straightening in a back-flung stop-thrust in case Cutter pivoted round to take him from behind. Cutter was forced to pitch hard to evade that damned fend, and, balanced on one leg, he threw the dagger in his left hand, side-arm, launching the weapon straight for the man's shadowed face—

Sparks as – impossibly – the man batted the flying weapon aside.

A new knife already in that hand, Cutter made to launch yet another attack – then he skidded on his heels and leaned back into an all-out defence as the man came forward, his heavy knives whirling a skein before him.

Two of those? Two?

'Wait!' Cutter cried out. 'Wait! Rallick? *Rallick?*'

The tjaluks withdrew. Blood spattered down from the one in the right hand – where the palm had been laid open. Dark eyes glittered from beneath the hood.

'Rallick – it's me. Cut— Crokus! Crokus Younghand!'

'As I'd first thought,' came the rumbling reply, 'only to change my mind, in a hurry. But now, yes, it is you. Older – gods, I have indeed been away a long time.'

'I cut your hand – I'm sorry—'

'Not half as sorry as me, Crokus. You are in the Guild now, aren't you? Who has trained you? Not Seba Krafar, that's for sure. I don't recognize the style at all—'

'What? No, no Guild. Not anything like that, Rallick. I've been – wait, you said you've been gone? From Darujhistan? Where? How long? Not since that night behind Coll's? But—'

'Aye,' Rallick cut in, 'it's you all right.'

'Gods below,' Cutter said, 'but it's so good to see you, Rallick Nom. I mean, if I'd known it was you at first – you shouldn't come up on a man from behind like that. I could've killed you!'

The assassin stood studying him.

Suddenly trembling, Cutter sheathed his knives, then began looking around for the one he'd thrown. 'Two of those pig-choppers – who else would use those? I should've realized when I saw the first one. I'm so sorry, Rallick. Instincts took over. They just . . . took over.'

'You did not heed my warning, then.'

Years ago, those dark, angry words, but Cutter did not need to ask *what warning?* He remembered it all too well. 'I would have,' he said, pausing in his search.

'Truly, Rallick. I went with the Malazans, you see, and Apsalar. Fiddler, Kalam, the four of us, to Seven Cities. Where everything . . . changed.'

'When did you return, Crokus?'

'Today. Tonight.' He glanced ruefully at the entrance to the Phoenix Inn. 'I've not even gone inside yet. It's . . . changed – aye, that word is already starting to haunt me.' He resumed his hunt. 'I suppose I should have expected it – where in Hood's name did that knife go, dammit?'

Rallick leaned back against a wall. 'The one you aimed at my throat?'

'Yes – I'm so—'

'Yes, you're sorry. Well, you won't find it down there. Try my left shoulder.'

'Oh, the thickness of blood! Darujhistan and her hundred thousand hearts and each and every one beats for none other than this hale, most generous resident of the Phoenix Inn! Seated here at this most grand of tables – although surely Meese should attend to this wobbly leg – nay, not mine, though that would be delicious indeed and well beyond common service in said establishment – with – where was Kruppe? Oh yes, with nary fell company to jiggle awake the night! Tell prescient Kruppe, yon friends, why the glowing faces belied by fretful eyes? Did Kruppe not promise boons galore? Pressures eased? Panics prevented? Purses packed with precious baubles all aglitter? Drink up – oh, humble apologies, we shall order more anon, 'tis a promise most pertinent should one elect to toast this, that and, perchance, t'other!'

'We got news,' Scorch said, looking surprised by his own words, 'and if you'd just shut your trap, you'd hear about it too.'

'News! Why, Kruppe is news personified. Details, analysis, reactions from common folk in the street, all in the blink of an eye and the puff of a single breath, who needs more? This new madness we must witness now weekly and all the bolts of burlap wasted on which some purple fool blathers all manner of foul gossip, why, 'tis nothing but rags for the ragman, or wipes for the arse-wipes or indeed blots for the blotters bless their feminine wiles – Kruppe rails at this elevation of circumstance and incidence! A profession, the fops now claim, as if baying hounds need certification to justify their slavering barks and snarls! Whatever happened to common decency? To decent commonry? What's decent is rarely common – that is true enough, while the obverse is perverse in all prickly irony, would you not agree? Kruppe would, being such an agreeable sort—'

'We found Torvald Nom!'

Kruppe blinked at Leff, then at Scorch, then – seeing perhaps the disbelief mirrored in the face of the latter – back to Leff. 'Extraordinary! And did you horribly hand him over to hirsute Gareb the Lender?'

Scorch growled under his breath.

'We worked out a better deal,' said Leff, licking his lips. 'Torvald will pay Gareb back, in full, and, you see, to do so he had to pay *us* for the privilege, right? So, Torvald pays us, Gareb pays us. We get paid twice!'

Kruppe lifted one pudgy finger – on which, he saw with momentary dismay, there was a smear of something unrecognizable – 'A moment, please. Torvald has both returned and bought you off? Then why is it Kruppe buying the drinks this night? Ah, allow Kruppe to answer his own question! Why, because Torvald *is yet* to pay off trusting Leff and Scorch, yes? He begged, yes, for one night. One night! And all would be well and such!'

'How'd you guess?'

Kruppe smiled. 'Dear foolish friends, should Gareb hear of this any time soon – should he, yes, learn that you had the notorious Torvald Nom in your very grasp, why, you will find your names on the very list you hold, thus forcing you to turn in yourselves to great reward, which will avail you nothing when Gareb hides and quarters poor Scorch and Leff. Ah, calamities await!'

'Torvald Nom was once our partner,' said Leff, though now sweating in earnest. 'He gave us his word, he did. And if he goes back on it, well, doing wrong to Scorch and Leff is never a good idea, for anybody. So you keep that in mind, too, Kruppe, if you go blabbing to Gareb or some such thing.'

'Beru forbid. Kruppe would do no such thing, dearest temperamental friends! Nay, Kruppe's fear relates back to those new rags abounding in the grubby hands of urchins at every street corner these days, such a plague upon Darujhistan! Said rags are nefariously quick and diabolical with their gossip, and who can know the multitude of dubious sources? Kruppe worries what the morrow's rag will proclaim!'

'Damned well better proclaim nothing,' snarled Scorch, looking terrified and belligerent all at once.

'Now, blessed friends,' Kruppe said with a perfunctory but flourished wave of his hands, 'we must end this debacle for tonight! Dread circumstance hovers. Kruppe senses stupendous events imminently . . . imminent. A taste upon the air, a flutter in the wind, a flicker in the lantern light, a waver in watery pools of ale, a thump upon the stairs . . . a rattling exposure of front doors – ho! Noms and flowers! Knives and bleeders! Faces most ashen and dismayed! Begone from Kruppe's table, recent wumplings of desultory concourse! Reunion most precious awaits!'

Rallick was leaning heavily against Cutter by the time they reached the entrance to the Phoenix Inn. *Gods, if I've killed him – my friend – gods, no—*

Pushing open the door he half dragged Rallick inside.

And saw, behind the counter, Meese. Beyond her, Irilta. And there, to his left, frozen in mid-step and staring with wide eyes—

'Sulty! Rallick's hurt – we need a room – and help—'

All at once Meese was pulling the assassin from Cutter's arms. 'Hood's breath, he's cut to pieces!'

'I'm sorry—' Cutter began.

But Irilta was now there, taking his face between hands that smelled of ale and chopped garlic. Lips suddenly looming large as she planted a full kiss on his mouth, tongue briefly writhing in like a worm down a hole.

Cutter reeled back, then found Sulty in his arms, grasping him tight – tight with arms astonishingly strong after a dozen or so years of trays and pitchers – so tight all the air was pushed from his lungs.

'He'll live,' pronounced Meese from where she crouched over Rallick, who was lying on the floor behind the counter. 'Once we stop the bleeding. He musta been jumped by three or four, by the looks.' Straightening, she dropped the bloody dagger on the counter. A crowd was gathering, and heads now tilted in for a closer look at that foreign-made weapon.

'Malazan!' hissed someone.

Pulling himself from Sulty's arms, Cutter pushed through. 'Give me room! Don't touch that knife! It's mine.'

'Yours?' demanded Irilta. 'What's that supposed t'mean, Crokus?'

'He came up on me from behind – all quiet – like a killer. I thought I was defending myself – it was all a mistake – you sure he's going to be all right, Meese?'

'You was that scrawny thief years back!' said a man with a vaguely familiar face, his expression flitting between disbelief and accusation.

'Crokus, Irilta said,' added the man beside him. 'Did something the night the Moon came down, I heard. Knocked over a pillar or something. You remember, Scorch, don't you?'

'I make a point of remembering only what I need to, Leff. Though sometimes other stuff sticks, too. Anyway, he was a pickpocket, one of Kruppe's lads.'

'Well he ain't any more, is he?' Scorch said in a half-snarl. 'Now he's a Guild assassin!'

'No I'm not!' shouted Cutter – all at once feeling like the ungainly youth he had been years ago. Furious at his own burning face he swung to Meese. 'Where's everybody else? I mean—'

Meese held up a hand – on which there was some of Rallick's blood – and said, 'He's waiting, Crokus. At his usual table – go on. Hey,' she shouted to the crowd, 'give him a way through! Go back t'your tables!'

Just like that, Cutter reflected, he had made things a shambles. His grand return. Everything. Reaching out as he passed, he retrieved his knife – not meeting Meese's eyes as he did so. Then, as bodies pulled back, he saw—

There, at his usual table, the small round man with greasy hair and beaming, cherubic smile. Filthy frilly cuffs, a faded and stained red waistcoat. A glistening pitcher on the puddled tabletop, two tankards.

Just a thief. A pickpocket. A raider of girls' bedrooms. Wasn't I the breathless one? A wide-eyed fool. Oh, Kruppe, look at you. If anybody wasn't going to change, it's you.

Cutter found himself at the table, collapsing into the waiting chair, reaching for the tankard. 'I gave up on my old name, Kruppe. It's now Cutter. Better suited, don't you think?' *Then why do I feel like weeping?* 'Especially after what I did to Rallick just now.'

Kruppe's brows lifted. 'Kruppe sympathizes, oh yes he does. Life stumbles on – although the exception is none other than Kruppe himself, for whom life *dances*. Extraordinary, how such truth rubs so many so wrongly; why, can one's very existence prove sufficient for such inimical outrage? Seems it can, oh yes, most certainly. There are always those, dear friend, for whom a wink is an insult, a smile a taunt. For whom humour alone is cause for suspicion, as if laughter was sly contempt. Tell Kruppe, dear Cutter, do you believe that we are all equal?'

'Equal? Well—'

'A laudable notion, we can both agree, yes? Yet' – and he raised one rather unclean finger – 'is it not true that, from one year to the next, we each ourselves are capable of changes so fundamental that our present selves can in no reasonable way be considered equal to our past selves? If the rule does not apply even within our own individual lives, how can one dare hope to believe that it pertains collectively?'

'Kruppe, what has all this—'

'Years past, Cutter who was once named Crokus, we would not have a discussion such as this, yes? Kruppe sees and sees very well. He sees sorrow and wisdom both. Pain and still open wounds. Love found and love lost. A certain desperation that still spins like a coin – which way will it fall? Question as yet unanswered, a future as yet undecided. So, old friend now returned, let us drink, thus yielding the next few moments to companionable silence.' And with that Kruppe collected his tankard and lifted it high.

Sighing, Cutter did the same.

'The spinning coin!'

And he blanched. 'Gods below, Kruppe!'

'Drink, friend! Drink deep the unknown and unknowable future!'

And so he did.

The wheel had stopped spinning, milky water dripping down its sides to gather in the gutter surrounding it. The bright lanterns had been turned well down, sinking the room into soft light, and she now walked towards her bed, drying her hands with a towel.

In a day or two she would fire up the kiln.

It was late and this was no time to be thinking the heavy, turgid thoughts that now threatened to reach up and take hold of her weary mind. Regret has a flavour and it is stale, and all the cups of tea in the world could do nothing to wash it away.

The scratching at the door brought her round – some drunk at the wrong house, no doubt. She was in no mood to answer.

Now knuckles, tapping with muted urgency.

Tiserra tossed the towel down, rubbed absently at her aching wrist, then collected one of the heavier stirring sticks from the glaze table and approached the door. 'Wrong house,' she said loudly. 'Go on, now!'

A fist thumped.

Raising the stick, Tiserra unlatched the door and swung it back.

The man stepping into the threshold was wearing a stupid grin.

One she knew well, had known for years, although it had been some time since she had last seen it. Lowering the stick, she sighed. 'Torvald Nom. You're late.'

'Sorry, love,' he replied. 'I got waylaid. Slavers. Ocean voyages. Toblakai, dhenrabi, torture and crucifixion, a sinking ship.'

'I had no idea going out for a loaf of bread could be so dangerous.'

'Well,' he said, 'the whole mess started with me hearing about a debt. One I didn't know I had. That bastard Gareb set me up, said I owed him when I didn't, but that's not something one can argue, not without an advocate – which we couldn't afford—'

'I know all about Gareb,' Tiserra replied. 'His thugs visited here often enough once you disappeared, and yes, I did need an advocate – to get Gareb to back off.'

'He was threatening you?'

'He claimed that your debt was my debt, dear husband. Of course that's nonsense. Even after I won that challenge, he had me followed around. For months. Suspected you were in hiding somewhere and I was delivering food and the like, I suppose. I can't tell you how much fun that was. Why can't I, Torvald? Because it wasn't. Fun, that is. Not fun at all.'

'I'm home now,' Torvald said, trying the smile again. 'Wealthy, too. No more debt – I'm clearing that in the morning, straight away. And no more low-grade temper for your clay either. And a complete replenishment of your herbs, tinctures and such – speaking of which, just to be safe we should probably put together a ritual or two—'

'Oh, really? You've been stealing again, haven't you? Tripped a few wards, did you? Got a bag of coins all glowing with magic, have you?'

'And gems and diamonds. It was only proper, love, honest. A wrongful debt dealt with wrongfully, the two happily cancelling each other out, leaving everything rightful!'

She snorted, then stepped back and let him inside. 'I don't believe I'm buying all this.'

'You know I never lie to you, Tis. Never.'

'So who did you rob tonight?'

'Why, Gareb, of course. Cleaned him out, in fact.'

Tiserra stared at him. 'Oh, husband.'

'I know, I'm a genius. Now, about those wards – as soon as he can, he'll bring in some mages to sniff out the whereabouts of his loot.'

'Yes, Torvald, I grasp the situation well enough. You know where the secret hole is – drop the bag in there, if you please, while I get started on the rest.'

But he had not moved. 'Still love me?' he asked.

Tiserra turned and met his eyes. 'Always, y'damned fool. Now hurry.'

Glories unending this night in Darujhistan! And now the dawn stirs awake, a light to sweep aside the blue glow of the unsleeping city. See the revellers stumbling towards their beds or the beds of newfound friends or even a stranger's bed, what matter the provenance of love? What matter the tangled threads of friendship so stretched and knotted?

What matter the burdens of life, when the sun blazes into the sky and the gulls stir from their posts in the bay, when crabs scuttle for deep and dark waters? Not every path is well trod, dearest friends, not every path is set out with even pave-stones and unambiguous signs.

Rest eyes in the manner of a thief who is a thief no longer, as he looks with deepest compassion down upon the sleeping face of an old friend, there in a small room on the upper floor of the Phoenix Inn; and sees too a noble councilman snoring slouched in yon chair. While in the very next room sits an assassin who is, perhaps, an assassin no longer, dull-eyed with pain as he ponders all manner of things, in fashions sure to be mysterious and startling, were any able to peek into his dark mind.

Elsewhere, a child long ago abandoned by his mother frets in his sleep, pursued by a nightmare face with the absurd name of Snell attached to it.

And two guards run, hearts pounding, from the gate to the estate as alarms ring loud and urgent, for an evil man has lost all his ill-won wealth – a fact as sure to pluck his talons as a torturer's pliers, since evil only thrives in a well of power, and when the coin of cruelty is stolen away, why, so too vanishes the power.

A fingerless man stumbles home, god-blessed and blood oozing from battered knuckles, while his wife sleeps without dreams, her expression so peaceful even the most unsentimental sculptor could do naught but weep.

And, in a street unworthy of any particular notice, stands an ox, thinking about breakfast. What else is there, after all, when love and friendship and power, and regret and loss and reunion fierce enough to tear away all that might have been bittersweet, when all – *all* – is gone and done with, what else is there, but the needs of the stomach?

Eat! Dine on pleasures and taste sweet life!

Inconsequential? Bah!

As Kruppe ever says, it is a wise ox that gets the yoke.

Chapter Six

'The miracle of hindsight is how it transforms great military geniuses of the past into incompetent idiots, and incompetent idiots of the present into great military geniuses. There is the door, and be sure to take all your pompous second-guessing delusions with you . . .'

EMPEROR KELLANVED
ON THE OCCASION OF THE CONQUEST OF
FALARI'S GRAND COUNCIL
(THE TRIAL OF CRUST)

There had been an earthquake. A spine of rock nearly a league long had simply dropped away, opening an inlet to the sea. There were no silts churned up by this cataclysm, for the spine was a lifeless conglomeration of obsidian and pumice, legacy of past eruptions. At its apex, the inlet was sharply angled, the sides sheer rock. That angle widened on its way out to the sea, flanked at the mouth by twin upthrusts of rock a quarter-league apart.

The inlet's floor was inclined. The water at the apex was no more than fifteen spans deep, crystal clear, revealing a jumble of blockish stones and white bones cluttering the bottom – remnants of tholos tombs and the K'Chain Che'Malle that had been interred within them.

Ruins were visible on both sides of the cut, including a mostly toppled Jaghut tower. In the sky above a tortured rack of hills, just to the north, hovered the stain of a gate, a mottled scar in the air itself. All that bled from it now was pain, a sour, unyielding stench that seemed as thirsty as the ravaged landscape stretching out on all sides.

Traveller stood staring up at the gate for a long time. Two days now from the spot where he had washed up and he had yet to find fresh water. The blood of the bear that had attacked him had sustained him for a time, but that had been salty nectar, and now he suffered.

There had been enough conspiracies intent on achieving his death, over the course of his life thus far, to have made a lesser man long since despair, tumbling into madness or suicide in one last surrender to the hunger of gods and mortals. It would be, perhaps, rather just if he was to fail now for lack of the most basic staples needed to keep one alive.

But he would not surrender, for he could hear a god's laughter, as ironic as a loving whisper in his ear. Somewhere inland, he was sure, this blasted waste would crumble into sweeps of dusty earth, and then grasses, a wind-stirred prairie and steppes. If only he could hold on long enough to reach it.

He had skinned the bear and now carried the hide in a wrapped bundle slung from one shoulder. Although not particularly attractive, it provided a scent disguising his own, and one that would send most carnivores scurrying. Conversely, he would need to stalk game – assuming he ever found any – from upwind, but that would have been true even without the skin.

He was on the coast of Morn. Far from where he had intended to make landfall here on the Genabackan continent. A long walk awaited him, but there was nothing new in that prospect. Nor, he had to admit, in the threat of failure.

Facing inland, Traveller set out, boots crunching on black, bubbled glass. The morning sun reflected from the mottled surface in blinding flashes, and the heat swirled up around him until he was sheathed in sweat. He could see the far end, a few thousand paces distant – or thought he could, knowing well how the eyes could be deceived – a darker stretch, like a raised beach of black sand drawn across the horizon, with nothing visible beyond.

Some time later he was certain that the ridge was not an illusion. A wind-banked, undulating heap of crushed obsidian, a diamond glitter that cut into his eyes. As he drew closer, he thought he could hear faint moaning, as of some as yet unfelt wind. And now he could see beyond, another vast stretch of featureless plain, with no end visible through the shimmering heat.

Ascending the rise, boots sinking deep into the sand, Traveller heard the moaning wind once more, and he looked up to see that something had appeared on the plain directly ahead. A high-backed throne, the figure seated upon it a blurred cast of shadows. Standing perhaps ten paces to the right was a second figure, this one wrapped in a dark grey cloak, the hood pulled back to reveal a wind-burned profile and a shock of black hair cut short.

From behind the throne now emerged Hounds, padding forward, their paws kicking up puffs of dust that drifted in their wake. Baran, Gear, Blind. Shan and Rood and two others Traveller had never seen before. Bone-white, both of them, with onyx eyes. Leaner than the others, longer-necked, and covered in scars that displayed a startling dark blue skin beneath the short white hair. Moving as a pair, they ranged out to the far right – inland – and lifted noses to the air. The other Hounds came straight for Traveller.

He walked down to meet them.

Shan was the first to arrive, pulling up along one side, then slinking like a cat around his back to come up on the other. He settled his left hand on her sleek black neck. Ancient Baran was next, and Traveller reached out to set his other hand against one muscled cheek, feeling the skein of seamed scars from centuries of savage combat, the hint of crushing molars beneath the ragged but soft skin. Looking into the beast's light brown eyes, he found he could not hold the gaze for long – too much sorrow, too much longing for peace for which he could give no benison. Baran leaned his head into that caress, and then rasped a thick tongue against Traveller's forearm.

With the huge beasts all round him now – excepting the two white ones – Traveller approached the throne. As he drew nearer, Cotillion finally faced him.

'You look terrible, old friend.'

Traveller smiled, not bothering to respond in kind. Cotillion's face betrayed exhaustion, beyond anything he had ever seen when the man had been mortal, when he had been named Dancer, when he had shared the rule of an empire. Where were the gifts of godhood? What was their value, when to grasp each one was to flinch in pain and leak blood from the hands?

'You two,' Traveller said, eyes settling now on Shadowthrone, 'banish my every regret.'

'That won't last, I'm sure,' hissed the god on his throne. 'Where is your army, First Sword? I see only dust in your wake.'

'While you sit here, claiming dominion over a wasteland.'

'Enough of the mutual appreciation. You are beset, old friend – hee hee, how often do I use those words, eh? Old friends, oh, where are they now? How far fallen? Scattered to the winds, stumbling hopelessly unguided and blind—'

'You never had that many friends, Kellanved.'

'Beset, I was saying. By nightfall you will be dead of dehydration – it is four days or more to the first spring on the Lamatath Plain.'

'I see.'

'Of course, no matter where you happen to be when you finally die, *your* old friend is bound to come find you.'

'Yes, I am sure he will.'

'To gloat in victory.'

'Hood does not gloat.'

'Well, that's a disappointing notion. So, he will come to not gloat, then. No matter. The point is, *you will have lost.*'

'And my success or lack thereof matters to you, Kellanved?'

Cotillion replied. 'Surprisingly, yes it does.'

'Why?'

That blunt question seemed to take both gods aback for a moment. Then Shadowthrone snorted. 'Does it matter? Hardly. Not at all, in fact. We are here to help you, you damned oaf. You stubborn, obstinate, belligerent fool. Why I ever considered you an old friend entirely escapes me! You are too stupid to have been one, ever! Look, even Cotillion is exasperated by your dimwittedness.'

'Mostly amused, actually,' Cotillion corrected, now grinning at Traveller. 'I was just reminded of our, ah, discussions in the command tent when on campaign. Perhaps the most telling truth of old friendships is in how their dynamics never change.'

'Including your smarmy postulations,' said Shadowthrone drily. 'Listen, you, Traveller or however you call yourself now. My Hounds will guide you to your salvation – hah, how often has that been said? In the meantime, we will give you skins of water, dried fruit and the like – the myriad irritating needs of mortality, I seem to recall. Vaguely. Whatever.'

'And what do you seek in return for this gift?'

A dozen heartbeats passed with no reply forthcoming.

Traveller's face slowly descended into a dangerous frown. 'I will not be swayed from my task. Not even delayed—'

'No, of course not.' Shadowthrone waved an ephemeral hand. 'The very opposite, in fact. We urge you. We exhort you. Make haste, set true your course, seek out your confrontation. Let nothing and no one stand in your way.'

Traveller's frown deepened.

A soft laugh from Cotillion. 'No need. He speaks true, First Sword. It is our pleasure to enable you, in this particular matter.'

'I will not bargain with him.'

'We know.'

'I am not sure you fully understand—'

'We do.'

'I mean to kill Hood. I mean to kill the God of Death.'

'Best of luck to you!' said Shadowthrone.

More silence.

Cotillion then came forward, carrying supplies that had not been there a moment ago. He set them down. 'Shan will lead the way,' he said quietly, stepping back.

Traveller glanced over at the two new Hounds. 'And those ones?'

Cotillion followed his gaze, looking momentarily troubled before he shrugged. 'Hard to say. They just sort've . . . showed up—'

'I summoned them, of course!' said Shadowthrone. 'The white one is named Pallid. The whiter one is named Lock. Seven is the desired number, the necessary number.'

'Shadowthrone,' Cotillion said, 'you did not summon them.'

'I must have! Why else would they be here? I'm sure I did, at some point. A wish, perhaps, whilst staring upward at the stars. Or a desire, yes, of such overwhelming power that even the Abyss could not deny me!'

'The others seem to have accepted them,' Cotillion noted, shrugging again.

'Has it occurred to you,' said Traveller, softly, to the god standing before him, 'that they might be the fabled Hounds of Light?'

'Really? Why would you think that?' And in that moment, when Cotillion met his eyes and winked, all the exhaustion – the very immortality of ascendancy itself – vanished, and Traveller saw once more – after what seemed a lifetime – the man he had once called his friend.

Yet he could not bring himself to smile, to yield any response at all to that gesture and the invitation it offered. He could not afford such . . . weakness. Not now, perhaps never again. Certainly, not with what these two old friends had become. *They are gods, and gods are not to be trusted.*

Reaching down, he collected the skins and the knapsack. 'Which one drove the bear to the coast?' he asked.

'Gear. You needed food, or you would not have got even this far.'

'I was very nearly its supper, Cotillion.'

'We have always had faith in you, First Sword.'

The next – and probably last – question Traveller had for the god was the most difficult one to voice. 'And which of you wrecked my ship and killed my crew?'

Cotillion's brows lifted. 'Not us. Dassem, we would not do that.'

Traveller studied the god's eyes – always softer than one might have expected, but he had long since grown used to that – and then he turned away. 'All right.'

Pallid and Lock fell in as reluctant, desultory rearguard as the Hounds escorted Traveller inland. Shadowthrone had managed to turn his throne round so that he could watch the First Sword and his entourage slowly dwindle into the northeast.

Standing nearby, Cotillion lifted his hands and looked down upon the palms, seeing the glistening sweat pooling there. 'That was close.'

'Eh? What was?'

'If he had decided we were behind the shipwreck, well, I don't like to think what would have happened here.'

'Simple, Cotillion. He would have killed us.'

'And the Hounds would not have interceded.'

'Except perhaps my newest pets! No old loyalties there! Hee hee!'

'Close,' said Cotillion again.

'You could have just told him the truth. That Mael wanted him and wanted him badly. That we had to reach in and drag him out – he would have been far more thankful with all that.'

'Gratitude is a useless luxury in this instance, Shadowthrone. No distractions, remember? Nothing and no one to turn Traveller from his fated destiny. Leave Mael for another time.'

'Yes, very good. A detail we can offer Traveller when our need for him is immediate and, er, pressing. We delved, following the suggestion he set us this day, in this place, and lo! Why, none other than the Elder God of the Seas was to blame! Now get over here and draw that damned sword and hack these enemies to pieces!'

'That is not the delving we need to do right now,' Cotillion said.

'Well, of course not. We already know! What need delving?'

Cotillion faced Shadowthrone. 'Mael could have killed him easily enough, don't you think? Instead, he set out to *delay* Traveller. We need to think on that. We need to figure out why.'

'Yes, I am beginning to see. Suspicions awakened – I was momentarily careless, unmindful. Delay, yes, why? What value?'

'I just realized something.'

'What? Quick, tell me!'

'It doesn't matter what Mael had in mind. It won't work.'

'Explain!'

'Mael assumes a quarry on the run, after all . . .'

'Yes, he must, of course, no other possibility. Mael doesn't get it! The idiot! Hee hee! Now, let's get out of this ash-heap, my throat's getting sore.'

Cotillion stared after the Hounds and their charge, squinting against the bright sunlight. 'Timing, Shadowthrone . . .'

'Perfection.'

'So far.'

'We will not fail.'

'We'd better not.'

'Which among our newfound allies do you imagine the weak link?'

Cotillion glanced back at Shadowthrone. 'Well, *you*, of course.'

'Apart from me, I mean.'

Cotillion stared. Shadowthrone waited. Fidgeting on his throne.

Midnight at the lone tavern of Morsko provided Nimander with memories he would never lose. Slack-eyed, black-mouthed villagers staggering forward, colliding with him and the others. Stained bottles thrust into their faces. Eyes smeared with something murky and yellowed. The drink was potent enough to numb tongues, if the exhorting moans were in truth invitations to imbibe.

Even without Clip's earlier warning, Nimander was not inclined to accept such hospitality; nor, he saw with some relief, were any of his kin. They stood, still crowded at the entrance, bemused and uneasy. The pungent air of the low-ceilinged chamber was sweet, overlaying strains of acrid sweat and something like living decay.

Skintick moved up alongside Nimander and they both watched as Clip – Desra at his side – made his way to the counter. 'A simple jug of wine? Anywhere in this place? Not likely.'

Nimander suspected Skintick was right. All he could see, at every table, in every hand, was the same long-necked flask with its blackened mouth.

The moans were louder now, cacophonous like the lowing of beasts in an abattoir. Nimander saw one man – an ancient, bent, emaciated creature – topple face first on to the wood-slatted floor, audibly smashing his nose. Someone close by stepped back, crushing the hapless man's fingers under a heel.

'So, where is the priest?' Nenanda asked from behind Nimander and Skintick. 'It was his invitation, after all.'

'For once, Nenanda,' Skintick said without turning, 'I am pleased to have you standing here, hand on sword. I don't like this.'

'None here can hurt us,' Nenanda pronounced, yet his tone made it plain he was pleased by Skintick's words. 'Listen to me,' he said, 'while Clip is not close by – he holds us all in contempt.'

Nimander slowly turned round, as Skintick said, 'We'd noticed. What do you make of that, brother?'

'He sees what he chooses to see.'

Nimander saw that Kedeviss and Aranatha were listening, and the faint doe-like expression on the latter's face was suddenly gone, replaced by a chilling emptiness that Nimander knew well. 'It is no matter,' Nimander said, sudden sweat prickling awake beneath his clothes. 'Leave it, Nenanda. It is no matter.'

'But it is,' Nenanda retorted. 'He needs to know. Why we survived our battles, when all the others fell. He needs to *understand*.'

'That's over with, now,' Nimander insisted.

'No,' said Skintick, 'Nenanda is right this time, Nimander. He is right. Clip wants to take us to this dying god, after all. Whatever he plans disregards us, as if we did not exist. Voiceless—'

'Useless,' cut in Nenanda.

Nimander looked away. More villagers were collapsing, and those on the floorboards had begun twitching, writhing in pools of their own waste. Sightless eyes rolled ecstatically in sunken sockets. 'If I have made us . . . voiceless, I am sorry.'

'Enough of that rubbish,' Skintick said conversationally.

'I agree,' said Nenanda said. 'I didn't before – I was angry with you, Nimander, for not telling this so-called Mortal Sword of Darkness. Telling him about us, who we were. What we've been through. So I tried to do it myself, but it's no use. Clip doesn't listen. Not to anyone but himself.'

'What of Desra?' Nimander asked.

Nenanda snorted. 'She covets her own mystery.'

That was a sharp observation from Nenanda, surprising Nimander. But it was not an answer to what he had meant with his question.

Skintick, however, understood. 'She remains one of us, Nimander. When the need arrives, you need not doubt her loyalty.'

Kedeviss spoke then, with dry contempt. 'Loyalty is not one of Desra's virtues, brothers. Set no weight upon it.'

Skintick sounded amused when he asked, 'Which of Desra's virtues *should* we set weight upon, then, Kedeviss?'

'When it comes to self-preservation,' she replied, 'Desra's judgement is precise. Never wrong, in fact. She makes surviving the result of profound clarity – Desra sees better and sharper than any of us. *That* is her virtue.'

Clip was on his way back, Desra now clinging to his left arm as might a woman struggling against terror.

'The Dying God is about to arrive,' Clip said. He had put away his chain and rings, and from his palpable unease there now rose, like a dark cloud, the promise of violence. 'You should all leave. I don't want to have to cover you, if this turns bad. I won't have the time, nor will I accept blame if you start dying. So, for all our sakes, get out of here.'

It was, Nimander would recall later, the moment when he could have stepped forward, could have looked into Clip's eyes, unwavering, revealing his own defiance and the promise behind it. Instead, he turned to the others. 'Let's go,' he said.

Nenanda's eyes widened, a muscle twitching one cheek. Then he spun about and marched out of the tavern.

With an expression that might have been shame, Skintick reached out to prise Desra away from Clip, then guided her out. Aranatha met Nimander's eyes and nodded – but the meaning of the gesture eluded him, given the vast emptiness in her eyes – then she and Kedeviss exited the taproom.

Leaving Nimander and Clip.

'It pleases me,' said Clip, 'that you take orders as well as you do, Nimander.

And that the others still choose to listen to you. Not,' he added, 'that I think that will last much longer.'

'Do not confront this dying god,' Nimander said. 'Not here, not now.'

'Excellent advice. I have no intention of doing so. I simply would see it.'

'And if it is not pleased by being seen by one such as you, Clip?'

He grinned. 'Why do you think I sent you to safety? Now, go, Nimander. Back to our rooms. Comfort your frightened rabbits.'

Outside, beneath a glorious sweep of bright stars, Nimander found his kin in a tight huddle in the centre of the main street. *Rabbits? Yes, it might look that way.* From the tavern they could hear the frenzied moaning reach a fierce pitch, and the sound was now echoing, seeming to roll back in from the hills and fields surrounding the village.

'Do you hear that?' Skintick asked. 'Nimander? Do you hear it? The scarecrows – they are singing.'

'*Mother Dark*,' breathed Kedeviss in horror.

'I want to see one of those fields,' Skintick suddenly said. 'Now. Who is with me?'

When no one spoke, Nimander said, 'You and me, Skintick. The rest to our rooms – Nenanda, stand vigil until we return.'

Nimander and Skintick watched as Nenanda purposefully led the others away. Then they set out into a side alley, feet thumping on the dusty, hard-packed ground. Another voice had joined all the others, emerging from the temple, a cry of escalating pain, a cry of such suffering that Nimander staggered, his legs like water beneath him. He saw Skintick stumble, fall on to his knees, then push himself upright once more.

Tears squeezed from his eyes, Nimander forced himself to follow.

Old house gardens to either side, filled with abandoned yokes, ploughs and other tools, the furrows overgrown with weeds like bleached hair in the starlight. *Gods, they've stopped eating. All is in the drink. It feeds them even as it kills them.*

That sepulchral wail was dwindling now, but it would rise again, he knew, with the next breath. Midnight in the tavern, the foul nectar was drunk down, and the god in terrible pain was summoned – the gate to his tormented soul forced open. Fed by immortal pain, the prostrate worshippers spasmed in ecstasy – he could see their blackened mouths, the writhing black tongues, the eyes in their smudge-pits; he could see that old man with the smashed nose and the broken fingers—

And Clip remained inside. Witness to the madness, to its twisted face, and when the eyes opened and fixed on his own—

'Hurry,' groaned Nimander as he came up against Skintick, but as he moved past his cousin reached out and grasped hold of his tunic, drawing Nimander to a halt.

They were at the edge of a field.

Before them, in the cold silver light, the rows of scarecrows were all in motion, limbs writhing like gauze-wrapped serpents or blind worms. Black blood was streaming down. The flowers of the horrid plants had opened, exuding clouds of pollen that flashed like phosphorescence, riding the currents of night air.

And Nimander wanted to rush into that field, into the midst of the crucified victims. He wanted to taste that pollen on his tongue, on the back of his throat. *He wanted to dance in the god's pain.*

Skintick, weeping, was dragging him back – though it seemed he was fighting his own battle, so taut were his muscles, so contradictory their efforts that they fell against one another. On to the ground.

Clawing on their bellies now, back down the dirt track.

The pollen – *the pollen is in the air. We have breathed it, and now – gods below – now we hunger for more.*

Another terrible shriek, the voice a physical thing, trying to climb into the sky – but there was nothing to grasp, no handholds, no footholds, and so it shot out to the sides, closing icy cold grips upon throats. And a voice, screaming into their faces.

You dance! You drink deep my agony! What manner of vermin are you! Cease! Leave me! Release me!

A thousand footsteps charging through Nimander's brain, dancers unending, unable to stop even had they wanted to, which they did not, no, let it go on, and on – gods, for ever!

There, in the trap of his mind, he saw the old man and his blood- and nectar-smeared face, saw the joy in the eyes, saw the suppleness of his limbs, his straightened back – every crippling knob and protuberance gone. Tumours vanished. He danced in the crowd, one with all the others, exalted and lost in that exaltation.

Nimander realized that he and Skintick had reached the main street. As the god's second cry died away, some sanity crept back into his mind. He pushed himself on to his feet, dragging Skintick up with him. Together, they ran, staggering, headlong for the inn – did salvation beckon? Or had Nenanda and the others fallen as well? Were they now dancing in the fields, selves torn away, flung into that black, turgid river?

A third cry, yet more powerful, more demanding.

Nimander fell, pulled down by Skintick's weight. Too late – they would turn about, rise, set out for the field – the pain held him in its deadly, delicious embrace – too late, now—

He heard the inn's door slam open behind them.

Then Aranatha was there, blank-eyed, dark skin almost blue, reaching down to grasp them both by their cloaks. The strength she kept hidden was unveiled suddenly, and they were being dragged towards the door – where more hands took them, tugged them inside—

And all at once the compulsion vanished.

Gasping, Nimander found himself lying on his back, staring up at Kedeviss's face, wondering at her calculating, thoughtful expression.

A cough from Skintick at his side. '*Mother Dark save us!*'

'Not her,' said Kedeviss. 'Just Aranatha.'

Aranatha, who flinches at shadows, ducks beneath the cry of a hunting hawk.

*She hides her other self behind a wall no power can surmount. Hides it. Until it's
needed.*

Yes, he could feel her now, an emanation of will filling the entire chamber. Assailed, but holding. As it would.

As it must.

Another cough from Skintick. 'Oh, dear . . .'

And Nimander understood. Clip was out there. Clip, face to face with the Dying God. Unprotected.

Mortal Sword of Darkness. Is that protection enough?

But he feared it was not. Feared it, because he did not believe Clip was the
Mortal Sword of anything. He faced Skintick. 'What do we do?'

'I don't know. He may already be . . . lost.'

Nimander glanced over at Aranatha. 'Can we make it to the tavern?'

She shook her head.

'We should never have left him,' announced Nenanda.

'Don't be an idiot,' Kedeviss snapped.

Skintick still sat on the floor, clawing periodically at his face, wracked with
shivers. 'What manner of sorcery afflicts this place? How can a god's blood do
this?'

Nimander shook his head. 'I have never heard of anything like what is happening here, Skintick. The Dying God. It bleeds *poison*.' He struggled to keep from
weeping. Everything seemed stretched thin, moments from tearing to pieces, a reality all at once in tatters, whipped away on mad winds.

Skintick's sigh was ragged. 'Poison. Then why do I thirst for more?'

There was no answer for that. *Is this a truth made manifest? Do we all feed on
the pain of others? Do we laugh and dance upon suffering, simply because it is
not our own? Can such a thing become addictive? An insatiable need?*

All at once the distant moaning changed pitch, became screams. Terrible, raw –
the sounds of slaughter. Nenanda was suddenly at the door, his sword out.

'Wait!' cried Kedeviss. 'Listen! That's not *him*. That's *them*! He's murdering
them all – do you want to help, Nenanda? Do you?'

Nenanda seemed to slump. He stepped back, shaken, lost.

The shrieks did not last long. And when the last one wavered, sank into silence, even the Dying God's cries had stilled. Beyond the door of the inn, there
was nothing, as if the village – the entire outside world – had been torn away.

Inside, none slept. Each had pulled away from the others, coveting naught but
their own thoughts, listening only to the all too familiar voice that was a soul's
conversation with itself. On the faces of his kin, Nimander saw, there was dull
shock, a bleakness to the staring, unseeing eyes. He felt the surrender of Aranatha's
will, her power, as the threat passed, as she withdrew once more so far inward that
her expression grew slack, almost lifeless, the shy, skittering look not ready to
awaken once more.

Desra stood at the window, the inside shutters pulled to either side, staring
out upon an empty main street as the night crawled on, leaving Nimander to

wonder at the nature of her internal dialogue – if such a thing existed, if she was not just a creature of sensation, riding currents of instinct, every choice re-framed into simple demands of necessity.

'There is cruelty in your thoughts.'

Phaed. *Leave me alone, ghost.*

'*Don't get me wrong. I approve. Desra is a slut. She has a slut's brain, the kind that confuses giving with taking, gift with loss, invitation with surrender. She is power's whore, Nimander, and so she stands there, waiting to see him, waiting to see this strutting murderer that she would take to her bed. Confusions, yes. Death with life. Desperation with celebration. Fear with need and lust with love.*'

Go away.

'*But you don't really want* that, *because then it would leave you vulnerable to that other voice in your head. The sweet woman murmuring all those endearing words – do I recall ever hearing such when she was alive?*'

Stop.

'*In the cage of your imagination, blissfully immune to all that was real – the cruel indifferences, yes – you make so much of so little, Nimander. A chance smile. A look. In your cage she lies in your arms, and this is the purest love, isn't it? Unsullied, eternal—*'

Stop, Phaed. You know nothing. You were too young, too self-obsessed, to see anything of anyone else, unless it threatened you.

'*And she was not a threat?*'

You never wanted me that way – don't be absurd, ghost. Don't invent—

'*I invent nothing! You were just too blinded to see what was right in front of you! And did she die at the spear of a Tiste Edur? Did she truly? Where was I at that moment, Nimander? Do you recall seeing me at all?*'

No, this was too much.

But she would not relent. '*Why do you think the idea of killing Sandalath was so easy for me? My hands were already stained—*

Stop!

Laughter, ringing through his head.

He willed himself to say nothing, waited for those chilling peals of mirth to dwindle, grow ever fainter.

When she spoke again in his mind there was no humour at all in her tone. '*Nenanda wants to replace you. He wants the command you possess, the respect the others hold for you. He will take it, when he sees his chance. Do not trust him, Nimander. Strike first. A knife in the back – just as you acted to stop me, so you must do again, and this time you cannot fail. There will be no Withal there to finish the task. You will have to do it yourself.*'

Nimander lifted his gaze, looked upon Nenanda, the straight back, the hand resting on pommel. *No, you are lying.*

'*Delude yourself if you must – but not for much longer. The luxury must be short-lived. You will need to show your . . . decisiveness, and soon.*'

And how many more kin do you want to see dead, Phaed?

'My games are done with. You ended them once and for all. You and the swordsmith. Hate me if you will, but I have talents, and I gift them to you, Nimander – you were the only one to ever listen to me, the only one to whom I opened my heart—'

Heart? That vile pool of spite you so loved to swim in – that was your heart?

'You need me. I give strength where you are weakest. Oh, make the bitch murmur of love, fill her mouth with all the right words. If it helps. But she cannot help you with the hard choices a leader must make. Nenanda believes he can do better – see it in his eyes, so quick to challenge.'

'It's growing light,' Desra said from the window. She turned. 'I think we should go out. To the tavern. It may be he is wounded. It may be he needs our help.'

'I recall him not asking for it,' growled Nenanda.

'He is not all-powerful,' said Desra, 'though he might affect such – it comes with being so young.'

Nimander stared across at her. Where did that insight come from?

'Clip is vulnerable?' Kedeviss asked in mock surprise. 'Be quick to take advantage of that, Desra.'

'The endless siege that is your envy grows wearisome, Kedeviss.'

Kedeviss paled at that and said nothing.

Oh, we are a vicious bunch, are we not? Nimander rubbed at his face, then said, 'Let's go, then, and see for ourselves what has become of him.'

Desra was first through the door.

Out into pale silvery light, a cerulean sky devoid of clouds, looking somehow speckled with grit. The harvested plants drooped in their racks, sodden with dew, the bulbs like swollen heads lined up in rows above the latticework. Nimander saw, as he paused out on the street, that the temple's doors were ajar.

Clip was lying on the wooden sidewalk in front of the tavern, curled up, so covered in dried blood that he might have been a figure moulded in black mud.

They set out towards him.

Clip's eyes were open, staring – Nimander wondered if he was dead, until he saw the slow rise and fall of his chest – but showing no awareness of anything, even as they closed round him, even as Nimander knelt in front of him.

Skintick moved up to the tavern doors, pushed them open and stepped inside. He staggered out a moment later, both hands covering his face as he stumbled out into the middle of the street and stood there, back to the others.

Slaughter. He slaughtered them all. Clip's sword was lying nearby, thick with gore, as if the entire weapon had been dragged through some enormous beast.

'They took something from him,' Aranatha said. 'Gone. Gone away.'

Nenanda broke into a jog, straight for the temple opposite.

'Gone for good?' Nimander asked Aranatha.

'I don't know.'

'How long can he live this way?'

She shook her head. 'Force food and water into him, keep his wounds clean . . .'

Long moments when no one spoke, when it seemed not a single question could be found, could be cleaned off and uttered in the name of normality.

Nenanda returned. 'They've fled, the priests, all fled. Where was the Dying God supposed to be?'

'A place named Bastion,' said Kedeviss. 'West of here, I think.'

'We need to go there,' Nimander said, straightening to face the others.

Nenanda bared his teeth. 'To avenge him.'

'To get him back,' Nimander retorted. 'To get back to him whatever they took.'

Aranatha sighed. 'Nimander . . .'

'No, we go to Bastion. Nenanda, see if there're any horses, or better yet, an ox and wagon – there was a large stable behind the inn.' He looked down at Clip. 'I don't think we have the time to walk.'

As the three women set out to collect the party's gear, followed for the moment by Nenanda, Nimander turned to study the tavern's entrance. He hesitated – even from here he could see something: dark sprawled shapes, toppled chairs, and now the buzz of flies spun out from the gloom within.

'Don't,' said Skintick behind him. 'Nimander. Don't.'

'I have seen dead people before.'

'Not like these.'

'Why?'

'They are all smiling.'

Nimander faced his closest friend, studied his ravaged face, and then nodded. After a moment he asked, 'What made the priests flee?'

'Aranatha, I think,' answered Skintick.

Nimander nodded, believing the same. They had taken Clip – even with all the dead villagers, the priests had taken Clip, perhaps his very soul, as a gift to the Dying God. But they could do nothing against the rest of them – not while Aranatha resisted. Fearing retribution, they fled in the night – away, probably to Bastion, to the protection of their god.

'Nimander,' said Skintick in a low, hollow voice, 'we are forced.'

'Yes.'

'Awakened once more.'

'Yes.'

'I had hoped . . . never again.'

I know, Skintick. You would rather smile and jest, as befits your blessed nature. Instead, the face you will turn towards what is to come . . . it will be no different from ours, and have we not all looked upon one another in those times? Have we not seen the mirrors we became to each other? Have we not recoiled?

Awakened.

What lay in the tavern was only the beginning. Merely Clip and his momentary, failing frenzy.

From this point on, what comes belongs to us.

To that, even Phaed was silent. While somewhere in the mists of his mind, so faint as to be almost lost, a woman wept.

It was a quirk of blind optimism that held that someone broken could, in time, heal, could reassemble all the pieces and emerge whole, perhaps even stronger for the ordeal. Certainly wiser, for what else could be the reward for suffering? The notion that did not sit well, with anyone, was that one so broken might remain that way – neither dying (and so removing the egregious example of failure from all mortal eyes) nor improving. A ruined soul should not be stubborn, should not cling to what was clearly a miserable existence.

Friends recoil. Acquaintances drift away. And the one who fell finds a solitary world, a place where no refuge could be found from loneliness when loneliness was the true reward of surviving for ever maimed, for ever weakened. Yet who would not choose that fate, when the alternative was pity?

Of course, pity was a virtually extinct sentiment among the Tiste Andii, and this Endest Silann saw as a rare blessing among his kind. He could not have suffered such regard for very long. As for the torment of his memories, well, it was truly extraordinary how long one could weather that assault. Yet he knew he was not unique in this matter – it was the burden of his entire people, after all. Sufficient to mitigate his loneliness? Perhaps.

Darkness had been silent for so long now, his dreams of hearing the whisper of his realm – of his birthplace – were less than ashes. It was no wonder, then, was it, that he now sat in the gloom of his chamber, sheathed in sweat, each trickle seeming to drink all warmth from his flesh. Yes, they had manifested Kurald Galain here in this city, an act of collective will. Yet it was a faceless power – Mother Dark had left them, and no amount of desire on their part could change that.

So, then, what is this?

Who speaks with such power?

Not a whisper but a shout, a cry that bristled with . . . what? *With affront. Indignation. Outrage. Who is this?*

He knew that he was not alone in sensing this assault – others must be feeling it, throughout Black Coral. Every Tiste Andii probably sat or stood motionless at this moment, heart pounding, eyes wide with fear and wonder. And, perhaps, *hope.*

Could it be?

He thought to visit the temple, to hear from the High Priestess herself . . . something, a pronouncement, a recognition proclaimed. Instead, he found himself staggering out of his room, hurrying up the corridor, and then ascending the stairs, round and round as if caught in a swirling fever. Out into his Lord's southfacing demesne – stumbling in to find Anomander Rake seated in his high-backed chair, facing the elongated window and, far below, crashing seas painted black and silver as deep, unknown currents thrashed.

'My Lord,' Endest gasped.

'Did I have a choice?' Anomander Rake asked, gaze still on the distant tumult.

'My Lord?'

'Kharkanas. Did you agree with her . . . assessment? Endest Silann? Did I not see true what was to come? Before Light's arrival, we were in a civil war. Vulnerable to the forces soon to be born. Without the blood of Tiamatha, I could never have enforced . . . peace. Unification.'

'Sire,' said Endest Silann, then found he could not go on.

Rake seemed to understand, for he sighed and said, 'Yes, a most dubious peace. For so many, the peace of death. As for unification, well, that proved woefully short-lived, did it not? Still, I wonder, if I had succeeded – truly succeeded – would that have changed her mind?'

'My Lord – something is happening.'

'Yes.'

'What must we do?'

'Ah, my friend, you are right to ask that. Never mind the High Priestess and her answer – always the same one with her, yes? Who cries the war cry of Kurald Galain? Let us seek the answer between her legs. Even that can grow tiresome, eventually. Although do not repeat my words to Spinnock Durav – I would not disaffect his occasional pleasure.'

Endest Silann wanted to shriek, wanted to lunge against his Lord, grasp him by the neck, and force out – force out what? He did not know. The Son of Darkness was, to his mind, the smartest creature – mortal, immortal, it mattered not – that he had ever met. His thoughts travelled a thousand tracks simultaneously, and no conversation with him could be predicted, no path deemed certain.

'I cannot give answer this time,' Anomander Rake then said. 'Nor, I am afraid, can Spinnock. He will be needed . . . elsewhere.' And now his head turned, and his eyes fixed upon Endest Silann. 'It must fall to you, again. Once more.'

Endest felt his soul recoil in horror, shrink back into whatever cave it had clawed out for itself somewhere down in the mined-out pit of his heart. 'Sire, I cannot.'

Anomander seemed to consider that for a time, ten thousand tracks danced across, on to something new that triggered faint surprise on his features. And he smiled. 'I understand. I will not ask again, then.'

'Then . . . then what – who? Sire – I do not—'

The wryness of Anomander Rake's tone jarred terribly with his words, 'Reborn into fury, oh, would that I could see that.' Then his voice grew sober. 'You were right – you cannot stand in my stead. Do not intercede in any way, Endest Silann. Do not set yourself between two forces, neither of which you can withstand. You may well feel the need, but defy it with all your will. You must not be lost.'

'Sire, I do not understand.'

But Anomander Rake raised one hand.

And yes, the emanation was gone. Darkness was silent once more. Whatever had come into their world had vanished.

Endest found he was trembling. 'Will – will it return, my Lord?'

The Son of Darkness studied him with strangely veiled eyes, then rose and walked over to the window. 'Look, the seas grow calm once more. A most worthy lesson, I think. Nothing lasts for ever. Not violence, not peace. Not sorrow, old friend, nor rage. Look well upon this black sea, Endest Silann, in the nights ahead. To calm your fears. To offer you guidance.'

And, just like that, he knew he was dismissed.

Bemused, frightened of a future he knew he was not intelligent enough to yet comprehend, he bowed, then departed. Corridors and stairs, and not so much as an echo remained. He recalled an old prayer, the one whispered before battle.

> Let Darkness receive my every breath
> With her own.
> Let our lives speak in answer unto death
> Never alone.

But now, at this moment, he had never felt *more* alone. The warriors no longer voiced that prayer, he well knew. Darkness did not wait to receive a breath, nor the last breath that bridged life and death. A Tiste Andii warrior fought in silence, and when he or she fell, they fell alone. More profoundly alone than anyone who was not Tiste Andii could comprehend.

A new vision entered his head then, jarring him, halting him halfway down the stairs. The High Priestess, back arching, crying out in ecstasy – or desperation, was there truly a difference?

Her search. Her answer that was no answer at all.

Yes, she speaks for us, does she not?

'He is troubled,' Salind murmured, only now shaking off the violent cold that had gripped her. 'The Redeemer stirred awake then, for some reason unknown and, to us, unknowable. But I felt him. He is most troubled . . .'

The half-dozen pilgrims gathered round the fire all nodded, although none possessed her percipience in these matters, too bound up still in the confused obstinacy of mortality's incessant demands, and, of course, there was the dread, now, the one that had stalked them every moment since the Benighted's abandonment, an abandonment they saw as a turning away, which was deemed just, because none there had proved worthy of Seerdomin and the protection he offered. Yes, he was right in denying them. They had all failed him. In some way as yet undetermined.

Salind understood all these notions, and even, to some extent – this alone surprising given her few years – comprehended the nature of self-abnegation that could give rise to them. People in great need were quick to find blame in themselves, quick to assume the burden of guilt for things they in truth had no control over and could not hope to change. It was, she had begun to understand, integral to the very nature of belief, of faith. A need that could not be answered by the self was then given over to someone or something greater than oneself, and this form of surrender was a lifting of a vast, terrible weight.

In faith could be found release. Relief.

And so this enormous contradiction is laid bare. The believers yield all, into the arms of the Redeemer – who by his very nature can release nothing, can find nothing in the way of relief, and so can never surrender.

Where then the Redeemer's reward?

Such questions were not for her. Perhaps indeed they were beyond answering. For now, there was before her a mundane concern, of the most sordid kind. A dozen ex-soldiers, probably from the Pannion Tenebrii, now terrorized the pilgrim encampment. Robbing the new arrivals before they could set their treasures upon the barrow. There had been beatings, and now a rape.

This informal gathering, presumably the camp's representatives, had sought her out, pleading for help, but what could she say to them? *We were wrong to believe in the Benighted. I am sorry. He was not what we thought he was. He looked into my eyes and he refused. I am sorry. I cannot help you.*

'You say the Redeemer is troubled, Priestess,' said the spokesman, a wiry middle-aged man who had once been a merchant in Capustan – fleeing west before the siege, a refugee in Saltoan who had seen with his own eyes the Expulsion, the night when the advance agents of the Pannion Domin were driven out of that city. He had been among the first of the pilgrims to arrive at the Great Barrow and now it seemed he would stay, perhaps for the rest of his life. Whatever wealth he had once possessed was now part of the barrow, now a gift to a god who had been a man, a man he had once seen with his own eyes. 'Surely this is because of Gradithan and his thugs. The Redeemer was a soldier in his life. Will he not reach out and smite those who prey upon his followers?'

Salind held out her hands, palms up. 'Friend, we do not converse. My only gift is this . . . sensitivity. But I do not believe that the source of the Redeemer's disquiet lies in the deeds of Gradithan and his cohorts. There was a burgeoning of . . . something. Not close at hand, yet of such power to make the ether tremble.' She hesitated, then said, 'It had the flavour of Kurald Galain – the warren of the Tiste Andii. And,' she frowned, 'something else that I have felt before. Many times, in fact. As if a storm raged far to the south, one that returns again and again.'

Blank faces stared at her.

Salind sighed. 'See the clouds roll in from the sea – can we halt their progress? Can we – any of us – drive back the winds and rain, the hail? No. Such forces are far above us, far beyond our reach, and they rage as they will, fighting wars in the heavens. This, my friends, is what I am feeling – when something ripples through the ether, when a storm awakens to the south, when the Redeemer shifts uneasy and is troubled.'

'Then we are nothing to him,' said the merchant, sorrow brimming in his eyes. 'I surrendered everything, all my wealth, for yet another indifferent god. If he cannot protect us, what is the point?'

She wished that she had an answer to such questions. Were these not the very grist of priestly endeavours? To grind out palatable answers, to hint of promising paths to true salvation? To show a benign countenance gifted by god-given wisdom, glowing as if fanned by sacred breath? 'It is my feeling,' she said, haltingly, 'that a faith that delivers perfect answers to every question is not a true faith, for its only purpose is to satisfy, to ease the mind and so end its questing.' She held up a hand to still the objections she saw awakened among these six honest, serious believers. 'Is it for faith to deliver peace, when on all sides inequity thrives – for it shall indeed thrive, when the blessed walk past blissfully blind, content in their own moral purity, in the peace filling their souls? Oh, you might then reach out a hand to the wretched by the roadside, offering them your own footprints, and you may see the blessed burgeon in number, grow into a multitude, until you are as an army. But there will be, will ever be, those who turn away from your hand. The ones who quest because it is in their nature to quest, who fear the seduction of self-satisfaction, who mistrust easy answers. Are these ones then to be your enemy? Does the army grow angered now? Does it strike out at the unbelievers? Does it crush them underfoot?

'My friends, is this not describing the terror this land has just survived?' Her eyes fixed on the merchant. 'Is this not what destroyed Capustan? Is this not what the rulers of Saltoan so violently rejected when they drove out the Pannion monks? Is this not what the Redeemer died fighting against?'

'None of this,' growled a woman, 'eases my daughter's pain. She was raped, and now there is nothing to be seen in her eyes. She has fled herself and may never return. Gradithan took her and destroyed her. Will he escape all punishment for such a thing? He laughed at me, when I picked up my daughter. When I stood before him with her limp in my arms, *he laughed at me.*'

'The Benighted must return,' said the merchant. 'He must defend us. He must explain to us how we failed him.'

Salind studied the faces before her, seeing the fear and the anger, the pain and the growing despair. It was not in her to turn them away, yet what could she do? She did not ask to become a priestess – she was not quite sure how it even happened. And what of her own pain? Her own broken history? What of the flesh she had once taken into her mouth? Not the bloody meat of a stranger, no. The First Born of the Tenescowri, Children of the Dead Seed, ah, they were to be special, yes, so special – willing to eat their own kin, and was that not proof of how special they were? What, then, of the terrible need that had brought *her* here?

'You must go to him,' said the merchant. 'We know where to find him, in Black Coral – I can lead you to him, Priestess. Together, we will demand his help – he was a Seerdomin, a chosen sword of the tyrant. *He owes us! He owes us all!*'

'I have tried—'

'I will help you,' insisted the merchant. 'I will show him our desire to mend our ways. To accord the Benighted the proper respect.'

Others nodded, and the merchant took this in and went on, 'We will help. All of us here, we will stand with you, Priestess. Once he is made to understand what is happening, once we confront him – there in that damned tavern with that damned Tiste Andii he games with – how can he turn away from us yet again?'

But what of fairness? What of Seerdomin and his own wounds? See the zeal in your fellows – see it in yourself, then ask: where is my compassion when I stand before him, shouting my demands?

Why will none of you defend yourselves?

'Priestess!'

'Very well.' And she rose, drawing her woollen robe tight about herself. 'Lead on, then, merchant, to where he may be found.'

A man huddled against the counter, sneezing fiercely enough to loosen his teeth, and while this barrage went on none at the table attempted to speak. Hands reached for tankards, kelyk glistened on lips and eyes shone murky and fixed with intent upon the field of battle.

Spinnock Durav waited for Seerdomin to make a move, to attempt something unexpected in the shoring up of his buckling defences – the man was always good for a surprise or two, a flash of tactical genius that could well halt Spinnock in his tracks, even make him stagger. And was this not the very heart of the contest, its bright hint of glory?

The sneezing fit ended – something that, evidently, came of too much kelyk. A sudden flux of the sinuses, followed by an alarmingly dark discharge – he'd begun to see stains, on walls and pavestones and cobbles, all over the city now. This foreign drink was outselling even ale and wine. And among the drinkers there were now emerging abusers, stumbling glaze-eyed, mouths hanging, tongues like black worms. As yet, Spinnock had not seen such among the Tiste Andii, but perhaps it was only a matter of time.

He sipped at his cup of wine, pleased to note that the trembling in his fingers had finally ceased. The eruption of power from Kurald Galain that had taken him so unawares had vanished, leaving little more than a vague unease that only slightly soured the taste of the wine. Strange disturbances these nights; who could say their portent?

The High Priestess might have an idea or two, he suspected, although the punctuation of every statement from her never changed, now, did it? Half smiling, he sipped again at his drink.

Seerdomin frowned and sat back. 'This is an assault I cannot survive,' he pronounced. 'The Jester's deceit was well played, Spinnock. There was no anticipating that.'

'Truly?' Spinnock asked. 'With these allies here?'

Seerdomin grimaced at the other two players, then grunted a sour laugh. 'Ah, yes, I see your point. That kelyk takes their minds, I think.'

'Sharpens, just so you know,' said Garsten, licking his stained lips. 'Although I'd swear, some nights it's more potent than other times, wouldn't you say so, Fuldit?'

'Eh? Yah, s'pose so. When you gonna move den, Seerdomin? Eh? Resto, bring us another bottle!'

'Perhaps,' muttered Seerdomin, 'it's *my* mind that's not sharp. I believe I must surrender.'

Spinnock said nothing, although he was disappointed – no, he was shaken. He could see a decent counter, had been assuming his opponent had seen it immediately, but had been busy seeking something better, something wilder. Other nights, Seerdomin's talent would burst through at moments like these – a fearless gambit that seemed to pivot the world on this very tabletop.

Perhaps if I wait a little longer—

'I yield,' said Seerdomin.

Words uttered, a crisis pronounced.

'Resto, bring us a pitcher, if you'd be so—' Seerdomin got no further. He seemed to jolt back into his chair, as if an invisible hand had just slammed into his chest. His eyes were on the tavern door.

Spinnock twisted in his seat to see that strangers had arrived at the Scour. A young woman wearing a rough-woven russet robe, her hair cut short – shorter even than the High Priestess's – yet the same midnight black. A pale face both soft and exquisite, eyes of deep brown, now searching through the gloom, finding at last the one she sought: Seerdomin. Behind her crowded others, all wearing little more than rags, their wan faces tight with something like panic.

The woman in the lead walked over.

Seerdomin sat like a man nailed to his chair. All colour had left his face a moment earlier, but now it was darkening, his eyes flaring with hard anger.

'Benighted—'

'This is my refuge,' he said. 'Leave. Now.'

'We—'

' "We"? Look at your followers, Priestess.'

She turned, in time to see the last of them rush out of the tavern door.

Seerdomin snorted.

Impressively, the young woman held her ground. The robe fell open – lacking a belt – and Spinnock Durav judged she was barely adolescent. A priestess? *Ah, the Great Barrow, the Redeemer.* 'Benighted,' she resumed, in a voice that few would find hard to listen to, indeed, at length, 'I am not here for myself. Those who were with me insisted, and even if their courage failed them at the end, this makes their need no less valid.'

'They came with demands,' Seerdomin said. 'They have no right, and they realized the truth of that as soon as they saw me. You should now do the same, and leave as they have.'

'I must try—'

Seerdomin surged to his feet, suddenly enough to startle Garsten and Fuldit despite their addled senses, and both stared up wide-eyed and frightened.

The priestess did not even flinch. 'I must try,' she repeated, 'for their sake, and for my own. We are beset in the camp—'

'No,' cut in Seerdomin. 'You have no right.'

'Please, will you just listen?'

The hard edge of those words clearly surprised Seerdomin. Garsten and Fuldit, collecting their tankards and bottles, quickly left the table.

Spinnock Durav rose, bowed slightly to both, and made for the exit. As he passed Resto – who stood motionless with a pitcher in his hand – he said under his breath, 'On my tab, please – this entire night. Seerdomin will have no thought of you when he leaves.'

Resto blinked up at him, then nodded.

In the darkness opposite the Scour's door, Spinnock Durav waited. He had half expected to see the pilgrims waiting outside, but the street was empty – they had fled indeed, at a run, probably all the way back to the camp. There was little spine in the followers of the Redeemer.

With at least one exception, he corrected himself as the priestess stepped outside.

Even from ten paces away, he saw her sag slightly, as if finding herself on suddenly watery legs. Tugging the robe tight round herself, she set off, three, four strides, then slowed and finally halted to turn and face Spinnock Durav.

Who came forward. 'My pardon, Priestess,' he said.

'Your friend took that pitcher for himself,' she said. 'Expect a long night. If you have a care you can collect him in a few bells – I'd rather he not spend a senseless night lying on that filthy floor.'

'I would have thought the possibility might please you,' Spinnock said.

She frowned. 'No. He is the Benighted.'

'And what does that mean?'

She hesitated, then said, 'Each day, until recently, he came to the Great Barrow and knelt before it. Not to pray, not to deliver a trinket.'

Confused, Spinnock Durav asked, 'What, then?'

'He would rather that remain a secret, I suspect.'

'Priestess, he is my friend. I see well his distress—'

'And why does that bother you so? More than a friend might feel – I can sense that. Most friends might offer sympathy, even more, but within them remains the stone thought that they are thankful that they themselves do not share their friend's plight. But that is not within you, not with this Seerdomin. No,' she drew a step closer, eyes searching, 'he answers a need, and so wounded as he now is, *you* begin to bleed.'

'Mother Dark, woman!'

She retreated at his outburst and looked away. 'I am sorry. Sir, the Benighted kneels before the Great Barrow and delivers unto the Redeemer the most precious gift of all. *Company*. Asking for nothing. He comes to relieve the Redeemer's loneliness.' She ran a hand back through her short hair. 'I sought to tell him something, but he would not hear me.'

'Can I—'

'I doubt it. I tried to tell him what I am sensing from the Redeemer. Sir, your friend is *missed*.' She sighed, turning away. 'If all who worship did so without need. If all came to their saviour unmindful of that title and its burden, if they came as friends—' she glanced back at him, 'what would happen then, do you think? I wonder . . .'

He watched her walk away, feeling humbled, too shaken to pursue, to root out the answers – the details – he needed most. To find out what he could do. For Seerdomin. For her.

For her?

Now, why should she matter? By the Abyss, what has she done to me?

And how in the Mother's name can Seerdomin resist her?

How many women had there been? He had lost count. It would have been better, perhaps, if he'd at least once elected to share his gift of longevity. Better, yes, than watching those few who'd remained with him for any length of time lose all their beauty, surrendering their youth, until there was no choice but for Kallor to discard them, to lock them away, one by one, in some tower on some windswept knoll. What else could he have done? They hobbled into lives of misery, and that misery was an affront to his sensibilities. Too much bitterness, too much malice in those hot, ageing eyes ever fixing upon him. Did he not age as well? True, a year for them was but a heartbeat for Kallor, but see the lines of his face, see the slow wasting of muscle, the iron hue of his hair . . .

It was not just a matter of choosing the slowest burning wood, after all, was it? And with that thought he kicked at the coals of the fire, watched sparks roil nightward. Sometimes, the urgent flames of the quick and the short-lived delivered their own kind of heat. Hard wood and slow burn, soft wood and smouldering reluctance before ashen collapse. Resinous wood and oh how she flared! Blinding, yes, a glory no man could turn from.

Too bad he'd had to kill every child he begat. No doubt that left most of his wives and lovers somewhat disaffected. But he had not been so cruel as to hesitate, had he? No. Why, he'd tear those ghastly babes from their mothers' arms not moments after they'd tumbled free of the womb, and was that not a true sign of mercy? No one grows attached to dead things, not even mothers.

Attachments, yes, now they were indeed a waste of time and, more relevantly, a weakness. To rule an empire – to rule a hundred empires – one needed a certain objectivity. All was to be used, to be remade howsoever he pleased. Why, he had launched vast construction projects to glorify his rule, but few understood that it was not the completion that mattered, but the work itself and all that it implied – his command over their lives, their loyalty, their labour. Why, he could work them for decades, see generations of the fools pass one by one, all working each and every day of their lives, and still they did not understand what it meant for them to give to him – to Kallor – so many years of their mortal existence, so much of it, truly, that any rational soul would howl at the cruel injustice of such a life.

This was, as far as he was concerned, the real mystery of civilization – and for all that he exploited it he was, by the end, no closer to understanding it. This willingness of otherwise intelligent (well, reasonably intelligent) people to parcel up and then bargain away appalling percentages of their very limited lives, all in service to someone else. And the rewards? Ah, some security, perhaps. The cement that is stability. A sound roof, something on the plate, the beloved offspring each one destined to repeat the whole travail. And was that an even exchange?

It would not have been so, for him. He knew that, had known it from the very first. He would bargain away nothing of his life. He would serve no one, yield none of his labour to the edification and ever-expanding wealth of some fool who imagined that his or her own part of the bargain was profound in its generosity, was indeed the most precious of gifts. That to work for him or her was a *privilege* – gods! The conceit of that! The lie, so bristling and charged in its brazen display!

Just how many rules of civil behaviour were designed to perpetuate such egregious schemes of power and control of the few over the many? Rules defended to the death (usually the death of the many, rarely that of the few) with laws and wars, with threats and brutal repression – ah, those were the days, were they not? How he had gloried in that outrage!

He would never be one of the multitude. And he had proved it, again and again, and again. And he would continue to prove it.

A crown was within reach. A kingship waited to be claimed. Mastery not over something as mundane as an empire – that game had grown stale long ago – but over a realm. An entity consisting of all the possible forces of existence. The power of earthly flesh, every element unbound, the coruscating will of belief, the skein of politics, religion, social accord, sensibilities, woven from the usual tragic roots of past ages golden and free of pain and new ages bright with absurd promise. While through it all fell the rains of oblivion, the cascading torrent of failure and death, suffering and misery, a god broken and for ever doomed to remain so – oh, Kallor knew he could usurp such a creature, leave it as powerless as his most abject subject.

All – *all of it* – within his reach.

He kicked again at the embers, the too-small branches that had made up this shortlived fire, saw countless twigs fall into white ash. A few picked bones were visible amidst the coals, all that remained of the pathetic creature he had devoured earlier this night.

A smear of clouds cut a swath across the face of the stars and the dust-veiled moon had yet to rise. Somewhere out on the plain coyotes bickered with the night. He had found trader tracks this past day, angling northwest-southeast. Well-worn wagon ruts, the tramping of yoked oxen. Garbage strewn to either side. Rather disappointing, all things considered; he had grown used to solitude, where the only sign of human activity had been the occasional grassfire on the western horizon – plains nomads and their mysterious ways – something to do with the bhederin herds and the needs for various grasses, he suspected. If they spied him they wisely kept their distance. His passing through places had a way of agitating ancient spirits, a detail he had once found irritating enough to hunt the things down and kill them, but no longer. Let them whine and twitch, thrash and moan in the grip of timorous nightmares, and all that. Let their mortal children cower in the high grasses until he was well and gone.

The High King had other concerns. And other matters with which he could occupy his mind.

He sat straighter, every sense stung awake by a burgeoning of power to the north. Slowly rising to his feet, Kallor stared into the darkness. Yes, something foaming awake, what might it be? And . . . yes, *another* force, and that one he well recognized – Tiste Andii.

Breath hissed between worn teeth. Of course, if he continued on this path he would have come full circle, back to that horrid place – what was its name? Yes, Coral. The whole mess with the Pannion Domin, oh, the stupidity! The pathetic, squalid idiocy of that day!

Could this be those two accursed hunters? Had they somehow swept round him? Were they now striking south to finally face him? Well, he might welcome that. He'd killed his share of dragons, both pure and Soletaken. *One at a time, of course. Two at once . . . that could be a challenge.*

For all this time, their pursuit had been a clumsy, witless thing. So easily fooled, led astray – he could have ambushed them countless times, and perhaps he should have done just that. At the very least, he might have come to understand the source of their persistent – yes, pathological – relentlessness. Had he truly angered Rake that much? It seemed ridiculous. The Son of Darkness was not one to become so obsessed; indeed, none of the Tiste Andii were, and was that not their fundamental weakness? This failing of will?

How he had so angered Korlat and Orfantal? Was it because he did not stay, did not elect to fight alongside all the doomed fools on that day? *Let the Malazans bleed! They were our enemies! Let the T'lan Imass betray Silverfox – she deserved it!*

It was not our war, Brood. Not our war, Rake. Why didn't you listen to me?

Bah, come and face me, then, Korlat. Orfantal. Come, let us be done with this rubbish!

The twin flaring of powers ebbed suddenly.

Somewhere far to the east the coyotes resumed their frantic cries.

He looked skyward, saw the gleam of the rising moon, its ravaged scowl of reflected sunlight and the blighted dust of its stirred slumber. *Look at you. Your face is my face, let us be truthful about that. Beaten and boxed about, yet we climb upright time and again, to resume our trek.*

The sky cares nothing for you, dear one. The stars don't even see you.

But you will march on, because it is what you do.

A final kick at the coals. Let the grasses burn to scar his wake, he cared not. No, he would not come full circle – he never did, which was what had kept him alive for this long. No point in changing anything, was there?

Kallor set out. Northward. There were, if he recalled, settlements, and roads, and a main trader track skirling west and north, out across the Cinnamon Wastes, all the way to Darujhistan.

Where he had an appointment to keep. A destiny to claim by right of sword and indomitable will.

The moon's light took hold of his shadow and made a mess of it. Kallor walked on, oblivious of such details.

Three scrawny horses, one neglected ox and a wagon with a bent axle and a cracked brake: the amassed inherited wealth of the village of Morsko comprised only these. Bodies left to rot on the tavern floor – they should have set fire to the place, Nimander realized. Too late now, too hard the shove away from that horrid scene. And what of the victims on their crosses, wrapped and leaking black ichors into the muddy earth? They had left them as well.

Motionless beneath a blanket in the bed of the wagon, Clip stared sightlessly at the sideboards. Flecks of the porridge they had forced down his throat that morning studded his chin. Flies crawled and buzzed round his mouth. Every now and then, faint trembling rippled through his body.

Stolen away.

Noon, the third day now on this well-made cobbled, guttered road. They had just passed south of the town of Heath, which had once been a larger settlement, perhaps a city, and might well return to such past glory, this time on the riches of kelyk, a dilute form of saemankelyk, the Blood of the Dying God. These details and more they had learned from the merchant trains rolling up and down this road, scores of wagons setting out virtually empty to villages and towns east of Bastion – to Outlook itself – then returning loaded with amphorae of the foul drink, wagons groaning beneath the weight, back to some form of central distribution hub in Bastion.

The road itself ran south of these settlements – all of which nested above the shoreline of Pilgrim Lake. When it came opposite a village there would be a junction, with a track or wend leading north. A more substantial crossroads marked the intersection of levelled roads to the reviving cities of Heath, Kel Tor and, somewhere still ahead, Sarn.

Nimander and his group did not travel disguised, did not pretend to be other than what they were, and it was clear that the priests, fleeing ahead of them, had delivered word to all their ken on the road and, from there, presumably into the towns and villages. At the junctions, in the ramshackle waystations and storage sheds, food and water and forage for the animals awaited them.

The Dying God – or his priests – had blessed them, apparently, and now awaited their pleasure in Bastion. The one who had sacrificed his soul to the Dying God was doubly blessed, and some final consummation was anticipated, probably leading to Clip's soul's being thoroughly devoured by an entity who was cursed to suffer for eternity. Thus accursed, it was little wonder the creature welcomed company.

All things considered, it was well that their journey had been one of ease and accommodation. Nimander suspected that his troupe would have been rather more pleased to carve their way through hordes of frenzied fanatics, assuming they could manage such a thing.

Having confirmed that Clip's comatose condition was unchanged, he climbed down from the wagon and returned to the scruffy mare he had been riding since Morsko. The poor beast's ribs had been like the bars of a cage under tattered vellum, its eyes listless and the tan coat patchy and dull. In the three days since, despite the steady riding, the animal had recovered somewhat under Nimander's ministrations. He was not particularly enamoured of horses in general, but no creature deserved to suffer.

As he climbed into the worn saddle he saw Skintick standing, stepping up on to the wagon's bench where Nenanda sat holding the reins, and shading his eyes to look southward across the empty plain.

'See something?'

A moment, then, 'Yes. Someone . . . walking.'

Up from the south? 'But there's nothing out there.'

Kedeviss and Aranatha rose in their stirrups.

'Let's get going,' Desra said from the wagon bed. 'It's too hot to be just sitting here.'

Nimander could see the figure now, tall for a human. Unkempt straggly grey hair fanned out round his head like an aura. He seemed to be wearing a long coat of chain, down to halfway between his knees and ankles, slitted in front. The hand-and-a-half grip of a greatsword rose above his left shoulder.

'An old bastard,' muttered Skintick, 'to be walking like that.'

'Could be he lost his horse,' said Nenanda disinterestedly. 'Desra is right – we should be going.'

Striding like one fevered under the sun, the stranger came ever closer. Something about him compelled Nimander's attention, a kind of dark fascination – for what, he couldn't quite name. A cascade of images tumbled through his mind. As if he was watching an apparition bludgeoning its way out from some hoary legend, from a time when gods struggled, hands about each other's throats, when blood fell as rain and the sky itself rolled and crashed against the shores of the Abyss. All this, riding across the dusty air between them as the old man came up to the road. All this, written in the deep lines of his gaunt visage, in the bleak wastelands of his grey eyes.

'He is as winter,' murmured Skintick.

Yes, and something . . . colder.

'What city lies beyond?' the man asked.

A startled moment when Nimander realized that the stranger had spoken Tiste Andii. 'Heath.'

The man turned, faced west. 'This way, then, lies Bastion and the Cinnamon Track.'

Nimander shrugged.

'You are from Coral?' the stranger asked, scanning the group. 'Is he still camped there, then? But no, I recognize none of you, and that would not be possible. Even so, tell me why I should not kill you all.'

That got Nenanda's attention, and he twisted in his seat to sneer down at the old man.

But Nimander's blood had turned to ice. 'Because, sir, you do not know us.'

Pale eyes settled on him. 'You have a point, actually. Very well, instead, I would travel with you. Ride, yes, in your wagon – I have worn my boots through crossing this wretched plain. Tell me, have you water, decent food?'

Nenanda twisted further to glare at Nimander. 'Turn this fool away. He can drink our dust.'

The old man regarded Nenanda for a moment, then came back to Nimander. 'Tie a leash on this one and we should be fine.' And he stepped up to the wagon and, setting a foot on a spoke of the rear wheel, pulled himself up. Where he paused, frowning as he studied the prostrate form of Clip. 'Is he ill?' he asked Desra. 'Are you caught with plague? No, not that – your kind rarely succumb to such things. Stop staring, child, and tell me what is wrong with this one.'

'None of your business,' she snapped, as Nimander had known she would. 'If you're going to crowd in then sit there, to give him some shade.'

Thin brows lifted, then a faint smile flickered across his withered, cracked lips. And without another word he moved to where Desra had indicated and settled down, stretching out his legs. 'Some water, darling, if you please.'

She stared at him for a moment, then pulled loose a skin and slid it over. 'That one's not water,' she said with a sweet smile. 'It's called kelyk. A local brew. Very popular.'

Nimander sat motionless, watching all this. He saw that Skintick and Nenanda were both doing the same.

To Desra's words, the old man grimaced. 'I'd rather water,' he said, but reached for the skin anyway. Tugged free the stopper, then sniffed.

And recoiled. 'Imperial dust!' he said in a growl. He replaced the stopper and flung the skin to the back of the wagon. 'If you won't spare water then never mind, bitch. We can settle your inhospitality later.'

'Desra,' said Nimander as he gathered his reins, 'give the man some water.'

'After he called me a bitch?'

'After you tried poisoning him with kelyk, yes.'

They set out on the road, westward. Two more days, said the last trader they had passed that morning. Past Sarn and the lesser lake. To Bastion, the city by the inland sea, a sea so filled with salt no sailor or fisher could drown in it, and where no fish could be found barring an enormous eel with the jaws of a wolf. Salt that had not been there a generation ago, but the world will change, amen.

The Abject Temple of Saemenkelyk awaited them in Bastion.

Two days, then, to meet the Dying God. And, one way or another, to wrest from it Clip's soul. Nimander did not think the priests would just step aside for that.

Riding his mount alongside the wagon, Nimander spoke to the old man. 'If you are going to Bastion, sir, you might want reconsider staying with us.'

'And why is that.' There was little in that tone even remotely interrogative.

'I don't think I can adequately explain why,' Nimander replied. 'You'll just have to take me at my word.'

Instead the old man unslung his weapon and set it between him and Clip, then he laced his long-fingered hands behind his head and settled back, closing his eyes. 'Wake me when it's time to eat,' he said.

The worn grip and nicked pommel of the greatsword, the broad cross-hilt and the scarred wooden scabbard all drew Nimander's attention. *He can still use that damned weapon, ancient as he is.*

Grim legends, the clangour of warring gods, yes, this gaunt warrior belonged to such things.

He collected his reins. 'As you like, stranger.' Nudging the mare into a trot, he glanced up to meet Skintick's gaze as he rode past. And saw none of the usual mocking pleasure. Instead, something wan, distraught.

True, there was not much to laugh about, was there?

My unhappy kin.

Onward, then, to Bastion.

A succession of ridges stepped down towards the basin of the valley, each marking a time when the river had been wider, its cold waters churning away from dying glaciers and meltwater lakes. Now, a narrow twisting gully threaded along the distant floor, fringed by cottonwoods. Standing upon the highest ridge, Traveller looked down to the next level, where a half-dozen tipis rose, not quite breaking the high ground skyline. Figures moving about, clothed in tanned hides and skins, a few dogs, the latter now padding out to the camp's edge closest to the slope, sharp ears and lifted noses alerted to his presence although not one barked.

A herd of horses foraged further down, a small, stocky steppe breed that Traveller had never seen before. Ochre flanks deepening to brown on the haunches, manes and tails almost black.

Down on the valley floor, some distance to the right, carrion birds were on the ground, perched on islands of dead flesh beneath the branches of cottonwoods. Other horses wandered there, these ones more familiar, trailing reins as they cropped the high grasses.

Two men walked out to the base of the slope. Traveller set out down towards them. His own escort of Hounds had left him this morning, either off on a hunt or gone for good – there was no telling which.

Sun-burnished faces watched him approach. Eyes nestled in wind-stretched epicanthic folds. Midnight-black hair in loosely bound manes, through which were threaded – rather sweetly – white blossoms. Long, narrow-bladed curved knives in beaded belts, the iron black except along the honed edges. Their clothing was beautifully sewn with red-dyed gut thread, studded here and there with bronze rivets.

The elder one, on the right, now held up both hands, palms outward, and said in archaic Daru, 'Master of the Wolf-Horses, welcome. Do not kill us. Do not rape our women. Do not steal our children. Leave us with no diseases. Leave us our g'athend horses-of-the-rock, our mute dogs, our food and our shelters, our weapons and our tools. Eat what we give you. Drink what we give you. Smoke what we give you. Thank us for all three. Grant your seed if a woman comes to you in the night, kill all vermin you find. Kiss with passion, caress with tenderness, gift us with the wisdom of your years but none of their bitterness. Do not judge and you will not be judged. Do not hate, do not fear, and neither will we hate or fear you. Do not invite your wolf-horses into our camp, lest they devour us and all our beasts. Welcome, then, wanderer, and we will tell you of matters, and show you other matters. We are the Kindaru, keepers of the horses-of-the-rock, the last clan left in all Lama Teth Andath – the grasses we have made so that trees do not reach high to steal the sky. Welcome. You need a bath.'

To such a greeting, Traveller could only stand, silent, bemused, torn between laughter and weeping.

The younger of the two men – perhaps in his mid-twenties – smiled wryly and said, 'The more strangers we meet, the more we add to our words of welcome. This is born of experience, most of it sad, unpleasant. If you mean us harm, we ask that you heed the words given you, and so turn away. Of course, if you mean to betray us, then there is nothing we can do. Deceit is not our way.'

Traveller grimaced. 'Deceit is everyone's way.'

Twin expressions of dismay, so similar that it was made clear they were father and son. 'Yes,' said the son, 'that is true. If we saw that you would enter our camp and be with us, yet plan betrayal, why, we would plan the same, and seek to deliver unto you first what you thought to deliver unto us.'

'You are truly the last camp left?'

'Yes, we are waiting to die. Our ways, our memories. And the g'athend will run free once more, until they too are gone – for the horses we keep are the last of their kind, too.'

'Do you ride them?'

'No, we worship them.'

Yet they spoke Daru – what strange history twisted and isolated these ones from all the others? What turned them away from farms and villages, from cities and riches? 'Kindaru, I humbly accept your welcome and will strive to be a worthy guest.'

Both men now smiled. And the younger one gestured with one hand.

A faint sound behind him made Traveller turn, to see four nomads rising as if from nowhere on the slope, armed with spears.

Traveller looked back at the father and son. 'You are all too familiar with strangers, I think.'

They walked down into the camp. The silent dogs, ranging ahead, were met by a small group of children all bedecked in white flowers. Bright smiles flashed up at Traveller, tiny hands taking his to lead him onward to the hearthfires, where women were now preparing a midday meal. Iron pots filled with some milky substance steamed, the smell pungent, sweet and vaguely alcoholic.

A low bench was set out, four-legged and padded, the woven coverlet a rainbow of coloured threads in zigzag patterns. The wooden legs were carved into horse heads, noses almost touching in the middle, the manes flowing in sweeping curves, all stained a lustrous ochre and deep brown. The artistry was superb, the heads so detailed Traveller could see the veins along the cheeks, the lines of the eyelids and the dusty eyes both opaque and depthless. There was only one such bench, and it was, he knew, to be his for the duration of his stay.

The father and son, and three others of the band, two women and a very old man, all sat cross-legged in a half-circle, facing him across the fire. The children finally released his hands and a woman gave him a gourd filled with the scalded milk, in which floated strips of meat.

'Skathandi,' said the father. 'Camped down by the water. Here to ambush us and steal our horses, for the meat of the g'athend is highly prized by people in the cities. There were thirty in all, raiders and murderers – we will eat their horses, but you may have one to ride if you desire so.'

Traveller sipped the milk, and as the steam filled his face his eyes widened. Fire in his throat, then blissful numbness. Blinking tears from his eyes, he tried to focus on the man who had spoken. 'You sprang the ambush, then. Thirty? You must be formidable warriors.'

'This was the second such camp we found. All slain. Not by us, friend. Someone, it seems, likes the Skathandi even less than we do.'

The father hesitated, and in the pause his son said, 'It was our thought that you were following that someone.'

'Ah.' Traveller frowned. 'Someone? There is but one – one who attacks Skathandi camps and slaughters everyone?'

Nods answered him.

'A demon, we think, who walks like a storm, dark with terrible rage. One who covers well his tracks.' The son made an odd gesture with one hand, a rippling of the fingers. 'Like a ghost.'

'How long ago did this demon travel past here?'

'Three days.'

'Are these Skathandi a rival tribe?'

'No. Raiders, preying on caravans and all who dwell on the Plain. Sworn, it is said, to a most evil man, known only as the Captain. If you see an eight-wheeled carriage, so high there is one floor above and a balcony with a golden rail – drawn, it is said, by a thousand slaves – then you will have found the palace of this Captain. He sends out his raiders, and grows fat on the trade of his spoils.'

'I am not following this demon,' said Traveller. 'I know nothing of it.'

'That is probably well.'

'It heads north?'

'Yes.'

Traveller thought about that as he took another sip of the appallingly foul drink. With a horse under him he would begin to make good time, but that might well take him right on to that demon, and he did not relish a fight with a creature that could slay thirty bandits and leave nary a footprint.

One child, who had been kneeling beside him, piling handfuls of dirt on to Traveller's boot-top, now clambered up on to his thigh, reached into the gourd and plucked out a sliver of meat, and waved it in front of Traveller's mouth.

'Eat,' said the son. 'The meat is from a turtle that tunnels, very tender. The miska milk softens it and removes the poison. One generally does not drink the miska, as it can send the mind travelling so far that it never returns. Too much and it will eat holes in your stomach and you will die in great pain.'

'Ah. You could have mentioned that earlier.' Traveller took the meat from the child. He was about to plop it into his mouth when he paused. 'Anything else I should know before I begin chewing?'

'No. You will dream tonight of tunnelling through earth. Harmless enough. All food has memory, so the miska proves – we cook everything in it, else we taste the bitterness of death.'

Traveller sighed. 'This miska, it is mare's milk?'

Laughter erupted.

'No, no!' cried the father. 'A plant. A root bulb. Mare milk belongs to foals and colts, of course. Humans have their own milk, after all, and it is not drunk by adults, only babes. Yours, stranger, is a strange world!' And he laughed some more.

Traveller ate the sliver of meat.

Most tender – indeed, delicious. That night, sleeping beneath furs in a tipi, he dreamt of tunnelling through hard-packed, stony earth, pleased by its surrounding warmth, the safety of darkness.

He was woken shortly before dawn by a young woman, soft of limb and damp with desire, who wrapped herself tight about him. He was startled when she prised open his mouth with her own and deposited a full mouthful of spit, strongly spiced with something, and would not pull away until he swallowed it down. By the time she and the drug she had given him were done, there was not a seed left in his body.

In the morning, Traveller and the father went down to the abandoned Skathandi horses. With help from the mute dogs they were able to capture one of the animals, a solid piebald gelding of sixteen or so hands with mischief in its eyes.

The dead raiders, he noted as his companion went in search among the camp's wreckage for a worthy saddle, had indeed been cut to pieces. Although the work of the scavengers had reduced most of the corpses to tufts of hair, torn sinew and broken bones, there was enough evidence of severed limbs and decapitations to suggest some massive edged weapon at work. Where bones had been sliced through, the cut was sharp with no sign of crushing.

The father brought over the best of the tack, and Traveller saw with surprise that it was a Seven Cities saddle, with Malazan military brands on the leather girth-straps.

He was just finishing cinching the straps tight – after the gelding could hold its breath no longer – when he heard shouting from the Kindaru camp, and both he and the father turned.

A rider had appeared on the same ridge that Traveller had come to yesterday, pausing for but a moment before guiding the mount down into the camp.

Traveller swung himself on to his horse and gathered the reins.

'See the beast she rides!' gasped the man beside him. 'It is a Jhag'athend! We are blessed! Blessed!' And all at once he was running back to the camp.

Traveller set heels to his gelding and rode after the man.

The rider was indeed a woman, and Traveller saw almost immediately that she was of Seven Cities stock. She looked harried, threadbare and worn, but a ferocious fire blazed in her eyes when they fell upon Traveller as he rode into the camp.

'Is there anywhere in the world where I won't run into damned Malazans?' she demanded.

Traveller shrugged. 'And I hardly expected to encounter an Ugari woman on the back of a Jhag stallion here on the Lamatath Plain.'

Her scowl deepened. 'I am told there's a demon travelling through here, heading north. Killing everyone in his path and no doubt enjoying every moment of it.'

'So it seems.'

'Good,' snapped the woman.

'Why?' Traveller asked.

She scowled. 'So I can give him his damned horse back, that's why!'

Book Two

Cold-Eyed Virtues

From her ribs and from the hair of women
Seen swimming sun-warmed rivers in summer's light,
From untroubled brows and eyes clear and driven
Gazing out from tower windows when falls the night

From hands cupped round pipe bowls alabaster carved
When veiled invitations coy as blossoms under shade
Invite a virgin's dance a rose-dappled love so starved
Where seen a coarse matron not yet ready to fade

And the tall bones of legs 'neath rounded vessels perched
Swaying lusty as a tropical storm above white coral sands
Where in all these gathered recollections I have searched
To fashion this love anew from soil worked well by my hands

And into the bower garland-woven petals fluttering down
Hovers the newfound woman's familiar unknown face
For on this earth no solitude is welcomed when found
And she who is gone must be in turn be replaced

And by the look in her eye I am a composite man
Assembled alike from stone, twig and stirred sediments
Lovers lost and all those who might have been
We neither should rail nor stoke searing resentments
For all the rivers this world over do flow in but one
Direction

LOVE OF THE BROKEN
BRENETH

Chapter Seven

'I can see your reasons, my love. But won't you get thirsty?'

INSCRIPTION FOUND BENEATH
CAPSTONE OF HOUSEHOLD WELL,
LAKEFRONT DISTRICT, DARUJHISTAN

As fast as his small feet could carry him, the small boy rushed through Two-Ox Gate and out on to the raised cobble road that, if he elected to simply hurry on, and on, would take him to the very edge of the world, where he could stand on the shore staring out upon a trackless ocean, so vast it swallowed the sun every night. Alas, he wasn't going that far. Out to the hills just past the shanty town to collect dung, a bag full, as much as he could carry balanced on his head.

It is said by wise and sentimental poets that a child's eyes see farther than an adult's, and who would – with even less than a moment's thought – claim otherwise? Beyond the ridge awaits a vista crowded with possibilities, each one deemed more improbable than the last by teeth-grinding codgers eager to assert a litany of personal failures should anyone care to hear, but no one does and if that isn't proof the world's gone to ruin then what is? But *improbabilities* is a word few children know, and even if they did, why, they would dismiss the notion with a single hand fluttering overhead as they danced to the horizon. Because it will not do to creep timorously into the future, no, one should leap, sail singing through the air, and who can say where one's feet will finally set down on this solid, unknown land?

The boy hurried on, tracked by the dull eyes of the lepers in front of their hovels, squatting forlorn and forgotten each in a nest of flies when flies with singular poignancy expound the proof of cold-legged indifference. And the scrawny half-wild dogs crept out to follow him for a time, gauging with animal hunger if this one might be weakened, a thing to be taken down. But the boy collected rocks and when a dog drew too close he let fly. Ducked tails and startled yelps and now the dogs vanished like ghosts beneath stilted shacks and down narrow, twisting lanes off the main road.

Overhead, the sun regarded all with its unblinking omnipotence, and went on stealing moisture from every surface to feed its unquenchable thirst. And there were long-legged birds prancing on the sewage flats just past Brownrun Bay, beaks darting down to snatch up fleas and whatnot, while lizard-ducks nested on floating shit islands further out, calling to one another their hissing announcement of each bell in perfect cadence with the city's water clocks and those sonorous chimes drifting out over the lake, although why lizard-ducks were obsessed with such artificial segmentation of time was a question as yet unanswered even after centuries of scholarly pursuit – not that the foul-smelling creatures gave a whit for the careers they had spawned, more concerned as they were with enticing up from the soupy water eels that would swallow their eggs, only to find the shells impervious to all forms of digestion, whilst the scaled monstrosities within prepared to peck their way free and then feed on eel insides unto gluttony.

What significance, then, such details of the natural world, when the boy simply walked on, his long hair bleached by the sun and stirred like a mane by the freshening breeze? Why, none other than the value of indifference, beneath which a child may pass unnoticed, may pass by free as a fluffed seed on the warm currents of summer air. With only a faint memory of his dream the night before (and yes, the one before that, too, and so on) of that face so vicious and the eyes so caustic as to burn him with their dark intentions, the face that might pursue him through each day with the very opposite of indifference, and see how deadly that forgetfulness might be for the child who hurried on, now on a dirt track winding its way up into the modest hills where baleful goats gathered beneath the occasional tree.

For the blessing of indifference might be spun on end, momentarily offering the grim option of curse, because one child's gift can well be another's hurt. Spare then a moment for the frightened beast named Snell, and all the cruel urges driving him to lash out, to torment the brother he never wanted. He too thrives on indifference, this squat, round-shouldered, swaggering tyrant before whom the wild dogs in the shanty town cowered in instinctive recognition that he was one of their own, and the meanest of the lot besides; while the boy, chest swelled with power, continued on, trailing his intended victim with something in his soul that went far beyond a simple beating this time, oh, yes. The thing inside, it spread black, hairy legs like a spider, his hands transformed there at the end of his wrists, oh, spiders, yes, hook-taloned and fanged and onyx-eyed, and they could close into bony fists if they so desired, or they could stab with venom – why not both?

He carried rocks as well. To wing at the lepers he passed, to laugh as they flinched or cried out in pain, and he rode their ineffectual curses all the way up the road.

While, all along the hillside, the sun had done its work, and the boy filled his bag with tinder-dry dung for this night's hearthfire. Bent over like an old man, he roved this way and that. This bounty would please the woman-who-was-not-his-mother, who mothered him as a mother should – although, it must be said, lacking something essential, some maternal instinct to awaken cogent realization that her adopted son lived in grave danger – and as the sack bulked in his grip, he thought to pause and rest for a time, there, up on the summit of the hill. So that he could look out over the lake, watch the beautiful sails of the feluccas and fisher boats.

Set free his mind to wander – oh, memories are made of moments such as this one.

And, alas, of the one soon to come.

But give him these moments of freedom, so precious for their rarity. Begrudge not this gift of indifference.

It could, after all, very well be his last day of such freedom.

Down on the track at the base of the hill, Snell has spied his quarry. The spiders at the ends of his wrists opened and closed their terrible black legs. And like a monster that wrings goats' necks for the pleasure of it, he clambers upward, eyes fixed on that small back and tousled head there at the edge of the ridge.

In a temple slowly drowning there sat a Trell entirely covered in drying, blackening blood, and in his soul there was enough compassion to encompass an entire world, yet he sat with eyes of stone. When it is all one can do to simply hold on, then to suffer is to weather a deluge no god can ease.

Beneath the blood, faint traceries of spider's web tattooing etched his dark brown hide. These stung like hot wires wrapped about his body, his limbs; wrapped everywhere and seeming to tighten incrementally with every shiver that took him.

Three times now he had been painted in the blood of Burn, the Sleeping Goddess. The web was proving a skein of resistance, a net trapping him on the inside, and keeping out the blessed gift of the goddess.

He would pass through Burn's Gate, into the molten fires of the underworld, and the priests had prepared for that, yet now it seemed they would fail in fashioning a means of protecting his mortal flesh. What then could he do?

Well, he could walk away from this place and its huddled, doleful priests. Find another way to cross a continent, and then an ocean. He could perhaps try another temple, try to bargain with another god or goddess. He could—

'We have failed you, Mappo Runt.'

He glanced over to meet the anguished eyes of the High Priest.

'I am sorry,' the old man went on. 'The web that once healed you is proving most . . . selfish. Claiming you for its own – Ardatha never yields her prizes. She has snared you, for purposes unknown to any but her. She is most hateful, I think.'

'Then I will wash this off,' Mappo said, climbing to his feet, feeling the blood crack, pluck hairs from his skin. The web sang agony through him. 'The one who healed me in Ardatha's name is here in the city – I think I had better seek her out. Perhaps I can glean from her the spider goddess's intent – what it is she would have me do.'

'I would not recommend that,' the High Priest said. 'In fact, Mappo, I would run away. Soon as you can. For now, at least, Ardatha's web does not seek to hold you back from the path you have chosen. Why risk a confrontation with her? No, you must find another way, and quickly.'

Mappo considered this advice for a time, then grunted and said, 'I see the wisdom in your words; thank you. Have you any suggestions?'

The expression drooped. 'Unfortunately, I have.' He gestured and three young acolytes crept forward. 'These ones will assist in scrubbing the blood from you. In the meantime, I will send a runner and, perchance, an arrangement can be fashioned. Tell me, Mappo Runt, are you rich?'

Sweetest Sufferance, who had been so named by a mother either resigned to the rigours of motherhood or, conversely, poisoned by irony, blinked rapidly as she was wont to do when returning to reality. She looked round bemusedly, saw her fellow survivors seated with her, the table in their midst a chaotic clutter of cups, tankards, plates, utensils and the remnants of at least three meals. Her soft brown eyes flicked from one item to the next, then slowly lifted, out past the blank-eyed faces of her companions, and took in the taproom of Quip's Bar.

Quip Younger was barely visible on the counter, sprawled across it with his upper body and head resting on one forearm. He slept with his mouth hanging open and slick with drool. Almost within reach of the man there squatted a rat on the counter, one front paw lifting every now and then as it seemed to study the face opposite and especially the gaping dark hole of Quip Younger's mouth.

A drunk was lying just inside the door, passed out or dead, the only other patron present this early in the morning (excepting the rat).

When she finally brought her attention back to her companions, she saw Faint studying her, one brow lifting.

Sweetest Sufferance rubbed at her round face, her cheeks reminding her, oddly enough, of the dough her mother used to knead just before the harvest festival, those big round cakes all glittering with painted honey that used to trap ants and it was her task to pick them off but that was all right because they tasted wonderful.

'Hungry again, aren't ya?'

'You can always tell,' Sweetest Sufferance replied.

'When you rub your cheeks, there's a look comes into your eyes, Sweetie.'

Faint watched as Master Quell hissed awake with a sound no different from the noise an alligator might make when one stepped too close. And glared round a moment before relaxing into a relieved slump. 'I was dreaming—'

'Yah,' cut in Faint, 'you're always dreaming, and when you ain't dreaming, you're doing, and now if only those two things were any different from each other, why, you'd actually get some rest, Master. Which we'd like to see, wouldn't we just.'

'Got you through, didn't I?'

'Losing five Shareholders in the process.'

'That's the risks y'take,' Quell said, grimacing. 'Hey, who's paying for all this?'

'You might've asked that once before. You are, of course.'

'How long we been here? Gods, my bladder feels like I'm about to pass a papaya.' And with that he reeled – wincing – upright, and tottered for the closet behind the bar.

The rat watched him pass with suspicious eyes, then crept a few waddles closer to Quip Younger's mouth.

Glanno Tarp jerked alive in his chair. 'No more bargains!' he snarled. 'Oh,' he then said, slouching back down. 'Somebody stopped bringing beer – can they do that? Sweetest, darling, I dreamt we was making love—'

'Me too,' she said. 'Only it wasn't a dream.'

Glanno's eyes widened. 'Really?'

'No, it was a nightmare. If you want another round, you'll have t'wake up Quip Younger.'

Glanno squinted over. 'He'll wake up when he can't breathe, soon as the rat goes for it. A silver council says he swallows instead of spitting out.'

At the voicing of a wager Reccanto Ilk's watery grey eyes sharpened and he said, 'I'll take that one. Only what if he does both? Swallows then chokes and spits out? When you say "swallows" you got to mean he chews if he has to.'

'Now that's quibblering again and when you never done that, Ilk? It's pointless you saying you want to wager when you keep rectivifying things.'

'The point is you're always too vague, Glanno, with these bets of yours. Y'need precision—'

'What I need is . . . well, I don't know what I need, but whatever it is you ain't got it.'

'I got it but I ain't giving it,' said Sweetest Sufferance. 'Not to none of you, anyhow. There's a man out there, oh, yes, and I'll find him one day and I'll put him in shackles and lock him in my room and I'll reduce him to a pathetic wreck. Then we'll get married.'

'The marriage prediceeds the wrecking,' Glanno said. 'So I might dream of you, darling, but that's as far as it'll ever go. That's called self-prevarication.'

'Are you sure?' Faint asked him, then, as the front door squealed open, she turned in her chair. An adolescent boy in a voluminous brown robe edged in warily, eyes like freshly laid turtle eggs. Lifting the robe he stepped gingerly over the drunk and padded across to their table and if he had a tail, why, Faint told herself, it'd be half wagging half slipping down between his legs.

'Mmm. Mmmm.'

'Would that be "Master"?' Faint asked.

The youth nodded, drew a deep breath, and tried again. 'Negotiation, for a delivery, yes?'

'Master Quell is peremptorily predispossessed,' Glanno Tarp said.

'Predisposed, he means,' Faint explained. 'What needs delivering, and where?'

'Not what. Who. Don't know where.'

'Tell you what,' Faint said, 'go get the who and bring him or her here and we'll take it from there, all right? There now, watch your step on your way out.'

Bobbing head, hurried departure.

'Since when you did the negotiating?' Reccanto asked her, squinting.

'You know,' Faint observed, 'any half-decent Denul healer could fix your bad eyes, Ilk.'

'What's it to you?'

'What it is to me is you nearly lopped my head off, you damned blind idiot – do I look like a snarling corpse?'

'Sometimes. Anyway, I figured it out at the last moment—'

'After I ducked and kicked you between the legs.'

'Right, corpses ain't that smart, so now that's settled. I was asking you a question.'

'He was,' chimed in Glanno Tarp. 'Look at us, we're short maybe six, seven – we can't be going nowhere any time soon.'

'Maybe not, but maybe it'll be a quick, easy one.'

The others all stared at her.

Faint relented. 'Fine. Besides, I was just standing in for Quell, who might never leave that closet.'

'Could be he's dead,' Sweetest Sufferance suggested.

'Internally explodicated,' said Glanno Tarp, 'and don't think I'm going in for a look.'

'There goes the rat!' hissed Reccanto Ilk.

They looked, watched, breathless.

A pause, nose twitching, then a scurry of small steps. Close now, close enough to flinch back at the reeking breath.

'Two councils it falls over dead.'

'Be more precise – it's gonna fall over dead some day, ain't it?'

'Gods below!'

The rat held its ground, edged a mite closer. Then gathered itself, stretched out its neck, and began drinking from the pool of slime with tiny, flickering laps of its slivery tongue.

'That's what I was thinking it was gonna do,' said Sweetest Sufferance.

'Liar.'

'So now he ain't never going to wake up,' said Reccanto, 'and I'm going to die here of thirst.'

The closet door creaked open and out staggered Master Quell, not looking at all refreshed. He hobbled over. 'That papaya's stuck – I need a healer—'

'Or a fruit seller,' Faint said. 'Listen, could be we got us a new contract.'

Quell's eyes bugged slightly, then he spun round and staggered back into the closet.

'Now see what you did!' snapped Reccanto.

'It's not *my* papaya, is it?'

So early in the morning, the streets of Darujhistan, barring those of markets, were ghostly, strewn with rubbish and yet somehow magical. The sun's golden light stroked every surface with a gentle artist's hand. The faint mists that had drifted in from the lake during the night now retreated once more, leaving the air crisp. In the poorer quarters, shutters opened on upper storeys and moments later the contents of chamber pots sailed out, splashing the alleys and any hapless denizen still lying drunk to the world, and moments later rats and such crept out to sample the fresh offerings.

The dolorous High Priest led Mappo Runt away from the temple quarter and down into the Lakefront District, skirting Second Tier Wall before cutting across towards the Gadrobi District – in essence taking the Trell back the way he had come the night before. As they walked, the city awoke around them, rubbed sleep from its eyes, then gawked at the shambling priest and his enormous, barbaric companion.

They eventually arrived upon a narrow, sloped street in which sat a massive, ornate carriage of a sort that Mappo had seen before, though he could not for the moment recall where. Six horses stood in their traces, looking bored. Someone had dumped feed all round them, and there was enough fresh dung scattered about to suggest that the animals had been left there a while.

The priest directed Mappo towards a nearby tavern. 'In there,' he said. 'The Trygalle Trade Guild has made a specialty of journeys such as the one you require. Of course, they are expensive, but that is hardly surprising, is it?'

'And one simply seeks out one such caravan, wherever one might find them? That sounds to be an ineffective business plan.'

'No, they have offices. Somewhere – not a detail I possess, I'm afraid. I only knew of this carriage because its arrival destroyed the front of my cousin's shop.' And, pointing to a nearby ruin, he smiled like a man who had forgotten what real smiling signified. Then he shrugged. 'All these twists of fate. Blessed by serendipity and all that. If you fail here, Mappo Runt, you will have a long, tedious walk ahead of you. So do not fail.' He then bowed, turned and walked away.

Mappo eyed the front of the tavern. And recalled when he had last seen that sort of carriage.

Tremorlor.

Shareholder Faint had just stood, stretching out all the alarming kinks in her back, when the tavern door opened and a monstrous figure pushed its way in, shoulders squeezing through the frame, head ducking. A misshapen sack slung over one shoulder, a wicked knife tucked in its belt. A damned Trell.

'Glanno,' she said, 'better get Master Quell.'

Scowling, the last driver left alive in their troupe rose and limped away.

She watched as the huge barbarian stepped over the drunk and made his way to the bar. The rat looked up and hastily retreated down the length of the counter. The Trell nudged Quip Younger's head. The barkeep coughed and slowly straightened, wiping at his mouth, blinking myopically as he lifted his gaze to take in the figure looming over him.

With a bleat he reeled back a step.

'Never mind him,' Faint called out. 'You want us, over here.'

'What I want,' the Trell replied in passable Daru, 'is breakfast.'

Head bobbing, Quip bolted for the kitchen, where he was met by a screeching woman, the piercing tirade dimming as soon as the door closed behind him.

Faint dragged a bench from the nearby wall – no chair in this dump would survive – and waved to it with a glance over to the barbarian. 'Come over, then. Sit, but just so you know, we're avoiding Seven Cities. There was a terrible plague there; no telling if it's run its course.'

'No,' the Trell rumbled as he approached, 'I have no desire to return to Seven Cities, or Nemil.'

The bench groaned as he settled on to it.

Sweetest Sufferance was eyeing the newcomer with a strangely avid intensity. Reccanto Ilk simply stared, mouth open, odd twitches of his scalp shifting his hairline up and down.

Faint said to the Trell, 'The truth of it is, we're really in no shape for anything . . . ambitious. Master Quell needs to put out a call for more shareholders, and that could hold us back for days, maybe a week.'

'Oh, that is unfortunate. It is said your Guild has an office here in Darujhistan—'

'It does, but I happen to know we're the only carriage available, for the next while. Where were you hoping to go, and how quickly?'

'Where is your Master, or are you the one who does the negotiating?'

At that moment Glanno finally succeeded in dragging Quell out from the water closet. The Master was pale, and shiny with sweat, and it seemed his legs weren't working very well. Faint met his slightly wild gaze. 'Better?' she asked.

'Better,' he replied in a gasp, as Glanno more or less carried him over to his chair. 'It was a damned kidney stone, it was. Size of a knuckle – I never thought . . . well, never mind. Gods, who is this?'

The Trell half rose to bow. 'Apologies. My name is Mappo Runt.' And he sat back down.

Faint saw Quell lick dry lips, and with a trembling hand reach for a tankard. He scowled to find it empty and set it back down. 'The most infamous Trell of them all. You lost him, didn't you?'

The barbarian's dark eyes narrowed. 'Ah, I see.'

'Where?' Quell's voice sounded half strangled.

'I need to get to a continent named Lether. To an empire ruled by Tiste Edur, and a cursed emperor. And yes, I can pay you for the trouble.'

Faint had never seen her master so rattled. It was fascinating. Clearly, Quell had recognized the Trell's name, which signified . . . well, something.

'And, er, did he face that emperor, Mappo? In ritual combat?'

'I do not think so.'

'Why?'

'I believe I would have . . . sensed such a thing—'

'The end of the world, you mean.'

'Perhaps. No, something else happened. I cannot say what, Master Quell. I need to know, will you take me there?'

'We're under-crewed,' Quell said, 'but I can drop by the office, see if there's a list of waiting prospects. A quick interview process. Say by this time tomorrow, I can have an answer.'

The huge warrior sighed. He glanced round. 'I have nowhere else to go, so I will stay here until then.'

'Sounds wise,' Quell said. 'Faint, you're with me. The rest of you, get cleaned up, see to the horses, carriage and all that. Then stay close by, keep Mappo company – he might have nasty tusks but he don't bite.'

'But I do,' said Sweetest Sufferance, offering the Trell an inviting smile.

Mappo stared at her a moment, then, rubbing at his face, he rose. 'Where's that breakfast, anyway?'

'Let's go, Faint,' said Quell, pushing himself upright with another wince.

'Can you make it?' she asked him.

A nod. 'Haradas is handling the office these days – she can heal me quick enough.'

'Good point. Hands on?'

There is, as a legion of morose poets well know, nothing inconsequential about love. Nor all those peculiarities of related appetites often confused for love, for example lust, possession, amorous worship, appalling notions of abject surrender where one's own will is bled out in sacrifice, obsessions of the fetishistic sort that might include earlobes or toenails or regurgitated foodstuffs, and indeed that adolescent competitiveness which in adults – adults who should of course know better but don't – is manifested as insane jealousy.

Such lack of restraint has launched and no doubt sunk an equal number of ships, if one took the long view of such matters, which in retrospect is not only advisable but, for all the sighs of worldly wind, probably the most essential survival trait of them all – but pray, let not this rounded self wallow unthinkingly into recounting a host of lurid tales of woe, loss and the like, nor bemoan his present solitude as anything other than a voluntary state of being!

Cast attention, then (with audible relief), upon these three for whom love heaves each moment like a volcano about to erupt, amidst the groan of continents, the convulsion of valleys and the furrowing of furrows – but no, honesty demands a certain revision to what steams and churns beneath the surface. Only two of the three thrash and writhe in the delicious agony of that-which-might-be-love, and the subject of their fixed attention is none other than the third in their quaint trio, who, being of feminine nature, is yet to decide and, now that she basks in extraordinary attention, may indeed *never* decide. And should the two ever vying for her heart both immolate themselves at some future point, ah well, there are plenty of eels in the muck, aren't there?

And these three, then, bound together in war and bound yet tighter in the calamity of desire long after the war was done with, now find themselves in the fair city of Darujhistan, two pursuing one and where the one goes so too will they, but she wonders, yes, just how far she can take them and let's see, shall we?

Being illiterate, she has scrawled her name on to a list, assuming her name can be pictographically rendered into something like a chicken heart's spasm the moment before death, and lo, did not her two suitors follow suit, competing even here in their expressions of illiterate extravagance, with the first devising a most elaborate sigil of self that might lead one to imagine his name's being Smear of Snail in Ecstasy, whilst the other, upon seeing this, set to with brush, scrivener's dust and fingernails to fashion a scrawl reminiscent of a serpent trying to cross a dance floor whilst a tribe importuned the fickle gods of rain. Both men then stood, beaming with pride in between mutual baring of teeth, while their love sauntered off to find a nearby stall where an old woman wearing seaweed on her head was cooking stuffed voles over a brazier of coals.

The two men hastened after her, both desperate to pay for her breakfast, or beat the old woman senseless, whichever their darling preferred.

Thus it was that High Marshal Jula Bole and High Marshal Amby Bole, along with the swamp witch named Precious Thimble, all late of the Mott Irregulars, were close at hand and, indeed, ready and willing newfound shareholders when Master Quell and Faint arrived at the office of the Trygalle Trade Guild. And while three was not quite the number Quell sought by way of replacements, they would just have to do, given Mappo Runt's terrible need.

So they would not have to wait until the morrow after all. Most *consequential* indeed.

Happy days!

Conspiracies are the way of the civilized world, both those real and those imagined, and in all the perambulations of move and countermove, why, the veracity of such schemes are irrelevant. In a subterranean, most private chamber in the estate of Councilman Gorlas Vidikas sat fellow Council members Shardan Lim and Hanut Orr in the company of their worthy host, and the wine had flowed like the fount of the Queen of Dreams – or if not dreams then at least irresponsible aspirations – throughout the course of the night just past.

Still somewhat inebriated and perhaps exhausted unto satiation by self-satisfaction, they were comfortably silent, each feeling wiser than their years, each feeling that wellspring of power against which reason was helpless. In their half-lidded eyes something was swollen and nothing in the world was unattainable. Not for these three.

'Coll will be a problem,' Hanut said.

'Nothing new there,' Shardan muttered, and the other two granted him soft, muted laughter. 'Although,' he added as he played with a silver candle snuffer, 'unless we give him cause for suspicion, there is no real objection he can legitimately make. Our nominee is well enough respected, not to mention harmless, at least physically.'

'It's just that,' Hanut said, shaking his head, 'by virtue of us as nominators, Coll will be made suspicious.'

'We play it as we discussed, then,' Shardan responded, taunting with death the nearest candle's flame. 'Bright-eyed and full of ourselves and brazenly awkward, eager to express our newly acquired privilege to propose new Council members. We'd hardly be the first to be so clumsy and silly, would we?'

Gorlas Vidikas found his attention wandering – they'd gone through all this before, he seemed to recall. Again and again, in fact, through the course of the night, and now a new day had come, and still they chewed the same tasteless grist. Oh, these two companions of his liked the sound of their own voices all too well. Converting dialogue into an argument even when both were in agreement, and all that distinguished the two was the word choices concocted in each reiteration.

Well, they had their uses none the less. And this thing he had fashioned here was proof enough of that.

And now, of course, Hanut once more fixed eyes upon him and asked yet again the same question, 'Is this fool of yours worth it, Gorlas? Why him? It's not as if we aren't approached almost every week by some new prospect wanting to buy our votes on to the Council. Naturally, it serves us better to string the fools along, gaining favour upon favour, and maybe one day deciding we own so much of them that it will be worth our while to bring them forward. In the meantime, of course, we just get richer and more influential *outside* the Council. The gods know, we can get pretty damned rich with *this* one.'

'He is not the type who will play the whore to our pimp, Hanut.'

A frown of distaste. 'Hardly a suitable analogy, Gorlas. You forget that you are the junior among us here.'

The one who happens to own the woman you both want in your beds. Don't chide me about whores and pimps, when you know what you'll pay for her. Such thoughts remained well hidden behind his momentarily chastened expression. 'He'll not play the game, then. He wants to attain the Council, and in return we shall be guaranteed his support when we make our move to shove aside the elder statesmen and their fossilized ways, and take the *real* power.'

Shardan grunted. 'Seems a reasonable arrangement, Hanut. I'm tired, I need some sleep.' And he doused the candle before him as he rose. 'Hanut, I know a new place for breakfast.' He smiled at Gorlas. 'I am not being rude in not inviting you, friend. Rather, I imagine your wife will wish to greet you this morning, with a breakfast you can share. The Council does not meet until mid-afternoon, after all. Take your leisure, Gorlas, when you can.'

'I will walk you both out,' he replied, a smile fixed upon his face.

Most of the magic Lady Challice Vidikas was familiar with was of the useless sort. As a child she had heard tales of great and terrible sorcery, of course, and had she not seen for herself Moon's Spawn? On the night when it sank so low its raw underside very nearby brushed the highest rooftops, and there had been dragons in the sky then, and a storm to the east that was said to have been fierce magic born of some demonic war out in the Gadrobi Hills, and then the confused madness behind Lady Simtal's estate. But none of this had actually affected her directly. Her life had slipped through the world so far as most people's did, rarely touched by anything beyond the occasional ministrations of a healer. All she had in her possession was a scattering of ensorcelled items intended to do little more than entrance and amuse.

One such object was before her now, on her dresser, a hemisphere of near-perfect glass in which floated a semblance of the moon, shining as bright as it would in the night sky. The details on its face were exact, at least from the time when the real moon's visage had been visible, instead of blurred and uncertain as it was now.

A wedding gift, she recalled, although she'd forgotten from whom it had come. One of the less obnoxious guests, she suspected, someone with an eye to romance in the old-fashioned sense, perhaps. A dreamer, a genuine well-wisher. At night, if she desired darkness in the room, the half-globe needed covering, for its reful-gent glow was bright enough to read by. Despite this inconvenience, Challice kept the gift, and indeed kept it close.

Was it because Gorlas despised it? Was it because, while it had once seemed to offer her a kind of promise, it had, over time, transformed into a symbol of some-thing entirely different? A tiny moon, yes, shining ever so bright, yet there it re-mained, trapped with nowhere to go. Blazing its beacon like a cry for help, with an optimism that never waned, a hope that never died.

Now, when she looked upon the object, she found herself feeling claustropho-bic, as if she was somehow sharing its fate. But *she* could not shine for ever, could she? No, her glow would fade, was fading even now. And so, although she pos-sessed this symbol of what might be, her sense of it had grown into a kind of fas-cinated resentment, and even to look upon it, as she was doing now, was to feel its burning touch, searing her mind with a pain that was almost delicious.

All because it had begun feeding a desire, and perhaps this was a far more pow-erful sorcery than she had first imagined; indeed, an enchantment tottering on the edge of a curse. The burnished light breathed into her, filled her mind with strange thoughts and hungers growing ever more desperate for appeasement. She was being enticed into a darker world, a place of hedonistic indulgences, a place unmindful of the future and dismissive of the past.

It beckoned to her, promising the bliss of the ever-present moment, and it was to be found, she knew, *somewhere out there.*

She could hear her husband on the stairs, finally deigning to honour her with his company, although after a night's worth of drinking and all the manly mutual rais-ing of hackles, verbal strutting and preening, he would be unbearable. She had not slept well and was, truth be told, in no mood for him (but then, she realized, she had been in no mood for him for some time, now – shock!), so she swiftly rose and went to her private changing room. A journey out into the city would suit her rest-lessness. Yes, to walk without purpose and gaze upon the detritus of the night's fes-tivities, to be amused by the bleary eyes and unshaven faces and the last snarl of exhausted arguments.

And she would take her breakfast upon a terrace balcony in one of the more el-egant restaurants, perhaps Kathada's or the Oblong Pearl, permitting her a view of the square and Borthen Park where servants walked watchdogs and nannies pushed two-wheeled prams in which huddled a new generation of the privileged, tucked inside nests of fine cotton and silk.

There, with fresh fruits and a carafe of delicate white wine, and perhaps even a pipe bowl, she would observe all the life meandering below, sparing a thought (just once and then done with) for the dogs she didn't want and the children she didn't have and probably would never have, given Gorlas's predilections. To think, for a time, in a musing way, of his parents and their dislike of her – convinced that she was barren, no doubt, but no woman ever got pregnant from that place, did she? – and of her own father, now a widower, with his sad eyes and the smile he struggled to fashion every time he looked upon her. To contemplate, yet again, the notion of pulling her father aside and warning him – about what? Well, her husband, for one, and Hanut Orr and Shardan Lim for that matter. Dreaming of a great triumvirate of tyranny and undoubtedly scheming to bring it about. But then, he would laugh, wouldn't he? And say how the young Council members were all the same, blazing with ambition and conviction, and that their ascension was but a matter of time, as unstoppable as an ocean tide, and soon they would come to realize that and cease their endless plans of usurpation. Patience, he would tell her, is the last virtue learned. *Yes, but often too late to be of any value, dear Father. Look at you, a lifetime spent with a woman you never liked, and now, free at last, you find yourself grey, a fresh stoop to your shoulders, and you sleep ten bells every night—*

Such thoughts and others whilst she refreshed herself and began selecting her attire for the day. And in the bedroom beyond she heard Gorlas sit on the bed, no doubt unlacing his boots, knowing well that she was here in the tiny chamber and clearly not caring.

And what then would Darujhistan offer up to her this bright day? Well, she would see, wouldn't she?

She turned from watching her students in the compound and, eyes alighting upon him, she scowled. 'Oh, it's you.'

'This is the new crop, then? Apsalar's sweet kiss, Stonny.'

Her scowl turned wry and she walked past him into the shade of the colonnade, where she sat down on the bench beside the archway, stretching out her legs. 'I won't deny it, Gruntle. But it's something I've been noticing – the noble-born children are all arriving lazy, overweight and uninterested. Sword skill is something their fathers want for them, as obnoxious to them as lyre lessons or learning numbers. Most of them can't even hold up the practice swords for longer than fifty heartbeats, and here it's expected I can work them into something worth more than snot in eight months. Apsalar's sweet kiss? Yes, I'll accept that. It *is* theft, all right.'

'And you're doing well by it, I see.'

She ran one gloved hand along her right thigh. 'The new leggings? Gorgeous, aren't they?'

'Stunning.'

'Black velvet doesn't work on any old legs, you know.'

'Not mine, anyway.'

'What do you want, Gruntle? I see the barbs have faded, at least. News was you were positively glowing when you came back.'

'A disaster. I need a new line of work.'

'Don't be ridiculous. It's the only thing you're remotely good at. Oafs like you need to be out there, chopping through the thick skulls of bandits and whatnot. Once you start staying put this city is doomed and it just so happens that I like living here, so the sooner you're back out on the trails the better.'

'I missed you too, Stonny.'

She snorted.

'Bedek and Myrla are well, by the way.'

'Stop right there.'

He sighed, rubbed at his face.

'I mean it, Gruntle.'

'Look, an occasional visit is all I'm asking—'

'I send money.'

'You do? That's the first I've heard of that. Not a mention from Bedek and from how they're doing, well, you can't be sending much, or very often.'

She glared at him. 'Snell meets me outside the door and the coins go right into his hands – I make sure, Gruntle. Anyway, how dare you? I made the adoption legal and so I don't owe them anything, damn you.'

'Snell. Well, that probably explains it. Next time try Myrla or Bedek, anyone but Snell.'

'You're saying the little shit is stealing it?'

'Stonny, they're barely scraping by, and, thinking on it, well, I know you well enough to know that, adoption or no, you won't see them starve – any of them, especially not your son.'

'Don't call him that.'

'Stonny—'

'The spawn of rape – I can see *his* face, right there in Harllo's own, looking up at me. I can see it clear, Gruntle.' And she shook her head, refusing to meet his eyes, and her legs had drawn up, tightly clenched, and all the bravado was gone as she clasped her arms tight about herself, and Gruntle felt his heart breaking yet again and there was nothing he could do, nothing he could say to make it any better, only worse.

'You'd better go,' she said in a tight voice. 'Come back when the world dies, Gruntle.'

'I was thinking about the Trygalle Trade Guild.'

Her head snapped round. 'Are you mad? Got a damned death wish?'

'Maybe I do.'

'Get out of my sight, then. Go on, run off and get yourself killed.'

'Your students look ready to keel over,' Gruntle observed. 'Repeated lunges aren't easy for anyone – I doubt any of them will be able to walk come the morrow.'

'Never mind them. If you're really thinking of signing on with the Trygalle, say it plain.'

'I thought you might talk me out of it.'

'Why would I bother? You got your life just like I got mine. We aren't married. We aren't even lovers—'

'Had any success in that area, Stonny? Someone might—'

'Stop this. Stop all of it. You're like this every time you come back from a bad one. All full of pity and damn near dripping with sanctimony while you try and try to convince me.'

'Convince you of what?'

'Being human, but I'm done with that. Stonny Menackis died years ago. What you're seeing now is a thief running a school teaching nothing to imps with piss in their veins. I'm just here to suck fools dry of their coin. I'm just here to lie to them about how their son or daughter is a champion duelist in the making.'

'So you won't be talking me out of signing with the Trygalle, then.' Gruntle turned to the archway. 'I see I do nothing good here. I'm sorry.'

But she reached out and grasped his forearm as he was about to leave. 'Don't,' she said.

'Don't what?'

'Take it from me, Gruntle, there's nothing good in a death wish.'

'Fine,' he said, then left.

Well, he'd messed it all up again. Nothing new in that, alas. *Should hunt down Snell, give him a shake or two. At the very least, scare the crap out of him. Get him to spill where he's been burying his hoard. No wonder he likes sitting on the threshold. Keeping an eye out, I suppose.*

Still, Gruntle kept coming back to all these unpleasant truths, the life he was busy wasting, the pointlessness of all the things he chose to care about – well, not entirely true. There was the boy, but then, the role of an occasional uncle could hardly be worth much, could it? What wisdom could he impart? Very little, if he looked back on the ruin of his life so far. Companions dead or lost, followers all rotting in the ground, the ash-heaps of past battles and decades spent risking his life to protect the possessions of someone else, someone who got rich without chancing anything worthwhile. Oh, Gruntle might charge for his services, he might even bleed his employers on occasion, and why not?

Which was why, come to think on it, the whole thing with the Trygalle Trade Guild was starting to make sense to him. A shareholder was just that, someone with a stake in the venture, profiting by their own efforts with no fat fool in the wings waiting with sweaty hands.

Was this a death wish? Hardly. Plenty of shareholders survived, and the smart ones made sure they got out before it was too late, got out with enough wealth to buy an estate, to retire into a life of blissful luxury. Oh, that was just for him, wasn't it? *Well, when you're only good at one thing, then you stop doing it, what's left but doing nothing?*

With some snivelling acolyte of Treach scratching at his door every night. *'The Tiger of Summer would roar, Chosen One. Yet here you lie indolent in silk bedding. What of battle? What of blood and the cries of the dying? What of chaos and the reek of spilled wastes, the curling up round mortal wounds in the slime and mud? What of the terrible strife from which you emerge feeling so impossibly alive?'*

Yes, what of it? *Let me lie here, rumbling this deep, satisfied purr. Until war finds me, and if it never does, well, that's fine by me.*

Bah, he was fooling nobody, especially not himself. He was no soldier, true enough, but it seemed mayhem found him none the less. The tiger's curse, that even when it is minding its own business a mob of beady-eyed fools come chanting into the jungle, beating the ground. Was that true? Probably not, since there was no reason for hunting tigers, was there? He must have invented the scene, or caught a glimpse of Treach's own dreaming. Then again, did not hunters beard beasts of all sorts in their dens and caves and burrows? After some fatuous excuse about perils to livestock or whatever, off the mob went, eager for blood.

Beard me, will you? Oh, please do – and all at once, he found his mood changed, mercurial and suddenly seething with rage.

He was walking along a street, close now to his abode, yet the passers-by had all lost their faces, had become nothing more than mobile pieces of meat, and he wanted to kill them all.

A glance down at his hands and he saw the black slashes of the tiger's barbs deep as dusty jet, and he knew then that his eyes blazed, that his teeth were bared, the canines glistening, and he knew, too, why the amorphous shapes he passed were shrinking from his path. If only one would come close, he could lash out, open a throat and taste the salty chalk of blood on his tongue. Instead, the fools were rushing off, cringing in doorways or bolting down alleys.

Unimpressed, disappointed, he found himself at his door.

She didn't understand, or maybe she did all too well. Either way, she'd been right in saying he did not belong in this city, or any other. They were all cages, and the trick he'd never learned was how to be at peace living in a cage.

In any case, peace was overrated – look at Stonny, after all. *I take my share, my fortune, and I buy them a new life – a life with servants and such, a house with an enclosed garden where he can be carried out and sit in the sun. The children properly schooled; yes, some vicious tutor to take Snell by the throat and teach him some respect. Or if not respect, then healthy terror. And for Harllo, a chance at a future.*

One should be all I need, and I can survive one, can't I? It's the least I can do for them. In the meantime, Stonny will take care of things – making sure the coin reaches Myrla.

Where did I see that damned carriage anyway?

He was at his door again, this time facing the street. Loaded with travel gear, with weapons and his fur-lined rain-cloak – the new one that smelled like sheep – and so it was clear that some time had passed, but the sort that was inconsequential, that did nothing but what needed doing, with no wasted thought. Nothing like hesitation, or the stolid weighing of possibilities, or the moaning back-and-forth that some might call wise deliberation.

Walking now, this too of little significance. Why, nothing had significance, until the moment when the claws are unsheathed, and the smell of blood gives bite to the air. And that moment waited somewhere ahead and he drew closer, step by step, because when a tiger decides it's time to hunt, it is time to hunt.

Snell came up behind his quarry, delighted by his own skill at stealth, at stalking the creature who sat in the high grasses all unknowing, proving that Harllo wasn't fit for the real world, the world where everything was a threat and needed taking care of lest it take care of you. It was the right kind of lesson for Snell to deliver, out here in the wilds.

He held in one hand a sack filled with the silver councils Aunt Stonny had brought, two linings of burlap and the neck well knotted so he could grip it tight. The sound the coins made when they struck the side of Harllo's head was most satisfying, sending a shock of thrill through Snell. And the way that hateful head snapped to one side, the small body pitching to the ground, well, that was a sight he would cherish.

He kicked at the unconscious form for a while, but without the grunts and whimpers it wasn't as much fun, so he left off. Then, collecting the hefty sack of dung, he set out for home. His mother would be pleased at the haul, and she'd plant a kiss on his forehead and he could bask for a time, and when someone wondered where Harllo had got to, why, he'd tell them he'd seen him down at the docks, talking with some sailor. When the boy didn't come home tonight, Myrla might send for Gruntle to go down and check the waterfront, where he'd find out that two ships had sailed that day, or three, and was there a new cabin boy on one of them? Maybe so, maybe not, who paid attention to such things?

Dismay, then, and worries, and mourning, but none of that would last long. Snell would become the precious one, the one still with them, the one they needed to take care of, protect and coddle. The way it used to be, the way it was supposed to be.

Smiling under the bright morning sun, with long-legged birds pecking mud on the flats out on the lake to his left, Snell ambled his way back home. A good day, a day of feeling so alive, so free. He had righted the world, the whole world.

The shepherd who found the small boy in the grasses of the summit overlooking the road into Maiten and then Two-Ox Gate was an old man with arthritic knees who knew his usefulness was coming to an end, and very soon indeed he would find himself out of work, the way the herdmaster watched him hobbling and leaning too much on his staff. Examining the boy, he was surprised to find him still alive, and this brought thoughts of what he might do with such an urchin in his care.

Worth the effort? He could bring his wife back here, with the cart, and together they could lift the body into the bed and wheel him back to their shack on the shore of the lake. Tend to him and see if he lived or died, feed him enough if it came to that, and then?

Well, he had thoughts, yes, plenty of thoughts on that. None of them pleasant, but then, whoever said the world was a pleasant place? Foundlings were fair game and that was a rule somewhere, he was sure of it, a rule, just like finding salvage on the beach. What you found you owned, and the money would do them good, besides.

He too concluded that it was a good day.

He remembered his childhood, running wild in the streets and alleys, clambering on to the rooftops at night to stare about in wonder at the infamous Thieves' Road. So inviting this romance of adventure under the moon's secret light, whilst slept all the dullards and might-be victims in the unlit rooms below.

Running wild, and for the child one road was as good as another, perhaps better so long as there was mystery and danger every step of the way. Even later, when that danger had become all too real, it had been for Cutter a life unfurling, revealing a heart saturated with wonder.

Romance was for fools, he now knew. No one valued the given heart, no one saw that sacrifice for the precious gift it was. No, just a thing to be grasped, twisted by uncaring hands, then wrung dry and discarded. Or a commodity and nothing more, never as desirable as the next one, the one in waiting, or the one held by someone else. Or, something far worse, a gift too precious to accept.

The nature of the rejection, he told himself, was irrelevant. Pain and grief arrived in singular flavours, bitter and lifeless, and too much of them rotted the soul. He could have taken other roads. Should have. Maybe walked Murillio's path, a new love every night, the adoration of desperate women, elegant brunches on balconies and discreet rendezvous beneath whispering leaves in some private garden.

Or how about Kruppe? A most wily master to whom he could have apprenticed himself yet further than he already had, in the art of high thievery, in the disposition of stolen items, in the acquisition of valuable information available to whoever was willing to pay and pay well. In the proper appreciation of wines, pastries and inappropriate attire. A lifetime of cherubic delight, but was there really room in the world for more than one Kruppe?

Assuredly not!

Was it preferable, then, this path of daggers, this dance of shadows and the taking of lives for coin without even a soldier's sanction (as if that mattered)? Rallick would not agree. And Murillio would shake his head, and Kruppe waggle his eyebrows, and Meese might grin and make another grab for his crotch, with Irilta looking on with motherly regard. And there'd be that glow in Sulty's eyes, tinged now with the bitter truth that she was no longer enough for one such as him, that she could only dream, that somehow his being an assassin set him upon such a high station that her lowly existence as a serving wench was beneath all notice. Where even his efforts at friendship were perceived as pity and condescension, sufficient to pitch her into tears at the wrong word, the missed glance.

How the time for dreams of the future seemed to slip past unnoticed, until in reviving them a man realized, with a shock, that the privilege was no longer his to entertain, that it belonged to those younger faces he saw on all sides, laughing in the tavern and on the streets, *running wild*.

'You have changed,' Murillio said from the bed where he reclined, propped up on pillows, his hair hanging unbound and unwashed, 'and I'm not sure it's for the better.'

Cutter regarded his old friend for a moment, then asked, 'What's better?'

'What's better. You wouldn't have asked that question, and certainly not in that way, the last time I saw you. Someone broke your heart, Crokus – not Challice D'Arle, I hope!'

Smiling, Cutter shook his head. 'No, and what do you know, I'd almost forgotten her name. Her face, certainly . . . and the name is Cutter now, Murillio.'

'If you say so.'

He just had, but clearly Murillio was worse for wear, not up to his usual standard of conversation. If he'd been making a point by saying that, well, maybe *Crokus* would've snatched the bait. *It's the darkness in my soul . . . no, never mind.*

'Seven Cities, was it? Took your time coming home.'

'A long journey, for the ship I was on. The north route, along the island chains, stuck in a miserable hovel of a port for two whole seasons – first winter storms, which we'd expected, then a spring filled with treacherous ice rafts, which we didn't – no one did, in fact.'

'Should have booked passage on a Moranth trader.'

Cutter glanced away. 'Didn't have a choice, not for the ship, nor for the company on it.'

'So you had a miserable time aboard?'

He sighed. 'Not their fault, any of them. In fact, I made good friends—'

'Where are they now, then?'

Cutter shrugged. 'Scattered about, I imagine.'

'Will we meet them?' Murillio asked.

He wondered at this line of questioning, found himself strangely irritated by Murillio's apparent interest in the people he had come back with. 'A few, maybe. Some stepped ashore only to leave again, by whatever means possible – so, not any of those. The others . . . we'll see.'

'Ah, I was just curious.'

'About what?'

'Well, which of your groups of friends you considered more embarrassing, I suppose.'

'Neither!'

'Sorry, I didn't mean to offend . . . Cutter. You're just seeming somewhat . . . restless, as if you'd rather be elsewhere.'

It's not that easy. 'It all feels . . . different. That's all. Bit of a shock, finding you nearly dead.'

'I imagine besting Rallick in a knife fight was rather shocking, as well.'

Cutter didn't much want to think about that. 'I could never have imagined that you'd lose a duel, Murillio.'

'Easy to do, when you're drunk and wearing no breeches.'

'Oh.'

'Actually, neither of those is relevant to my present situation. I was careless. Why was I careless? Because I'm getting old. Because it's all slowing down. *I'm* slowing down. Look at me, lying here, healed up but full of aches, old pains, and nothing but cold ashes in my soul. I've been granted a second chance and I intend to take it.'

'Meaning?'

Murillio shot him a look. Seemed about to say something, then changed his mind and said something else. 'I'm going to retire. True, I've not saved up much, but then, I should be able to live with more modest expectations, shouldn't I? There's a new duelling school in the Daru. I've heard it's doing rather well, long lists of applicants and all that. I could help out, a couple of days a week.'

'No more widows. No more clandestine trysts.'

'Precisely.'

'You'll make a good instructor.'

'Not likely,' he replied with a grimace, 'but I have no aspirations to be one, either. It's work, that's all. Footwork, forms, balance and timing – the more serious stuff they can get from someone else.'

'If you go in there talking like that,' Cutter said, 'you'll never get hired.'

'I've lost my ability to charm?'

Cutter sighed and rose from his chair. 'I doubt it.'

'What brought you back?' Murillio asked.

The question stopped him. 'A conceit, maybe.'

'What kind of conceit?'

The city is in danger. It needs me. 'Oh,' he said, turning to the door, 'the childish kind. Be well, Murillio – I think your idea is a good one, by the way. If Rallick drops by looking for me, tell him I'll be back later.'

He took the back stairs, went through the dank, narrow kitchen, and out into the alley, where the chill of the night just past remained in the air. He did need to speak to Rallick Nom, but not right now. He felt slightly punch-drunk. The shock of his return, he supposed, the clash inside himself between who he had once been and who he was now. He needed to get settled, to get the confusion from his mind. If he could begin to see clearly again, he'd know what to do.

Out into the city, then, to wander. Not quite *running wild*, was it?

No, those days were long gone.

The wound had healed quickly, reminding him that there had been changes – the powder of otataral he had rubbed into his skin only a few days ago, or so it seemed. To begin a night of murder now years past. The other changes, however, were proving far more disconcerting. He had lost so much time. Vanished from the world, and the world just went on without him. As if Rallick Nom had been dead, yes – no different from that, only now he was back, which wasn't how things should be. *Pull a stick from the mud and the mud closes in to swallow up the hole, until no sign remains that the stick ever existed.*

Was he still an assassin of the Guild? Not at the moment, and this truth opened to him so many possibilities that his mind reeled, staggered back to the simpler notion of descending into the catacombs, walking up to Seba Krafar and announcing his return; resuming, yes, his old life.

And if Seba was anything like old Talo, he would smile and say *welcome back, Rallick Nom.* From that moment the chances that Rallick would make it back out alive were virtually nonexistent. Seba would see at once the threat standing before him. Vorcan had favoured Rallick and that alone was sufficient justification for getting rid of him. Seba wanted no rivals – he'd had enough of those if Krute's tale of the faction war was accurate.

He had another option when it came to the Guild. Rallick could walk in and kill Seba Krafar, then announce he was interim Master, awaiting Vorcan's return. Or he could stay in hiding for as long as possible, waiting for Vorcan to make her own move. Then, with her ruling the nest once again, he could emerge out of the woodwork and those missing years would be as nothing, would be without meaning. That much he shared with Vorcan, and because of that she would trust no one but Rallick. He'd be second in command, and how could he not be satisfied with that?

Oh, this was an old crisis – years old now. His thought that Turban Orr would be the last person he killed had been as foolish then as it was now.

He sat on the edge of the bed in his room. From the taproom below he could hear Kruppe expounding on the glories of breakfast, punctuated by some muted no doubt savage commentary by Meese, and with those two it was indeed as if nothing had changed. The same could not be said for Murillio, alas. Nor for Crokus, who was now named Cutter – an assassin's name for certain, all too well suited to the man Crokus had become. *Now who taught him to fight with knives like that? Something of the Malazan style – the Claw, in fact.*

Rallick had been expecting Cutter to visit, had been anticipating the launch of a siege of questions. He would want to explain, wouldn't he? Try to justify his decisions to Rallick, even when there was no possible justification. *He didn't listen to me, did he? Ignored my warnings. Only fools think they can make a difference.* So, where was he? *With Murillio, I expect, holding off on the inevitable.*

A brief knock at the door and Irilta entered – she'd been living hard of late, he could see, and such things seemed to catch up faster with women than with men – though when men went they went quickly. 'Brought you breakfast,' she said, carrying a tray over. 'See? I remembered it all, right down to the honey-soaked figs.'

Honey-soaked figs? 'Thank you, Irilta. Let Cro – er, Cutter know that I'd like to see him now.'

'He went out.'

'He did? When?'

She shrugged. 'Not so long ago, according to Murillio.' She paused for a hacking cough that reddened her broad face.

'Find yourself a healer,' Rallick said when she was done.

'Listen,' she said, opening the door behind her, 'I ain't got no regrets, Rallick. I

ain't expecting any god's kiss on the other side, and ain't nobody gonna say of Irilta she didn't have no fun when she was alive, no sir.'

She added something else but since she was in the corridor and closing the
door Rallick didn't quite catch it. Might have been something like 'try chewin on
that lesson some . . .', but then, she'd never been the edgy one, had she?

He looked down at the tray, frowned, then picked it up and rose.

Out into the corridor, balancing it one-handed while he lifted the latch of the
next door along and walked into Murillio's room.

'This is yours,' Rallick said. 'Honey-soaked figs, your favourite.'

A grunt from Murillio on the bed. 'Explains these strips of spiced jerky – you
are what you eat, right?'

'You're not nearly as sweet as you think, then,' Rallick said, setting the tray
down. 'Poor Irilta.'

'Poor Irilta nothing – that woman's crowded more into her years than all the
rest of us combined, and so now she's dying but won't bother with any healer because, I think, she's ready to leave.' He shook his head as he reached for the first
glazed fig. 'If she knew you were pitying her, she'd probably kill you for real, Rallick.'

'Missed me, did you?'

A pause, a searching glance, then Murillio bit into the fig.

Rallick went and sat down in one of the two chairs crowding the room along
with the bed. 'You spoke to Cutter?'

'Somewhat.'

'I thought he'd come to see me.'

'Did you now?'

'The fact that he didn't shouldn't make me think he got scared, should it?'

Murillio slowly shook his head.

Rallick sighed. Then he said, 'Saw Coll last night – so our plan worked. He got
his estate back, got his name back, his self-respect. You know, Murillio, I didn't
think anything could work out so well. So . . . perfectly. How in Hood's name did
we ever manage such a thing?'

'That was a night for miracles all right.'

'I feel . . . lost.'

'Not surprising,' Murillio replied, reaching for another fig. 'Eat some of that
jerky – the reek is making me nauseated.'

'Better on my breath?'

'Well, I don't see us kissing any time soon.'

'I'm not hungry,' Rallick said. 'I was when I first woke up, I think, but that
faded.'

'Woke up – you slept all that time in the Finnest House? All tucked up in bed?'

'On stone, just inside the door. With Vorcan lying right beside me, apparently.
She wasn't there when I came round. Just an undead Jaghut.'

Murillio seemed to think about that for a while, then said, 'So, what now, Rallick Nom?'

'Wish I knew.'

'Baruk might need things done, like before.'

'You mean like guarding Cutter's back? Keeping an eye on Coll? And how long before the Guild learns I'm back? How long before they take me down?'

'Ah, the Guild. Well, I'd figured you'd just head straight in, toss a few dozen lifeless bodies around and resume your rightful place. With Vorcan back . . . well, it seems obvious to me what needs doing.'

'That was never my style, Murillio.'

'I know, but circumstances change.'

'Don't they just.'

'He'll be back,' Murillio said. 'When he's ready to talk to you. Keep in mind, he's gone and collected some new scars, deep ones. Some of them still bleeding, I think.' He paused, then said, 'If Mammot hadn't died, well, who knows what might have happened. Instead, he went off with the Malazans, to return Apsalar to her home – oh, I see you have no idea what I'm talking about. All right, let me tell you the story of how that night ended – after you left. Just eat that damned jerky, please!'

'You drive a damned hard bargain, friend.'

And for the first time that morning, he saw Murillio smile.

Her scent clung to the bedding, sweet enough to make him want to weep, and even some of her warmth remained, or maybe that was just the sun, the golden light streaming in from the window and carrying with it the vaguely disturbing sound of birds mating in the tree in the back yard. *No need to be so frantic, little ones. There's all the time in the world.* Well, he would be feeling that right now, wouldn't he?

She was working the wheel in the outer room, a sound that had once filled his life, only to vanish and now, at long last, return. As if there had been no sordid crimes of banditry and the slavery that came as reasonable punishment, as if there had been no rotting trench lying shackled alongside Teblor barbarians. No huge warrior hanging from a cross amidships, with Torvald trickling brackish water between the fool's cracked lips. No sorcerous storms, no sharks, no twisted realms to crawl in and out of. No dreams of drowning – no, all that had been someone else's life, a tale sung by a half-drunk bard, the audience so incredulous they were moments from rage, ready to tear the idiot to pieces at the recounting of just one more unlikely exploit. Yes, someone else's life. The wheel was spinning, as it always did, and she was working clay and giving it form, symmetry, beauty. Of course, she never did her best work the day after a night of lovemaking, as if she'd used up something essential, whatever it was that fed creativity, and sometimes he felt bad about that. She'd laugh and shake her head, dismissing his concerns, spinning the wheel yet harder.

He'd seen, on the shelves of the outer room, scores of mediocre pots. Should this fact bother him? It might have, once, but no longer. He had vanished from her life – no reason, however, for her to waste away in some lonely vigil or prolonged period of mourning. People got on with things, and so they should. Of course she'd taken lovers. Might still have them, in fact, and it had been something of a miracle that she'd been alone when he showed up – he'd half expected some over-muscled godling with tousled golden locks and the kind of jaw that just begged to be punched to answer the door.

'Maybe he's visiting his mother,' Torvald mumbled.

He sat up, swung his legs round and settled feet on the woven mat covering the floor. Noticed that flat pillows had been sewn on to the mat, stuffed with lavender that crackled under his feet. 'No wonder her feet smell nice.' Anyway, he didn't mind what she'd been up to all that time. Didn't even mind if she was still up to a few things now, though those things might make things a little crowded. 'Things, right.'

The day had begun, and all he needed to do was settle up certain matters and then he could resume his life as a citizen of Darujhistan. Maybe visit a few old friends, some members of his estranged family (the ones who'd talk to him, anyway), see the sites that'd make him the most nostalgic, and give some thought to what he was going to do with the rest of his life.

But first things first. Pulling on his foreign-cut clothes (the clean set, that had dried in a rather wrinkled state, alas), Torvald Nom made his way to the outer room. Her back was to him as she hunched over the wheel, legs pumping the pedals. He saw the large bowl of clean water where it always was, went over and splashed his face. Was reminded that he needed a shave – but now he could actually pay someone else to do such things. To the opportunistic shall come rewards. Someone had said that, once, he was sure.

'My sweetness!'

She half turned and grinned at him. 'Look how bad this is, Tor. See what you've done?'

'It's the temper, of course—'

'It's tired thighs,' she said.

'A common complaint?' he asked, walking alongside the shelves and leaning in to study a stack of misaligned plates.

'Pretty rare, actually. What you think you're seeing up there, husband, isn't. It's the new style everyone wants these days. Symmetry is dead, long live the clumsy and crooked. Every noble lady wants a poor cousin in the country, some aunt or great-aunt with stubby fingers who makes crockery for her kin, in between wringing chicken necks and husking gourds.'

'That's a complicated lie.'

'Oh, it's never actually stated, Tor, only implied.'

'I was never good at inferring what's implied. Unless it's implicitly inferred.'

'I've had precisely two lovers, Tor, and neither one lasted more than a few months. Want their names?'

'Do I know them?'

When she didn't reply he glanced over and found her looking at him. 'Ah,' he said wisely.

'Well, so long as you don't start squinting at everyone who comes in here or says hello to me on the street – if that's going to be the case, then I'd better tell you—'

'No, no, darling. In fact, the mystery is . . . intriguing. But that won't survive my actually knowing.'

'That's true. Which is why I won't be asking you about anything. Where you've been, what you've done.'

'But that's different!'

Her brows rose.

'No, really,' Torvald said, walking over. 'What I told you last night, I wasn't exaggerating.'

'If you say so.'

He could see that she didn't believe him. 'I am stung. Crushed.'

'You'd better get going,' Tiserra said, returning once more to the lump of clay on the wheel. 'You've got a debt to clear.'

'The loot's not sticky?'

'It's all clean as can be, I made sure. Unless Gareb's scratched secret sigils on every coin he owned he won't know either way. He might suspect, though.'

'I've got a good tale to explain all that, if necessary,' Torvald said. 'Foreign investments, unexpected wealth, a triumphant return.'

'Well, I'd tone down the new version, Tor.'

He regarded her, noting her amusement, and said nothing. What was the point? *That giant whose life I saved more than once, his name was Karsa Orlong. Do you think I could make up a name like that, Tis? And what about these shackle scars? Oh, it's the new style among the highborn, enforced humility and all that.*

Oh, it didn't matter anyway. 'I don't plan on meeting Gareb in person,' he said as he walked to the front door. 'I'll work through Scorch and Leff.'

The lump of wet clay slid off the wheel and splatted on the wall, where it clung for a moment, then oozed down to glom on to the floor.

Surprised, Torvald turned to his wife and saw the expression that he hadn't seen in . . . in . . . well, in quite a while. 'Wait!' he cried. 'That partnership is over with, I swear it! Darling, they're just acting as my go-between, that's all—'

'You start scheming with those two again, Torvald Nom, and I'll take out a contract on you myself.'

'They always liked you, you know.'

'Torvald—'

'I know, my love, I know. Don't worry. No more scheming with Scorch and Leff. That's a promise. We're rich now, remember?'

'The problem with lists,' Scorch said, 'is all the names on 'em.'

Leff nodded. 'That's the problem, all right. You got it dead on there, Scorch. All them names. They must've had some kind of meeting, don't you think? All the loansharks in some crowded, smoky room, lounging about with nubile women dropping grapes in their mouths, and some scribe with stained lips scratching away. Names, people down on their luck, people so stupid they'd sign anything, grab the coin no matter how insane the interest. Names, you got it, Scorch, a list of fools. Poor, dumb, desperate fools.'

'And then,' Scorch said, 'when the list is done, out it goes, for some other poor, dumb, desperate fools to take on.'

'Hey now, we ain't poor.'

'Yes we are. We been poor ever since Torvald Nom vanished on us. He was the brains – admit it, Leff. Now, you tried being the brains ever since and look where it's got us, with a damned list and all those names.'

Leff raised a finger. 'We got Kruppe, though, and he's already given us six of 'em.'

'Which we passed on and you know what that means? It means thugs kicking in the door in the middle of the night, delivering threats and maybe worse. People got hurt 'cause of us, Leff. Bad hurt.'

'They got hurt because they couldn't pay up. Unless you decide to run, and I do mean run, as in out of the city, as in hundreds of leagues away to some town or city with no connections to here, but people don't do that and why not? Because they're all caught up, tangled in the nets, and they can't see their way clear because they got husbands and wives and children and maybe it's hard but at least it's familiar, you know what I mean?'

'No.'

Leff blinked. 'I was just saying—'

'What did they think they were doing, to get caught up in nets – swimmin' the lake? Besides, not all of it's loans, is it? There's blackmail, too, which gives me a thought or two—'

'No way, Scorch. I don't want in on anything like that.'

'I'm just suggesting we talk to Tor about it, that's all. See what he conjures up in the way of plans and such.'

'Assuming Tor ever shows up.'

'He will, you'll see, Leff. He was our partner, wasn't he? And he's back.'

The conversation ended abruptly, for no reason obvious to either of them, and they stood looking at each other for a dozen heartbeats. They were opposite the entrance to the Phoenix Inn. It was morning, when they did their best thinking, but that had a way of dying quick, so that by late afternoon they would find themselves sitting somewhere, sluggish as tortoises in a hailstorm, arguing about nothing in particular with monosyllabic brevity and getting angrier by the moment.

Without another word they both set out for the Phoenix Inn.

Clumped inside, looking round – just to be sure – then heading over to where sat Kruppe, plump hands upraised and hovering like hooded snakes, then striking down to one of dozens of pastries heaped on numerous platters in front of him. Fingertip fangs spearing hapless sweets right and left, each one moving in a blur up to his mouth, gobbled up in a shower of crumbs one after another.

Mere moments later and half the offerings were gone. Kruppe's cheeks bulged, his jam-smeared lips struggling to close as he chewed and frantically swallowed, pausing to breathe loudly through his nose. Seeing Scorch and Leff approaching, he waved mutely, gesturing them into their seats.

'You're going to explode one day, Kruppe,' said Leff.

Scorch stared with his usual expression of rapt disbelief.

Kruppe finally managed to swallow everything down, and he raised his hands once more, left them to hover whilst he eyed his two guests. 'Blessed partners, is this not a wondrous morning?'

'We ain't decided yet,' Leff said. 'We're still waiting for Torvald – he had a runner find us down at the docks and said he'd meet us here. He's already changing things all round, like maybe he don't trust us. It's a blow, I tell you, Kruppe. A real blow.'

'Conflagration of suspicions climbing high into yon blue sky is quite unnecessary, shifty-eyed friends of wise Kruppe. Why, infamous and almost familiar offspring of House Nom is true to his word, and Kruppe asserts – with vast confidence – that the first name is about to be struck from dire list!'

'First? What about the six—'

'You've not heard? Oh, my. Each had flown, only moments before the cruel night-beaters closed in. Most extraordinary ill-luck.'

Scorch clawed at his face. 'Gods, we're back where we began!'

'That's impossible, Kruppe! Someone must've tipped 'em off!'

Kruppe's gnarled brows lifted, then waggled. 'Veracity of your discoveries is not in doubt, you will be pleased to hear. Thusly, you have succeeded in your task with said six, whilst they who compiled the list have, alas, not quite matched your rate of success. And so, how many remain? Twelve, yes? Not counting sleep-addled Torvald Nom, that is.'

'He ain't no sleep-addered or whatever,' Scorch said. 'In fact, he looked just fine yesterday.'

'Perhaps glorious reunion has sapped all verve, then. Kruppe assumed sleep-addered indeed, given the man's hapless and ineffectual perusal of this taproom – ah, at last he sees us!'

And both Scorch and Leff twisted round in their chairs to see Torvald Nom sauntering up and, noting the man's broad smile, they were instantly relieved and then, just as quickly, nervous.

'My apologies for being late,' Torvald said, dragging up another chair. 'I got a shave and the old woman threw in the buffing of my nails for free – said I was surprisingly handsome under all those whiskers and if that's not a good start to a day then what is? True, she was about a thousand years old, but hey, compliments don't have to be pretty, do they? And you're Kruppe. You must be – who else in this city tries to eat with his nose when his mouth is filled? I'm Torvald Nom.'

'Sit, newfound friend. Kruppe is generous enough this morning to disregard dubious observation regarding his eating habits and the habits of his orifices. Kruppe further observes that you, while once a poor destitute man, have suddenly acquired impressive wealth, so finely attired and groomed are you, and that with great relief friends Scorch and Leff are soon to pay a most propitious visit to one Gareb the Lender. And on this of all days, one suspects Gareb to be most gracious at repayment of said debt, yes?'

Torvald stared at Kruppe, evidently speechless with admiration.

Kruppe's left hand darted down, captured a puff pastry that indeed might have been trying to escape, and pushed it whole into his mouth. Beaming, he chewed.

'You got the money?' Leff asked Torvald.

'What? Oh. Here,' and he drew out a pouch. 'In full. Kruppe, you are witness to this, so don't try anything, Leff. Not you either, Scorch. Walk it straight over to Gareb's. Get the chit saying I'm cleared, too. Then come straight back here and I'll buy you all lunch.'

Scorch was looking back and forth between Torvald and Kruppe, and finally of the latter he asked, 'What was that you said about Gareb?'

Kruppe swallowed, licked his lips, and said, 'Why, only that a dastardly thief broke into his estate last night and stole his entire hoard. The poor man! And 'tis said the thief stole much more than that – why, the wife's dignity, too, or at least her innocence in so far as nonmarital intercourse is concerned.'

'Hold on,' Leff said. 'The thief slept with Gareb's wife? Where was Gareb?'

'At a moneylenders' meeting, Kruppe understands, discussing important matters and, no doubt, eating his fill of grapes and whatnot.'

'Well then,' Torvald Nom said, 'won't he be happy I've returned to repay my debt.'

'Won't he just!' said Kruppe, beaming once more.

Leff took the bag of coins and peered inside. 'All there?'

'All there,' Torvald replied.

Leff rose and said, 'Let's get this done with, Scorch.'

When the two were gone, Torvald Nom sat back in his chair and smiled at Kruppe.

Who smiled back.

And when that was done with, Kruppe collected another pastry and held it before his mouth, in order to more closely observe its delight, and perhaps torture it a moment before his mouth opened like a bear's jagged maw. Poised thus, he paused to glance over at Torvald Nom. 'Upstairs, dear sir, you shall find, if you so desire, a cousin of renown. Like you, suddenly returned to fair Darujhistan. None other than Rallick, among the Noms of House Nom one might presume a sheep blacker than you. Indeed, the very black of nadir, the Abyss, whilst you might reveal a lesser black, such as charcoal. Two sheep, then, in this very inn, of a very dark hue – why, could Kruppe but witness such a meeting!' And time now to lift an admonishing finger. 'But listen, dear friend Torvald Nom, most clandestine is Rallick's return, yes? Seal thy lips, I beg you!'

'He's in hiding? Who from?'

A flutter of pudgy fingers, like worms in a reef-bed. 'Quick, then, lest he depart on some fell errand. Kruppe will save your seat here against your return – he so looks forward to the sumptuous lunch for which Torvald will pay and pay happily!'

Torvald was suddenly sweating, and he fidgeted in the chair. 'The reunion can, er, wait. Really, why would I want to bother him right now? No, honest, Kruppe, and as for secret, well, I'll keep it just fine, provided you, er, do the same. Say nothing to Rallick, I mean. Let me . . . surprise him!'

'Rallick has little love for surprises, Torvald Nom, as you must surely know. Why, just last night he—'

'Just don't say anything, all right?'

'Oh, aren't conspiracies delicious? Kruppe will say nothing to no one, none to worry no matter what. This is a most solemn promise most solemnly promised! Now, old friend, be so good as to accost yon Meese o'er there – some wine to loosen the throats prior to vast meal, yes? Kruppe's mouth salivates and, perhaps, so too sniffles his nose – all in anticipation, yes?'

'If this is what I want, then I don't want it.'

'Oh, now that makes sense, Antsy. And if you happen to be a short bow-legged red-faced crab of a man, well, you'd rather be a short bow-legged red-faced crab of a—'

'You're an idiot, Bluepearl, and that don't change no matter what you want. What I'm saying is simple, right? Even you should grasp the meaning. A soldier retires, right? And looks to a life all simple and peaceful, but is it?'

'Is it which?'

'What?'

'Is it simple or is it peaceful?'

'It isn't and that's my point!'

'That wasn't your point. Your point was you don't want it and if that's the case, then head on over to the Malazan Embassy and throw yourself on the mercy of whoever and if they don't hang you they'll sign you up all over again.'

'The point was, I'd like being retired if I only could be!'

'I'm going to the cellar to check on stock.'

Antsy watched him leave, then snorted and shook his head. 'That man needs help.'

'So go help him,' Blend said from the next table over.

Antsy jumped in his seat, then glared at her. 'Stop doing that! Anyway, I didn't mean that kind of help. Oh, gods, my head aches.'

'Sometimes,' Blend said, 'I try to make myself as quiet as possible because that way the military marching band in my skull maybe won't find me.'

'Huh,' said Antsy, brows knitting. 'Never knew you played an instrument, Blend. Which one?'

'Pipes, drums, flute, rattle, horn, waxstring.'

'Really? All at once?'

'Of course. You know, I think I'd be annoyed if I headed upstairs and found Picker creeping out of Scillara's room right about now.'

'So stay sitting right there.'

'Well, it's only my imagination inventing the scene.'

'You sure?'

She lasted four or five heartbeats before swearing under her breath and rising.

Antsy watched her leave, then smiled. 'It's better,' he said to no one, 'when you don't have an imagination. Like me.' He paused, scowled. 'Mind, could be I could use one right about now, so I could figure out how and when them assassins are gonna try again. Poison. Magic. Knives. Crossbow quarrels in the night, through the window, right through the shutters, a perfect shot. Thump to the floor goes Antsy, the Hero of Mott Wood. A spear up through that floor just to finish him off, since they been tunnelling for weeks and was waiting, knowing he'd fall right there right then, aye.'

He sat, eyes wide, red moustache twitching.

Sitting in the shadows in the far corner, back resting against the wall, Duiker watched with wry amusement. Extraordinary, how some people survived and others didn't. The soldier's face was always the same once the mask fell away – a look of bemusement, the faint bewildered surprise to find oneself still alive, knowing all too well there was no good reason for it, nothing at all but the nudge of luck, the emptiness of chance and circumstance. And all the unfairness of the world made a bitter pool of the eyes.

A commotion from the back room and a moment later the narrow door opened and out walked the bard, grey hair tousled by sleep, eyes red even at this distance. A glance over at Antsy. 'There's lice in the mattress,' he said.

'I doubt they mind the company,' the ex-sergeant replied, levering himself upright and making for the stairs.

The bard stared after him for a moment, then headed over to the bar, where he poured himself a tankard of pungent, dark Rhivi beer. And came over to where Duiker sat.

'Historians and bards both,' he said, sitting down.

Duiker nodded, understanding well enough.

'But what you observe and what I observe, well, that can turn out quite differently. Then again, maybe the distinction is merely superficial. The older I get, the more I suspect just that. You describe events, seeing the great sweep of things. I look at the faces, rushing by so fast they might be no more than a blur if I don't take care. To see them true, to remember them all.'

'Where are you from?' Duiker asked.

The bard drank down a mouthful and set the tankard carefully before him. 'Korel, originally. But that was a long time ago.'

'Malazan invasion?'

An odd smile as the man studied the tankard on the table before him. His hands, however, remained in his lap. 'If you mean Greymane, then yes.'

'So which of the countless contradictory tales are true? About him, I mean.'

The bard shrugged. 'Never ask that of a bard. I sing them all. Lies, truths, the words make no distinction in what they tell, nor even the order they come in. We do as we please with them.'

'I've been listening to you these past few nights,' said Duiker.

'Ah, an audience of one. Thank you.'

'You've sung verses of *Anomandaris* I've never heard before.'

'The unfinished ones?' The bard nodded and reached for the tankard. ' "Black Coral, where stand the Tiste Andii . . ." He drank another mouthful.

'Have you come from there, then?'

'Did you know that there is no god or goddess in all the pantheon that claims to be the patron – or matron – of bards? It's as if we've been forgotten, left to our own devices. That used to bother me, for some reason, but now I see it for the true honour it represents. We have been made unique, in our freedom, in our responsibility. Is there a patron of historians?'

'Not that I'm aware of. Does this mean I'm free, too?'

'It's said you told the tale of the Chain of Dogs once, here in this very room.'

'Once.'

'And that you have been trying to write it down ever since.'

'And failing. What of it?'

'It may be that expositional prose isn't right for the telling of that story, Duiker.'

'Oh?'

The bard set the tankard to one side and slowly leaned forward, fixing the historian with grey eyes. 'Because, sir, you see their faces.'

Anguish welled up inside Duiker and he looked away, hiding his suddenly trembling hands. 'You don't know me well enough for such matters,' he said in a rasp.

'Rubbish. This isn't a personal theme here, historian. It's two professionals discussing their craft. It's me, a humble bard, offering my skills to unlock your soul and all it contains – everything that's killing it, moment by moment. You can't find your voice for this. Use mine.'

'Is that why you're here?' Duiker asked. 'Like some vulture eager to lap up my tears?'

Brows lifted. 'You are an accident. My reasons for being here lie . . . elsewhere. Even if I could explain more, I would not. I cannot. In the meantime, Duiker, let us fashion an epic to crush the hearts of a thousand generations.'

And now, yes, tears rolled down the lined tracks of the historian's face. And it took all the courage he still possessed to then nod.

The bard leaned back, retrieving his tankard. 'It begins with you,' he said. 'And it ends with you. Your eyes to witness, your thoughts alone. Tell me of no one's mind, presume nothing of their workings. You and I, we tell nothing, we but *show*.'

'Yes.' Duiker looked up, back into those eyes that seemed to contain – and hold sure – the grief of the world. 'What's your name, bard?'

'Call me Fisher.'

Chaur was curled up at the foot of the bed, snoring, twitching like a dreaming dog. Picker observed him for a moment before settling back on the mattress. How had she got here? Was that raw tenderness between her legs what she thought it was and if so then did Barathol remember as little of it as she did? Oh, too complicated to work out. She wasn't ready to be thinking of all those things, she wasn't ready to be thinking at all.

She heard someone moving down the hall. Then a muted conversation, punctuated by a throaty laugh that did not belong to Blend or anyone else Picker knew, meaning it was probably that woman, Scillara. Picker gasped slightly at a sudden recollection of holding the woman's breasts in her hands and hearing that laugh but up close and a lot more triumphant.

Gods, did I sleep with them all? Damn that Quorl Milk!

A wheeze from Chaur and she started guiltily – but no, she'd not do any such thing to an innocent like him. There were limits – there had to be limits.

A muffled knock on the door.

'Oh, come in, Blend.'

And in she came, light-footed as a cat, and her expression seemed filled up with something, on the verge of bursting.

No, not tears, please. 'I don't remember nothing, Blend, so don't start on me.'

Blend held back a moment longer, then erupted.

In howling laughter, bending over in convulsions.

Chaur sat up on the floor, blinking and smiling, then he too was laughing.

Picker glared at Blend, wanting to kill her. 'What's so damned funny?'

Blend managed to regain control over herself. 'They pretty much carried us all the way back. But then we woke up and we all had one thing and one thing only on our minds. They didn't stand a chance!'

'Gods below.' Then she stiffened. 'Not Chaur—'

'No, Scillara got him in here first.'

Chaur was still laughing, tears rolling down his face. He seemed to be losing control and all at once Picker felt alarmed. 'Stop now, Chaur! Stop!'

The wide empty eyes fixed on her, and all mirth vanished.

'Sorry,' she said. 'It's all right. Go down to the kitchen and get something to eat, Chaur, there's a lad.'

He rose, stretched, scratched himself, then left the room. He barked one last laugh somewhere near the stairs.

Picker rubbed at her face. 'Not Antsy, too. Don't tell me . . .'

Blend shrugged. 'Lust is blind, I suppose. And let's hope all memory of it stays that way. I fear all his fantasies came true last night . . . only he can't remember any of it!'

'I feel sick.'

'Oh, relax, it's what all those parts are made for, after all.'

'Where is Barathol?'

'Went out early. With Mallet for company. Looking for the Blacksmiths' Guild. You must remember his big, er, hands.'

'My kitten remembers, all right.'

Another snort from Blend. 'Meow.'

The grey gloom of the cellar seemed to defy the lantern's light, but Bluepearl was used to that, and he was only marginally surprised when the ghost shuffled out from the wall at the far end where rested a half-dozen casks still sealed by the monks' sigil. Sunk to his hips in the floor, the ghost paused and looked round, finally spying the Malazan standing near the steep stone steps.

The ghost waded closer. 'Is that you, Fellurkanath?'

'Fella what? You're dead, monk, and you've been dead for some time, I'd wager – who wears tricornered hats these days?'

'Oh,' the ghost moaned, clutching his face, 'K'rul has coughed me out. Why? Why now? I've nothing useful to tell, especially not to any foreigner. But he's stirring below, isn't he? Is that why? Am I to be the voice of dire warning? What do you care? It's already too late anyway.'

'Someone's trying to murder us.'

'Of course they are. You're squatting and they don't want company. You should broach a cask, one of these. That will tell you everything you need to know.'

'Oh, really now. Go away.'

'Who raised the floor and why? And look at this.' The ghost pushed his head back to reveal that his throat had been sliced open, all the way back to his spine. Gory, bloodless flesh and slashed veins and arteries vaguely silver in the dim light. 'Was this the ultimate sacrifice? Little do you know.'

'Do I need to get a necromancer down here?' Bluepearl demanded. 'Go away!'

'The living never heed the dead,' muttered the ghost, lowering his head and turning round to walk back towards the far wall. 'And that's just it. If we didn't know better, why, we'd be still alive. Think about that, if you dare.'

Vanishing into the heavy stones, and gone.

Bluepearl sighed, looked round until he found the bottle he was looking for. 'Hah, I knew we had one. Quorl Milk. Why should they get all the fun?'

The two men trundled just behind the woman, so eager they trod on her heels as they fought for some imagined dominant position. Faint had never seen anything so pathetic, and the way the witch played all innocent, even when she worked her two men just to keep trouble stirred up – all of it seemingly accidental, of course, but it wasn't accidental because Precious Thimble knew precisely what she was up to and as far as Faint was concerned that was cruel beyond all reason.

It didn't help, either, that the two men – evidently brothers – looked so much alike. With the same way of walking, the same facial expressions, the same tone of voice. If they were no different from each other, then why not just choose one and be done with it?

Well, she didn't expect any of them to last very long in any case. For most shareholders, the first trip was the deadliest one. It came with not knowing what to expect, with not reacting fast enough or just the right way. The first journey into the warrens killed over half first-timers. Which meant that Precious Thimble (who struck Faint as a survivor) might well have her choice taken from her, when either Jula or Amby Bole went down somewhere on the trail.

As they rounded the corner and came within sight of the carriage, Faint saw that Glanno Tarp was already seated up top. Various rituals had been triggered to effect repairs to the huge contrivance; the horses looked restless and eager to be away – as mad as the rest of them, they were. Off to one side and now watching Faint, Quell and their new shareholders approaching, stood Reccanto Ilk and

Sweetest Sufferance, and a third man – huge, round-shouldered, and tattooed in a pattern of—

'Uh oh,' said Master Quell.

That's the one, isn't it? The caravan guard, the one who survived the Siege of Capustan. What was his name again?

'This is not for you, Gruntle,' Master Quell said.

'Why not?'

'I've got some damned good reasons for saying no to you, and if you just give me a moment I'll come up with them.'

The man's feral smile revealed elongated canines.

'The Trell is inside,' Reccanto said. 'Want me to get him, Quell? We should get going, right?'

'Gruntle—'

'I'd like to sign on,' the caravan guard said, 'as a shareholder. Just like those re-cruits there behind you. Same stakes. Same rules.'

'When did you last take an order, Gruntle? You've been commanding guards for years now. You really think I want arguments with everything I say?'

'No arguments. I'm not interested in second-guessing you. As a shareholder, just another shareholder.'

The tavern door opened then and out walked Mappo Runt.

His glance slipped past Gruntle then swung back, eyes narrowing. Then he faced Master Quell. 'Is this one accompanying us? Good.'

'Well—'

The Trell moved up to the wagon and clambered up its side in a racket of squealing springs to take position behind Glanno Tarp. He looked back down. 'We'll probably need someone like him.'

'Like what?' asked the witch, Precious Thimble.

'Soletaken,' Mappo replied, shrugging.

'It's not quite like that,' Gruntle said quietly as he moved to join Mappo atop the carriage.

Master Quell stared after him, then, shaking himself, said, 'Everyone get aboard, then. You two Boles, you're facing astern. Witch, inside with me, where we can have ourselves a conversation. And you too, Mappo. We don't put passengers up top. Too risky.'

Faint swung herself up to sit beside Glanno Tarp.

Brakes were released. Glanno glanced back to scan the crowd clinging to vari-ous handholds on the roof behind him. Grinned, then snapped the reins.

The horses screamed, lunged.

The world exploded around them.

Blaze down, blessed sun, on this city of wonders where all is of consequence. Cast your fiery eye on the crowds, the multitudes moving to and fro on their ways of life. Flow warmth into the rising miasma of dreams, hopes, fears and loves that ever seethe skyward, rising in the breaths expelled, the sighs released, reflected from restive glances and sidelong regard, echoing eternal from voices in clamour.

See then this street where walks a man who had been young the last time he walked this street. He is young no longer, oh, no. And there in the next street, wandering a line of market stalls crowded with icons, figurines and fetishes from a thousand cults – most of them long extinct – walks a woman whose path had, years ago now, crossed that of the man. She too no longer feels young, and if desire possessed tendrils that could pass through stone and brick, that could wend through mobs of senseless people, why, might they then meet in some fateful place and there intertwine, weaving something new and precious as a deadly flower?

In another quarter of the city strides a foreigner, an impressive creature, tall and prominently muscled, very nearly sculpted, aye, with skin the perfect hue of polished onyx and eyes in which glittered flecks of hazel and gold, and many were the glances sliding over him as he passed. But he was not mindful of such things, for he was looking for a new life and might well find it here in this glorious, exotic city.

In a poor stretch of the Gadrobi District a withered, weathered woman, tall and thin, knelt in her narrow strip of garden and began placing flatstones into a pattern in the dark earth. So much of what the soil could give must first be prepared, and these ways were most arcane and mysterious, and she worked as if in a dream, while in the small house behind her still slept her husband, a knuckled monster filled with fear and hate, and his dreams were dark indeed for the sun could not reach the places in his soul.

A woman lounged on the deck of a moored ship in the harbour. Sensing fell kin somewhere in the city and, annoyed, giving much thought to what she would do about it. If anything, anything at all. Something was coming, however, and was she not cursed with curiosity?

An ironmonger held a conversation with his latest investor, who was none other than a noble Councillor and reputedly the finest duellist in all Darujhistan, and therein it was decided that young and most ambitious Gorlas Vidikas would take charge of the iron mines six leagues to the west of the city.

A rickety wagon rocked along the road well past Maiten yet still skirting the lake, and in its bed amidst filthy blankets was the small battered form of a child, still unconscious but judged, rightly so, that he would live. The poor thing.

This track, you see, led to but one place, one fate. The old shepherd had done well and had already buried his cache of coins beneath the stoop behind the shack where he lived with his sickly wife, who had been worn out by seven failed pregnancies, and if there was bitter spite in the eyes she fixed upon the world is it any wonder? But he would do good by her in these last tired years, yes, he would, and he set to one side one copper coin that he would fling to the lake spirits at dusk – an ancient, black-stained coin bearing the head of a man the shepherd didn't recognize – not that he would, for that face belonged to the last Tyrant of Darujhistan.

The wagon rolled on, on its way to the mines.

Harllo, who so loved the sun, was destined to wake in darkness, and mayhap he was never again to see the day's blessed light.

Out on the lake the water glittered with golden tears.

As if the sun might relinquish its hard glare and, for just this one moment, weep for the fate of a child.

Chapter Eight

When can he not stand alone
Where in darkness no shadows are cast
Whose most precious selves deny the throne
While nothing held in life will last a moment longer
Than what's carved into the very bones
But this is where you would stand
In his place and see all bleak and bridled
An array of weapons each one forged
For violence

When can he not stand alone
Where darkness bleeds into the abyss so vast
Whose every yearning seeks a new home
While each struggle leaves the meek to the stronger
And the fallen lie scattered like stones
But this is the life you would take in hand
To guide him 'cross the path so broken so riddled
Like the weapon of your will now charged
In cold balance

When can he not stand alone
Where in darkness every shadow is lost
Whose weary selves cut away and will roam
While nothing is left but this shielded stranger
Standing against the wind's eternal moans
But this is your hero who must stand
Guarding your broken desires the ragged flag unfurled
Rising above the bastion to see your spite purged
In his silence

ANOMANDARIS, BOOK III, VERSES 7–10
FISHER KEL TATH

he swath of ground where all the grasses had been worn away might
have marked the passing of a herd of bhederin, if not for the impossibly wide ruts left behind by the enormous studded wheels of a wagon,

and the rubbish and occasional withered corpse scattered to either side. Vultures and crows danced among the detritus.

Traveller sat slouched in the Seven Cities saddle atop the piebald gelding. Nearby, at the minimum distance that his horse would accept, was the witch, Samar Dev, perched like a child above the long-legged, gaunt and fierce Jhag horse whose name was, she had said, Havok. The beast's true owner was somewhere ahead, perhaps behind the Skathandi and the Captain's monstrous carriage, or beyond it. Either way, she was certain a clash was imminent.

'He dislikes slavers,' she had said earlier, as if this explained everything.

No demon, then, but a Toblakai of true blood, a detail that sent pangs of regret and pain through Traveller, for reasons he kept to himself – and though she had seen something of that anguish in his face it appeared she would respect his privacy. Or perhaps feared its surrender, for Samar Dev was a woman, he suspected, prone to plunging into vast depths of emotion.

She had, after all, travelled through warrens to find the trail of the one ahead of them on this plain, and such an undertaking was not embraced on a whim. *All to deliver a horse.* He knew enough to leave it at that, poor as it might be as justification for such extremity. The Kindaru had accepted the reason with sage nods, seeing nothing at all unusual in any of it – the horse was a sacred beast, after all, a Jhag, brother to their cherished horses-of-the-rock. They possessed legends with similar themes, and indeed they had spent half the night recounting many of them – and now they had found themselves a new one. Master of the Wolf-Horses met a woman so driven as to be his own reflection, and together they rode into the north, having drawn their threads through the last camp of the Kindaru, and were now entwined each with the other and both with the Kindaru, and though this was a tale not yet done it would nevertheless live on, for as long as lived the Kindaru themselves.

He had noted the grief in Samar Dev's weary, weathered face, as the many wounds delivered – in all innocence – by the Kindaru slowly sank deeper, piercing her heart, and now compassion swirled dark and raw in her eyes, although the Kindaru were far behind them now. It was clear, brutally so, that both she and Traveller had collected a new thread to twist into their lives.

'How far ahead?' she asked.

'Two days at the most.'

'Then he might have found them by now, or they him.'

'Yes, it's possible. If this Skathandi Captain has an army, well, even a Toblakai can die.'

'I know that,' she replied. Then added, 'Maybe.'

'And there are but two of us, Samar Dev.'

'If you'd rather cut away from this trail, Traveller, I will not question your decision. But I need to find him.'

He glanced away. 'His horse, yes.'

'And other things.'

Traveller considered for a time. He studied the broad, churned-up track. A thousand or five thousand; when people were moving in column it was always difficult to tell. The carriage itself would be a thing worth seeing, however, and the direction just happened to be the one he needed to take. The prospect of being forced into a detour was unacceptable. 'If your friend is smart, he won't do anything overt. He'll hide, as best one can on these plains, until he sees an advantage – though what that advantage might be, against so many, I can't imagine.'

'So you will stay with me for a while longer?'

He nodded.

'Then I should tell you some things, I think.'

They guided their horses on to the track and rode at the trot.

Traveller waited for her to continue.

The sun's heat reminded him of his homeland, the savannahs of Dal Hon, although in this landscape there were fewer flies, and of the enormous herds of countless kinds of beasts – and the ones that hunted them – there was little sign. Here on the Lamatath there were bhederin, a lone breed of antelope, hares, wolves, coyotes, bears and not much else. Plenty of hawks and falcons overhead, of course – but this place did not teem as one might expect and he wondered about that.

Had the conflagration at Morn wiped everything out? Left a blasted landscape slow to recover, into which only a few species drifted down from the north? Or were the K'Chain Che'Malle rabid hunters, indulging in a slaughterfest that did not end until they themselves were extinct?

'What do you know of the Emperor of a Thousand Deaths?'

He glanced across at her. 'Not much. Only that he cannot be killed.'

'Right.'

He waited.

Locusts crawled across the dusty track amidst shredded blades of grass, as if wondering who had beaten them to it. Somewhere high above a raptor loosed a piercing cry, the kind intended to panic a bird in flight.

'His sword was forged by the power of the Crippled God. Possessing levels of sorcery to which the wielder can reach, each time, only by dying – fighting and dying with that weapon in his hands. The Emperor, a poor ravaged creature, a Tiste Edur, knew that death was but an illusion. He knew, I am certain of it, that he was cursed, so terribly cursed. That sword had driven him mad.'

Traveller imagined that such a weapon would indeed drive its wielder insane. He could feel sweat on the palms of his hands and shifted the reins into his right hand, settling the other on his thigh. His mouth felt unaccountably dry.

'He needed champions. Challengers. Sometimes they would kill him. Sometimes more than once. But as he came back again and again, ever stronger, in the end the challenger would fall. And so it went.'

'A terrible fate,' Traveller muttered.

'Until one day some ships arrived. On board, yet more champions from distant lands. Among them, Karsa Orlong, the Toblakai. I happened to be with him, then.'

'I would hear the story behind such a partnership.'

'Maybe later. There was someone else, another champion. His name was Icarium.'

Traveller slowly twisted in his saddle, studied the woman across from him. Some unconscious message told the gelding to halt.

Samar's Jhag horse continued on for a few steps, then she reined it in and turned to meet Traveller's eyes. 'I believe, if Icarium had met the Emperor, well, the dying would still be going on, spreading like a wildfire. An entire continent . . . pretty much incinerated. Who knows, perhaps the entire world.'

He nodded, not trusting himself to speak.

'Instead,' Samar Dev said, 'Karsa was sent for first.'

'What happened?'

Her smile was sad. 'They fought.'

'Samar Dev,' Traveller said, 'that makes no sense. The Toblakai still lives.'

'Karsa killed the Emperor. With finality.'

'How?'

'I have some suspicions. I believe that, somewhere, somehow, Karsa Orlong spoke with the Crippled God – not a pleasant conversation, I'm sure. Karsa rarely has those.'

'Then the Emperor of a Thousand Deaths—'

'Gone, delivered unto a final death. I like to believe Rhulad thanked Karsa with his last breath.'

If there was need for such a thought she was welcome to it. 'And the sword? Does the Toblakai now carry it as his own?'

She collected her reins and nudged her mount onward. 'I don't know,' she said. 'Another reason why I have to find him.'

You are not alone in that, woman. 'He bargained with the Crippled God. He *replaced* the Emperor.'

'Did he?'

He urged his horse forward, came up alongside her once more. 'What other possibility is there?'

And to that she grinned. 'Ah, but that is where I know something you don't, Traveller. I know Karsa Orlong.'

'What does that mean?'

'It's his favourite game, you see, pretending to be so . . . obvious. Blunt, lacking all subtlety, all decorum. Just a savage, after all. The only possibility is the obvious one, isn't it? That's why I don't believe that's what he's done.'

'You don't wish to believe, you mean. Now I will speak plain, Samar Dev. If your Toblakai wields the sword of the Crippled God, he shall have to either yield it or draw it against me. Such a weapon must be destroyed.'

'You set yourself as an enemy of the Crippled God? Well, you're hardly alone in that, are you?'

He frowned. 'I did not then,' he said, 'nor do I desire to do so now. But he goes too far.'

'Who are you, Traveller?'

'I played the game of civilization once, Samar Dev. But in the end I remain as I am, a savage.'

'Too many have put themselves into Karsa Orlong's path,' she said. 'They do not stand there long.' A pause, and then, 'Civilized or barbarian – those are but words – the cruel killer can wear all the costumes he wants, can pretend to great causes and hard necessities. Gods below, it all sickens me, the way you fools carry on. Over the whole damned world it's ever the same.'

He answered this rant with silence, for he believed it *was* ever the same, and that it would never change. Animals remained just that, whether sentient or not, and they fought, they killed, they died. Life was suffered until it was over, and then . . . *then what?*

An end. It had to be that. It *must* be that.

Riding on, now, no words between them. Already past the telling of stories, the recounting of adventures. All that mattered, for each of them, was what lay ahead.

With the Toblakai named Karsa Orlong.

Some time in his past, the man known as the Captain had been a prisoner to someone. At some point he had outlived his usefulness and had been staked out on the plain, wooden spikes driven through his hands, his feet, hammered to the hard earth to feed the ants, to feed all the carrion hunters of Lamatath. But he'd not been ready to die just then. He had pulled his hands through the spikes, had worked his feet free, and had crawled on elbows and knees half a league, down into a valley where a once-mighty river had dwindled to a stream fringed by cottonwoods.

His hands were ruined. His feet could not bear his weight. And, he was convinced, the ants that had crawled into his ears had never left, trapped in the tunnels of his skull, making of his brain a veritable nest – he could taste their acidic exudations on his swollen, blackened tongue.

If the legend was true, and it was, hoary long-forgotten river spirits had squirmed up from the mud beneath the exposed bank's cracked skin, clawing like vermin to where he huddled fevered and shivering. To give life was no gift for such creatures; no, to give was in turn to take. As the king feeds his heir all he needs to survive, so the heir feeds the king with the illusion of immortality. And the hand reaches between the bars of one cage, out to the hand reaching between the bars of the other cage. They exchange more than just touch.

The spirits fed him life. And he took them into his soul and gave them a new home. They proved, alas, restless, uncivil guests.

The journey and the transformation into a nomadic tyrant of the Lamatath Plains was long, difficult, and miraculous to any who could have seen the wretched, maimed creature the Captain had once been. Countless tales spun like dust-devils about him, many invented, some barely brushing the truth.

His ruined feet made walking an ordeal. His fingers had curled into hooklike things, the bones beneath calcifying into unsightly knobs and protrusions. To see his hands was to be reminded of the feet of vultures clutched in death.

He rode on a throne set on the forward-facing balcony of the carriage's second tier, protected from the midday sun by a faded red canvas awning. Before him walked somewhere between four hundred and five hundred slaves, yoked to the carriage, each one leaning forward as they strained to pull the enormous wheeled palace over the rough ground. An equal number rested in the wagons of the entourage, helping the cooks and the weavers and the carpenters until their turn came in the harnesses.

The Captain did not believe in stopping. No camps were established. Motion was everything. Motion was eternal. His two wings of cavalry, each a hundred knights strong, rode in flanking positions, caparisoned in full banded armour and ebony cloaks, helmed and carrying barbed lances, the heads glinting in the sunlight. Behind the palace was a mobile kraal of three hundred horses, his greatest pride, for the bloodlines were strong and much of his wealth (that which he did not attain through raiding) came from them. Horse-traders from far to the south sought him out on this wasteland, and paid solid gold for the robust destriers.

A third troop of horse warriors, lighter-armoured, ranged far and wide on all sides of his caravan, ensuring that no enemy threatened, and seeking out possible targets – this was the season, after all, and there were – rarely these days, true enough – bands of savages eking out a meagre existence on the grasslands, including those who bred grotesque mockeries of horses, wide-rumped and bristle-maned, that if nothing else proved good eating. These ranging troops included raiding parties of thirty or more, and at any one time the Captain had four or five such groups out scouring the plains.

Merchants had begun hiring mercenary troops, setting out to hunt him down. But those he could not buy off he destroyed. His knights were terrible in battle.

The Captain's kingdom had been on the move for seven years now, rolling in a vast circle that encompassed most of the Lamatath. This territory he claimed as his own, and to this end he had recently dispatched emissaries to all the bordering cities – Darujhistan, Kurl and Saltoan to the north, New Callows to the southwest, Bastion and Sarn to the northeast – Elingarth to the south was in the midst of civil war, so he would wait that out.

In all, the Captain was pleased with his kingdom. His slaves were breeding, providing what would be the next generation drawing his palace. Hunting parties carried in bhederin and antelope to supplement the finer foodstuffs looted from passing caravans. The husbands and wives of his soldiers brought with them all the necessary skills to maintain his court and his people, and they too were thriving.

So like a river, meandering over the land, this kingdom of his. The ancient, half-mad spirits were most pleased.

Though he never much thought about it, the nature of his tyranny was, as far as he was concerned, relatively benign. Not with respect to foreigners, of course, but then who gave a damn for them? Not his blood, not his adopted kin, not his responsibility. And if they could not withstand his kingdom's appetites, then whose fault was that? Not his.

Creation demands destruction. Survival demands that something else fails to survive. No existence was truly benign.

Still, the Captain often dreamed of finding those who had nailed him to the ground all those years ago – his memories of that time were maddeningly vague. He could not make out their faces, or their garb. He could not recall the details of their camp, and as for who and what he had been before that time, well, he had no memory at all. Reborn in a riverbed. He would, when drunk, laugh and proclaim that he was but eleven years old, eleven from that day of rebirth, that day of beginning anew.

He noted the lone rider coming in from the southwest, the man pushing his horse hard, and the Captain frowned – the fool had better have a good reason for abusing the beast in that manner. He didn't appreciate his soldiers posturing and seeking to make bold impressions. He decided that, if the reason was insufficient, he would have the man executed in the traditional manner – trampled into bloody ruin beneath the hoofs of his horses.

The rider drew up alongside the palace, a servant on the side platform taking the reins of the horse as the man stepped aboard. An exchange of words with the Master Sergeant, and then the man was climbing the steep steps to the ledge surrounding the balcony. Where, his head level with the Captain's knees, he bowed.

'Sire, Fourth Troop, adjudged ablest rider to deliver this message.'

'Go on,' said the Captain.

'Another raiding party was found, sire, all slain in the same manner as the first one. Near a Kindaru camp this time.'

'The Kindaru? They are useless. Against thirty of my soldiers? That cannot be.'

'Troop Leader Uludan agrees, sire. The proximity of the Kindaru was but coincidental – or it was the raiding party's plan to ambush them.'

Yes, that was likely. The damned Kindaru and their delicious horses were getting hard to find of late. 'Does Uludan now track the murderers?'

'Difficult, sire. They seem to possess impressive lore and are able to thoroughly hide their trail. It may be that they are aided by sorcery.'

'Your thought or Uludan's?'

A faint flush of the man's face. 'Mine, sire.'

'I did not invite your opinion, soldier.'

'No, sire. I apologize.'

Sorcery – the spirits within should have sensed such a thing anywhere on his territory. Which tribes were capable of assembling such skilled and no doubt numerous warriors? Well, one obvious answer was the Barghast – but they did not travel the Lamatath. They dwelt far to the north, along the edges of the Rhivi Plain, in fact, and north of Capustan. There should be no Barghast this far south. And if, somehow, there were . . . the Captain scowled. 'Twenty knights shall accompany you back to the place of slaughter. You then lead them to Uludan's troop. Find the trail no matter what.'

'We shall, sire.'

'Be sure Uludan understands.'

'Yes, sire.'

And understand he would. The knights were there not just to provide a heavier adjunct to the troop. They were to exact whatever punishment the sergeant deemed necessary should Uludan fail.

The Captain had just lost sixty soldiers. Almost a fifth of his total number of light cavalry.

'Go now,' he said to the rider, 'and find Sergeant Teven and send him to me at once.'

'Yes, sire.'

As the man climbed back down, the Captain leaned back in his throne, staring down at the dusty backs of the yoked slaves. Kindaru there, yes. And Sinbarl and the last seven or so Gandaru, slope-browed cousins of the Kindaru soon to be entirely extinct. A shame, that – they were strong bastards, hard-working, never complaining. He'd set aside the two surviving women and they now rode a wagon, bellies swollen with child, eating fat grubs, the yolk of snake eggs and other bizarre foods the Gandaru were inclined towards. Were the children on the way pure Gandaru? He did not think so – their women rutted anything with a third leg, and far less submissively than he thought prudent. Even so, one or both of those children might well be his.

Not as heirs, of course. His bastard children held no special rights. He did not even acknowledge them. No, he would adopt an heir when the time came – and, if the whispered promises of the spirits were true, that could be centuries away.

His mind had stepped off the path, he realized.

Sixty slain soldiers. Was the kingdom of Skathandi at war? Perhaps so.

Yet the enemy clearly did not dare face him here, with his knights and the entire mass of his army ready and able to take the field of battle. Thus, whatever army would fight him was small—

Shouts from ahead.

The Captain's eyes narrowed. From his raised vantage point he could see without obstruction that a lone figure was approaching from the northwest. A skin of white fur flapped in the breeze like the wing of a ghost-moth, spreading out from the broad shoulders. A longsword was strapped to the man's back, its edges oddly rippled, the blade itself a colour unlike any metal the Captain knew.

As the figure came closer, as if expecting the massed slaves to simply part before him, the Captain's sense of scale was jarred. The warrior was enormous, easily half again as tall as the tallest Skathandi – taller even than a Barghast. A face seemingly masked – no, tattooed, in a crazed broken glass or tattered web pattern. Beneath that barbaric visage, the torso was covered in some kind of shell armour, pretty but probably useless.

Well, the fool – huge or not – was about to be trampled or pushed aside. Motion was eternal. Motion was – a sudden spasm clutched at the Captain's mind, digging fingers into his brain – the spirits, thrashing in terror – shrieking—

A taste of acid on his tongue—

Gasping, the Captain gestured.

A servant, who sat behind him in an upright coffin-shaped box, watching through a slit in the wood, saw the signal and pulled hard on a braided rope. A horn blared, followed by three more.

And, for the first time in seven years, the kingdom of Skathandi ground to a halt.

The giant warrior strode for the head of the slave column. He drew his sword. As he swung down with that savage weapon, the slaves began screaming.

From both flanks, the ground shook as knights charged inward.

More frantic gestures from the Captain. Horns sounded again and the knights shifted en masse, swung out wide to avoid the giant.

The sword's downward stroke had struck the centre spar linking the yoke harnesses. Edge on blunt end, splitting the spar for half its twenty-man length. Bolts scattered, chains rushed through iron loops to coil and slither on to the ground.

The Captain was on his feet, tottering, gripping the bollards of the balcony rail. He could see, as his knights drew up into ranks once more, all heads turned towards him, watching, waiting for the command. But he could not move. Pain lanced up his legs from the misshapen bones of his feet. He held on to the ornate posts with his feeble hands. Ants swarmed in his skull.

The spirits were gone.

Fled.

He was alone. He was empty.

Reeling back, falling into his throne.

He saw one of his sergeants ride out, drawing closer to the giant, who now stood leaning on his sword. The screams of the slaves sank away and those suddenly free of their bindings staggered to either side, some falling to their knees as if subjecting themselves before a new king, a usurper. The sergeant reined in and, eyes level with the giant's own, began speaking.

The Captain was too far away. He could not hear, and he needed to – sweat poured from him, soaking his fine silks. He shivered as fever rose through him. He looked down at his hands and saw blood welling from the old wounds – opened once more – and from his feet as well, pooling in the soft padded slippers. He remembered, suddenly, what it was like to think about dying, letting go, surrendering. There, yes, beneath the shade of the cottonwoods—

The sergeant collected his reins and rode at the canter for the palace.

He drew up, dismounted in a clatter of armour and reached up to remove his visored helm. Then he ascended the steps.

'Captain, sir. The fool claims that the slaves are now free.'

Staring into the soldier's blue eyes, the grizzled expression now widened by disbelief, by utter amazement, the Captain felt a pang of pity. 'He is the one, isn't he?'

'Sir?'

'The enemy. The slayer of my subjects. I feel it. The truth – I see it, I feel it. I taste it!'

The sergeant said nothing.

'He wants my throne,' the Captain whispered, holding up his bleeding hands. 'Was that all this was for, do you think? All I've done, just for him?'

'Captain,' the sergeant said in a harsh growl. 'He has ensorcelled you. We will cut him down.'

'No. You do not understand. *They're gone!*'

'Sir—'

'Make camp, Sergeant. Tell him – tell him he is to be my guest at dinner. My guest. Tell him . . . tell him . . . my guest, yes, just that.'

The sergeant, a fine soldier indeed, saluted and set off.

Another gesture with one stained, dripping, mangled hand. Two maids crept out to help him to his feet. He looked down at one. A Kindaru, round and plump and snouted like a fox – he saw her eyes fix upon the bleeding appendage at the end of the arm she supported, and she licked her lips.

I am dying.

Not centuries. Before this day is done. Before this day is done, I will be dead. 'Make me presentable,' he gasped. 'There shall be no shame upon him, do you see? I want no pity. He is my heir. He has come. At last, he has come.'

The maids, both wide-eyed with fear now, helped him inside.

And still the ants swarmed.

The horses stood in a circle facing inward, tails flicking at flies, heads lowered as they cropped grass. The oxen stood nearby, still yoked, and watched them. Kedeviss, who leaned with crossed arms against one of the wagon's wheels, seemed to be watching the grey-haired foreigner with the same placid, empty regard.

Nimander knew just how deceptive that look could be. Of them all – these paltry few left – she saw the clearest, with acuity so sharp it intimidated almost everyone subject to it. The emptiness – if the one being watched finally turned to meet those eyes – would slowly fade, and something hard, unyielding and immune to obfuscation would slowly rise in its place. Unwavering, ever sharpening until it seemed to pierce the victim like nails being hammered into wood. And then she'd casually look away, unmindful of the thumping heart, the pale face and the beads of sweat on the brow, and the one so assailed was left with but one of two choices: to fear this woman, or to love her with such savage, demanding desire that it could crush the heart.

Nimander feared Kedeviss. And loved her as well. He was never good with choices.

If Kallor sensed that regard – and Nimander was certain he did – he was indifferent to it, preferring to divide his attention between the empty sky and the empty landscape surrounding them. When he wasn't sleeping or eating. An unpleasant guest, peremptory and imperious. He would not cook, nor bother cleansing his plate afterwards. He was a man with six servants.

Nenanda was all for banishing the old man, driving him away with stones and pieces of dung, but Nimander found something incongruous in that image, as if it was such an absurd impossibility that it had no place even in his imagination.

'He's weakening,' Desra said at his side.

'We're soon there, I think,' Nimander replied. They were just south of Sarn, which had once been a sizeable city. The road leading to it had been settled all along its length, ribbon farms behind stalls, shops and taverns. The few residents left were an impoverished lot, skittish as whipped dogs, hacking at hard ground that had been fallow too long – at least until they saw the travellers on the main road, whereupon they dropped their hoes and hurried away.

The supplies left at the T-intersection had been meticulously packed into wooden crates, the entire pile covered in a tarp with its corners staked. Ripe fruits, candied sugar-rocks dusted in salt, heavy loaves of dark bread, strips of dried eel, watered wine and three kinds of cheese – where all this had come from, given the wretched state of the farms they'd passed, was a mystery.

'He would kill us as soon as look at us,' Desra said, her eyes now on Kallor. 'Skintick agrees.'

'What manner of man is he?'

Nimander shrugged. 'An unhappy one. We should get going.'

'Wait,' said Desra. 'I think we should get Aranatha to look at Clip.'

'Aranatha?' He looked round, found the woman sitting, legs folded under her like a fawn's, plucking flowers from the sloped bank of the road. 'Why? What can she do?'

Desra shook her head, as if unable to give her reasons. Or unwilling.

Sighing, Nimander said, 'Go ahead, ask her, then.'

'It needs to come from you.'

Why? 'Very well.' He set out, a dozen strides taking him to where Aranatha sat. As his shadow slipped over her she glanced up and smiled.

Smiles so lacking in caution, in diffidence or wry reluctance, always struck him as a sign of madness. But the eyes above it, this time, were not at all vacuous. 'Do you feel me, Nimander?'

'I don't know what you mean by that, Aranatha. Desra would like you to examine Clip. I don't know why,' he added, 'since I don't recall you possessing any specific skills in healing.'

'Perhaps she wants company,' Aranatha said, rising gracefully to her feet.

And he was struck, as if slapped across the face, by her beauty. Standing now so close, her breath so warm and so strangely dark. *What is happening to me? Kedeviss and now Aranatha.*

'Are you all right, Nimander?'

'Yes.' *No.* 'I'm fine.' *What awakens in me? To deliver both anguish and exaltation?*

She placed a half-dozen white flowers in his hand, smiled again, then walked over to the wagon. A soft laugh from Skintick brought him round.

'There's more of that these days,' his brother said, gazing after Aranatha. 'If we are to be an incongruous lot, and it seems we are, then it follows that we confound each other at every turn.'

'You are speaking nonsense, Skintick.'

'That is my task, isn't it? I have no sense of where it is we're heading – no, I don't mean Bastion, nor even the confrontation that I think is coming. I mean *us*, Nimander. Especially you. The less control you have, the greater your talent for leadership seems to become, the qualities demanded of such a person – like those flowers in your hand, petals unfolding.'

Nimander grimaced at this and scowled down at the blossoms. 'They'll be dead shortly.'

'So may we all,' Skintick responded. 'But . . . pretty while it lasts.'

Kallor joined them as they prepared to resume the journey. His weathered face was strangely colourless, as if drained of blood by the incessant wind. Or whatever memories haunted him. The flatness in his eyes suggested to Nimander that the man was without humour, that the notion was as alien to him as mending the rips in his own clothes. 'Are you all finally done with your rest?' Kallor asked, noting the flowers still in Nimander's hand with a faint sneer.

'The horses needed it,' Nimander said. 'Are you in a hurry? If so, you could always go ahead of us. When you stop for the night we'll either catch up with you or we won't.'

'Who would feed me, then?'

'You could always feed yourself,' Skintick said. 'Presumably you've had to do that on occasion.'

Kallor shrugged. 'I will ride the wagon,' he said, heading off.

Nenanda had collected the horses and now led them over. 'They all need reshoeing,' he said, 'and this damned road isn't helping any.'

A sudden commotion at the wagon brought them all round, in time to see Kallor flung backward from the side rail, crashing heavily on the cobbles, the look on his face one of stunned surprise. Above him, standing on the bed, was Aranatha, and even at that distance they could see something dark and savage blazing from her eyes.

Desra stood near her, mouth hanging open.

On the road, lying on his back, Kallor began to laugh. A rasping, breathy kind of laugh.

With a bemused glance at Skintick and Nenanda, Nimander walked over.

Aranatha had turned away, resuming her ministrations with Clip, trickling water between the unconscious man's lips. Tucking the flowers under his belt, Nimander pulled himself on to the wagon and met Desra's eyes. 'What happened?'

'He helped himself to a handful,' Desra replied tonelessly, nodding towards Aranatha. 'She, er, pushed him away.'

'He was balanced on a wheel spoke?' Skintick asked from behind Nimander.

Desra shook her head. 'One hand on the rail. She just . . . *sent him flying.*'

The old man, his laughter fading away, was climbing to his feet. 'You damned Tiste Andii,' he said, 'no sense of adventure.'

But Nimander could see that, despite Kallor's seeming mirth, the grizzled warrior was somewhat shaken. Drawing a deep breath and wincing at some pain in his ribs, he moved round to the back of the wagon and once more climbed aboard, this time keeping his distance from Aranatha.

Nimander leaned on the rail, close to Aranatha. 'Are you all right?' he asked.

Glancing up, she gave him another one of those appallingly innocent smiles. 'Can you feel me now, Nimander?'

Was the *idea* of water enough to create an illusion so perfect that every sense was deceived? The serpent curl of the One River, known as Dorssan Ryl, encircled half the First City of Kharkanas. Before the coming of light there was no reflection from its midnight surface, and to settle one's hand in its ceaseless flow was to feel naught but a cooler breath against the skin as the current sighed round the intrusion. 'Water in Darkness, dreams in sleep' – or so wrote one of Mad Poets of the ninety-third century, during the stylistic trend in poetry characterized by brevity, a style that crashed in the following century during the period of art and oratory known as the Flowering Bright.

Water in perfect illusion . . . was this fundamentally no different from real water? If the senses provide all that defines the world, then were they not the arbiters of reality? As a young acolyte, fired with passions of all sorts, Endest Silann had argued bell after bell with his fellow students over such matters. All those 'Essence of truth, senses will lie' themes that seemed so important then, before every universe exploded in the conflagration of creation, shoving all those bright, flaring candles over the table edge, down into the swirling sea of wax where every notion, every idea, melted into one and none, into the scalding sludge that drowned everyone no matter how clever, how wise, how *poetic*.

What am I thinking of these days? Naught but the nonsense of my wasted youth. 'Certainty scours, a world without wonder.' Ah, then, perhaps those terse poets had stumbled on to something after all. Is this what obsesses me now? A suspicion that all the truths that matter lie somewhere in a soul's youth, in those heady days when words and thoughts could still shine – as if born from nothing solely for our personal edification.

Generation upon generation, this does not change. Or so it comforts us to believe. Yet I wonder, now, does that stretch of delight grow shorter? Is it tightening, cursed into a new kind of brevity, the one with ignorance preceding and cynicism succeding, each crowding the precious moment?

What then the next generation? Starved of wonder, indifferent to the reality or the unreality of the water flowing past, caring only whether they might drift or drown. And then, alas, losing the sense of difference between the two.

There was no one, here in his modest chamber, to hear his thoughts. No one, indeed, who even cared. Deeds must tumble forward, lest all these witnesses grow bored and restless. And if secrets dwelt in the lightless swirl of some unseen, unimagined river, what matter when the effort to delve deep was simply too much? *No, better to . . . drift.*

But worries over the mere score of young Tiste Andii growing now in Black Coral was wasted energy. He had no wisdom to offer, even if any of them was inclined to listen, which they weren't. The old possessed naught but the single virtue of surviving, and when nothing changed, it was indeed an empty virtue.

He remembered the great river, its profound mystery of existence. Dorssan Ryl, into which the sewers poured the gritty, rain-diluted blood of the dead and dying. The river, proclaiming its reality in a roar as the rain lashed down in torrents, as clouds, groaning, fell like beasts on to their knees, only to fold into the now-raging currents and twist down into the black depths. All this, swallowed by an illusion.

There had been a woman, once, and yes, he might have loved her. Like the hand plunged into the cool water, he might have been brushed by this heady emotion, this blood-whispered obsession that poets died for and over which people murdered their dearest. And he recalled that the last time he set eyes upon her, down beside Dorssan Ryl, driven mad by Mother's abandonment (many were), there was nothing he recognized in her eyes. To see, there in a face he had known, had adored, that appalling absence – she was gone, never to return.

So I held her head under, watched those staring, uncomprehending eyes grow ever wider, filling with blind panic – and there! At the last moment, did I not see – a sudden light, a sudden—

Oh, this was a nightmare. He had done nothing, he had been too much the coward. And he had watched her leave, with all the others so struck by loss, as they set out on a hopeless pilgrimage, a fatal search to find Her once again. What a journey that must have been! Before the last crazed one fell for the final time, punctuating a trail of corpses leagues long. A crusade of the insane, wandering into the nowhere.

Kharkanas was virtually an empty city after they'd gone. Anomander Rake's first lordship over echoing chambers, empty houses. There would be many more.

A calm, then, drifting on like flotsam in the stream, not yet caught by the rushes, not yet so waterlogged that it vanished, tumbled like a severed moon into the muddy bed. Of course it couldn't last. One more betrayal was needed, to shatter the world once and for all.

The night just past Endest Silann, making his way to a back storeroom on the upper level, came upon the Son of Darkness in a corridor. Some human, thinking the deed one of honour, had hung a series of ancient Andii tapestries down both walls of the passage. Scenes of Kharkanas, and one indeed showing Dorssan Ryl – although none would know if not familiar with that particular vantage point, for the river was but a dark slash, a talon curled round the city's heart. There was no particular order, arrayed so in ignorance, and to walk this corridor was to be struck by a collage of images, distinct as memories not one tethered to the next.

Anomander Rake had been standing before one, his eyes a deep shade of amber. Predatory, fixed as a lion's before a killing charge. On the faded tapestry a figure stood tall amidst carnage. The bodies tumbled before him all bled from wounds to the back. Nothing subtle here, the weaver's outrage dripped from every thread. White-skinned, onyx-eyed, sweat-blackened hair braided like hanging ropes. Slick swords in his hands, he looked out upon the viewer, defiant and cold. In the wracked sky behind him wheeled Locqui Wyval with women's heads, their mouths open in screams almost audible.

'He did not mean it,' said Anomander Rake.

But he did. 'Your ability to forgive far surpasses mine, Lord.'

'The body follows the head, but sometimes it's the other way round. There was a cabal. Ambitious, hungry. They used him, Endest, they used him badly.'

'They paid for it, didn't they?'

'We all did, old friend.'

Endest Silann looked away. 'I so dislike this hallway, Lord. When I must walk it, I look neither left nor right.'

Rake grunted. 'It is indeed a gauntlet of recrimination.'

'Reminders, Lord, of the fact that some things never change.'

'You must wrest yourself loose, Endest. This despondency can . . . ravage the soul.'

'I have heard there is a river that empties into Coral Bay. Eryn or Maurik. Which seems depthless.'

Anomander Rake, still studying the tapestry, nodded.

'Spinnock Durav has seen it, walked its shores. He says it reminds him of Dorssan Ryl . . . his childhood.'

'Yes, there are some similarities.'

'I was thinking, if I could be spared . . .'

His Lord glanced over and smiled. 'A pilgrimage? Of course, Endest. If, that is, you can return before a month passes.'

Ah, are we so close, then? 'I will not stay long, Lord. Only to see, with my own eyes, that is all.'

The glance had become something more focused, and the amber glare had dimmed to something like . . . *like mud.* 'I fear you may be disappointed. It is but a deep river. We cannot touch the past, old friend.' He looked back once more on the tapestry. 'And the echoes we imagine we hear, well, they *deceive.* Do not be surprised, Endest, if you find nothing you seek, and everything you fear.'

And what is it, Lord, that you think I seek? I would not ask what you think I fear for you know the answer to that one. 'I thought the walk might do me some good.'

'And so it shall.'

Now, the next day, he sat in his chamber. A small leather pack of supplies rested beside the door. And the thought of a walk, a long one, up rugged mountainsides beneath hard sunlight, no longer seemed so appetizing. Age did such things, feeding the desire then starving the will. And what, after all, would seeing the river achieve?

A reminder of illusions, perhaps, a reminder that, in a realm for ever beyond reach, there stood the ruin of a once-great city, and, flowing round it, Dorssan Ryl, living on, ceaseless in its perfect absence, in playing its game of existence. A river of purest darkness, the life water of the Tiste Andii, and if the children were gone, well, what difference did that make?

Children will leave. Children will abandon the old ways, and the old fools with all their pointless advice can mutter and grumble to empty spaces and nod at the answering echoes. Stone and brickwork make ideal audiences.

No, he would make this journey. He would defy the follies of old age, unmeasured and unmocked under the eyes of the young. A solitary pilgrimage.

And all these thoughts, seeming so indulgent and wayward, will perhaps reveal their worth then, driving dire echoes forward to that future moment of revelation. Hah. Did he believe such things? Did he possess the necessary faith?

'Ask no question, the river shall answer.'

'Question the river, find the answer.'

The Mad Poets spent lifetimes waging profound wars in their rendered prose. Achieving what? Why, the implosive obliteration of their tradition.

Summarize that in two clauses.

'I need you to make a journey.'

Spinnock Durav managed a smile. 'When, Lord?'

Anomander Rake stretched out his legs until his boots were very nearly in the flames of the hearth. 'Soon, I think. Tell me, how goes the game?'

He squinted at the fire. 'Not well. Oh, I win each time. It's just that my finest opponent does poorly of late. His mind is on other matters, unfortunately. I am not pressed, and this removes much of the pleasure.'

'This would be Seerdomin.'

Spinnock glanced up, momentarily surprised. *But of course,* he told himself, *he is the Son of Darkness, after all. They may well call him the Ghost King, but I doubt there is a single detail he does not know in Black Coral. They will not heed that until they make a terrible mistake and then it will be too late.* 'Seerdomin, yes. The Benighted.'

A faint smile from Anomander Rake. 'Itkovian was a most extraordinary man. This newborn cult interests me, and I am not so sure it would have pleased him. He saw himself as a soldier, a failed one at that – the fall of Capustan devastated him.' He paused for a moment, clearly remembering, then he said, 'They were but a mercenary company, modest in complement – nothing like the Crimson Guard. I dare say even the Crimson Guard would have failed to hold Capustan.'

Spinnock Durav remained silent, attentive. He had been away during that time. Another journey on behalf of his Lord. *Hunting a dragon, of all things.* Conversations like the one he'd found at the end of that quest were not worth repeating.

'He could forgive everyone but himself.'

No wonder you liked him.

Anomander Rake sighed. 'I cannot say how long you will need, Spinnock. As long, perhaps, as you can manage.'

As the significance of that statement settled into Spinnock Durav he felt an uncharacteristic flash of dismay. Angry at himself, he slowly settled his hands on the arms of the chair, fingers curling round the smooth wood, hoping he'd left nothing in his expression. *This is what I do and will do. Until my end. She is young, so young – oh, there's no point in thinking about . . . about any of that. About her at all.* Was he able to keep the anguish from his eyes? What thoughts – doubts – rustled through his Lord now as he watched his old friend? Feeling defeated, Spinnock Durav glanced over at Anomander Rake.

The ruler of Black Coral sat frowning at his smouldering boots.

So, how long has he been thus? 'I have always . . . managed, Lord.'

'Yes, you have. I am curious. What so afflicts Seerdomin?'

'A crisis of faith, I think.' *Life like Kef Tanar, this skipping across paths. He does it so well, this man whom I have never defeated in our tabletop wars, not in ten thousand years. But I can stay with you, Lord, at least this far.* 'He has ceased

making his daily pilgrimage. Among those living out there, there have grown . . .
expectations. Which, it seems, he is unable to meet.'

'You tread carefully, Spinnok Durav. That is unlike you.'

'I do not possess all the details yet.'

'But you shall.'

'Eventually, yes.'

'And then?'

Spinnock looked across at Rake. 'I will do what needs doing.'

'Best hurry, then.'

Ah, yes, I see now.

'The Redeemer is a most helpless god,' Anomander Rake said after a time. 'Unable to refuse, unable to give. A sea sponge swallowing the entire sea. Then the next one and the one after that. Can it simply go on for ever? But for Itkovian, I would think not.'

'Is that a sort of faith, Lord?'

'Perhaps it is. Is his ability to forgive truly endless? To take on the pain and guilt of others for all eternity? I admit, I have some serious difficulties with this cult's root tenets – oh, as I said, I greatly admired Itkovian, the Shield Anvil of the Grey Swords. I even understand, to some extent, his gesture with the Kron T'lan Imass. As the Redeemer, however . . . I cannot but wonder at a god so willing to assume the crimes and moral flaws of its followers, while in turn demanding nothing – no expectation of a change in behaviour, no threat of punishment should they continue to transgress. Absolution – yes, I grasp the notion, but absolution is not the same as redemption, is it? The former is passive. The latter demands an effort, one with implicit sacrifice and hardship, one demanding all the higher qualities of what we call virtues.'

'Yet he is called the Redeemer.'

'Because he takes on the task of redemption for all who come to him, all who pray to him. And yes, it is an act of profound courage. But he does not expect the same of his people – he appears to possess no expectations whatsoever.'

This was most loquacious of his Lord, evidence of a long, careful condensation of thought, of considerable energy devoted to the nature of the cult clinging to the very edge of Black Coral and Night, all of which seemed . . . unusual. 'He leads by example, then.'

A sudden glitter of interest in Anomander Rake's eyes and he studied Spinnock Durav intently. 'Has any one follower stumbled on to that possibility, Spinnock Durav?'

'I do not know. I, er, don't think so – but, Lord, I am too far outside all of it at the moment.'

'If the Redeemer cannot deny, then he is trapped in a state of imbalance. I wonder, what would be needed to redress that imbalance?'

Spinnock Durav found his mouth dry, and if he'd built proud castles of comprehension, if he'd raised sound fortifications to guard his assumptions, and arrayed vast armies to argue his case and to shift and align and manoeuvre to defend his cherished notions – if he had done all this to then sit in comfort, secure in his place in this conversation – if this was indeed a game of Kef Tanar, then in one simple question posed, his foe had crashed his empire to ruin.

What would be needed to redress that imbalance?

A man who refuses.

You tell me time is short, my Lord. You lead me to elucidate what bothers me – for you can see that something does – and then, amidst the lofty clouds of religious discussion, you lash a lightning bolt down, striking my very heart.

If I am to do something, I must do it soon.

My Lord, my awe of you is unbounded. My love for you and the compassion you so delicately unveil leads me into this willingness, to storm without hesitation what you would have me storm, to stand for as long as needed, for it is what you need.

'It is well I am immune to heat,' Anomander Rake said, 'for I have scorched my boots most severely.'

And so the fire grows round you, yet you do not flinch.

I will not fail you, my Lord.

'Endest Silann is upon the mountain road now,' Anomander Rake said, rising. 'And Crone has returned but soon must wing away again. I shall ask her to send a few grandchildren to guard him on his journey. Unless, of course, you think it might offend Endest Silann should he see them wheeling overhead?'

'It might, Lord, but that should not change your decision.'

A faint smile. 'Agreed. Send my regards to the priestess, Spinnock.'

Until that moment, he had not known he was going to visit the High Priestess – who had scoured away her very name in service to her role in the Temple of Darkness, to make of her ever-open legs an impersonal act, that made her body a vessel and nothing more – but he now knew that he needed to do just that. Kurald Galain was a most troubled warren right now. Storms rumbled within it, drumming every thread of power. Energies crackled. *Making her insatiable. So, she will want me – but that is not what concerns Anomander Rake. There is something else. I must go to her, and I don't even know why.*

But he does.

Spinnock Durav found himself sitting alone in the small chamber. The fire was down to coals. The air smelled of burned leather.

The High Priestess of the Temple of Dark had cut her hair even shorter, making her disturbingly boyish as she pushed him on to his back, straddling him with her usual eagerness. Normally, he would now begin to slow her down, providing a force of resistance defying her impatience, and so drawing out her pleasure. This time, however, he let her have her way. This was all incidental. Since that unknown force had trembled through Kurald Galain, all the priestesses had been frantic in their desire, forcing male Tiste Andii into the temple and the rooms with the plush beds. If the rumours were true, then even the occasional human was dragged in for the same needful interrogation.

But no answers could be found in the indulgences of the flesh, and perhaps all this was a kind of metaphorical revelation of that raw truth, one that extended far beyond the temple and the prescriptions of priestesses. Yet, did he want answers from Salind? From that young human woman who could not be more than twenty years of age? From another High Priestess?

He had seen too much, had lived too long. All she faced ahead and all the experiences still awaiting her – they belonged to her age, and should indeed be shared – if at all – by one of similar years. He had no desire to be a mentor, for the student soon grows past the need of one (if the mentor has done his job well), and then it is the mentor who rails against the notion of equality, or of being surpassed. But the impossibility of the notion went further. She would never surpass him. Instead, she would grow old all too quickly, and the sensibilities of her life, a life so truncated, could never match his.

Korlat had not hesitated with the Malazan sergeant Whiskeyjack – Spinnock had heard the tragic tale, bound up as it was in the conquest of Black Coral and the fall of the Pannion Domin. And the prolonged absence of both Korlat and her brother, Orfantal. Nevertheless, Whiskeyjack had been a man late in his years – he had lived most of a life. And who could say if the union could have lasted? When, in a terribly short span of years, Korlat would have seen her beloved descend into decay, his back bent, hands atremble, memory failing.

Spinnock could almost imagine the end of that, as, broken-hearted, Korlat would face a moment with a knife in her hands, contemplating the mercy of ending her husband's life. Was this a thing to look forward to? *Do we not possess enough burdens as it is?*

'If not for your desire I could feel in my nest,' said the woman now lying beneath him, 'I would think you disinterested, Spinnock Durav. You have not been with me here, it seems, and while it's said a man's sword never lies, now I truly wonder if that is so.'

Blinking, he looked down into her face. A most attractive face, one that both suited the nature of her devotion and yet seemed far too innocent – too open – for this life of uninhibited indulgence. 'I am sorry,' he said. 'I waited for you to . . . leave.'

She pushed out from under him, sat up and ran her long-fingered hands through the brush of her hair. 'We fail in that of late,' she said.

Ah, so that is the reason for your desperation, your avidness.

'It will return,' she said. 'It must. Something . . . changes, Spin.'

He stared at her unblemished back, the graceful curve of her spine, the slight rounding on her hips that he knew to be soft and cool to the touch. The angle of her shoulders bespoke either temporary satiation or a more prolonged weariness. 'Our Lord sends his regards.'

She turned to look down at him, brows lifted in surprise. 'He does? That would be a first.'

Spinnock frowned. *Yes, it would. I hadn't thought of that.* 'I will be leaving soon.'

Her eyes hardened. 'Why does he treat you so? As if he possessed you, to do with as he pleases.'

'I stand in his stead.'

'But you are not the Son of Darkness.'

'No, that is true.'

'One day you are going to die in his stead.'

'I am.'

'And then he will need to find another fool.'

'Yes.'

She glared down at him, then turned and swiftly rose. Black skin polished in the glow of the lanterns – nothing boylike now, a figure all curves and softened planes. Spinnock smiled. 'I will miss you as well.'

Faint surrender as she sighed. And when she faced him again, there was nothing veiled in her eyes. 'We do what we can.'

'Yes.'

'No, you don't understand. The Temple – my priestesses. We try as Anomander Rake tries, both of us, seeking to hold on to some meaning, some purpose. He imagines it can be found in the struggles of lesser folk – of humans and all their miserable squabbles. He is wrong. We know this and so too does he. The Temple, Spin, chooses another way. The rebirth of our Gate, the return of Mother Dark, into our lives, our souls.'

'Yes. And?'

Something crumpled in her expression. 'We fail as he does. We know and he knows. The Son of Darkness does not send me his regards.'

Then . . . he said 'priestess'.

But he didn't mean this one. Spinnock sat up, reached down to the floor where his clothes were lying. 'High Priestess,' he said, 'what can you tell me of the Cult of the Redeemer?'

'What?'

He looked up, wondered at the alarm in her eyes. After a moment he shook his head. 'No, I am not interested in forgiveness. Embracing the T'lan Imass killed the man – what would embracing us do to his soul?'

'I care not to think, Spin. Oh, he was glorious in his way – for all the blood that was needlessly spilled because of it – still . . . glorious. If you speak not of our burdens, then I do not understand your question.'

'It is newborn, this cult. What shape will it take?'

She sighed again – most extraordinary and further proof of her exhaustion. 'As you say, very young indeed. And like all religions, its shape – it future – will be found in what happens now, in these first moments. And that is a cause for concern, for although pilgrims gather and give gifts and pray, no organization exists. Nothing has been formulated – no doctrine – and all religions need such things.'

He rubbed at his jaw, considering, and then nodded.

'Why does this interest you?' she asked.

'I'm not sure, but I appreciate your expertise.' He paused, stared down at the clothes in his hands. He had forgotten something, something important – what might it be?

'I was not wrong,' she observed, still watching him. 'You are not yourself, Spin. Have you finally come to resent your Lord's demands?'

'No.' *Perhaps, but that is not worthy of consideration – the flaw would be mine, after all.* 'I am fine, High Priestess.'

She snorted. 'None of us are that, Spin,' she said as she turned away.

As his gaze dropped he saw his sword and belt lying on the floor. Of course – he had forgotten his ritual. He collected the weapon and, as the High Priestess threw on her robes, carried it over to the table and set it down. From the belt's stiff leather pouch he removed a small sponge, a metal flask of eel oil, and a much-stained pad of sharkskin.

'Ah,' said the High Priestess from the doorway, 'all is right with the world again. Later, Spin.'

'Yes, High Priestess,' he replied, electing to ignore her sarcasm. And the need it so poorly disguised.

Rain had rushed in from the sea, turning the paths into rivers of mud. Salind sat in the makeshift shed, legs curled up beneath her, shivering as water dripped down through holes in the roof. More people had come scratching at her door, but she had turned them all away.

She'd had enough of being a High Priestess. All her heightened sensitivities to the whims of the Redeemer were proving little more than a curse. What matter all these vague emotions she sensed from the god? She could do nothing for him.

This should not have surprised her, and she told herself that what she was feeling wasn't hurt, but something else, something more impersonal. Perhaps it was her grieving for the growing list of victims as Gradithan and his sadistic mob continued to terrorize the camp – so much so that some were planning to leave as soon as the road dried out. Or her failure with the Benighted. The expectations settling upon her, in the eyes of so many people, were too vast, too crushing. She could not hope to answer them all. And she was finding that, in truth, she could answer none of them.

Words were empty in the face of brutal will. They were helpless to defend whatever sanctity might be claimed, for a person's self, for their freedom to choose how they would live, and with whom. Empathy haunted her. Compassion opened wounds which only a hardening of the soul could in the future prevent, and this she did not want – she had seen too many faces, looked into too many eyes, and recoiled from their coldness, their delight in vicious judgement.

The righteous will claim sole domain on judgement. The righteous are the first to make hands into fists, the first to shout down dissenters, the first to bully others into compliance.

I live in a village of the meek, and I am the meekest of them all. There is no glory in being helpless. Nor is there hope.

Rain lashing down, a drumming roar on the slatted, angled roof, the sound of a deluge that filled her skull. *That the Redeemer will embrace is neither just nor unjust. No mortal can sanction their behaviour in the Redeemer's name. How dare they so presume?* Miserable faces marching past, peering in through the cracks in her door. And she wanted to rail at them all. *You damned fools. Absolution is not enough!* But they would then look upon her, moon-eyed and doleful, desperate that every question yield an answer, clinging to the notion that one suffered for a reason and knowledge of that reason would ease the suffering.

Knowledge, Salind told herself, eases nothing. It just fills spaces that might otherwise flood with despair.

Can you live without answers? All of you, ask that of yourself. Can you live without answers? Because if you cannot, then most assuredly you will invent your own answers and they will comfort you. And all those who do not share your view will by their very existence strike fear and hatred into your heart. What god blesses this?

'I am no High Priestess,' she croaked, as water trickled down her face.

Heavy boots splashing in the mud outside. The door was tugged back and a dark shape blotted out the pale grey light. 'Salind.'

She blinked, trying to discern who so spoke to her with such . . . such compassion. 'Ask me nothing,' she said. 'Tell me less.'

The figure moved, closing the door in a scrape of sodden grit that filled the shed with gloom once more. Pausing, standing, water dripping from a long leather cloak. 'This will not do.'

'Whoever you are,' Salind said, 'I did not invite you in. This is my home.'

'My apologies, High Priestess.'

'You smell of sex.'

'Yes, I imagine so.'

'Do not touch me. I am poison.'

'I – I have no desire to . . . touch you, High Priestess. I have walked this village – the conditions are deplorable. The Son of Darkness, I well know, will not long abide such poverty.'

She squinted up at him. 'You are the Benighted's friend. The only Tiste Andii for whom humans are not beneath notice.'

'Is this what you believe of us, then? That is . . . unfortunate.'

'I am ill. Please go away, sir.'

'My name is Spinnock Durav. I might have told you that when last we met – I do not recall and clearly neither do you. You . . . challenged me, High Priestess.'

'No, I rejected you, Spinnock Durav.'

There might have been something like wry amusement in his tone as he replied, 'Perhaps the two are one and the same.'

She snorted. 'Oh, no, a perennial optimist.'

He reached down suddenly and his warm palm pressed against her forehead. She jerked back. Straightening, he said, 'You are fevered.'

'Just go.'

'I will, but I intend to take you with me—'

'And what of everyone else so afflicted in this camp? Will you carry them all out? Or just me, just the one upon whom you take pity? Unless it is not pity that drives you.'

'I will have healers attend the camp—'

'Do that, yes. I can wait with the others.'

'Salind—'

'That's not my name.'

'It isn't? But I was—'

'I simply chose it. I had no name. Not as a child, not until just a few months ago. I had no name at all, Spinnock Durav. Do you know why I haven't been raped yet? Most of the other women have. Most of the children, too. But not me. Am I so ugly? No, not in the flesh – even I know that. It's because I was a Child of the Dead Seed – do you know the meaning of that, Tiste Andii? My mother crawled half-mad on a battlefield, reaching beneath the jerkins of dead soldiers until she found a member solid and hard. Then she took it into herself and, if she were blessed, it would spill into her. A dead man's seed. I had plenty of brothers and sisters, a family of aunts and a mother who in the end rotted to some terrible disease that ate her flesh – her brain was long gone by then. I have not been raped, because I am untouchable.'

He stared down at her, evidently shocked, horrified into dumb silence.

She coughed, wishing she did not get sick so often – but it had always been this way. 'You can go now, Spinnock Durav.'

'This place festers.' And he moved forward to pick her up.

She recoiled. 'You don't understand! I'm sick because *he's* sick!'

He halted and she finally could make out his eyes, forest green and tilted at the corners, and far too much compassion gleamed in that regard. 'The Redeemer? Yes, I imagine he is. Come,' and he took her up, effortlessly, and she should have struggled – should have been free to choose – but she was too weak. Pushing him away with her hands was a gesture, a desire, transformed into clutching help-lessly at his cloak. Like a child.

A child.

'When the rains stop,' he murmured, his breath no doubt warm but scalding against her fevered cheek, 'we shall rebuild. Make all this new. Dry, warm.'

'Do not rape me.'

'No more talk of rape. Fever will awaken many terrors. Rest now.'

I will not judge. Not even this life of mine. I will not – there is weakness in the world. Of all sorts. All sorts . . .

Stepping outside with the now unconscious woman in his arms, Spinnock Durav looked round. Figures on all sides, both hooded and bareheaded in the rain, water streaming down.

'She is sick,' he said to them. 'She needs healing.'

No one spoke in reply.

He hesitated, then said, 'The Son of Darkness will be informed of your . . . difficulties.'

They began turning away, melting into the grey sheets. In moments Spinnock found himself alone.

He set out for the city.

The Son of Darkness will be informed . . . but he knows already, doesn't he? He knows, but leaves it all to . . . to whom? Me? Seerdomin? The Redeemer him-self?

'Give my regards to the priestess.'

Her, then, this frail thing in my arms. I will attend to her, because within her lies the answer.

Gods, the answer to what?

Boots uncertain in the slime and mud, he made his careful way back. Night awaited.

And, rising up from the depths of his memories, the fragment of some old poem, '*The moon does not rain, but it weeps.*' A fragment, yes, it must be that. Alas, he could not recall the rest and so he would have to settle with the phrase – although it truth it was anything but settling.

I could ask Endest – ah, no, he is gone from us for the time being. The High Priestess, perhaps. She knows every Tiste Andii poem ever written, for the sole purpose of sneering at every one of them. Still.

The words haunted him, mocked him with their ambiguity. He preferred things simple and straightforward. Solid like heroic sculpture – those marble and alabaster monuments to some great person who, if truth be known, was nowhere near as great as believed or proclaimed, and indeed looked nothing like the white polished face above the godlike body – *oh, Abyss take me, enough of this!*

In the camp, in the wake of the Tiste Andii's departure with the High Priestess half dead in his arms, the bald priest, short and bandy-legged and sodden under rain-soaked woollen robes, hobbled up to Gradithan. 'You saw?'

The ex-soldier grunted. 'I was tempted, you know. A sword point, right up back of his skull. Shit-spawned Tiste Andii bastard, what in Hood's name did he think, comin' here?'

The priest – a priest of some unknown god somewhere to the south, Bastion, perhaps – made tsk-tsking sounds, then said, 'The point is, Urdo—'

'Shut that mouth of yours! That rank ain't for nobody no more, you under-stand? Never mind the asshole thinkin' he's the only one left, so's he can use it like it was his damned name or something. Never mind, cos he'll pay for that soon enough.'

'Humble apologies, sir. My point was, she's gone now.'

'What of it?'

'She was the Redeemer's eyes – his ears, his everything in the mortal world – and now that Tiste Andii's gone and taken her away. Meaning we can do, er, as we please.'

At that, Gradithan slowly smiled. Then said in a low, easy voice, 'What've we been doin' up to now, Monkrat?'

'While she was here, the chance remained of awakening the Benighted to his holy role. Now we need not worry about either of them.'

'I was never worried in the first place,' the once-Seerdomin said in a half-snarl. 'Go crawl back into your hole, and take whatever boy with you as you fancy – like you say, nothing stopping us now.'

After the horrid creature scurried off, Gradithan gestured to one of his lieutenants. 'Follow that Andii pig back into Night,' he said. 'But keep your distance. Then get word to our friends in the city. It's all taken care of at the Barrow – that's the message you tell 'em, right? Go on and get back here before dawn and you can take your pick of the women – one you want to keep for a while if you care to, or strangle beneath you for all I give a shit. Go!'

He stood in the rain, feeling satisfied. Everything was looking up, and up. And by squinting, why, he could almost make out that cursed tower with its disgusting dragon edifice – aye, soon it would all come down. Nice and bloody, like.

And though he was not aware of it – not enough to find cause for the sudden shiver that took him – he turned away from that unseeing regard, and so unknowingly broke contact with sleepy, cold, reptilian eyes that could see far indeed, through rain, through smoke, through – if so desired – stone walls.

Carved edifice Silanah was not. Sleepless, all-seeing protector and sentinel, beloved of the Son of Darkness, and possessed of absolute, obsidian-sharp judgement, most assuredly she was all that. And terrible in wrath? Few mortals could even conceive the truth and the capacity of the implacably just.

Which was probably just as well.

'Mercy in compassion, no dragon lives.'

When skill with a sword was but passing, something else was needed. Rage. The curse was that rage broke its vessel, sent fissures through the brittle clay, sought out every weakness in the temper, the mica grit that only revealed itself in the edges of the broken shards. No repairs were possible, no glue creeping out when the fragments were pressed back together, to be wiped smooth with a fingertip.

Nimander was thinking about pottery. Web-slung amphorae clanking from the sides of the wagon, the horrid nectar within – a species of rage, perhaps, little different from what had coursed through his veins when he fought. Rage in battle was said to be a gift of the gods – he had heard that belief uttered by that Malazan marine, Deadsmell, down in the hold of the Adjunct's flagship, during one of those many nights when the man had made his way down into the dark belly, jug of rum swinging by an ear in one hand.

At first Nimander had resented the company – as much as did his kin – but the Malazan had persisted, like a sapper undermining walls. The rum had trickled down throats, loosened the hinges of tongues, and after a time all those fortifications and bastions had stretched open their doorways and portals.

The rum had lit a fire in Nimander's brain, casting flickering red light on a host of memories gathered ghostly round the unwelcoming hearth. There had been a keep, somewhere, a place of childhood secure and protected by the one they all called *Father*. Ridged spines of snow lining the cobbled track leading to the embrasure gate, a wind howling down from grey mountains – a momentary abode where scores of children scurried about wild as rats, with the tall figure of Anomander Rake wandering the corridors in godlike indifference.

What had there been before that? Where were all the mothers? That memory was lost, entirely lost.

There had been a priest, an ancient companion of the Son of Darkness, whose task it had been to keep the brood fed, clothed, and healthy. He had looked upon them all with eyes filled with dismay, no doubt understanding – long before any of them did – the future that waited them. Understanding well enough to with-hold his warmth – oh, he had been like an ogre to them all, certainly, but one who, for all his bluster, would never, ever do them harm.

Knowing this, they had abused their freedom often. They had, more than once, mocked that poor old man. They had rolled beakers into his path when he walked past, squealing with delight when his feet sent them flying to bounce and shatter, or, better yet, when he lost his balance and thumped down on his backside, wincing in pain.

Such a cruel fire, lighting up all these ghastly recollections. Deadsmell, in his sleepy, seemingly careless way, had drawn out their tale. From that keep hidden in the fastness of some remote range of mountains to the sudden, startling arrival of a stranger – the aged, stooped Tiste Andii who was, it was learned with a shock, Anomander's very own brother. And the arguments echoing from their father's private chambers, as brothers fought over unknown things – decisions past, decisions to come, the precise unfolding of crimes of the soul that led to harsh accusations and cold, cold silences.

Days later, peace was struck, somehow, in the dark of night. Their father came to them then, to tell them how Andarist was taking them all away. To an island, a place of warmth, of stretches of soft sand and pellucid waters, of trees crowded with fruit. And there, standing in the background during this imparting of a new future, was old Endest Silann, his face ravaged by some extremity of emotion – no more beakers underfoot, no more taunts and elusive imps racing to escape imagined pursuits (he never pursued, never once reached to snatch one of them, never raised a hand, never even raised his voice; he was nothing but a focus for their irreverence – an irreverence they would not dare turn upon their father). He had had his purpose and he had weathered it and now he wept as the children were drawn together and a warren was opened, a portalway into an unknown, mysterious new world where anything was possible.

Andarist led them through.

They would learn new things. The weapons awaiting them.

A stern teacher, not one to mock, oh no, that was quickly made clear when a casual cuff against the side of Skintick's head sent him flying – a cuff to answer some muttered derision, no doubt.

The games ended. The world turned suddenly serious.

They came to love that old man. Loved him far too much, as it turned out, for where Anomander might well have proved capable of pushing back the horrors of adulthood and its terrible world, Andarist was not.

Children made perfect soldiers, perfect killers. They had no sense of mortality. They did not fear death. They took bright pleasure in destruction, even when that destruction involved taking a life. They played with cruelty to watch the results. They understood the simplicity of power found there in the weapon held in the hand.

See a bored child with a stick – and see how every beast nearby flees, understanding well what is now possible and, indeed, probable. See the child, eyes scanning the ground, swinging the stick down to crush insects, to thrash flowers, to wage a war of mayhem. Replace the stick with a sword. Explain how guilt need not be considered when the ones who must die are the enemy.

Unleash them, these children with the avid eyes.

Good soldiers. Andarist had made them good soldiers. What child, after all, does not know rage?

But the vessel breaks.

The vessel breaks.

The Dying God, Nimander now believed, was a child. The mad priests poured him full, knowing the vessel leaked, and then drank of that puerile seepage. Because he was a child, the Dying God's thirst and need were without end, never satiated.

As they journeyed along the road, ever westward, they found themselves between planted fields. Here the scarecrows were truly dead, used up. Withered, webbed in black scraps of cloth, stiffly rocking in the wind. Poured out, these lives, and Nimander now saw these fields as bizarre cemeteries, where some local aberration of belief insisted that the dead be staked upright, that they ever stand ready for whatever may come.

Watchers of this road and all the fools who travelled it.

Once, on Drift Avalii, almost a year before the first attacks, two half-dead Dal Honese had washed up on the rocky coast. They had been paddling to the island of Geni, for reasons unexplained, in an ancient dugout. Both were naked, as they had used up every scrap of cloth from their garments to stuff into the cracks in the hull – too many cracks, it turned out, and the beleaguered craft eventually sank, forcing the two men to swim.

The Lord's nudge brought them to Drift Avalii, and somehow they avoided the murderous reefs and rocks girdling the island.

Dwellers in the dark jungles of their homeland, they were from a tribe obsessed with its own ancestors. The dead were not buried. The dead were made part of the mud walls of the village's huts. When one in a family died, a new room would be begun, at first nothing but a single wall projecting outward. And in that wall was the corpse, clay-filled eye sockets, nose, ears, mouth. Clay like a new skin upon face, limbs, torso. Upright, in cavorting poses as if frozen in a dance. Two more kin needed to die before the room was complete and ready to be roofed with palm fronds and the like.

Some houses were big as castles, sprawled out at ground level in a maze of chambers, hundreds of them, dark and airless. In this way, the dead never left. They remained, witnessing all, eternal in judgement – this pressure, said the two refugees, could drive one insane, and often did.

The jungle resisted farming. Its soil disliked taming. The huge trees were impervious to fire and could turn the edge of an iron axe. Villages were growing too massive, devouring land, while every cleared area around them was exhausted. Rival tribes suffered the same, and before too long wars were unleashed. The dead ancestors demanded vengeance for transgressions. Murdered kin – whose bodies had been stolen and so could not be properly taken care of – represented an open wound, a crime that needed answering.

Blood back and forth, said the two refugees. *Blood back and forth, that is all. And when the enemy began destroying villages, burning them to the ground . . .*

No answer to the madness but flight.

Nimander thought about all this as he led his mare by the reins along the dusty road. He had no ancestors to haunt him, no ancestors to demand that he do this and that, that he behave in this way but not in that way. Perhaps this was freedom, but it left him feeling strangely . . . lost.

The two Dal Honese had built a new boat and paddled away – not back home, but to some unknown place, a place devoid of unblinking ghosts staring out from every wall.

Rocking sounds came from the wagon and he turned to see Kallor swinging down on the near side, pausing to adjust his cloak of chain, then walking until he was alongside Nimander.

'Interesting use of corpses,' he said.

'What use would that be?' Skintick asked with a glance back towards them.

'To frighten the crows? Not that any right-minded crow would look twice at those foul plants – they're not even native to this world, after all.'

Nimander saw Skintick's brows rise. 'They aren't?'

Kallor scratched at his beard and, since it seemed he wasn't in any hurry to reply, Skintick faced forward once more.

'Saemankelyk,' said Nimander. 'The Dying God . . . who will be found in Bastion.'

The grey-haired warrior grunted. 'Nothing changes.'

'Of course it changes,' Skintick retorted without turning round. 'It keeps getting worse.'

'That is an illusion,' Kallor replied. 'You Tiste Andii should know that. Your sense of things getting worse comes from growing older. You see more, and what you see wars with your memories of how things used to be.'

'Rubbish. Old farts like you say that because it suits you. You hope it freezes us in our tracks so we end up doing nothing, which means your precious status quo persists just that much longer – enough for you to live out your life in whatever comfort you think you've earned. You won't accept culpability for anything, so you tell us that nothing ever changes.'

'Ah, the fire of youth. Perhaps one day, pup, you'll be old – assuming your stupidity doesn't get you killed first – and I'll find you, somewhere. You'll be sitting on the stone steps of some abandoned temple or, worse, some dead king's glorious monument. Watching the young people rush by. And I'll settle down beside you and ask you: "What's changed, old man?" And you will squint, chew your gums for a time, then spit on to the cobbles shaking your head.'

'Plan on living for ever, Kallor?'

'Yes, I do.'

'What if your stupidity gets you killed?'

Kallor's grin was feral. 'It hasn't yet.'

Skintick glanced back again, eyes bright, and all at once he laughed. 'I am changing my mind about you.'

'The Dying God has stolen Clip's soul,' Nimander said. 'We're going to get it back.'

'Good luck.'

'I suppose we will need it.'

'I'm not the kind who helps, Nimander,' Kallor said. 'Even kin of Rake. Maybe,' he added, 'especially kin of Rake.'

'What makes you think—'

The man interrupted with a snort. 'I see him in all of you – excepting the empty one you call Clip. You are heading to Coral. Or you were, before this detour was forced upon you. Tell me, what do you imagine will happen when you find your glorious patron? Will he reach out one perfect hand to brush your brows, to bless the gift of your existence? Will you thank him for the privilege of being alive?'

'What do you know about it?' Nimander demanded, feeling the heat rise to flush his face.

'Anomander Rake is a genius at beginning things. It's finishing them he has trouble with.'

Ah, that stings of truth. Kallor, you have just prodded my own soul. A trait I inherited from him, then? That makes too much sense. 'So, when I speak to him of you, Kallor, he will know your name?'

'Were we acquaintances? Yes, we were. Did we delight in each other's company? You will have to ask him that one. Caladan Brood was simpler, easier to manage. Nothing but earth and stone. As for K'azz, well, I'll know more when I finally meet the bastard.'

'I do not know those names,' Nimander said. 'Caladan Brood. K'azz.'

'It's of no real significance. We were allies in a war or three, that is all. And perhaps one day we will be allies once more, who can say? When some vast enemy forces us once again into the same camp, all on the same side.' He seemed to think about that for a moment, then said, 'Nothing changes.'

'Are you then returning to Coral – where waits our father?'

'No. The dust I kicked up last time will need a few centuries to settle, I expect.' He was about to add something more when his attention was pulled away, and he stepped across Nimander's path – forcing him to halt – to walk to the road's edge, facing north.

'I'd spotted that,' Skintick muttered, also stopping.

Fifty or so paces from the road, just beyond a strip of the alien plants and its row of wrapped effigies, was a ruin. Only one of the walls of the squarish, tower-like structure rose above man-height. The stones were enormous, fitted without mortar. Trees of a species Nimander had never seen before had rooted on top of the walls, snaking long, thick ropes down to the ground. The branches were skeletal, reaching horizontally out to the sides, clutching mere handfuls of dark, leathery leaves.

Nenanda had stopped the wagon and all were now studying the ruin that had so captured Kallor's attention.

'Looks old,' Skintick said, catching Nimander's eye and winking.

'Jaghut,' Kallor said. And he set out towards it. Nimander and Skintick followed.

In the field, the furrows of earth were bleached, dead, and so too the ghastly plants. Even the terrible clouds of insects had vanished.

Kallor stepped between two corpses, but there was not enough room so he reached out to either side and pushed the stakes over. Dust spat from the bases as the scarecrows sagged, then, pulling free, fell to the ground. The warrior continued on.

'We can hope,' said Skintick under his breath as he and Nimander followed through the gap.

'For what?' Nimander asked.

'That he decides he doesn't like this Dying God. And makes up his mind to do something about it.'

'You believe he is that formidable?'

Skintick shot him a glance. 'When he said he was allied with Anomander and those others, it didn't sound as though he meant he was a soldier or minor officer in some army, did it?'

Nimander frowned, then shook his head.

Skintick hissed wordlessly through his teeth, and then said, 'Like . . . equals.'

'Yes, like that. But it doesn't matter, Skin – he won't help us.'

'I wasn't hoping for that. More like him deciding to do something for his own reasons, but something that ends up solving our problem.'

'I'd wager no coins on that, Skin.'

Drawing closer to the ruin, they fell silent. Decrepit as it was, the tower was imposing. The air around it seemed grainy, somehow brittle, ominously cold despite the sun's fierce heat.

The highest of the walls revealed a section of ceiling just below the uppermost set of stones, projecting without any other obvious support to cast a deep shadow upon the ground floor beneath it. The facing wall reached only high enough to encompass a narrow, steeply arched doorway. Just outside this entrance and to one side was a belly-shaped pot in which grew a few straggly plants with drooping flowers, so incongruous amid the air of abandonment that Nimander simply stared down at them, disbelieving.

Kallor walked up to the entrance, drew off a scaled gauntlet and wrapped it against the root-tracked frame. 'Will you greet us?' he demanded in a loud voice.

From within a faint shuffling sound, and then a thin, rasping reply: 'Must I?'

'The ice is long gone, Jaghut. The plains beyond are dry and empty. Even the dust of the T'lan Imass has blown away. Would you know something of the world you have ignored for so long?'

'Why? Nothing changes.'

Kallor turned a pleased smirk upon Nimander and Skintick and then faced the dark doorway once more. 'Will you invite us in, Jaghut? I am the High—'

'I know who you are, O Lord of Futility. King of Ashes. Ruler of Dead Lands. Born to glory and cursed to destroy it every time. Killer of Dreams. Despoiler of—'

'All right, enough of all that. I'm not the one living in ruins.'

'No, but you ever leave them in your wake, Kallor. Come in, then, you and your two Others. I greet you as guests and so will not crush the life from you and devour your souls with peals of laughter. No, instead, I will make some tea.'

Nimander and Skintick followed Kallor into the darkness within.

The air of the two-walled chamber was frigid, the stones sheathed in amber-streaked hoarfrost. Where the other two walls should have been rose black, glimmering barriers of some unknown substance, and to look upon them too long was to feel vertiginous – Nimander almost pitched forward, drawn up only by Skintick's sudden grip, and his friend whispered, 'Never mind the ice, cousin.'

Ice, yes, it was just that. Astonishingly transparent ice—

A figure crouched at a small hearth, long-fingered hands working a blackened kettle on to an iron hook above the coals. 'I ate the last batch of cookies, I'm afraid.' The words drifted out inflectionless from beneath a broad-brimmed black felt hat. 'Most people pass by, when they pass by. Seeing nothing of interest. None draw close to admire my garden.'

'Your garden?' Skintick asked.

'Yes. Small, I know. Modest.'

'The pot with the two flowers.'

'Just so. Manageable – anything larger and the weeding would drive me mad, you see.'

'Taking up all your time,' Kallor commented, looking round.

'Just so.'

A long stone altar provided the Jaghut with his bed, on which pale furs were neatly folded. A desk sat nearby, the wood stained black, the chair before it high-backed and padded in deerskin. On a niche set in the highest wall squatted a three-legged silver candlestick, oxidized black. Beeswax candles flickered in guttered pools. Leaning near the altar was an enormous scabbarded greatsword, the cross-hilt as long as a child's arm. Cobwebs coated the weapon.

'You know my name,' Kallor said. 'But I have not yet heard yours.'

'That is true.'

Something dangerous edged into Kallor's voice as he said, 'I would know the name of my host.'

'Once, long ago, a wolf god came before me. Tell me, Kallor, do you understand the nature of beast gods? Of course not. You are only a beast in the unfairly pejorative sense – unfair to beasts, that is. How is it, then, that the most ancient gods of this world were, one and all, beasts?'

'The question does not interest me, Jaghut.'

'What of the answer?'

'You possess one?'

The hands reached out and lifted the kettle from the hook as steam rushed up round the long fingers. 'This must now steep for a time. Am I unusual in my penchant for evading such direct questions? A trait exclusive to Jaghut? Hardly. Knowledge may be free; my voice is not. I am a miser, alas, although I was not always this way.'

'Since I see little value in this particular matter,' said Kallor, 'I would not bargain with you.'

'Ah, and what of the Others with you? Might not they be interested?'

Clearing his throat, Skintick said, 'Venerable one, we possess nothing of worth to one such as you.'

'You are too modest, Tiste Andii.'

'I am?'

'Each creature is born from one not its kind. This is a wonder, a miracle forged in the fires of chaos, for chaos indeed whispers in our blood, no matter its particular hue. If I but scrape your skin, so lightly as to leave but a momentary streak, that which I take from you beneath my nail contains every truth of you, your life, even your death, assuming violence does not claim you. A code, if you will, seemingly precise and so very ordered. Yet chaos churns. For all your similarities to your father, neither you nor the one named Nimander – nor any of your brothers and sisters – is identical to Anomander Dragnipurake. Do you refute this?'

'Of course not—'

'For each kind of beast there is a first such beast, more different from its parents than the rest of its kin, from which a new breed in due course emerges. Is this firstborn then a god?'

'You spoke of a wolf god,' Skintick said. 'You began to tell us a story.'

'So I did. But you must be made to understand. It is a question of essences. To see a wolf and know it as pure, one must possess an image in oneself of a pure wolf, a perfect wolf.'

'Ridiculous,' Kallor grunted. 'See a strange beast and someone tells you it is a wolf – and from this one memory, and perhaps a few more to follow, you have fashioned your image of a wolf. In my empires, philosophers spewed such rubbish for centuries, until, of course, I grew tired of them and had them tortured and executed.'

A strange muffled noise came from the hunched-over Jaghut. Nimander saw the shoulders shaking and realized the ancient was laughing.

'I have killed a few Jaghut,' Kallor said; not a boast, simply a statement. A warning.

'The tea is ready,' the Jaghut said, pouring dark liquid into four clay cups that Nimander had not noticed before. 'You might wonder what I was doing when the wolf god found me. I was fleeing. In disguise. We had gathered to imprison a tyrant, until our allies turned upon us and resumed the slaughter. I believe I may be cursed to ever be in the wrong place at the wrong time.'

'T'lan Imass allies,' Kallor said. 'Too bad they never found you.'

'Kron, the clan of Bek'athana Ilk who dwelt in the Cliffs Above the Angry Sea. Forty-three hunters and a Bonecaster. They found me.'

Skintick squatted to pick up two of the cups, straightening to hand one to Nimander. The steam rising from the tea was heady, hinting of mint and cloves and something else. The taste numbed his tongue.

'Where is mine?' Kallor demanded. 'If I must listen to this creature I will drink his tea.'

Smiling, Skintick pointed down to where the cups waited on the ground.

Another soft laugh from the Jaghut. 'Raest was the name of the Tyrant we defeated. One of my more obnoxiously arrogant offspring. I did not mourn his fall. In any case, unlike Raest, I was never the strutting kind. It is a sign of weakness to shine blinding bright with one's own power. Pathetic diffidence. A need that undermines. I was more . . . secure.'

He had Kallor's attention now. 'You killed forty-three T'lan Imass and a bonecaster?'

'I killed them all.' The Jaghut sipped from his own cup. 'I have killed a few T'lan Imass,' he said, the intonation a perfect mimicry of Kallor's own claim a few moments past. 'Tell me, then, do you like my abode? My garden?'

'Solitude has driven you mad,' Kallor said.

'You would know all about that now, wouldn't you, O Lord of Failures? Partake of the tea, lest I take offence.'

Teeth bared, Kallor bent down to retrieve his cup.

The Jaghut's left hand shot out, closing about Kallor's wrist. 'You wounded that wolf god,' he said.

Nimander stared as he saw the old man struggle to twist free of that grip. Veins standing out on his temple, jaw muscles bunching beneath the beard. But there was no pulling loose. There was no movement at all from that withered, green hand.

'When you laid waste to your realm,' the Jaghut continued. 'You wounded it terribly.'

'Release me,' Kallor said in a rasp. And with his other hand he reached back for the grip of his sword.

All at once the Jaghut's hand fell away.

Kallor staggered back and Nimander saw a white impression of fingers encircling the old warrior's wrist. 'This is not how a host behaves. You force me to kill you.'

'Oh, be quiet, Kallor. This tower was an Azath once. Shall I awaken it for you?'

Wondering, Nimander watched as Kallor backed towards the entrance, eyes wide in that weathered, pallid face, the look of raw recognition dawning. 'Gothos, what are you doing here?'

'Where else should I be? Now remain outside – these two Tiste Andii must go away for a while.'

Heat was spreading fast, out from Nimander's stomach. He cast a wild look at Skintick, saw his friend sinking slowly to his knees. The empty cup in his hand fell away, rolled briefly on the damp ground. Nimander stared at the Jaghut. 'What have you done?'

'Only what was necessary.'

With a snarl Kallor spun round and stalked from the chamber. Over his shoulder he said, 'I will not wait long.'

Nimander's eyes were drawn once more to the walls of ice. Black depths, shapes moving within. He staggered, reached out his hands—

'Oh, don't step in there—'

And then he was falling forward, his hands passing into the wall before him, no resistance at all.

'Nimander, do not—'

Blackness.

Desra wandered round the wagon, drawing up to halt beside the ox. She set a hand on its back, felt the beast's heat, the rippling with every twitch shedding the biting flies. She looked down into the animal's eye, saw with a start how delicate its lashes. *'You must take the world as it is.'* Andarist's last words to her, before the world took him.

It wasn't hard. People either had strength or they didn't. The weak ones left her disgusted, welling with dark contempt. If they chose at all it was ever the wrong choice. They let the world break them time and again, then wondered – dull-eyed as this ox – why it was so cruel. But it wasn't the world that was the problem, was it? It was stepping into the stampede's path over and over again. It was learning nothing from anything. *Nothing.*

There were more weak people than strong ones. The weak were legion. Some just weren't smart enough to cope with anything beyond meeting immediate needs: the field to sow, the harvest to bring on to the threshing floor, the beasts of burden to feed. The child to raise, the coin for the next jug of ale, the next knuckle bag of d'bayang. They didn't see beyond the horizon. They didn't even see the next valley over. The world outside was where things came from, things that caused trouble, that jarred the proper order of life. They weren't interested in thinking. Depths were frightening, long roads a journey without purpose where one could end up lost, curling up to die in the ditch.

She had seen so many of the weak ones. They died unjustly in their thousands. Tens of thousands. They died because they worshipped ignorance and believed this blind god could make them safe.

Among the strong, only a few were worth paying attention to. Most were bullies. Their threats were physical or they were emotional, but the effect was the same – to make the victim feel weak. And it was the self-appointed task of these bullies to convince as many people as possible that they were inherently weak, and their lives ones of pathetic misery. Once this was done, the bully would then say: *do as I say and I will keep you safe. I will be your strength . . . unless you anger me. If you anger me I will terrorize you. I might even kill you.* There were plenty of these bastards, pig-eyed and blustery little boys in big bodies. Or fish-eyed nasty bitches – although these ones, after proving to their victims how weak they were, would then lap up all the spilled blood. Delicate tongues flicking in and out. You had the physical bullies and the emotional bullies, and they both revelled in destroying lives.

No, she had no time for them. But there were others whose strength was of a much rarer kind. Not easy to find, because they revealed nothing. They were quiet. They often believed themselves to be much weaker than they were. But when pushed too hard, they surprised themselves, finding that they would not back away another step, that a wall had risen in their souls, unyielding, a barrier that could not be passed. To find one such as this was the most precious of discoveries.

Desra had played the bully more than once, as much from boredom as from anything else. She'd lapped up her share of blood.

She might well do the same with this one named Clip – if he ever returned to them, and there was no guarantee of that. Yes, she would use him and people like him, who imagined themselves strong but were, in truth, weak – or so she would prove, eventually. Certainly, their blood didn't taste any purer, any sweeter.

She had made her discovery, after all, of one whose strength was absolute. Before whom she herself felt weak but in a most pleasant, most satisfying way – one to whom she might surrender whatever she chose without fearing he would one day use it against her. Not this one.

Not Nimander Golit.

Desra saw Kallor emerge from the ruin, his agitation plain to see. Armour rustling, he marched between the scarecrows and up on to the road. Reaching the wagon, he pulled himself up with a worn boot on a wooden spoke, then paused to stare down at Clip. 'You should throw this fool away,' he said to Aranatha, who sat holding a thin cloth stretched out over the unconscious figure.

She smiled in answer and said nothing.

Desra frowned at Kallor. 'Where are the others?'

'Yes,' he replied with a sneer, 'the *others*.'

'Well?'

He lifted himself over the slats. 'The Jaghut decided to use them – unfortunately for them.'

Use?

Nenanda swung round from where he sat on the bench. 'What Jaghut?' he demanded.

But Desra was already turning away, rushing down through the ditch and on to the withered field. Between the toppled scarecrows—

So who is this Dying God?

Skintick, who knew himself well, who knew that his imagination was the deadliest weapon he used against himself, who knew how, in any situation, he might laugh – a plunge into the depths of absurdity, a desperate attempt to save his sanity – now found himself awakening on a dusty platform, no more than twelve paces across, of limestone. It was surrounded by olive trees, a grove of ancient twisted boles and dark leathery leaves, the fruit clustered in abundance. A warm wind slid over his naked form, making the sun's heat – at least to begin with – less oppressive than it should have been. The air smelled of salt.

The stumps of columns encircled the platform. They had been painted the deep hue of wine, but that had begun to flake away, exposing raw yellow rock.

Who is this Dying God?

His head aching, Skintick slowly sat up, shielding his eyes from the glare, but the sun's light rebounded from the stone and there was no relief. Groaning, he pushed himself to his feet, stood tottering. Gods, the pain in his head! Pulsing, exploding in blinding flashes behind his eyes.

Who is this Dying—

There were corpses huddled beneath the trees – mostly bones and rotted cloth, tufts of hair, skin-stretched skulls. Once brightly coloured clothes, strange shoes, the glitter of buttons and jewellery, gold on bared teeth.

The sun felt . . . *evil*. As if its heat, its light, was somehow killing him, lancing through his flesh, tearing through his brain. He was growing ever sicker.

There was, he suddenly understood, no one left alive on this world. Even the trees were dying. The oceans were burning away and death was everywhere. It could not be escaped. The sun had become a murderer.

Who is this—

You could dream of the future. You could see it as but a recognizable continuation of what can be seen around you at this moment. See it as progress, a driven force with blinding glory at the very end. Or each moment as the pinnacle, at least until the next higher peak resolved itself. A farmer sows to feed the vision of fruition, of abundance, and the comfort that comes with a predictable universe reduced to this upcoming season. Drip libations to remind the gods that order exists.

You could dream of, at least, a place for your son, your daughter. Who would wish to deliver a child into a world of mayhem, of inescapable annihilation? And did it matter if death arrived as a force beyond the control of anyone, or as the logical consequence of wilful stupidity? No it did not, when there was no one left to ponder such questions.

Fury and folly. Someone here had played the ultimate practical joke. Seeded a world with life, witnessed its burgeoning, and then nudged the sun to anger. Into a deadly storm, a momentary cough of poison light, and the season of life ended. Just so.

Who is—

The god dies when the last believer dies. Rising up bloated and white, sinking down into unseen depths. Crumbling into dust. Expelled in a gust of hot wind.

Venomous spears lanced through Skintick's brain, shearing through every last tether that remained. And suddenly he was free, launching skyward. Free, yes, because nothing mattered any more. The hoarders of wealth, the slayers of children, the rapists of the innocent, all gone. The decriers of injustice, the addicts of victimization, the endlessly offended, gone.

Nothing was fair. *Nothing. And that is why you are dying, dear god. That is why. How can you do anything else? The sun rages!*

Meaningless!

We all die. Meaningless!

Who—

A hard slap and he was jolted awake. A seamed, tusked face hovered over him. Vertical pupils set in grey, the whites barely visible. *Like a damned goat.*

'You,' the Jaghut said, 'are a bad choice for this. Answering despair with laughter like that.'

Skintick stared up at the creature. He couldn't think of anything to say.

'There is a last moment,' Gothos continued, 'when every sentient creature alive realizes that it's over, that not enough was done, that hindsight doesn't survive dying. Not enough was done – you Tiste Andii understood that. Anomander Rake did. He realized that to dwell in but one world was madness. To survive, you must spread like vermin. Rake tore his people loose from their complacency. And for this he was cursed.'

'I saw – I saw a world dying.'

'If that is what you saw, then so it is. Somewhere, somewhen. On the paths of the Azath, a distant world slides into oblivion. Potential snuffed out. What did you feel, Skintick?'

'I felt . . . free.'

The Jaghut straightened. 'As I said, a bad choice.'

'Where – where is Nimander?'

Sounds at the doorway—

Desra rushed into the chamber. She saw Skintick, saw him slowly sitting up. She saw what must be the Jaghut, the hood drawn back to reveal that greenish, unhuman visage, the hairless pate so mottled it might have been a mariner's map of islands, a tortured coastline, reefs. He stood tall in his woollen robes.

But nowhere could she find Nimander.

The Jaghut's eyes fixed on her for a moment, and then he faced one of the walls of ice.

She followed that gaze.

Staggering into darkness he was struck countless times. Fists pounded, fingers raked ragged furrows through his skin. Hands closed about his limbs and pulled.

'This one is mine!'

'No, mine!'

All at once voices cried out on all sides and a hand closed about Nimander's waist, plucked him into the air. The giant figure carrying him ran, feet thumping like thunder, up a steep slope, rocks scurrying down, first a trickle, then a roar of cascading stones, with screams in their wake.

Choking dust blinded him.

A sharp-edged crest crunching underfoot, and then a sudden even steeper descent, down into a caldera. Grey clouds rising in plumes, sudden coruscating heat foul with gases that stung his eyes, burned in his throat.

He was flung on to hot ash.

The giant creature loomed over him.

Through tears Nimander looked up, saw a strangely child-like face peering down. The forehead sloped back behind an undulating brow-ridge from which the eyebrows streamed down in thick snarls of pale, almost white hair. Round, smooth cheeks, thick lips, a pug nose, a pale bulging wattle beneath the rounded chin. Its skin was bright yellow, its eyes emerald green.

It spoke in the language of the Tiste Andii. 'I am like you. I too do not belong here.'

The voice was soft, a child's voice. The giant slowly blinked, and then smiled, revealing a row of daggerlike fangs.

Nimander struggled to speak. 'Where – who – all those people . . .'

'Spirits. Trapped like ants in amber. But it is not amber. It is the blood of dragons.'

'Are you a spirit?'

The huge head shook in a negative. 'I am an Elder, and I am lost.'

'Elder.' Nimander frowned. 'You call yourself that. Why?'

A shrug like hills in motion. 'The spirits have so named me.'

'How did you come to be here?'

'I don't know. I am lost, you see.'

'And before this place?'

'Somewhere else. I built things. Of stone. But each house I built then vanished – I know not where. It was most . . . frustrating.'

'Do you have a name?'

'Elder?'

'Nothing else?'

'Sometimes, I would carve the stone. To make it look like wood. Or bone. I remember . . . sunsets. Different suns, each night, different suns. Sometimes two. Sometimes three, one fierce, the others like children. I would build another house, if I could. I think, if I could do that, I would stop being lost.'

Nimander sat up. He was covered in volcanic dust, so fine it shed from him like liquid. 'Build your house, then.'

'Whenever I begin, the spirits attack me. Hundreds, then thousands. Too many.'

'I stepped through a wall of ice.' The memory was suddenly strong. 'Omtose Phellack—'

'Oh, ice is like blood and blood is like ice. There are many ways in. None out.

You do not belong here because you are not yet dead. You are lost, like me. We should be friends, I think.'

'I can't stay—'

'I am sorry.'

Panic seethed to life in Nimander. He stood, sinking to his shins in the hot ash. 'I can't – Gothos. Find me. *Gothos!*'

'I remember Gothos.' A terrible frown lowered the Elder's brows. 'He would appear, just before the last stone was set. He would look upon my house and pronounce it adequate. Adequate! Oh, how I hated that word! My sweat, my blood, and he called them adequate! And then he would walk inside and close the door, and I would place the last stone, and the house would vanish! I don't think I like Gothos.'

'I don't blame you,' Nimander said, unwilling to voice his suspicion that Gothos's arrival and the vanishing of the houses were in fact connected; that indeed the Jaghut came to *collect* them. *This Elder builds the Houses of the Azath.*

And he is lost.

'Tell me,' Nimander said, 'do you think there are others like you? Others, out there, building houses?'

'I don't know.'

Nimander looked round. The jagged walls of the cone enclosed the space. Enormous chunks of pumice and obsidian lay half buried in the grey dust. 'Elder, do the spirits ever assail you here?'

'In my pit? No, they cannot climb the sides.'

'Build your house here.'

'But—'

'Use the rim as your foundation.'

'But houses have corners!'

'Make it a tower.'

'A house . . . within the blood of dragons? But there are no sunsets.'

A house within the blood of dragons. What would happen? What would change? Why do the spirits deny him this? 'If you are tired of being lost,' Nimander said, 'build a house. But before you are done, before you set that last stone, walk into it.' He paused and looked round, then grunted a laugh. 'You won't have any choice; you will be building the thing from the inside out.'

'But then who will finish it?'

Nimander looked away. He was trapped here, possibly for ever. If he did as Gothos did, if he remained inside the house to await its completion, he might find a way out. He might walk those hidden pathways. And in so doing, he would doom this creature to eternity here. This child, this mason.

And that I cannot do. I am not like Gothos. I am not that cruel.

He heard laughter in his head. Phaed, shrieking with laughter. Then she said, *'Don't be an idiot. Take the way out. Leave this fool to his building blocks! He's pathetic!'*

'I will set the last stone,' Nimander said. 'Just make sure it's small enough for me to lift and push into place.' And he looked up, and he saw that the giant was smiling, and no, it no longer looked like a child, and in its eyes something shone and its light flowed down, bathed Nimander.

'I am different,' the Elder said in a deep, warm voice, *'when I build.'*

'Get him out,' Desra said.

'I cannot.'

'Why?'

The Jaghut blinked like a lizard. 'I don't know how. The gate is Omtose Phellack, but the realm beyond is something else, something I want nothing to do with.'

'But you made this gate – and gates open from both sides.'

'I doubt he could ever find it,' the Jaghut said. 'Even assuming anyone lets him get close.'

'Anyone? Who's in there with him?'

'A few million miserable wretches.'

Desra glared at Skintick. 'How could you let this happen?'

He was weeping and could only shake his head.

'Do not blame this one,' the Jaghut said. 'Do not blame anyone. Accidents happen.'

'You drugged us,' Skintick suddenly accused him, his voice harsh with grief.

'Alas, I did. And I had my reasons for doing so . . . which seem to have failed. Therefore I must be more . . . direct, and oh how I dislike being direct. When next you see Anomander, tell him this from me: he chose wisely. Each time, he chose wisely. Tell him, then, that of all whom I ever met, there is but one who has earned my respect, and he is that one.'

A sudden sob from Skintick.

Desra felt strangely shaken by the Jaghut's words.

'And,' the Jaghut then added, 'for you. Do not trust Kallor.'

Feeling helpless, useless, she stepped closer to the wall of ice, squinted into its dark depths.

'Careful, woman. That blood pulls hard on you Tiste.'

And yes, she could feel that, but it was nothing to trust, nothing to even pay attention to – it was the lie she had always known, the lie of something better just ahead, of all the questions answered, just ahead. *Another step, one more. One more.* Time's dialogue with the living, and time was a deceitful creature, a liar. Time promised everything and delivered nothing.

She stared into the darkness, and thought she saw movement, deep, deep within.

'No Jaghut is to be trusted,' Kallor said, glaring at the lowering sun. 'Especially not Gothos.'

Aranatha studied the ancient warrior with an unwavering gaze, and though he would not meet her sister's eyes, it was clear to Kedeviss that Kallor felt himself under siege. A woman's attention, devastating barrage of inexorable calculation – even a warrior flinched back.

But these were momentary distractions, she knew. Something had happened. Desra had rushed into the ruin and not returned. Nenanda stood fidgeting, eyes on the crumbled edifice.

'Some gods are born to suffer,' Kallor said. 'You'd be better off heading straight to Coral. Unleash Anomander Rake against that Dying God, if getting this Clip back is so important to you. At the very least you'll have your vengeance.'

'And is vengeance so important?' Kedeviss asked.

'Often it's all there is,' Kallor replied, still squinting westward.

'Is that why they're after you?'

He turned, studied her. 'And who would be after me?'

'Someone. That much seems obvious. Am I wrong?'

Aranatha spoke from the wagon, 'You are not, sister. But then, he has always been hunted. You can see it in his eyes.'

'Be glad that you remain marginally useful to me,' Kallor said, turning away once more.

Kedeviss saw Nenanda glaring at the warrior's back.

How much time had passed? Days, perhaps weeks. Nimander stood, watching the mason build his tower. Shaping stone with fists, with round hammerstones found somewhere, with leather-wrapped wooden mallets to edge the pumice facing he had decided to add to 'lighten the walls'.

To accommodate the giant, the tower needed to be huge, four storeys or more to the ceiling. '*Made with the blood of dragons, the glass of what flowed, the pumice of what foamed with dying breaths. A tower, yes, but also a monument, a grave marker. What will come of this? I know not. You were clever, Nimander, with this idea. Too clever to stay here. You must leave, when the tower vanishes, you must be within it. I will stay.*'

They repeated that argument again and again, and each time Nimander prevailed, not through brilliant reasoning, not through appealing to the Elder's selfish desires (because it turned out he didn't have any), but only through his refusal to surrender.

He had nothing awaiting him, after all. Nenanda could lead the others through – he was finding his own kind of wisdom, his restraint, and with Skintick and Kedeviss to guide him, he would do well. Until such time as they reached Coral.

Nimander had lost too many battles – he could see that in himself. Could feel every scar, still fresh, still wounding. This place would give him time to heal, if such a thing were possible. How long? *Why not eternity?*

A chorus of wails surrounded them, an army of spirits grovelling in the ash and dust at the base of the volcanic cone. Bemoaning the end of the world – as if this world suited them just fine, when clearly it didn't, when each one dreamed of reclaiming flesh and bone, blood and breath. They sought to assail the slope but somehow failed again and again.

Nimander helped when he could, carrying tools here and there, but mostly he sat in the soft dust, seeing nothing, hearing only the cries from beyond the tower's growing wall, feeling neither thirst nor hunger, slowly emptying of desire, ambition, everything that might once have mattered.

Around him the darkness deepened, until the only light came from some preternatural glow from the pumice. The world closing in . . .

Until—

'One stone remains. This stone. The base of this low window, Nimander, within your reach. I will help you climb outside – then push the stone through, like this – but tell me, please, why can we not both leave here? I am within the tower. So are you. If I set the stone—'

'Elder,' cut in Nimander. 'You are almost done here. Where is Gothos?'

A look of surprise. 'I don't know.'

'He does not dare this realm, I think.'

'Perhaps that is true.'

'I don't even know if this will work – if it will create for you a way out.'

'I understand, Nimander. Remain inside with me. Let me set this stone.'

'I don't know where this tower will take you,' Nimander replied. 'Back to your realm, wherever that is, perhaps – but not my home. Nothing I know. Besides, you carved this to be pushed into place from outside – the angles—'

'I can reshape it, Nimander.'

I cannot go with you. 'In finding out where you are, Elder, I become lost. You are the mason, the maker of the houses. It is your task. You do not belong here.'

'Nor do you.'

'Don't I? There are Tiste Andii spirits out there. And Tiste Edur. Even Liosan. The ones who fell in the first wars, when dragons burst through every gate to slay, to die. Listen to them out there! They have made peace with one another – a miracle, and one I would be happy to share.'

'You are not a ghost. They will take you. They will fight over you, a beginning of a new war, Nimander. They will tear you to pieces.'

'No, I will reason with them—'

'You cannot.'

Despair stirred awake in Nimander, as he saw the truth of the Elder's words. Even here, he was not welcome. Even here he would bring destruction. *Yet, when they tear me limb from limb, I will die. I will become just like them. A short war.* 'Help me through the window,' he said, pulling himself up on to the rough ledge.

'As you wish. I understand, Nimander.'

Yes, perhaps you do.

'Nimander.'

'Yes?'

'Thank you. For this gift of creation.'

'Next time you meet Gothos,' Nimander said as his friend pushed him through the portal, 'punch him in the face for me, will you?'

'Yes, another good idea. I will miss you. You and your good ideas.'

He fell through on to a thick powdery slope, hastily reaching up to grip the window's edge to keep from sliding. Behind and below voices cried out in sudden hunger. He could feel their will churning up to engulf him.

A heavy scrape from the window and out came the final stone, end first, grinding as it was forced through. Catching Nimander by surprise. The weight pushed against his fingers where he held tight and he swore in pain as the tips were crushed, pinned – tearing one hand free left nails behind, droplets of blood spattering. He scrabbled for another handhold, then, voicing a scream, he tore loose his other arm.

Gods, how was he going to manage this? With two mangled hands, with no firm footing, with a mob surging frantic up the slope behind him?

Inexorable, the stone ground its way out. He brought a shoulder beneath it, felt the massive weight settling. His arms began to tremble.

Far enough now, yes, and he reached with one hand, began pushing to one side the nearest end of the blood-slick chunk of obsidian. He could see the clever angles now, the planes and how everything would somehow, seemingly impossibly, slide into perfect position. Push, some more – not much – almost in place—

Thousands, hundreds of thousands – a storm of voices, screams of desperation, of dismay, of terrible horror – *too much! Please, stop! Stop!*

He was weakening – he would not make it – he could not hold on any longer – with a sob he released his grip and in the last moment, tottering, he pushed with both hands, setting the stone – and then he was falling back, down, swallowed in cascading ash, stones, scouring chunks of rough pumice. Down the slope he tumbled, buried beneath ever more rubble. Hot. Suffocating. Blind. Drowning – and one flailing hand was grasped, hard, by one and then two hands – small – a woman's hands.

His shoulder flared in pain as that grip tightened, pulled him round. The collapsing hillside tugged at him, eager to take him – he understood its need, he sympathized, yes, and wanted to relent, to let go, to vanish in the crushing darkness.

The hands dragged him free. Dragged him by one bloody arm. The storm of voices raged anew, closer now and closing fast. Cold fingertips scrabbled against his boots, nails clawing at his ankles and oh he didn't care, let them take him, let them—

He tumbled down on to damp earth. Gloom, silence but for harsh breaths, a surprised grunt from nearby.

Rolling on to his back, coughing through a mouth caked in ash. Eyes burning—

Desra knelt over him, her head down, her face twisted in pain as she held her arms like two broken wings in her lap. Skintick, rushing close to crouch beside him.

'I thought – she—'

'How long?' Nimander demanded. 'How could you have waited so long? Clip—'

'What? It's been but moments, Nimander. Desra – she came in, she saw into the ice – saw you—'

Fire burned his fingers, flicked flames up his hands and into his wrists, sizzling fierce along the bones. Fresh blood dripped from dust-caked wounds where nails had been. 'Desra,' he moaned. 'Why?'

She looked up, fixed him with hard eyes. 'We're not finished with you yet, Nimander,' she said in a rasp. 'Oh no, not yet.'

'You damned fool,' Gothos said. 'I was saving that one for later. And now he's free.'

Nimander twisted round. 'You cannot just *collect* people! Like shiny stones!'

'Why not? My point is, I needed that one. There is now an Azath in the blood of dragons—'

'The spilled blood – the blood of dead dragons—'

'And you think the distinction is important? Oh, me and my endless folly!' With sharp gestures he raised his hood once more, then turned to settle down on a stool, facing the hearth, his position a perfect match to the moment Nimander, Skintick and Kallor had first entered this place. 'You idiot, Nimander. Dragons don't play games. Do you understand me? *Dragons play no games.* Ah, I despair, or I would if I cared enough. No, instead, I will make some ashcakes. Which I will not share.'

'It's time to leave,' Skintick said.

Yes, that much was obvious.

'They're coming now,' Kallor said.

Kedeviss looked but could not see any movement in the gloom of the ruin's entrance.

'It's too late to travel – we'll have to camp here. Make us a fine meal, Aranatha. Nenanda, build a fire. A house of sticks to set aflame – that'll make Gothos wince, I hope. Yes, entice him out here tonight, so that I can kill him.'

'You can't kill him,' Aranatha said, straightening in the wagon bed.

'Oh, and why not?'

'I need to talk to him.'

Kedeviss watched her kin descend from the wagon, adjust her robes, then stride towards the ruin – where Skintick had appeared, helping Nimander, whose hands were dark with blood. Behind them, Desra.

'That bitch sister of yours is uncanny,' Kallor said in a growl.

Kedeviss saw no need to comment on that.

'She speaks with Gothos – why? What could they possibly say to each other?'

Shrugging, Kedeviss turned away. 'I think I will do the cooking tonight,' she said.

Dying, the Captain stared across at the giant warrior with the shattered face. Woven carpets beneath each of them, the one on which sat the Captain now sodden with blood – blood that seemed to flow for ever, as if his body was but a valve, broken, jammed open, and out it came, trickling down from wounds that would never close. He was, he realized, back where he began. Opulence surrounded him this time, rather than grit and mud and dust on the edge of a dried riverbed, but did that make any real difference? Clearly it didn't.

Only the dying could laugh at that truth. There were many things, he now understood, to which only the dying could respond with honest mirth. Like this nemesis warrior sitting cross-legged, hunched and glowering opposite him.

A small brazier smouldered between them, perched on three legs. On the coals rested a squat kettle, and the spiced wine within steamed to sweeten the air of the chamber.

'You shall have to knock out some of the inner walls,' the captain said. 'Have the slaves make you a new bed, one long enough, and other furniture besides.'

'You are not listening,' the giant said. 'I lose my temper when people do not listen.'

'You are my heir—'

'No. I am not. Slavery is an abomination. Slavery is what people who hate do to others. They hate themselves. They hate in order to make themselves different, better. You. You told yourself you had the right to own other people. You told yourself they were less than you, and you thought shackles could prove it.'

'I loved my slaves. I took care of them.'

'There is plenty of room for guilt in the heart of hate,' the warrior replied.

'This is my gift—'

'Everyone seeks to give me gifts. I reject them all. You believe yours is wondrous. Generous. You are nothing. Your empire is pathetic. I knew village dogs who were greater tyrants than you.'

'Why do you torment me with such words? I am dying. You have killed me. And yet I do not despise you for that. No, I make you my heir. I give you my kingdom. My army will take your commands. Everything is yours now.'

'I don't want it.'

'If you do not take it, one of my officers will.'

'This kingdom cannot exist without the slaves. Your army will become nothing more than one more band of raiders, and so someone will hunt them down and destroy them. And all you sought to build will be forgotten.'

'You torment me.'

'I tell you the truth. Let your officers come to kill me. I will destroy them all. And I will scatter your army. Blood to the grass.'

The Captain stared at this monster, and knew he could do nothing. He was sinking back against his heap of pillows, every breath shallower than the last. Swathed in robes and furs, he was none the less cold. 'You could have lied,' he whispered.

The man's last words. Karsa studied the dead face for a moment longer. Then he thumped against the panel door to his left.

It opened a crack.

'Everyone leave this carriage,' Karsa commanded. 'Take whatever you want – but you do not have much time.'

Then he settled back once more. Scanned the remnants of the lavish feast he had devoured – while the Captain had simply watched, smug as a rich father even as he died. But Karsa was not his son. Not his heir, no matter what the fool desired. He was Toblakai. A Teblor, and far to the north waited his people.

Was he ready for them?

He was.

Would they be ready for him? Probably not.

A long walk awaited him – there was not a single horse in this paltry kingdom that could accommodate him. He thought back to his youth, to those bright days of hard drama, crowded with omens, when every blade of grass was saturated with significance – but it was the young mind that fashioned such things. Not yet bleached by the sun, not yet worn down by the wind. Vistas were to be crossed. Foes were to be vanquished with harsh barks of fierce triumph, blood spraying in the air.

Once, long ago it seemed now, he had set out to find glory, only to discover that it was nothing like what he had imagined it to be. It was a brutal truth that his companions then had understood so much better than he had, despite his being War Leader. Nevertheless, they had let themselves be pulled into his wake, and for this they had died. The power of Karsa's own will had overwhelmed them. What could be learned from that?

Followers will follow, even unto their own deaths. There was a flaw to such people – the willingness to override one's own instinct for self-preservation. And this flaw invited exploitation, perhaps even *required* it. Confusion and uncertainty surrendered to simplicity, so comforting, so deadly.

Without followers this Captain would have achieved nothing. The same the world over. Wars would disintegrate into the chaos of raids, skirmishes, massacres of the innocent, the vendetta of blood-feuds, and little else. Monuments would never be raised. No temples, no streets and roads, no cities. No ships, no bridges. Every patch of ploughed land would shrink to what a few could manage. Without followers, civilization would never have been born.

He would tell his people all this. He would make them not his followers, but his companions. And together they would bring civilization to ruin, whenever and wherever they found it. Because, for all the good it created, its sole purpose was to breed followers – enough to heave into motion forces of destruction, spreading a tide of blood at the whim of those few cynical tyrants born to lead. Lead, yes, with lies, with iron words – *duty, honour, patriotism, freedom* – that fed the wilfully stupid with grand purpose, with reason for misery and delivering misery in kind.

He had seen the enemy's face, its twin masks of abject self-sacrifice and cold-eyed command. He had seen leaders feed on the flesh of the bravely fallen. *And this is not the Teblor way. It shall not be my way.*

The sounds of looting from the rooms around him were gone now. Silence on all sides. Karsa reached down and used a hook to lift the kettle from the coals and set it down on the small table amidst the foodstuffs, the silver plates and the polished goblets.

Then he kicked the brazier over, scattering coals on to the beautifully woven carpets, into the silks and woollen blankets, the furs. He waited to see flames ignite.

When the first ones began, Karsa Orlong rose and, hunched over to clear the panel door, he made his way out.

Darkness in the world beyond the camp's cookfires. A mad profusion of stars overhead. Arrayed in a vast semicircle facing the enormous carriage was the kingdom of the Captain. Karsa Orlong stood in front of the throne on the balcony.

'The slaves are free,' he said in a loud voice that carried to everyone. 'The officers will divide the loot, the horses and all the rest – an equal share for all, slaves and free, soldier and crafter. Cheat anyone and I will kill you.'

Behind him on the carriage, flames licked out from the countless windows and vents. Black smoke rose in a thickening column. He could feel the heat gusting against his back.

'Come the dawn,' he said, 'everyone will leave. Go home. Those without a home – go find one. And know that the time I give you now is all that you will ever have. For when next you see me, when you are hiding there in your cities, I will come as a destroyer. Five years or twenty – it is what you have, what I give you. Use it well. All of you, *live well*.'

And that such a farewell should be received, not as a benediction, but as a threat, marked well how these people understood Karsa Orlong – who came from the north, immune to all weapons. Who slew the Captain without even touching him. Who freed the slaves and scattered the knights of the realm with not a single clash of swords.

The god of the Broken Face came among them, as each would tell others for the years left to them. And, so telling, with eyes wide and licking dry lips, they would reach in haste for the tankard and its nectar of forgetfulness.

Some, you cannot kill. Some are deliverers of death and judgement. Some, in wishing you a full life, promise you death. There is no lie in that promise, for does not death come to us all? And yet, how rare the one to say so. No sweet euphemism, no quaint colloquialism. No metaphor, no analogy. There is but one true poet in the world, and he speaks the truth.

Flee, my friends, but there is nowhere to hide. Nowhere at all.

See your fate, there in his Broken Face.

See it well.

Horses drawn to a halt on a low hilltop, grasses whispering unseen on all sides.

'I once led armies,' Traveller said. 'I was once the will of the Emperor of Malaz.'

Samar Dev tasted bitterness and leaned to one side and spat.

The man beside her grunted, as if acknowledging the gesture as commentary. 'We served death, of course, in all that we did. For all our claims otherwise.

Imposing peace, ending stupid feuds and tribal rivalries. Opening roads to merchants without fear of banditry. Coin flowed like blood in veins, such was the gift of those roads and the peace we enforced. And yet, behind it all, *he* waited.'

'All hail civilization,' Samar Dev said. 'Like a beacon in the dark wilderness.'

'With a cold smile,' Traveller continued, as if not hearing her, 'he waits. Where all the roads converge, where every path ends. He waits.'

A dozen heartbeats passed, with nothing more said.

To the north something burned, lancing bright orange flames into the sky, lighting the bellies of churning clouds of black smoke. *Like a beacon . . .*

'What burns?' Traveller wondered.

Samar Dev spat again. She just couldn't get that foul taste out of her mouth. 'Karsa Orlong,' she replied. 'Karsa Orlong burns, Traveller. Because that is what he does.'

'I do not understand you.'

'It's a pyre,' she said. 'And he does not grieve. The Skathandi are no more.'

'When you speak of Karsa Orlong,' Traveller said, 'I am frightened.'

She nodded at that admission – a response he probably could not even see. The man beside her was an honest one. In many ways as honest as Karsa Orlong.

And on the morrow these two would meet.

Samar Dev well understood Traveller's fear.

Chapter Nine

The bulls ever walk alone to the solitude
Of their selves
Swaggering in their coats of sweaty felt
Every vein swollen
Defiant and proud in their beastly need
Thunderous in step
Make way make way the spurting swords
Slay damsel hearts
Cloven the cut gaping wide – so tender an attitude!
And we must swoon
Before red-rimmed eyes you'll find no guilt
In the self so proven
And the fiery charge of most fertile seed
Sings like gods' rain
Make way make way another bold word
The dancer's sure to misstep
In the rushing drums of the multitude

Dandies of the Promenade
Seglora

Expectation is the hoary curse of humanity. One can listen to words, and see them as the unfolding of a petal or, indeed, the very opposite: each word bent and pushed tighter, smaller, until the very packet of meaning vanishes with a flip of deft fingers. Poets and tellers of tales can be tugged by either current, into the riotous conflagration of beauteous language or the pithy reduction of the tersely colourless.

As with art, so too with life. See a man without fingers standing at the back of his house. He is grainy with sleep that yields no rest, no relief from a burdensome world (and all that), and his eyes are strangely blank and might be shuttered too as he stares out on the huddled form of his wife as she works some oddity in her vegetable patch.

This one is terse. Existence is a most narrow aperture indeed. His failing is not in being inarticulate through some lack of intellect. No, this mind is most finely honed. But he views his paucity of words – in both thought and dialogue – as a virtue, sigil of rigid manhood. He has made brevity an obsession, an addiction, and in his endless paring down he strips away all hope of emotion and with it empathy. When language is lifeless what does it serve? When meaning is rendered down what veracity holds to the illusion of depth?

Bah! to such conceits! Such anal self-serving affectation! Wax extravagant and let the world swirl thick and pungent about you! Tell the tale of your life as you would live it!

A delighted waggle of fingers now might signal mocking cruelty when you are observing this fingerless man who stands silent and expressionless as he studies his woman. Decide as you will. *His woman.* Yes, the notion belongs to him, artfully whittled from his world view (one of expectation and fury at its perpetual failure). Possession has its rules and she must behave within the limits those rules prescribe. This was, to Gaz, self-evident, a detail that did not survive his own manic editing.

But what was Thordy doing with all those flat stones? With that peculiar pattern she was building there in the dark loamy soil? One could plant nothing beneath stone, could one? No, she was sacrificing fertile ground, and for what? He didn't know. And he knew that he might never know. As an activity, however, Thordy's diligent pursuit was a clear transgression of the rules, and he might have to do something about that. Soon.

Tonight he would beat a man to death. Exultation, yes, but a cold kind. Flies buzzing in his head, the sound rising like a wave, filling his skull with a hundred thousand icy legs. He would do that, yes, and this meant he didn't have to beat his wife – not yet, anyway; a few more days, maybe a week or so – he would have to see how things went.

Keep things simple, give the flies not much to land on, that was the secret. The secret to staying sane.

The wedges of his battered fingerless hands burned with eager fire.

But he wasn't thinking much of anything at all, was he? Nothing to reach his face, his eyes, the flat line of his mouth. Sigil of manhood, this blank façade, and when a man has nothing else at least he could have that. And he would prove it to himself again and again. Night after night.

Because this is what artists did.

Thordy was thinking of many things, none of them particularly relevant – or so she would have judged if pressed to examination, although of course there was no one who might voice such a challenge, which was just as well. Here in her garden she could float, as aimless as a leaf blown down on to a slow, lazy river.

She was thinking about freedom. She was thinking about how a mind could turn to stone, the patterns solid and immovable in the face of seemingly unbearable pressures, and the way dust trickled down faint as whispers, unnoticed by any. And she was thinking of the cool, polished surface of these slate slabs, the waxy feel of them, and the way the sun reflected soft, milky white and not at all painful to rest eyes upon. And she was remembering the way her husband talked in his sleep, a pouring forth of words as if whatever dam held them back in his wakefulness was kicked down and out gushed tales of gods and promises, invitations and bloodlust, the pain of maimed hands and the pain of maiming that those hands delivered.

And she noted the butterflies dancing above the row of greens just off to her left, almost within reach if she stretched out a dirt-stained hand, but then those orange-winged sprites would wing away though she posed them no threat. Because life was uncertain and danger waited in the guise of peaceful repose.

And her knees ached and nowhere in her thoughts could be found expectation – nowhere could be found such hard-edged proof of reality as the framework of what waited somewhere ahead. No hint at all, even as she laid down stone after stone. It was all outside, you see, all outside.

The clerk at the office of the Guild of Blacksmiths had never once in his life wielded hammer and tongs. What he did wield demanded no muscles, no weight of impetus atop oaken legs, no sweat streaming down to sting the eyes, no gusts of scalding heat to singe the hairs on the forearms. And so, in the face of a true blacksmith, the clerk gloried in his power.

That pleasure could be seen in his small pursed lips turned well down at each end, could be caught in his watery eyes that rested everywhere and nowhere; in his pale hands holding a wooden stylus like an assassin's dagger, the tip stained blue by ink and wax. He sat on his stool behind the broad counter that divided the front room as if guarding the world's wealth and every promise of paradise that membership in this most noble Guild offered its hallowed, upright members (and the fat man winks).

So he sat, and so Barathol Mekhar wanted to reach over the counter, pluck the clerk into the air, and break him in half. Over and over again, until little more than a pile of brittle tailings remained heaped on the scarred counter, with the stylus thrust into it like a warrior's sword stabbing a barrow.

Dark was the amusement in Barathol's thoughts as the clerk shook his head yet again.

'It is simple – even for you, I'm sure. The Guild demands credentials, specifically the sponsorship of an accredited Guild member. Without this, your coin is so much dross.' And he smiled at this clever pun voiced to a smith.

'I am new to Darujhistan,' Barathol said, again, 'and so such sponsorship is impossible.'

'Yes it is.'

'As for apprenticeship—'

'Also impossible. You say you have been a blacksmith for many years now and I do not doubt such a claim – the evidence is plain before me. This of course makes you over-qualified as an apprentice and too old besides.'

'If I cannot be apprenticed how can I get a sponsor?'

A smile of the lips and shake of the head. A holding up of the palms. 'I don't make the rules, you understand.'

'Can I speak to anyone who might have been involved in devising these rules?'

'A blacksmith? No, alas, they are all off doing smithy things, as befits their profession.'

'I can visit one at his or her place of work, then. Can you direct me to the nearest one?'

'Absolutely not. They have entrusted me with the responsibilities of operating the administration of the Guild. If I were to do something like that I would be disciplined for dereliction of duty, and I am sure you do not want that on your conscience, do you?'

'Actually,' said Barathol, 'that is a guilt I can live with.'

The expression hardened. 'Honourable character is an essential prerequisite to becoming a member of the Guild.'

'More than sponsorship?'

'They are balanced virtues, sir. Now, I am very busy today—'

'You were sleeping when I stepped in.'

'It may have appeared that way.'

'It appeared that way because it was that way.'

'I have no time to argue with you over what you may or may not have perceived when you stepped into my office—'

'You were asleep.'

'You might have concluded such a thing.'

'I did conclude it, because that is what you were. I suppose that too might result in disciplinary measures, once it becomes known to the members.'

'Your word against mine, and clearly you possess an agenda, one that reflects poorly on your sense of honour—'

'Since when does honesty reflect poorly on one's sense of honour?'

The clerk blinked. 'Why, when it is vindictive, of course.'

Now it was Barathol's turn to pause. And attempt a new tack. 'I can pay an advance on my dues – a year's worth or more, if necessary.'

'Without sponsorship such payment would be construed as a donation. There is legal precedent to back that interpretation.'

'You'd take my coin and give me nothing in return?'

'That is the essence of a charitable donation, is it not?'

'I don't think it is, but never mind that. What you are telling me is that I cannot become a member of the Guild of Blacksmiths.'

'Membership is open to all blacksmiths wishing to work in the city, I assure you. Once you have been sponsored.'

'Which makes it a closed shop.'

'A what?'

'The Malazan Empire encountered closed shops in Seven Cities. They broke them wide open. I think even some blood was spilled. The Emperor was not one to cringe before professional monopolies of any sort.'

'Well,' the clerk said, licking his slivery lips, 'thank all the gods the Malazans never conquered Darujhistan!'

Barathol stepped outside and saw Mallet waiting across the street, eating some kind of flavoured ice in a broad-leaf cone. The morning's heat was fast melting the ice, and purple water was trickling down the healer's pudgy hand. His lips were similarly stained.

Mallet's thin brows rose as the blacksmith approached. 'Are you now a proud if somewhat poorer member of the Guild?'

'No. They refused me.'

'But why? Can you not take some kind of exam—'

'No.'

'Oh . . . so now what, Barathol?'

'What? Oh, I'll open up a smithy anyway. Independent.'

'Are you mad? They'll burn you out. Smash up your equipment. Descend on you in a mob and beat you to death. And that's just on opening day.'

Barathol smiled. He liked Malazans. Despite everything, despite the countless mistakes the Empire had made, all the blood spilled, he liked the bastards. Hood knew, they weren't nearly as fickle as the natives of his homeland. Or, he added wryly, the citizens of Darujhistan. To Mallet's predictions he said, 'I've handled worse. Don't worry about me. I plan on working here as a blacksmith, whether the Guild likes it or not. And eventually they will have to accept me as a member.'

'That won't feel very triumphant if you're dead.'

'I won't be. Dead, that is.'

'They'll try to stop anyone doing business with you.'

'I am very familiar with Malazan weapons and armour, Mallet. My work meets military standards in your old empire, and as you know, those are set high.' He glanced across at the healer. 'Will the Guild scare you off? Your friends?'

'Of course not. But remember, we're retired.'

'And being hunted by assassins.'

'Ah, I'd forgotten about that. You have a point. Even so, Barathol, I doubt us few Malazans can keep you in business for very long.'

'The new embassy has a company of guards.'

'True.'

'And there are other Malazans living here. Deserters from the campaigns up north—'

'That's true, too, though they tend to hide from us – not that we care. In fact, we'd rather get their business at the bar. What's the point in grudges?'

'Those that come to me will be told just that, then, and so we can help each other.'

Mallet tossed the sodden cone away and wiped his hands on his leggings. 'They tasted better when I was a young brat – although they were more expensive since a witch was needed to make the ice in the first place. Here, of course, it's to do with some of the gases in the caverns below.'

Barathol thought about that for a moment as he looked upon the healer with his purple lips and saw, for the briefest moment, how this man had been when he was a child, and then he smiled once more. 'I need to find a suitable location for my smithy. Will you walk with me, Mallet?'

'Glad to,' the healer replied. 'Now, I know the city – what precisely are you looking for?'

And so Barathol told him.

And oh how Mallet laughed and off they went into the city's dark chambers of the heart, where blood flowed in a roar and all manner of deviousness was possible. If the mind was so inclined. A mind such as Barathol Mekhar's when down – *down!* – was thrown the ghastly gauntlet!

The ox, the selfsame ox, swung its head back and forth as it pulled the cartload of masonry into the arched gateway, into blessed shade for a few clumping strides, and then out into the bright heat once more – delicate blond lashes fluttering – to find itself in a courtyard and somewhere close was sweet cool water, the sound as it trickled an invitation, the smell soft as a kiss upon the broad glistening nose with its even more delicate blond hairs, and up rose the beast's massive head and would not the man with the switch have pity on this weary, thirsty ox?

He would not. The cart needed unloading first and so the ox must stand, silently yearning, jaws working the cud of breakfast with loud, thick sounds of suction and wetly clunking molars, and the flies were maddening but what could be done about flies? Nothing at all, not until the chill of night sent them away and so left the ox to sleep, upright in bovine majesty beneath stars (if one was lucky) which, perhaps, was where the flies slept.

Of course, to know the mind of an ox is to waste inordinate amounts of time before recognizing the placid civility of a herbivore's sensibilities. Lift gaze, then, to the two vaguely shifty characters edging in through the gate – not workers struggling to and fro in the midst of the old estate's refurbishment; not clerks nor servants; not masons nor engineers nor inspectors nor weight-gaugers nor measurers. To all appearances malingerers, skulkers, but in truth even worse than that—

Twelve names on the list. One happily struck off. Eleven others found and then escaped like the slippery eels they no doubt were, being hunted by debt, ill luck and the vagaries of a clearly malicious universe intent on delivering misery and whatnot. But no matter such failure among the thugs sent out to enforce collection or deliver punishment – not the problem of these men, now, was it?

Bereft of all burdens, blessed with exquisite freedom, Scorch and Leff were here, in this soon-to-be-opulent estate that was even now rising from the dust of neglect and decay to enshroud like a cloak of jewels the mysterious arrival of a nobleborn – a woman, it was rumoured, all veiled, but see the eyes! *Eyes of such beauty! Why, imagine them widening as I reach down—*

Scorch and Leff, edging in nervously, barely emerging from the shadow of the arched gate. Peering round, as if lost, as if moments from running off with stolen chunks of masonry or an armload of bricks or even a bag of iron wedges—

'Ho – you two! What do you want here?'

Starting guiltily. Scorch staring wide-eyed at the grizzled foreman walking up to them – a Gadrobi so bowlegged he looked to be wading hip-deep through mud. Leff ducking his head as if instinctively dodging an axe – which said a lot about his life thus far, didn't it – and then stepping one small pace forward and attempting a smile that fared so poorly it could not even be described as a grimace.

'Is there a castellan we could talk to?' Leff asked.

'About what?'

'Gate guards,' Leff said. 'We got lots of qualifications.'

'Oh. Any of them relevant?'

'What?'

Leff looked at Scorch and saw the panic spreading like a wildfire on his friend's face. A match to his own growing dismay – madness, thinking they could just step up another rung on the ladder. Madness! 'We . . . we could walk her dogs, I mean?'

'You could? I suppose you could, if the Mistress had any.'

'Does she?' Leff asked.

'Does she what?'

'Have any. Dogs we could walk.'

'Not even ones you can't walk.'

'We can guard the gate!' Scorch shouted. 'That's what we're here for! To get hired on, you see, as estate guards. And if you don't think we can swing a sword or use a crossbow, why, you don't know us at all, do you?'

'No, you're right,' the foreman replied. 'I don't.'

Leff scowled. 'You don't what?'

'Stay here,' the old man said, turning away, 'while I get Castellan Studlock.'

As the foreman waded away through the dust – watched with longing by the ox beside the rubble heap – Leff turned on Scorch. 'Studlock?'

Scorch shrugged helplessly. 'I ain't never heard of him. Why, have you?'

'No. Of course not. I'd have remembered.'

'Why?'

'Why? Are you a Hood-damned idiot?'

'What are we doing here, Leff?'

'Torvald said no, remember? To everything. He's too good for us now. So we'll show him. We'll get hired on this fancy estate. As guards. With uniforms and polished buckles and those braided peace-straps for our swords. And so he'll curse himself that he didn't want us no more, as partners or anything. It's his wife, I bet – she never liked us at all, especially you, Scorch, so that's what you've done to us and I won't forget any time soon neither so don't even think otherwise.'

He shut his mouth then and stood at attention since the foreman was returning and at his side pitter-pattered a figure so wrapped up in swaddles of cotton it took three steps for every pendulum pitch forward from the foreman. The feet beneath the ragged hem were small enough to be cloven hoofs. A hood covered the castellan's head and in the shadow of the hood's broad mouth there was something that might have been a mask. Gloved hands were drawn up in a way that reminded Leff – and, a moment later, Scorch – of a praying mantis, and if this was the estate castellan then someone had knocked the world askew in ways unimaginable to either Leff or Scorch.

The foreman said, 'Here they are, sir.'

Were there eyes in the holes of that smooth mask? Who could tell? But the head shifted and something told both men – like spider legs dancing up their spines – that they were under scrutiny.

'So true,' Castellan Studlock said in a voice that made Leff think of gravel under the fingernails while Scorch thought about the way there was always one gull that bullied all the rest and if the others just ganged up, why, equality and freedom would belong to everyone! 'So true,' said the swaddled, masked man (or woman, but then the foreman had said 'sir', hadn't he), 'there is need for estate guards. The Mistress will be arriving today, in fact, from the out-country. Proper presentation is desired.' The castellan paused and then leaned forward from the waist and Leff saw the red glint of unhuman eyes in the holes of the mask. 'You, what is your name?'

'Leff Bahan, sir, is my name.'

'You have been eating raw lake conch?'

'What? Er, not recently.'

A wrapped finger darted upward and wagged slowly back and forth. 'Risky. Please, open your mouth and stick out your tongue.'

'What? Er, like this?'

'That is fine, very fine, yes. So.' The castellan leaned back. 'Greva worms. You are infected. Pustules on your tongue. Dripping sinuses, yes? Itchy eyelids – the eggs do that, and when they hatch, why, the worms will crawl out from the corners of your eyes. Raw lake conch, tsk tsk.'

Leff clawed at his face. 'Gods, I need a healer! I gotta go—'

'No need. I will happily see your ailment treated – you must be presentable to the Mistress, yes, each standing at attention on either side of the gate. Well attired, hale of complexion and parasite-free. A small barracks is being readied. It will be necessary to hire at least three more to complete the requirements – do you have reliable friends capable of such work?'

'Er,' said Scorch when it was obvious that Leff had momentarily lost his facility for speech, 'we might. I could go and see . . .'

'Excellent, and your name is?'

'Scorch. Er, we got references—'

'No need. I am confident in my ability to judge character, and I have concluded that you two, while not to be considered vast of intellect, are nevertheless inclined to loyalty. This here will mark an advancement in your careers, I am sure, and so you will be diligent as befits your secret suspicion that you have exceeded your competence. All this is well. Also, I am pleased to note that you do not possess any parasites of a debilitating, unsightly sort. So, Scorch, go yonder and find us one, two or three additional guards. In the meantime, I will attend to Leff Bahan.'

'Right. Yes sir, I will do just that!'

The foreman was standing nearby, smirking. Neither Scorch nor a stunned Leff noticed this detail, and yes, they should have.

'A woman needs her secrets,' said Tiserra, lifting up an eggshell-thin porcelain cup and holding it in front of the bright sunlight. 'This one is good, darling. No flaws.' And the hag in the stall grinned, head bobbing.

Torvald Nom nodded happily, then licked his lips. 'Isn't this fun?' he said. 'Fine crockery to go into our new kitchen and the fancy oven on its four legs and all. Real drapes. Plush furniture, colourful rugs. We can get the storage shed re-built, too. Bigger, solid—'

Tiserra set the cup down and moved directly in front of him. 'Husband.'

'Yes?'

'You're trying too hard.'

'I am? Well, it's like a dream, you see, being able to come back home. Do all these things for you, for us. It still doesn't feel real.'

'Oh, that's not the problem,' she said. 'You are already getting bored, Torvald Nom. You need more than just tagging along at my side. And the coin won't last for ever – Beru knows I don't make enough for the both of us.'

'You're saying I need to get a job.'

'I will tell you a secret – just one, and keep in mind what I said earlier: we women have many secrets. I'm feeling generous today, so listen well. A woman is well pleased with a mate. He is her island, if you will, solid, secure. But sometimes she likes to swim offshore, out a way, floating facing the sun if you will. And she might even dive from sight, down to collect pretty shells and the like. And when she's done, why, she'll swim back to the island. The point is, husband, she doesn't want her mate's company when swimming. She needs only to know the island waits there.'

Torvald blinked, then frowned. 'You're telling me to get lost.'

'Leave me my traipsing through the market, darling. No doubt you have manly tasks to pursue, perhaps at a nearby tavern. I'll see you at home this evening.'

'If that's how you want it, then of course I will leave you to it, sweetness – and yes, I could do with a wander. A man has secrets, too!'

'Indeed.' And she smiled. 'Provided they're not the kind that, if I find out, I will have to hunt you down and kill you.'

He blanched. 'No, of course not! Nothing like that!'

'Good. See you later, then.'

And, being a brave man, a contented man (more or less), Torvald Nom happily fled his wife, as brave, contented men are wont to do the world over. *Need to plough that field behind the windbreak, love. Going to head out now and drop the nets. Better sand down that tabletop. Time to go out and rob somebody, sweetness.* Yes, men did as they did, just as women did as *they* did – mysterious and inexplicable as those doings might be.

And, so thinking, it was not long before Torvald Nom found himself walking into the Phoenix Inn. A man looking for work in all the wrong places.

Scorch arrived a short time later, pride and panic warring in his face, and my, how that pride blazed as he strutted up to where Torvald Nom was sitting.

Back at the estate Castellan Studlock brought Leff into an annexe to one side of the main building, where after some rummaging in crates stuffed with straw the muffled figure found a small glass bottle and presented it to Leff.

'Two drops into each eye. Two more on to the tongue. Repeat two more times today and three times a day until the bottle is empty.'

'That will kill them worms in my head?'

'The Greva worms, yes. I cannot vouch for any others.'

'I got more worms in my head?'

'Who can say? Do your thoughts squirm?'

'Sometimes! Gods below!'

'Two possibilities,' Studlock said. 'Suspicion worms or guilt worms.'

Leff scowled. 'You saying it's worms cause those things? Guilt and suspicion? I ain't never heard anything like that.'

'Are you sometimes gnawed with doubt? Do notions take root in your mind? Do strange ideas slither into your head? Are you unaccountably frightened at the sight of a fisher's barbed hook?'

'Are you some kind of healer?'

'I am what one needs me to be. Now, let us find you a uniform.'

Torvald Nom was rehearsing what he would tell his wife. Carefully weighing each word, trying out in his mind the necessary nonchalance required to deftly avoid certain details of his newfound employment.

'It's great that we're all working together again,' Scorch said, ambling happily at his side. 'As estate guards, no less! No more strong-arm work for smelly criminals. No more hunting down losers to please some vicious piranha. No more—'

'Did this castellan mention the wages?'

'Huh? No, but it's bound to be good. Must be. It's demanding work—'

'Scorch, it may be lots of things, but "demanding" isn't one of them. We're there to keep thieves out. And since all three of us have been thieves ourselves at one time or another, we should be pretty damned good at it. We'd better be, or we'll get fired.'

'We need two more people. He wanted three more and all I got was you. So, two more. Can you think of anybody?'

'No. What family?'

'What?'

'This Mistress – what House does she belong to?'

'Don't know.'

'What's her name?'

'No idea.'

'She's from the countryside?'

'Think so.'

'Well, has any noble died recently that might have pulled her in? Inheritance, I mean?'

'How should I know? You think I bother keeping track of who's dead in that crowd? They ain't nothing to me, is my point.'

'We should've asked Kruppe – he'd know.'

'Well we didn't and it don't matter at all. We got us legitimate work, the three of us. We're on our way to being, well, legitimate. So just stop questioning everything, Tor! You're going to ruin it!'

'How can a few reasonable questions ruin anything?'

'It just makes me nervous,' Scorch replied. 'Oh, by the way, you can't see the castellan.'

'Why? Who else would I talk to about getting hired?'

'No, that's not what I mean. I mean you can't see him. All wrapped up in rags. With a hood, and gloves, and a mask. That's what I mean. His name is Studlock.'

'You can't be serious.'

'Why not? That's his name.'

'The castellan is bundled like a corpse and you don't find that somewhat unusual?'

'Could be afraid of the sun or something. No reason to be suspicious. You never met any strange people in your day, Tor?'

And Torvald Nom glanced across at Scorch, and found he had no reply to that at all.

'I see you have found another candidate,' Studlock said. 'Excellent. And yes, he will do nicely. Perhaps as the Captain of the House Guard?'

Torvald started. 'I haven't said a word yet and already I'm promoted?'

'Comparative exercise yields confidence in this assessment. Your name is?'

'Torvald Nom.'

'Of House Nom. Might this not prove a conflict of interest?'

'Might it? Why?'

'The Mistress is about to assume the vacant seat on the Council.'

'Oh. Well, I have virtually no standing in the affairs of House Nom. There are scores of us in the city, of course, with ties stretching everywhere, including off-continent. I, however, am not involved in any of that.'

'Were you cast out?'

'No, nothing so, er, extreme. It was more a question of . . . interests.'

'You lack ambition.'

'Precisely.'

'That is a fine manicure, Torvald Nom.'

'Er, thank you. I could recommend . . .' but that notion dwindled into a painful silence and Torvald tried hard to not glance down at the castellan's bandaged fingers.

At this moment Leff appeared from round the other side of the main house. His lips and his eyes were bright orange.

Scorch grunted. 'Hey, Leff. Remember that cat you sat on in that bar once?'

'What of it?'

'Nothing. Was just reminded, the way its eyes went all bulgy and crazed.'

'What's that supposed to mean?'

'Nothing. Was just reminded, is all. Look, I brought Tor.'

'I see that,' snarled Leff. 'I can see just fine, thank you.'

'What's wrong with your eyes?' Torvald Nom asked.

'Tincture,' said Leff. 'I got me a case of Greva worms.'

Torvald Nom frowned. 'Humans can't get Greva worms. Fish get Greva worms, from eating infected conch.'

Leff's bulging orange eyes bulged even more. Then he spun to face the castellan.

Who shrugged and said, 'Jurben worms?'

Torvald Nom snorted. 'The ones that live in the caverns below? In pockets of green gas? They're as long as a man's leg and nearly as thick.'

The castellan sighed. 'The spectre of misdiagnosis haunts us all. I do apologize, Leff. Perhaps your ailments are due to some other malady. No matter, the drops will wash out in a month or two.'

'I'm gonna have squished cat eyes for another month?'

'Preferable to Greva worms, I should think. Now, gentlemen, let us find the house clothier. Something black and brocaded in gold thread, I should imagine. House colours and all that. And then, a brief summary of your duties, shifts, days off and the like.'

'Would that summary include wages?' Torvald Nom asked.

'Naturally. As captain you will be paid twenty silver councils per week, Torvald Nom. Scorch and Leff, as guards, at fifteen. Acceptable?'

All three quickly nodded.

He felt slightly shaky on his feet, but Murillio knew that had nothing to do with any residue of weakness left by his wound. This weakness belonged to his spirit. As if age had sprung on to his back with claws digging into every joint and now hung there, growing heavier by the moment. He walked hunched at the shoulders and this seemed to have arrived like a new habit, or perhaps it was always there and only now, in his extremity, had he become aware of it.

That drunken pup's sword thrust had pierced something vital indeed, and no Malazan healer or any other kind of healer could mend it.

He tried forcing confidence into his stride as he made his way down the crowded street, but it was not an easy task. *Half drunk. Breeches at my ankles. Worthwhile excuses for what happened that night. The widow Sepharla spitting venom once she sobered up enough to realize what had happened, and spitting it still, it seems. What had happened, yes. With her daughter. Oh, not rape – too much triumph in the girl's eyes for that, though her face glowed with delight at her escort's charge to defend her honour. Once the shock wore off. I should never have gone back to explain—*

But that was yesterday's nightmare, all those sparks raining down on the domestic scene with its airs of concern, every cagey word painting over the cracks in savage, short jabs of the brush. What had he expected? What had he gone there to find? Reassurance?

Maybe. I guess I arrived with my own brush.

Years ago, he would have smoothed everything over, almost effortlessly. A murmur here, a meeting of gazes there. Soft touch with one hand, the barest hint of pressure. Then again, years ago, *it would never have happened in the first place. That drunken fool!*

Oh, he'd growled those three words often in his head. But did they refer to the young man with the sword, or to himself?

Arriving at the large duelling school, he made his way through the open gate and emerged into the bright sunlight of the training ground. A score of young, sweating, overweight students scraped about in the dust, wooden weapons clattering. Most, he saw at once, lacked the necessary aggression, the killer's instinct. They danced to avoid, prodding the stick points forward with a desultory lack of commitment. Their footwork, he saw, was abysmal.

The class instructor was standing in the shade of a column in the colonnaded corridor just beyond. She was not even observing the mayhem in the compound, intent, it seemed, on some loose stitching or tear in one of her leather gauntlets.

Making his way along one side of the mob getting lost in clouds of white dust, Murillio approached the instructor. She noted him briefly then returned her attention to the gauntlet.

'Excuse me,' Murillio said as he arrived. 'Are you the duelling mistress?'

'I am.' She nodded without looking at the students, where a couple of fights had started for real. 'How am I doing so far?'

Murillio glanced over and studied the fracas for a moment. 'That depends,' he said.

She grunted. 'Good answer. What can I do for you? Do you have some grandson or daughter you want thrown in there? Your clothes were expensive . . . once. As it looks, I doubt you can afford this school, unless of course you're one of those stinking rich who make a point of dressing all threadbare. Old money and all that.'

'Quite a sales pitch,' Murillio observed. 'Does it actually work?'

'Classes are full. There's a waiting list.'

'I was wondering if you need help. With basic instruction.'

'What school trained you then?'

'Carpala.'

She snorted. 'He took one student every three years.'

'Yes.'

And now she looked at him with an intensity he'd not seen before. 'Last I heard, there were seven students of his left in the city.'

'Five, actually. Fedel tumbled down a flight of stairs and broke his neck. He was drunk. Santbala—'

'Was stabbed through the heart by Gorlas Vidikas – the brat's first serious victory.'

Murillio grimaced. 'Not much of a duel. Santbala had gone mostly blind but was too proud to admit it. A cut on the wrist would have given Gorlas his triumph.'

'The young ones prefer killing to wounding.'

'It's what duelling has come to, yes. Fortunately, most of your students here are more likely to stab themselves than any opponent they might one day face, and such wounds are rarely fatal.'

'Your name?'

'Murillio.'

She nodded as if she'd already guessed. 'And you're here because you want to teach. If you'd taken up teaching when Carpala was still alive—'

'He would have hunted me down and killed me, yes. He despised schools. In fact, he despised duelling. He once said teaching the rapier was like putting a poisonous snake into a child's hand. He drew no pleasure from instruction and was not at all surprised when very nearly every one of his prize students either got themselves killed or wasted away as drunkards or worse.'

'You did neither.'

'No, that's true. I chased women.'

'Only now they're too fast for you?'

'Something like that.'

'I am Stonny Menackis. This school exists to make me rich, and yes, it's working. Tell me, will you be sharing your old master's hatred of teaching?'

'Not as vehemently, I imagine. I don't expect to take any pleasure in it, but I will do what's needed.'

'Footwork.'

He nodded. 'Footwork. The art of running away. And forms, the defensive cage, since that will keep them alive. Stop-hits to the wrist, knee, foot.'

'Non-lethal.'

'Yes.'

She sighed and straightened. 'All right. Assuming I can afford you.'

'I'm sure you can.'

She shot him a quizzical glance, and then added, 'Don't think about chasing me, by the way.'

'I am finished with all that, or, rather, it's finished with me.'

'Good—'

At this moment they both noticed that an old woman had come up to them.

Stonny's voice was suddenly . . . different, as she said, 'Myrla. What are you doing here?'

'I've been looking for Gruntle—'

'That fool went off with the Trygalle – I warned him and now he's going to get himself killed for no good reason!'

'Oh. It's Harllo, you see . . .'

'What about him?'

The old woman was flinching at everything Stonny said and Murillio suspected he would have done the same in the face of such a tone. 'He's gone missing.'

'What? For how long?'

'Snell said he saw him, two days back. Down at the docks. He's never not come home at day's end – he's only five—'

'Two days!'

Murillio saw that Stonny's face had gone white as death and a sudden terror was growing in her eyes. *Two days!*

'Snell says—'

'You stupid woman – Snell is a liar! A damned thief!'

Myrla stepped back under the onslaught. 'He gave us the coin you brought—'

'After I nearly had to strangle him, yes! What's Snell done to Harllo? *What's he done?*'

Myrla was weeping now, wringing her arthritic hands. 'Said he done nothing, Stonny—'

'A moment,' cut in Murillio, physically stepping between the two women as he saw Stonny about to move forward, gloved hand lifting. 'A child's gone missing? I can put out the word – I know all sorts of people. Please, we can do this logically – down at the docks, you said? We'll need to find out which ships left harbour in the last two days – the trading season's only just starting, so there shouldn't be many. His name is Harllo, and he's five years old—' *Gods below, you send him out into the streets and he's only five?* 'Can you give me a description? Hair, eyes, the like.'

Myrla was nodding, even as tears streamed down her lined cheeks and her entire body trembled. She nodded and kept on nodding.

Stonny spun round and rushed away, boots echoing harshly down the corridor.

Murillio stared after her in astonishment. 'Where – what?'

'It's her son, you see,' said Myrla between sobs. 'Her only son, only she don't want him and so he's with us but Snell he has bad thoughts and does bad things sometimes only not this, never this bad, he wouldn't do anything this bad to Harllo, he wouldn't!'

'We'll find him,' said Murillio. *One way or the other, Lady's pull bless us, and bless the lad.* 'Now, please, describe him and describe him well – what he normally does each day – I need to know that, too. Everything you can tell me, Myrla. Everything.'

Snell understood, in a dim but accurate way, how others, wishing only the best in him, could have their faith abused at will, and even should some truth be dragged into the light, well, it was then a matter of displaying crushed self-pity, and the great defender would take him into her arms – as mothers do.

Can we hope that on rare occasions, perhaps late at night when the terrors crept close, he would think about how things he'd done could damage his mother's faith, and not just in him, but in herself as well? The son, after all, is but an extension of the mother – at least so the mother believed, there in some inarticulate part of her soul, unseen yet solid as an iron chain. Assail the child and so too the mother is assailed, for what is challenged is her life as a mother, the lessons she taught or didn't teach, the things she chose not to see, to explain away, to pretend were otherwise than what they were.

Weep for the mother. Snell won't and he never would, saving all his future to weep exclusively for himself. The creeping terrors awakened startling glimmers of thought, of near-empathy, but they never went so far as to lead to any self-recognition, or compassion for the mother who loved him unconditionally. His nature was the kind that took whatever was given to him as if it was a birthright, all of it, for ever and ever more.

Rage at injustice came when something – anything – was withheld. Things he righteously deserved, and of course he deserved everything he wanted. All that he wanted he reached for, and oh such fury if those things eluded his grasp or were then taken away!

In the absence of what might be imposed, a child will fashion the structure of the world as it suits itself. Created from a mind barely awake – and clearly not even that when it came to introspection – that world becomes a strange place indeed. But let us not rail at the failings of nearby adults tied by blood or whatever. Some children are born in a cage – it's already there, in their skulls – and it's a dark cage.

He was wandering the streets, fleeing all the cruel questions being flung at him. They had no right to accuse him like that. Oh, when he was all grown up, nobody would be allowed to get after him like this. He'd break their faces. He'd step on their heads. He'd make them afraid, every one of them, so he could go on doing whatever he liked. He couldn't wait to get older and that was the truth.

And yet, he found himself heading for Two-Ox Gate. He needed to know, after all. Was Harllo still lying there? He hadn't hit him so hard, had he? Enough to kill him? Only if Harllo had been born weak, only if something was wrong with him from the start. And that wouldn't be a surprise, would it? Harllo's own mother had thrown him away, after all. So, if Harllo was lying dead in the grasses on that hilltop, why, it wasn't Snell's fault, was it? Something would have killed him sooner or later.

So that was a relief, but he'd better go and find out for sure. What if Harllo hadn't died at all? What if he was out there somewhere, planning murder? He could be spying on Snell right now! With a knife he'd found, or a knotted stick. Quick, cunning, able to dart out of sight no matter how fast Snell spun round on the street – he was out there! Waiting, stalking.

Snell needed to prove things, and that was why he was running through Maiten, where the stink of Brownrun Bay and the lepers was nearly enough to make him retch – and hah! Listen to them scream when struck by the bigger stones he threw at them! He was tempted to tarry for a time, to find one of the uglier ones he could stone again and again until the cries just went away, and wouldn't that be a mercy? Better than rotting away.

But no, not yet, maybe on the way back, after he'd stood for a time, looking down at the flyblown corpse of Harllo – that would be the perfect conclusion to this day, after all. His problems solved. Nobody hunting him in the shadows. He'd throw stones fast and hard then, a human catapult – *smack!* Crush the flimsy skull!

Maybe he wasn't grown up yet, but he could still do things. *He could take lives.*

He left the road, made his way up the hill. This was the place all right – how could he forget? Every detail was burned into his brain. The first giant tapestry in the history of Snell. *Slaying his evil rival, and see the dragons wheeling in the sky above the lake – witnesses!*

The slope unaccountably tired him, brought a tremble to his legs. Just nervousness, of course. His shins stung as he rushed through the grasses, and came to the place.

No body.

Sudden terror. Snell looked round, on all sides – he was out there! Wasn't hurt at all! He'd probably faked the whole thing, biting down on his pain with every kick. Hiding, yes, just to get Snell in trouble and when Gruntle came back there'd be Hood to pay! Gruntle who made Harllo his favourite because Harllo did things to help out but wasn't it Snell who brought back that last sack of fuel? It was! Of course Gruntle wasn't there to see that, was he? So he didn't know anything because if he did—

If he did he'd kill me.

Cold, shivering in the lake wind, Snell ran back down the hill. He needed to get home, maybe not right home, but somewhere close – so he could jump Harllo when he showed up to tell his lies about what had happened. Lies – Snell had no bag of coins, did he? Harllo's mother's coins, hah, wasn't that funny? She was rich enough anyway and Snell deserved that money as much as anyone else – he reached up and tenderly touched the swelling on his left cheek. The bitch had hit him, all to steal back the money. Well, she'd pay one day, yes, she would.

One day, yes, he'd be all grown up. And then . . . *look out!*

It had taken the death of a once-famous duellist before people started treating Gorlas Vidikas as an adult, but now he was a man indeed, a feared one, a member of the Council. He was wealthy but not yet disgustingly rich, although that was only a matter of time.

Fools the world over worshipped gods and goddesses. But coin was the only thing worth worshipping, because to worship it was to see it grow – more and ever more – and all that he took for himself he took from someone else and this was where the real conquest happened. Day by day, deal by deal, and winning these games was proof of true faith and worship, and oh how deliciously satisfying.

Fools dropped coins into collection bowls. The rich cleaned those bowls out and this was the true division of humanity. But more than that: the rich decided how many coins the fools had to spare and how did that rate as power? Which side was preferable? As if the question needed asking.

Coin purchased power, like a god blessing the devout, but of both power and wealth there could never be enough. As for the victims, well, there could never be enough of them either. Someone was needed to clean the streets of the Estate District. Someone was needed to wash clothes, bedding and the like. Someone was needed to make the damned things in the first place! And someone was needed to fight the wars when the rich decided they wanted still more of whatever was out there.

Gorlas Vidikas, born to wealth and bred to title, found life to be good. But it could be better still and the steps to improvement were simple enough.

'Darling wife,' he now said as she was rising to leave, 'I must take a trip and will not return until tomorrow or even the day after.'

She paused, watching in a distracted way as the servants closed in to collect the dishes from the late breakfast – calloused hands darting in like featherless birds – and said, 'Oh?'

'Yes. I have been granted the overseer title of an operation out of the city, and I must visit the workings. Thereafter, I must take ship to Gredfallan Annexe to finalize a contract.'

'Very well, husband.'

'There was no advance notice of any of this,' Gorlas added, 'and, alas, I had extended invitations to both Shardan and Hanut to dine with us this evening.' He paused to smile at her. 'I leave them in your capable hands – please do extend my apologies.'

She was staring down at him in a somewhat disconcerting way. 'You wish me to host your two friends tonight?'

'Of course.'

'I see.'

And perhaps she did at that – yet was she railing at him? No. And was there perhaps the flush of excitement on her cheeks now? But she was turning away so he could not be sure. And walking, hips swaying in that admirable way of hers, right out of the room.

And there, what was done . . . was done.

He rose and gestured to his manservant. 'Make ready the carriage, I am leaving immediately.'

Head bobbing, the man hurried off.

Someone was needed to groom the horses, to check the tack, to keep the carriage clean and the brakes in working order. Someone was needed to ensure he had all he needed in the travel trunks. And, as it happened, someone was needed for other things besides. Like spreading the legs as a reward for past favours, and as a future debt when it was time to turn everything round.

They could take his wife. He would take them, one day – everything they owned, everything they dreamed of owning. After tonight, he would own one of them or both of them – both for certain in the weeks to come. Which one would produce Gorlas's heir? He didn't care – Challice's getting pregnant would get his parents off his back at the very least, and might well add the reward of satisfying her – and so wiping that faint misery from her face and bringing an end to all those irritating sighs and longing faraway looks out of the windows.

Besides, she worshipped money too. Hood knew she spent enough of it, on precious trinkets and useless indulgences. Give her a child and then three or four more and she'd be no further trouble and content besides.

Sacrifices needed to be made. *So make it, wife, and who knows, you might even be smiling when it's done with.*

A bell and a half later the Vidikas carriage was finally clearing Two-Ox Gate and the horses picked up their pace as the road opened out, cutting through the misery of Maiten (and where else should the lost and the hopeless go but outside the city walls?) which Gorlas suffered with closed shutters and a scent ball held to his nose.

When he ruled he'd order a massive pit dug out on the Dwelling Plain and they would drag all these wasted creatures out there and bury the lot of them. It was simple enough – can't pay for a healer and that's just too bad, but look, we won't charge for the burial.

Luxuriating in such thoughts, and other civic improvements, Gorlas dozed as the carriage rumbled onward.

Challice stood alone in her private chambers, staring at the hemisphere of glass with its trapped moon. What would she lose? Her reputation. Or, rather, that reputation would change. Hanut grinning, Shardan strutting in that knowing way of his, making sure his secret oozed from every pore so that it was anything but a secret. Other men would come to her, expecting pretty much the same. And maybe, by then, there would be no stopping her. And maybe, before too long, she'd find one man who decided that what he felt was love, and she would then begin to unveil her plan – the only plan she had and it certainly made sense. Eminently logical, even reasonable. Justifiable.

Sometimes the beast on its chain turns on its master. Sometimes it goes for his throat, and sometimes it gets there.

But it would take time. Neither Shardan Lim nor Hanut Orr would do – both needed Gorlas even though their triumvirate was a partnership of convenience. Any one of them would turn on the other if the situation presented itself – but not yet, not for a long while, she suspected.

Could she do this?

What is my life? Here, look around – what is it? She had no answer to that question. She was like a jeweller blind to the notion of value. Shiny or dull, it didn't matter. Rare or abundant, the only difference lay in desire and how could one weigh that, when the need behind it was the same? The same, yes, in all its sordid hunger.

She could reduce all her needs to but one. She could do that. She would have to, to stomach what was to come.

She felt cold, could see the purple tracks through the pallid white skin of her arms as her blood flowed turgidly on. She needed to walk in sunlight, to feel the heat, and know that people would look upon her as she passed – on her fine cape of ermine with its borders of black silk sewn with silvered thread; on the bracelets on her wrists and down at her ankles – too much jewellery invited the thief's snatching hand, after all, and was crass besides. And her long hair would glisten with its scented oils, and there would be a certain look in her eyes, lazy, satiated, seductively sealed away so that it seemed she took notice of nothing and no one, and this was, she well knew, a most enticing look in what were still beautiful eyes—

She found herself looking into them, there in the mirror, still clear even after half a carafe of wine at breakfast and then the pipe of rustleaf afterwards, and she had a sudden sense that the next time she stood thus, the face staring back at her would belong to someone else, another woman wearing her skin, her face. A stranger far more knowing, far wiser in the world's dismal ways than this one before her now.

Was she looking forward to making her acquaintance?

It was possible.

The day beckoned and she turned away – before she saw too much of the woman she was leaving behind – and set about dressing for the city.

'So, you're the historian who survived the Chain of Dogs.'

The old man sitting at the table looked up and frowned. 'Actually, I didn't.'

'Oh,' said Scillara, settling down into the chair opposite him – her body felt strange today, as if even fat could be weightless. Granted, she wasn't getting any heavier, but her bones were wearing plenty and there was a sense of fullness, of roundness, and for some reason all of this was making her feel sexually charged, very nearly brimming over with a slow, sultry indolence. She drew out her pipe and eyed the Malazan opposite. 'Well, I'm sorry to hear that.'

'It's a long story,' he said.

'Which you're relating to that ponytailed bard.'

He grunted. 'So much for privacy.'

'Sounds to be a good thing, getting it all out. When he found out I was in Sha'ik's camp in Raraku, he thought to cajole details out of me. But I was barely conscious most of that time, so I wasn't much help. I told him about Heboric, though.'

And Duiker slowly straightened, a sudden glint in his eyes burning away all the sadness, all the weariness. 'Heboric?'

Scillara smiled. 'Fisher said you might be interested in that.'

'I am. Or,' he hesitated, 'I think I am.'

'He died, I'm afraid. But I will tell you of it, if you'd like. From the night we fled Sha'ik.'

The light had dimmed in Duiker's eyes and he looked away. 'Hood seems determined to leave me the last one standing. All my friends . . .'

'Old friends, maybe,' she said, pulling flame into the bowl. 'Plenty of room for new ones.'

'That's a bitter consolation.'

'We need to walk, I think.'

'I'm not in the mood—'

'But I am and Barathol is gone and your partners are upstairs chewing on conspiracies. Chaur is in the kitchen eating everything in sight and Blend's fallen in love with me and sure, that's amusing and even enjoyable for a time, but for me it's not the real thing. Only she's not listening. Anyway, I want an escort and you're elected.'

'Really, Scillara—'

'Being old doesn't mean you can be rude. I want you to take me to the Phoenix Inn.'

He stared at her for a long moment.

She drew hard on her pipe, swelled her lungs to thrust her ample breasts out and saw how his gaze dropped a fraction or two. 'I'm looking to embarrass a friend, you see,' she said, then released the lungful of smoke towards the black-stained rafters.

'Well,' he sourly drawled, 'in that case . . .'

'Rallick's furious,' Cutter said as he sat down, reaching for the brick of cheese to break off a sizeable chunk which he held in his left hand, an apple in his right. A bite from the apple was quickly followed by one from the cheese.

'Kruppe commiserates. Tragedy of destiny, when destiny is that which one chooses given what one is given. Dear Cutter might have retained original name had he elected a life in, say, Murillio's shadow. Alas, Cutter in name is cutter in deed.'

Cutter swallowed and said, 'Hold on. I wasn't making a point of walking in Rallick's shadow. Not anybody's shadow – in fact, the whole idea of "shadow" makes me sick. If one god out there has truly cursed me, it's Shadowthrone.'

'Shifty Shadowthrone, he of the sourceless shade, a most conniving, dastardly god indeed! Chill is his shadow, cruel and uncomfortable is his throne, horrid his Hounds, tangled his Rope, sweet and seductive his innocent servants! But!' And Kruppe held aloft one plump finger. 'Cutter would not speak of walking in shadows, why, not anyone's! Even one which sways most swayingly, that cleaves most cleavingly, that flutters in fluttering eyelashes framing depthless dark eyes that are not eyes at all, but pools of unfathomable depth – and is she sorry? By Apsalar she is not!'

'I hate you sometimes,' Cutter said in a grumble, eyes on the table, cheese and apple temporarily forgotten in his hands.

'Poor Cutter. See his heart carved loose from yon chest, flopping down like so much bloodied meat on this tabletop. Kruppe sighs and sighs again in the deep of sympathy and extends, yes, this warm cloak of companionship against the cold harsh light of truth this day and on every other day! Now, kindly pour us more of this herbal concoction which, whilst tasting somewhat reminiscent of the straw and mud used to make bricks, is assured by Meese to aid in all matters of digestion, including bad news.'

Cutter poured, and then took another two bites, apple and cheese. He chewed for a time, then scowled. 'What bad news?'

'That which is yet to arrive, of course. Will honey aid this digestive aid? Probably not. It will, one suspects, curdle and recoil. Why is it, Kruppe wonders, that those who claim all healthy amends via rank brews, gritty grey repasts of the raw and unrefined, and unpalatable potions, and this amidst a regime of activities invented solely to erode bone and wear out muscle – all these purveyors of the pure and good life are revealed one and all as wan, parched well nigh bloodless, with vast fists bobbing up and down in the throat and watery eyes savage in righteous smugitude, walking like energized storks and urinating water pure enough to drink all over again? And pass if you please to dear beatific Kruppe, then, that last pastry squatting forlorn and alone on yon pewter plate.'

Cutter blinked. 'Sorry. Pass what?'

'Pastry, dear lad! Sweet pleasures to confound the pious worshippers of suffering! How many lives do each of us have, Kruppe wonders rhetorically, to so constrain this one with desultory disciplines so efficacious that Hood himself must bend over convulsed in laughter? This evening, dear friend of Kruppe, you and I will walk the cemetery and wager which buried bones belong to the healthy ones and which to the wild cavorting headlong maniacs who danced bright with smiles each and every day!'

'The healthy bones would be the ones left by old people, I'd wager.'

'No doubt no doubt, friend Cutter, a most stolid truth. Why, Kruppe daily encounters ancient folk and delights in their wide smiles and cheery well-mets.'

'They're not all miserable, Kruppe.'

'True, here and there totters a wide-eyed one, wide-eyed because a life of raucous abandon is behind one and the fool went and survived it all! Now what, this creature wonders? Why am I not dead? And you, with your three paltry decades of pristine boredom, why don't you just go somewhere and die!'

'Are you being hounded by the aged, Kruppe?'

'Worse. Dear Murillio moans crabby and toothless and now ponders a life of inactivity. Promise Kruppe this, dear Cutter – when you see this beaming paragon here before you falter, dribble at the mouth, mutter at the clouds, wheeze and fart and trickle and all the rest, do bundle Kruppe up tight in some thick impervious sack of burlap, find a nearby cliff and send him sailing out! Through the air! Down on to the thrashing seas and crashing rocks and filmy foams – Kruppe implores you! And listen, whilst you do so, friend Cutter, sing and laugh, spit into my wake! Do you so promise?'

'If I'm around, Kruppe, I'll do precisely as you ask.'

'Kruppe is relieved, so relieved. Aaii, last pastry revolts in nether gut – more of this tea, then, to yield the bitumen belch of tasteless misery on earth. And then, shortly anon, it will be time for lunch! And see who enters, why, none other than Murillio, newly employed and flush and so eager with generosity!'

Iskaral Pust's love was pure and perfect, except that his wife kept getting in the way. When he leaned left she leaned right; when he leaned right she leaned left. When he stretched his neck she stretched hers and all he could see was the mangled net of her tangled hair and beneath that those steely black eyes too knowing for her own good and for his, too, come to that.

'The foolish hag,' he muttered. 'Can't she see I'm leaning this way and that and bobbing up and down only because I feel like it and not because the High Priestess is over there amply presenting her deliciously ample backside – knowing well, yes she does, how I squirm and drool, pant and palpitate, the temptress, the wilful vixen! But no! Every angle and this horrid nemesis heaves into view, damning my eyes! Maybe I can cleverly send her off on an errand, now there's an idea.' He smiled and leaned forward, all the armour of his charm trembling and creaking in the face of the onslaught of her baleful stare. 'Sweet raisin crumpet, the mule needs grooming and tender care in the temple stables.'

'Does it now?'

'Yes. And since you're clearly not busy with anything at the moment, you could instead do something useful.'

'But I am doing something useful, dearest husband.'

'Oh, and what's that, tender trollop?'

'Why, I am sacrificing my time to keep you from making a bigger fool of yourself than is normal, which is quite a challenge, I assure you.'

'What stupidity is she talking about? Love oyster, whatever are you talking about?'

'She's made her concession that you are who you claim to be. And that's the only thing keeping her from tossing us both out on our scrawny behinds. You and me and the mule and the gibbering bhokarala – assuming she can ever manage to get them out of the cellar. I'm a witch of the spider goddess and the High Priestess back there is not at all happy about that. So I'm telling you, O rotted apple of my eye, if I let you try and jump her we're all done for.'

'She talks so much it's a wonder her teeth don't fall out. But wait! Most of them already have! Shh, don't laugh, don't even smile. Am I smiling? Maybe, but it's the indulgent kind, the kind that means well or if not well then nothing at all though wives the world over, when seeing it, go into apoplectic rage for no good reason at all, the cute, loveable dearies.' He sighed and leaned back, trying to peer under her right armpit, but the peripheral vision thing turned that into a hairy nightmare. Flinching, he sighed again and rubbed at his eyes. 'Go on, wife, the mule is pining and your sweet face is all he longs for – to kick! Hee hee! Shh, don't laugh! Don't even smile!' He looked up. 'Delicious wrinkled date, why not take a walk, out into the sunshine in the streets? The gutters, more like, hah! The runnels of runny sewage – take a bath! Piss up one of those lampposts and not a dog in Darujhistan would dare the challenge! Hah! But this smile is the caring kind, yes, see?'

The High Priestess Sordiko Qualm cavorted up to where they sat – this woman didn't walk, she went as much sideways as forward, a snake of seduction, an enchantress of nonchalance; gods, a man could die just watching! Was that a whimper escaping him? Of course not, more likely Mogora's armpit coming up for air made that gasping, squelching sound.

'I would be most pleased,' the High Priestess said in that well-deep voice that purred like every temptation imaginable all blended into one steaming stew of invitation, 'if you two indulged in mutual suicide.'

'I could fake mine,' Iskaral Pust whispered. 'Then she'd be out of our way – I know, High Priestess of all my fantasies, I can see how you wage war against your natural desires, your blazing hunger to get your hands on me! Oh, I know I'm not as handsome as some people, but I have power!'

Sighing, Sordiko Qualm cavorted away – but no, from behind it was more a saunter. Approaching was a cavort, leaving was a saunter. 'Sordiko Saunter Qualm Cavort, she comes and goes but never quite leaves, my love of loves, my better love than that excuse for love I once thought was real love but let's face it love it wasn't, not like this love. Why, this love is the big kind, the swollen kind, the towering kind, the rutting gasping pumping exploding kind! Oh, I hurt myself.'

Mogora snorted. 'You wouldn't know real love if it bit you in the face.'

'Keep that armpit away from me, woman!'

'You've turned this temple into a madhouse, Iskaral Pust. You turn every temple you live in into a madhouse! So here we are, contemplating mutual murder, and what does your god want from us? Why, nothing! Nothing but waiting, always waiting! Bah, I'm going shopping!'

'At last!' Iskaral crowed.

'And you're coming with me, to carry my purchases.'

'Not a chance. Use the mule.'

'Stand up or I'll have my way with you right here.'

'In the holy vestry? Are you insane?'

'Rutting blasphemy. Will Shadowthrone be pleased?'

'Fine! Shopping, then. Only no leash this time.'

'Then don't get lost.'

'I wasn't lost, you water buffalo, I was escaping.'

'I'd better get the leash again.'

'And I'll get my knife!'

Oh, how marriage got in the way of love! The bonds of mutual contempt drawn tight until the victims squeal, but is it in pain or pleasure? Is there a difference? But that is a question not to be asked of married folk, oh no.

And in the stables the mule winks at the horse and the horse feels breakfast twisting in her gut and the flies, well, they fly from one lump of dung to another, convinced that each is different from the last, fickle creatures that they are, and there is no wisdom among the fickle, only longing and frustration, and the buzz invites the next dubious conquest smelling so fragrant in the damp straw.

Buzz buzz.

Amidst masses of granite and feverish folds of bedrock veined with glittering streaks, the mining operation owned by Humble Measure was an enormous pit facing a cliff gouged with caves and tunnels. Situated equidistant between Darujhistan and Gredfallan Annexe and linked by solid raised roads, the mine and its town-sized settlement had a population of eight hundred. Indentured workers, slaves, prisoners, work chiefs, security guards, cooks, carpenters, potters, rope makers, clothes makers and menders, charcoal makers, cutters and nurses, butchers and bakers – the enterprise seethed with activity. Smoke filled the air. Old women with bleeding hands clambered through the heaps of tailings collecting shreds of slag and low-quality chunks of coal. Gulls and crows danced round these rag-clad, hunched figures.

Not a single tree was left standing anywhere within half a league of the mine. Down on a slope on the lakeside was a humped cemetery in which sat a few hundred shallow graves. The water just offshore was lifeless and stained red, with a muddy bottom bright orange in colour.

Scented cloth held to his face, Gorlas Vidikas observed the operation which he now managed, although perhaps "managed" was the wrong word. The day to day necessities were the responsibility of the camp workmaster, a scarred and pock-faced man in his fifties with decades-old scraps of raw metal still embedded in his hands. He hacked out a cough after every ten words or so, and spat thick yellow mucus down between his bronze-capped boots.

'The young 'uns go the fastest, of course.' *Cough, spit.* 'Our *moles* or so we call 'em, since they can squeeze inta cracks no grown-up can get through,' *cough, spit,* 'and this way if there's bad air it's none of our stronger workers get killed.' *Cough* . . . 'We was havin' trouble gettin' enough young 'uns for a time there, until we started buyin' 'em from the poorer fam'lies both in and outa the city – they got too many runts t'feed, ye see? An' we got special rules for the young 'uns – nobody gets their hands on 'em, if you know what I mean.

'From them it goes on up. A miner lasts maybe five years, barring falls and the like. When they get too sick we move 'em outa the tunnels, make 'em shift captains. A few might get old enough for foreman – I was one of them, ye see. Got my hands dirty as a lad and 'ere I am and if that's not freedom I don't know what is, hey?'

This workmaster, Gorlas Vidikas silently predicted, would be dead inside three years. 'Any trouble with the prisoners?' he asked.

'Nah, most don't live long enough to cause trouble. We make 'em work the deadlier veins. It's the arsenic what kills 'em, mostly – we're pullin' gold out too, you know. Profit's gone up three thousand per cent in the past year. E'en my share I'm looking at maybe buying a small estate.'

Gorlas glanced across at this odious creature. 'You married?'

Cough, spit. 'Not yet,' and he grinned, 'but you know what a rich man can buy, hey?'

'As part of what I am sure will be an exceptional relationship,' Gorlas said, *where I profit from your work,* 'I am prepared to finance you on such an estate. A modest down payment on your part, at low interest . . .'

'Really? Why, noble sir, that would be fine. Yessy, very fine. We can do that all right.'

And when you kick off with no heirs I acquire yet another property in the Estate District. 'It is my pleasure,' he said with a smile. 'Those of us who have done well in our lives need to help each other whenever we can.'

'My thoughts too, 'bout all that. My thoughts exactly.'

Smoke and stenches, voices ringing through dust, oxen lowing as they strained with overloaded wagons. Gorlas Vidikas and the dying workmaster looked down on the scene, feeling very pleased with themselves.

Harllo squirmed his way out from the fissure, the hand holding the candle stretched out in front of him, and felt a calloused grip wrap round his narrow wrist. The candle was taken and then Bainisk was pulling Harllo out, surprisingly tender but that was Bainisk, a wise veteran all of sixteen years old, half his face a streak of shiny scar tissue through which peered the glittering blue of his eyes – both of which had miraculously escaped damage. He was grinning now as he helped Harllo on to his feet.

'Well, Mole?'

'Iron, raw and cold and wide across as three of my hands laid flat.'

'The air?'

'I'm here, aren't I?'

Laughing, Bainisk slapped him on the back. 'You've earned the afternoon. Back to Chuffs you go.'

Harllo frowned. 'Please, can't I stay on here?'

'Venaz giving you more trouble?'

'Bullies don't like me,' Harllo said.

'That's 'cause you're smart. Now listen, I warned him off once already and once is all the warning I give and he knows that so he won't be bothering you. We need our moles happy and in one piece. It's a camp law. I'm in charge of Chuffs, right?'

Harllo nodded. 'Only you won't be there, will you? Not this afternoon.'

'Venaz is in the kitchen today. It'll be all right.'

Nodding, Harllo collected his small sack of gear, which was a little heavier than usual, and set out for upside. He liked the tunnels, at least when the air wasn't foul and burning his throat. Surrounded by so much solid stone made him feel safe, protected, and he loved most those narrowest of cracks that only he could get through – or the few others like him, still fit with no broken bones and still small enough. He'd only cracked one finger so far and that was on his right hand which he used to hold the candle and not much else. He could pull himself along with his left, his half-naked body slick with sweat despite the damp stone and the trickles of icy water.

Exploring places no one had ever seen before. Or dragging the thick snaking hoses down into the icy pools then calling out for the men on the pumps to get started, and in the candle's fitful flickering light he'd watch the water level descend and see, sometimes, the strange growths on the stone, and in the crevices the tiny blind fish that – if he could reach – he slid into his mouth and chewed and swallowed, so taking something of this underworld into himself, and, just like those fish, at times he didn't even need his eyes, only his probing fingers, the taste and smell of the air and stone, the echoes of water droplets and the click-click of the white roaches skittering away.

Earlier this morning he'd been sent down a crevasse, ropes tied to his ankles as he was lowered like a dead weight, down, down, three then four knots of rope, before his outstretched hands found warm, dry rock, and here, so far below ground, the air was hot and sulphurous and the candle when he lit it flared in a crossflow of sweet rich air.

In the yellow light he looked round and saw, sitting up against a wall of the crevasse not three paces away, a corpse. Desiccated, the face collapsed and the eye sockets shrunken holes. Both legs were shattered, clearly from a fall, the shards sticking through the leathery skin.

Furs drawn up like a blanket, and close to within reach of one motionless, skeletal hand was a rotted bag now split open, revealing two antler picks, a bone punch and a groundstone mallet. A miner, Harllo realized, just like him. A miner of long, long ago.

Another step closer, eyes on those wonderful tools which he'd like to take, and the corpse spoke.

'As you please, cub.'

Harllo lunged backward. His heart pounded wild in the cage of his chest. 'A demon!'

'Patron of miners, perhaps. Not a demon, cub, not a demon.'

The candle had gone out with Harllo's panicked retreat. The corpse's voice, sonorous, with a rhythm like waves on a sandy beach, echoed out from the pitch black darkness.

'I am Dev'ad Anan Tol, of the Irynthal Clan of the Imass, who once lived on the shores of the Jhagra Til until the Tyrant Raest came to enslave us. Sent us down into the rock, where we all died. Yet see, I did not die. Alone of all my kin, I did not die.'

Harllo shakily fumbled with the candle, forcing the oiled wick into the spring spark tube. Three quick hissing pumps of the sparker and flame darted up.

'Nice trick, that.'

'The tube's got blue gas, not much and runs out fast so it needs refilling. There's bladders upside. Why didn't you die?'

'I have had some time to ponder that question, cub. I have reached but one conclusion that explains my condition. The Ritual of Tellann.'

'What made the evil T'lan Imass! I heard about that from Uncle Gruntle! Undead warriors at Black Coral – Gruntle saw them with his own eyes! And they kneeled and all their pain was taken from them by a man who then died since there was so much pain he took from them and so they built a barrow and it's still there and Gruntle said he wept but I don't believe that because Gruntle is big and the best warrior in the whole world and nothing could make him weep nothing at all!' And Harllo had to stop then so that he could regain his breath. And still his heart hammered like hailstones on a tin roof.

From the Imass named Dev'ad Anan Tol, silence.

'You still there?' Harllo asked.

'Cub. Take my tools. The first ever made and by my own hand. I was an inventor. In my mind ideas bred with such frenzy that I lived in a fever. At times, at night, I went half mad. So many thoughts, so many notions – my clan feared me. The bonecaster feared me. Raest himself feared me, and so he had me thrown down here. To die. And my ideas with me.'

'Should I tell everyone about you? They might decide to lift you out, so you can see the world again.'

'The world? That tiny flame you hold has shown me more of the world than I can comprehend. The sun . . . oh, the sun . . . that would destroy me, I think. To see it again.'

'We have metal picks now,' Harllo said. 'Iron.'

'Skystone. Yes, I saw much of it in the tunnels. The Jaghut used sorcery to bring it forth and shape it – we were not permitted to witness such things. But I thought, even then, how it might be drawn free, without magic. With heat. Drawn out, given shape, made into useful things. Does Raest still rule?'

'Never heard of any Raest,' said Harllo. 'Bainisk rules Chuffs and Workmaster rules the mine and in the city there's a council of nobles and in faraway lands there're kings and queens and emperors and empresses.'

'And T'lan Imass who kneel.'

Harllo glanced up the shaft – he could hear faint voices, echoing down. 'They want to pull me back up. What should I tell them about this place?'

'The wrong rock, the white grit that sickens people. Foul air.'

'So no one else comes down here.'

'Yes.'

'But then you'll be alone again.'

'Yes. Tell them, too, that a ghost haunts this place. Show them the ghost's magical tools.'

'I will. Listen, could be I might sneak back down here, if you like.'

'Cub, that would be most welcome.'

'Can I bring you anything?'

'Yes.'

'What?'

'Splints.'

And now Harllo was making his way back to daylight, and in his extra-heavy bag there clunked the tools of the corpse. Antler and bone hardened into stone, tines jabbing at his hip.

If Venaz found out about them he might take them, so Harllo knew he had to be careful. He had to hide them somewhere. Where nobody went or looked or picked through things. Plenty to think about, he had.

And he needed to find something called "splints". Whatever they were.

She insisted on taking his arm as they walked towards the Phoenix Inn, down from the Estate District, through Third Tier Wall, and into the Daru District. 'So many people,' she was saying. 'This is by far the biggest city I've ever been in. I think what strikes me is how many familiar faces I see – not people I actually know, just people who look like people I've known.'

Duiker thought about that, and then nodded. 'The world is like that, aye.'

'Is it now? Why?'

'I have no idea, Scillara.'

'Is this all the wisdom you can offer?'

'I even struggled with that one,' he replied.

'All right. Let's try something else. I take it you see no point in history.'

He grunted. 'If by that you mean that there is no progress, that even the notion of progress is a delusion, and that history is nothing more than a host of lessons nobody wants to pay attention to, then yes, there is no point. Not in writing it down, not in teaching it.'

'Never mind, then. You choose.'

'Choose what?'

'Something to talk about.'

'I don't think I can – nothing comes to mind, Scillara. Well, I suppose I'd like to know about Heboric.'

'He was losing his mind. We were trying to get to Otataral Island, where he wanted to give something back, something he once stole. But we never made it. Ambushed by T'lan Imass. They were going after him and the rest of us just got in the way. Me, Cutter, Greyfrog. Well, they also stole Felisin Younger – that seemed to be part of the plan, too.'

'Felisin Younger.'

'That's the name Sha'ik gave her.'

'Do you know why?'

She shook her head. 'I liked her, though.'

'Sha'ik?'

'Felisin Younger. I was training her to be just like me, so it's no wonder I liked her.' And she gave him a wide smile.

Duiker answered with a faint one of his own – hard indeed to be miserable around this woman. Better if he avoided her company in the future. 'Why the Phoenix Inn, Scillara?'

'As I said earlier, I want to embarrass someone. Cutter, in fact. I had to listen to him for months and months, about how wonderful Darujhistan is, and how he would show me this and that. Then as soon as we arrive he ducks away, wanting nothing to do with us. Back to his old friends, I suppose.'

She was being offhand, but Duiker sensed the underlying hurt. Perhaps she and Cutter had been more than just companions. 'Instead,' he said, 'you found us Malazans.'

'Oh, we could have done much worse.'

'Barathol had kin,' said Duiker. 'In the Bridgeburners. An assassin. Seeing your friend was like seeing a ghost. For Picker, Antsy . . . Blend. Bluepearl. The old marines.'

'One of those familiar faces belonging to someone you don't know.'

He smiled again. 'Yes.' *Oh, yes, Scillara, you are clever indeed.*

'And before you know it, some old marine healer is out doing whatever he can to help Barathol Mekhar. Only there's this history – the stuff that doesn't matter – with our blacksmith friend. Having to do with Aren and the—'

'Red Blades, aye.'

She shot him a look. 'You knew?'

'We all know. The poor bastard. Getting such a raw deal in his own homeland. Things like that, well, we can sympathize with, because we have our histories. The kind that can't be ignored because they've put us right where we are, right here, a continent away from our home.'

'Progress?'

'That remains to be seen. And here we are. Phoenix Inn.'

She stood studying the decrepit sign for a long moment. 'That's it? It's a dump.'

'If the story is accurate, Kalam Mekhar himself went in there once or twice. So did Sorry, who later took the name of Apsalar, and that was where young Crokus met her – who is now known as Cutter, right? Putting it all together isn't easy. Mallet was there for most of that. In there,' he added, 'you might even find a man named Kruppe.'

She snorted. 'Cutter talked about him. Some oily fence and ex-thief.'

'Ambassador at large during the Pannion War. The man who stood down Caladan Brood. Single-handedly confounding most of the great leaders on the continent.'

Her eyes had widened slightly. 'Really? All that? Cutter never mentioned any of that.'

'He wouldn't have known, Scillara. He went off with Fiddler, Kalam and Apsalar.'

'That's a tale I'm slowly putting together myself,' she said. 'Apsalar. The woman Cutter loves.'

Ah.

'Let's go, then.'

And they set out across the street.

'The kid's been snatched, is my guess,' Murillio concluded, settling back in his chair. 'I know, Kruppe, it's one of those things that just happens. Tanners grab children, trader ships, fishing crews, pimps and temples, they all do given the chance. So I know, there may not be much hope—'

'Nonsense, Murillio loyal friend of Kruppe. In appealing to this round self you have displayed utmost wisdom. Moreover, Kruppe applauds this new profession of yours. Instructor yes, in all fine points of fine pointiness – the art of duelling is writ bold in blood, yes? Bold too is this Stonny Menackis, old partner to none other than Gruntle of the Barbs, and was there not a third? A long-armed man who did not return from Capustan? And was his name not Harllo? Kruppe must plumb deeper depths of memory to be certain of such details, yet his instinct cries out *true!* And how can such a voice be denied?'

Cutter rubbed at the bristle on his chin. 'I could head back down to the ship I came in on, Murillio. Talk to the dock waifs and the old women under the piers.'

'I'd appreciate that, Cutter.'

'Kruppe suspects a whispery warming of heart in dear Murillio for his new employer – ah, does Kruppe flinch at vehement expostulation? Does he wince at savage denial? Why, the answer is no to both!'

'Leave off that, Kruppe,' Murillio said. 'The lad's her son.'

'Left in the care of others – is she so cold of heart, then? Do you rise to extraordinary challenge, mayhap? The best kind, of course, ever the best kind.'

'There's a story there,' Murillio said. 'Not all women make good mothers, true enough. But she doesn't seem that kind. I mean, well, she struck me as someone with fierce loyalties. Maybe. Oh, I don't know. It'd be nice to find the runt, that's all.'

'We understand, Murillio,' Cutter said.

'Rely upon Kruppe, dearest friend. All truths will yield themselves in the fullness of revelatory revelation, anon. But wait, fortuitous reunion of another sort beckons,' and he leaned forward, small eyes fixing upon Cutter. Eyebrows waggled.

'You're scaring me—'

'Terror shall burgeon imminently for poor Cutter.'

'What are you—'

A hand settled on his shoulder, soft, plump.

Cutter closed his eyes and said, 'I've got to stop sitting with my back to the door.'

Murillio rose, suddenly formal as he bowed to someone standing behind Cutter. 'Historian. We have met once or—'

'I recall,' the man replied, moving round into Cutter's sight as he collected two chairs from a nearby table. *Thank the gods, not his hand.*

'Please do thank Mallet again—'

'I will,' the historian replied. 'In the meantime, I'm not the one who should be doing the introductions.' Those weary, ancient eyes fixed on Cutter. 'You're Cutter, yes?'

He twisted to look at the woman standing behind his chair. Seated as he was, his eyes were level with a pair of breasts covered in tight-fitting linen. And he knew them well. It was a struggle to lift his gaze higher. 'Scillara.'

'You call that an introduction?' she asked, dragging up the other chair the historian had pulled close. She wedged herself in on Cutter's right and sat down. 'I've never seen bones picked so clean on a plate before,' she observed, her eyes on the leavings of lunch.

Kruppe wheezed upright. He began waving his hands. 'Kruppe hastens with proper welcome to this grand company to already beloved Scillara of the Knowing Eyes and other assorted accoutrements of charm Kruppe would dearly wish to knowingly eye, if not for the dastardly demands of decorum. Welcome, cries Kruppe, even as he slumps back – *oof!* – exhausted by his enthusiasm and dimpled with desire.'

Murillio bowed to Scillara. 'I won't be as crass as dimpled Kruppe. I am Murillio, an old friend of Cro— Cutter's.'

She began repacking her pipe with rustleaf. 'Cutter spoke often of your charm, Murillio, when it comes to women,' and she paused to smile.

Murillio sat back down a tad hard and Cutter saw, wryly amused, that he looked more awake now than he had in days, perhaps since the stabbing.

Kruppe was fanning his flushed face. Then he raised a hand. 'Sulty! Sweet creature, the finest wine in the house! No, wait! Go down the street to the Peacock and buy us a bottle of *their* finest wine! The finest wine in their house, yes! Is something wrong, Meese? Kruppe meant no insult, honest! Sulty, be on with you, child! Meese, why—'

'No more,' cut in Murillio, 'unless you want to pile on ever more insults to our faithful proprietor, until she comes over here and kills you outright.'

'Dire misunderstanding! Enthusiasm and—'

'Dimples, we know.'

Cutter spoke up, 'Scillara was a camp follower in Sha'ik's rebel city in Raraku. Er, not a follower like that, I mean—'

'Yes I was,' she said. 'Just that.' She struck sparks to the bowl. 'Plaything to soldiers. In particular, Malazans. Renegades from Korbolo Dom's turncoat army. His Dogslayers. I was then plucked from what would have been a short, benumbed existence by a Malazan priest with no hands, who dragged me across half of Seven Cities, along with Cutter here.' She sent a stream of smoke upward, then continued. 'Just inland of the Otataral Sea, we got jumped. The priest was cut down. Cutter got disembowelled and I had a baby – no real connection between the two, by the way, apart from bad timing. Some villagers found us and saved us – the son of Osserc showed up for that – and that's how we collected Barathol Mekhar and Chaur, making up for the two we'd lost in the ambush.

'Now, normally I don't tell long-winded tales like this one, but what I gave you was necessary for you to understand a few important things. One: I left the baby in the village, with no regrets. Two: Cutter, who was with us because The Rope thought Felisin Younger needed protecting, nearly died and is now living with a feeling of having failed at his task, since Felisin was taken from us. Three: Cutter also has a broken heart, and no matter how much fun we eventually had, him and me, it's clear that I can't help him with that. And finally, four: he's embarrassed by me because he probably thinks I'm too fat and he thinks you'll all be thinking the same thing, too.'

All three men facing her fervently shook their heads at that, while Cutter sat head in hands.

Sulty arrived to slam down a thick-based dusty clay bottle and two more goblets. 'Three councils, Kruppe!'

Kruppe set three silver coins into her hand without a whimper.

After a long moment, the historian sighed, reached out and uncorked the bottle. He sniffed the mouth. Brows lifted. 'Empty the rubbish in your cups, please.'

They did and Duiker poured.

'Cutter,' said Murillio.

'What?'

'You were disembowelled? Gods below, man!'

'Kruppe struggles to taste the wonder of this wondrous vintage, so gasted of flabber is he at said horrendous tale. The world is most cruel, yet salvation unfolds at the last, blessed be all the gods, goddesses, spirits, marsupials and amphibians and indeed all the rest. Made drunk by punches is poor Kruppe, rocked this way, knocked that, buffeted askew in every direction at once very nearly unto exploding. Beloved Scillara, you tell a most awkward tale, and tell it badly. Despite this, see us here, each one reeling at said poorly told revelations!'

'Perhaps excessive in my efforts at summarizing, I'll grant you,' Scillara allowed. 'But I thought: best to push through the uncomfortable stage, and now here we are, relaxed and eager to quaff down this fine wine. I have decided I like the Phoenix Inn.'

Duiker rose. 'My task complete, I shall—'

'Sit back down, old man,' she said. 'If I have to slap the life back into you I will. Less painful, one hopes, partaking of our company this day, don't you think?'

The historian slowly sat back down.

Kruppe gusted out a sigh. 'Pity us men at this table, we are outnumbered!'

'I take it Cutter's told nothing,' Scillara observed. 'Not even how we almost drowned when the moon broke up and fell out of the sky. Saved by a dragon.'

'I will indeed stay,' said Duiker, 'provided you back up and tell us all this properly, Scillara.'

'As you like.'

'From the moment you first met Heboric.'

'This will take all night,' she said. 'And I'm hungry.'

'Murillio will be delighted to purchase our suppers,' declared Kruppe.

'For once you are right,' Murillio said.

'I don't think you're too fat,' said Cutter. 'I don't think anything like that, Scillara.' *Too good, yes. And why don't you see how Barathol looks at you? As for me, well, Apsalar was smart enough to get away and I won't begrudge her that. In fact, I doubt there's a woman low enough for me anywhere in the world.*

Was that too self-pitying? No, just realistic, he decided.

Oh, and by the way, everyone, that dragon is wearing silks and biding her time aboard her damned ship, right there in Darujhistan harbour . . . Oh, and did I mention that the city is in imminent danger?

The bottle of wine was done and Sulty was sent off for another one. Meese was quickly appeased by the orders for supper and the knowledge that, eventually, the swill she stocked would be broached and consumed to excess.

As Scillara told her tale.

While Cutter's mind, sodden with alcohol, wandered through all those thoughts that were anything but self-pitying. *Not a woman anywhere . . .*

Lady Challice Vidikas sat at one end of the table, Shardan Lim on her left, Hanut Orr to her right. For this night she wore emerald green silks, the short coat tight-fitting, collarless to expose her unadorned, powdered throat and low-cut to reveal her scented breasts. Her hair was tied up, speared through with silver pins. Rouge blushed her cheeks. Kohl thickened her lashes. Earrings depended from her ears in tumbling, glittering array, the green of emerald and the blue of sapphire. The coat's short sleeves revealed her bared arms, the skin soft, smooth, slightly plump, unstained by the sun. Leggings of brushed kid leather covered her lower limbs and on her feet was the latest style of sandals, the one with a high peglike heel.

Amber wine glimmered in crystal goblets. Candlelight painted soft and gold every detail in a pool that faded into gloom beyond the three at the table, so that the servants moved in shadows, appearing only to clear dishes, rearrange settings, and deliver yet more food.

She but picked at her meal, wanting to be somewhat drunk for what would come at the end of this night. The only question she was unable to answer was . . . *which one first?*

Oh, there was sexual excitement – she could not deny that. Both men were hale and attractive, though in very different ways. And both equally obnoxious, but she thought she could live with that. For certain, her heart would play no role in what was to come, no giving over, no confusion that might lead to conflicted feelings, or feelings of any sort.

She could keep this simple. Everyone made use of what they had, didn't they, especially when what they had proved desirable to others. This was how power accrued, after all. One man here, right or left, would have her this night – had they already decided which one between them? A toss of the knuckles. A wager in flesh. She was not sure – the evening was early yet and thus far she'd seen no overt signs of competition.

Hanut spoke, 'Shardan and I have been discussing you all afternoon, Lady Challice.'

'Oh? How flattering.'

'It was on the night of my uncle's murder, wasn't it? At Lady Simtal's estate – you were there.'

'I was, yes, Hanut.'

'That night, young Gorlas Vidikas saved your life.'

'Yes.'

'And so won your heart,' said Shardan Lim, smiling behind his goblet as he sipped.

'You make it sound an easy thing,' she said, 'winning my heart.'

'Then gratitude made a good start,' Shardan observed as Hanut settled back as if willing to listen and venture nothing else – at least for now. 'He was very young, as were you. An age when charms seemed to flash blindingly bright.'

'And I was dazzled,' she said.

'Gorlas did very well by it, I should say. One hopes he daily expresses his gratitude . . . when he is here, I mean. All the proper, entirely unambiguous gestures and the like.'

Hanut Orr stirred. 'For too long, Lady Vidikas, the House of Orr and the House of D'Arle have been at odds on the Council. Generations of that, and, as far as I am concerned, for no good reason. I find myself wishing, often, that your father would meet me, to make amends, to forge something new and lasting. An alliance, in fact.'

'An ambitious goal, Hanut Orr,' said Challice. *Unfortunately, my father thinks you are a preening, fatuous ass. A true Orr, in other words.* 'And you are most welcome, I'm sure, to make such an overture. I wish you the Lady's tug.'

'Ah, then I have your blessing in such an endeavour?'

'Of course. Will that impress my father? That remains to be seen.'

'Surely he cherishes you dearly,' Shardan Lim murmured. 'How could he not?'

I have this list . . . 'The House of Vidikas was ever a modest presence in the Council,' she said. 'A long, unbroken succession of weak men and women singularly lacking in ambition.'

Hanut Orrr snorted and reached for his goblet. 'Excepting the latest, of course.'

'Of course. My point is, my father ascribes little weight to the desires of House Vidikas, and I am now part of that house.'

'Do you chafe?'

She fixed her gaze on Shardan Lim. 'A bold question, sir.'

'My apologies, Lady Vidikas. Yet I have come to cherish you and so only wish you happiness and contentment.'

'Why would you imagine I felt otherwise?'

'Because,' Hanut Orr drawled, 'you've been knocking back the wine this night like a tavern harlot.' And he rose. 'Thank you, Lady Vidikas, for a most enjoyable evening. I must, alas, take my leave.'

Struggling against anger, she managed a nod. 'Of course, Councillor Orr. Forgive me if I do not see you out.'

He smiled. 'Easily done, milady.'

When he was gone, Shardan swore softly under his breath. 'He was angry with you.'

'Oh?' The hand that raised the goblet to her lips was, she saw, trembling.

'Hanut wants your father to come to him, not the other way round. He won't be a squirming pup to anyone.'

'A pup is never strong enough to make the first move, Shardan Lim. He misunderstood my challenge.'

'Because it implies a present failing on his part. A failing of his nerve.'

'Perhaps it does, and that should make him angry with me? How, precisely, does that work?'

Shardan Lim laughed and as he stretched out it was clear that, free now of Hanut Orr's shadow, he was like a deadly flower opening to the night. 'You showed him up for the self-important but weak-willed bully that he is.'

'Unkind words for your friend.'

Shardan Lim stared down at his goblet as he drank a mouthful. Then he said in a growl, 'Hanut Orr is no friend of mine.'

The wine was making her brain feel strangely loose, untethered. She no longer even tasted each sip, there had been so many of them, the servant a silent ghost slipping in to refill her goblet. 'I think he believes otherwise.'

'I doubt it. It was some damned conspiracy with House Orr that saw my father assassinated. And now it seems my family is snared, trapped, and the games just go on and on.'

This was a most unexpected side of the man and she did not know how to respond to it. 'Such honesty humbles me, Shardan Lim. For what it is worth, I will keep what I have heard this night to myself.'

'No need, but thank you anyway. In fact, I'd rather your husband well understood how things stand. Hanut Orr is a dangerous man. House Lim and House Vidikas share many things, principal among them the stigma of disrespect on the Council. Contempt, even. I have been curious,' and now the look he turned upon her was sharp, searching. 'This venture of your husband's, ever pushing for this ironmonger of his to attain membership in the Council – what does Gorlas play at?'

She blinked in confusion. 'I'm sorry, I have no idea.'

'Might you find out? For me?'

'I am not sure if I can – Gorlas does not confide in me on such matters.'

'Does he confide in you at all?' He went on without waiting for her reply (not that she had one). 'Lady Vidikas – Challice – he is wasting you, do you understand? I see this – gods, it leaves me furious! You are an intelligent woman, a beautiful woman, and he treats you like one of these silver plates. Just one more possession, one more piece in his hoard.'

She set her goblet down. 'What do you want from me, Shardan Lim? Is this some sort of invitation? A conspiracy of love? Trysts behind my husband's back? While he travels here and there, you and I meeting up in some squalid inn? Getting intimate with each other's bodies, then lying back and making pointless plans, endlessly lying to each other about a future together?'

He stared across at her.

All the servants had with uncharacteristic discreetness vanished into the side chambers, the kitchens, anywhere but this dining room. Even the wine server had disappeared. It occurred to Challice that Shardan's manservant had probably been free with coin among the house staff and that sly, silent man was now outside in the courtyard, passing a pipe to eager-eyed menials, and they were all laughing, snickering, rolling their eyes and worse.

Too late, she realized, to change any of that. To scour the lurid thoughts from their petty minds.

'You describe,' Shardan Lim finally said, 'a most sordid arrangement, with all the cynicism of a veteran in such matters. And that I do not believe. You have been faithful, Challice. I would not so care for you otherwise.'

'Oh? Have you been spying on me, then?' It was a mocking question that lost its carefree aura as the man voiced no denial, and she suddenly felt chilled to the bone. 'Following another man's wife around does not seem an honourable thing to do, Shardan Lim.'

'Love has no honour.'

'Love? Or obsession? Is it not your own hunger for possession that has you coveting a woman owned by another man?'

'He does not own you. That is my point, Challice. Such notions of ownership are nothing but twisted lies disguised as love. I have no interest in owning you. Nor in stealing you away – if I had I would have found an excuse to duel your husband long ago, and I would have killed him without compunction. For you. To give you back your life.'

'With you at the grieving widow's side? Oh, that would look odd now, wouldn't it? Me leaning on the arm of the man who murdered my husband. And you talk to me of freedom?' She was, she realized, shocked sober. By what this man was revealing to her; by the stunning depth of his depraved desire.

'Giving you back your life, I said.'

'I will ask you again: what do you want?'

'To show you what it means to be free. To cut your chains. Take me to your bed if you so desire. Or don't. Send me out of here with your boot to my backside. The choice is yours. I want you to feel your freedom, Challice. In your soul – let it burn, bright or dark as you like, but let it *burn!* Filling you entirely.'

Her breaths came fast, shallow. Oh, this was a most unanticipated tactic of his. *Give me nothing, woman. No, give it to yourself instead. Make use of me. As proof. Of your freedom. Tonight you can make yourself free again. The way it felt when you were younger, when there was no husband weighing down your arm. Before the solemn shackles were slipped on.* A most extraordinary invitation indeed. 'Where are my servants?'

'Away for the rest of the night, Lady Vidikas.'

'Just like Hanut Orr. Does he sit in some tavern right now, telling everyone—'

'I arranged nothing with that bastard. And you must realize, he will talk whether anything happens or not. To wound you. Your reputation.'

'My husband will then hear of it, even though nothing has happened.'

'And should you stand before Gorlas and deny the rumours, will he believe you, Challice?'

No. He wouldn't want to. 'He will not accept being cuckolded.'

'He will smile because he doesn't care. Until it serves him to challenge one of us, me or Hanut, to a duel. On a point of honour. He is a fine duellist. A cruel one at that. He disregards all rules, all propriety. Victory is all that matters and if that means flinging sand into his opponent's eyes he will do just that. A very dangerous man, Challice. I would not want to face him with rapiers bared. But I will if I have to.' Then he shook his head. 'But it won't be me.'

'No?'

'It will be Hanut Orr. That is the man he wants for you. He's given you to Hanut Orr – another reason he stormed off, since he finally understood that I would not permit it.'

'So in Gorlas's stead this night you have defended my honour.'

'And failed, because Hanut is skewering your reputation even as we speak. When I said you can make use of me, Challice, I meant it. Even now, here, you can tell me to seek out Hanut – yes, I can guess where he is right now – and call him out. I can kill him for you.'

'My reputation . . .'

'Is already ruined, Lady Vidikas, and I am truly sorry for that. Tell me what you would have me do. Please.'

She was silent. It was getting difficult to think clearly. Consequences were crashing down like an avalanche and she was buried, all air driven from her lungs. Buried, yes, in what had not even happened.

Yet.

'I will try this freedom of yours, Shardan Lim.'

He rose, one hand settling on the grip of his rapier. 'Milady.'

Oh, how noble. Snorting, she rose. 'You've taken hold of the wrong weapon.'

His eyes widened. Was the surprise real or feigned? Was there a glimmer of triumph in those blue, blue eyes? She couldn't find it at all.

And that frightened her.

'Shardan . . .'

'Milady?'

'Make no wishes for a future. Do you understand me?'

'I do.'

'I will not free my heart only to chain it anew.'

'Of course you won't. That would be madness.'

She studied him a moment longer, and received nothing new for that effort. 'I am glad I am not drunk,' she said.

And he bowed.

Making, in that one gesture, this night of adultery so very . . . noble.

Night seeps into Darujhistan, a thick blinding fog in which people stumble or hide as they walk the alleys and streets. Some are drawn like moths to the lit areas and the welcoming eternal hiss of gas from the wrought iron poles. Others seek to move as one with the darkness, at least until some damned piece of crockery snaps underfoot, or a pebble is sent skittering. And everywhere can be seen the small glitter of rodent eyes, or heard the slither of tails.

Light glows through shutters and bubbled glass windows, but never mind the light and all peaceful slumber and discourse and all the rest such illumination might reveal! Dull and witless the expectations so quickly and predictably surrendered!

A woman in whose soul burned freedom black and blazing arches her back as only the second man in her life slides deep into her and something ignites in her mind – Gorlas ever used his fingers in this place, after all, and fingers cannot match – *gods below!*

But leave that now – truly, imagination suffices to wax eloquent all the clumsy shifting about and strange sounds and the fumbling for this and that, and then that – no more! Out into the true darkness, yes, to the fingerless man stalking his next victim.

To a new estate and Captain Torvald Nom of the House Guard, moments from leaving for the night with all security in the so-capable hands of Scorch and Leff (yes, he worked hard on that), who pauses to watch a black two-person carriage trundle into the courtyard, and whose eyes thin to verymost slits of suspicion and curiosity and a niggling feeling of . . . something, as a cloaked, hooded figure steps into view and slides like a bad thought up the stairs and into the main house. *Who . . .* ponder no longer, Torvald Nom! On your way, yes, back home to your loving and suitably impressed wife. Think of nothing but that and that alone and be on your way!

A guard with occasional chest pains is questioning patrons of a bar, seeking witnesses who might have seen someone set out to follow that local man into the alley in order to beat him to death and would no one step forward on behalf of that hapless victim? Might do, aye, ifn any of us liked him, y'see . . .

In a crypt (irrationally well lit, of course) sits a man plotting the downfall of the city, starting with a handful of Malazans, and he sits most contented in the absence of shadows or any other ambivalence imposed upon reality.

Out in Chuffs, as moles sleep in their tiny cots, Bainisk sits down beside Harllo's bed to hear more stories about Darujhistan, for Bainisk was born in Chuffs and has never left it, you see, and his eyes glow as Harllo whispers about riches and all sorts of wonderful foods and great monuments and statues and blue fire everywhere and before long both are asleep, Harllo in his lumpy bed and Bainisk on the floor beside it, and across the way Venaz sees this and sneers to display his hatred of both Bainisk and Bainisk's new favourite when Venaz used to be his best, but Bainisk was a betrayer, a liar and worse and someday Harllo would pay for that—

Because Harllo was right. He was a boy who drew bullies like a lodestone and this was a cruel fact and his kind were legion and it was a godly blessing how so many survived and grew up to wreak vengeance upon all those people not as smart as they were, but even that is a bitter reward and never quite as satisfying as it might be.

Back to Darujhistan, with relief, as a Great Raven launches herself skyward from the tower of Baruk's estate, watched with evil satisfaction by a squat, overweight demon staring out from a spark-spitting chimney mouth.

And this was a night like any other, a skein of expectations and anticipations, revelations and perturbations. Look around. Look around! On all sides, day and night, light and dark! Every step taken with the firm resolve to believe in the solid ground awaiting it. Every step, one after another, again and again, and no perilous ledge yawns ahead, oh no.

Step and step, now, step and step—

Chapter Ten

Will you come and tell me when the music ends
When the musicians are swallowed in flames
Every instrument blackening and crumbling to ash
When the dancers stumble and sprawl their diseased limbs
rotting off and twitching the skin sloughing away

Will you come and tell me when the music ends
When the stars we pushed into the sky loose their roars
And the clouds we built into visible rage do now explode
When the bright princes of privilege march past with dead smiles
falling from their faces a host of deceiving masks

Will you come and tell me when the music ends
When reason sinks into the morass of superstition
Waging a war of ten thousand armies stung to the lash
When we stop looking up even as we begin our mad running
into stupidity's nothingness with heavenly choirs screaming

Will you come and tell me when the music ends
When the musicians are no more than black grinning sticks
Every instrument wailing its frantic death cry down the road
When the ones left standing have had their mouths cut off
leaving holes from which a charnel wind eternally blows

Will you come and tell me when the music ends
The fire is eating my breath and agony fills this song
When my fingers crack on the strings and fall from my hands
And this dance twists every muscle like burning rope
while your laughter follows down my crumpling corpse

Won't you come and tell me when the music ends
When I can leap away and face one god or a thousand
Or nothing at all into this blessed bliss of oblivion
When I can prise open this box and release cruel and bitter fury
at all the mad fools crowding the door in panicked flight

Watch me and watch me with eyes wide and shocked
With disbelief with horror with indignant umbrage to upbraid

And the shouted *Nays* are like drumbeats announcing a truth
The music ends my friends, my vile, despicable friends, and see me –
see me slam the door slam it hard – in all your faces!

THE MUSIC ENDS
FISHER KEL TATH

H is boots crunched on waterworn stones slick with mist as he made his way to the water's edge. The steep slopes of the surrounding mountainsides were verdant, thick rainforest, crimson-barked trees towering high, beards of moss hanging from toppled trunks.

Endest Silann leaned on his stolid walking stick, the muscles of his legs trembling. He looked round as he slowly regained his breath. It was chilly, the sun's arc just slipping past the western peaks, and shadow swallowed the river valley.

Black water rushed by and he felt its cold – no need to squat down, no need to slide a hand into the tugging current. This dark river was, he could see now, nothing like Dorssan Ryl. How could he have expected otherwise? The new is ever but a mangled echo of the old and whatever whispers of similarity one imagined do naught but sting with pain, leaving one blistered with loss. Oh, he had been a fool, to have journeyed all this way. Seeking what? Even that he could not answer.

No, perhaps he could. *Escape. Brief, yes, but escape none the less.* The coward flees, knowing he must return, wishing that the return journey might kill him, take his life as it did the old everywhere. *But listen! You can shape your soul – make it a bucket, a leaking one that you carry about. Or your soul can be a rope, thick and twisted, refusing to break even as it buckles to one knot after another. Choose your image, Endest Silann. You are here, you've made it this far, haven't you? And as he told you . . . not much farther to go. Not much farther at all.*

He smelled woodsmoke.

Startled, alarmed, he turned away from the rush of the river. Faced upstream whence came the late afternoon breeze. There, in distant gloom, the muted glow of a campfire.

Ah, no escape after all. He'd wanted solitude, face to face with intractable, indifferent nature. He'd wanted to feel . . . irrelevant. He'd wanted the wildness to punch him senseless, leave him humiliated, reduced to a wretch. Oh, he had wanted plenty, hadn't he?

With a sour grunt, Endest Silann began walking upstream. At the very least, the fire would warm his hands.

Thirty paces away, he could see the lone figure facing the smoky flames. Huge, round-shouldered, seated on a fallen log. And Endest Silann smiled in recognition.

Two trout speared on skewers cooked above the fire. A pot of simmering tea sat with one blackened shoulder banked in coals. Two tin cups warmed on the flat rock making up one side of the hearth.

Another log waited opposite the one on which sat the warlord, Caladan Brood, who slowly twisted round to watch Endest Silann approach. The broad, oddly bestial face split into a wry smile. 'Of all the guests I imagined this night, old friend, you did not come to mind. Forgive me. You took your time since beginning your descent into this valley, but for that I will happily make allowances – but do not complain if the fish is overcooked.'

'Complaints are far away and will remain so, Caladan. You have awakened my appetite – for food, drink and, most of all, company.'

'Then sit, make yourself comfortable.'

'So you did indeed disband your army after the siege,' said Endest Silann, making his way over to settle himself down. 'There were rumours. Of course, my master said nothing.'

'See me now,' said the warlord, 'commanding an army of wet stones, and yes, it proves far less troublesome than the last one. Finally, I can sleep soundly at night. Although, matching wits with these trout has challenged me mightily. There, take one of those plates, and here – beware the bones, though,' he added as he set a fish on the plate.

'Alone here, Caladan Brood – it makes me wonder if you are hiding.'

'It may be that I am, Endest Silann. Unfortunately, hiding never works.'

'No, it never does.'

Neither spoke for a time as they ate their supper. The trout was indeed overdone but Endest Silann said nothing, for it was delicious none the less.

If Anomander Rake was a mystery shrouded in darkness, then Caladan Brood was one clothed in geniality. Spare with words, he nevertheless could make virtually anyone feel welcome and, indeed, appreciated. Or rather, he could when the pressures of command weren't crouched on his shoulders like a damned mountain. This night, then, Endest Silann well understood, was a gift, all the more precious in that it was wholly unexpected.

When the meal was done, night's arrival closed out the world beyond the fire's light. The rush of the river was a voice, a presence. Water flowed indifferent to the heave and plunge of the sun, the shrouded moon and the slow spin of the stars. The sound reached them in a song without words, and all effort to grasp its meaning was hopeless, for, like the water itself, one could not grasp hold of sound. The flow was ceaseless and immeasurable and just as stillness did not in fact exist, so too true, absolute silence.

'Why are you here?' Endest Silann asked after a time.

'I wish I could answer you, old friend, and Burn knows the desire to ease the burden is almost overwhelming.'

'You are assuming, Caladan, that I am ignorant of what awaits us.'

'No, I do not do that – after all, you have sought a pilgrimage, out to this river – and among the Tiste Andii, this place has proved a mysterious lure. Yet you ask why I am here, and so your knowledge must be . . . incomplete. Endest Silann, I cannot say more. I cannot help you.'

The old Tiste Andii looked away, off into the dark where the river sang to the night. So, others had come here, then. Some instinctive need drawing them, yes, to the ghost of Dorssan Ryl. He wondered if they had felt the same disappointment as he had upon seeing these black (but not black enough) waters. *It is not the same. Nothing ever is, beginning with ourselves.* 'I do not,' he said, 'believe much in forgiveness.'

'What of restitution?'

The question stunned him, stole his breath. The river rushed with the sound of ten thousand voices and those cries filled his head, spread into his chest to grip his heart. Cold pooled in his gut. *By the Abyss . . . such . . . ambition.* He felt the icy trickle of tears on his fire-warmed cheeks. 'I will do all I can.'

'He knows that,' Caladan Brood said with such compassion that Endest Silann almost cried out. 'You might not believe this now,' the huge warrior continued, 'but you will find this pilgrimage worthwhile. A remembrance to give strength when you need it most.'

No, he did not believe that now, and could not imagine ever believing it. Even so . . . the *ambition.* So appalling, so breathtaking.

Caladan Brood poured the tea and set a cup into Endest's hands. The tin shot heat into his chilled fingers. The warlord was standing beside him now.

'Listen to the river, Endest Silann. Such a peaceful sound . . .'

But in the ancient Tiste Andii's mind that sound was a wailing chorus, an overwhelming flood of loss and despair. The ghost of Dorssan Ryl? No, this was where that long dead river emptied out, feeding the midnight madness of its history into a torrent where it swirled with a thousand other currents. Endless variations on the same bitter flavour.

And as he stared into the flames he saw once more the city dying in a conflagration. Kharkanas beneath the raging sky. Blinding ash like sand in the eyes, smoke like poison in the lungs. Mother Darkness in her fury, denying her children, turning away as they died and died. And died.

Listen to the river. Remember the voices.

Wait, as does the warlord here. Wait, to see what comes.

The smell of the smoke remained long after the fire was done. They rode in on to charred ground and blackened wreckage. Collapsed, crumbled inward, the enormous carriage still reared like a malignant smoking pyre in the centre of stained earth. Detritus was scattered about to mark the disintegration of the community. Yet, although the scene was one of slaughter, there were no bodies. Trails set off in all directions, some broader than others.

Samar Dev studied the scene for a time, then watched as Traveller dismounted to walk over to the edge of the camp, where he began examining some of the tracks leading away. He was an odd man, she decided. Quiet, self-contained, a man used to being alone, yet beneath it all was a current of . . . yes, mayhem. As if it was his own solitude that kept the world safe.

Once, long ago now, she had found herself in the company of another warrior equally familiar with that concept. But there the similarity ended. Karsa Orlong, notwithstanding that first journey into the besieged fortress outside Ugarat, thrived on an audience. *Witness*, he would say, in full expectation of just that. He wanted his every deed observed, as if each set of eyes existed solely to mark Karsa Orlong, and the minds behind them served, to the exclusion of all else, to recount to all what he had done, what he had said, what he had begun and what he had ended. *He makes us his history. Every witness contributes to the narrative – the life, the deeds of Toblakai – a narrative to which we are, each of us, bound.*

Chains and shackles snaked out from the burned carriage. Empty, of course. And yet, despite this, Samar Dev understood that the survivors of this place remained slaves. Chained to Karsa Orlong, their liberator, chained to yet another grim episode in his history. *He gives us freedom and enslaves us all. Oh, now there is irony. All the sweeter for that he does not mean to, no, the very opposite each and every time. The damned fool.*

'Many took horses, loaded down with loot,' Traveller said, returning to his mount. 'One trail heads north, the least marked – I believe it belongs to your friend.'

My friend.

'He is not far ahead of us now, and still on foot. We should catch up to him today.'

She nodded.

Traveller studied her for a moment. He then swung himself on to his horse and collected the reins. 'Samar Dev, I cannot work out what happened here.'

'He did,' she replied. 'He happened here.'

'He killed no one. From what you have told me, well, I thought to find something else. It is as if he simply walked up to them and said, "It's over."' He frowned across at her. 'How can that be?'

She shook her head.

He grunted, guiding his horse round. 'The scourge of the Skathandi has ended.'

'It has.'

'My fear of your companion has . . . deepened. I am ever more reluctant to find him.'

'But that will not stop you, will it? If he carries the Emperor's Sword . . .'

He did not reply. He didn't need to.

They set out at a canter. Northward.

The wind cut across from the west, sun-warmed and dry. The few clouds scudding past overhead were thin and shredded. Ravens or hawks circled, wheeling specks, and Samar Dev thought of flies buzzing the corpse of the earth.

She spat to clear away the taste of woodsmoke.

A short time later they came upon a small camp. Three men, two pregnant women. The fear in their eyes warred with abject resignation as Samar Dev and Traveller came up and reined in. The men had not sought to flee, proof of the rarest kind of courage – the women were too burdened to run, so the men had stayed and if that meant death, then so be it.

Details like these ever humbled Samar Dev.

'You are following the Toblakai,' Traveller said, dismounting. They stared, saying nothing. Traveller half turned and gestured for Samar Dev. Curious, she slipped down.

'Can you see to the health of the women?' he asked her in a low voice.

'All right,' she said, then watched as the Dal Honese warrior led the three men off to one side. Bemused, Samar Dev approached the women. Both, she saw, were far along in their pregnancies, and then she noted that both seemed . . . not quite human. Furtive eyes the hue of tawny grasses, a kind of animal wariness along with the resignation she had noted earlier, but now she understood it as the fatalism of the victim, the hunted, the prey. Yes, she could imagine seeing such eyes in the antelope with the leopard's jaws closed on its throat. The image left her feeling rattled.

'I am a witch,' she said. 'Shoulder Woman.'

Both remained sitting. They stared in silence.

She edged closer and crouched down opposite them. They bore features both human and animal, as if they represented some alternative version of human beings. Dark-skinned, slope-browed, with broad mouths full-lipped and probably – when not taut with anxiety – unusually expressive. Both looked well fed, essentially healthy. Both emanated that strange completeness that only pregnant women possessed. When everything outward faced inward. In a less generous moment she might call it *smugness* but this was not such a moment. Besides, there was in those auras something animal that made it all seem proper, natural, as if this was exclusively and precisely what women were for.

Now *that* notion irritated her.

She straightened and walked over to where Traveller stood with the men. 'They are fine,' she said.

His brows rose at her tone, but he said nothing.

'So,' she asked, 'what secrets have they revealed?'

'The sword he carries was made of flint, or obsidian. Stone.'

'Then he rejected the Crippled God. No, I'm not surprised. He won't do what's expected. Ever. It's part of his damned religion, I suspect. What now, Traveller?'

He sighed. 'We will catch up with him anyway.' A brief smile. 'With less trepidation now.'

'There's still the risk,' she said, 'of an . . . argument.'

They returned to their horses.

'The Skathandi king was dying,' Traveller explained as they both rode out from the camp. 'He bequeathed his kingdom to your friend. Who then dissolved it, freeing all the slaves, warning off the soldiers. Taking nothing for himself. Nothing at all.'

She grunted.

Traveller was silent for a moment and then he said, 'A man like that . . . well, I am curious. I would like to meet him.'

'Don't expect hugs and kisses,' she said.

'He will not be pleased to see you?'

'I have no idea, although I am bringing him his horse, which should count for something.'

'Does he know how you feel about him?'

She shot him a look, and then snorted. 'He may think he does but the truth is *I* don't know how I feel about him, so whatever he's thinking it's bound to be wrong. Now that we're closing in, I'm the one getting more nervous. It's ridiculous, I know.'

'It seems your examination of those two women has soured your mood. Why?'

'I don't know what you wanted me to do about them. They were pregnant, not in labour. They looked hale enough, better than I expected in fact. They didn't need me poking and prodding. The babies will be born and they will live or they will die. Same for the mothers. It's just how things are.'

'My apologies, Samar Dev. I should not have so ordered you about. Were I in your place, I too would have been offended by the presumption.'

Was that what had annoyed her? Possibly. Equally likely, her mute acquiescence, the doe-eyed ease with which she had fallen into that subservient role. *As when I was with Karsa Orlong. Oh, I think I now step on to the thinnest crust of sand above some bottomless pit. Samar Dev discovers her very own secret weaknesses. Was she foul of mood earlier? See her now.*

A talent, a sensitivity – *something* – clearly told Traveller to say nothing more.

They rode on, the horses' hoofs thumping the taut drum of the earth. The warm wind slid dry as sand. In a low, broad depression on their left stood six pronghorn antelope, watching them pass. Rust-red slabs of flat rock tilted up through the thin ground along the spines of hills. Long-billed birds of some kind perched on them, their plumage the same mix of hues. 'It is all the same,' she murmured.

'Samar Dev? Did you speak?'

She shrugged. 'The way so many animals are made to match their surroundings. I wonder, if all this grass suddenly grew blood red, how long before the markings on those antelope shift into patterns of red? You'd think it could never be the other way round, but you would be wrong. See those flowers – the bright colours to attract the right insects. If the right insects don't come to collect the pollen the flower dies. So, brighter is better. Plants and animals, it goes back and forth, the whole thing inseparable and dependent. Despite this, nothing stays the same.'

'True, nothing ever stays the same.'

'Those women back there . . .'

'Gandaru. Kin to the Kindaru and Sinbarl – so the men explained.'

'Not true humans.'

'No.'

'Yet true to themselves none the less.'

'I imagine so, Samar Dev.'

'They broke my heart, Traveller. Against us, they don't stand a chance.'

He glanced across at her. 'That is quite a presumption.'

'It is?'

'We are riding towards a Tartheno Toblakai, belonging to a remnant tribe isolated somewhere in northern Genabackis. You tell me that Karsa Orlong intends to deliver destruction to all the "children" of the world – to us, in other words. When you speak of this, I see fear in your eyes. A conviction that he will succeed. So now, tell me, against one such as Karsa Orlong and his kind, do we stand a chance?'

'Of course we do, because we can fight back. What can these gentle Gandaru manage? Nothing. They can hide, and when that fails they are killed, or enslaved. Those two women were probably raped. Used. Vessels for human seed.'

'Barring the rape, every animal we hunt for food possesses the same few choices. Hide or flee.'

'Until there is no place left to hide.'

'And when the animals go, so too will we.'

She barked a laugh. 'You might believe so, Traveller. No, we won't go that way. We'll just fill the empty lands with cattle, with sheep and goats. Or break up the ground and plant corn. There is no stopping us.'

'Except, perhaps, for Karsa Orlong.'

And there, then, was the truth of all this. Karsa Orlong pronounced a future of destruction, extinction. *And she wished him well.*

'There,' Traveller said in a different voice, and he rose in his stirrups. 'He didn't travel too far after all—'

From Havok's saddle, Samar Dev could now see him. He had halted and was facing them, a thousand paces distant. Two horses stood near him, and there were humps in the grass of the knoll, scattered like ant hills or boulders but, she knew, neither of those. 'He was attacked,' she said. 'The idiots should have left well enough alone.'

'I'm sure their ghosts concur,' Traveller said.

They cantered closer.

The Toblakai looked no different from the last time she had seen him – there on the sands of the arena in Letheras. As sure, as solid, as undeniable as ever. '*I shall kill him . . . once.*' And so he did. Defying . . . everything. Oh, he was looking at her now, and at Havok, with the air of a master summoning his favourite hunting dog.

And suddenly she was furious. 'This wasn't obligation!' she snapped, savagely reining in directly in front of him. 'You abandoned us – there in that damned foreign city! "Do this when the time is right", and so I did! *Where the Hood did you go? And*—'

And then she yelped, as the huge warrior swept her off the saddle with one massive arm, and closed her in a suffocating embrace, and the bastard was laughing and even Traveller – curse the fool – was grinning, although to be sure it was a hard grin, mindful as he clearly was of the half-dozen bodies lying amidst blood and entrails in the grasses.

'Witch!'

'Set me down!'

'I am amazed,' he bellowed, 'that Havok suffered you all this way!'

'Down!'

So he dropped her. Jarring her knees, sending her down with a thump on her backside, every bone rattled. She glared up at him.

But Karsa Orlong had already turned away and was eyeing Traveller, who remained on his horse. 'You – are you her husband then? She must have had one somewhere – no other reason for her forever refusing me. Very well, we shall fight for her, you and me—'

'Be quiet, Karsa! He's not my husband and no one's fighting for me. *Because I belong to no one but me!* Do you understand? Will you *ever* understand?'

'Samar Dev has spoken,' said Traveller. 'We met not long ago, both journeying on this plain. We chose to ride as companions. I am from Dal Hon, on the continent of Quon Tali—'

Karsa grunted. 'Malazan.'

An answering nod. 'I am called Traveller.'

'You hide your name.'

'What I hide merely begins with my name, Karsa Orlong.'

The Toblakai's eyes thinned at that.

'You bear the tattoos,' Traveller went on, 'of an escaped slave of Seven Cities. Or, rather, a recaptured one. Clearly, the chains did not hold you for long.'

Samar Dev had picked herself up and was now brushing the dust from her clothes. 'Are these Skathandi?' she asked, gesturing at the bodies. 'Karsa?'

The giant turned away from his study of the Malazan. 'Idiots,' he said. 'Seeking vengeance for the dead king – as if I killed him.'

'Did you?'

'No.'

'Well,' she said, 'at least now I will have a horse of my own.'

Karsa walked over to Havok and settled a hand on his neck. The beast's nostrils flared and the lips peeled back to reveal the overlong fangs. Karsa laughed. 'Yes, old friend, I smell of death. When was it never thus?' And he laughed again.

'Hood take you, Karsa Orlong – what happened?'

He frowned at her. 'What do you mean, Witch?'

'You killed the Emperor.'

'I said I would, and so I did.' He paused, and then said, 'And now this Malazan speaks as if he would make me a slave once more.'

'Not at all,' said Traveller. 'It just seems as if you have lived an eventful life, Toblakai. I only regret that I will probably never hear your tale, for I gather that you are not the talkative type.'

Karsa Orlong bared his teeth, and then swung up into the saddle. 'I am riding north,' he said.

'As am I,' replied Traveller.

Samar Dev collected both horses and tied a long lead to the one she decided she would not ride, then climbed into the saddle of the other – a russet gelding with a broad back and disinterested eyes. 'I think I want to go home,' she pronounced. 'Meaning I need to find a port, presumably on the western coast of this continent.'

Traveller said, 'I ride to Darujhistan. Ships ply the lake and the river that flows to the coast you seek. I would welcome the company, Samar Dev.'

'Darujhistan,' said Karsa Orlong. 'I have heard of that city. Defied the Malazan Empire and so still free. I will see it for myself.'

'Fine then,' Samar Dev snapped. 'Let's ride on, to the next pile of corpses – and with you for company, Karsa Orlong, that shouldn't be long – and then we'll ride to the next one and so on, right across this entire continent. To Darujhistan! Wherever in Hood's name that is.'

'I will see it,' Karsa said again. 'But I will not stay long.' And he looked at her with suddenly fierce eyes. 'I am returning home, Witch.'

'To forge your army,' she said, nodding, sudden nerves tingling in her gut.

'And then the world shall witness.'

'Yes.'

After a moment, the three set out, Karsa Orlong on her left, Traveller on her right, neither speaking, yet they were histories, tomes of past, present and future. Between them, she felt like a crumpled page of parchment, her life a minor scrawl.

High, high above them, a Great Raven fixed preternatural eyes upon the three figures far below, and loosed a piercing cry, then tilted its broad black-sail wings and raced on a current of chill wind, rushing east.

She thought she might be dead. Every step she took was effortless, a product of will and nothing else – no shifting of weight, no swing of legs nor flexing of knees. Will carried her where she sought to go, to that place of formless light where the white sand glowed blindingly bright beneath her, at the proper distance had she been standing. Yet, looking down, she saw nothing of her own body. No limbs, no torso, and nowhere to any side could she see her shadow.

Voices droned somewhere ahead, but she was not yet ready for them, so she remained where she was, surrounded in warmth and light.

Pulses, as from torches flaring through thick mist, slowly approached, disconnected from the droning voices, and she now saw a line of figures drawing towards her. Women, heads tilted down, long hair over their faces, naked, each one heavy with pregnancy. The torch fires hovered over each one, fist-sized suns in which rainbow flames flickered and spun.

Salind wanted to recoil. She was a Child of a Dead Seed, after all. Born from a womb of madness. She had nothing for these women. She was no longer a priestess, no longer able to confer the blessing of anyone, no god and least of all herself, upon any child waiting to tumble into the world.

Yet those seething orbs of flame – she knew they were the souls of the unborn, the not-yet-born, and these mothers were walking towards her, with purpose, with need.

I can give you nothing! Go away!

Still they came on, faces lifting, revealing eyes dark and empty, and seemed not to see her even as, one by one, they walked *through* Salind.

Gods, some of these women were not even human.

And as each one passed through her, she felt the life of the child within. She saw the birth unfolding, saw the small creature with those strangely wise eyes that seemed to belong to every newborn (except, perhaps, her own). And then the years rushing on, the child growing, faces taking the shape they would carry into old age—

But not all. As mother after mother stepped through her, futures flashed bright, and some died quickly indeed. Fraught, flickering sparks, ebbing, winking out, darkness rushing in. And at these she cried out, filled with anguish even as she understood that souls travelled countless journeys, of which only one could be known by a mortal – so many, in countless perturbations – and that the loss belonged only to others, never to the child itself, for in its inarticulate, ineffable wisdom, understanding was absolute; the passage of life that seemed tragically short could well be the perfect duration, the experience complete—

Others, however, died in violence, and this was a crime, an outrage against life itself. Here, among these souls, there was fury, shock, denial. There was railing, struggling, bitter defiance. No, some deaths were as they should be, but others were not. From somewhere a woman's voice began speaking.

'Bless them, that they not be taken.

'Bless them, that they begin in their time and that they end in its fullness.

'Bless them, in the name of the Redeemer, against the cruel harvesters of souls, the takers of life.

'Bless them, Daughter of Death, that each life shall be as it is written, for peace is born of completion, and completion denied – completion of all potential, all promised in life – is a crime, a sin, a consignation to eternal damnation. Beware the takers, the users! The blight of killers!

'They are coming! Again and again, they harvest the souls—'

That strange voice was shrieking now, and Salind sought to flee but all will had vanished. She was trapped in this one place, as mother after mother plunged into her, eyes black and wide, mouths gaping in a chorus of screams, wailing terror, heart-crushing fear, for their unborn children—

All at once she heard the droning voices again, summoning her, inviting her into . . . into what?

Sanctuary.

With a cry tearing loose from her throat, Salind pulled away, raced towards those voices—

And opened her eyes. Low candlelight surrounded her. She was lying on a bed. The voices embraced her from all sides and, blinking, she sought to sit up.

So weak—

An arm slipped behind her shoulders, helped her rise as pillows were pushed underneath. She stared up at a familiar, alien face. 'Spinnock Durav.'

He nodded.

Others were rising into view now. Tiste Andii women, all in dark shapeless robes, eyes averted as they began filing out of the chamber, taking their chanting song with them.

Those voices – so heavy, so solid – they truly belonged to these women? She was astonished, half disbelieving, and yet . . .

'You almost died,' Spinnock Durav said. 'The healers called you back – the priestesses.'

'But – why?'

His smile was wry. 'I called in a favour or two. But I think, once they attended you, there was more to it. An obligation, perhaps. You are, after all, a sister priestess – oh, betrothed to a different ascendant, true enough, but that did not matter. Or,' and he smiled again, 'so it turned out.'

Yes, but why? Why did you bring me back? I don't want—oh, she could not complete that thought. Understanding now, at last, how vast the sin of suicide – of course, it would not have been that, would it? To have simply slipped away, taken by whatever sickness afflicted her. Was it not a kind of wisdom to surrender?

'No,' she mumbled, 'it isn't.'

'Salind?'

'To bless,' she said, 'is to confer a hope. Is that enough? To make sacred the wish for good fortune, a fulfilled life? What can it achieve?'

He was studying her face. 'High Priestess,' he now said, haltingly, as if truly attempting an answer, 'in blessing, you purchase a moment of peace, in the one being blessed, in the one for whom blessing is asked. Perhaps it does not last, but the gift you provide, well, its value never fades.'

She turned her head, looked away. Beyond the candles, she saw a wall crowded with Andiian hieroglyphs and a procession of painted figures, all facing one way, to where stood the image of a woman whose back was turned, denying all those beseeching her. A mother rejecting her children – she could see how the artist had struggled with all those upturned faces, the despair and anguish twisting them – painted in tears, yes.

'I must go back,' she said.

'Back? Where?'

'The camp, the place of the pilgrims.'

'You are not yet strong enough, High Priestess.'

Her words to him had stripped away his using her chosen name. He was seeing her now as a High Priestess. She felt a twinge of loss at that. But now was not the time to contemplate the significance of such things. Spinnock Durav was right – she was too weak. Even these thoughts exhausted her. 'As soon as I can,' she said.

'Of course.'

'They are in danger.'

'What would you have me do?'

She finally looked back at him. 'Nothing. This belongs to me. And Seerdomin.'

At the mention of that name the Tiste Andii winced. 'High Priestess—'

'He will not reject me again.'

'He is missing.'

'What?'

'I cannot find him. I am sorry, but I am fairly certain he is no longer in Black Coral.'

'No matter,' she said, struggling to believe her own words. 'No matter. He will come when he is needed.' She could see that Spinnock Durav was sceptical, but she would not berate him for that. 'The Redeemer brought me to the edge of

death,' she said, 'to show me what was needed. To show me why I was needed.'
She paused. 'Does that sound arrogant? It does, doesn't it?'

His sigh was ragged. He stood. 'I will return to check on you, High Priestess.
For now, sleep.'

Oh, she had offended him, but how? 'Wait, Spinnock Durav—'

'It is all right,' he said. 'You have misread me. Well, perhaps not entirely. You
spoke of your god showing you what was needed – something we Tiste Andii
ever yearn for but will not ever achieve. Then you doubt yourself. Arrogance?
Abyss below, High Priestess. Is this how you feel when the Redeemer *blesses*
you?'

Then she was alone in the chamber. Candle flames wavering in the wake of
Spinnock Durav's departure, the agitated light making the figures writhe on the
walls.

Still the mother stood, turned away.

Salind felt a twist of anger. *Bless your children, Mother Dark. They have suffered long enough. I say this in gratitude to your own priestesses, who have given
me back my life. I say it in the name of redemption. Bless your children, woman.*

The candles settled once more, flames standing tall, immune to Salind's meek
agitations. Nowhere in this room was there darkness and that, she realized, was
answer enough.

The old blood splashed on the walls was black, eager to swallow the lantern's
light. Dust still trickled down from stress fractures in the canted ceiling, reminding Seerdomin that half a mountain stood above him. The keep's upper levels
were crushed, collapsed, yet still settling even after all this time. Perhaps, some
time soon, these lower tunnels would give away, and the massive ruin atop the
hollowed-out cliff would simply tilt and slide into the sea.

In the meantime, there were these unlit, wending, buckled corridors, a chaotic
maze where no one belonged, and yet boot prints tracked the thick, gritty dust.
Looters? Perhaps, although Seerdomin well knew there was little to be found in
these lower levels. He had walked these routes many times, doing what he could
for the various prisoners of the Pannion Seer, though it was never enough – no,
never enough.

If there was a curse, a most vicious kind of curse, whereby a decent person
found him or herself in inescapable servitude to a creature of pure, unmitigated
evil, then Seerdomin had lived it. Decency was not exculpable. Honour purchased no abeyance on crimes against humanity. And as for duty, well, it increasingly seemed the sole excuse of the morally despicable. He would offer up
none of these in defence of the things he had done at his master's behest. Nor
would he speak of duress, of the understandable desire to stay alive under the
threat of deadly coercion. None of these was sufficient. When undeniable crimes
had been committed, justification was the act of a coward. *And it was our cowardice that permitted such crimes in the first place.* No tyrant could thrive
where every subject said *no*.

The tyrant thrives when the first fucking fool salutes.

He well understood that many people delighted in such societies – there had been fellow Seerdomin, most of them in fact, who revelled in the fear and the obedience that fear commanded. And this was what had led him here, trailing an old palace retainer of the Seer who had made his furtive way into the ruins of the old keep. No, not a looter. A sordid conspiracy was afoot, Seerdomin was certain of that. Survivors of one nightmare seeking to nurture yet another. That man would not be alone once he reached his destination.

He closed the shutter to the lantern once more and continued on.

Malazan soldiers had died here, along with the Pannion's own. Seguleh had carved through the ranks of palace guard. Seerdomin could almost hear the echoes of that slaughter, the cries of the dying, the desperate pleading against cruel mischance, the stinging clash of weapons. He came to a set of steps leading down. Rubble had been cleared away. From somewhere below came the murmur of voices.

They had set no guard, proof of their confidence, and as he stealthily descended he could make out the glow of lanterns emanating from the cell down below.

This chamber had once been home to the one called Toc the Younger. Chained against one wall, well within reach of the Seer's monstrous mother. Seerdomin's paltry gifts of mercy had probably stung like droplets of acid on the poor man. Better to have left him to go entirely mad, escaping into that oblivious world where everything was so thoroughly broken that repair was impossible. He could still smell the reek of the K'Chain matron.

The voices were becoming distinguishable – three, maybe four conspirators. He could hear the excitement, the sweet glee, along with the usual self-importance, the songs of those who played games with lives – it was the same the world over, in every history, ever the same.

He had crushed down his outrage so long ago, it was a struggle to stir it into life once more, but he would need it. Sizzling, yet hard, controlled, peremptory. Three steps from the floor, still in darkness, he slowly drew out his tulwar. It did not matter what they were discussing. It did not even matter if their plans were pathetic, doomed to fail. It was the very act that awakened in Seerdomin the heart of murder, so that it now drummed through him, thunderous with contempt and disgust, ready to do what was needed.

When he first stepped into the chamber, none of the four seated at the table even noticed, permitting him to take another stride, close enough to send his broad-bladed weapon through the first face that lifted towards him, cutting it in half. His return attack was a looping backswing, chopping through the neck of the man to the right, who, in lurching upright, seemed to offer his throat to that slashing edge like a willing sacrifice. As his head tumbled away, the body stumbling as it backed over the chair, Seerdomin grasped one edge of the table and flipped it into the air, hammering it into the man on the left, who fell beneath the table's weight. Leaving one man directly opposite Seerdomin.

Pleading eyes, a hand scrabbling at the ornate dagger at the belt, backing away—

Not nearly fast enough, as Seerdomin moved forward and swung his heavy tulwar down, cutting through the upraised forearms and carving into the man's upper chest, through clavicle and down one side of the sternum. The edge jammed at the fourth rib, forcing Seerdomin to kick the corpse loose. He then turned to the last conspirator.

The old palace retainer. Spittle on his lips, the reek of urine rising like steam. 'No, please—'

'Do you know me, Hegest?'

A quick nod. 'A man of honour – what you have done here—'

'Defies what you would expect of an honourable man, and it is that very expectation that frees you to scheme and plot. Alas, Hegest, your expectation was wrong. Fatally so. Black Coral is at peace, for the first time in decades – freed of terror. And yet you chafe, dreaming no doubt of your old station, of all the excesses you were privileged to possess.'

'I throw myself upon the mercy of the Son of Darkness—'

'You can't throw yourself that far, Hegest. I am going to kill you, here, now. I can do it quick, or slow. If you answer my questions, I will grant you the mercy you have never spared others. If you refuse, I will do to you as you have done to many, many victims – and yes, I well remember. Which fate will it be, Hegest?'

'I will tell you everything, Seerdomin. In exchange for my life.'

'Your life is not the coin of this deal.'

The man began weeping.

'Enough of that,' Seerdomin growled. 'Today, I am as you once were, Hegest. Tell me, did the tears of your victims soften your heart? No, not once. So wipe your face. And give me your answer.'

And so the man did, and Seerdomin began asking his questions.

Later, and true to his word, Seerdomin showed mercy, in so far as that word meant anything when taking someone else's life, and he well knew it didn't mean much. He cleaned his weapon on Hegest's cloak.

Was he any different, then, from these fools? There were countless avenues he could take that would lead him to assert otherwise, each one tortured and malign with deceit. Without doubt, he told himself as he made his way out, what he had done ended something, whereas what these fools had been planning was the beginning of something else, something foul and sure to spill innocent blood. By this measure, his crime was far the lesser of the two. So why, then, did his soul feel stained, damaged?

Cogent reasoning could lead a man, step by logical step, into horror. He now carried with him a list of names, the sordid details of a scheme to drive out the Tiste Andii, and while he knew it was destined to fail, to leave it free was to invite chaos and misery. And so he would have to kill again. Quietly, revealing nothing to anyone, for this was an act of shame. For his kind, for humans and their stupid, vicious inclinations.

Yet he did not want to be the hand of justice, for that hand was ever bloody and often indiscriminate, prone to excesses of all sorts.

The cruellest detail among all that he had learned this night was that this web of conspiracy reached out to the pilgrim camp. Hegest had not known who the players were out there, but it was clear that they were important, perhaps even essential. Seerdomin would have to go back to the camp and the very thought sickened him.

Salind, the High Priestess, was she one of the conspirators? Was this act of usurpation at its heart a religious one? It would not be the first time that a religion or cult ignited with the fires of self-righteous certainty and puritanical zeal, leading to ghastly conflict, and had he not heard – more than once – the bold assertion that the Son of Darkness held no claim upon the region outside Night? An absurd notion, yes, an indefensible one, the very kind fanatics converged upon, clenched fists held high in the air.

He had, for a time, nurtured the belief that he was not unique in his appreciation for the rule of the Tiste Andii, and his respect for the wisdom displayed again and again by the Son of Darkness. The gift of peace and stability, the sure, unambiguous rules of law imposed by a people whose own civilization spanned tens of thousands of years – even longer if the rumours were at all accurate. How could any human begrudge this gift?

Many did, it was now clear. The notion of freedom could make even peace and order seem oppressive, generate the suspicion of some hidden purpose, some vast deceit, some unspecified crime being perpetrated beyond human ken. That was a generous way of looking at it; the alternative was to acknowledge that humans were intrinsically conflicted, cursed with acquisitive addictions of the spirit.

He reached the steep ramp leading to the well-hidden entrance to the tunnels, rats skittering from his path, and emerged into the warmer, drier air of Night. Yes, he would have to go to the pilgrim camp, but not now. This would demand some planning. Besides, if he could excise the cancer in the city, then the conspirators out there would find themselves isolated, helpless and incapable of achieving anything. He could then deal with them at his leisure.

Yes, that was a better course. Reasonable and methodical, as justice should be. He was not deliberately avoiding such a journey.

Satisfied with these arguments, Seerdomin set out to begin his night of slaughter, and here, in this city, night was without end.

The rats watched him set off. They could smell the blood on him, and more than one had been witness to the slaughter far below, and certain of these now ambled away from the ruin, heading for the world of daylight beyond the shroud.

Summoned, yes, by their master, the one known as Monkrat, an amusing enough name, implicitly contemptuous and derisive. What none of the man's associates truly understood was the truth underlying that name. *Monkrat, yes. The Monk of Rats, priest and wizard, conjuror and binder of spirits. Laugh and snicker if you like . . . at your peril.*

The liberators had found an enemy, and something would have to be done about that.

The city of Bastion crouched above the vast dying lake, its stolid, squat walls blackened and streaked with some kind of oil. The shanties and hovels surrounding the wall had been burned and then razed, the charred wreckage strewn down the slope leading to the cobbled road. Smoke hung above the battlements, thick and surly.

Cradling his battered hands – the reins looped loose about them – Nimander squinted up at the city and its yawning gates. No guards in sight, not a single figure on the walls. Except for the smoke the city looked lifeless, abandoned.

Riding at his side in the front of their modest column, Skintick said, 'A name like "Bastion" invites images of ferocious defenders, bristling with all manner of weapons, suspicious of every foreigner climbing towards the gates. So,' he added with a sigh, 'we must be witness here to the blessed indolence of Saemankelyk, the Dying God's sweet blood.'

Memories of his time in the company of the giant mason still haunted Nimander. It seemed he was cursed with occurrences devoid of resolution, every life crossing his path leaving a swirling wake of mysteries in which he flailed about, half drowning. The Jaghut, Gothos, only worsened matters, a creature of vast antiquity seeking to make use of them, somehow, for reasons he had been too uninterested to explain.

Since we failed him.

The smell of rotting salt filled the air and they could see the bleached flats stretching out from the old shoreline, stilted docks high and dry above struggling weeds, fisher boats lying on their sides farther out. Off to their left, inland, farmsteads were visible amidst rows of scarecrows, but it looked as if there was nothing still living out there – the plants were black and withered, the hundreds of wrapped figures motionless.

They drew closer to the archway, and still there was no one in sight.

'We're being watched,' Skintick said.

Nimander nodded. He felt the same. Hidden eyes, avid eyes.

'As if we've done just what they wanted,' Skintick went on, his voice low, 'by delivering Clip, straight to their damned Abject Temple.'

That was certainly possible. 'I have no intention of surrendering him – you know that.'

'So we prepare to wage war against an entire city? A fanatic priesthood and a god?'

'Yes.'

Grinning, Skintick loosened the sword at his side.

Nimander frowned at him. 'Cousin, I don't recall you possessing such bloodlust.'

'Oh, I am as reluctant as you, Nimander. But I feel we've been pushed long enough. It's time to push back, that's all. Still, that damage to your hands worries me.'

'Aranatha did what she could – I will be fine.' He did not explain how the wounding felt more spiritual than physical. Aranatha had indeed healed the crushed bones, the mangled flesh. Yet he still cradled them as if crippled, and in his dreams at night he found himself trapped in memories of that heavy block of obsidian sliding over his fingertips, the pain, the spurting blood – and he'd awaken slick with sweat, hands throbbing.

The very same hands that had strangled Phaed – almost taking her life. The pain felt like punishment, and now, in the city before them, he believed that once more they would know violence, delivering death with terrible grace.

They reined in before the gate's archway. Sigils crowded the wooden doors, painted in the same thick, black dye that marred the walls to either side.

Nenanda spoke from the wagon's bench. 'What are we waiting for? Nimander? Let's get this over with.'

Skintick twisted in the saddle and said, 'Patience, brother. We're waiting for the official welcoming party. The killing will have to come later.'

Kallor climbed down from the back of the wagon and walked up to the gate. 'I hear singing,' he said.

Nimander nodded. The voices were distant, reaching them in faint waves rippling out from the city's heart. There were no other sounds, as one would expect from a crowded, thriving settlement. And through the archway he could see naught but empty streets and the dull faces of blockish buildings, shutters closed on every window.

Kallor had continued on, into the shadow of the gate and then out to the wide street beyond, where he paused, his gaze fixed on something to his left.

'So much for the welcoming party,' Skintick said, sighing. 'Shall we enter, Nimander?'

From behind them came Aranatha's melodic voice. 'Be warned, cousins. This entire city is the Abject Temple.'

Nimander and Skintick both turned at that.

'Mother bless us,' Skintick whispered.

'What effect will that have on us?' Nimander asked her. 'Will it be the same as in the village that night?'

'No, nothing like that has awakened yet.' Then she shook her head. 'But it will come.'

'And can you defend us?' Nenanda asked.

'We will see.'

Skintick hissed under his breath and then said, 'Now that's reassuring.'

'Never mind,' Nimander replied. Wincing, he tightened his grip on the reins and with a slight pressure of his legs he guided his horse into the city.

The others lurched into motion behind him.

Coming to Kallor's side Nimander followed the old man's gaze down the side street and saw what had so captured his attention. The ruin of an enormous mechanism filled the street a hundred paces down. It seemed to have come from the sky, or toppled down from the roof of the building nearest the outer wall – taking most of the facing wall with it. Twisted iron filled its gaping belly, where flattened, riveted sheets had been torn away. Smaller pieces of the machine littered the cobbles, like fragments of armour, the iron strangely blue, almost gleaming.

'What in the Abyss is that?' Skintick asked.

'Looks K'Chain Che'Malle,' Kallor said. 'But they would offer up no gods, dying or otherwise. Now I am curious,' and so saying he bared his teeth in a smile not directed at anyone present – which was, Nimander decided, a good thing.

'Aranatha says the entire city is sanctified.'

Kallor glanced over. 'I once attempted that for an entire empire.'

Skintick snorted. 'With you as the focus of worship?'

'Of course.'

'And it failed?'

Kallor shrugged. 'Everything fails, eventually.' And he set out for a closer examination of the ruined machine.

'Even conversation,' muttered Skintick. 'Should we follow him?'

Nimander shook his head. 'Leave him. If the city is a temple, then there must be an altar – presumably somewhere in the middle.'

'Nimander, we could well be doing everything they want us to do, especially by bringing Clip to that altar. I think we should find an inn, somewhere to rest up. We can then reconnoitre and see what awaits us.'

He thought about that for a moment, and then nodded. 'Good idea. Lead the way, Skin, see what you can find.'

They continued on down the main street leading from the gate. The tenements looked lifeless, the shops on the ground level empty, abandoned. Glyphs covered every wall and door, spread out from every shuttered window to as far as a hand could reach if someone was leaning out. The writing seemed to record a frenzy of revelation, or madness, or both.

A half-dozen buildings along, Skintick found an inn, closed up like everything else, but he dismounted and approached the courtyard gates. A push swung them wide and Skintick looked back with a smile.

The wagon's hubs squealed in well-worn grooves in the frame of the gate as Nenanda guided it in. The compound beyond was barely large enough to accommodate a single carriage on its circular lane that went past, first, the stables, and then the front three-stepped entrance to the hostelry. A partly subterranean doorway to the left of the main doors probably led into the taproom. In the centre of the round was a stone-lined well – stuffed solid with bloating corpses.

Skintick's smile faded upon seeing this detail. Dead maggots ringed the well. 'Let's hope,' he said to Nimander, 'there's another pump inside . . . drawing from a different source.'

Nenanda had set the brake and he now dropped down, eyeing the bodies. 'Previous guests?'

'It's what happens when you don't pay up.'

Nimander dismounted and shot Skintick a warning look, but his cousin did not notice – or chose not to, for he then continued, 'Or all the beds were taken. Or some prohibition against drinking anything but kelyk – it clearly doesn't pay to complain.'

'Enough,' said Nimander. 'Nenanda, can you check the stables – see if there's feed and clean water. Skintick, let's you and I head inside.'

A spacious, well-furnished foyer greeted them, with a booth immediately to the right, bridged by a polished counter. The narrow panel door set in its back wall was shut. To the left was a two-sided cloakroom and beside that the sunken entranceway into the taproom. A corridor was directly ahead, leading to rooms, and a steep staircase climbed to the next level where, presumably, more rooms could be found. Heaped on the floor at the foot of the stairs was bedding, most of it rather darkly stained.

'They stripped the rooms,' observed Skintick. 'That was considerate.'

'You suspect they've prepared this place for us?'

'With bodies in the well and ichor-stained sheets? Probably. It's reasonable that we would stay on the main street leading in, and this was the first inn we'd reach.' He paused, looking round. 'Obviously, there are many ways of readying for guests. Who can fathom human cultures, anyway?'

Outside, Nenanda and the others were unpacking the wagon.

Nimander walked to the taproom entrance and ducked to look inside. Dark, the air thick with the pungent, bittersweet scent of kelyk. He could hear Skintick making his way up the stairs, decided to leave him to it. One step down, on to the sawdust floor. The tables and chairs had all been pushed to one side in a haphazard pile. In the open space left behind the floor was thick with stains and coagulated clumps that reminded Nimander of dung in a stall. Not dung, however; he knew that.

He explored behind the bar and found rows of dusty clay bottles and jugs, wine and ale. The beakers that had contained kelyk were scattered on the floor, some of them broken, others still weeping dark fluid.

The outer door swung open and Nenanda stepped inside, one hand on the grip of his sword. A quick look round, then he met Nimander's gaze and shrugged. 'Was you I heard, I guess.'

'The stables?'

'Well enough supplied, for a few days at least. There's a hand pump and spout over the troughs. The water smelled sour but otherwise fine – the horses didn't hesitate, at any rate.' He strode in. 'I think those bodies in the well, Nimander – dead of too much kelyk. I suspect that well was in fact dry. They just used to it dump the ones that died, as they died.'

Nimander walked back to the doorway leading into the foyer.

Desra and Kedeviss had carried Clip inside, setting him on the floor. Skintick was on the stairs, a few steps up from the mound of soiled bedding. He was leaning on one rail, watching as the two women attended to Clip. Seeing Nimander, he said, 'Nothing but cockroaches and bedbugs in the rooms. Still, I don't think we should use them – there's an odd smell up there, not at all pleasant.'

'This room should do,' Nimander said as he went over to look down at Clip. 'Any change?' he asked.

Desra glanced up. 'No. The same slight fever, the same shallow breathing.'

Aranatha entered, looked round, then went to the booth, lifted the hinged counter and stepped through. She tried the latch on the panel door and when it opened, she disappeared into the back room.

A grunt from Skintick. 'In need of the water closet?'

Nimander rubbed at his face, flexed his fingers to ease the ache, and then, as Nenanda arrived, he said, 'Skintick and I will head out now. The rest of you . . . well, we could run into trouble at any time. And if we do one of us will try to get back here—'

'If you run into trouble,' Aranatha said from the booth, 'we will know it.'

Oh? How? 'All right. We shouldn't be long.'

They had brought all their gear into the room and Nimander now watched as first Desra and then the other women began unpacking their weapons, their fine chain hauberks and mail gauntlets. He watched as they readied for battle, and said nothing as anguish filled him. None of this was right. It had never been right. And he could do nothing about it.

Skintick edged his way round the bedding and, with a tug on Nimander's arm, led him back outside. 'They will be all right,' he said. 'It's us I'm worried about.'

'Us? Why?'

Skintick only smiled.

They passed through the gate and came out on to the main street once more. The mid-afternoon heat made the air sluggish, enervating. The faint singing seemed to invite them into the city's heart. An exchanged glance; then, with a shrug from Skintick, they set out.

'That machine.'

'What about it, Skin?'

'Where do you think it came from? It looked as if it just . . . appeared, just above one of the buildings, and then dropped, smashing everything in its path, ending with itself. Do you recall those old pumps, the ones beneath Dreth Street in Malaz City? Withal found them in those tunnels he explored? Well, he took us on a tour—'

'I remember, Skin.'

'I'm reminded of those machines – all the gears and rods, the way the metal components all meshed so cleverly, ingeniously – I cannot imagine the mind that could think up such constructs.'

'What is all this about, Skin?'

'Nothing much. I just wonder if that thing is somehow connected with the arrival of the Dying God.'

'Connected how?'

'What if it was like a skykeep? A smaller version, obviously. What if the Dying God was *inside* it? Some accident brought it down, the locals pulled him out. What if that machine was a kind of throne?'

Nimander thought about that. A curious idea. Andarist had once explained that skykeeps – such as the one Anomander Rake claimed as his own – were not a creation of sorcery, and indeed the floating fortresses were held aloft through arcane manipulations of technology.

K'Chain Che'Malle, Kallor had said. Clearly, he had made the same connection as had Skintick.

'Why would a god need a machine?' Nimander asked.

'How should I know? Anyway, it's broken now.'

They came to a broad intersection. Public buildings commanded each corner, the architecture peculiarly utilitarian, as if the culture that had bred it was singularly devoid of creative flair. Glyphs made a mad scrawl on otherwise unadorned walls, some of the symbols now striking Nimander as resembling that destroyed mechanism.

The main thoroughfare continued on another two hundred paces, they could see, opening out on to an expansive round. At the far end rose the most imposing structure they had seen yet.

'There it is,' Skintick said. 'The Abject . . . altar. It's where the singing is coming from, I think.'

Nimander nodded.

'Should we take a closer look?'

He nodded again. 'Until something happens.'

'Does being attacked by a raving mob count?' Skintick asked.

Figures were racing into the round, naked but with weapons in their hands that they waved about over their heads, their song suddenly ferocious, as they began marching towards the two Tiste Andii.

'Here was I thinking we were going to be left alone,' Nimander said. 'If we run, we'll just lead them back to the inn.'

'True, but holding the gate should be manageable, two of us at a time, spelling each other.'

Nimander was the first to hear a sound behind him and he spun round, sword hissing from the scabbard.

Kallor.

The old warrior walked towards them. 'You kicked them awake,' he said.

'We were sightseeing,' said Skintick, 'and though this place is miserable we kept our opinions to ourselves. In any case, we were just discussing what to do now.'

'You could stand and fight.'

'We could,' agreed Nimander, glancing back at the mob. Now fifty paces away and closing fast. 'Or we could beat a retreat.'

'They're brave right now,' Kallor observed, stepping past and drawing his two-handed sword. As he walked he looped the plain, battered weapon over his head, a few passes, as if loosening up his shoulders. Suddenly he did not seem very old at all.

Skintick asked, 'Should we help him?'

'Did he ask for help, Skin?'

'No, you're right, he didn't.'

They watched as Kallor marched directly into the face of the mob.

And all at once that mob blew apart, people scattering, crowding out to the sides as the singing broke up into wails of dismay. Kallor hesitated for but a moment, before resuming his march. In the centre of a corridor now that had opened up to let him pass.

'He just wants to see that altar,' Skintick said, 'and he's not the one they're bothered with. Too bad,' he added, 'it might have been interesting to see the old badger fight.'

'Let's head back,' Nimander said, 'while they're distracted.'

'If they let us.'

They turned and set off at an even, unhurried pace. After a dozen or so strides Skintick half turned. He grunted, then said, 'They've left us to it. Nimander, the message seems clear. To get to that altar, we will have to go through them.'

'So it seems.'

'Things will get messy yet.'

Yes, they would.

'So, do you think Kallor and the Dying God will have a nice conversation? Observations on the weather. Reminiscing on the old tyrannical days when everything was all fun and games. Back when the blood was redder, its taste sweeter. Do you think?'

Nimander said nothing, thinking instead of those faces in that mob, the black stains smeared round their mouths, the pits of their eyes. Clothed in rags, caked with filth, few children among them, as if the kelyk made them all equal, regardless of age, regardless of any sort of readiness to manage the world and the demands of living. They drank and they starved and the present was the future, until death stole away that future. A simple trajectory. No worries, no ambitions, no dreams.

Would any of that make killing them easier? No.

'I do not want to do this,' Nimander said.

'No,' Skintick agreed. 'But what of Clip?'

'I don't know.'

'This kelyk is worse than a plague, because its victims invite it into their lives, and then are indifferent to their own suffering. It forces the question – have we any right to seek to put an end to it, to destroy it?'

'Maybe not,' Nimander conceded.

'But there is another issue, and that is mercy.'

He shot his cousin a hard look. 'We kill them all for their own good? Abyss take us, Skin—'

'Not them – of course not. I was thinking of the Dying God.'

Ah . . . well. Yes, he could see how that would work, how it could, in fact, make this palatable. If they could get to the Dying God without the need to slaughter hundreds of worshippers. 'Thank you, Skin.'

'For what?'

'We will sneak past them.'

'Carrying Clip?'

'Yes.'

'That won't be easy – it might be impossible, in fact. If this city is the temple, and the power of the Dying God grants gifts to the priests, then they will sense our approach no matter what we do.'

'We are children of Darkness, Skintick. Let us see if that still means something.'

Desra pulled her hand from Clip's brow. 'I was wrong. He's getting worse.' And she straightened and looked across to Aranatha. 'How are they?'

A languid blink. 'Coming back, unharmed.'

Something was wrong with Aranatha. Too calm, too . . . empty. Desra always considered her sister to be vapid – oh, she wielded a sword with consummate elegance, as cold a killer as the rest of them when necessity so demanded – but there was a kind of pervasive disengagement in Aranatha. Often descending upon her in the midst of calamity and chaos, as if the world in its bolder mayhem could bludgeon her senseless.

Making her unreliable as far as Desra was concerned. She studied Aranatha for a moment longer, their eyes meeting, and when her sister smiled Desra answered with a scowl and turned to Nenanda. 'Did you find anything to eat in the taproom? Or drink?'

The warrior was standing by the front door, which he held open with one hand. At Desra's questions he glanced back. 'Plenty, as if they'd just left – or maybe it was a delivery, like the kind we got on the road.'

'Someone must be growing proper food, then,' said Kedeviss. 'Or arranging its purchase from other towns and the like.'

'They've gone to a lot of trouble for us,' Nenanda observed. 'And that makes me uneasy.'

'Clip is dying, Aranatha,' Desra said.

'Yes.'

'They're back,' Nenanda announced.

'Nimander will know what to do,' Desra pronounced.

'Yes,' said Aranatha.

She circled once, high above the city, and even her preternatural sight struggled against the eternal darkness below. Kurald Galain was a most alien warren, even in this diffused, weakened state. Passing directly over the slumbering mass of Silanah, Crone cackled out an ironic greeting. Of course there was no visible response from the crimson dragon, yet the Great Raven well knew that Silanah sensed her wheeling overhead. And no doubt permitted, in a flash of imagery, the vision of jaws snapping, bones and feathers crunching as delicious fluids spurted – Crone cackled again, louder this time, and was rewarded with a twitch of that long, serpentine tail.

She slid on to an updraught from the cliff's edge, then angled down through it on a steep dive towards the low-walled balcony of the keep.

He stood alone, something she had come to expect of late. The Son of Darkness was closing in, like an onyx flower as the bells of midnight rang on, chime by chime to the twelfth and last, and then there would be naught but echoes, until even these faded, leaving silence. She crooked her wings to slow her plummet, the keep still rushing up to meet her. A flurry of beating wings and she settled atop the stone wall, talons crunching into the granite.

'And does the view ever change?' Crone asked.

Anomander Rake looked down, regarded her for a time.

She opened her beak to laugh in silence for a few heartbeats. 'The Tiste Andii are not a people prone to sudden attacks of joy, are they? Dancing into darkness? The wild cheerful cavort into the future? Do you imagine that our flight from his rotting flesh was not one of rapturous glee? Pleasure at being born, delight at being alive? Oh, I have run out of questions for you – it is indeed now a sad time.'

'Does Baruk understand, Crone?'

'He does. More or less. Perhaps. We'll see.'

'Something is happening to the south.'

She bobbed her head in agreement. 'Something, oh yes, something all right. Are the priestesses in a wild orgy yet? The plunge that answers *everything*! Or, rather, postpones the need for answers for a time, a time of corresponding bliss, no doubt. But then . . . reality returns. Damn reality, damn it to the Abyss! Time for another plunge!'

'Travel has soured your mood, Crone.'

'It is not in my nature to grieve. I despise it, in fact. I rail against it! My sphincter explodes upon it! And yet, what is it you force upon me, your old companion, your beloved servant?'

'I have no such intention,' he replied. 'Clearly, you fear the worst. Tell me, what have your kin seen?'

'Oh, they are scattered about, here and there, ever high above the petty machinations of the surface crawlers. We watch as they crawl this way and that. We watch, we laugh, we sing their tales to our sisters, our brothers.'

'And?'

She ducked her head, fixed one eye upon the tumultuous black seas below. 'This darkness of yours, Master, breeds fierce storms.'

'So it does.'

'I will fly high above the twisting clouds, into air clear and cold.'

'And so you shall, Crone, so you shall.'

'I dislike it when you are generous, Master. When that soft regard steals into your eyes. It is not for you to reveal compassion. Stand here, yes, unseen, unknowable, that I might hold this in my mind. Let me think of the ice of true justice, the kind that never shatters – listen, I hear the bells below! How sure that music, how true the cry of iron.'

'You are most poetic this day, Crone.'

'It is how Great Ravens rail at grief, Master. Now, what would you have me do?'

'Endest Silann is at the deep river.'

'Hardly alone, I should think.'

'He must return.'

She was silent for a moment, head cocked. Then she said, 'Ten bells have sounded.'

'Ten.'

'I shall be on my way, then.'

'Fly true, Crone.'

'I pray you tell your beloved the same, Master, when the time is nigh.'

He smiled. 'There is no need for that.'

Chapter Eleven

Who are you to judge whether she is old
or young, and if she is lifting the bucket
or lowering it down into this well?
And is she pretty or plain as undyed linen,
is she a sail riding the summer wind
bright as a maiden's eye above waves of blue?
Does her walk sway in pleasure and promise
of bracing dreams as if the earth could sing
fertile as joyous butterflies in a flowered field,
or has this saddle stretched slack in cascades
of ripe fruit and rides no more through
blossomed orchards? Who then are you
to cage in presumptuous iron the very
mystery that calls us to life where hovers
the brimming bucket, ever poised between
dark depths and choral sunlight – she is beauty
and this too is a criminal exhortation, and
nothing worthwhile is to be found in your
regard that does little more than stretch
this frayed rope – so shame!
Dismissal delivers vicious wounds and she
walks away or walks to with inner cringing.
Dare not speak of fairness, dare not indulge
cruel judgement when here I sit watching
and all the calculations between blinks
invite the multitude to heavy scorn and see
that dwindling sail passing for ever beyond you
as is her privilege there on the sea of flowers
all sweet fragrance swirling in her wake –
it will never *ever* reach you – and this is
balance, this is measure, this is the observance
of strangers who hide their tears
when turning away.

Young Men Against a Wall
Nekath of One Eye Cat

No purer artist exists or has ever existed than a child freed to imagine. This scattering of sticks in the dust, that any adult might kick through without a moment's thought, is in truth the bones of a vast world, clothed, fleshed, a fortress, a forest, a great wall against which terrible hordes surge and are thrown back by a handful of grim heroes. A nest for dragons, and these shiny smooth pebbles are their eggs, each one home to a furious, glorious future. No creation was ever raised as fulfilled, as brimming, as joyously triumphant, and all the machinations and manipulations of adults are the ghostly recollections of childhood and its wonders, the awkward mating to cogent function, reasonable purpose; and each façade has a tale to recount, a legend to behold in stylized propriety. Statues in alcoves fix sombre expressions, indifferent to every passer-by. Regimentation rules these creaking, stiff minds so settled in habit and fear.

To drive children into labour is to slaughter artists, to scour deathly all wonder, the flickering dart of imagination eager as finches flitting from branch to branch – all crushed to serve grown-up needs and heartless expectations. The adult who demands such a thing is dead inside, devoid of nostalgia's bright dancing colours, so smooth, so delicious, so replete with longing both sweet and bitter – dead inside, yes, and dead outside, too. Corpses in motion, cold with the resentment the undead bear towards all things still alive, all things still warm, still breathing.

Pity these ones? Nay, never, never so long as they drive on hordes of children into grisly labour, then sup languid of air upon the myriad rewards.

Dare this round self descend into hard judgement? This round self does dare! A world built of a handful of sticks can start tears in the eyes, as the artist on hands and knees sings a score of wordless songs, speaks in a hundred voices, and moves unseen figures across the vast panorama of the mind's canvas (pausing but once to wipe nose on sleeve). He does so dare this! And would hasten the demise of such cruel abuse.

Even a serpent has grandiose designs, yet must slither in minute increments, struggling for distances a giant or god would scorn. Tongue flicking for the scent, this way and that. Salvation is the succulent fruit at hunt's end, the sun-warmed bird's egg, the soft cuddly rat trapped in the jaws.

So searches the serpent, friend to the righteous. So slides the eel through the world's stirred muck, whiskers a-probing. Soon, one hopes, soon!

Young Harllo was not thinking of justice, nor of righteous freedom, nor was he idly fashioning glittering worlds from the glistening veins of raw iron, or the flecks of gold in the midst of cold, sharp quartzite. He had no time to kneel in some overgrown city garden building tiny forts and reed bridges over run-off tracks left by yesterday's downpour. No, for Harllo childhood was over. Aged six.

At this moment, then, he was lying on a shelf of hard, black stone, devoured by darkness. He could barely hear the workers far above, although rocks bounced their way down the crevasse every now and then, echoing with harsh barks from the floor far below.

The last time here he had dangled from a rope, and there had been no careless rain of stones – any one of which could crush his skull. And on his descent back then, his outstretched arms had encountered no walls, leading him to believe the crevasse was vast, opening out perhaps into a cavern. This time, of course, there was no rope – Harllo should not even be here and would probably be switched once he was found out.

Bainisk had sent him back to Chuffs at shift's end. And that was where he ought now to be, hurriedly devouring his bowl of watery soup and husk of black bread, before stumbling off to his cot. Instead, he was climbing down this wall, without light to ensure that he would not be discovered by those working above.

Not a cavern after all. Instead, a pocked, sheer cliff-face – and those gaping holes were all oddly regular, rectangular, although not until Harllo reached this balcony ledge did he comprehend that he was climbing down the face of some buried building. He wanted to slip into one of these windows and explore, but he had promised to deliver *splints* to the Bone Miner below, and that was what he would do.

Careful questioning had led him to a definition of "splints", but he could not find sticks suitable for the purpose of fixing the Miner's shattered legs. Either too feeble and small, or not straight enough; and besides, all the wood brought to the camp was too well guarded. Instead, he had gone to the tailings heaps, where all manner of garbage was thrown. Eyed suspiciously by the old women who'd sold children and grandchildren to the mine yet found they could not sever their ties – thus dooming themselves to this fringe-world at camp's edge – Harllo had picked through the rubbish.

Often, and especially from the run-off tunnels pumped through layers of sandstone, miners would find piles of bones from long dead creatures. Bones heavy and solid and almost impossible to break. Skulls and the like were sold to collectors – scholars with squinty eyes and too much coin and time for their own good. The pieces already fractured off, broken up and forming a kind of gravel, went to the herbalists for their gardens and the mock-healers for potions and pastes – or so Bainisk called them, *mock-healers*, with a sneer – *ground-up bone's good only for constipation!* This left the oversized long bones – which for some reason were believed to be cursed.

Out on the heaps he found two that seemed to have been from the same kind of beast. After some examination and comparison, he confirmed that he had a right one and a left one. They were heavy, thick and ridged, and he hoped they would do.

Between shifts at the main tunnel there was a half-bell when no one was under rock, and Harllo, sweating beneath the weight of the bones, hurriedly carried them in; then, finding an abandoned side-passage, he stashed them along with some lengths of rope and leather laces. That had been before his shift, and now here he was, trying to do what he had promised.

Those long leg bones were strapped to his back. His neck and shoulders were raw from the ropes and more than once he had thought the swinging of the heavy bones would tug him away from the wall, but he had held on, this far at least.

And now, lying on this balcony ledge, Harllo rested.

If someone went looking for him and didn't find him, an alarm would be raised. Always two possibilities when someone went missing. Flight, or lost in the tunnels. Searches would set out in both directions, and some old woman would say how she saw him at the heaps, collecting bones and who knew what else. Then someone else would recall seeing Harllo carrying something back to the main tunnel mouth in between shifts – and Venaz would say that Harllo was clearly up to something, since he never came back for his meal. Something against the rules! Which would put Bainisk in a bad situation, since Bainisk had favoured him more than once. Oh, this was all a mistake!

Groaning, he slipped over the edge, cautious with his handholds, and resumed his journey down.

And, not two man-heights down from the balcony, his groping feet found another ledge, followed immediately by another – a staircase, angling steeply down the wall. One hand maintaining contact with the seamless stone, Harllo worked his way down, step by step.

He did not recall noticing any of this his first time down here. Of course, the candlelight had been feeble – which made easier catching the glitter of gold and the like – and he had gone straight back to the rope. And hadn't his mind been awhirl? A talking Imass! Down here for maybe hundreds of years – with no one to talk to and nothing to look at, oh, how miserable that must have been.

So. He should not be resenting doing all this for the Bone Miner. A few switches to the back wasn't much to pay for this mercy.

He reached the floor and paused. So dark! 'Hello? It's me! Dev'ad Anan Tol, can you hear me?'

'I can. Follow, then, the sound of my voice. If such a thing is possible—'

'It is . . . I think. Scratch the rock you're sitting on – I'll feel that under my feet—'

'That,' said the Imass, 'is an impressive talent.'

'I'm good when I can't see. Vibrations, it's called.'

'Yes. Can you feel this then?'

'I'm getting closer, yes. I think I can start a lantern here. Shuttered so it won't spread out.' He crouched down, the ends of the long bones thunking behind him, and untied the small tin lantern from his belt. 'This one's called a pusher. You can fix it on to a pole and push it ahead. If the wick dims fast then you know it's bad air. Wait.' A moment later and soft golden light slanted like a path, straight to where sat the Bone Miner. Harllo grinned. 'See, I was almost there, wasn't I?'

'What is it that you carry, cub?'

'Your *splints*. And rope and string.'

'Let me see those . . . bones. Yes, give them to me—' And he reached out skeletal hands to grasp the splints as soon as Harllo came close enough. A low grating gasp from the Imass, then soft muttering. 'By the Shore of Jaghra Til, I had not thought to see . . . . cub, my tools . . . for this. The gift is not in balance.'

'I can try to find some better ones—'

'No, child. The imbalance is the other way. These are emlava, a male, his hind long bones. True, they twist and cant. Still . . . yes . . . possible.'

'Will they work as splints then?'

'No.'

Harllo sagged.

The Imass rumbled a low laugh. 'Ah, cub. Not splints. No. *Legs.*'

'So you can walk again? Oh, I'm glad!'

'If indeed I was somehow caught in the Ritual of Tellann, yes, I think I can fashion . . . from these . . . why do you fret so, cub?'

'I had to sneak down here. If they find out I'm missing . . .'

'What will happen?'

'I might be beaten – not so much as to make me useless. It won't be so bad.'

'You should go, then, quickly.'

Harllo nodded, yet still he hesitated. 'I found a building, a buried building. Was that where you lived?'

'No. It was a mystery even to the Jaghut Tyrant. Countless empty rooms, windows looking out upon nothing – blank rock, pitted sandstone. Corridors leading nowhere – we explored most of it, I recall, and found nothing. Do not attempt the same, cub. It is very easy to get lost in there.'

'I better go,' said Harllo. 'If I can come down here again—'

'Not at risk of your hide. Soon, perhaps, I will come to you.'

Harllo thought of the consternation such an event would bring, and he smiled. A moment later he shuttered the lantern and set off for the stairs.

From sticks a fortress, a forest, a great wall. From sticks, a giant, rising up in the darkness, and to look into the pits of its eyes is to see twin tunnels into rock, reaching down and down, reaching back and back, to the very bones of the earth.

And so he rises, to look upon you – Harllo imagines this but none of it in quite this way. Such visions and their deadly promise belong to the adults of the world. To answer what's been done. What's been done.

And in the city every building wears a rictus grin, or so it might seem, when the stone, brick, plaster and wood breathe in the gloom of dusk, and the gas lanterns are yet to be set alight, and all the world is ebbing with shadows drawing together to take away all certainty. The city, this artifice of cliffs and caves, whispers of madness. Figures scurry for cover, rats and worse peer out curious and hungry, voices grow raucous in taverns and other fiery sanctuaries.

Is this the city of the day just past? No, it is transformed, nightmare-tinged, into a netherworld so well suited to the two figures walking – with comfort and ease – towards the gate of an estate. Where stand two guards, nervous, moments from warning the strangers off – for the Lady of the House was in residence and she valued her privacy, yes, she did. Or so it must be assumed, and Scorch and Leff, having discussed the matter at length, were indeed convinced that, being a Lady, she valued all those things few others could afford, including . . . er, privacy.

They held crossbows because who could say what might creep into view and besides, the heavy weapons were so comforting to cradle when clouds devoured the stars and the moon had forgotten to rise and the damned lanterns still weren't lit. True enough, torches in sconces framed the arched gateway but this did little more than blind the two guards to the horrors lurking just beyond the pool of light.

Two such horrors drew closer. One was enormous, broad-shouldered and oddly short-legged, his hair shaggy as a yak's. He was smiling – or, that is, his teeth gleamed and perhaps it was indeed a smile, perhaps not. His companion was almost as tall, but much thinner, almost skeletal. Bald, the high dome of his forehead bore a tattooed scene of some sort within an elaborate oval frame of threaded gold stitched through the skin. His teeth, also visible, were all capped in silver-tipped gold, like a row of fangs. He wore a cloak of threadbare linen so long it dragged behind him, while his looming companion was dressed like a court jester – bright greens, oranges and reds and yellows – and these were just the colours of his undersized vest. He wore a billowy blouse of sky-blue silk beneath the vest, the cuffs of the sleeves stiff and reaching halfway between wrist and elbow. A shimmering black kerchief encircled his ox-like neck. He wore vermilion pantaloons drawn tight just beneath the knees, and calf-high snug moccasins.

'I think,' muttered Scorch, 'I'm going to be sick.'

'Stop there!' Leff barked. 'State your business if you have any – but know this, the Mistress is seeing no one.'

'Excellent!' said the huge one in a thunderous voice. 'There will be no delay then in her granting us audience. If you please, O orange-eyed one, do inform the Mistress that Lazan Door and Madrun have finally arrived, at her service.'

Leff sneered, but he was wishing that Torvald Nom hadn't gone off for supper or a roll with his wife or whatever, so he could pass all this on to him and not have to worry about it any more. Standing here at the gate, yes, that was within his abilities. 'Train your weapon on 'em, Scorch,' he said. 'I'll go find the castellan.'

Scorch shot him a look of raw terror. 'There's two, Leff, but only one quarrel! Leave me yours.'

'Fine, but I'd like to see you get two off with them only ten paces away. If they rushed you, why, you'd be lucky to get just one off.'

'Still, it'll make me feel better.'

'Now now, gentlemen,' the big one said, all too smoothly, 'there's no need for concern. I assure you, we are expected. Is this not the estate of Lady Varada? I do believe it is.'

'Varada?' hissed Scorch to Leff. 'Is that her name?'

'Shut it,' Leff snapped under his breath. 'You're making us look like idiots!' He carefully set his crossbow down and drew out the gate key. 'Nobody move unless it's to go away – not you, Scorch! Stay right there. I'll be right back.'

After he slipped out of sight, closing and locking the gate behind him, Scorch faced the two strangers once more. He managed a smile. 'Nice get-up, that,' he said to the jester. 'You a court clown or something? Sing us a song. How 'bout a riddle? I ain't any good at riddles but I like hearing 'em and the way when I do my thinking, trying to figure 'em out, my whole brain just goes white, sorta. Can you juggle? I like juggling, tried it once, got up to two at a time – that took weeks, let me tell you. Weeks. Juggling demands discipline all right, and maybe it looks easier to other people, but you and I know, well, just how talented you have to be to do it. Do you dance, too, or stand on your head—'

'Sir,' the giant cut in, 'I am not a jester. Nor a juggler. Nor a riddler, nor singer, nor dancer.'

'Oh. Colour-blind?'

'Excuse me?'

'The guard,' said the other man, the thin one, in a voice even thinner, 'has misconstrued your attire, Madrun. Local fashion is characteristically mundane, unimaginative. Did you not so observe earlier?'

'So I did. Of course. A clash of cultures—'

'Just so!' cried Scorch. 'Your clothes, yes, a clash of cultures all right – good way of describing it. You a puppetmaster, maybe? I like puppet shows, the way they look so lifelike, even the ones with wrinkled apples for heads—'

'Not a puppeteer, alas,' cut in Madrun with a heavy sigh.

The gate creaked open behind Scorch and he turned to see Leff and Studlock step through. The castellan floated past and hovered directly in front of the two strangers.

'Well, you two took your time!'

Madrun snorted. 'You try digging your way out of a collapsed mountain, Studious. Damned earthquake came from nowhere—'

'Not quite,' said Studlock. 'A certain hammer was involved. I admit, in the immediate aftermath I concluded that never again would I see your miser— your memorable faces. Imagine my surprise when I heard from a caravan merchant that—'

'Such rumours,' interjected the one Scorch rightly assumed was named Lazan Door, 'whilst no doubt egregiously exaggerated and so potentially entertaining, can wait, yes? Dear Studious, who dreamed of never again seeing our pretty faces, you have a new Mistress, and she is in need of compound guards. And, as we are presently under-employed, why, destinies can prove seamless on occasion, can't they?'

'So they can, Lazan. Yes, compound guards. You see, we have gate guards already. And a captain as well, who is presently elsewhere. Now, if you two will follow me, we can meet the Mistress.'

'Excellent,' said Madrun.

Scorch and Leff moved well aside as the trio filed in through the gate. Leff then locked it and turned to Scorch.

'We never got no audience with the Mistress!'

'We been snubbed!'

Leff collected his crossbow again. 'It's because we're on the lowest rung, that's why. The lowest . . . again! And here we thought we were climbing! Sure, Tor did some climbing, captain and all. But look at us – not even compound guards and we got here first!'

'Well,' said Scorch, 'if we'd a known there was a difference – gate and compound – we would've pushed for that, right? We was ill-informed – look at you, after all.'

'What's that supposed to mean?'

'You got orange eyes, Leff!'

'That was a different kind of ill-informed.'

'That's what you think.'

'If you're so smart, Scorch, you coulda asked about being compound guards!'

'If it was just me, I would have!'

'If it was just you, Studlock never would've hired you at all, except maybe to clean out the latrines!'

'At least then I'd be *inside* the gate!'

Well, he had a point there. Leff sighed, stared out on the street. 'Look, there's the lantern crew.'

'Let's shoot 'em!'

'Sure, if you want us to get fired, Scorch, is that what you want?'

'I was only joking, Leff.'

There were looks that killed, and then there were looks that conducted torture. Excoriating skin with incremental, exquisite slices that left blood welling to the surface. That plucked eyeballs and pulled until all the tendons stretched, upon which those long wet ligaments were knotted together so that both eyes sat on the bridge of the nose. Torture, yes, delivered in cold pleasure, in clinical regard.

It was hardly surprising, then, that Torvald Nom devoured his supper in haste, forgetting to chew, and so was now afflicted with terrible indigestion, struggling to keep from groaning as he helped Tiserra clean the plates and whatnot; and the ominous silence stretched on, even as she cast sidelong looks of blood-curdling excision all unconvincingly dressed up as companionable, loving glances.

It was time to return to the estate for the evening. These precious deadly moments of domestic tranquillity – fraught as all such moments were with all that was left unspoken, the topics unbidden yet ever lurking, the hidden pitfalls and explosive nuances or even more explosive lack thereof – why, they had to come, alas, to an end, as considerations of career and professional responsibility returned once more to the fore.

'My sweet, I must leave you now.'

'Oh, must you?'

'Yes. Until midnight, but don't feel the need to wait up.'

'I've had a busy day. Two new orders. I doubt I'll be awake when you return, darling.'

'I'll try to be quiet.'

'Of course you will.'

Perfunctory kiss.

Just so, the pleasant exchanges to conclude the repast just past, but of course such words were the flourishes of feint and cunning sleight of hand. Beneath the innocence, Torvald well understood, there was this: 'My sweet, I will run not walk back to the estate now.'

'Oh, your stomach is upset? Let's hope you heave all over your two gate guards when you get there.'

'Yes. And suddenly it'll be midnight and like a doomed man I will count the steps to the gallows awaiting me at home. Pray to Beru and every other ascendant the world over that you're asleep when I get here, or at least feigning sleep.'

'I've had a busy day, husband, just thinking of all the things I'd like to do to you for breaking that promise. And when you get home, why, I'll be dreaming dreadful scenes, each one adding to that pleasant smile on my slumbering visage.'

'I shall attempt to sleep on no more than a hand's span of bed, stiff as a planed board, not making a sound.'

'Yes, you will. Darling.'

And the perfunctory kiss, smooch smooch.

Blue light painted the streets through which Torvald Nom now hurried along, blue light and black thoughts, a veritable bruising of dismay, and so the buildings to each side crowded, leaned in upon him, until he felt he was squirting – like an especially foul lump of excrement – through a sewer pipe. Terrible indeed, a wife's disappointment and, mayhap, disgust.

The princely wages were without relevance. The flexible shifts could barely earn a begrudging nod. The sheer impressive legality of the thing yielded little more than a sour grunt. And even the fact that Torvald Nom now held the title of Captain of the House Guard, while Scorch and Leff were but underlings among a menagerie of underlings (yes, he had exaggerated somewhat), had but granted him a temporary abeyance of the shrill fury he clearly deserved – and it waited, oh, it waited. He knew it. She knew it. And he knew she was holding on to it, like a giant axe, poised above his acorn of a head.

Yes, he'd given up slavery for this.

Such was the power of love, the lure of domestic tranquillity and the fending off of lonely solitude. Would he have it any other way?

Ask him later.

Onward, and there before him the estate's modest but suitably maintained wall, and the formal gate entranceway, its twin torches flaring and flickering, enough to make the two shapes of his redoubtable underlings look almost . . . attentive.

Not that either of them was watching the street. Instead, it seemed they were arguing.

'Stay sharp there, you two!' Torvald Nom said in his most stentorian voice, undermined by the punctuation of a loud, gassy belch.

'Gods, Tor's drunk!'

'I wish. Supper didn't agree with me. Now, what's your problem? I heard you two snapping and snarling from the other side of the street.'

'We got two new compound guards,' said Leff.

'Compound guards? Oh, you mean guarding the compound—'

'That's what I said. What else do compound guards guard if not compounds? Captains should know that kind of stuff, Tor.'

'And I do. It's just the title confused me. Compound needs guarding, yes, since the likelihood of someone getting past you two is so . . . likely. Well. So, you've met them? What are they like?'

'They're friends of Studlock – who they call Studious,' said Scorch, his eyes widening briefly before he looked away and squinted. 'Old friends, from under some mountain.'

'Oh,' said Torvald Nom.

'That collapsed,' Scorch added.

'The friendship? Oh, the mountain, you mean. It collapsed.'

Leff stepped closer and sniffed. 'You sure you're not drunk, Tor?'

'Of course I'm not drunk! Scorch is talking a lot of rubbish, that's all.'

'Rubble, not rubbish.'

'Like that, yes! Oh, look, Leff, just open the damned gate, will you? So I can meet the new compound guards.'

'Look for them in the compound,' Scorch advised.

Oh, maybe his wife was right, after all. Maybe? Of course she was. These two were idiots and they were also his friends and what did that say about Torvald Nom? No, don't think about that. *Besides, she's already done the necessary thinking about that, hasn't she?*

Torvald hastened through the gateway. Two strides into the compound and he halted. *Studious? Studious Lock? The Landless? Studious Lock the Landless, of One Eye Cat?*

'Ah, Captain, well timed. Permit me to introduce our two new estate guards.'

Torvald flinched as Studlock drifted towards him. Hood, mask, eerie eyes, all bound up in rags to cover up what had been done to him back in his adopted city – yes, but then, infamy never stayed hidden for long, did it? 'Ah, good evening, Castellan.' This modest, civil greeting was barely managed, croaking out from an all too dry mouth. And he saw, with growing trepidation, the two figures trailing in Studlock's wake.

'Captain Torvald Nom, this gaily clad gentleman is Madrun, and his ephemerally garbed companion is Lazan Door. Both hail from the north and so have no local interests that might conflict with their loyalties – a most important requirement, as you have been made aware, for Lady Varada of House Varada. Now, I have seen to their kit and assigned quarters. Captain, is something wrong?'

Torvald Nom shook his head. Then, before he could think – before his finely honed sense of propriety could kick in – he blurted out: 'But where are their masks?'

The shaggy haired giant frowned. 'Oh,' he said, 'that is most unfortunate. Reassure me once more, Studious, please.'

The castellan's pause was long, and then one rag-tied hand fluttered. 'Reputations, alas, are what they are, Madrun. Evidently, our captain here has travelled some. One Eye Cat? Let us hope he never wandered close to that foul, treacherous den of thieves, murderers and worse—'

'Never been there,' Torvald Nom said, hastily, licking his lips. 'But the tales of the, er, the ones hired to oust the Malazan Fist . . . and, er, what happened afterwards—'

'Outrageous lies,' said Lazan Door in his breathy, wispy voice, 'such as are invariably perpetrated by those with a vested interest in the illusion of righteousness. All lies, Captain. Foul, despicable, ruinous lies. I assure you we completed our task, even unto pursuing the Fist and his cadre into the very heart of a mountain—'

'You and Madrun Badrun, you mean. Studious Lock, on the other hand, was . . .' And only then did Torvald Nom decide that he probably shouldn't be speaking, probably shouldn't be revealing quite the extent of his knowledge. 'The tale I heard,' he added, 'was garbled, second and maybe even third hand, a jumble of details and who can separate truth from fancy in such things?'

'Who indeed,' said the castellan with another wave of one hand. 'Captain, we must trust that the subject of our past misadventures will not arise again, in any company and in particular that of our two intrepid gate guards.'

'The subject is now and for ever more closed,' affirmed Torvald Nom. 'Well, I'd best get to my office. To work on, um, shift scheduling – it seems we now have our night shift pretty much filled. As for the daytime—'

'As stated earlier,' cut in the castellan, 'the necessity for armed vigilance during the day is simply non-existent. Risk assessment and so forth. No, Captain, we have no need for more guards. Four will suffice.'

'Good, that will make scheduling easier. Now, it was a pleasure meeting you, Lazan Door, Madrun Badrun.' And, with disciplined march, Torvald Nom crossed the compound, making for his tiny office in the barracks annexe. Where he shut the flimsy door and sat down in the chair behind the desk which, in order to reach it, demanded that he climb over the desk itself. Slumping down, hands holding up his head, he sat. Sweating.

Was Lady Varada aware of any of this . . . this background, back there where the ground still steamed with blood and worse? Well, she'd hired Studlock, hadn't she? But that didn't mean anything, did it? He'd crunched down his name, and even that name wasn't his real name, just something the idiots in One Eye Cat gave him, same as Madrun Badrun. As for Lazan Door, well, that one might be real, original even. And only one of them was wearing a mask and that mask was some local make, generic, not painted with any relevant sigils or whatever. So, she might not know a thing! She might be completely blind, unsuspecting, unaware, unprepared, uneverything!

He climbed back over his desk, straightened and smoothed out his clothing as best he could. It shouldn't be so hard, the captain seeking audience with the Mistress. Perfectly reasonable. Except that the official route was through the castellan, and that wouldn't do. No, he needed to be cleverer than that. In fact, he needed to . . . *break in*.

More sweat, sudden, chilling him as he stood between the desk and the office door, a span barely wide enough to turn round in.

So, Lazan Door and Madrun Badrun would be patrolling the compound. And Studious Lock the Landless, well, he'd be in his own office, there on the main floor. Or even in his private chambers, sitting there slowly unravelling or undressing or whatever one wanted to call it.

There was a window on the back wall of the annexe. Plain shutters and simple inside latch. From there he could clamber on to the roof, which was close enough to the side wall of the main building to enable him to leap across and maybe find a handhold or two, and then he could scramble up to the next and final level, where dwelt the Lady. It was still early so she wouldn't be asleep or in any particular state of undress.

Still, how would she react to her captain's intruding so on her privacy? Well, he could explain he was testing the innermost security of the estate (and, in finding it so lacking, why, he could press for hiring yet more guards. Normal, reasonable, sane guards this time. No mass murderers. No sadists. No one whose humanness was questionable and open to interpretation. He could, then, provide a subtle counterbalance to the guards they already had).

It all sounded very reasonable, and diligent, as befitted a captain.

He worked his way round and opened the office door. Leaned out to make sure the barracks remained empty – of course it did, they were out there guarding things! He padded across to the back window. Unlatched it and eased out the shutters. Another quick, darting look, outside this time. Estate wall not ten paces opposite. Main building to his left, stables to his right. Was this area part of their rounds? It certainly should be. Well, if he moved fast enough, right this moment—

Hitching himself up on to the windowsill, Torvald Nom edged out and reached up for the eaves-trough. He tested his weight on it and, satisfied at the modest creak, quickly pulled himself up and on to the sloped roof. Reached back down and carefully closed the shutters.

He rolled on to his back and waited. He'd wait, yes, until the two monsters tramped past.

The clay tiles dug into his shoulder blades. Was that the scuff of boots? Was that the whisper of linen sweeping the cobbles? Was that – no, it wasn't, he wasn't hearing a damned thing. Where had his damned compound guards gone? He sat up, crept his way to the peak of the roof. Peered out on to the grounds – and there they were, playing dice against the wall to one side of the gate.

He could fire them for that! Why, even Studlock wouldn't be able to—

And there *he* was, Studious himself, floating across towards his two cohorts. And his voice drifted back to Torvald Nom.

'Any change in the knuckles, Lazan?'

'Oh yes,' the man replied. 'Getting worse. Options fast diminishing.'

'How unfortunate.'

Madrun Badrun grunted and then said, 'We had our chance. Go north or go south. We should've gone north.'

'That would not work, as you well know,' said Studious Lock. 'Where are your masks?'

Lazan Door flung the bone dice against the wall again, bent to study the results.

'We tossed 'em,' answered Madrun.

'Make new ones.'

'We don't want to, Studious, we really don't.'

'That goes without saying, but it changes nothing.'

Oh, Torvald suspected he could crouch here and listen to the idiots all night. Instead, he needed to take advantage of their carelessness. He eased back down the slope of the roof, lifted himself into a crouch, and eyed the main building – and, look, a balcony. Well, that wasn't wise, was it?

Now, could he make the leap without making any noise? Of course he could – he'd been a thief for years, a successful thief, too, if not for all the arrests and fines and prison time and slavery and the like. He paused, gauging the distance, deciding which part of the rail he'd reach for, then launched himself across the gap.

Success! And virtually no noise at all. He dangled for a moment, then pulled himself on to the balcony. It was narrow and crowded with clay pots snarled with dead plants. Now, he could work the locks and slip in on this floor, taking the inside route to the level above. That would be simplest, wouldn't it? Riskier scaling the outside wall, where a chance glance from any of the three fools still jabbering away just inside the gate might alight upon him. And the last thing he wanted was to see any of them draw swords (not that he recalled seeing them wearing any).

He tested the balcony door. Unlocked! Oh, things would indeed have to change. Why, he could just saunter inside and find himself—

'Please, Captain, take a seat.'

She was lounging in a plush chair, barely visible in the dark room. Veiled? Yes, veiled. Dressed in some long loose thing, silk perhaps. One long-fingered hand, snug in a grey leather glove, held a goblet. There was a matching chair opposite her.

'Pour yourself some wine – yes, there on the table. The failure of that route, from the roof of the annexe, is that the roof is entirely visible from the window of any room on this side of the house. I assume, Captain, you were either testing the security of the estate, or that you wished to speak with me in private. Any other alternatives, alas, would be unfortunate.'

'Indeed, Mistress. And yes, I was testing . . . things. And yes,' he added as, summoning as much aplomb as he could manage, he went over to pour himself a goblet full of the amber wine, 'I wished to speak with you in private. Concerning your castellan and the two new compound guards.'

'Do they seem . . . excessive?'

'That's one way of putting it.'

'I would not want to be discouraging.'

He sat down. 'Discouraging, Mistress?'

'Tell me, are my two gate guards as incompetent as they appear to be?'

'That would be quite an achievement, Mistress.'

'It would, yes.'

'It may surprise you,' Torvald Nom said, 'but they actually possess a nasty streak. And considerable experience. They have been caravan guards, enforcers, Guild thugs and bounty hunters. It's the formality of this present job that has them so . . . awkward. They will adjust in time.'

'Not too well, I hope.'

All right, Torvald Nom decided, she was talking about something and he had no idea what that something was. 'Mistress, regarding Studlock, Lazan and Madrun—'

'Captain, I understand you are estranged from House Nom. That is unfortunate. I always advise that such past errors be mended whenever possible. Reconciliation is essential to well-being.'

'I will give that some thought, Mistress.'

'Do so. Now, please make your way out using the stairs. Inform the castellan that I wish to speak to him – no, there will be no repercussions regarding your seeking a private conversation with me. In fact, I am heartened by your concern. Loyalty was ever the foremost trait of the family Nom. Oh, now, do finish your wine, Captain.'

He did, rather quickly. Then walked over and locked the balcony doors. A bow to Lady Varada, and then out into the corridor, closing the door behind him. A moment to figure out where the stairs were, and, feeling slightly numbed – was it the wine? No, it wasn't the wine – he descended to the ground floor and out through the formal entrance, striding across the compound to where stood the castellan and his two friends.

'Castellan Studlock,' Torvald Nom called out, pleased to see how all three looked up guiltily from their game. 'The Mistress wishes to see you immediately.'

'Oh? Of course. Thank you, Captain.'

Torvald watched him flit away, and then turned to Lazan Door and Madrun. 'Interesting technique you have here. I feel the need to describe your duties, since it appears the castellan forgot to. You are to patrol the compound, preferably at random intervals, employing a variety of routes to ensure that you avoid predictability. Be especially mindful of unlit areas, although I do not recommend you carry torches or lanterns. Any questions?'

Madrun was smiling. He bowed. 'Sound instruction, Captain, thank you. We shall commence our duties immediately. Lazan, collect up your scrying dice. We must attend to the necessary formalities of diligent patrol.'

Scrying dice? Gods below. 'Is it wise,' he asked, 'to rely upon the hoary gods to determine the night's flavour?'

Lazan Door cleared his throat then bared his metal fangs. 'As you say, Captain. Divination is ever an imprecise science. We shall be sure to avoid relying overmuch on such things.'

'Er, right. Good, well, I'll be in my office, then.'

'Again,' Madrun said, his smile broadening.

There was, Torvald decided as he walked away, nothing pleasant about that smile. About either of their smiles, in fact. Or anything else about those two. Or Studious Lock, for that matter – *Blood Drinker, Bile Spitter, Poisoner, oh, they had so many names for that one. How soon before he earns a few more? And Madrun Badrun? And Lazan Door? What is Lady Varada up to?*

Never mind, never mind. He had an office, after all. And once he crawled over the desk and settled down in the chair, why, he felt almost important.

The sensation lasted a few heartbeats, which was actually something of an achievement. Any few precious moments, yes, of not thinking about those three. Any at all.

Make new masks – now why should they do that? Renegade Seguleh are renegade – they can't ever go back. Supposedly, but then, what do any of us really know about the Seguleh? Make new masks, he said to them. Why?

What's wrong with normal advice? Wash that robe, Lazan Door, before the spiders start laying eggs. Choose no more than two colours, Madrun, and not ones that clash. Please. And what's with those moccasins?

Masks? Never mind the masks.

His stomach gurgled and he felt another rise of bilious gas. *'Always chew your food, Tor, why such a hurry? There's plenty of daylight left to play. Chew, Tor, chew! Nice and slow, like a cow, yes. This way nothing will disagree with you. Nothing disagrees with cows, after all.'*

So true, at least until the axe swings down.

He sat in his office, squeezed in behind the desk, in a most disagreeable state.

'She's poisoning him, is my guess.'

Scorch stared, as if amazed at such a suggestion. 'Why would she do that?'

'Because of you,' said Leff. 'She hates you, Scorch, because of the way you always got Tor into trouble, and now she thinks you're going to do it all over again, so that's why she's poisoning him.'

'That don't make any sense. If she was worried she wouldn't be killing him!'

'Not killing, just making sickly. You forget, she's a witch, she can do things like that. Of course, she'd do better by poisoning you.'

'I ain't touching nothing she cooks, that's for sure.'

'It won't help if she decides you're better off dead, Scorch. Gods, I am so glad I'm not you.'

'Me too.'

'What?'

'I'd have orange eyes and that'd be awful because then we'd both have orange eyes so looking at each other would be like looking at yourself, which I have to do all the time anyway but imagine double that! No thanks, is what I say.'

'Is that what you say?'

'I just said it, didn't I?'

'I don't know. I don't know what you just said, Scorch, and that's the truth.'

'Good, since what I had to say wasn't meant for you anyway.'

Leff looked round and no, he didn't see anyone else. Of course he didn't, there
was no point in looking.

'Besides,' said Scorch, 'you're the one who's been poisoned.'

'It wasn't no poison, Scorch. It was a mistake, a misdiagnosis. And it's fading—'

'No it ain't.'

'Yes. It is.'

'No. It ain't.'

'I'd stop saying that if I was you—'

'Don't start that one again!'

Blessed fates! Leave them to it, thy round self begs! The night stretches on, the
city wears its granite grin and shadows dance on the edge of darkness. Late-night
hawkers call out their wares, their services both proper and dubious. Singers sing
and the drunk drink and thieves do their thieving and mysteries thrive wherever
you do not belong and that, friends, is the hard truth.

Like rats we skitter away from the pools of light, seeking other matters, other
scenes both tranquil and foul.

Follow, oh, follow me!

Benefactor of all things cosmopolitan, bestower of blessings upon all matters human and humane (bless their hearts both squalid and generous, bless their
dreams and bless their nightmares, bless their fears and their loves and their
fears of love and love of fears and bless, well, bless their shoes, sandals, boots and
slippers and to walk in each, in turn, ah, such wonders! Such peculiar follies!),
Kruppe of Darujhistan walked the Great Avenue of sordid acquisitiveness, casting a most enormous, indeed gigantic shadow that rolled sure as a tide past all
these shops and their wares, past the wary eyes of shop owners, past the stands
of fruit and succulent pastries, past the baskets of berries and the dried fish and
the strange leafy things some people ate believing themselves to be masticators
of wholesomeness, past the loaves of bread and rounds of cheese, past the vessels
of wine and liquors in all assorted sizes, past the weavers and dressmakers, past
the crone harpist with nubs for fingers and only three strings left on her harp and
her song about the peg and the hole and the honey on the nightstand – ducking
the flung coins and so quickly past! – and the bolts of cloth going nowhere and
the breeches blocking the doorway and the shirts for men-at-arms and shoes
for the soulless and the headstone makers and urn-pissers and the old thrice-
divorced man who tied knots for a living with a gaggle of children in tow surely
bound by blood and thicker stuff. Past the wax-drippers and wick-twisters, the
fire-eaters and ashcake-makers, past the prostitutes – oozing each languorous
step with smiles of appreciation and fingers all aflutter and unbidden mysterious
sensations of caresses in hidden or at least out-of-reach places and see eyes
widen and appreciation flood through like the rush of lost youth and princely
dreams and they sigh and call out *Kruppe, you darling man! Kruppe, ain't you
gonna pay for that? Kruppe, marry every one of us and make us honest women!
Kruppe* – rushing quickly past, now, aaii, frightening prospect to imagine! A

bludgeon of wives (surely that must be the plural assignation)! A prattle of prostitutes!

Past this gate, thank the gods, and into the tunnel and out again and now civilization loomed austere and proper and this bodacious shadow strode alone, animated in its solitude, and yet this moment proved ample time to partake of past passages through life itself.

Out from one sleeve a berry-studded pastry, a ripe pompfruit, and a flask of minty wine; out from the other a new silver dinner knife with the Varada House monogram (my, where did this come from?), the polished blade – astonishing! – already glistening with a healthy dollop of butter streaked with honey – and so many things crowding these ample but nimble hands but see how one thing after another simply *vanished* into inviting mouth and appreciative palate as befitting all culinary arts when the subtle merging of flavours yielded exquisite masterpiece – butter, honey, and – oh! – jam, and pastry and cheese and fruit and smoked eel – agh! Voluminous sleeve betrays self! Wine to wash away disreputable (and most cruel) taste.

Hands temporarily free once more, to permit examination of new shirt, array of scented candles, knotted strings of silk, handsome breeches and gilt-threaded sandals soft as any one of Kruppe's four cheeks, and here a kid-gut condom – gods, where did that come from? Well, an end to admiration of the night's most successful shopping venture, and if that crone discovered but two strings left on her harp, well, imagine how the horse felt!

Standing now, at last, before most austere of austere estates. As the gate creaked open, inviting invitation and so invited Kruppe invited himself in.

Steps and ornate formal entranceway and corridor and more steps these ones carpeted and wending upward and another corridor and now the dark-stained door and – oh, fling aside those wards, goodness – inside.

'How did you – never mind. Sit, Kruppe, make yourself comfortable.'

'Master Baruk is so kind, Kruppe shall do as bid, with possibly measurable relief does he so *oof!* into this chair and stretch out legs, yes they are indeed stretched out, the detail subtle. Ah, an exhausting journey, Baruk beloved friend of Kruppe!'

A toad-like obese demon crawled up to nest at his feet, snuffling. Kruppe produced a strip of dried eel and offered it. The demon sniffed, then gingerly accepted the morsel.

'Are things truly as dire as I believe, Kruppe?'

Kruppe waggled his brows. 'Such journeys leave self puckered with dryness, gasping with thirst.'

Sighing, the High Alchemist said, 'Help yourself.'

Beaming a smile, Kruppe drew out from a sleeve a large dusty bottle, already uncorked. He examined the stamp on the dark green glass. 'My, your cellar is indeed well equipped!' A crystal goblet appeared from the other sleeve. He poured. Downed a mouthful then smacked his lips. 'Exquisite!'

'Certain arrangements have been finalized,' said Baruk.

'Most impressive, Baruk friend of Kruppe. How can such portentous events be measured, one wonders. If one was the wondering type. Yet listen – the buried gate creaks, dust sifts down, stones groan! Humble as we are, can we hope to halt such inevitable inevitabilities? Alas, time grinds on. All fates spin and not even the gods can guess how each will topple. The moon itself rises uncertain on these nights. The stars waver, rocks fall upward, wronged wives forgive and forget – oh, this is a time for miracles!'

'And is that what we need, Kruppe? Miracles?'

'Each moment may indeed seem in flux, chaotic and fraught, yet – and Kruppe knows this most surely – when all is set out, moment upon moment, then every aberration is but a modest crease, a feeble fold, a crinkled memento. The great forces of the universe are as a weight-stone upon the fabric of our lives. Rich and poor, modest and ambitious, generous and greedy, honest and deceitful, why, all is flattened! Splat! Crunch, smear, ooze! What cares Nature for jewelled crowns, coins a-stacked perilously high, great estates and lofty towers? Kings and queens, tyrants and devourers – all are as midges on the forehead of the world!'

'You advise an extended perspective. That is all very well, from an historian's point of view, and in retrospect. Unfortunately, Kruppe, to those of us who must live it, in the midst, as it were, it provides scant relief.'

'Alas, Baruk speaks true. Lives in, lives out. The sobs of death are the sodden songs of the world. So true, so sad. Kruppe asks this: witness two scenes. In one, an angry, bitter man beats another man to death in an alley in the Gadrobi District. In the other, a man of vast wealth conspires with equally wealthy compatriots to raise yet again the price of grain, making the cost of simple bread so prohibitive that families starve, are led into lives of crime, and die young. Are both acts of violence?'

The High Alchemist stood looking down at Kruppe. 'In only one of those examples will you find blood on a man's hands.'

'True, deplorable as such stains are.' He poured himself some more wine.

'There are,' said Baruk, 'countless constructs whereby the wealthy man might claim innocence. Mitigating circumstances, unexpected costs of production, the law of supply and demand, and so on.'

'Indeed, a plethora of justifications, making the waters so very murky, and who then sees the blood?'

'And yet, destitution results, with all its misery, its stresses and anxieties, its foul vapours of the soul. It can be said that the wealthy grain merchant wages subtle war.'

Kruppe studied the wine through the crystal. 'And so the poor remain poor and, mayhap, even poorer. The employed but scarcely getting by cling all the harder to their jobs, even unto accepting despicable working conditions – which in turn permits the employers to fill their purses unto bulging, thus satisfying whatever hidden pathetic inadequacies they harbour. A balance can be said to exist, one never iterated, whereby the eternal war is held in check, so as to avoid anarchy. Should the grain merchant charge too high, then revolution may well explode into life.'

'Whereupon everyone loses.'

'For a time. Until the new generation of the wealthy emerge, to begin once again their predations on the poor. Balance is framed by imbalances and so it seems such things might persist for all eternity. Alas, in any long view, one sees that this is not so. The structure of society is far more fragile than most believe. To set too much faith in its resilience is to know a moment of pristine astonishment at the instant of its utter collapse – before the wolves close in.' Kruppe raised one finger. 'Yet, witness all these who would grasp hold of the crown, to make themselves the freest and the wealthiest of them all. Oh, they are most dangerous in the moment, as one might expect. Most dangerous indeed. One is encouraged to pray. Pray for dust.'

'An end to it all.'

'And a new beginning.'

'I somehow expected more from you, my friend.'

Kruppe smiled, reached down and patted the demon's pebbly head. It blinked languidly. 'Kruppe maintains a perspective as broad as his waistline, which, as you know, is unceasing. After all, where does it begin and where does it end?'

'Any other momentous news?'

'Cities live in haste. Ever headlong. Nothing changes and everything changes. A murderer stalks Gadrobi District, but Kruppe suspects you know of that. Assassins plot. You know this too, friend Baruk. Lovers tryst or dream of said trysts. Children belabour unknown futures. People retire and others are retired, new careers abound and old nemeses lurk. Friendships unfold while others unravel. All in its time, most High Alchemist, all in its time.'

'You do not put me at ease, Kruppe.'

'Join me in a glass of this exquisite vintage!'

'There are a dozen wards sealing the cellar – twice as many as since your last visit.'

'Indeed?'

'You did not trip a single one.'

'Extraordinary!'

'Yes, it is.'

The demon belched and the heady fragrance of smoked eel wafted through the chamber. Even the demon wrinkled its nostril slits.

Kruppe produced, with a flourish, some scented candles.

An intestinal confusion of pipes, valves, copper globes, joins and vents dominated one entire end of the building's main front room. From this bizarre mechanism came rhythmic gasps (most suggestive), wheezes (inserting, as it were, a more realistic contribution) and murmurs and hissing undertones. Six nozzles jutted out, each one ready for a hose attachment or extension, but at the moment all shot out steady blue flame and this heated the crackling dry air of the chamber so that both Chaur and Barathol – working barebacked as they had been the entire day just done – were slick with sweat.

Most of the clutter in this decrepit bakery had now been removed, or, rather, transferred from inside to the narrow high-walled yard out the back, and Chaur was on his hands and knees using wet rags to wipe dust and old flour from the well-set pavestone floor. Barathol was examining the brick bases of the three humped ovens, surprised and pleased to find, sandwiched between layers of brick, vast slabs of pumice-stone. The interior back walls of the ovens each contained fixtures for the gas that had been used as fuel, with elongated perforated tubes projecting out beneath the racks. Could he convert these ovens to low-heat forges? Perhaps.

The old copper mixing drums remained, lining one half of the room's back wall, and would serve for quenching. He had purchased an anvil from an inbound caravan from Pale, the original buyer having, alas, died whilst the object was en route. A plains design, intended for portability – Rhivi, he had been informed – it was not quite the size he wanted or needed, but it would suffice for now. Various tongs and other tools came from the scrap markets on the west side of the city, including a very fine hammer of Aren steel (no doubt stolen from a Malazan army's weaponsmith).

On the morrow he would put in his first orders for wood, coke, coal, and raw copper, tin and iron.

It was getting late. Barathol straightened from his examination of the ovens and said to Chaur, 'Leave that off now, my friend. We're grimy, true, but perhaps an outside restaurant would accommodate us, once we show our coin. I don't know about you, but some chilled beer would sit well right now.'

Looking up, Chaur's smeared and smudged face split into a wide smile.

The front door was kicked open and both turned as a half-dozen disreputable men pushed in, spreading out. Clubs and mallets in their hands, they began eyeing the equipment. A moment later and a finely dressed woman strode through the milling press, eyes settling on Barathol, upon which she smiled.

'Dear sir, you are engaged in an illegal activity—'

'Illegal? That is a reach, I'm sure. Now, before you send your thugs on a rampage of destruction, might I point out that the valves are not only open but the threads have been cut. In other words, for now, the flow of gas from the chambers beneath this structure cannot be stopped. Any sort of damage will result in, well, a ball of fire, probably of sufficient size to incinerate a sizeable area of the district.' He paused, then added, 'Such wilful destruction on your part will be viewed by most as, um, illegal. Now, you won't face any charges since you will be dead, but the Guild that hired you will face dire retribution. The fines alone will bankrupt it.'

The woman's smile was long gone by now. 'Oh, aren't you the clever one. Since we cannot discourage you by dismantling your shop, we have no choice then but to focus our attention on yourselves.'

Barathol walked to the kneading counter and reached into a leather satchel, withdrawing a large round ball of fired clay. He faced the woman and her mob, saw a few expressions drain of blood, and was pleased. 'Yes, a Moranth grenado. Cusser, the Malazans call this one. Threaten myself or my companion here, and I will be delighted to commit suicide – after all, what have we to lose that you would not happily take from us, given the chance?'

'You have lost your mind.'

'You are welcome to that opinion. Now, the question is, have you?'

She hesitated, then snarled and spun on her heel. Waving her crew to follow her, out she went.

Sighing, Barathol returned the cusser to the satchel. *'In every thirteenth crate of twelve cussers each,'* Mallet had told him, *'there is a thirteenth cusser. Empty. Why? Who knows? The Moranth are strange folk.'*

'It worked this time,' he said to Chaur, 'but I doubt it will last. So, the first order of business is to outfit you. Armour, weapons.'

Chaur stared at him as if uncomprehending.

'Remember the smell of blood, Chaur? Corpses, the dead and dismembered?'

Sudden brightening of expression, and Chaur nodded vigorously.

Sighing again, Barathol said, 'Let's climb out over the back wall and find us that beer.'

He took the satchel with him.

Elsewhere in the city, as the tenth bell of the night sounded, a fingerless man set out for a new tavern, murder on his mind. His wife went out to her garden to kneel on stone, which she polished using oiled sand and a thick pad of leather.

A buxom, curvaceous woman – who drew admiring regard along with curdling spite depending on gender and gender preference – walked with one rounded arm hooked in the rather thinner seamed arm of a Malazan historian, who bore an expression wavering between disbelief and dismay. They strolled as lovers would, and since they were not lovers, the historian's bemusement only grew.

In the High Markets of the Estates District, south of the gallows, sauntered Lady Challice. Bored, stung with longing and possibly despoiled (in her own mind) beyond all hope of redemption, she perused the host of objects and items, none of which were truly needed, and watched as women just like her (though most were trailed by servants who carried whatever was purchased) picked through the expensive and often finely made rubbish eager as jackdaws (and as mindless? Ah, beware cruel assumptions!), and she saw herself as so very different from them. So . . . changed.

Not three hundred paces away from Lady Challice, wandering unmindful of where his steps took him, was Cutter, who had once been a thief named Crokus Younghand, who had once stolen something he shouldn't have, and, finding that he could not truly give it back, had then confused guilt and sympathy with the bliss of adoration (such errors are common), only to be released in the end by a young woman's open contempt for his heartfelt, honest admissions.

Well, times and people change, don't they just.

On a rooftop half a city away, Rallick Nom stood looking out upon the choppy sea of blue lights, at his side Krute of Talient, and they had much to discuss and this meant, given Rallick Nom's taciturnity, a long session indeed.

Krute had too much to say. Rallick weighed every morsel he fed back, not out of distrust, simply habit.

In a duelling school, long after the last of the young students had toddled out, Murillio sat under moonlight with Stonny Menackis as, weeping, she unburdened herself to this veritable stranger – which perhaps is what made it all so easy – but Stonny had no experience with a man such as Murillio, who understood what it was to listen, to bestow rapt, thorough and most genuine attention solely upon one woman, to draw all of her essence – so pouring out – into his own being, as might a hummingbird drinking nectar, or a bat a cow's ankle blood (although this analogy ill serves the tender moment).

And so between them unseen vapours waft, animal and undeniable, and so much seeps into flesh and bone and self that stunning recognition comes – when it comes – like the unlocking of a door once thought sealed for ever more.

She wept and she wept often, and each time it was somehow easier, somehow more natural, more comfortable and acceptable, no different, truly, from the soft stroke of his fingers through her short hair, the way the tips brushed her cheek to smooth away the tears – and oh, who then could be surprised by all this?

To the present, then, as the blurred moon, now risen, squints down upon a score of figures gathering on a rooftop. Exchanging hand signals and muttering instructions and advice. Checking weapons. A full score, for the targets were tough, mean, veterans with foreign ways. And the assault to come, well, it would be brutal, unsubtle, and, without doubt, thorough.

The usual crowd in K'rul's Bar, a dozen or so denizens choosing to be unmindful of the temple that once was – these quarried stone walls, stained with smoke and mute repositories for human voices generation upon generation, from droning chants and choral music to the howl of drunken laughter and the squeals of pinched women, these walls, then, thick and solid, ever hold to indifference in the face of drama.

Lives play out, lives parcel out portions framed by stone and wood, by tile and rafter, and each of these insensate forms have, in their time, tasted blood.

The vast, low-ceilinged main taproom with its sunken floor was once a transept or perhaps a congregation area. The narrow corridor between inset pillars along the back was once a colonnade bearing niches on which, long ago, stood funerary urns containing the charred, ashen remains of High Priests and Priestesses. The kitchen and the three storerooms behind it had once supplied sustenance to monks and the sanctioned blade-wielders, scribes and acolytes. Now they fed patrons, staff and owners.

Up the steep, saddled, stone steps to the landing on the upper floor, from which ran passages with sharply angled ceilings, three sides of a square with the fourth interrupted by the front façade of the building. Eight cell-like rooms fed off each of these passages, those on the back side projecting inward (supported by the pillars of the main floor colonnade) while the two to either side had their rooms against the building's outer walls (thus providing windows).

The cells looking out on to the taproom had had inside walls knocked out, so that eight rooms were now three rooms, constituting the offices. The interior windows were now shuttered – no glass or skin – and Picker was in the habit of throwing them wide open when she sat at her desk, giving her a clear view of the front third of the taproom, including the entranceway.

On this night, there were few guests resident in the inn's rooms. Barathol and Chaur had not yet returned. Scillara had taken Duiker into the Daru District. The bard was on the low dais in the taproom, plunking some airy, despondent melody that few of the twenty or so patrons listened to with anything approaching attention. A stranger from Pale had taken a corner room on the northeast corner and had retired early after a meagre meal and a single pint of Gredfallan ale.

Picker could see Blend at her station beside the front door, sunk in shadows as she sat, legs outstretched, her hands cradling a mug of hot cider – bizarre tastes, that woman, since it was sultry and steamy this night. People entering rarely even noticed her, marching right past without a glance down. Blend's talent, aye, and who could say if it was natural or something else.

Antsy was yelling in the kitchen. He'd gone in there to calm down the two cooks – who despised each other – and it turned out as it usually did, with Antsy at war with everyone, including the scullions and the rats cowering beneath the counter. In a short while utensils would start flying and Picker would have to drag herself down there.

Bluepearl was . . . somewhere. It was his habit to wander off, exploring the darker crooks and crannies of the old temple.

A night, then, no different from any other.

Bluepearl found himself in the cellar. Funny how often that happened. He had dragged out the fourth dusty cask from the crawlspace behind the wooden shelves. The first three he had sampled earlier in the week. Two had been vinegar, from which he could manage only a few swallows at a time. The other had been something thick and tarry, smelling of cedar or perhaps pine sap – in any case, he'd done little more than dip a finger in, finding the taste even fouler than the smell.

This time, however, he felt lucky. Broaching the cask, he bent close and tried a few tentative sniffs. Ale? Beer? But of course, neither lasted, did they? Yet this cask bore the sigil of the temple on the thick red wax coating the lid. He sniffed again. Definitely yeasty, but fresh, which meant . . . sorcery. He sniffed a third time.

He'd danced with all kinds of magic as a squad mage in the Bridgeburners. Aye, he had so many stories that even that sour-faced bard upstairs would gape in wonder just to hear half of them. Why, he'd ducked and rolled under the nastiest kinds, the sorceries that ripped flesh from bones, that boiled the blood, that made a man's balls swell up big as melons – oh, that time had been before he'd joined, hadn't it? Yah, the witch and the witch's daughter – never mind. What he was was an old hand.

· And this stuff – Bluepearl dipped a finger in and then poked it into his mouth –

oh, it was magic indeed. Something elder, hinting of blood (aye, he'd tasted the like before).

'Is that you, Brother Cuven?'

He twisted round and scowled at the ghost whose head and shoulders lifted into view through the floor. 'Do I look like Brother Cuven? You're dead, long dead. It's all gone, you hear? So why don't you go and do the same?'

'I smelled the blade,' murmured the ghost, beginning to sink back down. 'I smelled it . . .'

No, Bluepearl decided, it probably wasn't a good thing to be drinking this stuff. Not before some kind of analysis was made. Could be Mallet might help on that. Now, had he messed it up by opening the cask? Probably it would go bad now. So, he'd better take it upstairs.

Sighing, Bluepearl replaced the wooden stopper and picked up the cask.

In the corner room on the second level, the stranger who'd booked the room for this night finished digging out the last of the bars on the window. He then doused the lantern and moved across to the hallway door, where he crouched down, listening.

From the window behind him the first of the assassins climbed in.

Blend, her eyes half closed, watched as five men came in, moving in a half-drunken clump and arguing loudly about the latest jump in the price of bread, slurred statements punctuated by shoves and buffets, and wasn't it a wonder, Blend reflected as they staggered into the taproom, how people could complain about very nearly anything as if their lives depended on it.

These ones she didn't know, meaning they'd probably spied the torchlit sign on their way back from some other place, deciding that this drunk wasn't drunk enough, and she noted that they were better dressed than most – nobles, most likely, with all the usual bluster and airs of invincibility and all that. Well, they'd be spending coin here and that was what counted.

She took another sip of cider.

Antsy had his short sword out as he crept towards the back of the smallest of the three storerooms. That damned two-headed rat was back. Sure, nobody else believed him except maybe the cooks now since they'd both seen the horrid thing, but the only way to prove it to the others was to kill the bugger and then show it to everyone.

They could then pickle it in a giant jar and make of it a curio for the bar. It would be sure to pull 'em in. Two-headed rat caught in the kitchen of K'rul's Bar! Come see!

Oh, hold on . . . was that the best kind of advertising? He'd have to ask Picker about that.

First, of course, he needed to kill the thing.

He crept closer, eyes fixed on the dark gap behind the last crate to the left.

Kill the thing, aye. Just don't chop either head off.

Eleven figures crowded the corner room on the upper floor. Three held daggers, including the man crouched at the door. Four cradled crossbows, quarrels set. The last four – big men all – wielded swords and bucklers, and beneath their loose shirts there was fine chain.

The one at the door could now hear the argument in the taproom downstairs, accusations regarding the price of bread – a ridiculous subject, the man thought yet again, given how these ones were dressed like second and thirdborn nobles – but clearly no one had taken note of the peculiarity. Loud voices, especially drunk-sounding ones, had a way of filling the heads of people around them. Filling them with the wrong things.

So now everyone's attention was on the loud, obnoxious newcomers, and at least some of the targets were likely to be converging, having it in mind to maybe toss the fools out or at least ask them to tone it down and all that.

Almost time then . . .

Sitting on the stool on the dais, the bard let his fingers trail away from the last notes he had played, and slowly leaned back as the nobles now argued over which table to take. There were plenty to choose from so the issue was hardly worth all that energy.

He watched them for a long moment, and then set his instrument down and went over to the pitcher and tankard waiting to one side of the modest stage. He poured himself some ale, and then leaned against the wall, taking sips.

Picker rose from her chair as the door opened behind her. She turned. 'Mallet, that bunch of idiots who just came in.'

The healer nodded. 'There'll be trouble with them. Have you seen Barathol or Chaur? They were supposed to be coming back here – the Guild's probably caught wind of what he's up to by now. I'm thinking of maybe heading over, in case—'

Picker held up her hand, two quick signals that silenced Mallet. 'Listen to them,' she said, frowning. 'It's not sounding right.'

After a moment, Mallet nodded. 'We'd better head down.'

Picker turned and leaned on the sill, squinting at the shadows where Blend sat – and she saw those outstretched legs slowly draw back. 'Shit.'

It was an act. That conclusion arrived sudden and cold as a winter wind. Alarmed, Blend rose from her chair, hands slipping beneath her raincape.

As the outside door opened once more.

That damned rat had slipped beneath the door leading to the cellar – Antsy saw its slithery tail wriggle out of sight and swore under his breath. He could catch it on the stairs—

The cellar door swung open and there stood Bluepearl, carrying a dusty cask as if it was a newborn child.

'Did you see it?' Antsy demanded.

'See what?'

'The two-headed rat! It just went under the door!'

'Gods below, Antsy. Please, no more. There's no two-headed rat. Move aside, will you? This thing's heavy.'

And he shouldered past Antsy, out into the kitchen.

Three cloaked figures stepped in from outside K'rul's Bar, crossbows at the ready. The bolts snapped out. Behind the bar, Skevos, who was handling the shift this night, was driven back as a quarrel thudded into his chest, shattering his sternum. A second quarrel shot up towards the office window where Picker was leaning out and she lunged back, either struck or dodging there was no way to tell. The third quarrel caught Hedry, a serving girl of fifteen years of age, and spun her round, her tray of mugs tumbling over.

From closer to the dais, the five drunks drew knives and swords from beneath their cloaks and fanned out, hacking at everyone within reach.

Shrieks filled the air.

Stepping out from her table, Blend slid like smoke into the midst of the three figures at the doorway. Her knives flickered, slashed, opening the throat of the man directly in front of her, severing the tendons of the nearest arm of the man to her left. Ducking beneath the first man as he toppled forward, she thrust one of her daggers into the chest of the third assassin. The point punched through chain and the blade snapped. She brought the other one forward in an upper cut, stabbing between the man's legs. As he went down, Blend tore the knife free and spun to slash at the face of the second assassin. Throwing his head back to avoid the blade drove it into a low rafter. There was a heavy crunch and the man sagged on watery knees. Blend stabbed him through an eye.

She heard a fourth crossbow release and something punched her left shoulder, flinging her round. The arm below that shoulder seemed to have vanished – she could feel nothing – and she heard the knife clunk on the floor, even as the assassin, who had held back in the doorway, now rushed towards her, crossbow discarded and daggers drawn.

Mallet had opened the door at the moment that Picker – leaning out of the window – gave a startled yelp. A quarrel slammed into the wall not an arm's reach from the healer's head. Ducking, he threw himself out into the corridor.

As he half straightened, he saw figures pouring from round the corner to his left. Cords thrummed. One bolt punched into his stomach. The other ripped through his throat. He fell backward in a wash of blood and pain.

Lying on his back, hearing footfalls fast approach, Mallet reached up to his neck – he couldn't breathe – blood gushed down into his lungs, hot and numbing. Frantic, he summoned High Denul—

A shadow descended over him and he looked up into a passive young face, the eyes blank as a dagger lifted into view.

Kick open the gate, Whiskeyjack—

Mallet watched the point flash down.

A sting in his right eye, and then darkness.

Mallet's killer straightened, withdrawing the dagger, and he wondered, briefly, at the odd smile on the dead man's face.

Emerging from the kitchen, ducking beneath the low crossbeam of the doorway leading into the taproom, Bluepearl heard crossbows loose, heard screams, and then the hiss of swords whipped free of scabbards. He looked up.

A flung dagger pinned his right hand to the cask. Shouting at the fiery agony, he staggered back as two assassins rushed towards him. One with a knife, the other with a long, thin-bladed sword.

The attacker with the knife was in the lead, his weapon raised.

Bluepearl spat at him.

That pearlescent globule transmogrified in the air, expanding into a writhing ball of serpents. A dozen fanged jaws struck the assassin in the face. He screamed in horror, slashing at his own face with his knife.

Bluepearl sought to drop the cask, only to have its weight tug his arm downward – his hand still pinned – and he shrieked at the burst of agony.

He had time to look up and see the sword as it was thrust into his face. Into the side of his nose, the point punching deeper, upward, driving into his forebrain.

At the threshold to the cellar, Antsy heard the scrap erupt in the taproom. Whirling round, loosing twenty curses in fourteen different languages, readjusting his grip on his shortsword. Gods, it sounded like unholy slaughter out there. He needed a damned shield!

The cooks and scullions were rushing for the back door – and all at once there were screams from the alley beyond.

Antsy plunged into the storeroom on the left. To the crate at the far end, beneath the folds of burlap. He jimmied the lid open and plucked out three, four sharpers, stuffing them beneath his shirt. A fifth one for his left hand. Then he rushed back out into the kitchen.

One cook and two scullions – both girls – were running back inside, and Antsy saw cloaked forms crowding the back door. 'Down!' he screamed, throwing the sharper overhand, hard, straight past the two assassins in the doorway. The sharper struck the alley wall and exploded.

He saw red mist burst round the two visible assassins, like Hood's own haloes. They both slammed down face first. From the alley beyond, a chorus of terrible shrieks. Antsy drew out another sharper, ran to the doorway. Standing on the backs of the dead assassins, he leaned out and threw the grenado into the alley. Another snapping, fierce detonation. And there were no more cries out there.

'Chew on that, you fuckin' arseholes!'

Picker rolled across the floor in the wake of that first quarrel. She saw Mallet lunge into the corridor, saw the bolts take him down. Scrambling – knowing the healer was a dead man – she threw herself at the office door, slamming it shut even as footfalls rushed closer. Dropping the latch, a heartbeat before a heavy weight pounded into the solid barrier, she went to the crate at the foot of the desk.

Fumbled with the key for a moment – thundering thumps from the door behind her, mayhem in the taproom below – before working the lock free and flinging back the lid. She drew out her heavy crossbow and a clutch of quarrels.

She heard the echo of sharpers from the kitchen and grinned, but it was a cold grin.

On her feet once more, even as wood splintered on the door, she rushed back to the window – in time to see Blend knocked back by a bolt in her shoulder, and an assassin lunging after her from the doorway.

It was a damned good shot, her quarrel striking the man in the forehead, snapping his head back in a burst of blood, skull and brains.

Whirling round, she went back to the crate, found the lone sharper she'd stashed there, then back to the window, where she leapt up on to the sill, balanced in a crouch. Directly below was a table. Two bodies bled out beside it, legs tangled in the knocked-over chairs – two innocent patrons, two regulars who never did nobody any harm, good with tips, always a smile—

The door crashed open behind her. She twisted and threw the sharper, then dropped down from the sill. The crack of the grenado in the office, a gout of flames and smoke, as Picker landed on the tabletop.

It exploded beneath her. One of her knees slammed into her chin and she felt teeth crack as she fell to one side, thumping down on one of the corpses. She managed to hold on to the crossbow, although the quarrels scattered across the floor.

Spitting blood, she sat up.

Blend saw her attacker flung back, saw his head cave inward above his eyes. She crouched down, reaching up for the quarrel embedded in her left shoulder. The point was jammed into the cartilage between the bone of the upper arm and the shoulder's socket. Leaving it in there was probably worse than pulling the damned thing out. Gritting her teeth, she tugged the bolt free.

That made her pass out.

After pushing the surviving crew in the kitchen back out into the alley – now crowded with a dozen torn-up corpses – Antsy crossed the room, collecting the iron lid of a large cauldron along the way. At the entrance leading to the taproom he found Bluepearl, dead as dead could be in a pool of ale, and just beyond him knelt an assassin who seemed to have taken his dagger to his own face, which was now a sliced, shredded, eyeless mess. He was crooning some wordless melody from deep in his throat.

Antsy's backslash split the bastard's skull. Tugging the sword loose, he edged forward.

There'd been another sharper, from upstairs, and the crashing of furniture, but little else now. Moving in a crouch, sword ready, lid held like a shield, he worked his way round the near end of the bar.

There was Picker, on her knees directly ahead, reaching out for a quarrel on the floor and quickly loading her marine-issue weapon. Blend was lying motionless near the bar entrance.

Antsy hissed.

Picker looked up, met his eyes. She signalled with one hand, six gestures, and he nodded, answering with two.

Dripping ale and blood, a few soft groans here and there.

Soft footfalls on the landing at the top of the stairs.

Antsy set down his sword, drew out a sharper and showed it to Picker, who nodded and then quietly moved round, using the wreckage of the table for cover, and trained her crossbow on the stairs.

When he saw she was ready, Antsy lifted his makeshift shield to cover shoulder and head, then quickly stepped round to the foot of the stairs. And threw the grenado upward.

Two quarrels clanged off the cauldron lid, with enough force to knock it from his hand. At the same moment an assassin, having launched herself from halfway down the stairs, sailed down towards him.

Picker's quarrel caught the attacker somewhere in the midsection, convulsing her in mid-flight. She crashed down just as the sharper detonated near the landing.

And then Antsy, sword in hand once more, was rushing up those steps. Picker raced into his wake, drawing out her own sword. 'Get outa the way with that pigsticker!' she snarled. 'Cover me in close!' She pulled him back and round by one shoulder and pushed past.

Limbs twitching from a heap of bodies on the landing, and splashed blood on the walls – and movement beyond, somewhere in the corridor.

She scrambled over the dead and dying on the landing, pitched into the corridor and, seeing three assassins slowly picking themselves up from the floor, charged forward.

Short work cutting down the stunned attackers, with Antsy guarding her back.

Blend opened her eyes and wondered why she was lying on the floor. She attempted to lift her left arm and gasped as pain blossomed red and hot, leaving her half blind in its aftermath. Oh, now she remembered. With a low moan, she rolled on to her good side and worked herself into a sitting position, blinking sweat and worse from her eyes.

The bar door was open, one of the hinges broken.

In the street beyond, she saw at least a half-dozen cloaked figures, gathered and creeping closer.

Shit.

Desperate, she looked round for the nearest discarded weapon. Knowing she wouldn't have time, knowing they were going to cut her down once and for all. Still – she saw a knife and reached out for it.

The six assassins came at a sprint.

Someone slammed into them from one side, loosing a bellowing bawl like a wounded bull, and Blend stared as the huge man – *Chaur* – swung his enormous fists. Heads snapped back on broken necks, faces crumpled in sprays of blood—

And then Barathol was there, with nothing more than a knife, slashing into the reeling assassins, and Blend could see the fear in the blacksmith's eyes – fear for Chaur, dread for what might happen if the assassins recovered—

As they were now doing.

Blend pushed herself to her feet, collecting the dagger from the floor as she staggered forward—

And was shoved aside by Antsy. Hacking at the nearest assassin with his shortsword, a dented cauldron lid shielding his left side.

Chaur, his forearms slashed by desperate daggers, picked up an assassin and threw him down on to the cobbles. Bones snapped. Still bawling, he picked the broken form up by an ankle and swung him into the air, round, then loose – to collide with another assassin, and both went down. Barathol was suddenly above the first man, driving his boot heel down on his temple. Limbs spasmed.

Antsy pulled his sword from an assassin's chest and readied himself for his next target, then slowly straightened.

Leaning against the doorframe, Blend spat and said, 'All down, Sergeant.'

Barathol wrapped Chaur in a hug to calm the man down. Tears streaked Chaur's broad cheeks, and his fists were still closed, like massive bloody mauls at the ends of his arms. He had wet himself.

Blend and Antsy watched as the blacksmith hugged his friend tightly, with need and with raw relief, so exposed that both Malazans had to look away.

Picker came up behind Blend. 'You gonna live?' she asked.

'Good as new, as soon as Mallet—'

'No. Not Mallet, love.'

Blend squeezed shut her eyes. 'They caught us, Pick,' she said. 'They caught us good.'

'Aye.'

She glanced over. 'You got 'em all in the taproom? Damned impressive—'

'No, I didn't, but they're all down. Four of 'em, right at the foot of the stage. Looked like they rushed it.'

Rushed it? But who was up there . . . 'We lose our bard, then?'

'Don't know,' Picker said. 'Didn't see him.'

Rushed the stage . . .

'We lost Bluepearl, too.'

Blend slowly closed her eyes a second time. Oh, she was hurting, and a lot of that hurt couldn't get sewn up. *They caught us.* 'Picker.'

'They slaughtered everyone, Blend. People with nothing but bad luck being here tonight. Skevos. Hedry, Larmas, little Boothal. All to take us down.'

From up the street came a squad of City Guard, lanterns swinging.

For a scene such as Blend was looking out on right now, there should be a crowd of onlookers, the ones hungry to see injured, dying people, the ones who fed on such things. But there was no one.

Because this was Guild work.

'Some of us are still breathing,' Blend said. 'It's not good to do that. Leave some marines still breathing.'

'No, it's not good at all.'

Blend knew that tone. Still, she wondered. *Are we enough? Is there enough in us to do this? Do we still have what's needed?* They'd lost a healer and a mage this night. They'd lost the best of them. *Because we were careless.*

Antsy joined them as the guards closed in round Barathol and Chaur. 'Pick, Blend,' he said, 'I don't know about you two, but right now, gods below, I'm feeling old.'

A sergeant of the guard approached. 'How bad is it inside?'

No one seemed eager to reply.

Six streets away, a world away, Cutter stood in the front yard of a store selling headstones and crypt façades. An array of stylized deities, none of them temple-sanctioned as yet, beseeching blessings upon the future dead. Beru and Burn, Soliel and Nerruse, Treach and the Fallen One, Hood and Fanderay, Hound and tiger, boar and worm. The shop was closed and he looked upon stones still uncarved, awaiting names of loved ones. Against one of the low yard walls stood a row of marble sarcophagi, and against the wall opposite there were tall urns with their flared mouths, narrow necks and swollen bellies, reminding him of pregnant women . . . birth into death, wombs to hold all that remained of mortal flesh, homes to those who would answer the final question, the last question: *what lies beyond? What awaits us all? What shape the gate before me?* There were plenty of ways of asking it, but they all meant the same thing, and all sought the one answer.

One spoke of death often. The death of a friendship. The death of love. Each echoed with the finality that waited at the very end, but they were faint echoes, ghostly, acting out scenes in puppet shows swallowed in flickering shadows. *Kill a love. What lies beyond? Emptiness, cold, drifting ashes, yet does it not prove fertile? A place where a new seed is planted, finding life, growing into itself? Is this how true death is, as well?*

From the dust, a new seed . . .

A pleasing thought. A comforting thought.

The street behind him was modestly crowded, the last of the late night shoppers reluctant to close out this day. Maybe they had nothing to go home to. Maybe they hungered for one more purchase, in the forlorn hope that it would fill whatever emptiness gnawed deep inside.

None wandered into this yard, none wanted the reminder of what waited for them all. Why, then, had he found himself here? Was he seeking some kind of comfort, some reminder that for each and every person, no matter where, the same conclusion was on its way? One could walk, one could crawl, one could run headlong, but one could never turn round and head the other way, could never escape. That, even with the truism that all grief belonged to the living, the ones left behind – facing empty spaces where someone once stood – there could be found a kind of calm repose. *We walk the same path, some farther along, some further back, but still and for ever more the same path.*

There was, then, the death of love.

And there was, alas, its murder.

'Crokus Younghand.'

He slowly turned round. A woman stood before him, exquisitely dressed, a cloak of ermine about her shoulders. A heart-shaped face, languid eyes, painted lips, and yes, he knew this face. Had known it, a younger version, a child's version, perhaps, but now there was nothing of that child – not in the eyes, not even in the sad smile on those full lips. 'Challice D'Arle.'

Later, he would look back on this moment, on the dark warning contained in the fact that, when he spoke her name of old, she did not correct him.

Would such percipience have changed things? All that was to come?

Death and murder, seeds in the ashes, one does as one does. Sarcophagi gaped. Urns echoed hollow and dark. Stone faces awaited names, grief crouching at the gate.

Such was this night in the city of Darujhistan.

Such is this night, *everywhere.*

Chapter Twelve

Where will I stand
When the walls come down
East to the sun's rise
North to winter's face
South to where stars are born
West to the road of death

Where will I stand
When the winds wage war
Fleeing the dawn
Howling the breath of ice
Blistered with desert's smile
Dusty from crypts

Where will I stand
When the world crashes down
And on all sides
I am left exposed
To weapons illimitable
From the vented host

Will I stand at all
Against such forces unbarred
Reeling to every blow
Blinded by storms of pain
As all is taken from me
So cruelly taken away

Let us not talk of courage
Nor steel fortitude
The gifts of wisdom
Burn too hot to touch
The hunger for peace
Breaks the heart

Where will I stand
In the dust of a done life
Face bared to regrets

That flail the known visage
Until none but strangers
Watch my fall

NONE BUT STRANGERS
FISHER KEL TATH

The stately trees with their black trunks and midnight leaves formed a rough ring encircling Suruth Common. From the centre of the vast clearing, one could, upon facing north, see the towers of the Citadel, their slim lines echoing these sacred trees. Autumn had arrived, and the air was filled with the drifting filaments from the blackwood.

The great forges to the west lit crimson the foul clouds hanging over them, so that it seemed that one side of Kharkanas was ablaze. An eternal rain of ash plagued the massive, sprawling factories, nothing as sweet as the curled filaments to mark the coming of the cold season.

Within the refuge of Suruth Common, the blasted realm of the factories seemed worlds away. Thick beds of moss cloaked the pavestones of the clearing, muting Endest Silann's boots as he walked to the concave altar stone at the very heart. He could see no one else about – this was not the season for festivity. This was not a time for celebration of any sort. He wondered if the trees sensed him, if they were capable of focusing some kind of attention upon him, made aware by the eddies of air, the exudation of heat and breath.

He had read once a scholar's treatise describing the chemical relationship between plants and animals. The language had been clinical in the fashion of such academic efforts, and yet Endest recalled closing the book and sitting back in his chair. The notion that he could walk up to a plant, a tree, even a blackwood, and bless it with his own breath – a gift of lung-soured air that could enliven that tree, that could in truth deliver health and vigour, deliver life itself . . . ah, but that was a wonder indeed, one that, for a time, calmed the churning maelstrom that was a young man's soul.

So long ago, now, and he felt, at times, that he was done with giving gifts.

He stood alone in front of the ancient altar. The past night's modest rain had formed a shallow pool in the cup of the basalt. It was said the Andii came from the forests and their natural clearings. Born to give breath to the sacred wood, and that the first fall of his people occurred the moment they walked out, to set down the first shaped stone of this city.

How many failings had there been since? Suruth Common was the last fragment of the old forest left in all Kharkanas. Blackwood itself had fed the great forges.

He had no desire to look westward. More than the fiery glow disturbed him. The frenzy in those factories – they were making weapons. Armour. They were readying for war.

He had been sent here by the High Priestess. *'Witness,'* she had said. And so he would. The eyes of the Temple, the priesthood, must remain open, aware, missing nothing in these fraught times. That she had chosen him over others – or even herself – was not a measure of respect. His presence was political, his modest rank a deliberate expression of the Temple's contempt.

'Witness, Endest Silann. But remain silent. You are a presence, *do you understand?'*

He did.

They appeared almost simultaneously, one from the north, one from the east and one from the south. Three brothers. Three sons. This was to be a meeting of blood and yes, they would resent him, for he did not belong. Indeed, the Temple did not belong. Would they send him away?

The trees wept their promise of a new season of life – a season that would never come, for there was nowhere left for the filaments to take root – not for scores of leagues in any direction. The river would take millions, but even those fine black threads could not float on its waters, and so what the river took the river kept, buried in the dead silts of Dorssan Ryl. *Our breath was meant to give life, not take it away. Our breath was a gift, and in that gift the blackwood found betrayal.*

This was and is our crime, and it was and remains unforgivable.

'Good evening, priest,' said Andarist, who then added, 'Anomander, it seems you were right.'

'An easy prediction,' Anomander replied. 'The Temple watches me the way a rove of rhotes watch a dying ginaf.'

Endest blinked. The last wild ginaf vanished a century past and no longer did the silver-backed herds thunder across the south plains; and these days roves of rhotes winged above battlefields and nowhere else – and no, they did not starve. *Are you the last, Lord? Is this what you are saying? Mother bless me, I never know what you are saying. No one does. We share language but not meaning.*

The third brother was silent, his red eyes fixed upon the forges beneath the western sky.

'The clash between Drethdenan and Vanut Degalla draws to an end,' said Andarist. 'It may be time—'

'Should we be speaking of this?' Silchas Ruin cut in, finally turning to face Endest Silann. 'None of this is for the Temple. Especially not some pathetic third level acolyte.'

Anomander seemed uninterested in settling his attention upon Endest Silann. In the face of his brother's belligerence, he shrugged. 'This way, Silchas, perhaps we can insure the Temple remains . . . neutral.'

'By unveiling to it all that we intend? Why should the Temple hold to any particular faith in us? What makes the three of us more worthy of trust than, say, Manalle, or Hish Tulla?'

'There is an obvious answer to that,' said Andarist. 'Priest?'

He could refuse a reply. He could feign ignorance. He was naught but a third level acolyte, after all. Instead, he said, 'You three are not standing here trying to kill each other.'

Andarist smiled at Silchas Ruin.

Who scowled and looked away once again.

'We have things to discuss,' said Anomander. 'Andarist?'

'I have already sent representatives to both camps. An offer to mitigate. Veiled hints of potential alliances against the rest of you. The key will be in getting Drethdenan and Vanut into the same room, weapons sheathed.'

'Silchas?'

'Both Hish and Manalle have agreed to our pact. Manalle still worries me, brothers. She is no fool—'

'And Hish is?' laughed Andarist – a maddeningly easy laugh, given the treachery they were discussing.

'Hish Tulla is not subtle. Her desires are plain. It is as they all say: she does not lie. No, Manalle is suspicious. After all, I am speaking of the greatest crime of all, the spilling of kin's blood.' He paused, then faced Anomander, and suddenly his expression was transformed. Unease, something bewildered and lit with horror. 'Anomander,' he whispered, 'what are we doing?'

Anomander's features hardened. 'We are strong enough to survive this. You will see.' Then he looked at Andarist. 'The one who will break our hearts stands before us. Andarist, who chooses to turn away.'

'A choice, was it?' At the heavy silence that followed, he laughed again. 'Yes, it was. One of us . . . it must be, at least one of us, and I have no desire to walk your path. I have not the courage for such a thing. The courage, and the . . . cruel madness. No, brothers, mine is the easiest task – I am to do *nothing*.'

'Until I betray you,' said Silchas, and Endest was shocked to see the white-skinned Lord's wet eyes.

'There is no other way through,' said Andarist.

Centuries into millennia, Endest Silann would wonder – and never truly know – if all that followed was as these three had planned. Courage, Andarist had called it. And . . . cruel madness – by the Mother, yes – such destruction, the sheer audacity of the treachery – could they have *meant* all of that?

The next time Anomander had met Endest Silann had been on the bridge at the foot of the Citadel, and in his words he made it clear that he had not recognized him as the same man as the one sent to witness his meeting with his brothers. A strange carelessness for one such as Anomander. Although, unquestionably, the Lord had other things on his mind at that moment.

Endest Silann had delivered to the High Priestess his account of that fell meeting. And in relating the details of the betrayal, such as could be culled from what he had heard – all the implications – he had expected to see outrage in her face. Instead – and, he would think later with prescient symbolism – she had but turned away.

There had been no storms in the sky then. Nothing to hint of what would come. The blackwood trees of Suruth Common had lived for two millennia, maybe longer, and each season they shed their elongated seeds to the wind. Yet, when next he looked upon those stately trees, they would be on fire.

'You have grown far too quiet, old friend.'

Endest Silann looked up from the dying flames. Dawn was fast approaching. 'I was reminded . . . the way that wood crumbles into dissolution.'

'The release of energy. Perhaps a better way of seeing it.'

'Such release is ever fatal.'

'Among plants, yes,' said Caladan Brood.

Among plants . . . 'I think of the breath we give them – our gift.'

'And the breath they give back,' said the warlord, 'that burns if touched. I am fortunate, I think,' he continued, 'that I have no appreciation for irony.'

'It is a false gift, for with it we claim ownership. Like crooked merchants, every one of us. We give so that we can then justify taking it back. I have come to believe that this exchange is the central tenet of our relationship . . . with everything in the world. Any world. Human, Andii, Edur, Liosan. Imass, Barghast, Jaghut—'

'Not Jaghut,' cut in Caladan Brood.

'Ah,' said Endest Silann. 'I know little of them, in truth. What then was their bargain?'

'Between them and the world? I don't even know if an explanation is possible, or at least within the limits of my sorry wit. Until the forging of the ice – defending against the Imass – the Jaghut gave far more than they took. Excepting the Tyrants, of course, which is what made such tyranny all the more reprehensible in the eyes of other Jaghut.'

'So, they were stewards.'

'No. The notion of stewardship implies superiority. A certain arrogance.'

'An earned one, surely, since the power to destroy exists.'

'Well, the illusion of power, I would say, Endest. After all, if you destroy the things around you, eventually you destroy yourself. It is arrogance that asserts a kind of separation, and from that the notion that we can shape and reshape the world to suit our purposes, and that we can *use* it, as if it was no more than a living tool composed of a million parts.' He paused and shook his head. 'See? Already my skull aches.'

'Only with the truth, I think,' said Endest Silann. 'So, the Jaghut did not think of themselves as stewards. Nor as parasites. They were without arrogance? I find that an extraordinary thing, Warlord. Beyond comprehension, in fact.'

'They shared this world with the Forkrul Assail, who were their opposites. They were witnesses to the purest manifestation of arrogance and separation.'

'Was there war?'

Caladan Brood was silent for so long that Endest began to believe that no answer was forthcoming, and then he glanced up with his bestial eyes glittering in the ebbing flames of the hearth. ' "Was"?'

Endest Silann stared across at his old friend, and the breath slowly hissed from him. 'Gods below, Caladan. No war can last that long.'

'It can, when the face of the army is without relevance.'

The revelation was . . . monstrous. Insane. 'Where?'

The warlord's smile was without humour. 'Far away from here, friend, which is well. Imagine what your Lord might elect to do, if it was otherwise.'

He would intervene. He would not be able to stop himself.

Caladan Brood rose then. 'We have company.'

A moment later the heavy thud of wings sounded in the fading darkness above them, and Endest Silann looked up to see Crone, wings crooked now, riding shifting currents of air as she descended, landing with a scatter of stones just beyond the edge of firelight.

'I smell fish!'

'Wasn't aware your kind could smell at all,' Caladan Brood said.

'Funny oaf, although it must be acknowledged that our eyes are the true gift of perfection – among many, of course. Why, Great Ravens are plagued with excellence – and do I see picked bones? I do, with despondent certainty – you rude creatures have left me nothing!'

She hopped closer, regarding the two men with first one eye and then the other. 'Grim conversation? Glad I interrupted. Endest Silann, your Lord summons you. Caladan Brood, not you. There, messages delivered! Now I want food!'

Harak fled through Night. Old tumbled streets, the wreckage of the siege picked clean save for shattered blocks of quarried stone; into narrow, tortured alleys where the garbage was heaped knee-high; across collapsed buildings, scrambling like a spider. He knew Thove was dead. He knew Bucch was dead, and a half-dozen other conspirators. All dead. Killers had pounced. Tiste Andii, he suspected, some kind of secret police, penetrating the cells and now slaughtering every liberator they could hunt down.

He'd always known that the unhuman demon-spawn were far from the innocent, benign occupiers they played at, oh, yes, they were rife with deadly secrets. Plans of slavery and oppression, of tyranny, not just over Black Coral, but beyond, out to the nearby cities – wherever humans could be found, the Tiste Andii cast covetous eyes. And now he had proof.

Someone was after him, tracking with all the deliberate malice of a hunting cat – he'd yet to spy that murderer, but in a world such as Night that was not surprising. The Tiste Andii were skilled in their realm of Darkness, deadly as serpents.

He needed to reach the barrow. He needed to get to Gradithan. Once there, Harak knew he would be safe. They had to be warned, and new plans would have to be made. Harak knew that he might well be the last one left in Black Coral.

He stayed in the most ruined areas of the city, seeking to circle round or, failing that, get out through the inland gate that led into the forested hills – where the cursed Bridgeburners had made a stand, killing thousands with foul sorcery and Moranth munitions – why, the entire slope was still nothing more than shattered, charred trees, fragments of mangled armour, the occasional leather boot and, here and there in the dead soil, jutting bones. Could he reach that, he could find a path leading into Daylight and then, finally, he would be safe.

This latter option became ever more inviting – he was not too far from the gate, and these infernal shadows and the endless gloom here was of no help to him – the Tiste Andii could see in this darkness, after all, whilst he stumbled about half blind.

He heard a rock shift in the rubble behind him, not thirty paces away. Heart pounding, Harak set his eyes upon the gate. Smashed down in the siege, but a path of sorts had been cleared through it, leading out to the raised road that encircled the inland side of the city. Squinting, he could make out no figures lingering near that gate.

Twenty paces away now. He picked up his pace and, once on to the cleared avenue, sprinted for the opening in the wall.

Were those footfalls behind him? He dared not turn.

Run! Damn my legs – run!

On to the path, threading between heaps of broken masonry, and outside the city!

Onward, up the slope to the raised road, a quick, frantic scamper across it, and down into the tumbled rocks at the base of the ruined slope. Battered earth, makeshift grave mounds, tangled roots and dead branches. Whimpering, he clambered on, torn and scratched, coughing in the dust of dead pine bark.

And there, near the summit, was that sunlight? Yes. It was near dawn, after all. Sun – blessed light!

A quick glance back revealed nothing – he couldn't make out what might be whispering through the wreckage below.

He was going to make it.

Harak scrambled the last few strides, plunged into cool morning air, shafts of golden rays – and a figure rose into his path. A tulwar lashed out. Harak's face bore an expression of astonishment, frozen there as his head rolled from his shoulders, bounced and pitched back down the slope, where it lodged near a heap of bleached, fractured bones. The body sank down on to its knees, at the very edge of the old trench excavated by the Bridgeburners, and there it stayed.

Seerdomin wiped clean his blade and sheathed the weapon. Was this the last of them? He believed that it was. The city . . . cleansed. Leaving only those out at the barrow. Those ones would persist for a time, in ignorance that everything in Black Coral had changed.

He was weary – the hunt had taken longer than he had expected. Yes, he would rest now. Seerdomin looked about, studied the rumpled trenchwork the sappers had managed with little more than folding shovels. And he was impressed. A different kind of soldier, these Malazans.

But even this the forest was slowly reclaiming.

He sat down a few paces from the kneeling corpse and settled his head into his gloved hands. He could smell leather, and sweat, and old blood. The smells of his past, and now they had returned. In his mind he could hear echoes, the rustle of armour and scabbards brushing thighs. Urdomen marching in ranks, the visors on their great helms dropped down to hide their fevered eyes. Squares of Betaklites forming up outside the city, preparing to strike northward. Scalandi skirmishers and Tenescowri – the starving multitudes, desperate as bared teeth. He recalled their mass, shifting in vast heaves, ripples and rushes on the plain, the way each wave left bodies behind – the weakest ones, the dying ones – and how eddies would form round them, as those closest swung back to then descend on their hapless comrades.

When there was no one else, the army ate itself. And he had simply looked on, expressionless, wrapped in his armour, smelling iron, leather, sweat and blood.

Soldiers who had fought in a just war – a war they could see as just, anyway – could hold on to a sense of pride, every sacrifice a worthy one. And so fortified, they could leave it behind, finding a new life, a different life. And no matter how grotesque the injustices of the world around them, the world of the present, that veteran could hold on to the sanctity of what he or she had lived through.

But fighting an unjust war . . . that was different. If one had any conscience at all, there was no escaping the crimes committed, the blood on the hands, the sheer insanity of that time – when honour was a lie, duty a weapon that silenced, and courage itself was stained and foul. Suddenly, then, there was no defence against injustice, no sanctuary to be found in memories of a righteous time. And so anger seethed upward, filling every crack, building into rage. There was no way to give it a voice, no means of releasing it, and so the pressure built. When it finally overwhelmed, then suicide seemed the easiest option, the only true escape.

Seerdomin could see the logic of that, but logic was not enough. Anyone could reason themselves into a corner, and so justify surrender. It was even easier when courage itself was vulnerable to abuse and sordid mockery. Because, after all, to persist, to live on, demanded courage, and that was only possible when the virtue remained worthy of respect.

Seerdomin lifted his head and glared over at the decapitated corpse. 'Can you understand any of that, Harak? Can you grasp, now, finally, how the very existence of people like you gives me reason to stay alive? Because you give my rage a face, and my sword, well, it's hungry for faces.' It was either that, or the fury within him would devour his own soul. No, better to keep the face he slashed open someone else's, rather than his own. Keep finding them, one after another. Justice was so weak. The corrupt won, the pure of heart failed and fell to the wayside. Graft and greed crowed triumphant over responsibility and compassion. He could fight that, and that fight need not even be in his own name. He could fight for Black Coral, for the Tiste Andii, for humanity itself.

Even for the Redeemer – *no, that cannot be. What I do here can never be healed – there can be no redemption for me. Ever. You must see that. All of you must see that.*

He realized he was pleading – but to whom? He did not know. *We were put in an impossible situation, and, at least for us, the tyrant responsible is dead – has been punished. It could have been worse – he could have escaped retribution, escaped justice.*

There was trauma in war. Some people survived it; others were for ever trapped in it. For many of those, this circumstance was not a failing on their part. Not some form of sickness, or insanity. It was, in truth, the consequence of a profoundly moral person's inability to reconcile the conflicts in his or her soul. No healer could heal that, because there was nothing to heal. No elixir swept the malady away. No salve erased the scars. The only reconciliation possible was to make those responsible accountable, to see them face justice. And more often than not, history showed that such an accounting rarely ever took place. And so the veteran's wounds never mend, the scars never fade, the rage never subsides.

So Seerdomin had come to believe, and he well knew that what he was doing here, with weapon in hand, solved nothing of the conflict within him. For he was as flawed as anyone, and no matter how incandescent his rage, his righteous fury, he could not deliver pure, unsullied justice – for such a thing was collective, integral to a people's identity. Such a thing must be an act of society, of civilization. *Not Tiste Andii society – they clearly will not accept that burden, will not accede to meting out justice on behalf of us humans, nor should they be expected to. And so . . . here I am, and I hear the Redeemer weep.*

One cannot murder in the name of justice.

Irreconcilable. What he had been, what he was now. The things he did then, and all he was doing here, at this moment.

The would-be usurper knelt beside him, headless in sour symbolism. But it was a complicated, messy symbol. And he could find for himself but one truth in all of this.

Heads roll downhill.

It may be that in the belief of the possibility of redemption, people willingly do wrong. Redemption waits, like a side door, there in whatever court of judgement we eventually find ourselves. Not even the payment of a fine is demanded, simply the empty negotiation that absolves responsibility. A shaking of hands and off one goes, through that side door, with the judge benignly watching on. Culpability and consequences neatly evaded.

Oh, Salind was in a crisis indeed. Arguments reduced until the very notion of redemption was open to challenge. The Redeemer embraced, taking all within himself. Unquestioning, delivering absolution as if it was without value, worthless, whilst the reward to those embraced was a gift greater than a tyrant's hoard.

Where was justice in all of this? Where was the punishment for crimes committed, retribution for wrongs enacted? *There is, in this, no moral compass. No need for one, for every path leads to the same place, where blessing is passed out, no questions asked.*

The cult of the Redeemer . . . it is an abomination.

She had begun to understand how priesthoods were born, the necessity of sanctioned forms, rules and prohibitions, the mortal filter defined by accepted notions of justice. And yet, she could also see how profoundly dangerous such an institution could become, as arbiters of morality, as dispensers of that justice. Faces like hooded vultures, guarding the door to the court, choosing who gets inside and who doesn't. How soon before the first bag of silver changes hands? How soon before the first reprehensible criminal buys passage into the arms of the blind, unquestioning Redeemer?

She could fashion such a church, could formalize the cult into a religion, and she could impose a harsh, unwavering sense of justice. But what of the next generation of priests and priestesses? And the one after that, and the next one? How long before the hard rules make that church a self-righteous, power-mongering tyranny? How long before corruption arrives, when the hidden heart of the religion is the simple fact that the Redeemer embraces *everyone who comes before him*? A fact virtually guaranteed to breed cynicism in the priesthood, and from such cynicism secular acquisitiveness would be inevitable.

This loss was not just a loss of faith in the Redeemer. It was a loss of faith in religion itself.

Her prayers touched a presence, were warmed by the nearby breath of an immortal. And she pleaded with that force. She railed. Made demands. Insisted on explanations, answers.

And he took all her anger into his embrace, as he did everything else. And that was *wrong*.

There were two meanings to the word 'benighted'. The first was pejorative, a form of dour ignorance. The second was an honour conferred in service to a king or queen. It was this latter meaning that had been applied to Seerdomin, a title of respect.

There was a third definition, one specific to Black Coral and to Seerdomin himself. He dwelt in Night, after all, where Darkness was not ignorance, but profound wisdom, ancient knowledge, symbolic of the very beginning of existence, the first womb from which all else was born. He dwelt in Night, then, and for a time had made daily pilgrimages out to the barrow with its forbidden riches, a one-man procession of rebirth that Salind only now comprehended.

Seerdomin was, in truth, the least ignorant of them all. Had he known Itkovian in his life? She thought not. Indeed, it would have been impossible. And so whatever had drawn Seerdomin to the cult arrived later, after Itkovian's death, after his ascension. Thus, a personal crisis, a need that he sought to appease with daily prayers.

But . . . why bother? The Redeemer turned no one away. Blessing and forgiveness was a certainty. The bargaining was a sham. Seerdomin need only have made that procession once, and been done with it.

Had no one confronted him, he would still be making his daily pilgrimage, like an animal pounding its head against the bars of a cage – and, disregarded to one side, the door hanging wide open.

Was that significant? Seerdomin did not want the Redeemer's embrace. No, the redemption he sought was of a different nature.

Need drove her from the bed in the temple, out into Night. She felt weak, light-headed, and every step seemed to drain appalling amounts of energy into the hard cobbles underfoot. Wrapped in a blanket, unmindful of those she passed, she walked through the city.

There was meaning in the barrow itself, in the treasure that none could touch. There was meaning in Seerdomin's refusal of the easy path. In his prayers that asked either something the Redeemer could not grant, or nothing at all. There was, perhaps, a secret in the Redeemer's very embrace, something hidden, possibly even deceitful. He took in crimes and flaws and held it all in abeyance . . . until when? The redeemed's death? What then? Did some hidden accounting await each soul?

How much desperation hid within each and every prayer uttered? The hope for blessing, for peace, for the sense that something greater than oneself might acknowledge that hapless self, and might indeed alter all of reality to suit the self's desires. Were prayers nothing more than attempted bargains? A pathetic assertion of some kind of reciprocity?

Well, she would not bargain. No, she had questions, and she wanted answers. She *demanded* answers. If the faith that was given to a god came from nothing more than selfish desires, then it was no less sordid than base greed. If to hand over one's soul to a god was in fact a surrendering of will, then that soul was worthless, a willing slave for whom freedom – and all the responsibility that entailed – was anathema.

She found herself reeling through the gate, on to the road that Seerdomin once walked day after day. It had begun raining, the drops light, cool on her fevered forehead, sweet as tears in her eyes. Not much grew to either side of the road, not even the strange Andiian plants that could be found in the walled and rooftop gardens. The dying moon had showered this place in salt water, a downpour the remnants of which remained as white crust like a cracked skin on the barren earth.

She could smell the sea rising around her as she staggered on.

And then, suddenly, she stumbled into daylight, the sun's shafts slanting in from the east whilst a single grey cloud hung directly overhead, the rain a glittering tracery of angled streaks.

Bare feet slipping on the road's cobbles, Salind continued on. She could see the barrow ahead, glistening and freshly washed, with the mud thick and churned up round its base. There were no pilgrims to be seen – perhaps it was too early. *Perhaps they have all left.* But no, she could see smoke rising from cookfires in the encampment. *Have they lost their way, then? Is that surprising? Have I not suffered my own crisis of faith?*

She drew closer, gaze fixed now on the barrow.

Redeemer! You will hear me. You must hear me!

She fell on to her knees in the mud and its chill rippled up through her. The rain was past and steam now rose on all sides. Water ran in trickles everywhere on the barrow, a hundred thousand tears threading through all the offerings.

Redeemer—

A fist closed in the short hair at the back of her neck. She was savagely pulled upright, head yanked round. She stared up into Gradithan's grinning face.

'You should never have come back,' the man said. His breath stank of kelyk, and she saw the brown stains on his lips and mouth. His eyes looked strangely slick, like stones washed by waves. 'I am tempted, Priestess, to give you to my Urdomen – not that they'd have you.'

Urdomen. He was an Urdo, a commander of the fanatic élites. Now I begin to underst—

'But Monkrat might.'

She frowned. What had he been saying? 'Leave me,' she said, and was shocked at how thin and weak her voice sounded. 'I want to pray.'

He twisted his grip, forcing her round to face him, close enough to be lovers. 'Monkrat!'

Someone came up beside them.

'Get some saemankelyk. I'd like to see how well she dances.'

She could feel his hard knuckles pressing the back of her neck, twisting and ripping hair from its roots, pushing into the bruises he'd already made.

'I can give you nothing,' she said.

'Oh, but you will,' he replied. 'You'll give us a path,' and he turned her back to face the barrow, 'straight to him.'

She did not understand, and yet fear gripped her, and as she heard someone hurrying up, bottle swishing, her fear burgeoned into terror.

Gradithan tugged her head further back. 'You are going to drink, woman. Waste a drop and you'll pay.'

Monkrat came close, lifting the bottle with its stained mouth to her lips.

She sought to twist her face away but the Urdo's grip denied that. He reached up with his other hand and closed her nostrils.

'Drink, and then you can breathe again.'

Salind drank.

Finding her gone from her room, Spinnock Durav stood for a long moment, staring down at the rumpled mattress of the cot, noting the missing blanket, seeing that she'd left most of her clothes behind, including her moccasins. He told himself he should not be surprised. She had not much welcomed his attentions.

Still, he felt as if some cold, grinning bastard had carved a gaping hole in his chest. It was absurd, that he should have been careless enough, complacent enough, to find himself this vulnerable. A human woman of so few years – he was worse than some old man sitting on the temple steps and drooling at every young thing sauntering past. Love could be such a squalid emotion: burning bright in the midst of pathos, the subject of pity and contempt, it blazed with brilliant stupidity all the same.

Furious with himself, he wheeled about and strode from the room.

In a city of unending Night, no bell was too early for a drink. He left the temple and the keep, made his way down ghostly streets to the Scour.

Inside, Resto was behind the bar, red-eyed and scratching at his beard and saying nothing as Spinnock walked to the table at the back. Tavern-keepers knew well the myriad faces of misery, and unbidden he drew a tall tankard of ale, bringing it over with gaze averted.

Glaring at the other tables – all empty; he was the only customer – Spinnock collected the tankard and swallowed down half its foamy contents.

Moments after Resto delivered the third such tankard the door opened and in walked Seerdomin.

Spinnock felt a sudden apprehension. Even from there the man smelled of blood, and his face was a ravaged thing, aged and pallid, the eyes so haunted that the Tiste Andii had to look away.

As if unaware of his reaction, Seerdomin came to Spinnock's table and sat down opposite him. Resto arrived with a jug and a second tankard.

'She doesn't want my help,' Spinnock said.

Seerdomin said nothing as he poured ale into his tankard, setting the jug back down with a thump. 'What are you talking about?'

Spinnock looked away. 'I couldn't find you. I searched everywhere.'

'That desperate for a game?'

A game? Oh. Kef Tanar. 'You are looking at a pathetic old man, Seerdomin. I feel I must sacrifice the last of my dignity, here and now, and tell you everything.'

'I don't know if I'm ready for that,' the man replied. 'Your dignity is important to me.'

Spinnock flinched, and still would not meet Seerdomin's eyes. 'I have surrendered my heart.'

'Well. You can't marry her, though, can you?'

'Who?'

'The High Priestess – although it's about time you realized that she loves you in return, probably always has. You damned Andii – you live so long it's as if you're incapable of grasping on to things in the here and now. If I had your endless years . . . no, scratch out the eyes of that thought. I don't want them. I've lived too long as it is.'

Spinnock's mind was spinning. The High Priestess? 'No, she doesn't. Love me, I mean. I didn't mean her, anyway.'

'Gods below, Spinnock Durav, you're a damned fool.'

'I know that. I've as much as confessed it, for Hood's sake.'

'So you're not interested in making the High Priestess happier than she's been in a thousand years. Fine. That's your business. Some other woman, then. Careful, someone might up and murder her. Jealousy is deadly.'

This was too offhand for Seerdomin, too loose, too careless. It had the sound of a man who had surrendered to despair, no longer caring – about anything. Loosing every arrow in his quiver, eager to see it suddenly, fatally empty. This Seerdomin frightened Spinnock. 'What have you been up to?' he asked.

'I have been murdering people.' He poured another round, then settled back in his chair. 'Eleven so far. They saw themselves as liberators. Scheming the downfall of their Tiste Andii oppressors. I answered their prayers and liberated every one of them. This is my penance, Spinnock Durav. My singular apology for the madness of humanity. Forgive them, please, because I cannot.'

Spinnock found a tightness in his throat that started tears in his eyes. He could not so much as look at this man, dared not, lest he see all that should never be revealed, never be exposed. Not in his closest friend. Not in anyone. 'That,' he said, hating his own words, 'was not necessary.'

'Strictly speaking, you are right, friend. They would have failed – I lack no faith in your efficacy, especially that of your Lord. Understand, I did this out of a desire to prove that, on occasion, we are capable of policing our own. Checks and balances. This way the blood stains my hands, not yours. Giving no one else cause for hating you.'

'Those who hate need little cause, Seerdomin.'

The man nodded – Spinnock caught the motion peripherally.

There was a silence. The tale had been told, Spinnock recalled, more than once. How the Bridgeburner named Whiskeyjack – a man Anomander Rake called friend – had intervened in the slaughter of the Pannion witches, the mad mothers of Children of the Dead Seed. Whiskeyjack, a human, had sought to grant the Son of Darkness a gift, taking away the burden of the act. A gesture that had shaken his Lord to the core. *It is not in our nature to permit others to share our burden.*

Yet we will, unhesitatingly, take on theirs.

'I wonder if we blazed his trail.'

'What?'

Spinnock rubbed at his face, feeling slightly drunk. 'Itkovian's.'

'Of course you didn't. The Grey Swords—'

'Possessed a Shield Anvil, yes, but they were not unique in that. It's an ancient title. Are we the dark mirror to such people?' Then he shook his head. 'Probably not. That would be a grand conceit.'

'I agree,' Seerdomin said in a slurred growl.

'I love her.'

'So you claimed. And presumably she will not have you.'

'Very true.'

'So here you sit, getting drunk.'

'Yes.'

'Once I myself am drunk enough, Spinnock Durav, I will do what's needed.'

'What's needed?'

'Why, I will go and tell her she's a damned fool.'

'You'd fail.'

'I would?'

Spinnock nodded. 'She's faced you down before. Unflinchingly.'

Another stretch of silence. That stretched on, and on.

He was drunk enough now to finally shift his gaze, to fix his attention on Seerdomin's face.

It was a death mask, white as dust. 'Where is she?' the man asked in a raw, strained voice.

'On her way back out to the barrow, I should think. Seerdomin, I am sorry. I did not lie when I said I was a fool—'

'You were,' and he rose, weaving slightly before steadying himself with both hands on the back of his chair. 'But not in the way you think.'

'She didn't want my help,' Spinnock Durav said.

'And I would not give her mine.'

'Your choice—'

'You should not have listened, my friend. To her. *You should not have listened to her!'*

Spinnock stood as Seerdomin spun round and marched for the door. He was suddenly without words, numbed, stunned into confusion. *What have I done?*

What have I not done?

But his friend was gone.

In her irritation, Samar Dev discovered traits in herself that did not please. There was no reason to resent the manner in which her two companions found so much pleasure in each other's company. The way they spoke freely, unconstrained by decorum, unaffected even by the fact that they barely knew one another, and the way the subjects flowed in any and every direction, flung on whims of mood, swirling round heady topics like eddies round jagged rocks. Most infuriating of all, they struck on moments of laughter, and she well knew – *damn the gods, she was* certain – that neither man possessed such ease of humour, that they were so far removed from that characterization that she could only look on in stunned disbelief.

They spoke of their respective tribes, traded tales of sexual conquests. They spoke of weapons and neither hesitated in handing over his sword for the other to examine and, indeed, try a few experimental swings and passes with. Traveller told of a friend of old named Ereko, a Tartheno of such pure, ancient blood that he would have towered over Karsa Orlong had the two been standing side by side. And in that story Samar Dev sensed deep sorrow, wounds of such severity that it was soon apparent that Traveller himself could not venture too close, and so his tale of Ereko reached no conclusion. And Karsa Orlong did not press, revealing his clear understanding that a soul could bleed from unseen places and often all that kept a mortal going depended on avoiding such places.

He reciprocated in his speaking of the two companions who had accompanied him on an ill-fated raid into the settled lands of humans, Bairoth Gild and Delum Thord. Whose souls, Karsa blithely explained, now dwelt within the stone of his sword.

Traveller simply grunted at that detail, and then said, 'That is a worthy place.'

By the second day of this, Samar Dev was ready to scream. Tear her hair from her head, spit blood and curses and teeth and maybe her entire stomach by the time she was done. And so she held her silence, and held on to her fury, like a rabid beast chained to the ground. It was absurd. Pathetic and ridiculous, this crass envy she was feeling. Besides, had she not learned more about both men since their fateful meeting than she had ever known before? Like a tickbird flitting between two bull bhederin, her attention was drawn to first one, then the other. While the peace lasted it would do to say nothing, to make no commotion no matter how infuriated she happened to be.

They rode on, across the vast plain, along a worn caravan track angling into the Cinnamon Wastes. Those few merchant trains they met or overtook were singularly taciturn, the guards edgy, the traders unwelcoming. Just before dusk last night, four horsemen had passed close by their camp, and, after a long look, had ridden on without a word ventured.

Karsa had sneered and said, 'See that, Samar Dev? As my grandfather used to say, "The wolf does not smell the bear's anus."'

'Your grandfather,' Traveller had replied, 'was an observant man.'

'Mostly he was a fool, but even fools could spout tribal wisdom.' And he turned to Samar Dev again. 'You are safe, Witch.'

'From other people, yes,' she had growled in reply.

And the bastard had laughed.

The Cinnamon Wastes were well named. One species of deep-rooted grass quickly predominated, rust-red and hip-high, with serrated edges and thorny seed-pods on thin wavering stalks. Small red-banded lizards swarmed these grasses, tails whipping and rustling as they scattered from their path. The land levelled until not a single rise or hill was in sight.

Amidst this monotony, Traveller and Karsa Orlong seemed intent on wearing out their vocal cords.

'Few recall,' Traveller was saying, 'the chaos of the Malazan Empire in those early days. The madness only *began* with Kellanved, the Emperor. His first cadre of lieutenants were all Napan, each one secretly sworn to a young woman named Surly, who was heiress to the crown of the Nap Isles – in hiding ever since the Untan conquest.' He paused. 'Or so goes the tale. Was it true? Was Surly truly the last of the Napan royal line? Who can say, but it came in handy when she changed her name to Laseen and attained the throne of the Empire. In any case, those lieutenants were crocked, every one of them. Urko, Crust, Nok, all of them. Quick to fanaticism, willing to do anything and everything to advance the Empire.'

'The Empire, or Surly?' asked Karsa Orlong. 'Does it not seem just as likely that they were simply using Kellanved?'

'A fair suspicion, except that only Nok remained once Laseen became Empress. The others each . . . drowned.'

'Drowned?'

'Officially. That cause of death quickly became euphemistic. Put it this way. They *disappeared*.'

'There was someone else,' Samar Dev said.

'Dancer—'

'Not him, Traveller. There was the First Sword. There was Dassem Ultor, commander of all the Emperor's armies. He was not Napan. He was Dal Honese.'

Traveller glanced across at her. 'He fell in Seven Cities, shortly before Laseen took power.'

'Surly had him assassinated,' said Samar Dev.

Karsa Orlong grunted. 'Eliminating potential rivals – she needed to clear the path. That, Witch, is neither savage nor civilized. You will see such things in dirt-nosed tribes and in empires both. This truth belongs to power.'

'I would not dispute your words, Toblakai. Do you want to know what happened after you killed Emperor Rhulad?'

'The Tiste Edur quit the Empire.'

'How – how did you know that?'

He bared his teeth. 'I guessed, Witch.'

'Just like that?'

'Yes. They did not want to be there.'

Traveller said, 'I expect the Tiste Edur discovered rather quickly the curse of occupation. It acts like a newly opened wound, infecting and poisoning both the oppressors and the oppressed. Both cultures become malformed, bitter with extremes. Hatred, fear, greed, betrayal, paranoia, and appalling indifference to suffering.'

'Yet the Malazans occupied Seven Cities—'

'No, Samar Dev. The Malazans conquered Seven Cities. That is different. Kellanved understood that much. If one must grip hard in enemy territory, then that grip must be hidden – at the very cusp of local power. And so no more than a handful is being strictly controlled – everyone else, merchants and herders and farmers and tradefolk – everyone – are to be shown better circumstances, as quickly as possible. "Conquer as a rogue wave, rule in quiet ripples." The Emperor's own words.'

'This is what the Claw did, isn't it? Infiltrate and paralyse the rulers—'

'The less blood spilled, the better.'

Karsa Orlong barked a laugh. 'That depends,' he said. 'There are other kinds of conquest.'

'Such as?'

'Traveller, my friend, you speak of conquest as a means of increasing one's power – the more subjects and the more cities under your control is the measure of that power. But what of the power of destruction?'

Samar Dev found she was holding her breath, and she watched Traveller considering Karsa's words, before he said, 'There is nothing then to be gained.'

'You are wrong,' said Karsa, pausing to stretch his back. Havok's head tossed, a chopping motion like an axe blade. 'I have looked upon the face of civilization, and I am not impressed.'

'There is no flaw in being critical.'

'He's not just being critical,' said Samar Dev. 'He intends to destroy it. Civilization, I mean. The whole thing, from sea to sea. When Karsa Orlong is done, not a single city in the world will remain standing, isn't that right, Toblakai?'

'I see no value in modest ambitions, Witch.'

Traveller was quiet then, and the silence was like an expanding void, until even the moan of the incessant wind seemed distant and hollow.

Gods, how often have I wished him well? Even as the thought horrifies me – he would kill millions. He would crush every symbol of progress. From ploughs back to sticks. From bricks to caves. From iron to stone. Crush us all back into the ground, the mud of waterholes. And the beasts will hunt us, and those of us who remain, why, we will hunt each other.

Traveller finally spoke. 'I dislike cities,' he said.

'Barbarians both,' she muttered under her breath.

Neither man responded. Perhaps they hadn't heard. She shot each of them a quick glance, right and then left, and saw that both were smiling.

Riding onward, the day rustling in waves of red grass.

Until Traveller once again began speaking. 'The first law of the multitude is conformity. Civilization is the mechanism of controlling and maintaining that multitude. The more civilized a nation, the more conformed its population, until that civilization's last age arrives, when multiplicity wages war with conformity. The former grows ever wilder, ever more dysfunctional in its extremities; whilst the latter seeks to increase its measure of control, until such efforts acquire diabolical tyranny.'

'More of Kellanved?' Samar Dev asked.

Traveller snorted. 'Hardly. That was Duiker, the Imperial Historian.'

Through the course of the night just past, Nimander Golit had led his meagre troop through the city of Bastion. Children of Darkness, with Aranatha's quiet power embracing them, they had moved in silence, undetected as far as they could tell, for no alarms were raised. The city was a thing seemingly dead, like a closed flower.

At dusk, shortly before they set out, they had heard clattering commotion out on the main avenue, and went to the gates to watch the arrival into the city of scores of enormous wagons. Burdened with trade goods, the carters slack-faced, exhausted, with haunted eyes above brown-stained mouths. Bales of raw foodstuffs, casks of figs and oils, eels packed in salt, smoked bhederin, spiced mutton, and countless other supplies that had been eagerly pressed upon them in exchange for the barrels of kelyk.

There was cruel irony to be found in the sordid disinterest the locals displayed before such essential subsistence – most were past the desire for food. Most were starving in an ecstatic welter of saemankelyk, the black ink of a god's pain.

The Tiste Andii wore their armour. They wore their gear for fighting, for killing. Nimander did not need a glance back to know the transformation and what it did to the expressions on all but one of the faces of those trailing behind him. Skintick, whose smile had vanished, yet his eyes glittered bright, as if fevered. Kedeviss, ever rational, now wore a mask of madness, beauty twisted into something terrible. Nenanda, for all his postures of ferocity, was now ashen, colourless, as if the truth of desire soured him with poison. Desra, flushed with something like excitement. Only Aranatha was unchanged. Placid, glassy-eyed with concentration, her features somehow softer, blurred.

Skintick and Kedeviss carried Clip between them. Nenanda held over one shoulder the man's weapons, his bow and quiver, his sword and knife belt – all borne on a single leather strap that could be loosed in a moment should the need arise.

They had slipped past buildings in which worshippers danced, starved limbs waving about, distended bellies swaying – doors had been left open, shutters swung back to the night. Voices moaned in disjointed chorus. Even those faces that by chance turned towards the Tiste Andii as they moved ghostly past did not awaken with recognition, the eyes remaining dull, empty, unseeing.

The air was warm, smelling of rancid salt from the dying lake mixed with the heavier stench of putrefying corpses.

They reached the edge of the central square, looked out across its empty expanse. The altar itself was dark, seemingly lifeless.

Nimander crouched down, uncertain. There must be watchers. It would be madness to think otherwise. Could they reach the altar before some hidden mob rushed forth to accost them? It did not seem likely. They had not seen Kallor since his march to the altar the previous day. Nenanda believed the old man was dead. He believed they would find his body, cold and pale, lying on the tiled floor somewhere within the building. For some reason, Nimander did not think that likely.

Skintick whispered behind him, 'Well? It's nearing dawn, Nimander.'

What awaited them? There was only one way to find out. 'Let's go.'

All at once, with their first strides out into the concourse, the air seemed to swirl, thick and heavy. Nimander found he had to push against it, a tightness forming in his throat and then his chest.

'They're burning the shit,' Skintick hissed. 'Can you smell it? The kelyk—'

'Quiet.'

Fifteen, twenty paces now. Silence all around. Nimander set his eyes on the entrance to the altar, the steps glistening with dew or something far worse. The black glyphs seemed to throb in his eyes, as if the entire structure was breathing. He could feel something dark and unpleasant in his veins, like bubbles in his blood, or seeds, eager to burst into life. He felt moments from losing control.

Behind him, hard gasping breaths – they were all feeling this, they were all—

'Behind us,' grunted Nenanda.

And to the sides, crowds closing in from every street and alley mouth, slowly, dark shapes pushing into the square. *They look like the scarecrows, cut loose from their stakes – Mother's blessing—*

Forty strides, reaching the centre of the concourse. Every avenue closed to them now, barring that to the building itself.

'We're being herded,' said Kedeviss, her voice tight. 'They want us inside.'

Nimander glanced back, down upon the limp form of Clip, the man's head hanging and hair trailing on the ground. Clip's eyes were half open. 'Is he still alive?'

'Barely,' said Kedeviss.

Hundreds of figures drew yet closer, blackened eyes gleaming, mouths hanging open. Knives, hatchets, pitchforks and hammers dangled down from their hands. The only sound that came from them was the shuffle of their bared feet.

Twenty paces now from the steps. To the right and left, and in their wake, the worshippers in the front lines began lifting their weapons, then those behind them followed suit.

'Skintick,' said Nimander, 'take Clip yourself. Aranatha, his weapons. Desra, ward your sister. Kedeviss, Nenanda, prepare to rearguard – once we're inside, hold them at the entrance.'

Two against a thousand or more. Fanatics, fearless and senseless – *gods, we are unleashed.*

He heard a pair of swords rasp free of scabbards. The sound sliced through the air, and it was as if the cold iron touched his brow, startling him awake.

The crowd was close now, a bestial growl rising.

Nimander reached the first step. 'Now!'

They rushed upward. Skintick was immediately behind Nimander, Clip on his hunched back as he gripped one wrist and one thigh. Then Aranatha, flowing up the steps like an apparition, Desra in her wake. Nenanda and Kedeviss, facing the opposite way with swords held ready, backed up more slowly.

The front ranks of worshippers moaned and then surged forward.

Iron rang, clashed, thudded into flesh and bone. Nimander plunged through the entranceway. There was no light – every torch in its sconce had been capped – yet his eyes could penetrate the gloom, in time to see a score of priests rushing for him.

Shouting a warning, Nimander unsheathed his sword—

The fools were human. In this darkness they were half blind. He slashed out, saw a head roll off shoulders, the body crumpling. A back swing intercepted an arm thrusting a dagger at his chest. The sword's edge sliced through wrist bones and the severed hand, still gripping the weapon, thumped against his chest before falling away. Angling the sword point back across his torso, Nimander stabbed the one-handed priest in the throat.

In his peripheral vision he caught Clip's form rolling on to the floor as Skintick freed his arms to defend himself.

The sickly sound of edge biting meat echoed in the chamber, followed by the spatter of blood across tiles.

Nimander stop-thrust another charging priest, the point pushing hard between ribs and piercing the man's heart. As he fell he sought to trap the sword but Nimander twisted round and with a savage tug tore his weapon free.

A knife scraped the links of his chain hauberk beneath his left arm and he pulled away and down, cross-stabbing and feeling the sword punch into soft flesh. Stomach acids spurted up the blade and stung his knuckles. The priest folded round the wound. Nimander kicked hard into his leg, shin-high, breaking bones. As the man sagged away, he pushed forward to close against yet another one.

Sword against dagger was no contest. As the poor creature toppled, sobbing from a mortal wound, Nimander whipped his sword free and spun to meet the next attacker.

There were none left standing.

Skintick stood nearby, slamming his still bloodied sword back into the scabbard at his belt, then crouching to retrieve Clip. Desra, weapon dripping, hovered close to Aranatha who, unscathed, walked past, gaze fixed on the set of ornate doors marking some grand inner entranceway. After a moment Desra followed.

From the outer doors the frenzied sounds of fighting continued, human shrieks echoing, bouncing in crazed cacophony. Nimander looked back to see that Kedeviss and Nenanda still held the portal, blood and bile spreading beneath their boots to trace along the indents and impressions of the tiles. Nimander stared at that detail, transfixed, until a nudge from Skintick shook him free.

'Come on,' Nimander said in a rasp, setting out into Aranatha's wake.

Desra felt her entire body surging with life. Not even sex could match this feeling. A score of insane priests rushing upon them, and the three of them simply cut them all down. With barely a catch of breath – she had seen Nimander slaughter the last few, with such casual grace that she could only look on in wonder. Oh, he believed himself a poor swordsman, and perhaps when compared to Nenanda, or Kedeviss, he was indeed not their equal. Even so – *Bastion, your children should never have challenged us. Should never have pushed us to this.*

Now see what you've done.

She hurried after her brainless sister.

Skintick wanted to weep, but he knew enough to save that for later, for that final stumble through, into some future place when all this was over and done with, when they could each return to a normal life, an almost peaceful life.

He had never been one for prayers, especially not to Mother Dark, whose heart was cruel, whose denial was an ever-bleeding wound in the Tiste Andii. Yet he prayed none the less. Not to a god or goddess, not to some unknown force at ease with the gift of mercy. No, Skintick prayed for *peace*.

A world of calm.

He did not know if such a world existed, anywhere. He did not know if one such as he deserved that world. Paradise belonged to the innocent.

Which was why it was and would ever remain . . . empty.

And that *is what makes it a paradise.*

At the outer doors, the slaughter continued. Kedeviss saw Nenanda smiling, and had she the time, she would have slapped him. Hard. Hard enough to shake the glee from his eyes. There was nothing glorious in this. The fools came on and on, crushing each other in their need, and she and Nenanda killed them one by one by one.

Oh, fighting against absurd odds was something they were used to; something they did damnably well. That was no source of pride. Desperate defence demanded expedience and little else. And the Tiste Andii were, above all else, an expedient people.

And so blood spilled down, bodies crumpled at their feet, only to be dragged clear by the next ones to die.

She killed her twentieth worshipper, and he was no different from the nineteenth, no different from the very first one, back there on the steps.

Blood like rain. Blood like tears. It was all so pointless.

Nenanda began laughing.

Moments later, the worshippers changed their tactics. With frenzied screams they pushed forward en masse, and those Nenanda and Kedeviss mortally wounded were simply heaved ahead, dying, flailing shields of flesh and bone. As the mob drove onward, the two Tiste Andii were forced from the threshold—

And the attackers poured in with triumphant shrieks.

Nenanda stopped laughing.

Nimander was at the inner doorway when he heard the savage cries behind him. Spinning round, he saw Nenanda and Kedeviss retreating under an onslaught of maddened figures.

'Skintick!'

His cousin shifted Clip's body on to Nimander's shoulders, then turned and, drawing his sword once more, plunged into the melee.

Nimander staggered into the passageway.

Why? Why are we doing this? We deliver Clip to the Dying God, like a damned sacrifice. Ahead, he saw Desra and Aranatha approaching the far end, where it seemed there was another chamber. *The altar room – where he awaits us—* 'Stop!' he shouted.

Only Desra glanced back.

Aranatha strode within.

The reek of burning kelyk assailed Nimander and he stumbled as he moved forward beneath the slack, dragging weight of Clip's unconscious form. The raw glyphs swarmed on the walls to either side. Projecting busts of some past deity showed battered faces, sections crushed and others sheared off by recent demolition. Lone eyes leered down. Half-mouths smiled with a jester's crook. Passing by one after another.

Trembling, Nimander forced himself forward. He saw Desra stride after Aranatha.

The glyphs began weeping, and all at once he felt as if time itself was dissolving. Sudden blindness, the terrible sounds of fighting behind him diminishing, as if pulled far away, until only the rush of blood remained, a storm in his head.

Through which, faintly and then rising, came a child's voice. Singing softly.

Seerdomin emerged from Night, squinted against the mid-morning glare. Silver clouds ahead, heaped above the barrow like the sky's detritus. Rain slanted down on the mound.

Tulwar in his hand, he hurried on, boots slipping in the salt-crusted mud of the track.

She had gone out, alone.

Spinnock Durav – the only friend he had left – had professed his love for her. But he had not understood – yes, she would refuse his help. But such refusal must be denied. He should have comprehended that.

Gods below, this was not Seerdomin's fight. *She* was not his fight.

Yet he found himself driven on, cold with fear, feverish with dread, and everything that he saw around him seemed to scream its details, as if even the mundane truths could burn, could sting like acid in his eyes. Ruts and broken spokes, potsherds, pools of opaque water, exposed roots like the hackles of the earth – each one ferociously demanding his attention. *We are as it is*, they seemed to shout, *we are all there is! We are—*

Not his fight, but Spinnock had not understood. He was Tiste Andii. He was a creature of centuries and what was avoided one day could be addressed later – decades, millennia, *ages* later. In their eyes, nothing changed. Nothing *could* change. They were a fallen people. The dream of getting back up had faded to dust.

She had gone out. Alone. Out where the conspirators strutted in the light of day, insanely plotting the return of suffering. Where they abused the sanctuary of an indifferent god. Maybe she was now back among her kind – if that was true, then Spinnock Durav deserved to hear the truth of that.

A rat slithered into the ditch a few strides ahead. He drew closer to the filth of the encampment, its stench so foul not even the rain could wash it away.

Would he be challenged? He hoped so. If the conspirators hid themselves, he might have trouble rooting them out. And if *she* decided to hide, well, he would have to kick through every decrepit hut and shelter, into every leaking tent and rust-seized wagon.

Birdsong drifted down from the trees of the slope on the opposite side of the camp, the sound startlingly clear. Tendrils of smoke from rain-dampened hearths undulated upward, each one solid as a serpent in Seerdomin's eyes. He was, he realized, walking into their nest.

But Spinnock, you need not do this, you need not even know of this. This is a human affair, and if she is willing then yes, I will drag her free of it. Back to you. One can be saved and that should be enough.

He wondered if the Redeemer ever saw things that way. Taking one soul into his embrace with a thousand yearning others looking on – but no, he did not choose, did not select one over another. He took them all.

Seerdomin realized he did not care either way. This god was not for him. Redemption had never been his reason for kneeling before that barrow. *I was lonely. I thought he might be the same. Damn you, High Priestess, why didn't you just leave me alone?*

Not my mess.

Spinnock, you owe me, and you will never know. I will say nothing – let this rain wash the blood from my hands—

He had begun this march half drunk, but nothing of that remained. Now, everything was on fire.

Reaching the slope of the camp's main avenue, he began the ascent. The rain was fine as mist, yet he was quickly soaked through, steam rising from his forearms. The ground gave queasily beneath his boots with every step. He arrived at the crest leaning far forward, scrabbling in his haste.

Straightening, something flashed into his vision. He heard a snap, a crunch that exploded in his head, and then nothing.

Gradithan stood over the sprawled form of Seerdomin, staring down at the smashed, bloodied face. Monkrat crept closer and crouched down beside the body.

'He lives. He will drown in his blood if I do not roll him over, Urdo. What is your wish?'

'Yes, push him over – I want him alive, for now at least. Take his weapons, bind his limbs, then drag him to the Sacred Tent.'

Gradithan licked his lips, tasting the staleness of dried kelyk. He wanted more, fresh, bitter and sweet, but he needed his mind. Sharp, awake, aware of everything.

As Monkrat directed two of his Urdomen to attend to the Seerdomin, Gradithan set off for the Sacred Tent. Sanctified ground, yes, but only temporary. Soon, they would have the barrow itself. The barrow, and the ignorant godling within it.

Along the track, the once-worshippers of the Redeemer knelt as he passed. Some moaned in the dregs of the night's dance. Others stared at the mud in front of their knees, heads hanging, brown slime drooling down from their gaping mouths. Oh, this might seem like corruption, but Gradithan wasn't interested in such misconceptions.

The Dying God was more important than Black Coral and its morose overlords. More important than the Redeemer and his pathetic cult. The Dying God's song was a song of pain, and was not pain the curse of mortality?

He had heard of another cult, a foreign one, devoted to someone called the Crippled God.

Perhaps, Monkrat had ventured that morning, *there is a trend*.

There was something blasphemous in that observation, and Gradithan reminded himself that he would have to have the mage beaten – but not yet. Gradithan needed Monkrat, at least for now.

He entered the Sacred Tent.

Yes, she was still dancing, writhing now on the earthen floor, too exhausted perhaps to stand, yet the sensual motions were still powerful enough to take away Gradithan's breath. It did not matter any more that she had been a Child of the Dead Seed. No one could choose their parents, after all. Besides, she had been adopted now. By the Dying God, by the blessed pain and ecstasy it delivered.

Let her dance on, yes, until the gate was forced open.

Gradithan lifted his head, sniffed the air – oh, the blood was being spilled, the sacrifice fast closing on the threshold. *Close now.*

The Dying God bled. Mortal followers drank that blood. Then spilled it out, transformed, so that the Dying God could take it once more within himself. This was the secret truth behind all blood sacrifice. The god gives and the mortal gives

back. All the rest . . . nothing more than ornate dressing, nothing more than obfuscation.

Die, my distant friends. Die in your multitudes. We are almost there.

'You are dying.'

Seerdomin opened his eyes. An unfamiliar face stared down at him.

'You are bleeding into your brain, Segda Travos. They mean to abuse you. Torture you with terrible sights – the Urdo named Gradithan believes you a traitor.
He wants you to suffer, but you will defy him that pleasure, for you are dying.'

'Who – what . . .'

'I am Itkovian. I am the Redeemer.'

'I – I am sorry.'

The man smiled and Seerdomin could see how that smile belonged to these
gentle features, the kind eyes. Such compassion was . . . *wrong.*

'Perhaps it seems that way, but you are strong – your spirit is very strong,
Segda Travos. You believe I am without true compassion. You believe I embrace
suffering out of selfish need, to feed a hunger, an addiction.' Itkovian's soft eyes
shifted away. 'Perhaps you are right.'

Seerdomin slowly sat up. And saw a domed sky that glittered as if with millions upon millions of stars, a solid cluster vying for every space, so that every
splinter and whorl of darkness seemed shrunken, in retreat. The vision made his
head spin and he quickly looked down. And found he was kneeling on a ground
composed entirely of coins. Copper, tin, brass, a few sprinkles of silver, fewer still
of gold. Gems gleamed here and there. 'We are,' he said in an awed whisper,
'within your barrow.'

'Yes?' said Itkovian.

Seerdomin shot the god a quick glance. 'You did not know . . .'

'Is knowing necessary, Segda Travos?'

'I no longer use that name. Segda Travos is dead. I am Seerdomin.'

'Warrior Priest of the Pannion Seer. I see the warrior within you, but not the
priest.'

'It seems I am not much of a warrior any more,' Seerdomin observed. 'I was
coming to save her.'

'And now, my friend, you must fight her.'

'What?'

Itkovian pointed.

Seerdomin twisted round where he knelt. A storm was building, seeping up
into the dome of offerings, and he saw how the blackness engulfed those blazing
stars, drowning them one by one. Beneath the savage churning clouds there was a
figure. Dancing, and with each wild swing of an arm more midnight power spun
outward, up into the growing storm cloud. She seemed to be a thousand or more
paces away, yet grew larger by the moment.

He could see her mouth, gaping like a pit, from which vile liquid gushed out,
splashing down, spraying as she twirled.

Salind. Gods, what has happened to you?

'She wants me,' Itkovian said. 'It is her need, you see.'

'Her need?'

'Yes. For answers. What more can a god fear, but a mortal demanding answers?'

'Send her away!'

'I cannot. So, warrior, will you defend me?'

'I cannot fight that!'

'Then, my friend, I am lost.'

Salind came closer, and as she did so she seemed to lose focus in Seerdomin's eyes, her limbs smearing the air, her body blurring from one position to the next. Her arms seemed to multiply, and in each one, he now saw, she held a weapon. Brown-stained iron, knotted wood trailing snags of hair, daggers of obsidian, scythes of crimson bronze.

Above her stained, weeping mouth, her eyes blazed with insane fire.

'Redeemer,' whispered Seerdomin.

'Yes?'

'Answer me one question. I beg you.'

'Ask.'

And he faced the god. *'Are you worth it?'*

'Am I worth the sacrifice you must make? No, I do not think so.'

'You will not beg to be saved?'

Itkovian smiled. 'Will you?'

No. I never have. He rose to his feet, found that the tulwar remained in his hand. He hefted the weapon and eyed Salind. *Can I defy her need? Can I truly stand against that?* 'If not for your humility, Redeemer, I would walk away. If not for your . . . uncertainty, your doubts, your *humanity*.'

And, awaiting no reply from the god, he set out into her path.

The sudden hush within the Scour Tavern finally penetrated Spinnock Durav's drunken haze. Blinking, he tilted his head, and found himself looking up at his Lord.

Who said, 'It is time, my friend.'

'You now send me away?' Spinnock asked.

'Yes. I now send you away.'

Spinnock Durav reeled upright. His face was numb. The world seemed a sickly place, and it wanted in. He drew a deep breath.

'My request pains you – why?'

He could have told him then. He could have spoken of this extraordinary blessing of love. For a human woman. He could have told Anomander Rake of his failure, and in so doing he would have awakened the Son of Darkness to his sordid plight.

Had he done all of this, Anomander Rake would have reached a hand to rest light on his shoulder, and he would have said, *Then you must stay, my friend. For love, you must stay – go to her, now. Now, Spinnock Durav. It is the last gift within our reach. The last – did you truly believe I would stand in the way of that? That I would decide that my need was greater?*

Did you think I could do such a thing, when I come to you here and now because of my own love? For you? For our people?

Go to her, Spinnock Durav. Go.

But Spinnock Durav said nothing. Instead, he bowed before his Lord. 'I shall do as you ask.'

And Anomander Rake said, 'It is all right to fail, friend. I do not demand the impossible of you. Do not weep at that moment. For me, Spinnock Durav, find a smile to announce the end. Fare well.'

The killing seemed without end. Skintick's sword arm ached, the muscles lifeless and heavy, and still they kept coming on – faces twisted eager and desperate, expressions folding round mortal wounds as if sharp iron was a blessing touch, an exquisite gift. He stood between Kedeviss and Nenanda, and the three had been driven back to the second set of doors. Bodies were piled in heaps, filling every space of the chamber's floor, where blood and fluids formed thick pools. The walls on all sides were splashed high.

He could see daylight through the outer doors – the morning was dragging on. Yet from the passage at their backs there had been . . . nothing. Were they all dead in there? Bleeding out on the altar stone? Or had they found themselves somehow trapped, or lost with no answers – was Clip now dead, or had he been delivered into the Dying God's hands?

The attackers were running out of space – too many corpses – and most now crawled or even slithered into weapon range.

'Something's wrong,' gasped Kedeviss. 'Skintick – go – we can hold them off now. Go – find out if . . .'

If we're wasting our time. I understand. He pulled back, one shoulder cracking into the frame of the entranceway. Whirling, he set off along the corridor. When horror stalked the world, it seemed that every grisly truth was laid bare. Life's struggle ever ended in failure. No victory was pure, or clean. Triumph was a comforting lie and always revealed itself to be ephemeral, hollow and short-lived. This is what assailed the spirit when coming face to face with horror.

And so few understood that. So few . . .

He clawed through foul smoke, heard his own heartbeat slowing, dragging even as his breaths faded. *What – what is happening?* Blindness. Silence, an end to all motion. Skintick sought to push forward, only to find that desire was empty when without will, and when there was no strength, will itself was a conceit. Glyphs flowed down like black rain, on his face, his neck and his hands, streaming hot as blood.

Somehow, he fought onward, his entire body dragging behind him as if half dead, an impediment, a thing worth forgetting. He wanted to pull free of it, even as he understood that his flesh was all that kept him alive – yet he yearned for dissolution, and that yearning was growing desperate.

Wait. This is not how I see the world. This is not the game I choose to play – I will not believe in this abject . . . surrender.

It is what kelyk offers. The blood of the Dying God delivers escape – from everything that matters. The invitation is so alluring, the promise so entrancing.

Dance! All around you the world rots. Dance! Poison into your mouths and poison out from your mouths. Dance, damn you, in the dust of your dreams. I have looked into your eyes and I have seen that you are nothing. Empty.

Gods, such seductive invitation!

The recognition sobered him, abrupt as a punch in the face. He found himself lying on the tiles of the corridor, the inner doors almost within reach. In the chamber beyond darkness swirled like thick smoke, like a storm trapped beneath the domed ceiling. He heard singing, soft, the voice of a child.

He could not see Nimander, or Desra or Aranatha. The body of Clip was sprawled not five paces in, face upturned, eyes opened, fixed and seemingly sightless.

Trembling with weakness, Skintick pulled himself forward.

The moment he had bulled his way into the altar chamber, Nimander had felt something tear, as if he had plunged through gauze-thin cloth. From the seething storm he had plunged into, he emerged to sudden calm, to soft light and gentle currents of warm air. His first step landed on something lumpy that twisted beneath his weight. Looking down, he saw a small doll of woven grasses and twigs. And, scattered on the floor all round, there were more such figures. Some of strips of cloth, others of twine, polished wood and fired clay. Most were broken – missing limbs, or headless. Others hung down from the plain, low ceiling, twisted beneath nooses of leather string, knotted heads tilted over, dark liquid dripping.

The wordless singing was louder here, seeming to emanate from all directions. Nimander could see no walls – just floor and ceiling, both stretching off into formless white.

And dolls, thousands of dolls. On the floor, dangling from the ceiling.

'Show yourself,' said Nimander.

The singing stopped.

'Show yourself to me.'

'If you squeeze them,' said the voice – a woman's or a young boy's – 'they leak. I squeezed them all. Until they broke.' There was a pause, and then a soft sigh. 'None worked.'

Nimander did not know where to look – the mangled apparitions hanging before him filled him with horror now, as he saw their similarity to the scarecrows of the fields outside Bastion. *They are the same. They weren't planted rows, nothing made to deliver a yield. They were . . . versions.*

'Yes. Failing one by one – it's not fair. How did he do it?'

'What are you?' Nimander asked.

The voice grew sly, 'On the floor of the Abyss – yes, there *is* a floor – there are the fallen. Gods and goddesses, spirits and prophets, disciples and seers, heroes and queens and kings – the *junk* of existence. You can play there. I did. Do you want to? Do you want to play there, too?'

'No.'

'All broken, more broken than me.'

'They call you the Dying God.'

'All gods are dying.'

'But you are no god, are you?'

'Down on the floor, you never go hungry. Am I a god now? I must be. Don't you see? I ate so many of them. So many parts, pieces. Oh, their power, I mean. My body didn't need food. Doesn't need it, I mean, yes, that is fair to say. It is so fair to say. I first met him on the floor – he was exploring, he said, and I had travelled so far . . . so far.'

'Your worshippers—'

'Are mostly dead. More to drink. All that blood, enough to make a river, and the current can take me away from here, can bring me back. All the way back. To make her *pay for what she did*!'

Having come from chaos, it was no surprise that the god was insane. 'Show yourself.'

'The machine was broken, but I didn't know that. I rode its back, up and up. But then something happened. An accident. We fell a long way. We were terribly broken, both of us. When they dragged me out. Now I need to make a new version, just like you said. And you have brought me one. It will do. I am not deaf to its thoughts. I understand its chaos, its pains and betrayals. I even understand its arrogance. It will do, it will do.'

'You cannot have him,' said Nimander. 'Release him.'

'None of these ones worked. All the power just leaks out. How did he do it?'

One of these dolls. He is one of these dolls. Hiding in the multitude.

The voice began singing again. Wordless, formless.

He drew his sword.

'What are you doing?'

The iron blade slashed outward, chopping through the nearest figures. Strings cut, limbs sliced away, straw and grass drifting in the air.

A cackle, and then: 'You want to *find* me? How many centuries do you have to spare?'

'As many as I need,' Nimander replied, stepping forward and swinging again. Splintering wood, shattering clay. Underfoot he ground his heel into another figure.

'I'll be gone long before then. The river of blood you provided me – my way out. Far away I go! You can't see it, can you? The gate you've opened here. You can't even see it.'

Nimander destroyed another half-dozen dolls.

'Never find me! Never find me!'

A savage blur of weapons as Salind charged Seerdomin. Each blow he caught with his tulwar, and each blow thundered up his arm, shot agony through his bones.

He reeled back beneath the onslaught. Three steps, five, ten. It was all he could do to simply defend himself. And that, he knew, could not last.

The Redeemer wanted him to hold against this?

He struggled on, desperate.

She was moaning, a soft, yearning sound. A sound of *want*. Mace heads beat against his weapon, sword blades, the shafts of spears, flails, daggers, scythes – a dozen arms swung at him. Impacts thundered through his body.

He could not hold. He could not—

An axe edge tore into his left shoulder, angled up to slam into the side of his face. He felt his cheekbone and eye socket collapse inward. Blinded, Seerdomin staggered, attempting a desperate counter-attack, the tulwar slashing out. The edge bit into wood, splintering it. Something struck him high on his chest, snapping a clavicle. As his weapon arm sagged, suddenly lifeless, he reached across and took the sword with his other hand. Blood ran down from his shoulder – he was losing all strength.

Another edge chopped into him and he tottered, then fell on to his back.

Salind stepped up to stand directly over him.

He stared up into her dark, glittering eyes.

After a moment Nimander lowered his sword. The Dying God was right – this was pointless. 'Show yourself, you damned coward!'

Aranatha was suddenly at his side. 'He must be summoned,' she said.

'You expect him to offer us his name?'

The Dying God spoke. 'Who is here? *Who is here?*'

'I am the one,' answered Aranatha, 'who will summon you.'

'You do not know me. You cannot know me!'

'I know your path,' she replied. 'I know you spoke with the one named Hairlock, on the floor of the Abyss. And you imagined you could do the same, that you could fashion for yourself a body. Of wood, of twine, of clay –'

'*You don't know me!*'

'She discarded you,' said Aranatha, 'didn't she? The fragment of you that was left afterwards. Tainted, childlike, abandoned.'

'You cannot know this – you were not there!'

Aranatha frowned. 'No, I was not there. Yet . . . the earth trembled. Children woke. There was great need. You were the part of her . . . that she did not want.'

'*She will pay! And for you – I know you now – and it is too late!*'

Aranatha sighed. 'Husband, Blood Sworn to Nightchill,' she intoned, 'child of Thelomen Tartheno Toblakai, Bellurdan Skullcrusher, I summon you.' And she held out her hand, in time for something to slap hard into its grip. A battered, misshapen puppet dangled, one arm snapped off, both legs broken away at the knees, a face barely discernible, seemingly scorched by fire. Aranatha faced Nimander. 'Here is your Dying God.'

Around them the scene began dissolving, crumbling away.

'He does not speak,' Nimander said, eyeing the mangled puppet.

'No,' she said. 'Curious.'

'Are you certain you have him, Aranatha?'

She met his eyes, and then shrugged.

'What did he mean, that he *knew* you? And how – how did you know his name?'

She blinked, and then frowned down at the puppet she still held out in one hand. 'Nimander,' she whispered in a small voice, 'so much blood . . .'

Reaching out to Clip, Skintick dragged the man close, studied the face, the staring eyes, and saw something flicker to life. 'Clip?'

The warrior shifted his gaze, struggling to focus, and then he scowled. His words came out in an ugly croak. 'Fuck. What do you want?'

Sounds, motion, and then Nimander was there, kneeling on the other side of Clip. 'We seem,' he said, 'to have succeeded.'

'How?'

'I don't know, Skin. Right now, I don't know anything.'

Skintick saw Aranatha standing just near a massive block of stone – the altar. She was holding a doll or puppet of some sort. 'Where's Desra?' he suddenly asked, looking round.

'Over here.'

The foul smoke was clearing. Skintick lifted himself into a sitting position and squinted in the direction of the voice. In the wall behind the altar and to the left, almost hidden between columns, there was a narrow door, through which Desra now emerged. She was soaked in blood, although by the way she moved, none of it was her own. 'Some sort of High Priest, I suppose,' she said. 'Trying to protect a corpse, or what I think is a corpse.' She paused, and then spat on to the floor. 'Strung up like one of those scarecrows, but the body parts . . . all wrong, all sewn together—'

'The Dying God,' said Aranatha, 'sent visions of what he wanted. Flawed. But what leaked out tasted sweet.'

From the corridor Kedeviss and Nenanda arrived. They both looked round, their faces flat, their eyes bludgeoned.

'I think we killed them all,' said Kedeviss. 'Or the rest fled. This wasn't a fight – this was a slaughter. It made no sense—'

'Blood,' said Nimander, studying Clip – who remained lying before him – with something like suspicion. 'You are back with us?'

Clip swung his scowl on to Nimander. 'Where are we?'

'A city called Bastion.'

A strange silence followed, but it was one that Skintick understood. *The wake of our horror. It settles, thickens, forms a hard skin – something lifeless, smooth. We're waiting for it to finish all of that, until it can take our weight once more.*

And then we leave here.

'We still have far to go,' said Nimander, straightening.

In Skintick's eyes, his kin – his friend – looked aged, ravaged, his eyes haunted and bleak. The others were no better. None of them had wanted this. And what they had done here . . . it had all been for Clip.

'Blood,' said Clip, echoing Nimander, and he slowly climbed to his feet. He glared at the others. 'Look at you. By Mother Dark, I'd swear you've been rolling in the waste pits of some abattoir. Get cleaned up or you won't have my company for much longer.' He paused, and his glare hardened into something crueller. 'I smell murder. Human cults are pathetic things. From now on, spare me your lust for killing innocents. I'd rather not be reminded of whatever crimes you committed in the name of the Son of Darkness. Yes,' he added, baring his teeth, 'he has so much to answer for.'

Standing over him, weapons whirling, spinning. Seerdomin watched her with his one remaining eye, waiting for the end to all of this, an end he only faintly regretted. The failure, his failure, yes, that deserved some regret. But then, had he truly believed he could stop this apparition?

He said I was dying.

I'm dying again.

All at once, she was still. Her eyes like hooded lanterns, her arms settling as if the dance had danced its way right out of her and now spun somewhere unseen. She stared down at him without recognition, and then she turned away.

He heard her stumbling back the way she had come.

'That was long enough.'

Seerdomin turned his head, saw the Redeemer standing close. Not a large man. Not in any way particularly impressive. Hard enough, to be sure, revealing his profession as a soldier, but otherwise unremarkable. 'What made you what you are?' he asked – or tried to – his mouth filled with blood that frothed and spattered with every word.

The Redeemer understood him none the less. 'I don't know. We may possess ambition, and with it a self-image both grandiose and posturing, but they are empty things in the end.' Then he smiled. 'I do not recall being such a man.'

'Why did she leave, Redeemer?'

The answer was long in coming. 'You had help, I believe. And no, I do not know what will come of that. Can you wait? I may need you again.'

Seerdomin managed a laugh. 'Like this?'

'I cannot heal you. But I do not think you will . . . cease. Yours is a strong soul, Seerdomin. May I sit down beside you? It has been a long time since I last had someone to speak to.'

Well, here I bleed. But there is no pain. 'As long as I can,' he said, 'you will have someone to speak to.'

The Redeemer looked away then, so that Seerdomin could not see his sudden tears.

'He didn't make it,' Monkrat said, straightening.

Gradithan glowered down at Seerdomin's corpse. 'We were so close, too. I don't understand what's happened, I don't understand at all.'

He turned slightly and studied the High Priestess where she knelt on the muddy floor of the tent. Her face was slack, black drool hanging from her mouth. 'She used it up. Too soon, too fast, I think. All that wasted blood . . .'

Monkrat cleared his throat. 'The visions—'

'Nothing now,' Gradithan snapped. 'Find some more kelyk.'

At that Salind's head lifted, a sudden thirst burning in her eyes. Seeing this, Gradithan laughed. 'Ah, see how she worships now. An end to all those doubts. One day, Monkrat, *everyone* will be like her. Saved.'

Monkrat seemed to hesitate.

Gradithan turned back and spat on to Seerdomin's motionless, pallid visage. 'Even you, Monkrat,' he said. 'Even you.'

'Would you have me surrender my talents as a mage, Urdo?'

'Not yet. But yes, one day, you will do that. Without regrets.'

Monkrat set off to find another cask of kelyk.

Gradithan walked over to Salind. He crouched in front of her, leaned forward to lick the drool from her lips. 'We'll dance together,' he said. 'Are you eager for that?'

He saw the answer in her eyes.

High atop the tower, in the moment that Silanah stirred – cold eyes fixed upon the pilgrim encampment beyond the veil of Night – Anomander Rake had reached out to still her with the lightest of touches.

'Not this time, my love,' he said in a murmur. 'Soon. You will know.'

Slowly, the enormous dragon settled once more, eyes closing to the thinnest of slits.

The Son of Darkness let his hand remain, resting there on her cool, scaled neck. 'Do not fear,' he said, 'I will not restrain you next time.'

He sensed the departure of Spinnock Durav, on a small fast cutter into the Ortnal beyond Nightwater. Perhaps the journey would serve him well, a distance ever stretching between the warrior and what haunted him.

And he sensed, too, the approach of Endest Silann down along the banks of the river, his oldest friend, who had one more task ahead of him. A most difficult one.

But these were difficult times, he reflected.

Anomander Rake left Silanah then, beneath Darkness that never broke.

North and west of Bastion, Kallor walked an empty road.

He had found nothing worthwhile in Bastion. The pathetic remnant of one of Nightchill's lovers, a reminder of curses voiced long ago, a reminder of how time twisted everything, like a rope binding into ever tighter knots and kinks. Until what should have been straight was now a tangled, useless mess.

Ahead awaited a throne, a new throne, one that he deserved. He believed it was taking shape, becoming something truly corporeal. Raw power, brimming with unfulfilled promise.

But the emergence of the throne was not the only thing awaiting him, and he sensed well that much at least. A convergence, yes, yet another of those confounded cusps, when powers drew together, when unforeseen paths suddenly intersected. When all of existence could change in a single moment, in the solitary cut of a sword, in a word spoken or a word left unspoken.

What would come?

He needed to be there. In its midst. Such things were what kept him going, after all. Such things were what made life worth living.

I am the High King of Failures, am I not? Who else deserves the Broken Throne? Who else personifies the misery of the Crippled God? No, it will be mine, and as for all the rest, well, we'll see, won't we?

He walked on, alone once more. Satisfying, to be reminded – as he had been when travelling in the company of those pathetic Tiste Andii – that the world was crowded with idiots. Brainless, stumbling, clumsy with stupid certainties and convictions.

Perhaps, this time, he would dispense with empires. This time, yes, he would crush everything, until every wretched mortal scrabbled in the dirt, fighting over grubs and roots. Was that not the perfect realm for a broken throne?

Yes, and what better proof of my right to claim that throne? Kallor alone turns his back on civilization. Look on, Fallen One, and see me standing before you. Me and none other.

I vow to take it all down. Every brick. And the world can look on, awed, in wonder. The gods themselves will stare, dumbfounded, amazed, bereft and lost. Curse me to fall each and every time, will you? But I will make a place where no fall is possible. I will defeat that curse, finally defeat it.

Can you hear me, K'rul?

No matter. You will see what there is to see, soon enough.

These were, he decided, glorious times indeed.

Book Three

To Die
in the Now

Push it on to the next moment
Don't think now, save it
For later when thinking will show
Its useless face
When it's too late and worry is wasted
In the rush for cover

Push it past into that pocket
So that it relents its gnawing presence
And nothing is worth doing
In pointless grace
When all the valid suppositions
Smother your cries

Push it over into the deep hole
You don't want to know
In case it breaks and makes you feel
Cruel reminders
When all you could have done is now past
No don't bother

Push it well into the corner
It's no use, so spare me the grief
You didn't like the cost so bright, so high
The bloodiest cut
When all you sought was sweet pleasure
To the end of your days

Push it on until it pushes back
Shout your shock, shout it
You never imagined you never knew what
Turning away would do
Now wail out your dread in waves of disbelief
It's done it's dead

Push your way to the front
Clawing the eyes of screaming kin
No legacy awaits your shining children
It's killed, killed
Gone the future all to feed some holy glory
The world is over. Over.

SIBAN'S DYING CONFESSION
SIBAN OF AREN

Chapter Thirteen

We watched him approach from a league away
Staggering beneath the weight of all he held
In his arms
We thought he wore a crown but when he came near
The circlet was revealed as the skin of a serpent
Biting its tail
We laughed and shared the carafe when he fell
Cheering as he climbed back upright
In pleasing charm
We slowed into silence when he arrived
And saw for ourselves the burden he carried
Kept from harm
We held stern in the face of his relieved smile
And he said this fresh young world he had found
Was now ours
We looked on as if we were grand gods
Contemplating a host of undeserved gifts
Drawing knives
Bold with pride we cut free bloodied slices
And ate our fill
We saw him weep then when nothing was left
Backing away with eyes of pain and dismay
Arms falling
But wolves will make of any world a carcass
We simply replied with our natures revealed
In all innocence
We proclaimed with zeal our humble purity
Though now he turned away and did not hear
As the taste soured
And the betrayal of poison crept into our limbs
We watched him walk away now a league maybe more
His lonely march
His mourning departure from our kindness
His happy annihilation of our mindless selves
Snake-bit unto death

The Last Days of Our Inheritance
Fisher kel Tath

The vast springs of the carriage slammed down to absorb the thundering impact; then, as the enormous conveyance surged back up, Gruntle caught a momentary glimpse of one of the Bole brothers, his grip torn loose, wheeling through the grainy air. Arms scything, legs kicking, face wide with bemused surprise.

His tether snapped taut, and Gruntle saw that the idiot had tied it to one of his ankles. The man plunged down and out of sight.

The horses were screaming, manes whipping in their frantic heaves forward across stony, broken ground. Shadowy figures voiced muted cries as the beasts trampled them under hoof, and the carriage rocked sickeningly over bodies.

Someone was shrieking in his ear, and Gruntle twisted round on his perch on the carriage roof, to see the other Bole brother – Jula – tugging on the tether. A foot appeared – moccasin gone, long knobby toes splayed wide as if seeking a branch – and then the shin and lumpy knee. A moment later Amby reached up, found a handhold, and pulled himself back on to the roof. Wearing the strangest grin Gruntle had ever seen.

In the half-light the Trygalle carriage raced onward, plunging through seething masses of people. Even as they carved through like a ship cutting crazed seas, ragged, rotting arms reached up to the sides. Some caught hold only to have their arms torn from their sockets. Others were pulled off their feet, and these ones started climbing, seeking better purchase.

Upon which the primary function of the shareholders was made apparent. Sweetest Sufferance, the short, plump woman with the bright smile, was now snarling, whaling with a hatchet into an outreaching arm. Bones snapped like sticks and she shouted as she kicked into a leering desiccated face, hard enough to punch the head from the shoulders.

Damned corpses – they were riding through a sea of animated corpses, and it seemed that virtually every one of them wanted to book passage.

A large brutish shape reared up beside Gruntle. Barghast, hairy as an ape, filed blackened teeth revealed in a delighted grin.

Releasing one hand from the brass rung, Gruntle tugged loose one of his cutlasses, slashed the heavy blade into the corpse's face. It reeled away, the bottom half of the grin suddenly gone. Twisting further round, Gruntle kicked the Barghast in the chest. The apparition fell back. A moment later someone else appeared, narrow-shouldered, the top of its head an elongated pate with a nest of mousy hair perched on the crown, a wizened face beneath it.

Gruntle kicked again.

The carriage pitched wildly as the huge wheels rolled over something big. Gruntle felt himself swinging out over the roof edge and he shouted in pain as his hand was wrenched where it gripped a rung. Clawed fingers scrabbled against his thighs and he kicked in growing panic. His heel struck something that didn't yield and he used that purchase to launch himself back on to the roof.

On the opposite side, three dead men were now mauling Sweetest Sufferance, each one seemingly intent on some kind of rape. She twisted and writhed beneath them, chopping with her hatchets, biting at their withered hands and head-butting the ones that tried for a kiss. Reccanto Ilk then joined the fray, using a strange saw-toothed knife as he attacked various joints – shoulders, knees, elbows – and tossing the severed limbs over the side as he went.

Gruntle lifted himself on to his knees and glared out across the landscape. The masses of dead, he realized, were all moving in one direction, whilst the carriage cut obliquely into their path – and as the resistance before them built, figures converging like blood to a wound, forward momentum began inexorably to slow, the horses stamping high as they clambered over ever more undead.

Someone was shouting near the rear of the carriage, and Gruntle turned to see the woman named Faint leaning down over the side, yelling through the shuttered window.

Another heavy blow buffeted the carriage, and something demonic roared. Claws tore free a chunk of wood.

'Get us out of here!'

Gruntle could not agree more, as the demon suddenly loomed into view, reptilian arms reaching for him.

Snarling, he leapt to his feet, both weapons now in hand.

An elongated, fanged face lunged at him, hissing.

Gruntle roared back – a deafening sound – cutlasses lashing out. Edges slammed into thick hide, sliced deep into lifeless flesh, down to the bones of the demon's long neck.

He saw something like surprise flicker in the creature's pitted eyes, and then the head and half of the neck fell away.

Two more savage chops sent its forearms spinning.

The body plunged back, and even as it did so smaller corpses were scrambling on to it, as if climbing a ladder.

He now heard a strange sound ahead, rhythmic, like the clashing of weapons against shield rims. But the sound was too loud for that, too overwhelming, unless – Gruntle straightened and faced forward.

An army indeed. Dead soldiers, moving in ranks, in squares and wedges, marching along with all the rest – and in numbers unimaginable. He stared, struggling to comprehend the vastness of the force. As far as he could see before them . . . *Gods below, all of the dead, on the march – but where? To what war?*

The scene suddenly blurred, dispersed in fragments. The carriage seemed to slump under him. Darkness swept in, a smell of the sea, the thrash of waves, sand sliding beneath the wheels. The carriage side nearest him lurched into the bole of a palm tree, sending down a rain of cusser-sized nuts that pounded along the roof before bounding away. The horses stumbled, slowing their wild plunge, and a moment later everything came to a sinking halt.

Looking up Gruntle saw stars in a gentle night sky.

Beneath him the carriage door creaked open, and someone clambered out to vomit on to the sands, coughing and spitting and cursing.

Master Quell.

Gruntle climbed down, using the spokes of the nearest wheel, and, his legs feeling shaky under him, made his way to the sorceror.

The man was still on his hands and knees, hacking out the last dregs of whatever had been in his stomach. 'Oh,' he gasped. 'My aching head.'

Faint came up alongside Gruntle. She'd been wearing an iron skullcap but she'd lost it, and now her hair hung in matted strands, framing her round face. 'I thought a damned tiger had landed on us,' she said, 'but it was you, putting the terror into a demon. So it's true, those tattoos aren't tattoos at all.'

Glanno Tarp had dropped down, dodging to avoid the snapping teeth of the nearest horses. 'Did you see Amby Bole go flying? Gods, that was stupacular!'

Gruntle frowned. 'Stu – what?'

'Stupidly spectacular,' explained Faint. 'Or spectacularly stupid. Are you Soletaken?'

He glanced at her, then set off to explore.

A task quickly accomplished. They were on an island. A very small island, less than fifty paces across. The sand was crushed coral, gleaming silver in the starlight. Two palm trees rose from the centre. In the surrounding shallows, a thousand paces out, ribbons of reef ran entirely round the atoll, breaking the surface like the spine of a sea serpent. More islands were visible, few bigger than the one they were on, stretching out like the beads of a broken necklace, the nearest one perhaps three thousand paces distant.

As he returned he saw a corpse plummeting down from the carriage roof to thump in the sand. After a moment it sat up. 'Oh,' it said.

The Trell emerged from the carriage, followed by the swamp witch, Precious Thimble, who looked ghostly pale as she stumbled a few steps, then promptly sat down on the sand. Seeing Gruntle, Mappo walked over.

'I gather,' he said, 'we encountered something unexpected in Hood's realm.'

'I wouldn't know,' Gruntle replied. 'It was my first visit.'

'Unexpected?' Faint snorted. 'That was insane – all the dead in existence, on the march.'

'Where to?' Gruntle asked.

'Maybe not to, maybe *from*.'

From? In retreat? Now that was an alarming notion. *If the dead are on the run . . .*

'Used to be,' Faint mused, 'the realm of the dead was an easy ride. Peaceful. But in the last few years . . . something's going on.' She walked over to Master Quell. 'So, if that's not going to work, Quell, what now?'

The man, still on his hands and knees, looked up. 'You just don't get it, do you?'

'What?'

'We didn't even reach the damned *gate*.'

'But, then, what—'

'*There wasn't any gate!*' the mage shrieked.

A long silence followed.

Nearby, the undead man was collecting seashells.

Jula Bole's watery eyes fixed on Precious Thimble, dreamy with adoration. Seeing this, Amby did the same, trying to make his expression even more desirous, so that when she finally looked over she would see that he was the right one for her, the only one for her. As the moments stretched, the competition grew fierce.

His left leg still ached, from the hip right down to his toes, and he had only one moccasin, but at least the sand was warm so that wasn't too bad.

Precious Thimble was in a meeting with Master Quell and that scary barbed man, and the hairy giant ogre named Mappo. These were the important people, he decided, and excepting Precious Thimble he wanted nothing to do with them. Standing too close to those folk was never healthy. Heads explode, hearts burst – he'd seen it with his own eyes, back when he was a runt (but not nearly as much of a runt as Jula) and the family had decided at last to fight the Malazans who were showing up in their swamp like poison mushrooms. Buna Bole had been running things back then, before he got eaten by a toad, but it was a fact that Buna's next-to-closest brothers – the ones who wanted to get closer – all went and got themselves killed. Exploding heads. Bursting hearts. Boiling livers. It was the law of dodging, of course. Marshals and their submarshals were smart and smart meant fast, so when the arrows and quarrels and waves of magic flew, why, they dodged out of the way. Anybody round them, trying to be as smart but not smart at all and so just that much slower, well, they didn't dodge quick enough.

Jula finally sighed, announcing his defeat, and looked over at Amby. 'I can't believe I saved you.'

'I can't neither. I wouldn't of.'

'That's why I can't believe that's what I did. But then she's seen how brave I am, how generous and selfless. She's seen I'm better because she knows you wouldn't have done it.'

'Maybe I would've, and maybe she knows that, Jula. Besides, one of them sick smelly ones was trying to open the doors, and if it wasn't for me he'd of got in – and that's what she really saw.'

'You didn't scrape that one off on purpose.'

'How do you know?'

'Because you butted him with your face, Amby.'

Amby tested his nose again and winced, and then he sneered. 'She saw what she saw, and what she saw wasn't *you*.'

'She saw my hands, reaching down to drag you back up. She saw that.'

'She didn't. I made sure by covering them with, er, with my shirt.'

'You lie.'

'*You* lie.'

'No, you.'

'You!'

'You can say what you like, Amby, whatever you like. It was me saving you.'

'Pulling off my moccasin, you mean.'

'That was an accident.'

'Yeah, then where is it?'

'Fell off the side.'

'No it didn't. I checked your bag, Jula. You wasn't trying to save me at all, you was stealing my moccasin because it's your favourite moccasin. I want it back.'

'It's against the law to look in someone else's bag.'

'Swamp law. Does this look like a swamp?'

'That doesn't matter. You broke the law. Anyway, what you found was my spare moccasin.'

'Your one spare moccasin?'

'That's right.'

'Then why was it full of my love notes?'

'What love notes?'

'The ones me and her been writing back and forth. The ones I hid in my moccasin. Those ones, Jula.'

'What's obvious now is just how many times you been breaking the law. Because you been hiding your love notes – which you write to yourself and nobody else – you been hiding them in my spare moccasin!'

'Not that you'd ever look.'

'But I might, if I knew about it.'

'You didn't though, did you? Besides, you don't have a spare moccasin, because I stole it.'

'And that's why I stole it back!'

'You can't steal back what you didn't know was stolen in the first place. That's just stealing. And stealing's against the law.'

'Swamp law.'

'Your bag *is* a swamp.'

'Hahahahaha—'

And Amby grinned at his own joke, and then he too laughed. 'Hahahahaha—'

Faint tugged the stopper free and took a swig, then handed the skin to Sweetest Sufferance. 'Listen to those idiots,' she said.

'I don't want to,' Sweetest Sufferance replied. And then she shivered. 'That was the first time, you know, them trying to get in my trousers like that.'

'Cursed with rigor mortis, maybe.'

She snorted. 'You kidding me? Whatever they had down there wasn't even real, like maybe sticks tied on or something.' She drank down some wine, then sighed and looked round. 'Pretty.'

'Our tiny piece of paradise.'

'We can watch the sun come up, at least. That will be nice.' She was quiet for a moment, before resuming, 'When Reccanto showed up, I thought he was helping. But now I think he was just using the situation to get a few handfuls of his own.'

'Are you surprised, Sweetie? He's a man.'

'With bad eyes.'

'Bad eyes and bad hands.'

'I might have to murder him.'

'Hold on,' said Faint, taking the skin back. 'He *did* save you, cutting off arms and hands—'

'Eliminating the competition.'

'Defending your honour, Sweetie.'

'If you say so.'

Faint replaced the stopper. 'Gods below, Sweetie, what do you think we ran into back there?'

Sweetest Sufferance pursed her plump lips, long-lashed lids settling down over her eyes. 'Back in One Eye Cat, when I was a child, I was taken to a Dawn of Flies – you know, those ceremonies from the Temple of Hood, when all the priests paint themselves in honey—'

'In some places,' cut in Faint, 'they use blood.'

'So I've heard. In One Eye Cat, it was honey, so that the flies stuck. Flies and wasps, actually. Anyway, I was with my grandfather, who'd been a soldier in the Revenants—'

'Gods, it's been a long time since I last heard them mentioned!' Faint stared across at Sweetest Sufferance. 'Is this true? Your grandfather was with the Revenants?'

'So he always told it. When I was very young, I believed every word he said. When I was older, I didn't believe any of it. And now I'm still older, I've gone back to believing him. Things in his house, the carved flagstones, the broken masks he had on the wall . . . yes, Faint, I believe he was at that.'

'Commanded by a Seguleh—'

'An outlawed Seguleh, yes. Anyway, it was my grandfather who took me to watch his old company's patron temple and all the priests and priestesses doing their flies thing.'

'Wait. The Revenants were supposed to have all disappeared – taken by Hood himself, to serve him in the realm of the dead. So what was your grandfather doing living in One Eye Cat?'

'He lost his sword arm in a battle. He'd been left for dead, and by the time anyone found him it was too late for any serious healing. So they seared the stump and retired him out. Now, you going to let me tell my tale or not?'

'Yes, fine. Sorry.'

'He said the priests were getting it all wrong, with that honey. The flies and wasps weren't the important thing in the ceremony. It was the blood – honey, but that symbolized blood. The Revenants – who were as good as Hood's own warrior-priests, in the mortal world anyway – well, they were flagellants. Blood on the skin, life bled out to die on the skin – that was the important detail. It's why Hood cherishes dead soldiers more than any other of the countless dead that stumble through the gate. The Merchants of Blood, the army that will fight on the hidden plain called Defiance Last.' She paused, then licked her lips. 'That's what the

Dawn of Flies is about. A final battle, the dead gathered, on a hidden plain called Defiance Last.'

'So,' said Faint, feeling chilled by Sweetest Sufferance's story, 'maybe that's why Hood took the Revenants. Because that battle is coming.'

'Give me some more of that,' Sweetest Sufferance said, reaching for the wineskin.

Glanno Tarp nudged Reccanto Ilk. 'See 'em? They're talking about us. Well, me, mostly. It's gonna happen, Ilk, sooner or later, it's gonna happen.'

Reccanto Ilk squinted across at the man. 'What, they gonna kill you in your sleep?'

'Don't be an idiot. One a them's gonna ask me to forevermarry her.'

'And *then* she'll kill you in your sleep. And then we can all slice up your share.'

'You think I didn't see how you gropered Sweetie?'

'How could you? You was driving!'

'There ain't nothing that I don't see, Ilk. That's what makes me such a godiferous driver.'

'She's got the nicest handholds.'

'Watch what you're doing with my future foreverwife.'

'Could be Faint you end up with, which means I can do what I like with Sweetie.'

Glanno Tarp loosed a loud belch. 'We should make up something to eat. Breakfast, so when they're finished jawbering over there we can up and get on our way.'

'Wherever that is.'

'Wherever don't matter. Never has and never will.'

Reccanto Ilk grinned. 'Right. It ain't the destination that counts . . .'

And together they added, 'It's the journey!'

Faint and Sweetest Sufferance looked over, both scowling. 'Not that again!' Faint called. 'Just stop it, you two! Stop it or we'll kill you in your sleep!'

Reccanto Ilk nudged Glanno Tarp.

Mappo crouched, rocking on the balls of his broad feet, waiting for Master Quell to finish his muttered incantation against pain. He sympathized, since it was clear that the mage was suffering, his face pale and drawn, forehead slick with sweat, his hands trembling.

That anyone would choose such a profession, given the terrible cost, was a difficult notion to accept. Was coin worth this? He could not understand that sort of thinking.

What held real value in this world? In any world? Friendship, the gifts of love and compassion. The honour one accorded the life of another person. None of this could be bought with wealth. It seemed to him such a simple truth. Yet he knew that its very banality was fuel for sneering cynicism and mockery. Until such things were taken away, until the price of their loss came to be personal, in some terrible, devastating arrival into one's life. Only at that moment of profound extremity did the contempt wash down from that truth, revealing it bare, undeniable.

All the truths that mattered were banal.

Yet here was another truth. He had paid for this journey. His coin bought this man's pain. The exchange was imbalanced, and so Mappo grieved for Master Quell, and would not shy away from his own guilt. Honour meant, after all, a preparedness, a willingness to weigh and measure, to judge rightful balance with no hand tilting the scales.

And so, they all here were paying to serve Mappo's need, this journey through warrens. Another burden he must accept. If he could.

The formidable warrior sitting beside him stirred then and said, 'I think I see now why the Trygalle loses so many shareholders, Master Quell. By the abyss, there must be warrens where one can journey through in peace?'

Master Quell rubbed at his face. 'Realms resist, Gruntle. We are like a splash of water in hot oil. It's all I can do to not . . . bounce us off. Mages can push themselves into their chosen warrens – it's not easy, it's a game of subtle persuasion most of the time. Or a modest assertion of will. You don't want to blast a hole from one realm to the next, because that's likely to go out of control. It can devour a mage in an instant.' He looked up at them with bloodshot eyes. 'We can't do it that way.' He waved a weak hand at the carriage behind him. 'We arrive like an insult. We *are* an insult. Like a white-hot spear point, we punch through, race along our wild path, and all that we leave in our wake I need to make sure is, er, cauterized. Seared shut. Failing that, a rush of power explodes behind us, and that's a wave no mortal can ride for long.'

Precious Thimble spoke from behind Mappo. 'You must be High Mages, then, one and all.'

To her observation, Master Quell nodded. 'I admit, it's starting to trouble me, this way of travel. I think we're scarring the whole damned universe. We're making existence . . . bleed. Oh, just a seep here and there, amidst whatever throbs of pain reality might possess. In any case, that's why there's no peaceful path, Gruntle. Denizens in every realm are driven to annihilate us.'

'You said we did not even reach Hood's Gate,' the barbed man said after a moment. 'And yet . . .'

'Aye.' He spat on to the sand. 'The dead sleep no more. What a damned mess.'

'Find us the nearest land in our own world,' said Mappo. 'I will walk from there. Make my own way—'

'We stay true to the contract, Trell. We'll deliver you where you want to go—'

'Not at the price of you and your companions possibly dying – I cannot accept that, Master Quell.'

'We don't do refunds.'

'I do not ask for one.'

Master Quell rose shakily. 'We'll see after our next leg. For now, it's time for breakfast. There's nothing worse than heaving when there's nothing in the gut to heave.'

Gruntle also straightened. 'You have decided on a new path?'

Quell grimaced. 'Look around, Gruntle. It's been decided for us.'

Mappo rose and remained at Gruntle's side as Quell staggered to his crew, who were gathered round a brazier they had dragged out from the belly of the carriage. The Trell squinted at the modest plot of land. 'What did he mean?' he asked.

Gruntle shrugged. When he smiled at Mappo his fangs gleamed. 'Since I have to guess, Trell, I'd say we're going for a swim.'

And Precious Thimble snorted. 'Mael's realm. And you two thought Hood was bad.'

When she was four years old, Precious Thimble was given a breathing tube and buried in peat, where she remained for two days and one night. She probably died. Most of them did, but the soul remained in the dead body, trapped by the peat and its dark, sorcerous qualities. This was how the old witches explained things. A child must be given into the peat, into that unholy union of earth and water, and the soul must be broken free of the flesh it dwelt within, for only then could that soul travel, only then could that soul wander free in the realm of dreams.

She had few memories of that time in the peat. Perhaps she screamed, sought to thrash in panic. The ropes that bound her, that would be used to pull her free at dusk of the second day, had left deep burns on her wrists and her neck, and these burns had not come from the gentle, measured pressure when the witches had drawn her back into the world. It was also whispered that sometimes the spirits that lurked in the peat sought to steal the child's body, to make it a place of their own. And the witches who sat guarding the temporary grave told of times when the rope – its ends wrapped about their wrists – suddenly grew taut, and a battle would then begin, between the witches of the surface and the spirits of the deep. Sometimes, it was admitted, the witches lost, the ropes were gnawed unto breaking, and the child was pulled into the foul deep, emerging only once every year, on the Night of the Awakened. Children with blue-brown skin and hollowed-out eye sockets, with hair the colour of rust or blood, with long polished nails – walking the swamp and singing songs of the earth that could drive a mortal mad.

Had spirits come for her? The witches would not say. Were the burns on her skin the result of panic, or something else? She did not know.

Her memories of that time were few and visceral. The weight on her chest. The seeping cold. The taste of fetid water in her mouth, the stinging in her squeezed-shut eyes. And the sounds she could hear, terrible trickling sounds, like the rush of fluids in the veins of the earth. The thumps and crunches, the crackling approach of . . . things.

It was said there was no air in the peat. That not even her skin could breathe – and such breathing was necessary to all life. And so she must have died in truth.

Since then, at night when she slept, she could rise from her flesh, could hover, invisible, above her motionless body. And look down in admiration. She was beautiful indeed, as if something of the child she had been never aged, was immune to growing old. A quality that made men desperate to claim her, not as an equal, alas, but as a possession. And the older the man the greater the need.

When she had made this discovery, about herself and about the men who most desired her, she was disgusted. Why give this gorgeous body to such wrinkled, pathetic creatures? She would not. Ever. Yet she found it difficult to defend herself against such needy hunters of youth – oh, she could curse them into misery, she could poison them and see them die in great pain, but such things only led her to pity, the soft kind not the nasty kind, which made being cruel just that much harder.

She had found her solution in the two young Bole brothers. Barely out of their teens, neither one well suited to staying in the Mott Irregulars, for certain reasons over which she need not concern herself. And both of them gloriously in love with her.

It did not matter that they barely had a single brain between them. They were Boles, ferocious against mages' and magic of any kind, and born with the salamander god's gift of survival. They protected her in all the battles one could imagine, from out and out fighting to the devious predations of old men.

When she was done admiring her own body, she would float over to where they slept and look down upon their slack faces, on the gaping mouths from which snores groaned out in wheezing cadence, the threads of drool and the twitching eyelids. Her pups. Her guard dogs. Her deadly hounds.

Yet now, on this night with the tropical stars peering down, Precious Thimble felt a growing unease. This Trygalle venture she'd decided on – this whim – was proving far deadlier than she had expected. In fact, she'd almost lost one of them in Hood's realm. And losing one of them would be . . . bad. It would free the other one to close in and that she didn't want, not at all. And one guard dog wasn't nearly as effective as two.

Maybe, just maybe, she'd gone too far this time.

Gruntle opened his eyes, and watched as the faintly glowing emanation floated over to hover above the sleeping forms of the Bole brothers, where it lingered for a time before returning to sink back down into the form of Precious Thimble.

From nearby he heard the Trell's soft grunt, and then, 'What game does she play at, I wonder . . .'

Gruntle thought to reply. Instead, sleep took him suddenly, pouncing, tumbling his mind away and down, spitting him out like a mangled rat into a damp glade of high grass. The sun blazed down like a god's enraged eye. Feeling battered, misused, he rose on to all fours – a position that did not feel at all awkward, or strike him as unusual.

Solid jungle surrounded the clearing, from which came the sounds of countless birds, monkeys and insects – a cacophony so loud and insistent that a growl of irritation rose from deep in his throat.

All at once the nearest sounds ceased, a cocoon of silence broken only by the hum of bees and a pair of long-tailed hummingbirds dancing in front of an orchid – that both then raced off in a beating whirr of wings.

Gruntle felt his hackles rise, stiff and prickling on the back of his neck – too fierce for a human – and looking down he saw the sleek banded forelimbs of a tiger where his arms and hands should have been.

Another one of these damned dreams. Listen, Trake, if you want me to be just like you, stop playing these scenes for me. I'll be a tiger if that's what you want – just don't confine it to my dreams. I wake up feeling clumsy and slow and I don't like it. I wake up remembering nothing but freedom.

Something was approaching. *Things . . . three, no, five. Not big, not dangerous.* He slowly swung his head round, narrowing his gaze.

The creatures that came to the edge of the clearing were somewhere between apes and humans. Small as adolescents, lithe and sleek, with fine fur thickening at the armpits and crotch. The two males carried short curved batons of some sort, fire-hardened, with inset fangs from some large carnivore. The females wielded spears, one of them holding her spear in one hand and a broad flint axe head in the other, which she tossed into the clearing. The object landed with a thump, flattening the grasses, halfway between Gruntle and the band.

Gruntle realized, with a faint shock, that he knew the taste of these creatures – their hot flesh, their blood, the saltiness of their sweat. In this form, in this place and in this time, he had hunted them, had pulled them down, hearing their piteous cries as his jaws closed fatally round their necks.

This time, however, he was not hungry, and it seemed they knew it.

Awe flickered in their eyes, their mouths twisting into strange expressions, and all at once one of the women was speaking. The language trilled, punctuated by clicks and glottal stops.

And Gruntle understood her.

'*Beast of darkness and fire, hunter in dark and light, fur of night and motion in grasses, god who takes, see this our gift and spare us for we are weak and few and this land is not ours, this land is the journey for we dream of the shore, where food is plenty and the birds cry in the heat of the sun.*'

Gruntle found himself sliding forward, silent as a thought, and he was life and power bound in a single breath. Forward, until the axe blade was at his taloned paws. Head lowering, nostrils flaring as he inhaled the scent of stone and sweat, the edges where old blood remained, where grasses had polished the flint, the urine that had been splashed upon it.

These creatures wanted to claim this glade for their own.

They were begging permission, and maybe something more. Something like . . . *protection.*

'*The leopard tracks us and challenges you,*' the woman sang, '*but she will not cross your path. She will flee your scent for you are the master here, the god, the unchallenged hunter of the forest. Last night, she took my child – we have lost all our children. Perhaps we will be the last. Perhaps we will never find the shore again. But if our flesh must feed the hungry, then let it be you who grows strong with our blood.*

'Tonight, if you come to take one of us, take me. I am the eldest. I bear no more children. I am useless.' She hunched down then, discarding her spear, and sank into the grasses, where she rolled on to her back, exposing her throat.

They were mad, Gruntle decided. Driven insane by the terrors of the jungle, where they were strangers, lost, seeking some distant coastline. And as they journeyed, every night delivered horror.

But this was a dream. From some ancient time. And even if he sought to guide them to the shore they sought, he would awaken long before that journey was completed. Awaken, and so abandon them to their fates. And what if he grew hungry in this next moment? What if his instinct exploded within him, launching him at this hapless female, closing his jaws on her throat?

Was this where the notion of human sacrifice came from? When nature eyed them avid with hunger? When they had naught but sharpened sticks and a smouldering fire to protect them?

He would not kill them this night.

He would find something else to kill. Gruntle set off, into the jungle. A thousand scents filled him, a thousand muted noises whispered in the deep shadows. He carried his massive weight effortlessly, silent as he padded forward. Beneath the canopy the world was dusk and so it would ever remain, yet he saw everything, the flit of a green-winged mantis, the scuttle of woodlice in the humus, the gliding escape of a millipede. He slipped across the path of deer, saw where they had fed on dark-leaved shoots. He passed a rotted log that had been torn apart and pushed aside, the ground beneath ravaged by the questing snouts of boar.

Some time later, with night descending, he found the spoor he had been seeking. Acrid, pungent, both familiar and strange. It was sporadic, proof that the creature that left it was cautious, taking to the trees in its moments of rest.

A female.

He slowed his pace as he tracked the beast. All light was gone now, every colour shifted into hues of grey. If she discovered him she would flee. But then, the only beast that wouldn't was the elephant, and he had no interest in hunting that wise leviathan with its foul sense of humour.

Edging forward, one soft step at a time, he came upon the place where she had made a kill. A wapiti, its panic a bitter breath in the air. The humus scuffed by its tiny hoofs, a smear of blood on curled black leaves. Halting, settling down, Gruntle lifted his gaze.

And found her. She had drawn her prey up on to a thick branch from which lianas depended in a cascade of night blossoms. The wapiti – or what remained of it – was draped across the bole, and she was lying along the branch's length, lambent eyes fixed upon Gruntle.

This leopard was well suited to hunting at night – her coat was black on black, the spots barely discernible.

She regarded him without fear, and this gave Gruntle pause.

A voice then murmured in his skull, sweet and dark. *'Go on your way, Lord. There is not enough to share . . . even if I so desired, which of course I do not.'*

'I have come for you,' Gruntle replied.

Her eyes widened and he saw muscles coiling along her shoulders. *'Do all beasts know riders, then?'*

For a moment Gruntle did not comprehend her question, and then understanding arrived with sudden heat, sudden interest. *'Has your soul travelled far, my lady?'*

'Through time. Through unknown distances. This is where my dreams take me every night. Ever hunting, ever tasting blood, ever shying from the path of the likes of you, Lord.'

'I am summoned by prayer,' Gruntle said, knowing even as he said it that it was the truth, that the half-human creatures he had left behind did indeed call upon him, as if to invite the killer answered some innate refusal of random chance. He was summoned to kill, he realized, to give proof to the notion of fate.

'Curious idea, Lord.'

'Spare them, Lady.'

'Who?'

'You know of whom I speak. In this time, there is but one creature that can voice prayers.'

He sensed wry amusement. *'You are wrong in that. Although the others have no interest in imagining beasts as gods and goddesses.'*

'Others?'

'Many nights away from this place, there are mountains, and in them can be found fastnesses where dwell the K'Chain Che'Malle. There is a vast river that runs to a warm ocean, and on its banks can be found the pit-cities of the Forkrul Assail. There are solitary towers where lone Jaghut live, waiting to die. There are the villages of the Tartheno Toblakai and their tundra-dwelling cousins, the Neph Trell.'

'You know this world far better than I do, Lady.'

'Do you still intend to kill me?'

'Will you cease hunting the half-humans?'

'As you like, but you must know, there are times when this beast has no rider. There are times too, I suspect, when the beast you now ride also hunts alone.'

'I understand.'

She rose from her languid perch, and made her way down the trunk of the tree head first, landing lightly on the soft forest floor. *'Why are they so important to you?'*

'I do not know. Perhaps I pity them.'

'For our kind, Lord, there is no room for pity.'

'I disagree. It is what we can give when we ride the souls of these beasts. Hood knows, it's all we can give.'

'Hood?'

'The God of Death.'

'You come from a strange world, I think.'

Now this was startling. Gruntle was silent for a long moment, and then he asked, *'Where are you from, Lady?'*

'A city called New Morn.'

'I know of a ruin named Morn.'

'My city is no ruin.'

'Perhaps you exist in a time before the coming of Hood.'

'Perhaps.' She stretched, the glow of her eyes thinning to slits. *'I am leaving soon, Lord. If you are here when I do, the beast that remains will not take kindly to your presence.'*

'Oh? And would she be so foolish as to attack me?'

'And die? No. But I would not curse her with terror.'

'Ah, is that pity, then?'

'No, it is love.'

Yes, he could see how one could come to love such magnificent animals, and find the riding of their souls a most precious gift. *'I will go now, Lady. Do you think we will meet again?'*

'It does seem we share the night, Lord.'

She slipped away, and even Gruntle's extraordinary vision failed him from tracking her beyond a few strides. He swung about and padded off in the opposite direction. Yes, he could feel his own grip here weakening, and soon he would return to his own world. That pallid, stale existence, where he lived as if half blind, half deaf, deadened and clumsy.

He allowed himself a deep cough of anger, silencing the unseen denizens on all sides.

Until some brave monkey, high overhead, flung a stick at him. The thump as it struck the ground near his left hind leg made him start and shy away.

From the darkness overhead he heard chittering laughter.

The storm of chaos cavorted into his vision, consuming half the sky with a swirling madness of lead, grainy black and blazing tendrils of argent. He could see the gust front tearing the ground up in a frenzied wall of dust, rocks and dirt, growing ever closer.

Imminent oblivion did not seem so bad, as far as Ditch was concerned. He was being dragged by the chain shackled to his right ankle. Most of his skin had been scraped away – the white bone and cartilage of his remaining elbow, studded with grit, was visible within haloes of red. His knees were larger versions, and the shackle was slowly carving through his ankle and foot bones. He wondered what would happen when that foot was finally torn off – how it would feel. He'd lie there, motionless at last, perhaps watching that shackle tumble and twist and stutter away. He'd be . . . free.

The torment of this existence should not include pain. That was unfair. Of course, most of that pain was fading now – he was too far gone to curl and flinch, to gasp and sob – but the memories remained, like fire in his skull.

Pulled onward over loose stones, their sharp edges rolling up his back, gouging new furrows through the pulped meat, knuckling against the base of his skull to tear away the last few snarls of hair and scalp. And as the chain snagged, only to give and twist him round, he stared again and again upon that storm in their wake.

Songs of suffering from the groaning wagon somewhere ahead, an unending chorus of misery ever drifting back.

Too bad, he reflected, that the huge demon had not found him in the moments following his collapse, had not lifted him to its shoulder – not that it could carry any more than it already had been carrying. But even if it had done little more than drag him to one side, then the edge of the wagon's massive wheel would not have crushed his right arm and shoulder, grinding both into pulp until only threads of gristle were all that held it to his body. After that, all hopes – faint as they had been – of rising again to add his strength to the procession had vanished. He had become yet one more dead weight, dragged in the wake, adding to the suffering of those who trudged on.

Nearby, almost parallel to him, a huge chain sheathed in moss ended in the remnants of a dragon. Wings like tattered sails, spars snapped and dangling, the mostly skinless head dragged behind a shredded neck. When he had first seen it he had been shocked, horrified. Now, each time it came into view, he felt a wave of dread. That such a creature should have failed was proof of the desperate extremity now plaguing them.

Anomander Rake had stopped killing. The legion was failing. Annihilation edged ever closer.

Life fears chaos. It was ever thus. We fear it more than anything else, because it is anathema. Order battles against dissolution. Order negotiates cooperation as a mechanism of survival, on every scale, from a patch of skin to an entire menagerie of interdependent creatures. That cooperation, of course, may not of essence be necessarily peaceful – a minute exchange of failures to ensure greater successes.

Yes, as I am dragged along here, at the very end of my existence, I begin to understand . . .

See me, see this gift of contemplation.

Rake, what have you done?

A calloused hand closed about his remaining arm, lifted him clear of the ground, and he was being carried forward, closer to that crawling wagon.

'There is no point.'

'That,' replied a deep, measured voice, 'is without relevance.'

'I am not worth—'

'Probably not, but I intend to find you room on that wagon.'

Ditch hacked a ragged laugh. 'Just tear my foot off, good sir, and leave me.'

'No. There may be need for you, mage.'

Need? Now that was an absurd thing to say. 'Who are you?'

'Draconus.'

Ditch laughed a second time. 'I looked for you . . . seems centuries ago, now.'

'Now you have found me.'

'I thought you might know a way of escaping. Now, isn't that funny? After all, if you had, you would not still be here, would you?'

'That seems logical.'

An odd reply. 'Draconus.'

'What?'

'Are you a logical man?'

'Not in the least. Now, here we are.'

The sight that greeted Ditch as he was heaved round to face forward was, if anything, even more terrifying than anything else he had witnessed since arriving in the accursed realm of Dragnipur. A wall of bodies, projecting feet jammed amongst staring faces, the occasional arm hanging out, twitching, dripping sweat. Here a knee, there a shoulder. Tangles of sodden hair, fingers with dagger-long nails. Human, demon, Forkrul Assail, K'Chain Che'Malle, others of natures Ditch could not even identify. He saw one hand and forearm that appeared to be made entirely of metal, sockets and hinges and rods and a carapace of iron skin visible in mottled, pitted patches. Worse of all were the staring eyes, peering from faces that seemed to have surrendered every possible expression, leaving behind something slack and dull.

'Make space up top!' bellowed Draconus.

Cries of 'No room!' and 'Nowhere left!' greeted him.

Ignoring such protests, Draconus began climbing the wall of flesh. Faces twisted in rage and pain, eyes widened in affronted disbelief, hands clawed at him or beat him with fists, but the huge warrior was indifferent to all of it. Ditch could feel the man's enormous strength, an implacable certainty to every movement that bespoke something unconquerable. He was awed into silence.

Higher they climbed, and shadows raced in crazed patterns now in the churning glare of the storm, as if the natural gloom of the world clung close to its surface, and here, high above it, the air was clearer, sharper.

The rocking crawl of the wagon below was felt now in the swaying of the wall near the top, a motion groaned out in the slick shifting of flesh and in a wavering song of dull, rhythmic moans and grunts. The wall finally sloped inward, and Ditch was tugged over hummocks of skin, the bodies so tight-packed that the surface beneath him seemed solid, an undulating landscape, sheathed in sweat and flecks of ash and grime. Most of those lying here had settled on their stomachs, as if to stare at the sky – that would vanish for ever as soon as the next body arrived – was too much to bear.

Draconus rolled him into a depression between two backs, one facing one way, the other in the opposite direction. A man, a woman – the sudden contact with the woman's soft flesh as he was wedged against her startled an awakening in Ditch and he cursed.

'Take what you can, mage,' said Draconus.

Ditch heard him leaving.

He could make out distinct voices now, odd nearby sounds. Someone was scrabbling closer and Ditch felt a faint tug on his chain.

'Almost off, then. Almost off.'

Ditch twisted round to see who had spoken.

A Tiste Andii. He was clearly blind, and both sockets bore the terrible scarring of burns – only deliberate torture could be that precise. His legs were gone, stumps visible just below his hips. He was dragging himself up alongside Ditch, and the mage saw that the creature held in one hand a long sharpened bone with a blackened point.

'Plan on killing me?' Ditch asked.

The Tiste Andii paused, lifted his head. Straggly black hair framed a narrow, hollowed-out face. 'What sort of eyes do you have, friend?'

'Working ones.'

A momentary smile, and then he squirmed closer.

Ditch managed to shift round so that his ruined shoulder and arm were beneath him, freeing his undamaged arm. 'It's crazy, but I still intend to defend myself. Though death – if it even exists here – would be a mercy.'

'It doesn't,' replied the Tiste Andii. 'I could stab you for the next thousand years and do nothing more than leave you full of holes. Full of holes.' He paused and the smile flickered once more. 'Yet I must stab you anyway, since you've made a mess of things. A mess, a mess, a mess.'

'I have? Explain.'

'There's no point, unless you have eyes.'

'I have them, you damned fool!'

'But can they *see*?'

He caught the emphasis on the last word. Could he awaken magic here? Could he scrape something from his warren – enough to attenuate his vision? There was nothing to do but try. 'Wait a moment,' he said. Oh, the warren was there, yes, as impervious as a wall – yet he sensed something he had not expected. Cracks, fissures, things bleeding in, bleeding out.

The effects of chaos, he realized. *Gods, it's all breaking down!* Would there be a time, he wondered – an instant, in the very moment that the storm finally struck them – when he would find his warren within reach? Could he escape before he was obliterated along with everyone and everything else?

'How long, how long, how long?' asked the Tiste Andii.

Ditch found he could indeed scrape a residue of power. A few words muttered under his breath, and all at once he saw what had been hidden before – he saw, yes, the flesh he was lying on.

A mass of tattoos blanketed every exposed patch of skin, lines and images crossing from one body to the next, yet nowhere could he see solid areas – all was made up of intricate, delicate traceries, patterns within patterns. He saw borders that dipped and twisted. He saw elongated figures with stretched faces and misshapen torsos. Not a single body atop this massive wagon had been exempted – barring Ditch's own.

The Tiste Andii must have heard his gasp, for he laughed. 'Imagine yourself hovering . . . oh, say fifteen man-heights overhead. Fifteen man-heights. Overhead, overhead. Hovering in the air, just beneath the ceiling of nothingness, the ceiling of nothingness. Looking down upon all this, all this, all this. Aye, it looks awry to you from where you crouch, but from up there, from up there, from up there – you will see no mounds of flesh, no knobs of skin-stretched bones – you'll see no shadows at all – only the scene. The scene, yes, laid flat you'd swear. You'd swear it to every god and goddess you can think of. Flat! Laid flat, laid flat!'

Ditch struggled to comprehend what he was seeing – he did not dare attempt what the Tiste Andii had suggested, fearing the effort would drive him mad; no, he would not try to imagine himself plucked free of his flesh, his soul floating somewhere overhead. It was difficult enough to comprehend the obsession of this creation – a creation by a blind man. 'You've been up here for a long time,' Ditch finally said. 'Avoiding getting buried.'

'Yes and yes. I was among the first on the wagon. Among the first. Murdered by Draconus, because I sought to wrest Dragnipur from him – oh, Anomandaris Purake was not the first to try. I was. I was. I was. And if I had won the sword, why, my first victim would have been Anomandaris himself. Is that not a bitter joke, friend? It is, it is.'

'But this' – Ditch gestured with his one hand – 'it has to be a recent effort—'

'No, only the last layer, the last layer, the last layer.'

'What – what do you use for ink?'

'Clever question! From the wagon bloodwood, blackwood, the pitch and the pitch ever leaking out, ever sweating from the grain.'

'Could I hover high up, as you say,' asked Ditch, 'what scene would I see?'

'Wanderings, Holds, Houses, every god, every goddess, every spirit worth mentioning. Demon kings and demon queens. Dragons and Elders – oh, all there, all there. All there. Is this where you mean to stay, friend? Is this where you mean to stay?'

Ditch thought of this creature hunkered up against him, that bone needle pricking his skin. 'No. I plan on crawling round, as much as I can, never stopping. Leave me out of your scene.'

'You cannot do that! You will ruin everything!'

'Imagine me invisible, then. Imagine I don't even exist – I will stay out of your way.'

The sightless eyes were glistening and the Tiste Andii was shaking his head again and again.

'You will not have me,' Ditch said. 'Besides, it will all be ending soon.'

'Soon? How soon? How soon? How soon? How soon?'

'The storm looks to be no more than a league behind us.'

'If you will not join the scene,' the Tiste Andii said, 'I will push you off.'

'Draconus might not like that.'

'He will understand. He understands more than you, more than you, more and more and more than you!'

'Just let me rest,' said Ditch, 'for a while. I will then climb back down. I don't want to be up here when the end comes. I want to be standing. Facing the storm.'

'Do you really imagine the ritual will awaken all at once? Do you do you do you? The flower opens soon, but the night is long, and it will take that long, that long. For the flower to open. Open in the moment before dawn. Open in the moment. Draconus chose you – a mage – for the nexus. I need the nexus. You are the nexus. Lie there, be quiet, don't move.'

'No.'

'I cannot wait long, friend. Crawl about now if you like, but I cannot wait too long. A league away!'

'What is your name?' Ditch asked.

'What matter any of that?'

'For when I next speak to Draconus.'

'He knows me.'

'I don't.'

'I am Kadaspala, brother to Enesdia who was wife to Andarist.'

Andarist. That's one name I recognize. 'You wanted to murder the brother of your sister's husband?'

'I did. For what he did to them, what he did to them. For what he did to them!'

Ditch stared at the anguish in the man's ravaged face. 'Who blinded you, Kadaspala?'

'It was a gift. A mercy. I did not comprehend the truth of that, not the real truth of it, the real truth. No. Besides, I thought my inner sight would be enough – to challenge Draconus. To steal Dragnipur. I was wrong, wrong. I was wrong. The truth is a gift, a mercy.'

'Who blinded you?'

The Tiste Andii flinched, then seemed to curl into himself. Tears glistened in the pits of his sockets. 'I blinded myself,' Kadaspala whispered. 'When I saw what he'd done. What he'd done. To his brother. To my sister. To my sister.'

Suddenly, Ditch did not want to ask any more questions of this man. He pushed himself from between the two bodies. 'I am going to . . . explore.'

'Come back, mage. Nexus. Come back. Come back.'

We'll see.

With all this time to reflect on things, Apsal'ara concluded that her biggest mistake was not in finding her way into Moon's Spawn. Nor in discovering the vaults and the heaps of magicked stones, ensorcelled weapons, armour, the blood-dipped idols and reliquaries from ten thousand extinct cults. No, her greatest error in judgement had been in trying to stab Anomander Rake in the back.

He'd been amused at finding her. He'd not spoken of executing her, or even chaining in her some deep crypt for all eternity. He'd simply asked her how she had managed to break in. Curiosity, more than a little wonder, perhaps even some admiration. And then she went and tried to kill him.

The damned sword had been out of its scabbard faster than an eye-blink, the deadly edge slicing across her belly even as she lunged with her obsidian dagger.

Such stupidity. But lessons only became lessons when one has reached the state of humility required to heed them. When one is past all the egotistical excuses and explanations flung up to fend off honest culpability. It was nature to attack first, abjuring all notions of guilt and shame. Lash out, white with rage, then strut away convinced of one's own righteousness.

She had long since left such imbecilic posturing behind. A journey of enlightenment, and it had begun with her last mortal breath, as she found herself lying on the hard stone floor, looking up into the eyes of Anomander Rake, and seeing his dismay, his regret, his sorrow.

She could feel the growing heat of the storm, could feel its eternal hunger. Not long now, and then all her efforts would be for naught. The kinks of the chain finally showed some wear, but not enough, not nearly enough. She would be destroyed along with everyone else. She was not unique. She was, in fact, no different from every other idiot who'd tried to kill Rake, or Draconus.

The rain trickling down from the wagon bed was warmer than usual, foul with sweat, blood and worse. It streamed over her body. Her skin had been wet for so long it was coming away in ragged pieces, white with death, revealing raw red meat underneath. She was rotting.

The time was coming when she would have to drop down once more, emerge from under the wagon, and see for herself the arrival of oblivion. There would be no pity in its eyes – not that it had any – just the indifference that was the other face of the universe, the one all would have for ever turned away. The regard of chaos was the true source of terror – all the rest were but flavours, variations.

I was a child once. I am certain of it. A child. I have a memory, one memory of that time. On a barren bank of a broad river. The sky was blue perfection. The caribou were crossing the river, in their tens and tens of thousands.

I remember their up-thrust heads. I remember seeing the weaker ones crowded in, pushed down to vanish in the murky water. These carcasses would wash up down current, where the short-nosed bears and the wolves and eagles and ravens waited for them. But I stood with others. Father, mother, perhaps sisters and brothers – just others – my eyes on the vast herd.

Their seasonal migration, and this was but one of many places of crossing. The caribou often choose different paths. Still, the river had to be crossed, and the beasts would mill for half a morning on the bank, until they plunged into the current, until all at once they were flooding the river, a surging tide of hide and flesh, of breaths drawn in and gusted out.

Not even the beasts display eagerness when accosting the inevitable, when it seems numbers alone can possibly confuse fate, and so each life strikes, strives out into the icy flow. 'Save me.' That is what is written in their eyes. 'Save me above all the others. Save me, so that I may live. Give me this moment, this day, this season. I will follow the laws of my kind . . .'

She remembered that one moment when she was a child, and she remembered her sense of awe in witnessing the crossing, in that force of nature, that imposition of will, its profound implacability. She remembered, too, the terror she had felt.

Caribou are not just caribou. The crossing is not just this crossing. The caribou are all life. The river is the passing world. Life swims through, riding the current, swims, drowns, triumphs. Life can ask questions. Life – some of it – can even ask: how is it that I can ask anything at all? And: how is it that I believe that answers answer anything worthwhile? What value this exchange, this precious dialogue, when the truth is unchanged, when some live for a time while others drown, when in the next season there are new caribou while others are for ever gone?

The truth is unchanged.

Each spring, in the time of crossing, the river is in flood. Chaos swirls beneath the surface. It is the worst time.

Watch us.

The child had not wanted to see. The child had wailed and fled inland. Brothers and sisters pursued, laughing maybe, not understanding her fear, her despair. Someone pursued, anyway. Laughing, unless it was the river that laughed, and it was the herd of caribou that surged up from the bank and lunged forward, driving the watchers to scatter, shouting their surprise. Perhaps that was what had made her run. She wasn't sure.

The memory ended with her panic, her cries, her confusion.

Lying on the crossbeam, the wood sweating beneath her, Apsal'ara felt like that child once again. The season was coming. The river awaited her, in fullest flood, and she was but one among many, praying for fate's confusion.

A hundred stones flung into a pond will shatter the smooth surface, will launch a clash of ripples and waves until the eye loses all sense of order in what it sees. And this discordant moment perturbs the self, awakens unease in the spirit and leaves one restive. So it was that morning in Darujhistan. Surfaces had been shattered. People moved and every move betrayed agitation. People spoke and they were abrupt in their speech and they were short with others, strangers and dear ones alike.

A squall of rumours rode the turgid currents, and some held more truth than others, but all of them hinted of something unpleasant, something unwelcome and disorderly. Such sensibilities can grip a city and hold tight for days, sometimes weeks, sometimes for ever. Such sensibilities could spread like a plague to infect an entire nation, an entire people, leaving them habituated in their anger, perpetually belligerent, inclined to cruelty and miserly with their compassion.

Blood had been spilled in the night. More corpses than usual had been found in the morning, a score or more of them in the Estates District, delivering a thunderous shock to the coddled highborn citizens in their walled homes. Spurred by frantic demands for investigation, the City Guard brought in court mages to conduct magical examinations. Before long a new detail was whispered that widened eyes, that made citizens gasp. *Assassins! One and all – the Guild has been devastated!* And, following this, on a few faces, a sly smile of pleasure – quickly hidden or saved for private moments, since one could never be too careful. Still, the evil killers had clearly taken on someone nastier than them, and had paid for it with dozens of lives.

Some then grew somewhat more thoughtful – oh, they were rare enough to make one, well, depressed. None the less, for these there followed a rather ominous question: *precisely who is in this city who can with impunity cut down a score of deadly assassins?*

As chaotic as that morning was, what with official carriages and corpse-wagons rattling this way and that; with squads of guards and crowds of gawping onlookers and the hawkers who descended among them with sweetened drinks and sticky candies and whatnot; with all this, none made note of the closed, boarded-up K'rul's Bar with its freshly washed walls and flushed gutters.

It was just as well.

Krute of Talient stepped into his squalid room and saw Rallick Nom slouched in a chair. Grunting, Krute walked over to the niche that passed for a kitchen and set down the burlap sack with its load of vegetables, fruit and wrapped fish. 'Not seen you much of late,' he said.

'It's a foolish war,' Rallick Nom said without looking up.

'I'm sure Seba Krafar agrees with you this morning. They struck, in what they must have imagined was overwhelming force, only to get mauled. If this keeps up Seba will be Master in a Guild of one.'

'You sound foul of mood, Krute. Why does it matter to you that Seba is making mistakes?'

'Because I gave my life to the Guild, Rallick.' Krute stood with a turnip in one hand. After a moment he flung it into the basket beside the cask of fresh water. 'He's single-handedly destroying it. True, he'll be gone soon enough, but what will be left by then?'

Rallick rubbed at his face. 'Everyone's mood is sour these days, it seems.'

'What are we waiting for?'

Krute could not long hold Rallick's gaze when the assassin finally looked at him. There was something so . . . remorseless in those cold eyes, in that hard face that seemed carved to refute for ever the notion of a smile. A face that could not soften, could not relax into anything human. No wonder he'd been Vorcan's favourite.

Krute fidgeted with the food he'd purchased. 'You hungry?' he asked.

'What did you have in mind?'

'Fish stew.'

'In a few bells it'll be hot enough outside to melt lead.'

'That's what I'm cooking, Rallick.'

Sighing, the assassin rose and stretched. 'Think I'll take a walk instead.'

'As you like.'

At the door Rallick paused and glanced over, his expression suddenly wry. 'It wears off, doesn't it?'

Krute frowned. 'What does?'

Rallick did not reply, and moments later he was gone, the door closing behind him.

'What does?' Did I have any reason there to be so obtuse? Must have, though

*I can't think of one right now. Maybe just . . . instinctive. Yes, Rallick Nom, it
wears off. Fast.*

   *Things were easier before – should have recognized that back then. Should
have liked things just fine. Should have stopped gnawing.*

On her hands and knees, Thordy rubbed the ashes into the spaces between the set
stones, into every crack and fissure, every groove scoring the vaguely flat surfaces. Tiny bits of bone rolled under her fingertips. No ash was perfect unless it
came from nothing but wood, and this ash was made of more things than just
wood. The dry season had, she hoped, finally arrived. Otherwise she might have
to do this all over again, to keep the glyphs hidden, the pleasant, beautiful glyphs
with all the promises they whispered to her.

   She heard the back door swing open on its leather hinges and knew Gaz was
standing on the threshold, eyes hooded, watching her. His fingerless hands twitching at the ends of his arms, the ridge of knuckles marred and bright red, teeth-cut
and bone-gouged.

   He killed people every night, she knew, to keep from killing her. She was, she
knew, the cause of their deaths. Every one of them a substitute for what Gaz really wanted to do.

   She heard him step outside.

   Straightening, wiping the ash from her hands on her apron, she turned.

   'Breakfast leavings,' he muttered.

   'What?'

   'The house is full of flies,' he said, standing there as if struck rooted by the
sunlight. Red-shot eyes wandered about the yard as if wanting to crawl out from
his head and find shelter. Beneath that rock, or the bleached plank of grey wood,
or under the pile of kitchen scraps.

   'You need a shave,' she said. 'Want me to heat the water?'

   The haunted eyes flicked towards her – but there was nowhere to hide in that
direction, so he looked away once more. 'No, don't touch me.'

   She thought of holding the razor in her hand, settling its edge against his
throat. Seeing the runnels winding down through the lathered soap, the throb of
his pulse. 'Well,' she said, 'the beard hides how thin you've become. In the face,
anyway.'

   His smile was a threat. 'And you prefer that, wife?'

   'It's just different, Gaz.'

   'You can't prefer anything when you don't care, right?'

   'I didn't say that.'

   'You didn't have to. Why'd you make that stone thing – right there on the best
dirt?'

   'I just felt like it,' she replied. 'A place to sit and rest. Where I can keep an eye
on all the vegetables.'

   'In case they run away?'

   'No. I just like looking at them, that's all.' *They don't ask questions. They don't ask for much of anything at all. A few dribbles of water, maybe. A clear path to the sun, free of any weeds.*

They don't get suspicious. They don't think about murdering me.

'Have supper ready for dusk,' Gaz said, lurching into motion.

She watched him leave. Gritty ash made black crescents of her fingernails, as if she had been rooting through the remnants of a pyre. Which was appropriate, because she had, but Gaz didn't need to know things like that. He didn't need to know anything at all.

Be a plant, Gaz. Worry about nothing. Until the harvest.

The ox was too stupid to worry. If not for a lifetime of back-breaking labour and casual abuse, the beast would be content, existence a smooth cycle to match the ease of day into night and night into day and on and on for ever. Feed and cud aplenty, water to drink and salt to lick, a plague to eradicate the world's biting flies and ticks and fleas. If the ox could dream of paradise, it would be a simple dream and a simple paradise. To live simply was to evade the worries that came with complexity. This end was achieved at the expense, alas, of intelligence.

The drunks that staggered out of the taverns as the sun rose were in search of paradise and they had the sodden, besotted brains to prove it. Lying senseless in the durhang and d'bayang dens could be found others oozing down a similar path. The simplicity they would find was of course death, the threshold crossed almost without effort.

Unmindful (naturally) of any irony, the ox pulled a cart into an alley behind the dens where three emaciated servants brought out this night's crop of wasted corpses. The carter, standing with a switch to one side, spat out a mouthful of rustleaf juice and silently gestured to another body lying in the gutter behind a back door. In for a sliver, in for a council. Grumbling, the three servants went over to this corpse and reached for limbs to lift it from the cobblestones. One then gasped and recoiled, and a moment later so too did the others.

The ox was not flicked into motion for some time thereafter, as humans rushed about, as more arrived. It could smell the death, but it was used to that. There was much confusion, yet the yoked beast remained an island of calm, enjoying the shade of the alley.

The city guardsman with the morning ache in his chest brushed a hand along the ox's broad flank as he edged past. He crouched down to inspect the corpse.

Another one, this man beaten so badly he was barely recognizable as human. Not a single bone in his face was left unbroken. The eyes were pulped. Few teeth remained. The blows had continued, down to his crushed throat – which was the likely cause of death – and then his chest. Whatever weapon had been used left short, elongated patterns of mottled bruising. Just like all the others.

The guardsman rose and faced the three servants from the dens. 'Was he a customer?'

Three blank faces regarded him, then one spoke, 'How in Hood's name can we tell? His damned face is gone!'

'Clothing? Weight, height, hair colour – anyone in there last—'

'Sir,' cut in the man, 'if he was a customer he was a new one – he's got meat on his bones, see? And his clothes was clean. Well, before he spilled hisself.'

The guardsman had made the same observations. 'Might he have been, then? A new customer?'

'Ain't been none in the last day or so. Some casuals, you know, the kind who can take it or leave it, but no, we don't think we seen this one, by his clothes and hair and such.'

'So what was he doing in this alley?'

No one had an answer.

Did the guardsman have enough to requisition a necromancer? *Only if this man was well born. But the clothes aren't that high-priced. More like merchant class, or some mid-level official. If so, then what was he doing here in the dregs of Gadrobi District?* 'He's Daru,' he mused.

'We get 'em,' said the loquacious servant, with a faint sneer. 'We get Rhivi, we get Callowan, we get Barghast even.'

Yes, misery is egalitarian. 'Into the cart, then, with the others.'

The servants set to work.

The guardsman watched. After a moment his gaze drifted to the carter. He studied the wizened face with its streaks of rustleaf juice running down the stubbled chin. 'Got a loving woman back home?'

'Eh?'

'I imagine that ox is happy enough.'

'Oh, aye, that it is, sir. All the flies, see, they prefer the big sacks.'

'The what?'

The carter squinted at him, then stepped closer. 'The bodies, sir. Big sacks, I call 'em. I done studies and lots of thinking, on important things. On life and stuff. What makes it work, what happens when it stops and all.'

'Indeed. Well—'

'Every body in existence, sir, is made up of the same stuff. So small you can't see except with a special lens but I made me one a those. Tiny, that stuff. I call 'em *bags*. And inside each bag there's a wallet, floating in the middle like. And I figure that in that wallet there's notes.'

'I'm sorry, did you say notes?'

A quick nod, a pause to send out a stream of brown juice. 'With all the details of that body written on 'em. Whether it's a dog or a cat or a green-banded nose-worm. Or a person. And things like hair colour and eye colour and other stuff – all written on those notes in that wallet in that bag. They're instructions, you see, telling the bag what kind of bag it's supposed to be. Some bags are liver bags, some are skin, some are brain, some are lungs. And it's the mother and the father that sew up them bags, when they make themselves a baby. They sew 'em up, you see, with half and half, an' that's why brats share looks from both ma and da. Now this 'ere ox, it's got bags too that look pretty much the same, so's I been thinking of sewing its half with a human half – wouldn't that be something?'

'Something, good sir, likely to get you run out of the city – if you weren't stoned to death first.'

The carter scowled. 'That's the probbem wi' the world then, ain't it? No sense of adventure!'

'I have a very important meeting.'

Iskaral Pust, still wearing his most ingratiating smile, simply nodded.

Sordiko Qualm sighed. 'It is official Temple business.'

He nodded again.

'I do not desire an escort.'

'You don't need one, High Priestess,' said Iskaral Pust. 'You shall have me!' And then he tilted his head and licked his lips. 'Won't she just! Hee hee! And she'll see that with me she'll have more than she ever believed possible! Why, I shall be a giant walking penis!'

'You already are,' said Sordiko Qualm.

'Are? Are what, dearest? We should get going, lest we be late!'

'Iskaral Pust, I don't want you with me.'

'You're just saying that, but your eyes tell me different.'

'What's in my eyes,' she replied, 'could see me dangling on High Gallows. Assuming, of course, the entire city does not launch into a spontaneous celebration upon hearing of your painful death, and set me upon a throne of solid gold in acclamation.'

'What is she going on about? No one knows I'm even here! And why would I want a gold throne? Why would she, when she can have *me*?' He licked his lips again, and then revised his smile. 'Lead on, my love. I promise to be most officious in this official meeting. After all, I am the Magus of the House of Shadow. Not a mere High Priest, but a Towering Priest! A Looming Priest! I shall venture no opinions of whatever, unless invited to, of course. No, I shall be stern and wise and leave all the jabbering to my sweet underling.' He ducked and added, 'With whom I shall be underlinging very shortly!'

Her hands twitched oddly, most fetchingly, in fact, and then surrender cascaded in her lovely eyes, thus providing Iskaral Pust with the perfect image to resurrect late at night under his blankets with Mogora snoring through all the spider balls filled with eggs lodged up her nose.

'You will indeed be silent, Iskaral Pust. The one with whom I must speak does not tolerate fools, and I will make no effort to intercede should you prove fatally obnoxious.' She paused and shook her head. 'Then again, I cannot imagine you being anything but obnoxious. Perhaps I should retract my warning, in the hope that you will give such offence as to see you instantly obliterated. Whereupon I can then evict those foul bhokarala and your equally foul wife.' Sudden surprise. 'Listen to me! Those thoughts were meant to be private! Yours is a most execrable influence, Iskaral Pust.'

'Soon we shall be as peas in a pod! Those spiny, sharp pods that stick to everything, especially crotch hair if one is forced to wee in the bushes.' He reached out for her. 'Hand in hand gliding down the streets!'

She seemed to recoil, but of course that was only his delicate and fragile self-esteem and its niggling worries, quickly buried beneath the plastering of yet another ingratiating smile on his face.

They escaped the temple through a little used side postern gate, slamming it shut just in time to avoid the squall of bhokarala excitedly pursuing them down the corridor.

Wretched sunshine in the streets, Sordiko Qualm seemingly indifferent to such atmospheric disregard – why, not a single cloud in sight! Worse than Seven Cities, with not a crevasse to be found anywhere.

Miserable crowds to thread through, a sea of ill-tempered faces snapping round at the gentle prod of his elbows and shoulders as he hurried to keep pace with the long-legged High Priestess. 'Long legs, yes! Ooh. Ooh ooh ooh. Look at them scythe, see the waggle of those delicious—'

'Quiet!' she hissed over a shapely shoulder.

'Shadowthrone understood. Yes he did. He saw the necessity of our meeting, her and me. The consummation of Shadow's two most perfect mortals. The fated storybook love – the lovely innocent woman – but not too innocent, one hopes – and the stalwart man with his brave smile and warm thews. Er, brave thews and warm smile. Is "thews" even the right word? Muscled arms and such, anyway. Why, I am a mass of muscles, am I not? I can even make my ears flex, when the need presents itself – no point in showing off. She despises the strutting type, being delicate and all. And soon—'

'Watch that damned elbow, runt!'

'And soon the glory will be delivered unto us—'

'—a damned apology!'

'What?'

A hulking oaf of a man was forcing himself into Iskaral Pust's path, his big flat face looking like something one found at the bottom of a nightsoil bucket. 'I said I expect a damned apology, y'damned toad-faced ferret!'

Iskaral Pust snorted. 'Oh, look, a hulking oaf of a man with a big flat face looking like something one finds at the bottom of a nightsoil bucket wants *me* to apologize! And I will, good sir, as soon as you apologize for your oafishness and your bucket-face – in fact, apologize for existing!'

The enormous apish hand that reached for his throat was so apish that it barely possessed a thumb, or so Iskaral Pust would later report to his wide-eyed murmuring audience of bhokarala.

Naturally, he ignored that hand and did some reaching out of his own, straight into the oaf's crotch, where he squeezed and yanked back and forth and tugged and twisted, even as the brute folded up with a whimper and collapsed like a sack of melons on to the filthy cobbles, where he squirmed most pitifully.

Iskaral Pust stepped over him and hurried to catch up to Sordiko Qualm, who seemed to have increased her pace, her robes veritably flying out behind her.

'The rudeness of some people!' Iskaral Pust gasped.

They arrived at the gates of a modest estate close to Hinter's Tower. The gates were locked and Sordiko Qualm tugged on a braided rope, triggering chiming from somewhere within.

They waited.

Chains rattled on the other side of the gates, and a moment later the solid doors creaked open, streams of rust drifting down from the hinges.

'Not many visitors, I take it?'

'From this moment on,' said Sordiko Qualm, 'you will be silent, Iskaral Pust.'

'I will?'

'You will.'

Whoever had opened the gates seemed to be hiding behind one of them, and the High Priestess strode in without any further ceremony. Iskaral Pust rushed in behind her to avoid being locked out, as both gates immediately began closing. As soon as he was clear he turned to upbraid the rude servant. And saw, working a lever to one side, a Seguleh.

'Thank you, Therule,' said Sordiko. 'Is the Lady in the garden?'

There was no reply.

The High Priestess nodded and walked on, along a winding path through an overgrown, weedy courtyard, its walls covered in wisteria in full bloom. Sordiko paused upon seeing a large snake coiled in the sun on the path, then edged carefully round it.

Iskaral crept after her, eyes on the nasty creature as it lifted its wedge-shaped head, tongue flicking out in curiosity or maybe hunger. He hissed at it as he passed and was pleased at its flinch.

The estate's main house was small, elegant in a vaguely feminine way. Arched pathways went round it on both sides, vine-webbed tunnels blissfully draped in shadows. The High Priestess chose one and continued on towards the back.

As they drew closer they heard the murmur of voices.

The centre of the back garden was marked by a flagstone clearing in which stood a dozen full-sized bronze statues in a circle facing inward. Each statue wept water from its oddly shielded face down into the ringed trough it stood in, where water flowed ankle deep. The statues, Iskaral Pust saw with faint alarm as they drew closer, were of Seguleh, and the water that fell down did so from beneath masks sheathed in moss and verdigris. In the middle of the circle was a thin-legged, quaint table of copper and two chairs. In the chair facing them sat a man with long grey hair. There was blood-spatter on his plain shirt. A woman was seated with her back to them. Long, lustrous black hair shimmered, contrasting perfectly with the white linen of her blouse.

Upon seeing Sordiko Qualm and Iskaral Pust the man rose and bowed to his host. 'Milady, until next time.'

A second, sketchier bow to the High Priestess and Iskaral, and then he was walking past.

Sordiko Qualm entered the circle and positioned herself to the right of the now vacated chair. To Iskaral Pust's astonishment (and, a moment later, delight) she curtsied before her host. 'Lady Envy.'

'Do sit, my love,' Lady Envy replied. Then, as Iskaral Pust hovered into view, seeing at last her exquisite face, so perfect a match to that lovely hair, and the poise of her, er, pose, there in that spindly chair with her legs crossed revealing the underside of one shapely thigh just begging for a caress, she scowled and said, 'Perhaps I should get a sandbox installed for your foundling, High Priestess? Somewhere to play and soak up his drool.'

'We would, alas, have to bury him in it.'

'Interesting suggestion.'

Therule then arrived with another chair. The similarity between him and the statues was somewhat disquieting, and Iskaral Pust shivered as he quickly bowed to Lady Envy then perched himself on the chair.

'Her beauty challenges even that of the High Priestess! Why, imagine the two of them—'

'Iskaral Pust!' snapped Sordiko Qualm. 'I did instruct you to be quiet, did I not?'

'But I said nothing, my love! Nothing at all!'

'I am not your love, nor will I ever be.'

He smiled, and then said, 'I will play these two beauties off one another, driving both to spasms of jealousy with my charm, as it slides so easily from one to the other. Pluck here, brush there! Oh, this will be such a delight!'

'I am of a mind to kill him,' said Lady Envy to Sordiko Qualm.

'Alas, he is the Magus of Shadow.'

'You cannot be serious!'

'Oh yes!' cried Iskaral Pust. 'She is! Furthermore, it is most propitious that I am here, for I know something you do not!'

'Oh, goodness,' sighed Lady Envy. 'A beautiful morning thus shattered into ruin.'

'Who was he?' Iskaral demanded. 'That man who was here? Who was he?'

'Why should I tell you that?'

'In exchange – you satisfy my curiosity and I yours – and so we shall satisfy each other and how do you like that, Sordiko Qualm? Hah!'

Lady Envy rubbed at her temples for a moment, as if overwhelmed, and then said. 'That was the bard, Fisher kel Tath. A most unusual man. He . . . invites confession. There have been dire events in the city—'

'None so dire as what I would tell you!' said Iskaral Pust.

And now Sordiko was rubbing at her own brow.

'It's working!'

Lady Envy eyed him. 'If I grant you this exchange, Magus, will you then restrain yourself, thus permitting the High Priestess and me to conduct our conversation?'

'My restraint is guaranteed, Lady Envy. Of course, I make this promise only if you do the same.'

'Whatever do you mean?'

'Lady Envy, I arrived on a ship.'

'What of it?'

'A ship owned by a most delicious woman—'

'Oh, not another one!' moaned Sordiko Qualm.

'The poor thing,' said Lady Envy.

'Hardly.' Iskaral Pust leaned back in his chair, tilting it up on its legs so that his view could encompass both women. 'How I dream of such moments as this! See how they hang on my every word! I have them, I have them!'

'What is wrong with this man, High Priestess?'

'I could not begin to tell you.'

Iskaral Pust examined has hands, his fingernails – but that made him slightly nauseous, since the bhokarala were in the habit of sucking on his fingertips when he slept at night, leaving them permanently wrinkled, mangled and decidedly unpleasant, so he looked away, casually, and found himself staring at Therule, which wasn't a good idea either, so, over there, at that flower – safe enough, he supposed – until it was time at last to meet Lady Envy's extraordinary eyes. 'Yes,' he drawled, 'I see the similarity at last, although you were the victor in the war of perfection. Not by much, but triumphant none the less and for that I can only applaud and admire and all that. In any case, resident even at this very moment, on the ship, in the harbour, is none other than your beloved sister, Spite!'

'I thought so!' Lady Envy was suddenly on her feet, trembling in her ... excitement?

Iskaral Pust sniggered. 'Yes, I play at this until they play no more, and all truths are revealed, as sensibilities are rocked back and forth, as shock thunders through the cosmos, as the shadows themselves explode into all existence! For am I not the Magus of Shadow? Oh, but I am, I am!' He then leaned forward with an expression of gravid dismay. 'Are you not delighted, Lady Envy? Shall I hasten to her to forward your invitation to visit this wondrous garden? Instruct me as your servant, please! Whatever you wish, I will do! Of course I won't! I'll do whatever I want to. Let her think otherwise – maybe it'll bring some colour back to her face, maybe it'll calm the storm in her eyes, maybe it'll stop the water in this trough from boiling – impressive detail, by the way, now, what should I say next?'

Sordiko Qualm and Lady Envy never did get to their conversation that day.

Grainy-eyed and exhausted, Cutter went in search of somewhere to eat breakfast. Once his belly was full, he'd head back to the Phoenix Inn and collapse on his bed upstairs. This was the extent of his tactical prowess and even achieving that had been a struggle. He would be the last man to downplay the extraordinary variety of paths a life could take, and there were few blessings he could derive from having come full circle – from his journey and the changes wrought in himself between the Darujhistan of old and this new place – and yet the contrast with the fate that had taken Challice Vidikas had left him numbed, disorientated and feeling lost.

He found an empty table on the half-courtyard restaurant facing Borthen Park, an expensive establishment that reminded him he was fast running out of coin, and sat waiting for one of the servers to take note of him. The staff were Rhivi one and all, three young women dressed in some new obscure fashion characterized by long swishing skirts of linen streaked in indigo dye, and tight black leather vests with nothing underneath. Their hair was bound up in knotted braids, revealing bisected clam-shells stitched over their ears. While this latter affectation was quaint the most obvious undesirable effect was that twice one of the servers sauntered past him and did not hear his attempts to accost her. He resolved to stick out a leg the next time, then was shocked at such an ungracious impulse.

At last he caught the attention of one of them and she approached. 'A pot of tea, please, and whatever you're serving for breakfast.'

Seeing his modest attire, she glanced away as she asked, in a bored tone, 'Fruit breakfast or meat breakfast? Eggs? Bread? Honey? What kind of tea – we have twenty-three varieties.'

He frowned up at her. 'Er, you decide.'

'Excuse me?'

'What did you have this morning?'

'Flatcakes, of course. What I always have.'

'Do you serve those here?'

'Of course not.'

'What kind of tea did you drink?'

'I didn't. I drank beer.'

'Rhivi custom?'

'No,' she replied, still looking away, 'it's my way of dealing with the excitement of my day.'

'Gods below, just bring me something. Meat, bread, honey. No fancy rubbish with the tea, either.'

'Fine,' she snapped, flouncing off in a billow of skirts.

Cutter squeezed the bridge of his nose in an effort to fend off a burgeoning headache. He didn't want to think about the night just past, the bell after bell spent in that graveyard, sitting on that stone bench with Challice all too close by his side. Seeing, as the dawn's light grew, what the handful of years had done to her, the lines of weariness about her eyes, the lines bracketing her mouth, the maturity revealed in a growing heaviness, her curves more pronounced than they had once been. The child he had known was still there, he told himself, beneath all of that. In the occasional gesture, in the hint of a soft laugh at one point. No doubt she saw the same in him – the layers of hardness, the vestiges of loss and pain, the residues of living.

He was not the same man. She was not the same woman. Yet they had sat as if they had once known each other. As if they were old friends. Whatever childish hopes and vain ambitions had sparked the space between them years ago, they were deftly avoided, even as their currents coalesced into something romantic, something oddly nostalgic.

It had been the lively light ever growing in her eyes that most disturbed Cutter, especially since he had felt his own answering pleasure – in the hazy reminiscences they had played with, in the glow lifting between them on that bench that had nothing to do with the rising sun.

There was nothing right about any of this. She was married, after all. She was nobility – but no, that detail was without relevance, for what she had proposed had nothing to do with matters of propriety, was in no way intended to invite public scrutiny.

She is bored. She wants a lover. She wants what she could have had but didn't take. A second chance, that's what she wants.

Do second chances even exist?

This would be . . . sordid. Despicable. How could he even contemplate such a thing?

Maybe Apsalar saw all too well. Saw right into me, to the soul that was less than it should have been, to the will that was weak. I do not stand before a woman, do I? No, I fall into her arms. I change shape to fit each one, to make things snug, as if matching their dreams is the only path I know into their hearts.

Maybe she was right to walk away.

Was this all that Challice wanted? An amusing diversion to alleviate the drudgery of her comfortable life? He admitted to some suspicion that things were not that simple. There had been a darker current, as if to take him meant something more to Challice. Proof of her own descent, perhaps. Her own fall. Or something else, something even more pernicious.

The Rhivi server had brought him a pot of tea, a plate of fresh bread, a dipping jar of honey, and a bowl of diced fruit. He now stared at the array on the table in front of him, trying without success to recall the moment it had all arrived.

'I need you,' she had said, the words cutting through his exhaustion as the sky began to show its colour. 'Crokus. Cutter. Whatever name you want. I knew it the moment I saw you. I had been walking, most of the night, just walking. I didn't know it, but I was looking for someone. My life's become a question that I thought no one could answer. Not my husband, not anyone. And then, there you were, standing in this cemetery, like a ghost.'

Oh, he knew about ghosts, the way they could haunt one day and night. The way they found places to hide in one's own soul. Yes, he knew about ghosts. 'Challice—'

'You loved me once. But I was young. A fool. Now, I am neither young nor a fool. This time, I won't turn away.'

'Your husband—'

'Doesn't care what I do, or with whom I do it.'

'Why did you marry him then?'

She had looked away, and it was some time before she replied. 'When he saved my life, that night in the garden of Simtal's estate, it was as if he then owned it. My life. He owned it because he saved it. He wasn't alone in believing that, either. So did I. All at once, it was as if I no longer had any choice. He possessed my future, to do with as he pleased.'

'Your father—'

'Should have counselled me?' She laughed, but it was a bitter laugh. 'You didn't see it, but I was spoiled. I was obnoxious, Crokus. Maybe he tried, I don't really recall. But I think he was happy to see me go.'

No, this was not the Challice he had known.

'House Vidikas owns an annexe, a small building down by the docks. It's almost never used. There are two levels. On the main floor it's just storage, filled with the shipwright's leavings after the trader boat was finished. On the upper level is where the man lived while under contract. I've . . . seen it, and I have a key.'

Seen it? He wondered at her hesitation in that admission. But not for long. *She's used it before. She's using it still. For trysts just like the one she's talking about right now. Challice, why are you bothering with me?*

At his hesitation she leaned closer, one hand on his arm. 'We can just meet there, Crokus. To talk. A place where we can talk about anything, where there's no chance of being seen. We can just talk.'

He knew, of course, that such a place was not for talking.

And, this evening, he would meet her there.

What was he— 'Ow!'

The server had just cuffed him in the side of the head. Astonished, he stared up at her.

'If I go to all that work to make you a damned breakfast, you'd better eat it!'

'Sorry! I was just thinking—'

'It's easier when you're chewing. Now, don't make me have to come back here.'

He glared at her as she walked away. *If I was nobleborn she'd never have done that.* He caught the eye of a man sitting at a nearby table.

'You have a way with women, I see.'

'Hah hah.'

Events and moments can deliver unexpected mercy, and though she did not know it, such mercy was granted to Scillara at that instant, for she was not thinking of Cutter. Instead, she was sitting beside the Malazan historian, Duiker, fighting an instinct to close her arms round him and so in some small measure ease his silent grief. All that held her back, she knew, was the fear that he would not welcome her sympathy. That, and the distinct possibility that she was misreading him.

To live a hard life was to make solid and impregnable every way in, until no openings remained and the soul hid in darkness, and no one else could hear its screams, its railing at injustice, its long, agonizing stretches of sadness. Hardness without created hardness within.

Sadness was, she well knew, not something that could be cured. It was not, in fact, a failing, not a flaw, not an illness of spirit. Sadness was never without reason, and to assert that it marked some kind of dysfunction did little more than prove ignorance or, worse, cowardly evasiveness in the one making the assertion. As if happiness was the only legitimate way of being. As if those failing at it needed to be locked away, made soporific with medications; as if the causes of sadness were merely traps and pitfalls in the proper climb to blissful contentment, things to be edged round or bridged, or leapt across on wings of false elation.

Scillara knew better. She had faced her own sadness often enough. Even when she discovered her first means of escaping it, in durhang, she'd known that such an escape was simply a flight from feelings that existed legitimately. She'd just been unable to permit herself any sympathy for such feelings, because to do so was to surrender to their truth.

Sadness belonged. As rightful as joy, love, grief and fear. All conditions of being.

Too often people mistook the sadness in others for self-pity, and in so doing revealed their own hardness of spirit, and more than a little malice.

The taproom stank of blood, shit, piss and vomit. Blend was recovering in her bedroom upstairs, as close to death as she'd ever been, but the worst was past, now. Barathol and Chaur had gone down to the cellars below to help Picker and Antsy bury the bodies of their comrades. The blacksmith's grief at the death of his new friend, Mallet, was too raw for Scillara to face – he was in no way a hard man and this jarred her frail assembly of beliefs, for he should have been. Yet had she not seen the same breathless vulnerability when he'd struggled to bring Chaur back to life after the huge simpleton had drowned?

'He is . . .' Duiker began, and then frowned, 'a remarkable man, I think.'

Scillara blinked. 'Who?'

The historian shook his head, unwilling to meet her eyes. 'I should be getting drunk.'

'Never works,' she said.

'I know.'

They were silent again, moments stretching on.

We just stumbled into these people. A crazy contest at a restaurant. We were just getting to know them, to treasure each and every one of them.

Mallet was a healer. A Bridgeburner. In his eyes there had burned some kind of self-recrimination, a welter of guilt. A healer tortured by something he could not heal. A list of failures transformed into failings. Yet he had been a gentle man. That soft, oddly high voice – which they would never hear again.

For him, Barathol had wept.

Bluepearl was a mage. Amusingly awkward, kind of wide-eyed, which hardly fit all that he'd been through, because he too had been a Bridgeburner. Antsy had railed over the man's corpse, a sergeant dressing down a soldier so incompetent as to be dead. Antsy had been offended, indignant, even as anguish glittered in his bright blue eyes. '*You damned fool!*' he'd snarled. '*You Hood-damned useless idiotic fool!*' When he'd made to kick the body Picker had roughly pulled him back, almost off his feet, and Antsy had lurched off to slam the toe of one boot into the planks of the counter.

They looked older now. Picker, Antsy. Wan and red-eyed, shoulders slumped, not bothering to rinse the dried blood from their faces, hands and forearms.

Duiker alone seemed unchanged, as if these last deaths had been little more than someone pissing into a wide, deep river. His sadness was an absolute thing, and he never came up for air. She wanted to take him in her arms and *shake* the life back into him. Yet she would not do that, for she knew such a gesture would be a selfish one, serving only her own needs. As much, perhaps, as her initial impulse to embrace him in sympathy.

Because she too felt like weeping. For having dragged the historian out into the city – away from what had happened here the past night. For having saved his life.

When they'd first arrived back; when they'd seen the bodies on the street; when they'd stepped inside to look upon the carnage, Duiker had shot her a single glance, and in that she had read clearly the thought behind it. *See what you took me away from?* A thought as far away from the sentiment of gratitude that it might as well be in another realm.

The truth was obvious. He would rather have been here. He would rather have died last night. Instead, interfering bitch that she was, Scillara had refused him that release. Had instead left him in this sad life that would not end. That glance had been harder, more stinging, than a savage slap in the face.

She should have gone below. Should be standing there in that narrow, cramped cellar, holding Chaur's hand, listening to them all grieve, each in their own way. Antsy's curses. Picker at his side, so close as to be leaning on him, but otherwise expressionless beyond the bleakness of her glazed stare. Barathol and his glistening beard, his puffy eyes, the knotted muscles ravaging his brow.

The door opened suddenly, sending a shaft of daylight through suspended dust, and in stepped the gray-haired bard.

She and Duiker watched as the man shut the door behind him and replaced the solid iron bar in its slots – how he had ended up with that bar in his hands was a mystery, yet neither Scillara nor the historian commented.

The man approached, and she saw that he too had not bothered to change his clothes, wearing the old blood with the same indifference she had seen in the others.

There'd been a half-dozen bodies, maybe more, at the stage. A passing observation from Blend implicated the bard in that slaughter, but Scillara had trouble believing that. This man was gaunt, old. Yet her eyes narrowed on the blood spatter on his shirt.

He sat down opposite them, met Duiker's eyes, and said, 'Whatever they have decided to do, Historian, they can count me in.'

'So they did try for you, too,' said Scillara.

He met her gaze. 'Scillara, they attacked everyone in the room. They killed innocents.'

'I don't think they'll do anything,' said Duiker, 'except sell up and leave.'

'Ah,' the bard said, then sighed. 'No matter. I will not be entirely on my own in any case.'

'What do you mean?'

'I called in an old favour, Historian. Normally, I am not one to get involved in . . . things.'

'But you're angry,' Scillara observed, recognizing at last the odd flatness in the old man's eyes, the flatness that came before – *before cold killing. This poet has claws indeed. And now I look at him, he's not as old as I thought he was.*

'I am, yes.'

From below there came a splintering *crack* followed by shouts of surprise. All three at the table swiftly rose. Duiker leading the way, they ran to the kitchen, then down the narrow stairs to the cellar. Torchlight wavered at the far end of the elongated storage room, casting wild shadows on a bizarre scene. Pungent fluid sloshed on the earthen floor, seeming reluctant to drain, and in a half-circle stood the two Malazans, Barathol and Chaur, all facing one side wall where a large cask had shattered.

Antsy, Scillara surmised, had just kicked it.

Splitting it open, in a cascade of pickling juice, revealing to them all the object that liquid had so perfectly preserved.

Folded up with knees beneath chin, arms wrapped round the shins.

Still wearing a mask on which four linear, vertical barbs marked a row across the forehead.

The bard grunted. 'I'd often wondered,' he said under his breath, 'where the old ones ended up.'

The fluids were now seeping into the floor, along the edges of the freshly dug mounds.

A hundred stones, a cavort of ripples, the city in its life which is one life which is countless lives. To ignore is to deny brotherhood, sisterhood, the commonality that, could it be freed, would make the world a place less cruel, less vicious. But who has time for that? Rush this way, plunge that way, evade every set of eyes, permit no recognition in any of the faces flashing past. The dance of trepidation is so very tiresome.

Hold this gaze, if you dare, in the tracking of these tremulous ripples, the lives, *the lives!* See Stonny Menackis, wrought with recrimination, savaged by guilt. She sleeps badly or not at all (who would risk peering into her dark bedroom at night, for fear of seeing the gleam of staring eyes?). She trembles, her nerves like strings of fire, whilst poor Murillio stands apart, desperate to comfort her, to force open all that had now closed between them.

And in the courtyard a mob of unattended young savages whaled about with wooden swords and it's a miracle no one's yet lost an eye or dropped to the pavestones with a crushed trachea.

While, in a workroom not too far away, Tiserra sits at the potter's wheel and stares into space as the lump of clay spins round and round to the rhythm of her pumping foot – struck frozen, shocked by the stunning realization of the sheer depth of her love for her husband. A love so fierce that she is terrified, comprehending at last the extent of her vulnerability.

The sense is a wonder. It is delicious and terrifying. It is *ecstatic*.

Smile with her. Oh, do smile with her!

Whilst at this very moment, the object of Tiserra's devotion strides into the courtyard of the Varada estate, his new place of employment. His mind, which had been calm in the course of his walk from home, now stirs with faint unease. He had sent Scorch and Leff home, and he had stood at the gate watching them stumble off like undead, and this had made him think of moments of greatest danger – just before dawn was the moment to strike, if one intended such violence – but who would bother? What was this mysterious Lady Varada up to anyway?

A seat on the Council, true, but was that sufficient cause for assassination? And why was he thinking of such things at all? There'd been rumours – picked up at the drunk baker's stall – that the night just past should have belonged to the Assassins' Guild but had turned sour for the hired killers and oh, wasn't that re-grettable? A moment of silence then pass the dumplings, if you please.

Now he paused in the courtyard, seeing the latest employees, his peculiar charges, with their dubious pasts and potentially alarming motivations. Reunited, yes, with the castellan, with the infamous Studious Lock. Madrun and Lazan Door were tossing knuckles against the compound wall to his right. Technically, their shift was over, although Torvald Nom suspected that this game of theirs had been going on for some time. Another word of warning to them? No, his spir-its were already plunging, as they were wont to do when he awakened to a sense that something was being pulled over him, that he was being connived around – as his mother used to say when with one foot she pinned young Torvald to the floor and stared down at him as he squirmed and thrashed (mostly an act, of course; she weighed about as much as a guard dog, without the bite). Connived around, dear boy, and when I get to the bottom of things and all the trouble's on the table, why, who will I find hiding in the closet?

His sweet mother never quite mastered the extended metaphor, bless her.

Suddenly too despondent to so much as announce his arrival, Torvald Nom headed for his office, eager to climb over the desk and plant himself in the chair, where he could doze until the sounding of the lunch chime. At least the cooks she'd employed knew their business.

Leave him there, now, and ride one last ripple, out beyond the city, west along the lakeshore, out to a dusty, smoky pit where the less privileged laboured through their shortened lives to keep such creatures as Gorlas Vidikas and Humble Measure at the level of comfort and entitlement they held to be righteous. And, to be fair, they laboured as well to contribute to the general feeling of civilization, which is normally measured by technical wherewithal, a sense of progression and the notion of structural stability, little of which said labourers could themselves experience, save vicariously.

The child Harllo has been lashed ten times for being places he wasn't supposed to be, and this punishment was fierce enough to leave him prostrate, lying on his stomach on his cot with thick unguents slowly melting into the wounds on his back.

Bainisk had received a whip to his left shoulder which would result in the third such scar for dereliction of his responsibilities as overseer in Chuffs, and he now came to sit beside Harllo, studying his young charge in a silence that stretched.

Until at last Harllo said, 'I'm sorry, Bainisk—'

'Never mind that. I just want to know what you were up to. I didn't think you'd keep secrets from me, I really didn't. Venaz is saying "I told you so". He's saying you're no good, Mole, and that I should just push you on to the dredge crews.'

The young ones did not live long in the dredge crews. 'Venaz wants to be your best mole again.'

'I know that, only he's grown too big.'

'People like him never like people like me,' Harllo said. This was not a whine, just an observation.

'Because you're smarter than he is and his being older means nothing, means it's worse even, because in your head you're already past him, past us all, maybe. Listen, Harllo, I seen ones like you before, coming in, going through. They get beaten down, beaten stupid. Or they end up getting killed. Maybe they try to run, maybe they stand up to the pit bosses over something. Your smartness is what's going to ruin you, you understand?'

'Yes, Bainisk. I'm sorry.'

'Why'd you sneak back into the tunnels?'

He could tell him everything. At this moment, it seemed like the right thing to do. But Harllo no longer trusted himself with such feelings. Explaining was dangerous. It could get them all into even more trouble.

'You was carrying bones,' said Bainisk. 'Those bones, they're cursed.'

'Why?'

'They just are.'

'But why, Bainisk?'

'Because they were found where no bones belong, that's why. So far down it's impossible that anybody buried them – and besides, who'd bury dead animals? No, those bones, they're from demons that live in the rock and in the dark. Right down with the roots of the earth. You don't touch them, Harllo, and you never ever try putting them back.'

So this was what Bainisk suspected him of doing, then? 'I was . . . I was scared,' Harllo said. 'It was as if we were disturbing graves or something. And that's why there've been so many accidents lately—'

'Them accidents are because the new boss is pushing us too hard, into the tunnels with the cracked ceilings and the bad air – the kind of air that makes you see things that ain't real.'

'I think maybe that's what happened to me.'

'Maybe, but,' and he rose, 'I don't think so.'

He walked away then. Tomorrow, Harllo was expected to return to work. He was frightened of that, since his back hurt so, but he would do it, because it would make things easier for Bainisk who'd been punished when he shouldn't have been. Harllo would work extra hard, no matter the pain and all; he would work extra hard so Bainisk would like him again.

Because, in this place, with no one liking you, there didn't seem much point in going on.

Lying on his stomach, fresh into another year of life, Harllo felt no ripples reach him from the outside world. Instead, he felt alone. Maybe he'd lost a friend for ever and that felt bad, too. Maybe his only friend was a giant skeleton in the depths of the mines – who with new legs might have walked away, disappeared into the dark, and all Harllo had to remember him by was a handful of tools hidden beneath his cot.

For a child, thinking of the future was a difficult thing, since most thoughts of the future built on memories of the past, whether in continuation or serving as contrast, and a child held few memories of his or her past. The world was truncated forward and back. Measure it from his toes to the top of his head, tousle the mop of hair in passing, and when nothing else is possible, hope for the best.

In the faint phosphor glow streaking the rock, a T'lan Imass climbed to his feet and stood like someone who had forgotten how to walk. The thick, curved femurs of the emlava forced him into a half-lean, as if he was about to launch himself forward, and the ridged ball of the long bones, where it rested in the socket of each hip, made grinding sounds as he fought for balance.

Unfamiliar sorcery, this. He had observed how connecting tissue had re-knitted, poorly at first, to these alien bones, and he had come to understand that such details were a kind of conceit. The Ritual forced animation with scant subtlety, and whatever physical adjustments occurred proceeded at a snail's pace, although their present incompleteness seemed to have no effect on his ability to settle his weight on these new legs, even to move them into his first lurching step, then his second.

The grinding sounds would fade in time, he suspected, as ball and socket were worn into a match, although he suspected he would never stand as erect as he once had.

No matter. Dev'ad Anan Tol was mobile once more. And as he stood, a flood of memories rose within him in a dark tide.

Leading to that last moment, with the Jaghut Tyrant, Raest, standing before him, blood-smeared mace in one hand, as Dev'ad writhed on the stone floor, legs forever shattered.

No, he had not been flung from a ledge. Sometimes, it was necessary to lie.

He wondered if the weapons he had forged, so long ago now, still remained hidden in their secret place. Not far. After a moment, the T'lan Imass set out. Feet scraping, his entire body pitching from side to side.

Raest's unhuman face twisted indignant. Outraged. Slaves were ever slaves. None could rise to challenge the master. None could dare plot the master's downfall, none could get as close as Dev'ad had done. Yes, an outrage, a crime against the laws of nature itself.

'I break you, T'lan. I leave you here, in this pit of eternal darkness. To die. To rot. None shall know a word of your mad ambition. All knowledge of you shall fade, shall vanish. Nothing of you shall remain. Know this, could I keep you alive down here for ever, I would – and even that torture would not suffice. In my enforced indifference, T'lan, lies mercy.'

See me now. I have outlived you, Raest. And there, old friend, lies my mercy.

He came to the secret place, a deep crack in the wall, into which he reached. His hand closed about a heavy, rippled blade, and Dev'ad dragged the weapon out.

The T'lan knew stone, stone that was water and water that was stone. Iron belonged to the Jaghut.

He held up the sword he had made countless thousands of years ago. Yes, it had the form of flint, the ridges encircling every flake struck from the edge, the undulating modulations of parallel flaking and the twin flutes running the length to either side of a wavy dorsal spine. The antler base that formed the grip was now mineralized, a most comforting and pleasing weight.

The form of flint indeed. And yet this sword was made of iron, tempered in the holy fires of Tellann. Impervious to rust, to decay, the huge weapon was the hue of first night, the deep blue sky once the final light of the drowned sun had faded. In the moment of the stars' birth, yes, that was the colour of this blade.

He leaned it point down against the wall and reached into the crack again, drawing out a matching knife – hefty as a shortsword. The hide sheaths had long since rotted to dust, but he would make new ones soon.

The Tyrant of old was gone. Somewhere close, then, waited an empty throne.

Waiting for Dev'ad Anan Tol. Who had once been crippled but was crippled no longer.

He raised both weapons high, the dagger in his right hand, the sword in his left. Slashes of first night, in the moment of the stars' birth. Iron in the guise of stone, iron in the guise of stone that is water and water that is stone and stone that is iron. Jaghut tyranny in the hands of a T'lan Imass.

The gods are fools, alas, in believing every piece in the game is known. That the rules are fixed and accepted by all; that every wager is counted and marked, exposed and glittering on the table. The gods lay out their perfect paths to the perfect thrones, each one representing perfect power.

The gods are fools because it never occurs to them that not everyone uses paths.

Chapter Fourteen

Beneath the battered shield of the sky
The man sits in a black saddle atop a black horse
His hair long and grey drifting out round his iron helm
Knowing nothing of how he came to be here
Only that where he has come to be is nowhere
And where he must go is perhaps near
His beard is the hue of dirty snow
His eyes are eyes that will never thaw

Beneath him the horse does not breathe
Nor does the man and the wind moans hollow
Along the dents of his rusty scaled hauberk
And it is too much to shift about to the approach
Of riders one from his right the other from his left
On dead horses with empty eyes they rein in
Settle silent with strange familiarity
Flanking easy his natural command

Beneath these three the ground is lifeless
And within each ashes are stirred in the dirge
Of grim recollections that slide seeping into regret
But all is past and the horses do not move
And so he glances rightward with jaw clenching
Upon the one-eyed regard he once knew though not well
Answering the wry smile with sudden need
So he asks, 'Are they waiting, Corporal?'

'Bequeathed and loose on the dead plain, Sergeant,
And was this not what you wanted?'
To that he can but shrug and set gaze upon the other
'I see your garb and know you, sir, yet do not.'
Black beard and visage dark, a brow like cracked basalt
A man heavy in armour few could stand in
And he meets the observance with a grimace
'Then know, if you will, Brukhalian of the Grey Swords.'

Beneath these three thunder rides the unproven earth
Nothing sudden but growing like an awakening heart

And the echoes roll down from the shield overhead
As iron reverberates the charge of what must be
'So once more, the Bridgeburners march to war.'
To which Brukhalian adds, 'Too the Grey Swords who fell
And this you call Corporal was reborn only to die,
A new bridge forged between you and me, good sir.'

They turn then on their unbreathing mounts
To review the ranks arrayed in grainy mass on the plain
Onward to war from where and what they had once been
When all that was known is all that one knows again
And in this place the heather never blooms
The blood to be spilled never spills and never flows
Iskar Jarak, Bird That Steals, sits astride a black horse
And looks to command once more

> *SWORD AND SHIELD*
> FISHER KEL TATH

Bliss on a sun-warmed sandy beach, on a remote island, proves tedious to souls habituated to stimulation and excitement. The smaller the island, the faster the scene palls. So Gruntle concluded after completing his thirtieth circle round the white rim of the shore, finding himself fascinated by his own footprints, especially when a new set arrived to track his path. Dulled and insensate as he had become, it was a moment before it occurred to him to halt and turn round, to see the one who now followed.

Master Quell was sweating, gasping, fighting through the soft sand as he probably fought through all of life, one wheezing step at a time. He was sunburned on one side of his body, face and neck, bared forearm, ankle and foot, the result of falling asleep in an unwise position. That he had been pursuing Gruntle for some time was clear in that his footprints completed an entire circumlocution, leaving Gruntle to wonder why the man had not simply called out to capture his attention. Indeed, if Gruntle had not noticed the new trail upon his own, they might well have gone round all day, one pursuing, the other simply walking at a pace the pursuer could not achieve.

'A simple shout,' he said as the man drew closer.

'I did not, uh, want, uh, to call undue attention, uh, upon us.'

'You do not sound well.'

'I need to pee.'

'Then—'

'I can't. Well, I can, but intermittently. Generally when I'm not, er, thinking about it.'

'Ah. A healer could—'

'Yes, yes, I know. Never mind that. Listen—'

'Master Quell,' said Gruntle, 'this was not the way to avoid undue attention – everyone else is sitting right there in the shade of the carriage, and they have been watching us for some time. Me, at least. Why, the Bole brothers wave to me with every pass I make.'

They both glanced over and, sure enough, Jula and Amby waved.

Master Quell rubbed at his bicolour red and pasty face. 'I need an escort.'

'For what? To where?'

'Back to the realm of the dead. No, not in the carriage. Just you and me, Gruntle. I need to get a sense of what's going on. We need to just, er, slip in. A quick look round, then back out.'

'And then?'

Quell's brows lifted. 'Then? Well, we resume our journey, of course.'

'You want me to escort you into Hood's realm, as what, your bodyguard?'

The man bristled slightly. 'The shareholder agreement you have made with the Guild includes discretionary tasks as assigned by the Pilot.'

Gruntle shrugged. 'I was but wondering, Master Quell, what possible use I could be, given that the realm is awash with rabid masses of miserable corpses.'

'I said we'd go in quiet!'

'We could ask the passenger we picked up back there.'

'What? Oh, is he still here?'

'Under the palm trees.'

'Under them? Only a dead man could be so stupid. Fine, let's see what we can find out – but I still need to see some things for myself.'

The rest of the crew, along with Mappo, watched them walk over to the twin palm trees, edging into their shade to stand – nervously – before the gaunt, withered undead who was piling up coconuts into pyramids like catapult ammunition. Even as he worked, unmindful of his new guests, another nut thumped heavily on the sand nearby, making both Gruntle and Quell flinch.

'You,' said Quell.

The ghastly face peered up with shrunken eyes. 'Do you like these? Patterns. I like patterns.'

'Happy for you,' Quell muttered. 'How long have you been dead?'

'How long is a taproot?'

'What? Well, show it to me and I'll guess.'

'It's three times the length of the aboveground stalk. In the baraka shrub, anyway. Does the ratio hold for other plants? Should we find out?'

'No. Later, I mean. Look, you were marching with all the rest in Hood's realm. Why? Where were you all going? Or coming from? Was it Hood himself who summoned you? Does he command all the dead now?'

'Hood never commands.'

'That's what I thought, but—'

'Yet now he has.'

Quell's eyes widened. 'He has?'

'How wide is the sky? How deep is the ocean? I think about these things, all the time.'

Gruntle noted the Master gaping, like a beached fish, and so he asked, 'What was your name when you were alive, sir?'

'My name? I don't recall. Being alive, I mean. But I must have been, once. My name is Cartographer.'

'That sounds more like a profession.'

The corpse scratched his forehead, flakes of skin fluttering down. 'It does. An extraordinary coincidence. What were my parents thinking?'

'Perhaps you are but confused. Perhaps you were a cartographer, trained in the making of maps and such.'

'Then it was wise that they named me so, wasn't it? Clever parents.'

'What did Hood command of you, Cartographer?'

'Well, he said "Come" and nothing more. It wasn't a command to create confusion, or arguments regarding interpretation. A simple command. Even dogs understand it, I believe. Dogs and sharks. I have found seventeen species of shellfish on this beach. Proof that the world is round.'

Another nut thudded in the sand.

'We are perturbing this island with our presence,' said the cartographer. 'The trees are so angry they're trying to kill us. Of course, I am already dead.' He climbed to his feet, bits falling away here and there, and brushed sand and skin from his hands. 'Can we go now?'

'Yes,' said Master Quell, though his eyes were still a little wild. 'We're going back to Hood's realm and we're happy to take you with us.'

'Oh, no, I'm not going back there. It's not time.'

'Yes it is and yes you are,' said Master Quell.

'No it isn't and no I'm not. Hood issued a second command, one just to me. He said "Go" and so I did. It's not time. Until it is, I'm staying with you.'

'Everyone who rides the carriage,' Quell said in a growl, 'has to work for the privilege.'

'Yes, and I have begun.' And he gestured down at the coconut pyramids. 'You have netting bundled to the sides of the carriage, presumably to hold people on board. If we are to cross water, then we should place these nuts within said netting. As flotation devices, in case someone is washed overboard.' He made a heaving motion with his emaciated arms. 'With a line attached for retrieval.'

'That might work,' said Gruntle.

'Gods below,' Master Quell muttered. 'Fine, I'm not arguing with a dead man. Gruntle, draw your weapons. We're going now.'

'My weapons?'

'Just in case. And now, no more damned talking back!'

Quell fashioned a portal into Hood's warren that was but a thin, elongated slice, like a parting of curtains, from which cool lifeless breath gusted out, sweeping the sand into the air. Eyes stinging, Gruntle glanced back just before following the mage into the rent. And saw Amby and Jula wave.

They emerged on the summit of a hill, one of a long spine of hills, each one so similar to the next that they might be enormous barrows – although why there would be barrows in the realm of death Gruntle could not imagine.

In the valley before them the broad basin was a solid river of grey figures, tens of thousands on the march. Ragged pennons hung from standards as if impervious to the moaning wind. Weapons glinted in muted flashes.

'Gods below,' muttered Quell. 'He's assembling the entire host.'

'Looks that way,' agreed Gruntle, feeling like an idiot with his cutlasses in his hands. He slid them back into the underslung scabbards. 'Do we make our way down?'

'I'd rather not.'

'Good. Seen enough? Can we go now, Master Quell?'

'Look, a rider approaches.'

The horse was clearly as dead as the man who rode it, gaunt and withered, mottled where hair had worn off. Both wore armour, boiled leather tarnished and cracked, flapping on frayed leather thongs as they climbed the slope. A ragged cape lifted like a tattered wing behind the warrior. As they drew closer, Gruntle swore under his breath. 'He's wearing a mask – he's a damned Seguleh!' And he reached for his weapons—

'Gods' breath, Gruntle, don't do that!'

It was a struggle to lower his arms. Gruntle's blood felt hot as fire in his veins – the beast within him wanted to awaken, to show hackles lifted and fangs bared. The beast wanted to challenge this . . . *thing*. Trembling, he made no move as the rider drove his horse over the crest a dozen paces to their right, sawing the reins and wheeling the beast round to face them.

'Now this is living!' the Seguleh roared, tilting his head back to loose a manic laugh. Then he leaned forward on the saddle and cocked his head, long filthy hair swinging like ropes. 'Well,' he amended in an amused rumble, 'not quite. But close enough. Close enough. Tell me, mortals, do you like my army? I do. Did you know the one thing a commander must battle against – more than any enemy across the plain, more than any personal crisis of will or confidence, more than unkind weather, broken supply chains, plague and all the rest? Do you know what a commander wages eternal war with, my friends? I will tell you. The true enemy is *fear*. The fear that haunts every soldier, that haunts even the beasts they ride.' He lifted a gauntleted hand and waved to the valley below. 'But not with *this* army! Oh, no. Fear belongs to the living, after all.'

'As with the T'lan Imass,' said Gruntle.

The darkness within the mask's elongated eye-holes seemed to glitter as the Seguleh fixed his attention on Gruntle. 'Trake's cub. Now, wouldn't you like to cross blades with me?' A low laugh. 'Yes, as with the T'lan Imass. Is it any wonder the Jaghut recoiled?'

Master Quell cleared his throat. 'Sir,' he said, 'what need has Hood for an army? Will he now wage war against the living?'

'If only,' the Seguleh replied in a grunt. 'You don't belong here – and if you drag that infernal carriage of yours back here any time soon, I will seek you out myself.

And then Trake's spitting kitten here can fulfil his desperate desire, hah!' He twisted in his saddle. Other riders were approaching. 'Look at that, my watchdogs. "Be reasonable", indeed. Have I chopped these two interlopers to pieces? I have not. Constraint has been shown.' He faced Gruntle and Quell once more. 'You will confirm this, yes?'

'Beyond you goading Gruntle here,' Quell said, 'yes, I suppose we can.'

'It was a jest!' the Seguleh shouted.

'It was a threat,' Quell corrected, and Gruntle was impressed by the man's sudden courage.

The Seguleh tilted his head, as if he too was casting new measure upon the mage. 'Oh, trundle your wagon wherever you like, then, see if I care.'

Three riders mounted the summit and, slowing their horses to a walk, drew up to where waited the Seguleh, who now sat slumped like a browbeaten bully.

Gruntle started, took an involuntary step forward. 'Toc Anaster?'

The one-eyed soldier's smile was strained. 'Hello, old friend. I am sorry. There may come a time for this, but it is not now.'

Gruntle edged back, blunted by Toc Anaster's cold – even harsh – tone. 'I – I did not know.'

'It was a messy death. My memories remain all too sharp. Gruntle, deliver this message to your god: *not long now*.'

Gruntle scowled. 'Too cryptic. If you want me to pass on your words, you will have to do better than that.'

Toc Anaster's single eye – terrifying in its lifelessness – shifted away.

'He cannot,' said the middle horseman, and there was something familiar about the face behind the helm's cheekguards. 'I remember you from Capustan. Gruntle, chosen servant of Treach. Your god is confused, but it must choose, and soon.'

Gruntle shrugged. 'There is no point in bringing all this to me. Trake and me, we're not really on speaking terms. I didn't ask for any of this. I don't even want it—'

'Hah!' barked the Seguleh, twisting round to face the middle rider. 'Hear that, Iskar Jarak? Let me kill him!'

Iskar Jarak? I seem to recall he had a different name. One of those odd ones, common to the Malazan soldiery – what was it now?

'Save your wrath for Skinner,' Iskar Jarak calmly replied.

'Skinner!' roared the Seguleh, savagely wheeling his horse round. 'Where is he, then? I'd forgotten! Hood, you bastard – you made me forget! Where is he?' He faced the three riders. 'Does Toc know? Brukhalian, you? Someone tell me where he's hiding!'

'Who knows?' said Iskar Jarak. 'But there is one thing for certain.'

'What?' demanded the Seguleh.

'Skinner is not here on this hill.'

'Bah!' The Seguleh drove spurs into his horse's senseless flanks. The animal surged forward anyway, plunging off the hilltop and raging downslope like an avalanche.

Soft laughter from Brukhalian, and Gruntle saw that even Toc was grinning – though he still would not meet his eyes. That death must have been terrible indeed, as if the world had but one answer, one way of ending things, and whatever lessons could be gleaned from that did not ease the spirit. The notion left him feeling morose.

It was a common curse to feel unclean, but that curse would be unbearable if no cleansing awaited one, if not at the moment of dying, then afterwards. Looking upon these animated corpses, Gruntle saw nothing of redemption, nothing purged – guilt, shame, regrets and grief, they all swirled about these figures like a noxious cloud.

'If getting killed lands me with you lot,' he said, 'I'd rather do without.'

The one named Iskar Jarak leaned wearily over the large Seven Cities saddle horn. 'I sympathize, truly. Tell me, do you think we've all earned our rest?'

'Don't you?'

'You have lost all your followers.'

'I have.' Gruntle saw that Toc Anaster was now watching him, fixed, sharp as a dagger point.

'They are not here.'

He frowned at Iskar Jarak. 'And they should be, I suppose?'

Brukhalian finally spoke, 'It is just that. We are no longer so sure.'

'Stay out of Hood's realm,' said Toc Anaster. 'The gate is . . . closed.'

Master Quell started. 'Closed? But that's ridiculous! Does Hood now turn the dead away?'

Toc's single eye held on Gruntle. 'The borders are sealed to the living. There will be sentinels. Patrols. Intrusions will not be tolerated. Where we march you can't go. Not now, perhaps never. Stay away, until the choice is taken from you. *Stay away.*'

And Gruntle saw then, finally, the anguish that gripped Toc Anaster, the bone-deep fear and dread. He saw how the man's warning was in truth a cry to a friend, from one already lost, already doomed. *Save yourself. Just do that, and it will all be worth it – all we must do, the war we must seek. Damn you, Gruntle, give all this meaning.*

Quell must have sensed something of these fierce undercurrents, for he then bowed to the three riders. 'I shall deliver your message. To all the pilots of the Trygalle Trade Guild.'

The ground seemed to shift uneasily beneath Gruntle's boots.

'And now you had better leave,' said Brukhalian.

The hill groaned – and what Gruntle had imagined as some internal vertigo was now revealed as a real quaking of the earth.

Master Quell's eyes were wide and he held his hands out to the sides to stay balanced.

At the far end of the range of hills, a massive eruption thundered, lifting earth and stones skyward. From the ruptured mound something rose, clawing free, sinuous neck and gaping, snapping jaws, wings spreading wide—

The hill shivered beneath them.

The three riders had wheeled their horses and were now barrelling down the slope.

'Quell!'

'A moment, damn you!'

Another hill exploded.

Damned barrows all right! Holding dead dragons! 'Hurry—'

'Be quiet!'

The portal that split open was ragged, edges rippling as if caught in a storm.

The hill to their right burst its flanks. A massive wedge-shaped head scythed in their direction, gleaming bone and shreds of desiccated skin—

'Quell!'

'Go! I need to—'

The dragon heaved up from cascading earth, forelimbs tearing into the ground. The leviathan was coming for them.

No – it's coming for the portal – Gruntle grasped Master Quell and dragged him towards the rent. The mage struggled, shrieking – but whatever he sought to say was lost in the deafening hiss from the dragon as it lurched forward. The head snapped closer, jaws wide – and Gruntle, with Quell in his arms, threw himself back, plunging into the portal—

They emerged at twice the height of a man above the sandy beach, plummeting downward to thump heavily in a tangle of limbs.

Shouts from the others—

As the undead dragon tore through the rent with a piercing cry of triumph, head, neck, forelimbs and shoulders, then one wing cracked out, spreading wide in an enormous torn sail shedding dirt. The second wing whipped into view—

Master Quell was screaming, weaving frantic words of power, panic driving his voice ever higher.

The monstrosity shivered out like an unholy birth, lunged skyward above the island. Stones rained down in clouds. As the tattered tip of its long tail slithered free, the rent snapped shut.

Lying half in the water, half on hard-packed sand, Gruntle stared up as the creature winged away, still shedding dust.

Shareholder Faint arrived, falling to her knees beside them. She was glaring at Master Quell who was slowly sitting up, a stunned look on his face.

'You damned fool,' she snarled, 'why didn't you throw a damned harness on that thing? We just lost our way off this damned island!'

Gruntle stared at her. *Insane. They are all insane.*

There was a tension in his stance that she had not seen before. He faced east, across the vast sweeping landscape of the Dwelling Plain. Samar Dev gave the tea another stir then hooked the pot off the coals and set it to one side. She shot Karsa Orlong a look, but the Toblakai was busy retying the leather strings of one of his moccasins, aided in some mysterious way by his tongue which had curled into view from the corner of his mouth – the gesture was so childlike she wondered if he wasn't mocking her, aware as always that she was studying him.

Havok cantered into view from a nearby basin, his dawn hunt at an end. The other horses shifted nervously as the huge beast drew closer with head held high as if to show off the blood glistening on his muzzle.

'We need to find water today,' Samar Dev said, pouring out the tea.

'So we will,' Karsa replied, standing now to test the tightness of the moccasin. Then he reached beneath his trousers to make some adjustments.

'Reminding yourself it's there?' she asked. 'Here's your tea. Don't gulp.'

He took the cup from her. 'I know it's there,' he said. 'I was just reminding *you*.'

'Hood's breath,' she said, and then stopped as Traveller seemed to flinch.

He turned to face them, his eyes clouded, far away. 'Yes,' he said. 'Spitting something out.'

Samar Dev frowned. 'Yes what?'

His gaze cleared, flitted briefly to her and then away again. 'Something is happening,' he said, walking over to pick up the tin cup. He looked down into the brew for a moment, then sipped.

'Something is always happening,' Karsa said easily. 'It's why misery gets no rest. The witch says we need water – we can follow yon valley, at least for a time, since it wends northerly.'

'The river that made it has been dead ten thousand years, Toblakai. But yes, the direction suits us well enough.'

'The valley remembers.'

Samar Dev scowled at Karsa. The warrior was getting more cryptic by the day, as if he was being overtaken by something of this land's ambivalence. For the Dwelling Plain was ill named. Vast stretches of . . . nothing. Animal tracks but no animals. The only birds in the sky were those vultures that daily tracked them, wheeling specks of patience. Yet Havok had found prey.

The Dwelling Plain was a living secret, its language obscure and wont to drift like waves of heat. Even Traveller seemed uneasy with this place.

She drained the last of her tea and rose. 'I believe this land was cursed once, long ago.'

'Curses are immortal,' said Karsa in a dismissive grunt.

'Will you stop that?'

'What? I am telling you what I sense. The curse does not die. It persists.'

Traveller said, 'I do not think it was a curse. What we are feeling is the land's memory.'

'A grim memory, then.'

'Yes, Samar Dev,' agreed Traveller. 'Here, life comes to fail. Beasts too few to breed. Outcasts from villages and cities. Even the caravan tracks seem to wander half lost – none are used with any consistency, because the sources of water are infrequent, elusive.'

'Or they want to keep bandits guessing.'

'I have seen no old camps,' Traveller pointed out. 'There are no bandits here, I think.'

'We need to find water.'

'So you said,' Karsa said, with an infuriating grin.

'Why not clean up the breakfast leavings, Toblakai. Astonish me by being useful.' She walked over to her horse, collecting the saddle on the way. She could draw a dagger, she could let slip some of her lifeblood, could reach down into this dry earth and see what was there to be seen. Or she could keep her back turned, her self closed in. The two notions warred with each other. Curiosity and trepidation.

She swung the saddle on to the horse's broad back, adjusted the girth straps and then waited for the animal to release its held breath. Nothing likes to be bound. Not the living, perhaps not the dead. Once, she might have asked Karsa about that, if only to confirm what she already knew – but he had divested himself of that mass of souls trailing in his wake. Somehow, the day he killed the Emperor. Oh, two remained, there in that horrid sword of his.

And perhaps that was what was different about him, she realized. *Liberation. But then, has he not already begun collecting more?* She cinched the strap then half turned to regard the giant warrior, who was using sand to scrub the blackened pan on which she'd cooked knee-root, challenging the pernicious crust with a belligerent scowl. No, she could sense nothing – not as drawn in as she'd made herself. Thus, sensing nothing didn't mean anything, did it? Perhaps he had grown at ease with those victims dragged behind him everywhere he went.

A man like that should not smile. Should never smile, or laugh. He should be haunted.

But he was too damned arrogant to suffer haunting, a detail that invariably irritated her, even as she was drawn to it (and was that not irritating in itself?).

'You chew on him,' said Traveller, who had come unseen to her side and now spoke quietly, 'as a jackal does an antler. Not out of hunger so much as habit. He is not as complicated as you think, Samar Dev.'

'Oh yes he is. More so, in fact.'

The man grimaced as he set about saddling his own horse. 'A child dragged into the adult world, but no strength was lost. No weakening of purpose. He remains young enough,' Traveller said, 'to still be certain. Of his vision, of his beliefs, of the way he thinks the world works.'

'Oh, so precisely when will the world get round to kicking him good and hard between the legs?'

'For some, it never does.'

She eyed him. 'You are saying it does no good to rail against injustice.'

'I am saying do not expect justice, Samar Dev. Not in this world. And not in the one to come.'

'Then what drives you so, Traveller? What forces your every step, ever closer to whatever destiny waits for you?'

He was some time in answering, although she did not deceive herself into thinking that her words had struck something vulnerable. These men here with her, they were armoured in every way. He cinched the girth straps and dropped the stirrups. 'We have an escort, Samar Dev.'

'We do? The vultures?'

'Well, yes, there are those, too. Great Ravens.'

At that she squinted skyward. 'Are you sure?'

'Yes, but I was speaking of another escort.'

'Oh, then who? And why doesn't it show itself?'

Traveller swung himself astride his horse and gathered the reins. Karsa had completed packing the camp gear and was now bridling Havok. 'I have no answers to those questions, Samar Dev. I do not presume to know the minds of Hounds of Shadow.'

She saw Karsa Orlong glance over at that, but there was nothing revealed in his expression beyond simple curiosity.

Gods, he drives me mad!

'Do they hunt us?' Karsa asked.

'No,' Traveller replied. 'At least, not me, nor, I imagine, our witch here.'

Karsa mounted his Jhag horse. 'Today,' he announced, 'I shall not ride with you. Instead, I shall find these Hounds of Shadow, for I wish to see them for myself. And if they in turn see me alone, then they may choose to make plain their desires.'

'Now what is the point of that?' demanded Samar Dev.

'I have faced Hounds before,' he said. 'I am happy to invite them close, so they can smell the truth of that.'

'There is no need,' said Traveller. 'Karsa Orlong, the Hounds began as my escort – one in truth – granted me by Shadowthrone. They are not interested in you, I am sure of it.'

Samar Dev rounded on him. 'Then why did you suggest otherwise?'

He met her eyes and she saw him gritting his teeth, the muscles of his jaws binding. 'You were right, Witch,' he said, 'you know this warrior better than I.'

Karsa snorted a laugh.

They watched him ride off.

Samar Dev wanted to spit – the tea had left her mouth dry, bitter. 'He probably will at that,' she muttered, 'whether the Hounds like it or not.'

Traveller simply nodded.

Skintick knew precisely the day he died. The final terrible battle waged on Drift Avalii, with four of his closest companions falling, each just beyond his reach, beyond his own life which he would have sacrificed to take their place. And into the midst of the crumbling defence, Andarist had stepped forward, making of himself a lodestone to the attacking Tiste Edur.

The death of the man whom Skintick thought of as his father remained in his mind, like a scene painted by some chronicler of abject, pathetic moments. And in that sad, regretful face, he had seen all the kin who had fallen before, killed for no cause worth thinking about – or so it seemed at the time. The grey-skinned barbarians desired the throne – perhaps they were collecting such things, as if possession conferred a right, but what did it matter? These games were stupidity, every trophy an absurd icon symbolizing precisely nothing beyond the raging ego of the players.

Honourable souls had died for this, and, once the grief washed away, what was left but this building contempt for all of it? Defending this, fighting for that, winning in one moment only to lose in the next. Raw magic blistering flesh, javelins winging to thud into bodies, everything of value spilling out on to dusty cobbles and the ribbons of grass growing exuberant between them.

The things that died in him on that day would be deemed virtues by most. Duty had revealed its lie, shattering the sanctity of loyalty and honour. They'd fought for nothing. They could have retreated, holed up at the decrepit temple entrance, and simply waited for the arrival of the humans, first the assassins and then the one named Traveller and his followers. Traveller, who murdered everyone foolish enough to step into his path. Whose arrival made Andarist's death – and the deaths of his friends – meaningless.

How Skintick hated that man. Competence was no gift when it arrived too late.

He no longer believed in honesty either. To be told the truth was to feel the shackles snap shut on one's ankle. Truth was delivered with the expectation that it would force a single course of action – after all, how could one honourably turn away? Truth was used as a weapon, and all one could do in defence against such an assault was to throw up a wall of lies. Lies of acceptance, capitulation. Lies to oneself, too. That things mattered. That ideas had currency and symbols deserved the servitude of courageous fools. And that it all had meaning.

Nor was he a believer in courage. People relied on the bravery of others to reap whatever profits they imagined they had earned or deserved, but the blood spilled was never theirs, was it? No, it was clear now to Skintick. Virtues were lauded to ensure compliance, to wrap round raw, reprehensible servitude. To proclaim the sacrifice of others – each of whom stood in for those reaping the rewards and so were paid in suffering and pain.

So much for the majesty of patriotism.

He was having none of it, not any more, never again. And this was what made him dead now. And like anyone for whom nothing matters, he now found much of what he saw around him profoundly amusing. Snide commentary, derisive regard and an eye for the horror of true irony, these were the things he would now pursue.

Did Anomander Rake grieve for his dead brother? For Andarist, who had stood in his place? Did he spare a thought for his wretched spawn, so many of whom were now dead? Or was he now lolling fat and dissolute on whatever mockery he called his throne, reaping all the rewards of his brother's final sacrifice? *And that of my cousins? My closest friends, who each died to defend a possession so valuable to you that it rots in an empty temple? Remind me to ask you that question when we finally meet.*

Though he loved Nimander – indeed, loved them all in this pathetic band (save

Clip, of course) – Skintick could not help but observe with silent hilarity the desperate expectations of this journey's fated end. They all sought safety and, no doubt, a pat on the head for services rendered. They all wanted to be told that their sacrifices had meaning, value, were worthy of pride. And Skintick knew that he alone would be able to see the disdain veiled in the eyes of the Son of Darkness, even as he spouted all the necessary platitudes, before sending them off to their small rooms in some forgotten wing of whatever palace Rake now occupied.

And then what, my dearest kin? Shunted out on to the streets to wander in the dusk, as the presence of others slowly prises our band apart, until all we once were become memories thick with dust, barely worthy of the occasional reminiscence, some annual gathering in some tavern with a leaking roof, where we will see how we each have sagged with the years, and we'll get drunk swapping tales we all know by heart, even as the edges grow blunt and all the colours bleed out.

Desra lying on her back, her legs spread wide, but the numbness inside can't be pierced that way and she probably knows but habits never die, they just wear disguises. Nenanda will polish his weapons and armour every morning – we'll see him clanking round guarding everything and nothing, his eyes mottled with verdigris and rust. Aranatha sits in an overgrown garden, mesmerized for ten years and counting by a lone blossom beneath a tree; do we not envy the bliss in her empty eyes? Kedeviss? Well, she will chronicle our despair, our sordid demise. Rounding us up for the night in the tavern will be her one task with any meaning – at least to her – and she will silently rail at our turgid, insipid uninterest.

Nimander, ah, Nimander, what waits for you? One night, your vision will clear. One deadly, devastating night. You will see the blood on your hands, dear vicious Phaed's blood. And that of so many others, since you were the one we victimized by proclaiming you as our leader. And on that night, my friend, you will see that it was all for naught, and you will take your own life. A tower, a window ledge and a plummet down through the dark to achieve the incumbent poetic futility.

Skintick could not find himself in that future. He did not expect to complete this journey. He was not sure he even wanted to. The same chronicler who painted past scenes would paint the future ones, too. The same damned theme, reworked with all the obsessiveness of a visionary throttling the blind.

One thing was certain. He would permit no one to ever again abuse his virtues – even those few that remained, in their dishevelled state. They were not currency, not things to be measured, weighed against gold, gems, property or power. If the bastards wanted all that, they could sweat their own sweat and bleed their own blood to get it.

Take me as a knife and I will turn in your hand. I swear it.

'You are smiling,' Nimander observed. 'It pleases me to see that alive and well.'

Skintick glanced at him. The legacy of Bastion remained in the stains of old blood beneath the salt that now caked moccasins and leggings. No one had bothered cleaning their gear, so desperate was the need to leave that city. Something had changed in Nimander, however, beyond the horrors of saemenkelyk and the Dying God's altar. As if his sense of purpose had taken a fresh beating, like a new seedling trampled underfoot. How many times, Skintick wondered, could Nimander suffer that, before some fundamental poison altered his very nature? The vision he had of Nimander's final demise was dependent upon a certain sanctity of spirit's remaining, something precious and rare that would drive him to that last act of despair. If it was already dead, or twisted malign, then Nimander's fate would become truly unknown.

Has he found ambition? Is the poison of cynicism awakening in his beleaguered soul? This could change things, Skintick realized. *He might become someone I could choose to follow – yes, down that nasty path and why not? Let someone else suffer for our gains, for a change. Topple them into the dirt and see how they like the sweet reversal.*

Is he hard enough to play that game?

Am I hard enough to make use of him?

They had found a horse for Clip, but retained the wagon, at least for this journey northward along the edge of the dying salt lake. Nenanda was seated once more on the raised bench, reins in one hand, switch in the other. Aranatha sat with her legs dangling off the end of the wagon, eyes on the row of broken teeth that was Bastion's dwindling skyline, hazy and shimmering above the heat waves. Desra lounged in the wagon's bed, dozing among the casks of water and bundles of dried goods. Kedeviss rode flank off to the right, almost thirty paces away now, her horse picking its way along the old beach with its withered driftwood.

Clip rode far ahead, emphasizing his impatience. He'd not been much interested in hearing the tale of their doings since his collapse at the village – a failing on his part (as he evidently saw the suggestion) that he refused to entertain, although this clearly left a mysterious and no doubt troubling gap in his memory. He was, if anything, even more evasive than he had been before, and more than once Skintick had caught suspicion in the warrior's eyes when observing the rest of them. As if they had conspired to steal something from him, and had succeeded.

Skintick's distrust of the bastard was growing. It wasn't hard to hate Clip – absurdly easy, in fact – and such sentiments could well cloud his sense of the warrior with his endlessly spinning rings. Clip was, he now believed, one of those eager to abuse the virtues of others to achieve whatever private and entirely personal victory he sought. And if the effort left a half-dozen contemptible youths dead in his wake, what of it?

He could not but see the bloodstains they now wore; could not but have noticed the notched and nicked weapons they took files to during rest stops. Their damaged armour. And dazed and groggy as he had been upon awakening in the altar chamber, he could not have been blind to the scores of dead – the veritable slaughterhouse they had left behind. And yet still Clip saw them as barely worth his regard, beyond that malicious suspicion as it slowly flowered into paranoia, and what might that lead him to do?

To us?

Yes, one more fear to stalk me now, though I am dead.

'We will need to find a way through those mountains,' Nimander said, squinting ahead.

'God's Walk, Clip called them. An astounding fount of unexpected knowledge, our grateful friend.'

'Grateful? Ah, I see. Well, he wasn't there in spirit, was he?'

'No, too busy dancing from the spider's bite.'

'It does little good to try describing what happened,' Nimander said. 'To one who remains closed, words are thinner than webs, easily swept aside.'

'We should have lied.'

Nimander looked over, brows lifting.

Skintick grinned. 'Some wild tale of godly possession and insane fanatics eager to splash the world with their own blood. Us stumbling on to a path to paradise only to find we're not welcome. Double-crossing a simpleton god who misunderstood the notion of puppets – that they be made of followers, not himself. A tale of poisoned wine that was blood that was wine that was blood. Oh, and let's not forget our glorious slaughter, that improbable collection of lucky swings and pokes and the infernal bad luck of our attackers. And then—'

'Enough, Skin, please.'

'Why did we bother, Nimander? Bother saving him?'

Nimander's eyes remained on the distant mountains. 'Aranatha says he is needed. Necessary.'

'For what? And what would she know about it anyway?'

'I wish I could answer those questions, Skin.'

'I feel as if I am drowning in blood.'

Nimander nodded. 'Yes. I feel the same. I think we all do.'

'I don't think Anomander Rake has it in him to throw us a rope.'

'Probably not.'

This admission, so wise, shook Skintick. His fear was accurate – their leader had changed. *Does he even now see clearly? Yet, if that is so, where is his despair? I do not understand—*

'It feels like,' Nimander said, 'dying inside. That's what it feels like.'

'Don't say that, brother. Don't.'

'Why not?'

Only one of us can feel that way. Only one. I got there first, damn you! It's mine! Abruptly, he barked a laugh. 'No reason, in truth. No reason at all.'

'You are acting strangely, Skin, did you know that?'

He shrugged. 'We need to wash this blood off, Nimander.'

They rode on across the bleached salt flat. The day grew hotter.

Directly beneath the floor of the *terondai*, where blazed the black sun, a vast chamber had been carved out of the bedrock. When Anomander Rake, Lord of

Black Coral and Son of Darkness, wearied of the view from the keep's tower and
other high vantage points, he descended into this womb in the rock, where darkness remained absolute.

Such moments were rare, and even rarer that the Lord should summon Endest
Silann to meet him in the subterranean cavern. His legs still stiff from the long
trek back to the city, the castellan made his way down the steep, winding stairs,
until at last he reached the base. Enormous doors sealed the cave, scaled in beaten
silver in patterns suggesting the skin of dragons. Tarnished black, barring the
gleam of the scales' edges, the barrier was barely visible to Endest Silann's failing
eyes, and when he reached for the heavy latch he was forced to grope for a moment before his hand settled on the silver bar.

Cold air gusted around him as he pulled one of the doors open. A smell of raw
stone, acrid and damp, the sound of trickling water. He saw his Lord standing
near the centre, where an obelisk rose like a stalagmite from the floor. This basalt
edifice was carved square at the base, tapering to an apex at twice the height of a
Tiste Andii. On the side facing Rake there was an indent, moulded to match the
sword he carried on his back.

'It is not often,' said Anomander as Endest approached, 'that I feel the need to
ease the burden of Dragnipur.'

'Sire.'

He watched as Anomander unsheathed the dread sword and set it into the in-
dentation. At once the obelisk began sweating, thick, glistening beads studding the
smoothed surface, then racing down the sides. Something like thunder groaned
through the stone underfoot.

Endest Silann sighed, leaned on his walking stick. 'The stone, Lord, cannot
long withstand that burden.' *Yet you can, and this so few understand, so few
comprehend at all.*

'A few moments more,' Anomander Rake murmured.

'Sire, that was not a chastisement.'

A brief smile. 'But it was, old friend, and a wise one. Stone knows its own
weight, and the limits of what it can sustain. Be assured, I will not long abuse its
generosity.'

Endest Silann looked round, drawing in the sweet darkness, so pure, so perfect.
*It is almost as we once knew. Kharkanas, before she embraced Light, before the
ones born of ashes lifted themselves up and took swords in hand. Scabandari. Il-
gast Rend, Halyd Bahann. Esthala who dreamed of peace. Kagamandra Tulas
Shorn, who did not.*

'I have sent Spinnock Durav away.'

'Yes, I heard. Sire, I cannot—'

'I am afraid you have no choice, Endest.'

'The High Priestess—'

'Understands, and she will do all she can.'

So long ago now. Lord, your patience beggars that of gods.

'There was no purpose worthy enough to breathe life into our people, was there? It is not history that so assailed us, although many see it that way. The lessons of futility can be gathered by anyone with a mind so inclined. Every triumph hollow, every glory revealed at last to be ephemeral. But none of that gives cause to wither the spirit. Damage it, perhaps, yes, but the road we have walked down stands high above such things. Do you understand that, Endest?'

'I think I do, sire.'

'We were murdered by compromises. No, not those that followed the arrival of Light. Not those born of Shadow. These things were inevitable. They were, by their very nature, *necessary*.'

'Yes.'

'The day we accepted her turning away, Endest, was the day we ran the knives across our own throats.' Anomander Rake paused, and then said, 'We are an ancient, stubborn people.' He faced Endest Silann. 'See how long it has taken to bleed out?'

And then, to complete the unruly triumvirate, there was the brood of Osserc. Menandore, and that mess of mixed bloods to follow: Sheltatha Lore, Sukul Ankhadu, Brevith Dreda. The others, the ones outside all of that, how they watched on, bemused, brows darkening with anger. Draconus, you thought you could give answer to all of us. You were wrong.

Were you wrong? He found himself staring at Dragnipur, catching the faintest echo of rumbling wheels, the muted cries of the suffering, and there, yes, that seething storm of chaos drawing every closer.

'Without the blood of dragons,' Anomander Rake went on, 'we would all be dust, scattered on the winds, drifting between the stars themselves. Yes, others might see it differently, but that cold fever, so sudden in our veins, so fierce in our minds – the chaos, Endest – gave us the strength to persist, to cease fearing change, to accept all that was unknown and unknowable. And this is why you chose to follow us, each in our time, our place.'

The chaos in you, yes, a fire on the promontory, a beacon piercing the profound entropy we saw all around us. And yet, so few of you proved worthy of our allegiance. So few, Lord, and fewer with each generation, until now here you stand, virtually alone.

Tears were streaming from his eyes now, weeping as did the obelisk, as did the stone on all sides. *The one who was worth it. The only one.*

'You will find the strength within you, Endest Silann. Of that I have no doubt.'

'Yes, sire.'

'As shall I.' And with that the Son of Darkness reached out, reclaimed the sword Dragnipur. With familiar ease he slid the weapon into the scabbard on his back. He faced Endest and smiled as if the burden he had just accepted yet again could not drive others to their knees – gods, ascendants, the proud and the arrogant, all to their knees. Rake's legs did not buckle, did not even so much as tremble. He stood tall, unbowed, and in the smile he offered Endest Silann there was a certainty of purpose, so silent, so indomitable, so utterly appalling that Endest felt his heart clench, as if moments from rupturing.

And his Lord stepped close then, and with one hand brushed the wetness from one cheek.

He could see her dancing out there, amidst dust devils and shards of frost-skinned rock, through shafts of blistering sunlight and hazy swirls of spinning snow. Blood still streamed from his wounds and it seemed that would never cease – that this crimson flow debouched from some eternal river, and the blood was no longer his own, but that of the god standing beside him. It was an odd notion, yet it felt truthful even though he dared not ask the Redeemer, dared not hear the confirmation from the god's mouth.

The crazed weather whirled on out on that plain, and she moved through it effortlessly, round and round, this way and that, but not yet drawing closer, not yet coming for him once more.

'Why does she wait?' he asked. 'She must see that I cannot withstand another assault, that I will surely fall.'

'She would if she could,' the Redeemer replied.

'What holds her back?'

'Wounds must heal, memories of pain fade.'

Seerdomin rubbed at the grit on his face. There had been dirty rain, gusting up to where they stood, but it had since wandered back down into the basin, a rotted brown curtain dragged aimlessly away.

'Sometimes,' said the Redeemer, 'things leak through.'

Seerdomin grunted, then asked, 'From where?'

'Lives of the T'lan. So much was unleashed, so much forgotten only to be lived once again. There was anguish. There was . . . glory.'

He had not been there to witness that moment. The kneeling of the T'lan Imass. Such a thing was hard to imagine, yet it sent shivers through him none the less. A moment to shake every belief, when the world drew breath and . . . *held it*.

'Did you know what to expect?'

'They humbled me,' said the Redeemer.

I suspect it was you who humbled them, Itkovian – yes, a mortal back then, just a mortal. No, they were the ones struck mute, filled with awe and wonder. I do not know how I know that, but I do.

. . . things leak through.

'The madness of the weather comes from the memories of the T'lan Imass? Can you not summon them? Draw them up in ranks before you? Do you not think they would proudly accept such a thing? A way to pay you back for what you did? Redeemer, summon the spirits of the T'lan Imass – and that woman below will never reach you.'

'I cannot. I will not. Yes, they would accept that notion. Reciprocity. But I will not. What I gave I gave freely, a gift, not an exchange. Oh, they forced one upon me, at the end, but it was modest enough – or I was weak enough then not to resist it.'

'If you will not accept service,' Seerdomin then said, 'why do you seek it from me?'

'You are free to choose,' the Redeemer replied. 'Defend me, or step aside and see me fall.'

'That's hardly a choice!'

'True. Such things rarely are. I would send you back, but your body no longer functions. It lies on a heap of rubbish behind the pilgrim camp. Scavengers have fed, for your flesh is not poisoned as is that of the others thus disposed.'

Seerdomin grimaced, fixing eyes once more upon the High Priestess dancing on the plain. 'Thank you for the grisly details. If I stand aside – if I watch you die – then what will happen to me? To my spirit?'

'I do not know. If I am able, I will grieve for you then, as much as I do for the souls of all those I now hold within me.'

Seerdomin slowly turned and studied the god. 'If she takes you – all those T'lan Imass—'

'Will be helpless. They will succumb. All who are within me will succumb.'

'So much for standing aside.'

'Seerdomin. Segda Travos, you are not responsible for their fate. I am. This error is mine. I will not judge you harshly should you choose to yield.'

'Error. What error?'

'I am . . . defenceless. You sensed that from the very beginning – when you came to the barrow and there knelt, honouring me with your companionship. I possess no provision for judgement. My embrace is refused no one.'

'Then change that, damn you!'

'I am trying.'

Seerdomin glared at the god, who now offered a faint smile. After a moment, Seerdomin hissed and stepped back. 'You ask this of *me*? Are you mad? I am not one of your pilgrims! Not one of your mob of would-be priests and priestesses! *I do not worship you!*'

'Precisely, Segda Travos. It is the curse of believers that they seek to second-guess the one they claim to worship.'

'In your silence what choice do they have?'

The Redeemer's smile broadened. 'Every choice in the world, my friend.'

Countless paths, a single place sought by all. If she could be bothered, she could think on the innumerable generations – all that rose to stand with thoughts reaching into the night sky, or plunging into the mesmerizing flames of the campfire – the hunger did not change. The soul lunged, the soul crawled, the soul scraped and dragged and pitched headlong, and in the place it desired – *needed* – there was this: the bliss of certainty.

Conviction like armour, eyes shining like swords; oh, the bright glory that was the end to every question, every doubt. Shadows vanished, the world raged sudden white and black. Evil dripped with slime and the virtuous stood tall as giants. Compassion could be partitioned, meted out only to the truly deserving – the innocent and the blessed. As for all the rest, they could burn, for they deserved no less.

She danced like truth unleashed. The beauty of simplicity flowed pure and sweet through her limbs, rode the ebb and sweep of her sighing breath. All those agonizing uncertainties were gone, every doubt obliterated by the gift of saemenkelyk.

She had found the shape of the world, every edge clear and sharp and undeniable. Her thoughts could dance through it almost effortlessly, evading snags and tears, not once touching raw surfaces that might scrape, that might make her flinch.

The bliss of certainty delivered another gift. She saw before her a universe transformed, one where contradictions could be rightfully ignored, where hypocrisy did not exist, where to serve the truth in oneself permitted easy denial of anything that did not fit.

The minuscule mote of awareness that hid within her, like a snail flinching into its shell, was able to give shape to this transformation, well recognizing it as genuine revelation, the thing she had been seeking all along – yet in the wrong place.

Salind understood now that the Redeemer was a child god, innocent, yes, but not in a good way. The Redeemer possessed no certainty in himself. He was not all-seeing, but blind. From a distance the two might appear identical, there in that wide embrace, the waiting arms, the undefended openness. He forgave all because he could not see *difference*, could not even sense who was deserving and who was not.

Saemenkelyk brought an end to ambiguity. It divided the world cleanly, absolutely.

She must give that to him. It would be her gift – the greatest gift imaginable – to her beloved god. An end to his ambivalence, his ignorance, his helplessness.

Soon, the time would come when she would once again seek him. The pathetic mortal soul standing in her way would not frustrate her the next time she found her weapons – no, her righteous blades would cut and slash him to pieces.

The thought made her fling her arms into the air as she whirled. *Such joy!*

She had a gift. It was her duty to deliver it.

Whether you like it or not.

No, he could not refuse. If he did, why, she would have to kill him.

Bone white, the enormous beasts stood on the ridge, side on, their heads turned to watch Karsa Orlong as he cantered Havok ever closer. He sensed his horse tensing beneath him, saw the ears flick a moment before he became aware that he was being flanked by more Hounds – these ones darker, heavier, short-haired excepting one that reminded him of the wolves of his homeland, that tracked him with amber eyes.

'So,' Karsa murmured, 'these are the Hounds of Shadow. You would play games with me, then? Try for me, and when we're done few of you will leave this place, and none will be free of wounds, this I promise you. Havok, see the black one in the high grasses? Thinks to hide from us.' He grunted a laugh. 'The others will feint, but that black one will lead the true charge. My sword shall tap *her* nose first.'

The two white beasts parted, one trotting a dozen or so paces along the ridge, the other turning round and doing the same in the opposite direction. In the gap now between them, shadows swirled like a dust-devil.

Karsa could feel a surge of battle lust within him, his skin prickling beneath the fixed attention of seven savage beasts, yet he held his gaze on that smudge of gloom, where two figures were now visible. Men, one bare-headed and the other hooded and leaning crooked over a knobby cane.

The Hounds to either side maintained their distance, close enough for a swift charge but not so close as to drive Havok into a rage. Karsa reined in six paces from the strangers and eyed them speculatively.

The bare-headed one was plainly featured, pale as if unfamiliar with sunlight, his dark hair straight and loose, almost ragged. His eyes shifted colour in the sunlight, blue to grey, to green and perhaps even brown, a cascade of indecision that matched his expression as he in turn studied the Toblakai.

The first gesture came from the hooded one with the hidden face, a lifting of the cane in a half-hearted waver. 'Nice horse,' he said.

'Easier to ride than a dog,' Karsa replied.

A snort from the dark-haired man.

'This one,' said the hooded man, 'resists sorcery, Cotillion. Though his blood is old, I wonder, will all mortals one day be like him? An end to miracles. Nothing but dull, banal existence, nothing but mundane absence of wonder.' The cane jabbed. 'A world of bureaucrats. Mealy-minded, sour-faced and miserable as a reunion of clerks. In such a world, Cotillion, not even the gods will visit. Except in pilgrimage to depression.'

'Quaintly philosophical of you, Shadowthrone,' replied the one named Cotillion. 'But is this one really the right audience? I can almost smell the bear grease from here.'

'That's Lock,' said Shadowthrone. 'He was rolling in something a while ago.'

Karsa leaned forward on the strange saddle that Samar Dev had had fitted for Havok back in Letherii. 'If I am a clerk, then one prophecy will prove true.'

'Oh, and which one would that be?' Cotillion asked, seemingly amused that Karsa was capable of speech.

'The tyranny of the number counters will be a bloody one.'

Shadowthrone wheezed laughter, then coughed into the silence of the others and said, 'Hmmm.'

Cotillion's eyes had narrowed. 'In Darujhistan, a temple awaits you, Toblakai. A crown and a throne for the taking.'

Karsa scowled. 'Not more of that shit. I told the Crippled God I wasn't interested. I'm still not. My destiny belongs to me and none other.'

'Oh,' said Shadowthrone, cane wavering about once again, like a headless snake, 'we're not encouraging you to take it. Far from it. You on that throne would be . . . distressing. But he will drive you, Toblakai, the way hunters drive a man-eating lion. Straight into the spike-filled pit.'

'A smart lion knows when to turn,' Karsa said. 'Watch as the hunters scatter.'

'It is because we understand you, Toblakai, that we do not set the Hounds upon you. You bear your destiny like a standard, a grisly one, true, but then, its only distinction is in being obvious. Did you know that we too left civilization behind? The scribblers were closing in on all sides, you see. The clerks with their purple tongues and darting eyes, their shuffling feet and sloped shoulders, their bloodless lists. Oh, measure it all out! Acceptable levels of misery and suffering!' The cane swung down, thumped hard on the ground. '*Acceptable?* Who the fuck says *any* level is acceptable? What sort of mind thinks that?'

Karsa grinned. 'Why, a civilized one.'

'Indeed!' Shadowthrone turned to Cotillion. 'And you doubted this one!'

Cotillion grimaced. 'I stand corrected, Shadowthrone. If the Crippled God has not yet learned his lesson with this warrior, more lessons are bound to follow. We can leave him to them. And leave this Toblakai, too.'

'Barring one detail,' Shadowthrone said in a rasp. 'Toblakai, heed this warning, if you value that destiny you would seek for yourself. Do not stand in Traveller's path. *Ever.*'

Karsa's grin broadened. 'We are agreed, he and I.'

'You are?'

'I will not stand in his path, and he will not stand in mine.'

Shadowthrone and Cotillion were silent then, considering.

Leaning back, Karsa collected the lone rein. Havok lifted his head, nostrils flaring. 'I killed two Deragoth,' Karsa said.

'We know,' said Cotillion.

'Their arrogance was their soft underbelly. Easy to reach. Easy to plunge in my hands. I killed them because they thought me weak.'

Cotillion's expression grew mocking. 'Speaking of arrogance . . .'

'I was speaking,' said Karsa as he swung Havok round, 'of lessons.' Then he twisted in the saddle. 'You laugh at those coming to the Crippled God. Perhaps one day I will laugh at those coming to you.'

Cotillion and Shadowthrone, with the Hounds gathering close, watched the Toblakai ride away on his Jhag horse.

A thump of the cane. 'Did you sense the ones in his sword?'

Cotillion nodded.

'They were . . .' Shadowthrone seemed to struggle with the next word, '. . . *proud.*'

And again, Cotillion could do little more than nod.

Abruptly, Shadowthrone giggled, the sound making the two new Hounds flinch – a detail he seemed not to notice. 'Oh,' he crooned, 'all those poor clerks!'

'Is that a cloud on the horizon?'

At Reccanto Ilk's query, Mappo glanced up and followed the man's squinting gaze. He rose suddenly. 'That's more than a cloud,' he said.

Sweetest Sufferance, sitting nearby, grunted and wheezed herself upright, brushing sand from her ample behind. 'Master Qu – ellll!' she sang.

Mappo watched as the crew started scrabbling, checking the leather straps and fastening rings and clasps dangling from the carriage. The horses shifted about, suddenly restless, eyes rolling and ears flattening. Gruntle came up to stand beside the Trell. 'That's one ugly storm,' he said, 'and it looks to be bearing down right on us.'

'These people baffle me,' Mappo admitted. 'We are about to get obliterated, and they look . . . excited.'

'They are mad, Mappo.' He eyed the Trell for a long moment, then said, 'You must be desperate to have hired this mob.'

'Why is it,' Mappo asked, 'that Master Quell seemed indifferent to unleashing an undead dragon into this world?'

'Well, hardly indifferent. He said *oops!* At least, I think that's what I heard, but perhaps that was but my imagination. This Trygalle Guild . . . these carriages, they must be dragging things across realms all the time. Look at yon walking corpse.'

They did so, observing in silence as the desiccated figure, holding a collection of cast-off straps and rope, stood speculatively eyeing one of the carriage's spoked wheels.

The wind freshened suddenly, cooler, strangely charged.

One of the horses shrilled and began stamping the sand. After a moment the others caught the same feverish anxiety. The carriage rocked, edged forward. Master Quell was helping Precious Thimble through the door, hastening things at the end with a hard shove to her backside. He then looked round, eyes slightly wild, until he spied Mappo.

'Inside you go, good sir! We're about to leave!'

'Not a moment too soon,' Gruntle said.

Mappo set out for the carriage, then paused and turned to Gruntle. 'Please, be careful.'

'I will, as soon as I figure out what's about to happen. Quell! What warren are we using now? And hadn't you better get the way through opened?'

Quell stared at him. 'Get on the damned carriage!'

'Fine, but tell me—'

'You idiot!' shouted Faint from where she sat on the roof. 'Don't you get it?' And she jabbed a finger at the churning black cloud now almost towering over them. '*That's* our ride!'

'But – wait – how—'

'Climb aboard, you oaf, or drown!'

'Climb aboard,' shrieked Sweetest Sufferance, 'and maybe drown anyway!'

Gruntle saw that the corpse had tied itself to the wheel.

Gods below, what am I doing here?

A roar exploded on the reef and Gruntle whirled round to see the gust front's devastating arrival, a wall of thrashing, spume-crested water, rising, charging, lifting high to devour the entire island.

He lunged for the carriage. As he scrambled up the side of the carriage and fumbled for the lashing, Reccanto Ilk, squinting, asked, 'Is it here yet?'

The horses began screaming in earnest.

And all at once, the shortsighted idiot had his answer.

Chapter Fifteen

You would call us weak?
Fear talks out of the side of the mouth
Each item in your list is an attack
That turns its stab upon yourself
Displaying the bright terrors
That flaw the potential for wonder

You drone out your argument
As if stating naught but what is obvious
And so it is but not in the way you think
The pathos revealed is your paucity
Of wisdom disguised as plain speak
From your tower of reason

As if muscle alone bespoke strength
As if height measures the girth of will
As if the begotten snips thorns from the rose
As if the hearthfire cannot devour a forest
As if courage flows out lost monthly
In wasted streams of dead blood

Who is this to utter such doubt?
Priest of a cult false in its division
I was there on the day the mob awoke
Storming the temple of quailing half-men
You stood gape-jawed behind them
As your teachings were proved wrong

Shrink back from true anger
Flee if you can this burgeoning strength
The shape of the rage against your postulated
Justifications is my soldier's discipline
Sure in execution and singular in purpose
Setting your head atop the spike

LAST DAY OF THE MAN SECT
SEVELENATHA OF GENABARIS
(CITED IN 'TREATISE ON UNTENABLE PHILOSOPHIES
AMONG CULTS'
GENORTHU STULK)

Many children, early on, acquire a love of places they have never been. Often, such wonder is summarily crushed on the crawl through the sludge of murky, confused adolescence on to the flat, cracked pan of adulthood with its airless vistas ever lurking beyond the horizon. Oh, well, sometimes such gifts of curiosity, delight and adventure do indeed survive the stationary trek, said victims ending up as artists, scholars, inventors and other criminals bent on confounding the commonplace and the platitudes of peaceful living. But never mind them for now, since, for all their flailing subversions, nothing really ever changes unless in service to convenience.

Bainisk was still, in the sheltered core of his being, a child. Ungainly with growth, yes, awkward in a body in which he had not yet caught up, but he had yet to surrender his love of the unknown. And so it should be wholly understandable that he and young Harllo should have shared a spark of delight and wonder, the kind that wove tight between them so that not even the occasional snarl could truly sever the binding.

In the week following that fateful tear in the trust between them, Harllo had come to believe that he was once more truly alone in the world. Wounds scabbed over and scabs fell away to reveal faint scars that soon faded almost out of existence, and the boy worked on, crawling into fissures, scratching his way along fetid, gritty cracks in the deep rock. Choking at times on bad air, stung by blind centipedes and nipped by translucent spiders. Bruised by shifting stones, his eyes wide in the darkness as he searched out the glitter of ore on canted, close walls.

At week's end, however, Bainisk was with him once more, passing him a jug of silty lakewater as he backed out of a fissure and sat down on the warm, dry stone of the tunnel floor, and in this brief shared moment the tear slowly began to heal, reknitted in the evasiveness of their eyes that would not yet lock on to the reality of their sitting side by side – far beneath the world's surface, two beating hearts that echoed naught but each other – and this was how young boys made amends. Without words, with spare gestures that, in their rarity, acquired all the necessary significance. When Harllo was done drinking he passed back the jug.

'Venaz is on me all the time now,' Bainisk said. 'I tried it, with him again, I mean. But it's not the same. We're both too old for what we had, once. All he ever talks about is stuff that bores me.'

'He just likes hurting people.'

Bainisk nodded. 'I think he wants to take over my job. He argued over every order I gave him.'

'People like him always want to take over,' Harllo said. 'And most times when other people see it they back off and let them. That's what I don't get, Bainisk. It's the scariest thing of all.'

That last admission was uncommon between boys. The notion of being frightened. But theirs was not a normal world, and to pretend that there was nothing to fear was not among the few privileges they entertained. Out here, people didn't need reasons to hurt someone. They didn't need reasons for doing anything.

'Tell me about the city again, Mole.'

'There's a haunted tower. My uncle took me to see it once. He has big hands, so big that when he holds yours it's like your hand disappears and there's nothing in the world could pull you apart. Anyway, there's a ghost in that tower. Named Hinter.'

Bainisk set on him wide eyes. 'Did you see it? Did you see that ghost?'

'No, it was daytime. They're hard to see in daytime.'

'It's dark enough down here,' Bainisk said, looking round. 'But I ain't never seen a ghost.'

Harllo thought to tell him, then. It had been his reason for bringing up the story in the first place, but he found himself holding back yet again. He wasn't sure why. Maybe it was because the skeleton wasn't a true ghost. 'Sometimes,' he said, 'the dead don't go away. I mean, sometimes, they die but the soul doesn't, er, leave the body. It stays where it is, where it always was.'

'Was this Hinter like that?'

'No, he was a real ghost. A spirit with no body.'

'So what makes ghosts of some people but not others?'

Harllo shrugged. 'Don't know, Bainisk. Maybe spirits with a reason to stay are the ones that become ghosts. Maybe the Lord of Death doesn't want them, or lets them be so they can maybe finish doing what they need to do. Maybe they don't realize they're dead.' He shrugged again. 'That's what my uncle said. He didn't know either, and not knowing made him mad – I could tell by the way he held my hand tighter.'

'He got mad at a ghost?'

'Could be. That's what I figure, anyway. I didn't say nothing to make him mad, so it must have been the ghost. His not knowing what it wanted or something.'

Harllo could well recall that moment. Like Bainisk, he'd asked lots of questions, amazed that such a thing as a ghost could exist, could be hiding, watching them, thinking all its ghost thoughts. And Gruntle had tried to answer him, thought it was obviously a struggle. And when Harllo asked him if maybe his father – who was dead – might be a ghost out there somewhere far away, his uncle had said nothing. And when he asked if maybe his ghost father was still around because he was looking for his son, then Gruntle's big hand squeezed tight and then tighter for a breath or two, not enough to actually hurt Harllo, but close. And then the grip softened once more, and Gruntle took him off to buy sweets.

He'd probably seen Hinter, looking out through one of the gloomy windows of the tower. He'd probably wanted to tell Hinter to go away and never come back. Like bad fathers did. Because maybe Harllo's father wasn't dead at all, since one time his real mother had said something about *putting the bastard away*, and though Harllo didn't know the precise meaning of 'bastard' he'd heard it often enough to guess it was a word used for people no one liked having around.

But thinking about Gruntle made him sad, so instead he reached for the jug of water again and drank deep.

Bainisk watched him, and then rose. 'There's a new chute that's been cleared. I was thinking maybe you could climb it, if you was rested up enough.'

'Sure, Bainisk. I'm ready.'

They set out in silence. But this time the silence wasn't uncomfortable, and Harllo felt such a wave of relief when he realized this that his eyes welled up for a moment. Silly, really, and dangerous besides. When he had a moment when Bainisk wasn't looking, he quickly wiped his grimy cheeks and then dried the backs of his hands on his tunic.

Even had he been turned towards Harllo, Bainisk probably would not have noticed. His mind was stepping stealthily on to the worn stones of the path leading to Hinter's Tower, so that he could see the ghost for himself. What a thing that would be! To see with his own eyes something that he had never seen before!

There in that amazing city so far away. Where all manner of wonders jostled with the crowds on all the bright streets. Where ghosts argued with landlords over rent. Where people had so much food they got fat and had to be carried around. And people didn't hurt other people for no good reason, and people like Venaz got exactly what they deserved.

Oh yes, he did love that city, that place where he had never been.

Don't be absurd. The modestly pudgy man in the red waistcoat is not so crass as to fish for weeping multitudes in the rendition of this moment, nor so awkward with purple intent. Give Kruppe some credit, you who are so quick to cast aspersions like hooks into a crowded pool (caught something, did you? No, dear friend, do not crow your prowess, 'twas only this carp desperate to get out).

The water's reflection is not so smooth; oh, no, not so smooth.

Is Bainisk's city quaint, possibly even cute and heartwarming, in a softly tragic way? Not the point!

Some of us, you see (or don't), still dream of that city. Where none of us have ever been.

That, dear ones, is the point.

Second guessing is murder. Or, depending on one's point of view, suicide. Blend had found plenty of opportunity to consider such matters while lying bleeding on the floor of K'rul's Bar. It had been close, and without Mallet around the prospects of a thorough healing of her wounds was something she would just have to live without. The Councilman, Coll, had sent over a local cutter with passing skills in common Denul, and he had managed to half knit the ruptured flesh and stem the flow of blood, and then had taken needle and gut to suture the wounds. All of which left Blend propped up on her bed, barely able to move.

K'rul's Bar remained closed. What had once been a temple was now a crypt. From what Picker had told her, there wasn't a patch of raw earth in the cellars below that wasn't soft and queasy underfoot. The Elder God never had it so good.

Bluepearl and Mallet, both dead. The very idea of that left gaping holes that opened out beneath every thought, every feeling that leaked through her grim control. The bastards had survived decades of war, battle after battle, only to get cut down in their retirement by a mob of assassins.

The shock lingered, there in the echoes of empty rooms, the silences from all the wrong places, the bitter arguments that erupted between Antsy and Picker in the office or in the corridors. If Duiker remained resident – if he hadn't fled – he was silent, witnessing, as any historian would, every opinion strapped down into immobility. And, it seemed, thoroughly uninterested in whether she – or any of them – lived or died.

The sunlight creeping through the shutters told her it was day, possibly late afternoon, and she was hungry and maybe, just maybe, they'd all forgotten her. She'd heard the occasional thump from the main floor below, a few murmured conversations, and was contemplating finding something to pound on the floor when she heard steps approaching along the corridor. A moment later her door opened and in strode Scillara, bearing a tray.

Something sweet and avid curled up deep in Blend's gut, then squirmed at a succession of delicious thoughts. 'Gods, you're a sight. I was moments from slipping away, straight into Hood's hoary arms, but now, all at once—'

'You have reason to live, yes, all that. It's tapu – I hope you don't mind, but the only cuisine I know at all is Seven Cities, and little enough of that.'

'They've got you cooking now?'

'Pays my room and board. At least,' she added as she set the tray down on Blend's lap, 'no one's demanded I clear my tab.'

Blend looked down at the skewers of meat and vegetables and fruit. The pungent aroma of greenspice made her eyes water. 'Money can go piss itself,' she said.

Scillara's eyes widened.

Blend shrugged, reaching for the first skewer. 'We were never in this to get rich, love. It was just . . . something to do, a place to be. Besides, we're not going to hold our hands out when it comes to you and Barathol, and Chaur. Gods below, you dragging Duiker off on a date kept the old fool alive. And Barathol and Chaur arrived like a mailed fist – from what I hear, just in time, too. We may be idiots, Scillara, but we're loyal idiots.'

'I imagine,' Scillara said, pulling a chair close, 'the Assassins' Guild is not thinking of you as idiots at the moment. More like a hornet's nest they regret kicking. Regret?' She snorted. 'That's too mild a word. If you think you're reeling, consider the Guild Master right now.'

'He'll recover,' Blend said. 'Us? I'm not so sure. Not this time.'

Scillara's heavy-lidded eyes settled on Blend for a long moment, and then she said, 'Picker was badly shaken. Still is, in fact. Time and again I see the colour drain from her face, I see her knees go weak, and she reaches out to grab hold of something. Middle of the night, she's up and pacing the hallways – she acts like Hood's at her shoulder these days—'

'That's just it, though, isn't it? A few years ago and she'd be strapping on the armour and counting quarrels – we'd have to chain her down to keep her from charging off—'

'You don't get it, do you, Blend?'

'What?'

'Years ago, as you say, she was a soldier – so were you. A soldier lives with certain possibilities. Needs to keep in mind what might happen at any time. But you're all retired now. Time to put all that away. Time to finally relax.'

'Fine. It takes a while to get it all back—'

'Blend, Picker's the way she is right now because she almost lost *you*.'

In the silence that followed that statement, Blend's mind was awhirl. 'Then . . .'

'She can't bear to come in here and see you the way you are. So pale. So weak.'

'And that's what keeping her from hunting the killers down? That's ridiculous. Tell her, from me, Scillara, that all this going soft shit is, um, unattractive. Tell her, if she's not ready to start talking vengeance, then she can forget about me. We've never run from anything in our lives, and as soon as I'm back on my feet, I plan on a rat hunt the likes of which the Guild has never seen.'

'All right.'

'Is this what all the arguing's about? Her and Antsy?'

A nod.

'Find me a High Denul healer, will you? I'll pay whatever it takes.'

'Fine. Now eat.'

The corpse still smelled of fermented peaches. Laid out on a long table in one of the back rooms, the Seguleh might have been sleeping one off, and Picker expected the ghastly warrior's serenely closed eyes to flicker open at any moment. The thought sent shivers through her and she glanced over once more at Duiker.

'So, Historian, you've done some thinking on this, some jawing with that bard and that alchemist friend of yours. Tell us, what in Hood's name are all these pickled Seguleh doing in the cellar?'

Duiker frowned, rubbed at the back of his neck, and would not meet Picker's hard stare. 'Baruk didn't take the news well. He seemed . . . upset. How many casks have you examined?'

'There's twelve of the bastards, including this one. Three are women.'

Duiker nodded. 'They can choose. Warriors or not. If not, they cannot be challenged. Seems to relate to infant mortality.'

Picker frowned. 'What does?'

'Denul and midwifery. If most children generally survive, then mothers don't need to birth eight or ten of them in the hopes that one or two make it—'

'Well, that's the way it is everywhere.'

'Of course,' Duiker continued as if he had not heard her statement, 'some cultures have an overriding need to increase their population base. And this can impose strictures on women. There's a high attrition rate among the Seguleh. A duelling society by its very nature cuts down the survival rate once adulthood is reached. Young warriors in their prime – probably as deadly as a war, only this is a war that never ends. Still, there must be periods – cycles, perhaps – when young women are freed up to choose their own path.'

Picker's eyes settled on the corpse on the table while Duiker spoke. She tried to imagine such a society, wherein like bhederin cows all the women stood moaning as their tails were pushed to one side almost as soon as the last calf dropped out bleating on to the ground. It was madness. It was *unfair*. 'Good thing even Seguleh women wear masks,' she muttered.

'Sorry, what?'

She scowled across at the historian. 'Hides all the rage.'

'Oh, well, I don't know that the non-warrior women do – it never occurred to me to ask. But I see your point.'

'But is that enough?' she asked. 'Do so many warriors kill each other that it's necessary to demand that of the women?'

Duiker glanced at her, then away again.

The bastard's hiding some suspicions.

'I don't know, Picker. Could be. Their savagery is infamous.'

'How long do you think these ones have been down there? In the cellar, I mean, in those casks?'

'The seals are templar. Baruk suggests that the cult persisted, in some residual form, long after its presumed extinction.'

'Decades? Centuries?'

He shrugged.

'But what are they doing here in Darujhistan anyway? Those islands are right off the south end of the damned continent. Nearly a thousand leagues between them and this city.'

'I don't know.'

Yeah, right. Sighing, she turned away. 'Seen Antsy?'

'At the bar.'

'Typical. Depleting our stock.'

'Your indecision has left him despondent.'

'Stuff that, Duiker,' she snapped, walking from the room, leaving him there with that damned corpse. It was a contest which of them was the less forthcoming, in any case, and she was tired of the duck and dodge. Yet, something in all of that had lodged in her the suspicion that the Guild contract out on them was connected, somehow, with this old temple and all its grisly secrets. *Find the connection, and maybe find the piece of shit who put on the chop on us. Find him, or her, so I can shove a cusser up inside nice and deep.*

Antsy was leaning on the bar, glowering at nothing in particular, at least until he found a perfect victim in Picker as she walked up. 'Careful, woman,' he growled, 'I ain't in the mood.'

'Ain't in the mood for what?'

'For anything.'

'Except one thing.'

'Anything you might try on me, is what I meant. As for the other thing, well, I've already decided to go it alone if I have to.'

'So,' she leaned on the bar beside him, 'what are you waiting for, then?'

'Blend. Once she's back on her feet, Pick, she'll be hungry enough to take the fight to 'em.' He tugged on his moustache, then scowled at her. 'It's you I can't figure.'

'Antsy,' Picker said, sighing, 'much as I'd love to murder every damned assassin in this city, and the Guild Master, too, they're not the source of the problem. Someone hired them, only we don't know who, and we don't know why. We've been through this before. We're back right where we started, in fact, only this time we're down two.' She found she was trembling, and was unable to meet Antsy's stare. 'You know, I find myself wishing Ganoes Paran was here – if anybody could work out what's going on, it's the Captain.'

Antsy grunted. 'Master of the Deck, aye.' He drank down the last of his drink and straightened. 'Fine, let's go to the Finnest House, then – maybe he's in there, maybe he's not. Either way, it's doing something.'

'And leave Blend here on her own?'

'She's not alone. There's Duiker and Scillara. Not to mention that bard. There ain't nobody coming back to finish us, not in the daytime at least. We can be back before dusk, Pick.'

Still she hesitated.

Antsy stepped close. 'Listen, I ain't so stupid, I know what's goin' on in your head. But us just sitting here is us waiting for their next move. You know the marine doctrine, Corporal. It ain't our job to react – it's our job to hit first and make *them* do the reacting. Twice now they hit us – they do it again and we're finished.'

Despite the alcoholic fumes drifting off the man, his blue eyes were hard and clear, and Picker knew he was right, and yet . . . she was afraid. And she knew he could see it, was struggling with it – badly – since fear was not something he'd expect from her. *Not ever. Gods, you've become an old woman, Pick. Frail and cowering.*

They've killed your damned friends. They damn near killed your dearest love.

'I doubt he's there,' she said. 'Else he'd have been by. He's gone somewhere, Antsy. Might never be back and why would he? Wherever Paran's gone, he's probably busy – he's the type. Always in the middle of some damned thing.'

'All right,' Antsy allowed. 'Still, maybe there's some way we can, um, send him a message.'

Her brows rose. 'Now that's an idea, Antsy. Glad one of us is thinking.'

'Aye. Can we go now, then?'

They set out, making use of a side postern gate. Both wore cloaks, hiding armour and their swords, the weapons loose in their scabbards. Antsy also carried two sharpers, each in its own cloth sack, one knotted to his weapon harness and the other down at his belt. He could tug a grenado loose and fling it in its sack as one might throw a slingstone. It was his own invention, and he'd practised with a stone inside the sack, acquiring passable skill. Hood knew he was no sapper, but he was learning.

Nothing infuriated him more than losing a fight. True, they'd come out the other side, while pretty much all of the assassins had died, so it wasn't really a defeat, but it felt like one. Since retiring, his handful of Malazan companions had come to feel like family. Not in the way a squad did, since squads existed to fight, to kill, to wage war, and this made the tightness between the soldiers a strange one. Stained with brutality, with the extremes of behaviour that made every moment of life feel like a damned miracle. No, this family wasn't like that. They'd all calmed down some. Loosened up, left the nasty shit far behind. Or so they'd thought.

As he and Picker set out for Coll's estate and the wretched house behind its grounds, he tried to think back to when he'd had nothing to do with this kind of life, back to when he'd been a scrawny bow-legged runt in Falar. Bizarrely, his own mental image of his ten-year-old face retained the damned moustache and he was pretty sure he'd yet to grow one, but memories were messy things. Unreliable, maybe mostly lies, in fact. A scatter of images stitched together by invented shit, so that what had been in truth a time as chaotic as the present suddenly seemed like a narration, a story.

The mind in the present was ever eager to narrate its own past, each one its own historian, and since when were historians reliable on anything? *Aye, look at Duiker. He spun a fine tale, that one about Coltaine and the Chain of Dogs. Heartbreaking, but then those were always the best kind, since they made a person feel – when so much of living was avoiding feeling anything. But was any of it real? Aye, Coltaine got killed for real. The army got shattered just like he said. But any of the rest? All those details?*

No way of ever knowing. And it don't really matter in the end, does it?

Just like our own tales. Who we were, what we did. The narration going on, until it stops. Sudden, like a caught breath that never again lets out.

End of story.

The child with the moustache was looking at him, there in his head. Scowling, suspicious, maybe disbelieving. *'You think you know me, old man? Not a chance. You don't know a thing and what you think you remember ain't got nothing to do with me. With how I'm thinking. With what I'm feeling. You're farther away than my own da, that miserable, bitter tyrant neither of us could ever figure out, not you, not me, not even him. Maybe he's not us, but then he's not him, either.*

'Old man, you're as lost as I am and don't pretend no different. Lost in life . . . till death finds you.'

Well, this was why he usually avoided thinking about his own past. Better left untouched, hidden away, locked up in a trunk and dropped over the side to sink down into the depths. Problem was, he was needing to dredge up some things all over again. Thinking like a soldier, for one. Finding that nasty edge again, the hard way of looking at things. The absence of hesitation.

Gallons of ale wasn't helping. Just fed his despondency, his sense of feeling too old, too old for all of it, now.

'Gods below, Antsy, I can hear you grinding your teeth from over here. Whatever it is, looks like it's tasting awful.'

He squinted across at her. 'Expect me to be skippin' a dance down this damned street? We're in more trouble than we've ever been, Pick.'

'We've faced worse—'

'No. Because when we faced worse we was ready for it. We was trained to deal with it. Grab it by the throat, choke the life from it.' He paused, and then spat on to the cobbles before adding, 'I'm starting to realize what "retirement" really means. Everything we let go of, we're now scrabbling to get back, only it's outa reach. *It's fuckin' out of reach.*'

She said nothing, and that told Antsy she knew he was right; that she felt the same.

Scant comfort, this company.

They reached Coll's estate, went round towards the back wall. The journey from K'rul's Bar to here was already a blur in Antsy's mind, so unimportant as to be instantly worthless. He'd not registered a single figure amidst the crowds on the streets. Had they been tracked? Followed? Probably. 'Hood's breath, Pick, I wasn't checkin' if we picked up a sniffin' dog. See what I mean?'

'We did,' she replied. 'Two of 'em. Lowlifes, not actual assassins, just their dogs, like you say. They're keeping their distance – probably warned right off us. I doubt they'll follow us into the wood.'

'No,' Antsy agreed. 'They'd smell ambush.'

'Right, so never mind them.'

She led the way into the overgrown thicket behind the estate. The uneven forest floor was littered at the edges with rubbish, but this quickly dwindled as they pushed deeper into the shadowy, overgrown copse. Few people, it was obvious, wanted to set eyes on the Finnest House, to feel the chill of it looking right back at them. Attention from something as ghastly as that dark edifice was unwanted attention.

Thirty uneven strides in, they caught sight of the black half-stone half-wood walls, the wrinkled, scarred face of the house, shutters matted like rotted wicker, no light leaking through from anywhere. Vines snaked up the sides, sprawled out over the humped ground in the low-walled yard. The few trees in that yard were twisted and leafless, roots bared like bones.

'More lumps than last time I was here,' Picker observed as they made their way towards the gate.

Antsy grunted. 'No shortage of idiots tryin' t'get inside. Thinkin' they'll find treasure . . .'

'Secret short cuts to power,' she added. 'Magical items and crap.'

'An' all they got was an early grave.' He hesitated at the gate and glanced at Picker. 'Could be we end up the same way.'

'Stay on the path, that's the trick. Follow me.'

He fell into step close behind her as she set out along the narrow, winding track of tilted pavestones. Too close, as he trod on her heel and almost made her stumble. She shot him a vicious look over one shoulder before continuing on.

The sheer lack of anything untoward had Antsy's nerves overwrought by the time they reached the door. He watched as Picker lifted a gloved hand, made a

fist, hesitated, then thumped it hard against the black wood. The boom reverberated as if an abyss waited on the other side.

They waited. From here, all sounds of the city beyond this wood had vanished,
as if the normal world had ceased to exist, or, perhaps, the endless rush of life out
there held no relevance to what loomed before them now, this grotesque intrusion from another realm.

A dozen heartbeats. Picker made to pound once more on the door.

The clunk of a latch sounded dully through the thick wood, and a moment
later the door creaked back.

Paran had spoken of the lich resident in the Finnest House, the blasted creature
that had once been a Jaghut, but this was Antsy's first sight of it. Tall (gods how he
hated tall things), gaunt yet large-boned, adorned in a long ragged coat of black
chain. Bared head with long colourless hair hanging down from patches – where
the scalp was visible there was twisted scarring, and in one place something had
punctured through the skull, and within the uneven hole left behind there was
only darkness, as if the apparition's brain had simply withered away. Tusks in a
shattered face, the eyes shrunken back into shadows. All in all, Antsy was not inspired with confidence that this fell meeting would proceed in anything like a reasonable fashion.

'Lord Raest,' Picker said, bowing. 'I am a friend of Ganoes Paran. If you recall,
we met—'

'I know who you are, Corporal Picker,' the lich replied in a deep, resonant voice.

'This is Sergeant Antsy—'

'What do you want?'

'We need to find Ganoes Paran—'

'He is not here.'

'We need to get a message to him.'

'Why?'

Picker glanced at Antsy, then back up at Raest. 'Well, it's a complicated tale – can
we come inside?'

Raest's dead eyes held steady on her for a long moment, and then he asked, 'Do
you expect me to serve refreshments as well?'

'Er, no, that won't be necessary, Raest.'

The Jaghut stepped back.

Picker edged round him and halted a few steps in. Antsy pushed in behind her.
They stood in a vaulted entryway, raw black stone underfoot. Opposite the front
door there were twin doors and a narrow corridor off to the right and left. The air
was dry and warm, smelling of freshly turned earth – reminding Antsy of the cellar beneath K'rul's Bar.

'Been digging graves?' he asked, and then cursed himself, trying to ignore
Picker's wild stare.

Raest shut the door and faced them. 'What manner of refreshments were you
expecting, Sergeant Antsy? I am afraid I have nothing buried within the house. If
you like, however—'

'No that's fine,' Picker said hastily.

Antsy could only nod agreement. His mouth had dried up, tongue like a piece of leather gummed against the palate. And he needed to empty his bladder, but the thought of asking directions to the water closet was suddenly akin to demanding that the Jaghut hand over all his money or else.

Raest studied them in silence for a moment longer, and then said, 'Follow me, if you must.'

The lich's moccasin-wrapped feet made rasping sounds. Cloth rustled, the mail of the coat crackling, as Raest walked to the double doors and pushed them open.

Within was a main room bearing a stone fireplace directly opposite, wherein flames flickered cosily, and two deep, high-backed chairs to either side, sitting on a thick woven rug bearing arcane, geometric patterns barely visible in the general gloom. Large tapestries covered the walls to either side, one clearly Malazan in origin – probably Untan given the subject matter (some antiquated court event, significance long lost but no doubt relevant to House Paran); the other was local and depicted a scene from the Night of the Moon, when Moon's Spawn had descended to brush the highest buildings in the city; when dragons warred in the night sky, and Raest himself had attempted his assault upon Darujhistan. The image focused on the dragons, one black and silver-maned, the other muted bronze or brown. Jaws and talons were locked upon one another as they fought in midair, with the backdrop the base of Moon's Spawn and the silhouettes of rooftops and spires, all bordered in an intricate pattern of Great Ravens in flight.

'That's not bad,' Picker muttered, eyeing the work.

Antsy grunted, not one to ponder too much on artwork beyond identifying whatever scene it happened to be recording. Personally, he could not imagine a more useless talent, and thanked the gods he'd never been cursed with such creative misery. Most of his own memories of great events he had witnessed employed stick figures, and that was good enough for him. It did not occur to him that this was at all unusual.

Raest gestured to the two chairs. 'Sit down,' he said, the tone only vaguely related to an invitation. When they had done so, both angling their chairs to face the Jaghut, he said, 'Explain to me, if you will, how precisely you intend to send Ganoes Paran a message.'

'We have no idea,' Picker said, with a queasy smile. 'We were hoping you might have some suggestions.'

'I have many suggestions,' Raest replied, 'none of which are relevant to your request.'

Antsy slowly narrowed his eyes, but said nothing.

Picker opened her mouth a few times, breaking off a succession of possible responses, the repeated gaping reminding Antsy of netted fish on the deck of his da's fisher boat. *Unless I just made that up. All a lie, maybe. Maybe I seen a fish on some other deck. How can I be sure? How can—*

'One possibility occurs to me,' Raest said. 'It would, I suspect, require that one of you be an adept with the Deck of Dragons. Or possessing the potential thereof.'

'I see,' said Picker. 'Well, I've had a few brushes with the Deck.'

'You are an illustrator of Decks?'

'What? Oh, not that kind of brush. I mean, I've had my hands on 'em a few times.'

'Did such contact leave you damaged, Sergeant Picker?'

'Damaged how?'

'Are you, perhaps, now insane?'

She sat upright. 'Hang on, how in Hood's name would I even know if I was insane or not?'

'Precisely,' said Raest, and waited.

Antsy's gaze fixed once more on the Jaghut. 'Pick,' he finally growled.

She twisted to face him in exasperation. 'What is it now, Antsy?'

'This bastard's having us on.'

Her eyes bulged momentarily, and then she looked once more at the Jaghut.

Who shrugged. 'One needs to amuse oneself on occasion. Company is so very rare these days.'

'So when it arrives,' Antsy snapped, 'you treat it like dirt? Do you think maybe there's a connection atwixt the two, you hoary lich?'

'Like dirt? I think not. More like . . . with amiable contempt.'

'You got a few things to learn about people, Jaghut.'

'Undoubtedly, Sergeant Antsy. Alas, I find myself disinclined to make any effort in that direction.'

'Oh? And what direction do you make your efforts in?'

'When I discover one I will let you know, if it proves of any interest – to either me or, of course, you. In the meantime, I have no idea if communication is possible with Ganoes Paran. Perhaps if you informed me of your present crisis, I might be able to assist you in some way that does not involve precipitous, desperate acts that might ultimately inconvenience me.'

'Hood forbid we do that,' snarled Antsy.

'Hood is not one to forbid much of anything,' Raest observed.

'Can't think he much likes these Azath Houses,' Picker said, having recovered from her shock and irritation and, perhaps, indignation. 'All this trapping of souls and things like you, Raest.'

'I doubt I rate highly on Hood's wish list,' the undead Jaghut replied.

Antsy grunted a laugh. 'All right, I'm finally working out your sense of humour. And I thought Malazan marines were dry, Abyss below! Fine, Raest, let's play this game for real. If you can help us with our problem, we'll do something for you in return. If it's within our abilities, that is, so nothing like "get me outa here" or anything like that. But, you know, other stuff.'

'I do have a modest request. Very well, I accept the reciprocal engagement.'

Antsy grinned across at Picker, and then said to Raest, 'It's this. Someone's taken out a contract on us. We don't know why. We're thinking maybe Paran can work out who and what's got 'em so aggravated.'

The Jaghut stared.

Picker cleared her throat. 'Possible causes. One, we're Malazans. Veterans. We've made more than a few enemies on this continent. Two, we own K'rul's Bar, which used to be K'rul's Belfry, which used to be K'rul's Temple. In the cellar we just found thirteen pickled Seguleh, maybe centuries old, but looking fresh. Since they're, er, pickled.' She paused, drew a breath, and then continued, 'Three, well, I ain't got to three yet. The way I figure it, it's all got to do with K'rul – maybe some cultists want the temple back. Maybe someone put in an order for pickled Seguleh and wants 'em delivered.'

Antsy stared at her. 'Someone did what? Pick, that's the stupidest idea I've ever heard.'

'I wouldn't argue with that,' she said, 'only I'm desperate, and besides, I got a hunch those Seguleh are part of the problem.'

Antsy looked to Raest. 'So there it is. Got any suggestions or are you just going to stand there for ever?'

'Yes I am,' Raest replied, 'but that detail is not relevant. As for suggestions, I suggest you kill every assassin in the city.'

'Then whoever wants us dead just starts hiring thugs,' Picker said.

'Kill all thugs.'

Antsy tugged at his moustache. 'Ain't practical. There's only three of us left – it'd take years.'

'Kidnap the Guild Master and torture him or her to reveal the client. Then kill the client.'

'Killing the client makes sense to us,' Picker said, nodding. 'The kidnapping thing doesn't sound very feasible – we'd have to carve through a few hundred assassins to do it. Besides, we don't know where the Guild Master's hideout is. We could capture and torture an assassin to find that out, but they probably operate in cells which means whoever we get might not know a thing. The point is, we don't know who the client is. We need to find out.'

Raest said, 'Your suspicion that the K'rul Temple is central to this matter is probably accurate. Determining the specifics, however, would best be served by enlisting the assistance of the Master of the Deck.'

'That's what we wanted in the first place!' Antsy shouted.

'Extraordinary, isn't it?'

Antsy glared up at the infuriating lich, bit down a few retorts that might prove unwise. He drew a deep breath to calm himself, and then said in a nice, quiet tone, 'So let's see if we can send him a message, shall we?'

'Follow me,' Raest said.

Back into the corridor, turning right, five strides to a narrow door on the left that led into the squat round tower, up the spiral staircase, arriving into the upper level – a circular room with the walls bearing oversized painted renditions of the cards of the Deck of Dragons. Something twisted the eye in this chamber and Picker almost staggered.

'Gods below,' muttered Antsy. 'This place is magicked – makes me sick to the stomach.'

The images swirled, blurred, shifted in rippling waves that crossed from every conceivable direction, a clash of convergences inviting vertigo no matter where the eye turned. Picker found herself gasping. She squeezed shut her eyes, heard Antsy cursing as he backed out of the room.

Raest's dry voice drifted faintly into her head. 'The flux has increased. There appears to be some manner of . . . deterioration. Even so, Corporal Picker, if you focus your mind and concentrate on Ganoes Paran, the efficacy of your will may prove sufficient to anchor in place the Master's own card, which perhaps will awaken his attention. Unless of course he is otherwise engaged. Should your willpower prove unequal to the task, I am afraid that what remains of your sanity will be torn away. Your mind itself will be shredded by the maelstrom, leaving you a drooling wreck.' After a moment, he added, 'Such a state of being may not be desirable. Of course, should you achieve it, you will not care one way or the other, which you may consider a blessing.'

'Well,' she replied, 'that's just great. Give me a moment, will you?'

She tugged from her memory the captain's not unpleasant face, sought to fix it before her mind's eye. *Ganoes Paran, pay attention. Captain, wherever you are. This is Corporal Picker, in Darujhistan. Ganoes, I need to talk to you.*

She saw him now, framed as would a card be framed in the Deck of Dragons. She saw that he was wearing a uniform, that of the Malazan soldier he had once been – was that her memory, conjuring up her last sight of him? But no, he looked older. He looked beaten down, smeared in dust. Spatters of dried blood on his scarred leather jerkin. The scene behind him was one of smoke and ruination, the blasted remnants of rolling farmland, tracts defined by low stone walls, but nothing green in sight. She thought she could see bodies on that dead earth.

Paran's gaze seemed to sharpen on her. She saw his mouth move but no sound reached her.

Ganoes! Captain – listen, just concentrate back on me.

'—*not the time, Corporal. We've landed in a mess. But listen, if you can get word to them, try. Warn them, Picker. Warn them off.*'

Captain – someone's after the temple – K'rul's Temple. Someone's trying to kill us—

'—*jhistan can take care of itself, Pick. Baruk knows what to do – trust him. You need to find out who wants it. Talk to Kruppe. Talk to the Eel. But listen – pass on my warning, please.*'

Pass it on to who? Who are you talking about, Captain? And what was that about Kruppe?

The image shredded before her eyes, and she felt something like claws tear into her mind. Screaming, she sought to reel back, pull away. The claws sank deeper, and all at once Picker realized that there was intent, there was malice. Something had arrived, and it *wanted her.*

Shrieking, she felt herself being dragged forward, into a swirling madness, into the maw of something vast and hungry, something that wanted to feed on her. For a long, long time, until her soul was gone, devoured, until nothing of her was left.

Pressure and darkness on all sides, ripping into her. She could not move.

In the midst of the savage chaos, she felt and heard the arrival of a third presence, a force flowing like a beast to draw up near her – she sensed sudden attention, a cold-eyed regard, and a voice murmured close, 'Not here. Not now. There were torcs once, that you carried. There was a debt, still unpaid. Not now. Not here.'

The beast pounced.

Whatever had grasped hold of Picker, whatever was now feeding on her, suddenly roared in pain, in fury, and the claws tore free, slashed against its new attacker.

Snarls, the air trembling to thunder as two leviathans clashed.

Dwarfed, forgotten, small as an ant, Picker crawled away, leaking out her life in a crimson trail. She was weeping, shivering in the aftermath of the thing's feeding. It had been so . . . intractable, so horribly . . . indifferent. To who she was, to her right to her own life. *My soul . . . my soul was . . . food. That's all. Abyss below*—

She needed to find a way out. All round her chaos swarmed and shivered as the great forces battled on, there in her wake. She needed to tell Antsy things, important things. Kruppe. Baruk. And perhaps the most important detail of all. When they'd walked into the House, she had seen that the two bodies that had been lying on the floor on her last visit were gone. *Gone. Two assassins, said Paran.*

And one of them was Vorcan.

She's in the city. She's out there, Antsy—

Concentrate! The room. In the tower – find the room—

Crawling, weeping.

Lost.

Antsy loosed a dozen curses when Raest dragged Picker's unconscious body on to the landing. 'What did you do?'

'Alas,' the Jaghut said, stepping back as Antsy fell to his knees beside the woman, 'my warnings of the risk were insufficient.'

As Antsy set his hand upon Picker's brow he hissed and snatched it back. 'She's ice cold!'

'Yet her heart struggles on,' Raest said.

'Will she come back? Raest, you damned lich! *Will she come back?*'

'I don't know. She spoke, for a time, before the situation . . . changed. Presumably, she was speaking to Ganoes Paran.'

'What did she say?'

'Questions, for the most part. I was able, however, to glean a single name. Kruppe.'

Antsy bared his teeth. He set his hand again upon her forehead. Slightly warmer? Possibly, or this time he'd been expecting it, making it less of a shock. Hard to tell which. 'Help me get her back downstairs,' he said.

'Of course. And now, in return for my assistance, I will tell you what I seek from you.'

He glared up at the Jaghut. 'You can't be serious.'

'This time, I am, Sergeant Antsy. I wish to have a cat.'

A cat. 'To eat?'

'No, as a pet. It will have to be a dead cat, of course. Now, permit me to take her legs, whilst you take her arms. Perhaps some time before the hearth will revive her.'

'Do you think so?'

'No.'

This had all been his idea, and now look at what had happened. 'Picker,' he whispered. 'I'm sorry. I'm so sorry.'

'A white one,' said Raest.

'What?'

'A white cat. A dead white cat, Sergeant.'

Oh, aye, Raest. One stuffed lumpy with cussers. Here, catch, you damned bastard.

Shit, we're down to two now. Down to two . . .

'Never bargain with the dead. They want what you have and will give you what they have to get it. Your life for their death. Being dead, of course, whatever life they grab hold of just ends up slipping through their bony fingers. So you both lose.'

'That is rather generous of you, Hinter,' said Baruk. 'In fact, I do not recall you being so loquacious the last time we spoke.'

The apparition stood within the door frame of the tower. 'The struggle I face is between my desire to close my ghostly fingers about your throat, High Alchemist, and providing whatever service I can to this fair city. It must also be noted, the return of the Tyrant would also mark the end of what limited freedom I possess, for I would be quickly enslaved. And so, self-interest and altruism prove unlikely allies, yet sufficient to overwhelm my natural murderous urges.'

'The debate is moot,' Baruk replied, interlacing his fingers and resting his hands on his stomach, 'since I have no intention of coming within reach of your deadly grasp. No, I will remain here, in the yard.'

'Just as well,' Hinter replied. 'I haven't dusted in centuries.'

'There are forces in the city,' Baruk said after a moment, 'formidable, unpredictable forces. The threat—'

'Enough of that,' Hinter cut in. 'You know very well why most of those entities are in the city, since you invited them, High Alchemist. And as for the others on the way, well, few of those will surprise you much. They are . . . *necessary*. So, an end to your dissembling.'

'Not all of what approaches is my doing,' Baruk countered. 'Were you aware that both Lady Envy and Sister Spite are here right now? The daughters of Draconus were *not* invited, not by me at any rate. One is bad enough, but both . . .' he shook his head, 'I fear they will leave the entire city a smouldering heap of ashes, given the chance.'

'So do something to ensure that does not happen,' Hinter said airily.

'Any suggestions on that count?'

'None whatsoever.'

'Has either one paid you a visit?'

'You strain my altruism, High Alchemist. Very well, of course Lady Envy has visited, and more than once.'

'Does she know her sister is here?'

'Probably.'

'What does Envy want, Hinter?'

'What she has always wanted, High Alchemist.'

Baruk hissed under his breath and glanced away. 'She can't have it.'

'Then I suggest you pay her sister a visit. She resides aboard—'

'I know where she is, thank you. Now, have you heard of that self-proclaimed High Priest of the Crippled God who's now squatting in an abandoned Temple of Fener? And leads a congregation growing by the day?'

'No, I have not. But are you surprised?'

'The Fallen God is a most unwelcome complication.'

'The legacy of messing with things not yet fully understood – of course, those precipitous sorcerors all paid with their lives, which prevented everyone else from delivering the kind of punishment they truly deserved. Such things are most frustrating, don't you think?'

Baruk's gaze narrowed on the ghost in the doorway.

After a moment Hinter waved an ethereal hand. 'So many . . . legacies.'

'Point taken, Necromancer. As you can see, however, I am not one to evade responsibility.'

'True, else you would have come within my reach long ago. Or, indeed, chosen a more subtle escape, as did your fellow . . . mages in the Cabal, the night Vorcan walked the shadows . . .'

Baruk stared, and then sighed. 'I have always wondered at the sudden incompetence displayed by my comrades that night. Granted, Vorcan's skills were – are – impressive.' And then he fell silent for a moment. And thought about certain matters. 'Hinter, has Vorcan visited you?'

'No. Why would she?'

Baruk was suddenly chilled. 'She made no effort at . . . discussing anything with me that night.'

'Perhaps she knew how you would respond.'

'As she would have for Derudan as well.'

'No doubt.'

'But the others . . .'

Hinter said nothing.

Baruk felt sick inside. Matters had grown far too complicated in this city. Oh, he had known that they were walking a most narrow bridge, with the yawning abyss below whispering soft invitations of surrender. But it seemed the far end was ever dwindling, stretching away, almost lost in the mists. And every step he took seemed more tenuous than the last, as if at any moment the span beneath him might simply crumble into dust.

He could understand those others in the Cabal and the sudden, perfect escape that Vorcan represented. And he recalled that flat promise in her eyes on that night long ago now – it still haunted him, the ease of her betrayal, as if the contract offered by the Malazan Empire had simply provided her with an excuse for doing something she had always wanted to do: murder every other mage in the Cabal.

He might ask her why, but Vorcan was a woman who kept her own counsel. She owed him nothing and that had not changed.

'You had better go now,' Hinter said, cutting into his thoughts.

He blinked. 'Why?'

'Because your silence is boring me, High Alchemist.'

'My apologies, Hinter,' Baruk replied. 'One last thing, and then I will indeed leave. The risk of your enslavement is very real, and is not dependent on the actual return of the Tyrant – after all, there are agents in the city even now working towards that fell resurrection. They might well decide—'

'And you imagine they might succeed, High Alchemist?'

'It is a possibility, Hinter.'

The ghost was silent for a time, and then said, 'Your solution?'

'I would set one of my watchers on your tower, Hinter. To voice the alarm should an attempt be made on you.'

'You offer to intercede on my behalf, High Alchemist?'

'I do.'

'I accept, on condition that this does not indebt me to you.'

'Of course.'

'You would rather I remain . . . neutral, and this I understand. Better this than me as an enemy.'

'You were once a most formidable sorceror—'

'Rubbish. I was passable, and fatally careless. Still, neither of us would have me serving a most miserable cause. Send your watcher, then, but give me its name, lest I invite in the wrong servant.'

'Chillbais.'

'Oh,' said Hinter, '*him.*'

As he made his way back to his estate, Baruk recalled his lone meeting with Vorcan, only a few nights after her awakening. She had entered the chamber with her usual feline grace. The wounds she had borne were long healed and she had found a new set of clothes, loose and elegant, that seemed at complete odds with her chosen profession.

He had stood before the fireplace, and offered her a slight bow to hide a sudden tremble along his nerves. 'Vorcan.'

'I will not apologize,' she said.

'I did not ask you to.'

'We have a problem, Baruk,' she said, walking over to pour herself some wine, then facing him once more. 'It is not a question of seeking prevention – we cannot stop what is coming. The issue is how we will position ourselves for that time.'

'You mean, to ensure our continued survival.'

A faint smile as she regarded him. 'Survival is not in question. We three left in Cabal will be needed. As we were once, as we will be again. I am speaking more of our, shall we say, *level of comfort.*'

Anger flared within Baruk then. 'Comfort? What value that when we have ceased to be free?'

She snorted. 'Freedom is ever the loudest postulation among the indolent. And let's face it, Baruk, we *are* indolent. And now, suddenly, we face the end to that. Tragedy!' Her gaze hardened. 'I mean to remain in my privileged state—'

'As Mistress of the Assassins' Guild? Vorcan, there will be no need for such a Guild, no room for it.'

'Never mind the Guild. I am not interested in the Guild. It served, a function of the city, a bureaucratic mechanism. Its days are fast dwindling in number.'

'Is that why you sent your daughter away?'

A flicker of true annoyance in her eyes, and she looked away. 'My reasons are not of your concern in that matter, High Alchemist.' Her tone added, *And it's none of your business, old man.*

'What role, then,' Baruk asked, 'do you envision for yourself in this new Darujhistan?'

'A quiet one,' she replied.

Yes, quiet as a viper in the grass. 'Until such time, I imagine, as you see an opportunity.'

She drained her wine and set down the goblet. 'We are understood, then.'

'Yes,' he said, 'I suppose we are.'

'Do inform Derudan.'

'I shall.'

And she left.

The recollection left a sour taste in Baruk's mouth. Was she aware of the *other* convergences fast closing on Darujhistan? Did she even care? Well, she wasn't the only one who could be coy. One thing he had gleaned from that night of murder years ago: Vorcan had, somehow, guessed what was on its way. Even back then, she had begun her preparations . . . all to ensure her *level of comfort.* Sending her daughter away, extricating herself from the Guild. *And visiting her version of mercy upon the others in the Cabal. And if she'd got her way, she would now be the only one left alive.*

Think hard on that, Baruk, in the light of her professed intentions. Her desire to position herself.

Might she try again?

He realized he was no longer sure she wouldn't.

This is the moment for mirrors, and surely that must be understood by now. Polished, with the barest of ripples to twist the reflection, to make what one faces both familiar and subtly altered. Eyes locked, recognition unfolding, quiet horrors flowering. What looks upon you here, now, does not mock, denies the cogent wink, and would lead you by a dry and cool hand across the cold clay floor of the soul.

People will grieve. For the dead, for the living. For the loss of innocence and for the surrender of innocence, which are two entirely different things. We will grieve, for choices made and not made, for the mistakes of the heart which can never be undone, for the severed nerve-endings of old scars and those to come.

A grey-haired man walks through the Estate District. No more detailed description is necessary. The blood on his hands is only a memory, but some memories leave stains difficult to wash away. By nature, he observes. The world, its multitude of faces, its tide-tugged swirling sea of emotions. He is a caster of nets, a trailer of hooks. He speaks in the rhythm of poetry, in the lilt of song. He understands that there are wounds in the soul that must not be touched; but there are others that warm to the caress. He understands, in other words, the necessity of the tragic theme. The soul, he knows, will, on occasion, offer no resistance to the tale that draws blood.

Prise loose those old scars. They remind one what it is to grieve. They remind one what it is to live.

A moment for mirrors, a moment for masks. The two ever conspire to play out the tale. Again and again, my friends.

Here, take my hand.

He walks to an estate. The afternoon has waned, dusk creeps closer through the day's settling dust. Each day, there is a moment when the world has just passed by, leaving a sultry wake that hovers, suspended, not yet stirred by the awakening of night. The Tiste Edur worship this instant. The Tiste Andii are still, motionless as they wait for darkness. The Tiste Liosan have bowed their heads and turned away to grieve the sun's passing. In the homes of humans, hearthfires are stirred awake. People draw into their places of shelter and think of the night to come.

Before one's eyes, solidity seems poised, moments from crumbling into dissolution. Uncertainty becomes a law, rising supreme above all others. For a bard, this time is a minor key, a stretch of frailty, a pensive interlude. Sadness drifts in the air, and his thoughts are filled with endings.

Arriving at the estate, he is quickly and without comment escorted into the main house, down its central corridor and out into a high-walled garden where night flowers stream down the walls, drenched blossoms opening to drink in the gathering dusk. The masked bodyguard then leaves him, for the moment alone in the garden, and the bard stands motionless for a time, the air sweet and pungent, the sound of trickling water filling the enclosed space.

He recalls the soft songs he has sung here, unaccompanied by any instrument. Songs drawn from a hundred cultures, a dozen worlds. His voice weaving together the fragments of Shadow's arrival, drawing together the day just past and the night eager to arrive.

There were secrets in music and poetry. Secrets few knew and even fewer understood. Their power often stole into a listener subtle as the memory of scent on a drawn breath, less than a whisper, yet capable of transforming the one so gifted, an instinctual ecstasy that made troubles vanish, that made all manner of grandeur possible – indeed, within reach.

A skilled bard, a wise bard, knew that at certain moments in the course of a cycle of day and night, the path into the soul of a listener was smooth, unobstructed, a succession of massive gates that swung open to a feather's touch. This was the most precious secret of all. Dusk, midnight, and that strange period of sudden wakefulness known as the watch – yes, the night and its stealthy approach belonged to the heart.

Hearing a footfall behind him, he turns.

She stands, her long black hair shimmering, her face untouched by sun or wind, her eyes a perfect reflection of the violet blossoms adorning the walls. He can see through the white linen of her dress to the outlines of her body, roundness and curves and sweeps of aesthetic perfection – those forms and lines that murmured their own secret language to awaken desires in a man's soul.

Every sense, he knows, is a path into the heart.

Lady Envy watches him, and he is content to let her do so, as he in turn regards her.

They could discuss the Seguleh – the dead ones in the casks, the living ones serving in this estate. They could ponder all that they sensed fast approaching. He could speak of his anger, its quiet, deadly iron that was so cold it could burn at the touch – and she would see the truth of his words in his eyes. She might drift this way and that in this modest garden, brushing fingertips along trembling petals, and speak of desires so long held that she was almost insensate to the myriad roots and tendrils they had wrought through her body and soul, and he would perhaps warn her of the dangers they presented, the risk of failure that must be faced and, indeed, accepted – and she would sigh and nod and know well he spoke with wisdom.

Mocking flirtation, the jaw-dropping self-obsession, all the ways in which she amused herself when engaging with the mortals of this world, did not accompany Lady Envy to this garden. Not with this man awaiting her. Fisher kel Tath was not a young man – and there were times when she wondered if he was mortal at all, although she would never pry in search of truth – and he was not at all godlike with physical perfection. His gifts, if she could so crassly list them, would include his voice, his genius with the lyre and a dozen other obscure instruments, and the mind behind the eyes that saw all, that understood far too much of what he did see, that understood too the significance of all that remained and would ever remain hidden – yes, the mind behind the eyes and every faint hint he offered up to reveal something of that mind, its manner of observance, its stunning capacity for compassion that only blistering fools would call weakness.

No, this was one man whom she would not mock – could not, in fact.

They could have discussed many things. Instead, they stood, eyes meeting and held, and the dusk closed in with all its scents and secrets.

Storm the abyss and throw down a multitude of astounded gods! The sky cracks open from day into night, and then cracks yet again, revealing the flesh of space and the blood of time – see it rent and see it spray in glistening red droplets of dying stars! The seas boil and the earth steams and melts!

Lady Envy has found a lover.

Poetry and desire, fulminations one and the same and oh this is a secret to make thugs and brainless oafs howl at the night.

Has found a lover.

A lover.

'I dreamt I was pregnant.'

Torváld paused inside the door and hesitated just a little too long before saying, 'Why, that's great!'

Tiserra shot him a quizzical look from where she stood at the table bearing her latest throw of pottery. 'It is?'

'Absolutely, darling. You can go through all the misery of that without its being real. I can imagine your sigh of relief when you awoke and realized it was nothing but a dream.'

'Well, I certainly imagined yours, my love.'

He walked in and slumped down into a chair, stretching out his legs. 'Something strange is going on,' he said.

'It was just a passing madness,' she said. 'No need for you to fret, Tor.'

'I mean at the estate.' He rubbed at his face. 'The castellan spends all his time mixing up concoctions for diseases nobody has, and even if they did, his cures are liable to kill them first. The two compound guards do nothing but toss bones and that's hardly something you'd think renegade Seguleh would do, is it? And if that's not weird enough, Scorch and Leff are actually taking their responsibilities seriously.'

At that she snorted.

'No, really,' Torvald insisted. 'And I think I know why. They can smell it, Tiss. The strangeness. The Mistress went to the Council and claimed her place and there wasn't a whisper of complaint – or so I heard from Coll – and you'd think there'd be visitors now from various power blocs in the Council, everyone trying to buy her alliance. But . . . nothing. No one. Does that make sense?'

Tiserra was studying her husband. 'Ignore it, Tor. All of it. Your task is simple – keep it that way.'

He glanced up at her. 'I would, believe me. Except that all my instincts are on fire – as if some damned white-hot dagger is hovering at my back. And not just me, but Scorch and Leff, too.' He rose, began pacing.

'I haven't begun supper yet,' Tiserra said. 'It'll be awhile – why don't you go to the Phoenix Inn for a tankard or two? Say hello to Kruppe if you see him.'

'What? Oh. Good idea.'

She watched him leave, waited for a few dozen heartbeats to ensure that he'd found no reason to change his mind, and then went to one of the small trapdoors hidden in the floor, sprang the release and reached in to draw out her Deck of Dragons. She sat at the table and carefully removed the deerskin cover.

This was something she did rarely these days. She was sensitive enough to know that powerful forces were gathering in Darujhistan, making any field she attempted fraught with risk. Yet Tiserra, for all her advice to Torvald to simply ignore matters, well knew that her husband's instincts were too sharp to be summarily dismissed.

'Renegade Seguleh,' she muttered, then shook her head and collected up the Deck. Her version was Barukan, with a few cards of her own added, including one for The City – in this case, Darujhistan – and another – but no, she would not think of that one. Not unless she had to.

A tremor of fear rushed through her. The wooden cards felt cold in her hands. She decided on a spiral field and was not at all surprised when she set the centre card down and saw that it was The City, a silhouetted, familiar skyline at dusk, with the glow of blue fires rising up from below, each one like a submerged star. She studied it for a time, until those fires seemed to swim before her eyes, until the dusk the card portrayed began to flow into the world around her, one bleeding into the other, back and forth until the moment was fixed, time pinned down as if by a knife stabbed into the table. She was not seeking the future – prophecy was far too dangerous with all the converging powers – but the present. This very instant, each strand's point of attachment in the vast web that now spanned Darujhistan.

She set down the next card. High House Shadow, The Rope, Patron of Assassins. Well, that was not too surprising, given the latest rumours. Yet she sensed the relationship was more complicated than it at first appeared – yes, the Guild was active, was snarled in something far bloodier than they had anticipated. Too bad for them. Still, The Rope never played one game. There were others, beneath the surface. The obvious was nothing more than a veil.

The third card clattered on to the tabletop, and she found her hand would not rest, flinging out the next card and yet another. Three tightly bound, then. Three cards, forming their own woven nest. Obelisk, Soldier of Death, and Crown. These needed a frame. She set down the sixth card and grunted. Knight of Darkness – a faint rumble of wooden wheels, a chorus of moans drifting like smoke from the sword in the Knight's hands.

Thus, The Rope on one side, the Knight on the other. She saw that her hands were trembling. Three more cards quickly followed – another nest. King of High House Death, King in Chains, and Dessembrae, Lord of Tragedy. Knight of Darkness as the inside frame. She set down the other end and gasped. The card she wished she had never made. *The Tyrant.*

Closing the field. The spiral was done. City and Tyrant at beginning and end.

Tiserra had not expected anything like this. She was not seeking prophecy – her thoughts had been centred on her husband and whatever web he had found himself trapped in – no, not prophecy, nothing on such a grand scale as this . . .

I see the end of Darujhistan. Spirits save us, I see my city's end. This, Torvald, is your nest.

'Oh, husband,' she murmured, 'you are in trouble indeed . . .'

Her eyes strayed once more to The Rope. *Is that you, Cotillion? Or has Vorcan returned? It's not just the Guild – the Guild means nothing here. No, there are faces behind that veil. There are terrible deaths coming. Terrible deaths.* Abruptly, she swept up the cards, as if by that gesture alone she could defy what was coming, could fling apart the strands and so free the world to find a new future. As if things could be so easy. As if choices were indeed free.

Outside, a cart clunked past, its battered wheels crackling and stepping on the uneven cobbles. The hoofs of the ox pulling it beat slow as a dirge, and there came to her the rattle of a heavy chain, slapping leather and wood.

She wrapped the deck once more and returned it to its hiding place. And then went to another, this one made by her husband – perhaps indeed he'd thought to keep it a secret from her, but such things were impossible. She knew the creak of every floorboard, after all, and had found his private pit only days after he'd dug it.

Within, items folded within blue silk – the silk of the Blue Moranth. Tor's loot – she wondered again how he'd come by it. Even now, as she knelt above the cache, she could feel the sorcery roiling up thick as a stench, reeking of watery decay – the Warren of Ruse, no less, but then, perhaps not. *This, I think, is Elder. This magic, it comes from Mael.*

But then, what connection would the Blue Moranth have with the Elder God?

She reached down and edged back the silk. A pair of sealskin gloves, glistening as if they had just come up from the depths of some ice-laden sea. Beneath them, a water-etched throwing axe, in a style she had never seen before – not Moranth, for certain. A sea-raider's weapon, the inset patterns on the blue iron swirling like a host of whirlpools. The handle was an ivory tusk of some sort, appallingly oversized for any beast she could imagine. Carefully tucked in to either side of the weapon were cloth-wrapped grenados, thirteen in all, one of which was – she had discovered – empty of whatever chemical incendiary was trapped inside the others. An odd habit of the Moranth, but it had allowed her a chance to examine more closely the extraordinary skill involved in manufacturing such perfect porcelain globes, without risk of blowing herself and her entire home to pieces. True, she had heard that most Moranth munitions were made of clay, but not these ones, for some reason. Lacquered with a thick, mostly transparent gloss that was nevertheless faintly cerulean, these grenados were – to her eye – works of art, which made the destruction implicit in their proper use strike her as almost criminal.

Now, dear husband, why do you have these? Were they given to you, or did you – as is more likely – steal them?

If she confronted him, she knew, he would tell her the truth. But that was not something she would do. Successful marriages took as sacrosanct the possession of secrets. When so much was shared, certain other things must ever be held back. Small secrets, to be sure, but precious ones none the less.

Tiserra wondered if her husband foresaw a future need for such items. Or was this just another instance of his natural inclination to hoard, a quirk both charming and infuriating, sweet and potentially deadly (as all the best ones were).

Magic flowed in endless half-visible patterns about the porcelain globes – another detail she suspected was unusual.

Ensorcelled munitions – what were the Blue Moranth thinking?

Indeed, whatever were they thinking?

Two empty chairs faced Kruppe, a situation most peculiar and not at all pleasing. A short time earlier they had been occupied. Scorch and Leff, downing a fast tankard each before setting out to their place of employment, their nightly vigil at the gates of the mysterious estate and its mysterious lady. Oh, a troubled pair indeed, their fierce frowns denoting an uncharacteristic extreme of concentration. They'd swallowed down the bitter ale like water, the usual exchange of pleasant idiocies sadly muted. Watching them hurry out, Kruppe was reminded of two condemned men on the way to the gallows (or a wedding), proof of the profound unfairness of the world.

But fairness, while a comforting conceit, was an elusive notion, in the habit of swirling loose and wild about the vortex of the self, and should the currents of one collide with those of another, why, fairness ever revealed itself as a one-sided coin. In this fell clash could be found all manner of conflict, from vast continent-spanning wars to neighbours feuding over a crooked fence line.

But what significance these philosophical meanderings? Nary effect upon the trudging ways of life, to be sure. Skip and dance on to this next scene of portentous gravity, and here arriving hooded as a vulture through the narrow portal of the Phoenix Inn, none other than Torvald Nom. Pausing just within the threshold, answering Sulty's passing greeting with a distracted smile, and then to the bar, where Meese has already poured him a tankard. And in reaching over to collect it, Torvald's wrist is grasped, Meese pulling him close for a few murmured words of possible import, to which Torvald grimaces and then reluctantly nods – his response sufficient for Meese to release him.

Thus sprung, Torvald Nom strode over to smiling Kruppe's table and slumped down into one of the chairs. 'It's all bad,' he said.

'Kruppe is stunned, dear cousin of Rallick, at such miserable misery, such pessimistic pessimism. Why, scowling Torvald has so stained his world that even his underlings have been infected. Look, even here thy dark cloud crawls darkly Kruppe's way. Gestures are necessary to ward off sour infusion!' And he waved his hand, crimson handkerchief fluttering like a tiny flag. 'Ah, that is much better. Be assured, Torvald Kruppe's friend, that "bad" is never as bad as bad might be, even when it's very bad indeed.'

'Rallick left a message for me. He wants to see me.'

Kruppe waggled his brows and made an effort at leaning forward, but his belly got in the way so he settled back again, momentarily perturbed at what might be an expanding girth – but then, it was in truth a question of angles, and thus a modest shift in perspective eased his repose once more, thank the gods – 'Unquestionably Rallick seeks no more than a cheery greeting for his long lost cousin. There is, Kruppe proclaims, no need for worry.'

'Shows what little you know,' Torvald replied. 'I did something terrible once. Horrible, disgusting and evil. I scarred him for life. In fact, if he does track me down, I expect he'll kill me. Why d'you think I ran away in the first place?'

'A span of many years,' said Kruppe, 'weakens every bridge, until they crumble at a touch, or if not a touch, then a frenzied sledgehammer.'

'Will you speak to him for me, Kruppe?'

'Of course, yet, alas, Rallick has done something terrible and horrible and disgusting and evil to poor Kruppe, for which forgiveness is not possible.'

'What? What did he do?'

'Kruppe will think of something. Sufficient to wedge firmly the crowbar of persuasion, until he cannot but tilt helpless and desperate for succour in your direction. You need only open wide your arms, dear friend, when said moment arrives.'

'Thanks, Kruppe, you're a true friend.' And Torvald drank deep.

'No truer, no lie, 'tis true. Kruppe blesses you, alas, with none of the formal panoply accorded you by the Blue Moranth – oh, had Kruppe been there to witness such extraordinary, indeed singular, honorificals! Sulty, sweet lass, is it not time for supper? Kruppe withers with need! Oh, and perhaps another carafe of vintage—'

'Hold it,' Torvald Nom cut in, his eyes sharpening. 'What in Hood's name do you know about *that*, Kruppe? And how? Who told you – no one could've told you, because it was secret in the first place!'

'Calmly, please, calmly, Kruppe's dearest friend.' Another wave of the handkerchief, concluded by a swift mop as sweat had inexplicably sprung to brow. 'Why, rumours—'

'Not a chance.'

'Then, er, a dying confession—'

'We're about to hear one of those, yes.'

Kruppe hastily mopped some more. 'Source escapes me at the moment, Kruppe swears! Why, are not the Moranth in a flux—'

'They're *always* in a damned flux, Kruppe!'

'Indeed. Then, yes, perturbations among the Black, upon gleaning hints of said catechism, or was it investiture? Something religious, in any case—'

'It was a blessing, Kruppe.'

'Precisely, and who among all humans more deserved such a thing from the Moranth? Why, none, of course, which is what made it singular in the first place, thus arching the exoskeletal eyebrows of the Black, and no doubt the Red and Gold and Silver and Green and Pink – are there Pink Moranth? Kruppe is unsure. So many colours, so few empty slots in Kruppe's brain! Oh, spin the wheel and let's see explosive mauve flash into brilliant expostulation and why not? Yes, 'twas the Mauve Moranth so verbose and carelessly so, although not so carelessly as to reveal anything to anyone but Kruppe and Kruppe alone, Kruppe assures you. In fact, so precise their purple penchant for verbosity that even Kruppe's recollection of the specific moment is lost – to them and to Kruppe himself. Violate a Violet if you dare, but they're not telling. Nor is Kruppe!' And he squeezed out a stream of sweat from his handkerchief, off to one side, of course, which unfortunately coincided with Sulty's arrival with a plate of supper.

Thus did Kruppe discover the virtue of perspiratory reintegration, although his subsequent observation that the supper was a tad salty was not well received, not well received at all.

Astoundingly, Torvald quickly lost all appetite for his ale, deciding to leave (rudely so) in the midst of Kruppe's meal.

Proof that manners were not as they once were. But then, they never were, were they?

Hasty departure to echo Torvald Nom's flight back into the arms of his wife, out into the dusk when all paths are unobstructed, when nothing of reality intrudes with insurmountable obstacles and possibly deadly repercussions. In a merchant house annexe down at the docks, in the second floor loft above a dusty storeroom with sawdust on the floor, a wellborn young woman straddles a once-thief on the lone narrow cot with its thin, straggly mattress, and in her eyes darkness unfolds, is revealed to the man savage and naked – raw enough to startle in him a moment of fear.

Indeed. *Fear.* At the moment, Cutter could not reach past that ephemeral chill, could not find anything specific – what Challice's eyes revealed was all-consuming, frighteningly desperate, perhaps depthless and insatiable in its need.

She was unmindful of him – he could see that. In this instant he had become a weapon on which she impaled herself, ecstatic with the forbidden, alive with betrayal. She stabbed herself again and again, transformed into something private, for ever beyond his reach, and, yes, without doubt these were self-inflicted wounds, hinting of an inwardly directed contempt, perhaps even disgust.

He did not know what to think, but there was something alluring in being faceless, in being that weapon – and this truth shivered through him as dark as all that he saw in her eyes.

Apsalar, is this what you feared? If it is, then I understand. I understand why you fled. You did it for both of us.

With this thought he arched, groaning, and spilled into Challice Vidikas. She gasped, lowered herself on to him. Sweat on sweat, waves of heat embracing them.

Neither spoke.

From outside, gulls cried to the dying sun. Shouts and laughter muted by walls, the faint slap of waves on the broken crockery-cluttered shore, the creak of pulleys as ships were loaded and off-loaded. From outside, the world as it always was.

Cutter was now thinking of Scillara, of how this was a kind of betrayal – no different from Challice's own. True, Scillara had said often enough that theirs was a love of convenience, unbound by expectations. She'd insisted on that distance, and if there had been moments of uncontrolled passion in their lovemaking, it was the selfish kind, quickly plucked apart once they were both spent. He also suspected that he had hurt her – with their landing in his city, some part of him had sought to sever what they had had aboard the ship, as if by closing one chapter every thread was cut and the tale began anew.

But that wasn't possible. All breaks in the narrative of living had more to do with the limits of what could be sustained at any one time, the reach of temporary exhaustion. Memory did not let go; it remained the net dragged in one's wake, with all sort of strange things snarled in the knotted strands.

He had behaved unfairly, and that had hurt her and, indeed, hurt their friendship. And now it seemed he had gone too far, too far to ever get back what he now realized was precious, was *truer* than everything he was feeling now, here beneath this woman.

It's said joy's quick crash was weighted in truth. All at once Challice, sprawled prone atop him, felt heavier.

In her own silence, Challice of House Vidikas was thinking back to that morning, to one of those rare breakfasts in the company of her husband. There had been sly amusement in his expression, or at least the tease of that emotion, making his every considerate gesture slightly mocking, as if in sitting facing one another at the table they were but acting out clichéd roles of propriety. And finding, it seemed, a kind of comfort in the ease of their mutual falsehoods.

She suspected that some of Gorlas's satisfaction involved a bleed-over into her private activities, as if it pleased him to take some credit for her fast-receding descent into depravity; that his unperturbed comfort was in fact supportive, something to be relied upon, a solid island she could flail back to when the storm grew too wild, when her swimming in the depths took on the characteristics of drowning.

Making her so-called private activities little more than extensions of his possession. In owning her he was free to see her used and used up elsewhere. In fact, she had sensed a sexual tension between them that had not been there since . . . that had *never* been there before. She was, she realized, making herself more desirable to him.

It seemed a very narrow bridge that he chose to walk. Some part of her, after all, was her own – belonging to no one else no matter what they might believe – and so she would, ultimately, be guided by her own decisions, the choices she made that would serve her and none other. Yes, her husband played a most dangerous game here, as he might well discover.

He had spoken, in casual passing, of the falling out between Shardan Lim and Hanut Orr, something trivial and soon to mend, of course. But moments were strained of late, and neither ally seemed eager to speak to Gorlas about any of it. Hanut Orr had, however, said some strange things, offhand, to Gorlas in the few private conversations they'd had – curious, suggestive things, but no matter. It was clear that something had wounded Hanut Orr's vaunted ego, and that was ever the danger with possessing such an ego – its constant need to be fed, lest it deflate to the prods of sharp reality.

Sharden Lim's mood, too, had taken a sudden downward turn. One day veritably exalted, the next dour and short-tempered.

Worse than adolescents, those two. You'd think there was a woman involved . . .

Challice had affected little interest, finding, to her own surprise, that she was rather good at dissembling, at maintaining the necessary pretensions. The Mistress of the House, the pearlescent prize of the Master, ever smooth to the touch, as delicate as a porcelain statue. Indifferent to the outside world and all its decrepit, smudged details. This was the privilege of relative wealth, after all, encouraging the natural inclination to manufacture a comforting cocoon. Keeping out the common indelicacies, the mundane miseries, all those raw necessities, needs, wants, all those crude stresses that so strained the lives of normal folk.

Only to discover, in gradual increments of growing horror, that the world within was little different; that all those grotesque foibles of humanity could not be evaded – they just reared up shinier to the eye, like polished baubles, but no less cheap, no less sordid.

In her silence, Challice thought of the gifts of privilege, and oh wasn't she privileged indeed? A rich husband getting richer, one lover among his closest allies (and that was a snare she might use again, if the need arose), and now another – one Gorlas knew virtually nothing about. At least, she didn't think he did.

Sudden rapid flutter of her heart. *What if he has someone following me?* The possibility was very real, but what could she do about it? And what might her husband do when he discovered that her most recent lover was not a player in his game? That he was, in fact, a stranger, someone clearly beyond his reach, his sense of control. Would he then realize that she too was now beyond his control?

Gorlas might panic. He might, in truth, become murderous.

'Be careful now, Cro— Cutter. What we have begun is very dangerous.'

He said nothing in reply, and after a moment she pushed herself off him, and rose to stand beside the narrow bed. 'He would kill you,' she continued, looking down on him, seeing once again how the years had hardened his body, sculpted muscles bearing the scars of past battles. His eyes, fixed on her own, regarded her with thoughts and feelings veiled, unknowable.

'He's a duellist, isn't he?'

She nodded. 'One of the best in the city.'

'Duels,' he said, 'don't frighten me.'

'That would be a mistake, Cutter. In any case, given your . . . station, it's doubtful he'd bother with anything so formal. More like a half-dozen thugs hired to get rid of you. Or even an assassin.'

'So,' he asked, 'what should I do about it?'

She hesitated, and then turned away to find her clothes. 'I don't know. I was but warning you, my love.'

'I would imagine you'd be even more at risk.'

She shrugged. 'I don't think so. Although,' she added, 'a jealous man is an unpredictable man.' Turning, she studied him once more. 'Are you jealous, Cutter?'

'Of Gorlas Vidikas?' The question seemed to surprise him and she could see him thinking about it. 'Title and wealth, yes, that would be nice. Being born into something doesn't mean it's deserved, of course, so maybe he hasn't earned all his privileges, but then, maybe he has – you'd know more of that than I would.'

'That's not what I meant. When he takes me, when he makes love to me.'

'Oh. Does he?'

'Occasionally.'

'Make love? Or just make use of you?'

'That is a rather rude question.'

Years ago, he would have leapt to his feet, apologies tumbling from him in a rush. Now, he remained on the bed, observing her with those calm eyes. Challice felt a shiver of something in her, and thought it might be fear. She had assumed a certain . . . control. Over all of this. Over him. And now she wondered. 'What,' he now asked, 'do you want from me, Challice? Years and years of this? Meeting in dusty, abandoned bedrooms. Something you can own that Gorlas does not? It's not as if you'll ever leave him, is it?'

'You once invited me to run away with you.'

'If I did,' he said, 'you clearly said no. What has changed?'

'I have.'

His gaze sharpened on her. 'So now . . . you would? Leave it all behind? The estate, the wealth?' He waved languidly at the room around them. 'For a life of this? Challice, understand: the world of most people is a small world. It has more limitations that you might think—'

'And you think it's that different among the nobleborn?'

He laughed.

Fury hissed through her, and to keep from lashing out she quickly began dressing. 'It's typical,' she said, pleased at her calm tone. 'I shouldn't have been surprised. The lowborn always think we have it so easy, that we can do anything, go anywhere. That our every whim is answered. They don't think—' she spun to face him, and watched his eyes widen as he comprehended her anger, '—*you* don't think that people like me can suffer.'

'I never said that—'

'You *laughed*.'

'Where are you going now, Challice? You're going back to your home. Your estate, where your handmaids will rush to attend to you. Where another change of clothes and jewellery awaits. After a languid bath, of course.' He sat up, abruptly. 'The ship's carpenter who stayed in this room here, well, he did so because he had nowhere else to go. This was *his* estate. Temporary, dependent on the *whim* of House Vidikas, and when his reason for being here was done out he went, to find somewhere else to live – if he was lucky.' He reached for his shirt. 'And where will I go now? Oh, out on to the streets. Wearing the same clothes I arrived in, and that won't change any time soon. And tonight? Maybe I can wheedle another night in a room at the Phoenix Inn. And if I help in the kitchen I'll earn a meal and if Meese is in a good mood then maybe even a bath. Tomorrow, the same challenges of living, the same questions of "what next?"' He faced her and she saw amused irony in his expression, which slowly faded. 'Challice, I'm not saying you're somehow immune to suffering. If you were, you wouldn't be here, would you? I spoke of limited worlds. They exist everywhere, but that doesn't mean they're all identical. Some are a damned sight more limited than others.'

'You had choices, Cutter,' she said. 'More choices than I ever had.'

'You could have told Gorlas no when he sought your hand in marriage.'

'Really? Now that reveals one thing in you that's not changed – your naïveté.'

He shrugged. 'If you say so. What next, Challice?'

His sudden, seemingly effortless dismissal of the argument took her breath away. *It doesn't matter to him. None of it. Not how I feel, not how I see him.* 'I need to think,' she said, inwardly flailing.

He nodded as if unsurprised.

'Tomorrow evening,' she said, 'we should meet again.'

A half-grin as he asked, 'To talk?'

'Among other things.'

'All right, Challice.'

Some thoughts, possessing a frightening kind of self-awareness, knew to hide deep beneath others, riding unseen the same currents, where they could grow unchallenged, unexposed by any horrified recognition. One could always sense them, of course, but that was not the same as slashing through all the obfuscation, revealing them bared to the harsh light and so seeing them wither into dust. The mind ran its own shell-game, ever amused at its own sleight of hand misdirection – in truth, this was how one tended to live, from moment to moment, with the endless exchange of denials and deference and quick winks in the mirror, even as inner proclamations and avowals thundered with false willpower and posturing conviction.

Does this lead one into unease?

Challice Vidikas hurried home, nevertheless taking a circuitous route as now and then whispers of paranoia rose in faint swells to the surface of her thoughts.

She was thinking of Cutter, this man who had once been Crokus. She was thinking of the significance in the new name, the new man she had found. She was thinking, also (there, beneath the surface), of what to do with him.

Gorlas would find out, sooner or later. He might confront her, he might not. She might discover that he knew only by arriving one afternoon at the loft in the annexe, and finding Cutter's hacked, lifeless corpse awaiting her on the bed.

She knew she was trapped – in ways a free man like Cutter could never comprehend. She knew, as well, that the ways out were limited, each one chained to sacrifices, losses, abandonments, and some . . . despicable. Yes, that was the only word for them.

Despicable. She tasted the word anew, there in her mind. Contemplated whether she was in fact capable of living with such a penance. *But why would I? What would I need to see done, to make me see myself in that way?*

How many lives am I willing to destroy, in order to be free?

The question itself was despicable, the stem to freedom's blessed flower – to grasp hold was to feel the stab of countless thorns.

Yet she held tight now, riding the pain, feeling the slick blood welling up, running down. She held tight, to feel, to taste, to know what was coming . . . if . . . *if I decide to accept this.*

She could wait for Gorlas to act. Or she could strike first.

A corpse lying on the bed. A mangled rose lying on the floor.

Cutter was not Crokus – she could see that, yes, very clearly. Cutter was . . . *dangerous.* She recalled the scars, the old knife wounds, sword wounds even, perhaps. Others that might have been left by the punch of arrows or crossbolts. He had fought, he had taken lives – she was certain of it.

Not the boy he'd once been. *But this man he now is . . . can he be used? Would he even blink if I so asked?*

Should I ask? Soon? Tomorrow?

Thus exposed, one must recoil indeed, but these were deep-run thoughts, nowhere near the surface. They were free to flow, free to swirl round unseen, if as detached from all reality. But they weren't, were they? Detached from all reality.

Oh, no, they were not.

Does this lead one into unease?

On a surge of immense satisfaction, Barathol Mekhar's rather large fist smashed into the man's face, sending him flying back through the doorway of the smithy. He stepped out after him, shaking the stinging pain from his hand. 'I will be pleased to pay the Guild's annual fees, sir,' he said, 'when the Guild decides to accept my membership. As for demanding coin while denying my right to run my business, well, you have just had my first instalment.'

A smashed nose, blood pouring forth, eyes staring up from a puffiness burgeoning to swallow up his features, the Guild agent managed a feeble nod.

'You are welcome,' Barathol continued, 'to come back next week for the next one, and by all means bring a few dozen of your associates – I expect I'll be in an even more generous mood by then.'

A crowd had gathered to watch, but the blacksmith was disinclined to pay them any attention. He rather wanted word to get out, in fact, although from what he'd gathered his particular feud was already a sizzling topic of conversation, and no doubt his words just spoken would be quoted and misquoted swift as a plague on the hot winds.

Turning about, he walked back into his shop.

Chaur stood near the back door, wearing his heavy apron with its spatter of burn holes revealing the thick weave of aesgir grass insulation beneath the leather – the only plant known that did not burn, even when flung into a raging fire. Oversized gloves of the same manufacture covered his hands and forearms, and he was holding tongs that gripped a fast-cooling curl of bronze. Chaur's eyes were bright and he was smiling.

'Best get that back into the forge,' Barathol said.

As expected, business was slow. A campaign had begun, fomented by the Guild, that clearly involved the threat of a blacklist that could – and would – spread to other guilds in the city. Barathol's customers could find themselves unable to purchase things they needed from a host of other professions, and that of course would prove devastating. And as for Barathol's own material requirements, most doors had already begun closing in his face. He was forced to seek out alternatives in the black market, never·a secure option.

As his friend Mallet had predicted, Malazans resident in the city had been indifferent to all such extortions and warnings against taking Barathol's custom. There was, evidently, something in their nature that resisted the notion of threats, and in fact being told they could not do something simply raised their hackles and set alight a stubborn fire in their eyes. That such a response could prove a curse had been driven home with the slaughter at K'rul's – and the grief that followed remained deeply embedded in Barathol, producing within him a dark, cold rage. Unfortunately for the latest agent from the Guild of Blacksmiths, something of that fury had transferred itself into Barathol's instinctive reaction to the man's demand for coin.

Even so, he had not come to Darujhistan to make enemies. Yet now he found himself in a war. Perhaps more than one at that. No wonder, then, his foul mood.

He made his way into the work yard, where the heat from the two stoked forges rolled over him in a savage wave. His battle axe needed a new edge, and it might do to fashion a new sword – something he could actually wear·in public.

Barathol's new life in Darujhistan was proving anything but peaceful.

Bellam Nom was, in Murillio's estimation, the only student of the duelling school worthy of the role. Fifteen years of age, still struggling with the awkwardness of his most recent growth spurt, he approached his studies with surprising determination. Even more astonishing, the lad actually *wanted* to be here.

In the prolonged absence of Stonny Menackis's attention, it had fallen to Murillio to assume most of the school's responsibilities, and he was finding this very distant relation of Rallick (and Torvald) in every respect a Nom, which alone encouraged a level of instruction far beyond what he gave the others. The young man stood before him sheathed in sweat, as the last of class hurried out through the compound gate, the echoes of their voices quickly fading, and Murillio sensed that Bellam was far from satisfied with the torturously slow pace of the day's session.

'Master,' he now said, 'I have heard of an exercise, involving suspended rings. To achieve the perfect lunge, piercing the hole and making no contact with the ring itself—'

Murillio snorted. 'Yes. Useful if you happen to be in a travelling fair or a circus. Oh, for certain, Bellam, point control is essential in fencing with the rapier – I wouldn't suggest otherwise. But as an exercise, I am afraid its value is limited.'

'Why?'

Murillio eyed the young man for a moment, and then sighed. 'Very well. The exercise requires too many constraints, few of which ever occur in the course of a real fight. You achieve point control – useful point control, I mean – when it's made integral to other exercises. When it's combined with footwork, distance, timing and the full range of defence and offence demanded when facing a real, living opponent. Spearing rings is all very impressive, but the form of concentration it demands is fundamentally *different* from the concentration necessary in a duel. In any case, you can spend the next two months mastering the art of spearing a ring, or two months mastering the art of staying alive against a skilled enemy, and not just staying alive, but presenting a true threat to that enemy, in turn.' He shrugged. 'Your choice, of course.'

Bellam Nom grinned suddenly and Murillio saw at once how much he looked like his oh-so-distant cousin. 'I still might try it – in my own time, of course.'

'Tell you what,' Murillio said. 'Master spearing a suspended ring at the close of a mistimed lunge, an off-balance recovery to your unarmed side, two desperate parries, a toe-stab to your opponent's lead foot to keep him or her from closing, and a frantic stop-thrust in the midst of a back-pedalling retreat. Do that, and I will give you my second best rapier.'

'How long do I have?'

'As long as you like, Bellam.'

'Extra time with an instructor,' said a voice from the shaded colonnade to one side, 'is not free.'

Murillio turned and bowed to Stonny Menackis. 'Mistress, we were but conversing—'

'You were giving advice,' she cut in, 'and presenting this student with a challenge. The first point qualifies as instruction. The second is an implicit agreement to extracurricular efforts on your part at some time in the future.'

Bellam's grin had broadened. 'My father, Mistress, will not hesitate to meet any extra expense, I assure you.'

She snorted, stepping out from the gloom. 'Any?'

'Within reason, yes.'

She looked terrible. Worn, old, her clothes dishevelled. If Murillio had not known better, he would judge her as being hungover, a condition of temporary, infrequent sobriety to mark an alcoholic slide into fatal oblivion. Yet he knew she was afflicted with something far more tragic. Guilt and shame, self-hatred and grief. The son she didn't want had been taken from her – to imagine that such a thing could leave her indifferent was to not understand anything at all.

Murillio said to Bellam, 'You'd best go now.'

They watched him walk away.

'Look at him,' Stonny muttered as he reached the gate, 'all elbows and knees.'

'That'll pass,' he said.

'A stage, is it?'

'Yes.' And of course he knew this particular game, the way she spoke of Harllo by not speaking of him, of the life that might await him, or the future taken away from him, stolen by her cruel denial. She would inflict this on herself again and again, at every opportunity. Seemingly innocent observations, each one a masochistic flagellation. For this to work, she required someone like Murillio, who would stand and listen and speak and pretend that all this was normal – the back and forth and give and take, the blood pooling round her boots. She had trapped him in this role – using the fact of his adoration, his love for her – and he was no longer certain that his love could survive such abuse.

The world is small. And getting smaller.

He had walked the pauper pits south of the city, just outside the wall between the two main trader gates. He had looked upon scores of recent unclaimed dead. It was, in fact, becoming something of a ritual for him, and though he had only secondhand descriptions of Harllo, he did his best, since no one who knew the boy would accompany him. Not Stonny, not Myrla nor Bedek. On occasion, Murillio had been forced to descend into one of the pits to make closer examination of some small body, a soft, lime-dusted face, eyes lidded shut as if in sleep or, on occasion, scrunched in some last moment of pain, and these mute, motionless faces now paraded in his dreams at night, a procession of such sorrow that he awoke with tears streaming from his eyes.

He told Stonny none of this. He'd said nothing of how his and Kruppe's enquiries among the sailors and fisherfolk had failed to find any evidence of someone press-ganging a five-year-old boy. And that every other possible trail thus far had turned up nothing, not even a hint or remote possibility, leaving at last the grim likelihood of some fell mishap, unreported, uninvestigated – just another dead child abandoned long before death's arrival, known only in the records of found corpses as the "twice-dead".

'I am thinking of signing over my stakes in this school,' Stonny now said. 'To you.'

Startled, he turned to stare at her. 'I won't accept.'

'Then you'd be a fool – as if I didn't already know that. You're better suited. You're a better teacher. I barely managed any interest in this from the very start – it was always the coin – and now I find I could not care less. About the school, the students – even promising ones like Nom there. I don't care about anything, in fact.'

Including you, Murillio. Yes, he heard that unspoken addition without the need for her to actually say it aloud. Well, she would of course want to push him away. Much as she needed him to play those self-wounding games with her, she needed even more the solitude necessary for complete self-destruction. Isolation was more than a simple defence mechanism; it also served to prepare one for more severe punishments, possibly culminating in suicide. On another level, she would view her desire to drive him off as an act of mercy on her part. But that was a most irritating form of self-pity.

He had given his heart to the wrong woman. *Timing, Bellam Nom, is everything. With sword in hand.*

With love in hand.

Oh, well. I'd figured it out with a rapier, at least.

'Don't make that decision just yet,' he said. 'I have one more thing I can try.' *It won't be pleasant, but you don't need to know that.*

Stonny simply turned away. 'I'll see you tomorrow, then.'

Many adults, in the indurated immobility of years, acquire a fear of places they have never been, even as they long for something different in their lives, something new. But this new thing is a world of the fantastical, formless in answer to vague longings, and is as much defined by absence as presence. It is a conjuration of emotions and wishful imaginings, which may or may not possess a specific geography. Achieving such a place demands a succession of breaks with one's present situation, always a traumatic endeavour, and upon completion, why, sudden comes the fear.

Some do not choose the changes in their lives. Some changes no one in their right mind would ever choose. In K'rul's Bar, a once-soldier of the Malazan Empire stands tottering over the unconscious form of her lover, whilst behind her paces Antsy, muttering self-recriminations under his breath, interrupted every now and then with a stream of curses in a half-dozen languages.

Blend understood all that had motivated Picker to attempt what she had done. This did little to assuage her fury. The very same High Denul healer that had just attended to her had set to a thorough examination of Picker as soon as Antsy had returned with his charge lying in the bed of a hired oxcart, only to pronounce that there was nothing to be done. Either Picker would awaken or she wouldn't. Her spirit had been torn loose and now wandered lost.

The healer had left. In the main room below, Duiker and Scillara sat in the company of ghosts and not much else.

Although still weak, Blend set out to collect her weapons and armour. Antsy followed her into the corridor.

'What're you planning?' he demanded, almost on her heels as she went into her own room.

'I'm not sure,' she replied, laying out her chain hauberk on the bed, then pulling off her shirt to find the padded undergarment.

Antsy's eyes bugged slightly as he stared at her breasts, the faint bulge of her belly, the sweet—

Blend tugged on the quilted shirt and then returned to the hauberk. 'You'll need to wrap me,' she said.

'Huh? Oh, aye. Right. But what about me?'

She regarded him for a moment. 'You want to help?'

He half snarled in reply.

'All right,' she said. 'Go find a couple of crossbows and plenty of quarrels. You're going to cover me, for as long as that's possible. We don't walk together.'

'Aye, Blend.'

She worked the hauberk over her head and pushed her arms through the heavy sleeves.

Antsy went to the equipment trunk at the foot of the bed and began rummaging through its contents, looking for the swaths of black cloth to bind the armour close and noiseless about Blend's body. 'Gods below, woman, what do you need all these clothes for?'

'Banquets and soirées, of course.'

'You ain't never been to one in your life, woman.'

'The possibility always exists, Antsy. Yes, those ones, but make sure the draw-strings are still in them.'

'How do you expect to find the nest?'

'Simple,' she said. 'Don't know why we didn't think of it before. The name Picker said, the one that Jaghut heard.' She selected a matched pair of Wickan longknives from her store of weapons and strapped the belt on, low on her hips, offered Antsy a hard grin. 'I'm going to ask the Eel.'

Chapter Sixteen

And these things were never so precious
Listen to the bird in its cage as it speaks
In a dying man's voice; when he is gone
The voice lives to greet and give empty
Assurances with random poignancy

I do not know if I could live with that
If I could armour myself as the inhuman beak
Opens to a dead man's reminder, head cocked
As if channelling the ghost of the one
Who imagines an absence of sense, a vacuum awaiting

The cage is barred and nightly falls the shroud
To silence the commentary of impossible apostles
Spirit godlings and spanning abyss, impenetrable cloud
Between the living and the dead, the here and the gone
Where no bridge can smooth the passage of pain

And these things were never so precious
Listening to the bird as it speaks and it speaks
And it speaks, the one who has faded away
The father departed knowing the unknown
And it speaks and it speaks and it speaks
In my father's voice

CAGED BIRD
FISHER KEL TATH

There was no breath to speak of. Rather, what awoke him was the smell
of death, dry, an echo of pungent decay that might belong to the carcass of a beast left in the high grasses, desiccated yet holding its reek
about itself, close and suffocating as a cloak. Opening his eyes, Kallor found himself staring up at the enormous, rotted head of a dragon, its massive fangs and
shredded gums almost within reach.

The morning light was blotted out and it seemed the shade cast by the dragon
roiled with all its centuries of forgotten breath.

As the savage thunder of Kallor's heartbeat eased, he slowly edged to one side – the dragon's viper head tilting to track his movement – and carefully stood, keeping his hands well away from the scabbarded sword lying on the ground beside his bedroll. 'I did not,' he said, scowling, 'ask for company.'

The dragon withdrew its head in a crackling of dried scales along the length of its serpent neck; settled back between the twin cowls of its folded wings.

He could see runnels of dirt trickling down from creases and joins on the creature's body. One gaunt forelimb bore the tracery of fine roots in a colourless mockery of blood vessels. From the shadowed pits beneath the gnarled brow ridges there was the hint of withered eyes, a mottling of grey and black that could hold no display of desire or intent; and yet Kallor felt that regard raw as sharkskin against his own eyes as he stared up at the undead dragon.

'You have come,' he said, 'a long way, I suspect. But I am not for you. I can give you nothing, assuming I wanted to, which I do not. And do not imagine,' he added, 'that I will bargain with you, whatever hungers you may still possess.'

He looked about his makeshift camp, saw that the modest hearth with its fistful of coals still smouldered from the previous night's fire. 'I am hungry, and thirsty,' he said. 'You can leave whenever it pleases you.'

The dragon's sibilant voice spoke in Kallor's skull. *'You cannot know my pain.'*

He grunted. 'You cannot *feel* pain. You're dead, and you have the look of having been buried. For a long time.'

'The soul writhes. There is anguish. I am broken.'

He fed a few clumps of dried bhederin dung on to the coals, and then glanced over. 'I can do nothing about that.'

'I have dreamt of a throne.'

Kallor's attention sharpened with speculation. 'You would choose a master? That is unlike your kind.' He shook his head. 'I scarcely believe it.'

'Because you do not understand. None of you understand. So much is beyond you. You think to make yourself the King in Chains. Do not mock my seeking a master, High King Kallor.'

'The Crippled God's days are numbered, Eleint,' said Kallor. 'Yet the throne shall remain, long after the chains have rusted to dust.'

There was silence between them then, for a time. The morning sky was clear, tinted faintly red with the pollen and dust that seemed to seethe up from this land. Kallor watched the hearth finally lick into flames, and he reached for the small, battered, blackened pot. Poured the last of his water into it and set the pot on the tripod perched above the fire. Swarms of suicidal insects darted into the flames, igniting in sparks, and Kallor wondered at this penchant for seeking death, as if the lure for an end was irresistible. Not a trait he shared, however.

'I remember my death,' the dragon said.

'And that's worth remembering?'

'The Jaghut were a stubborn people. So many saw naught but the coldness in their hearts—'

'Misunderstood, were they?'

'They mocked your empire, High King. They answered you with scorn. It seems the wounds have not healed.'

'A recent reminder, that's all,' Kallor replied, watching the water slowly awaken. He tossed in a handful of herbs. 'Very well, tell me your tale. I welcome the amusement.'

The dragon lifted its head and seemed to study the eastern horizon.

'Never wise to stare into the sun,' Kallor observed. 'You might burn your eyes.'

'It was brighter then – do you recall?'

'Perturbations of orbit, or so believed the K'Chain Che'Malle.'

'So too the Jaghut, who were most diligent in their observations of the world. Tell me, High King, did you know they broke peace only once? In all their existence – no, not the T'lan Imass – that war belonged to those savages and the Jaghut were a most reluctant foe.'

'They should have turned on the Imass,' Kallor said. 'They should have annihilated the vermin.'

'Perhaps, but I was speaking of an earlier war – the war that destroyed the Jaghut long before the coming of the T'lan Imass. The war that shattered their unity, that made of their lives a moribund flight from an implacable enemy – yes, long before and long after the T'lan Imass.'

Kallor considered that for a moment, and then he grunted and said, 'I am not well versed in Jaghut history. What war was this? The K'Chain Che'Malle? The Forkrul Assail?' He squinted at the dragon. 'Or, perhaps, you Eleint?'

There was sorrow in its tone as the dragon replied, 'No. There were some among us who chose to join in this war, to fight alongside the Jaghut armies—'

'Armies? Jaghut armies?'

'Yes, an entire people gathered, a host of singular will. Legions uncountable. Their standard was rage, their clarion call injustice. When they marched, swords beating on shields, time itself found measure, a hundred million hearts of edged iron. Not even you, High King, could imagine such a sight – your empire was less than a squall to that terrible storm.'

For once, Kallor had nothing to say. No snide comment to voice, no scoffing refutation. In his mind he saw the scene the dragon had described, and was struck mute. To have witnessed such a thing!

The dragon seemed to comprehend his awe. 'Yes again, High King. When you forged your empire, it was on the dust of that time, that grand contest, that most bold assault. We fought. We refused to retreat. We failed. We fell. So many of us fell – should we have believed otherwise? Should we have held to our faith in the righteousness of our cause, even as we came to believe that we were doomed?'

Kallor stared across at the dragon, the tea in the pot steaming away. He could almost hear the echoes of tens of millions, hundreds of millions, dying on a plain so vast even the horizons could not close it in. He saw flames, rivers of blood, a sky solid with ash. In creating this image, he had only to draw upon his own fury of destruction, then multiply it a thousand fold. The notion took his breath, snatched it from his lungs, and his chest filled with pain. 'What,' he managed, 'who? What enemy could vanquish such a force?'

'Grieve for the Jaghut, High King, when at last you sit on that throne. Grieve for the chains that bind all life, that you can never break. Weep, for me and my fallen kin – who did not hesitate to join a war that could not be won. Know, for ever in your soul, Kallor Eidorann, that the Jaghut fought the war no other has dared to fight.'

'Eleint . . .'

'Think of these people. Think of them, High King. The sacrifice they made for us all. Think of the Jaghut, and an impossible victory won in the heart of defeat. Think, and then you will come to understand all that is to come. Perhaps, then, you alone will know enough to honour their memory, the sacrifice they made for us all.

'High King, the Jaghut's only war, their greatest war, was against Death itself.'

The dragon turned away then, spreading its tattered wings. Sorcery blossomed round the huge creature, and it lifted into the air.

Kallor stood, watching the Eleint rise into the cinnamon sky. A nameless dead dragon, that had fallen in the realm of Death, that had fallen and in dying had simply . . . *switched sides*. No, there could be no winning such a war. 'You damned fool,' he whispered at the fast receding Eleint. 'All of you, damned fools.' *Bless you, bless you all.*

Gothos, when next we meet, this High King owes you an apology.

On withered cheeks that seemed cursed to eternal dryness, tears now trickled down. He would think long and think hard, now, and he would come to feelings that he'd not felt in a long time, so long that they seemed foreign, dangerous to harbour in his soul.

And he would wonder, with growing unease, at the dead Eleint who, upon escaping the realm of Death, would now choose the Crippled God as its new master.

A throne, Emperor Kellanved once said, *is made of many parts*. And then he had added, *any one of which can break, to the king's eternal discomfort*. No, it did no good to simply sit on a throne, deluding oneself of its eternal solidity. He had known that long before Kellanved ever cast an acquisitive eye on empire. But he was not one for resonant quotations.

Well, everyone has a few flaws.

In a dark pool a score of boulders rise clear of the lightless, seemingly lifeless surface. They appear as islands, no two connected in any obvious way, no chain of uplifted progression to hint at some mostly submerged range of mountains, no half-curl to mark a flooded caldera. Each stands alone, a bold proclamation.

Is this how it was at the very beginning? Countless scholars struggled to make sense of it, the distinct existences, the imposition of order in myriad comprehensions. Lines were drawn, flags splashed with colours, faces blended into singular philosophies and attitudes and aspects. *Here there is Darkness, and here there is Life. Light, Earth, Fire, Shadow, Air, Water. And Death.* As if such aspects began as pure entities, unstained by contact with any of the others. And as if *time* was the enemy, forcing the inevitable infections from one to another.

Whenever Endest Silann thought about these things, he found himself trapped in a prickly, uneasy suspicion. In his experience, purity was an unpleasant concept, and to imagine worlds defined by purity filled him with fear. An existence held to be pure was but the physical corollary of a point of view bound in certainty. Cruelty could thrive unfettered by compassion. The pure could see no value among the impure, after all. Justifying annihilation wasn't even necessary, since the inferiority was ever self-evident.

Howsoever all creation had begun, he now believed, those pure forms existed as nothing more than the raw materials for more worthy elaborations. As any alchemist knew, transformation was only possible as a result of admixture. For creation to thrive, there must be an endless succession of catalysts.

His Lord had understood that. Indeed, he had been driven to do all that he had done by that very comprehension. And change was, for so many, terrifying. For so much of existence, Anomander Rake had fought virtually alone. Even his brothers had but fallen, bound by the ties of blood, into the chaos that followed.

Was Kharkanas truly the first city? The first, proudest salutation to order in the cosmos? Was it in fact even true that Darkness preceded all else? What of the other worlds, the rival realms? And, if one thought carefully about that nascent age of creation, had not the admixture already begun? Was there not Death in the realms of Darkness, Light, Fire and all the rest? Indeed, how could Life and Death exist in any form of distinction without the other?

No, he now believed that the Age of Purity was but a mythical invention, a convenient separation of all the forces necessary for all existence. Yet was he not witness to the Coming of Light? To Mother Dark's wilful rejection of eternal stasis? Did he not with his own eyes see the birth of a sun over his blessed, precious city? How could he not have understood, at that moment, how all else would follow, inevitably, inexorably? That fire would awaken, that raging winds would howl, that waters would rise and the earth crack open? That death would flood into their world in a brutal torrent of violence? That Shadow would slide between things, whispering sly subversions of all those pristine absolutes?

He sat alone in his room, in the manner of all old men when the last witness has wandered off, when nothing but stone walls and insensate furniture gathered close to mock his last few aspirations, his last dwindling reasons for living. In his mind he witnessed yet again, in a vision still sharp, still devastating, Andarist staggering into view. Blood on his hands. Blood painted in the image of a shattered tree upon his grief-wracked face – oh, the horror in his eyes could still make Endest Silann reel back, wanting none of this, this curse of witnessing—

No, better stone walls and insensate furniture. All the errors in Andarist's life, now crowding with jabbering madness in those wide, staring eyes.

Yes, he had reeled back once that stare fixed his own. Some things should never be communicated, should never be cast across to slash through the heavy curtains one raised to keep whatever was without from all that was within, slashing through and lodging deep in the soul of a defenceless witness. *Keep your pain to yourself, Andarist! He left you to this – he left you thinking you wiser than you were. Do not look so betrayed, damn you! He is not to blame!*

I am not to blame.

To break Shadow is to release it into every other world. Even in its birth, it had been necessarily ephemeral, an illusion, a spiral of endless, self-referential tautologies. Shadow was an argument and the argument alone was sufficient to assert its existence. To stand within was a solipsist's dream, seeing all else as ghostly, fanciful delusion, at best the raw matter to give Shadow shape, at worst nothing more than Shadow's implicit need to define itself – *Gods, what is the point of trying to make sense of such a thing? Shadow is, and Shadow is not, and to dwell within it is to be neither of one thing nor of any other.*

And your children, dear Shadow, took upon themselves the strength of Andian courage and Liosan piety, and made of that blend something savage, brutal beyond belief. So much for promises of glory.

He found he was sitting with his head in his hands. History charged, assailing his weary defences. From the image of Andarist he next saw the knowing half-smile of Silchas Ruin, on the dawn when he walked to stand beside Scabandari, as if he knew what was to come, as if he was content with accepting all that followed, and doing so to spare his followers from a more immediate death – as Liosan legions ringed the horizon, soldiers singing that horrifying, haunting song, creating a music of heartbreaking beauty to announce their march to slaughter – sparing his people a more immediate death, granting them a few more days, perhaps weeks, of existence, before the Edur turned on their wounded allies on some other world.

Shadow torn, rent into pieces, drifting in a thousand directions. *Like blowing upon a flower's seed-head, off they wing into the air!*

Andarist, broken. Silchas Ruin, gone.

Anomander Rake, standing alone.

This long. This long . . .

The alchemist knows: the wrong catalyst, the wrong admixture, ill-conceived proportions, and all pretence of control vanishes – the transformation runs away, unchained, burgeons to cataclysm. *Confusion and fear, suspicion and then war, and war shall breed chaos. And so it shall and so it does and so it ever will.*

See us flee, dreaming of lost peace, the age of purity and stasis, when we embraced decay like a lover and our love kept us blind and we were content. So long as we stayed entertained, we were content.

Look at me.

This is what it is to be content.

Endest Silann drew a deep breath, lifted his head and blinked to clear his eyes. His master believed he could do this, and so he would believe his master. There, as simple as that.

Somewhere in the keep, priestesses were singing.

A hand reached up and grasped hard. A sudden, powerful pull tore loose Apsal'ara's grip and, snarling curses, she tumbled from the axle frame and thumped heavily on the sodden ground.

The face staring down at her was one she knew, and would rather she did not. 'Are you mad, Draconus?'

His only response was to grasp her chain and begin dragging her out from under the wagon.

Furious, indignant, she writhed across the mud, seeking purchase – anything to permit her to right herself, to even, possibly, resist. Stones rolled beneath the bite of her fingernails, mud grated and smeared like grease beneath her elbows, her knees, her feet. And still he pulled, treating her with scant, bitter ceremony, as if she was nothing more than a squalling cut-purse – *the outrage!*

Out from the wagon's blessed gloom, tumbling across rock-studded dirt – chains whipping on all sides, lifting clear and then falling back to track twisting furrows, lifting again as whoever or whatever was at the other end heaved forward another single, desperate step. The sound was maddening, pointless, infuriating.

Apsal'ara rolled upright, gathering a length of chain and glaring across at Draconus. 'Come closer,' she hissed, 'so I can smash your pretty face.'

His smile was humourless. 'Why would I do that, Thief?'

'To please me, of course, and I at least deserve that much from you – for dragging me out here.'

'Oh,' he said, 'I deserve many things, Apsal'ara. But for the moment, I will be content with your attention.'

'What do you want? We can do nothing to stop this. If I choose to greet my end lounging on the axle, why not?'

They were forced to begin walking, another step every few moments – much slower now, so slow the pathos stung through to her heart.

'You have given up on your chain?' Draconus asked, as if the manner in which he had brought her out here was of no import, easily dismissed now.

She decided, after a moment, that he was right. At the very least, there'd been some . . . drama. 'Another few centuries,' she said, shrugging, 'which I do not have. Damn you, Draconus, there is nothing to see out here – let me go back—'

'I need to know,' he cut in, 'when the time comes to fight, Apsal'ara – will you come to my side?'

She studied him. A well-featured man, beneath that thick, black beard. Eyes that had known malice long since stretched to snapping, leaving behind a strange bemusement, something almost regretful, almost . . . *wise*. Oh, this sword's realm delivered humility indeed. 'Why?' she demanded.

His heavy brows lifted, as if the question surprised him. 'I have seen many,' he said, haltingly, 'in my time. So many, appearing suddenly, screaming in horror, in anguish and despair. Others . . . already numbed, hopeless. Madness arrives to so many, Apsal'ara. . . .'

She bared her teeth. Yes, she had heard them. Above the places where she hid. Out to the sides, beyond the incessant rains, where the chains rolled and roped, fell slack then lifted once more, where they crossed over, one wending ever farther to one side, cutting across chain after chain – as the creature at the end staggered blind, unknowing, and before too long would fall and not rise again. The rest would simply step over that motionless chain, until it stretched into the wagon's wake and began dragging its charge.

'Apsal'ara, you arrived spitting like a cat. But it wasn't long before you set out to find a means of escape. And you would not rest.' He paused, and wiped a hand across his face. 'There are so few here I have come to . . . admire.' The smile Draconus then offered her was defenceless, shocking. 'If we must fall, then I would choose the ones at my side – yes, I am selfish to the last. And I am sorry for dragging you out here so unceremoniously.'

She walked alongside him, saying nothing. Thinking. At last, she sighed. 'It is said that only one's will can fight against chaos, that no other weapons are possible.'

'So it is said.'

She shot him a look. 'You know me, Draconus. You know . . . I have strength. Of will.'

'You will fight long,' he agreed, nodding. 'So very long.'

'The chaos will want my soul. Will seek to tear it apart, strip away my awareness. It will rage all around me.'

'Yes,' he said.

'Some of us are stronger than others.'

'Yes, Apsal'ara. Some of us are stronger than others.'

'And these you would gather close about you, that we might form a core. Of resistance, of stubborn will.'

'So I have thought.'

'To win through to the other side? Is there an *other side*, Draconus?'

'I don't know.'

'You don't know,' she repeated, making the words a snarl. 'All my life,' she said, 'I have chosen to be alone. In my struggles, in my victories and my failings. Draconus, I will face oblivion in the same way. I must – we *all* must. It does nothing to stand together, for we each fall alone.'

'I understand. I am sorry, then, Apsal'ara, for all this.'

'There is no *other side*, Draconus.'

'No, probably not.'

She drew up more of her chain, settled its crushing weight on to her shoulders, and then pulled away from the man, back towards the wagon. No, she could not give him anything, not when hope itself was impossible. He was wrong to admire her. To struggle was her own madness, resisting something that could not be resisted, fighting what could not be defeated.

This foe would take her mind, her self, tearing it away piece by piece – and she might sense something of those losses, at least to begin with, like vast blanks in her memory, perhaps, or an array of simple questions she could no longer answer. But before long, such knowledge would itself vanish, and each floating fragment would swirl about, untethered, alone, unaware that it had once been part of something greater, something whole. Her life, all her awareness, scattered into frightened orphans, whimpering at every strange sound, every unseen tug from the surrounding darkness. From woman to child, to helpless babe.

She knew what was coming. She knew, too, that in the end there was a kind of mercy to that blind ignorance, to the innocence of pieces. Unknowing, the orphans would dissolve away, leaving nothing.

What mind could not fear such a fate?

'Draconus,' she whispered, although she was far from his side now, closing in on the wagon once more, 'there is no other side of chaos. Look at us. Each chained. Together, and yet alone. See us pass the time as we will, until the end. You made this sword, but the sword is only a shape given to something far beyond you, far beyond any single creature, any single *mind*. You just made it momentarily manageable.'

She slipped into the gloom behind the lead wheel. Into the thick, slimy rain.

'Anomander Rake understands,' she hissed. 'He understands, Draconus. More than you ever did. Than you ever will. The world within Dragnipur must die. That is the greatest act of mercy imaginable. The greatest sacrifice. Tell me, Draconus, would you relinquish your power? Would you crush down your selfishness, to choose this . . . this emasculation? This sword, your cold, iron grin of vengeance – would you see it become lifeless in your hands? As dead as any other hammered bar of iron?'

She ducked beneath the lead axle and heaved the chain on her shoulders up and on to the wooden beam. Then climbed up after it. 'No, Draconus, you could not do that, could you?'

There had been pity in Rake's eyes when he killed her. There had been sorrow. But she had seen, even then, in that last moment of locked gazes, how such sentiments were tempered.

By a future fast closing in. Only now, here, did she comprehend that.

You give us chaos. You give us an end to this.

And she knew, were she in Anomander Rake's place, were she the one possessing Dragnipur, she would fail in this sacrifice. The power of the weapon would seduce her utterly, irrevocably.

None other. None other but you, Anomander Rake.

Thank the gods.

He awoke to the sting of a needle at the corner of one eye. Flinching back, gasping, scrabbling away over the warm bodies. In his wake, that blind artist, the mad Tiste Andii, Kadaspala, face twisted in dismay, the bone stylus drawing back.

'Wait! Come back! Wait and wait, stay and stay, I am almost done! I am almost done and I must be done before it's too late, before it's too late!'

Ditch saw that half his mangled body now bore tattoos, all down one side – wherever skin had been exposed whilst he was lying unconscious atop the heap of the fallen. How long had he been lying there, insensate, whilst the insane creature stitched him full of holes? 'I told you,' he said, 'not me. *Not me!*'

'Necessary. The apex and the crux and the fulcrum and the heart. He chose you. I chose you. Necessary! Else we are all lost, we are all lost, we are all lost. Come back. Where you were and where you were, lying just so, your arm over, the wrist – the very twitch of your eye—'

'I said *no!* Come at me again, Kadaspala, and I will choke the life from you. I swear it. I will crush your neck to pulp. Or snap your fingers, every damned one of them!'

Lying on his stomach, gaping sockets seeming to glare, Kadaspala snatched his hands back, hiding them beneath his chest. 'You must not do that and you must not do that. I was almost finished with you. I saw your mind went away, leaving me your flesh – to do what was needed and what was needed is still needed, can't you understand that?'

Ditch crawled further away, well beyond the Tiste Andii's reach, rolling and then sinking down between two demonic forms, both of which shifted sickeningly beneath his weight. 'Don't come any closer,' he hissed.

'I must convince you. I have summoned Draconus. He is summoned. There will be threats, they come with Draconus, they always come with Draconus. I have summoned him.'

Ditch slowly lowered himself down on to his back. There would be no end to this, he knew. Each time his mind fell away, fled to whatever oblivion it found, this mad artist would crawl to his side, and, blind or not, he would resume his work. *What of it? Why should I really care? This body is mostly destroyed now, anyway. If Kadaspala wants it – no, damn him, it is all I have left.*

'So many are pleased,' the Tiste Andii murmured, 'to think that they have become something greater than they once were. It is a question of sacrifices, of which I know all there is to know, yes, I know all there is to know. And,' he added, somewhat breathlessly, 'there is of course more to it, more to it. Salvation—'

'You cannot be serious.'

'It is not quite a lie, not quite a lie, my friend. Not quite a lie. And truth, well, truth is never as true as you think it is, or if it is, then not for long not for long not long for long.'

Ditch stared up at the sickly sky overhead, the flashes of reflected argent spilling through what seemed to be roiling clouds of grey dust. Everything felt imminent, something hovering at the edge of his vision. There was a strangeness in his mind, as if he was but moments from hearing some devastating news, a fatal illness no healer could solve; he knew it was coming, knew it to be inevitable, but the details were unknown and all he could do was wait. Live on in endless anticipation of that cruel, senseless pronouncement.

If there were so many sides to existing, why did grief and pain overwhelm all else? Why were such grim forces so much more powerful than joy, or love, or even compassion? And, in the face of that, did dignity really provide a worthy response? It was but a lifted shield, a display to others, whilst the soul cowered behind it, in no way ready to stand unmoved by catastrophe, especially the personal kind.

He felt a sudden hatred for the futility of things.

Kadaspala was crawling closer, his slithering stalking betrayed in minute gasps of effort, the attempts at stealth pathetic, almost comical.

Blood and ink, ink and blood, right, Kadaspala? The physical and the spiritual, each painting the truth of the other.

I will wring your neck, I swear it.

He felt motion, heard soft groans, and all at once a figure was crouching down beside him. Ditch opened his eyes. 'Yes,' he said, sneering, 'you were summoned.'

'Just how many battles, wizard, are you prepared to lose?'

The question irritated him, but then it was meant to. 'Either way, I have few left, don't I?'

Draconus reached down and dragged Ditch from between the two demons, roughly throwing him on to his stomach – no easy thing, since Ditch was not a small man, yet the muscles behind that effort made the wizard feel like a child.

'What are you doing?' Ditch demanded, as Draconus placed his hands to either side of the wizard's head, fingers lacing below his jaw.

Ditch sought to pull his head back, away from that tightening grip, but the effort failed.

A sudden wrench to one side. Something in his neck broke clean, a crunch and snap that reverberated up into his skull, a brief flare of what might have been pain, then . . . nothing.

'What have you done?'

'Not the solution I would have preferred,' Draconus said from above him, 'but it was obvious that argument alone would not convince you to cooperate.'

Ditch could not feel his body. Nothing, nothing at all beneath his neck. *He broke it – my neck, severed the spinal cord. He – gods! Gods!* 'Torment take you, Elder God. Torment take your soul. An eternity of agony. Death of all your dreams, sorrow unending among your kin – may they too know misery, despair – all your—'

'Oh, be quiet, Ditch. I haven't the time for this.'

The scene before Ditch's eyes rocked then, swung wild and spun, as Draconus dragged him back to where he had been lying before, to where Kadaspala needed him to be. *The apex, the crux, the heart, the whatever. You have me now, Tiste Andii.*

And yes, I did not heed your threat, and look at me now. True and true, you might say, Ditch never learns. Not about threats. Not about risks. And no, nothing – nothing – about creatures such as Draconus. Or Anomander Rake. Or any of them, who do what they have to do, when it needs doing.

'Hold your face still,' Kadaspala whispered close to one ear. 'I do not want to blind you, I do not want to blind you. You do not want to be blind, trust me, you do not want to be blind. No twitching, this is too important, too too too important and important, too.'

The stab of the stylus, a faint sting, and now, as it was the only sensation he had left, the pain shivered like a blessing, a god's merciful touch to remind him of his flesh – that it still existed, that blood still flowed beneath the skin.

The healer, Ditch, has devastating news.

But you still have your dignity. You still have that.

Oh yes, he still has his dignity. See the calm resignation in these steady eyes, the steeled expression, the courage of no choice.

Be impressed, won't you?

The south-facing slopes of God's Walk Mountains were crowded with ruins. Shattered domes, most of them elliptical in shape, lined the stepped tiers like broken teeth. Low walls linked them, although these too had collapsed in places, where run-off from the snow-clad peaks had cut trenches and gullies like gouges down the faces, as if the mountains themselves were eager to wash away the last remnants of the long-dead civilization.

Water and earth will heal what needs healing. Water and earth, sun and wind, these will take away every sign of wilful assertion, of cogent imposition. Brick crumbles to rubble, mortar drifts away as grit on the breeze. These mountains, Kedeviss knew, *will wash it all away.*

The notion pleased her, and in these sentiments she was little different from most Tiste Andii – at least those she knew and had known. There was a secret delight in impermanence, in seeing arrogance taken down, whether in a single person or in a bold, proud civilization. Darkness was ever the last thing to remain, in the final closing of eyelids, in the unlit depths of empty buildings, godless temples. When a people vanished, their every home, from the dishevelled hovel of the destitute to the palaces of kings and queens, became nothing but a sepulchre, a tomb host to nothing but memories, and even these quickly faded.

She suspected that the dwellers of the village, there at the foot of the nearest mountain, on the edge of a lake in headlong retreat, knew nothing about the sprawling city whose ruins loomed above them. A convenient source of cut stone and oddly glazed bricks and nothing more. And of course, whatever little knowledge they had possessed, they had surrendered it all to Saemenkelyk, for it was clear as the troupe drew closer that the village was lifeless, abandoned.

Against the backdrop of the mountains, the figure of Clip – striding well ahead of the rest of them – looked appropriately diminished, like an ant about to tackle a hillside. Despite this, Kedeviss found her gaze drawn to him again and again. *I'm not sure. Not sure about him.* Distrust came easy, and even had Clip been all smiles and eager generosity, still she would have her suspicions. They'd not done well with strangers, after all.

'I have never,' said Nimander as he walked at her side, 'seen a city like that.'

'They certainly had a thing about domes,' observed Skintick behind them. 'But let's hope that some of those channels still run with fresh water. I feel salted as a lump of bacon.'

Crossing the dead lake had been an education in human failure. Long lost nets tangled on deadheads, harpoons, anchors, gaffs and more shipwrecks than seemed reasonable. The lake's death had revealed its treachery in spiny ridges and shoals, in scores of mineralized tree trunks, still standing from the day some dam high in the mountains broke to send a deluge sweeping down into a forested valley. Fisher boats and merchant scows, towed barges and a few sleek galleys attesting to past military disputes, the rusted hulks of armour and other things less identifiable – the lake bed seemed a kind of concentrated lesson on bodies of water and the fools who dared to navigate them. Kedeviss imagined that, should a sea or an ocean suddenly drain away to nothing, she would see the same writ large, a clutter of loss so vast as to take one's breath away. What meaning could one pluck free from broken ambition? *Avoid the sea. Avoid risks. Take no chances. Dream of nothing, want less.* An Andian response, assuredly. Humans, no doubt, would draw down into thoughtful silence, thinking of ways to improve the odds, of turning the battle and so winning the war. For them, after all, failure was temporary, as befitted a short-lived species that didn't know any better.

'I guess we won't be camping in the village,' Skintick said, and they could see that Clip had simply marched through the scatter of squatting huts, and was now attacking the slope.

'He can walk all night if he likes,' Nimander said. 'We're stopping. We need the rest. Water, a damned bath. We need to redistribute our supplies, since there's no way we can take the cart up and over the mountains. Let's hope the locals just dropped everything like all the others did.'

A bath. Yes. But it won't help. We cannot clean our hands, not this time.

They passed between sagging jetties, on to the old shore by way of a boat-launch ramp of reused quarry stones, many of which had been carved with strange symbols. The huts rested on solid, oversized foundations, the contrast between ancient skill and modern squalor so pathetic it verged on the comical, and Kedeviss heard Skintick's amused snort as they wended their way between the first structures.

A rectangular well dominated the central round, with more perfectly cut stone set incompetently in the earth to form a rough plaza of sorts. Discarded clothing and bedding was scattered about, bleached by salt and sun, like the shrunken remnants of people.

'I seem to recall,' Skintick said, 'a child's story about flesh-stealers. Whenever you find clothes lying on the roadside and in glades, it's because the stealers came and took the person wearing them. I never trusted that story, though, since who would be walking round wearing only a shirt? Or one shoe? No, my alternative theory is far more likely.'

Nimander, ever generous of heart, bit on the hook. 'Which is?'

'Why, the evil wind, of course, ever desperate to get dressed in something warm, but nothing ever fits so the wind throws the garments away in a fit of fury.'

'You were a child,' Kedeviss said, 'determined to explain everything, weren't you? I don't really recall, since I stopped listening to you long ago.'

'She stabs deeps, Nimander, this woman.'

Nenanda had drawn up the cart and now climbed down, stretching out the kinks in his back. 'I'm glad I'm done with that,' he said.

Moments later Aranatha and Desra joined them.

Yes, here we are again. With luck, Clip will fall into a crevasse and never return.

Nimander looked older, like a man whose youth has been beaten out of him. 'Well,' he said with a sigh, 'we should search these huts and find whatever there is to find.'

At his command the others set out to explore. Kedeviss remained behind, her eyes still on Nimander, until he turned about and regarded her quizzically.

'He's hiding something,' she said.

He did not ask whom she meant, but simply nodded.

'I'm not sure why he feels the need for us, 'Mander. Did he want worshippers? Servants? Are we to be his cadre in some political struggle to come?'

A faint smile from Nimander. 'You don't think, then, he collected us out of fellowship, a sense of responsibility – to take us back . . . to our "Black-Winged Lord"?'

'Do you know,' she said, 'he alone among us has never met Anomander Rake. In a sense, he's not taking us to Anomander Rake. We're taking *him*.'

'Careful, Kedeviss. If he hears you you will have offended his self-importance.'

'I may end up offending more than that,' she said.

Nimander's gaze sharpened on her.

'I mean to confront him,' she said. 'I mean to demand some answers.'

'Perhaps we should all—'

'No. Not unless I fail.' She hoped he wouldn't ask for her reasons on this, and suspected, as she saw his smile turn wry, that he understood. A challenge by all of them, with Nimander at the forefront, could force into the open the power struggle that had been brewing between Clip and Nimander, one that was now played out in gestures of indifference and even contempt – on Clip's part, at any rate, since Nimander more or less maintained his pleasant, if slightly morbid, passivity, fending off Clip's none too subtle attacks as would a man used to being under siege. Salvos could come from any direction, after all. *So carry a big shield, and keep smiling.*

She wondered if Nimander even knew the strength within him. He could have become a man such as Andarist had been – after all, Andarist had been more of a father to him than Anomander Rake had ever been – and yet Nimander had grown into a true heir to Rake, his only failing being that he didn't know it. And perhaps that was for the best, at least for the time being.

'When?' he asked now.

She shrugged. 'Soon, I think.'

A thousand paces above the village, Clip settled on one of the low bridging walls and looked down at the quaintly sordid village below. He could see his miserable little army wandering about at the edges of the round, into and out of huts.

They were, he decided, next to useless. If not for concern over them, he would never have challenged the Dying God. Naturally, they were too ignorant to comprehend that detail. They'd even got it into their heads that they'd saved his life. Well, such delusions had their uses, although the endless glances his way – so rank with hopeful expectation – were starting to grate.

He spun the rings. *Clack-clack . . . clack-clack . . .*

Oh, I sense your power, O Black-Winged Lord. Holding me at bay. Tell me, what do you fear? Why force me into this interminable walk?

The Liosan of old had it right. Justice was unequivocal. Explanations revealed the cowardice at the core of every criminal, the whining expostulations, the succession of masks each one tried on and discarded in desperate succession. The *not-my-fault* mask. The *it-was-a-mistake* mask. *You-don't-understand* and *see-me-so-helpless* and *have-pity-I'm-weak* – he could see each expression, perfectly arranged round eyes equally perfect in their depthless pit of self-pity (*come in there's room for everyone*). Mercy was a flaw, a sudden moment of doubt to undermine the vast, implacable structure that was true justice. The masks were meant to stir awake that doubt, the last chance of the guilty to squirm free of proper retribution.

Clip had no interest in pity. Acknowledged no flaws within his own sense of justice. The criminal depends upon the compassion of the righteous and would use that compassion to evade precisely everything that criminal deserved. Why would any sane, righteous person fall into such a trap? It permitted criminals to thrive (since they played by different rules and would hold no pity or compassion for those who might wrong *them*). No, justice must be pure. Punishment left sacrosanct, immune to compromise.

He would make it so. For his modest army, for the much larger army to come. His people. The Tiste Andii of Black Coral. *We shall rot no longer. No more dwindling fires, drifting ashes, lives wasted century on century – do you hear me, O Lord? I will take your people, and I will deliver justice.*

Upon this world.

Upon every god and ascendant who ever wronged us, betrayed us, scorned us.

Watch them reel, faces bloodied, masks awry, the self-pity in their eyes dissolving – and in its place the horror of recognition. That there is no escape this time. That the end has arrived, for every damned one of them.

Yes, Clip had read his histories. He knew the Liosan, the Edur, he knew all the mistakes that had been made, the errors in judgement, the flaws of compassion. He knew, too, the true extent of the Black-Winged Lord's betrayal. Of Mother Dark, of all the Tiste Andii. *Of those you left in the Andara. Of Nimander and his kin.*

Your betrayal, Anomander Rake, of me.

The sun was going down. The rings clacked and clacked, and clacked. Below, the salt pan was cast in golden light, the hovels crouched on the near shoreline blessed picturesque by distance and lack of detail. Smoke from a cookfire now rose from their midst. Signs of life. Flames to beat back the coming darkness. But it would not last. It never lasted.

The High Priestess pushed the plate away. 'That's it,' she said. 'Any more and I will burst.' A first level acolyte ducked in to take the plate, scurrying off with such haste that she almost spilled the towering heap of cracked crayfish shells.

Leaning back, the High Priestess wiped the melted butter from her fingers. 'It's typical,' she said to the half-dozen sisters seated at the table, 'the nets drag up a sudden, unexpected bounty, and what do we do? Devour it entire.'

'Kurald Galain continues to yield surprises,' said the Third Sister; 'why not expect more to come?'

'Because, dearest, nothing lasts for ever. Surrounding Kharkanas, there once stood forests. Until we chopped them down.'

'We were young—'

'And that would be a worthy defence,' the High Priestess cut in, 'if we have not, here in our old age, just repeated the stupidity. Look at us. Come the morrow all our clothes will cease to fit. We will discover, to our horror, bulges where none existed before. We see pleasure as an excuse for all manner of excess, but it is a most undisciplined trait. Now, sermon ended. Someone pour the tea.'

More first level acolytes slithered in.

A rustling of small bells at the corridor door preceded the arrival of a temple guardian. The woman, clad in scale armour and ringed leather, marched up to halt beside the High Priestess. She lowered the grille face-piece on her helm and leaned close to whisper – lips unseen and so unreadable to any – a brief message.

The High Priestess nodded, and then gestured the guardian away. 'Second and Third Sister, remain in your seats. You others, take your tea to the Unlit Garden. Sixth Sister, once there you can stop hiding that flask and top up everyone else, yes?'

Moments later, only three women remained in the chamber, as even the acolytes had been sent away.

The door opened again and the guardian reappeared, this time escorting an old woman, human, who tottered on two canes to support her massive weight. Sweat darkened the cloth of her loose clothing round her armpits and cleavage and on the bulging islands of her hips. Her expression was one of anxiety and discomfort.

Unbidden, Third Sister rose and pulled a bench away from one wall, positioning it in the woman's path.

'Please do sit,' said the High Priestess, thinking, alas, of the two dozen blind crayfish she'd just eaten, each almost half the size of a lobster, served up drenched in melted butter. *Pleasure until pain, and we then rail at our misfortune.*

With muttered thanks, the woman lowered herself on to the bench. 'Please to introduce myself,' she said in a wheeze. 'I am the Witch—'

'I know,' the High Priestess interrupted, 'and that title will suffice here, as must my own. Yours has been a trying journey, and so I can only assume you come with word of a crisis.'

A quick nod. 'The cult of the Redeemer, High Priestess, has become . . . corrupted.'

'And what is the agency of that corruption?'

'Well, but that is complicated, you see. There was a High Priestess – oh, she was a reluctant owner of that title, and all the duties that came with it. Yet none could deny her natural authority—'

'"Natural authority,"' said the High Priestess. 'I like that phrase. Sorry, do go on.'

'Outlaws have usurped the pilgrim camp. There is some concentrated form of the drink called kelyk – I do not know if you are familiar with it?'

'We are, yes.'

Another quick nod. 'Saemankelyk. The word comes from a dialect common south of God's Walk Mountains. "Saeman" means "Dying God" and "kelyk" means—'

'Blood.'

A sigh. 'Yes.'

Second Sister cleared her throat, and then said, 'Surely you do not mean to suggest that the meaning is literal?'

The witch licked her lips – an instinctive gesture rather than anything ironic – and said, 'I have applied some . . . arts, er, to examining this Saemankelyk. There are unnatural properties, that much is certain. In any case, the outlaws have made addicts of the pilgrims. Including Salind, the Redeemer's High Priestess.'

Third Sister spoke. 'If this foul drink is in any way blessed, then one might well see its poisonous influence as a corruption of the Redeemer's worshippers. If one kneels before Saemenkelyk . . . well, one cannot kneel before *two* masters, can one?'

Not without physically splitting in half, no. 'Witch, what is it you wish of us?'

'This corruption, High Priestess. It could . . . spread.'

Silence round the table.

It was clear now to the High Priestess that the witch had given this meeting considerable thought, until arriving at the one suggestion she considered most likely to trigger alarm. *As if we Tiste Andii are but taller, black-skinned versions of humans. As if we could so easily be . . . stolen away.*

Emboldened, the witch resumed. 'High Priestess, Salind – she needs help. We need help. There was a warrior, one among you, but he has disappeared. Now that Seerdomin is dead, I sought to find him. Spinnock Durav.'

The High Priestess rose. 'Come with me, Witch,' she said. 'Just you and me. Come, it's not far.'

The old woman levered herself upright, confusion in her small eyes.

To a side passage, a narrow corridor of twenty paces, and then down a short flight of stairs, the air still smelling of fresh-chiselled basalt, into a large but low-vaulted octagonal chamber devoid of any furniture, the floor of which was inlaid with onyx tesserae, irregular in shape and size. A journey of but a few moments for most people; yet for the witch it was an ordeal, striking the High Priestess with the poignancy of the old woman's desperation – that she should so subject herself to such a struggle. The trek from her home through the city to the keep must have been an epic undertaking.

These thoughts battered at the High Priestess's impatience, and so she weathered the delay saying nothing and without expression on her smooth, round face.

As soon as the witch tottered into the chamber, she gasped.

'Yes, you are clearly an adept,' observed the High Priestess. 'There are nodes of power in this temple. Kurald Galain, the cleansing darkness.' She could see that the witch was breathing hard and fast, and there was a look of wonder on that sweat-sheathed face. 'Do not be alarmed at what you feel inside,' she said. 'By entering here, you have drawn Kurald Galain into your body, in your breaths, through the very pores of your skin. The sorcery is now within you.'

'B-but . . . why? Why have you done this to me?'

'I could sense the labouring of your heart, Witch. Your trek to my temple would have been your last—'

'Oh, I knew that!' snapped the witch.

The sudden irritation shocked the High Priestess for a moment. She reassessed this woman tottering before her. 'I see. Then . . .'

'Then *yes*, I prayed my sacrifice would be worth it. Salind is so precious – what has been done to her is despicable. Is . . . *evil*.'

'Then you have not come in the name of the Redeemer, have you?'

'No. I came for a friend.'

A friend. 'Witch, Spinnock Durav is no longer in Black Coral. It grieves me to hear of Seerdomin's death. And it grieves me more to learn of Salind's fate. Tell me, what else are you feeling?'

The witch was hunched over, as if in visceral pain. 'Fine,' she hissed reluctantly. 'I can see that there is no risk of the poison spreading. I never thought there was.'

'I know that,' said the High Priestess, her voice soft.

'But I needed to bargain for your help.'

'That is ever the assumption among you humans. Do you know, when the delegates from the Free Cities came to treat with us, when the Rhivi and the man who pretended to be Prince K'azz D'Avore of the Crimson Guard came to us – they all thought to bargain. To buy our swords, our power. To *purchase* our alliance. Lord Anomander Rake but lifted one hand – before any of them could even so much as say one beseeching word. And he said this: "We are the Tiste Andii. Do not seek to bargain with us. If you wish our help, you will ask for it. We will say yes or we will say no. There will be no negotiations."'

The witch was staring across at her.

The High Priestess sighed. 'It is not an easy thing for a proud man or woman, to simply *ask*.'

'No,' whispered the witch. 'It's not.'

Neither spoke then for a dozen heartbeats, and then the witch slowly straightened. 'What have you done to me?'

'I expect Kurald Galain has done its assessment. Your aches are gone, yes? Your breathing has eased. Various ailments will disappear in the next few days. You may find your appetite . . . diminished. Kurald Galain prefers forces in balance.'

The witch's eyes were wide.

The High Priestess waited.

'I did not ask for such things.'

'No. But it did not please me to realize that your journey to my temple would prove fatal.'

'Oh. Then, thank you.'

The High Priestess frowned. 'Am I not yet understood?'

'You are,' replied the witch, with another flash of irritation, 'but I have my own rules, and I will voice my gratitude, whether it pleases you or not.'

That statement earned a faint smile and the High Priestess dipped her head in acknowledgement.

'Now, then,' said the witch after yet another brief stretch of silence, 'I ask that you help Salind.'

'No.'

The witch's face darkened.

'You have come here,' said the High Priestess, 'because of a loss of your own faith. Yes, you would have the Temple act on behalf of Salind. It is our assessment that Salind does not yet need our help. Nor, indeed, does the Redeemer.'

'Your . . . assessment?'

'We are,' said the High Priestess, 'rather more aware of the situation than you might have believed. If we must act, then we will, if only to preempt Silanah – although, I admit, it is no easy thing attempting to measure out the increments of an Eleint's forbearance. She could stir at any time, at which point it will be too late.'

'Too late?'

'Yes, for Salind, for the usurpers, for the pilgrim camp and all its inhabitants.'

'High Priestess, who is Silanah? And what is an Eleint?'

'Oh, I am sorry. That was careless of me. Silanah commands the spire of this keep – she is rather difficult to miss, even in the eternal gloom. On your return to your home, you need but turn and glance back, and up, of course, and you will see her.' She paused, and then added, 'Eleint means dragon.'

'Oh.'

'Come, let us return to the others. I am sure more tea has been brewed, and we can take some rest there.'

The witch seemed to have run out of commentary, and now followed meekly as the High Priestess strode from the chamber.

The return journey did not take nearly as long.

It should have come as no surprise to Samar Dev when Karsa Orlong rode back into the camp at dusk at the end of the third day since leaving them. Riding in, saying nothing, looking oddly thoughtful.

Unscathed. As if challenging the Hounds of Shadow was no greater risk than, say, herding sheep, or staring down a goat (which, of course, couldn't be done – but such a detail would hardly stop the Toblakai, would it? And he'd win the wager, too). No, it was clear that the encounter had been a peaceful one – perhaps predicated on the Hounds' fleeing at high speed, tails between their legs.

Slipping down from Havok's back, Karsa walked over to where sat Samar Dev beside the dung fire. Traveller had moved off thirty or so paces, as it was his habit to attend to the arrival of dusk in relative solitude.

The Toblakai crouched down. 'Where is the tea?' he asked.

'There isn't any,' she said. 'We've run out.'

Karsa nodded towards Traveller. 'This city he seeks. How far away?'

Samar Dev shrugged. 'Maybe a week, since we're going rather slowly.'

'Yes. I was forced to backtrack to find you.' He was silent for a moment, look-ing into the flames, and then he said, 'He does not seem the reluctant type.'

'No, you're right. He doesn't.'

'I'm hungry.'

'Cook something.'

'I will.'

She rubbed at her face, feeling the scrape of calluses from her hands, and then tugged at the knots in her hair. 'Since meeting you,' she said, 'I have almost for-gotten what it is to be clean – oh, Letheras was all right, but we were pretty much in a prison, so it doesn't really count. No, with you it's just empty wastelands, blood-soaked sands, the occasional scene of slaughter.'

'You sought me out, Witch,' he reminded her.

'I delivered your horse.' She snorted. 'Since you two are so clearly perfect for each other, it was a matter of righting the cosmic balance. I had no choice.'

'You just want me,' he said, 'yet whenever we are together, you do nothing but second-guess everything. Surrender, woman, and you can stop arguing with your-self. It has been a long time since I spilled my seed into a woman, almost as long as since you last felt the heat of a man.'

She could have shot back, unleashed a flurry of verbal quarrels that would, in-evitably, all bounce off his impervious barbarity. 'You'd be gentle as a desert bear, of course. I'd probably never recover.'

'There are sides of me, Witch, that you have not seen, yet.'

She grunted.

'You are ever suspicious of being surprised, aren't you?'

A curious question. In fact, a damned tangle of a question. She didn't like it. She didn't want to go near it. 'I was civilized, once. Content in a proper city, a city with an underground sewer system, with Malazan aqueducts and hot water from pipes. Hallways between enclosed gardens and the front windows to channel cool air through the house. Proper soap to keep clothes clean. Songbirds in cages. Chilled wine and candied pastries.'

'The birds sing of imprisonment, Samar Dev. The soap is churned by inden-tured workers with bleached, blistered hands and hacking coughs. Outside your cool house with its pretty garden there are children left to wander in the streets. Lepers are dragged to the edge of the city and every step is cheered on by a hail of stones. People steal to eat and when they are caught their hands are cut off. Your city takes water from farms and plants wither and animals die.'

She glared across at him. 'Nice way to turn the mood, Karsa Orlong.'

'There was a mood?'

'Too subtle, was it?'

He waved a dismissive hand. 'Speak your desires plain.'

'I was doing just that, you brainless bhederin. Just a little . . . comfort. That's all. Even the illusion would have served.'

Traveller returned to the fire. 'We are about to have a guest,' he said.

Samar Dev rose and searched round, but darkness was fast swallowing the plain. She turned with a query on her lips, and saw that Karsa had straightened and was looking skyward, to the northeast. And there, in the deepening blue, a dragon was gliding towards them.

'Worse than moths,' Traveller muttered.

'Are we about to be attacked?'

He glanced at her, and shrugged.

'Shouldn't we at least scatter or something?'

Neither warrior replied to that, and after a moment Samar Dev threw up her hands and sat down once more beside the fire. No, she would not panic. Not for these two abominations in her company, and not for a damned dragon, either. Fine, let it be a single pass rather than three – what was she, an ant? She picked up another piece of dung and tossed it into the fire. *Moths? Ah, I see. We are a beacon, are we, a wilful abrogation of this wild, empty land. Whatever. Flap flap on over, beastie, just don't expect scintillating discourse.*

The enormous creature's wings thundered as the dragon checked its speed a hundred paces away, and then it settled almost noiselessly on to the ground. Watching it, Samar Dev's eyes narrowed. 'That thing's not even alive.'

'No,' Karsa and Traveller said in unison.

'Meaning,' she continued, 'it shouldn't be here.'

'That is true,' Traveller said.

In the gloom the dragon seemed to regard them for a moment, and then, in a blurring dissolution, the creature *sembled*, until they saw a tall, gaunt figure of indeterminate gender. Grey as cobwebs and dust, pallid hair long and ropy with filth, wearing the remnants of a long chain hauberk, unbelted. An empty, splintered scabbard hung from a baldric beneath the right arm. Leggings of some kind of thick hide, scaled and the hue of forest loam, reached down to grey leather boots that rose to just below the knees.

No light was reflected from the pits of its eyes. It approached with peculiar caution, like a wild animal, and halted at the very edge of the firelight. Whereupon it lifted both hands, brought them together into a peak before its face, and bowed.

In the native tongue of Ugari, it said, 'Witch, I greet you.'

Samar Dev rose, shocked, baffled. Was it some strange kind of courtesy, to address her first? Was this thing in the habit of ignoring ascendants as if they were nothing more than bodyguards? And from her two formidable companions, not a sound.

'And I greet you in return,' she managed after a moment.

'I am Tulas Shorn,' it said. 'I scarce recall when I last walked this realm, if I ever have. The very nature of my demise is lost to me, which, as you might imagine, is proving disconcerting.'

'So it would, Tulas Shorn. I am Samar Dev—'

'Yes, the one who negotiates with spirits, with the sleeping selves of stream and rock, crossroads and sacred paths. Priestess of Burn—'

'That title is in error, Tulas Shorn—'

'Is it? You are a witch, are you not?'

'Yes, but—'

'You do not reach into warrens, and so force alien power into this world. Your congress is with the earth, the sky, water and stone. You are a priestess of Burn, chosen among those of whom she dreams, as are others, but you, Samar Dev, she dreams of often.'

'How would you know that?'

Tulas Shorn hesitated, and then said, 'There is death in dreaming.'

'You are Tiste Edur,' said Karsa Orlong, and, baring his teeth, he reached for his sword.

'More than that,' said Traveller, 'one of Hood's own.'

Samar Dev spun to her two companions. 'Oh, really! Look at you two! Not killed anything in weeks – how can you bear it? Planning on chopping it into tiny pieces, are you? Well, why not fight for the privilege first?'

Traveller's eyes widened slightly at her outburst.

Karsa's humourless smile broadened. 'Ask it what it wants, then, Witch.'

'The day I start taking orders from you, Karsa Orlong, I will do just that.'

Tulas Shorn had taken a step back. 'It seems I am not welcome here, and so I shall leave.'

But Samar Dev's back was up, and she said, 'I welcome you, Tulas Shorn, even if these ones do not. If they decide to attack you, I will stand in their way. I offer you all the rights of a guest – it's my damned fire, after all, and if these two idiots don't like it they can make their own, preferably a league or two away.'

'You are right,' Traveller said. 'I apologize. Be welcome, then, Tulas Shorn.'

Karsa shrugged. 'I suppose,' he said, 'I've killed enough Edur. Besides, this one's already dead. I still want to know what it wants.'

Tulas Shorn edged in warily – a caution that seemed peculiarly out of place in a corpse, especially one that could veer into a dragon at any moment. 'I have no urgent motivations, Tartheno Toblakai. I have known solitude for too long and would ease the burden of being my only company.'

'Then join us,' Karsa said, returning to crouch at the fire. 'After all,' he added, 'perhaps one day I too will tire of my own company.'

'Not any time soon, I would wager,' said the Tiste Edur.

Traveller snorted a laugh, and then looked shocked with himself.

Samar Dev settled down once more, thinking of Shorn's words. *There is death in dreaming.* Well, she supposed, there would be at that. Then why did she feel so . . . rattled? *What were you telling me, Tulas Shorn?*

'Hood has released you?' Traveller asked. 'Or was he careless?'

'Careless?' The Tiste Edur seemed to consider the word. 'No, I do not think that. Rather, an opportunity presented itself to me. I chose not to waste it.'

'So now,' said Traveller, eyes fixed on the withered face enlivened only by reflected firelight, 'you wing here and there, seeking what?'

'Instinct can set one on a path,' Tulas Shorn said, 'with no destination in mind.' It raised both hands and seemed to study them. 'I have thought to see life once more, awakened within me. I do not know if such a thing is even possible. Samar Dev, is such a thing possible? Can she dream me alive once more?'

'Can she – what? I don't know. Call me a priestess if you like, but I don't worship Burn, which doesn't make me a very good priestess, does it? But if she dreams death, then she dreams life, too.'

'From one to the other is generally in one direction only,' Traveller observed. 'Hood will come for you, Tulas Shorn; sooner or later, he will come to reclaim you.'

For the first time, she sensed evasiveness in the Tiste Edur as it said, 'I have time yet, I believe. Samar Dev, there is sickness in the Sleeping Goddess.'

She flinched. 'I know.'

'It must be expunged, lest she die.'

'I imagine so.'

'Will you fight for her?'

'I'm not a damned priestess!' She saw the surprise on the faces of Karsa and Traveller, forced herself back from the ragged edge of anger. 'I wouldn't know where to start, Tulas Shorn.'

'I believe the poison comes from a stranger's pain.'

'The Crippled God.'

'Yes, Samar Dev.'

'Do you actually think it can be healed?'

'I do not know. There is physical damage and then there is spiritual damage. The former is more easily mended than the latter. He is sustained by rage, I suspect. His last source of power, perhaps his only source of power whilst chained in this realm.'

'I doubt he's in the negotiating mood,' Samar Dev said. 'And even if he was, he's anathema to the likes of me.'

'It is an extraordinary act of courage,' said Tulas Shorn, 'to come to know a stranger's pain. To even consider such a thing demands a profound dispensation, a willingness to wear someone else's chains, to taste their suffering, to see with one's own eyes the hue cast on all things – the terrible stain that is despair.' The Tiste Edur slowly shook its head. 'I have no such courage. It is, without doubt, the rarest of abilities.'

None spoke then for a time. The fire ate itself, indifferent to witnesses, and in its hunger devoured all that was offered it, again and again, until night and the disinterest of its guests left it to starve, until the wind stirred naught but ashes.

If Tulas Shorn sought amiable company, it should have talked about the weather.

In the morning, the undead Soletaken was gone. And so too were Traveller's and Samar Dev's horses.

'That was careless of us,' Traveller said.

'He was a guest,' Samar Dev said, baffled and more than a little hurt by the betrayal. They could see Havok, standing nervously some distance off, as if reluctant to return from his nightlong hunting, as if he had been witness to something unpleasant.

There was, however, no sign of violence. The picket stakes remained where they had been pounded into the hard ground.

'It wanted to slow us down,' Traveller said. 'One of Hood's own, after all.'

'All right,' Samar Dev glared across at a silent Karsa Orlong, 'the fault was all mine. I should have left you two to chop the thing to bits. I'm sorry.'

But Karsa shook his head. 'Witch, goodwill is not something that needs an apology. You were betrayed. Your trust was abused. If there are strangers who thrive on such things, they will ever remain strangers – because they have no other choice. Pity Tulas Shorn and those like it. Even death taught it nothing.'

Traveller was regarding the Toblakai with interest, although he ventured no comment.

Havok was trotting towards them. Karsa said, 'I will ride out, seeking new mounts – or perhaps the Edur simply drove your beasts off.'

'I doubt that,' Traveller said.

And Karsa nodded, leaving Samar Dev to realize that he had offered the possibility for her sake, as if in some clumsy manner seeking to ease her self-recrimination. Moments later, she understood that it had been anything but clumsy. It was not her inward chastisement that he spoke to; rather, for her, he was giving Tulas Shorn the benefit of the doubt, although Karsa possessed no doubt at all – nor, it was clear, did Traveller.

Well then, I am ever the fool here. So be it. 'We'd best get walking, then.'

In setting out, they left behind a cold hearth ringed in stones, and two saddles.

Almost two leagues away, high in the bright blue sky, Tulas Shorn rode the freshening breeze, the tatters of its wings rapping in the rush of air.

As it had suspected, the trio had made no effort to hunt down the lost horses. Assuming, as they would, that the dragon had simply obliterated the animals.

Tulas Shorn had known far too much death, however, to so casually kill innocent creatures. No, instead, the dragon had taken them, one in each massive clawed foot, ten leagues to the south, almost within sight of a small, wild herd of the same breed – one of the last such wild herds on the plain.

Too many animals were made to bow in servitude to a succession of smarter, crueller masters (and yes, those two traits went together). Poets ever wailed upon witnessing fields of slaughter, armies of soldiers and warriors frozen in death, but Tulas Shorn – who had walked through countless such scenes – reserved his sorrow, his sense of tragedy, for the thousands of dead and dying horses, war dogs, the oxen trapped in yokes of siege wagons mired in mud or shattered, the beasts that bled and suffered through no choice of their own, that died in a fog of ignorance, all trust in their masters destroyed.

The horse knows faith in the continuation of care from its master; that food and water will be provided, that injuries will be mended, that the stiff brush will stroke its hide at day's end. And in return it serves as best it can, or at least as best it chooses. The dog understands that the two-legged members of its pack cannot be challenged, and believes that every hunt will end in success. These were truths.

A master of beasts must be as a parent to a host of unruly but trusting children. Stolid, consistent, never wanton in cruelty, never unmindful of the faith in which he or she is held. Oh, Tulas Shorn was not unaware of the peculiarity of such convictions, and had been the subject of mockery even among fellow Tiste Edur.

Although such mockery had invariably faded when they had seen what had been achieved by this strange, quiet warrior with the Eleint-tainted eyes.

Gliding high above the Lamatath Plain, now scores of leagues south of the witch and her companions, Tulas Shorn could taste something in the air, so ancient, so familiar, that if the dragon had still possessed functioning hearts, why, they would have thundered. Pleasure, perhaps even anticipation.

How long had it been?

Long.

What paths did they now wander down?

Alien ones, to be sure.

Would they remember Tulas Shorn? The first master, the one who had taken them raw and half-wild and taught them the vast power of a faith that would never know betrayal?

They are close, yes.

My Hounds of Shadow.

If he'd had a single moment, a lone instant of unharried terror, Gruntle might have conjured in his mind a scene such as might be witnessed from someone in a passing ship – some craft beyond the raging storm, at the very edge of this absurd insanity. Hands gripping the ratlines, deck pitching wild in the midst of a dishevelled sea, and there, yes . . . *something impossible.*

An enormous carriage thrashing through a heaving road of foam, frenzied horses ploughing through swollen, whipped waves. And figures, clinging here and there like half-drowned ticks, and another, perched high on the driver's bench behind the maddened animals, from whom endless screams pealed forth, piercing the gale and thunder and surge. Whilst on all sides the storm raged on, as if in indignant fury; the winds howled, rain slashing the air beneath bulging, bruised clouds; and the sea rose up in a tumult, spray erupting in tattered sheets.

Yes, the witness might well stare, agape. Aghast.

But Gruntle had no opportunity for such musing, no sweet luxury of time to disconnect his mind's eye from this drenched, exhausted and battered body strapped tight to the roof of the carriage, this careering six-wheeled island that seemed ever tottering on the edge of obliteration. To draw one more breath was the only goal, the singular purpose of existence. Nothing else was remotely relevant.

He did not know if he was the last one left – he had not opened his eyes in an eternity – and even if he was, why, he knew he would not hold out much longer. He convulsed yet again, but there was nothing left in his stomach – gods, he had never felt so sick in all his life.

The wind tore at his hair – he'd long since lost his helm – savage as clawed fingers, and he ducked lower. Those unseen fingers then grabbed a handful and pulled his head up.

Gruntle opened his eyes and found himself staring into a crazed face, the features so twisted that he could not for a moment recognize who was accosting him – some lost sailor from a drowned ship? Flung aboard the carriage as gods rolled in helpless laughter? – but no, it was Faint, and that expression was not abject terror. It was wild, gut-wrenching hilarity.

She tugged on the rings attached to the iron rails and managed to pull herself yet closer, enough to dip her head down beside his, and in the half-sheltered cave their arms created her voice seemed to come from his own skull. 'I thought you were dead! So pale, like a damned cadaver!'

And this left her convulsed with laughter? 'I damn well wish I was!' he shouted back.

'We've known worse!'

Now, he'd heard that a dozen times since this venture began, and he had begun to suspect it was one of those perfect lies that people voiced to stay sane no matter what madness they found themselves in. 'Has Quell ever done anything like this before?'

'Like what? This is the Trygalle Trade Guild, shareholder! *This is what we do, man!*'

And when she began laughing again, he planted a hand on her head and pushed her away. Faint retreated, back along the rail, and Gruntle was alone once more.

How long had it been? Days. Weeks. Decades. He desperately needed fresh water – whatever rain reached his face was as salty as the sea. He could feel himself weakening – even could he find something to eat, he would never hold it down. Outrageous, to think that he could die here, body flopping about on its straps, slowly torn apart by the storm. Not with a weapon in hand, not with a defiant bellow tearing loose from his throat. Not drenched in hot blood, not staring his killer in the eye.

This was worse than any demise he might imagine. As bad as some unseen disease – the sheer helplessness of discovering that one's own body could fail all on its own. He could not even roar to the heavens with his last breath – the gesture would flood his mouth, leave him choking, defiance flung straight back at him, right back down his own throat.

More screaming – laughter? No, this was *screaming*.

What now?

Gruntle snatched a breath and then looked up.

Walls of water on all sides – he flinched – and then a swell heaved them skyward, the carriage twisting, pitching. Rings squealed as he was tossed up, until sharp, savage tugs from the straps snatched him back down.

But he had seen – yes – all his companions – their wide eyes, their gaping mouths – and he had seen, too, the object of their terror.

They were racing, faster than any wave, straight for a towering cliff face.

'Land ho!' shrieked Glanno Tarp from his perch.

Explosions of foam at the cliff's base appeared with every lift of the waves. Jagged spires of black rock, reefs, shoals and all those other names for killers of people and ships. And carriages. All looming directly ahead, a third of a league away and closing fast.

Can those horses climb straight up a cliff face? Sounds ridiculous – but I won't put it past them. Not any more.

Even so, why is everyone screaming?

A moment later Gruntle had his answer. Another upward pitch, and this time he twisted round and glanced back, into their wake – no reason, at least, he didn't think there was, but the view, surely, could not be as horrifying as what lay ahead.

And he saw another wall of water, this one high as a damned mountain.

Its sickly green flank picked up the carriage and then the horses, and began carrying them into the sky. So fast that the water streamed from the roof, from every flattened shareholder, and even the rain vanished as higher they went, into the gut of the clouds.

He thought, if he dared open his eyes, he would see stars, the ferment above, to the sides, and indeed below – but Gruntle's nerve had failed him. He clung, eyes squeezed shut, flesh dry and shivering in the bitter cold of the wind.

More sound than a mortal brain could comprehend – thunder from beneath, animal squeals and human shrieks, the swollen thrash of blood in every vein, every artery, the hollow howl of wind in his gaping mouth.

Higher, and higher still—

And wasn't there a cliff dead ahead?

He could not look.

Everyone thought that Reccanto Ilk was the one with the bad eyes, and that was a most pleasing misindirection as far as Glanno Tarp was concerned. Besides, he was fine enough with things within, oh, thirty or so paces. Beyond that, objects acquired a soft-edged dissolidity, became blocks of vague shape, and the challenge was in gauging the speed at which they approached, and, from this, their distance and relative size. The carriage driver had taken this to a fine art indeed, with no one the wiser.

Which, in this instance at least, was of no help at all.

He could hear everyone screaming behind him, and he was adding plenty all on his own, even as the thought flashed in his mind that Reccanto Ilk was probably shrieking in ignorance – simply because everyone else was – but the looming mass of the rotted cliff-face was a most undenimissable presence, and my how big it was getting!

The horses could do naught but run, in what must have seemed downhill for the hapless beasts, even as the wave's surge reared ever higher – all sorts of massomentum going on here, Glanno knew, and no quibblering about it, either.

What with pitch and angle and cant and all that, Glanno could now see the top of the cliff, a guano-streaked lip all wavy and grimacing. Odd vertical streaks depended down from the edge – what were those? Could be? Ladders? How strange.

Higher still, view expandering, the sweep of the summit, flat land, and globs of glimmering light like melted dollops of murky wax. Something towering, a spire, a tower – yes, a towering tower, with jagged-teeth windows high up, blinking in and out – all directly opposite now, almost level—

Something pounded the air, pounded right into his bones, rattling the roots of his insipid or was it inspired grin – something that tore the wave apart, an upward charging of spume, a world splashed white, engulfing the horses, the carriage, and Glanno himself.

His mouth was suddenly full of seawater. His eyes stared through stinging salt. His ears popped like berries between finger and thumb, *ploop ploop*. And oh, that hurt!

The water rushed past, wiping clean the world – and there, before him – were those buildings?

Horses were clever. Horses weren't half blind. They could find something, a street, a way through, and why not? Clever horses.

'Yeaagh!' Glanno thrashed the reins.

Equine shrills.

The wheels slammed down on to something hard for the first time in four days.

And, with every last remnant of axle grease scrubbed away, why, those wheels locked up, a moment of binding, and then the carriage leapt back into the air, and Glanno's head snapped right and left at the flanking blur of wheels spinning past at high speed.

Oh.

When the carriage came back down again, the landing was far from smooth.

Things exploded. Glanno and the bench he was strapped to followed the horses down a broad cobbled street. Although he was unaware of it at the time, the carriage behind them elected to take a sharp left turn on to a side street, just behind the formidable tower, and, skidding on its belly, barrelled another sixty paces down the avenue before coming to a rocking rest opposite a squat gabled building with a wooden sign swinging wildly just above the front door.

Glanno rode the bench this way and that, the reins sawing at his fingers and wrists, as the horses reached the end of the rather short high street, and boldly leapt, in smooth succession, a low stone wall that, alas, Glanno could not quite manage to clear on his skidding bench. The impact shattered all manner of things, and the driver found himself flying through the air, pulled back down as the horses, hoofs hammering soft ground, drew taut the leather harness, and then whipped him round as they swung left rather than leaping the next low stone wall – and why would they? They had found themselves in a corral.

Glanno landed in deep mud consisting mostly of horse shit and piss, which was probably what saved his two legs, already broken, from being torn right off. The horses came to a halt beneath thrashing rain, in early evening gloom, easing by a fraction the agony of his two dislocated shoulders, and he was able to roll mostly on to his back, to lie unmoving, the rain streaming down his face, his eyes closed, with only a little blood dripping from his ears.

Outside the tavern, frightened patrons who had rushed out at the cacophony in the street now stood getting wet beneath the eaves, staring in silence at the wheelless carriage, from the roof of which people on all sides seemed to be falling, whereupon they dragged themselves upright, bleary eyes fixing on the tavern door, and staggered whenceforth inside. Only a few moments afterwards, the nearest carriage door opened with a squeal, to unleash of gush of foamy seawater, and then out stumbled the occupants, beginning with a gigantic tattooed ogre.

The tavern's patrons, one and all, really had nothing to say.

Standing in the highest room of the tower, an exceedingly tall, bluish-skinned man with massive, protruding tusks, curved like the horns of a ram to frame his bony face, slowly turned away from the window, and, taking no notice of the dozen servants staring fixedly at him – not one of whom was remotely human – he sighed and said, 'Not again.'

The servants, reptilian eyes widening with comprehension, then began a wailing chorus, and this quavering dirge reached down through the tower, past chamber after chamber, spiralling down the spiral staircase and into the crypt that was the tower's hollowed-out root. Wherein three women, lying motionless on stone slabs, each opened their eyes. And in doing so, a crypt that had been in darkness was dark no longer.

From the women's broad, painted mouths there came a chittering sound, as of chelae clashing behind the full lips. A conversation, perhaps, about hunger. And need. And dreadful impatience.

Then the women began shrieking.

High above, in the topmost chamber of the tower, the man winced upon hearing those shrieks, which grew ever louder, until even the fading fury of the storm was pushed down, down under the sea's waves, there to drown in shame.

In the tavern in the town on the coast called the Reach of Woe, Gruntle sat with the others, silent at their table, as miserable as death yet consumed with shaky relief. Solid ground beneath them, dry roof overhead. A pitcher of mulled wine midway between.

At the table beside them, Jula and Amby Bole sat with Precious Thimble – although she was there in flesh only, since everything else had been battered senseless – and the two Bole brothers were talking.

'The storm's got a new voice. You hear that, Jula?'

'I hear that and I hear you, Amby. I hear that in this ear and I hear you in that ear, and they come together in the middle and make my head ache, so if you shut up then one ear's open so the sound from the other can go right through and sink into that wall over there and that wall can have it, 'cause I don't.'

'You don't – hey, where'd everyone go?'

'Down into that cellar – you ever see such a solid cellar door, Amby? Why, it's as thick as the ones we use on the pits we put wizards in, you know, the ones nobody can open.'

'It was you that scared 'em, Jula, but look, now we can drink even more and pay nothing.'

'Until they all come back out. And then you'll be looking at paying a whole lot.'

'I'm not paying. This is a business expense.'

'Is it?'

'I bet. We have to ask Master Quell when he wakes up.'

'He's awake, I think.'

'He don't look awake.'

'Nobody does, exceptin' us.'

'Wonder what everyone's doing in the cellar. Maybe there's a party or something.'

'That storm sounds like angry women.'

'Like Mother, only more than one.'

'That would be bad.'

'Ten times bad. You break something?'

'Never did. You did.'

'Someone broke something, and those mothers are on the way. Sounds like.'

'Sounds like, yes.'

'Coming fast.'

'Whatever you broke, you better fix it.'

'No way. I'll just say you did it.'

'I'll say I did it first – no, you did it. I'll say you did it first.'

'I didn't do—'

But now the shrieking storm was too loud for any further conversation, and to Gruntle's half-deadened ears it did indeed sound like voices. Terrible, inhuman voices, filled with rage and hunger. He'd thought the storm was waning; in fact, he'd been certain of it. But then everyone had fled into the cellar—

Gruntle lifted his head.

At precisely the same time that Mappo did.

Their eyes met. And yes, both understood. *That's not a storm.*

Chapter Seventeen

My finest student? A young man, physically perfect.

To look upon him was to see a duellist by any known measure. His discipline was a source of awe; his form was elegance personified. He could snuff a dozen candles in successive lunges, each lunge identical to the one preceding it. He could spear a buzzing fly. Within two years I could do nothing more for him for he had passed my own skill.

I was, alas, not there to witness his first duel, but it was described to me in detail. For all his talent, his perfection of form, for all his precision, his muscle memory, he revealed one and only one flaw.

He was incapable of fighting a real person. A foe of middling skill can be profoundly dangerous, in that clumsiness can surprise, ill-preparation can confound brilliant skills of defence. The very unpredictability of a real opponent in a life and death struggle served my finest student with a final lesson.

It is said the duel lasted a dozen heartbeats. From that day forward, my philosophy of instruction changed. Form is all very well, repetition ever essential, but actual blood-touch practice must begin within the first week of instruction. To be a duellist, one must duel. The hardest thing to teach is how to survive.

TREVAN AULT
2ND CENTURY, DARUJHISTAN

Gather close, and let us speak of nasty little shits. Oh, come now, we are no strangers to the vicious demons in placid disguises, innocent eyes so wide, hidden minds so dark. Does evil exist? Is it a force, some deadly possession that slips into the unwary? Is it a thing separate and thus subject to accusation and blame, distinct from the one it has used? Does it flit from soul to soul, weaving its diabolical scheme in all the unseen places, snarling into knots tremulous fears and appalling opportunity, stark terrors and brutal self-interest?

Or is the dread word nothing more than a quaint and oh so convenient encapsulation of all those traits distinctly lacking moral context, a sweeping generalization embracing all things depraved and breathtakingly cruel, a word to define that peculiar glint in the eye – the voyeur to one's own delivery of horror, of pain and anguish and impossible grief?

Give the demon crimson scales, slashing talons. Tentacles and dripping poison. Three eyes and six slithering tongues. As it crouches there in the soul, its latest abode in an eternal succession of abodes, may every god kneel in prayer.

But really. Evil is nothing but a word, an objectification where no objectification is necessary. Cast aside this notion of some external agency as the source of inconceivable inhumanity – the sad truth is our possession of an innate proclivity towards indifference, towards deliberate denial of mercy, towards disengaging all that is moral within us.

But if that is too dire, let's call it evil. And paint it with fire and venom.

There are extremities of behaviour that seem, at the time, perfectly natural, indeed reasonable. They are arrived at suddenly, or so it might seem, but if one looks the progression reveals itself, step by step, and that is a most sad truth.

Murillio walked from the duelling school, rapier at his hip, gloves tucked into his belt. Had he passed anyone who knew him they might be forgiven for not at first recognizing him, given his expression. The lines of his face were drawn deep, his frown a clench, as if the mind behind it was in torment, sick of itself. He looked older, harder. He looked to be a man in dread of his own thoughts, a man haunted by an unexpected reflection in a lead window, a silvered mirror, flinching back from his own face, the eyes that met themselves with defiance.

Only a fool would have stepped directly into this man's path.

In his wake, a young student hesitated. He had been about to call out a greeting to his instructor; but he had seen Murillio's expression, and, though young, the student was no fool. Instead, he set out after the man.

Bellam Nom would not sit in any god's lap. Mark him, mark him well.

There had been fervent, breathless discussion. Crippled Da was like a man reborn, finding unexpected reserves of strength to lift himself into the rickety cart, with Myrla, her eyes bright, fussing over him until even he slapped her hands away.

Mew and Hinty stared wide-eyed, brainless as toddlers were, faces like sponges sucking in everything and understanding none of it. As for Snell, oh, it was ridiculous, all this excitement. His ma and da were, he well knew, complete idiots. Too stupid to succeed in life, too thick to realize it.

They had tortured themselves and each other over the loss of Harllo, their mutual failure, their hand-in-hand incompetence that made them hated even as they wallowed in endless self-pity. Ridiculous. Pathetic. The sooner Snell was rid of them the better, and at that thought he eyed his siblings once again. If Ma and Da just vanished, why, he could sell them both and make good coin. They weren't fit for much else. Let someone else wipe their stinking backsides and shove food into their mouths – damned things choked half the time and spat it out the other half, and burst into tears at the lightest poke.

But his disgust was proving a thin crust, cracking as terror seethed beneath, the terror born of remote possibilities. Da and Ma were going to a temple, a new temple, one devoted to a god as broken and useless as Bedek himself. The High Priest, who called himself a prophet, was even more crippled. Nothing worked below his arms, and half his face sagged and the eye on that side had just dried up since the lids couldn't close and now it looked like a rotten crab apple – Snell had seen it for himself, when he'd stood at the side of the street watching as the Prophet was being carried by his diseased followers to the next square, where he'd croak out yet another sermon predicting the end of the world and how only the sick and the stupid would survive.

No wonder Da was so eager. He'd found his god at last, one in his own image, and that was usually the way, wasn't it? People don't change to suit their god; they change their god to suit them.

Da and Ma were on their way to the Temple of the Crippled God, where they hoped to speak to the Prophet himself. Where they hoped to ask the god's blessing. Where they hoped to discover what had happened to Harllo.

Snell didn't believe anything would come of that. But then, he couldn't be sure, could he? And that was what was scaring him. What if the Crippled God knew about what Snell had done? What if the Prophet prayed to it and was told the truth, and then told Da and Ma?

Snell might have to run away. But he'd take Hinty and Mew with him, selling them off to get some coin, which he'd need and need bad. Let someone else wipe their stinking . . .

Yes, Ma, I'll take care of them. You two go, see what you can find out.

Just look at them, so filled with hope, so stupid with the idea that something else will solve all their problems, swipe away their miseries. The Crippled God: how good can a god be if it's crippled? If it can't even heal itself? That Prophet was getting big crowds. Plenty of useless people in the world, so that was no surprise. And they all wanted sympathy. Well, Snell's family deserved sympathy, and maybe some coin, too. And a new house, all the food they could eat and all the beer they could drink. In fact, they deserved maids and servants, and people who would think for them, and do everything that needed doing.

Snell stepped outside to watch Ma wheeling Da off down the alley, clickety-click.

Behind him Hinty was snuffling, probably getting ready to start bawling since Ma was out of sight and that didn't happen often. Well, he'd just have to shut the brat up. A good squeeze to the chest and she'd just pass out and things would get quiet again. Maybe do that to both of them. Make it easier wrapping them up in some kind of sling, easier to carry in case he decided to run.

Hinty started crying.

Snell spun round and the runt looked at him and her crying turned into shrieks.

'Yes, Hinty,' Snell said, grinning, 'I'm coming for ya. I'm coming for ya.'
And so he did.

Bellam Nom had known that something was wrong, terribly so. The atmosphere in the school was sour, almost toxic. Hardly conducive to learning about duelling, about everything one needed to know about staying alive in a contest of blades.

On a personal, purely selfish level, all this was frustrating, but one would have to be an insensitive bastard to get caught up in that kind of thinking. The problem was, something had broken Stonny Menackis. Broken her utterly. And that in turn had left Murillio shattered, because he loved her – no doubt about that, since he wouldn't have hung around if he didn't, not with the way she was treating him and everyone else, but especially him.

It hadn't been easy working out what was wrong, since nobody was talking much, but he'd made a point of lingering, standing in shadows as if doing little more than cooling himself off after a bell's worth of footwork in the sunlight. And Bellam Nom had sharp ears. He also had a natural talent, one it seemed he had always possessed: he could read lips. This had proved useful, of course. People had a hard time keeping secrets from Bellam.

Master Murillio had reached some sort of decision, and walked as one driven now, and Bellam quickly realized that he did not need to employ any stealth while trailing him – an entire legion of Crimson Guard could be marching on the man's heels and he wouldn't know it.

Bellam was not certain what role he might be able to play in whatever was coming. The only thing that mattered to him was that he be there when the time came.

Mark him well. These are the thoughts of courage, unquestioning and uncompromising, and this is how heroes come to be. Small ones. Big ones. All kinds. When drama arrives, they are there. Look about. See for yourself.

He seemed such an innocuous man, so aptly named, and there was nothing in this modest office that might betray Humble Measure's ambitions, nor his bloodthirsty eagerness in making use of Seba Krafar and his Guild of Assassins.

Harmless, then, and yet Seba found himself sweating beneath his nondescript clothes. True, he disliked appearing in public, particularly in the light of day, but that unease barely registered when in the presence of the Master Ironmonger.

It's simple. I don't like the man. And is that surprising? Despite the fact that he's provided the biggest contract I've seen, at least as head of the Guild. Probably the Malazan offer Vorcan took on was bigger, but only because achieving it was impossible, even for that uncanny bitch.

Seba's dislike was perhaps suspect, even to his own mind, since it was caught up in the grisly disaster of Humble Measure's contract. Hard to separate this man from the scores of assassins butchered in the effort (still unsuccessful) to kill those damned Malazans. And this particular subject was one that would not quite depart, despite Humble Measure's casual, dismissive wave of one soft hand.

'The failing is of course temporary,' Seba Krafar said. 'Hadn't we best complete it, to our mutual satisfaction, before taking on this new contract of yours?'

'I have reconsidered the K'rul Temple issue, at least for the moment,' said Humble Measure. 'Do not fear, I am happy to add to the original deposit commensurate with the removal of two of the subjects, and should the others each fall in turn, you will of course be immediately rewarded. As the central focus, however, I would be pleased if you concentrated on the new one.'

Seba Krafar was never able to meet anyone's gaze for very long. He knew that most would see that as a weakness, or as proof that Seba could not be trusted, but he always made a point of ensuring that what he had to say was never evasive. This blunt honesty, combined with the shying eyes, clearly unbalanced people, and that was fine with Seba. Now, if only it worked on this man. 'This new one,' he ventured, 'is political.'

'Your specialty, I gather,' said Humble Measure.

'Yes, but one that grows increasingly problematic. The noble class has learned to protect itself. Assassinations are not as easy as they once were.'

The Ironmonger's brows lifted. 'Are you asking for more money?'

'Actually, no. It's this: the Guild is wounded. I've had to promote a dozen snipes months ahead of their time. They're not ready – oh, they can kill as efficiently as anyone, but most of them are little more than ambitious thugs. Normally, I would cull them, ruthlessly, but at the moment I can't afford to.'

'This requires, I assume, certain modifications to your normal tactics.'

'It already has. Fifteen of my dead from K'rul Bar were my latest promotions. That's left the rest of them rattled. An assassin without confidence is next to useless.'

Humble Measure nodded. 'Plan well and execute with precision, Master Krafar, and that confidence will return.'

'Even that won't be enough, unless we succeed.'

'Agreed.'

Seba was silent for a moment, still sweating, still uneasy. 'Before I accept this latest contract,' he said, 'I should offer you a way out. There are other, less bloody ways of getting elected to the Council. It seems money is not a problem, and given that—' He stopped when the man lifted a hand.

Suddenly, there was something new in Humble Measure's eyes, something Seba had not seen before, and it left him chilled. 'If it was my desire to buy my way on to the Council, Master Krafar, I would not have summoned you here. That should be obvious.'

'Yes, I suppose—'

'But I have summoned you, yes? Therefore, it is reasonable to assume my desires are rather more complicated than simply gaining a seat on the Council.'

'You want this particular councillor dead.'

Humble Measure acknowledged this with a brief closing of his eyes that somehow conveyed a nod without his having to move his head. 'We are not negotiating my reasons, since they are none of your business and have no relevance to the task itself. Now, you will assault this particular estate, and you will kill the councillor and everyone else, down to the scullery maid and the terrier employed to kill rats.'

Seba Krafar looked away (but then, he'd been doing that on and off ever since he'd sat down). 'As you say. Should be simple, but then, these things never are.'

'Are you saying that you are not up to this?'

'No, I'm saying that I have learned to accept that nothing is simple, and the simpler it looks the more complicated it probably is. Therefore, this will need careful planning. I trust you are not under any pressure to get on to the Council in a hurry? There're all kinds of steps needed in any case, sponsorships or bloodline claims, assessment of finances and so on . . .' He fell silent after, in a brief glance, he noted the man's level look. Seba cleared his throat, and then said, 'Ten days at the minimum. Acceptable?'

'Acceptable.'

'Then we're done here.'

'We are.'

'The disposition provided us by the Malazan embassy is unacceptable.'

Councillor Coll fixed a steady regard on Hanut Orr's smooth-shaven face, and saw nothing in it but what he had always seen. Fear, contempt, misdirection and outright deceit, the gathered forces of hatred and spite. 'So you stated,' he replied. 'But as you can see, the meeting has finished. I do my best to leave matters of the Council in the chamber. Politicking is a habit that can fast run away with you, Councillor.'

'I do not recall seeking your advice.'

'No, just my allegiance. Of the two, you elected the wrong one, Councillor.'

'I think not, since it is the only relevant one.'

'Yes,' Coll smiled, 'I understood you well enough. Now, if you will excuse me—'

'Their explanation for why they needed to expand the embassy is flimsy – are you so easily duped, Councillor Coll? Or is it just a matter of filling your purse to buy your vote?'

'Either you are offering to bribe me, Councillor Orr, or you are suggesting that I have been bribed. The former seems most unlikely. Thus, it must be the latter, and since we happen to be standing in the corridor, with others nearby – close enough to hear you – you leave me no choice but to seek censure.'

Hanut Orr sneered. 'Censure? Is that the coward's way of avoiding an actual duel?'

'I accept that it is such a rare occurrence that you probably know little about it. Very well, for the benefit of your defence, allow me to explain.'

A dozen or more councillors had now gathered and were listening, expressions appropriately grave.

Coll continued, 'I hereby accept your accusation as a formal charge. The procedure now is the engagement of an independent committee that will begin investigating. Of course, said investigation is most thorough, and will involve the detailed auditing of both of our financial affairs – yes, accuser and accused. Such examination inevitably . . . propagates, so that all manner of personal information comes to light. Once all pertinent information is assembled, my own advocates will review your file, to determine whether a countercharge is appropriate. At this point, the Council Judiciary takes over proceedings.'

Hanut Orr had gone somewhat pale.

Coll observed him with raised brows. 'Shall I now seek censure, Councillor?'

'I was not suggesting you were taking bribes, Councillor Coll. And I apologize if my carelessness led to such an interpretation.'

'I see. Were you then offering me one?'

'Of course not.'

'Then, is our politicking done here?'

Hanut Orr managed a stiff bow, and then whirled off, trailed after a moment by Shardan Lim and then, with studied casualness, young Gorlas Vidikas.

Coll watched them depart.

Estraysian D'Arle moved to his side and, taking him by the arm, led him towards a private alcove – the ones designed precisely for extra-chamber politicking. Two servants delivered chilled white wine and then quickly departed.

'That was close,' Estraysian murmured.

'He's young. And stupid. A family trait? Possibly.'

'There was no bribe, was there?'

Coll frowned. 'Not as such. The official reasons given are just as Orr claimed. Flimsy.'

'Yes. And he was not privy to the unofficial ones.'

'No. Wrong committee.'

'Hardly an accident. That ambitious trio's been given places on every meaningless committee we can think of – but that's not keeping them busy enough, it seems. They still find time to get in our way.'

'One day,' said Coll, 'they will indeed be as dangerous as they think they are.'

Outside the building, standing in the bright sun, the three ambitious young counsellors formed a sort of island in a sea of milling pigeons. None took note of the cooing on all sides.

'I'll have that bastard's head one day,' said Hanut Orr. 'On a spike outside my gate.'

'You were careless,' said Shardan Lim, doing little to disguise his contempt.

Stung, Orr's gloved hand crept to the grip of his rapier. 'I've had about enough of you, old friend. It's clear you inherited every mewling weakness of your predecessor. I admit I'd hoped for something better.'

'Listen to you two,' said Gorlas Vidikas. 'Bitten by a big dog so here you are snapping at each other, and why? Because the big dog's *too* big. If he could see you now.'

Hanut Orr snorted. 'So speaks the man who can't keep his wife on a tight enough leash.'

Was the perfect extension of the metaphor deliberate? Who can say? In any case, to the astonishment of both Orr and Lim, Gorlas Vidikas simply smiled, as if appreciative of the riposte. He made a show of brushing dust from his cuffs. 'Well then, I will leave you to . . . whatever, as I have business that will take me out of the city for the rest of the day.'

'That Ironmonger will never get on the Council, Vidikas,' Shardan Lim said. 'There's no available seat and that situation's not likely to change any time soon. This partnership of yours will take you nowhere and earn you nothing.'

'On the contrary, Shardan. I am getting *wealthy*. Do you have any idea how essential iron is to this city? Ah, I see that such matters are beneath you both. So be it. As a bonus, I am about to acquire a new property in the city as well. It has been and will continue to be a most rewarding partnership. Good day to you, sirs.'

There was no denying Seba Krafar's natural air of brutality. He was a large, bearish man, and though virtually none of the people he pushed past while crossing the market's round knew him for the Master of the Assassin's Guild, they none the less quickly retreated from any confrontation; and if any might, in their own natural belligerence, consider a bold challenge to this rude oaf, why, a second, more searching glance disavowed them of any such notions.

He passed through the press like a heated knife through pig fat, a simile most suited to his opinion of humanity and his place within it. One of the consequences of this attitude, however, was that his derisive regard led to a kind of arrogant carelessness. He took no notice whatsoever of the nondescript figure who fell into his wake.

The nearest cellar leading down into the tunnels was at the end of a narrow, straight alley that led to a dead end. The steps to the cellar ran along the back of the last building on the left. The cellar had once served as a storage repository for coal, in the days before the harnessing of gas – back when the notion of poisoning one's own air in the name of brainless convenience seemed reasonable (at least to people displaying their lazy stupidity with smug pride). Now, the low-ceilinged chamber squatted empty and sagging beneath three levels of half-rotted tenement rooms in symbolic celebration of modernity.

From the shutterless windows babies cried to the accompaniment of clanking cookware and slurred arguments, sounds as familiar to Seba Krafar as the rank air of the alley itself. His thoughts were busy enough to justify his abstracted state. Fear warred with greed in a mutual, ongoing exchange of masks which were in fact virtually identical, but never mind that; the game was ubiquitous enough, after all. Before too long, in any case, the two combatants would end up supine with exhaustion. Greed usually won, but carried fear on its back.

So much for Seba Krafar's preoccupations. Even without them, it was unlikely he would have heard the one on his trail, since that one possessed unusual talents, of such measure that he was able to move up directly behind the Master Assassin, and reach out with ill intent.

A hand closed on Seba's neck, fingers like contracting claws of iron pressing nerves that obliterated all motor control, yet before the assassin could collapse (as his body wanted to do) he was flung halfway round and thrown up against a grimy stone wall. And held there, moccasined feet dangling.

He felt a breath along one cheek, and then heard whispered words.

'Pull your watchers off K'rul's Bar. When I leave here, you will find a small sack at your feet. Five councils. The contract is now concluded – I am buying it out.' The tip of a knife settled beneath Seba's right eye. 'I trust five councils are sufficient. Unless you object.'

'No, not at all,' gasped Seba. 'The Malazans are safe – at least from the Guild. Of course, that just means the client will seek, er, other means.'

'Yes, about your client.'

'I cannot—'

'No need to, Seba Krafar. I am well aware of the Master Ironmonger's particular obsession.'

'Lucky you,' Seba said in a growl – gods, whoever this was still held him off the ground, and that grip did not waver. 'Because,' he added – for he was still a brave man – 'I'm not.'

'If you were,' said the man, 'you would not be so eager to take his coin, no matter how much he offered.'

'Since you put it that way, perhaps those five councils down there could buy him an accident.'

'Generous offer, but suicidal on your part. No, I do not hire people to do my dirty work.'

Through gritted teeth – feeling was returning to his limbs, like sizzling fire – Seba said, 'So I've gathered.'

'We're done here,' the man said.

'Unless you've other pressing business,' Seba managed, and felt a slackening of that grip, and, vague beneath his feet, the greasy cobblestones.

'Very well,' said the voice, 'you've actually managed to impress me, Seba Krafar. Reach up to that old lantern hook, there on your left – you can hold yourself up until the strength returns to your legs. It wouldn't do anything to your already damaged dignity to have you fall now. Stay facing the wall for ten steady breaths, eyes closed. I don't want to have to change my mind about you.'

'First impressions are never easy to live up to,' said Seba, 'but I'll do my best.'

The hand pulled away, then returned to give his shoulder a gentle pat.

He stood, forehead pressed against the wall, eyes closed, and counted ten slow breaths. Somewhere round the third one, he caught the stench – oh, more than just muscles let loose below his neck, and now he understood the man's comments on dignity. *Yes, plopping down on my arse would've been most unpleasant.*

Sweat ran down both sides of his face. Glancing straight down, he saw the small bag with its measly five coins. 'Shit,' he muttered, 'I forgot to write him a receipt.'

Fisher waited at the mouth of the alley, until he saw the Master Assassin delicately bend down to retrieve the bag.

Agreement consummated.

The Master Assassin, he was certain, would bother them no more. As for Humble Measure, well, that man's downfall would require something considerably more complicated. But there was time.

And this is the lesson here, dear friends. Even a man such as Fisher kel Tath, for all his formidable, mysterious qualities, was quite capable of grievous errors in judgement.

Time then to return to K'rul's Bar. Perhaps Picker had found her way back, into that cool flesh that scarcely drew breath. If not, why, Fisher might have to do something about that. Lost souls had a way of getting into trouble.

Was this sufficient cause for his own carelessness? Perhaps. Leaving the round and its crowds, he walked into the narrow, shady Avenue of the Bullocks, threading between the few hurrying passers-by – at night, this street was notorious for muggings, and indeed, was it not but two days ago that the City Guard found yet another battered corpse? There, before those very steps leading to a shop selling square nails, rivets and wooden frames on which to hang skinned things and other works worthy of display. Even during the day this track was risky. It was the shadows, you see—

And out from one stepped a small, toad-visaged apparition wearing a broad grin that split the very dark, somewhat pocked face, reminding one of a boldly slashed overripe melon. Seemingly balanced on this creature's head was a bundle of bow-gut – no, it was hair – in which at least three spiders nested.

'You,' hissed the man, his eyes bright and then shifty, and then bright once more.

'None other,' said Fisher, with the faintest of sighs.

'Of course not.' The head tilted but the hair did not slide off. 'Another idiot – this city's full of them! "None other." What kind of thing to say is that? If some other, why, I'd not have leapt into his path, would I? Best keep this simple.' The head righted itself, spiders adjusting their perches to match. 'I bring word from my brilliant not-all-there master.' A sudden whisper: 'Brilliant, yes, a word used most advisedly; still, use it once and we're done with it for ever.' He then raised his voice once more. 'When all this is done—'

'Excuse me,' cut in Fisher. 'When all what is done?'

'This, of course! Foolish Iskaral – keep it simple! Simpler, even! Listen, dear middling bard, when all this is done, eke out the eel – no, wait – er, seek out the eel. Seal? Damn, I had the message memorized and everything! Peek at – eat an eel – seek and peek the bleak earl – perk the veal, deal the prick – oh, Hood's breath! What was it again? And I had the gall to call him brilliant! He should've sent Sordiko Qualm, yes, so I could've followed the glorious rocking ship of her sweet hips—' and he wagged his head side to side, side to side, eyes glazing, 'slib-slab, slib-slab, oh!'

'Thank you,' Fisher said as the man began muttering under his breath and pausing every now and then to lick his lips, 'for, er, the message. I assure you, I understand.'

'Of course you do – you're a man, aren't you? Gods, that a simple casual stride could so reduce one to gibbering worship – why, who needs gods and goddesses when we have arses like that?'

'Indeed, who? Now, since you have successfully delivered your message from your master, may I proceed on my way?'

'What? Naturally. Go away. You're a damned distraction, is what you are.'

A tilt of the head, and the bard was indeed on his way once more.

The mob outside the newly consecrated Temple of the Fallen One, or the Crippled God, or indeed the name by which most knew it – the Temple of Chains – was thick and strangely rank. More than natural sweat as might be squeezed out by the mid-morning sun, this was the human rendering of desperation, made even sicklier with obsequious anticipation.

Yet the door to the narrow-fronted temple remained shut, evidently barred from within. Offerings were heaped up against it – copper and tin coins as well as links of chain and the odd clasp and cheap jewellery.

Bedek on his cart and Myrla standing before him, gripping the handles, found themselves in the midst of trembling alcoholics, the pock-scarred, the lame and the deformed. Milky eyes stared, as if cataracts were punishment for having seen too much – all other eyes were filled with beseeching need, the hunger for blessing, for even the passing brush of a twisted hand if it belonged to the Prophet. Misshapen faces lifted up, held fixedly upon that door. Once within the press, and unable to get any closer, the stink became unbearable. The breath of rotting teeth and consumptive dissolution. From his low perch, Bedek could see nothing but shoulders and the backs of heads. Whimpering, he plucked at his wife's tunic.

'Myrla. *Myrla!*'

The look she turned on him was both savage and . . . small, and with a shock Bedek suddenly saw her – and himself – as meaningless, insignificant, worthless. They were, he realized, no better than anyone else here. Each of them seeking to be singled out, to be guided out, to be raised up from all the others. Each dreaming of coming into glorious focus in the eyes of a god – eyes brimming with pity and knowledge, eyes that understood injustice and the unfairness of existence. A god, yes, to make them right. *To make us all – each and every one of us – right. Whole.*

But Bedek had held no such notions. They were not why he was here. He and Myrla were different. From all of these people. They, you see, had lost a child.

The door would remain locked, they learned, until at least midday. Sometimes even later. And even then, the Prophet might not emerge. If he was communing with his own pain, they were told, he might not be seen for days.

Yes, but did he *bless* people? Did he *help* people?

Oh, yes. Why, I saw a man in terrible pain, and the Prophet took it all away.

He healed the man?

No, he smothered him. Delivered his spirit – now at peace – into the hands of the Fallen One. If you are in pain, this is where you can end your life – only here, do you understand, can you be sure your soul will find a home. There, in the loving heart of the Fallen One. Don't you want to find your legs again? Other side of life, that's where you'll find them.

And so Bedek came to understand that, perhaps, this Crippled God could not help them. Not with finding Harllo. And all at once he wanted to go home.

But Myrla would have none of that. The yearning was unabated in her eyes, but it had been transformed, and what she sought now had nothing to do with Harllo. Bedek did not know what that new thing might be, but he was frightened down to the core of his soul.

Snell struggled to form a sling to take the runts, both of whom were lying senseless on the floor. He had checked to see they were both breathing, since he'd heard that making them black out could sometimes kill them – if he'd held them tight for too long – though he'd been careful. He was always careful when doing that, though if one of them did die, why, he would say it went to sleep and just never woke up and that happened, didn't it, with the little ones? And then he'd cry because that was expected.

Poor thing, but it'd always been weak, hadn't it? So many children were weak. Only the strong ones, the smart ones, survived. It's what the world was like, after all, and the world can't be changed, not one bit.

There was a man in the Daru High Market who always dressed well and had plenty of coin, and it was well known he'd take little ones. Ten, twenty silver councils, boy or girl, it didn't matter which. He knew people, rich people – he was just the middleman, but you dealt with him if you didn't want no one to find out anything, and if there were any small bodies left over, well, they never ever showed up to start people asking questions.

It would be a bit of a walk, especially with both Mew and Hinty, and that's why he needed to work out a sling of some sort, like the ones the Rhivi mothers used. Only, how did they do that?

The door opened behind him and Snell whirled in sudden terror.

The man standing in the threshold was familiar – he'd been with Stonny Menackis the last time she'd visited – and Snell could see at once that dear Snell was in trouble. Ice cold fear, a mouth impossibly dry, a pounding heart.

'They're just sleeping!'

The man stared. 'What have you done with them, Snell?'

'Nothing! Go away. Da and Ma aren't here. They went to the Chains Temple. Come back later.'

Instead, the man stepped inside. One gloved hand casually flung Snell back, away from the motionless girls on the floor. The blow rocked Snell, and as if a stopper had been jarred loose fear poured through him. As the man knelt and drew off a glove to set a palm against Mew's forehead, Snell scrabbled to the back wall.

'I'm gonna call the guards – I'm gonna scream—'

'Shut your damned face or I'll do it for you.' A quick, heavy look. 'I've not yet started with you, Snell. Everything comes back to you. On the day Harllo went missing, on that day, Snell . . .' He lifted his hand and straightened. 'Are they drugged? Tell me how you did this.'

He meant to keep lying, but all at once he thought that maybe if he told the truth about this, the man might believe the lies he used afterwards, on the other stuff. 'I just squeeze 'em, when they cry too much, that's all. It don't hurt them none, honest.'

The man had glanced at the stretch of burlap lying beside Mew. Maybe he was putting things together, but nothing could be proved, could it? It would be all right. It would be—

Two quick strides and those hands – one gloved and the other bare and scarred – snagged the front of Snell's tunic. He was lifted into the air until his eyes were level with the man's. And Snell saw in those deadly eyes something dark, a lifeless whisper that could flatten out at any moment, and all thoughts of lying whimpered away.

'On that day,' the man said, 'you came back with a load of sun-dried dung. Something you'd never done before, and have never done since. No, your mother said it was Harllo who did such things. Harllo, who at five fucking years old did more to help this family than you ever have. Who collected that dung, Snell?'

Snell had widened his eyes as wide as they could go. He made his chin tremble. 'Harllo,' he whispered, 'but I never hurt him – I swear it!'

Oh, he hadn't wanted to lie. It just came out.

'Past Worrytown or Two-Ox Gate?'

'The gate. Two-Ox.'

'Did you go with him or did you follow him? What happened out there, Snell?'

And Snell's eyes betrayed him then, a flicker too instinctive to stop in time – down to where Mew and Hinty were lying.

The man's eyes flattened just as Snell had feared they might.

'I never killed him! He was breathing when I left him! If you kill me they'll find out – they'll arrest you – you'll go the gallows – you can't kill me – don't!'

'You knocked him out and left him there, after stealing the dung he'd collected. The hills beyond Two-Ox Gate.'

'And I went back, a couple of days – the day after – and he was gone! He's just run off, that's all—'

'A five-year-old boy doing everything he could to help his family just ran off, did he? Or did you drive him off, Snell?'

'I never did – he was just gone – and that's not my fault, is it? Someone maybe found him, maybe even adopted him.'

'You are going to tell your parents everything, Snell,' the man said. 'I will be back tonight, probably late, but I will be back. Don't even think of running—'

'He won't,' said a voice from the door.

The man turned. 'Bellam – what—'

'Master Murillio, I'll stay here and keep an eye on the fucker. And when his parents show up, well, he'll spill it all out. Go on, Master, you don't need to worry about anything happening back here.'

The man – Murillio – was silent for a time, seeming to study the rangy boy who stood, arms folded, leaning against the doorway's frame.

And then he set Snell down and stepped back. 'I won't forget this, Bellam.'

'It'll be fine, Master. I won't beat the bones out of him, much as I'd like to, and much as he obviously deserves it. No, he's going to sit and play with his little sisters – soon as they come round—'

'A splash of water should do it.'

'After a splash, then. And not only is Snell going to play with them, but he's going to make a point of losing every game, every argument. If they want him to stand on his head while picking his arsehole, why, that's what Snell will do. Right, Snell?'

Snell had met older boys just like this one. They had calm eyes but that was just to fix you good when you weren't expecting nothing. He was more frightened of this Bellam than he'd been of Murillio. 'You hurt me and I'll get my friends after you,' he hissed. 'My street friends—'

'And when they hear the name Bellam Nom they'll cut you loose faster than you can blink.'

Murillio had found a clay bowl into which he now poured some water.

'Master,' said Bellam, 'I can do that. You got what you needed from him – at least a trail, a place to start.'

'Very well. Until tonight then, Bellam, and thank you.'

After he'd left, Bellam shut the door and advanced on Snell, who once more cringed against the back wall.

'You said—'

'We do that, don't we, when it comes to grown-ups.'

'Don't touch me!'

'No grown-ups anywhere close, Snell – what do *you* like to do when they're not around? Oh, yes, that's right. You like to torment everyone smaller than you. That sounds a fun game. I think I'll play, and look, you're smaller than me. Now, what torment shall we do first?'

In leaving them for the time being, all grim concern regarding anything unduly cruel can be thankfully dispensed with. Bellam Nom, being cleverer than most, knew that true terror belonged not to what did occur, but to what *might* occur. He was content to encourage Snell's own imagination into the myriad possibilities, which was a delicate and precise form of torture. Especially useful in that it left no bruises.

Bullies learn nothing when bullied in turn; there are no lessons, no about-face in their squalid natures. The principle of righteous justice is a peculiar domain where propriety and vengeance become confused, almost indistinguishable. The bullied bully is shown but the other side of the same fear he or she has lived with all his or her life. The about-face happens there, on the outside, not the inside. Inside, the bully and everything that haunts the bully's soul remains unchanged.

It is an abject truth, but conscience cannot be shoved down the throat.

If only it could.

Moths were flattened against the walls of the narrow passageway, waiting for something, probably night. As it was a little used route to and from the Vidikas estate, frequented twice a day at specific times by deliveries to the kitchen, Challice had taken to using it with all the furtive grace of the insouciant adulteress that she had become. The last thing she expected was to almost run into her husband there in the shadows midway through.

Even more disconcerting, it was clear that he had been awaiting her. One hand holding his duelling gloves as if about to slap them across her cheek, yet there was an odd smile on his face. 'Darling,' he said.

She halted before him, momentarily struck dumb. It was one thing to play out the game at breakfast, a table between them cluttered with all the false icons of a perfect and perfectly normal marriage. Their language then was such a smooth navigation round all those deadly shoals that it seemed the present was but a template of the future, of years and years of this; not a single wound stung to life, no tragic floundering on the jagged shallows, sailors drowning in the foam.

He stood before her now, tall with a thousand sharp edges, entirely blocking her path, his eyes glittering like wrecker fires on a promontory. 'So pleased I found you,' he said. 'I must head out to the mining camp – no doubt you can hear the carriage being readied behind you.'

Casual words, yet she was startled, like a bird; flash of fluttering, panicked wings in the gloom as she half turned to register the snort of horses and the rustle of traces from the forecourt behind her. 'Oh,' she managed, then faced him once more. Her heart's rapid beat began slowing down.

'Even here,' Gorlas said, 'there is a sweet flush to your cheeks, dear. Most becoming.'

She could almost feel the brush of fingertips to grant benediction to the compliment. A moth, startled awake by the clash of currents in the dusty air, wings dry as talc as it fluttered against her face. She flinched back. 'Thank you,' she said.

This was just another game, of course. She realized that now. He did not want things to get messy, not here, not any time soon. She told herself this with certainty, and hoped it was true. But then, why not an explosive shattering? Freeing him, freeing her – wouldn't that be healthier in the end? *Unless his idea of freeing himself is to kill me. Such things happen, don't they?*

'I do not expect to be back for at least three days. Two nights.'

'I see. Be well on your journey, Gorlas.'

'Thank you, darling.' And then, without warning, he stepped close, his free hand grasping her right breast. 'I don't like the thought of strangers doing this,' he said, his voice low, that odd smile still there. 'I need to picture the face, one I know well. I need a sense of the bastard behind it.'

She stared into his eyes and saw only a stranger, calculating, as clinical and cold as a dresser of the dead – like the one who'd come to do what was needed with the corpse of her mother, once the thin veil of sympathy was tossed aside like a soiled cloth and the man set to work.

'When I get back,' he continued, 'we'll have a talk. One with details. I want to know all about him, Challice.'

She knew that what she said at this precise moment would echo in her husband's mind for virtually every spare moment in the course of the next three days and two nights, and by the time he returned her words would have done their work in transforming him – into a broken thing, or into a monster. She could say *All right*, as if she was being forced, cornered, and whatever immediate satisfaction he felt would soon twist into something dark, unpleasant, and she would find herself across from a vengeful creature in three days' time. She might say *If you like*, and he would hear that as defiance and cruel indifference – as if for her his needs were irrelevant, as if she would oblige out of pity and not much else. No, in truth she had few choices in what she might utter at this moment. In an instant, as he awaited her response, she decided on what she would say and when it came out it was calm and assured (but not too much so). 'Until then, husband.'

He nodded, and she saw the pupils of his eyes dilate. She caught his quickened breathing, and knew her choice had been the right one. Now, the next three days and two nights, Gorlas would be as one on fire. With anticipation, with his imagination unleashed and playing out scenarios, each one a variation on a single theme.

Yes, Gorlas, we are not done with each other yet, after all.

His hand withdrew from her breast and, with a courtly bow, he stepped to one side to permit her to pass.

She did so.

Murillio hired a horse for the day; with tack included, the rental amounted to three silver councils along with a twenty-council deposit. Of that, the animal was worth perhaps five, certainly not much more. Slope-backed, at least ten years old, worn out, beaten down, the misery in the beast's eyes stung Murillio to sympathy and he was of half a mind to forgo the deposit and leave the animal in the hands of a kindly farmer with plenty of spare pasture.

He rode at a slow, plodding walk through the crowded streets, until he reached Two-Ox Gate. Passing through the archway's shadow, he collected the horse into a steady trot on the cobbled road, passing laden wagons and carts and the occasional Gadrobi peasant struggling beneath baskets filled with salted fish, flasks of oil, candles and whatever else they needed to make bearable living in a squalid hut along the roadside.

Once beyond the leper colony, he began scanning the lands to either side, seeking the nearest active pasture. A short distance on he spied sheep and goats wandering the slope of a hillside to his right. A lone shepherd hobbled along the ridge, waving a switch to keep the flies off. Murillio pulled his mount off the road and rode towards him.

The old man noticed his approach and halted.

He was dressed in rags, but the crook he carried looked new, freshly oiled and polished. His eyes were smeared with cataracts from too many years in the bright sunlight, and he squinted, wary and nervous, as Murillio drew up and settled back in the saddle.

'Hello, good shepherd.'

A terse nod answered him.

'I am looking for someone—'

'Nobody but me here,' the old man replied, flicking the switch before his face.

'This was a few weeks back. A young boy, up here collecting dung, perhaps.'

'We get 'em, out from the city.'

The furtiveness was ill-disguised. The old man licked his lips, switched at flies that weren't there. There were secrets here, Murillio realized. He dismounted. 'You know of this one,' he said. 'Five years old. He was hurt, possibly unconscious.'

The shepherd stepped back as he approached, half raised the crook. 'What was I supposed to do?' he demanded. 'The ones that come out here, they got nothing. They live in the streets. They sell the dung for a few coppers. I got no help here, we just working for somebody else. We go hungry every winter – what was I supposed to do?'

'Just tell me what happened,' said Murillio. 'You do that and maybe I'll just walk away, leave you be. But you're a bad liar, old man, and if you try again I might get angry.'

'We wasn't sure he was gonna live – he was beat up near dead, sir. Woulda died if we hadn't found him, took care of him.'

'And then?'

'Sold him off. It's hard enough, feedin' ourselves—'

'To who? Where is he?'

'Iron mines. The Eldra Holdings, west of here.'

Murillio felt a chill grip his heart. 'A five-year-old boy—'

'Moles, they call 'em. Or – so I heard.'

He returned to the horse. Lifted himself into the saddle and roughly pulled the beast round. Rode hard back to the road.

A thousand paces along, the horse threw a shoe.

The ox lumbered along at the pace of a beast for which time was meaningless, and perhaps in this it was wise indeed. Walking beside it, the man with the crop twitched its flank every now and then, but this was habit, not urgency. The load of braided leather was not a particularly onerous burden, and if the carter timed things right, why, he might wangle himself a meal at the camp before the long return journey back to the city. At least by then the day would be mostly done and the air would've cooled. In this heat, neither man nor beast was in any hurry.

Hardly surprising, then, that the lone traveller on foot caught up with them before too long, and after a brief conversation – a few words to either side of the jangle of coins – the load on the cart grew heavier, yet still not enough to force a groan from the ox. This was, after all, the task of its life, the very definition of its existence. In truth, it had little memory of ever being free, of ever trundling along without something to drag behind it, or the endless reverberation in its bones as wheels clunked across cobbles, slipping into and out of worn ruts in the stone.

Languid blinks, the storm of flies that danced in the heat, twitching tail and spots of blood on the fetlocks, and pulling something from one place to another. And at its side, squinting red-shot eyes, a storm of flies dancing, spots of blood here and there from midges and whatnot, and taking something from one place to another. Ox and driver, parallel lives through meaningless years. A singular variation, now, the man sitting with legs dangling off the cart, his boots worn and blisters oozing, and the dark maelstrom in his eyes that was for neither of them, and no business of theirs besides.

The ornate, lacquered, leaf-sprung carriage that rumbled past them a league from the camp had its windows shuttered against the heat and dust.

The man in the back had watched its approach. The carter watched it pass. The ox saw it moving away in front of it at a steady pace that it could never match, even had it wanted to, which it didn't.

Snell was nobody's fool, and when the ball of bound multicoloured twine rolled close to the door and Hinty stared at it, expecting its miraculous return to her pudgy, grimy hands, why, Snell obliged – and as soon as he was at the door, he darted outside and was gone.

He heard Bellam's shout, but Snell had a good head start and besides, the stupid idiot wouldn't just leave the runts behind, would he? No, Snell had made good his escape, easy as that, because he was clever and jerks could threaten him all the time but he won in the end, he always won – proof of his cleverness.

Up the street, into an alley, under the broken fence, across the narrow yard – chickens scattering from his path – and on to the stacked rabbit pens, over the next fence, into Twisty Alley, twenty strides up and then left, into the muddy track where a sewage pipe leaked. Nobody'd go down this pinched passageway, what with the stench and all, but he did, piss soaking through his worn moccasins, and then he was out on to Purse Street, and freedom.

Better if he'd stolen the runts to sell. Better still if he'd still had his stash of coins. Now, he had nothing. But nobody would catch him now. There were some older boys with connections to the gang that worked Worrytown, lifting what they could from the trader wagons that crowded through. If Snell could get out there, he'd be outside the city, wouldn't he? They could hunt for ever and not find him.

And he could make himself rich. He could rise in the ranks and become a pack leader. People would be scared of him, terrified even. Merchants would pay him just to not rob them. And he'd buy an estate, and hire assassins to kill Bellam Nom and Stonny Menackis and Murillio. He'd buy up his parents' debts and make them pay *him* every month – wouldn't that be something? It'd be perfect. And his sisters he could pimp out and eventually he'd have enough money to buy a title of some sort, get on the Council, and proclaim himself King of Darujhistan, and he'd order new gallows built and execute everyone who'd done him wrong.

He rushed through the crowds, his thoughts a world away, a future far off but almost in reach.

His feet were clipped out from under him and he fell hard: numbing shock from one shoulder and his hip. Bellam Nom stood over him, breathing hard but grinning. 'Nice try,' he said.

'Mew and Hinty! You left them—'

'Locked up, yes. That's what slowed me down.' And he reached down, grasped Snell's arm and yanked him to his feet, twisting hard enough to make him yelp in pain.

Bellam dragged Snell back the way he'd come.

'I'm going to kill you one day,' Snell said, then winced as Bellam's grip tightened on his arm.

'It's what people like you rely on, isn't it?'

'What?'

'That none of us are as nasty as you. That we'll have qualms about, say, skinning you alive. Or shattering your kneecaps. Gouging out your eyes. You want to kill me? Fine, just don't be surprised if I get to you first, Snell.'

'You can't murder—'

'Can't I? Why not? You seem to think you can, whenever you like, whenever the chance arises. Well, I'm not Stonny Menackis. I'm not Murillio, either. They're . . . civilized folk. No, Snell, I'm more like you, only I'm older and better at it.'

'If you did anything to me, Murillio would have to go after you. Like you say, he's not like us. Or Stonny. She'd cut you to pieces. Yes, it'd be Stonny, once Da asked her to, and he would.'

'You're making a big assumption, Snell.'

'What?'

'That they'd ever figure out it was me.'

'I'll warn them – as soon as they come back – I'll warn them about you—'

'Before or after you make your confession? About what you did to poor Harllo?'

'That was different! I didn't do nothing on purpose—'

'You hurt him, probably killed him, and left his body for the birds. You kept it all a secret, Snell. Hood knows, if I asked nicely enough, your da might just hand you over to me and good riddance to you.'

Snell said nothing. There was true terror inside him now. So much terror it filled him up, spilled out through his pores, and out from between his legs. This Bellam was a monster. He didn't feel anything for nobody. He just wanted to hurt Snell. A monster. A vicious demon, yes, a demon. Bellam was everything that was wrong with . . . with . . . everything.

'I'll be good,' Snell whimpered. 'You'll see. I'll make it right, all of it.'

But these were lies, and both of them knew it. Snell was what he was, and no amount of cuddling and coddling would change that. He stood, there in the mind, as if to say: *we are in your world. More of us than you imagine. If you knew how many of us there are, you'd be very, very frightened. We are here. Now, what are you going to do with us?* Snell was what he was, yes, and so, too, was Bellam Nom.

When he was dragged in through the narrow door of a nondescript shop at the near end of Twisty Alley, Snell suddenly recoiled – he knew this place. He knew—

'What you got yourself there, Bellam?'

'A fresh one, Goruss, and I'll let him go cheap.'

'*Wait!*' Snell shrieked, and then a heavy hand clamped over his mouth and he was pulled into the gloom, smelling rank sweat, feeling a breath on his cheek as the ogre named Goruss leaned in close.

'A screamer, iz he?'

'A nasty little shit, in fact.'

'We'll work that outer 'im.'

'Not this one. He'd stab his mother just to watch the blood flow. 'Sprobably left a trail of tortured small animals ten leagues long, buried in little holes in every back yard of the neighbourhood. This is one of those, Goruss.'

'Eighteen silver?'

'Slivers?'

'Yah.'

'All right.'

Snell thrashed about as he was carried off into a back room, then down steps and into an unlit cellar that smelled of piss-soaked mud. He was gagged and bound and thrown into a low iron cage. Goruss then went back up the stairs, leaving Snell alone.

In the front room, Goruss sat down across from Bellam. 'Ale, nephew?'

'Too early for me, Uncle.'

'How long you want me to hold him?'

'Long enough to shit everything out of him. I want him so scared he breaks inside.'

'Give him a night, then. Enough to run through all his terrors, but not so much he gets numb. Shit, nephew, I don't deal in anybody under, oh, fifteen years old, and we do careful interviewing and observing, and only the completely hopeless ones get shipped to the rowing benches. And even then, they get paid and fed and signed out after five years – and most of them do good after that.'

'I doubt Snell knows any of that, Uncle. Just that children are dragged into this shop and they don't come back out.'

'Must look that way.'

Bellam smiled. 'Oh, it does, Uncle, it does.'

'Not seen him in days.'

Barathol just nodded, then walked over to the cask of water to wash the grime off his forearms and hands. Chaur sat on a crate nearby, eating some local fruit with a yellow skin and pink, fleshy insides. Juice dribbled down his stubbled chin.

Scillara gave him a bright smile as she wandered into the front room. The air smelled brittle and acrid, the way it does in smithies, and she thought now that, from this moment on, the scent would accompany her every recollection of Barathol, this large man with the gentle eyes. 'Had any more trouble with the Guilds?' she asked.

He dried himself off and flung the cloth to one side. 'They're making it hard, but I expected that. We're surviving.'

'So I see.' She kicked at a heap of iron rods. 'New order?'

'Swords. The arrival of the Malazan embassy's garrison has triggered a new fad among the nobles. Imperial longswords. Gave trouble to most of the local sword-smiths.' He shrugged. 'Not me, of course.'

Scillara settled down in the lone chair and began scraping out her pipe. 'What's so special about Malazan longswords?'

'The very opposite, actually. The local makers haven't quite worked out that they have to reverse engineer to get them right.'

'Reverse engineer?'

'The Malazan longsword's basic design and manufacture is originally Untan, from the imperial mainland. Three centuries old, at least, maybe older. The empire still uses the Untan foundries and they're a conservative bunch.'

'Well, if the damned things do what they're supposed to do, why make changes?'

'That seems to be the thinking, yes. The locals have gone mad folding and re-folding, trying to capture that rough solidity, but the Untan smiths are in the habit of working iron not hot enough. It's also red iron that they're using – the Untan Hills are rotten with it even though it's rare everywhere else.' He paused, watching as she lit her pipe. 'This can't be of any real interest to you, Scillara.'

'Not really, but I do like the sound of your voice.' And she looked up at him through the smoke, her eyes half veiled.

'Anyway, I can make decent copies and the word's gone out. Eventually, some swordsmith will work things out, but by then I'll have plenty of satisfied customers and even undercutting me won't be too damaging.'

'Good,' she said.

He studied her for a moment, and then said, 'So, Cutter's gone missing, has he?'

'I don't know about that. Only that I've not seen him in a few days.'

'Are you worried?'

She thought about it, and then thought some more. 'Barathol, that wasn't my reason for visiting you. I wasn't looking for someone to charge in as if Cutter's been kidnapped or something. I'm here because I wanted to see you. I'm lonely – oh, I don't mean anybody'll do, either, when I say that. I just wanted to see you, that's all.'

After a moment, he shrugged and held out his hands. 'Here I am.'

'You won't make it easy, will you?'

'Scillara, look at me. Please, look. Carefully. You're too fast for me. Cutter, that historian, even that Bridgeburner, you leave them all spinning in your wake. Given my choice, I'd rather go through the rest of my life beneath the notice of everyone. I'm not interested in drama, or even excitement.'

She stretched out her legs. 'And you think I am?'

'It's life that you're full of.' Barathol frowned and then shook his head. 'I'm not very good at saying what I mean, am I?'

'Keep trying.'

'You can be . . . overwhelming.'

'Typical, put on a little fat and suddenly I'm too much for him.'

'You're not fat and you know it. You have,' he hesitated, 'shape.'

She thought to laugh, decided that it might come out too obviously hurt, which would make him feel even worse. Besides, her comment had been little more than desperate misdirection – she'd lost most of the weight she'd put on during her pregnancy. 'Barathol, has it not occurred to you that maybe I am as I am because behind it all there's not much else?'

His frown deepened.

Chaur dropped down from the crate and came over. He patted her on the head with a sticky hand and then hurried off into the yard.

'But you've lived through so much.'

'And you haven't? Gods below, you were an officer in the Red Blades. What you did in Aren—'

'Was just me avoiding a mess, Scillara. As usual.'

'What are we talking about here?'

His eyes shied away. 'I'm not sure. I suppose, now that Cutter's left you . . .'

'And Duiker's too old and Picker's a woman and that's fun but not serious – for me, at least – I've found myself in need of another man. Chaur's a child, in his head, that is. Leaving . . . you.'

The harsh sarcasm of her voice stung him and he almost stepped back. 'From where I'm standing,' he said.

'Well,' she said, sighing, 'it's probably what I deserve, actually. I have been a bit . . . loose. Wayward. Looking, trying, not finding, trying again. And again. From where you're standing, yes, I can see that.'

'None of that would matter to me,' Barathol then said. 'Except, well, I don't want to be just another man left in your wake.'

'No wonder you've devoted your life to making weapons and armour. Problem is, you're doing that for everyone else.'

He said nothing. He simply watched her, as, she realized, he had been doing for some time now. All at once, Scillara felt uncomfortable. She drew hard on her pipe. 'Barathol, you need some armour of your own.'

And he nodded. 'I see.'

'I'm not going to make promises I can't keep. Still, it may be that my waywardness is coming to an end. People like us, who spend all our time looking, well, even when we *find* it we usually don't realize it – until it's too late.'

'Cutter.'

She squinted up at him. 'He had no room left in his heart, Barathol. Not for me, not for anyone.'

'So he's just hiding right now?'

'In more ways than one, I suspect.'

'But he's broken your heart, Scillara.'

'Has he?' She considered. 'Maybe he has. Maybe I'm the one needing armour.' She snorted. 'Puts me in my place, doesn't it.' And she rose.

Barathol started. 'Where are you going?'

'What? I don't know. Somewhere. Nowhere. Does it matter?'

'Wait.' He stepped closer. 'Listen to me, Scillara.' And then he was silent, on his face a war of feelings trying to find words. After a moment, his scowl deepened. 'Yesterday, if Cutter had just walked in here to say hello, I'd have taken him by the throat. Hood, I'd have probably beaten him unconscious and tied him up in that chair. Where he'd stay – until you dropped by.'

'Yesterday.'

'When I thought I had no chance.'

She was having her own trouble finding words. 'And now?'

'I think . . . I've just thrown on some armour.'

'The soldier . . . unretires.'

'Well, I'm a man, and a man never learns.'

She grinned. 'That's true enough.'

And then she leaned close, and as he slowly raised his arms to take her into an embrace she almost shut her eyes – all that relief, all that anticipation of pleasure, even joy – and the hands instead grasped her upper arms and she was pushed suddenly to one side. Startled, she turned to see a squad of City Guard crowding the doorway.

The officer in the lead had the decency to look embarrassed.

'Barathol Mekhar? By city order, this smithy is now under temporary closure, and I am afraid I have to take you into custody.'

'The charge?'

'Brought forward by the Guild of Smiths. Contravention of proper waste disposal. It is a serious charge, I'm afraid. You could lose your business.'

'I don't understand,' Barathol said. 'I am making use of the sewage drains – I spill nothing—'

'The common drain, yes, but you should be using the industrial drain, which runs alongside the common drain.'

'This is the first I have heard of such a thing.'

'Well,' said a voice behind the guards, 'if you were a member of the Guild, you'd know all about it, wouldn't you?'

It was a woman who spoke, but Scillara could not see past the men in the doorway.

Barathol threw up his hands. 'Very well, I am happy to comply. I will install the proper pipes—'

'You may do so,' said the officer, 'once the charges are properly adjudicated, fines paid, and so forth. In the meantime, this establishment must be shut down. The gas valves must be sealed. Materials and tools impounded.'

'I see. Then let me make some arrangement for my helper – somewhere to stay and—'

'I am sorry,' cut in the officer, 'but the charge is against both you and your apprentice.'

'Not precisely,' said the unseen woman. 'The blacksmith cannot have an apprentice unless he is a member of the Guild. The two are colluding to undermine the Guild.'

The officer's expression tightened. 'As she said, yes. I'm not here to prattle on in the language of an advocate. I do the arrest and leave one of my guards to oversee the decommissioning of the establishment by a qualified crew.'

'A moment,' said Barathol. 'You are arresting Chaur?'

'Is that your apprentice's name?'

'He's not my apprentice. He's a simpleton—'

'Little more than a slave, then,' snapped the unseen official of the Guild. 'That would be breaking a much more serious law, I should think.'

Scillara watched as two men went to the yard and returned with a wide-eyed, whimpering Chaur. Barathol attempted to console him, but guards stepped in between them and the officer warned that, while he didn't want to make use of shackles, he would if necessary. So, if everyone could stay calm and collected, they could march out of here like civilized folk. Barathol enquired as to his right to hire an advocate and the officer replied that, while it wasn't a right as such, it was indeed a privilege Barathol could exercise, assuming he could afford one.

At that point Scillara spoke up and said, 'I'll find one for you, Barathol.'

A flicker of relief and gratitude in his eyes, replaced almost immediately by his distress over the fate of Chaur, who was now bawling and tugging his arms free every time a guard sought to take hold of him.

'Let him alone,' said Barathol. 'He'll follow peacefully enough – just don't grab him.'

And then the squad, save one, all marched out with their prisoners. Scillara fell in behind them, and finally saw the Guild official, a rather imposing woman whose dignity was marred by the self-satisfied smirk on her face.

As Scillara passed behind the woman, she took hold of her braid and gave it a sharp downward tug.

'Ow!' The woman whirled, her expression savage.

'Sorry,' Scillara said. 'Must have caught on my bracelet.'

And as Scillara continued on down the street, she heard, from the squad officer: 'She's not wearing any bracelet.'

The Guild woman hissed and said, 'I want her—'

And then Scillara turned the corner. She did not expect the officer to send anyone in pursuit. The man was doing his job and had no interest in complicating things.

'And there I was,' she muttered under her breath, 'about to trap a very fine man in my messed-up web. Hoping – praying – that he'd be the one to untangle my life.' She snorted. 'Just my luck.'

From rank superstitions to scholarly treatises, countless generations had sought understanding of those among them whose minds stayed undeveloped, childlike or, indeed, seemingly trapped in some other world. God and demon possession, stolen souls, countless chemical imbalances and unpleasant humours, injuries sustained at birth or even before; blows to the head as a child; fevers and so on. What could never be achieved, of course (barring elaborate, dangerous rituals of spirit-walking), was to venture into the mind of one thus afflicted.

It would be easy to assume an inner world of simple feelings, frightening unknowns and the endless miasma of confusion. Or some incorporeal demon crouched down on every thought, crushing the life from it, choking off every possible passage to awareness. Such assumptions, naturally, are but suppositions, founded only on external observation: the careful regard of seemingly blank eyes and stupid smiles, repetitive behaviour and unfounded fears.

Hold tight, then, this hand, on this momentary journey into Chaur's mind.

The world he was witness to was a place of objects, some moving, some never moving, and some that were still but could be moved if one so willed it. These three types were not necessarily fixed, and he well knew that things that seemed destined to immobility could suddenly come awake, alive, in explosive motion. Within himself, Chaur possessed apprehensions of all three, in ever shifting forms. There was love, a deeply rooted object, from which came warmth, and joy, and a sense of perfect well-being. It could, on occasion, reach out to take in another – someone or something on the outside – but, ultimately, that was not necessary. The love was within him, its very own world, and he could go there any time he liked. This was expressed in a rather dreamy smile, an expression disengaged with everything on the outside.

Powerful as it was, love was vulnerable. It could be wounded, jabbed into recoiling pain. When this happened, another object was stirred awake. It could be called *hate*, but its surface was mottled with fear and anger. This object was fixed as deeply in his soul as was love, and the two needed each other even if their relationship was strained, fraught. Prodded into life by love's pain, hate opened eyes that could only look outward – never to oneself, never even to the identity known as Chaur. Hate blazed in one direction and one only – to the outer world with its objects, some moving, some not, some that might do either, shifting from one to the next and back again.

Hate could, if it must, make use of Chaur's body. In lashing out, in a frenzied reordering of the world. To bring it back into the right shape, to force an end to whatever caused love its pain.

All of this depended upon observation, but such observation did not rely overmuch on what he saw, or heard, smelled, touched or tasted. Hate's secret vision was much sharper – it saw colours that did not exist for others, and those colours were, on an instinctive level, encyclopedic. Seeing them, hate knew *everything*. Knew, indeed, far beyond what a normal mind might achieve.

Was this little more than a peculiar sensitivity to nonverbal communication? Don't ask Chaur. He is, after all, in his own world.

His object called hate had a thing about blood. Its hue, the way it flowed, the way it smelled and tasted, and this was a bizarre truth: his hate *loved* blood. To see it, to immerse oneself in it, was to feel joy and warmth and contentment.

The guards flanking Chaur, walking at ease and with modest thoughts of their own, had no inkling of all that swirled in the seemingly simple mind of their prisoner. Who walked, limbs loose and swinging now that the natural tension that had bound up the huge man's neck and shoulders had eased away – clearly, the oaf had forgotten all the trouble he was in, had forgotten that they were all walking to a gaol, that soon Chaur would find himself inside a cage of stolid black iron bars. All those thick walls enclosing the simpleton's brain were clearly back in place.

Not worth a second glance.

And so there were none to see the hate-filled eyes peering out through every crack, every murder hole, every arrow slit – a thousand, ten thousand glittering eyes, seeing everything, the frenzied flicking as immobile objects were observed, gauged and then discarded; as others were adjudged potentially useful as things that, while unmoving, could be made to move. Seeing all, yes, absorbing and processing at speeds that would stun one of normal intelligence – because this was something different, something alien, something almost perfect in its own way, by its own rules, by all the forces it could assemble, harbour, and then, when the time was appropriate, unleash upon a most unsuspecting world.

The simple ones aren't simple. The broken ones aren't broken. They are rearranged. For better, for worse? Such judgements are without relevance. After all, imagine a world where virtually every mind is simpler than it imagines itself to be, or is so utterly broken that it is itself unaware of its own massive, stunning dysfunction. In such a world, life goes on, and madness thrives. Stupidity repeats. Behaviours destroy and destroy again, and again, yet remain impervious to enlightenment. Crimes against humanity abound, and not one victimizer can even comprehend one day becoming victim; not a single cruel soul understands that cruelty delivered yields cruelty repaid tenfold. It is enough to eat today and let tomorrow's children starve. Wealth ever promises protection against the strictures of an unkind, avaricious world, and yet fails to deliver on that promise every single time, be the slayer disease, betrayal or the ravaging mobs of revolution. Wealth cannot comprehend that the very avarice it fears is its own creation, the toxic waste product of its own glorious exaltation. Imagine such a world, then – oh, don't bother. Better to pity poor, dumb Chaur.

Who, without warning, exploded into motion. Placid thoughts in guardian skulls shattered into oblivion as fists smashed, sending each man flying out to the side. As dulled senses of something awry shot the first spurt of chemical alarm through the nearest of the remaining guards, Chaur reached him, picked him up by belt and neck, and threw him against a happily immobile stone wall on the right. The officer and the last guard both began their whirl to confront the still mostly unknown threat, and Chaur, smiling, was there to meet them. He had in his left hand – gripped by one ear – a heavy amphora, which he had collected from a stall to his left, and he brought this object round to crash into the officer. Clay shards, a shower of pellet grain, and in their midst a crumpling body. The last guard, one hand tugging at his sword, mouth open to begin a shout of alarm, saw in his last conscious moment Chaur and his broad smile, as the simpleton, with a roundhouse swing, drove his fist into the side of the man's head, collapsing the helm on that side and sending the headpiece flying. In a welter of blood from ear and temple, the guard fell to the ground, alive but temporarily unwilling to acknowledge the fact.

And Chaur stood now facing Barathol, with such pleased, excited eyes that the blacksmith could only stare back, speechless, aghast.

Gorlas Vidikas stepped out from the carriage and paused to adjust his leggings, noting with faint displeasure the discordant creases sitting in that sweaty carriage had left him with, and then glanced up as the sickly foreman wheezed his way over.

'Noble sir,' he gasped, 'about the interest payments – I've been ill, as you know—'

'You're dying, you fool,' Gorlas snapped. 'I am not here to discuss your problems. We both know what will happen should you default on the loan, and we both know – I should trust – that you are not long for this world, which makes the whole issue irrelevant. The only question is whether you will die in your bed or end up getting tossed out on your backside.' After a moment, he stepped closer and slapped the man on his back, triggering a cloud of dust. 'You've always got your shack here at camp, yes? Come now, it's time to discuss other matters.'

The foreman blinked up at him, with all that pathetic piteousness perfected by every loser the world over. Better, of course, than the dark gleam of malice – the stupid ones were quick to hate, once they'd got a sense of how they'd been duped – no, best keep this one making all those mewling *help-me* faces.

Gorlas smiled. 'You can stay in your lovely new home, friend. I will withhold the interest payments so you can leave this world in peace and comfort.' And oh, wasn't this such extraordinary favour? This concession, this grave sacrifice, why, it would not be remiss if this idiot fell to his knees in abject gratitude, but never mind that. A second thump on the back, this one triggering a coughing fit from the old man.

Gorlas walked to the edge of the vast pit and surveyed the bustling hive of activity below. 'All is well?'

The foreman, after hacking out a palmful of yellow phlegm, hobbled up to stand hunched beside him, wiping a hand on a caked trouser leg. 'Well enough, sir, yes, well enough indeed.'

See how his mood has improved? No doubt eaten up with worry all morning, the poor useless bastard. Well, the world needed such creatures, didn't it? To do all the dirty, hard work, and then thank people like Gorlas for the privilege. *You're so very welcome, you stupid fool, and see this? It's my smile of indulgence. Bask and bask well – it's the only thing I give away that's truly free.*

'How many losses this week?'

'Three. Average, sir, that's average as can be. One mole in a cave-in, the others died of the greyface sickness. We got the new vein producing now. Would you believe, it's red iron!'

Gorlas's brows lifted, 'Red iron?'

A quick, eager nod. 'Twice the price at half-weight, that stuff. Seems there's growing demand—'

'Yes, the Malazan longswords everyone's lusting after. Well, this will make it easier to order one, since up to now only one smith had the skill to make the damned weapons.' He shook his head. 'Ugly things, if you ask me. Curious thing is, we don't get red iron round here – not till now, that is – so how was the fool making such perfect copies?'

'Well, noble sir, there's an old legend 'bout how one can actually turn regular iron into the red stuff, and do it cheap besides. Maybe it ain't just a legend.'

Gorlas grunted. Interesting. Imagine finding out that secret, being able to take regular iron, toss in something virtually worthless, and out comes red iron, worth four times the price. 'You've just given me an idea,' he murmured. 'Though I doubt the smith would give up the secret – no, I'd have to pay. A lot.'

'Maybe a partnership,' the foreman ventured.

Gorlas scowled. He wasn't asking for advice. Still, yes, a partnership might work. Something he'd heard about that smith . . . some Guild trouble. Well, could be Gorlas could smooth all that over, for a consideration. 'Never mind,' he said, a tad overloud, 'it was just a notion – I've already discarded it as too complicated, too messy. Let's forget we ever discussed it.'

'Yes, sir.'

But was the foreman looking oddly thoughtful? Might be necessary, Gorlas reflected, to hasten this fool's demise.

From up the road behind them, a trader's cart was approaching.

Stupid, really. He'd elected his riding boots, but the things were ancient, worn, and it seemed his feet had flattened out some since he'd last used them, and now he had enormous blisters, damned painful ones. And so, for all his plans of a stentorian, impressive arrival at the camp, full of dour intent and an edge of bluster, to then be ameliorated by a handful of silver councils, a relieved foreman sending a runner off to retrieve the wayward child, Murillio found himself on the back of a rickety cart, covered in dust and sweating in the midst of a cloud of flies.

Well, he would just have to make the best of it, wouldn't he? As the ox halted at the top of the ridgeline, the old man walking slow as a snail over to where stood the eponymous foreman beside some fancy noble – now both looking their way – Murillio eased himself down, wincing at the lancing pain shooting up his legs, thinking with dread of the long walk back to the city, his hand holding Harllo's tiny one, with darkness crawling up from the ditches to either side – a long, long walk indeed, and how he'd manage it was, truth be told, beyond him.

Soldiers knew about blisters, didn't they? And men and women who worked hard for a living. To others, the affliction seemed trivial, a minor irritation – and when there were years between this time and the last time one had suffered from them, it was easy to forget, to casually dismiss just how debilitating they truly were.

Raw leather rubbed at each one like ground glass as he settled his weight back down. Still, it would not do to hobble over, and so, mustering all his will, Murillio walked, one careful step at a time, to where the foreman and the nobleman stood discussing things with the carter. As he drew closer, his gaze narrowed on the highborn one, a hint of recognition . . . but where? When?

The carter had been told by the foreman where to take the supplies, and off he went, with a passing nod at Murillio.

The foreman was squinting curiously, and as Murillio drew up before them he spat to one side and said, 'You look lost, sir. If you've the coin you can buy a place at the workers' table – it's plain fare but fillin' enough, though we don't serve nothing but weak ale.' He barked a laugh. 'We ain't no roadside inn, are we?'

Murillio had thought long on how he would approach this. But he had not expected a damned nobleman in this particular scene, and something whispered to him that what should have been a simple negotiation, concluded by paying twice the going rate for a five-year-old boy, might now turn perilously complicated. 'Are you the foreman of the camp, sir?' he asked, after a deferential half-bow to the nobleman. At the answering nod, Murillio continued, 'Very good. I am here in search of a young boy, name of Harllo, who was sold to your camp a few weeks back.' He quickly raised a gloved hand. 'No, I have no desire to challenge the propriety of that arrangement. Rather, I wish to purchase the boy's freedom, and so deliver him back to his, er, terribly distressed parents.'

'Do ye now?' The foreman looked over at the nobleman.

Yes, Murillio thought he might know this young man.

'You are the one named Murillio,' the nobleman said, with an odd glitter in his gaze.

'You have the better of me—'

'That goes without saying. I am the principal investor of this operation. I am also a councillor. Gorlas Vidikas of House Vidikas.'

Murillio bowed a second time, as much to hide his dismay as in proper deference. 'Councilman Vidikas, it is a pleasure meeting you.'

'Is it? I very much doubt that. It took me a few moments to place you. You were pointed out, you see, a couple years back, at some estate fete.'

'Oh? Well, there was a time when I was—'

'You were on a list,' Gorlas cut in.

'A what?'

'A hobby of a friend of mine, although I doubt he would have seen it as a hobby. In fact, if I was so careless as to use that word, when it came to his list, he'd probably call me out.'

'I am sorry,' Murillio said, 'but I'm afraid I do not know what you are talking about. Some sort of list, you said?'

'Likely conspirators,' Gorlas said with a faint smile, 'in the murder of Turban Orr, not to mention Ravyd Lim – or was it some other Lim? I don't recall now, but then, that hardly matters. No, Turban Orr, and of course the suspicious suicide of Lady Simtal – all on the same night, in her estate. I was there, did you know that? I saw Turban Orr assassinated with my own eyes.' And he was in truth smiling now, as if recalling something yielding waves of nostalgia. But his eyes were hard, fixed like sword points. 'My friend, of course, is Hanut Orr, and the list is his.'

'I do recall attending the Simtal fete,' Murillio said, and in his mind he was re-living those moments after leaving the Lady's bedchamber – leaving her with the means by which she could take her own life – and his thoughts, then, of every-thing he had surrendered, and what it might mean for his future. Appropriate, then, that it should now return to crouch at his feet, like a rabid dog with fangs bared. 'Alas, I missed the duel—'

'It was no duel, Murillio. Turban Orr was provoked. He was set up. He was assassinated, in plain view. Murder, not a duel – do you even comprehend the difference?'

The foreman was staring back and forth between them with all the dumb be-wilderment of an ox.

'I do, sir, but as I said, I was not there to witness the event—'

'You call me a liar, then?'

'Excuse me?' Gods below, ten years past and he would have handled this with perfect grace and mocking equanimity, and all that was ruffled would be smoothed over, certain debts accepted, promises of honouring those debts not even needing explicit enunciation. Ten years past and—

'You are calling me a liar.'

'No, I do not recall doing so, Councillor. If you say Turban Orr was assassi-nated, then so be it. As for my somehow conspiring to bring it about, well, that is itself a very dangerous accusation.' Oh, he knew where this was leading. He had known for some time, in fact. It was all there in Gorlas Vidikas's eyes – and Murillio now recalled where he had last seen this man, and heard of him. Gorlas enjoyed duelling. He enjoyed killing his opponents. Yes, he had attended one of this bastard's duels, and he had seen—

'It seems,' said Gorlas, 'we have ourselves a challenge to honour here.' He gave a short laugh. 'When you retracted your accusation, well, I admit I thought you were about to tuck your tail between your legs and scuttle off down the road. And perhaps I would've let you go at that – it's Hanut's obsession, after all. Not mine.'

Murillio said nothing, understanding how he had trapped himself, with the foreman to witness the fact that the demand for a duel had come from him, not Gorlas Vidikas. He also understood that there had been no chance, none at all, that Gorlas would have let him go.

'Naturally,' continued the councillor, 'I have no intention of withdrawing my accusation – so either accept it or call me out, Murillio. I have vague recollections that you were one judged a decent duellist.' He scanned the track to either side. 'This place seems well suited. Now, a miserable enough audience, granted, but—'

'Excuse me,' cut in the foreman, 'but the day's shift bell is about to sound. The crews can get a perfect view, what with you two on the ridgeline – if you'd like.'

Gorlas winked over at Murillio as he said, 'By all means we shall wait, then.'

The foreman trundled down the path into the pit, to ensure that the crew captains were told what was going on. They'd enjoy the treat after a long day's work in the tunnels.

As soon as the foreman was out of earshot, Gorlas grinned at Murillio. 'Now, anything more we should talk about, now that we've got no witness?'

'Thank you for the invitation,' Murillio said, tightening the straps of his glove. 'Turban Orr didn't deserve an honourable death. Hanut is your friend? Tell me, do you enjoy sleeping with vipers, or are you just stupid?'

'If that was an attempt to bring me to a boil, it was pathetic. You truly think I don't know all the tricks leading up to a duel? Gods below, old man. Still, I am pleased by your admission – Hanut will be delighted to hear that his suspicions were accurate. More important, he will find himself in my debt.' And then he cocked his head. 'Of course, the debt will be all the greater if I let you live. A duel unto wounding – leaving your fate in Hanut's hands. Yes, that would be perfect. Well, Murillio, shall it be wounding?'

'If you like,' Murillio said.

'Are your boots pinching?'

'No.'

'You seem in discomfort, Murillio, or is that just nerves?'

Bells clanged in the pit below. Distant shouts, and out from the tunnel mouths spewed filthy figures looking barely human at this distance. Runners raced down the lines. Word was getting out.

'What's this Harllo boy to you, anyway?'

Murillio glanced back to Gorlas. 'You married Estraysian D'Arle's daughter, didn't you? She's made herself very . . . popular, of late, hasn't she? Alas, I am starting to understand why – you're not much of a man, are you, Gorlas?'

For all the councillor's previous bravado, he paled in the late afternoon light.

'It's terrible, isn't it,' Murillio went on, 'how every sordid detail, no matter how private and personal, so easily leaves the barricaded world of the wellborn and races like windblown seeds among all us common folk, us lowborn. Why, whatever happened to decency?'

The rapier rasped its way out of the sheath and the point lifted towards Murillio. 'Draw your weapon, old man.'

Krute of Talient stepped inside. He saw Rallick Nom standing by the window, but it was shuttered closed. The man might as well be standing facing a wall. Oh, he was a strange one indeed, stranger now than he'd ever been before. All that silence, all that sense of something being very much . . . wrong. In his head? Maybe. And that was a worrying thought – that Rallick Nom might not be right any more.

'It's confirmed,' said Krute, setting down the burlap sack filled with the makings for supper. 'One contract dissolved, a new one accepted. Stinks of desperation, doesn't it? Gods, Seba's even called me back and that's an invitation no sane man would refuse.' He paused, eyeing his friend, and then said, 'So you may not be seeing much of me from now on. From what I've gathered, this new one's pretty straightforward, but it's the kind that'll shake up the precious bloods.'

'Is it now?' Rallick asked, expressionless.

'Listen,' said Krute, knowing he was betraying his nerves, 'I couldn't say no, could I? It's fine enough living off your coin, but that's hard on a man's pride. I've got a chance to get back into the middle of things again. I've got a chance to walk with the Guild again. Rallick, I got to take it, you understand?'

'Is it that important to you, Krute?'

Krute nodded.

'Then,' said Rallick, 'I had best leave your company.'

'I'm sorry about that – it's my being . . . what's that word again?'

'Compromised.'

'Exactly. Now, if you'd made your move on Seba, well, we wouldn't be in this situation, would we? It's the waiting that's been so hard.'

'There are no plans to replace Seba Krafar,' said Rallick. 'I am sorry if I have unintentionally misled you on that count. This is not to say we're uninterested in the Guild.' He hesitated. 'Krute, listen carefully. I can leave you some coin – enough for a while, a half-year's worth, in fact. Just decline Seba's invitation – you don't know what you're getting into—'

'And you do? No, Rallick, the point is, if I don't know it's because I've been pushed out of things.'

'You should be thankful for that.'

'I don't need any patronizing shit from you, Rallick Nom. You're all secrets now, nothing but secrets. But you'll live here, with me, and eat what I cook, and what about me? Oh, right, on the outside again, this time with you. Well, I can't live like that, so you'd better go. Don't think ill of me – I won't tell Seba about you.'

'Can I not buy your retirement, Krute?'

'No.'

Rallick nodded and then walked to the door. 'Guard yourself well, Krute.'

'You too, Rallick.'

Emerging from the tenement building's narrow back door, Rallick Nom stepped out into the rank, rubbish-filled alley. His last venture into the world had seen him very nearly killed by Crokus Younghand, and of his time spent recovering at the Phoenix Inn, it was clear that no one who'd known of his presence had said a thing – not Kruppe, nor Coll, nor Murillio, nor Meese or Irilta; the Guild had not sniffed out his ignominious return. Even that wayward cousin of his, Torvald, had said nothing – although why that man had so vigorously avoided him was both baffling and somewhat hurtful.

Anyway, in a sense, Rallick remained invisible.

He paused in the alley. Still light, a ribbon of brightness directly above. It felt odd, to be outside in the day, and he knew it would not be long before someone caught sight of him, recognizing his face – eyes widening with astonishment – and word would race back to Seba Krafar. And then?

Well, the Master would probably send one of his lieutenants to sound Rallick out – what did he want? What did he expect from the Guild? There might be an invitation as well, the kind that was deadly either way. Accept it and walk into an ambush. Reject it and the hunt would begin. There were few who could take down Rallick one on one, but that wouldn't be the preferred tactic in any case. No, it would be a quarrel to the back.

There were other places he could hide – he could probably walk right back into the Finnest House. But then, Krute was not the only one getting impatient. Besides, Rallick had never much liked subterfuge. He'd not used it when he'd been active in the Guild, after all – except when he was working, of course.

No, the time had come to stir things awake. And if Seba Krafar's confidence had been rattled by a handful of rancorous Malazans, well, he was about to be sent reeling.

The notion brought a faint smile to Rallick's lips. *Yes, I am back.*

He set out for the Phoenix Inn.

I am back, so let's get this started, shall we?

Echoing alarms at the blurred border between the Daru and Lakefront districts, a half-dozen streets behind them now as Barathol – holding Chaur's hand as he would a child's – dragged the giant man through the late afternoon crowds. They had passed a few patrols, but word had yet to outdistance the two fugitives, although it was likely that this flight would, ultimately, prove anything but surreptitious – guards and bystanders both could not help but recall the two huge foreigners, one onyx-skinned, the other the hue of stained rawhide, rushing past.

Barathol had no choice but to dispense with efforts at stealth and subterfuge. Chaur was bawling with all the indignant outrage of a toddler justly punished, astonished to discover that not all things were cute and to be indulged by adoring caregivers – that, say, shoving a sibling off a cliff was not quite acceptable behaviour.

He had tried calming Chaur down, but simple as Chaur was, he was quick to sense disapproval, and Barathol had been unthinking and careless in expressing that disapproval – well, rather, he had been shocked into carelessness – and now the huge child would wail unto eventual exhaustion, and that exhaustion was still a long way off.

Two streets away from the harbour, three guards thirty paces behind them suddenly raised shouts, and now the chase was on for real.

To Barathol's surprise, Chaur fell silent, and the smith pulled him up alongside him as they hurried along. 'Chaur, listen to me. Get back to the ship – do you understand? Back to the ship, to the lady, yes? Back to Spite – she'll hide you. To the ship, Chaur, understand?'

A tear-streaked face, cheeks blotchy, eyes red, Chaur nodded.

Barathol pushed him ahead. 'Go. On your own – I'll catch up with you. Go!'

And Chaur went, lumbering, knocking people off their feet until a path miraculously opened before him.

Barathol turned about to give the three guards some trouble. Enough to purchase Chaur the time he needed, at least.

He managed that well enough, with fists and feet, with knees and elbows, and if not for the arrival of reinforcements, he might even have won clear. Six more guards, however, proved about five too many, and he was wrestled to the ground and beaten half senseless.

The occasional thought filtered weakly through the miasma of pain and confusion as he was roughly carried to the nearest gaol. He'd known a cell before. It wasn't so bad, so long as the jailers weren't into torture. Yes, he could make a tour of gaol cells, country to country, continent to continent. All he needed to do was start up a smithy without the local Guild's approval.

Simple enough.

Then these fragmented notions went away, and the bliss of unconsciousness was unbroken, for a time.

' 'Tis the grand stupidity of our kind, dear Cutter, to see all the errors of our ways, yet find in ourselves the inability to do anything about them. We sit, dumbfounded by despair, and for all our ingenuity, our perceptivity, for all our extraordinary capacity to see the truth of things, we hunker down like snails in a flood, sucked tight to our precious pebble, fearing the moment it is dislodged beneath us. Until that terrible calamity, we do nothing but cling.

'Can you even imagine a world where all crimes are punished, where justice is truly blind and holds out no hands happy to yield to the weight of coin and influence? Where one takes responsibility for his or her mistakes, acts of negligence, the deadly consequences of indifference or laziness? Nay, instead we slip and duck, dance and dodge, dance the dodge slip duck dance, feet ablur! Our selves transformed into shadows that flit in chaotic discord. We are indeed masters of evasion – no doubt originally a survival trait, at least in the physical sense, but to have such instincts applied to the soul is perhaps our most egregious crime against morality. What we will do so that we may continue living with ourselves. In this we might assert that a survival trait can ultimately prove its own antithesis, and in the cancelling out thereof, why, we are left with the blank, dull, vacuous expression that Kruppe now sees before him.'

'Sorry, what?'

'Dear Cutter, this is a grave day, I am saying. A day of the misguided and the misapprehended, a day of mischance and misery. A day in which to grieve the unanticipated, this yawning stretch of too-late that follows fell decisions, and the stars will plummet and if we truly possessed courage we would ease ourselves with great temerity into that high, tottering footwear of the gods, and in seeing what they see, in knowing what they have come to know, we would at last comprehend the madness of struggle, the absurdity of hope, and off we would stumble, wailing our way into the dark future. We would weep, my friend, we would weep.'

'Maybe I have learned all about killing,' Cutter said in a mumble, his glazy eyes seemingly fixed on the tankard in his hand. 'And maybe assassins don't spare a thought as to who deserves what, or even motivations. Coin in hand, or love in the heart – reward has so many . . . flavours. But is this what she really wants? Or was that some kind of careless . . . burst, like a flask never meant to be opened – shatters, everything pours out – staining your hands, staining . . . everything.'

'Cutter,' said Kruppe in a low, soft but determined tone. '*Cutter.* You must listen to Kruppe, now. You must listen – he is done with rambling, with his own bout of terrible, grievous helplessness. Listen! Cutter, there are paths that must not be walked. Paths where going back is impossible – no matter how deeply you would wish it, no matter how loud the cry in your soul. Dearest friend, you must—'

Shaking himself, Cutter rose suddenly. 'I need a walk,' he said. 'She couldn't have meant it. That future she paints . . . it's a fairy tale. Of course it is. Has to be. No, and no, and no. But . . .'

Kruppe watched as the young man walked away, watched as Cutter slipped through the doorway of the Phoenix Inn, and was gone from sight.

'Sad truth,' Kruppe said – his audience of none sighing in agreement – 'that a tendency towards verbal excess can so defeat the precision of meaning. That intent can be so well disguised in majestic plethora of nuance, of rhythm both serious and mocking, of this penchant for self-referential slyness, that the unwitting simply skip on past – imagining their time to be so precious, imagining themselves above all manner of conviction, save that of their own witty perfection. Sigh and sigh again.

'See Kruppe totter in these high shoes – nay, even his balance is not always precise, no matter how condign he may be in so many things. Totter, I say, as down fall the stars and off wail the gods and helplessness is an ocean in flood, ever rising – but we shall not drown alone, shall we? No, we shall have plenty of company in this chill comfort. The guilty and the innocent, the quick and the thick, the wise and the dumb, the righteous and the wicked – the flood levels all, faces down in the swells, oh my.

'Oh my . . .'

A miracle, better than merely recounted second or third hand, but witnessed. Witnessed: the four bearers would have carried their charge directly past, but then – see – a gnarled, feeble hand reached out, damp fingertips pressing against Myrla's forehead.

And the bearers – who were experienced in such random gestures of deliverance – halted.

She stared up into the Prophet's eyes and saw terrible pain, a misery so profound it purified, and knowledge beyond anything her useless, dross-filled mind could comprehend. 'My son,' she gasped. 'My son . . . my self – oh my heart—'

'Self, yes,' he said, fingers pressing against her forehead like four iron nails, pinning her guilt and shame, her weakness, her useless stupidity. 'I can bless that. So I shall. Do you feel my touch, dear woman?'

And Myrla could not but nod, for she did feel it, oh, yes, she felt it.

From behind her Bedek's quavering voice drifted past. 'Glorious One – our son has been taken. Kidnapped. We know not where, and we thought, we thought . . .'

'Your son is beyond salvation,' said the Prophet. 'He has the vileness of knowledge within his soul. I can sense how you two merged in his creation – yes, your blood was his poison of birth. He understands compassion, but he chooses it not. He understands love, but uses it as a weapon. He understands the future, and knows it does not wait for anyone, not even him. He is a living maw, your son, a living maw, which all of the world must feed.'

The hand withdrew, leaving four precise spots of ice on Myrla's forehead – every nerve dead there, for ever more. 'Even the Crippled God must reject such a creature. But you, Myrla, and you, Bedek, I bless. I bless you both in your lifelong blindness, your insensitive touch, the fugue of your malnourished minds. I bless you in the crumpling of the two delicate flowers in your hands – your two girls – for you have made of them versions no different from you, no better, perhaps much worse. Myrla. Bedek. I bless you in the name of empty pity. Now go.'

And she staggered back, stumbled into the cart, knocking it and Bedek over. He cried out, falling hard on to the cobbles, and a moment later she landed on top of him. The snap of his left arm was loud in the wake of the now-resumed procession of bearers and Prophet, the swirling press of begging worshippers sweeping in, stepping without care, without regard. A heavy boot stamped down on Myrla's hip and she shrieked as something broke, lancing agony into her right leg. Another foot collided with her face, toenails slashing one cheek. Heels on hands, fingers, ankles.

Bedek caught a momentary glimpse upward, to see the face of a man desperate to climb over them, for they were in his way and he wanted to reach the Prophet, and the man looked down, his pleading expression transforming into one of black hate. And he drove the point of his boot into Bedek's throat, crushing the trachea.

Unable to breathe past the devastation that had once been his throat, Bedek stared up with bulging eyes. His face deepened to a shade of blue-grey, and then purple. The awareness in the eyes flattened out, went away, and away.

Still screaming, Myrla dragged herself over her husband – noting his stillness but otherwise uncomprehending – and pulled herself through a forest of hard, shifting legs – shins and knees, jabbing feet, out into a space, suddenly open, clear, the cobbles slick beneath her.

Although she was not yet aware of them, four spots of gangrene were spreading across her forehead – she could smell something foul, horribly foul, as though someone had dropped something in passing, somewhere close; she just couldn't see it yet. The pain of her broken hip was now a throbbing thing, a deadweight she dragged behind her, growing ever more distant in her mind.

We run from our place of wounding. No different from any other beast, we run from our place of wounding. Run, or crawl, crawl or drag, drag or reach. She realized that even such efforts had failed her. She was broken everywhere. She was dying.

See me! I have been blessed. He has blessed me.
Bless you all.

He could barely stand, and now he must duel. Murillio untied his coin pouch and tossed it towards the foreman who had just returned, gasping and red-faced. The bag landed in a cloud of dust, a heavy thud. 'I came for the boy,' Murillio said. 'That's more than he's worth – do you accept the payment, foreman?'

'He does not,' said Gorlas. 'No, I have something special in mind for little Harllo.'

'He's not part of any of this—'

'You just made him so, Murillio. One of your clan, maybe even a whelp of one of your useless friends in the Phoenix Inn – your favoured hangout, yes? Hanut knows everything there is to know about you. No, the boy's in this, and that's why you won't have him. I will, to do with as I please.'

Murillio drew his rapier. 'What makes people like you, Gorlas?'

'I could well ask the same of you.'

Well, a lifetime of mistakes. And so we are perhaps more alike than either of us would care to admit. He saw the foreman bend down to collect the purse. The odious man hefted it and grinned. 'About those interest payments, Councillor . . .'

Gorlas smiled. 'Why, it seems you can clear your debt after all.'

Murillio assumed his stance, point extended, sword arm bent slightly at the elbow, left shoulder thrown back to reduce the plane of his exposed torso. He settled his weight, gingerly, down through the centre of his hips.

Smiling still, Gorlas Vidikas moved into a matching pose, although he was leaning slightly forward. Not a duellist ready to retreat, then. Murillio recalled that from the fight he'd seen the very end of, the way Gorlas would not step back, unwilling to yield ground, unwilling to accept that sometimes pulling away earned advantages. No, he would push, and push, surrendering nothing.

He rapped Murillio's blade with his own, a contemptuous batting aside to gauge response.

There was none. Murillio simply resumed his line.

Gorlas probed with the rapier's point, jabbing here and there round the bell hilt, teasing and gambling with the quillons that could trap his blade, but for Murillio to do so he would have to twist and fold his wrist – not much, but enough for Gorlas to make a darting thrust into the opened guard, and so Murillio let the man play with that. He was in no hurry; footsore and weary as he was, he suspected he would have but one solid chance, sooner or later, to end this. Point to lead kneecap, or down to lead boot, or a flicking slash into wrist tendons, crippling the sword arm – possibly for ever. Or higher, into the shoulder, stop-hitting a lunge.

Gorlas pressed, closing the distance, and Murillio stepped back.

And that *hurt*.

He could feel wetness in his boots, that wretched clear liquid oozing out from the broken blisters.

'I think,' ventured Gorlas, 'there's something wrong with your feet, Murillio. You move like a man standing on nails.'

Murillio shrugged. He was past conversation; it was hard enough concentrating through the stabs of pain.

'Such an old-style stance you have, old man. So . . . upright.' Gorlas resumed the flitting, wavering motions of his rapier, minute threats here and there. He had begun a rhythmic rocking back and forth on the balls of his feet, attempting to lull Murillio into that motion.

When he finally launched into his attack, the move was explosive, lightning fast.

Murillio tracked the feints, caught and parried the lunge, and snapped out a riposte – but he was stepping back as he did so, and his point snipped the cloth of Gorlas's sleeve. Before he could ready himself, the younger duellist extended his attack with a hard parrying beat and then a second lunge, throwing his upper body far forward – closing enough to make Murillio's retreat insufficient, as was his parry.

Sizzling fire in his left shoulder. Staggering back, the motion tugging the point free of his flesh, Murillio righted himself and then straightened. 'Blood drawn,' he said, voice tightened by pain.

'Oh, that,' said Gorlas, resuming his rocking motion once more, 'I've changed my mind.'

One insult too many. I never learn.

Murillio felt his heart pounding. The scar of his last, near-fatal wounding seemed to be throbbing as if eager to reopen. He could feel blood pulsing down from his pierced shoulder muscle, could feel warm trickles running down the length of his upper arm to soak the cloth at his elbow.

'Blood drawn,' he repeated. 'As you guessed, I am in no shape to duel beyond that, Gorlas. We were agreed, before a witness.'

Gorlas glanced over at his foreman. 'Do you recall, precisely, what you heard?'

The old man shrugged. 'Thought there was something about wounding . . .'

Gorlas frowned.

The foreman cleared his throat. '. . . but that's all. A discussion, I think. I heard nothing, er, firmed up between you.'

Gorlas nodded. 'Our witness speaks.'

A few hundred onlookers in the pit below were making restless sounds. Murillio wondered if Harllo was among them.

'Ready yourself,' Gorlas said.

So, it was to be this way. A decade past Murillio would have been standing over this man's corpse, regretful, of course, wishing it all could have been handled peacefully. And that was the luxury of days gone past, that cleaner world, while everything here, now, ever proved so . . . messy.

I didn't come here to die this day. I'd better do something about that. I need to survive this. For Harllo. He resumed his stance. Well, he was debilitated, enough to pretty much ensure that he would fight defensively, seeking only ripostes and perhaps a counterattack – taking a wound to deliver a death. All of that would be in Gorlas's mind, would shape his tactics. Time, then, to surprise the bastard.

His step and lunge was elegant, a fluid forward motion rather quick for a man his age. Gorlas, caught on the forward tilt of his rocking, was forced to jump a half-step back, parrying hard and without precision. His riposte was wild and inaccurate, and Murillio caught it with a high parry of his own, following through with a second attack – the one he had wanted to count from the very first – a fully extended lunge straight for his opponent's chest – heart or lungs, it didn't matter which—

But somehow, impossibly, Gorlas had stepped close, inside and to one side of that lunge – his half-step back had not been accompanied by any shift in weight, simply a repositioning of his upper body, and this time his thrust was not at all wild.

Murillio caught a flash along the length of Daru steel, and then he could not breathe. Something was pouring down the front of his chest, and spurting up into his mouth.

He felt part of his throat tearing from the inside out as Gorlas slashed his blade free and stepped to the right.

Murillio twisted round to track him, but the motion lost all control, and he continued on, legs collapsing under him, and now he was lying on the stony ground.

The world darkened.

He heard Gorlas say something, possibly regretful, but probably not.

Oh, Harllo, I am so sorry. So sorry—

And the darkness closed in.

He was rocked momentarily awake by a kick to his face, but that pain quickly flushed away, along with everything else.

Gorlas Vidikas stood over Murillio's corpse. 'Get that carter to take the body back,' he said to the foreman, bending down to clean his blade on the threadbare silk sleeve of his victim's weapon arm. 'Have him deliver it to the Phoenix Inn, rapier and all.'

From the pit below, people were cheering and clanging their tools like some ragtag mob of barbarians. Gorlas faced them and raised his weapon in salute. The cheering redoubled. He turned back to the foreman. 'An extra tankard of ale for the crews tonight.'

'They will toast your name, Councillor!'

'Oh, and have someone collect the boy for me.'

'It's his shift in the tunnels, I think, but I can send someone to get him.'

'Good, and they don't have to be gentle about it, either. But make sure – nothing so bad he won't recover. If they kill him, I will personally disembowel every one of them – make sure they understand.'

'I will, Councillor.' The foreman hesitated. 'I never seen such skill, I never seen such skill – I thought he had you—'

'I'm sure he thought so, too. Go find that carter, now.'

'On my way, Councillor.'

'Oh, and I'll take that purse, so we're clear.'

The foreman rushed over to deliver it. Feeling the bag's weight for the first time, Gorlas raised his brows – a damned year's wages for this foreman, right here – probably all Murillio had, cleaned right out. Three times as much as the interest this fool owed him. Then again, if the foreman had stopped to count out the right amount, intending to keep the rest, well, Gorlas would have two bodies to dispose of rather than just one, so maybe the old man wasn't so stupid after all.

It had, Gorlas decided, been a good day.

And so the ox began its long journey back into the city, clumping along the cobbled road, and in the cart's bed lay the body of a man who might have been precipitous, who might indeed have been too old for such deadly ventures, but no one could say that his heart had not been in the right place. Nor could anyone speak of a lack of courage.

Raising a most grave question – if courage and heart are not enough, what is?

The ox could smell blood, and liked it not one bit. It was a smell that came with predators, with hunters, notions stirring the deepest parts of the beast's brain. It could smell death as well, there in its wake, and no matter how many clumping steps it took, that smell did not diminish, and this it could not understand, but was resigned to none the less.

There was no room in the beast for grieving. The only sorrow it knew was for itself. So unlike its two-legged masters.

Flies swarmed, ever unquestioning, and the day's light fell away.

Chapter Eighteen

He is unseen, one in a crowd whom none call
Do not slip past that forgettable face
Crawl not inside to find the unbidden rill
As it flows in dark horror from place to place

He is a common thing, in no way singular
Who lets no one inside the uneven steps
Down those eyes that drown the solitary star
We boldly share in these human depths

Not your brother, not anyone's saviour
He will loom only closer to search your clothes
Push aside the feeble hand that seeks to stir
Compassion's glow (the damp, dying rose)

He has plucked his garden down to bone
And picked every last bit of warm flesh
With fear like claws and nervous teeth when alone
He wanders this wasteland of cinder and ash

I watch in terror as he ascends our blessed throne
To lay down his cloak of shame like a shroud
And beckons us the illusion of a warm home
A sanctuary beneath his notice, one in a crowd

He finds his power in our indifference
Shredding the common to dispense with congress
No conjoined will to set against him in defiance
And one by one by one, he kills us

A KING TAKES THE THRONE
(CARVED ON THE POET'S WALL,
ROYAL DUNGEONS, UNTA)

With a twist and a snarl, Shan turned on Lock. The huge white-coated beast did not flinch or scurry, but simply loped away, tongue lolling as if in laughter. A short distance off, Pallid watched. Fangs still bared, Shan slipped off into the high grasses once more.

Baran, Blind, Rood and Gear had not slowed during this exchange – it had happened many times before, after all – and they continued on, in a vaguely crescent formation, Rood and Gear on the flanks. Antelope observed them from a rise off to the southwest – the barest tilt of a head from any of the Hounds and they would be off, fast as their bounding legs could take them, their hearts a frenzied drum-roll of bleak terror.

But the Hounds of Shadow were not hunting this day. Not antelope, not bhederin, nor mule deer nor ground sloth. A host of animals that lived either in states of blessed anonymity or states of fear had no need to lurch from the former into the latter – at least not because of the monstrous Hounds. As for the wolves of the plains, the lumbering snub-nosed bears and the tawny cats of the high grasses, there were none within ten leagues – the faintest wisp of scent had sent them fleeing one and all.

Great Ravens sailed high above the Hounds, minute specks in the vaulted blue.

Shan was displeased with the two new companions, these blots of dirty white with the lifeless eyes. Lock in particular irritated her, as it seemed this one wanted to travel as she did, close by her side, sliding unseen, ghostly and silent. Most annoying of all, Lock was Shan's able match in such skill.

But she had no interest in surrendering her solitude. Ambush and murder were best served alone, as far as she was concerned. Lock complicated things, and Shan despised complications.

Somewhere, far behind them, creatures pursued. In the profoundly long history of the Hounds of Shadow, they had been hunted many times. More often than not, the hunters came to regret the decision, whether a momentary impulse or an instinctive need; whether at the behest of some master or by the hatred in their souls, their desire usually proved fatal.

Occasionally, however, being hunted was such exquisite pleasure that the Hounds never turned the game. Let the chase go on, and on. Dance from the path of that rage, all that blind need.

All things will cast a shadow. If light blazes infernal, a shadow can grow solid, outlines sharp, motion rippling within. Shape is a reflection, but not all reflections are true. Some shadows lie. Deception born of imagination and imagination born of fear, or perhaps it is the other way round and fear ignites imagination – regardless, shadows will thrive.

In the dark conjurings of a sentient mind, all that is imagined can be made real. The beast, and the shadow it casts. The beast's shadow, and the light from which it is born. Each torn away, made distinct, made into things of nightmare.

Philosophers and fools might claim that light is without shape, that it finds its existence in painting the shape of other things, as wayward as the opening of an

eye. That, in the absence of such things, it slants unseen, indeed, invisible. Without other things to strike upon, it does not cavort, does not bounce, does not paint
and reflect. Rather, it flows eternal. If this is so, then light is unique in the universe.

But the universe holds to one law above all others: *nothing is unique.*

Fools and philosophers have not, alas, seen the light.

Conjure the shape of beasts, of Hounds and monsters, fiends and nightmares.
Of light, of dark, and of shadow. A handful of clay, a gifted breath of life, and
forces will seethe in the conflicts inscribed upon their souls.

The Deragoth are the dark, and in their savage solidity would claim ownership
of the shadows they cast. Lock and Pallid, however, are the light that gave the Deragoth shape, without whom neither the Deragoth nor the Hounds of Shadow
would exist. If the hunters and the hunted so will, one day the beasts shall come
together, baleful in mutual regard, perhaps even eager to annihilate one another,
and then, in a single instant of dumbfounded astonishment, vanish one and all.
Ha hah.

Not all instincts guide one to behaviours of survival. Life is mired in stupidity,
after all, and the smarter the life, the stupider it can be. The Hounds of Shadow
were neither brilliant nor brainless. They were, in fact, rather clever.

Salutations to this triparate universe, so mutually insistent. And why not? It
doesn't even exist, except in the caged mind that so needs simplification.

A mind, mused Cotillion, *like mine.*

He glanced across at his companion. *But not his. When you stand at the centre
of the game, no questions arise. How can that be? What is it like, to be the
storm's eye? What happens, dear Shadowthrone, when you blink?*

'This,' muttered Shadowthrone, 'was unexpected.'

'A damned complication,' Cotillion agreed. 'We need the Hounds there, just to
ensure nothing goes awry.'

Shadowthrone snorted. 'It always goes awry. Gods below, I've had to use that
mad High Priest again.'

'Iskaral Pust.' After a moment, Cotillion realized he was smiling. He quickly
cast away that expression, since if Shadowthrone saw it he might well go apoplectic. 'Lovely as she is, Sordiko Qualm is not insurance enough, not for this, anyway.'

'Nor is Pust!' snapped Shadowthrone.

They watched the Hounds drawing closer, sensed the beasts' collective curiosity
at this unplanned intercession. Their task now, after all, was simple. Straightforward, even.

Cotillion glanced back over his shoulder, eyes narrowing on the gaunt figure
walking towards them. Well, not precisely – the stranger was on his way to a
damned reunion, and what would come of that?

'Too many histories, too many half-truths and outright lies.' Shadowthrone
snarled every word of that statement. 'Pups of the Tiste Edur – any one will do, it
seems, if they know the old commands. But now . . .'

'According to my, er, research, its name is Tulas Shorn, and no, I do not know the gender and what seems to be left of it doesn't look as if it will provide enough detail to decide either way.'

Shadowthrone grunted, and then said, 'At least it's sembled – oh, how I hate dragons! If vermin had a throne, they'd be on it.'

'Everywhere there's a mess, they're in the middle of it, all right. Eleint, Soletaken – hardly a difference, when it comes to trouble.'

'The chaos of their blood, Cotillion. Imagine how dull it would be without them . . . and I so cherish dullness.'

If you say so.

'So,' Shadowthrone resumed, 'how does all this fit with your ridiculously convoluted theories?'

'They're only convoluted because they are without substance – if you'll kindly excuse that inadvertent pun. Light, Dark, Shadow. Hounds of this and that and that. These beasts may exist only because of semantics.'

Shadowthrone snorted. 'You don't have to clean up after them – the only possible excuse for such an idiotic suggestion. They smell, they slaver and slobber, they scratch and they lick, Cotillion. Oh, and they tear things to pieces. When it suits them.'

'Because we expect them to.'

'Really now.'

'Listen – what was the mess behind the origin of the Deragoth? Wild beasts from the dusty aeons of past ages, seven left in all the world, and the First Emperor – who was anything but – chooses them as the repositories of his divided soul. All very well, but then we have the Hounds of Shadow, and, presumably, the Hounds of Light—'

'They're just damned albinos, Cotillion, a detail probably irrelevant, and besides, there're only two of them—'

'That we know of, and we know of them only because they wandered into our realm – why? What or who summoned them?'

'I did, of course.'

'How?'

Shadowthrone shrugged. 'I mused out loud on the need for . . . replacements.'

'And that constitutes summoning? I believe I have also heard you musing on the "need" for a breathlessly beautiful Queen of Shadow, a slave to your every desire—'

'You were hiding behind the curtain! I knew it!'

'The point is, where is she?'

The question was left unanswered, as Tulas Shorn had arrived, halting ten paces before them. 'It seems,' the undead Tiste Edur said, 'my Hounds have found new . . . pets.'

'Saw his head off, Cotillion,' Shadowthrone said. 'I hate him already.'

Shan slid up beside Cotillion, eyes fixed on Tulas Shorn. A moment later Baran, Rood, Blind and Gear arrived, padding round the rulers of the Realm of Shadow, and onward to encircle the Tiste Edur.

Who held out his hands, as if inviting the beasts to draw close.

None did.

'They preferred you living, I think,' Cotillion observed. 'The dead surrender so much.'

'If only my sentiments were dead,' Tulas Shorn said, then sighed as it lowered its hands to its sides once more. 'Still, it pleases me to see them. But two are missing.'

At that Cotillion glanced round. 'Well, you're right.'

'Killed?'

'Killed,' confirmed Shadowthrone.

'Who?'

'Anomander Rake.'

At the name Tulas Shorn started.

'Still around,' said Shadowthrone, 'yes. Hee hee. Houndslayer.'

'And neither of you strong enough to avenge the slayings, it seems. I am astonished that my Hounds have accepted such feeble masters.'

'I thought it was pets. No matter. Ganrod and Doan died because they were precipitate. Blame poor training. I do.'

'I am of a mind to test you,' said Tulas Shorn after a moment.

'You want the Throne of Shadow, do you?'

'My first rule was cut short. I have learned since—'

'Hardly. You died.' Shadowthrone waved one ephemeral hand. 'Whatever you learned, you did not learn well enough. Obviously.'

'You seem certain of that.'

'He is,' said Cotillion.

'Is it simply megalomania, then, that so afflicts him?'

'Well, yes, but that's beside the point.'

'And what is the point?'

'That you clearly have not learned anything worthwhile.'

'And why do you say that?'

'Because you've just said that you were of a mind to test us.'

Tulas Shorn cocked its head. 'Do you imagine the Hounds will defend you?'

'These ones? Probably not.'

'Then—' But the rest of his statement was left unfinished, as Lock and Pallid arrived, heads low, hackles upright like spines, to flank Shadowthrone and Cotillion. Upon seeing them, Tulas Shorn stepped back. 'By the Abyss,' it whispered, 'have you two lost your minds? They cannot be here – they must not be among you—'

'Why?' Cotillion demanded, leaning forward in sudden interest.

But the Tiste Edur simply shook its head.

The two bone-white Hounds looked barely restrained, moments from exploding into a deadly charge. The hate was avid in their eyes.

'Why?' Cotillion asked again.

'The . . . implacability of forces – we think to tame, but the wildness remains. Control is a delusion in the mind of self-proclaimed *masters*.' And that last word dripped with contempt. 'The leash, you fools, is *frayed* – don't you understand anything at all?'

'Perhaps—'

Tulas Shorn lifted both hands again, but this time in a warding gesture. 'We'd thought the same, once. We'd deceived ourselves into thinking we were the masters, that every force bowed to our command. And what happened? *They destroyed everything!*'

'I don't—'

'Understand! *I see that!* They are conjurations – manifestations – they exist to warn you. They are the proof that all that you think to enslave *will turn on you.*' And it backed away. 'The end begins again, it begins again.'

Cotillion stepped forward. 'Light, Dark and Shadow – these three – are you saying—'

'Three?' Tulas Shorn laughed with savage bitterness. 'What then of Life? Fire and Stone and Wind? What, you fools, of the Hounds of Death? Manifestations, I said. *They will turn – they are telling you that! That is why they exist! The fangs, the fury – all that is implacable in nature – each aspect but a variation, a hue in the maelstrom of destruction!*'

Tulas Shorn was far enough away now, and the Tiste Edur began veering into a dragon.

As one, all seven Hounds surged forward – but they were too late, as the enormous winged creature launched skyward, rising on a wave of appalling power that sent Cotillion staggering back; that blew through Shadowthrone until he seemed half shredded.

The Soletaken dragon rose higher, as if riding on a column of pure panic, or horror. Or dismay. A pillar reaching for the heavens. Far above, the Great Ravens scattered.

Recovering, Cotillion turned on Shadowthrone. 'Are we in trouble?'

The ruler of High House Shadow slowly collected himself back into a vaguely human shape. 'I can't be sure,' he said.

'Why not?'

'Why, because I blinked.'

Up ahead, the Hounds had resumed their journey. Lock loped a tad too close alongside Shan and she snarled the beast off.

Tongue lolled, jaw hanging in silent laughter.

So much for lessons in hubris.

There were times, Kallor reflected, when he despised his own company. The day gloried in its indifference, the sun a blinding blaze tracking the turgid crawl of the landscape. The grasses clung to the hard earth the way they always did, seeds drifting on the wind as if on sighs of hope. Tawny rodents stood sentinel above warren holes and barked warnings as he marched past. The shadows of circling hawks rippled across his path every now and then.

Despising himself was, oddly enough, a comforting sensation, for he knew he was not alone in his hate. He could recall times, sitting on a throne as if he and it had merged into one, as immovable and inviolate as one of the matching statues outside the palace (any one of his innumerable palaces), when he would feel the oceanic surge of hate's tide. His subjects, tens, hundreds of thousands, each and every one wishing him dead, cast down, torn to pieces. Yet what had he been but the perfect, singular representative of all that they despised within themselves? Who among them would not eagerly take his place? Casting down foul judgements upon all whose very existence offended?

He had been, after all, the very paragon of acquisitiveness. Managing to grasp what others could only reach for, to gather into his power a world's arsenal of weapons, and reshape that world in hard cuts, to make of it what he willed – not one would refuse to take his place. Yes, they could hate him; indeed, they *must* hate him, for he embodied the perfection of success, and his very existence mocked their own failures. And the violence he delivered? Well, watch how it played out in smaller scenes everywhere – the husband who cannot satisfy his wife, so he beats her down with his fists. The streetwise adolescent bully, pinning his victim to the cobbles and twisting the hapless creature's arm. The noble walking past the starving beggar. The thief with the avaricious eye – no, none of these are any different, not in their fundamental essence.

So, hate Kallor even as he hates himself. Even in that, he will do it better. Innate superiority expressed in all manner of ways. See the world gnash its teeth – he answers with a most knowing smile.

He walked, the place where he had begun far, far behind him now, and the place to where he was going drawing ever closer, step by step, as inexorable as this crawling landscape. Let the sentinels bark, let the hawks muse with wary eye. Seeds ride his legs, seeking out new worlds. He walked, and in his mind memories unfolded like worn packets of parchment, seamed and creased, scurried up from the bottom of some burlap sack routed as rats, crackling as they opened up in a rain of flattened moths and insect carcasses.

Striding white-faced and blood-streaked down a jewel-studded hallway, dragging by an ankle the corpse of his wife – just one in a countless succession – her arms trailing behind her limp as dead snakes, their throats slashed open. There had been no warning, no patina of dust covering her eyes when she fixed him with their regard that morning, as he sat ordering the Century Candles in a row on the table between them. As he invited her into a life stretched out, the promise of devouring for ever – no end to the feast awaiting them, no need to ever exercise anything like restraint. They would speak and live the language of excess. They would mark out the maps of interminable expansion, etching the ambitions they could now entertain. Nothing could stop them, not even death itself.

Some madness had afflicted her, like the spurt and gush of a nicked artery – there could be no other cause. Madness it had been. Insanity, to have flung away so much. Of what he offered her. So much, yes, of *him*. Or so he had told himself at the time, and for decades thereafter. It had been easier that way.

He knew now why she had taken her own life. To be offered *everything* was to be shown what she herself was capable of – the depthless reach of her potential depravity, the horrors she would entertain, the plucking away of every last filament of sensitivity, leaving her conscience smooth, cool to the touch, a thing maybe alive, maybe not, a thing nothing could prod awake. She had seen, yes, just how far she might take herself . . . and had then said *no*.

Another sweet packet, unfolding with the scent of flowers. He knelt beside Vaderon, his war horse, as the animal bled out red foam, its one visible eye fixed on him, as if wanting to know: was it all worth this? What has my life purchased you, my blood, the end of my days?

A battlefield spread out on all sides. Heaps of the dead and the dying, human and beast, Jheck and Tartheno Toblakai, a scattering of Forkrul Assail each one surrounded by hundreds of the fallen, the ones protecting their warleaders, the ones who failed in taking the demons down. And there was no dry ground, the blood was a shallow sea thickening in the heat, and more eyes looked upon nothing than scanned the nightmare seeking friends and kin.

Voices cried, but they seemed distant – leagues away from Kallor where he knelt beside Vaderon, unable to pull his gaze from that one fixating eye. Promises of brotherhood, flung into the crimson mud. Silent vows of honour, courage, service and reward, all streaming down the broken spear shaft jutting from the animal's massive, broad chest. And yes, Vaderon had reared to take that thrust, a thrust aimed at Kallor himself, because this horse was too stupid to understand anything.

That Kallor had begun this war, had welcomed the slaughter, the mayhem.

That Kallor, this master now kneeling at its side, was in truth a brutal, despicable man, a bag of skin filled with venom and spite, with envy and a child's selfish snarl that in losing took the same from everyone else.

Vaderon, dying. Kallor, dry-eyed and damning himself for his inability to weep. To feel regret, to sow self-recrimination, to make promises to do better the next time round.

I am as humankind, he often told himself. *Impervious to lessons. Pitiful in loss and defeat, vengeful in victory. With every possible virtue vulnerable to exploitation and abuse by others, could they claim dominion, until such virtues became hollow things, sweating beads of poison. I hold forth goodness and see it made vile, and do nothing, voice no complaint, utter no disavowal. The world I make I have made for one single purpose – to chew me up, me and everyone else. Do not believe this bewildered expression. I am bemused only through stupidity, but the clever among me know better, oh, yes they do, even as they lie through my teeth, to you and to themselves.*

Kallor walked, over one shoulder a burlap sack ten thousand leagues long and bulging with folded packets. So different from everyone else. Ghost horses run at his side. Wrist-slashed women show bloodless smiles, dancing round the rim of deadened lips. And where dying men cry, see his shadow slide past.

'I want things plain,' said Nenanda. 'I don't want to have to work.' And then he looked up, belligerent, quick to take affront.

Skintick was bending twigs to make a stick figure. 'But things aren't plain, Nenanda. They never are.'

'I know that, just say it straight, that's all.'

'You don't want your confusion all stirred up, you mean.'

Nimander roused himself. 'Skin—'

But Nenanda had taken the bait – and it was indeed bait, since for all that Skintick had seemed intent on his twigs, he had slyly noted Nenanda's diffidence. 'Liars *like* confusion. Liars and thieves, because they can slip in and slip out, when there's confusion. They want your uncertainty, but there's nothing uncertain in what *they* want, is there? That's how they use you – you're like that yourself sometimes, Skintick, with your clever words.'

'Wait, how can they use me if I am them?'

Desra snorted.

Nenanda's expression filled with fury and he would have risen, if not for Aranatha's gentle hand settling on his arm, magically dispelling his rage.

Skintick twisted the arms of the tiny figure until they were above the knotted head with its lone green leaf, and held it up over the fire so that it faced Nenanda. 'Look,' he said, 'he surrenders.'

'Do not mock me, Skintick.'

'On the contrary, I applaud your desire to have things simple. After all, either you can cut it with your sword or you can't.'

'There you go again.'

The bickering would go on half the night, Nimander knew. And as it went on it would unravel, and Skintick would increasingly make Nenanda into a thick-witted fool, when he was not anything of the sort. But words were indeed ephemeral, able to sleet past all manner of defences, quick to cut, eager to draw blood. They were the perfect weapons of deceit, but they could also be, he well knew, the solid pavestones of a path leading to comprehension – or what passed for comprehension in this murky, impossible world.

There were so many ways to live, one for every single sentient being – and perhaps for the non-sentient ones too – that it was a true miracle whenever two could meet in mutual understanding, or even passive acceptance. Proof, Skintick had once said, of life's extraordinary flexibility. *But then*, he had added, *it is our curse to be social creatures, so we've little choice but to try to get along.*

They were camped on a broad terrace above the last of the strange ruins – the day's climb had been long, dusty and exhausting. Virtually every stone in the rough gravel filling the old drainage channels proved to be some sort of fossil – pieces of what had once been bone, wood, tooth or tusk – all in fragments, pieces. The entire mountainside seemed to be some sort of midden, countless centuries old, and to imagine the lives needed to create so vast a mound was to feel bewildered, weakened with awe. Were the mountains behind this one the same? Was such a thing even possible?

Can't you see, Nenanda, how nothing is simple! Not even the ground we walk upon. How is this created! Is what we come from and where we end up any different! No, that was badly put. Make it simpler. What is this existence!

As Nenanda might answer, it does a warrior no good to ask such questions.

Leave us this headlong plunge, leave to the moment to come that next step, even if it's over an abyss. There's no point in all these questions.

And how might Skintick respond to that? *Show a bhederin fear and watch it run off a cliff. What killed it? The jagged rocks below, or the terror that made it both blind and stupid?* And Nenanda would shrug. *Who cares? Let's just eat the damned thing.*

This was not the grand conflict of sensibilities one might think it was. *Just two heads on the same coin, one facing right on this side, the other facing left on the other side. Both winking.*

And Desra would snort and say, *Keep your stupid words, I'll take the cock in my hand over words any time.*

Holding on for dear life, Skintick would mutter under his breath, and Desra's answering smile fooled no one. Nimander well remembered every conversation among his followers, his siblings, his family, and remembered too how they could repeat themselves, with scant variation, if all the cues were triggered in the right sequence.

He wondered where Clip had gone to – somewhere out beyond this pool of fire-light, perhaps listening, perhaps not. Would he hear anything he'd not heard before? Would anything said this night alter his opinion of them? It did not seem likely. They bickered, they rapped against personalities and spun off either laughing or infuriated. Prodding, skipping away, ever seeking where the skin was thinnest above all the old bruises. All just fighting without swords, and no one ever died, did they?

Nimander watched Kedeviss – who had been unusually quiet thus far – rise and draw her cloak tighter about her shoulders. After a moment, she set off into the dark.

Somewhere in the crags far away, wolves began howling.

Something huge loomed just outside the flickering orange light, and Samar Dev saw both Karsa and Traveller twist round to face it, and then they rose, reaching for their weapons. The shape shifted, seemed to wag from side to side, and then – at the witch's eye level had she been standing – a glittering, twisting snout, a broad flattened halo of fur, the smear of fire in two small eyes.

Samar Dev struggled to breathe. She had never before seen such an enormous bear. If it reared, it would tower over even Karsa Orlong. She watched that uplifted head, the flattened nose testing the air. The creature, she realized, clearly relied more on smell than on sight. *I thought fire frightened such beasts – not summoned them.*

If it attacked, things would happen . . . fast. Two swords flashing into its lunge, a deafening bellow, talons scything to sweep away the two puny attackers – and then it would come straight for her. She could see that, was certain of it. The bear had come for her.

De nek okral. The words seemed to foam up to the surface of her thoughts, like things belched from the murky depths of instinct. 'De nek okral,' she whispered.

The nostrils flared, dripping.

And then, with a snuffling snort, the beast drew back, out of the firelight. A crunch of stones, and the ground trembled as the animal lumbered away.

Karsa and Traveller moved their hands away from their weapons, and then both eased back down, resuming their positions facing the fire.

The Toblakai warrior found a stick and dropped it into the flames. Sparks whirled skyward, bright with liberation, only to wink out. His expression looked thoughtful.

Samar Dev glanced down at her trembling hands, and then slipped them beneath the woollen blanket she had wrapped about herself.

'Strictly speaking,' said Traveller, 'not an okral. De nek . . .' He raised his brows. ' "Short nose?" '

'How should I know?' Samar Dev snapped.

His brows lifted higher.

'I don't know where those words came from. They just . . . arrived.'

'They were Imass, Samar Dev.'

'Oh?'

'*Okral* is the word for a plains bear, but that was no plains bear – too big, legs too long—'

'I would not,' said Karsa, 'wish to be chased by that beast, even on horseback. That animal was built for running its prey down.'

'But it was not hunting,' said Traveller.

'I don't know what it was doing,' Karsa conceded with a loose shrug. 'But I am glad it changed its mind.'

'From you two,' Samar said, 'it would have sensed no fear. That alone would have made it hesitate.' Her voice was harsh, almost flinging the words out. She was not sure why she was so angry. Perhaps naught but the aftermath of terror – a terror that neither companion had the decency to have shared with her. They made her feel . . . diminished.

Traveller was still studying her, and she wanted to snarl at him. When he spoke, his tone was calm. 'The old gods of war are returning.'

'War? The god of war? That was Fener, wasn't it? The Boar.'

'Fener, Togg, Fanderay, Treach, and,' he shrugged, 'De nek Okral – who can say how many once existed. They arose, I would imagine, dependent on the environment of the worshippers – whatever beast was supreme predator, was the most savage—'

'But none were,' cut in Karsa Orlong. 'Supreme. That title belonged to us two-legged hunters, us bright-eyed killers.'

Traveller continued to stare at Samar Dev. 'The savagery of the beasts reflected the savagery in the souls of the worshippers. In war, this is what was shared. Boar, tigers, wolves, the great bears that knew no fear.'

'Is this what Fener's fall has done, then?' Samar Dev asked. 'All the hoary, forgotten ones clambering back to fight over the spoils? And what has that to do with that bear, anyway?'

'That bear,' said Traveller, 'was a god.'

Karsa spat into the fire. 'No wonder I have never before seen such a beast.'

'They once existed,' said Traveller. 'They once ruled these plains, until all that they hunted was taken from them, and so they vanished, as have so many other proud creatures.'

'The god should have followed them,' said Karsa. 'There are too many faces of war as it is.'

Samar Dev grunted. 'That's rich coming from you.'

Karsa eyed her over the flames, and then grinned, the crazed tattoos seeming to split wide open on his face. 'There need be only one.'

Yours. Yes, Toblakai, I understand you well enough. 'I have one true fear,' she said. 'And that is, when you are done with civilization, it will turn out that you as master of everything will prove no better than the ones you pulled down. That you will find the last surviving throne and plop yourself down on it, and find it all too much to your liking.'

'That is an empty fear, Witch,' said Karsa Orlong. 'I will leave not one throne to sit on – I will shatter them all. And if, when I am done, I am the last left standing – in all the world – then I will be satisfied.'

'What of your people?'

'I have listened too long to the whispers of Bairoth Gild and Delum Thord. Our ways are but clumsier versions of all the other ways in which people live – their love of waste, their eagerness to reap every living thing as if belonged to them, as if in order to prove ownership they must destroy it.' He bared his teeth. 'We think no differently, just slower. Less . . . efficiently. You will prattle on about progress, Samar Dev, but progress is not what you think it is. It is not a tool guided by our hands – not yours, not mine, not Traveller's. It is not something we can rightly claim as our destiny. Why? Because in truth we have no control over it. Not your machines, Witch, not a hundred thousand slaves shackled to it – even as we stand with whips in hand.'

Now Traveller had turned slightly and was studying the Toblakai with that same curious wonder that she had seen before. 'What then,' he asked, 'is progress, Karsa Orlong?'

The Toblakai gestured into the night sky. 'The crawl of the stars, the plunge and rise of the moon. Day, night, birth, death – progress is the passage of reality. We sit astride this horse, but it is a beast we can never tame, and it will run for ever – we will age and wither and fall off, and it cares not. Some other will leap aboard and it cares not. It may run alone, and it cares not. It outran the great bears. The wolves and their worshippers. It outran the Jaghut, and the K'Chain Che'Malle. And still it runs on, and to it we are nothing.'

'Then why not let us ride it for a time?' Samar Dev demanded. 'Why not leave us that damned illusion?'

'Because, woman, we ride it to hunt, to kill, to destroy. We ride it as if it is our right and our excuse both.'

'And yet,' said Traveller, 'is that not precisely what you intend, Karsa Orlong?'

'I shall destroy what I can, but never shall I claim to own what I destroy. I will be the embodiment of progress, but emptied of greed. I shall be like nature's fist: blind. And I shall prove that ownership is a lie. The land, the seas, the life to be found there. The mountains, the plains, the cities, the farms. Water, air. We own none of it. This is what I will prove, and by proving it will make it so.'

He leaned forward then and gathered up in his hands a heap of dusty earth. The Toblakai rose to his feet, and dropped the soil on to the fire, snuffing out the flames. Darkness took them all, as if but awaiting this moment. Or, she thought with a chill, as if it has always been there. *The light blinded me, else I would have seen it.*

As I do now.

God of war, what did you want with me!

With an ear-piercing scream the enkaral crashed down on to Pearl, talons slashing through flesh, dagger fangs closing on the back of the demon's neck. Grunting, he reached up and closed one hand about the winged beast's throat, the other forcing its way beneath the enkaral's upper jaw – fingers sliced into shreds as he reached ever farther and then began prising the mouth back open. The fangs of the lower jaw sank deeper into the muscles of Pearl's neck, and still he pushed. As this was going on, the talons never ceased their frantic rending along the demon's lower back, seeking to hook round his spine, seeking to tear loose that column – but the chains and shackles snarled its efforts, as did Pearl's twisting to evade each stabbing search through his muscles.

Finally, as his grip on the beast's throat tightened, he could hear the desperate squeal of its breath, and the jaws weakened. Something crunched and all at once Pearl was able to rip the jaws free of his neck. He staggered forward, dragging the huge beast round, both hands closing on its scaled throat – and more things collapsed inside that crushing grip.

The enkaral flailed about, legs kicking wildly now, talons scoring furrows on Pearl's thighs. He forced the beast down on to the ground. The thrashing slowed, and then, with a spasm, the creature went limp.

Pearl slowly rose, flinging to carcass to one side; a thud, the slap and rustle of chains. The demon then glanced over to the figure walking alongside it. 'Did I anger it somehow, Draconus?'

The man squinted, shifting the weight of his chains over his other shoulder before replying, 'No, Pearl. Madness took it, that's all. You just happened to be near.'

'Oh,' said Pearl. And then the demon sighed. 'Then it is good it was me and not something . . . smaller.'

'Can you continue, Pearl?'

'I can, yes. Thank you for asking.'

'Not much longer, I should think.'

'No, not much longer,' agreed Pearl. 'And then?'

'We will see, won't we?'

'Yes, that is true. Draconus?'

'Pearl?'

'I think I will welcome an end – is that a terrible thing for me to say?'

The man shook his head, his expression hinting that he might be in pain. 'No, my friend, it is not.'

Fully one half of the sky was now a seething argent storm. Thunder rolled from the horizon behind them, as the very ground was ripped up, annihilated – their world had acquired an edge, raw as a cliff, and that cliff was drawing closer as vast sections sheared away, as the raging abyss swallowed the toppling stone columns one by one.

And it occurred to Draconus, then, that each of them here, seemingly alone, each with his or her own shackle, his or her own chain, had finally, at long last, come together.

We are an army. But an army in retreat. See the detritus we leave in our wake, the abandoned comrades. See the glaze of our eyes, this veil of numbed exhaustion – when at last we tear it aside, we will find the despair we have harboured for so long, like a black poisoned fruit under a leaf – all revealed as we look into each other's eyes.

Was the comfort found in mutual recognition of any true worth? Here, at the last? When the common ground is failure? *Like a field of corpses after a battle. Like a sea of skulls rolling in the tide. Is not the brotherhood too bitter to bear?*

And now, he wanted to . . . to what? Yes, to rage, but first, *let me close my eyes. Just for a moment. Let me find, again, my will—*

'Draconus?'

'Yes, Pearl?'

'Do you hear drums? I hear drums.'

'The thunder—' and then he stopped, and turned round, to look back at that fulminating, crazed horizon. '*Gods below.*'

Chaos had found a new way to mock them. With legions in ranks, weapons and armour blazing, with standards spitting lightning into the sky. Emerging in an endless row, an army of something vaguely human, shaped solely by intent, in numbers unimaginable – they did not march so much as flow, like a frothing surge devouring the ground – and no more than a league away. Lances and pike heads flashing, round shields spinning like vortices. Drums like rattling bones, rushing to swarm like maddened wasps.

So close . . . has the hunger caught fresh our scent – does the hunger now rush to us, faster than ever before?

Is there something in that storm . . . that knows what it wants?

'I do not understand,' said Pearl. 'How can chaos take shapes?'

'Perhaps, friend, what we are seeing is the manifestation of what exists in all of us. Our secret love of destruction, the pleasure of annihilation, our darkest glee. Perhaps when at last they reach us, we shall realize that they are us and we are them.' *That Dragnipur has but cut us in two, and all chaos seeks is to draw us whole once more.*

Oh, really now, Draconus, have you lost your mind?

'If they are the evil in our souls, Pearl, then there can be no doubt as to their desire.'

'Perhaps not just our souls,' mused Pearl, wiping blood from his eyes. 'Perhaps every soul, since the beginning of creation. Perhaps, Draconus, when each of us dies, the evil within us is torn free and rushes into the realm of Chaos. Or the evil is that which survives the longest . . .'

Draconus said nothing. The demon's suggestions horrified him, and he thought – oh, he was thinking, yes – that Pearl had found a terrible truth. Somewhere among those possibilities.

Somewhere among them . . . I think . . . there is a secret. An important secret. Somewhere . . .

'I do not want to meet my evil self,' said Pearl.

Draconus glanced across at him. 'Who does?'

Ditch was dreaming, for dreaming was his last road to freedom. He could stride, reaching out to the sides, reshaping everything. He could make the world as he wanted it, as it should be, a place of justice, a place where he could be a god and look upon humanity as it truly was: a mob of unruly, faintly ridiculous children. Watch them grasp things when they think no one's looking. Watch them break things, hurt things, steal. Listen to their expostulations of innocence, their breathless list of excuses, listen to how they repent and repent and repent and then go and do the same damned things all over again. Children.

With all his godly powers, he would teach them about consequences, that most terrible of lessons, the one resisted the longest. He would teach them because he had learned in the only way possible – with scars and broken bones, with sickness in the soul tasting of fear, with all the irreparable damage resulting from all his own thoughtless decisions.

There could be wonder and joy among children, too. Too easy to see naught but gloom, wasn't it? Wonder and joy. Naïve creations of beauty. He was not blind to such things, and, like any god, he understood that such gifts were pleas for mercy. An invitation to indulge that reprehensible host of flaws. Art and genius, compassion and passion, they were as islands assailed on all sides. But no island lived for ever. The black, writhing, worm-filled seas ever rose higher. And sooner or later, the hungry storms ate their fill.

Nature might well struggle for balance. And perhaps the egregious imbalance Ditch thought he perceived in his kind was but an illusion, and redress waited, stretched out to match the extremity. A fall as sudden and ferocious as the rise.

In his state of dreaming, it did not occur to him that his dreams were not his own, that this harsh cant of judgement belonged to a tyrant or even a god, or to one such as himself if madness had taken hold. But he was not mad, and nor was he a tyrant, and for all his natural inclination (natural to almost everyone) to wish for true justice he was, after all, wise enough to know the vulnerability of moral notions, the ease with which they were corrupted. Was he dreaming, then, the dreams of a god?

Blind as Kadaspala was, he could sense far too much of Ditch's visions – he could feel the incandescent rage in the flicker of the man's eyelids, the heat of his breath, the ripples of tautness washing over his face. Oh, this unconscious wizard stalked an unseen world, filled with outrage and fury, with the hunger for retribution.

There were so many paths to godhood. Kadaspala was certain of that. So many paths, so many paths. Refuse to die, refuse to surrender, refuse to die and refuse to surrender and that was one path, stumbled on to without true intent, without even wanting it, and these gods were the bemused ones, the reluctant ones. They were best left alone, for to prod them awake was to risk apocalypse. Reluctant power was the deadliest power of them all, for the anger behind it was long stoked. Long stoked and stoked long and long, so best leave them leave them leave them alone.

Other gods were called into being and the nature of that call took countless forms. A convulsion of natural forces, until the very sludge awakens. Wherever discordant elements clashed, the possibility was born. Life. Intent. Desire and need. But these too were accidental things, in as much as anything could be accidental when all the particles necessary for creation abounded, as they surely did. There were other ways of calling a god into being.

Gather a host of words, a host of words. Gather a host of words. Make them, make them, make them what? Physical, yes, make them physical, from the empty ether to the incision in clay, the stain on stone, the ink on skin. Physical, because the physical created – by its very nature before the eye (or the inner eye) – created and created *patterns*. And they could be played with played with played with. In numbers and sigils, in astral proportions. They could be coded inside codes inside codes until something is rendered, something both beautiful and absolute. Beautiful in its absoluteness. In its absolution, in its absolved essence, a thing of beauty.

Understand, won't you, the truth of patterns, how pattern finds truth in the tension of juxtaposition, in the game of meaning meaning the game which is the perfect pattern of language in the guise of imperfection – but what value any of this any of this any of this?

The value is the body of text (hah, the body – the *bodies*) that in its absoluteness becomes sacred, and in sacredness becomes all that it portrays in its convivial ordering of the essentially meaningless. Patterns where none existed before. Creation from nothing. Awakening from absence of self. And what is the word the beautiful word the precious word and the perfect word that starts the game starts everything everything everything?

Why, the word is *birth*.

Bodies of text, all these bodies, all this flesh and the ink and the words and the words oh the words. Bodies and bodies, patterns inside patterns, lives and lives and lives all dreaming . . . all dreaming one dream.

One dream. One dream one dream one one one dream. One.

A dream of justice.

'Let the cosmos quake,' Kadaspala whispered as he etched sigil inside sigil inside sigil, as he wove language and meaning, as the ink rode the piercing and flowed beneath skin pocket by pocket. 'Quake and quiver, whimper and quaver. A god oh a god yes a god now a god soon a god a god awakens. Lives and lives cut down one and all, cut down, yes, by judgement's sharp edge – did we deserve it? Did we earn the punishment? Are any of us innocent, any of us at all? Not likely not likely not likely. So, lives and lives and none none none of us did not receive precisely what we deserved.

'Do you understand? Godling, to you I speak. Listen listen listen well. We are what you come from. The punished, the punished, the victims of justice, the victims of our own stupidity, yes, and who could say that none of us have learned our lesson? Who can say that? Look oh look oh look where we are! Godling, here is your soul, writ in flesh, in flesh, writ here by Kadaspala, who was once blind though he could see and now can see though he is blind. And am I not the very definition of sentience? Blind in life, I can see in death – the definition of mortality, my darling child, heed it and heed it come the moment you must act and decide and stand and sit in judgement. Heed and heed, godling, this eternal flaw.

'And what, you will wonder, is written upon your soul? What is written here? Here upon the flesh of your soul? Ah, but that is the journey of your life, godling, to learn the language of your soul, to learn it to learn it even as you live it.

'Soon, birth arrives. Soon, life awakens.

'Soon, *I make a god.*'

And even now, the god dreams of justice. For, unlike Ditch, Kadaspala is indeed mad. His code struck to flesh is a code of laws. The laws from which the god shall be born. Consider that, consider that well.

In the context of, say, mercy . . .

She was out there, down in the basin, on her knees, head hanging, her torso weaving back and forth to some inner rhythm. After studying her yet again, Seerdomin, with a faint gasp, tore his gaze away – something it was getting ever harder to manage, for she was mesmerizing, this child-woman, this fount of corruption, and the notion that a woman's fall could be so alluring, so perfectly sexual, left him horrified. By this language of invitation. By his own darkness.

Behind him, the Redeemer murmured, 'Her power grows. Her power over you, Segda Travos.'

'I do not want to be where she is.'

'Don't you?'

Seerdomin turned and eyed the god. 'Self-awareness can be a curse.'

'A necessary one.'

'I suppose so,' he conceded.

'Will you still fight her, Segda Travos?'

'I think so, yes.'

'Why?'

Seerdomin bared his teeth. 'Don't you start with me, Redeemer. The enemy never questions motivations – the enemy doesn't chew the ground out beneath its own feet.' He jabbed a finger back at the woman kneeling in the basin. 'She has no questions. No doubts. What she has instead is strength. Power.'

'That is true,' said the Redeemer. 'All of it. It is why those haunted by uncertainty must ever retreat. They cannot stand before the self-righteous. Instead, they must slink away, they must hide, they must slip behind the enemy's lines—'

'Where every damned one of them is hunted down and silenced – no, Redeemer, you forget, I *lived* in a tyranny. I kicked in doors. I dragged people away. Do you truly believe unbelievers will be tolerated? Scepticism is a criminal act. Wave the standard or someone else will, and they'll be coming for you. Redeemer, I have looked in the eyes of my enemy, and they are hard, cold, emptied of everything but hate. I have, yes, seen my own reflection – it haunts me still.'

No further words were exchanged then. Seerdomin looked back down to that woman, the High Priestess who had once been Salind. She was naught but a tool, now, a weapon of some greater force's will, its hunger. The same force, he now suspected, that drove nations to war, that drove husbands to kill wives and wives to kill husbands. That could take even the soul of a god and crush it into subservience.

When will you rise, Salind? When will you come for me?

This was not the afterlife he had imagined. *My fighting should be over. My every need made meaningless, the pain of thoughts for ever silenced.*

Is not death's gift indifference? Blissful, perfect indifference?

She swayed back and forth, gathering strength as only the surrendered could do.

Monkrat walked through the pilgrim camp. Dishevelled as it had once been, now it looked as if a tornado had ripped through it. Tents had sagged; shacks leaned perilously close to collapse. There was rubbish everywhere. The few children still alive after being so long abandoned watched him walk past with haunted eyes peering out from filth-streaked faces. Sores ate into their drawn lips. Their bellies were swollen under the rags. There was nothing to be done for them, and even if there was, Monkrat was not the man to do it. In his mind he had left humanity behind long ago. There was no kinship to nip at his heart. Every fool the world over was on his or her own, or they were slaves. These were the only two states of being – every other one was a lie. And Monkrat had no desire to become a slave, as much as Gradithan or Saemenkelyk might want that.

No, he would remain his own world. It was easier that way. Ease was important. Ease was all that mattered.

Soon, he knew, he would have to escape this madness. Gradithan's ambitions had lost all perspective – the curse of kelyk. He talked now incessantly of the coming of the Dying God, the imminent end of all things and the glorious rebirth to follow. People talking like that disgusted Monkrat. They repeated themselves so often it soon became grossly obvious that their words were wishes and the wish was that their words might prove true. Round and round, all that wasted breath. The mind so liked to go round and round, so liked that familiar track, the familiarity of it. Round and round, and each time round the mind was just that much stupider. Increment by increment, the range of thoughts narrower, the path underfoot more deeply trenched – he had even noted how the vocabulary diminished, as uneasy notions were cast away and all the words associated with them, too. The circular track became a mantra, the mantra a proclamation of stupid wishes that things could be as they wanted them, that in fact they *were* as they wanted them.

Fanaticism was so popular. There had to be a reason for that, didn't there? Some vast reward to the end of thinking, some great bliss to the blessing of idiocy. Well, Monkrat trusted none of that. He knew how to think for himself and that was all he knew so why give it up? He'd yet to hear an argument that could convince him – but of course, fanatics didn't use arguments, did they? No, just that fixed gaze, the threat, the reason to fear.

Aye, he'd had enough. Gods below, he was actually longing for the city where he had been born. There in the shadow of Mock's Hold, and that blackwater bay of the harbour where slept a demon, half buried in mud and tumbled ballast stones. And who knew, maybe there was no one left there to recognize him – and why would they in any case? His old name was on the toll of the fallen, after all, and beside it was *Blackdog Wood, 1159 Burn's Sleep*. The Bridgeburners were gone, dead, destroyed in Pale with the remnants mopped up here at Black Coral. But he'd been a casualty long before then, and the years since then had been damned hard – no, it wasn't likely that he'd be recognized.

Yes, Malaz City sounded sweet now, as he walked this wretched camp's main street, the squalling of gulls loud in his ears.

Gradithan, you've lost it.

There won't be any vengeance on the Tiste Andii. Not for me, not for you. It was a stupid idea and now it's gone too far.

History wasn't worth reliving. He understood that now. But people never learned that – they never fucking learned that, did they? Round and round.

A fallen pilgrim stumbled out from between two hovels, brown-smeared chin and murky eyes swimming in some dubious rapture painting its lie behind them. He wanted to kick the brainless idiot between the legs. He wanted to stomp on the fool's skull and see the shit-coloured sludge spill out. He wanted every child to watch him do it, too, so they'd realize, so they'd run for their lives.

Not that he cared.

'High Priestess.'

She looked up, then rose from behind her desk, came round with a gathering of her robes, and then bowed. 'Son of Darkness, welcome. Did we have anything arranged?'

His smile was wry. 'Do we ever?'

'Please,' she said, 'do come in. I will send for wine and—'

'No need on my account, High Priestess.' Anomander Rake walked into the small office, eyed the two chairs and then selected the least ornate one to sit down in. He stretched out his legs, fingers lacing together on his lap, and eyed her speculatively.

She raised her arms, 'Shall I dance?'

'Shall I sing?'

'Abyss take me, no. Please.'

'Do sit down,' said Rake, indicating the other chair.

She did so, keeping her back straight, a silent question lifting her eyebrows.

He continued watching her.

She let out a breath and slumped back. 'All right, then. I'm relaxing. See?'

'You have ever been my favourite,' he said, looking away.

'Your favourite what?'

'High Priestess, of course. What else might I be thinking?'

'Well, that is the eternal question, isn't it?'

'One too many people spend too much time worrying about.'

'You cannot be serious, Anomander.'

He seemed to be studying her desk – not the things scattered on its surface, but the desk itself. 'That's too small for you,' he pronounced.

She glanced at it. 'You are deceived, alas. It's my disorganization that's too big. Give me a desk the size of a concourse and I'll still fill it up with junk.'

'Then it must be your mind that is too big, High Priestess.'

'Well,' she said, 'there is so little to think about and so much time.' She fluttered a hand. 'If my thoughts have become oversized it's only out of indolence.' Her gaze sharpened. 'And we have become so indolent, haven't we?'

'She has been turned away for a long time,' Anomander Rake said. 'That I allowed all of you to turn instead to me was ever a dubious enterprise.'

'You made no effort to muster worship, Son of Darkness, and that is what made it dubious.'

One brow lifted. 'Not my obvious flaws?'

'And Mother Dark is without flaws? No, the Tiste Andii were never foolish enough to force upon our icons the impossibility of perfection.'

' "Icons," ' said Anomander Rake, frowning as he continued studying the desk.

'Is that the wrong word? I think not.'

'And that is why I rejected the notion of worship.'

'Why?'

'Because, sooner or later, the believers shatter their icons.'

She grunted, and thought about that for a time, before sighing and nodding. 'A hundred fallen, forgotten civilizations, yes. And in the ruins all those statues . . . with their faces chopped off. The loss of faith is ever violent, it seems.'

'Ours was.'

The statement stung her. 'Ah, we are not so different then, after all. What a depressing realization.'

'Endest Silann,' he said.

'Your stare is making the legs of my desk tremble, Lord Rake – am I so unpleasant that you dare not rest eyes upon me?'

He slowly turned his head and settled his gaze upon her.

And seeing all that was in his eyes almost made her flinch, and she understood, all at once, the mercy he had been giving her – with his face turned away, with his eyes veiled by distraction. But then she had asked for his regard, as much out of vanity as the secret pleasure of her attraction to him – she could not now break this connection. Marshalling her resolve, she said, 'Endest Silann, yes. The reason for this visit. I understand.'

'He is convinced he was broken long ago, High Priestess. We both know it is not true.'

She nodded. 'He proved that when he sustained Moon's Spawn beneath the sea – proved it to everyone but himself.'

'I reveal to him my confidence,' said Rake, 'and each time he . . . contracts. I cannot reach through, it seems, to bolster what I know is within him.'

'Then it is his faith that is broken.'

He grimaced, made no reply.

'When the time comes,' she said, 'I will be there. To do what I can. Although,' she added, 'that may not be much.'

'You need not elaborate on the efficacy of your presence, High Priestess. We are speaking, as you said, of faith.'

'And there need be no substance to it. Thank you.'

He glanced away once more, and this time the wry smile she had seen before played again across his features. 'You were always my favourite,' he said.

'Me, or the desk you so seem to love?'

He rose and she did the same. 'High Priestess,' he said.

'Son of Darkness,' she returned, with another bow.

And out he went, leaving in his wake a sudden absence, an almost audible clap of displacement – but no, that was in her mind, a hint of something hovering there behind her memory of his face, his eyes and all that she had seen there.

Mother Dark, hear me. Heed me. You did not understand your son then. You do not understand him now.

Don't you see? This was all Draconus's doing.

'This ain't right,' gasped Reccanto Ilk, each word spraying blood. 'When it comes to screaming women, they should be leaving the bar, not trying to get in!'

The ragged hole the shrieking, snarling, jaw-snapping women had torn through the tavern's door was jammed with arms, stretching, fingers clutching, all reaching inward in a desperate attempt to tear through the barrier. Claws stabbed into the Trell's tattooed shoulders and he ducked his head lower, grunting as the demons battered at the door, planks splintering – but that Trell was one strong bastard, and he was holding 'em back, as he had been doing since that first rush that nearly saw Reccanto's precious head get torn off.

Thank whatever gods squatted in the muck of this damned village that these demons were so stupid. Not one had tried either of the shuttered windows flanking the entrance, although with that barbed hulk, Gruntle, waiting at one of 'em with his cutlasses at the ready, and Faint and the Bole brothers at the other, at least if them demons went and tried one of 'em they'd be cut to pieces in no time. Or so Reccanto hoped, since he was hiding under a table and a table wasn't much cover, or wouldn't be if them demons was nasty enough to tear apart Gruntle and Faint and the Boles and the Trell, and Sweetest Sufferance, too, for that matter.

Master Quell and that swampy witch, Precious Thimble, were huddled together at the back, at the barred cellar door, doing Hood knew what. Glanno Tarp was missing – he'd gone with the horses when they went straight and the carriage went left, and Reccanto was pretty sure that the idiot had gone and killed himself bad. Or worse.

As for that corpse, Cartographer, why, the last Ilk had seen of it it was still lashed to a wheel, spinning in a blur as the damned thing spun off its axle and bounded off into the rainy night. Why couldn't the demons go after it? A damned easier fight—

Repeated blows were turning the door into a shattered wreck, and one of the arms angled down to slash deep gouges across Mappo's back, making the Trell groan and groaning wasn't good, since it meant Mappo might just give up trying to hold 'em back and in they'd come, straight for the man hiding under the table. It wasn't fair. Nothing was fair and what was fair about that, dammit?

He drew out his rapier and clutched the grip in one shaky hand. A lunge from the knees – was such a thing possible? He was about to find out. Oh, yes, he'd skewer one for its troubles, just watch. And if the other two (he was pretty sure there were three of 'em) ripped him up then fine, just fine. A man could only do so much.

Gruntle was shouting something at Mappo, and the Trell bellowed a reply, drawing his legs up under himself as if about to dive to one side – thanks a whole lot, you ogre! – and then all at once Mappo did just that, off to the right, slamming into the legs of the Boles and Faint and taking all three down with him.

An explosion of wood splinters and thrashing arms, clacking fangs, unclean hair and terribly unreasonable expressions, and the three screeching women plunged in.

Two were brought up short pretty fast, as their heads leapt up in gouts of greenish uck and their bodies sprawled in a thrashing mess.

Even as this was happening, the third woman charged straight for Reccanto. He shrieked and executed his lunge from the knees, which naturally wasn't a lunge at all. More like a flèche, a forward flinging of his upper body, arm and point extended, and as he overbalanced and landed with a bone-creaking thump on the floorboards the rapier's point snagged on something and the blade bowed alarmingly and so he let go, so that it sprang up, then back down, the pommel crunching the top of Reccanto's head, not once, but twice, each time driving his face into the floor, nose crackling in a swirl of stinging tears and bursting into his brain the horrid stench of mouse droppings and greasy dirt – immediately replaced by a whole lot of flowing blood.

It was strangely quiet, and, moaning, Reccanto rolled on to his side and lifted himself up on one elbow.

And found himself staring into the blank, horrible eyes of the woman who'd charged him. The rapier point had driven in between her eyes, straight in, so far that he should be able to see it coming back out from somewhere beneath the back of her skull – but it wasn't there. Meaning—

'She broke it!' he raged, clambering on to his feet. 'She broke my damned rapier!'

The demonic woman was on her knees, head thrust forward, mouth still stretched open, the weight of her upper body resting on the knocked-over chair that had served as pathetic barricade. The other two, headless, still thrashed on the floor as green goo flowed. Gruntle was studying that ichor where it slathered the broad blades of his cutlasses.

Mappo, the Boles and Faint were slowly regaining their feet.

Sweetest Sufferance, clutching a clay bottle, staggered up to lean against Reccanto. 'Too bad about your rapier,' she said, 'but damn me, Ilk, that was the neatest flèche I ever did see.'

Reccanto squinted, wiped blood from his streaming nose and lacerated lips, and then grinned. 'It was, wasn't it. The timing of a master—'

'I mean, how could you have guessed she'd trip on one of them rolling heads and go down on her knees skidding like that, straight into your thrust?'

Tripped? Skidded? 'Yes, well, like I said, I'm a master duellist.'

'I could kiss you,' she continued, her breath rank with sour wine, 'except you went and pissed yourself and there's limits t'decency, if you know what I mean.'

'That ain't piss – we're all still sopping wet!'

'But we don't quite smell the way you do, Ilk.'

Snarling, he lurched away. Damned overly sensitive woman! 'My rapier,' he moaned.

'Shattered inside her skull, I'd wager,' said Gruntle, 'which couldn't have done her brain any good. Nicely done, Reccanto.'

Ilk decided it was time to strut a little.

Whilst Reccanto Ilk walked round like a rooster, Precious Thimble glanced over worriedly at the Boles, and was relieved to see them both apparently unharmed. They hadn't been paying her enough attention lately and they weren't paying her any now either. She felt a tremor of unease.

Master Quell was thumping on the cellar door. 'I know you can hear me,' he called. 'You, hiding in there. We got three of 'em – is there more? Three of 'em killed. Is there more?'

Faint was checking her weapons. 'We got to go and find Glanno,' she said. 'Any volunteers?'

Gruntle walked over, pausing to peer out of the doorway. 'The rain's letting off – looks as if the storm's spent. I'll go with you, Faint.'

'I was asking for volunteers – I wasn't volunteering myself.'

'I'll go!' said Amby.

'I'll go!' said Jula.

And then they glared at each other, and then grinned as if at some private joke, and a moment later both burst out laughing.

'What's so funny?' Precious Thimble demanded, truly bewildered this time. *Have they lost their minds? Assuming they have minds, I mean.*

Her harsh query sobered them and both ducked, avoiding her stare.

The cellar door creaked open, drawing everyone's attention, and a bewhiskered face poked out, eyes wide and rolling. 'Three, ya said? Ya said three?'

The dialect was Genabackan, the accent south islander.

'Ya got ah three? Deed?'

Quell nodded. 'Any more lurking about, host?'

A quick shake of the head, and the tavern keep edged out, flinching when he saw the slaughtered bodies. 'Oh, darlings,' he whispered, 'ahm so soory. So soory!'

'You know them?' Quell asked. 'You know what they were?'

More figures crowded behind the keep, pale faces, frightened eyes. To Quell's questions the whiskered man flinched. 'Coarsed,' he said in a rasp. 'Our daughters . . . coarsed.'

'Cursed? When they come of age, right?'

A jerky nod, and then the man's eyes widened on the wizard. 'You know it? You know the coarse?'

'How long have you had it, host? Here, in this village – how long have you had the curse?'

'Foor yars now. Foor yars.' And the man edged out. 'Aai, their heeds! Ya cart erf their heeds!' Behind him the others set up a wailing.

Precious Thimble met Quell's eyes and they exchanged a nod. 'Still about, I'd say,' Precious said under her breath.

'Agreed. Should we go hunting?'

She looked round once more. Mappo was dragging the first naked, headless corpse out through the doorway. The green blood had blackened on the floor and left tarry streaks trailing the body. 'Let's take that Trell with us, I think.'

'Good idea.' Quell walked up to the tavern keep. 'Is there a constable in this village? Who rules the land – where in Hood's name are we anyway?'

Owlish blinks of the eyes. 'Reach of Woe is war ye are. Seen the toower? It's war the Provost leeves. Yull wan the Provost, ah expeect.'

Quell turned away, rubbed at his eyes, then edged close to Precious Thimble. 'We're agreed, then, it's witchery, this curse.'

'Witch or warlock,' she said, nodding.

'We're on the Reach of Woe, a wrecker coast. I'd wager it's the arrival of strangers that wakes up the daughters – they won't eat their kin, will they?'

'When the frenzy's on them,' said Precious Thimble, 'they'll eat anything that moves.'

'That's why the locals bolted, then, right. Fine, Witch, go collect Mappo – and this time, tell him he needs to arm himself. This could get messy.'

Precious Thimble looked over at the last body the Trell was now dragging outside. 'Right,' she said.

Flanked by the Boles, Jula on his right, Amby on his left, Gruntle walked back down to the main street, boots squelching in the mud. The last spits of rain cooled his brow. Oh, he'd wanted a nastier fight. The problem with mindless attackers was their mindlessness, which made them pathetically predictable. And only three of the damned things—

'I was going first,' said Amby.

'No, I was,' said Jula.

Gruntle scowled. 'Going where? What are you two talking about?'

'That window back there,' said Jula, 'at the tavern. If'n the girlies got in through the door, I was goin' out through the window – only we couldn't get the shutters pulled back—'

'That was your fault,' said Amby. 'I kept lifting the latch and you kept pushing it back down.'

'The latch goes down to let go, Amby, you idiot.'

'No it goes up – it went up, I saw it—'

'And then back down—'

'Up.'

'Then down.'

Gruntle's sudden growl silenced them both. They were now following the hoof prints and various furrows of things being dragged in the wake of the animals. In the squat houses to either side, muted lights flickered through thick-glassed windows. The sound of draining water surrounded them, along with the occasional distant rumble of thunder. The air mocked with the freshness that came after a storm.

'There they are,' said Amby, pointing. 'Just past that low wall. You see them, Gruntle? You see them?'

A corral. The wreckage of the carriage high bench was scattered along the base of the stone wall.

Reaching it, they paused, squinted at the field of churned-up mud, the horses huddled at the far end – eyeing them suspiciously – and there, something sprawled near the middle. A body. Far off to the left was one of the carriage wheels.

Gruntle leading the way, they climbed the wall and set out for Glanno Tarp.

As they drew closer, they could hear him talking.

'. . . and so she wasn't so bad, compared to Nivvy, but it was years before I surrealized not all women talked that way, and if I'd a known, well, I probably would never have agreed to it. I mean, I have some decency in me, I'm sure of it. It was the way she carried on pretending she was nine years old, eyes so wide, all those cute things she did which, when you think about, was maybe cute some time, long ago, but now – I mean, her hair was going grey, for Hood's sake – oh, you found me. Good. No, don't move me just yet, my legs is broke and maybe a shoulder too, and an arm, wrist, oh, and this finger here, it's sprained. Get Quell – don't go moving me without Quell, all right? Thanks. Now, where was I? Nivvy? No, that stall keeper, Luft, now she didn't last, for the reasons I experplained before. It was months before I found me a new woman – well, before Coutre found me, would be more reaccurate. She'd just lost all her hair . . .'

The carriage wheel had moved slightly. Gruntle had caught the motion out of the corner of his eye and, leaving Glanno babbling on to the Boles, who stood looking down with mouths hanging open, he set out for it.

He sheathed his cutlasses and heaved at the wheel. It resisted until, with a thick slurping sound, it lifted clear of the mud and Gruntle pushed it entirely upright.

Cartographer was a figure seemingly composed entirely of clay, still bound by the wrists and ankle to the spokes. The face worked for a time, pushing out lumps of mud from its mouth, and then the corpse said, 'It's the jam-smeared bread thing, isn't it?'

'Look at that,' Quell said.

Precious Thimble made a warding gesture and then spat thrice, up, down, straight ahead. 'Blackdog Swamp,' she said. 'Mott Wood. This was why I left, dammit! That's the problem with Jaghut, they show up everywhere.'

Behind them, Mappo grunted but otherwise offered no comment.

The tower was something between square and round, the corners either weathered down by centuries and centuries of wind or deliberately softened to ease that same buffeting, howling wind. The entranceway was a narrow gloomy recess beneath a mossy lintel stone, the moss hanging in beards that dripped in a curtain of rainwater, each drop popping into eroded hollows on the slab of the landing.

'So,' said Quell with brittle confidence, 'the village Provost went and moved into a Jaghut tower. That was brave—'

'Stupid.'

'Stupidly brave, yes.'

'Unless,' she said, sniffing the air. 'That's the other problem with Jaghut. When they build towers, they live in them. For ever.'

Quell groaned. 'I was pretending not to think that, Witch.'

'As if that would help.'

'It helped me!'

'There's two things we can do,' Precious Thimble announced. 'We can turn right round and ignore the curse and all that and get out of this town as fast as possible.'

'Or?'

'We can go up to that door and knock.'

Quell rubbed at his chin, glanced back at a silent Mappo, and then once more eyed the tower. 'This witchery – this curse here, Precious, that strikes when a woman comes of age.'

'What about it? It's a damned old one, a nasty one.'

'Can you break it?'

'Not likely. All we can hope to do is make the witch or warlock change her or his mind about it. The caster can surrender it a whole lot more easily than someone else can break it.'

'And if we kill the caster?'

She shrugged. 'Could go either way, Wizard. Poof! Gone. Or . . . not. Anyway, you're stepping sideways, Quell. We were talking about this . . . this Provost.'

'Not sideways, Witch. I was thinking, well, about you and Sweetest Sufferance and Faint, that's all.'

All at once she felt as if she'd just swallowed a fistful of icy knuckles. Her throat ached, her stomach curdled. 'Oh, shit.'

'And since,' Quell went on remorselessly, 'it's going to be a day or two before we can effect repairs – at best – well . . .'

'I think we'd better knock,' she said.

'All right. Just let me, er, empty my bladder first.'

He walked off to the stone-lined gutter to his left. Mappo went off a few paces in the other direction, to rummage in his sack.

Precious Thimble squinted up at the tower. 'Well,' she whispered, 'if you're a Jaghut – and I think you are – you know we're standing right here. And you can smell the magic on our breaths. Now, we're not looking for trouble, but there's no chance you don't know nothing about that curse – we need to find that witch or warlock, you see, that nasty villager who made up this nasty curse, because we're stuck here for a few days. Understand? There's three women stuck here. And I'm one of them.'

'You say something?' Quell asked, returning.

'Let's go,' she said as Mappo arrived, holding an enormous mace.

They walked to the door.

Halfway there, it swung open.

'My mate,' said the Provost, 'is buried in the yard below.' He was standing at the window, looking out over the tumultuous seas warring with the shoals.

Quell grunted. 'What yard?' He leaned forward and peered down. 'What yard?'

The Provost sighed. 'It was there two days ago.' He turned from the window and eyed the wizard.

Who did his best not to quail.

Bedusk Pall Kovuss Agape, who called himself a Jaghut Anap, was simply gigantic, possibly weighing more than Mappo and at least a head and a half taller than the Trell. His skin was blue, a deeper hue than any Malazan Napan Quell could recall seeing. The blue even seemed to stain the silver-tipped tusks jutting from his lower jaw.

Quell cleared his throat. He needed to pee again, but that would have to wait. 'You lost her long ago?'

'Who?'

'Er, your mate?'

Bedusk Agape selected one of the three crystal decanters on the marble table, sniffed at its contents, and then refilled their goblets. 'Have you ever had a wife, Wizard?'

'No not that I'm aware of.'

'Yes, it can be like that at times.'

'It can?'

The Jaghut gestured towards the window. 'One moment there, the next . . . gone.'

'Oh, the cliff.'

'No, no. I was speaking of my wife.'

Quell shot Precious Thimble a helpless look. Off near the spiral staircase, Mappo stood examining an elaborate eyepiece of some kind, mounted on a spike with a peculiar ball-hinge that permitted the long black metal instrument to be swivelled about, side to side and up and down. The damned Trell was paying attention to all the wrong things.

Precious Thimble looked back at Quell with wide eyes.

'Loss,' stammered the wizard, 'is a grievous thing.'

'Well of course it is,' said Bedusk Agape, frowning.

'Um, not always. If, for example, one loses one's, er, virginity, or a favourite shiny stone, say . . .'

The red-rimmed eyes stayed steady, unblinking.

Quell wanted to squeeze his legs together – no, better, fold one over the other – lest his snake start drooling or, worse, spitting.

Precious Thimble spoke in a strangely squeaky voice, 'Jaghut Anap, the curse afflicting this village's daughters—'

'There have been twelve in all,' said Bedusk Agape. 'Thus far.'

'Oh. What happened to the other nine?'

The Jaghut flicked his gaze over to her. 'You are not the first trouble to arrive in the past few years. Of course,' he added, after sipping his wine, 'all the young girls are now sent to the next village along this coast – permanently, alas, which does not bode well for the future of this town.'

'I thought I saw women down in the tavern cellar,' said Precious Thimble.

'Bearing a child prevents the settling of the curse. Mothers are immune. Therefore, if you or your fellow female companions have at any time produced a child, you need not worry.'

'Um,' said Precious Thimble, 'I don't think any of us qualify.'

'How unfortunate,' said Bedusk.

'So how is it you got elected Provost?' Quell asked. 'Just curious, you see – I'm the nosy type, that's all. I didn't mean anything—'

'I believe it was a collective attempt to ameliorate my grief, my solitude. None would deny, I now expect, that such an invitation was ill-conceived.'

'Oh? Why?'

'Well, had I remained in my isolation, this terrible curse would not exist, I am afraid.'

'It's your curse, then?'

'Yes.'

A long moment of silence. From near the staircase, Mappo slowly turned to face them.

'Then you can end it,' said Quell.

'I could, yes, but I shall not.'

'Why?'

'Because you are not that important.'

Quell crossed his legs. 'May I ask, what happened to your mate?'

'We argued. I lost. I buried her.'

There seemed to be, at least to the wizard's thinking, something missing in that answer. But he was getting distracted by his bladder. He couldn't think straight.

'So,' said Precious Thimble in a thin voice, 'if you lose an argument to someone, you then kill them?'

'Oh, I didn't say she was dead.'

Mappo spoke from where he still stood, 'She is now, Jaghut.'

Bedusk Agape sighed. 'That does seem likely, doesn't it?'

'How long,' the Trell asked, 'was she pinned down? Your mate?'

'Nine years or so.'

'And the argument?'

'I sense a certain belligerence in you, Trell.'

'Belligerence, Jaghut?' Mappo bared his fangs in a cold grin. 'Your senses have dulled with disuse, I think.'

'I see. And you imagine you can best me?'

'I was asking you about the argument.'

'Something trivial. I have forgotten the details.'

'But you found yourself alone, at least until the villagers took pity on you and elected you their Provost. And then . . . you fell in love?'

Bedusk Agape winced.

Precious Thimble gasped. 'Oh! I see now. Oh, it's like that. She spurned you. You got mad, again, only this time you couldn't very well bury the whole village—'

'Actually, I considered it.'

'Um, well, you decided not to, then. So, instead, you worked up a curse, on her and all her young pretty friends, since they laughed at you or whatever. You turned them all into Tralka Vonan. Blood Feeders.'

'You cannot hope to break my curse, Witch,' said Bedusk. 'Even with the wizard's help, you will fail.' The Jaghut then faced Mappo. 'And you, Trell, even if you manage to kill me, the curse will not die.' He refilled his goblet for the third time. 'Your women will have a day or so before the curse takes effect. In that time, I suppose, they could all endeavour to become pregnant.'

All at once Quell sat straighter.

But when he saw Precious Thimble's expression, his delighted smile turned somewhat sheepish.

Down on the narrow strand of what had once been beach, at the foot of the raw cliff, waves skirled foam-thick tendrils through the chunks of clay and rock and black hairy roots, gnawing deep channels and sucking back into the sea milky, silt-laden water. The entire heap was in motion, settling, dissolving, sections collapsing under the assault of the waves.

Farther down the beach the strand reemerged, the white sand seemingly studded with knuckles of rust, to mark the thousands of ship nails and rivets that had been scattered in profusion along the shoreline. Fragments of wood formed a snagged barrier higher up, and beyond that, cut into the cliff face, weathered steps led up to a hacked-out cave mouth.

This cave was in fact a tunnel, rising at a steep angle up through the bowels of the promontory, to open out in the floor of the village's largest structure, a stone and timbered warehouse where the wreckers off-loaded their loot after the long haul of the carts from the cliff base. A tidy enterprise, all things considered, one that gave employment to all the folk of the village – from tending the false fires to rowing the deep-hulled boats out to the reef, where the stripping down of the wrecks took place, along with clubbing survivors and making sure they drowned. The local legend, concocted to provide meagre justification for such cruel endeavours, revolved around some long-ago pirate raids on the village, and how someone (possibly the Provost, who had always lived here, or the locally famous Gacharge Hadlorn Who Waits – but he left so there was no way to ask him) had suggested that, since the sea was so eager to deliver murderers to this shore, why could it not also deliver death to the would-be murderers? And so, once the notion was planted, the earth was tilled, with mallet and pick and flint and fire, and the days of fishing for a living off the treacherous shoals soon gave way to a far more lucrative venture.

Oh, the nets were cast out every now and then, especially in the calm season when the pickings got slim, and who could deny the blessing of so many fish these days, and fat, big ones at that? Why, it wasn't so long ago that they'd damned near fished out the area.

The beach was comfortable with half-eaten corpses rolling up on to the sands, where crabs and gulls swarmed. The beach helped pick the bones clean and then left them to the waves to bury or sweep away. On this fast-closing night, however, something unusual clawed its way to the shore. Unusual in that it still lived. Crabs scuttled from its path as fast as their tiny legs could manage.

Water sluiced from the figure as it heaved itself upright. Red-rimmed eyes scanned the scene, fixing at last on the steps and the gaping mouth of the cave. After a moment, it set out in that direction, leaving deep footprints that the beach hastened to smooth away.

———

'Do you really think I can't see what's going on in your skull, Quell? You're right there, first in line, with the three of us lying in a row, legs spread wide. And in you dive, worse than a damned dog on a tilted fence post. Reccanto waiting for his turn, and Glanno, and Jula and Amby and Mappo here and Gruntle and probably that damned undead—'

'Hold on a moment,' growled the Trell.

'Don't even try,' Precious Thimble snapped.

They were marching back to the tavern, Precious Thimble in the lead, the other two hastening to keep up. That she was tiny and needed two steps for every one of theirs seemed irrelevant.

'Then again,' she went on, 'maybe that Jaghut will go and jump the queue, and by the dawn we'll all be planted with some ghastly monster, half Trell, half Jaghut, half pissy wizard, half—'

'Twins?' asked Quell.

She swung a vicious glare back at him. 'Oh, funny.'

'Anyway,' added Quell, 'I'm pretty sure that's not how things like that work—'

'How would you know? No, me and Sweetest and Faint, we're out of here as soon as we can get our gear together – you can collect us somewhere down the road. This damned village can go to Hood, with Bedusk Pall Kovuss Agape in the lead. They're damned wreckers anyway, and if anybody deserves cursing to damnation, it's them.'

'I wouldn't disagree there,' said Mappo.

'Stop trying to get under my skirt, Trell.'

'What? I wasn't—'

Quell cut in with a snort. 'You don't wear skirts, Witch. Though if you did, it'd be so much easier—'

Now she spun round. 'What would be, Quell?'

He'd halted and now backed up. 'Sorry, did I think that out loud?'

'You think the curse on this village is bad, you just wait and see what I can come up with!'

'All right, we take your point, Precious. Relax. You three just go, right? We'll get the carriage fixed up and find you, just like you said.'

She whirled about once more and resumed her march.

Gruntle saw the three in the street, closing fast on the entrance to the tavern. He shouted to catch their attention and hurried over.

'Master Quell, your driver is a heap of broken bones back there, but he's still breathing.'

'Well, he should have let go of the damned reins,' Quell said in a growl. 'And now I got to do healing and that takes time. That's just great – how am I supposed to fix the carriage? Why can't anybody else do anything useful around here? You, Witch – go and heal Glanno—'

'I can't do that! Oh, I can set splints and spit on wounds to chase infection away, but it's sounding as if he needs a whole lot more than that. Right, Gruntle?'

The tattooed warrior shrugged. 'Probably.'

'Don't even try,' she snarled at him, and then stalked into the tavern.

Gruntle stared after her. 'What did she mean? Try what?'

'Getting under her skirt,' said Quell.

'But she doesn't wear—'

'That's not the point,' the wizard cut in. 'You're thinking like a man. That's your mistake. It's all our mistakes, in fact. It's why we're standing out here, three men, no women. If we'd gone and said, why, Precious, we wouldn't even think of it, you know what she'd say then? "What's wrong with me? Am I too ugly or something?" and we'd be in trouble all over again!'

Gruntle glanced bemusedly at Mappo, who, rather cryptically, simply nodded.

Quell straightened his still-wet clothes. 'Lead me to him, then, Gruntle.'

At one end of the corral there was a stable and next to it, a loading platform built of weathered planks that marked one end of a huge, solidly built warehouse. Jula and Amby had helped Glanno sit up, and Cartographer, cut loose from the wheel, was staggering in circles as he plucked and scraped manure off his face, neck, and rotted clothes.

Glanno had reached the eleventh love of his life, some woman named Herboo Nast, '. . . who wore a fox round her neck – not just its fur, you understand, the actual animal, paws trussed up in berbraided silk, gamuzzled in leather, but it was the beast's eyes I remember most – that look. Panic, like it'd just realized it was trapped in its worst nightlymare. Not that she wasn't good-looking, in that goatlike way of hers – you know, those long curly hairs that show up under their chin after a certain age – did I mention how I liked my women experientialled? I do. I most certainly do. I wanna see decades and decades of miserable livin' in their eyes, so that when I arrive, why, it's like a fresh spring rain on a withered daisy. Which one was I talking about? Fox, goat, panic, trussed up, right, Herboo Nast—'

He stopped then, so abruptly that neither Jula nor Amby noticed the sudden, ominous silence, and just kept on with the smiles and nods with which they had accompanied Glanno's monologue, and they were still smiling and nodding when the figure that had appeared on the warehouse loading platform – the one whose arrival had so thoroughly stunned Glanno Tarp's flapping tongue – walked up to halt directly in front of all three, as the horses bolted for the most distant corner of the corral in a drumroll of hoofs.

'No losses so far and that's good,' said Quell as he and Gruntle walked towards the corral.

'I didn't know you were a practitioner of Denul,' Gruntle said.

'I'm not, not really, I mean. I have elixirs, unguents, salves, and some of those are High Denul, for emergencies.'

'Like now.'

'Maybe. We'll see.'

'Broken legs—'

'Doesn't need legs to drive the carriage, does he? Besides, he might decline my services.'

'Why would he do that?'

'Healing expenses cut into his share. He could come out of this owing the Guild rather than the other way round.' He shrugged. 'Some people refuse.'

'Well,' said Gruntle, 'he said to get you, so I don't think he's going to refuse, Master Quell.'

They reached the low stone wall and then halted.

'Who in Hood's name is that?' Gruntle asked, squinting at the tall ragged figure standing with the Bole brothers.

Quell grunted, and then said, 'Well, and it's just a guess, mind you, but I'd say that that's the Provost's wife.'

'He's married to a Jaghut?'

'Was, until he buried her, but then the yard collapsed into the sea, taking her with it. And now she's back and I'd wager a trip's profit she's not in the best of moods.' And then he smiled up at Gruntle. 'We can work all this out. Oh, yes, we can work all this out, now.'

This confidence was shattered when Jula and Amby Bole suddenly took it upon themselves to attack the Jaghut. Bellowing, they flung themselves at her, and all three figures lurched about as they struggled, clawed, scratched and bit, until finally they lost their footing and toppled in a multilimbed mass that slopped heavily in the muck.

Quell and Gruntle scrambled over the wall and raced for them.

Glanno Tarp was shrieking something, his words unintelligible as he sought to crawl away from the scrap.

From the Jaghut woman sorcery erupted, a thundering, deafening detonation that lit up the entire corral and all the buildings nearby. Blinking against the sudden blindness, Gruntle staggered in the mud. He heard Quell fall beside him. The coruscating, actinic light continued to bristle, throwing everything into harsh shadows.

Glanno Tarp resumed his shrieks.

As vision returned, Gruntle saw, to his astonishment, that both Boles still lived. In fact, they had each pinned down an arm and were holding tight as the Jaghut woman thrashed and snarled.

Drawing his cutlasses, Gruntle made his way over. 'Jula! Amby! *What are you doing!*'

Two mud-smeared faces looked up, and their expressions were dark, twisted with anger.

'A swamp witch!' Jula said. 'She's one of them swamp witches!'

'We don't like swamp witches!' added Amby. 'We *kill* swamp witches!'

'Master Quell said this one can help us,' said Gruntle. 'Or she would have, if not for you two jumping her like that!'

'Cut her head off!' said Jula. 'That usually works!'

'I'm not cutting her head off. Let her go, you two—'

'She'll attack us!'

Gruntle crouched down. 'Jaghut – stop snarling – listen to me! If they let you go, will you stop fighting?'

Eyes burned as if aflame. She struggled some more, and then ceased all motion. The blazing glare dimmed, and after a few deep, rattling breaths, she nodded. 'Very well. Now get these two fools off me!'

'Jula, Amby – let go of her—'

'We will, once you cut her head off!'

'Do it now, Boles, or I will cut *your* heads off.'

'Do Amby first!'

'No, Jula first!'

'I've got two cutlasses here, boys, so I'll do it at the same time. How does that suit you?'

The Boles half lifted themselves up and glared across at each other.

'We don't like it,' said Amby.

'So leave off her, then.'

They rolled to the sides, away from the Jaghut woman, and she pulled her arms loose and clambered to her feet. The penumbra of sorcery dimmed, winked out. Breathing hard, she spun to face the Bole brothers, who'd rolled in converging arcs until they collided and were now crouched side by side in the mud, eyeing her like a pair of wolves.

Clutching his head, Master Quell stumbled up to them. 'You idiots,' he gasped. 'Jaghut, your husband's cursed this village. Tralka Vonan. Can you do anything about that?'

She was trying to wipe the mud from her rotted clothes. 'You're not from around here,' she said. 'Who are you people?'

'Just passing through,' Quell said. 'But our carriage needs repairs – and we got wounded—'

'I am about to destroy this village and everyone in it – does that bother you?'

Quell licked his muddy lips, made a face, and then said, 'That depends if you're including us in your plans of slaughter.'

'Are you pirates?'

'No.'

'Wreckers?'

'No.'

'Necromancers?'

'No.'

'Then,' she said, with another glare at the Boles, 'I suppose you can live.'

'Your husband says even if he dies, the curse will persist.'

She bared stained tusks. 'He's lying.'

Quell glanced at Gruntle, who shrugged in return and said, 'I'm not happy with the idea of pointless slaughter, but then, wreckers are the scum of humanity.'

The Jaghut woman walked towards the stone wall. They watched her.

'Master Quell,' said Glanno Tarp, 'got any splints?'

Quell shot Gruntle another look. 'Told you, the cheap bastard.'

At last the sun rose, lifting a rim of fire above the horizon on this the last day of the wrecker village on the Reach of Woe.

From a window of the tower, Bedusk Pall Kovuss Agape stood watching his wife approaching up the street. 'Oh,' he murmured, 'I'm in trouble now.'

In the moments before dawn, Kedeviss rose from her blankets and walked out into the darkness. She could make out the shape of him, sitting on a large boulder and staring northward. Rings spun on chains, glittering like snared stars.

Her moccasins on the gravel scree gave her away and she saw him twist round to watch her approach.

'You no longer sleep,' she said.

To this observation, Clip said nothing.

'Something has happened to you,' she continued. 'When you awoke in Bastion, you were . . . changed. I thought it was some sort of residue from the possession. Now, I am not so sure.'

He put away the chain and rings and then slid down from the boulder, landing lightly and taking a moment to straighten his cloak. 'Of them all,' he said in a low voice, 'you, Kedeviss, are the sharpest. You see what the others do not.'

'I make a point of paying attention. You've hidden yourself well, Clip – or whoever you now are.'

'Not well enough, it seems.'

'What do you plan to do?' she asked him. 'Anomander Rake will see clearly, the moment he sets his eyes upon you. And no doubt there will be others.'

'I was Herald of Dark,' he said.

'I doubt it,' she said.

'I was Mortal Sword to the Black-Winged Lord, to Rake himself.'

'He didn't choose you, though, did he? You worshipped a god who never answered, not a single prayer. A god who, in all likelihood, never even knew you existed.'

'And for that,' whispered Clip, 'he will answer.'

Her brows rose. 'Is this a quest for vengeance? If we had known—'

'What you knew or didn't know is irrelevant.'

'A Mortal Sword serves.'

'I said, Kedeviss, I was a Mortal Sword.'

'No longer, then. Very well, Clip, what are you now?'

In the grainy half-light she saw him smile, and something dark veiled his eyes. 'One day, in the sky over Bastion, a warren opened. A machine tumbled out, and down—'

She nodded. 'Yes, we saw that machine.'

'The one within brought with him a child god – oh, not deliberately. No, the mechanism of his sky carriage, in creating gates, in travelling from realm to realm, by its very nature cast a net, a net that captured this child god. And dragged it here.'

'And this traveller – what happened to him?'

Clip shrugged.

She studied him, head cocked to one side. 'We failed, didn't we?'

He eyed her, as if faintly amused.

'We thought we'd driven the Dying God from you – instead, we drove him deeper. By destroying the cavern realm where he dwelt.'

'You ended his pain, Kedeviss,' said Clip. 'Leaving only his . . . hunger.'

'Rake will destroy you. Nor,' she added, 'will we accompany you to Black Coral. Go your own way, godling. We shall find our own way there—'

He was smiling. 'Before me? Shall we race, Kedeviss – me with my hunger and you with your warning? Rake does not frighten me – the Tiste Andii do not frighten me. When they see me, they will see naught but kin – until it is too late.'

'Godling, if in poring through Clip's mind you now feel you understand the Tiste Andii, I must tell you, you are wrong. Clip was a barbarian. Ignorant. A fool. He knew nothing.'

'I am not interested in the Tiste Andii – oh, I will kill Rake, because that is what he deserves. I will feed upon him and take his power into me. No, the one I seek is not in Black Coral, but within a barrow outside the city. Another young god – so young, so helpless, so naïve.' His smile returned. 'And he knows I am coming for him.'

'Must we then stop you ourselves?'

'You? Nimander, Nenanda, all you *pups*? Now really, Kedeviss.'

'If you—'

His attack was a blur – one hand closing about her throat, the other covering her mouth. She felt her throat being crushed and scrabbled for the knife at her belt.

He spun her round and flung her down to the ground, so hard that the back of her head crunched on the rocks. Dazed, her struggles weakened, flailed, fell away.

Something was pouring out from his hand where it covered her mouth, something that numbed her lips, her jaws, then forced its way into her mouth and down her throat. Thick as tree sap. She stared up at him, saw the muddy gleam of the Dying God's eyes – dying no longer, now freed – and thought: *what have we done?*

He was whispering. 'I could stop now, and you'd be mine. It's tempting.'

Instead, whatever oozed from his hand seemed to burgeon, sliding like a fat, sleek serpent down her throat, coiling in her gut.

'But you might break loose – just a moment's worth, but enough to warn the others, and I can't have that.'

Where the poison touched, there was a moment of ecstatic need, sweeping through her, but that was followed almost instantly by numbness, and then something . . . darker. She could smell her own rot, pooling like vapours in her brain.

He is killing me. Even that knowledge could not awaken any strength within her.

'I need the rest of them, you see,' he was saying. 'So we can walk in, right in, without anyone suspecting anything. I need my way in, that's all. Look at Nimander.' He snorted. 'There is no guile in him, none at all. He will be my shield. *My shield.*'

He was no longer gripping her neck. It was no longer necessary.

Kedeviss stared up at him as she died, and her final, fading thought was: *Nimander . . . guileless! Oh, but you don't . . .* And then there were nothing.

The nothing that no priest dared speak of, that no holy scripture described, that no seer or prophet set forth in ringing proclamation. The nothing, this nothing, it is the soul in waiting.

Comes death, and now the soul waits.

Aranatha opened her eyes, sat up, then reached out to touch Nimander's shoulder. He awoke, looked at her with a question in his eyes.

'He has killed Kedeviss,' she said, the words soft as a breath.

Nimander paled.

'She was right,' Aranatha went on, 'and now we must be careful. Say nothing to anyone else, not yet, or you will see us all die.'

'*Kedeviss.*'

'He has carried her body to a crevasse, and thrown her into it, and now he makes signs on the ground to show her careless steps, the way the edge gave way. He will come to us in shock and grief. Nimander, you must display no suspicion, do you understand?'

And she saw that his own grief would sweep all else aside – at least for now – which was good. Necessary. And that the anger within him, the rage destined to come, would be slow to build, and as it did she would speak to him again, and give him the strength he would need.

Kedeviss had been the first to see the truth – or so it might have seemed. But Aranatha knew that Nimander's innocence was not some innate flaw, not some fatal weakness. No, his innocence was a choice he had made. The very path of his life. And he had his reasons for that.

Easy to see such a thing and misunderstand it. Easy to see it as a failing, and to then believe him irresolute.

Clip had made this error from the very beginning. And so too this Dying God, who knew only what Clip believed, and thought it truth.

She looked down and saw tears held back, waiting for Clip's sudden arrival with his tragic news, and Aranatha nodded and turned away, to feign sleep.

Somewhere beyond the camp waited a soul, motionless as a startled hare. This was sad. Aranatha had loved Kedeviss dearly, had admired her cleverness, her percipience. Had cherished her loyalty to Nimander – even though Kedeviss had perhaps suspected the strange circumstances surrounding Phaed's death, and had seen how Phaed and her secrets haunted Nimander still.

When one can possess loyalty even in the straits of full, brutal understanding, then that one understands all there is to understand about compassion.

Kedeviss, you were a gift. And now your soul waits, as it must. For this is the fate of the Tiste Andii. Our fate. We will wait.

Until the wait is over.

Endest Silann stood with his back to the rising sun. And to the city of Black Coral. The air was chill, damp with night's breath, and the road wending out from the gates that followed the coastline of the Cut was a bleak, colourless ribbon that snaked into stands of dark conifers half a league to the west. Empty of traffic.

The cloak of eternal darkness shrouding the city blocked the sun's stretching rays, although the western flanks of the jumbled slope to their right was showing gilt edges; and far off to the left, the gloom of the Cut steamed white from the smooth, black surface.

'There will be,' said Anomander Rake, 'unpleasantness.'

'I know, Lord.'

'It was an unanticipated complication.'

'Yes, it is.'

'I will walk,' said Rake, 'until I reach the tree line. Out of sight, at least until then.'

'Have you waited too long, Lord?'

'No.'

'That is well, then.'

Anomander Rake rested a hand on Endest's shoulder. 'You have ever been, my friend, more than I deserve.'

Endest Silann could only shake his head, refuting that.

'If we are to live,' Rake went on, 'we must take risks. Else our lives become deaths in all but name. There is no struggle too vast, no odds too overwhelming, for even should we fail – should we fall – we will know that we have lived.'

Endest nodded, unable to speak. There should be tears streaming down his face, but he was dry inside – his skull, behind his eyes, all . . . dry. Despair was a furnace where everything had burned up, where everything was ashes, but the heat remained, scalding, brittle and fractious.

'The day has begun.' Rake withdrew his hand and pulled on his gauntlets. 'This walk, along this path . . . I will take pleasure in it, my friend. Knowing that you stand here to see me off.'

And the Son of Darkness set out.

Endest Silann watched. The warrior with his long silver hair flowing, his leather cloak flaring out. Dragnipur a scabbarded slash.

Blue seeped into the sky, shadows in retreat along the slope. Gold painted the tops of the tree line where the road slipped in. At the very edge, Anomander Rake paused, turned about and raised one hand high.

Endest Silann did the same, but the gesture was so weak it made him gasp, and his arm faltered.

And then the distant figure swung round.

And vanished beneath the trees.

Book Four

Toll the Hounds

Like broken slate
We take our hatred
And pile it high
Rolling with the hills
A ragged line to map
Our rise and fall
And I saw suffused
With the dawn
Crows aligned in rows
Along the crooked wall
Come to feed

Bones lie scattered
At the stone's foot
The heaped ruin
Of past assaults
The crows face each way
To eye the pickings
On both sides
For all its weakness
The world cannot break
What we make
Of our hatred

I watched the workers
Carry each grey rock
They laboured
Blind and stepped
Unerringly modest paths
Piece by sheared piece
They built a slaughter
Of innocent others
While muttering as they might
Of waves of weather
And goodly deeds

WE THE BUILDERS
HANASP TULAR

Chapter Nineteen

Pray you never hear an imprecise breath
Caught in its rough web
Every god turns away at the end
And not a whisper sounds
Do not waste a lifetime awaiting death
Caught in its rough web
It hovers in the next moment you must attend
As your last whisper sounds
Pray you never hear an imprecise breath

ROUGH WEB
FISHER

The soul knows no greater anguish than to take a breath that begins in love and ends with grief.

Time unravels now. Event clashes upon event. So much to recount, pray this sad-eyed round man does not falter, does not grow too breathless. History has its moments. To dwell within one is to understand nothing. We are rocked in the tumult, and the awareness of one's own ignorance is a smothering cloak that proves poor armour. You will flinch with the wounds. We shall all flinch.

As might a crow or an owl, or indeed a winged eel, hover now a moment above this fair city, its smoke haze, the scurrying figures in the streets and lanes, the impenetrable dark cracks of narrow alleyways. Thieves' Road spreads a tangled web between buildings. Animals bawl and wives berate husbands and husbands bellow back, night buckets gush from windows down into the guttered alleys and – in some poorer areas of the Gadrobi District – into streets where pedestrians duck and dodge in the morning ritual of their treacherous journeys to work, or home. Clouds of flies are stirred awake with the dawn's light. Pigeons revive their hopeless struggle to walk straight lines. Rats creep back into their closed-in refuges after yet another night of seeing far too much. The night's damp smells are burned off and new stinks arise in pungent vapours.

And on the road, where it passes through the leper colony west of the city, a weary ox and a tired old man escort a burdened cart on which lies a canvas-wrapped figure, worn riding boots visible.

Ahead awaits Two-Ox Gate.

Hover no longer. Plummet both wings and spirit down to the buzzing flies, the animal heat sweet and acrid, the musty closeness of the stained burlap. The old man pausing to wipe sweat from his lined brow with its array of warts and moles, and his knees ache and there is dull pain in his chest.

Of late, he has been carting corpses round day and night, or so it seems. Each one made him feel older, and the glances he has been casting at the ox are tainted with an irrational dislike, wavering in its intensity, as if the beast was to blame for . . . for something, though he knows not what.

The two guards at the gate were leaning against a wall, staying cool in the shade that would dwindle as the day rolled on overhead. Upon seeing the jutting boots one of the men stepped forward. 'Hold, there. You'll find plenty of cemeteries and pits outside the walls – we don't need more—'

'A citizen of the city,' said the old man. 'Killt in a duel. By Councillor Vidikas, who said to send him back to his friends – the dead man's friends, I mean.'

'Oh, right. On your way, then.'

Crowded as a city can be, an ox drawing a corpse-laden cart will find its path clear, for reasons involving a host of instinctive aversions, few of which made much sense. To see a dead body was to recoil, mind spinning a dust-devil of thoughts – *that is not me – see the difference between us! That is not me, that is not me. No one I know, no one I have ever known. That is not me . . . but . . . it could be.*

So easily, it could be.

Remonstrance of mortality is a slap in the face, a stinging shock. It is a struggle for one to overcome this moment, to tighten the armour about one's soul, to see bodies as nothing but objects, unpleasant, to be disposed of quickly. Soldiers and undertakers fashion macabre humour to deflect the simple, raw horror of what they must see, of that to which they are witness. It rarely works. Instead, the soul crawls away, scabbed, wounded, at peace with nothing.

A soldier goes to war. A soldier carries it back home. Could leaders truly comprehend the damage they do to their citizens, they would never send them to war. And if, in knowing, they did so anyway – to appease their hunger for power – then may they choke on the spoils for ever more.

Ah, but the round man digresses. Forgive this raw spasm of rage. A friend lies wrapped in canvas on the bed of a cart. Death is on its way home. Forgive.

Wending through Gadrobi District, life parted its stream, voices dimmed, and it was some time after the passing through of death that those voices arose once more in its wake. Curtains of flies repeatedly billowed open and closed again, until it seemed the ox pulled a stage of a thousand acts, each one the same, and the chorus was a bow wave of silence.

Journey on, comes the prayer of all, journey on.

At last, the old man finds his destination and draws the ox up opposite the doors, halting the beast with a tug on its yoke. He spends a moment brushing dust from his clothes, and then heads inside the Phoenix Inn.

It has been a long night. He hobbles to a table and catches the eye of one of the servers. He orders a tankard of strong ale and a breakfast. Stomach before business. The body's not going anywhere, is it?

He did not know if it was love; he suspected he did not understand that word. But there was something inside Cutter that felt . . . sated. Was it just physical, these tangled pitches and rolls and the oil of sweat, breaths hot in his face with the scent of wine and rustleaf? Was it just the taste of the forbidden, upon which he fed as might a bat on nectar? If so, then he should have felt the same when with Scillara, perhaps even more so, since without question Scillara's skills in that area far eclipsed those of Challice, whose hunger whispered of insatiable needs, transforming her lovemaking into a frantic search that found no appeasement, no matter how many times she convulsed in orgasm.

No, something was indeed different. Still, he was troubled, wondering if this strange flavour came from the betrayal they committed time and again. A married woman, the sordid man's conquest. Had he become such a man? Well, he supposed that he had, but not in the manner of those men who made a career of seducing and stealing the wives of other men. And yet, there was a sense, an extraordinary sense, he admitted, of dark pleasure, savage delight, and he could see just how addictive such living could become.

Even so, he was not about to pursue the headlong pitch of promiscuity. There remained a part of him that thirsted for an end – or, rather, a continuation: love and life made stable, forces of reassurance and comfort. He was not about to toss Challice aside and seek out a new lover. He was, he told himself, not Murillio, who could travel with practised ease from bedroom to bedroom – and see where it had got *him*, damn near murdered by some drunken suitor.

Oh, there was a lesson there, yes. At least it seemed that Murillio had heeded it, if the rumours of his "retirement" were accurate. *And what about me? Have I taken note? It seems not. I still go to her, I still plunge into this betrayal. I go to her, so hungry, so desperate, it is as if we have remade ourselves into perfect reflections. Me and Challice. Hand in hand in our descent.*

Because it makes the fall easier, doesn't it?

There was nothing to stop Gorlas Vidikas from exacting vengeance. He would be entirely within his rights to hunt them both down and murder them, and a part of Cutter would not blame him if he did just that.

He was thinking such thoughts as he walked to the annexe warehouse, but they did little to assail his anticipation. Into each other's arms again, desire hot as a fever in their mouths, their hands, their groins. Proof, to Cutter's mind, of the claims of some scholars that humans were but animals – clever ones, but animals none the less. There was no room for thinking, no space for rationality. Consequences thinned to ethereal ghosts, snatched in with the first gasp and flung away in the next. Only the moment mattered.

He made no effort to disguise himself, no effort to mask the destination of his journey, and he well knew how the locals around the warehouse watched him, with that glittering regard that was envy and disgust and amusement in equal parts; much as they had watched Challice perhaps only moments earlier, although in her case lust probably warred with all the other emotions. No, this affair was a brazen thing, and that in itself somehow made it all the more erotic.

There was heat in his mind as he used his key to open the office door, and when he stepped within he could smell her perfume in the dusty air. Through the office and into the cavernous warehouse interior, and then to the wooden steps leading to the loft.

She must have heard his ascent, for she was standing facing the door when he arrived.

Something in her eyes stopped him.

'You have to save me,' she said.

'What has happened?'

'Promise you'll save me, my love. Promise!'

He managed a step forward. 'Of course. What's—'

'He knows.'

The heat of desire evaporated. He was suddenly cold inside.

Challice drew closer and in her face he saw an expression he struggled to identify, and when he did the cold turned into ice. *She is . . . excited.*

'He will kill you. And me. He'll kill us both, Crokus!'

'As is his right—'

In her eyes a sudden fear, and she fixed him with it for a long moment before turning round. 'Maybe *you* have no problem with dying,' she hissed as she walked to the bed, where she faced him again. 'But I have!'

'What do you want me to do?'

'You know what to do.'

'What we *should* do,' he said, 'is run. Take what you can and let's just run. Find some other city—'

'No! I don't want to leave here! I *like* it here! I like the way I live, Crokus!'

'It was just a day or two ago, Challice, that you were lying in my arms and talking about escaping—'

'Just dreams – that wasn't real. I mean, the dream wasn't real. Wasn't realistic – just a stupid dream. You can't take any notice of what I say after we've . . . been together. I just come out with any old thing. Crokus, we're in trouble. We have to do something – we have to do it *now*.'

You just come out with any old thing, do you, Challice? But it's only after we've been together that you say you love me.

'He'll kill me,' she whispered.

'That doesn't sound like the Gorlas you've been describing.'

She sat down on the bed. 'He confronted me. Yesterday.'

'You didn't mention—'

She shook her head. 'It seemed, well, it seemed it was just the usual game. He said he wanted to know about you, and I said I'd tell him when he got back – he's at the mines right now. And then, and then, walking here just now – O gods! I suddenly understood! Don't you see? *He was asking about the man he planned to kill!*'

'So he plans to kill me. What of it, Challice?'

She bared her teeth, and it was an expression so brutal, so ugly, that Cutter was shocked. 'I said I *understood*. First you. Then he'll come back to me, so he can tell me what he did to you. In every detail. He will use every word like a knife – until he pulls out the real one. And then he'll cut my throat.' She looked up at him. 'Is that what you want? Does his killing me matter to you, Crokus?'

'He won't kill you—'

'You don't know him!'

'It sounds as if you don't, either.' At her glare, he added, 'Look, assume he'll take pleasure in killing me, and he will. And then, even more pleasure in telling you all about it – yes? We're agreed on that?'

She nodded, a single motion, tight.

'But if he then kills you, what has he got? Nothing. No, he'll want you to do it again, with someone else. Over and over again, and each time it'll turn out the same – he kills your lover, he tells you about it. He doesn't want all that to end. The man's a duellist, right, one who likes killing his opponents. This way, he can lawfully do it to as many men as you care to collect, Challice. He wins, you win—'

'How can you say *I win*!'

'—because,' he finished, 'neither of you gets bored.'

She stared at him as if he had just kicked in some invisible door hidden inside her. And then recovered. 'I don't want you to die, Crokus. Cutter – I keep forgetting. It's *Cutter* now. A dangerous name. An *assassin's* name. Careful, or someone might think there's something real behind it.'

'Which is it, Challice? You don't want me to die. Or am I the man I pretend to be? What is it, exactly, you're trying to appeal to?'

'But I love you!'

And there was that word again. And whatever it meant to her probably was not what it meant to him – not that he knew what it meant to him, of course. He moved to one side, as if intent on circling the bed even if it took him through the outer wall, then halted and ran his hands through his hair. 'Have you been leading me to this moment all along?'

'What?'

He shook his head. 'Just wondering out loud. It's not important.'

'I want my life as it is, Cutter, only without him. I want you instead of him. That's how I want it.'

What would Murillio say in this situation? But no, I'm not Murillio.

Still . . .

He'd be out through this window in a heartbeat. Duels with wronged husbands? Hood's breath! He faced her. 'Is that what you want?'

'I just told you it was!'

'No, that's not what I meant. I meant . . . oh, never mind.'

'You have to do it. For me. For us.'

'He's at the mines west of the city? For how much longer?'

'Two days at least. You can go out there.'

And suddenly she was standing in front of him, hands on the sides of his face, her body pressing hard, and he stared down into her dilated eyes.

Excitement.

I used to think . . . that look – this look . . . I used to think . . .

'My love,' she whispered. 'It has to be done. You see that, don't you?'

But it was always this, just this. Leading up to this moment. Where she was taking me – or have I got it all wrong?

'Challice—'

But her mouth was on his now, and she swallowed down all his words, until none were left.

Spin round and rush back. Murillio still lies in the dust, a crowd mechanically cheering in the pit below. The day draws to a close, and a youth named Venaz gathers his gang of followers and sets out for the tunnel called Steep.

Not much need be said about Venaz. But let us give him this. Sold to the mine by his stepfather – dear Ma too drunk to even lift her head when the collectors showed up and if she heard the clinking of coins, well, her thoughts would have crawled the short distance to the moment when she could buy another bottle, and no further. That had been four years ago.

The lesson that a child is not loved, not even by the one who bore it, delivers a most cruel wound. One that never heals, but instead stretches scar tissue over the mind's eye, so that for that orphan's entire life the world beyond is tainted, and it sees what others do not, and is blinded by perpetual mistrust to all that the heart feels. Such was Venaz, but to know is not to excuse, and we shall leave it there.

Venaz's pack consisted of boys a year or so younger than him. They vied with each other for position in the pecking order and were as vicious individually as they were in a group. They were just versions of him, variations only on the surface. They followed and would do anything he told them to, at least until he stumbled, made a mistake. And then they would close in like half-starved wolves.

Venaz walked emboldened, excited, delighted at this amazing turn of events. The Big Man wanted Harllo and not to pat him on the head either. No, there would be even more blood spilled on this day, and if Venaz could work it right, why, he might be the one to spill it – at the Big Man's nod, that's all it would take, and maybe the Big Man would see how good Venaz could be. Good enough, maybe, to recruit him into his own household. Every noble needed people like Venaz, to do the ugly stuff, the bad stuff.

They reached the slope leading to the mouth of the tunnel. Three grown-ups were trying to fix the axle of a cart and they looked up when Venaz arrived.

'Where's Bainisk?' Venaz asked.

'New vein,' one of them replied. 'He in trouble again?'

'He got his moles with him?' It felt good being so important he didn't have to answer the man's question.

Shrugs all round.

Venaz scowled. 'Has he got his moles with him?'

The one who'd spoken slowly straightened. His backhanded slap caught Venaz by surprise, and was hard enough to knock the boy back. He was then grabbed and thrown on to the stony ground. The man stood over him. 'Watch your mouth.'

Venaz sat up, glaring. 'You ain't seen what just happened? Up on the ridge?'

Another grunted. 'We heard 'bout something.'

'A duel – the Big Man killed someone!'

'So what?'

'And then he called for Harllo! He wants Harllo! And I come to get him and you're stopping me and when he hears—'

He got no further as the man who had struck him now grasped him by the throat and dragged him to his feet. 'He won't hear nothing, Venaz. You think we give a fuck about Vidikas having a fuckin' duel? Killin' some poor bastard for what? Our entertainment?'

'He's turnin' blue, Haid. Better loosen yer grip some.'

Venaz gasped an agonizing lungful of air.

'Get it right, lad,' Haid went on, 'Vidikas *owns* us. We're pieces of meat to him, right? So he puts out a call for one of us and for what? Why, to chew it up, that poor piece of meat. And what, you think that's a fuckin' good idea? Get outa my sight, Venaz, but you can count on me rememberin' this.'

The pack was huddled together now, white-faced, but among some of them there was something rather more calculating. Was this the moment to usurp Venaz?

The three men went back to working on the axle. Venaz, his colour returning to normal, dusted himself off and then set out in a stiff-legged march towards the tunnel mouth. His pack fell in behind him.

As they plunged into the cool gloom Venaz wheeled. 'That was Haid and Favo and Dule, right? Remember them names. They're on my list now, all three of them. They're on my list.'

Faces nodded.

And those who had been weighing their chances each realized that the moment had passed. They'd been too slow. Venaz had a way of recovering, and fast, scary fast. He was, they reminded themselves yet again, going places, without a doubt.

Harllo slid along the vein, feeling with his bared stomach the purity of the black silver and, yes, it *was* silver and where had it come from when all they'd been working for so long was copper up on the skins and iron down deep? But it felt so beautiful, this silver. Better than gold, better than anything.

Wait till he told Bainisk and Bainisk told the foreman! They'd be heroes. They might even get extra portions at supper, or a cup of watered wine!

The chute was narrow, so small they'd need moles for weeks before it got worked out big enough to take the pickers, so there was a good chance that Harllo would be seeing – and feeling – a lot more of this silver, every day, maybe.

And all that trouble from before would go away, just like that – he knew it would—

'Harllo!'

The voice whispered up from somewhere behind his feet, reminding him that he was still head down and that could be dangerous. He might pass out and not even know it. 'I'm all right, Bainisk! I found—'

'Harllo! Get back here right now!'

A shiver ran through Harllo. Bainisk's voice didn't sound right. It sounded . . . scared.

But that wouldn't last, would it? Not with the silver—

'Hurry!'

Moving backwards was never easy. He pushed with his hands, squirmed and pressed his toes against the hard stone and then extended his heels. There were leather pads tied to his feet for this purpose, but it still hurt. Like a caterpillar, gathering up and then pushing, bit by bit, working his way back up the chute.

All at once hands grasped his ankles and he was being roughly dragged.

Harllo cried out as his chin struck an obstruction and when he lifted his head up the top crunched on rock, scraping away skin and hair. 'Bainisk! What—'

He fell free of the chute, thumping down. The hands released his ankles and now grasped his upper arms, lifting him to his feet.

'Bainisk—'

'Shhh! Word's come down – someone came to find you – from the city.'

'What?'

'Vidikas killed him – in a duel – and now he's called for you to be brought to him. It's bad, Harllo. I think he's going to kill you!'

But this was too much to hear, too much all at once – someone had come – who? Gruntle! And Vidikas had . . . had killed him. *No. He couldn't have – he didn't—*

'Who was he?' he asked.

'I don't know. Listen, we're going to escape, you and me, Harllo – do you understand?'

'But how can we—'

'We're going deeper in, to the Settle—'

'But that's not safe—'

'There are huge cracks on that side – some of them, they got to go right up and out, lakeside. We get there, and then along the shoreline, all the way back to the city!'

They had been hissing back and forth, and now they heard shouts echoing down from the main passage.

'Venaz – that figures, doesn't it? Come on, Harllo, we got to go *now*!'

They set out, each with a lantern, Bainisk taking a coil of rope as well, down through the fresh workings – there was no one there yet, as first the air had been bad and then there'd been flooding and only the shift before the last of the hoses was snaked out to see how much more water was seeping back in. After fifty or so paces they were ankle-deep in icy water and flows slicked the side walls and drops rained down from the ceiling. The farther in they went, the more cracks they saw – everywhere, all sides, above and below – proof that they were reaching the Settle, where half a cliff was sinking towards the lake. The rumours were that it was only days from collapse.

The tunnel descended in irregular shelves, and now the water was at Harllo's thighs, numbingly cold. Both were gasping.

'Bainisk – will this go back up?'

'It will, if the water's not too deep, it will, I promise.'

'Why – why are you doing this? You should've just handed me over.'

Bainisk was some time before answering. 'I want to see it, Harllo.'

'You want to see what?'

'The city. I – I just want to see it, that's all. When I heard, well, it was as if everything fell into place. This was the time – our best chance – this close to the Settle.'

'You'd been thinking about this.'

'Yes. Harllo, I *never* stop thinking about this.'

'The city.'

'The city.'

Something clanged somewhere behind them – still distant, but closer than expected.

'Venaz! They're after us – shit – come on, Harllo, we got to hurry.'

The water reached Harllo's hips. He was having trouble working his legs. He kept stumbling. Twice he almost let his lantern sink down too far. Their desperate gasping echoed on all sides, along with sloshing water.

'Bainisk, I can't—'

'Drop your light – just take hold of my shirt – I'll pull you. Don't let go.'

Groaning, Harllo let the lantern sink into the water. A sudden hiss, something cracking. When he released the handle the lantern vanished into the blackness. He took hold of Bainisk's ragged shirt.

They continued on, Harllo feeling his legs trailing behind him but only from the hips – below that there was nothing. A strange lassitude flowed into him, taking away the icy cold. Bainisk was chest-deep now, whimpering as he sought to keep the lantern held high.

They stopped.

'The tunnel goes under,' said Bainisk.

'Issallright, Bainisk. We gan stop now.'

'No, hold on to this ledge. I'm going under. I won't be long. I promise.'

He set the lantern on a narrow ledge. And then he sank down and was gone.

Harllo was alone. It would be much easier to let go, to relax his aching hands. Venaz was coming, he'd be here soon. And then it would be over. The water was warm now – that might be one way to escape them. Do what Bainisk had just done. Just sink away, vanish.

He wasn't wanted, he knew. Not by his mother, not by anyone. And the one who'd come to find him, well, that man had died for that. And that wasn't right. Nobody should go and die for Harllo. Not Gruntle, not Bainisk, not anybody. So, no more of any of that – he could let go—

Foaming water, thrashing, gasps and coughs. An icy hand clutched at Harllo.

'We can get through! Harllo – the tunnel on the other side – it slopes upward!'

'I can't—'

'You have to! The city, Harllo, you have to show it to me – I'd be lost. I need you, Harllo. *I need you.*'

'All right, but . . .' He was about to tell Bainisk the truth. About the city. That it wasn't the paradise he'd made it out to be. That people starved there. That people did bad things to each other. But no, that could wait. It'd be bad to talk about those things right now. 'All right, Bainisk.'

They left the lantern. Bainisk uncoiled some of the rope and tied the end about Harllo's waist, fumbling with numbed hands on the knot. 'Take a few deep breaths first,' he said. 'And then one more, deep as you can.'

The plunge into the dark left Harllo instantly disoriented. The rope round his waist pulled him down and then into the face of the current. He opened his eyes and felt the thrill of shock from the icy flow. Strange glowing streaks flashed past, possibly from the rock itself, or perhaps they were but ghosts lurking behind his eyes. At first he sought to help Bainisk, flailing with his arms and trying to kick, but after a moment he simply went limp.

Either Bainisk would pull them both through, or he wouldn't. Either way was fine.

His mind began to drift, and he so wanted to take a breath – he couldn't hold back much longer. His lungs were burning. The water would be cool, cool enough to quench that fire for ever more. Yes, he could do that.

Cold bit into his right hand – *what?* And then his head was lifted above the surface. And he was sucking in icy lungfuls of air.

Darkness, the rush and gurgle of water flowing past, seeking to pull him back, back and down. But Bainisk was tugging him along, and it was getting shallower as the tunnel widened. The black, dripping ceiling seemed to be sagging, forming a crooked spine overhead. Harllo stared up at it, wondering how he could see at all.

And then he was being dragged across broken stone.

They halted, lying side by side.

Before too long, the shivering began. Racing into Harllo like demonic possession, a spirit that shook through him with rabid glee. His teeth chattered uncontrollably.

Bainisk was plucking at him. Through clacking teeth he said, 'Venaz won't stop. He'll see the lantern – he'll know. We got to keep going, Harllo. It's the only way to get warm again, the only way to get away.'

But it was so hard to climb to his feet. His legs still didn't work properly. Bainisk had to help him and he leaned heavily on the bigger boy as they staggered skidding upslope along the scree-scattered path.

It seemed to Harllo that they walked for ever, into and out of faint light. Sometimes the slope pitched downward, only to slowly climb yet again. Pain throbbed in Harllo's legs now, but it was welcome – life was returning, filled with its stubborn fire, and now he wanted to live, now it mattered more than anything else.

'Look!' Bainisk gasped. 'At what we're walking on – Harllo, look!'

Phosphorescent mould limned the walls, and in the faint glow Harllo could make out the vague shapes of the rubble underfoot. Broken pottery. Small fragments of burned bone.

'It's got to lead up,' Bainisk said. 'To some cave. The Gadrobi used them to bury their ancestors. A cave overlooking the lake. We're almost there.'

Instead, they reached a cliff ledge.

And stood, silent.

A vertical section of rock had simply plummeted away, leaving a broad gap. The bottom of the fissure was swallowed in black, from which warm air rose in dry gusts. Opposite them, ten or more paces across, a slash of diffuse light revealed the continuation of the tunnel they had been climbing.

'We'll climb down,' said Bainisk, uncoiling the rope and starting to tie a knot at one end. 'And then back up. We can do this, you'll see.'

'What if the rope's not long enough? I can't see the bottom, Bainisk.'

'We'll just find more handholds.' Now he was tying a loop at the other end which he then set round a knoblike projection. 'I'll throw a snake back up to dislodge this, so we can take the rope with us for the climb up the other side. Now, you go first.' He tossed the rest of the rope over the edge. They heard it snap out to its full length. Bainisk grunted. 'Like I said, we can find handholds.'

Harllo worked his way over the side, gripping hard the wet rope – it wanted to slide through, but if that happened he knew he was dead, so he held tight. His feet scrambled, found shallow ledges running at an angle across the cliff-face. Not much, but they eased the strain. He began working his way down.

He was perhaps three body-lengths down when Bainisk began following. The rope began swaying unpredictably, and Harllo found his feet slipping from their scant purchases again and again, each time resulting in a savage tug on his arms.

'Bainisk!' he hissed. 'Wait! Let me go a little farther down first – you're throwing me about.'

'Okay. Go on.'

Harllo found purchase again and resumed the descent.

If Bainisk started up again he no longer felt the sways and tugs. The rope was getting wetter, which meant that he was reaching its end – the water was soaking its way down. And then he reached the sodden knot. Sudden panic as he sought to find projections in the wall for his feet. There were very few – the stone was almost sheer.

'Bainisk! I'm at the knot!' He craned his neck to look down. Blackness, unrelieved, depthless. 'Bainisk! Where are you?'

Since Harllo's first call, Bainisk had not moved. The last thing he wanted to do was accidentally dislodge the boy, not after they'd made it this far. And, truth be told, he was experiencing a growing fear. This wall was too even – no cracks, the strata he could feel little more than ripples at a steeply canted angle. They would never be able to hold on once past the rope – and there was nothing he could use to slip the loop round.

They were, he realized, in trouble.

Upon hearing Harllo's last call – the boy reaching the knot – he readied himself to resume his descent.

And there was a sharp upward tug on the rope.

He looked up. Vague faces peering over, hands and more hands reaching to close on the rope. Venaz – yes, there he was, grinning.

'Got you,' he murmured, low and savage. 'Got you both, Bainisk.'

Another tug upward.

Bainisk drew his knife one-handed. He reached down to cut the rope beneath him, and then hesitated, looking up once more at Venaz's face.

Maybe that had been his own, only a few years ago. That face, so eager to take over, to rule the moles. Well, Venaz could have them. He could have it all.

Bainisk reached up with the knife, just above his fist where it held tight. And he sliced through.

Dig heels in, it will not help. We must wing back to the present. For everything to be understood, every facet must flash alight at least once. Earlier, the round man begged forgiveness. Now, he pleads for trust. His is a sure hand, even if it trembles. Trust.

A bard sits opposite an historian. At a nearby table in K'rul's Bar, Blend watches Scillara unfolding coils of smoke from her mouth. There is something avid in that gaze, but every now and then a war erupts in her eyes, when she thinks of the woman lying in a coma upstairs. When she thinks of her, yes. Blend has taken to sleeping in the bed with Picker, has taken to trying all she could think of to awaken sensation once more in her lover. But nothing has worked. Picker's soul is lost, wandering far from the cool, flaccid flesh.

Blend hates herself now, as she senses her soul ready to move on, to seek the blessing of a new life, a new body to explore and caress, new lips to press upon her own.

But this is silly. Scillara's amiability was ever casual. She was a woman who preferred a man's charms, such as they were. And truth be told, Blend had played in that crib more than once herself. So why now has this lust awakened? What made it so wild, so needy?

Loss, my dear. Loss is like a goad, a stinging shove that sets one lunging forward seeking handholds, seeking ecstasy, delicious surrender, even the lure of self-destruction. The bud cut at the stem throws its last energy into one final flowering, one glorious exclamation. *The flower defies*, to quote in entirety an ancient Tiste Andii poem. Life runs from death. It must, it cannot help it. *Life runs*, to quote a round man's epitome of poetic brevity.

Slip into Blend's mind, ease in behind her eyes, and watch as she watches, feel as she feels, if you dare.

Or try Antsy, there at the counter on which are arrayed seven crossbows, twelve flatpacks of quarrels amounting to one hundred and twenty darts, six shortswords, three throwing axes of Falari design, a Genabarii broadsword and buckler, two local rapiers with fancy quillons – so fancy the weapons were snagged together and Antsy had spent an entire morning trying to separate them, with no luck – and a small sack containing three sharpers. He is trying to decide what to wear.

But the mission they were about to set out on was meant to be peaceful, so he should just wear his shortsword as usual, peace-strapped as usual, everything as usual, in fact. But then there were assassins out there who wanted Antsy's head on a dagger point, so maybe keeping things usual was in fact suicidal. So he should strap on at least two shortswords, throw a couple of crossbows over his shoulders and hold the broadsword in his right hand and the twin rapiers in his left, with a flatpack tied to each hip, the sharper sack at his belt, and a throwing axe between his teeth – no, that's ridiculous, he'd break his jaw trying that. Maybe an extra shortsword, but then he might cut his own tongue out the first time he tried saying anything and he was sure to try saying something eventually, wasn't he?

But he could run the scabbards for all six shortswords through his belt, and end up wearing a skirt of shortswords, but that'd be all right, wouldn't it? But then, where would he carry the sharpers? One knock against a pommel or hilt and he'd be an expanding cloud of whiskers and weapon bits. And what about the crossbows? He'd need to load them all up but keep everything away from the releases, unless he wanted to end up skewering all his friends with the first stumble.

What if—

What's that? Back to Blend, please? Flesh against flesh, the weight of full breasts in hands, one knee pushing up between parted thighs, sweat a blending of sweet oils, soft lips trying to merge, tongues dancing eager and slick as—

'I can't wear alla this!'

Scillara glanced over. 'Really, Antsy? Didn't Blend say that about a bell ago?'

'What? Who? Her? What does she know?'

To that entirely unself-conscious display of irony, Blend could only raise her brows when she caught Scillara's eye.

Scillara smiled in response, then drew again on her pipe.

Blend glanced over at the bard, and then said to Antsy, 'We're safe out there now, anyway.'

Eyes bulging, Antsy stared at her in disbelief. 'You'd take the word of some damned minstrel? What does he know?'

'You keep asking what does anyone know, when it's obvious that whatever they know you're not listening to anyway.'

'What?'

'Sorry, that so confused me I doubt I could repeat it. The contract's cancelled – Fisher said so.'

Antsy wagged his head from side to side. 'Fisher said so!' He jabbed a finger at the bard. 'He's not Fisher – not the famous one, anyway. He's just stolen the name! If he was famous he wouldn't be just sittin' there, would he? Famous people don't do that.'

'Really?' the bard who called himself Fisher asked. 'What are we supposed to do, Antsy?'

'Famous people do famous things, alla time. Everybody knows that!'

'The contract has been bought out,' the bard said. 'But if you want to dress as if preparing for a single-handed assault on Moon's Spawn, you go right ahead.'

'Rope! Do I need rope? Let me think!' And to aid in this process Antsy began pacing, moustache twitching.

Blend wanted to pull a boot off and push her foot between Scillara's thighs. No, she wanted to crawl right in there. Staking a claim. With a hiss of frustration she stood, hesitated, and then went to sit down at the bard's table. She fixed him with an intense stare, to which he responded with a raised brow.

'There're more songs supposedly composed by Fisher than anyone else I'd ever heard of.'

The man shrugged.

'Some of them are a hundred years old.'

'I was a prodigy.'

'Were you now?'

Duiker spoke. 'The poet is immortal.'

She turned to face him. 'Is that some kind of general, ideological statement, Historian? Or are you talking about the man sharing this table with you?'

Antsy cursed suddenly and then said, 'I don't need any rope! Who put that into my head? Let's get going – I'm taking this shortsword and a sharper and anybody gets too close to me or looks suspicious they can eat the sharper for breakfast!'

'We'll stay here,' Duiker said when Blend hesitated. 'The bard and me. I'll look in on Picker.'

'All right. Thanks.'

Antsy, Blend and Scillara set out

The journey took them from the Estates District and into Daru District, along the Second Tier Wall. The city had fully awakened now, and in places the crowds were thick with the endless machinery of living. Voices and smells and needs and wants, hungers and thirsts, laughter and irritation, misery and joy, and the sunlight fell on everything it could reach and shadows retreated wherever they could.

Temporary barriers blocked the three foreigners here and there – a cart jammed sideways in a narrow street, a cart-horse dropped dead with its legs sticking up, half a family pinned under the upended cart. A swarm of people round a small collapsed building, stealing every dislodged brick and shard of lumber, and if anyone had been trapped in it, alas, no one was looking for them.

Scillara walked like a woman bred to be admired. And oh, yes, people noticed. In other circumstances, Blend – being another woman – might have resented that, but then she'd made a career out of not being noticed; and besides, she counted herself among the admirers.

'Friendly people, these Darujhistanii,' said Scillara as they finally swung south from the wall, heading for the southwest corner of the district.

'They're smiling,' said Blend, 'because they want a roll with you. And clearly you haven't noticed the wives and such, all looking as if they swallowed something sour.'

'Maybe they did.'

'Oh they did, all right. The truth that men are men, that's what they've swallowed.'

Antsy snorted. 'What else would men be but men? Your problem, Blend, is you see too much, even when it's not there.'

'Oh, and what have you been noticing, Antsy?'

'Suspicious people, that's what.'

'What suspicious people?'

'The ones who keep staring at us, of course.'

'That's because of Scillara – what do you think we've just been talking about?'

'Maybe they are, maybe they ain't. Maybe they're assassins, lookin' to jump us.'

'That old man back there who got his ear boxed by his wife was an assassin? What kind of Guild are they running here?'

'You don't know she was his wife,' Antsy retorted. 'And you don't know but that was a signal to somebody on a roof. We could be walking right into an ambush!'

'Of course,' agreed Blend, 'that woman was his mother, because Guild rules state that Ma's got to come along to make sure he's got the hand signals down, and that he eats all his lunch and his knives are sharp and he's tied up his moccasins right so he doesn't trip in the middle of his murderous lunge at Sergeant Antsy.'

'I ain't so lucky he trips,' Antsy said in a growl. 'In case you ain't noticed, Blend, it's been a run of the Lord's push for us. Oponn's got it in for me, especially.'

'Why?' Scillara asked.

'Because I don't believe in the Twins, that's why. Luck – it's all bad. Oponn only pulls now to push later. If you've been pulled, it don't end there. Never does. No, you can expect the push to come any time and all you know for sure is it's gonna come, that push. Every time. In fact, we're all as good as dead.'

'Well,' said Scillara, 'I can't argue with that. Sooner or later, Hood takes us all, and that's the only certainty there is.'

'Aren't you two cheerful this morning,' Blend observed. 'Look, here we are.'

They had arrived at the Warden Barracks, suitably sombre and foreboding.

Blend saw an annexe fronting the blockish building with the barred windows and set out towards it, the other two following.

A guard lounging outside the door watched them approach, and then said, 'Check your weapons at the front desk. You here to visit someone?'

'No,' snorted Antsy, 'we've come to break 'im out!' And then he laughed. 'Haha.'

No one found the joke at all amusing, especially after the sharper was found and correctly identified. Antsy then made the mistake of getting belligerent, in the midst of five or six stern-visaged constabulary, which led to a scuffle and then an arrest.

When all was said and done, Antsy found himself in a lock-up with three drunks, only one of whom was conscious – singing some old Fisher classic in a broken-hearted voice – and a fourth man who seemed to be entirely mad, convinced as he was that everyone he saw was wearing a mask, which was hiding something demonic, horrible, bloodthirsty. He'd been arrested for trying to tear off a merchant's face and he eyed Antsy speculatively before evidently deciding that the red-whiskered foreigner looked too tough to take on, at least while he was still awake.

The sentence was three days long, provided Antsy proved a model prisoner. Any trouble and it could stretch out some more.

As a result of all this, it was some time before Scillara and Blend managed to gain permission to see Barathol Mekhar. They met him in a holding cell while two guards stood flanking the single door, shortswords drawn.

Noting this, Scillara said, 'Making friends in here, are you?'

The blacksmith looked somewhat shamefaced as he shrugged. 'I had no intention of resisting the arrest, Scillara. My apprentice, alas, decided otherwise.' Anxiety tightened his features as he asked, 'Any news of him? Has he been captured? Is he hurt?'

Scillara shrugged. 'We've not seen or heard anything like that, Barathol.'

'I keep telling them here, he's only a child in his head. It was my responsibility, all of it. But he went and broke some bones and noses, and they're pretty annoyed about that.'

Blend cleared her throat. Something was going back and forth between Barathol and Scillara and it made her uneasy. 'Barathol, we can pay the fine to the Guild, but that scrap you had, that one's more serious.'

He nodded morosely. 'Hard labour, yes. Six months or so.' There was the twitch of a grin. 'And guess who I will be working for?'

'Who?'

'Eldra Foundry. And in six months I'll earn my ticket as a smith, since that's allowed. Some kind of rehabilitation programme.'

Scillara's throaty laugh straightened up both guards. 'Well, that's one way to get there, I suppose.'

He nodded. 'I went about it all wrong, it seems.'

'I'm not sure,' said Scillara. 'Is the Guild happy with that? I mean, it's sort of a way round them, isn't it?'

'They've no choice. Every Guild in the city has to comply, barring, I suppose, the Assassins' Guild. Obviously, for most prisoners six months working in a trade might earn them an apprentice grade of some sort – but there's no limit to how fast you can advance. Just pass the exams and that's that.'

Scillara looked ready to burst out laughing. Even Barathol was struggling.

Blend sighed and then said, 'I'll go settle the fine. Consider it a loan.'

'Much appreciated, Blend, and thank you.'

'Remembering Kalam,' she replied, heading out. Neither guard paid her any attention. But she was used to that.

A bhokaral answered the door. High Alchemist Baruk stared down at it for a long moment before concluding that this was nothing more than a bhokaral. Not a demon, not Soletaken. Just a bhokaral, its little wizened face scrunched up in belligerent regard, spiky ears twitching. When it made to close the postern door again Baruk stepped forward and held it open.

Sudden outrage and indignation. Hissing, spitting, making faces, the bhokaral shook a fist at Baruk and then fled down the corridor.

The High Alchemist closed the door behind him and made his way along the corridor. He could now hear other bhokarala, a cacophony of bestial voices joining in with the first one, raising an alarm that echoed through the temple. At a branching of the passageway he came upon an old Dal Honese woman tearing apart a straw broom. She glared up at Baruk and snapped something in some tribal tongue, then made squiggly gestures with the fingers of her left hand.

The High Alchemist scowled. 'Retract that curse, Witch. Now.'

'You'll not be so bold when the spiders come for you.'

'Now,' he repeated, 'before I lose my temper.'

'Bah! You're not worth the effort anyway!' And all at once she collapsed into a heap of spiders that scurried in all directions.

Baruk blinked, and then quickly stepped back. But none of the creatures skittered his way. Moments later they had inexplicably vanished, although not a single crack or seam was visible.

'High Alchemist.'

He looked up. 'Ah, High Priestess. I did knock—'

'And a bhokaral let you in, yes. They're in the habit of doing that, having chased away most of my acolytes.'

'I wasn't aware bhokarala were in the habit of infestation.'

'Yes, well. Have you come to speak to me or the chosen . . . mouthpiece of Shadowthrone?'

'I do not believe you have been entirely usurped, High Priestess.'

'Your generosity is noted.'

'Why is there a witch of Ardatha in your temple?'

'Yes, why? Come with me.'

The Magus of Shadow – *gods below* – was sitting on the floor in the altar chamber, sharpening knives. A dozen such weapons were scattered round him, each one of a different design. '. . . tonight,' he was muttering, 'they all die! Cut throats, cleaved hearts, pierced eyeballs, pared-back fingernails. Mayhem and slaughter. Clippings—' and then he glanced up, started guiltily, licked his lips once and suddenly smiled. 'Welcome, High Barukness. Isn't it a lovely day?'

'High Alchemist Baruk, Magus. And no, it is not a lovely day. What are you doing?'

His eyes darted. 'Doing? Nothing, can't you see that?' He paused. 'Can't he smell them? Close, oh so close! It's going to be a mess and whose fault will that be? A real mess – nothing to do with Iskaral Pust, though! I am perfect.' He attempted an expression of innocence. 'I am perfect . . . ly – perfectly – fine.'

Baruk could not help himself, turning to Sordiko Qualm. 'What was Shadowthrone thinking?'

The question clearly depressed her. 'I admit to a crisis of faith, High Alchemist.'

Iskaral Pust leapt to his feet. 'Then you must pray, my love. To me, since Shadowthrone sees through my eyes, hears through ears, smells through my nose.' His crossed his eyes and added in a different tone, 'Farts through my bung-hole, too, but that would be too offensive to mention.' He struggled to correct his gaze and smiled again. 'Sordiko, my sweetness, there are very special, very secret prayers. And, er, rituals. See me after this man has left, there's no time to waste!'

Bhokarala were creeping into the chamber. A score of them, moving with pointless stealth, all converging on Iskaral Pust – who seemed entirely unaware of them as he winked at Sordiko Qualm.

'High Priestess,' said Baruk, 'you have my sympathy.'

'I have news from Shadowthrone,' Iskaral Pust said. 'This is why I have summoned you, Baruchemist.'

'You did not summon me.'

'I didn't? But I must have. At least, I was supposed to.' He tilted his head. 'He's another idiot, nothing but idiots on all sides. There's just me and Sordiko darling, against the world. Well, we shall triumph!'

'Shadowthrone?' Baruk prompted.

'What? Who? Oh, him.'

'Through your mouth.'

'Brilliance shall pass, yes yes. Let me think, let me think. What was that message again? I forget. Wait! Wait, hold on. It was . . . what was it? Set a watch on the Urs Gate. That's it, yes. Urs Gate Or was it Foss Gate? Raven Gate? Worry Gate? Cutter Gate? Two-Ox?'

'Yes,' said Baruk, 'that's all of them.'

'Urs, yes, it must have been. Urs.'

Sordiko Qualm looked ready to weep.

Baruk rubbed at his eyes, and then nodded. 'Very well. I shall take my leave then.' He bowed to the High Priestess.

The bhokarala rushed in. Each stole a knife and then, with shrieks, they raced away clutching their prizes.

Iskaral Pust stared agape, and then pulled at the two snarls of hair above his ears. 'Evil!' he screamed. 'They knew! They knew all my plans! How? *How?*'

'Now, what shall I do with you?'

Chaur watched her with doleful eyes. He had been crying again, his eyes puffy, two runnels of snot streaking down to his reddened, chapped lips.

'We must assume,' Spite continued, 'that Barathol is unavoidably indisposed – of course, at the moment all we can do is assume, since in truth we have no idea what's happened to him. One thing is obvious, and that is that he cannot come here. If he could he would have, right? Come to collect you, Chaur.'

He was moments from bawling again. The simple mention of Barathol threatened to set him off.

Spite tapped her full lips with one long, perfectly manicured finger. 'Unfortunately, I will need to leave here soon. Can I trust you to stay here, Chaur? Can I?'

He nodded.

'Are you sure?'

He nodded again, and then wiped his nose, rather messily.

She frowned. 'Dear me, you're a sight. Do you realize it is nothing more than certain pathways in your brain that are in disarray? A practitioner of High Denul could work wonders for you, Chaur. It's a thought, isn't it? Oh, I know, you don't have "thoughts" as such. You have . . . impulses, and confusion, and these two make up the man known as Chaur. And, barring times such as this one, you are mostly happy, and perhaps that is not something to be fiddled with. The gods know, happiness is a precious and rare commodity, and indeed it seems that the more intelligent and perceptive the individual, the less happy they generally are. The cost of seeing things as they are, I expect.

'Then, of course, there is my sister. My smiling murderess sibling. My vicious, ice-cold, treacherous kin. She happens to be almost as intelligent as me, and yet she is immune to unhappiness. A quality, I suspect, of her particular insanity.

'Anyway, Chaur, you will need to remain here, staying out of sight. For I must pay my sister a visit. For a word or two. Soon, yes?'

He nodded.

'Now, let's get you cleaned up. I wouldn't want to upset Barathol and neither would you, I'm sure.'

Now, Chaur was good at understanding people most of the time. He was good at nodding, too. But on occasion understanding and nodding did not quite match. This was such a time.

But more of that later.

The carter failed to complete his breakfast, as it did not take long for someone to take note of the wrapped corpse, and then to bring word in to Meese that some fool had left a body in the bed of the cart outside the inn – hardly the kind of positive advertisement any inn might welcome, even the Phoenix. Swearing, Meese went out to see for herself, and something about those boots looked familiar. With a suddenly cold heart, she pulled the canvas back from Murillio's face.

Things happened quickly then: wretched comprehension, word's swift rush, and finally, the dusty, lifeless place in the soul that was grief. Abject sense of uselessness, the pummelling assault that is shock. The carter was cornered by Irilta and, seeing the strait he'd found himself in, the old man was quick to tell everyone all he knew.

The short, round man at the back of the room rose then with a sober expression and quietly took charge. He told Irilta and Meese to carry the body to a spare room upstairs, which they did with heartrending tenderness. Word was sent out to Coll. As for the others, well, everyone returned to the Phoenix Inn eventually, and so the ordeal of relaying the bad news would not end soon, and each time the emotions would well up once more. The living felt this new burden and they could see that the next few days would be without pleasure, without ease, and already everyone felt exhausted, and not even Kruppe was immune.

A dear friend is dead, and there is nothing just in death. When the moment arrives, it is always too soon. The curse of incompletion, the loss that can never be filled. Before too long, rising like jagged rocks from the flood, there was anger.

The carter was made to explain again about the visit to a mining camp, the duel over some boy, and the victor's instructions that the body be returned to the Phoenix Inn. That was all he knew, he swore it, and for the moment none but Kruppe – wise Kruppe, clever Kruppe – comprehended who that boy must have been.

Must he now visit a certain duelling school? Possibly.

The ordeal of the burden, the dread weight of terrible news – the witnessing of another crushed spirit, oh, this was a fell day indeed. A most sad, fell day.

And on this night, widows will weep, and so shall we.

Two men are converging on the Phoenix Inn. Which one arrives first changes everything. If the redressing of balance truly existed beyond nature – in the realm of humanity, that is – then Rallick Nom would have been the first to hear of his friend's death; and he would have set out, hard-eyed, to take upon himself a new burden, for although vengeance salved certain spiritual needs, cold murder delivered terrible damage to the soul. Of course, he had done this once before, in the name of another friend, and so in his mind he felt he could be no more lost than he already was.

Alas, that particular flavour of redress was not to be.

Troubled by a host of thoughts, Cutter approached the entrance to the Phoenix Inn. He noted an old carter leading an ox away, but had no reason to give it any further consideration. As soon as he walked inside, he sensed that something was wrong. Irilta was behind the bar with a bottle in her hand – not, he saw, to pour drinks for customers, but to lift it to her mouth, tilt it back and take punishing mouthfuls. Her eyes were red, startling in a pallid face.

Few people were speaking, and those who were did so in muted tones.

Meese was nowhere to be seen, but Cutter noticed Kruppe, sitting at his table with his back to the room – something he had never before seen him do. A dusty bottle of expensive wine was before him, four goblets set out. Kruppe was slowly filling the one opposite the chair on his right.

His unease deepening, Cutter walked over. He pulled out that chair and sat down.

There was no sign of Kruppe's usual affability in his visage. Grave, colourless, bleak. In his eyes, raw anguish. 'Drink, my young friend,' he said.

Cutter saw that the remaining two goblets were empty. He reached out. 'This is the expensive stuff, isn't it? What's happened, Kruppe?'

'Honourable Murillio is dead.'

The statement felt like a body blow, punching the breath from Cutter's chest. He could not move. Pain surged up through the numbness, sank down again only to return once more. Over and over again.

'A duel,' said Kruppe. 'He went to retrieve a lost child. The Eldra Mines west of the city.'

Something jerked inside Cutter, but he could make no sense of it. A recognition? Of what? 'I thought – I thought he'd given all that up.'

'Given what up, my friend? The desire to do right?'

Cutter shook his head. 'Duelling. I meant . . . duelling.'

'To effect the release of young Harllo. The mine's owner was there, or one of them at least. History comes round, as it is known to do.' Kruppe sighed. 'He was too old for such things.'

And now came the question, and it was asked in a dull tone, a voice emptied of everything. 'Who killed him, Kruppe?'

And the round man flinched, and hesitated.

'Kruppe.'

'This will not do—'

'Kruppe!'

'Ah, can such forces be resisted? Gorlas Vidikas.'

And that was that. He'd known, yes, Cutter had known. The mine . . . Eldra . . . the history. *He knows about me. He wanted to punish me. He killed Murillio to hurt me. He killed a fine . . . a fine and noble man. This – this must stop.*

'Sit down, Cutter.'

I mean to stop this. Now. It's what she wants, anyway.

'Coll is coming,' Kruppe said. 'And Rallick Nom – Crokus, leave this to Rallick—'

But he was already moving, eyes on the door. Irilta stood watching and something in her face caught his attention. There was dark hunger in her eyes – as if she knew where he was going, as if she knew – 'Cutter,' she said in a rasp, 'get the bastard. *Get him.*'

And then he was outside. The day's brilliance was like a slap, rocking his head. He gasped, but breathing still wasn't easy. Pressures assailed him, and rage rose in his mind, a nightmare leviathan with gaping mouth, and its howl filled his skull.

Deafening Cutter to the world.

The day is stripped down, time itself torn away, the present expanding, swallowing everything in sight. It is an instant and that instant feels eternal.

Recall this day's beginning. A single breath, drawn in with love—

Bellam Nom took a length of braided hide, made loops at both ends. He crouched down in front of Mew. 'See this loop, Mew? Take it in your hands – I'm going to hold on to the other end, all right? We're going out. You just keep hold of the rope, all right?'

Round-eyed Mew nodded.

'Don't worry,' said Bellam, 'I'll walk slowly.' He then went to Hinty and picked the girl up, taking her weight in the crook of his left arm. Her thin arms wrapped about his neck and her wet nose brushed his cheek. Bellam smiled down at Mew. 'Ready?'

Another nod.

They set out.

Snell was still with the old bodymonger, and Bellam had no interest in retrieving him just yet. He had no idea what had happened to Myrla and Bedek, but he left a message scrawled out with charcoal on the surface of the lone table, telling them where he'd taken Mew and Hinty.

Murillio should have been back by now. Bellam was getting worried. He couldn't wait around any longer.

They walked slowly through the crowds. Twice Mew was inadvertently tugged loose from the rope, but both times Bellam was able to retrieve her. They left the unofficial neighbourhood slum known as the Trench and after some time they arrived at the duelling school.

Bellam set Hinty down in the warm-up area, instructed Mew to remain with her little sister, then set out to find Stonny Menackis.

She was sitting on a stone bench in the shade-swallowed colonnade running along the back end of the practice yard, her long legs stretched out, her eyes on nothing. When she heard him approach she glanced up. 'Classes cancelled. Go away.'

'I'm not here for any lessons,' Bellam said, surprised at the harsh judgement in his own voice.

'Get out,' she said, 'before I beat you senseless.'

'Too many people, Stonny, are stepping in for you, doing what you're supposed to be doing. It's not fair.'

She scowled. 'What are you talking about?'

'Murillio hasn't come back?'

'Everybody leaves.'

'He found Harllo.'

'What?'

He saw interest flaring to life in her dark eyes. 'He found him, Stonny. Working in a mining camp. He went to get him back. But he hasn't returned. Something's happened, something bad – I can feel it.'

She stood. 'Where is this camp? How did he end up there?'

.'Snell.'

She stared. 'I'm going to kill that little bastard.'

'No, you're not. He's taken care of. We've got a new problem.'

At that moment a small figured stepped into the corridor, stared at them.

Stonny frowned. 'Mew? Where's your ma and da? Where's Hinty?'

Mew started crying, and then rushed towards Stonny who had no choice but to take the child into her arms.

'They've gone missing,' said Bellam. 'I was taking care of them, waiting, but they never showed up. Stonny, I don't know what to do with them. I need to get home – my own parents must be going crazy with worry.'

She spun round, still holding Mew, and her face was savage. 'I need to get Harllo! Take them to your home!'

'No. Enough of this. Take responsibility for them, Stonny. Once I let my parents know I'm all right, I'll go and find Murillio. Take responsibility. You owe it to Myrla and Bedek – they did it for you. For years.'

He thought she would strike him, saw the fury warring in her eyes. He stepped back. 'Hinty's in the warm-up, probably sleeping – she does that a lot. Oh, and they're hungry.'

He left them then.

It took the words of a young man – no, a boy – to do what Gruntle could not do. It took a barrage of blunt, honest words, smashing through, against which she had no real defence.

She stood, Mew in her arms, feeling as if her soul had been blasted open, and all that was left was a hollow shell, slowly refilling. Refilling with . . . something. 'Oh,' she whispered, *'Harllo.'*

Shardan Lim was waiting for Challice when she returned home. He rose from the ornate bench but did not approach, instead standing, watching her with an odd expression.

'This,' she said, 'is unexpected.'

'No doubt. Forgive me for intruding on your . . . busy schedule.'

There was no genuine remorse to back his apology, however, and she felt a trembling of her nerves. 'What do you want, Councillor?'

'Are we not past titles, Challice?'

'That depends.'

'Perhaps you're right. Even so, after we're done here there'll be no need for formalities between us.'

Should she call for the guard? What would he do? *Why, he'd laugh.*

Shardan Lim walked closer. 'Pour yourself some wine. Pour yourself a lot of wine, if you like. I must tell you, I am not at all pleased at having been so unceremoniously discarded. It seems you find adultery to your taste, and your appetite has grown. Out of control? I think, yes, out of control.'

'You forced open the door,' she said, 'and now complain that I've left the room?'

His thin colourless lips curved in a smile. 'Something like that. I'm not ready for you to leave just yet.'

'And I am to have no say in the matter?'

His brows lifted. 'Dear Challice. You surrendered such privileges long ago. You let your husband use you – not in any normal way, but still, you let him use you. You let me do the same, and now some lowborn thief, and who knows how many others. Make no protest now – it will sound hollow even to you, I'm sure.'

'It's still my life.' But the words sounded thin, too brittle to stretch very far over the misshapen, ugly truth.

He did not bother with a response, but looked across to a divan.

'You'll have to drag me,' she said, 'so the reality will be plain, so plain you won't be able to pretend this is anything but the rape it is.'

He looked disappointed. 'Wrong again, Challice. You are going to walk over there and undress. You are going to the lie back and spread your legs. It should be easy now; you've done it often enough. Your lowborn lover is going to have to share you, I'm afraid. Before long, I expect you'll not even be able to tell the difference.'

How could he force her to do such things? She did not understand, although – without doubt – he did. Yes, Shardan Lim understood things far too well.

She walked to the divan.

She was still sore, achy, from the morning's lovemaking. Before long, that ache would be deeper, more raw than it was now. Pain and pleasure, yes, entwined like lovers. She could feed them both again and again, for ever and again.

And so she would. Until the time came when she . . . awakened.

Crokus, never mind my husband. There is no point. I will tell you that the next time. I promise.

I promise.

Shardan Lim used her then, but in the end it was he who did not understand, after all. And when she thanked him afterwards, he seemed taken aback. As he hurried to dress and depart, she remained lying on the divan, amused at his confusion, at peace with the way of things now.

And she thought of her glass globe with its trapped moon, that gift of a youth long lost, and she smiled.

In a near tropical city, the dead are quickly dressed. A distraught Coll, half-mad with grief, arrived in a carriage. Meese came down from the room where she had sat with the body, and Coll sent one of his aides to crack open the family crypt.

There would be no delays permitted. Grief was transformed into fury when Coll discovered who had been responsible for Murillio's death.

'First blood drawn's never enough for Vidikas. He likes killing – under any other circumstances he'd be on his way to the High Gallows. Damn these antiquated duelling laws. The time's come to outlaw duels – I will address the Council—'

'Such a thing will not pass,' Kruppe said, shaking his head. 'Coll knows this as well as does Kruppe.'

Coll stood like a man trapped, cornered. 'Where's Rallick?' he asked in a growl.

Sighing, Kruppe poured the second to last goblet full and handed it to Coll. 'He will be here soon, Kruppe believes. Such is this day, in no hurry to end, and will any of us sleep this night? Kruppe already dreads the impending solitude. Ah, here is Rallick.'

They watched as Irilta stumbled to the assassin, very nearly collapsing into Rallick's arms. His expression of shock quickly darkened as she spoke, her voice muffled since her face was pressed against his shoulder – but not so muffled that he did not comprehend.

His gaze lifted, met Kruppe's, and then Coll's.

There was no one else left in the bar – the poisoned atmosphere had driven away even the most insensate drinkers. Sulty and Chud the new cook stood in the doorway leading to the kitchen, Sulty quietly weeping.

Kruppe poured the last goblet and then sat down, his back to the scene. Coll slumped down beside Kruppe, draining down the wine with the practised ease of an alcoholic reacquainting himself with his deadly passion, but Kruppe had chosen this wine with such risks in mind – its headiness was an illusion, the taste of alcohol a clever combination of spices and nothing more. This was, Kruppe understood, but a temporary solution. He knew Coll well, understood the self-serving cycle of self-pity that now loomed before the man, sauntering in wearing that familiar smirk, like an old, deadly lover. She would open wide her arms, now, to fold Coll in once more – the days and nights ahead would be difficult indeed.

After a long moment Rallick joined them, and although he remained standing he reached down for the goblet. 'Crokus should be here,' he said.

'He was, but he has left.'

Coll started. 'Left? Did Murillio mean so little to him that he'd just walk away?'

'He left,' said Kruppe, 'to find Gorlas Vidikas.'

Coll swore and rose. 'The fool – Vidikas will slice him to pieces! Rallick—'

And the assassin was already setting the goblet back down and turning away.

'Wait!' snapped Kruppe in a tone that neither man had ever heard before – not from Kruppe, at least. 'Both of you! Take up that wine again, Rallick.' And now he too rose. 'There is the memory of a friend and we will drink to it. Here, now. Rallick, you will not catch Crokus, you will not make it in time. Listen well to Kruppe, both of you. Vengeance need not be rushed—'

'So Rallick should just let Vidikas kill yet another friend of ours?'

Kruppe faced the assassin. 'Do you lack faith as well, Rallick Nom?'

'That is not the point,' the man replied.

'You cannot halt what has already happened. He has already walked this path. You discovered that, did you not? Outside this very inn.'

Coll rubbed at his face, as if waiting to find the numbness a bellyful of wine should have given him. 'Is Crokus truly—'

'He has a new name,' Rallick interrupted, finally nodding. 'One he has clearly earned the hard way.'

'Cutter, yes,' said Kruppe.

Coll looked back and forth between the two of them, and then thumped back down into his chair. All at once he looked a century old, shoulders folding in as he reached for the bottle and refilled his goblet. 'There will be repercussions. Vidikas is . . . not alone. Hanut Orr, Shardan Lim. Whatever happens is going to ripple outward – gods below, this could get messy.'

Rallick grunted. 'Hanut Orr and Shardan Lim. I can get in their way when the time comes.'

Coll's eyes flashed. 'You've got Cutter's back. Good. We can take care of this – you can, I mean. I'm useless – I always was.' He sank back, the chair creaking, and looked away. 'What's with this wine? It's doing nothing.'

'Murillio,' said Kruppe, 'would not be pleased at you standing drunk when his body is carried into the crypt. Honour him, Coll, now and from now on.'

'Fuck off,' he replied.

The back of Rallick Nom's gloved hand snapped hard against Coll's face, rocking him back. He surged upright, outraged, reaching for the ornate knife at his belt. The two men stood glaring at each other.

'Stop this!'

A bottle smashed against the floor, the contents spraying the feet of Coll and Rallick, and both turned as Meese snarled, 'There you go, Coll, lap it up and choke to death! In the meantime, how 'bout the rest of us pay our respects and walk him to the crypt – the undertaker's cart's arrived. It's time – not for any of you, but for him. For Murillio. You chew up this day and it'll haunt you for ever. And Hood's breath, so will I.'

Coll ducked his head and spat blood, and then said, 'Let's get this done, then. For Murillio.'

Rallick nodded.

Behind the bar, Irilta was suddenly sick. The sounds of her gagging and coughing silenced everyone else.

Coll looked shamefaced.

Kruppe rested a hand on the man's shoulder. And all at once the councillor was weeping, so broken that to bear witness was to break deep within oneself. Rallick turned away then, both hands lifting to his face.

Survivors do not mourn together. They each mourn alone, even when in the same place. Grief is the most solitary of all feelings. Grief isolates, and every ritual, every gesture, every embrace, is a hopeless effort to break through that isolation.

None of it works. The forms crumble and dissolve.

To face death is to stand alone.

How far can a lost soul travel? Picker believed she had begun in some distant frozen world, struggling thigh-deep through drifts of snow, a bitter wind howling round her. Again and again she fell, crusted ice scraping her flesh raw – for she was naked, her fingers blackening from the tips as they froze into solid, dead things. Her toes and then her feet did the same, the skin splitting, the ankles swelling.

Two wolves were on her trail. She did not know how she knew this, but she did. Two wolves. God and Goddess of War, the Wolves of Winter. They scented her as they would a rival – but she was no ascendant, and certainly no goddess. She had worn torcs once, sworn to Treach, and this now marked her.

War could not exist without rivals, without enemies, and this was as true in the immortal realm as it was in the mortal one. The pantheon ever reflects the nature of its countless aspects. The facets deliver unerring truths. In winter, war was the lifeless chill of dead flesh. In summer, war rotted in fetid, flyblown clouds. In autumn, the battlefield was strewn with the dead. In spring, war arose anew in the same fields, the seeds well nurtured in rich soil.

She fought through a dark forest of black spruce and firs. Her fingers dropped off one by one. She stumbled on stumps. The winter assailed her, the winter was her enemy, and the wolves drew ever closer.

Through a mountain pass, then; brief flashes of awareness and each time they arrived, lifting her out of oblivion, she found the landscape transformed. Heaped boulders, eskers, ragged peaks towering overhead. A tortured, twisted trail, suddenly pitching sharply downward, stunted pines and oaks to either side. Bestial howls voicing their rage high above, far behind her now.

A valley below, verdant and rank, a jungle nestled impossibly close to the high ranges and the whipping snow-sprayed winds – or perhaps she had traversed continents. Her hands were whole, her bare feet sinking into warm, wet loam. Insects spun and whirred about her.

From the thicket came an animal cough, a cat's heavy growl.

And another hunter had found her.

She hurried on, as if some other place awaited her, a sanctuary, a cave that she could enter, to emerge upon some other side, reborn. And now she saw, rising haphazardly from the moss and humus and mounds of rotted trunks, swords, blades encrusted, cross-hilts bedecked in moss, pommels green with verdigris. Swords of all styles, all so corroded and rusted that they would be useless as weapons.

She heard the cat's cough again, closer this time.

Panic flitted through her.

She found a clearing of high swaying grasses, a sea of emerald green that she plunged into, pushing her way across.

Something thrashed into her wake, a swift, deadly rush.

She screamed, fell to the ground.

Snapping, barking voices surrounded her, answered by a snarl from somewhere close behind her. Picker rolled on to her back. Humanlike figures crowded her, baring their teeth and making stabbing gestures with fire-hardened spears towards a leopard crouched down not three paces from where she was lying. The beast's ears were flattened back, its eyes blazing. Then, in a flash, it was gone.

Picker pushed herself to her feet, and found that she towered over these people, and yet they were one and all adults – even through the fine pelt of hair covering them she could see that. Five females, four males, and the females were the more robust between them, with wide hips and deep rib cages.

Luminous brown eyes fixed upon her with something like worship, and then the spears were brought around and she was being prodded along, on to a trail cutting across the path she had been taking. *So much for worship.* Those spears threatened, and she saw something black smeared on the points. *I'm a prisoner. Terrific.*

They hurried down the trail, a trail never meant for one as tall as Picker, and she found branches scraping across her face again and again. Before long they reached another clearing, this one at the foot of a cliff. A wide, low rock shelf projected over a sloping cave-mouth from which drifted woodsmoke. Two ancients were squatting at the entrance, both women, with a gaggle of children staring out behind them.

There was none of the expected squealing excitement from the children – indeed, no sounds were uttered at all, and Picker felt a sudden suspicion: these creatures were not the masters of their domain. No, they behaved as would prey. She saw stones to either side of the cave, heaped up to be used to make a barricade come the dusk.

Her captors drove her into the cave. She was forced to bend over to keep from scraping her head on the pitched, blackened ceiling. The children fled to either side. Beyond the flickering light from the lone hearth the cave continued on into darkness. Coughing in the smoke, she stumbled forward, round the fire, and into the depths. The shafts of the spears urged her on. The floor of packed earth beneath her feet was free of rubble, but the slope was getting ever steeper and she felt herself sliding, losing purchase.

Suddenly the shafts pressed hard against her and shoved.

Shouting in alarm, Picker pitched forward, slid on the damp floor as if it was layered in grease. She fought to grasp hold of something, but nothing touched her flailing hands – and then the floor vanished beneath her, and she was falling.

Harllo's sudden unexpected plummet ended quickly amidst sharp-edged boulders. Gashes ripped across his back, one thigh and the ankle of the same leg. The impact left him stunned. He vaguely heard something strike the rocks nearby, a terrible snapping, crunching sound.

Eventually, he stirred. The pain from the wounds was fierce, and he could feel blood trickling down, but it seemed he'd broken no bones. He crawled slowly to where he'd heard Bainisk land, and heard ragged breathing.

When his probing hands touched warm flesh, he found it wet, broken. And at the brush of his fingertips it flinched away.

'Bainisk!'

A low groan, and then a gasp.

'Bainisk, it's me. We made it down – we got away.'

'Harllo?' The voice was awful in its weakness, its pain. 'Tell me . . .'

He pulled himself up along Bainisk, his eyes making out a rough shape. He found Bainisk's face, tilted towards him, and Harllo drew himself on to his knees, and then he eased up his friend's head – feeling strange shards moving under his hands, beneath Bainisk's blood-matted hair – and then, as gently as he could manage, he settled the head on to his lap.

'Bainisk.'

The face was crushed along one side. It was a miracle that he could speak at all. 'I dreamed,' he whispered. 'I dreamed of the city. Floating on the lake . . . going wherever the waves go. Tell me, Harllo, tell me about the city.'

'You'll see it soon enough—'

'Tell me.'

Harllo stroked his friend's brow. 'In the city . . . Bainisk, oh, in the city, there's shops and everybody has all the money they need and you can buy whatever you want. There's gold and silver, beautiful silver, and the people are happy to give it away to anyone they like. No one ever argues about anything – why should they? There's no hunger, no hurts, no hurts of any kind, Bainisk. In the city every child has a mother and a father . . . and the mother loves her son for ever and ever and the father doesn't rape her. And you can just pick them for yourself. A beautiful mother, a strong, handsome father – they'd be so happy to take care of you – you'll see, you'll see.

'They'd see how good you are. They'd see right through to your heart, and see it pure and golden, because all you ever wanted to do was to help out, because you were a burden to them and you didn't want that, and maybe if you helped enough they'd love you, and want you to be with them, to live with them. And when it didn't work, well, it just means you have to work harder. Do more, do everything.

'Oh, Bainisk, the city . . . there are mothers . . .'

He stopped then, for Bainisk had stopped breathing. He was perfectly still, his whole broken-up body folded over the sharp rocks, his head so heavy in Harllo's lap.

Leave them there, now.

The city, ah, the city. As dusk closes in, the blue fires awaken. Figures stand in a cemetery surrounded by squat Daru crypts, and they are silent as they watch the workers sealing the door once more. Starlings flit overhead.

Down at the harbour a woman steps lithely on to the dock and breathes deep the squalid air, and then sets out to find her sister.

Scorch and Leff stand nervously at the gate of an estate. They're not talking much these nights. Within the compound, Torvald Nom paces. He is not sure if he should go home. The night has begun strange, heavy, and his nerves are a mess. Madrun and Lazan Door are throwing knuckles against a wall, while Studious Lock stands on a balcony, watching.

Challice Vidikas sits in her bedroom, holding a glass globe and staring at the trapped moon within its crystal clear sphere.

In a room above a bar Blend sits beside the motionless form of her lover, and weeps.

Below, Duiker slowly looks up as Fisher, cradling a lute, begins a song.

In the Phoenix Inn, an old, worn-out woman, head pounding, shambles to her small cubicle and sinks down on to the bed. There were loves in the world that never found voice. There were secrets never unveiled, and what would have been the point of that? She was no languid beauty. She was no genius wit. Courage failed her again and again, but not this time, as she drew sharp blades lengthways up her wrists, at precise angles, and watched as life flowed away. In Irilta's mind, this last gesture was but a formality.

Passing through Two-Ox Gate, Bellam Nom sets out on the road. From a hovel among the lepers he hears someone softly sobbing. The wind has died, the smell of rotting flesh hangs thick and motionless. He hurries on, as the young are wont to do.

Much farther down the road, Cutter rides on a horse stolen from Coll's stable. His chest is filled with ashes, his heart a cold stone buried deep.

He drew a breath, sometime earlier that day, filled with love.

And then released it, black with grief.

Both seem to be gone now, vanished within him, perhaps never to return. And yet, hovering there before his mind's eye, he sees a woman.

Ghostly, wrapped in black, dark eyes fixed upon his own.

Not this path, my love.

He shakes his head at her words. Shakes his head.

Not my path, my love.

But he rides on.

I will give you my breath, my love. To hold.

Hold it for me, as I hold yours. Turn back.

Cutter shakes his head again. 'You left me.'

No, I gave you a choice, and the choice remains. My love, I gave you a place to come to, when you are ready. Find me. Come find me.

'This first.'

Take my breath. But not this one, not this one.

'Too late, Apsalar. It was always too late.'

The soul knows no greater anguish than to take a breath that begins with love and ends with grief. But there are other anguishes, many others. They unfold as they will, and to dwell within them is to understand nothing.

Except, perhaps, this. In love, grief is a promise. As sure as Hood's nod. There will be many gardens, but this last one to visit is so very still. Not meant for lovers. Not meant for dreamers. Meant only for a single figure, there in the dark, standing alone.

Taking a single breath.

Chapter Twenty

In hollow grove and steeple chamber
The vine retreats and moss rolls inside
The void from whence it came
In shallow grave and cloven crypt
The bones shiver and shades flee
Into the spaces between breaths
In tilted tower and webslung doorway
Echoes still and whispers will die
Men in masks rap knuckles 'gainst walls
In dark cabinets and beneath bed slats
Puppets clack limbs and painted eyes widen
To the song pouring down from hills
And the soul starts in its cavern drum
Battered and blunted to infernal fright
This is the music of the beast
The clamour of the world at bay
Begun its mad savage charge
The hunt commences my friends
The Hounds are among us.

PRELUDE
TOLL THE HOUNDS
FISHER

Faces of stone, and not one would turn Nimander's way. His grief was too cold for them, too strange. He had not shown enough shock, horror, dismay. He had taken the news of her death as would a commander hearing of the loss of a soldier, and only Aranatha – in the single, brief moment when she acknowledged anyone or anything – had but nodded in his direction, as if in grim approval.

Skintick's features were tight with betrayal, once the stunned disbelief wore off, and the closeness he had always felt with Nimander now seemed to have suddenly widened into a chasm no bridge could span. Nenanda had gone so far as to half draw his sword, yet was torn as to who most deserved his blade's bite: Clip or Nimander. Clip for his shrug, after showing them the crumbled edge of the cliff where she must have lost her footing. Or Nimander, who stood dry-eyed and said nothing. Desra, calculating, selfish Desra, was the first to weep.

Skintick expressed the desire to climb down into the crevasse, but this was a sentimental gesture he had drawn from his time among humans – the need to observe the dead, perhaps even to bury Kedeviss's body beneath boulders – and his suggestion was met with silence. The Tiste Andii held no regard for corpses. There would be no return to Mother Dark, after all. The soul was flung away, to wander for ever lost.

They set out shortly thereafter, Clip in the lead, continuing on through the rough pass. Clouds swept down the flanks of the peaks, as if the mountains were shedding their mantles of white, and before long the air grew cold and damp, thin in their lungs, and all at once the clouds swallowed the world.

Stumbling on the slick, icy stone, Nimander trudged on in Clip's wake – although the warrior was no longer even visible, there was only one possible path. He could feel judgement hardening upon his back, an ever thickening succession of layers, from Desra, from Nenanda, and most painfully from Skintick, and it seemed the burdens would never relent. He longed for Aranatha to speak up, to whisper the truth to them all, but she was silent as a ghost.

They were now all in grave danger. They needed to be warned, but Nimander could guess the consequences of such a revelation. Blood would spill, and he could not be certain that it would be Clip's. Not now, not when Clip could unleash the wrath of a god – or whatever it was that possessed the warrior.

Kedeviss had brought to him her suspicions down in the village beside the lake bed, giving firm shape to what he had already begun to believe. Clip had awakened but at a distance, as if behind a veil. Oh, he had always shown his contempt for Nimander and the others, but this was different. Something fundamental had changed. The new contempt now hinted of hunger, avarice, as if Clip saw them as nothing more than raw meat, awaiting the flames of his need.

Yet Nimander understood that Clip would only turn upon them if cornered, if confronted. As Kedeviss had done – even when Nimander had warned her against such a scene. No, Clip still needed them. *His way in.* As for what would happen then, not even the gods knew. Lord Anomander Rake did not suffer upstarts. He was never slowed by indecisiveness, and in delivering mercy even the cruellest miser could not match his constraint. And as for Clip's claim to be some sort of emissary from Mother Dark, well, that had become almost irrelevant, unless the god within the warrior was seeking to usurp Mother Dark herself.

This notion disturbed Nimander. The goddess was, after all, turned away. Her leaving had left a void. Could something as alien as the Dying God assume the Unseen Crown? Who would even kneel before such an entity?

It was hard to imagine Anomander Rake doing so, or any of the other Tiste Andii that Nimander and his kin had known. Obedience had never been deemed a pure virtue among the Tiste Andii. To follow must be an act born of deliberation, of clear-eyed, cogent recognition that the one to be followed has earned the privilege. So often, after all, formal structures of hierarchy stood in place of such personal traits and judgements. A title or rank did not automatically confer upon the one wearing it any true virtue, or even worthiness to the claim.

Nimander had seen for himself the flaws inherent in that hierarchy. Among the Malazans, the renegade army known as the Bonehunters, there had been officers whom Nimander would not follow under any circumstances. Men and women of incompetence – oh, he'd seen how such fools were usually weeded out, through the informal justice system practised by the common soldier, a process often punctuated by a knife in the back, which struck Nimander as a most dangerous habit. But these were human ways, not those of the Tiste Andii.

If Clip and the Dying God that possessed him truly believed they could usurp Mother Dark, and indeed her chosen son, Anomander Rake, as ruler of the Tiste Andii, then that conceit was doomed. And yet, he could not but recall the poisonous lure of Saemenkelyk. There could be other paths to willing obedience.

And that is why I can say nothing. Why Aranatha is right. We must lull Clip into disregarding us, so that he continues believing we are fools. Because there is the chance, when the moment arrives, that I alone will be standing close enough. To strike. To catch him – them – unawares.

It may be that Anomander Rake and the others in Black Coral will have nothing to fear from Clip, from the Dying God. It may be that they will swat them down with ease.

But we cannot be sure of that.

In truth, I am afraid . . .

'I can see water.'

Startled, Nimander glanced back at Skintick, but his cousin would not meet his eyes.

'Where the valley dips down, eastward – I think that is the Cut that Clip described. And along the north shore of it, we will find Black Coral.'

Clip had halted on an outcropping and was staring down into the misty valley. They had left most of the cloud in their wake, descending beneath its ceiling. Most of the range was now on their left, westward, the nearest cliff-face grey and black and broken only by a dozen or so mountain sheep wending their way along a seam.

Skintick called out to the warrior, 'That looks to be a long swim across, Clip.'

The man turned, rings spinning on their chain. 'We will find a way,' he said. 'Now, we should continue on, before it gets too dark.'

'What is your hurry?' Skintick asked. 'The entire trail down is bound to be treacherous, especially in this half-light. What would be the point in taking a tumble and . . .' Skintick went no further.

And breaking a neck.

In the uncomfortable silence that followed, only the clack of the rings carried on, like a man chewing stones.

After a moment, Clip stepped back from the ledge and set out down the path once more.

Nimander made to follow but Skintick grasped his arm, forcing him round.

'Enough,' Skintick growled, and Nenanda moved up beside him, Desra joining them. 'We want to know what's going on, Nimander.'

Nenanda spoke. 'She didn't just fall – do you think we're fools, Nimander?'

'Not fools,' he replied, and then hesitated, 'but you must play at being fools . . . for a little longer.'

'He killed her, didn't he?'

At Skintick's question Nimander forced himself to lock gazes with his cousin, but he said nothing.

Nenanda gave a sudden hiss and whirled to glare at Aranatha, who stood nearby. 'You must have sensed something!'

Her brows arched. 'Why do you say that?'

He seemed moments from closing on her with a hand upraised, but she too did not flinch, and after a moment a look a sheer helplessness crumpled Nenanda's face and he turned from them all.

'He's not what he was,' said Desra. 'I've felt it – he's . . . uninterested.'

Of course she was speaking of Clip. Indeed they were not fools, none of them. Still Nimander said nothing. Still he waited.

Skintick could no longer hold Nimander's gaze. He glanced briefly at Desra and then stepped back. 'Fools, you said. We must play at being fools.'

Nenanda faced them once more. 'What does he want with us? What did he ever want? Dragging us along as if we were but his pets.' His eyes fixed on Desra. 'Flinging you on your back every now and then to keep the boredom away – and now you're saying what? Only that he's become bored by the distraction. Well.'

She gave no sign that his words wounded her. 'Ever since he awakened,' she said. 'I don't think boredom is a problem for him, not any more. And that doesn't make sense.'

'Because,' added Skintick, 'he's still contemptuous of us. Yes, I see your point, Desra.'

'Then what does he want with us?' Nenanda demanded again. 'Why does he still need us at all?'

'Maybe he doesn't,' said Skintick.

Silence.

Nimander finally spoke. 'She made a mistake.'

'Confronted him.'

'Yes.' He stepped away from Skintick, setting his gaze upon the descent awaiting them. 'My authority holds no weight,' he said. 'I told her to stay away – to leave it alone.'

'Leave it to Anomander Rake, you mean.'

He faced Skintick again. 'No. That is too much of an unknown. We – we don't know the situation in Black Coral. If they're . . . vulnerable. We don't know anything of that. It'd be dangerous to assume someone else can fix all this.'

They were all watching him now.

'Nothing has changed,' he said. 'If he gets even so much as a hint – it must be us to act first. We choose the ground, the right moment. Nothing has changed – do you all understand me?'

Nods. And odd, disquieting expressions on every face but Aranatha's – he could not read them. 'Am I not clear enough?'

Skintick blinked, as if surprised. 'You are perfectly clear, Nimander. We should get moving, don't you think?'

What – what has just happened here? But he had no answers. Uneasy, he moved out on to the trail.

The rest fell in behind him.

Nenanda drew Skintick back, slowing their progress, and hissed, 'How, Skin? How did he do that? We were there, about to – I don't know – and then, all of a sudden, he just, he just—'

'Took us into his hands once more, yes.'

'How?'

Skintick simply shook his head. He did not think he could find the right words – not for Nenanda, not for the others. *He leads. In the ways of leading, the ways the rest of us cannot – and can never – understand.*

I looked into his eyes, and I saw such resolve that I could not speak.

Absence of doubt? No, nothing so egotistic as that. Nimander has plenty of doubts, so many that he's lost his fear of them. He accepts them as easily as anything else. Is that the secret? Is that the very definition of greatness?

He leads. We follow – he took us into his hands, again, and each one of us stood, silent, finding in ourselves what he had just given us – that resolve, the will to go on – and it left us humbled.

Oh, do I make too much of this? Are we all no more than children, and these the silly, meaningless games of children?

'He killed Kedeviss,' muttered Nenanda.

'Yes.'

'And Nimander will give answer to that.'

Yes.

Monkrat squatted in the mud and watched the line of new pilgrims edge closer to the camp. Most of their attention, at least to begin with, had been on the barrow itself – on that emperor's ransom of wasted wealth – but now, as they approached the decrepit ruin, he could see how they hesitated, as something of the wrongness whispered through. Most were rain-soaked, senses dulled by long, miserable journeys. It would take a lot to stir their unease.

He watched the sharpening of their attention, as details resolved from the gloom, the mists and the woodsmoke. The corpse of the child in the ditch, the rotting swaths of clothes, the broken cradle with four crows crowding the rail, looming over the motionless, swaddled bundle. The weeds now growing up on the path leading to and from the barrow. Things were not as they should be.

Some might beat a quick retreat. Those with a healthy fear of corruption. But so many pilgrims came with the desperate hunger that was spiritual need – it was what made them pilgrims in the first place. They were lost and they wanted to be found. How many would resist that first cup of kelyk, the drink that welcomed, the nectar that stole . . . everything?

Perhaps more than among those who had come before – as they saw the growing signs of degradation, of abandonment of all those qualities of humanity the Redeemer himself honoured. Monkrat watched them hesitate, even as the least broken of the kelykan shuffled into their midst, each offering up a jug of the foul poison.

'The Redeemer has drunk deep!' they murmured again and again.

Well, not yet. But that time was coming, of that Monkrat had little doubt. At which point . . . he shifted about slightly and lifted his gaze to the tall, narrow tower rising into the dark mists above the city. No, he couldn't make her out from here, not with this sullen weather sinking down, but he could feel her eyes – eternally open. Oh, he knew that damned dragon of old, could well recall his terror as the creature sailed above the treetops in Blackdog and Mott Wood, the devastation of her attacks. If the Redeemer fell, *she* would assail the camp, the barrow, everything and everyone. There would be fire, a fire that needed no fuel, yet devoured all.

And then Anomander Rake himself would arrive, striding through the wreckage with black sword in his hands, to take the life of a god – whatever life happened to be left.

Shivering in the damp, he rose, pulling his tattered raincape about himself. Gradithan was probably looking for him, wanting to know what Monkrat's countless sets of eyes in the city might have seen – not that there was much to report. The Tiste Andii weren't up to much, but then they never were, until such time as necessity stirred them awake. Besides, he'd woken up with a headache, a dull throb just behind the eyes – it was the weather, pressure building in his sinuses. And even the rats in the camp were proving elusive, strangely nervous, skittish when he sought to snare them to his will.

He wasn't interested in seeing Gradithan. The man had moved from opportunist to fanatic alarmingly fast, and while Monkrat had no problem understanding the former, he was baffled by the latter. And frightened.

The best way to avoid Gradithan was to wander down into Black Coral. The blessing of darkness was far too bitter for the worshippers of Saemenkelyk.

He worked his way into the ankle-deep river of mud that was the trail leading into Night.

From somewhere nearby a cat suddenly yowled and Monkrat started as he sensed a wave of panic sweep through every rat within hearing. Shaking himself, he continued on.

A moment later he realized someone was walking behind him – a pilgrim, perhaps, smart enough to elect to avoid the camp, someone now looking for an inn, all thoughts of salvation riding the tide out in waves of revulsion.

'No believer should arrive willing.' So said that High Priestess, Salind, before Gradithan destroyed her. Monkrat recalled being confused by that statement back then. Now, he wasn't. Now, he understood precisely what she'd meant.

Worship born of need could not but be suspect, fashioned from self-serving motives as it was. *'Someone wanting their bowl filled will take whatever is poured
into it.'* No, revelation could not be sought, not through willing deprivation or
meditation. It needed to arrive unexpected, even undesired. *'Do not trust an easy
believer.'* Aye, she'd been a strange High Priestess, all right.

He remembered one night, when—

A knife edge pressed cold against his throat.

'Not a move,' hissed a voice behind him, and it was a moment before Monkrat
realized that the words had been spoken in Malazan.

'Figured I wouldn't recognize you, soldier?'

Cold sweat cut through the steamy heat beneath his woollen clothes. His
breath came in gasps. 'Hood's breath, if you're gonna kill me just get it done with!'

'I'm sore tempted, I am.'

'Fine, do it then – I've got a curse ready for you—'

The Malazan snorted, and dogs started barking. 'That'd be a real mistake.'

Monkrat's headache had redoubled. He felt something trickling down from his
nostrils. The air was rank with a stench he struggled to identity. Bestial, like an
animal's soaked pelt. 'Gods below,' he groaned. 'Spindle.'

'Aye, my fame precedes me. Sorry I can't recall your name, or your squad,
even. But you were a Bridgeburner – that much I do remember. Vanished up
north, listed as dead – but no, you deserted, ran out on your squadmates.'

'What squadmates? They were all killed. My friends, all killed. I'd had enough,
Spindle. We were getting chewed to pieces in that swamp. Aye, I walked. Would
it have been better if I'd stayed, only to die here in Black Coral?'

'Not everyone died here, soldier—'

'That's not what I heard. The Bridgeburners are done, finished.'

After a moment the knife fell away.

Monkrat spun round, stared at the short, bald man, wearing that infamous
hairshirt – and Hood's breath, *it stank.* 'Which has me wondering – what are you
doing here? Alive? Out of uniform?'

'Dujek looked at us – a handful left – and just went and added our names to the
list. He sent us on our way.'

'And you—'

'I decided on the pilgrimage. The Redeemer – I saw Itkovian myself, you see.
And I saw Capustan. I was here when the barrow went up – there's a sharper of
mine in that heap, in fact.'

'A *sharper*?'

Spindle scowled. 'You had to have been there, soldier.'

'Monkrat. That's my name now.'

'Wipe the blood from your nose, Monkrat.'

'Listen, Spindle – hear me well – you want nothing to do with the Redeemer.
Not now. You didn't kill me, so I give you that – my warning. Run, run fast. As
far away from here as you can.' He paused. 'Where'd you come from anyway?'

'Darujhistan. It's where we settled. Me and Antsy, Bluepearl, Picker, Blend,
Captain Paran. Oh, and Duiker.'

'Duiker?'

'The Imperial Historian—'

'I know who he is – was – whatever. It's just, that don't fit, him being there, I mean.'

'Aye, he didn't fit well at all. He was on the Chain of Dogs.'

Monkrat made a gesture. Fener's blessing.

Spindle's eyes widened. He sheathed his knife. 'I've worked up a thirst, Monkrat.'

'Not for kelyk, I hope.'

'That shit they tried to force on me back there? Smelled like puke. No, I want beer. Ale. Wine.'

'We can find that in Black Coral.'

'And you can tell me what's happened – to the Redeemer.'

Monkrat rubbed at the bristle on his chin, and then nodded. 'Aye, I will.' He paused. 'Hey, you remember the red dragon? From Blackdog?'

'Aye.'

'She's here – and when it gets bad enough with the Redeemer, well, she'll spread her wings.'

'No wonder I got so edgy when I arrived. Where's she hiding, then?'

Monkrat grimaced. 'In plain sight. Come on, see for yourself.'

The two ex-soldiers set out for Black Coral.

The clouds closed in, thick as curtains of sodden sand. In the camp, new dancers spun and whirled through the detritus, while a handful of terrified pilgrims fled back up the trail.

Rain arrived in a torrent, the water rushing down the flanks of the barrow, making it glisten and gleam until it seemed it was in motion. Shivering, moments from splitting wide open. From the clouds, thunder rattled like iron-shod spears, a strange, startling sound that drew denizens of Black Coral out into the streets, to stare upward in wonder.

The water in the black bowls surrounding the High Priestess trembled in answer to that reverberation. She frowned as a wave of trepidation rolled through her. The time was coming, she realized. She was not ready, but then, for some things, one could never be ready. The mind worked possibilities, countless variations, in a procession that did nothing but measure the time wasted in waiting. And leave one exhausted, even less prepared than would have been the case if, for example, she had spent that period in an orgy of hedonistic abandon.

Well, too late for regrets – she shook her head. *Oh, it's never too late for regrets. That's what regrets are all about, you silly woman.* She rose from the cushion and spent a moment shaking out the creases in her robe. Should she track down Endest Silann?

Another heavy clatter of thunder.

Of course he felt it, too, that old priest, the deathly charge growing ever tauter – he didn't need her to remind him, rushing in all hysterical foam to gush round the poor man's ankles. The absurd image made her smile, but it was a wry smile, almost bitter. She had worked hard at affecting the cool repose so essential to the role of High Priestess, a repose easily mistaken for wisdom. But how could a woman in her position truly possess wisdom, when the very goddess she served had rejected her and all that she stood for? Not wisdom, but futility. Persistent, stubborn futility. If anything, what she represented was a failure of the intellect, and an even graver one of the spirit. Her worship was founded on denial, and in the absence of a true relationship with her goddess, she – like all those who had come before her – was free to invent every detail of that mock relationship.

The lie of wisdom is best hidden in monologue. Dialogue exposes it. Most people purporting to wisdom dare not engage in dialogue, lest they reveal the paucity of their assumptions and the frailty of their convictions. Better to say nothing, to nod and look thoughtful.

Was that notion worth a treatise? Yet another self-indulgent meander for the hall of scrolls? How many thoughts could one explore? Discuss, weigh, cast and count? *All indulgences. The woman looking for the next meal for her child has no time for such things. The warrior shoulder to shoulder in a line facing an enemy can only curse the so-called wisdom that led him to that place. The flurry of kings and their avaricious terrors. The brutal solidity of slights and insults, grievances and disputes. Does it come down to who will eat and who will not? Or does it come down to who will control the option? The king's privilege in deciding who eats and who starves, privilege that is the taste of power, its very essence, in fact?*

Are gods and goddesses any different?

To that question, she knew Anomander Rake would but smile. He would speak of Mother Dark and the necessity of every decision she made – even down to the last one of turning away from her children. And he would not even blink when stating that his betrayal had forced upon her that final necessity.

She would walk away then, troubled, until some stretch of time later, when, in the solitude of her thoughts, she would realize that, in describing the necessities binding Mother Dark, he was also describing his very own necessities – all that had bound him to his own choices.

His betrayal of Mother Dark, she would comprehend – with deathly chill – had been *necessary.*

In Rake's mind, at any rate. And everything had simply followed on from there, inevitably, inexorably.

She could hear the rain lashing down on the temple's domed roof, harsh as arrows on upraised shields. The sky was locked in convulsions, a convergence of inimical elements. A narrow door to her left opened and one of her priestesses hurried in, then abruptly halted to bow. 'High Priestess.'

'Such haste,' she murmured in reply, 'so unusual for the temple historian.'

The woman glanced up, and her eyes were impressively steady. 'A question, if I may.'

'Of course.'

'High Priestess, are we now at war?'

'My sweetness – old friend – you have no idea.'

The eyes widened slightly, and then she bowed a second time. 'Will you summon Feral, High Priestess?'

'That dour creature? No, let the assassin stay in her tower. Leave her to lurk or whatever it is she does to occupy her time.'

'Spinnock Durav—'

'Is not here, I know that. I know that.' The High Priestess hesitated, and then said, 'We are now at war, as you have surmised. On countless fronts, only one of which – the one here – concerns us, at least for the moment. I do not think weapons need be drawn, however.'

'High Priestess, shall we prevail?'

'How should I know?' Those words snapped out, to her instant regret as she saw her old friend's gaze harden. 'The risk,' she said, in a quieter tone, 'is the gravest we have faced since . . . well, since Kharkanas.'

That shocked the temple historian – when nothing else had, thus far. But she recovered and, drawing a deep breath, said, 'Then I must invoke my role, High Priestess. Tell me what must be told. All of it.'

'For posterity?'

'Is that not my responsibility?'

'And if there will be no posterity? None to consider it, naught but ashes in the present and oblivion in place of a future? Will you sit scribbling until your last moment of existence?'

She was truly shaken now. 'What else would you have me do?'

'I don't know. Go find a man. Make fearful love.'

'I must know what has befallen us. I must know why our Lord sent away our greatest warrior, and then himself left us.'

'Countless fronts, this war. As I have said. I can tell you intent – as I understand it, and let me be plain, I may well not understand it at all – but not result, for each outcome is unknown. And each must succeed.'

'No room for failure?'

'None.'

'And if one should fail?'

'Then all shall fail.'

'And if that happens . . . ashes, oblivion – that will be our fate.'

The High Priestess turned away. 'Not just ours, alas.'

Behind her, the historian gasped.

On all sides, water trembled in bowls, and the time for the luxurious consideration of possibilities was fast fading. Probably just as well.

'Tell me of redemption.'

'There is little that I can say, Segda Travos.'

Seerdomin snorted. 'The god known as the Redeemer can say nothing of redemption.' He gestured to that distant quiescent figure kneeling in the basin. 'She gathers power – I can smell it. Like the rot of ten thousand souls. What manner of god does she now serve? Is this the Fallen One? The Crippled God?'

'No, although certain themes are intertwined. For followers of the Crippled God, the flaw is the virtue. Salvation arrives with death, and it is purchased through mortal suffering. There is no perfection of the spirit to strive towards, no true blessing to be gained as a reward for faith.'

'And this one?'

'As murky as the kelyk itself. The blessing is surrender, the casting away of all thought. The self vanishes within the dance. The dream is shared by all who partake of pain's nectar, but it is a dream of oblivion. In a sense, the faith is antilife. Not in the manner of death, however. If one views life as a struggle doomed to fail, then it is the failing that becomes the essence of worship. He is the Dying God, after all.'

'They celebrate the act of dying?'

'In a manner, yes, assuming you can call it celebration. More like enslavement. Worship as self-destruction, perhaps, in which all choice is lost.'

'And how can such a thing salve the mortal soul, Redeemer?'

'That I cannot answer. But it may be that we shall soon find out.'

'You do not believe I can protect you – at least in that we're in agreement. So, when I fall – when I fail – the Dying God shall embrace me as it will you.' He shook his head. 'I am not unduly worried about me. I fear more the notion of what eternal dying can do to redemption – that seems a most unholy union.'

The Redeemer simply nodded and it occurred to Seerdomin that the god had probably been thinking of little else. A future that seemed sealed into fate, an end to what was, and nothing glorious in what would follow.

He rubbed at his face, vaguely dismayed at the weariness he felt. Here, disconnected from his body, from any real flesh and bone, it was his spirit that was exhausted, battered down. And yet . . . *and yet, I will stand. And do all I can. To defend a god I have chosen not to worship, against a woman who dreamt once of his embrace, and dreams of the same now – with far deadlier intent.* He squinted down at her, a form almost shapeless in the gathering gloom beneath gravid, leaden clouds.

After a moment raindrops splashed against his helm, stained his forearms and his hands. He lifted one hand, and saw that the rain was black, thick, wending like slime.

The sky was raining kelyk.

She raised her head, and the distance between them seemed to vanish. Her eyes shone with fire, a slow, terrible pulse.

Gods below . . .

Like the worn ridge of a toothless jaw, the Gadrobi Hills rose into view, spanning the north horizon. Kallor halted to study them. An end to this damned plain, to this pointless sweep of grasses. And there, to the northwest, where the hills sank back down, there was a city.

He could not yet see it. Soon.

The temple would be nondescript, the throne within it a paltry thing, poorly made, an icon of insipid flaws. A broken fool once named Munug would writhe before it, in obeisance, the High Priest of Pathos, the Prophet of Failure – enough thematic unity, in fact, to give any king pause. Kallor allowed himself a faint smirk. Yes, he was worthy of such worship, and if in the end he wrested it body and soul from the Crippled God, so be it.

The temple his domain, the score of bent and maimed priests and priestesses his court, the milling mob outside, sharing nothing but chronic ill luck, his subjects. This, he decided, had the makings of an immortal empire.

Patience – it would not do, he realized, to seek to steal the Fallen One's worshippers. There was no real need. The gods were already assembling to crush the Crippled fool once and for all. Kallor did not think they would fail this time. Though no doubt the Fallen One had a few more tricks up his rotted sleeve, not least the inherent power of the cult itself, feeding as it did on misery and suffering – two conditions of humanity that would persist for as long as humans existed.

Kallor grunted. 'Ah, fuck patience. The High King will take this throne. Then we can begin the . . . negotiations.'

He was no diplomat and had no interest in acquiring a diplomat's skills, not even when facing a god. There would be conditions, some of them unpalatable, enough to make the hoary bastard choke on his smoke. Well, too bad.

One more throne. The last he'd ever need.

He resumed walking. Boots worn through. Dust wind-driven into every crease of his face, the pores of his nose and brow, his eyes thinned to slits. The world clawed at him, but he pushed through. Always did. Always would.

One more throne. Darujhistan.

Long ago, in some long-lost epoch, people had gathered on this blasted ridge overlooking the flattened valley floor, and had raised the enormous standing stones that now leaned in an uneven line spanning a thousand paces or more. A few had toppled here and there, but among the others Samar Dev sensed a belligerent vitality. As if the stones were determined to stand sentinel for ever, even as the bones of those who'd raised them now speckled the dust that periodically scoured their faces.

She paused to wipe sweat from her forehead, watching as Traveller reached the crest, and then moved off into the shade of the nearest stone, a massive phallic menhir looming tall, where he leaned against it with crossed arms. To await her, of course – she was clearly slowing them down, and this detail irritated her. What she lacked, she understood, was manic obsession, while her companions were driven and this lent them the vigour common to madmen. Which, she had long since decided, was precisely what they were.

She missed her horse, the one creature on this journey that she had come to feel an affinity with. An average beast, a simple beast, normal, mortal, sweetly dull-eyed and pleased by gestures of care and affection.

Resuming her climb, she struggled against the crumbled slope, forcing her legs between the sage brushes – too weary to worry about slumbering snakes and scorpions, or hairy spiders among the gnarled, twisted branches.

The thump of Havok's hoofs drummed through the ground, halting directly above her at the top of the slope. Scowling, she looked up.

Karsa's regard was as unreadable as ever, the shattered tattoo like a web stretching to the thrust of the face behind it. He leaned forward on his mount's neck and said, 'Do we not feed you enough?'

'Hood take you.'

'Why will you not accept sharing Havok's back, Witch?'

Since he showed no inclination to move, she was forced to work to one side as she reached the crest, using the sage branches to pull herself on to the summit. Where she paused, breathing hard, and then she held up her hands to her face, drawing in the sweet scent of the sage. After a moment she glanced up at the Toblakai. A number of responses occurred to her, in a succession of escalating viciousness. Instead of voicing any of them, she sighed and turned away, finding her own standing stone to lean against – noting, with little interest, that Traveller had lowered his head and seemed to be muttering quietly to himself.

This close to the grey schist, she saw that patterns had been carved into its surface, wending round milky nodules of quartz. With every dawn, she realized, this side of the stone would seem to writhe as the sun climbed higher, the nodes glistening. And the purpose of all that effort? Not even the gods knew, she suspected.

History, she realized, was mostly lost. No matter how diligent the recorders, the witnesses, the researchers, most of the past simply no longer existed. Would never be known. The notion seemed to empty her out somewhere deep inside, as if the very knowledge of loss somehow released a torrent of extinction within her own memories – moments swirling away, never to be retrieved. She set a finger in one groove etched into the stone, followed its serpentine track downward as far as she could reach, then back up again. The first to do so in how long?

Repeat the old pattern – ignorance matters not – just repeat it, and so prove continuity.

Which in turn proves what?

That in living, one recounts the lives of all those long gone, long dead, even forgotten. Recounts in the demands of necessity – to eat, sleep, make love, sicken, fade into death – and the urges of blessed wonder – a finger tracking the serpent's path, a breath against stone. Weight and presence and the lure of meaning and pattern.

By this we prove the existence of the ancestors. That they once were, and that one day we will be the same. I, Samar Dev, once was. And am no more.

Be patient, stone, another fingertip will come, to follow the track. We mark you and you mark us. Stone and flesh, stone and flesh . . .

Karsa slid down from Havok, paused to stretch out his back. He had been thinking much of late, mostly about his people, the proud, naïve Teblor. The ever-tightening siege that was the rest of the world, a place of cynicism, a place where virtually every shadow was painted in cruelty, in countless variations on the same colourless hue. Did he truly want to lead his people into such a world? Even to deliver a most poetic summation to all these affairs of civilization?

He had seen, after all, the poison of such immersion, when observing the Tiste Edur in the city of Letheras. Conquerors wandering bewildered, lost, made useless by success. An emperor who could not rule even himself. And the Crippled God had wanted Karsa to take up that sword. With such a weapon in his hands, he would lead his warriors down from the mountains, to bring to an end all things. To become the living embodiment of the suffering the Fallen One so cherished.

He had not even been tempted. Again and again, in their disjointed concourse, the Crippled God had revealed his lack of understanding when it came to Karsa Orlong. He made his every gift to Karsa an invitation to be broken in some fashion. *But I cannot be broken.* The truth, so simple, so direct, seemed to be an invisible force as far as the Crippled God was concerned, and each time he collided with it he was surprised, dumbfounded. Each time, he was sent reeling.

Of course, Karsa understood all about being stubborn. He also knew how such a trait could be fashioned into worthy armour, while at other times it did little more than reveal a consummate stupidity. Now, he wanted to reshape the world, and he knew it would resist him, yet he would hold to his desire. Samar Dev would call that 'stubborn', and in saying that she would mean 'stupid'. Like the Crippled God, the witch did not truly understand Karsa.

On the other hand, he understood her very well. 'You will not ride with me,' he said now as she rested against one of the stones, 'because you see it as a kind of surrender. If you must rush down this torrent, you will decide your own pace, as best you can.'

'Is that how it is?' she asked.

'Isn't it?'

'I don't know,' she replied. 'I don't know anything. I had some long forgotten god of war track me down. Why? What meaning was I supposed to take from that?'

'You are a witch. You awaken spirits. They scent you as easily as you do them.'

'What of it?'

'Why?'

'Why what?' she demanded.

'Why, Samar Dev, did you choose to become a witch?'

'That's – oh, what difference does that make?'

He waited.

'I was . . . curious. Besides, once you see that the world is filled with forces – most of which few people ever see, or even think about – then how can you not want to explore? Tracing all the patterns, discovering the webs of existence – it's no different from building a mechanism, the pleasure in working things out.'

He grunted. 'So you were curious. Tell me, when you speak with spirits, when you summon them and they come to you without coercion – why do you think they do that? Because, like you, they are curious.'

She crossed her arms. 'You're saying I'm trying to find significance in something that was actually pretty much meaningless. The bear sniffed me out and came for a closer look.'

He shrugged. 'These things happen.'

'I'm not convinced.'

'Yes,' he smiled, 'you are truly of this world, Samar Dev.'

'What's that supposed to mean?'

He turned back to Havok and stroked the beast's dusty neck. 'The Tiste Edur failed. They were not thorough enough. They left the cynicism in place, and thought that through the strength of their own honour, they could defeat it. But the cynicism made their honour a hollow thing.' He glanced back at her. 'What was once a strength became an affectation.'

She shook her head, as if baffled.

Traveller moved to join them, and there was something haggard in his face. Seeing this odd, inexplicable transformation, Karsa narrowed his gaze on the man for a moment. Then he casually looked away.

'Perhaps the bear came to warn you,' he said to Samar Dev.

'About what?'

'What else? War.'

'*What war?*'

The shout made Havok shift under his hand, and he reached up to grasp the beast's wiry mane. Calming the horse, he then vaulted on to its back. 'Why, the one to come, I would think.'

She glared across at Traveller, and seemed to note for the first time the change that had come over him.

Karsa watched her take a step closer to Traveller. 'What is it? What has happened? What war is he talking about?'

'We should get moving,' he said, and then he set out.

She might weep. She might scream. But she did neither, and Karsa nodded to himself and then reached down one arm. 'This torrent,' he muttered, 'belongs to him, not us. Ride it with me, Witch – you surrender nothing of value.'

'I don't?'

'No.'

She hesitated, and then stepped up and grasped hold of his arm.

When she was settled in behind him, Karsa tilted to one side and twisted round slightly to grin at her. 'Don't lie. It feels better already, does it not?'

'Karsa – what has happened to Traveller?'

He collected the lone rein and faced forward once more. 'Shadows,' he said, 'are cruel.'

Ditch forced open what he thought of as an eye. His eye. Draconus stood above the blind Tiste Andii, Kadaspala, reaching down and dragging the squealing creature up with both hands round the man's scrawny neck.

'You damned fool! It won't work that way, don't you see that?'

Kadaspala could only choke in reply.

Draconus glowered for a moment longer, and then flung the man back down on to the heap of bodies.

Ditch managed a croaking laugh.

Turning to skewer Ditch with his glare, Draconus said, 'He sought to fashion a damned god here!'

'And it shall speak,' Ditch said, 'in my voice.'

'No, *it shall not.* Do not fall into this trap, Wizard. Nothing must be fashioned of this place—'

'What difference? We all are about to die. Let the god open its eyes. Blink once or twice, and then give voice . . .' he laughed again, 'the first cry also the last. Birth and death with nothing in between. Is there anything more tragic, Draconus? Anything at all?'

'Dragnipur,' said Draconus, '*is nobody's womb.* Kadaspala, this was to be a cage. To keep Darkness in and Chaos out. One last, desperate barrier – the only gift we could offer. A gate that is denied its wandering must find a home, a refuge – a fortress, even one fashioned from flesh and bone. The pattern, Kadaspala, was meant to defy Chaos – two antithetical forces, as we discussed—'

'That will fail!' The blind Tiste Andii was twisting about at Draconus's feet, like an impaled worm. 'Fail, Draconus – we were fools, idiots. We were mad to think mad to think mad to *think* – give me this child, this wondrous creation – give me—'

'Kadaspala! The pattern – nothing more! Just the pattern, damn you!'

'Fails. Shatters. Shatters and fails shattering into failure. Failure failure failure. We die and we die and we die and we die!'

Ditch could hear the army marching in pursuit, steps like broken thunder, spears and standards clattering like a continent of reeds, the wind whistling through them. War chants erupting from countless mouths, no two the same, creating instead a war of discordance, a clamour of ferocious madness. The sound was more horrible than anything he had ever heard before – no mortal army could start such terror in a soul as this one did. And above it all, the sky raged, actinic and argent, seething, wrought through with blinding flashes from some descending devastation, ever closer descending – and when at last it struck, *the army will charge. Will sweep over us.*

Ditch looked about with his one eye – only to realize that it was still shut, gummed solid, that maybe he had no eye left at all, and that what he was seeing through was the pattern etched in black ink on his eyelid. *The god's eye? The pattern's eye? How is it I can see at all?*

Draconus stood facing their wake, the convulsing figure at his feet forgotten for the moment.

Such studied belligerence, such a heroic pose, the kind that should be sculpted in immortal bronze. Heroism that needed the green stains of verdigris, the proof of centuries passed since last such noble forces existed in the world – any world, whatever world; no matter, details unimportant. The statue proclaims the great age now lost, the virtues left behind.

Civilizations made sure their heroes were dead before they honoured them. Virtue belonged to the dead, not the living. Everyone knew this. Lived with this, this permanent fall from grace that was the present age. The legacy squandered, because this was what people did with things they themselves have not earned.

He studied Draconus, and the man seemed to darken, blur, become strangely indistinct. Ditch gasped, and in the next instant Draconus was once more as he had always been.

So little of his mind was left, so little of what could be called his *self*, and these moments of clarity were fast diminishing. Was there irony to be found, should the chaos reach him only to find him already gone?

Draconus was suddenly crouched down beside him. 'Ditch, listen to me. He's made you the nexus – you were meant to be the god's eyes – no, its brain – your pattern, the one upon your skin . . .'

Ditch grunted, amused. 'Each soul begins with a single word. He's written that word – on me. Identity is only a pattern. The beginning form. The world – life and experience – is Kadaspala, etching and etching the fine details. By life's end, who can even make out that first word?'

'It is within you,' said Draconus, 'to break that pattern, Ditch. Hold on to a part of yourself, hold tight to it – you may need it—'

'No, *you* may need it, Draconus.'

'There can be no child-god. Not fashioned of this *nightmare* – can't you understand that? It would be a horrid, terrible thing. Kadaspala is mad—'

'Yes,' agreed Ditch, 'most unfortunate. Mad. Not a good beginning, no.'

'Hold on, Ditch.'

'It's just a word.'

Draconus stared down into that painted eye. Then he rose, gathering up his chains, and moved out of Ditch's limited range of vision.

Kadaspala crawled close. 'He only wants to escape escape escape. But you but you but you are the knot the knot. Snapping tight! No one gets away. No one gets away. No one gets away. Hold still hold still and hold still until he awakens and he will awaken and so he will. Awaken. My child. The word, you see, the word is the word is the word. The word is *kill*.'

Ditch smiled. Yes, he'd known that. He had.

'Wait, sweet knot, and wait wait wait. Everything will make sense. Everything. Promise promise I promise and I do promise – for I have seen into the future. I know what's coming. I know all the plans. Her brother died and he should not have had to do that, no. No, he shouldn't have had to do that. I do this for her for her for her. Only for her.

'Knot, I do this for her.'

Kill, thought Ditch, nodding, *kill, yes, I understand. I do. Kill, for her. Kill.* And he found that the word itself, yes, the word itself, knew how to smile.

Even as the ashes rained down.

Beneath a sprawl of stars, Precious Thimble stood by the side of the track, watching the carriage approach. The repairs looked makeshift even in the gloom and the entire contraption rocked and wobbled. She saw Glanno Tarp perched on the high bench, his splinted legs splayed wide, and the horses tossed their heads, ears flattened and eyes rolling.

Figures walked to either side. Mappo and Gruntle on the left, Reccanto Ilk, the Boles and that wretched Cartographer on the right. Master Quell, presumably, was inside.

Beside Precious, Faint muttered something under her breath and then climbed to her feet. 'Wake up, Sweetest, they're finally here.'

From the town known as Reach of Woe, half a league distant, not a single glimmer of light showed.

Precious approached Gruntle. 'What happened back there?'

He shook his head. 'You truly do not want to know, Witch.'

'Why do Jaghut bother getting married at all?' Reccanto asked, his face pale as the moon. 'Gods below, that was the most pettytracted nefoaminous argument I ever seen! 'Twas still in full swing when we hightailed it outa there.'

'Blaggered?' said Faint. 'The carriage can barely crawl, Ilk.'

'Ain't nothing so tensifying as running for your life at a snail's pace, let me tell you, but if it wasn't for Master's protecterives we'd be nothing but flops of hairy skin and chunks of meat like everyone else back there.'

Precious Thimble shivered and made a warding gesture.

Master Quell emerged from the carriage after forcing open an ill-hung door. He was sheathed in sweat. 'What a damned world this is,' he said raggedly.

'I thought we were on an island,' Jula said, frowning.

'We heading back to sea?' Precious asked Quell.

'Not a chance – the carriage wouldn't hold. We need to find a more civil place to hole up.'

She watched him walk off the track to find a private place where he could groan and sigh as he emptied his bladder, or at least tried to – he never wandered far enough. 'You need a practitioner of High Denul,' she called after him.

'As you say, Witch, as you say. . . .'

Cartographer had found a stick from somewhere and was scraping out patterns on the dirt of the road a dozen paces ahead. Precious Thimble squinted at him. 'What's that thing doing?'

No one seemed to have an answer.

After a long pause, Sweetest Sufferance spoke. 'Either of you other girls feeling a tad bloodthirsty?'

Well, that woke everyone else up fast enough, Precious Thimble observed a short while later, still struggling with her own panic. That damned lardball was still half convulsed in laughter, and Precious was of a mind to stick a knife in one of those teary eyes, and she doubted anyone would try to stop her.

Master Quell reappeared. 'What's so funny, Sweetest? Oh, never mind.' He surveyed everyone else with a pinched, uncomfortable expression, like a man who'd sat on a cork. 'The night stinks – anybody else noticed that? I was thinking of Rashan, but now I'm not so sure.'

'You need only take me as far as a port,' said Mappo. 'I can find my own way from there.'

Quell squinted at him. 'We'll deliver you as agreed, Trell—'

'The risks—'

'Are why we charge as much as we do. Now, no more about that, and don't even think of just cancelling the contract – we'd take that as a grievous insult, a slur on our good name. We'll get you there, Trell, even if it's on one wheel behind a three-legged horse.'

Cartographer tottered back to them. 'If it pleases,' he said, attempting a smile that Precious decided was too ghoulish to describe without descending into insanity, 'I have outlined a solution.'

'Sorry I missed it,' said Quell.

'He meant that literally,' said Precious, pointing up the road.

Quell in the lead, they walked up to observe the faint scouring on the pale dust of the track.

'What in Hood's name is that?'

'A map, of course.'

'What kind of map?'

'Our journey to come.'

Reccanto Ilk squatted to study the effort, and then shook his head. 'I can't even make out the island we're on. This is a stupid map, Cartogopher.' He straightened and nodded to the others. 'That's what you get tryin' to work with a dead man. I swear, common sense is the first to go when you turn into the walking dead – why is that?'

The Bole brothers looked thoughtful, as if working on possible answers. Then, noticing each other's frown, both broke into smiles. Amby snorted then had to wipe goo from his upper lip with the back of one hand.

'I must be mad,' Precious whispered.

Quell asked, 'This is some kind of gate you've drawn here, Cartographer?'

'Absent of investiture, but yes. I have no power to give it. But then, you do.'

'Maybe,' Quell mused, 'but I don't recognize anything you've drawn, and that makes me nervous.'

Cartographer walked along one side and pointed a withered finger down at the far end of the map. 'Do you see this straight, wide groove? All the rest funnels into this path, the path we need to take. The best maps show you the right direction. The best maps are the ones that lead you to a specific destination.'

Reccanto Ilk scratched at his head, looking bewildered. 'But that's what maps are for – what's he glommering on about?'

'Not all maps,' corrected Cartographer, with a shake of his head – and nothing, Precious concluded, could ever be as solemn as a dead man's shake of the head. 'Objective rendition is but one form in the art of cartography, and not even the most useful one.'

'If you say so,' said Master Quell. 'I'm still uneasy.'

'You have few other options, Wizard. The carriage is damaged. The marital argument is even now extending beyond the town's limits and will soon engulf this entire island in a conflagration of disputing versions of who-said-what.'

'He's smarter than he was before,' observed Faint.

'That's true,' said Reccanto.

'I gather more of myself, yes,' said Cartographer, giving them all another ghastly smile.

Flinches all around.

'How come,' asked Quell, 'you never showed this talent before?'

The corpse straightened. 'I have displayed numerous talents on this journey, each one appropriate to the situation at the time. Have you forgotten the coconuts?'

Faint rolled her eyes and said, 'How could we forget the coconuts?'

'Besides,' resumed Cartographer, 'as an uninvited guest, I feel a pressing need to contribute to the enterprise.' One ragged hand gestured at the scribbles on the track. 'Invest power into this, Master Quell, and we can be on our way.'

'To somewhere we can stop for a time?'

Cartographer shrugged. 'I am not able to predict the situations awaiting us, only that in general they are not particularly threatening.'

Quell looked as if he needed to piss again. Instead, he turned back to the carriage. 'Everyone on board. Precious, you're with me again. Same for you, Mappo.' He paused. 'The rest of you, get ready.'

'For what?' Gruntle asked.

'For anything, of course.'

Reccanto, still strutting after his extraordinary on-the-knees skewering lunge, slapped one hand on the huge warrior's back. 'Don't fret, friend, you'll get used to all this eventually. Unless,' he added, 'it kills you first.'

Cartographer held up some ropes. 'Who will kindly tie me to a wheel?'

Night sweeps across the Dwelling Plain. Along the vast vault of the sky the stars are faint, smudged, as if reluctant to sharpen to knife points amidst the strangely heavy darkness. The coyotes mute their cries for this night. Wolves flee half blind in formless terror, and some will run until their hearts burst.

South of the western tail of the Gadrobi Hills, a lone chain-clad figure pauses in his journey, seeing at last the faint bluish glow that is the ever-beating heart of the great, legendary city.

Darujhistan.

Three leagues west of him, three more strangers gaze upon that selfsame glow, and in the eyes of one of them – unseen by the others – there is such dread, such anguish, as would crush the soul of a lesser man. His gauntleted hand steals again and again to the leather-wrapped grip of his sword.

He tells himself that vengeance answered is peace won, but even he does not quite believe that. Beyond the city awaiting him, the future is a vast absence, a void he now believes he will never see, much less stride into.

Yet, for all the tumultuous, seething forces of will within these arrayed strangers, none among them is the cause for the night's thick, palpable silence.

Less than a league north of the three strangers, seven Hounds are arrayed along a ridge, baleful eyes fixed upon the glow of the city.

The beasts possess the capacity to detect a rabbit's rapid heartbeat half a league away, so they hear well the tolling of the twelfth bell, announcing the arrival of midnight in the city of Darujhistan.

And as one, the seven Hounds lift their massive heads, and give voice to a howl.

The stars are struck into blazing sparks overhead. The High King halts in mid-stride, and the ancient, stubborn blood in his veins and arteries suddenly floods cold as ice. For the first time in this journey, Kallor knows a moment of fear.

Havok's long head snaps up and the beast skitters to one side. Astride the animal, Samar Dev makes a desperate grab for Karsa, lest she be thrown to the ground, and she can feel the sudden tautness of every muscle in the huge warrior.

Ahead of them, Traveller pauses, his shoulders hunching as if those all too close howls even now lash at his back. Then he shakes himself, and marches on.

Atop a cornice of a gate facing the south plain, a squat toad-like demon lifts its head, pointed ears suddenly alert.

Then, as the howls slowly fade, the demon settles once more.

Although now, at last, it can feel, rising up from the very earth, rising up to shiver along its bones, the rumble of heavy paws on distant ground.

Drawing closer, ever closer.

In the city behind Chillbais, the twelfth bell clangs its sonorous note. Another season's grand fete is almost gone. One more day in the name of Gedderone. One more night to close the riot of senseless celebration.

Dance, and dance on.

Because, as everyone knows, all that you see about you will last, well . . . for ever!

Chapter Twenty-One

My friend, this is not the place
The cut flowers lie scattered on the path
And the light of the moon glistens
In what the stems bleed

In the day just for ever lost
I watched a black wasp darting into the face
Of a web, and the spider she dropped
Only to be caught in midair

Footfalls leave no trace
In the wake of a hungry creature's wrath
You can only lie in hope, dreaming
She lightly touched ground

And danced away like a breath
Hiding beneath leaves nodding in place
While the hunter circles and listens
But pray nothing is found

My friend, this is not your face
So pale and still never again to laugh
When the moon's light fell and then stopped
Cold as silver in the glade

Look back on the day, it's for ever lost
Stare into the night, where things confound
The web stretches empty, wind keening
In threads of absent songs

(SONG OF) OLD FRIEND
FISHER

Voluminous in wonder, but, be assured, terse in grief. Consider the woodsman standing facing the forest, axe in hand. In a moment he will stride forward. Consider now the first line of trees, rooted, helpless against what comes.

The seep of trickling water round roots does not quicken. The sweet warmth of sunlight on leaves does not blaze into urgent flame. The world and its pace cannot change. What is to be done? Why, there is nothing to be done. The woodsman swings his axe with blinding speed and splendid indifference, and he hears not the chorus of cries.

Is this fancy worthless? For some, perhaps many, it must be. But know this, empathy is no game.

Twist back time. Dusk still gathers, but it is early yet and so it is a weak gathering. A lone rider draws up on a ridge overlooking a mining camp. Up here the sun's light remains. Dust streams gold and nothing wants to settle. In the shadowy pit below figures seethe back and forth.

He is finally seen. An old man works his way up the path. A runner hurries to the main building squatting atop a levelled heap of tailings.

It begins.

'Another guest? Come for the boy? What's so damned special about that boy?' But Gorlas Vidikas wasn't much interested in any answers to those questions, especially since this runner was in no position to explain much of anything, having been sent direct from the foreman. He rose and pulled on his cloak, then collected up his fine deerskin gloves, and set out. Would he have the pleasure of killing yet another fool? He dearly hoped so.

Was it that pompous old bastard, Coll? That would be ideal, and who could say, maybe the ghost of Lady Simtal would stir awake at the man's last gasp, to howl her delight at this most perfect vengeance, this long-awaited conclusion to the vile treachery of her last fete. Of course, that was mostly Hanut Orr's business, and maybe Shardan Lim's as well, but Gorlas welcomed the sudden unexpected currency he would reap in reward for killing at least two of the old conspirators.

Coll's death would also leave open a seat on the Council. Gorlas smiled at the thought as he climbed the slatted wooden steps up towards the ridge where it wound behind and above the main building. Humble Measure would offer up his own reward for such a thing, no doubt one that would make the gratitude of Hanut and Shardan seem like a pauper's grudging gift. He had a sudden, odd image then of a half-dozen such paupers – beggars and worse – gathered in some abandoned building, squatting on damp earth as they passed round a pathetic slab of grainy bread and a mouldy lump of cheese. And, as he looked on like some unseen ghost, he had the sense that the circle was somehow . . . incomplete.

Someone is missing. Who's missing?

He shook himself then, dispelling the scene, and found that he had halted just below the landing, one hand on the rail at his side. At that last moment, as the image burst apart, he thought he had caught a glimpse of something – a corpse twisting beneath a thick branch, the face swinging round to meet his own – then gone.

Gorlas found his mouth unaccountably dry. Had some god or spirit sent him a vision? Well, if something or someone had, it was a poor one, for he could make no sense of it, none at all.

He tugged on his gloves and resumed the climb, emerging out into the blessed sunlight where everything was painted gold. Yes, the wealth of the world was within reach. He'd never understood poor people, their stupidity, their lack of ambition, their laziness. So much within reach – couldn't they see that? And then how dare they bitch and complain and cast him dark looks, when he went and took all that he could? Let them fall to the wayside, let them tumble underfoot. He was going where he wanted to be and if that meant pushing them out of the way, or crushing them down, so be it.

Why, he could have been born in the damned gutter, and he'd still be where he was today. It was his nature to succeed, to win. The fools could keep their resentment and envy. Hard work, discipline, and the courage to grasp opportunity when it presented itself – these were all the things most people lacked. What they didn't lack, not in the least, was the boundless energy to complain. Bitterness was a waste of energy, and, like acid, it ate the vessel that held it.

As he came round the curve of the ridge he saw at once that the man awaiting him was not Coll. Nor, Gorlas realized, was he a stranger. *Gods below, can this be? Oponn, is it you so blessing me now? Pull me forward, Lady. Shove him closer, Lord.*

The young man (well, they were of the same age, but not in Gorlas's eyes) saw him approach and slowly dismounted, stepping round the horse and positioning himself in the centre of the path facing Gorlas.

'She was not foolish enough to send you here, was she?'

'You know me, then.'

Gorlas smiled. 'I watched you once, only a few days back, from across a street. You looked guilty, did you know that? You looked like a coward – what is your name? I want to know your name, so I can be precise when I tell her what I've done to you . . . and your corpse.'

The man stood unmoving, arms at his sides. 'I am not here for Challice,' he said.

'If you want to think it was all your idea, fine. But I should tell you, I know her well – far better than you. She's been working on you, filling your head – she's pretty much led you here by the hand, even if you're too thick to realize it. Of course, she probably didn't want anyone too smart, since a clever man would have seen through her deadly scheming. A clever man would have walked away. Or run.'

The man tilted his head slightly. 'What is the value of all this, Gorlas Vidikas?'

Gorlas sighed, glanced back at the foreman, who stood watching and listening – yes, something would have to be done about that – and then faced the man once more. 'Since you're too much the coward to actually tell me your name, I will just have to slice off your face, to take back to her as proof. Look at you, you're not even wearing a sword. Foreman! Do we still have Murillio's rapier? I forget, did that go back with him?'

'Not sure, sir – want me to go and look?'

'Well, find the waif a sword. Anything will do – it's not as if he knows how to use it in any case. And hurry, before we lose the light and the mob down there gets bored waiting.' He smiled at the man. 'They've got bloodthirsty of late – my fault, that—'

'Yes, about Murillio . . .'

'Ah, is that why you've come? The duel was fairly fought. He simply could not match my skill.'

'Where is the boy?'

'So he's the reason you're here? This is getting difficult to believe. The child's not some orphaned prince or something, is he? Rather, *was* he?'

'Was?'

'Yes. He's dead, I'm afraid.'

'I see.'

'So, still interested?' Gorlas asked. 'Of course, that's not really relevant any more, because I want you to stay. I suppose you can try to run, but I assure you, you'll be cut down before you get astride that fine horse – a horse I will welcome in my stables. Tell me, are you a better duellist than Murillio was? You'll have to be. Much better.'

The foreman had gone halfway down the trail before yelling instructions, and now a youth was scurrying up cradling a sword – not Murillio's, but something found in one of the workings from the look of it. Thin, tapered to a point that was slightly bent. Iron, at least, but the patina was a thick crust over the blade's spine, and both edges were severely notched. The handle, Gorlas saw as the foreman – breath wheezing – delivered it, wasn't even wrapped.

'Sorry about the lack of grip,' Gorlas said. 'But really, you should have come prepared.'

'How did it feel,' the man asked, 'killing an old man?'

'The duel was fair—'

'Agreed to the death? I doubt that, Vidikas.'

'I dislike the lack of respect in using my last name like that – especially when you won't even tell me your name.'

'Well, your wife calls you Useless, so if you'd prefer that . . .'

Gorlas flung the weapon at the man's feet, where it skidded in a puff of golden dust. 'On guard,' he ordered in a rasp. 'To the death.'

The man made no move to pick up the weapon. He stood as he had before, head tipped a fraction to one side.

'You are a coward in truth,' Gorlas said, drawing his rapier. 'Cowards do not deserve to be treated with honour, so let us dispense with convention—'

'I was waiting for you to say that.'

The foreman, standing off to one side, still struggling with the ache in his chest from a labouring heart, was in the process of licking his gritty lips. Before he had finished that instinctive flicker, the scene before him irrevocably changed.

And Gorlas Vidikas was falling forward, landing hard. His rapier rolled from his hand to catch up in the grass lining the track. Dust puffed up, then slowly settled.

The stranger – had he even moved? the foreman was unsure – now turned to him and said, 'You heard him dispense with the rules of the duel, correct?'

The foreman nodded.

'And, think back now, good sir, did you even once hear me voice a formal challenge?'

'Well, I was part of the way down the trail for a moment—'

'But not beyond range of hearing, I'm sure.'

'Ah, no, unless you did whisper something—'

'Think back. Gorlas was babbling on and on – could I have said anything even if I'd wanted to?'

'True enough, thinking on it.'

'Then are we satisfied here?'

'Ain't for me to say that either way,' the foreman replied. 'It's the man this one was working for.'

'Who, being absent, will have to rely solely upon your report.'

'Er, I suppose so.'

The man shrugged. 'Do as you see fit, then.' He glanced down into the pit. 'You get the feeling they're about to start cheering,' he said.

'They ain't decided.'

'No?'

'They ain't decided if whoever replaces Vidikas is gonna be any better, you see?'

'Because, in their experience, they're all the same.'

The foreman nodded. 'Didn't think you was nobleborn.'

'No, I'm not.'

'No, you're pretty much like them below. Like me, even.'

'I suppose so.' The man walked to the body of Gorlas Vidikas, bent down to roll it on to its back, and the foreman saw the two knife handles, blades buried to the hilts, jutting from Gorlas's chest.

He decided to lick his lips again, and somehow the dust suddenly tasted sweeter. 'Know anything 'bout property law, any chance?'

'Sorry, what?'

'Like, if I was paying on a loan to this man—'

'No, no idea. Though I imagine if you just sit tight, maybe wait to see if anybody ever shows up to collect, well, that would hardly be considered illegal. Would it now?'

'No, seems proper enough to me,' the foreman agreed.

The man worked the knives back out, wiped the blood off on the stained, rumpled cloak. 'Did he tell true about Harllo?'

'What? Oh. He did. The lad tried to escape, and was killed.'

The man sighed, and then straightened. 'Ah, shit, Murillio,' he muttered. 'I'm sorry.'

'Wait – this Harllo – was he that important? I mean—' and the foreman gestured, to encompass not only the corpse lying on the road, but the one that had been there the day before as well, 'all this killing. Who *was* Harllo?'

The man walked to his horse and swung himself into the saddle. He collected the reins. 'I'm not sure,' he said after a moment's consideration. 'The way it started, well, it seemed . . .' he hesitated, and then said, 'he was a boy nobody loved.'

Bitter and scarred as he was, even the foreman winced at that. 'Most of 'em are, as end up here. Most of 'em are.'

The man studied him from the saddle.

The foreman wondered – he didn't see much in the way of triumph or satisfaction in that face looking down at him. He wasn't sure what he was seeing, in fact. Whatever it was, it didn't fit.

Collecting the reins, the stranger drew the horse round and set off up the road. Heading back to the city.

The foreman coughed up a throatful of rank phlegm, then stepped forward and spat down, quite precisely, on to the upturned face of Gorlas Vidikas. Then he turned round. 'I want three guards and the fastest horses we got!'

He watched the runner scramble.

From the pit below rose the occasional snatch of harsh laughter. The foreman understood that well enough, and so he nodded. 'Damn and below, I'll give 'em all an extra flagon of ale anyway.'

Cutter rode for a time as dusk surrendered to darkness. The horse was the first to sense a loss of will, as the rider on its back ceased all efforts at guiding its pace. The beast dropped from a canter to a trot, then a walk, and then it came to rest and stood at the edge of the road, head lowering to snag a tuft of grass.

Cutter stared down at his hands, watched as the reins slithered free. And then he began to weep. For Murillio, for a boy he had never met. But most of all, he wept for himself.

Come to me, my love. Come to me now.

A short time later, three messengers thundered past – paying him no heed at all. The drum of horse hoofs was slow to fade, and the clouds of dust left in their wake hung suspended, lit only by starlight.

Venaz the hero, Venaz who followed orders, and if those meant something vicious, even murderous, then that was how it would be. No questions, no qualms. He had returned up top in grim triumph. Another escape thwarted, the message sweetly delivered. Even so, he liked being thorough. In fact, he'd wanted to make sure.

And so, in keeping with his new privileges as head of the moles, when he collected a knotted climbing rope and set off back into the tunnels, he was not accosted. He could do as he liked now, couldn't he? And when he returned, carrying whatever proof he could find of the deaths of Bainisk and Harllo, then Gorlas

Vidikas would see just how valuable he was, and Venaz would find a new life for himself.

Good work led to good rewards. A simple enough truth.

Whatever flood had filled part of the passage deep in the Settle had mostly drained away, easing his trek to the crevasse. When he reached it he crouched at the edge, listening carefully – to make certain that no one was still alive, maybe scuffling about in the pitch blackness down below. Satisfied, he worked Bainisk's rope off the knob of stone and replaced it with his own, then sent the rest of the coil tumbling over the edge.

Venaz set his lantern to its lowest setting and tied half a body-length of twine to the handle, and the other end to one ankle. He let the lantern down, and then followed with his legs. He brought both feet together, the rope in between, and edged further over until they rested on a knot. Now, so long as the twine didn't get fouled with the rope, he'd be fine.

Moving with great caution, he began his descent.

Broken, bleeding bodies somewhere below, killed by rocks – not by Venaz, since he'd not even cut the rope. Bainisk had done that, the fool. Still, Venaz could still take the credit – nothing wrong with that.

Even with the knots, the slow going was making his arms and shoulders ache. He didn't really have to do this. But maybe it would be the one deed that made all the difference in the eyes of Gorlas Vidikas. Nobles looked for certain things, mysterious things. They were born with skills and talents. He needed to show the man as much as he could of his own talents and all that.

The lantern clunked below him and he looked down to see the faint blush of dull light playing across dry, jagged stones. A few moments later he was standing, somewhat uneasily as the rocks shifted about beneath him. He untied the lantern and put away the twine, and then twisted the wick up a couple of notches. The circle of light widened.

He saw Bainisk's feet, the worn soles of the moccasins, the black-spattered shins, both of which were snapped and showing the split ends of bones. But there was no flowing blood. Bainisk was dead as dead come.

He worked his way closer and stared down at the smashed face, slightly startled by the way it seemed fixed in a smile.

Venaz crouched. He would collect Bainisk's belt-pouch, where he kept all his valuables – the small ivory-handled knife that Venaz so coveted; the half-dozen coppers earned as rewards for special tasks; the one silver coin that Bainisk had cherished the most, as it showed on one face a city skyline beneath a rainbow or some sort of huge moon filling the sky – a coin, someone had said, from Darujhistan, but long ago, in the time of the Tyrants. Treasures now belonging to Venaz.

But he could not find the pouch. He rolled the body over, scanned the blood-smeared rocks beneath and to all sides. No pouch. Not even fragments of string.

He must have given it to Harllo. Or maybe he'd lost it somewhere back up the passage – if Venaz didn't find it down here he could make a careful search on his way back up top.

Now, time to find the other boy, the one he'd hated almost from the first. Always acted like he was smarter than everyone else. It was that look in his eyes, as if he knew he was better, so much better it was easy to be nice to all the stupider people. Easy to smile and say nice things. Easy to be helpful and generous.

Venaz wandered out from Bainisk's body. Something was missing – and not just Harllo's body. And then, after a moment, he realized what it was. The rest of the damned rope, which should have fallen close to the cliff base, close to Bainisk. The damned rope was gone – *and so was Harllo.*

He worked his way along the crevasse and after twenty or so steps he reached the edge of the floor, which he discovered wasn't a floor at all, but a plug, a bridge of fallen rock. The crevasse dropped away an unknown depth, and the air rising from below was hot and dry. Frightened by the realization that he was standing on something that could collapse and fall away at any moment, Venaz hurried back in the other direction.

Harllo was probably badly hurt. He must have been. Unless . . . maybe he had been already down, standing, holding the damned rope, just waiting for Bainisk to join him. Venaz found his mouth suddenly dry. He'd been careless. That wouldn't go down well, would it? This could only work out right if he tracked the runt down and finished him off. The thought sent a cold tremor through him – he'd never actually killed somebody before. Could he even do it? He'd have to, to make everything right.

The plug sloped slightly upward on the other side of Bainisk's body, and each chunk of stone was bigger, the spaces between them whistling with winds from below. Terrifying grating sounds accompanied his every tender step.

Fifteen paces on, another sudden drop-off. Baffled, Venaz worked his way along the edge. He reached the facing wall – the other side of the crevasse – and held high the lantern. In the light he saw an angular fissure, two shelves of bedrock where one side had shifted faster and farther than the other – he could even see where the broken seams continued between the shelves. The drop had been about a body's height, and the fissure – barely a forearm wide – angled sharply into a kind of chute.

Bainisk would never have squeezed into that crack. But Harllo could, and did – it was the only way off the plug.

Venaz retied the lantern, and then forced himself into the fissure. A tight fit. He could only draw half-breaths before the cage of his ribs met solid, unyielding stone. Whimpering, he pushed himself deeper, but not so deep as to get stuck – no, to climb he'd need at least one arm free. By crabbing one leg sideways and squirming with his torso, he moved himself into a position whereby he could hitch himself up in increments. The dry, baked feel of the stone began as a salvation. Had it been wet he would simply have slid back down again and again. Before he'd managed two man-heights, however, he was slick with sweat, and finding streaks of the same above him, attesting to Harllo's own struggles. And he found that the only way he could hold himself in place between forward hitches was to take the deepest breath he could manage, turning his own chest into a wedge, a plug. The rough, worn fabric of his tunic was rubbing his skin raw.

How much time passed? How long this near vertical passage? Venaz lost all sense of such details. He was in darkness, a world of stone walls, dry gusts of air along one flank, a right arm that screamed with fatigue. He bled. He oozed sweat. He was a mass of scrapes and gouges. But then the fissure widened in step fractures, each one providing a blessed ledge on which to finally rest his quivering muscles. Widening, becoming a manageable chute. He was able to draw in deep breaths, and the creaking ache of his ribs slowly faded. He continued on, and before long he reached a new stress fracture, this one cutting straight into the bedrock, perpendicular to the chute.

Venaz hesitated, and then worked his way into it, to see how far it went – and almost instantly he smelled humus, faint and stale, and a little farther in he arrived at an almost horizontal dip where forest detritus had settled. Behind that heady smell there was something else – acrid, fresh. He brightened the lantern and held it out before him. A steep slope of scree rose along the passage, and even as he scanned it there was the clatter of stones bouncing down to patter amidst the dried leaves and dead moss.

He hurried to the base of the slide and peered upward.

And saw Harllo – no more than twenty man-heights above him, flattened on the scree, pulling himself upward with feeble motions.

Yes, he had smelled the boy.

Venaz smiled, and then quickly shuttered the lantern. If Harllo found out he was being chased still, he might try to kick loose a deadly slide of the rubble – of course, if he did that it'd take him down with it. Harllo wasn't stupid. Any wrong move on this slide and they'd both die. The real risk was when he reached the very top, pulling clear. Then there could be real trouble for Venaz.

And smell that downward draught – that was fresh, clean air. Smelling of reeds and mud. The lake shore.

Venaz thought about things, and thought some more. And then settled on a plan. A desperate, risky one. But really, he had no choice. No matter what, Harllo would hear him on this climb. Fine, then, let him.

He laughed, a low, throaty laugh that he knew would travel up the stones like a hundred serpents, coiling with icy poison round Harllo's heart. Laughed, and then crooned, 'Harrrllo! Found youuu!'

And he heard an answering cry. A squeal like a crippled puppy underfoot, a whimper of bleak terror. And all of this was good.

Panic was what he wanted. Not the kind that would make the boy scrabble wildly – since that might just send him all the way back down – but the kind that would, once he gained the top, send him flying out into the night, to run and run and run.

Venaz abandoned the lantern and began climbing.

The chase was torturous. Like two worms they snaked up the dusty slabs of shale. Desperate flight and pursuit were both trapped in the stuttering beating of hearts, the quaking gasps of needful lungs. All trapped inside, for their limbs could move but slowly, locked in an agonizing tentativeness. Minute slides froze them both, queasy shifts made them spread arms and legs wide, breaths held, eyes squeezed shut.

Venaz would have to kill him. For all of this, Harllo would die. There was no other choice now, and Venaz found it suddenly easy to think about choking the life from the boy. His hands round Harllo's chicken neck, the face above them turning blue, then grey. Jutting tongue, bulging eyes – yes, that wouldn't be hard at all.

Sudden scrambling above, a skitter of stones, and then Venaz realized he was alone on the slide. Harllo had reached the surface, and thank the gods, he was *running*.

Your one mistake, Harllo, and now I'll have you. Your throat in my hands.

I have you.

The soft whisper of arrivals once more awakens, even as figures depart. From places of hiding, from refuges, from squalid nests. Into the streams of darkness, shadowy shapes slide unseen.

Thordy watched as the killer who was her husband set out from the cage of lies they called, with quaint irony, their home. As his chopping footfalls faded, she walked out to her garden, to stand at the edge of the pavestone circle. She looked skyward, but there was no moon as yet, no bright smudge to bleach the blue glow of the city's gaslight.

A voice murmured in her head, a heavy, weighted voice. And what it told her made her heart slow its wild hammering, brought peace to her thoughts. Even as it spoke, in measured tones, of a terrible legacy of death.

She drew the one decent kitchen knife they possessed, and held the cold flat of the blade against one wrist. In this odd, ominous stance, she waited.

In the city, at that moment, Gaz walked an alley. Wanting to find someone. Anyone. To kill, to beat into a ruin, smashing bones, bursting eyes, tearing slack lips across the sharp stumps of broken teeth. Anticipation was such a delicious game, wasn't it?

In another home, this one part residence, part studio, Tiserra dried her freshly washed hands. Every sense within her felt suddenly raw, as if scraped with crushed glass. She hesitated, listening, hearing naught but her own breathing, this frail bellows of life that now seemed so frighteningly vulnerable. Something had begun. She was, she realized, terrified.

Tiserra hurried to a certain place in the house. Began a frantic search. Found the hidden cache where her husband had stored his precious gifts from the Blue Moranth.

Empty.

Yes, she told herself, her husband was no fool. He was a survivor – it was his greatest talent. Hard won at that – nowhere near that treacherous arena where

Oponn played push and pull. He'd taken what he needed. He'd done what he could.

She stood, feeling helpless. This particular feeling was not pleasant, not pleasant at all. It promised that the night ahead would stretch out into eternity.

Blend descended to the main floor, where she paused. The bard sat on the edge of the stage, tuning his lyre. Duiker sat at his usual table, frowning at a tankard of ale that his hands were wrapped round as if he was throttling some hard, unyielding fate.

Antsy – Antsy was in gaol. Scillara had wandered out a few bells earlier and had not returned. Barathol was spending his last night in his own cell – he'd be on a wagon headed out to some ironworks come the dawn.

Picker was lying on a cot upstairs, eyes closed, breaths shallow and weak. She was, in truth, gone. Probably never to return.

Blend drew on her cloak. Neither man paid her any attention.

She left the bar.

Ever since the pretty scary woman had left earlier – how long, days, weeks, years, Chaur had no idea – he had sat alone, clutching the sweating lance a dead man wearing a mask had once given C'ur, and rocking back and forth. Then, all at once, he wanted to leave. Why? Because the gulls outside never stopped talking, and the boat squeaked like a rat in a fist, and all the slapping water made him need to pee.

Besides, he had to find Baral. The one face that was always kind, making it easy to remember. The face that belonged to Da and Ma both, just one face, to make it easier to remember. Without Baral, the world turned cold. And mean, and nothing felt solid, and trying to stay together when everything else wasn't was so hard.

So he dropped the lance, rose and set out.

To find Baral. And yes, he knew where to find him. How he knew no one could say. How he thought, no one could imagine. How deep and vast his love, no one could conceive.

Spite stood across the street from the infernal estate that was the temporary residence of her infernal sister, and contemplated her next move, each consideration accompanied by a pensive tap of one finger against her full, sweetly painted lips.

All at once that tapping finger froze in mid-tap, and she slowly cocked her head. 'Oh,' she murmured. And again, 'Oh.'

The wind howled in the distance.

But, of course, there was no wind, was there?

'Oh.'
And how would this change things?

A guard, ignoring once more the dull ache in his chest and the occasional stab of pain shooting down his left arm, walked out from the guard annexe to begin his rounds, making his way to the Lakefront District and the wall that divided it from the Daru District – the nightly murders had begun clustering to either side of that wall. Maybe this time he'd be lucky and see something – someone – and everything would fall into place. Maybe.

He had put in a requisition for a mage, a necromancer, in fact, but alas the wheels of bureaucracy ground reluctantly in such matters. It would probably take the slaying of someone important before things could lurch into motion. He really couldn't wait for that. Finding this killer had become a personal crusade.

The night was strangely quiet, given that it marked the culmination of the Gedderone Fete. Most people were still in the taverns and bars, he told himself, even as he fought off a preternatural unease, and even as he noted the taut expressions of those people he passed, and the way they seemed to scurry by. Where was the revelry? The delirious dancing? *Early yet*, he told himself. But those two words and everything behind them felt oddly flat.

He could hear a distant storm on the plains south of the city. Steady thunder, an echoing wind, and he told himself he was feeling that storm's approach. Nothing more, just the usual *fizz* in the air that preceded such events.

He hurried on, grimacing at the ache in his chest, still feeling the parting kiss of his wife on his lips, the careless hugs of his children round his waist.

He was a man who would never ask for sympathy. He was a man who sought only to do what was right. Such people appear in the world, every world, now and then, like a single refrain of some blessed song, a fragment caught on the spur of an otherwise raging cacophony.

Imagine a world without such souls.

Yes, it should have been harder to do.

After a rather extended time of muted regard fixed dully upon a sealed crypt, four mourners began their return journey to the Phoenix Inn, where Meese would make a grim discovery – although one that, in retrospect, did not in fact shock her as much as it might have.

Before they had gone five hundred paces, however, Rallick Nom drew to a sudden halt. 'I must leave you now,' he said to the others.

'Kruppe understands.'

And the assassin narrowed his gaze upon the short, solemn-faced man.

'Where,' Rallick asked, 'will this go, Kruppe?'

'The future, my friend, is ever turned away, even when it faces us.'

To this bizarre, unlikely truism, Coll grunted, 'Gods below, Kruppe—'

But Rallick had already completed his own turning away and was walking towards the mouth of an alley.

'I got a sick feeling inside,' Meese said.

Coll grunted a second time and then said, 'Let's go. I need to find me another bottle – this time with something in it that actually does something.'

Kruppe offered him a beatific smile. Disingenuous? *Really now.*

Seba Krafar, Master of the Assassins' Guild, surveyed his small army of murderers. Thirty-one in all. Granted, absurd overkill, but even so he found himself not quite as comfortable – or as confident – as such numbers should have made him. 'This is ridiculous,' he muttered under his breath. And then he gestured.

The mob shifted into three distinct groups, and then each hurried off in a different direction, to close on the target at the appointed time.

Come the morning, there'd be a newly vacated seat on the Council. Blood-drenched, true, but it would hardly be the first time for that, would it?

Shardan Lim saw before him a perfect future. He would, if all went well, finally step out from Hanut Orr's shadow. And into his own shadow he'd drag Gorlas Vidikas. They would be sharing a woman, after all, and there would be no measured balance in that situation, since Gorlas was next to useless when it came to satisfying Challice. So Gorlas would find that his wife's happiness was dependent not upon him, but upon the other man sharing her pleasure – Shardan Lim – and when the first child arrived, would there be any doubt as to its progeny? An heir of provable bloodline, the perfect usurpation of House Vidikas.

He had set out alone this night, making his casual way to the Vidikas estate, and he now stood opposite the front gate, studying the modest but well-constructed building. There were hints of Gadrobi in the style, he saw. The square corner tower that was actually higher than it looked, its rooms abandoned to dust and spiders – virtually identical edifices could still be found here and there in the Gadrobi District, and in the hills to the east of the city. Vines covered three of the four walls, reaching up from the garden. If the tower had been a tree it would be dead, centuries dead. Hollowed out by rot, the first hard wind would have sent it thrashing down. This deliberate rejection was no accident. Gadrobi blood among the nobles was an embarrassment. It had always been that way and it always would be.

When Shardan owned this estate, he would see it torn down. His blood was pure Daru. Same as Challice's own.

He heard horses approach at a dangerously fast canter, up from the lower city, and a few moments later three riders appeared, sharply reining in before the estate's gate.

Frowning, Shardan Lim stepped out and quickly approached.

Private guards of some sort, looking momentarily confused as they dismounted. Their horses were lathered, heads dipping as they snorted out phlegm.

'You three,' Shardan called out, and they turned. 'I am Councillor Shardan Lim, and I am about to visit the Vidikas estate. If you carry a message for Lady Challice, do permit me to deliver it.' As he drew closer, he offered the three men a comradely smile. 'She is a delicate woman – having three sweaty men descend on her wouldn't do. I'm sure you understand—'

'Forgive me, Councillor,' one of the men said, 'but the news we deliver is bad.'

'Oh? Come now, no more hesitation.'

'Gorlas Vidikas is dead, sir. He was killed in a duel earlier today. We were instructed to ride to his widow first, and hence on to Eldra Iron Mongery. It means we got to go right back the way we come, but the foreman insisted. As a courtesy. As the proper thing to do.'

Shardan Lim simply stared at the man, his thoughts racing.

'Weren't no duel,' growled one of the other men.

'What's that?' Shardan demanded. 'You there, step out. What did you just say?'

The man was suddenly frightened, but he moved into the councillor's line of sight, managed a quick bow and then said, 'He was assassinated, sir. The foreman kept saying it was all legitimate, but we saw it, sir, with our own eyes. Two knives—'

'Two knives? *Two knives?* Are you certain?'

'Because of the other duel, you see, sir. It was revenge. It was murder. Councillor Vidikas killed another man, then this other one shows up. Then out flash those knives – so fast you couldn't even see 'em, and Councillor Vidikas topples over, stone dead, sir. Stone dead.'

'This is all sounding familiar,' Shardan Lim said. 'Listen to me, you three. One of you, ride to the Orr estate and inform Councillor Hanut Orr. The other two, go on to Eldra, as you will. I will inform Lady Challice. Then, the three of you, find a decent inn for the night and tell the proprietor to treat you well, and to bill House Lim. Go on, now.'

There was some discussion as to who would go where, and which inn they'd rendezvous at when the tasks were done, and then the three men rode off.

Thunder to the south, getting closer. He could hear the wind but it was yet to arrive. Shardan Lim walked up to the gate, pulled on the braided chime in its elongated niche. While he waited for the doorman to arrive, he thought about how he would deliver this grim news. He would need a grave countenance, something more fitting than the dark grin he was even now fighting.

She was a widow now. Vulnerable. There was no heir. Cousins and half-relations might well creep out of the woodwork, mediocre but grasping with sudden ambition. Proclaiming ascendancy in the Vidikas bloodline and so asserting their newly conceived rights to claim stewardship over the entire House. Without strong allies at her side, she'd be out before the week was done.

Once Hanut Orr heard the report, and gleaned whatever he could from the particular details, his mind would fill with the desire for vengeance – and more than a little fear along with it, Shardan was sure. And he would not even think of Challice, not at first, and the opportunities now present. The next day or two would be crucial, and Shardan would have to move sure and fast to position himself at her side and leave no room for Hanut Orr once the man's own ambitions awakened.

An eye-slot scraped to one side, then closed again with a snap. The gate opened. 'House Vidikas welcomes Councillor Lim,' said the doorman from his low bow, as if addressing Shardan's boots. 'The Lady is being informed of your arrival. If you will kindly follow me.'

And in they went.

She hesitated, facing the wardrobe, studying the array of possible shifts to draw on over her mostly naked body. Most were intended to cover other clothes, as befitted a modest noblewoman engaged in entertaining guests, but the truth was, she couldn't be bothered. She had been about to go to sleep, or at least what passed for sleep of late, lying flat and motionless on her bed.

Alone whether her husband was there or not. Staring upward in the grainy darkness. Where the only things that could stir her upright included another goblet of wine, one more pipe bowl or a ghostly walk in the silent garden.

Those walks always seemed to involve searching for something, an unknown thing, in fact, and she would follow through on the desire even as she knew that what she sought no garden could hold. Whatever it was did not belong to the night, nor could it be found in the spinning whirls of smoke, or the bite of strong drink on her numbed tongue.

She selected a flowing, diaphanous gown, lavender and wispy as wreaths of incense smoke, pulling it about her bared shoulder. A broad swath of the same material served to gather it tight about her lower torso, beneath her breasts, firm against her stomach and hips. The thin single layer covering her breasts hid nothing.

Shardan Lim was showing his impatience. His crassness. He was even now in the sitting room, sweaty, his eyes dilated with pathetic needs. He was nothing like what he pretended to be, once the façade of sophisticated lechery was plucked aside. The charm, the sly winks, the suave lie.

This entire damned world, she knew, consisted of nothing but thin veneers. The illusion of beauty survived not even a cursory second look. Cheap and squalid, this was the truth of things. He could paint it up all he liked, the stains on the sheets remained.

Barefooted, she set out to meet him. Imagining the whispers of the staff, the maids and servants, the guards – never within range of her hearing, of course. That would not do. Propriety must be maintained at all costs. They'd wait for her to pass, until she was out of sight. It was their right, after all, their reward for a lifetime of servitude, for all that bowing and scraping, for all the gestures meant to convince her and people like her that she was in fact superior to them. The noble bloods, the rich merchants, the famous families and all the rest.

When the truth was, luck and mischance were the only players in the game of success. Privilege of birth, a sudden harmony of forces, a sudden inexplicable balance later seen as a run of good fortune. Oh, they might strut about – *we all might* – and proclaim that talent, skill and cunning were the real players. But Challice held the belief that even the poor, the destitute, the plague-scarred and the beleaguered might possess talents and cunning, only to find their runs of fortune nonexistent, proper rewards for ever beyond reach.

Servants bowed, and that they needed to do so was proof of just how flimsy the delusion of superiority was.

She opened the door and walked with dignity into the sitting room. 'Councillor Lim, have you been left here alone? No one to provide you with refreshments? This is unacceptable—'

'I sent her away,' he cut in, and she saw that his expression was strange, conflicted by something but in a most peculiar way.

'You have not even poured yourself some wine. Allow me—'

'No, thank-you, Lady Challice. Although, perhaps, I should pour you one. Yes.'

And he went over to select a decanter and then a goblet. She watched the amber wine slosh into the crystal, and then flow over before he righted the decanter. He stared down at the goblet for a moment, and then faced her. 'Lady Challice, I have terrible news.'

Then why do you struggle so not to smile? 'Ah. Speak on, then, Councillor.'

He stepped forward. 'Challice—'

All at once, she sensed that something was deeply awry. He was too excited with his news. He was hungry to see its effect on her. He had no interest in using her body this night. And here she had arrived dressed like a fancy whore. 'Forgive me,' she said, stepping back and attempting to draw the shift more modestly about her.

He barely registered the gesture. 'Challice. Gorlas has been murdered. Your husband is dead.'

'Murdered? But he's still out at the mining camp. He's—' and then she stopped, stunned at how disbelief could so swiftly become certainty.

'Assassinated, out at the camp,' Shardan Lim said. 'Was it a contract? I can't imagine who would . . .' And then he too fell silent, and the regard he fixed upon her now was suddenly sharp, piercing.

She could not face the question he looked ready to ask, and so she went to collect the goblet, unmindful of the wine spilling over her hand, and drank deep.

He had moved to one side and still he said nothing as he watched her.

Challice felt light-headed, unbalanced. She was having trouble thinking. Feelings and convictions, which arrived first? Truths and dreads – she was finding it hard to breathe.

'Challice,' Shardan Lim whispered, suddenly standing close. 'There were other ways. You could have come to me. If this comes out, you will hang – do you understand me? It will take your father down – the entire House D'Arle. The whole Council will be rocked to its very foundations. Hood's breath, Challice – if anyone discovers the truth—'

She turned to him and her voice was flat as she said, 'What truth? What are you talking about, Councillor? My husband has been murdered. I expect you and the Council to conduct an investigation. The assassin must be found and punished. Thank you for taking upon yourself the difficult task of informing me. Now, please, leave me, sir.'

He was studying her as if he had never truly seen her before, and then he stepped away and shook his head. 'I'd no idea, Challice. That you were this . . .'

'That I was what, Councillor?'

'It may be . . . ah, that is, you are within your rights to claim the seat on the Council. Or arrange that someone of your own choosing—'

'Councillor Lim, such matters must wait. You are being insensitive. Please, will you now leave?'

'Of course, Lady Challice.'

When he was gone, she stood unmoving, the goblet still in one hand, the spilled wine sticky under her fingers.

A formal investigation. And yes, it would be thorough. Staff would be questioned. Improprieties revealed. Shardan Lim himself . . . yes, it would be occurring to him about now, as he walked the street, and he might well change his destination – no longer back to his house, but to the Orr estate. To arrange, with growing desperation, the covering of his own tracks.

But none of this affected her. Shardan Lim's fate was meaningless.

She had succeeded. She had achieved precisely what she wanted, the very thing she had begged him to do. For her. For them. But no, for her.

He had killed her husband. Because she had asked him to. And it was now almost certain that he would hang for it. Shardan would talk, pointing the finger so that all eyes shifted away from him, and his accusation would be all fire, blazing with deadly details. And as for her, why, she'd be painted as a foolish young woman. Playing with lowborn but astoundingly ignorant of just how vicious such creatures could be, when something or someone stood in their way. When obsessive love was involved, especially. Oh, she'd been playing, but that nasty young lowborn thug had seen it differently. And now she would have to live with the fact that her idle game had led to her husband's murder. Poor child.

Her father would arrive, because he was the sort of father to do just that. He would raise impenetrable walls round her, and personally defend every portico, every bastion. Aim the knife of innuendo towards her and he would step into its path. He would retaliate, ferociously, and the sly sceptics would quickly learn to keep their mouths shut, if they valued their heads.

She would be the eye of the storm, and feel not even a single drop of rain, nor sigh of wind.

Challice set the goblet down. She walked out into the corridor and proceeded without haste back to her bedroom, where she collected the glass globe with its imprisoned moon. And then left once more, this time to the square tower, with its rooms crowded with antique Gadrobi furniture slowly rotting to dust, with its musty draughts sliding up and down the stairs.

I have killed him. I have killed him.

I have killed him

Hanut Orr adjusted his sword-belt and checked his rapier yet again. He had come close to beating the hapless mine guard to glean every last detail of the events surrounding the assassination of Gorlas Vidikas, and he now believed he had a fair idea of the grisly story behind it. The echoes tasted sour, personal. Once he learned where the first man's body had been delivered, he knew where this night would take him.

He assembled his four most capable guards and they set out into the city.

Two knives to the chest. Yes, the past never quite went away, did it? Well, finally, he would be able to deliver his long-delayed vengeance. And when he was done there, he would find the one man who was at the centre of all of this. Councillor Coll would not see the dawn.

He dispatched two of his men to Coll's estate. *Watch. Any strangers show up, they don't reach the damned gate. We are at war tonight. Be ready to kill, am I understood?*

Of course he was. These hard men were no fools.

He knew that damned mob in the Phoenix Inn. He knew every one of Coll's decrepit, lowborn friends, and he intended to kill them all.

Down from the Estates District and into the Daru District. Not far.

Two streets from the Phoenix Inn he halted his two remaining men. 'You'll watch the front entrance, Havet. Kust, I want you to walk in and make a show – it won't have to be much, they'll smell you out fast enough. I have the alley, for when somebody bolts. Both of you, keep an eye out for a short, fat man in a red waistcoat. If you get a chance, Havet, cut him down – that shouldn't be hard. There's two tough-looking women who run the place – they're fair targets as well if they head outside. I'm not sure who else will be in that foul nest – we'll find out soon enough. Now, go.'

They went one way. He went another.

Torvald Nom grunted and gasped as he pulled himself on to the estate roof. Sitting at his desk had been driving him mad. He needed to be out, roving round, keeping an eye on everything. On *everything*. This was a terrible night and nothing had happened yet. He missed his wife. He wished he was back home, and with the coming storm he'd be drenched by the time he stumbled into that blessed, warm abode. Assuming he ever made it.

He worked his way along the edge so that he could see down into the forecourt. And there they were, Madrun and Lazan Door, throwing knuckles against the wall to the left of the main gate. He heard the door of the house open directly beneath him and saw the carpet of light unfold on the steps and pavestones, and the silhouette of the man standing in the doorway was instantly recognizable. Studlock, Studious Lock. Not moving at all, just watching, but watching what?

Knuckles pattered, bounced on stone, then settled, and the two compound guards hunched down over them to study the cast.

That's what he's watching. He's watching the throws.

And Torvald Nom saw both men slowly straighten, and turn as one to face the man standing in the doorway.

Who must have stepped back inside, softly closing the door.

Oh, shit.

There was a scuffle somewhere behind him and Torvald Nom spun round. It was too damned dark – where was the moon? Hiding somewhere behind the storm clouds, of course, and he glanced up. And saw a sweep of bright stars. *What clouds? There aren't any clouds. And if that's thunder, then where's the lightning? And if that's the howl of wind, why is everything perfectly still?* He wasn't sure now if he'd actually heard anything – nothing was visible on the roof, and there were no real places to hide either. He was alone up here.

Like a lightning rod.

He tried a few deep breaths to slow the frantic beat of his heart. At least he'd prepared himself. All his instincts strumming like taut wires, he'd done all he could.

And it's not enough. Gods below, it's not enough!

Scorch looked startled, but then he always looked startled.

'Relax,' hissed Leff, 'you're driving me to distraction.'

'Hey, you hear something?'

'No.'

'Exactly.'

'What's that supposed to mean? We ain't hearing nothing. Good. That means there's nothing to hear.'

'They stopped.'

'Who stopped?'

'Them, the ones on the other side of the gate, right? They stopped.'

'Well, thank Hood,' said Leff. 'Those knuckles was driving me crazy. Every damned night, on and on and on. Click clack click clack, gods below. I never knew Seguleh were such gamblers – it's a sickness, you know, an addiction. No wonder they lost their masks – probably in a bet. Picture it. "Ug, got nuffin but this mask, and m'luck's boot to change, 'sgot to, right? So, I'm in – look, 'sa good mask! Ug." '

'That would've been a mistake,' Scorch said, nodding. 'If you don't want nobody to know you're bluffing, what better way than to wear a mask? So, they lost 'em and it's been downhill ever since. Yeah, that makes sense, but it's got me thinking, Leff.'

' 'Bout what?'

'Well, the Seguleh. Hey, maybe they're *all* bluffing!'

Leff nodded back. This was better. Distract the fidgety idiot. All right, maybe things didn't feel quite right. Maybe there was a stink in the air that had nothing to do with smell, and maybe he had sweat trickling down under his armour, and he was keeping his hand close to the sword at his belt and eyeing the crossbow leaning against the gate. Was it cocked? It was cocked.

Click clack click clack. Come on, boys, start 'em up again, before you start making me *nervous.*

Cutter halted the horse and sat, leaning forward on the saddle, studying the ship moored alongside the dock. No lights showed. Had Spite gone to bed this early? That seemed unlikely. He hesitated. He wasn't even sure why he had come here. Did he think he'd find Scillara?

That was possible, but if so it was a grotesque desire, revealing an ugly side to his nature that he did not want to examine for very long, if at all. He had pretty much abandoned her. She was a stranger to Darujhistan – he should have done better. He should have been a friend.

How many more lives could he ruin? If justice existed, it was indeed appropriate that he ruin himself as well. The sooner the better, in fact. Grief and self-pity seemed but faint variations on the same heady brew that was self-indulgence – did he really want to drown Scillara in his pathetic tears?

No, Spite would be better – he'd get three words out and she'd start slapping him senseless. *Get over it, Cutter. People die. It wasn't fair, so you put it right. And now you feel like Hood's tongue after a night of slaughter. Live with it. So wipe your nose and get out there. Do something, be someone and stay with it.*

Yes, that was what he needed right now. A cold, cogent regard, a wise absence of patience. In fact, she wouldn't even have to say anything. Just seeing her would do.

He swung down from the saddle and tied the reins to a bollard, then crossed the gangplank to the deck. Various harbour notices had been tacked to the mainmast. Moorage fees and threats of imminent impoundment. Cutter managed a smile, imagining a scene of confrontation in the near future. Delightful to witness, if somewhat alarming, provided he stayed uninvolved.

He made his way below. 'Spite? You here?'

No response. Spirits plunging once more, he tried the door to the main cabin, and found it unlocked. Now, that was strange. Drawing a knife, he edged inside, and waited for his eyes to adjust to the gloom. Nothing seemed untoward, no signs of disarray – so there had been no roving thief, which was a relief. As he stepped towards the lantern hanging from a hook, his foot struck something that skidded a fraction.

Cutter looked down.

His lance – the one that dead Seguleh horseman had given him, in that plague-stricken fort in Seven Cities. He recalled seeing it later, strapped to the back of a floating pack amidst wreckage in the waves. He recalled Spite's casual retrieval. He had since stashed the weapon beneath his bunk. So, what was it doing here?

And then he noted the beads of what looked like sweat glistening on the iron blade.

Cutter reached down.

The copper sheathing of the shaft was warm, almost hot. Picking the lance up, he realized, with a start, that the weapon was *trembling*. 'Beru fend,' he whispered, 'what is going on here?'

Moments later he was back on the deck, staring over at his horse as the beast tugged at the reins, hoofs stamping the thick tarred boards of the dock. Its ears were flat, and it looked moments from tearing the bollard free – although of course that was impossible. Cutter looked down to find he was still carrying the lance. He wondered at that, but not for long, as he heard a sudden, deafening chorus of howls roll through the city. All along the shoreline, nesting birds exploded upward in shrieking panic, winging into the night.

Cutter stood frozen in place. *The Hounds.*

They're here.

Grisp Falaunt had once been a man of vast ambitions. Lord of the single greatest landholding anywhere on the continent, a patriarch of orchards, pastures, groves and fields of corn stretching to the very horizon. Why, the Dwelling Plain was unclaimed, was it not? And so he could claim it, unopposed, unobstructed by prohibitions.

Forty-one years later he woke one morning stunned by a revelation. The Dwelling Plain was unclaimed because it was . . . useless. Lifeless. Pointless. He had spent most of his life trying to conquer something that was not only unconquerable, but capable of using its very indifference to annihilate every challenger.

He'd lost his first wife. His children had listened to his promises of glorious inheritance and then had simply wandered off, each one terminally unimpressed. He'd lost his second wife. He'd lost three partners and seven investors. He'd lost his capital, his collateral and the shirt on his back – this last indignity courtesy of a crow that had been hanging round the clothes line in a most suspicious manner.

There comes a time when a man must truncate his ambitions, cut them right down, not to what was possible, but to what was manageable. And, as one grew older and more worn down, manageable became a notion blurring with minimal, as in how could a man exist with the minimum of effort? How little was good enough?

He now lived in a shack on the very edge of the Dwelling Plain, offering a suitable view to the south wastes where all his dreams spun in lazy dust-devils through hill and dale and whatnot. And, in the company of a two-legged dog so useless he needed to hand-feed it the rats it was supposed to kill and eat, he tended three rows of root crops, each row barely twenty paces in length. One row suffered a blight of purple fungus; another was infested with grub-worm; and the one between those two had a bit of both.

On this gruesome night with its incessant thunder and invisible lightning and ghost wind, Grisp Falaunt sat rocking on his creaking chair on his back porch, a jug of cactus spit in his lap, a wad of rustleaf bulging one cheek and a wad of durhang the other. He had his free hand under his tunic, as would any man keeping his own company with only a two-legged dog looking on – but the mutt wasn't paying him any attention anyway, which, all things considered, was a rare relief these nights when the beast mostly just stared at him with oddly hungry eyes. No, old Scamper had his eyes on something to the south, out there in the dark plain.

Grisp hitched the jug up on the back of a forearm and tilted in a mouthful of the thick, pungent liquor. Old Gadrobi women in the hills still chewed the spiny blades after hardening the insides of their mouths by eating fire, and spat out the pulp in bowls of water sweetened with virgin's piss. The mixture was then fermented in sacks of sewn-up sheep intestines buried under dung heaps. And there, in the subtle cascade of flavours that, if he squeezed shut his watering eyes, he could actually taste, one could find the bouquets marking every damned stage in the brewing process. Leading to an explosive, highly volatile cough followed by desperate gasping, and then—

But Scamper there had sharpened up, as much as a two-legged dog could, anyway. Ears perking, seeming to dilate – but no, that was the spit talking – and nape hairs snapping upright in fierce bristle, and there was his ratty, knobby tail, desperately snaking down and under the uneven haunches – and gods below, Scamper was whimpering and crawling, piddling as he went, straight for under the porch – look at the damned thing go! With only two legs, too!

Must be some storm out there—

And, looking up, Grisp saw strange baleful fires floating closer. In sets of two, lifting, weaving, lowering, then back up again. How many sets? He couldn't count. He could have, once, long ago, right up to twenty, but the bad thing about cactus spit was all the parts of the brain it stamped dead underfoot. Seemed that counting and figuring was among them.

Fireballs! Racing straight for him!

Grisp screamed. Or, rather, tried to. Instead, two wads were sucked in quick succession to the back of his throat, and all at once he couldn't breathe, and could only stare as a horde of giant dogs attacked in a thundering charge, straight across his three weepy rows, leaving a churned, uprooted, trampled mess. Two of the beasts made for him, jaws opening. Grisp had rocked on to the two back legs of the chair with that sudden, shortlived gasp, and now all at once he lost his balance, pitching directly backward, legs in the air, even as two sets of enormous jaws snapped shut in the place where his head had been a heartbeat earlier.

His shack erupted behind him, grey shards of wood and dented kitchenware exploding in all directions.

The thumping impact when he hit the porch sent both wads out from his mouth on a column of expelled air from his stunned lungs. The weight of the jug, two fingers still hooked through the lone ear, pulled him sideways and out of the toppled chair on to his stomach, and he lifted his head and saw that his shack was simply gone, and there were the beasts, fast dwindling as they charged towards the city.

Groaning, he lowered his head, settling his forehead on to the slatted boards, and could see through the crack to the crawlspace below, only to find Scamper's two beady eyes staring back up at him in malevolent accusation.

'Fair 'nough,' he whispered. 'Time's come, Scamper old boy, for us to pack up 'n' leave. New pastures, hey? A world before us, just waitin' wi' open arms, just—'

The nearest gate of the city exploded then, the shock wave rolling back to flatten

Grisp once more on the floorboards. He heard the porch groan and sag under him and had one generous thought for poor Scamper – who was scrambling as fast as two legs could take him – before the porch collapsed under him.

Like a dozen bronze bells, hammered so hard they tore loose from their frames and, in falling, dragged the bell towers down around them, the power of the seven Hounds obliterated the gate, the flanking unfinished fortifications, the guard house, the ring-road stable, and two nearby buildings. Crashing blocks of stone, wooden beams, bricks and tiles, crushed furniture and fittings, more than a few pulped bodies in the mix. Clouds of dust, spurts of hissing flame from ruptured gas pipes, the ominous subterranean roar of deadlier eruptions—

Such a sound! Such portentous announcement! The Hounds have arrived, dear friends. Come, yes, come to deliver mayhem, to reap a most senseless toll. Violence can arrive blind, without purpose, like the fist of nature. Cruel in disregard, brutal in its random catastrophe. Like a flash flood, like a tornado, a giant dust-devil, an earthquake – so blind, so senseless, so without intent!

These Hounds . . . they were nothing like that.

Moments before this eruption, Spite, still facing the estate of her venal bitch of a sister, reached a decision. And so she raised her perfectly manicured hands, up before her face, and closed them into fists. Then watched as a deeper blot of darkness formed over the estate, swelling ever larger until blood-red cracks appeared in the vast shapeless manifestation.

In her mind, she was recalling a scene from millennia past, a blasted landscape of enormous craters – the fall of the Crippled God, obliterating what had been a thriving civilization, leaving nothing but ashes and those craters in which magma roiled, spitting noxious gases that swirled high into the air.

The ancient scene was so vivid in her mind that she could scoop out one of those craters, half a mountain's weight of magma, slap it into something like a giant ball, and then position it over the sleepy estate wherein lounged her sleepy, unsuspecting sister. And, now that it was ready, she could just . . . *let go*.

The mass descended in a blur. The estate vanished – as did those nearest to it – and as a wave of scalding heat swept over Spite, followed by a wall of lava thrashing across the street and straight for her, she realized, with a faint squeal, that she too was standing far too close

Ancient sorceries were messy, difficult to judge, harder yet to control. She'd let her eponymous tendencies affect her judgement. Again.

Undignified flight was the only option for survival, and as she raced up the alley she saw, standing thirty paces ahead, at the passageway's mouth, a figure.

Lady Envy had watched the conjuration at first with curiosity, then admiration, and then awe, and finally in raging jealousy. That spitting cow *always* did things better! Even so, as she watched her twin sister bleating and scrambling mere steps ahead of the gushing lava flow, she allowed herself a most pitiless smile.

Then released a seething wave of magic straight into her sister's slightly prettier face.

Spite never thought ahead. A perennial problem, a permanent flaw – that she hadn't killed herself long ago was due only to Envy's explicit but casual-seeming indifference. But now, if the cow really wanted to take her on, at last, to bring an end to all this, well, that was just dandy.

As her sister's nasty magic engulfed her, Spite did the only thing she could do under the circumstances. She let loose everything she had in a counterattack. Power roared out from her, clashed and then warred with Envy's own.

They stood, not twenty paces apart, and the space between them raged like the heart of a volcano. Cobbles blistered bright red and melted away. Stone and brick walls rippled and sagged. Faint voices shrieked. Slate tiles pitched down into the maelstrom as roofs tilted hard over on both sides.

Needless to say, neither woman heard a distant gate disintegrate, nor saw the fireball that followed, billowing high into the night. They did not even feel the thunderous reverberations rippling out beneath the streets, the ones that came from the concussions of subterranean gas chambers igniting one after another.

No, Spite and Envy had other things on their minds.

There could be no disguising a sudden rush to the estate gate by a dozen black-clad assassins. As five figures appeared from an alley mouth directly opposite Scorch and Leff, three others, perched on the rooftop of the civic building to the right of the alley, sent quarrels hissing towards the two lone guards. The remaining four, two to a side, sprinted in from the flanks.

The facing attack had made itself known a moment too soon, and both Scorch and Leff had begun moving by the time the quarrels arrived. This lack of coordination could be viewed as inevitable given the scant training these assassins possessed, since this group was, in fact, little more than a diversion, and thus comprised the least capable individuals among the attackers.

One quarrel glanced off Leff's helm. Another was deflected by Scorch's chain hauberk, although the blow, impacting his left shoulder blade, sent him stumbling.

The sky to the west lit up momentarily, and the cobbles shook as Leff reached his crossbow, managed a skidding turn and loosed the quarrel into the crowd of killers fast closing.

A bellow of pain and one figure tumbled, weapons skittering.

Scorch scrabbled for his own crossbow, but it looked to Leff as if he would not ready it in time, and so with a shout he drew his shortsword and leapt into the path of the five attackers.

Scorch surprised him, as a quarrel sped past to thud deep into a man's chest, punching him back and fouling up the assassin behind him. Leff shifted direction and went in on that side, slashing with his sword at the tangled figure – a thick, heavyset woman – and feeling the edge bite flesh and then bone.

Shapes darted in on his left – but all at once Scorch was there.

Things got a bit hot then.

Torvald Nom was looking for a way down when the tiles beneath his boots trembled to the sounds of running feet. He spun round to find four figures charging towards him. Clearly, they had not been expecting to find anyone up here, since none carried crossbows. In the moment before they reached him, he saw in their hands knives, knotted clubs and braided saps.

The nearest one wobbled suddenly – a bolt was buried deep in his right temple – and then fell in a sprawl.

Torvald threw himself to one side and rolled – straight over the roof edge. Not quite what he had planned, and he desperately twisted as he fell, knowing that it wouldn't help in the least.

He had tucked into his belt two Blue Moranth sharpers.

Torvald could only close his eyes as he pounded hard on to the pavestones. The impact threw him back upward on a rising wave of stunning pain, but the motion seemed strangely slow, and he opened his eyes – amazed that he still lived – only to find that the world had turned into swirling green and blue clouds, thick, wet.

No, not clouds. He was inside a bulging, sloshing sphere of water. Hanging suspended now, as it rolled, taking him with it, out into the courtyard.

From the rooftop, which he was able to look up at as the misshapen globe tumbled him over and over, he saw an assassin pitch over the edge in a black spray of blood – and then he was looking at Madrun and Lazan Door, wielding two curved swords each, cutting through a mob that even now scattered in panic.

At that moment sorcery ignited the courtyard, rolling in a spitting, raging wave that swept up the main building's front steps and collided with the door, shattering it and the lintel above. Clouds of dust tumbled out, and three vague shapes rushed in, disappearing inside the house. A fourth one skidded to a halt at the base of the cracked steps, spun round and raised gloved hands. More magic, shrieking as it darted straight for the two unmasked Seguleh and those few assassins still standing. The impact sent bodies flying.

Torvald Nom, witnessing all this through murky water and discovering a sudden need to breathe, lost sight of everything as the globe heaved over one last time, even as he heard water draining, splashing down out to the sides, and watched the blurred pavestones beneath him draw closer.

All at once he found himself lying on the courtyard, drenched, gasping for air. He rolled over on to his back, saw a spark-lit, fiery black cloud tumble through the sky directly overhead – and that was curious, wasn't it?

Detonations from within the estate. A sudden scream, cut bloodily short. He looked over to where Lazan Door and Madrun had been. Bodies crowded up against the inside wall, like a handful of black knuckles, and their bouncing, skid-ding journey was at an end, every knuckle settled and motionless.

Someone was approaching. Slow, steady steps, coming to a rest beside him.

Blinking, Torvald Nom looked up. 'Cousin! Listen! I'm sorry, all right? I never meant it, honest!'

'What in Hood's name are you going on about, Tor?' Rallick Nom was wiping blood from his tjaluk knives. 'I'd swear you were scared of me or something.'

'I didn't mean to steal her, Rallick. That's no lie!'

'Tiserra?'

Torvald stared up at his cousin, wide-eyed, his heart bounding like an antelope with a hundred starving wolves on its stumpy tail.

Rallick made a face. 'Tor, you idiot. We were what, seven years old? Sure, I thought she was cute, but gods below, man, any boy and girl who start holding hands at seven and are still madly in love with each other twenty-five years later – that's not something to mess with—'

'But I saw the way you looked at us, year after year – I couldn't stand it, I couldn't sleep, I knew you'd come for me sooner or later, I knew . . .'

Rallick frowned down at him. 'Torvald, what you saw in my face was envy. Yes, such a thing can get ugly, but not with me. I watched in wonder, in admira-tion. Dammit, I loved you both. Still do.' He sheathed his weapons and reached down with a red-stained hand. 'Good to see you, cousin. Finally.'

Torvald took that hand, and suddenly – years of guilt and fear shedding away – the whole world was all right. He was pulled effortlessly to his feet. 'Hang on,' he said, 'what are you doing here?'

'Helping out, of course.'

'Taking care of me—'

'Ah, that was incidental, in truth. I saw you on the rooftop earlier. There'd be a few trying that way. Anyway, you did a nice job of catching their attention.'

'That quarrel through that one's head was from you?'

'At that range, I never miss.'

They turned then as Studious Lock, limping, emerged from the wreckage of the main entrance. And behind him strode the Lady of the house. She was wear-ing leather gloves that ran up to the elbow on which dagger-sheaths had been riv-eted. Her usual voluminous silks and linens had been replaced by tight-fitting, fighting clothes. Torvald squinted thoughtfully.

Studious Lock was making his way towards the heap of bodies.

Lady Varada saw Rallick and Torvald and approached.

Rallick bowed. 'Did the mage give you any trouble, Mistress?'

'No. Is the rooftop clear?'

'Of course.'

'And Seba?'

'Probably scampering for his warren as fast as his legs can take him.' Rallick paused. 'Mistress, you could walk back in—'

'And who is left in my Guild, Rallick? Of any worth, I mean.'

'Krute, perhaps. Myself. Even Seba would manage, so long as he was responsible for a single cell and nothing more.'

Torvald was no fool, and as he followed this conversation, certain things fell into place. 'Lady Varada,' he said. 'Er, Mistress Vorcan, I mean. You knew this was coming, didn't you? And you probably hired me, and Scorch and Leff, because you believed we were useless, and, er, expendable. You wanted them to get through – you wanted them all in here, so you could wipe them out once and for all.'

She regarded him for a moment, one eyebrow lifting, and then turned away and headed back to her house.

Torvald made to pursue her but Rallick reached out a hand and held him back. 'Cousin,' he said in a low voice, 'she was Mistress of the Assassins' Guild. Do you think she's anything like us? Do you really think she gives a damn if we live or die?'

Torvald glanced over at Rallick. 'Now who's the fool, cousin? No, you're right, about me and Scorch and Leff – and those fallen Seguleh over there – she doesn't care. But you, Rallick, that's different. Are you blind? Soon as she stepped out, her eyes went to you, and all the stiffness relaxed, and she came over to make sure you weren't wounded.'

'You can't be serious.'

'And you can't be so stupid, can you?'

At that moment the main gates crashed open and two bloody figures staggered in.

'We was attacked!' Scorch shouted in outrage.

'We killed 'em all,' Leff added, looking round wildly, 'but there could be more!'

Torvald noted his cousin's expression and softly laughed, drawing Rallick's attention once more. 'I got some wine in my office,' Torvald said. 'We can sit and relax and I can tell you some things about Scorch and Leff—'

'This is not the night for that, Tor – are you deaf?'

Torvald scowled, then thumped at the side of his head. Both sides. 'Sorry, got water in my ears. Even you here, you sound to me like you're under a bucket.'

The thumping worked, at least for one ear, and he could hear now what everyone else was listening to.

Screams, all through the city. Buildings crashing down. Echoing howls. Recalling the fireball he'd seen, he looked skyward. No stars in sight – the sky was filled with smoke, huge bulges underlit by wildfires in the city. 'Gods below!'

Harllo ran down the road. His knees were cut and deeply scored by his climb up the slope of scree, and blood ran down his shins. Stitches bit into his sides and every muscle was on fire. And Venaz was so close behind him that he could hear his harsh gasps – but Venaz was older, his legs were longer, and it would be soon now, no matter how tired he sounded.

To have come so far, and everything was about to end . . . but Harllo would not weep. Would not plead or beg for his life. Venaz was going to beat him to death. It was as simple as that. There was no Bainisk to stand in the way, there were no rules of the camp. Harllo was not a mole any more; he was of no use to anyone.

People like him, big and small, died all the time. Killed by being ignored, killed because nobody cared what happened to them. He'd walked the streets of Daru- jhistan often enough to see for himself, to see that the only thing between those huddled shapes and himself was a family that didn't even want him, no matter how hard he worked. They were Snell's parents, and Snell was what they'd made between them, and nothing in the world could cut through those tethers.

That was why they let Snell play with Harllo, and if he played using fists and feet and something went bad, well, that stuff happened all the time, didn't it? That's why they never came to get him. And the one man who did, Gruntle, who always looked down at him with sad eyes, he was dead now, too, and it was this fact that eased Harllo's mind. He was happy to go where Gruntle had gone. He would take hold of that giant scarred hand and know that, finally, he was safe.

'I got you! I got you!'

A hand snagged at the back of his shirt, missed.

Harllo threw himself forward – maybe one last spurt – away, fast as he could—

The hand caught a handful of tunic, and Harllo stumbled, and then a thin sweaty arm wrapped tight round his neck, lifting him from his feet.

The forearm pressed against his throat. He could not breathe. And all at once Harllo did not want to die.

He flailed, but Venaz was too big, too strong.

Harllo was forced down to the stony surface of the road, then pushed over on his back as Venaz straddled him and closed both hands round his neck.

The face glaring down at him was flushed with triumph. Sweat ran muddy streaks down it; something had cut one cheek and white threads of cave-worms clustered round the wound – they'd lay eggs and that cut would become a huge welt, until it burst and the grubs crawled out, and the scar left behind would never go away and Venaz would be ugly for the rest of his life.

'Got you got you got you,' Venaz whispered, his eyes bright. 'And now you die. Now you die. Got you and now you die.'

Those hands squeezed with savage strength.

He fought, he scratched, he kicked, but it was hopeless. He felt his face swell, grow hot. The darkness flushed red.

Something cracked hard and Venaz was reeling back, his grip torn loose. Hands closed on Harllo's upper arms and dragged him a short distance away. Gasping, he stared up at a strange face – another boy – who now stepped past him, advancing on Venaz.

Who had scrambled upright, nose streaming blood. 'Who the shit are—'

The stranger flung himself at Venaz, and both went down.

Coughing, tears streaming, Harllo forced himself on to his hands and knees. The two boys were about the same size, and they were of that age when a real fight had a deadly edge. They fought as would rabid dogs. Clawing into faces, seeking eye sockets, or inside the mouth to tear aside one entire cheek. They bit, gouged, used their elbows and knees as they rolled about on the roadside.

Something snapped, like a green sapling, and someone howled in terrible pain.

Harllo climbed to his feet, and he found he was holding a large round stone in his hands.

Venaz had broken the stranger's left arm, and he was now working himself on top, fists raining down into the other boy's face – who did what he could to protect it with his one working arm, but half of those fists got through, smashing into the face beneath.

Harllo stepped up behind Venaz, who was straddling the stranger. He looked down, seeing him as the stranger must have done when Harllo was the one lying on the ground, being murdered. He raised the rock, and then drove it down on to the top of Venaz's skull.

The impact made him lose his grip on the stone and he saw it roll off to one side, leaving a shallow dent in Venaz's head.

Venaz seemed to be in the midst of a coughing fit, a barely human stuttering sound bursting from his throat. He pushed himself off the other boy and rose wobbling to his feet. When he turned to stare at Harllo, he was smiling, the teeth bright shards between gushing streams of blood from his nose. His eyes had filled and were now opaque. He lost his balance and reeled to one side, only to lose his footing on the edge of the road and plunge into the grassy ditch.

Harllo went to stare down at him. Venaz was still smiling, lying on his back, his cut and bruised hands making strange circular motions. He had soiled himself and the stench made Harllo step back, away, to walk over and kneel down beside the other boy.

Who was sitting up, cradling his broken arm, hair hanging over his face.

'Hello,' said Harllo, 'who are you?'

Hanut Orr stood in the shadows behind the Phoenix Inn, waiting for the first of the cowardly bastards to come rushing out from the kitchen door. His man must be inside by now, stirring things up. Not long, then.

He ducked at the sound of ferocious howls echoing through the city, and then a thundering concussion somewhere to the south – but close – and he stepped out to the centre of the alley. Some shambling figure walking past had to shift quickly to one side to avoid colliding with him.

'Watch it,' Hanut snapped, and then he looked up into the slash of night visible between the buildings, as it suddenly lit red and orange.

It was pretty much the last thing he ever saw.

As soon as he was past the fool, Gaz whirled round, his right fingerless hand lashing out to crack with a crunch against the base of his victim's neck. Bone against bone, and it was not knuckles that broke – they were by now too scarred, too calcined, for that. No, what snapped was Hanut Orr's neck.

Gaz was swinging with his other hand even as the body crumpled, his left pounding into the man's forehead, flinging the head back like a bulbous seed pod on a broken stalk. Slap went the body, head bouncing once and then lolling way too far to one side.

He stared down, and then moaned. This was no drunk who'd been leaning against a wall behind the inn. He should have noted the man's tone when he'd warned him off.

This was a highborn.

Gaz found he was breathing fast. A rapid pounding in his chest, a sudden heat flooding through him. His knuckles throbbed.

'Thordy,' he whispered, 'I'm in deep trouble. *Thordyyyy . . .*'

He looked up and down the alley, saw no one, and then set off, stiff-legged, leaning far forward, his fingerless hands drawn up under his chin. He was going home. Yes, he had to get home, and be there all night, yes, he'd been there all night—

In trouble in trouble I'm in trouble now. Mages and necromancers, guards everywhere – listen to the alarms – they're found him already! Oh oh oh trouble, Thordy, so much trouble . . .

Councillor Coll had pushed him back on to the bar, then down on to its battered surface. The severe arch forced by the position had Hanut Orr's thug groaning in pain.

'Is he waiting, then?' Coll asked, leaning close. 'Your shitface boss – is he waiting outside?'

The man understood loyalty, and he understood the demands of raw survival, and of course there was no contest between the two. He managed a nod and gasped, 'Alley. He's in the alley. There's another man, other side of the street out front.'

'And who are you all looking for?'

'Any – uh – any one of you. No, wait. The assassin, the one with the two knives – the one who just killed Gorlas Vidikas.'

The man saw Coll's broad, oddly puffy face twist into a frown, and the heavy weight pressing down on his chest – keeping him pinned on the countertop – eased back.

'Meese, this one moves, kill him.'

The woman with the absurd two-handed mace stepped up, eyes flat and lifeless as they fixed on the thug. 'Give me a reason,' she said.

The thug simply shook his head and stayed right where he was, leaning now against the rail.

He watched as Coll shambled over to where stood the short, round man in the red waistcoat. They spoke for a time, in tones so low the man had no chance of overhearing their conversation. And then Coll went behind the bar and emerged a moment later with an antique broadsword that looked like a perfect fit in those huge hands. Trailed by the fat man, he marched out into the kitchen, presumably for the back door.

Well, Hanut Orr was an arrogant tyrant. So he got what he wanted and a whole lot more. Things like that happen.

The man suddenly recalled that he'd spilled nothing about the two men waiting outside Coll's estate. Well, this could work out just fine, so long as he managed to get out of this damned inn before Coll got ambushed at his gate.

Damned noisy in the city tonight – ah, yes, the last night of Gedderone Fete. Of course it was noisy, and dammit, he wanted to be out there himself, partying, dancing, squeezing soft flesh, maybe picking a fight or two – but ones he could win, of course. Nothing like this crap—

All at once Coll and the fat man were back, both looking confused.

'Sulty dear,' sang out the fat man, and one of the serving wenches looked over – they all had themselves a quiet, nervous audience among the half-dozen others in the tavern, and so numerous sets of eyes watched as she headed over. She was just rounding the nearest table when the fat man said, 'It would appear that Hanut Orr has met an untimely end – before we even arrived, alas for Coll's sake. Best summon a guard—'

She made a face. 'What? Out there? In the damned streets? Sounds like ten thousand wolves have been let loose out there, Kruppe!'

'Sweet Sulty, Kruppe assures you no harm will come to you! Kruppe assures, yes, and will warmly comfort too upon your triumphant return!'

'Oh now that's incentive,' and she turned round and headed for the front door. And the man was close enough to hear her add under her breath, 'Incentive to throw myself into the jaws of the first wolf I see . . .'

But out she went.

The guard with the loving family and the aching chest was at the intersection just on this side of the wall one street away from the Phoenix Inn – and hurrying with genuine alarm towards the sounds of destruction to the south (the other raging fire in the Estate District was not his jurisdiction) – when he heard someone shouting at him and so turned, lifting high his lantern.

A young woman was waving frantically.

He hesitated, and then flinched at a howl so loud and so close he expected to see a demon standing at his shoulder. He jogged towards the woman.

'For Hood's sake!' he shouted. 'Get yourself inside!'

He saw her spin round and scamper for the entrance to the Phoenix Inn. As he drew closer a flash of motion from a facing alley mouth almost drew him round, but when he shot the bull's eye in that direction, he saw no one. He hurried on, breathing hard as he climbed the steps and went inside.

A short time and a tumble of words later, he followed Councillor Coll and Kruppe into the alley, where they gathered round the corpse of yet another councillor. Hanut Orr, apparently.

Wincing at the tightness that was closing like a vice round his ribcage, the guard slowly squatted to examine the wounds. Only two blows – which didn't sound like his man – but then, the look of those wounds . . . 'I think he's killed another one,' he muttered. 'Not long ago either.' He looked up. 'And you two saw nothing?'

Coll shook his head.

Kruppe – a man the guard had always regarded askance, with considerable suspicion, in fact – hesitated.

'What? Speak, you damned thief.'

'Thief? Aaii, such an insult! Kruppe was but observing with most sharp eye the
nature of said wounds upon forehead and back of neck.'

'That's how I know it's the same man as has been killing dozens over the last
few months. Some kind of foreign weapon—'

'Foreign? Not at all, Kruppe suggests. Not at all.'

'Really? Do go on.'

'Kruppe suggests, most vigilant and honourable guard, that 'twas hands alone
did this damage. Knuckles and no more, no less.'

'No, that's wrong. I've seen the marks a fist makes—'

'But Kruppe did not say "fist". Kruppe was being more precise. Knuckles, yes?
As in knuckles unencumbered by fingers . . .'

The guard frowned, and then looked once more at that bizarre elongated dent
in Hanut Orr's forehead. He suddenly straightened. 'Knuckles . . . but no fingers.
But . . . I know that man!'

'Indeed?' Kruppe beamed. 'Best make haste then, friend, and beware on this
night of all nights, do beware.'

'What? Beware what – what are you talking about?'

'Why, the Toll, friend. Beware the Toll. Now go quickly – we shall take this
poor body inside, until the morning when proper arrangements are, er, arranged.
Such a multitude of sorrows this night! Go, friend, hunt down your nemesis! This
is the very night for such a thing!'

Everything was pulsing in front of the guard's eyes, and the pain had surged
from his chest into his skull. He was finding it hard to even so much as think.
But . . . yes, he knew that man. Gods, what was his name?

It would come to him, but for now he hurried down the alley, and out into yet
another bizarrely empty street. The name would come to him, but he knew
where the bastard lived, he knew that much and wasn't that enough for now? It
was.

Throbbing, pounding pulses rocked the brain in his skull. Flashes of orange
light, flushes of dry heat against his face – gods, he wasn't feeling right, not right
at all. There was an old cutter down the street from where he lived – after tonight,
he should pay her a visit. Lances of agony along his limbs, but he wasn't going to
stop, not even for a rest.

He had the killer. Finally. Nothing was going to get in his way.

And so onward he stumbled, lantern swinging wildly.

Gaz marched up to the door, pushed it open and halted, looking round. The stupid woman hadn't even lit the hearth – where the fuck was she? He made his way
across the single room, three strides in all, to the back door, which he kicked
open.

Sure enough, there she was, standing with her back to him, right there in front of that circle of flat stones she'd spent days and nights arranging and rearranging. As if she'd lost her mind, and the look in her eyes of late – well, they were in so much trouble now.

'Thordy!'

She didn't even turn round, simply said, 'Come over here, husband.'

'Thordy, there's trouble. I messed up. We messed up – we got to think – we got to get out of here, out of the city – we got to run—'

'We're not running,' she said.

He came up beside her. 'Listen, you stupid woman—'

She casually raised an arm and slid something cold and biting across his throat. Gaz stared, reached up his battered, maimed hands, and felt hot blood streaming down from his neck. 'Thordy?' The word bubbled as it came out.

Gaz fell to his knees, and she stepped up behind him and with a gentle push sent him sprawling face down on to the circle of flat stones.

'You were a good soldier,' she said. 'Collecting up so many lives.'

He was getting cold, icy cold. He tried to work his way back up, but there was no strength left in him, none at all.

'And me,' she went on, 'I've been good too. The dreams – he made it all so simple, so obvious. I've been a good mason, husband, getting it all ready . . . for you. For him.'

The ice filling Gaz seemed to suddenly reach in, as deep inside him as it was possible to go, and he felt something – something that was his, and his alone, something that called itself *me* – convulse and then shriek in terror and anguish as the cold devoured it, ate into it, and piece after piece of his life simply vanished, piece after piece after—

Thordy dropped the knife and stepped back as Hood, the Lord of Death, High King of the House of the Slain, Embracer of the Fallen, began to physically manifest on the stone dais before her. Tall, swathed in rotting robes of muted green, brown, and black. The face was hidden but the eyes were dull slits faintly lit in the midst of blackness, as was the smeared gleam of yellow tusks.

Hood now stood on the blood-splashed stones, in a decrepit garden in the district of Gadrobi, in the city of Darujhistan. Not a ghostly projection, not hidden behind veils of shielding powers, not even a spiritual visitation.

No, this was *Hood, the god.*

Here, now.

And in the city on all sides, the howling of the Hounds rose in an ear-shattering, soul-flailing crescendo.

The Lord of Death had arrived, to walk the streets in the City of Blue Fire.

The guard came on to the decrepit street facing the ramshackle house that was home to the serial murderer, but he could barely make it out through the pulsing waves of darkness that seemed to be closing in on all sides, faster and faster, as if he was witness to a savage, nightmarish compression of time, day hurtling into night into day and on and on. As if he was somehow rushing into his own old age, right up to his final mortal moment. A roaring sound filled his head, excruciating pain radiating out from his chest, burning with fire in his arms, the side of his neck. His jaws were clenched so tight he was crushing his own teeth, and every breath was agony.

He made it halfway to the front door before falling to his knees, doubling up and sinking down on to his side, the lantern clunking as it struck the cobbles. And suddenly he had room for a thousand thoughts, all the time he could have wanted, now that he'd taken his last breath. So many things became clear, simple, acquiring a purity that lifted him clear of his body—

And he saw, as he hovered above his corpse, that a figure had emerged from the killer's house. His altered vision revealed every detail of that ancient, unhuman visage within the hood, the deep-etched lines, the ravaged map of countless centuries. Tusks rising from the lower jaw, chipped and worn, the tips ragged and splintered. And the eyes – *so cold, so . . . haunted* – all at once the guard knew this apparition.

Hood. The Lord of Death had come for him.

He watched as the god lifted his gaze, fixing him with those terrible eyes.

And a voice spoke in his head, a heavy voice, like the grinding of massive stones, the sinking of mountains. 'I have thought nothing of justice. For so long now. It is all one to me. Grief is tasteless, sorrow an empty sigh. Live an eternity in dust and ashes and then speak to me of justice.'

To this the guard had nothing to say. He had been arguing with death night after night. He had been fighting all the way from the Phoenix Inn. Every damned step. He was past that now.

'So,' continued Hood, 'here I stand. And the air surrounding me, the air rushing into my lungs, it lives. I cannot prevent what comes with my every step here in the mortal world. I cannot be other than what I am.'

The guard was confused. Was the Lord of Death *apologizing*?

'But this once, I shall have my way. *I shall have my way.*' And he stepped forward, raising one withered hand – a hand, the guard saw, missing two fingers. 'Your soul shines. It is bright. Blinding. So much honour, so much love. Compassion. In the cavern of loss you leave behind, your children will be less than all they could have been. They will curl round scars and the wounds will never quite heal, and they will learn to gnaw those scars, to lick, to drink deep. This will not do.'

The guard convulsed, spinning down back into the corpse on the cobbles. He felt his heart lurch, and then pound with sudden ease, sudden, stunning vigour. He drew a deep breath, the air wondrous, cool, sweeping away the last vestige of pain – sweeping everything away.

All that he had come to, in those last moments – that scintillating clarity of vision, the breathtaking understanding of *everything* – now sank beneath a familiar cloud, settling grey and thick, where every shape was but hinted at, where he was lost. As lost as he had been, as lost as any and every mortal soul, no matter how blustery its claims to certainty, to faith. And yet . . . and yet *it was a warm cloud*, shot through with precious things: his love for his wife, his children; his wonder at their lives, the changes that came to them day by day.

He found he was weeping, even as he climbed to his feet. He turned to look at the Lord of Death, in truth not expecting to see the apparition which must surely come only to the dead and dying, and then cried out in shock.

Hood looked solid, appallingly real, walking down the street, eastward, and it was as if the webs binding them then stretched, the fabric snapping, wisping off into the night, and with each stride that took the god farther away the guard felt his life returning, an awareness of breathtaking solidity – in this precise moment, and in every one that would follow.

He turned away – and even that was easy – and settled his gaze upon the door, which hung open, and all that waited within was dark and rotted through with horror and madness.

The guard did not hesitate.

With this modest and humble man, with this courageous, honourable man, Hood saw true. And, for just this once, the Lord of Death had permitted himself to care.

Mark this, a most significant moment, a most poignant gesture.

Thordy heard boots on the warped floorboards of the back porch and she turned to see a city guardsman emerge from her house, out through the back door, holding a lantern in one hand.

'He is dead,' she said. 'The one you have come here for. Gaz, my husband.' She pointed with a blood-slick knife. 'Here.'

The guard walked closer, sliding back one of the shutters on the lantern and directing the shaft of light until it found and held on the motionless body lying on the stones.

'He confessed,' she said. 'So I killed him, with my own hand. I killed this . . . monster.'

The guardsman crouched down to study the corpse. He reached out and gently slipped one finger under the cuff of one of Gaz's sleeves, and raised up the battered, fingerless hand. He sighed then, and slowly nodded.

As he lowered the arm again and began straightening, Thordy said, 'I understand there is a reward.'

He looked across at her.

She wasn't sure what she saw in his expression. He might be horrified, or amused, or cynically drained of anything like surprise. But it didn't matter much. She just wanted the money. She needed the money.

Becoming, for a time, the mason of the Lord of the Slain entailed a fearsome responsibility. But she hadn't seen a single bent copper for her troubles.

The guardsman nodded. 'There is.'

She held up the kitchen knife.

He might have flinched a bit, maybe, but what mattered now would be Thordy seeing him nod a second time.

And after a moment, he did just that.

A god walked the streets of Darujhistan. In itself, never a good thing. Only fools would happily, eagerly invite such a visitation, and such enthusiasm usually proved short-lived. That this particular god was the harvester of souls meant that, well, not only was his manifestation unwelcome, but his gift amounted to unmitigated slaughter, rippling out to overwhelm thousands of inhabitants in tenement blocks, in the clustered hovels of the Gadrobi District, in the Lakefront District – but no, such things cannot be glanced over with a mere shudder.

Plunge then, courage collected, into this welter of lives. Open the mind to consider, cold or hot, all manner of judgement. Propriety is dispensed with, decency cast aside. This is the eye that does not blink, but is such steely regard an invitation to cruel indifference? To a hardened, compassionless aspect? Or will a sliver of honest empathy work its way beneath the armour of desensitized excess?

When all is done, dare to weigh thine own harvest of feelings and consider this one challenge: if all was met with but a callous shrug, then, this round man invites, shift round such cruel, cold regard, and cast one last judgement. Upon thyself.

But for now . . . *witness*:

Skilles Naver was about to murder his family. He had been walking home from Gajjet's Bar, belly filled with ale, only to have a dog the size of a horse step out in front of him. A blood-splashed muzzle, eyes burning with bestial fire, the huge flattened head swinging round in his direction.

He had frozen in place. He had pissed himself, and then shat himself.

A moment later a high wooden fence surrounding a vacant lot further up the street – where a whole family had died of some nasty fever a month earlier – suddenly collapsed and a second enormous dog appeared, this one bone white.

Its arrival snatched the attention of the first beast, and in a surge of muscles the creature lunged straight for it.

They collided like two runaway, laden wagons, the impact a concussion that staggered Skilles. Whimpering, he turned and ran.

And ran.

And now he was home, stinking like a slop pail, and his wife was but half packed – caught in the midst of a treacherous flight, stealing the boys, too. His boys. His little workers, who did everything Skilles told them to (and Beru fend if they didn't or even talked back, the little shits) and the thought of a life without them – without his perfect, private, very own slaves – lit Skilles into a white rage.

His wife saw what was coming. She pushed the boys into the corridor and then turned to give up her own life. Besk the neighbour the door next over was collecting the boys for some kind of escape to who knew where. Well, Skilles would just have to hunt him down, wouldn't he? It wasn't as if puny rat-faced Surna was going to hold him back for long, was it?

Just grab her, twist that scrawny neck and toss the waste of space to one side—

He didn't even see the knife, and all he felt of the murderous stab was a prick under his chin, as the thin blade shot up through his mouth, deflected inward by his upper palate, and sank three fingers deep straight into the base of his brain.

Surna and her boys didn't have to run after all.

Kanz was nine years old and he loved teasing his sister who had a real temper, as Ma always said as she picked up pieces of broken crockery and bits of hated vegetables scattered all over the floor, and the best thing was prodding his sister in the ribs when she wasn't looking, and she'd spin round, eyes flashing with fury and hate – and off he'd run, with her right on his heels, out into the corridor, pell-mell straight to the stairs and then down and round and down fast as he could go with her screeching behind him.

Down and round and down and—

—and he was flying through the air. He'd tripped, missed his grip on the rail, and the ground floor far below rushed up to meet him.

'You two will be the death of each other!' Ma always said. Zasperating! She said that too—

He struck the floor. Game over.

Sister's quick temper went away and never returned after that night. And Ma never again voiced the word 'zasperating'. Of course it did not occur to her that its sudden vanishing from her mind was because her little boy had taken it with him, the last word he'd thought. He'd taken it, as would a toddler a doll, or a blanket. For comfort in his dark new world.

Benuck Fill sat watching his mother wasting away. Some kind of cancer was eating her up inside. She'd stopped talking, stopped wanting anything; she was like a sack of sticks when he picked her up to carry her to the washtub to wipe down all the runny stuff she leaked out these days, these nights. Her smile, which had told him so much of her love for him, and her shame at what she had become – that horrible loss of dignity – had changed now into something else: an open mouth, lips withered and folded in, each breath a wheezing gasp. If that was a smile then she was smiling at death itself and that was hard for him to bear. Seeing that. Understanding it, what it meant.

Not long now. And Benuck didn't know what he would do. She had given him life. She had fed him, held him, kept him warm. She had given him words to live by, rules to help him shape his life, his self. She wasn't clever, very, or even wise. She was just an average person, who worked hard so that they could live, and worked even harder when Da went to fight in Pale where he probably died though they never found out either way. He just never came back.

Benuck sat wringing his hands, listening to her breathing, wishing he could help her, fill her with his own breath, fill her right up so she could rest, so she'd have a single, final moment when she didn't suffer, one last moment of painless life, and then she could let go . . .

But here, unseen by any, was the real truth. His mother had died eight days ago. He sat facing an empty chair, and whatever had broken in his mind had trapped him now in those last days and nights. Watching, washing, dressing. Things to do for her, moments of desperate care and love, and then back to the watching and there was no light left in her eyes and she made no sign she heard a thing he said, all his words of love, his words of thanks.

Trapped. Lost. Not eating, not doing anything at all.

Hood's hand brushed his brow then and he slumped forward in his chair, and the soul of his mother, that had been hovering in anguish in this dreadful room all this time, now slipped forward for an eternal embrace.

Sometimes, the notion of true salvation can start the eyes.

Avab Tenitt fantasized about having children with him in his bed. Hadn't happened yet, but soon he would make it all real. In the meantime he liked tying a rope round his neck, a damned noose, in fact, while he masturbated under the blankets while his unsuspecting wife scrubbed dishes in the kitchen.

Tonight, the knot snagged and wouldn't loosen. In fact, it just got tighter and tighter the more he struggled with it, and so as he spilled out, so did his life.

When his wife came into the room, exhausted, her hands red and cracked by domestic travails, and on her tongue yet another lashing pending for her wastrel husband, she stopped and stared. At the noose. The bloated, blue and grey face above it, barely recognizable, and it was as if a thousand bars of lead had been lifted from her shoulders.

Let the dogs howl outside all night. Let the fires rage. She was free and her life ahead was all her own and nobody else's. For ever and ever again.

A week later a neighbour would see her pass on the street and would say to friends that evening how Nissala had suddenly become beautiful, stunning, in fact, filled with vitality, looking years and years younger. Like a dead flower suddenly reborn, a blossom fierce under the brilliant warm sunlight.

And then the two gossipy old women would fall silent, both thinking the same dark thoughts, the delicious what-if and maybe-she notions that made life so much fun, and gave them plenty to talk about, besides.

In the meantime, scores of children would stay innocent for a little longer than they would have otherwise done.

Widow Lebbil was a reasonable woman most of the time. But on occasion this gentle calm twisted into something malign, something so bound up in rage that *it overwhelmed its cause. The same thing triggered her incandescent fury, the same thing every time.*

Fat Saborgan lived above her, and around this time every night – when decent people should be sleeping though truth be told who could do that on this insane night when the mad revelry in the streets sounded out of control – he'd start running about up there, back and forth, round and round, this way and that.

Who could sleep below that thunder?

And so she worked her way out of bed, groaning at her aching hips, took one of her canes and, standing on a rickety chair, pounded against the ceiling. Her voice was too thin, too frail – he'd never hear if she yelled up at him. Only the cane would do. And she knew he heard her, she knew he did, but did it make any difference?

No! Never!

She couldn't go on with this. She couldn't!

Thump thump scrape thump scrape thump thump – and so she pounded and pounded and pounded, her arms on fire, her shoulders cramping. Pounded and pounded.

Saborgan should indeed have heard the widow's protest, but, alas, he was lost in his own world, and he danced with the White-Haired Empress, who'd come from some other world, surely, to his very room and the music filled his head and was so sweet, so magical, and her hands were soft as doves held as gently as he could manage in his own blunted, clumsy fingers. And soft and frail as her hands were, the Empress led, tugging him back and forth so that he never quite regained his balance.

The White-Haired Empress was very real. She was in fact a minor demon, conjured and chained into servitude in this ancient tenement on the very edge of the Gadrobi District. Her task, from the very first, had been singular, a geas set upon her by the somewhat neurotic witch dead now these three centuries.

The White-Haired Empress was bound to the task of killing cockroaches, in this one room. The manner in which she did so had, over decades and decades, suffered a weakening of strictures, leaving the now entirely loony demon the freedom to improvise.

This mortal had huge feet, his most attractive feature, and when they danced he closed his eyes and silently wept, and she could guide those feet on to every damned cockroach skittering across the filthy floor. Step crunch step crunch – there! A big one – get it! Crunch and smear, crunch and smear!

In this lone room, barring the insects who lived in terror, there was pure, unmitigated joy, delicious satisfaction, and the sweetest love.

It all collapsed at around the same time as the floor. Rotted crossbeams, boards and thick plaster descended on to Widow Lebbil and it was as much the shock as the weight of the wreckage that killed her instantly.

Poor Saborgan, losing his grip on the wailing Empress, suffered the stunning implosion of a cane driven up his anus – oh, even to recount is to wince! – which proved a most fatal intrusion indeed. As for the Empress herself, well, after a moment of horrific terror her geas shattered, releasing her at last to return to her home, the realm of the Cockroach Kings (oh, very well, the round man just made up that last bit. Forgive?). Who knows where she went? The only thing for certain is that she danced every step of the way.

The vague boom of a collapsing floor in a squalid tenement building somewhere overhead went unnoticed by Seba Krafar, Master of the Assassins' Guild, as he staggered down the subterranean corridor, seeking the refuge of his nest.

Would the disasters never end? It had all started with that damned Rallick Nom cult, and then, almost before the dust settled on that, their first big contract ran up against the most belligerent, vicious collection of innkeepers imaginable. And the one that followed?

He suspected he was the only survivor. He'd left his crossbowmen to cover his retreat and not one of them had caught up with him; and now, with gas storage caverns igniting one after another, well, he found himself in an abandoned warren of tunnels, rushing through raining dust, coughing, eyes stinging.

All ruined. Wrecked. He'd annihilated the entire damned Guild.

He would have to start over.

All at once, the notion excited him. Yes, he could shape it himself – nothing to inherit. A new structure. A new philosophy, even.

Such . . . possibilities.

He staggered into his office, right up to the desk, which he leaned on with both hands on its pitted surface. And then frowned at the scattering of scrolls, and saw documents strewn everywhere on the floor – what in Hood's name?

'Master Krafar, is it?'

The voice spun him round.

A woman stood with her back resting against the wall beside the doorway. A cocked crossbow was propped beside her left boot, quarrel head resting on the packed earthen floor. Her arms were crossed.

Seba Krafar scowled. 'Who in Hound's name are you?'

'You don't know me? Careless. My name is Blend. I'm one of the owners of K'rul's.'

'That contract's cancelled – we're done with you. No more—'

'I don't care. It's simple – I want the name. The one who brought you the contract. Now, you can give it to me without any fuss, and I will walk out of here and that's the last you'll see of me, and all your worries will be at an end. The Guild removed from the equation. Consider it a gift, but now it's time for you to earn it.'

He studied her, gauging his chances. She didn't look like much. There was no way she'd reach that crossbow in time – two quick strides and he'd be right in her face. With two knives in her gut. And then he'd send a note to Humble Measure and claim one more down – leaving what, two or three left? He'd get paid well for that, and Hood knew he needed the coin if he was going to start over.

And so he attacked.

He wasn't sure what happened next. He had his knives out, she was right there in front of him, and then her elbow smashed into his face, shattering his nose and blinding him with pain. And somehow both thrusts he sent her way, one seeking the soft spot just beneath her sternum, the other striking lower down, both failed. One blocked, the other missing entirely, dagger point driving into the wall she'd been leaning against.

The blow to his face turned his knees to water, but only for the briefest of moments, for Seba Krafar was a bull of a man, a brawler. Damage was something to shake off and then just get on with it, and so, shoulder hunching, he attempted a slanting slash, trying to gut the bitch right then and there.

Something hard hammered his wrist, sending the dagger flying, and bones cracked in his arm. As he stumbled back, tugging the other knife from the wall, he attempted a frantic thrust to keep her off him. She caught his wrist and her thumb was like an iron nail, impaling the base of his palm. The knife dropped from senseless fingers. She then took that arm and twisted it hard round, pushing his shoulder down and so forcing his head to follow.

Where it met a rising knee.

An already broken nose struck again, struck even harder, in fact, is not something that can be shaken off. Stunned, not a sliver of will left in his brain, he landed on his back. Some instinct made him roll, up against the legs of his desk, and he heaved himself upright once more.

The quarrel took him low on the right side, just above his hip, glancing off the innominate and slicing messily through his liver.

Seba Krafar sagged back down, into a slump with his back against the desk.

With streaming eyes he looked across at the woman.

Malazan, right. She'd been a soldier once. No, she'd been a Bridgeburner. He used to roll his eyes at that. A Bridgeburner? So what? Just some puffed up ooh-ah crap. Seba was an assassin. Blood kin to Talo Krafar and now there was a monster of a man—

Who'd been taken down by a quarrel. Killed like a boar in a thicket.

She walked over to stand before him. 'That was silly, Seba. And now here you are, face broken and skewered. That's your liver bleeding out there, I think. Frankly, I'm amazed you're not already dead, but lucky for you that you aren't.' She crouched and held up a small vial. 'If I pour this into that wound – once I pluck out the bolt, that is, and assuming you survive that – well, there's a good chance you'll live. So, should I do that, Seba? Should I save your sorry arse?'

He stared at her. Gods, he hurt everywhere.

'The name,' she said. 'Give me the name and you've got a chance to survive this. But best hurry up with your decision. You're running out of time.'

Was Hood hovering? In that buried place so far beneath the streets? Well, of course he was.

Seba gave her the name. He even warned her off – don't mess with that one, he's a damned viper. There's something there, in his eyes, I swear—

Blend was true to her word.
So Hood went away.

The cascade of sudden deaths, inexplicable and outrageous accidents, miserable ends and terrible murders filled every abode, every corner and every hovel in a spreading tide, a most fatal flood creeping out through the hapless city on all sides. No age was spared, no weight of injustice tipped these scales. Death took them all: well born and destitute, the ill and the healthy, criminal and victim, the unloved and the cherished.

So many last breaths: coughed out, sighed, whimpered, bellowed in defiance, in disbelief, in numbed wonder. And if such breaths could coalesce, could form a thick, dry, pungent fugue of dismay, in the city on this night not a single globe of blue fire could be seen.

There were survivors. Many, many survivors – indeed, more survived than died – but alas, it was a close run thing, this measure, this fell harvest.

The god walked eastward, out from Gadrobi District and into Lakefront, and, from there, up into the Estates.

This night was not done. My, not done at all.

Unseen in the pitch black of this moonless, smoke-wreathed night, a massive shape sailed low over the Gadrobi Hills, westward and out on to the trader's road. As it drew closer to the murky lights of Worrytown, the silent flier slowly dropped lower until its clawed talons almost brushed the gravel of the road.

Above it, smaller shapes beat heavy wings here and there, wheeling round, plummeting and then thudding themselves back up again. These too uttered no calls in the darkness.

To one side of the track, crouched in high grasses, a coyote that had been about to cross the track suddenly froze.

Heady spices roiled over the animal in a warm, sultry gust, and where a moment earlier there had been black, shapeless clouds sliding through the air, now there was a figure – a man-thing, the kind the coyote warred with in its skull, fear and curiosity, opportunity and deadly betrayal – walking on the road.

But this man-thing, it was . . . different.

As it came opposite the coyote, its head turned and regarded the beast.

The coyote trotted out. Every muscle, every instinct, cried out for a submissive surrender, and yet as if from some vast power outside itself, the coyote held its head high, ears sharp forward as it drew up alongside the figure.

Who reached down to brush gloved fingers back along the dome of its head.

And off the beast bounded, running as fast as it legs could carry it, out into the night, the vast plain to the south.

Freed, blessed, beneficiary of such anguished love that it would live the rest of its years in a grassy sea of joy and delight.

Transformed. No special reason, no grim purpose. No, this was a whimsical touch, a mutual celebration of life. Understand it or stumble through. The coyote's role is done, and off it pelts, heart bright as a blazing star.

Gifts to start the eyes.

Anomander Rake, Son of Darkness, walked between the shanties of Worrytown. The gate was ahead, but no guards were visible. The huge doors were barred.

From beyond, from the city itself, fires roared here and there, thrusting bulging cloaks of spark-lit smoke up into the black night.

Five paces from the gates now, and something snapped and fell away. The doors swung open. And, unaccosted, unnoticed, Anomander Rake walked into Darujhistan.

Howls rose like madness unleashed.

The Son of Darkness reached up and unsheathed Dragnipur.

Steam curled from the black blade, twisting into ephemeral chains that stretched out as he walked up the wide, empty street. Stretched out to drag behind him, and from each length others emerged and from these still more, a forest's worth of iron roots, snaking out, whispering over the cobbles.

He had never invited such a manifestation before. Reining in that bleed of power had been an act of mercy, to all those who might witness it, who might comprehend its significance.

But on this night, Anomander Rake had other things on his mind.

Chains of smoke, chains and chains and chains, so many writhing in his wake that they filled the breadth of the street, that they snaked over and under and spilled out into side streets, alleys, beneath estate gates, beneath doors and through windows. They climbed walls.

Wooden barriers disintegrated – doors and sills and gates and window frames. Stones cracked, bricks spat mortar. Walls bowed. Buildings groaned.

He walked on as those chains grew taut.

No need yet to lean forward with each step. No need yet to reveal a single detail to betray the strength and the will demanded of him.

He walked on.

Throughout the besieged city, mages, witches, wizards and sorcerors clutched the sides of their heads, eyes squeezing shut as unbearable pressure closed in. Many fell to their knees. Others staggered. Still others curled up into tight foetal balls on the floor, as the world groaned.

Raging fires flinched, collapsed into themselves, died in silent gasps.

The howl of the Hounds thinned as if forced through tight valves.

In a slag-crusted pit twin sisters paused as one in their efforts to scratch each other's eyes out. In the midst of voluminous clouds of noxious vapours, knee deep in magma that swirled like a lake of molten sewage, the sisters halted, and slowly lifted their heads.

As if scenting the air.

Dragnipur.

Dragnipur.

Down from the Estates, into that projecting wedge that was Daru, and hence through another gate and on to the main avenue in Lakefront, proceeding parallel to the shoreline. As soon as he reached the straight, level stretch of that avenue, the Son of Darkness paused.

Four streets distant on that same broad track, Hood, Lord of Death, fixed his gaze on the silver-haired figure who seemed to have hesitated, but only for a moment, before resuming its approach.

Hood felt his own unease, yet onward he strode.

The power of that sword was breathtaking, even for a god. *Breathtaking.*

Terrifying.

They drew closer, in measured steps, and closer still.

The Hounds had fallen silent. In the wake of crushed fires, smoke billowed low, barely lit by fitful blue gaslight. Piercing in and out of the black clouds, Great Ravens circled, advanced, and retreated; and moments before the two figures reached each other, the huge birds began landing on roof edges facing down into the street, in rows and clusters, scores and then hundreds.

They were here.

To witness.

To know. To believe.

And, perchance, to feed.

Only three strides between them now. Hood slowed his steps. 'Son of Darkness,' he said, 'I have reconsidered—'

And the sword lashed out, a clean arc that took the Lord of Death in the neck, slicing clean through.

As Hood's head pitched round inside its severed cloth sack, the body beneath it staggered back, dislodging what it had lost.

A heavy, solid crunch as the god's head struck the cobbles, rolling on to one cheek, the eyes staring and lifeless.

Black blood welled up from the stump of neck. One more step back, before the legs buckled and the Lord of Death fell to his knees and then sat back.

Opposite the dead god, Anomander Rake, face stretching in agony, sought to remain standing.

Whatever weight descended upon him at this moment was invisible to the mortal eye, unseen even by the thousand Great Ravens perched and leaning far forward on all sides, but its horrendous toll was undeniable.

The Son of Darkness, Dragnipur in one hand, bowed and bent like an old man. The sword's point grated and then caught in the join between four cobbles. And Anomander Rake began to lean on it, every muscle straining as his legs slowly gave way – no, he could not stand beneath this weight.

And so he sank down, the sword before him, both hands on the cross-hilt's wings, head bowed against Dragnipur, and these details alone were all that distinguished him from the god opposite.

They sat, on knees and haunches, as if mirrored images. One leaning on a sword, forehead pressed to the gleaming, smoke-wreathed blade. The other decapitated, hands resting palm up on the thighs.

One was dead.

The other, at this moment, profoundly . . . vulnerable.

Things noticed.

Things were coming, and coming fast.

And this night, why, it is but half done.

Chapter Twenty-Two

He slid down the last of the trail and he asked of me,
'Do you see what you expected?'
And this was a question breaking loose, rolling free.
Out from under stones and scattered
Into thoughts of what the cruel fates would now decree.

He settled back in the dust and made his face into pain,
'Did you see only what you believed?'
And I looked down to where blood had left its stain
The charge of what's given, what's received
Announcing the closing dirge on this long campaign.

'No,' I said, 'you are not what I expected to see.'
Young as hope and true as love was my enemy,
'The shields were burnished bright as a sun-splashed sea,
And drowning courage hath brought me to this calamity.
Expectation has so proved the death of me.'

He spoke to say, 'You cannot war against the man you were,
And I cannot slay the man I shall one day become,
Our enemy is expectation flung backward and fore,
The memories you choose and the tracks I would run.
Slayer of dreams, sower of regrets, all that we are.'

Soldier at the End of his Days
(FRAGMENT)
Des'Ban of Nemil

They did not stop for the night. With the city's fitful glow to the north, throbbing crimson, Traveller marched as would a man possessed. At times, as she and Karsa rode on ahead to the next rise to fix their gazes upon that distant conflagration, Samar Dev feared that he might, upon reaching them, simply lash out with his sword. Cut them both down. So that he could take Havok for himself, and ride hard for Darujhistan.

Something terrible was happening in that city. Her nerves were on fire. Her skull seemed to creak with some kind of pervasive pressure, building with each onward step. She felt febrile, sick to her stomach, her mouth dry as dust, and she held on to Karsa Orlong's muscled girth as if he was a mast on a storm-wracked ship. He had said nothing for some time now, and she did not have the courage to break that grim silence.

Less than a league away, the city flashed and rumbled.

When Traveller reached them, however, it was as if they did not exist. He was muttering under his breath. Vague arguments, hissed denials, breathless lists of bizarre, disconnected phrases, each one worked out as if it was a justification for something he had done, or something he was about to do. At times those painful phrases sounded like justifications for both. Future blended with the past, a swirling vortex with a tortured soul at its very heart. She could not bear to listen.

Obsession was a madness, a fever. When it clawed its way to the surface, it was terrible to behold. It was impossible not to see the damage it did, the narrowness of the treacherous path one was forced to walk, as if between walls of thorns, jutting knife blades. One misstep and blood was drawn, and before long the poor creature was a mass of wounds, streaked and dripping, blind to everything but what waited somewhere ahead.

And what if he found what he sought? What if he won through in his final battle – whatever that might be? What then for Traveller?

It will kill him.

His reason for living . . . gone.

Gods below, I will not bear witness to such a scene. I dare not.

For I have my own obsessions . . .

Traveller marched on in dark argument. She and Karsa rode Havok, but even this frightening beast was starting, shying as if something was bodily pushing against it. Head tossed, hoofs stamped the packed ground.

Finally, after the horse almost reared, Karsa uttered a low snarl and reined in. 'Down, Witch,' he said – as Traveller once more stalked past – 'we will walk from here.'

'But Havok—'

'Can fend for himself. When I need him, we shall find each other once more.'

They dismounted. Samar stretched her back. 'I'm exhausted. My head feels like a wet pot in a kiln – about to explode. Karsa—'

'Stay here if you will,' he said, eyes on Traveller's back. 'I will go on.'

'Why? Wherever he's going, it's his battle, not yours. You cannot help him. You must not help him, Karsa – you see that, don't you?'

He grimaced. 'I can guard his back—'

'Why? We have journeyed together out of convenience. And that's done, now. Can't you feel it? It's done. Take one wrong step – cross his path – and he will drag out that sword.' She brought her hands up and pressed hard against her eyelids. Flashes of fire ignited her inner world. No different from what she was seeing in the city before them. She dropped her hands and blinked blearily at the Toblakai. 'Karsa, in the name of mercy, let's turn away. Leave him to . . . whatever's in Darujhistan.'

'Witch, we have been following a trail.'

'Sorry, what?'

'A trail.' He glanced down at her. 'The Hounds.'

She looked again at the city, even as a fireball ripped upward and moments later thunder rolled through the ground at their feet. *The Hounds. They're tearing that city apart.* 'We can't go there! We can't walk into *that!*'

In answer Karsa bared his teeth. 'I do not trust those beasts – are they there to protect Traveller? Or hunt him down in some deadly game in the streets?' He shook his head. 'I'll not clip his heels, Witch. We'll keep a respectable distance, but I *will* guard his back.'

She wanted to scream. *You stupid, stubborn, obstinate, thick-skulled bastard!* 'So who guards *our* backs?'

Sudden blackness welled up inside her mind and she must have reeled, for a moment later Karsa was holding her up, genuine concern in his face. 'What ails you, Samar?'

'You idiot, *can't you feel it?*'

'No,' he replied.

She thought he lied then, but had no energy to challenge him. That blackness had seemed vast, depthless, a maw eager to devour her, swallow her down. And, most horrifying of all, something about it was seductive. Slick with sweat, her legs shaky beneath her, she held on to Karsa's arm.

'Stay here,' he said quietly.

'No, it makes no difference.'

He straightened suddenly, and she saw that he was facing the way they had come. 'What – what is it?'

'That damned bear – it's back.'

She twisted round. Yes, there, perhaps a hundred paces away, a huge dark shape. Coming no closer.

'What's it want with me?' she asked in a whisper.

'If you stay, you may find out, Witch.'

'No, I said. We'll follow Traveller. It's decided.'

Karsa was silent for a moment, and then he grunted. 'I am thinking . . .'

'What?'

'You wanted to know, earlier, who would be guarding our backs.'

She frowned, and then loosed a small gasp and squinted once more at that monstrous beast. It was just . . . hovering, huge head slowly wagging from side to side, pausing occasionally to lift its snout in their direction. 'I wouldn't trust that, Karsa, I wouldn't trust that at all.'

He shrugged.

But still she resisted, glaring now into the vault of night overhead. 'Where's the damned moon, Karsa? *Where in the Abyss is the damned moon!*'

Kallor was certain now. Forces had converged in Darujhistan. Clashing with deadly consequence, and blood had been spilled.

He lived for such things. Sudden opportunities, unexpected powers stumbling, falling within reach. Anticipation awakened within him.

Life thrust forth choices, and the measure of a man or woman's worth could be found in whether they possessed the courage, the brazen decisiveness, to grasp hold and not let go. Kallor never failed such moments. Let the curse flail him, strike him down; let defeat batter him again and again. He would just get back up, shake the dust off, and begin once more.

He knew the world was damned. He knew that the curse haunting him was no different from history's own progression, the endless succession of failures, the puerile triumphs that had a way of falling over as soon as one stopped looking. Or caring. He knew that life itself corrected gross imbalances by simply folding everything over and starting anew.

Too often scholars and historians saw the principle of convergence with narrow, truncated focus. In terms of ascendants and gods and great powers. But Kallor understood that the events they described and pored over after the fact were but concentrated expressions of something far vaster. Entire ages converged, in chaos and tumult, in the anarchy of Nature itself. And more often than not, very few comprehended the disaster erupting all around them. No, they simply went on day after day with their pathetic tasks, eyes to the ground, pretending that everything was just fine.

Nature wasn't interested in clutching their collars and giving them a rattling shake, forcing their eyes open. No, Nature just wiped them off the board.

And, truth be told, that was pretty much what they deserved. Not a stitch more. There were those, of course, who would view such an attitude aghast, and then accuse Kallor of being a monster, devoid of compassion, a vision stained indelibly dark and all that rubbish. But they would be wrong. Compassion is not a replacement for stupidity. Tearful concern cannot stand in the stead of cold recognition. Sympathy does not cancel out the hard facts of brutal, unwavering observation. It was too easy, too cheap, to fret and wring one's hands, moaning with heartfelt empathy – it was damned self-indulgent, in fact, providing the perfect excuse for doing precisely nothing while assuming a pious pose.

Enough of that.

Kallor had no time for such games. A nose in the air just made it easier to cut the throat beneath it. And when it came to that choice, why, he *never* hesitated. As sure as any force of Nature, was Kallor.

He walked, shins tearing and uprooting tangled grasses. Above him, a strange, moonless night with the western horizon – where the sun had gone down long ago – convulsing with carmine flashes.

Reaching a raised road of packed gravel, he set out, hastening his pace towards the waiting city. The track dipped and then began a long, stretched-out climb. Upon reaching the summit, he paused.

A hundred paces ahead someone had set four torches on high poles where four paths met, creating a square with the flaring firelight centred on the crossroads. There were no buildings in sight, nothing to give reason for such a construction. Frowning, he resumed walking.

As he drew closer, he saw someone sitting on a marker stone, just beneath one of the torches. Hooded, motionless, forearms resting on thighs, gauntleted hands draped down over the knees.

Kallor felt a moment of unease. He scraped through gravel with one boot and saw the hood slowly lift, the figure straightening and then rising to its feet.

Shit.

The stranger reached up and tugged back the hood, then walked to position himself in the centre of the crossroads.

In the wake of recognition, dismay flooded through Kallor. 'No, Spinnock Durav, not this.'

The Tiste Andii unsheathed his sword. 'High King, I cannot let you pass.'

'Let him fight his own battles!'

'This need not be a battle,' Spinnock replied. 'I am camped just off this road. We can go there now, sit at a fire and drink mulled wine. And, come the morning, you can turn round, go back the other way. Darujhistan, High King, is not for you.'

'You damned fool. You know you cannot best me.' He glared at the warrior, struggling. A part of him wanted to . . . *gods* . . . a part of him wanted to weep. 'How many of his loyal, brave followers will he see die? And for what? Listen to me, Spinnock. I have no real enmity against you. Nor Rake.' He waved one chain-clad hand in the air behind him. 'Not even those who pursue me. Heed me, please. I have always respected you, Spinnock – by the Abyss, I railed at how Rake used you—'

'You do not understand,' the Tiste Andii said. 'You never did, Kallor.'

'You're wrong. *I have nothing against any of you!*'

'Korlat—'

'Did you think it was my intention to murder Whiskeyjack? Do you think I just cut down honourable men and loyal soldiers out of spite? You weren't even there! It was Silverfox who needed to die, and that is a failure we shall all one day come to rue. Mark my words. Ah, gods, Spinnock. *They got in my way, damn you! Just as you're doing now!*'

Spinnock sighed. 'It seems there will be no mulled wine this night.'

'Don't.'

'I am here, High King, to stand in your way.'

'You will die. I cannot stay my hand – everything will be beyond control by then. Spinnock Durav, please! This does not need to happen.'

The Tiste Andii's faint smile nearly broke Kallor's heart. *No, he understands. All too well. This will be his last battle, in Rake's name, in anyone's name.*

Kallor drew out his sword. 'Does it occur, to any of you, what these things do to *me*? No, of course not. The High King is cursed to fail, but never to fall. The High King is but . . . what? Oh, the physical manifestation of ambition. Walking proof of its inevitable price. Fine.' He readied his two-handed weapon. 'Fuck you, too.'

With a roar that ripped like fire from his throat, Kallor charged forward, and swung his sword.

Iron rang on iron.

Four torches lit the crossroads. Four torches painted two warriors locked in battle. Would these be the only witnesses? Blind and miserably indifferent with their gift of light?

For now, the answer must be *yes*.

The black water looked cold. Depthless, the blood of darkness. It breathed power in chill mists that clambered ashore to swallow jagged, broken rocks, fallen trees. Night itself seemed to be raining down into this sea.

Glittering rings spun and clicked, and Clip slowly turned face Nimander and the others. 'I can use this,' he said. 'The power rising from this water, it is filled with currents of pure Kurald Galain. I can use this.'

'A Gate?'

'Well, at least one of you is thinking. A Gate, yes, Nimander. A Gate. To take us to Black Coral.'

'How close?' Skintick asked.

Clip shrugged. 'Close enough. We will see. At the very least, within sight of the city walls.'

'So get on with it,' said Nenanda, his words very nearly a snarl.

Smiling, Clip faced the Cut once more. 'Do not speak, any of you. I must work hard at this.'

Nimander rubbed at his face. He felt numb, haunted by exhaustion. He moved off to sit on a boulder. Just up from the steep shoreline, thick moss blunted everything, the stumps of rotted trees, the upended roots, the tumbled black stones. The night air clung to him, cold and damp, reaching in to his bones, closing tight about his heart. He listened to the soft lap of the water, the suck and gurgle among the rocks. The smell was rich with decay, the mists sweet with brine.

He could feel the cold of the boulder seeping through, and his hands ached.

Clip spun his chain, whirled the two rings, one gold, one silver, and round and round they went. Apart from that he stood motionless, his back to them all.

Skintick settled down beside Nimander. Their eyes met and Skintick shrugged a silent question, to which Nimander replied with a faint shake of his head.

He'd thought he'd have a few more days. To decide things. The when. The how. The options if they should fail. Tactics. Fall-back plans. So much to think about, but he could speak to no one, could not even hint of what he thought must be done. Clip had stayed too close to them on this descent, as if suspicious, as if deliberately forcing Nimander to say nothing.

There was so much he needed to tell them, and so much that he needed to hear. Discussions, arguments, the weighing of risks and contingencies and coordination. All the things demanded of one who would lead; but his inability to give voice to his intentions, to deliver orders at the end of a long debate, had made him next to useless.

By his presence alone, Clip had stopped Nimander in his tracks.

In this game of move and countermove, Clip had outwitted him, and that galled. The moment the charade was shattered, there would be chaos, and in that scene Clip held the advantage. He had only himself to worry about, after all.

No, Nimander had no choice but to act alone, to trust in the others to follow.

He knew they were watching him, his every move, studying his face for any telltale expression, for every silent message, and this meant he had to hold himself in check. He had to guard himself against revealing anything, lest one of them misunderstand and so make a fatal mistake, and all of this was wearing him down.

Something lifted noisily from the black water. A span of darkness, vertical, its upper edges dripping, fast dissolving.

'Follow me,' Clip gasped. 'Quickly!'

Nimander rose and tugged Skintick back – 'Everyone, stay behind me' – and, seeing Clip lunge forward and vanish within the Gate, he hurried forward.

But Nenanda reached the portal before him, rushing in even as he drew his sword.

Cursing under his breath, Nimander darted after him.

The Gate was collapsing. Someone shrieked in his wake.

Nimander staggered on slippery, uneven bedrock, half blinded by streaks of luminescence that scattered like cut webs. He heard a gasping sound, almost at his feet, and a moment later stumbled against something that groaned.

Nimander reached down, felt a body lying prone. Felt something hot and welling under one palm – the slit of a wound, the leaking of blood. 'Nenanda?'

Another gasp, and then, 'I'm sorry, Nimander – I saw – I saw him reaching for his dagger, even as he stepped through – I saw – he knew, he knew you were following, you see – he—'

From somewhere ahead there came a hollow laugh. 'Do you imagine me an idiot, Nimander? Too bad it wasn't you. It should have been you. But then, this way it's just one more death for you to carry along.'

Nimander stared but could see nothing. 'You still need us!'

'Maybe, but it's too risky to have you so close. When I see a viper, I don't invite it into my belt-pouch. So, wander lost in here . . . for ever, Nimander. It won't feel very different from your life before this, I expect.'

'The god within you,' Nimander said, 'is a fool. My Lord will cut it down and you with it, Clip. You don't know him. You don't know a damned thing!'

Another laugh, this one much farther away.

Nimander wiped the tears from his cheeks with his free forearm. Beneath his palm, the pulse of blood from the wound had slowed.

Too many failures. Too many defeats.

A soul carries a vessel of courage. It cannot be refilled. Every thing that takes from it leaves less behind.

What do I have left?

Whatever it was, the time had come to drink deep, to use it all. One last time. Nimander straightened.

'Desra? Skintick? Anyone?'

His words drew echoes, and they were the only replies he received.

Nimander drew his sword, and then set out. In the direction of that mocking laughter.

Ribbons of light swam in the air on all sides.

He encountered no walls, felt no wayward currents of air. The folded bedrock beneath his feet undulated randomly, angling neither upward nor downward for long, uneven enough to make him stumble every now and then, and once to land on his knees with a painful, stinging jolt.

Lost. Not a single sound to betray where Clip might be now.

Yes, this was a clever end for Nimander, one that must have given Clip moments of delicious anticipation. Lost in darkness. Lost to his kin. To his Lord, and to a future that now would never arrive. So perfect, so precise, this punishment—

'Enough of that, you pathetic creature.'

Phaed.

'They're here, you fool. As lost as you.'

What? Who? Leave me be. I told you, I'm sorry. For what happened to you, for what I tried to do. I'm sorry—

'Too late for that. Besides, you don't understand. I lived in fear. I lived in perpetual terror. Of everything. Of all of you. That I'd be found out. Can you imagine, Nimander, what that was like? To live was torture, to dread an end even worse. Oh, I knew it was coming. It had to. People like me win for only so long, before someone notices – and then his face fills with disgust, and he crushes me underfoot.

'Or throws me out of a window.'

Please, no more—

'They're here. Desra, Skintick. Sweet Aranatha. Find them.'

How?

'I can't do this for you. Shouts will go unheard. There are layers to this place. Layers and layers and layers. You could have walked right through one of them and known nothing. Nimander Golit, the blood of our Lord is within you. The blood of Eleint, too – is that the secret? Is that the one weapon Clip did not know you possess? How could he know? How could anyone? We have suppressed it within ourselves for so long now—'

Because Andarist told us to!

'Because Andarist told us to. Because he was bitter. And hurting. He thought he could take his brother's children and make them his own, more his own than Rake's.'

Nenanda—

'Had the thinnest blood of all. We knew that. You knew it, too. It made him too predictable. It killed him. Brother, father, son – these layers are so precious, aren't they? Look on them again, my lover, my killer, but this time . . . with a dragon's eyes.'

But, Phaed, I don't know how! How do I do that?

She had no answer. No, it would never be that simple, would it? Phaed was not an easy memory, not a gentle ghost. Nor his wise conscience. She was none of that.

Just one more kin whose blood stained Nimander's hands.

He had stopped walking. He stood now, surrounded by oblivion.

'My hands,' he whispered. And then slowly lifted them. 'Stained,' he said. 'Yes, stained.'

The blood of kin. The blood of Tiste Andii. *The blood of dragons.*

That shines like beacons. That call, summon, can cast outward until—

A woman's hand reached out as if from nowhere, closing round one of his own in a cold grip.

And all at once she was before him, her eyes like twin veils, parting to reveal a depthless, breathtaking love.

He gasped, vertiginous, and almost reeled. 'Aranatha.'

She said, 'There is little time, brother. We must hurry.'

Still holding his hand, she set off, pulling him along as she might a child.

But Nimander was of no mind to complain.

He had looked into her eyes. He had seen it. That love. He had seen it.

And more, he had understood.

The Dying God, he was coming. Pure as music, bright as truth, solid as certainty. A fist of power, driving onward, smashing everything in its path, until that fist uncurled and the hand opened, to close round the soul of the Redeemer. A weaker god, a god lost in its own confusion.

Salind would be that fist, she would be that hand. Delivering a gift, from which a true and perfect faith would emerge. *This is the blood of redemption. You will understand, Redeemer. Drink deep the blood of redemption, and dance.*

The song is glory, and glory is a world we need never leave. And so, my beloved Itkovian, dance with me. Here, see me reaching for you—

Supine on the muddy floor of Gradithan's hut, Salind leaked thick black mucus from her mouth and nose, from the tear ducts of her eyes. Her fingernails were black, and more inky fluid oozed out of them. She was naked, and as he knelt beside her Gradithan had paused, breathing hard, his eyes fixed on the black milk trickling down from the woman's nipples.

Standing wrapped in his raincape close to the doorway, Monkrat looked on with flat eyes, his face devoid of expression. He could see how Gradithan struggled against the sudden thirst, the desire that was half childlike and half sexual, as he stared down at those leaking breasts. The bastard had already raped her, in some twisted consummation, a sacrifice of her virginity, so the only thing that must have been holding the man back was some kind of overriding imperative. Monkrat was not happy thinking about that.

Gradithan lifted Salind's head with one hand and tugged open her mouth with the other. He reached for the jug of saemankelyk. 'Time,' he muttered, 'and time, time, time, the time. Is now.' He tipped the jug and the black juice poured into Salind's gaping, stained mouth.

She swallowed, and swallowed, and it seemed she would never stop, that her body was depthless, a vessel with no bottom. She drank down her need, and that need could never find satiation.

Monkrat grunted. He'd known plenty of people like that. It was a secret poorly kept once you knew what to look for, there in their eyes. Hope and expectation and hunger and the hint of spiteful rage should a single demand be denied. They had a way of appearing, and then never leaving. Yes, he'd known people like that.

And, well, here was their god, shining from Salind's eyes. Everyone needed a god. Slapped together and shaped with frantic hands, a thing of clay and sticks. Built up of wants and all those unanswerable questions that plagued the mortal soul. Neuroses carved in stone. Malign obsessions given a hard, judgemental face – he had seen them, all the variations, in city after city, on the long campaigns of the Malazan Empire. They lined the friezes in temples; they leered down from balustrades. Ten thousand gods, one for every damned mood, it seemed. A pantheon of exaggerated flaws.

Salind was convulsing now, the black poison gushing from her mouth, thick as honey down her chin, and hanging in drop-heavy threads like some ghastly beard.

When she smiled, Monkrat flinched.

The convulsions found a rhythm, and Gradithan was pushed away as she undulated upright, a serpent rising, a thing of sweet venom.

Monkrat edged back, and before Gradithan could turn to him the ex-Bridgeburner slipped outside. Rain slanted down into his face. He paused, ankle-deep in streaming mud, and drew up his hood. That water had felt clean. If only it could wash all of this away. Oh, not the camp – it was already doing that – but everything else. Choices made, bad decisions stumbled into, years of useless living. Would he ever do anything right? His list of errors had grown so long he felt trapped by some internal pell-mell momentum. Dozens more awaited him—

A bedraggled shape emerged from the rain. Grizzled face, a sopping hairshirt. Like some damned haunt from his past, a ghoul grinning with dread reminders of everything he had thrown away.

Spindle stepped up to Monkrat. 'It's time.'

'For what? Aye, we got drunk, we laughed and cried and all that shit. And maybe I told you too much, but not enough, I'm now thinking, if you believe you can do a damned thing about all this. It's a god we're talking about here, Spin. *A god.*'

'Never mind that. I been walking through this shit-hole. Monkrat, there's *children* here. Just . . . abandoned.'

'Not for long. They're going to be taken. Used to feed the Dying God.'

'Not if we take 'em first.'

'Take them? Where?'

Spindle bared his teeth, and only now did Monkrat comprehend the barely restrained fury in the man facing him. 'Where? How about *away*? Does that sound too complicated for you? Maybe those hills west of here, in the woods. You said it was all coming down. If we leave 'em they'll all die, and I won't have it.'

Monkrat scratched at his beard. 'Now ain't that admirable of you, but—'

The hard angled point of a shortsword pressed the soft flesh below Monkrat's chin. He scowled. The bastard was fast, all right, and old Monkrat was losing his edge.

'Now,' hissed Spindle, 'you either follow Gredithick around—'

'Gradithan.'

'Whatever. You either follow him like a pup, or you start helping me round up the runts still alive.'

'You're giving me a choice?'

'Kind of. If you say you want to be a pup, then I'll saw off your head, as clumsily as I can.'

Monkrat hesitated.

Spindle's eyes widened. 'You're in a bad way, soldier—'

'I ain't a soldier no more.'

'Maybe that's your problem. You've forgotten things. Important things.'

'Such as?'

Spindle grimaced, as if searching for the right words, and Monkrat saw in his mind a quick image of a three-legged dog chasing rabbits in a field. 'Fine,' Spindle finally said in a grating tone. 'It had to have happened to you at least once. You and your squad, you come into some rotten foul village or hamlet. You come to buy food or maybe get your tack fixed, clothes mended, whatever. But you ain't there to kill nobody. And so you get into a few conversations. In the tavern. The smithy. With the whores. And they start talking. About injustices. Bastard land-holders, local bullies, shit-grinning small-time tyrants. The usual crap. The corruption and all that. You know what I'm talking about, Monkrat?'

'Sure.'

'So what did you do?'

'We hunted the scum down and flayed their arses. Sometimes we even strung 'em up.'

Spindle nodded. 'You did justice, is what you did. It's what a soldier can do, when there's nobody else. We got swords, we got armour, we got all we need to terrorize anybody we damned well please. But Dassem taught us – he taught every soldier in the Malazan armies back then. Sure, we had swords, but who we used 'em on was up to us.' The point of the shortsword fell away. 'We was *soldiers*, Monkrat. We had the chance – the privilege – of doing the right thing.'

'I deserted—'

'And I was forced into retirement. Neither one changes what we were.'

'That's where you're wrong.'

'Then listen to this.' The shortsword pressed against his throat again. 'I can still deliver justice, and if need be I'll do it right now and right here. By cutting a coward's head off.'

'Don't talk to me about cowardice!' Monkrat snapped. 'Soldiers don't talk that ever! You just broke the first rule!'

'Someone turns his back on being a soldier – on what it means in the soul – that's cowardice. You don't like the word, don't live it.'

Monkrat stared into the man's eyes, and hated what he saw there. He sagged.

'Best get on with it then, Spin. I got nothing left. I'm used up. What do you do when the soldier inside you dies before you do? Tell me.'

'You go through the motions, Monkrat. You just follow me. Do as I do. We start there and worry about the rest later.'

Monkrat realized that Spindle was still waiting. *'Do what's right,'* Dassem told us. Gods, even after all this time he still remembered the First Sword's words. *'That's a higher law than the command of any officer. Higher even than the Emperor's own words. You are in a damned uniform but that's not a licence to deliver terror to everyone – just the enemy soldier you happen to be facing. Do what is right, for that armour you wear doesn't just protect your flesh and bone. It defends honour. It defends integrity. It defends justice. Soldiers, heed me well. That armour defends humanity. And when I look upon my soldiers, when I see these uniforms, I see compassion and truth. The moment those virtues fail, then the gods help you, for no armour is strong enough to save you.'*

'All right, Spin. I'll follow you.'

A sharp nod. 'Dassem, he'd be proud. And not surprised, no, not surprised at all.'

'We have to watch out for Gradithan – he wants those virgins. He wants their blood, for when the Dying God arrives.'

'Yeah? Well, Gredishit can chew on Hood's arsehole. He ain't getting 'em.'

'A moment ago I was thinking, Spin . . .'

'Thinking what?'

'That you was a three-legged dog. But I was wrong. You're a damned Hound of Shadow is what you are. Come on. I know where they all huddle to stay outa the rain.'

Seerdomin adjusted the grip on his sword and then glanced back at the Redeemer. The god's position was unchanged. Kneeling, half bent over, face hidden behind his hands. A position of abject submission. Defeat and despair. Hardly an inspiring standard to stand in front of, hardly a thing to fight for, and Seerdomin could feel the will draining from him as he faced once more the woman dancing in the basin.

Convulsing clouds overhead, an endless rain of kelyk that turned everything black. The drops stung and then numbed his eyes. He had ceased to flinch from the crack of lightning, the stuttering crash of thunder.

He had fought for something unworthy once, and had vowed *never again*. Yet here he was, standing between a god of unimaginable power and a god not worth believing in. One wanted to feed and the other looked ready to be devoured – why should he get in the way of the two?

A wretched gasp from the Redeemer snapped him round. The rain painted Itkovian black, ran like dung-stained water down the face he had lifted skyward. 'Dying,' he murmured, so faint that Seerdomin had to step closer to catch the word. 'But no end is desired. Dying, for all eternity. Who seeks this fate? For himself? Who yearns for such a thing? Can I . . . can I help him?'

Seerdomin staggered back, as if struck by a blow to his chest. *That – Beru* fend – *that is not a proper question! Not against this . . . this thing. Look to yourself, Redeemer! You cannot heal what does not want healing! You cannot mend what delights in being broken!* 'You cannot,' he growled. 'You cannot help it, Redeemer. You can only fall to it. Fall, vanish, be swallowed up.'

'He wants me. She wants me. She gave him this want, do you see? Now they share.'

Seerdomin turned to gaze upon the High Priestess. She was growing more arms, each bearing a weapon, each weapon whirling and spinning in a clashing web of edged iron. Kelyk sprayed from the blades, a whirling cloud of droplets. Her dance was carrying her closer.

The attack was beginning.

'Who,' Seerdomin whispered, 'will share this with *me*?'

'Find her,' said the Redeemer. 'She remains, deep inside. Drowning, but alive. Find her.'

'Salind? She is nothing to me!'

'She is the fire in Spinnock Durav's heart. She is his life. Fight not for me. Fight not for yourself. Fight, Seerdomin, for your friend.'

A sob was wrenched from the warrior. His soul found a voice, and that voice wailed its anguish. Gasping, he lifted his sword and set his eyes upon the woman cavorting in her dance of carnage. *Can I do this? Spinnock Durav, you fool, how could you have fallen so?*

Can I find her?

I don't know. I don't think so.

But his friend had found love. Absurd, ridiculous love. His friend, wherever he was, deserved a chance. For the only gift that meant a damned thing. The only one.

Blinking black tears from his eyes, Seerdomin went down to meet her.

Her howl of delight was a thing of horror.

A soldier could discover, in one horrendous, crushing moment, that everything that lay at the heart of duty was a lie, a rotted, fetid mass, feeding like a cancer on all that the soldier was; and that every virtue was rooted in someone else's poison.

Look to the poor fool at your side. Know well there's another poor fool at your back. This is how far the world shrinks down, when everything else melts in front of your eyes – too compromised to sustain clear vision, the brutal, uncluttered recognition of the lie.

Torn loose from the Malazan Empire, from Onearm's Host, the bedraggled clutch of survivors that was all that remained of the Bridgeburners had dragged their sorry backsides to Darujhistan. They found for themselves a cave where they could hide, surrounded by a handful of familiar faces, to remind them of what had pushed them each step of the way, from the past to the present. And hoping it would be enough to take them into the future, one hesitant, wayward step at a time.

Slash knives into the midst of that meagre, vulnerable clutch, and it just falls apart.

Mallet. Bluepearl.

Like blindfolded goats dragged up to the altar stone.

Not that goats needed blindfolds. It's just no fun looking into a dying animal's eyes.

Picker fell through darkness. Maybe she was flesh and bone. Maybe she was nothing but a soul, torn loose and now plummeting with naught but the weight of its own regrets. But her arms scythed through bitter cold air, her legs kicked out to find purchase where none existed. And each breath was getting harder to snatch from that rushing blast.

In the dream-world every law could be twisted round, bent, folded. And so, as she sensed the unseen ground fast approaching, she spun herself upright and slowed, sudden and yet smooth, and moments later she landed lightly on uneven bedrock. Snail shells crunched underfoot; she heard the faint snap of small rodent bones.

Blinking, gasping one breath after another deep into her lungs, she simply stood for a time, knees slightly flexed, hands out to her sides.

She could smell an animal stench, thick, as if she found herself in a den in some hillside.

The darkness slowly faded. She saw rock walls on which scenes had been pecked, others painted in earthy hues. She saw the half-shells of gourds crowding the rough floor on both sides – she had landed upon a sort of path, reaching ahead and behind, perhaps three paces wide. Before her, six or seven paces away, it ended in a stone wall. Behind her, the trail blended into darkness. She looked once more at the objects cluttering the flanks. In each gourd there was thick, dark liquid. She knew instinctively that it was blood.

The image etched into the wall in front, where the path ended, now snared her attention, and slowly its details began to resolve. A carriage or wagon, a swarm of vague shapes all reaching up for it on both sides, with others hinted at in its wake. A scene of frenzy and panic, the figure sitting on the bench holding reins that seemed to whip about – but no, her mind was playing tricks in this faint light, and that sound, as of wheels slamming and rocking and spinning over broken ground, was only her lunging heart, the rush of blood in her ears.

But Picker stared, transfixed.

A soldier with nothing left to believe in is a terrible thing to behold. When the blood on the hands is unjust blood, the soul withers.

Death becomes a lover, and that love leads to but one place. Every time, but one place.

Friends and family watch on, helpless. And in this tragic scene, the liars, the cynical bearers of poison, they are nowhere to be found.

Endest Silann had once been a priest, a believer in forces beyond the mortal realm; a believer in the benign regard of ancestors, spirits, each one a moral lodestone that cut through the dissembling, the evasions of responsibility, the denials of culpability – a man of faith, yes, in the traditional sense of the word. But these things no longer found harbour in his soul. Ancestors dissolved into the ground, leaving nothing but crumbling flecks of bone in dark earth. Spirits offered no gifts and those still clinging to life were bitter and savage, too often betrayed, too often spat upon, to hold any love for anyone.

He now believed that mortals were cursed. Some innate proclivity led them again and again on the same path. Mortals betrayed every gift granted them. They betrayed the giver. They betrayed their own promises. Their gods, their ancestors, their children – everywhere, betrayal.

The great forests of Kharkanas had been cut down; the squalid dying islands of growth left behind had each one fallen to fire or blight. The rich soils washed down into the rivers. The flesh of the land was stripped back to reveal bedrock bones. And hunger stalked the children. Mothers wailed, fathers tried on hardened masks of resolve, but before any of this both had looked out upon the ravaged world with affronted disbelief – someone's to blame, someone always is, but by the Abyss, do not look at *me*!

But there was nowhere else to look. Mother Dark had turned away. She had left them to fates of their own devising, and in so doing, she had taken away their privilege of blaming someone else. Such was a godless world.

One might think, then, that a people might rise to fullest height, stand proud, and accept the notion of potential culpability for each decision made or not made. Yes, that would be nice. That would be something to behold, to feed riotous optimism. But such a moment, such stature, never came. Enlightened ages belonged to the past or waited for the future. Such ages acquired the gloss of iconic myth, reduced to abstractions. The present world was real, filled with the grit of reality and compromise. People did not stand tall. They ducked.

There was no one about with whom Endest Silann could discuss all this. No one who might – just might – understand the significance of what he was thinking.

Rush headlong. Things are happening. Standing stones topple one against another and on and on. Tidal surges lift ever higher. Smoke and screams and violence and suffering. Victims piled in heaps like the plunder of cannibals. This is the meat of glee, the present made breathless, impatience burning like acid. Who has time to comprehend?

Endest Silann stood atop the lesser tower of the keep. He held out one hand, knuckles to the earth, as black rain pooled in the cup of his palm.

Was the truth as miserable as it seemed?

Did it all demand that one figure, one solitary figure, rise to stand tall? To face that litany of destruction, the brutality of history, the lie of progress, the desecration of a home once sacred, precious beyond imagining? One figure? Alone?

Is his own burden not enough? Why must he carry ours? Why have we done this to him? Why, because it's easier that way, and we so cherish the easy paths, do we not? The least of effort defines our virtues. Trouble us not, for we dislike being troubled.

The children are hungry. The forests are dead, the rivers poisoned. Calamity descends again and again. Diseases flower like mushrooms on corpses. And soon we will war over what's left. As we did in Kharkanas.

He will take this burden, but what does that mean? That we are freed to stay unchanging? Freed to continue doing nothing?

The black water overflowed the cup, spilled down to become rain once more.

Even the High Priestess did not understand. Not all of it, no. She saw this as a single, desperate gambit, a cast of the knuckles on which rode everything. But if it failed, well, there'd be another game. New players, the same old tired rules. The wealth wagered never lost its value, did it? The heap of golden coins will not crumble. It will only grow bigger yet.

Then, if the players come and go, while the rules never change, does not that heap in fact command the game? Would you bow to this god of gold? This insensate illusion of value?

Bow, then. Press forehead to the hard floor. But when it all goes wrong, show me no affronted disbelief.

Yes, Anomander Rake would take that burden, and carry it into a new world. But he would offer no absolution. He would deliver but one gift – an undeserved one – and that was *time.*

The most precious privilege of all. *And what, pray tell, shall we do with it?*

Off to his left, surmounting a much higher tower, a dragon fixed slitted eyes upon a decrepit camp beyond the veil of Night. No rain could blind it, no excuse could brave its unwavering regard. Silanah watched. And waited.

But the waiting was almost over.

Rush then, to this feast. Rush, ye hungry ones, to the meat of glee.

The wall had never been much to begin with. Dismantled in places, unfinished in others. It would never have withstood a siege for any length of time. Despite its execrable condition, the breach made by the Hounds of Shadow was obvious. An entire gate was gone, filled with the flame-licked wreckage of the blockhouses and a dozen nearby structures. Figures now clambered in its midst, hunting survivors, fighting the flames.

Beyond it, vast sections of the city – where heaving clouds of smoke lifted skyward, lit bright by raging gas-fires – suddenly ebbed, as if Darujhistan's very breath had been snatched away. Samar Dev staggered, fell to her knees. The pressure closing about her head felt moments from crushing the plates of her skull. She cried out even as Karsa crouched down beside her.

Ahead, Traveller had swung away from the destroyed gate, seeking instead another portal to the east, through which terrified refugees now spilled out into the ramshackle neighbourhood of shanties, where new fires had erupted from knocked-down shacks and in the wake of fleeing squatters. How Traveller intended to push his way through that mob—

'Witch, you must concentrate.'

'What?'

'In your mind, raise a wall. On all sides. Make it strong, give it the power to withstand the one who has arrived.'

She pulled away from his hand. 'Who? Who has arrived? By the spirits, I can't stand—'

He slapped her, hard enough to knock her down. Stunned, she stared up at him.

'Samar Dev, I do not know who, or what – it is not the Hounds. Not even Shadowthrone. *Someone is there, and that someone blazes. I – I cannot imagine such a being—*'

'A god.'

He shrugged. 'Build your walls.'

The pressure had eased and she wondered at that, and then realized that Karsa had moved round, placing himself between her and the city. She saw sweat running down the Toblakai's face, streaming like rain. She saw the tightness in his eyes. 'Karsa—'

'If we are to follow, you and me both, then you must do this. Build walls, Witch, and hurry.'

His gaze lifted to something behind her and all at once she felt a breath of power at her back, gusting against her, sinking past clothes, past skin, through flesh and then deep into her bones. She gasped.

The pressure was pushed back, left to rage against immense barriers now shielding her mind.

She climbed to her feet.

Side by side, they set out after Traveller.

He was cutting across a ragged strip of fallow field, dust rising with each stride, making for the gate at a sharp angle.

The surging mob of people blocking the portal seemed to melt back, and she wondered what those refugees had seen in Traveller's face as he marched straight for them. Whatever it had been, clearly it was not something to be challenged.

A strange, diffuse light now painted the city, the uneven wall, the domes, minarets and spires visible behind it. From a thousand throats erupted a moaning wail. Of shock, of dread. She saw faces lift, one by one. She saw eyes widen.

Grunting, Karsa glanced back, and then halted. 'Gods below!'

She spun. The giant bear loomed twenty or so paces back, its outline limned by a silver light – and that light—

The moon had finally clambered free of the horizon – but it was . . . *Queen of Dreams—*

'Shattered,' Karsa said. 'The moon has shattered. Faces in the Rock, what has happened?'

What rose now into the sky was a mass of fragments, torn apart amidst a cloud of thin rings of dust. It had expanded in its eruption and was now twice its normal size. Huge chunks were visibly spiralling away from the centre. The light it cast was sickly yet astonishingly bright.

The monstrous bear had half turned and was lifting its snout towards that devastated world, as if it was capable of smelling death across the span of countless leagues.

Karsa tugged at Samar Dev. 'He's in the city, Witch. We cannot lose him.'
She permitted him to drag her along, her hand enveloped by his.

Perched in a niche close to the gate, Chillbais tracked the one known as Traveller. The demon was shaking uncontrollably. The bellowing of Hounds, the detonations of entire buildings, the arrival of the Son of Darkness and the slaying of a god – oh, any of these could have been sufficient cause for such quivering terror. Even that ruined moon thrusting skyward to the south. Alas, however, it was none of these that had elicited the winged toad's present state of abject extremity.

No, the source was threading through the crowd at the gate, now passing beneath the arch. The one named Traveller. Oh, he held in so much of himself, a will of such breathtaking intensity that Chillbais imagined it could, if the man so desired, reach into the heavens, close about all those spinning pieces in the sky, and remake the entire moon.

But this was not a healing power. This was not a benign will.

The Hounds howled anew, announcing all that they had sensed, all that they even now reeled away from. Goaded, they lashed out in all directions, killing with mindless frenzy. And once more madness was unleashed upon the hapless people of Darujhistan.

Oh, the master would be furious at this loss of control. Most furious.

Chillbais opened his mouth and managed an impossibly broad grin. A smile to the crazed night sky. The demon worked its way out of the niche and flapped its wings a few times to work out the folds. Then it sprang into the air.

Plunging into the milling crowd was not part of the plan, and the panic that ensued seemed out of all proportion to this modest demon's unexpected arrival. After some hectic moments, Chillbais succeeded in flapping upward once more, bruised and scraped, scratched and scuffed, winging his way to the estate of his master.

Eager to deliver a message.

He is here! He is here! Dassem Ultor is here!

Can I leave now?

Both Karsa and Samar Dev had witnessed the demon's plight, but neither made comment, even as it winged back up to vanish over the wall. They were rushing, Karsa Orlong imposing enough to clear a path, straight for the gate.

A short time later they stumbled through, out on to a broad avenue into which citizens streamed from every conceivable direction.

They saw Traveller sixty or so paces ahead, reaching an intersection oddly empty of refugees. Those figures nearest it were running in blind panic.

Traveller had halted. A solitary figure, bathed in the light of the shattered moon.

A Hound trotted into view on the warrior's left. A mangled, headless torso hung in its jaws, still draining thick blood. Its lambent eyes were on Traveller, who had not moved, although it was clear that he was tracking the beast with his gaze.

Karsa unsheathed his sword and quickened his pace. Samar Dev, her heart pounding, hurried after him.

She saw the Toblakai slow suddenly, and then stop, still thirty paces from the intersection, and a moment later she saw why.

Cotillion was walking up to Traveller. Another Hound – the black one – had appeared to guard the god's other flank.

Behind them a distant building suddenly crashed down, and in the heart of that thunder there was the sound of two beasts locked in mortal combat, neither yielding. Frail screams echoed in fragile counterpoint.

Traveller waited. Cotillion came to stand directly in front of him, and began to speak.

Samar Dev wanted to rush forward, at least to a spot from where she could overhear the god, catch whatever response Traveller delivered. But Karsa's hand held her back, and he shook his head, saying in a murmur, 'This is not for us, Witch.'

Traveller seemed to be refusing something, stepping back, looking away.

Cotillion pressed on.

'He does not want it,' Karsa said. 'Whatever he asks, Traveller does not want it.'

Yes, she could see that. 'Please, I need to—'

'No.'

'Karsa—'

'What drives you is want, not need.'

'Fine, then! I'm a nosy bitch – just leave me to it—'

'No. This is between them, and so it must remain. Samar Dev, answer me this. If you could hear what they say, if you comprehended all that it might mean, would you be able to stay silent?'

She bristled, and then hissed in frustration. 'I'm not very good at doing that, am I? All right, Karsa – but what if I did say something? What harm would that do?'

'Leave him,' said Karsa. 'Leave him free to choose for himself.'

Whatever Cotillion was saying seemed to strike like physical blows, which Traveller absorbed one after another, still looking away – still clearly unable to meet the god's eyes.

The Hound with the chewed-up torso was now eating it with all the mindless intensity common to carnivores filling their stomachs. The other beast had half turned away and seemed to be listening to that distant fight.

Cotillion was unrelenting.

For the god, for Traveller, and for Samar Dev and Karsa Orlong, the world beyond this scene had virtually vanished. A moment was taking portentous shape, hewn one piece at a time, like finding a face in the heart of a block of stone. A moment that spun on some kind of decision, one that Traveller must make, here, now, for it was obvious that Cotillion had placed himself in the warrior's path, and would not step to one side.

'Karsa – if this goes wrong—'

'I have his back,' said the Toblakai in a growl.

'But what if—'

An inhuman cry from Traveller cut through her words, cut through every thought, slashing like a knife. Such a forlorn, desperate sound – it did not belong to him, could not, but he had thrust out one arm, as if to shove Cotillion aside.

They stood too far apart for that. Yet Cotillion, now silent, simply stepped away from Traveller's path.

And the warrior walked past, but now it was as if each boot needed to be dragged forward, as if Traveller now struggled against some terrible, invisible tide. That ferocious obsession seemed to have come untethered – he walked as would a man lost.

Cotillion watched him go, and she saw him lift a forearm to his eyes, as if he did not want the memory of this, as if he could wipe it away with a single, private gesture.

Although she did not understand, sorrow flooded through Samar Dev. Sorrow for whom? She had no answer that made sense. She wanted to weep. For Traveller. For Cotillion. For Karsa. *For this damned city and this damned night.*

The Hounds had trotted off.

She blinked. Cotillion too had disappeared.

Karsa shook himself, and then led her onward once more.

The pressure was building, leaning in on her defences. She sensed cracks, the sifting of dust. And as they stumbled along in Traveller's wake, Samar Dev realized that the warrior was marching straight for the nexus of that power.

The taste of fear was bitter on her tongue.

No, Traveller, no. Change your mind. Change it, please.

But he would not do that, would he? Would not. Could not. *The fate of the fated, oh, that sounds clumsy, and yet . . . what else can it be called? This force of inevitability, both willed and unwilling, both unnecessary and inexorable. The fate of the fated.*

Walking, through a city trapped in a nightmare, beneath the ghoulish light of a moon in its death-throes. Traveller might as well be dragging chains, and at the ends of those chains, none other than Karsa Orlong and Samar Dev. And Traveller might as well be wearing his own collar of iron, something invisible but undeniable heaving him forward.

She had never felt so helpless.

In the eternity leading up to the moment of the Lord of Death's arrival, the world of Dragnipur had begun a slow, deadly and seemingly unstoppable convulsion. Everywhere, the looming promise of annihilation. Everywhere, a chorus of desperate cries, bellowing rage and hopeless defiance. The raw nature of each chained thing was awakened, and each gave that nature voice, and each voice held the flavour of sharp truth. Dragons shrilled, demons roared, fools shrieked in hysteria. Bold heroes and murderous thugs snatched deep breaths that made ribs creak, and then loosed battle cries.

Argent fires were tumbling down from the sky, tearing down through clouds of ash. An army of unimaginable size, from which no quarter was possible, had begun a lumbering charge, and weapons clashed the rims of shields and this white, rolling wave of destruction seemed to surge higher as if seeking to merge with the stormclouds.

Feeble, eroded shapes dragged along at the ends of chains now flopped blunted limbs as if to fend off the fast closing oblivion. Eyes rolled in battered skulls, remnants of life and of knowledge flickering one last time.

No, nothing wanted to die. When death is oblivion, life will spit in its face. If it can.

The sentient and the mindless were now, finally, all of one mind.

Shake awake all reason. These gathered instincts are not the end but the means. Rattle the chains if you must, but know that that which binds does not break, and the path is never as wayward as one might believe.

Ditch stared with one eye into the descending heavens, and knew terror, but that terror was not his. The god that saw with the same eye filled Ditch's skull with its shrieks. *Born to die! I am born to die! I am born to die! Not fair not fair not fair!* And Ditch just rattled a laugh – or at least imagined that he did so – and replied, *We're all born to die, you idiot. Let the span last a single heartbeat, let it last a thousand years. Stretch the heartbeat out, crush down the centuries, it's no different. They feel the same, when the end arrives.*

Gods, they feel the same!

No, he was not much impressed by this godling cowering in his soul. Kadaspala was mad, mad to think such a creation could achieve anything. Etch deep into its heart this ferocious hunger to *kill*, and then reveal the horror of its helplessness – oh, was that not cruel beyond all reason? Was that not its own invitation into insanity?

Kadaspala, you have but made versions of yourself. You couldn't help it – yes, I see that.

But, damn you, my flesh belonged to me. Not you.

Damn you—

But curses meant nothing now. Every fate was now converging. *Hah hah, take that, you pious posers, and you arrogant shits, and all you whining victims – see what comes! It's all the same, this end, all the same!*

And here he was, trapped in the greater scheme. His skin a piece of a tapestry. And its grand scene? A pattern he could never read.

The demon Pearl stood wearing bodies from which a forest of iron roots swept down in loops and coils. It could carry no more, and so it stood, softly weeping, its legs like two failing trunks that shook and trembled. It had long since weighed the value of hatred. For the High Mage Tayschrenn, who first summoned it and bound it to his will. For Ben Adaephon Delat, who unleashed it against the Son of

Darkness; and for Anomander Rake himself, whose sword bit deep. But the value was an illusion. Hate was a lie that in feeding fills the hater with the bliss of satiation, even as his spirit starves. No, Pearl did not hate. Life was a negotiation between the expected and the unexpected. One made do.

Draconus staggered up. 'Pearl, my friend, I have come to say goodbye. And to tell you I am sorry.'

'What saddens you?' the demon asked.

'I am sorry, Pearl, for all of this. For Dragnipur. For the horror forged by my own hands. It was fitting, was it not, that the weapon claimed its maker? I think, yes, it was. It was.' He paused, and then brought both hands up to his face. For a moment it seemed he would begin clawing his beard from the skin beneath it. Instead, the shackled hands fell away, down, dragged by the weight of the chains.

'I too am sorry,' said Pearl. 'To see the end of this.'

'What?'

'So many enemies, all here and not one by choice. Enemies, and yet working together for so long. It was a wondrous thing, was it not, Draconus? When necessity forced each hand to clasp, to work as one. A wondrous thing.'

The warrior stared at the demon. He seemed unable to speak.

Apsal'ara worked her way along the top of the beam. It was hard to hold on, the wagon pitching and rocking so with one last, useless surge forward, and the beam itself thick with the slime of sweat, blood and runny mucus. But something was happening at the portal, that black, icy stain beneath the very centre of the wagon.

A strange stream was flowing into the Gate, an intricate pattern ebbing down through the fetid air from the underside of the wagon's bed. Each tendril was inky black, the space around it ignited by a sickly glow that pulsed slower than any mortal heart.

Was it Kadaspala's pathetic god? Seeking to use the tattooist's insane masterpiece as if it was a latticework, a mass of rungs, down which it could clamber and so plunge through the Gate? Seeking to *escape*?

If so, then she intended to make use of it first.

Let the cold burn her flesh. Let pieces of her simply fall away. It was a better end than some snarling manifestation of chaos ripping out her throat.

She struggled ever closer, her breath sleeting out in crackling plumes that sank down in sparkling ice crystals. It reminded her of her youth, the nights out on the tundra, when the first snows came, when clouds shivered and shed their diamond skins and the world grew so still, so breathless and perfect, that she felt that time itself was but moments from freezing solid – to hold her for ever in that place, hold her youth, hold tight her dreams and ambitions, her memories of the faces she loved – her mother, her father, her kin, her lovers. No one would grow old, no one would die and fall away from the path, and the path itself, why, it would never end.

Leave me in mid-step. My foot never to settle, never to edge me forward that much closer to the end of things. Yes, leave me here. At the very heart of possibilities, not one of which will crash down. No failures to come, no losses, no regrets to kiss upon the lips – I will not feel the cold.

I will not feel the cold—

She cried out in the frigid, deathly air. Such pain – how could she ever get close enough?

Aspal'ara drew herself up, knees beneath her. And eyed that pattern, just there, a body's length away and still streaming down. If she launched herself from this place, simply threw herself forward, would that flowing net catch her?

Would it simply shatter? Or flow aside, opening up to permit the downward plunge of a body frozen solid, lifeless, eyes open but seeing nothing?

She had a sudden thought, shivering up through her doubts, her fears. And, with aching limbs, she began dragging up the length of her chains, piling the links on the beam in front of her.

Was the Gate's cold of such power that it could snap these links? If she heaved the heap into that Gate, as much as she could, *would the chains break?*

And then?

She snarled. *Yes, and then what? Run like a hare, leave the wagon far behind, flee the legions of chaos?*

And when the Gate itself is destroyed, where will I run then? Will this world even exist?

She realized then that such questions did not matter. To be free, even if only for a moment, would be enough.

Apsal'ara, the Mistress of Thieves. How good was she? Why, she slipped the chains of Dragnipur!

She continued piling up links of the chains, her breaths coming in agonized, lung-numbing gasps.

Draconus stumbled away from Pearl's side. He could not bear the emotions the demon stirred to life within him. He could not understand such a power to forgive, never mind the sheer madness of finding something worthwhile in this cursed realm. And to see Pearl standing there, almost crushed beneath the twitching, dripping bodies of fallen comrades, no, that too was too much.

Kadaspala had failed. The pattern was flawed; it had no power to resist what was about to assail them. It had been a desperate gambit, the only kind Draconus had left, and he could not even rail at the blind, legless Tiste Andii. *None of us were up to this.*

The moment Rake ceased killing things, we were doomed.

And yet, he found he had no rage left in him when he thought of Anomander Rake. In fact, he had begun to understand, even sympathize, with that exhausted desire to end things. To end *everything*. The delusion was calling it a game in the first place. That very founding principle had assured ultimate failure. Bored gods and children with appalling power, these were the worst sorts of arbiters in this scheme of existence. They fought change even as they forced it upon others; they sought to hold all they claimed even as they struggled to steal all they could from rivals. They proclaimed love only to kill it in betrayal and spite.

Yes, Draconus understood Rake. Any game that played with grief was a foul thing, an abomination. *Destroy it. Bring it all down, Rake. Rake, my heir, my son in spirit, my unknown and unknowable inheritor. Do as you must.*

I stand aside.

Oh, bold words.

When the truth is, I have no choice.

The force that suddenly descended upon the realm of Dragnipur was of such magnitude that, for an instant, Draconus believed the chaos had finally reached them, and he was driven to his knees, stunned, half blinded. The immense pressure bore down, excruciating, and Draconus ducked his head, covered it with his arms, and felt his spine bowing beneath a crushing presence.

If there was sound, he heard nothing. If there was life, he saw only darkness. If there was air, he could not draw it into his lungs. He felt his bones groaning—

The torture eased with the settling of a skeletal, long-fingered hand on his right shoulder.

Sounds rose once more, strangely muted. A renewed storm of wailing terror and dismay. In front of Draconus the world found its familiar details, although they seemed ghostly, ephemeral. He was able, at last, to breathe deep – and he tasted death.

Someone spoke above him. 'He is indeed a man of his word.'

And Draconus twisted round, lifted his gaze – the hand on his shoulder rasping away with a rustle of links – and stared up at the one who had spoken. At Hood, the Lord and High King of the Dead.

'No!' Draconus bellowed, rising only to stagger back, almost tripping on his chains. 'No! What has he done? By the Abyss, what has Rake done?'

Hood half raised his arms and seemed to be staring down at the manacles enclosing his gaunt wrists.

Disbelief collapsed into shock, and then raw horror. This made no sense. Draconus did not understand. He could not – gods – he could not believe—

He spun round, then, and stared at the legions of chaos – oh, they had been pushed back, a league or more, by the arrival of this singular creature, by the power of Hood. The actinic stormclouds had tumbled in retreat, building anew and seeming to thrash in frustration – yes, an interlude had been purchased. But – 'Wasted. All wasted! Why? This has achieved *nothing*! Hood – you were betrayed. Can you not see that? No—' Draconus clutched at his head. 'Rake, oh Rake, what did you want of this? How could think it would achieve anything?'

'I have missed you, Draconus,' Hood said.

And he twisted round once more, glaring at the god. Jaghut. Yes, the mad, unknowable Jaghut. 'You damned fool! You *asked* for this, didn't you? Have you lost your mind!?'

'A bargain, old friend,' Hood replied, still studying the chains on his wrists. 'A . . . gamble.'

'What will happen? When chaos claims you? When chaos devours the realm of death itself? You have betrayed the gods, all of them. You have betrayed all life. When you fall—'

'Draconus,' Hood cut in with a sigh, reaching up now to pull back the hood, revealing that withered Jaghut face, the clawed lines of eternal sorrow. 'Draconus, my friend,' he said softly, 'surely you do not think I have come here alone?'

He stared at the god, for a moment uncomprehending. And then – he caught a distant roar of sound, edging in from three of the four horizons, and those indistinct skylines were now . . . *seething*.

As the armies of the dead marched at the behest of their Lord.

From one side, a score of riders was fast approaching.

'Hood,' Draconus said, numbed, baffled, 'they are unchained.'

'So they are.'

'This is not their fight.'

'Perhaps. That is, as yet, undecided.'

Draconus shook his head. 'They cannot be here. They cannot fight the enemy – those dead, Hood, *all they have left* is their identities, each soul, barely holding on. *You cannot do this to them! You cannot ask this of them!*'

The god was now eyeing the wagon. 'All I shall ask,' he said, 'of the fallen, Draconus, is that they choose. Of their own will. After this, I shall ask nothing of them. Ever again.'

'So who will claim the dead?'

'Let the gods see to their own.'

The coldness of that response staggered Draconus. 'And what of those who worship no gods?'

'Yes, what of them?'

'What's that supposed to mean?'

'After this,' Hood said, still studying the wagon, 'the dead will not be my concern. Ever again.'

The approaching riders rode rotted, skeletal mounts. Ragged capes flailed out behind the warriors. From the advancing armies, countless standards wavered and pitched about amidst up-thrust spearheads. The numbers were indeed unimaginable. Broken fragments of war songs arrived like tatters of wind. The realm groaned – Draconus could not comprehend the weight that must now be crushing down the weapon's wielder. Could Draconus have withstood it? He did not know. But then, perhaps even at this moment Anomander Rake himself was dying, bones snapping, blood spurting . . .

But there was more. Here, before his eyes.

All the creatures chained to the wagon had ceased pulling the enormous edifice – for the first time in millennia, the wagon had *stopped rolling*. And those creatures stood or knelt, staring outward, silent, perhaps disbelieving, as legions of the dead closed in. A flood, an ocean of iron and bone—

The riders arrived. Strangers all to Draconus. Six trotted their withered mounts closer. One of them was masked, and he had seen those masks before – a host slain in succession by Anomander Rake. *Seguleh.* The marks upon this one told Draconus that he was looking upon the Second. Had he challenged the First? Or had someone challenged him?

The Second was the first to speak. 'This is the sorry shit-hole you want us to fight for, Hood? Flinging ourselves into the maw of chaos.' The masked face seemed to scan the huddled, bedraggled creatures in their chains. 'What are these, that we must now die again for? That we must cease for? Miserable wretches, one and all! Useless fools, bah! Hood, you ask too much.'

The Lord of Death did not even face the Seguleh as he replied, 'Do you now change your mind, Knight?'

'No,' he said. 'I was just complaining.' He drew out a pair of notched, rust-stained swords. 'You know me better than that. Still, oh, how I wanted Skinner. To lose him this way – by the Tyrant, it *galls*.'

'That is why,' said Hood, 'you will not lead the Dead into this war.'

'What? I am the Knight of Death! The damned bony fist himself! I demand—'

'Oh, do be quiet, Second,' sighed the Lord of Death. 'Other tasks await you – and you will not rue them, I am sure. Iskar Jarak, will you command in the Knight's stead? At the head of the spear, driving into the very heart of the enemy?'

The one so addressed had the look of a veteran among veterans. Grey-bearded, scarred, wearing threadbare, faded colours over his plain chain hauberk. Grey and magenta, bordered in black. At Hood's request he faced the Jaghut. 'We will harden the point,' he said. 'With Malazans. At the very tip, my Bridgeburners. Dujek on my left flank, Bult on the right with the Seventh and his Wickans.' He then twisted in the saddle to regard another soldier. 'Brukhalian and his Grey Swords to the right of Bult.'

Brukhalian nodded. 'I find honour in that, Iskar Jarak.'

'Skamar Ara, your Jacuruku legions to the left of Dujek. Hood, listen well. Beyond the spear, so many of the rest are so much dross. Their will is weakened by countless millennia – they will march into the face of the enemy, but they will not last.'

'Yes,' said Hood.

'Just so you know,' said Iskar Jarak. 'Just so you know.'

'Return now to your forces,' Hood commanded. 'Iskar Jarak, send to me the one-eyed outrider. And Bult, find my Soldier, the one once named Baudin. There are things still to do.'

Draconus watched as the commanders rode off, with only the Seguleh remaining, swords sheathed once more. 'Hood,' he said, 'what is happening here? You will ask the dead to fight for us? They will fail. They will earn oblivion and naught else. They cannot succeed, Hood. The chaos pursuing Dragnipur will not be denied – do you understand what I'm telling you?'

The Knight snorted. 'It is you who does not understand, Elder. Long before he was Lord of the Fallen, he was *Jaghut*. Lords of the Last Stands, hah! Sentinels of the Sundered Keeps. Devourers of the Forlorn Hope – you, Elder, who stood time and again against the Tiste Andii, the Tiste Edur – you, who walked the ashes of

Kharkanas itself – understand me. The dour Tiste Andii and the suicidal Edur, they are as *nothing* to the miserable madness of the Jaghut!'

During this tirade, Hood continued to stare at the wagon, at its towering, tottering heap of bodies. And then the Lord of the Dead spoke. 'I often wondered what it looked like, this Hold creaking on its wooden wheels . . . a pathetic thing, really. Crude, clumsy.' He faced Draconus, rotted skin curling back from the tusks. 'Now, *turn it around.*'

Chapter Twenty-Three

Ask what the dead face
Snatching the curtain aside
These stony tracks into blind worlds
Where to grope is to recall
All the precious jewels of life

Ask what the dead see
In that last backward glance
These fetish strings knots left untied
Where every sinew strains
To reach and touch once more

Ask what the dead know
When knowing means nothing
Arms full and heaped with baubles
As if to build a home anew
In places we've never been

Ask but the dead do not answer
Behind the veil of salty rain
Skirl now amid the rotted leavings
When the worms fall away
To that wealth of silence

THE LOST TREASURES OF INDAROS
FISHER KEL TATH

Eyes rolling white, the ox ran for its life. Cart skidding and bouncing, tilting on one wild wheel as the moaning beast hurtled round a corner and raced down a cobbled street.

Even the gods could not reach through that thick-boned pate of skull, down into the tender knot of terror in its murky brain. Once prodded awake, incessant need blurred the world beyond, reducing all to a narrow tunnel with salvation at the far, far end. Why, who could comprehend such extremity? Not mortal kin, much less a god with its eternally bemused brow – to regard such fitful interludes, blank-eyed and mind rushing past like a flash flood, what would be the value of that, after all?

The beast is what it is. Four-legged, two-legged. Panic will use as many limbs as are available to it, and a few more besides. Panic will ride a wheeled cart, and thunder on dung-smeared hoofs. Panic will scrabble up the very walls as one horrendous Hound after another slinks past.

The night air stinks and that stink fills the nostrils with all the frenzied flags of a ship floundering on shoals. Smoke and blood, bile and piss. But, mostly, blood.

And then there were the screams. Ringing out everywhere, so many of them cutting off in mid-shriek, or, even more chilling, in strangled gurgle. Mothers never before heard such a multitude of beseeching calls! And who could say if the ox was not bellowing for its own, for that sweet teat, the massive hulk looming overhead, with all its sure scents and briny warmth? Alas, the beast's mam was long since sent off to pull the great cart beyond the veil, and even could she come lumbering back at the desperate call of her get, what might she achieve in the face of a Hound?

No, solitary flight this must remain. For each and all. Ox, horse, dog, cat, mouse and rat, lizard and gnat. And people of all sorts. Old men with limps, old men who never limped in their lives but did so now. Women of all ages, sizes and dispositions, who would have limped could it have earned the necessary sympathy. Yet when even the rooftops hold no succour, why bother riding this bouncing cart of headlong panic? Best to simply flop down in abject surrender, with but a few tugs to rearrange the lie of one's dress or whatnot. Let the men soil themselves in their terror – they never washed enough as it was.

Nobles fled ignobly, the fallen fairly flew as if on winged feet, thieves blustered and bullies whined and wheedled, guards in their blind fear observed nothing and soldiers fled every clash of iron, tooth and claw. Fools with nothing stood their ground. Gamblers danced and whores bluffed – and inside a Temple of Shadow deliciously feminine acolytes squealed and darted from the path of a screaming Magus atop his charging mule, straight through the grand altar room, censers flying with tails of uncoiling serpentine smoke and heads with glowing coal eyes in myriad profusion. In the mule's careering wake, winged bhokarala shrieked and flitted about flinging gobs of snot and segmented cones of hairy dung at every fleeing female, while spiders swarmed up from the old long-forgotten blood drain at the base of the altar stone, a veritable carpet of seething jerky sticklegs, glistening abdomens, patterned thoraxes and beady Dal Honese eyes by the thousands, nay tens of thousands! And was it any wonder the Magus and the mule pelted right across the chamber, the doors at the far end exploding open as if of their own accord?

Even as the High Priestess – stumbling out from behind a curtain like a woman tossed from the throes of manic lovemaking, with stubble-rubbed chin and puffy lips high and low and breasts all awry and great molten swells of pale flesh swaying to and fro – plunging, yes, into the midst of that crawling black carpet of spite and venom, and so no wonder she began a dance riotous in its frenzy but let's face it, even Mogora was too shocked, too disbelieving, to sink a forest of fangs into such sweet meat – and the bhokarala swooped down to scoop up handfuls of yummy spiders and *crunch crunch* into their maws and if spiders could scream, why, they did so then, even as they foamed in swirling retreat back down the drain.

Mule and Magus drumrolled down the colonnade and out through another shattered set of doors, out into the moody alleyway with its huddled mass of hiding refugees, who now scattered at the arrival of this dread apparition, and the squall of bhokarala swirling out behind it.

Now, wing swift as a burning moth across the city, back to the ox as it lumbered along in heart-pounding, chest-heaving exhaustion – pursued by an angry cart and who knew what else – and found itself fast approaching the collapsed ruin of an enormous building of some sort. . . .

Serendipity serves as the quaintest description of the fickle mayhem delivered by the Hounds of Shadow. Shortly following the breach of the gate, Baran pelted westward in pursuit of Pallid, as that bone-white beast broke from the pack with untoward designs in another part of the stricken city.

Pallid was unaware that it was being hunted as it discovered a dozen city guards rushing down the centre of the street, heading for the destroyed gate. The monstrous beast lunged into their midst, lashing out with slavering jaws. Armour collapsed, limbs were torn away, weapons spun through the air. Screams erupted in a welter of slaughter.

Even as Pallid crushed in its jaws the head of the last guard, Baran arrived in an avalanche. The impact boomed like thunder as Pallid was struck in the side, the caged bell of its chest reverberating as both beasts skidded and then struck the wall of a large building.

The solid, fortified entranceway was punched inward. Stone shards tore through the three people unlucky enough to be stationed in the front room. The huge blocks framing the doors tumbled down, bouncing like knuckle bones, crushing one of the wounded men before he could even scream. The remaining two, lacerated and spilling blood, were pushed back by the broad front desk, and pinned against the far wall. Both died within moments, bones and organs macerated.

Rolling, snapping and growling, the two Hounds shattered that desk, and the grillework attached to it sailed upward to crack on the ceiling, which had already begun sagging as its supports and braces gave way. With terrible groans, the entire front of the structure dragged itself down, and now screams rose through the dust, muted and pitiful.

Another wall collapsed under the impact of the beasts, and beyond it was a corridor and bars lining cells, and two more guards who sought to flee down the aisle's length – but this entire room was coming down, the iron bars snapping out from their frames, locks shattering. Prisoners vanished beneath splintered wooden beams, plaster and bricks.

Rearing back on to its hind legs, knocked over by another charge from Baran, Pallid smashed into one cell. The prisoner within it pitched down and rolled up against one side as the Hounds, locked once more, knocked down the back wall and, kicking and snarling, rolled into the space beyond – an alleyway already half filled with falling masonry as the entire gaol broke apart.

The lone prisoner scrambled back to his feet and rushed into the Hounds' wake—

But not in time, as the floor above dropped down to fill the cell.

In the alley Pallid had managed to close its jaws about Baran's shoulder, and with a savage surge sent the beast wheeling through the air to crunch into what remained of the wall on that side – and this too folded inward beneath the impact of Baran's thrashing weight.

From the wreckage of the first cell, a section of plaster and mortared brick lifted up, and as it tumbled back the prisoner – covered in dust, bruised and bleeding – began to climb free.

Pallid, hearing these sounds – the gasps and coughs, the scrambling – wheeled round, eyes blazing.

And Barathol paused, legs still pinned, and stared into those infernal orbs, and knew that they were the last things he would ever see.

Pallid gathered its legs for its charge. Its smeared, torn lips stretched back to reveal its massive fangs, and then it sprang forward—

Even as a figure hurtled bodily into its side, striking it low, beneath its right shoulder, hard enough to twist the animal round as it flew in midair.

Barathol flung himself back and as much to one side as he could manage, as the Hound's crimson-splashed head pounded side-on into the rubble, its flailing body following.

Picking himself up from the ground, Chaur looked over at Barathol, and then showed him a bright red smile, even as he dragged free the huge war-axe he had collected from the smithy – Barathol's very own weapon. As Pallid clambered back upright, Chaur threw the axe in Barathol's direction, and then picked up a chunk of stone.

Barathol shrieked, desperate to tear himself free, as the white Hound, snarling, spun to face Chaur with fury incandescent in its eyes.

From the rubble farther down the alley, Baran was working free, but it would not arrive in time. Not for Chaur.

Kicking, heedless of tearing flesh, Barathol fought on.

Chaur threw his stone the instant the white Hound charged.

It struck the beast's snout dead-on.

A yelp of agony, and then the beast's momentum slammed it into Chaur, sent him flying across the alley to crunch sickeningly against the opposite wall. When he fell to the grimy cobbles, he did not move.

Barathol dragged his legs loose, leaving trails of blood and pieces of meat. He rolled, grasping hold of the axe handle, and then heaved himself to his feet.

Pallid's huge head turned.

Baran broke clear into the alley.

The white Hound looked over, and, with another snarl, the beast pivoted round and fled.

A moment later Baran flashed past.

Barathol sagged back on wobbly legs. Drawing in one cold breath after another, he turned his gaze once more upon the motionless body opposite. With a sob, he dragged himself to his feet and stumbled over.

In the strange, mysterious places within the brain, places that knew of themselves as Chaur, a black flood was seeping in, and one by one those places began to drown. Fitful sparks ebbed, and once gone did not light again. His state of unconsciousness slipped into something deeper, a kind of protective oblivion that mercifully hid from Chaur the fact that he was dying.

His expression was serene, save for the slow sag along one side of his face, and when Barathol rolled back his eyelids, the pupil of the eye on that side was vastly dilated.

Weeping, the blacksmith pulled Chaur's head and upper body on to his thighs. The rest of the world, the explosions, the screams, the thunder of battle, all fell away, and it was some time before Barathol realized that someone was clambering out of the rubble that was the gaol. A staccato cascade of curses in Falari, Malazan, Dobri and Daru. Blinking, the blacksmith lifted his gaze.

'Antsy – here, please, I need your help! Please. He's hurt.'

The ex-Bridgeburner was covered in dust but otherwise unscathed. 'I lost my damned sword. I lost my damned crossbow. I lost my damned sharpers. I lost my—'

'Antsy! Hood's breath, please help me – we need to find a healer. High Denul – there must be one in the city. *There must be!*'

'Well, there's Mallet, but he's – shit, he's dead. I forgot. Can't believe I forgot.' Antsy crouched down and studied Chaur for a moment, and then he shook his head. 'He's done for, Barathol. Cracked skull, bleeding into his brain – you can always tell, when one side of the face goes—'

'I know all that, damn you. We need a healer! Think, Antsy – there must be *someone*.'

'Maybe, but not close – we got to cross half the city, Barathol, and with them Hounds—'

'Never mind the Hounds.' The blacksmith gathered Chaur up into his arms and straightened.

Antsy stared. 'You can't carry him—'

'Then help me!'

'I'm trying! Let me think.'

At that moment they both heard the clumping of hoofs, the clack of wooden wheels on cobbles. And they turned to the alley mouth.

Behold, the ox. Too weary to run. Even the cart in its wake clumped in exhaustion. Stolid legs trembled. Mucus slathered down in a gleaming sheet that dragged dusty tendrils between the beast's front hoofs. The painful clarity of panic was fading, dulling its eyes once more, and when the two man-things arrived and set down a third body on the bed of the cart, why, this was old business as far as the ox was concerned. At last, the world had recovered its sanity. There were tasks to be done, journeys to complete. Salvation sweeter than mam's milk.

Tired but content, the beast fell in step beside the man-things.

The two cousins stood on the rooftop, looking out over the city. Conflagrations lit the night sky. A section of the Gadrobi District was aflame, with geysers of burning gas spouting high into the air. A short time earlier a strange atmospheric pressure had descended, driving down the fires – nothing was actually spreading, as far as could be determined, and the detonations had grown more infrequent. Even so, there was no one fighting the flames, which was, all things considered, hardly surprising.

In the courtyard below, Studious Lock was fussing about over the fallen compound guards, both of whom had been dragged out on to pallets. Miraculously, both still lived, although, having survived the assassins, there remained the grave chance that they would not survive Studlock's ministrations. Scorch and Leff had set themselves the task of patrolling outside the estate, street by alley by street by alley, round and round, crossbows at the ready and in states of high excitement.

'These Hounds,' said Rallick, 'are most unwelcome.'

'It seems walls don't stop them either. Any idea why they're here?'

When Rallick did not reply, Torvald glanced over and saw that his cousin was staring up at the shattered moon.

Torvald did not follow his gaze. That mess unnerved him. Would those spinning chunks now begin raining down? Rallick had noted earlier that most of the fragments seemed to heading the other way, growing ever smaller. There was another moon that arced a slower path that seemed to suggest it was farther away, and while it appeared tiny its size was in fact unknown. For all anyone knew, it might be another world as big as this one, and maybe now it was doomed to a rain of death. Anyway, Torvald didn't much like thinking about it.

'Rallick—'

'Never mind, Tor. I want you to stay here, within the walls. I doubt there will be any trouble – the Mistress has reawakened her wards.'

'Tiserra—'

'Is a clever woman, and a witch besides. She'll be fine, and mostly will be worrying about you. Stay here, cousin, until the dawn.'

'What about you?'

Rallick turned about then, and a moment later Torvald sensed that someone else had joined them, and he too swung round.

Vorcan stood, wrapped in a thick grey cloak. 'The High Alchemist,' she said to Rallick, 'suggested we be close by . . . in case we are needed. The time, I believe, has come.'

Rallick nodded. 'Rooftops and wires, Mistress?'

She smiled. 'You make me nostalgic. Please, take the lead.'

And yes, Torvald comprehended all the subtle layers beneath those gentle words, and he was pleased. *Leave it my cousin to find for himself the most dangerous woman alive. Well, then again, maybe I found myself the second most, especially if I forget to buy bread on my way home.*

Edging round the corner of the wall, an alley behind them, a street before them, Scorch and Leff paused. No point in being careless now, even though there'd be no attack from any assassins any time soon, unless of course they did breed fast as botflies, and Scorch wasn't sure if Leff had been joking with that, not sure at all.

The street was empty. No refugees, no guards, no murderous killers all bundled in black.

Most important of all: no Hounds.

'Damn,' hissed Leff, 'where are them beasts? What, you smell badder and worster than anyone else, Scorch? Is that the problem here? Shit, I want me a necklace of fangs. And maybe a paw to hang at my belt.'

'A paw? More like a giant club making you walk tilted over. Now, that'd be funny to see, all right. Worth getting a knock or two taking one of 'em down, just to see that. A Hound's paw, hah hah.'

'You said you wanted a skull!'

'Wasn't planning to wear it, though. To make me a boat, just flip it upside down, right? I could paddle round the lake.'

'Skulls don't float. Well, maybe yours would, being cork.'

They set out on to the street.

'I'd call it *Seahound*, what do you think?'

'More like *Sinkhound*.'

'You don't know anything you think you know, Leff. That's your problem. Always has been, always will be.'

'Wish there'd been twenty more of them assassins.'

'There were, just not attacking us. We was the diversion, that's what Tor said.'

'We diverted 'em, all right.'

At that moment a Hound of Shadow slunk into view, not twenty paces away. Its sides were heaving, strips of flesh hanging down trailing threads of blood. Its mouth was crusted with red foam. It swung its head and eyed them.

In unison, Scorch and Leff lifted their crossbows into vertical positions, and spat on the barbed heads. Then they slowly settled the weapons back down, trained on the Hound.

Nostrils flaring, the beast flinched back. A moment later and it was gone.

'Shit!'

'I knew you smelled bad, damn you! We almost had it!'

'Wasn't me!'

'It's no fun wandering around with you, Scorch, no fun at all. Every chance we get, you go and mess it all up.'

'Not on purpose. I like doing fun stuff as much as you do, I swear it!'

'Next time,' muttered Leff. 'We shoot first and argue later.'

'Good idea. Next time. We'll do it right the next time.'

Beneath a moon that haunted him with terrifying memories, Cutter rode Coll's horse at a slow trot down the centre of the street. In one hand he gripped the lance, but it felt awkward, too heavy. Not a weapon he'd ever used, and yet something made him reluctant to abandon it.

He could hear the Hounds of Shadow, unleashed like demons in his poor city, and this too stirred images from the past, but these were bittersweet. For *she* was in them, a presence dark, impossibly soft. He saw once more every one of her smiles, rare as they had been, and they stung like drops of acid on his soul.

He had been so lost, from the very morning he awoke in the monastery to find her gone. Oh, he'd delivered his brave face, standing there beside a god and unwilling to see the sympathy in Cotillion's dark eyes. He had told himself that it was an act of courage to let her go, to give her the final decision. Courage and sacrifice.

He no longer believed that. There was no sacrifice made in being abandoned. There was no courage in doing nothing. Regardless of actual age, he had been so much younger than her. Young in that careless, senseless way. When thinking felt hard, unpleasant, until one learned to simply shy away from the effort, even as blind emotions raged, one conviction after another raised high on the shining shield of truth. Or what passed for truth; and he knew now that whatever it had been, truth it was not. Blustery, belligerent stands, all those pious poses – they seemed so childish now, so pathetic. *I could have embraced the purest truth. Still, nobody would listen. The older you get, the thicker your walls. No wonder the young have grown so cynical. No wonder at all.*

Oh, she stood there still, a dark figure in his memories, the flash of eyes, the beginnings of a smile even as she turned away. And he could forget nothing.

At this moment, Challice, having ascended to the top of the estate tower – that ghoulish Gadrobi embarrassment – now stepped out on to the roof, momentarily buffeted by a gust of smoke. She held in her hands the glass globe in which shone the prisoner moon, and she paused, lifting her gaze, and stared in wonder at the destruction now filling a third of the sky.

But she had left him with bad habits. Terrible ones, and they had proceeded to shape his entire life. Cutter remembered the expression on Rallick's face – the shock and the dismay – as he looked down at the knife buried in his shoulder. The *recognition* – yes, Cutter was Apsalar's creation, through and through. Yes, another man had been lost.

It seemed wryly fitting that the moon was breaking into pieces in the night sky, but to find amusement in such a poignant symbol was proving a struggle. He did not possess Rallick's hardness, the layers of scar tissue worn like armour. And, for

all that she had given him, Cutter was not her perfect reflection. He could not silence the anguish he felt inside, the legacy of delivering murder, making the notion
of justice as unpalatable as a prisoner's gruel. And these were things she did not feel.

He rode on.

The Hounds knew him, he was sure of that, and if that meant anything on this
night, then he had no reason to fear them.

The occasional refugee darted across his path. Like ousted rats, the desperate
hunt for cover filled their minds, and the faces flashing past seemed empty of anything human. Survival was a fever, and it left eyes blank as those of a beached
fish. Witnessing this, Cutter felt his heart breaking.

This is my city. Darujhistan. Of the Blue Fires. It does not deserve this.

No, he did not fear the Hounds of Shadow. But he now despised them. The
devastation they were delivering was senseless, a pointless unleashing of destruction. He did not think Cotillion had anything at all to do with that. This stank of
Shadowthrone, the fickleness, the cruel indifference. He had freed his beasts to
play. In blood and snapped bones. In flames and collapsed tenements. All this
fear, all this misery. *For nothing.*

Awkward or not, the lance felt reassuring in his hand. Now, if only Shadowthrone would show himself, why, he'd find a place to plant the damned thing.

There, within its tiny, perfect world, the moon shone pure, unsullied. There had
been a time, she realized, when she too had been like that. Free of stains, not yet
bowed to sordid compromise, feeling no need to shed this tattered skin, these
glazed eyes.

Women and men were no different in the important things. They arrived with
talents, with predispositions, with faces and bodies either attractive to others or
not. And they all made do, in all the flavours of living, with whatever they possessed. And there were choices, for each and every one of them. For some, a few
of those choices were easier than others, when the lure of being desirable was not
a conceit, when it reached out an inviting hand and all at once it seemed to offer
the simplest path. So little effort was involved, merely a smile and thighs that did
not resist parting.

But there was no going back. These stains didn't wash off. The moon shone
pure and beautiful, but it remained for ever trapped.

She stared up into the sky, watched how fragments spun out from a fast-
darkening core. The momentum seemed to have slowed, and indeed, she thought
she could see pieces falling back, inward, whilst dust flattened out, as if transformed into a spear that pierced all that was left of the moon.

The dust dreams of the world it had once been.

But the dust, alas, does not command the wind.

Cutter knew now that he had – since her – taken into his arms two women as if
they were capable of punishing him, each in turn. Only one had succeeded, and

he rode towards her now, to stand before her and tell her that he had murdered her husband. Not because she had asked him to, because, in truth, she did not have that sort of hold over him, and never would. No, Gorlas Vidikas was dead for other reasons, the specifics of which were not relevant.

She was free, he would say. To do as she pleased. But whatever that would be, he would tell her, her future would not – could never – include him.

'See, there he is, at her side. What gall! Kills her husband and now she hangs on his arm. Oh, made for each other, those two. And may Hood find them the deepest pit, and soon.'

He could face that down, if need be. But he would not subject her to such a fate. Not even for love could he do that.

He had returned to his city, only to lose it for ever.

This journey to Challice would be his last. By dawn he would be gone. Darujhistan would not miss him.

She looked down once more at the imprisoned moon cupped in her hands. And here, she realized, was her childhood in all its innocence. Frozen, timeless, and for ever beyond her reach. She need only let her gaze sink in, to find all that she had once been. Cursed with beauty, blessed with health and vigour, the glow of promise—

Dust of dreams, will you now command the wind?

Dust of dreams, is it not time to set you free?

It was easy, then, to climb up on to the low wall, to stare down at the garden flagstones far below. Easy, yes, to set it all free.

Together, they plummeted through the smoky air, and when they struck, the globe shattered, the tiny moon flung loose to sparkle briefly in the air. Before twinkling out.

Dreams will not linger, but their dust rides the winds for ever.

Kruppe is no stranger to sorrow. The round man need only look at his own waistline to grasp the tragedies of past excesses, and understand that all the things that come to pass will indeed come to pass. Heart so heavy he must load it into a wheelbarrow (or nearly so), and with not a single sly wink to offer, he leaves the grim confines of the Phoenix Inn and commences the torrid trek to the stables, where he attends to his sweet-natured mule, deftly avoiding its snapping bites and lashing kicks.

The moon's face has broken apart into a thousand glittering eyes. Nothing can hide and all is seen. All can see that there is nothing left to hide. Dread clash is imminent.

The vast pressure snuffs blazing fires as would a thumb and finger a candlewick, *snuff!* Here and there and elsewhere, too. But this blessing is borne with harsh, cruel burden. A god has died, a pact been sealed, and in a street where onlookers now gather at the very edges, a most honourable man sits hunched over his knees, head bowed low. The wind takes ethereal chains emerging from the sword in his hands, and tugs them, tears at them, shreds them into ghostly nothings that drift up only to vanish in the smoke enwreathing the city.

Will he rise again?

Can he answer this final challenge?

What sort of man is this? This white-maned Tiste Andii whose hands remain stained with a brother's blood, a people's vast loss?

Ah, but look closely. The core burns still, hot and pure, and it gathers unto itself, bound by indomitable will. He will take the wounds of the heart, for Anomander Rake is the sort of man who sees no other choice, who accepts no other choice.

Still. For the moment, grant him a few more moments of peace.

The round man rides out into Darujhistan.

There are temptations, and to some they can prove, ah, overwhelming. If need be, the round man can prove a most blunt barrier.

Just ask the man with the hammer.

As a warrior walked alone – in his wake a Toblakai and a witch, on the flanks three, now four Hounds of Shadow – an ox and cart drew to a halt outside an estate. The two men leading it separated, one heading to the back of the cart to set a trembling hand upon a chest – terrified that he might find it still, silent – and a moment later a faint sob broke free, but it was one of relief. The other man hurried up to the postern gate and tugged on a braided cord.

He ducked upon hearing the heavy flap of feathered wings overhead, and glared upward, but saw nothing but a thick, impenetrable layer of smoke. He twitched as he waited, muttering under his breath.

The door creaked open.

'Master Baruk! I am glad it's you and not one of your damned servants – getting past them is impossible. Listen, we have a hurt man – bad hurt – who needs healing. We'll pay—'

'Sergeant—'

'Just Antsy these days, sir.'

'Antsy, I am so sorry, but I must refuse you—'

At that, Barathol came round the cart and marched up, his hands curling into fists for a moment, before loosening as he reached towards the huge axe slung across his back. But these gestures were instinctive – he was not even aware of them, and when he spoke it was in a tone of despairing fury. 'His skull is fractured! He'll die without healing – *and I will not accept that!*'

Baruk held up both hands. 'I was about to leave – I cannot delay any longer. Certain matters demand my immediate attention—'

'He needs—'

'I am sorry, Barathol.'

And the alchemist was backing through the gate once more. The panel clicked shut.

Antsy snatched and tugged at his moustache in agitation, and then reached out to restrain Barathol, who seemed about to kick down that door. 'Hold on, hold on – I got another idea. It's desperate, but I can't think of anything else. Come on, it's not far.'

Barathol was too distraught to say anything – he would grasp any hope, no matter how forlorn. Face ashen, he went back to the ox, and when Antsy set out, he and the ox and the cart bearing the body of Chaur followed.

In the stricken man's mind, few sparks remained. The black tide was very nearly done. Those flickers that knew themselves as Chaur had each lost touch with the others, and so wandered lost. But then, some of them had known only solitary existences throughout their lives – crucial sparks indeed – for ever blind to pathways that might have awakened countless possibilities.

Until one, drifting untethered, so strangely freed, now edged forward along a darkened path it had never before explored, and the track it burned remained vibrant in its wake. And then, in a sudden flaring, that spark found another of its kind.

Something stirred then, there in the midst of an inner world fast dying.

Awareness.

Recognition.

A tumbling complexity of thoughts, connections, relationships, meanings.

Flashing, stunned with its own existence, even as the blackness closed in on all sides.

Cutting down an alley away from Baruk's estate, Antsy, ten paces in the lead, stumbled suddenly on something. Swearing, he glanced back at the small object lying on the cobbles, and then bent down to collect it, stuffing the limp thing into his cloak.

He swore again, something about a *stink, but what's a dead nose gonna know or care?* And then he resumed walking.

They arrived at an estate that Barathol recognized. Coll's. And Antsy returned to help lead the suddenly uneasy ox down the side track, to that primordial thicket behind the garden wall. Beneath the branches the gloom was thick with flying moths, their wings a chorus of dry whispering. Fog crawled between the boles of twisted trees. The air was rich with a steamy, earthy smell.

Tears ran down Barathol's cheeks, soaked his beard. 'I told him to stay on the ship,' he said in a tight, distraught voice. 'He usually listens to me. He's not one to disobey, not Chaur. Was it Spite? Did she force him out?'

'What was he doing at the gaol?' Antsy asked, just to keep his friend talking for reasons even he could not explain. 'How did he even find it, unless someone led him there? It's all a damned mystery.'

'He saved my life,' said Barathol. 'He was coming to break me out – he had my axe. Chaur, you fool, why didn't you just leave it all alone?'

'He couldn't do that,' said Antsy.

'I know.'

They arrived at the edge of the clearing, halting just beyond a low, uneven stone wall almost buried beneath vines. The gateway was an arch of rough stone veined with black roots. The house beyond showed a blackened face.

'Let's do this, then,' said Antsy in a growl, coming round to the back of the cart. 'Before the ox bolts—'

'What are we doing?'

'We're carrying him up the path. Listen, Barathol, we got to stay on that path, you understand? Not one step off it, not one. Understand?'

'No—'

'This is the Finnest House, Barathol. It's an Azath.'

The ex-sergeant seemed to be standing within a cloud of rotting meat. Moths swarmed in a frenzy.

Confused, frightened, Barathol helped Antsy lift Chaur's body from the cart bed, and with the Falari in the lead and walking backwards – one tender step at a time – they made their way up the flagstone path.

'You know,' Antsy said between gasps – for Chaur was a big man, and, limp as he was, it was no easy thing carrying him – 'I was thinking. If the damned moon can just break apart like that, who's to say that can't happen to our own world? We could just be—'

'Be quiet,' snapped Barathol. 'I don't give a shit about the moon – it's been trying to kill me for some time. Careful, you're almost there.'

'Right, set him down then, easy, on the stones . . . aye, that'll do.'

Antsy stepped up to the door, reached for the knife at his belt and then swore. 'I lost my knife, too. I can't believe this!' He made a fist and pounded against the wood.

The sound that made was reminiscent of punching a wall of meat. No reverberation, no echoes.

'Ow, that hurt.'

They waited.

Sighing, Antsy prepared to knock a second time, but then something clunked on the other side of the barrier, and a moment later the door swung back with a loud squeal.

The tall, undead monstrosity filled the doorway. Empty, shadow-drowned eye sockets regarded them – or not; it was impossible to tell.

Antsy shifted from one foot to the other. 'You busy, Raest? We need to make use of the hallway floor behind you—'

'Oh yes, I am very busy.'

The Falari blinked. 'Really?'

'Dust breeds. Cobwebs thicken. Candle wax stains precious surfaces. What do you want?'

Antsy glanced back at Barathol. 'Oh, a corpse with a sense of humour, what do you know? And surprise, it's so *droll*.' He faced the Jaghut again and smiled. 'In case you ain't noticed, the whole city has gone insane – that's why I figured you might be suffering some—'

'I am sorry,' cut in Raest, 'is something happening?'

Antsy's eyes bulged slightly. 'The Hounds of Shadow are loose!'

Raest leaned forward as if to scan the vicinity, and then settled back once more. 'Not in my yard.'

Antsy clawed through his hair. 'Trust me, then, it's a bad night – now, if you'd just step back –'

'Although, come to think of it, I did have a visitor earlier this evening.'

'What? Oh, well, I'm happy for you, but –'

Raest lifted one desiccated hand and pointed.

Antsy and Barathol turned. And there, in the yard, there was a fresh mound of raw earth, steaming. Vines were visibly snaking over it. 'Gods below,' the Falari whispered, making a warding gesture with one hand.

'A T'lan Imass with odd legs,' said Raest. 'It seemed to harbour some dislike towards me.' The Jaghut paused. 'I can't imagine why.'

Antsy grunted. 'It should've stayed on the path.'

'What do T'lan Imass know of footpaths?' Raest asked. 'In any case, it's still too angry for a conversation.' Another pause. 'But there's time. Soldier, you have been remiss. I am therefore disinclined to yield the floor, as it were.'

'Like Hood I have!' And Antsy reached beneath his tunic and tugged out a bedraggled, half-rotted shape. 'I found you your damned white cat!'

'Oh, so you have. How sweet. In that case,' Raest edged back, 'do come in.'

Barathol hesitated. 'What will this achieve, Antsy?'

'He won't die,' the ex-sergeant replied. 'It's like time doesn't exist in there. Trust me. We can find us a proper healer tomorrow, or a month from now – it don't matter. S'long as he's breathing when we carry him across the threshold. So, come on, help me.' He then realized he was still clutching the dead cat, and so he went up to the Jaghut and thrust the ghastly thing into most welcoming arms.

'I shall call it Tufty,' said Raest.

The black tide ceased its seemingly inexorable crawl. A slow, shallow breath held half drawn. A struggling heart hovered in mid-beat. And yet that spark of aware-ness, suddenly emboldened, set out on a journey of exploration and discovery. So many long-dark pathways . . .

Dragnipur has drunk deep, so deep.

Dragnipur, sword of the father and slayer of the same. Sword of Chains, Gate of Darkness, wheeled burden of life and life ever flees dissolution and so it must! Weapon of edges, caring naught who wields it. Cut indifferent, cut blind, cut when to do so is its very purpose, its perfect function.

Dragnipur.

Dread sisterly feuds dwindled in significance – something was proffered, something was almost within reach. Matters of final possession could be worked out later, at leisure in some wrought-iron, oversized bathtub filled to the brim with hot blood.

Temporary pact. Expedience personified, Spite quelled, Envy in abeyance.

In their wake a crater slowly sagged, edges toppling inward, heat fast dissipating. The melted faces of buildings turned glassy in rainbow hues. For now the brilliance of these colours was but hinted at in this moon-glow. But that reflected light had begun a thousand new games, hinting at something far deadlier. Still to come, still to come.

Everywhere in the city, fires ebbed.

The pressure of Dragnipur Unsheathed starves the flames of destruction. Darkness is anathema to such forces, after all.

Yes, salvation found, in a weapon let loose.

The sisters were mad, but not so mad as to fail to grasp the pleasing irony of such things.

Quell the violence.

Invite murder.

He was in no condition to resist them – not both of them – extraordinary that such an alliance had not occurred long before this night. But sibling wounds are the festering kind, and natures at war are normally blind to every pacifying gesture. What was needed was the proper incentive.

Alas, it did not occur to either twin that their father understood all too well the potential danger of his daughters forged together in alliance. And in shaping them – as carefully, as perfectly as he shaped Dragnipur itself – he had done what he could to mitigate the risk.

And so, as they walked side by side up the street, in Spite's mind she had already begun scheming her fateful stab into her sister's back. While Envy amused herself with virtually identical thoughts, roles reversed, naturally.

First things first, however.

They would kill Anomander Rake.

For Dragnipur has drunk deep, so very deep . . .

'Karsa, *please.*'

Ashes drifted in the air, amidst foul smoke. Distant screams announced tragic scenes. The last night of the Gedderone Fete was sinking into misery and suffering.

'There is nothing to be done, Samar Dev. But we will do this – we will *witness*. We will withstand the cost of that, if we can.'

She had not expected such uncertainty in the Toblakai. Always a stranger to humility, or so he seemed to her. He had not even drawn his flint sword.

They were twenty-five paces behind Traveller. They could see an angled gate arching over the broad street as it sloped upward, a hundred paces ahead. But the warrior they tracked had slowed his steps. There was something – someone – in the centre of the street in front of Traveller. And silent crowds on both sides – crowds that flinched back as the Hounds lumbered into view; flinched, but did not flee.

Something held them in place, something stronger than fear.

Samar Dev sensed the pressure sliding past, like a wind sweeping round her, drawing inward once more – straight into that huddled figure, who now, at last, stirred.

Traveller stood, six or so paces away from the stranger, and watched in silence as the man slowly straightened.

Tiste Andii.

Silver-haired. In his hands, a sword trailing ghostly chains . . . *oh . . . spirits below, oh, no—*

Traveller spoke. 'He said you would stand in my way.' That voice carried, strong as waves surging against a dark shore.

Samar Dev's heart stuttered.

When Anomander Rake replied, his words were cold, solid and unyielding, 'What else did he tell you?'

Traveller shook his head. 'Where is he?' he demanded. 'I can feel – he's close. Where is he?'

Not Cotillion. A different 'he' this time. The one Traveller seeks. The one he has ever sought.

'Yes,' said Rake. 'Close.'

Thick, flapping sounds, drifting in from the smoky night sky. She looked up in alarm and saw Great Ravens. Landing upon roof ledges. Scores, hundreds, silent but for the beat of air beneath crooked wings. Gathering, gathering, along the arched gate and the sections of wall to either side. Landing everywhere, *so long as it's a place from which they can see.*

'Then stand aside,' commanded Traveller.

'I cannot.'

'Dammit, Rake, you are not my enemy.'

The Son of Darkness tilted his head, as if receiving a compliment, an unexpected gift.

'Rake. You have *never* been my enemy. You know that. Even when the Empire . . .'

'I know, Dassem. I know.'

'He said this would happen.' There was dismay in that statement, and resignation.

Rake made no reply.

'He said,' continued Dassem, 'that you would not yield.'

'No, I will not yield.'

'Please help me, Rake, help me to understand . . . *why?*'

'I am not here to help you, Dassem Ultor.' And Samar Dev heard genuine regret in that admission. The Son of Darkness closed both hands about the long grip of Dragnipur and, angling the pommel upward and to his right, slowly widened his stance. 'If you so want Hood,' he said, *'come and get him.'*

Dassem Ultor – the First Sword of the Malazan Empire – *who was supposed to be dead. As if Hood would even want this one* – Dassem Ultor, the one they had known as Traveller, unsheathed his sword, the water-etched blade flashing as if lapped by molten silver. Samar Dev's sense of a rising wave now burgeoned in her mind. *Two forces. Sea and stone, sea and stone.*

Among the onlookers to either side, a deep, soft chant had begun.

Samar Dev stared at those arrayed faces, the shining eyes, the mouths moving in unison. *Gods below, the cult of Dessembrae. These are cultists – and they stand facing their god.*

And that chant, yes, it was a murmuring, it was the cadence of deep water rising. Cold and hungry.

Samar Dev saw Anomander Rake's gaze settle briefly on Dassem's sword, and it seemed a sad smile showed itself, in the instant before Dassem attacked.

To all who witnessed – the cultists, Samar Dev, Karsa Orlong, even unto the five Hounds of Shadow and the Great Ravens hunched on every ledge – that first clash of weapons was too fast to register. Sparks slanted, the night air rang with savage parries, counterblows, the biting crunch of edges against cross-hilts. Even their bodies were but a blur.

And then both warriors staggered back, opening up the distance between them once more.

'Faces in the Rock,' hissed Karsa Orlong.

'Karsa—'

'No. Only a fool would step between these two.'

And the Toblakai sounded . . . *shaken.*

Dassem launched himself forward again. There were no war cries, no bellowed curses, not even the grunts bursting free as ferocious swings hammered forged iron. But the swords had begun singing, a dreadful, mournful pair of voices rising in eerie syncopation. Thrusts, slashes, low-edged ripostes, the whistle of a blade cutting through air where a head had been an instant earlier, bodies writhing to evade counterstrokes, and sparks rained, poured, from the two combatants, bounced like shattered stars across the cobbles.

They did not break apart this time. The frenzied flurry did not abate, but went on, impossibly on. Two forces, neither yielding, neither prepared to draw a single step back.

And yet, for all the blinding speed, the glowing shower spraying out like the blood of iron, Samar Dev saw the death blow. She saw it clear. She saw its undeniable truth – and somehow, *somehow*, it was *all wrong.*

Rake wide-legged, angling the pommel high before his face with Dragnipur's point downward – as if to echo his opening stance – and higher still, and Dassem, his free hand joining the other upon his sword's grip, throwing his entire weight into a crossways slash – the warrior bodily lifting as if about to take to the air and close upon Rake with an embrace, and his swing met the edge of Dragnipur at a full right angle – a single moment shaping a perfect cruciform fashioned by the two weapons' colliding, and then the power of Dassem's blow slammed Dragnipur back—

Driving its inside edge into Anomander Rake's forehead, and then down through his face.

His gauntleted hands sprang away from the handle, yet Dragnipur remained jammed, seeming to erupt from his head, as he toppled backward, blood streaming down to flare from the tip as the Son of Darkness crashed down on his back.

Even this impact did not dislodge Dragnipur. The sword shivered, and now there was but one song, querulous and fading in the sudden stillness.

Blood boiled, turned black. The body lying on the cobbles did not move. Anomander Rake was dead.

Dassem Ultor slowly lowered his weapon, his chest heaving.

And then he cried out, in a voice so filled with anguish that it seemed to tear a jagged hole in the night air. This unhuman scream was joined by a chorus of shrieks as the Great Ravens exploded into flight, lifting like a massive feathered veil that whirled above the street, and then began a spinning descent. Cultists flinched away and crouched against building walls, their wordless chant drowned beneath the caterwauling cacophony of this black, glistening shroud that swept down like a curtain.

Dassem staggered back, and then pitched drunkenly to one side, his sword dragging in his wake, point skirling a snake track across the cobbles. He was brought up short by a pitted wall, and he sagged against it, burying his face in the shelter of a crooked arm that seemed to be all that held him upright.

Broken. Broken. They are broken.

Oh, gods forgive them, they are broken.

Karsa Orlong shocked her then, as he twisted to one side and pointedly spat on to the street. 'Cheated,' he said. 'Cheated!'

She stared at him, aghast. She did not know what he meant – but no, she did. Yes, she did. 'Karsa, what just happened?' *Wrong. It was wrong.* 'I saw – I saw—'

'You saw true,' he said, baring his teeth, his gaze fixed upon that fallen body. 'As did Traveller, and *see what it has done to him.*'

The area surrounding the corpse of Anomander Rake churned with Great Ravens – although not one drew close enough to touch the cooling flesh – and now the five Hounds of Shadows, not one spared of wounds, closed in to push the birds aside, as if to form a protective circle around Anomander Rake.

No, not him. The sword . . .

Unease stirred awake in Samar Dev. 'This is not over.'

A beast can sense weakness. A beast knows the moment of vulnerability, and opportunity. A beast knows when to strike.

The moon died and, in dying, began its torturous rebirth. The cosmos is indifferent to the petty squabbles of what crawls, what whimpers, what bleeds and what breathes. It has flung out its fates on the strands of immutable laws, and in the skirling unravelling of millions of years, tens of millions, each fate will out. In its time, it will out.

Something massive had arrived from the depths of the blackness beyond and struck the moon a short time back. An initial eruption from the impact had briefly showered the moon's companion world with fragments, but it was the shock wave that delivered the stricken moon's death knell, and this took time. Deep in the core, vast tides of energy opened immense fissures. Concussive forces shattered the crust. Energy was absorbed until nothing more could be borne. The moon blew apart.

Leave it to the flit of eager minds to find prophetic significance. The cosmos does not care. The fates will not crack a smile.

From a thousand sources, now, reflected sunlight danced wild upon the blue, green and ochre world far below. Shadows were devoured, darkness flushed away. Night itself broke into fragments.

In the city of Darujhistan, light was everywhere, like a god's fingers. Brushing, prodding, poking, driving down into alleys that had never seen the sun. And each assault shattered darkness and shadow both. Each invasion *ignited*, in a proclamation of power.

Dearest serendipity, yet not an opportunity to be ignored, no. Not on this night. Not in the city of Darujhistan.

Pallid and Lock, their bone-white hides sprayed in crimson, their skin hanging in strips in places, with horrid puncture wounds red-rimmed black holes in their necks and elsewhere, padded side by side down the main avenue running parallel to the lake shore. Hurting, but undaunted.

Light bloomed, ran like water across their path.

Light tilted shafts down between buildings, and some of these flashed, and from those flashes more Hounds emerged.

Behold, the Hounds of Light have arrived.

What, the world shifts unexpectedly? Without hint, without inkling? How terrible, how unexpected! How perfectly . . . natural. Rules abound, laws carved into stones, but they are naught but delusions. Witness the ones who do not care. See the mocking awareness in their fiery eyes. Rail at the unknown, even as jaws open wide for the warbling throat.

But give the round man no grief. He spreads wide pudgy hands. He shrugs. He saves his sly smile for . . . why, for thee!

Venasara and Cast were the first to join Pallid and Lock. Cast was almost twice the weight of Lock, while Venasara still bore the signs of the ordeals of raising a squabble of young. Ultama soon arrived, long-limbed, sleek, broad head held low at the end of a sinewy neck. Ultama's oversized upper canines jutted down. The exposed portions of the fangs, dagger-length, gleamed white.

At an intersection ahead waited Jalan, Grasp and Hanas, the youngest three of the pack, hackles high and eyes flashing with vicious excitement.

Gait and then Ghennan were the last to arrive, the lord and the lady of the pack, more silver than white, with scarred muzzles misshapen by centuries of dread battle. These two wore thick collars of black leather scattered with pearls and opals – although far fewer than had once adorned these proud bands.

Ten in number. Each one a match for any Hound of Shadow.

Of whom there were, ah, but five.

No one stepped into the path of these beasts. They were coming to claim a prize for their master.

Dragnipur. A sword of perfect justice.

Such perfect justice.

High in the sky above the city, tilting, sliding and dipping to avoid each shaft of infernal light, an undead dragon tracked the Hounds of Light.

Tulas Shorn was not pleased, even as something flowed sweet as a stream through its mind. A kind of blessing, alighting with faint, lilting notes of wonder.

Tulas Shorn had never known that Hood, Lord of the Slain, could prove so . . . generous.

Or perhaps it was nothing more than Shorn's damned cousin's talent for anticipating the worst.

As an Elder might observe, there is nothing worse than a suspicious dragon.

Do not grieve. Hold close such propensities for a while longer. The time will come.

Some gifts are evil. Others are not, but *what* they are remains to be discovered.

Rest easy for the next few moments, for there is more to tell.

Iskaral Pust rode like a madman. Unfortunately, the mule beneath him had decided that a plodding walk would suffice, making the two of them a most incongruous pair. The High Priest flung himself back and forth, pitched from side to side. His feet kicked high, toes skyward, then lashed back down. Heels pounded insensate flanks in a thumping drumroll entirely devoid of rhythm. Reins flailed about but the mule had chewed through the bit and so the reins were attached to nothing but two mangled stumps that seemed determined to batter Pust senseless.

He tossed about as if riding a goaded bull. Spraying sweat, lips pulled back in a savage grimace, the whites visible round his bugged-out eyes.

The mule, why, the mule walked. Clump clump (pause) clump (pause) clump clump. And so on.

Swirling just above Iskaral Pust's head, and acrobatically avoiding the bit-ends, flapped the squall of bhokarala. Like oversized gnats, and how that mule's tail whipped back and forth! She sought to swat them away, but in the spirit of gnathood the bhokarala did not relent, so eager were they to claim the very next plop of dung wending its way out beneath that tail. Over which they'd fight tooth, talon and claw.

Swarming in mule and rider's wake was a river of spiders, flowing glittering black over the cobbles.

At one point three white Hounds tramped across the street not twenty paces distant. A trio of immensely ugly heads swung to regard mule and rider. And to show that it meant business, the mule propped up its ears. Clump clump (pause) clump clump clump.

The Hounds moved on.

It does no good to molest a mule.

Alas, as Iskaral Pust and his placid mount were moments from discovering, there were indeed forces in the world that could confound both.

And here then, at last, arrives the shining, blazing, astonishing nexus, the penultimate pinnacle of this profound night, as bold Kruppe nudges his ferocious war-mule into the path of one Iskaral Pust, mule, and sundry spiders and bhokarala.

Mule sees mule. Both halt with a bare fifteen paces between them, ears at bristling attention.

Rider sees rider. Magus grows dangerously still, eyes hooded. Kruppe waves one plump hand in greeting.

Bhokarala launch a midair conference that results in one beast landing awkwardly on the cobbles to the left of the High Priest, whilst the others find windowsills, projections, and the heads of handsome gargoyles on which to perch, chests heaving and tongues lolling.

The spiders run away.

Thus, the tableau is set.

'Out of my way!' screeched Iskaral Pust. 'Who is this fool and how dare he fool with me? I'll gnash him! I'll crush him down. I'll feint right and dodge left and we'll be by in a flash! Look at that pathetic mule – he'll never catch us! I got a sword to claim. Mine, yes, mine! And then won't Shadowthrone grovel and simper! Iskaral Pust, High Priest of Dragnipur! Most feared swordsman in ten thousand worlds! And if you think you've seen justice as its most fickle, you just wait!' He then leaned forward and smiled. 'Kind sir, could you kindly move yourself and yon beast to one side? I must keep an appointment, you understand. Hastily, in fact.' Then he hissed, 'Go climb up your own arse, you red-vested ball of lard that someone rolled across a forest floor! Go! Scat!'

'Most confounding indeed,' Kruppe replied with his most beatific smile. 'It seems we are in discord, in that you seek to proceed in a direction that will inevitably collide with none other than Kruppe, the Eel of Darujhistan. Poor priest, it is late. Does your god know where you are?'

'Eel? Kruppe? Collide? Fat and an idiot besides, what a dastardly combination, and on this of all nights! Listen, take another street. If I run into this Crappy Eel I'll be sure to let him know you're looking for him. It's the least I can do.'

'Hardly, but no matter. I am Kruppe the Crappy Eel, alas.'

'So fine, we've run into each other. Glad that's over with. Now let me pass!'

'Kruppe regrets that any and every path you may seek shall be impeded by none other than Kruppe himself. Unless, of course, you conclude that what you seek is not worth the effort, nor the grief certain to follow, and so wisely return to thy shadowy temple.'

'You don't know what I want so it's none of your damned business what I want!'

'Misapprehensions abound, but wait, does this slavering fool even understand?'

'What? I wasn't supposed to hear that? But I did! I did, you fat idiot!'

'He only thought he heard. Kind priest, Kruppe assures you, you did not hear but mishear. Kind priest? Why, Kruppe is too generous, too forgiving by far, and hear hear! Or is it here here? No matter, it's not as if this grinning toad will understand. Why, his mule's got a sharper look in its eye than he has. Now, kindly priest, it's late and you should be in bed, yes? Abjectly alone, no doubt. Hmm?'

Iskaral Pust stared. He gaped. His eyes darted, alighting on the bhokaral squatting on the cobbles beside him as it made staring, gaping, darting expressions. 'My worshippers! Of course! You! Yes, you! Gather your kin and attack the fat fool! Attack! Your god commands you! Attack!'

'Mlawhlaooblossblayowblagmilebbingoblaiblblafblablallblayarblablabnablah-blallblah!'

'What?'

'Bla?'

'Bla?'

'Yarb?'

'Bah! You're stupid and useless and ugly!'

'Blabluablablablahllalalabala, too!'

Iskaral Pust scowled at it.

The bhokaral scowled back.

'Rat poison!' Pust hissed. And then smiled.

The Bhokaral offered him a dung sausage. And then smiled.

Oh, so much for reasoned negotiation.

Iskaral Pust's warbling battle cry was somewhat strangled as he leaned forward, perched high in the stirrups, hands reaching like a raptor's talons, and the mule reluctantly stumped forward.

Kruppe watched this agonizingly slow charge. He sighed. 'Really now. It comes to this? So be it.' And he kicked his war-mule into motion.

The beasts closed, step by step. By step.

Iskaral Pust clawed the air, weaving and pitching, head bobbing. Overhead, the bhokarala screamed and flew in frenzied circles. The High Priest's mule flicked its tail.

Kruppe's war-mule edged to the right. Pust's beast angled to *its* right. Their heads came alongside, and then their shoulders. Whereupon they halted.

Snarling and spitting, Iskaral Pust launched himself at Kruppe, who grunted a surprised *oof!* Fists flew, thumbs jabbed, jaws snapped – the High Priest's crazed attack – and the Eel threw up his forearms to fend it off, only to inadvertently punch Pust in the nose with one pudgy hand. Head rocked back, a stunned gasp. Attack renewed.

They grappled. They toppled, thumping on to the cobbles in a flurry of limbs.

The bhokarala joined in, diving from above with screeches and snarls, swarming the two combatants before beginning to fight with each other. Fists flying, thumbs jabbing, jaws snapping. Spiders swept in from all sides, tiny fangs nipping everything in sight.

The entire mass writhed and seethed.

The two mules walked a short distance away, then turned in unison to watch the proceedings.

Best leave this egregious scene for now.

Honest.

When the two women appeared some distance down a side avenue, dressed in diaphanous robes, and approached side by side with elegant grace – like noble-born sisters out for a late night stroll – the Great Ravens scattered, shrieking, and the Hounds of Shadow drew up, hackles rising and lips stretching back to reveal glistening fangs.

Even at this distance, Samar Dev could feel the power emanating from them. She stepped back, her chest tightening. 'Who in Hood's name are they?'

When Karsa did not reply she glanced over to see that he was watching a lone horseman coming up from the lakefront. This rider held a lance and the moment her eyes alit upon that weapon she drew a sharp, ragged breath. *Gods, now what!*

The horse's hoofs echoed like a cracked temple bell.

Ignoring the rider, the Hounds of Shadow set out in the direction of the two women. The five enormous beasts moved warily, heads held low.

At this moment, High Alchemist Baruk stood beside his carriage in the estate compound. It might have seemed to the servants and guards watching that he was studying the crazed night sky, but none of these worthies was positioned to see anything of his face.

The man was weeping.

He did not see the shattered moon. Nor the wreaths of low smoke drifting past. In truth, he saw nothing that anyone else could possibly see, for his vision was turned inward, upon memories of friendship, upon burdens since accepted, and, through it all, there was a rising flood of *something* – he could not be certain, but he believed it was humility.

In the course of a life, sacrifices are made, dire legacies accepted. Burdens are borne upon a humble back, or they ride the shoulders of bitter martyrs. These are the choices available to the spirit. There was no doubt, none at all, as to which one had been chosen by the Son of Darkness.

A great man was dead. So much, cruelly taken away on this sour night.

And he had lost a friend.

It availed him nothing that he understood, that he accepted that so many other choices were made, and that he had his own role still to play out in this tragic end.

No, he simply felt broken inside.

Everything seemed thin, fragile. All that he felt in his heart, all that he saw with his eyes. So very fragile.

Yes, the moon died, but a rebirth was coming.

Could he hold to that?

He would try.

For now, however, all he could manage was these tears.

Baruk turned to his carriage, stepped inside. The door was shut behind him as he settled on the cushioned bench. He looked across to his guest, but could say nothing. Not to this one, who had lost so much more than he had. *So much more.*

The gates were opened and the carriage set out, its corner lanterns swinging.

Cutter dismounted, leaving the horse to wander where it would. He walked forward, indifferent to the presence of the Hounds – they seemed intent on something else in any case – and indifferent as well to the Great Ravens as they drove onlookers away with beaks eager to stab and slash. His eyes were on the body lying on the cobbles.

He walked past a woman who stood beside a towering warrior who was drawing loose a two-handed flint sword as he stared at something in the direction from whence Cutter had just come.

None of these details could drag Cutter's attention from the body, and that gleaming black sword so brutally driven into the head and face. He walked until he stood over it.

The woman moved up beside him. 'That weapon in your hands – it's not—'

'We are in trouble,' Cutter said.

'What?'

He could not believe what he was seeing. Could not accept that the Lord of Moon's Spawn was lying here, one eye closed, the other open and staring sightlessly. Killed by his own sword. Killed . . . *taken.* By Dragnipur. 'How did this happen? Who could have . . .'

'Dassem Ultor.'

He finally looked at her. She was Seven Cities, that much he could see at once. Older than Cutter by a decade, maybe more. 'The name's familiar, but . . .' He shrugged.

She pointed to one side and Cutter turned.

A man was crouched, slumped against a wall, a sword propped up beside him. He had buried his face in his arms. Cutter's eyes went back to that sword. *I've seen that thing before . . . but where? When?*

'He was known to us,' said the woman, 'as Traveller.'

Memories rushed through Cutter, leaving in their wake something cold, lifeless. 'It's not the same,' he whispered. 'Vengeance. Or grief. Your choice.' He drew an uneven breath. 'That sword – it was forged by Anomander Rake. It was his weapon. Before Dragnipur. He left it with his brother, Andarist. And then I . . . I . . . *Beru fend* . . .'

The giant warrior now twisted round. 'If you would protect that body,' he said in a growl, 'then ready that spear.'

The two women had halted a street away, their path blocked by a half-circle of Hounds, with less than twenty paces separating the parties.

Seeing those women, Cutter frowned. 'Spite,' he muttered. 'Did you guess? Or was it just some damned itch?'

'Samar Dev,' snapped the giant. '*Witch!* Get Traveller on his feet! I will need him!'

'*Damn you!*' screamed the woman beside Cutter. '*What is it?*'

But there was no need for an answer. For she saw now, as did Cutter.

More Hounds, these ones pale as ghosts, a pack twice the number of the Hounds of Shadow. Loping up the street from Lakefront, moments from a charge.

'It's the sword,' said the woman named Samar Dev. 'They've come for the sword.'

Cutter felt his limbs turn to ice, even as the lance in his hands flared with heat.

'Give me room,' said the giant, lumbering forward into a clear space.

Against ten Hounds? Are you mad?

Cutter moved out to the left of the warrior. The witch rushed over to Traveller.

The lance trembled. It was getting too hot to hold, but what else did he have? Some damned daggers – against these things? *Gods, what am I even doing here?*

But he would stand. He would die here, beside a giant – who was just as doomed. And for what? *There is nothing . . . there is nothing in my life. To explain any of this.* He glared at the white Hounds. *It's just a sword. What will you even do with it? Chew the handle? Piss on the blade?* He looked across at the huge warrior beside him. 'What's your name at least?'

The giant glanced at him. 'Yes,' he said with a sharp nod. 'I am Karsa Orlong of the Teblor. Toblakai. And you?'

'Crokus. Crokus Younghand.' He hesitated, then said, 'I was once a thief.'

'Be one again,' said Karsa, teeth bared, 'and steal me a Hound's life this night.'

Shit. 'I'll try.'

'That will do,' the Toblakai replied.

Thirty paces away now. And the white Hounds fanned out, filled the street in a wall of bleached hide, rippling muscle and rows of fangs.

A gust of charnel wind swept round Cutter; something clattered, rang sharp on cobbles, and then a hand swept down—

The Hounds of Light charged.

As, on the side street to the left, the daughters of Draconus unleashed their warrens in a howling rush of destruction that engulfed the five beasts before them.

Scything blade of notched iron, driving Spinnock Durav back. Blood sprayed with each blow, links of ringed armour pattered on the ground. So many tiny broken chains, there was a trail of them, marking each step of the warrior's rocking, reeling retreat. When his own sword caught Kallor's frenzied blows, the reverberation ripped up Spinnock's arm, seeming to mash his muscles into lifeless pulp.

His blood was draining away from countless wounds. His helm had been battered off, that single blow leaving behind a fractured cheekbone and a deaf ear.

Still he fought on; still he held Kallor before him.

Kallor.

There was no one behind the High King's eyes. The berserk rage had devoured the ancient warrior. He seemed tireless, an automaton. Spinnock Durav could find no opening, no chance to counterattack. It was all he could do to simply evade each death blow, to minimize the impacts of that jagged edge, to turn the remaining fragments of his hauberk into the blade's inexorable path.

Spreading bruises, cracked bones, gaping gouges from which blood welled, soaking his wool gambon, he staggered under the unceasing assault.

It could not last.

It had already lasted beyond all reason.

Spinnock blocked yet another slash, but this time the sound his sword made was strangely dull, and the grip suddenly felt loose, the handle shorn from the tine – the pommel was gone. With a sobbing gasp, he ducked beneath a whistling blade and then pitched back—

But Kallor pressed forward, giving him no distance, and that two-handed sword lashed out yet again.

Spinnock's parry jolted his arm and his weapon seemed to blow apart in his hand, tined blade spinning into the air, the fragments of the grip a handful a shards falling from his numbed fingers.

The back-slash caught him across his chest.

He was thrown from his feet, landing hard on the slope of the ditch, where he sagged back, blood streaming down his front, and closed his eyes.

Kallor's rasping breaths drew closer.

Sweat dripped on to Spinnock's face, but still he did not open his eyes. He had felt it. A distant death. Yes, he had felt it, as he feared he might. So feared that he might. And, of all the deeds he had managed here at these crossroads, all that he had done up until this moment, not one could match the cost of the smile that now emerged on split, bleeding lips.

And this alone stayed Kallor's sword from its closing thrust. Stayed it . . . for a time.

'What,' Kallor asked softly, 'was the point, Spinnock Durav?'

But the fallen warrior did not answer.

'You could never win. You could never do anything but die here. Tell me, damn you, *what was the fucking point?*'

The question was a sob, the anguish so raw that Spinnock was startled into opening his eyes, into looking up at Kallor.

Behind the silhouette with its halo of tangled, sweat-matted hair, the heaving shoulders, he saw Great Ravens, a score or more, flying up from the south.

Closer and closer.

With an effort, Spinnock focused on Kallor once more. 'You don't understand,' he said. 'Not yet, Kallor, but you will. Someday, you will.'

'He does not deserve you!'

Spinnock frowned, blinked to clear his eyes. 'Oh, Kallor . . .'

The High King's face was ravaged with grief, and all that raged in the ancient man's eyes – well, none of it belonged. Not to the legend that was Kallor. Not to the nightmares roiling round and round his very name. Not to the lifeless sea of ashes in his wake. No, what Spinnock saw in Kallor's eyes were things that, he suspected, no one would ever see again.

It was, of sorts, a gift.

'Kallor,' he said, 'listen to me. Take this as you will, or not at all. I – I am sorry. That you are driven to this. And . . . and may you one day show your true self. May you, one day, be redeemed in the eyes of the world.'

Kallor cried out, as if struck, and he staggered back. He recovered with bared teeth. 'My true self? Oh, you damned fool! You see only what you want to see! In this last moment of your pathetic, useless life! May your soul rage for eternity in the heart of a star, Tiste Andii! May you yearn for what you can never have! For all infernal eternity!'

Spinnock had flinched back at the tirade. 'Do you now curse me, High King?' he asked in a whisper.

Kallor's face looked ready to shatter. He dragged a forearm across his eyes. 'No,' he said. 'Of course not. I will kill you clean. For what you have shown me this night – I have never before faced such a defence.' And then he paused, edging forward again, his eyes burning in their pits. 'You had chances, Spinnock Durav. To strike back. You could have wounded me – yes, you could have . . .'

'I was not here to do that, Kallor.'

The High King stared, and a glint of comprehension lit in his face. 'No,' he said. 'You only needed to delay me.'

Spinnock closed his eyes once more and settled his head back. 'For a time. You may never accept this, but it was for your own good. It's a mess over there. In that city. My Lord wanted you kept away.'

Kallor snarled. 'How generous in his mercy is your Lord.'

'Yes,' sighed Spinnock, 'he was ever that.'

Silence, then.

Not a sound. A dozen laboured heartbeats. Another dozen. Finally, some odd unease forced Spinnock to open his eyes yet again, to look upon Kallor.

Who stood, head bowed.

'Yes,' said Spinnock, in true sorrow, 'he is gone.'

Kallor did not lift his gaze. He did not move at all.

'And so,' continued Spinnock, 'I have stood here. In his stead. One last time.' He paused. 'And yes, it makes my death seem . . . easier—'

'Oh shut up, will you? I am thinking.'

'About what?'

Kallor met his eyes and bared his teeth. 'That bastard. *The bold, brazen bastard!*'

Spinnock studied the High King, and then he grunted. 'Well, that's it, then.'

'I don't ever want to see you again, Spinnock Durav. You are bleeding out. I will leave you to that. I hear it's quieter, easier – but then, what do I know?'

The Tiste Andii watched him set off then, up the road, to that fair city that even now bled with its own terrible wounds.

Too late to do anything, even if he'd wanted to. But, Spinnock Durav now suspected, Kallor might well have done nothing. He might have stood aside. 'High King,' he whispered, 'all you ever wanted was a throne. But trust me, you don't want Rake's. No, proud warrior, that one you would not want. I think, maybe, you just realized that.'

Of course, when it came to Kallor, there was no way to know.

The Great Ravens were descending now, thumping heavily on to the blood-splashed, muddy surface of the road.

And Spinnock Durav looked skyward then, as the dark forms of two dragons sailed past, barely a stone's throw above the ground.

Racing for Kallor.

He saw one of the dragons suddenly turn its head, eyes flashing back in his direction, and the creature pitched to one side, coming round.

A moment later the other dragon reached Kallor, catching him entirely unawares, talons lashing down to grasp the High King and lift him into the air. Wings thundering, the dragon carried its charge yet higher. Faint screams of fury sounded from the man writhing in that grasp.

Dragon and High King dipped behind a hill to the north.

One of the Great Ravens drew up almost at Spinnock's feet.

'Crone!' Spinnock coughed and spat blood. 'I'd have thought . . . Darujhistan . . .'

'Darujhistan, yes. I'd have liked to. To honour, to witness. To remember, and to weep. But our Lord . . . well, he had thoughts of you.' The head tilted. 'When we saw you, lying there, Kallor looming as he so likes to do, ah, we thought we were too late – we thought we had failed our Lord – and you. We thought – oh, never mind.'

The Great Raven was panting.

Spinnock knew that this was not exhaustion he was seeing in the ancient bird. *You can shed no tears, yet tears take you none the less. The extremity, the terrible distress.*

The dragon that had returned now landed on the grasses to the south of the track. Sembling, walking towards Spinnock and Crone and the haggle of Crone's kin.

Korlat.

Spinnock would have smiled up at her, but he had lost the strength for such things, and so he could only watch as she came up to him, using one boot to shunt a squawking Crone to one side. She knelt and reached out a hand to brush Spinnock's spattered cheek. Her eyes were bleak. 'Brother . . .'

Crone croaked, 'Just heal him and be done with it – before he gasps out his last breath in front of us!'

She drew out a quaint flask. 'Endest Silann mixed this one. It should suffice.' She tugged loose the stopper and gently set the small bottle's mouth between Spinnock's lips, and then tilted it to drain the contents, and he felt that potent liquid slide down his throat. Sudden warmth flowed through him.

'Sufficient, anyway, to carry you home.' And she smiled.

'My last fight in his name,' said Spinnock Durav. 'I did as he asked, did I not?'

Her expression tightened, revealed something wan and ravaged. 'You have much to tell us, brother. So much that needs . . . explaining.'

Spinnock glanced at Crone.

The Great Raven ducked and hopped a few steps away. 'We like our secrets,' she cackled, 'when it's all we have!'

Korlat brushed his cheek again. 'How long?' she asked. 'How long did you hold him back?'

'Why,' he replied, 'I lit the torches . . . dusk was just past . . .'

Her eyes slowly widened. And she glanced to the east, where the sky had begun, at last, to lighten.

'Oh, Spinnock . . .'

A short time later, when she went to find his sword where it was lying in the grasses, Spinnock Durav said, 'No, Korlat. Leave it.'

She looked at him in surprise.

But he was not of a mind to explain.

Above the Gadrobi Hills, Kallor finally managed to drag free his sword, even as the dragon's massive head swung down, jaws wide. His thrust sank deep into the soft throat, just above the jutting avian collar bones. A shrill, spattering gasp erupted from the Soletaken, and all at once they were plunging earthward.

The impact was thunder and snapping bones. The High King was flung away, tumbling and skidding along dew-soaked grass. He gained his feet and spun to face the dragon.

It had sembled. Orfantal, on his face an expression of bemused surprise, was struggling to stand. One arm was broken. Blood gushed down from his neck. He seemed to have forgotten Kallor, as he turned in the direction of the road, and slowly walked away.

Kallor watched.

Orfantal managed a dozen steps before he fell to the ground.

It seemed this was a night for killing Tiste Andii.

His shoulders were on fire from the dragon's puncture wounds, which might well have proved fatal to most others, but Kallor was not like most others. Indeed, the High King was unique.

In his ferocity. In his stubborn will to live.

In the dry furnace heat of the hatred that ever swirled round him.

He set out once more for the city.

As dawn finally parted the night.

Kallor.

Chapter Twenty-Four

'There is no struggle too vast, no odds too overwhelming,
for even should we fail – should we fall – we will know
that we have lived.'

ANOMANDER RAKE
SON OF DARKNESS

The continent-sized fragments of the shattered moon sent reflected sunlight down upon the world. The fabric of Night, closed so tight about the city of Black Coral, began at last to fray. The web that was this knotted manifestation of Kurald Galain withered under the assault. Shafts broke through and moonlight painted buildings, domes, towers, walls and the long-dead gardens they contained. Silvery glow seeped into the dark waters of the bay, sending creatures plunging to the inky blackness of the depths.

New world, young world. So unexpected, so premature, this rain of death.

Endest Silann could feel every breach as he knelt on the cold mosaic floor of the temple's Grand Vestry. He had once held the waters back from Moon's Spawn. He had once, long, long ago, guided his Lord to the fateful, final encounter with Mother Dark herself. He had clasped the hand of a dying High Priestess, sharing with her the bleak knowledge that nothing awaited her, nothing at all. He had stood, gods, so long ago now, staring down at his blood-covered hands, above the body of a sweet, gentle woman, Andarist's wife. While through the high window, the flames of dying Kharkanas flickered crimson and gold.

The Saelen Gara of the lost Kharkanan forestlands had believed that the moon was Father Light's sweet seduction, innocent maiden gift to Mother Dark. To remind her of his love, there in the sky of night. But then, they had also believed the moon was but the backside of Father Light's baleful eye, and could one rise up and wing the vast distance to that moon, they would discover that it was but a lens, and to look through was to see other worlds for whom the moon was not the moon at all, but the sun. The Saelen Gara talespinner would grin then, and make odd motions with his hands. 'Perspective,' he'd say. 'You see? The world changes according to where you stand. So choose, my children, choose and choose again, where you will make your stand . . .'

Where you will make your stand. The world changes.

The world changes.

Yes, he had held back the sea. He had made Moon's Spawn into a single held breath that had lasted months.

But now, ah, *now*, his Lord had asked him to hold back Light itself.

To save not a fortress, but a city. Not a single breath to hold, but the breath of Kurald Galain, an Elder Warren.

But he was old, and he did not know . . . he did not know . . .

Standing twenty paces away, in a niche of the wall, the High Priestess watched. Seeing him struggle, seeing him call upon whatever reserves he had left. Seeing him slowly, inexorably, fail.

And she could do nothing.

Light besieged Dark in the sky overhead. A god in love with dying besieged a child of redemption, and would use that child's innocence to usurp this weakened island of Kurald Galain – to claim for itself the very Throne of Darkness.

For she has turned away.

Against all this, a lone, ancient, broken warlock.

It was not fair.

Time was the enemy. But then, she told herself with wry bitterness, time was always the enemy.

Endest Silann could not drive back every breach. She had begun to feel the damage being wrought upon Night, upon the Tiste Andii in this city. It arrived like a sickness, a failing of internal balances. She was weakening.

We are all weakening.

An old, broken man. He was not enough, and they had all known – everyone except the one who mattered the most. *Lord Rake, your faith blinded you. See him, kneeling there – there, my Lord, is your fatal error in judgement.*

And without him – without the power here and now to keep everything away – without that, your grand design will collapse into ruin.

Taking us with it.

By the Abyss, taking us all.

It seemed so obvious now. To stand in Rake's presence was to feel a vast, unassailable confidence. That he could gauge all things with such precision as to leave one in awe, in disbelief and in wonder.

The plans of the Son of Darkness never went awry. Hold to faith in him, and all shall settle into place.

But how many plans worked out precisely because of our faith in him? How many times did we – did people like Endest Silann and Spinnock Durav – do things beyond their capability, simply to ensure that Rake's vision would prove true? And how many times can he ask that of them, of us?

Anomander Rake wasn't here.

No, he was *gone*.

For ever gone.

Where then was that solid core of confidence, which they might now grasp tight? In desperation, in pathetic need?

You should never have left this to us. To him.

The sickness in her soul was spreading. And when she succumbed, the last bulwark protecting every Tiste Andii in Black Coral would give way.

And they would all die. For they were the flesh of Kurald Galain.

Our enemies feed on flesh.

Lord Anomander Rake, you have abandoned us.

She stood in the niche as if it was a sarcophagus. Fevered, watching Endest Silann slowly crumple there in the centre of that proud, diffident mosaic spanning the floor.

You failed us.

And now we fail you.

With a gasp of agony, Apsal'ara lunged backward along the beam. The skin of her hands and forearms had blackened. She kicked in desperate need, pushing herself still farther from that swirling vortex of darkness. Sliding on her back, over the grease of sweat, bile and blood. Steam rose from her arms. Her fingers were twisted like roots—

The pain was so vast it was almost exquisite. She writhed, twisted in its grip, and then pitched down from the beam. Chains rapped against the sodden wood. Her weight pulled them down in a rattle and she heard something *break*.

Thumping on to ash-smeared clay.

Staring as she held up her hands. Seeing frost-rimed shackles, and, beneath them, broken links.

She had felt the wagon rocking its way back round. Horror and disbelief had filled her soul, and the need to do something had overwhelmed her, trampling all caution, trampling sanity itself.

And now, lying on the cold, gritty mud, she thought to laugh.

Free.

Free with nowhere to run. With possibly dead hands – and what good was a thief with dead, rotting hands?

She struggled to uncurl her fingers. Watched the knuckles crack open like charred meat. Red fissures gaped. And, as she stared, she saw the first droplets of blood welling from them. Was that a good sign?

'Fire is life,' she intoned. 'Stone is flesh. Water is breath. Fire is life. Stone is water is flesh is breath is life. Pluck a flower from a field and it will not thrive. Take and beauty dies, and that which one possesses becomes worthless. I am a thief. I take but do not keep. All I gain I cast away. I take your wealth only because you value it.

'I am Apsal'ara, Mistress of Thieves. Only you need fear me, you who lust to own.'

She watched her fingers slowly straighten, watched flakes of skin lift and then fall away.

She would survive this. Her hands had touched Darkness, and lived still.

As if it mattered.

Even here, beneath the wagon, the dread sounds of war surrounded her. Chaos closed in on all sides. Souls died in numbers beyond counting, and their cries revealed a loss so far past comprehension that she refused to contemplate it. The death of honourable souls. The immense sacrifice wasted. No, none of this bore thinking about.

Apsal'ara rolled on to her side, and then on to her knees and elbows.

She began crawling.

And then gasped anew, as a familiar voice filled her head.

'Mistress of Thieves. Take the eye. The eye of the god. Apsal'ara, steal the eye . . .'

Trembling – wondering – how? How could he reach so into her mind? He could do so only if . . . only if—

Apsal'ara gasped a third time.

And so . . . once in pain, once in wonder, and once in . . . *in hope.*

She resumed crawling.

Pluck your flower. I am coming for you.

Oh yes, I am coming for you.

With each soul consumed, the power of chaos grew. Hunger surged with renewed strength, and the beleaguered defenders fell back another step.

But they were running out of steps.

The indomitable legions surrounded the now stationary wagon and its dwindling ring of souls. The countless dead who had answered Hood's final summons were melting away, most of them too ancient to call upon memories of strength, to even remember that will alone held power. In standing against the enemy, they had done little more than marginally slow the advance of chaos, as all that remained of them was ripped apart, devoured.

Some, however, were made of sterner things. The Grey Swords, delivered unto Hood by the loss of Fener, fought with grim ferocity. Commanding them, Brukhalian was like a deep-rooted standing stone, as if capable of willing himself immovable, unconquerable. He had, after all, done this before. The company fought and held for a time – an impressive length of time – but now their flanks were under assault, and there was nothing to do but retreat yet closer to the enormous wagon with its heap of bodies.

A score of Seguleh, all that remained of the Second's forces, formed one impossibly thin link with the Grey Swords. Each one had fallen to Anomander Rake, and this knowledge alone was sufficient, for it burned like acid, it stung like shame. They wore their masks, and as they fought, the painted slashes, the sigils of rank, began to fade, worn away by the fires of chaos, until upon each warrior the mask gleamed pure. As if here, within the world of this sword, some power could yield to greater truths. *Here,* Dragnipur seemed to say, *you are all equal.*

The Grey Swords' other flank closed up with another knot of soldiers – the Bridgeburners, into which remnants of other Malazan forces were falling, drawing upon the elite company's ascendant power, and upon the commander now known as Iskar Jarak.

The Bridgeburners were arrayed in a half-circle that slowly contracted under the brunt of the assault. Grey Swords on one flank, and the last of the Chained on the other, where a huge demon formed the point of a defiant wedge that refused to buckle. Tears streamed down the demon's face, for even as it fought, it grieved for those lost. And such grief filled Pearl's heart unto bursting. Pearl did not fight for itself, nor for the wagon, nor even the Gate of Darkness, the Wandering Hold. The demon fought for its comrades, as would a soldier pushed beyond breaking, pushed until there was nowhere else to go.

In the ash-swarmed sky above, chained dragons, Loqui Wyval and Enkarala tore swaths through the tumbling, descending storm clouds. Lightning lashed out to enwreathe them, slowly tearing them to pieces. Still they fought on. The Enkarala would not relent for they were mindless in their rage. The Loqui Wyval found strength in hearts greater than their modest proportions – no, they were not dragons; they were lesser kin – but they knew the power of mockery, of disdain. For the Enkarala, chaos itself was a contemptible thing. The dragons, many of whom had been chained since the time of Draconus, were indifferent to the Gate, to all the other squalid victims of this dread sword. They did not fight on behalf of any noble cause. No, each one fought alone, for itself, and they knew that survival had nothing to do with nobility. No alliance was weighed, no thought of fighting in concert brushed the incandescent minds of these creatures. Nothing in their nature was designed to accommodate aught but singular battle. A strength and a curse, but in these fiery, deadly clouds, that strength was failing, and the very nature of the dragons was now destroying them.

The battle raged. Annihilation was a deafening scream that drove all else from the minds of the defenders. They made their will into weapons, and with these weapons they slashed through the misshapen, argent foe, only to find yet more rising before them, howling, laughing, swords thundering on shields.

Toc had no idea where this damned horse had come from, but clearly some breathtaking will fired its soul. In its life it had not been bred for war, and yet it fought like a beast twice its weight. Kicking, stamping, jaws snapping. A Wickan breed – he was fairly certain of that – a creature of appalling endurance, it carried him into the fray again and again, and he had begun to suspect that he would fail before the horse did.

Humbling – no, *infuriating*.

He struggled to control it as he sought to lunge once more into that wall of chaotic rage. Getting to be a miserable habit, all this dying and dying again. Of course, this would be the final time, and a better man than he would find some consolation in that. A better man, aye.

Instead, he railed. He spat into the eye of injustice, and he fought on, even as his one eyeless socket itched damnably, until it seemed to be sizzling as if eating its way into his brain.

He lost his grip on the reins, and almost pitched from the saddle as the horse galloped away from the front line of the Bridgeburners. He loosed a stream of curses – he wanted to die at their sides, he needed to – no, he was not one of them, he could not match their power, their ascendant ferocity – he had seen Trotts there, and Detoran. And so many others, and there was Iskar Jarak himself, although why Whiskeyjack had come to prefer some Seven Cities name – in place of his real one – made no sense to Toc. Not that he was of any stature to actually ask the man – gods, even had he been, he couldn't even have got close, so tightly were the Bridgeburners arrayed around the soldier.

And now the stupid horse was taking him farther and farther away.

He saw, ahead, the Lord of Death. Standing motionless, as if contemplating guests at a damned picnic. The horse carried Toc straight for the hoary bastard, who slowly turned at the very last moment, as the horse skidded to a halt in a spray of ashes and mud.

Hood glanced down at the spatter on its frayed robes.

'Don't look at me!' Toc snarled as he collected up the reins once more. 'I was trying to get the beast going the other way!'

'You are my Herald, Toc the Younger, and I have need of you.'

'To do what, announce your impending nuptials? Where is the skeletal hag, anyway?'

'You have a message to deliver—'

'Deliver where? How? In case you haven't noticed, we're in a little trouble here, Hood. Gods, my eye – agh, I mean, the missing one – it's driving me mad!'

'Yes, your missing eye. About that—'

At that instant, Toc's horse reared in sudden terror, as a churning cloud lunged down like an enormous fist, engulfing a dying dragon directly overhead.

Swearing, his voice rising in terror, Toc fought to regain control of the beast as cloud and dragon tumbled to one side – the dragon pulled down to the thrashing legions, which closed in and swarmed it. In moments the dragon was gone.

The horse skittered and then settled—

Only to have it bolt once more, as in a burst of cold, bitter air, something else arrived.

What good could ever come of acceding to the suggestions of a corpse? This was the sort of question Glanno Tarp was good at asking, only he'd forgotten this time and it was funny how blind gibbering terror could do that. Warrens and warrens and portals and Gates and places nobody in their right minds might want to visit no matter how special the scenery – and no, dammit, he didn't know where they'd just ended up, but he could tell – oh yes, he could tell all right – that it wasn't a nice place.

Horses shrilling (but then, they always did that when arriving), carriage slapping down on to gritty mud in a chorus of outraged creaks, splinters and calam-cophony, slewing this way and that – and the sky was coming down in giant balls of mercury and there were dragons up there and wyval and Hood knew what else—

Chains sawing back and forth, to the sides and straight up, all emerging from the ghastliest wagon Glanno had ever seen – loaded with more bodies than seemed reasonable, much less possible.

So of course he froze up all the brakes – what else was he supposed to do? And then bodies were flying past. Sweetest Sufferance, curled up into a soft flouncy bouncy ball that landed bouncily and rolled and rolled. That snarling hulk Grun-tle, twisting in the air so that he could land on all fours – *meow* – and Faint, far less elegant for all her bountiferous beauty, going splat on her face all spread-eagled, silly girl. Amby and Jula flew past embraced like lovers, at least until the ground showed up and got between them. Reccanto Ilk fetched up beside Glanno, cracking the backrest of the bench.

'You idiot! We ain't tied ourselves! It was just dark and dark and nothing else and now you just go and drop us into—'

'Wasn't me, you clumsy pig!'

This argument didn't survive the fullest comprehension of their surroundings.

Reccanto Ilk slowly sat up. 'Holy shit.'

Glanno leapt to his feet. 'Cartographer!' But he'd forgotten about his splints. Yelping, he tottered, and then pitched forward on to the backs of the first two horses. They deftly stepped to either side so that he could fall a little more before getting tangled in all the crap down there, whereupon the horses eagerly moved back in an effort to crush him into the kind of pulp that could never again whip the reins.

Reccanto scrabbled to drag him back on to the bench. The splint bindings helped, although Glanno did plenty of shrieking in pain – at least he wasn't being crushed. Moments later he fetched up again on the splintered bench.

A wretched dead-looking Jaghut was walking up to Cartographer, who, lashed to a wheel, had come to rest with his head down, eyeing the Jaghut's muddy boots. 'I had begun to wonder,' the Jaghut said, 'if you had become lost.'

Pushing Reccanto aside, Glanno worked his way round to witness this fateful meeting – oh yes, that had to be Hood himself. Why, a damned family reunione-bration!

Cartographer's upside-down smile seemed to send a nearby rider's horse into yet another panic, and the soldier swore impressively as he fought to quell the beast. 'My Lord,' Cartographer was saying, 'we both know, surely, that what goes around comes around.' And then he struggled feebly at his bindings. 'And around,' he added despondently.

Gruntle, who had staggered up to join them, now growled deep in his chest and then went to the carriage door, thumping it with a fist. 'Master Quell!'

Hood turned to the warrior. 'That will not be necessary, Treach-spawn. My sole requirement was that you arrive here. Now, you need only leave once more. Cartographer will guide you.'

Sweetest Sufferance was dragging a dazed Faint back up on to the carriage, displaying surprising strength, although the effort made her eyes bulge alarmingly. Glanno nudged Reccanto and nodded towards Sweetest. 'That face remind you of anything?'

Reccanto squinted, and then sniggered.

'You're both dead,' she hissed.

Amby and Jula bobbed into view to either side of her, grinning through smears of mud.

Inside the carriage, Mappo started to open the door but Quell snapped out a shaky hand to stay him. 'Gods, don't do that!'

Precious Thimble had curled up on the floor at their feet, rocking and moaning.

'What awaits us outside?' the Trell asked.

Quell shook his head. He was bone white, face glistening with sweat. 'I should've guessed. The way that map on the road narrowed at the far end. Oh, we've been used! Duped! Gods, I think I'm going to be sick—'

'Damned Trygalle,' muttered Toc. More confused than he had ever been by this sudden, inexplicable arrival. How did they manage to arrive *here*? And then he saw Gruntle. 'Gods below, it's you!'

Someone was being loudly sick inside the carriage.

Gruntle stared up at Toc, and then frowned.

Ah, I guess I don't look like Anaster any more. 'We shared—'

'Herald,' said Hood. 'It is time.'

Toc scowled, and then scratched at his eye socket. 'What? You're sending me with them?'

'In a manner of speaking.'

'Then I'm to rejoin the living?'

'Alas, no, Toc the Younger. You are dead and dead you will remain. But this shall mark your final task as my Herald. Another god claims you.'

Toc prepared to dismount but the Lord of Death lifted a hand. 'Ride in the carriage's wake, *close* in its wake. For a time. Now, Herald, listen well to my last message. The blood is needed. The blood is needed . . .'

Gruntle had stopped listening. Even the vague disquiet he'd felt when that one-eyed rider had accosted him was fast vanishing beneath a flood of battle lust. He stared out at the enemy, watched the defenders wither away.

A war that could not be won by such sorry souls – a war that begged for a champion, one who would stand until the very end.

Another growl rumbled from him, and he stepped away from the carriage, reaching for his cutlasses.

'Whoa there, y'damned manx!'

The bark startled him and he glared up at Glanno Tarp, who smiled a hard smile. 'Shareholders can't just walk away – we'd have to plug ya fulla arrows. Get back aboard, stripy, we're leaving all over again!'

There could be but one outcome, and Draconus had known that all along. He had sensed nothing of the Trygalle's arrival, nor even its departure, with Toc riding in its wake. Whatever occurred behind him could not reach through to awaken his senses.

One outcome.

After all, Dragnipur had never offered salvation. Iron forged to bind, a hundred thousand chains hammered into the blade, layers upon layers entwined, folded, wrapped like rope. Draconus, surrounded in the molten fires of Burn's heart, drawing forth chains of every metal that existed, drawing them out link by glowing link. Twisted ropes of metal on the anvil, and down came the hammer. The *one* hammer, the only tool that could forge such a weapon – and he remembered its vast weight, the scalding grip that lacerated his alien hand.

Even in her dreaming, Burn had been most displeased.

Chains upon chains. Chains to bind. Bind Darkness itself, transforming the ancient forest through which it had wandered, twisting that blackwood into a wagon, into huge, tottering wheels, into a bed that formed a horizontal door – like the entrance to a barrow – above the portal. Blackwood, to hold and contain the soul of Kurald Galain.

He remembered. Sparks in countless hues skipping away like shattered rainbows. The deafening ringing of the hammer and the way the anvil trembled to every blow. The waves of heat flashing against his face. The bitter taste of raw ore, the stench of sulphur. *Chains! Chains and chains, pounded down into glowing impressions upon the blade, quenched and honed and into Burn's white heart and then – it begins again. And again.*

Chains! Chains to bind!

Bind the Fallen!

And now, unbelievably, impossibly, Draconus had felt that first splintering. Chains had broken.

So it ends. I did not think, I did not imagine—

He had witnessed his Bound companions falling away, failing. He had seen the chaos descend upon each one, eating through flesh with actinic zeal, until shackles fell to the ground – until the iron bands held nothing. *Nothing left.*

I never meant – I never wanted such an end – to any of you, of us.

No, I was far too cruel to ever imagine an end. An escape.

Yet now, witness these thoughts of mine. Now, I would see you all live on, yes, in these chains, but not out of cruelty. Ah, no, not that. Abyss take me, I would see you live out of mercy.

Perhaps he wept now. Or these scalding tears announced the crushing end of hysterical laughter. No matter. They were all being eaten alive. *We are all being eaten alive.*

And Dragnipur had begun to come apart.

When the chaos disintegrated the wagon, destroyed the door, and took hold of the Gate, the sword would shatter and chaos would be freed of this oh-so-clever trap, and Draconus's brilliant lure – his eternal snare eternally leading chaos on *and away from everything else* – would have failed. He could not contemplate what would happen then, to the countless succession of realms and worlds, and of course he would not be there to witness the aftermath in any case. But he knew that, in his last thoughts, he would feel nothing but unbearable guilt.

So, chaos, at least unto one victim, what you deliver is indeed mercy.

He had begun walking forward, to join the other Bound, to stand, perhaps, at Pearl's side, until the end came.

The echo of that snapping chain haunted him. *Someone's broken loose. How?* Even the Hounds of Shadow could only slip free by plunging into Kurald Galain's black heart. Their chains did not break. Dragnipur's essential integrity had not been not damaged.

But now . . . someone's broken loose.

How?

Chains and chains and chains to bind—

A bony hand closed on his shoulder and dragged him back.

Snarling, Draconus half turned. 'Let go, damn you! I will stand with them, Hood – I must, can't you see that?'

The Lord of Death's hand tightened, the nails biting, and Hood slowly pulled him closer. 'The fray,' the god said in a rasp, 'is not for you.'

'You are not my master—'

'Stand with me, Draconus. It's not yet time.'

'For what?' He struggled to tear free, but a Jaghut's strength could be immense, and barring the bloody removal of his entire shoulder, Draconus could do nothing. He and the Lord of Death stood alone, not twenty paces from the motionless wagon.

'Consider this,' said Hood, 'a request for forgiveness.'

Draconus stared. 'What? Who asks my forgiveness?'

Hood, Lord of the Dead, should have been the last to fall to Dragnipur. Whatever the Son of Darkness intended, its final play was found in the slaying of this ancient god. Such was the conviction of Draconus. A mad, pointless gamble, the empty purchase of time already consumed, at the wasting of countless souls, an entire realm of the dead.

As it turned out, Draconus was wrong.

There was one more. One more.

Arriving with the power of a mountain torn apart in a long, deafening, crushing detonation. Argent clouds were shredded, whipped away in dark winds. The legions pressing on all sides recoiled, and the thousand closing paces so viciously won were lost in an instant. Dragons screamed. Voices erupted as if dragged out from throats – the pressure, the pain, the stunning power—

Chaos flinched, and then, slowly, began to gather itself once more.

No single force could defeat this enemy. Destruction was its own law, and even as it devoured itself it would devour everything else. Chaos, riding the road of Darkness, ever to arrive unseen, from sources unexpected, from places where one never thought to look, much less guard against.

The sword and all within it was dying, now, at last; dying.

Hood's hand had left his shoulder, and Draconus sagged down on to his knees. One more.

And, yes, he knew who was now among them.

Should he laugh? Should he seek him out, mock him? Should he close hands about his throat so that they could lock one to the other until the descent of oblivion?

No, he would do none of this.

Who asks for my forgiveness?

Had he the strength, he would have cried out.

Anomander Rake, you need not ask. That begging, alas, must come from me. This was Mother Dark I snared here. Your mother—

And so, what will you now do?

A heartbeat later, a faint gasp escaped Draconus, and he lifted his head, opened his eyes once more. 'Rake?' he whispered.

Draconus slowly rose. And turned. To face the wagon.

To witness.

The Second watched yet another Seguleh fall. He then dragged his horse round, to glare with dead eyes at a tall, ornate carriage, as its train of screaming horses lunged forward. Figures pitched to one side, holding on for dear life as a fissure tore open – into which those horses vanished.

Hood's Herald – that one-eyed soldier – drove heels to his tattered mount, following.

And the Lord of Death's voice drifted through the Second. *'It seems you are needed after all, as you suspected. Now go – and know this, old friend, you have served me well.*

'I am the god of death no longer.

'When you have done this last thing, your service is at an end. And then, well, Skinner awaits . . .'

The Second tilted back his masked, helmed head and howled in glee. Sheathing his swords, he rode hard after the carriage.

He saw the Herald vanish.

And the fissure began to close.

The Second drove his long-dead Jaghut stallion into that dying portal—

And left the realm of Dragnipur. The other Seguleh were doomed anyway, and though in this last battle they had each redeemed something of their shame in dying to a foreigner, that was no reason to fall at their sides.

The Second did not stay long in the wake of the others as they thundered through unknown warrens, no, not long at all. For he had been summoned. Summoned, yes, by a weapon in need—

Riding a seething storm of fiery winds, plunging through, his horse's sheaves of armour clattering, its hoofs ringing sharp on cobbles, the Second saw what he sought, and he swept his hand down—

'I'll take that,' laughed a hollow, metallic voice. And the lance was torn from Cutter's hand. In an array of flapping tatters of hide, frayed straps and mangled buckles, the undead Seguleh who had, long ago now, once given him the weapon, now readied the lance, even as the masked warrior charged straight towards the white Hounds.

'Skinner!' he roared. 'I'm coming for you! But first, these guys . . .'

Karsa Orlong sidestepped at the sudden arrival of some armoured warrior riding a monstrous, dead horse. Seeing the newcomer ride to meet the Hounds, he snarled and set off after him.

The lance angled down on the left side and so the Toblakai went to the rider's right, eyes fixing on a Hound that clearly intended an attack on the horseman's unprotected side.

Two beasts and two warriors all met at once.

The rider's lance drove into a Hound's throat just beneath the jaw, surging upward through the base of the skull, severing the spinal cord on its way to obliterate the back of the animal's brain. The serrated lance head erupted from the skull in an explosion of grey pulp, blood and bone shards.

Karsa swung down, two-handed, as the other Hound arrived alongside the rider and reared to close jaws on the stranger's right thigh. Flint blade sliced down through the spine, chopping halfway through a neck thick as a horse's, before jamming – the Hound's forward momentum, now pitching downward, dragged the weapon and Karsa with it as the animal slammed the cobbles.

At that instant the rider's Jaghut horse collided chest to chest with a third hound. Bones shattered. The impact sent the rider over his horse's head, dragging his lance free as he went. He struck and rolled off the back of the Hound – which seemed stunned, as the undead horse stumbled back.

Pulled down on to his knees, Karsa ducked the snapping attack of another Hound – and then the beast was past, as were all the others. The Toblakai rose, took two quick strides and thrust his sword into the chest of the dazed third Hound. Howling in pain, it staggered away from Karsa's blade, blood fountaining out in the path of the withdrawing sword. The stranger had recovered and he now sank the lance into the gut of the writhing animal, the lance head tearing messily through soft tissue, fluids spilling down.

Something flashed in the eye-holes of the twin-scarred mask. 'Well done, To-blakai! Now let's chase down the others!'

The two warriors swung round.

Cutter stared as seven Hounds swept round Karsa and the Seguleh. Now he didn't even hold a lance – *dammit* – and he unsheathed a pair of knives as one of the beasts made straight for him.

A hand grasped the back of his shirt and yanked him back. Yelling in alarm, Cutter stumbled into someone's short, brawny arms. He caught a momentary glimpse of a weathered face, eyes bulging, red moustache twitching beneath a bulbous nose—

Do I know this man?

And the one who had thrown him clear now lumbered forward, lifting an enormous two-handed axe. Barathol—

'Wrong place for us!' growled the man holding Cutter, and they began backing up.

Barathol recognized this beast – the one Chaur had tangled with, the one that had broken his friend's skull. He almost sang his joy as he launched himself into its path, axe sweeping in a savage diagonal arc, low to high, as the Hound arrived, snarling, monstrous—

The axe edge bit deep into the beast's lower jaw – another single instant's delay and he would have caught its neck. As it was, the blow hammered the Hound's head to one side.

The beast's chest struck Barathol.

As if he'd been standing in the path of a bronze-sheathed battering ram, he was flung back, cartwheeling through the air, and was unconscious before he landed, fifteen paces behind the body of Anomander Rake.

The Hound had skidded, stumbled, wagging its head – its right mandible was broken, a row of jagged molars jutting out almost horizontal, blood splashing down.

For this battle, the beast was finished.

In the moment that Karsa and the stranger whirled round, a shadow swept over them, and both flinched down in the midst of a sudden wind, reeking of rot, gusting past—

Tips of its wings clattering along the facings of buildings to either side, a dragon sailed above the street, talons striking like vipers. Each one closing round a Hound in a crushing, puncturing embrace, lifting the screaming animals into the air. The dragon's head snapped down, jaws engulfing another—

And then the dragon thundered its wings and lifted skyward once more, carrying away three Hounds.

The creature's attack had lasted but a handful of heartbeats, in the moment that Cutter was dragged back into Antsy's arms – the Falari half carrying him in his charge towards the door of the shopfront to the right – and Barathol, his gaze fixed solely upon the hated Hound attacking him, swung his axe.

These three did not even see the dragon.

Samar Dev stared wide-eyed at the dragon as it heaved back into the sky with its three howling, snarling victims.

She was crouched over the motionless form of Traveller, Dassem Ultor, wielder of Vengeance, slayer of the Son of Darkness, who now lifted a sorrow-racked visage, bleak, broken – and then reached out and grasped her, tugged her close.

'Not my choice! Do not blame me, woman! Do you hear? Do not!'

Then his eyes widened and he dragged her down on to the cobbles, covered her with his own body.

As two behemoths collided not three paces distant.

A white Hound.

And a bear, a god, a beast forgotten in the passing of the world.

It had arrived a moment after the Hound, and its massive forearms wrapped round in a crushing embrace, lifting the Hound into the air – and clear of Samar Dev and Dassem – before both creatures slammed into and through the building's front wall.

Rubble crashed down, tumbling chunks of masonry striking Dassem's broad back as he pulled himself and Samar away from the collapsing façade. Somewhere within that building, bear and Hound fought in a frenzy.

Leaving, now, two Hounds of Light, unopposed, and they reached the corpse of Anomander Rake. Jaws closed about a thigh and his body was dragged upward. The second beast circled, as if contemplating its own bite – but the sword still lodged in the Tiste Andii's skull was pitching about as the first animal sought to carry away its prize, and wise caution kept it back.

The Seguleh threw his lance from fifteen paces away. The weapon sank into the side of the circling Hound, knocking it down – to be up again in an instant, snarling and snapping at the jutting shaft.

Karsa, whose longer strides had sent him ahead of the Second, voiced a Teblor battle cry – an ancient one, heard only when the elders spun their tales of ancient heroes – and the Hound gripping Rake's corpse flinched at the sound.

Releasing its hold on that torn, gashed leg, it lunged towards the attacking Toblakai.

Two javelins struck the animal from its left. Neither lodged, but it was enough to sting its attention, and the Hound's head pitched round to confront the new attackers.

Two young Teblor women stood on the other side of the avenue, each calmly readying another javelin in her atlatl. Between them stood a large, mangy dog, tensed, fangs bared, its growl so low it might as well have been coming up from the earth below.

The Hound hesitated.

Karsa charged towards it, blade whistling through the air—

The beast broke and ran – and the Toblakai's sword sliced off its stubby tail and nothing else.

The Hound howled.

Shifting round, Karsa advanced on the other animal – it had dragged the lance loose and now it too was fleeing, leaving a trail of blood.

The Seguleh reclaimed his gore-smeared weapon.

Karsa hesitated, and then he moved to stand over the body of Anomander Rake. 'They are beaten,' he said.

The masked face swung round. Dead eyes in rimmed slits regarded him. 'It has been a long time since I last heard that war cry, Toblakai. Pray,' the warrior added, 'I never hear it again!'

Karsa's attention, however, was drawn to the Teblor women, and the dog that now advanced, its own stubbed tail wagging.

Staring at the animal, watching its limping approach, Karsa Orlong struggled against a sob. He had sent this dog home. Half dead, fevered and weak from blood loss, it had set out – so long ago now, so long ago. He looked up at the Teblor women, neither of whom spoke. It was difficult to see through the tears – did he know these two? No, they looked too young.

They looked . . .

Down the side street, the five Hounds of Shadow had been driven back, unable to hold their ground against the combined sorceries of Spite and Envy. The magic slashed their hides. Blood sprayed from their snouts. And on all sides, forces sought to crush them down, destroy them utterly.

Writhing, battered, they fell back, step by step.

And the Daughters of Draconus drew ever closer to their prize.

Their father's sword.

A birthright long denied them. Of course, both Envy and Spite understood the value of patience. Patience, yes, in the fruition of their desires, their needs.

The Hounds could not match them, not in power, nor in savage will.

The long wait was almost over.

The sisters barely registered the quiet arrival of a carriage well behind the Hounds. Alas, the same could not be said for the one who stepped out from it and swung strangely bestial eyes towards them.

That steady, deadly regard reached through indeed.

They halted their advance. Sorceries died away. The Hounds, shedding blood that steamed in the dawn's light, limped back in the direction of the fallen wielder of Dragnipur.

Envy and Spite hesitated. Desires were stuffed screaming back into their tiny lockboxes. Plans hastily, bitterly readjusted. Patience . . . ah, patience, yes, awakened once more.

Oh well, maybe next time.

The vicious battle within the shell of the mostly demolished building had ended. Heart fluttering with fear, Samar Dev cautiously approached. She worked her way over the rubble and splintered crossbeams, edged past an inner wall that had remained mostly intact, and looked then upon the two motionless leviathans.

A faint cry rose from her. Awkwardly, she made her way closer, and a moment later found herself half sitting, half slumped against a fragmented slab of plastered wall, staring down at the dying bear's torn and shredded head.

The Hound was gasping as well, its back end buried beneath the giant bear, red foam bubbling from its nostrils, each breath shallower and wetter than the one before, until finally, with a single, barely audible sigh, it died.

Samar Dev's attention returned to the god that had so haunted her, ever looming, ever testing the air . . . seeking . . . what? '*What?*' she asked it now in a hoarse whisper. 'What did you want?'

The beast's one remaining eye seemed to shift slightly inside its ring of red. In it, she saw only pain. And loss.

The witch drew out her knife. Was this the thing to do? Should she not simply let it go? Let it leave this unjust, heartless existence? The last of its kind. Forgotten by all . . .

Well, I will not forget you, my friend.

She reached down with the knife, and slipped the blade into the pool of blood beneath the bear's head. And she whispered words of binding, repeating them over and over again, until at last the light of life departed the god's eye.

Clutching two Hounds with a third one writhing in his mouth, Tulas Shorn could do little more than shake the beasts half senseless as the dragon climbed ever higher above the mountains north of Lake Azure. Of course, he could do one more thing. He could drop them from a great height.

Which he did. With immense satisfaction.

'*Wait! Wait! Stop it! Stop!*'

Iskaral Pust climbed free of the ruckus – the mound of thrashing, snarling, spitting and grunting bhokarala, the mass of tangled, torn hair and filthy robes and prickly toes that was his wife, and he glared round.

'You idiots! He isn't even here any more! Gah, it's too late! Gah! That odious, slimy, putrid lump of red-vested dung! No, get that away from me, ape.' He leapt to his feet. His mule stood alone. 'What good are you?' he accused the beast, raising a fist.

Mogora climbed upright, adjusting her clothes. She then stuck out her tongue, which seemed to be made entirely of spiders.

Seeing this, Iskaral Pust gagged. 'Gods! No wonder you can do what you do!'

She cackled. 'And oh how you beg for more!'

'Aagh! If I'd known, I'd have begged for something else!'

'Oh, what would you have begged for, sweetie?'

'A knife, so I could cut my own throat. Look at me. I'm covered in bites!'

'They got sharp teeth, all right, them bhokarala—'

'Not them, month-old cream puff. These are spider bites!'

'You deserve even worse! Did you drug her senseless? There's no other way she'd agree to—'

'Power! I have power! It's irresistible, everybody knows that! A man can look like a slug! His hair can stick out like a bhederin's tongue! He can be knee-high and perfectly proportioned – he can stink, he can eat his own earwax, none of it matters! If he has *power*!'

'Well, that's what's wrong with the world, then. It's why ugly people don't just die out.' And then she smiled. 'It's why you and me, we're made for each other! Let's have babies, hundreds of babies!'

Iskaral Pust ran to his mule, scrabbled aboard, and fled for his life.

The mule walked, seemingly unmindful of the rider thrashing and kicking about on its back, and at a leisurely saunter, Mogora kept pace.

The bhokarala, which had been cooing and grooming in a reconciliatory love fest, now flapped up into the air, circling over their god's head like gnats round the sweetest heap of dung ever beheld.

Approaching thunder startled Picker from her reverie within the strange cave, and she stared upon the carved rock wall, eyes widening to see the image of the carriage blurring as if in motion.

If the monstrosity was indeed pounding straight for her, moments from exploding into the cavern, then she would be trampled, for there was nowhere to go in the hope of evading those rearing horses and the pitching carriage behind them.

An absurd way for her soul to die—

The apparition arrived in a storm of infernal wind, yet it emerged from the wall ghostly, almost transparent, and she felt the beasts and the conveyance tear through her – a momentary glimpse of a manic driver, eyes wide and staring, both legs jutting out straight and splayed and apparently splinted. And still others, on the carriage roof and tossing about on the ends of straps from the sides, expressions stunned and jolted. All of this, sweeping through her, and past—

And a rider lunged into view directly before her, sawing the reins – and this man and his mount were real, solid. Sparks spat out from skidding hoofs, the horse's eyeless head lifting. Picker staggered back in alarm.

Damned corpses! She stared up at the rider, and then swore. 'I know you!'

The one-eyed man, enwreathed in the stench of death, settled his horse and looked down upon her. And then he said, 'I am Hood's Herald now, Corporal Picker.'

'Oh. Is that a promotion?'

'No, a damned sentence, and you're not the only one I need to visit, so enough of the sardonic shit and listen to me—'

She bridled. 'Why? What am I doing here? What's Hood want with me that he ain't already got? Hey, take a message back to him! I want to—'

'I cannot, Picker. Hood is dead.'

'He's *what*?'

'The Lord of Death no longer exists. Gone. For ever more. Listen, I ride to the gods of war. Do you understand, torc-bearer? *I ride to all the gods of war.*'

Torc-bearer? She sagged. 'Ah, shit.'

Toc the Younger spoke then, and told her all she needed to know.

When he was done, she stared, the blood drained from her face, and watched as he gathered the reins once more and prepared to leave.

'Wait!' she demanded. 'I need to get out of here! How do I do that, Toc?'

The dead eye fixed upon her one last time. He pointed at the gourds resting on the stone floor to either side of Picker. 'Drink. Live up to your name. Pick one, Picker.'

'Are you mad? You just told me where that blood's come from!'

'Drink, and remember all that I have told you.'

And then he was gone.

Remember, yes, she would do that. *'Find the Toblakai. Find the killer and re-mind him . . . remind him, do you understand me? Then, torc-bearer, lead him to war.*

'*Lead him to war . . .*'

There had been more, much more. None of it anything she could hope to for-get. 'All I wanted to do was retire.'

Cursing under her breath, she walked over to the nearest gourd, crouched down before it. *Drink. It's blood, dammit!*

Drink.

To stand in the heart of Dragnipur, to stand above the very Gate of Darkness, this was, for Anomander Rake, a most final act. Perhaps it was desperation. Or a sac-rifice beyond all mortal measure.

A weapon named Vengeance, or a weapon named Grief – either way, where he had been delivered by that sword was a world of his own making. And all the choices that might have been were as dust on the bleak trail of his life.

He was the Son of Darkness. His people were lost. There was, for him, room to grieve, here at the end of things, and he could finally turn away, as his mother had done so long ago. Turn away from his children. As every father must one day do, in that final moment that was death. The notion of forgiveness did not even occur to him, as he stood on the mound of moaning, tattooed bodies.

He was, after all, not the begging sort.

The one exception was Draconus. Ah, but those circumstances were unique, the crime so faceted, so intricately complicated, that it did no good to seek to prise loose any single detail. In any case, the forgiveness he asked for did not demand an answer. All that mattered was that Draconus be given those words. He could do with them as he pleased.

Anomander Rake stood, eyes fixed heavenward, facing that seething conflagration, the descending annihilation, and he did not blink, did not flinch. For he felt its answer deep within him, in the blood of T'iam, the blood of chaos.

He would stand, then, for all those he had chained here. He would stand for all the others as well. And for these poor, broken souls underfoot. He would stand, and face that ferocious chaos.

Until the very last moment. The very last moment.

Like a mass of serpents, the tattoos swarmed beneath him.

Kadaspala had waited for so long. For this one chance. Vengeance against the slayer of a beloved sister, the betrayer of Andarist, noble Andarist, husband and brother. Oh, he had come to suspect what Anomander Rake intended. Sufficient reparation? All but one Tiste Andii would answer 'yes' to that question. All but one.

Not Kadaspala! No, not me! Not me not me! Not me not me not me!

I will make you fail. In this, your last gesture, your pathetic attempt at reconciliation – I will make you fail!

See this god I made? See it? See it see it!

No, you did not expect that expect that expect that, did you now? Did you now?

Nor the knife in its hand. Nor the knife in its hand!

Teeth bared, blind Kadaspala twisted on to his back, the better to see the Son of Darkness, yes, the better to see him. Eyes were not necessary and eyes were not necessary. To see the bastard.

Standing so tall, so fierce, almost within reach.

Atop the mountain of bodies, the moaning bridge of flesh and bone, the sordid barrier at Dark's door, this living ward – so stupid so stupid! Standing there, eyes lifting up, soul facing down and down and downward – will she sense him? Will she turn? Will she see? Will she understand?

No to all of these things. For Kadaspala has made a god a god a god he has made a god and the knife the knife the knife—

Anomander Rake stands, and the map awakens, its power and his power, awakening.

Wandering Hold, wander no longer. Fleeing Gate, flee no more. This is what he will do. This is the sacrifice he will make, oh so worthy so noble so noble yes and clever and so very clever and who else but Anomander Rake so noble and so clever?

All to fail!

Child god! It's time! Feel the knife in your hand – feel it! Now lift it high – the fool sees nothing, suspects nothing, knows nothing of how I feel, how I do not forget will never forget will never forget and no, I will never forget!

Reach high.

Stab!

Stab!

Stab!

Storm of light, a scattered moon, a rising sun behind bruised clouds from which brown, foul rain poured down, Black Coral was a city under siege, and the Tiste Andii within it could now at last feel the death of their Lord, and with him the death of their world.

Was it fair, to settle the burden of long-dead hope upon one person, to ask of that person so much? Was it not, in fact, cowardice? He had been their strength. He had been their courage. And he had paid the Hound's Toll for them all, centuries upon centuries, and not once had he turned away.

As if to stand in his mother's stead. As if to do what she would not.

Our Lord is dead. He has left us.

A people grieved.

The rain descended. Kelyk ran in bitter streams on the streets, down building walls. Filled the gutters in mad rush. Droplets struck and sizzled black upon the hide of Silanah. This was the rain of usurpation, and against it they felt helpless.

Drink deep, Black Coral.

And dance, yes, dance until you die.

Monkrat struggled his way up the muddy, root-tangled slope with the last two children in his arms. He glanced up to see Spindle crouched at the crest, smeared in clay, looking like a damned gargoyle. But there was no glee in the staring eyes, only exhaustion and dread.

The unnatural rain had reached out to this broken, half-shattered forest. The old trenches and berms were black with slime, the wreckage of retaining walls reminding him of rotting bones and teeth, as if the hillside's flesh had been torn away to reveal a giant, ravaged face, which now grinned vacuously at the grey and brown sky.

The two ex-Bridgeburners had managed to find an even twenty children, four of them so close to death they'd weighed virtually nothing, hanging limp in their arms. The two men had worked through the entire night ferrying them up to the entrenchments, down into the tunnels where they could be out of the worst of the rain. They had scrounged blankets, some food, clean water in clay jugs.

As Monkrat drew closer Spindle reached down to help him scrabble over the edge. The scrawny girls dangled like straw dolls, heads lolling, as Monkrat passed each one up to Spindle, who stumbled away with them, sloshing through the muddy rivulet of the trench.

Monkrat sagged, stared down at the ground to keep the rain from his eyes and mouth as he drew in deep breaths.

A lifetime of soldiering, aye, the kind that made miserable slogs like this one old news, as familiar as a pair of leaking leather boots. So what made this one feel so different?

He could hear someone crying in the tunnel, and then Spindle's voice, soothing, reassuring.

And gods, how Monkrat wanted to weep.

Different, aye, so very different.

'Soldiers,' he muttered, 'come in all sorts.'

He'd been one kind for a long time, and had grown so sick of it he'd just walked away. And now Spindle showed up, to take him and drag him inside out and make him into a different kind of soldier. And this one, why, it felt right. It felt proper. He'd no idea . . .

He looked over as Spindle stumbled into view. 'Let's leave it at this, Spin,' he begged. 'Please.'

'I want to stick a knife in Gradithan's face,' Spindle growled. 'I want to cut out his black tongue. I want to drag the bastard up here so every one of them tykes can see what I do to him—'

'You do that and I'll kill you myself,' Monkrat vowed, baring his teeth. 'They seen too much as it is, Spin.'

'They get to see vengeance—'

'It won't feel like vengeance to them,' Monkrat said, 'it'll just be more of the same fucking horror, the same cruel madness. You want vengeance, do it in private, Spindle. Do it down there. But don't expect my help – I won't have none of it.'

Spindle stared at him. 'That's a different row of knots you're showing me here, Monkrat. Last night, you was talking it up 'bout how we'd run him down and do him good—'

'I changed my mind, Spin. These poor runts did that.' He hesitated. 'You did that, making me do what we just done.' He then laughed harshly. 'Fancy this, I'm feeling . . . redeemed. Now ain't that ironic, Spin.'

Spindle slowly settled back against the trench wall, and then sank down until he was sitting in the mud. 'Shit. How about that. And I walked all this way, looking for just what you done and found here. I was needing something, I thought they was answers . . . but I didn't even know the right questions.' He grimaced and spat. 'I still don't.'

Monkrat shrugged. 'Me neither.'

'But you been redeemed.' And that statement was almost bitter sounding.

Monkrat struggled with his thoughts. 'When that hits you – me, when it hit me, well, what it's feeling like right now, Spin, it's like redemption finds a new meaning. It's when you don't need answers no more, because you know that anybody promising answers is fulla crap. Priest, priestess, god, goddess. Fulla crap, you understanding me?'

'That don't sound right,' Spindle objected. 'To be redeemed, someone's got to do the redeeming.'

'But maybe it don't have to be someone else. Maybe it's just doing something, being something, someone, and feeling that change inside – it's like you went and redeemed yourself. And nobody else's opinion matters. And you know that you still got all them questions, right ones, wrong ones, and maybe you'll be able to find an answer or two, maybe not. But it don't matter. The only thing that matters is you now know ain't nobody else has got a damned thing to do with it, with any of it. *That's* the redemption I'm talking about here.'

Spindle leaned his head back and closed his eyes. 'Lucky you, Monkrat. No, I mean that. I do.'

'You idiot. I was rotting here, seeing everything and doing nothing. If I now ended up someplace else, it's all because of you. Shit, you just done what a real priest should do – no fucking advice, no bullshit wisdom, no sympathy, none of that crap. Just a damned kick in the balls and get on with doing what you know is right. Anyway, I won't forget what you done, Spin. I won't ever forget.'

Spindle opened his eyes, and Monkrat saw an odd frown on the man's face as he stared skyward.

And then he too looked up.

A lone figure walked towards the Temple of Darkness, moccasins whispering on the slick cobbles. One hand was held up, from which thin delicate chains whirled round and round, the rings at their ends flashing. Thick rain droplets burst apart in that spinning arc, spraying against the face and the half-smile curving the lips.

Someone within that building was resisting. Was it Rake himself? Clip dearly hoped so, and if it was true, then the so-called Son of Darkness was weak, pathetic, and but moments from annihilation. Clip might have harboured demands and accusations once, all lined up and arrayed like arrows for the plucking. Bowstring thrumming, barbed truths winging unerringly through the air to strike home again and again. Yes, he had imagined such a scene. Had longed for it.

What value hard judgement when there was no one to hurt with it? Where was satisfaction? Pleasure in seeing the wounds? No, hard judgement was like rage. It thrived on victims. And the delicious flush of superiority in the delivery.

Perhaps the Dying God would reward him, for he so wanted victims. He had, after all, so much rage to give them. *Listen to me, Lord Rake. They slaughtered everyone in the Andara. Everyone! And where were you, when your worshippers were dying? Where were you? They called upon you. They begged you.*

Yes, Clip would break him. He owed his people that much.

He studied the temple as he approached, and he could sense familiarity in its lines, echoes of the Andara, and Bluerose. But this building seemed rawer, cruder, as if the stone inadvertently mimicked rough-hewn wood. Memories honoured? Or elegance forgotten? No matter.

An instant's thought shattered the temple doors, and he felt the one within recoil in pain.

He ascended the steps, walked through the smoke and dust.

Rings spinning, kelyk streaming.

The domed roof was latticed with cracks, and the rain poured down in thick, black threads. He saw a woman standing at the back, her face a mask of horror. And he saw an old man down on his knees in the centre of the mosaic floor, his head bowed.

Clip halted, frowned. *This* was his opponent? This useless, broken, feeble thing?

Where was Anomander Rake?

He . . . he is not here. He is not even here! I am his Mortal Sword! And he is not even here!

He screamed in fury. And power lashed out, rushing in a wall that tore tesserae from the broad floor as it ripped its way out from him, that shattered the pillars ringing the chamber so that they toppled back like felled trees. That engulfed the puny old man—

Endest Silann groaned under the assault. Like talons, the Dying God's power sank deep into him, shredding his insides. This was too vast to resist. He yielded ground, pace hastening, moments from a rout, a terrified, fatal flight—

But there was nowhere to go. If he fell now, every Tiste Andii in Black Coral would be lost. Saemenkelyk would claim them all, and the city itself would succumb to that dread stain. Kurald Galain would be corrupted, made to feed an alien god's mad hunger for power.

And so, amidst a broken chorus of snapping bones and splitting flesh, Endest Silann held on.

Desperate, searching for a source of strength – anything, anyone – but Anomander Rake was gone. He had raged with power like a pillar of fire. He had been indomitable, and in reaching out a hand to settle firm on a shoulder, he could make his confidence a gift. He could make the ones who loved him do the impossible.

But now, he was gone.

And Endest Silann was alone.

He felt his soul withering, dying under this blistering assault.

And, from some vast depth, the old man recalled . . . a river.

Defiant of all light, deep, so deep where ran the currents – currents that no force could contain. He could slip into those sure streams, yes, if he but reached down . . .

But the pain, it was so fierce. It demanded all of him. He could not claw free of it, even as it devoured him.

The river – if he could but reach it –

The god possessing Clip laughed. Everything was within his grasp. He could feel his cherished High Priestess, so lovingly usurped from the Redeemer's clutches, so thoroughly seduced into the mindless dance of oblivion, the worship of wasted lives – she was defeating the Redeemer's lone guardian – he was falling back step by step, a mass of wounds, a dozen of them clearly fatal, and though somehow he still stood, still fought, he could not last much longer.

The god wanted the Redeemer. A more worthy vessel than the one named Clip, which was so venal in its thoughts, so miserable in its hurts. No better than a child burned by neglect, and now all it dreamed of was lashing out.

It believed it had come to confront its father, but there was no father here. There never had been. It had believed it was chosen to deliver justice, but the one named Clip – who had never seen justice – did not understand its true meaning, which ever belonged solely and exclusively within the cage of one's own soul.

No, the god's need for Clip was coming to an end. This vessel would be given over to Saemenkelyk, no different from all the others. To dance, to lie above the High Priestess and gush black semen into her womb – a deed without pleasure, for all pleasure was consumed by the Dying God's own blood, by the sweet kelyk. And she would swell with the immortal gifts a thousand times, ten thousand times.

The sweetest poison, after all, is the one eagerly shared.

The god advanced on the kneeling old man. Time to kill the fool.

Aranatha's hand was cool and dry in Nimander's grasp as she led him through an unknown realm that left him blind, stumbling, like a dog beaten senseless, the leash of that hand tugging him on and on.

'Please,' he whispered, 'where are we going?'

'To battle,' she replied, and her voice was almost unrecognizable.

Nimander felt a tremor of fear. Was this even Aranatha? Perhaps some demon had taken her place – yet the hand, yes, he knew it. Unchanged, so familiar in its ethereal touch. Like a glove with nothing in it – but no, he could feel it, firm, solid. Her hand, like everything else about her, was a mystery he had come to love.

The kiss she had given him – what seemed an eternity ago – he could feel it still, as if he had tasted something alien, something so far beyond him that he had no hope of ever understanding, of ever recognizing what it might be. A kiss, sweet as a blessing – but had it been Aranatha who had blessed him?

'Aranatha—'

'We are almost there – oh, will you defend me, Nimander? I can but reach through, not far, with little strength. It is all I have ever been able to do. But now . . . she insists. She *commands*.'

'Who?' he asked, suddenly chilled, suddenly shivering. 'Who commands you?'

'Why, Aranatha.'

But then – 'Who – who are you?'

'Will you defend me, Nimander? I do not deserve it. My errors are legion. My hurt I have made into your curse, a curse upon every one of you. But we are past apologies. We stand in the dust of what's done.'

'Please—'

'I do not think enough of me can reach through – not against *him*. I am sorry. If you do not stand in his way, I will fall. I will fail. I feel in your blood a whisper of . . . someone. Someone dear to me. Someone who might have withstood *him*.

'But he does not await us. He is not there to defend me. What has happened? Nimander, I have only you.'

The small hand, that had felt dry and cool and so oddly reassuring in its remoteness, now felt suddenly frail, like thin porcelain.

She does not guide me.

She holds on.

He sought comprehension from all that she had said. *The blood of someone dear. She cannot reach through, not enough to make her powerful enough against Clip, against the Dying God. She – she is not Aranatha.*

'Nimander, I have only you.'

'We stand in the dust of what's done.'

'Nimander, we have arrived.'

Tears streamed down Seerdomin's ravaged face. Overwhelmed by the helplessness, by the futility of his efforts against such an enemy, he rocked to every blow, staggered in retreat, and if he was laughing – and gods, he was – there was no humour in that terrible sound.

He'd hadn't much pride to begin with – or so he had made his pose, there before the Redeemer, one of such humility – but no soldier with any spine left did not hold to a secret conviction of prowess. And although he had not lied when he'd told himself he was fighting for a god he did not believe in, well, a part of him was unassailed by that particular detail. As if it'd make no difference. And in that was revealed the secret pride he had harboured.

He would surprise her. He would astonish her by resisting far beyond what she could have anticipated. He would fight the bitch to a standstill.

How grim, how noble, how poetic. Yes, they would sing of the battle, all those shining faces in some future temple of white, virgin stone, all those shining eyes so pleased to share heroic Seerdomin's triumphant glory.

He could not help but laugh.

She was shattering him piece by pathetic piece. It was a wonder any part of his soul was left that could still recognize itself.

See me, Spinnock Durav, old friend. Noble friend. And let us share this laugh.

At my stupid posing.

I am mocked, friend, by my own pride. Yes, do laugh, as you so wanted to do each and every time you defeated me on our tiny field of battle, there on the stained table in that damp, miserable tavern.

You did not imagine how I struggled to hold on to that pride, defeat after defeat, crushing loss after crushing loss.

So now, let us cast aside our bland masks. Laugh, Spinnock Durav, as you watch me lose yet again.

He had not even slowed her down. Blades smashed into him from all sides, three, four at a time. His broken body did not even know where to fall – her attacks were all that kept him standing.

He'd lost his sword.

He might even have lost the arm and hand that had been wielding it. There was no telling. He had no sense beyond this knot of mocking knowledge. This lone inner eye unblinkingly fixed on its pathetic self.

And now, at last, she must have flung away all her weapons, for her hands closed round his throat.

He forced his eyes open, stared into her laughing face—

Oh.

I understand now. It was you laughing.

You, not me. You I was hearing. Yes, I understand now—

That meant that he, why, he'd been weeping. So much for mockery. The truth was, there was nothing left in him but self-pity. *Spinnock Durav, look away now. Please, look away.*

Her hands tightening round his throat, she lifted him from the ground, held him high. So she could watch his face as she choked the last life from him. Watch, and laugh in his face of tears.

The High Priestess stood with hands to her mouth, too frightened to move, watching the Dying God destroy Endest Silann. He should have crumbled by now, he should have melted beneath that onslaught. And indeed it had begun. Yet, somehow, unbelievably, he still held on.

Making of himself a final, frail barrier between the Tiste Andii and this horrendous, insane god. She cowered in its shadow. It had been hubris, mad hubris, to have believed they could withstand this abomination. Without Anomander Rake, without even Spinnock Durav. And now she sensed every one of her kin being driven down, unable to lift a hand in self-defence, lying with throats exposed, as the poison rain flooded the streets, bubbled in beneath doors, through windows, eating the tiles of roofs as if it was acid, to stream down beams and paint brown every wall. Her kin had begun to feel the thirst, had begun to desire that deadly first sip – as she had.

And Endest Silann held the enemy back.

Another moment.

And then yet another—

In the realm of Dragnipur, every force had ceased fighting. Every force, every face – Draconus, Hood, Iskar Jarak, the Chained, the burning eyes of the soldiers of chaos – all turned to stare at the sky above the wagon.

And at the lone figure standing tall on the mound of bodies.

Where something extraordinary had begun.

The tattooed pattern had lifted free of the tumbled, wrinkled canvas of skins – as if the layer that had existed for all to see was now revealed as but one side, one facet, one single dimension, of a far greater manifestation. Which now rose, unfolding, intricate as a perfect cage, a web of gossamer, glistening like wet strokes of ink suspended in the air around Anomander Rake.

He slowly raised his arms.

Lying almost at Rake's feet, Kadaspala twisted in a frenzy of joy. Revenge and revenge and yes, revenge.

Stab! Dear child! Now stab, yes and stab and stab—

Ditch, all that remained of him, stared with one eye. He saw an elongated, tattoo-swarmed arm lifting clear, saw the knife in its hand, hovering like a rearing serpent behind Rake's back. And none of this surprised him.

The child-god's one purpose. The child-god's reason to exist.

And he was its eye. There to look upon its soul inward and outward. To feel its heart, and that heart overflowed with life, with exultation. To be born and to live was such a gift! To see the sole purpose, to hold and drive the knife deep—

And then?

And then . . . *it all ends.*

Everything here. All of them. These bodies so warm against me. All, betrayed by the one their very lives have fed. Precious memories, host of purest regrets – but what, above all else, must always be chained to each and every soul? Why, regrets, of course. For ever chained to one's own history, one's own life story, for ever dragging that creaking, tottering burden . . .

To win free of those chains of regret is to shake free of humanity itself. And so become a monster.

Sweet child god, will you regret this?

'No.'

Why not?

'There . . . there will be no time.'

Yes, no time. For anyone. Anything. This is your moment of life – your birth, your deed, your death. By this you must measure yourself, in this handful of breaths.

Your maker wants you to kill.

You are born now. Your deed awaits. Your death hovers just beyond it. Child god, what will you do?

And he felt the god hesitate. He felt it awaken to its own self, and to the freedom that such awakening offered. Yes, its maker had sought to shape it. Sire to child, an unbroken stream of hate and vengeance. To give its own imminent death all the meaning it demanded.

Fail in this, and that death will have no meaning at all.

'Yes. But, if I die without achieving what I am made to do—'

The god could sense the power that had lifted clear now rushing down from this extraordinary Tiste Andii with the silver hair, rushing down along the traceries of the countless bodies – travelling the strands of the vast web. Down, and down, into that Gate.

What was he doing?

And Ditch smiled as he answered. *Friend, know this for certain. Whatever Anomander Rake now attempts to do, he does not do it for himself.*

And that statement stunned this child god.

Not for himself? Was such a thing possible? Did one not ever choose, first and foremost, for oneself?

For most, yes, that is true. And when these ones pass, they are quickly forgotten. Their every achievement grows tarnished. The recognition comes swift, that they were not greater than anyone else. Not smarter, not braver. Their motives, ah, such sordid things after all. For most, I said, but not this one. Not Anomander Rake.

'I see. Then, my mortal friend, I . . . I shall do no less.'

And so, that long arm writhed round, twisting, and the knife stabbed down, down into Kadaspala's chest.

The blind Tiste Andii shrieked, and his blood poured over the packed bodies.

Slain by his own child. And the web drank deep its maker's blood.

Someone crawled alongside Ditch. He struggled to focus with his one dying and *dying* eye. A broad face, the skin flaking off in patches, long thick hair of black slashed through with red. She held a flint knife in one hand.

'Take it,' he whispered. 'Take it quick—'

And so she did.

Agonizing pain, fire stabbing deep into his skull, and then . . . everything began to fade.

And the child god, having killed, now dies.

Only one man wept for it, red tears streaming down. Only one man even knew what it had done.

Was it enough?

Apsal'ara saw Anomander Rake pause, and then look down. He smiled. 'Go, with my blessing.'

'Where?'

'You will know soon enough.'

She looked deep into his shining eyes, even as they darkened, and darkened, and darkened yet more. Until she realized what she was seeing, and a breath cold as ice rushed over her. She cried out, recalling where she had felt that cold before—

And Apsal'ara, Mistress of Thieves, tossed him the bloody eye of the god.

He caught it one-handed.

'A keepsake,' she whispered, and then rolled clear.

For this wagon was no place to be. Not with what was about to happen.

The pattern sank down, through the heaped forms, even as the Gate of Darkness rose up to meet it.

Wander no longer.

Anomander Rake, still standing, head tilted back, arms raised, began to dissolve, shred away, as the Gate took hold of him, as it fed upon him, upon the Son of Darkness. Upon what he desired, what he *willed to be.*

Witnessing this, Draconus sank down to his knees.

He finally understood what was happening. He finally understood what Anomander Rake had planned, all along – this, this wondrous thing.

Staring upward, he whispered, 'You ask my forgiveness? When you unravel what I have done, what I did so long ago? When you heal what I wounded, when you mend what I broke?' He raised his voice to a shout. 'Rake! There is no forgiveness you must seek – not from me, gods below, *not from any of us!*'

But there was no way to know if he had been heard. The man that had been Anomander Rake was scattered into the realm of Kurald Galain, on to its own long-sealed path that might – just might – lead to the very feet of Mother Dark.

Who had turned away.

'Mother Dark,' Draconus whispered. 'I believe you must face him now. You must turn to your children. I believe your son insists. He demands it. Open your eyes, Mother Dark. See what he has done! For you, for the Tiste Andii – but not for himself. See! See and know what he has done!'

Darkness awakened, the pattern grasping hold of the Gate itself, and sinking, sinking down, passing beyond Dragnipur, leaving for ever the dread sword—

In the Temple of Shadow, in the city of Black Coral that drowned in poison rain, Clip and the god within him stood above the huddled form of Endest Silann.

This game was over. All pleasure in the victory had palled in the absurd, stubborn resistance of the old man.

The rings spun, round and round from one hand, as he drew a dagger with the other. Simple, messy, yes, but succinct, final.

And then he saw the floor suddenly awaken with black, seething strands, forming a pattern, and icy cold breath rose in a long sigh. The sheets of spilling rain froze the instant each droplet of water reached the cold air, falling to shatter on the heaved cobbles and broken tesserae. And that cold lifted yet higher.

The Dying God frowned.

The pattern was spreading to cover the entire floor of the altar chamber, swarming outward. It looked strangely misshapen, as if the design possessed more dimensions than were visible.

The entire temple trembled.

Crouched on a berm at the crest of a forested slope, Spindle and Monkrat stared up at the sky directly above Black Coral. As a strange mazelike pattern appeared in the air, burgeoning out to the sides even as it began sinking down on to the city.

They saw the moment when a tendril of that pattern touched the sleeping dragon perched on its spire, and they saw it spread its wings out in massive unfolding crimson fans, saw its head lifting on its long neck, jaws opening.

And Silanah roared.

A sound that deafened. A cry of grief, of rage, of unleashed *intent*.

It launched itself into that falling pattern, that falling sky, and sailed out over the city.

Spindle laughed a vicious laugh. 'Run, Gradithan. Run all you like! That fiery bitch is hunting you!'

Aranatha stepped through, Nimander following. Gasping, he tore his hand free – for her grip had become a thing of unbearable cold, burning, too deadly to touch.

He stumbled to one side.

She had halted at the very edge of an enormous altar chamber. Where a bizarre, ethereal pattern was raining down from the domed ceiling, countless linked filaments of black threads, slowly descending, even as other tendrils rose from the floor itself.

And Nimander heard her whisper, 'The Gate. How . . . oh, my dearest son . . . *oh, Anomander . . .* '

Clip stood in the centre of the chamber, and he turned round upon the arrival of Aranatha and Nimander.

The rings spun out on their lengths of chain – and then stopped, caught in the pattern, the chains shivering taut.

Sudden agony lit Clip's face.

There was a snap as the looped chain bit through his index finger – and the rings spun and whirled up and away, speared in the pattern. Racing along every thread, ever faster, until they were nothing but blurs, and then even that vanished.

Nimander stepped past Aranatha and leapt forward, straight for Clip.

Who had staggered to one side, looking down – as if seeking his severed finger somewhere at his feet. On his face, shock and pain, bewilderment—

He had ever underestimated Nimander. An easy mistake. Mistakes often were.

So like his sire, so slow to anger, but when that anger arrived . . . Nimander grasped Clip by the front of his jerkin, swung him off his feet and in a single, ferocious surge sent him sprawling, tumbling across the floor.

Awakening the Dying God. Blazing with rage, it regained its feet and whirled to face Nimander.

Who did not even flinch as he prepared to advance to meet it, unsheathing his sword.

A fluttering touch on his shoulder stayed him.

Aranatha – *who was no longer Aranatha* – stepped past him.

But no, her feet were not even touching the floor. She rose yet higher, amidst streams of darkness that flowed down like silk, and she stared down upon the Dying God.

Who, finding himself face to face with Mother Dark – with the Elder Goddess in the flesh – *quailed*. Shrinking back, diminished.

She does not reach through – not any more. She is here. Mother Dark is here.

And Nimander heard her say, 'Ah, my son . . . *I accept*.'

The Gate of Darkness wandered no more. Was pursued no longer. The Gate of Darkness had found a new home, in the heart of Black Coral.

Lying in a heap of mangled flesh and bone, dying, Endest Silann rose from the river – thing of memory and of truth, that had kept him alive for so long – and opened his eyes. The High Priestess knelt at his side, one hand brushing his cheek. 'How,' she whispered, 'how could he ask this of you? How could he know—'

Through his tears, he smiled. 'All that he has ever asked of us, of me, and Spinnock Durav, and so many others, he has given us in return. Each and every time. This . . . this is his secret. Don't you understand, High Priestess? We served the one who served us.'

He closed his eyes then, as he felt another presence – one he had never imagined he would ever feel again. And in his mind, he spoke, 'For you, Mother, he did this. For us, he did this. He has brought us all home. *He has brought us all home.*'

And she replied in his mind then, her voice rising from the depths below, from the river where he had found his strength. His strength to hold, one last time. As his Lord had asked him to. As his Lord had known he would do. She said, *I understand. Come to me, then.*

The water between us, Endest Silann, is clear.

The water is clear.

As the ruined, lifeless remnant that had once been Seerdomin was flung to one side, Salind prepared to resume her attack, at last upon the Redeemer himself—

The god who had once been Itkovian – silent, wondering witness to a defence of unimaginable courage – now lifted his head. He could feel a presence. More than one. A mother. A son. Apart for so long, and now they were entwined in ways too mysterious, too ineffable, to grasp. And then, in a flood, he was made to comprehend the truth of gifts, the truth of redemption. He gasped.

'I am . . . shown. I am shown . . .'

And down he marched to meet her.

'Thank you, Anomander Rake, for this unexpected gift. My hidden friend. And . . . fare you well.'

The Redeemer, on his barrow of worthless wealth, need not stand outside, need not face Darkness. No, he could walk forward now, into that realm.

Down through the thinning, watery rain to where she stood, uncertain, trembling, on the very edge of abandonment.

He took Salind into his embrace.

And, holding her close, he spoke these words: *'Bless you, that you not be taken. Bless you, that you begin in your time and that you end in its fullness. Bless you, in the name of the Redeemer, in my name, against the cruel harvesters of the soul, the takers of life. Bless you, that your life and each life shall be as it is written, for peace is born of completion.'*

Against this, the Dying God had no defence. In this embrace, the Dying God came to believe that he had not marched to the Redeemer, but that the Redeemer had summoned him. An invitation he could not have seen, nor recognized. To heal what none other could heal.

Here in this pure Darkness. At the very Gate of Mother Dark, there was, in fact, no other possible place for rebirth.

The Dying God simply . . . *slipped away.*

And Salind, why, she felt soft in his arms.

The Redeemer leaves judgement to others. This frees him, you see, to cleanse all.

And the water is clear between them.

The ashes drifted down upon a still, silent scene. The legions of chaos were gone from Dragnipur, their quarry vanished. The wagon stood motionless, riven with fissures. Draconus looked round and he could see how few of the Chained were left. So many obliterated, devoured. His gaze settled for a moment upon the patch of ground where the demon Pearl had made its stand, where it had fallen, defiant to the very end.

He saw the soldier named Iskar Jarak, sitting astride his horse and staring up at the place where Anomander Rake had been, there on top of the now motionless, silent bodies – not one of whom bore any remnant of the vast tattoo.

Draconus walked up to stand beside him. 'You knew him, didn't you?'

Iskar Jarak nodded. 'He called me a friend.'

Draconus sighed. 'I wish I could say the same. I wish . . . I wish I could have known him better than I did.' He heard someone approaching and turned to see Hood. 'Lord of Death, now what? We remain chained; we cannot leave as did the Bridgeburners and the Grey Swords. There are too few of us to pull the wagon, even had we anywhere to go. I see, I understand what Rake has done, and I do not hold him any ill will. But now, I find myself wishing I had joined the others. To find an end to this—'

Iskar Jarak grunted and then said, 'You spoke true, Draconus, when you said you did not know him well.'

Draconus scowled. 'What do you mean?'

'He means,' said Hood, 'we now come to the final act in this bargain. He has been true to his word, but now what comes is out of his hands. He wrought a promise, yes, but will that suffice?'

'Shame on you, Hood,' said Iskar Jarak, gathering up the reins. 'There is not a fool out there who would betray the Son of Darkness, not in this, not even now – though he has left us, though he has returned to his Mother's realm.'

'You chastise me, Iskar Jarak?'

'I do.'

The Jaghut snorted. 'Accepted,' he said.

Barathol sat on the cobbles, feeling as if every bone in his body was fractured, as if every muscle was bruised. He wanted to throw up, but struggled against the impulse, lest the convulsions kill him. He glanced yet again at that sprawled corpse with the sword embedded in its face and skull. He could see the broad, deep puncture wounds on one thigh, where the Hound had picked it up. No blood leaked from them.

Antsy came over and crouched down. 'Look at what we run into here. There's beast blood everywhere, and you, y'damned idiot, you stood down one of them monsters – with a damned axe!'

'Help me up, will you?'

Antsy stared, then sighed. 'We'd need the ox for that – you're big as a bhederin. Fine, I'll squat here and you try using me like I was a ladder, but don't blame me if my knees buckle.'

Another carriage had drawn up a short time earlier, and before it stood the High Alchemist Baruk – the one who'd turned them away – and beside him a warrior with Barghast blood, an enormous hammer strapped to his back. This one walked up to stare down at the dead Tiste Andii.

Barathol pulled himself upright, Antsy grunting under his weight, and then straightened with a soft word of thanks. He glanced over to study the others still remaining. The Toblakai warrior and the woman who seemed to be his companion. The two other Toblakai, young women – possibly even children – who might have been sisters, and a large dog bearing more scars than seemed possible. Great Ravens still lined the roof edges, or huddled like black, demonic gnomes on the street itself, silent as wraiths.

The dawn's golden sunlight streamed through the smoke hanging over the city, and he could hear nothing of the normal wakening bustle that should have already begun filling Darujhistan's streets.

Beyond this immediate gathering, others were appearing. Citizens, guards, blank-faced and empty of words, numb as refugees, none drawing too close but seemingly unwilling to leave.

The High Alchemist was standing a respectful distance away from the Barghast and the dead Tiste Andii, watching with sorrow-filled eyes. He then spoke, 'Caladan Brood, what he sought must—'

'Wait,' rumbled the Barghast. 'It must wait.' He bent down then, reached out and grasped hold of the black-bladed sword. And, with little ceremony, he worked the weapon loose, and then straightened once more.

It seemed everyone present held their breath.

Caladan Brood stared down at the weapon in his hands. Then, Barathol saw, the warrior's mouth twisted into a faint snarl, filed teeth gleaming. And he turned round and walked to the carriage, where he opened the side door and tossed the sword inside. It clanged, thumped. The door clicked shut.

The Barghast glared about, and then pointed. 'That ox and cart.'

'Caladan—'

'I will have my way here, Baruk.' His bestial eyes found Barathol. 'You, help me with him.'

Barathol bit back every groan as he took hold of the Tiste Andii's feet, watching as Brood forced his hands beneath the corpse's shoulders, down under the arms. Together, they lifted the body.

Antsy had brought the cart close and he now stood beside the ox, his expression miserable.

They laid the body of Anomander Rake on the slatted bed with its old blood stains. Brood leaned over it for a long moment. And then he drew himself upright once more and faced the High Alchemist. 'I shall build him a barrow. West of the city.'

'Caladan, please, that can wait. We have to—'

'No.' He moved to where Antsy stood and with one hand pushed the Falari away from the ox, grasping hold of the yoke. 'I will do this. None other need be burdened with this journey. It shall be Caladan Brood and Anomander Rake, together one last time.'

And so the ox began its fateful walk. A warrior at its side, the corpse of another in the cart.

The procession was forced to halt but once, not ten paces from where it started, as a short, round man in a red waistcoat had positioned himself directly in its path. Caladan Brood looked up, frowned.

The short, round man then, with surprising grace, bowed, before backing to one side.

Brood said nothing, simply tugging the ox into motion once again.

It was said that he had saved Darujhistan. Once, years ago, and now again. The Lord of Moon's Spawn, who on this night brought darkness down, darkness and cold, down upon the raging fires. Who somehow crushed the life from a growing conflagration of destruction. Saving the lives of everyone. It was said he single-handedly banished the demon Hounds. It was said, upon the instant of his death, the heart of the moon broke. And proof of that still lingered in the sky.

Who killed him? No one was sure. Rumours of Vorcan's return fuelled speculation of some vicious betrayal. A Malazan contract. A god's blind rage. But clearly it was fated, that death, for did not the worshippers of Dessembrae emerge from their temple last night? Was that not a time for the Lord of Tragedy? Oh, but it was, yes, it surely was.

And so, unbidden, people came out on to the streets. They lined the route taken by Caladan Brood to await his passing, the warrior, the ox, the cart. And when he did, he was watched in silence; and when the procession had passed, the people fell into his wake, becoming a river of humanity.

On this morning, Darujhistan was like no other city. No hawkers called out their wares. Market stalls remained shut. No fisher boats slipped their moorings and set out on the mirror waters of the lake. Looms stayed motionless, spindles unspun. And, from every temple, bells began their toll. Discordant, sonorous, building like a broken echo, as if the city itself had found a voice, and that voice, so filled with the chaos of grief, would now speak for every citizen, for the priests and priestesses, for the very gods in their temples.

Amidst the clanging bells, Great Ravens rose into the smoky sky, wheeling above rooftops, forming a caterwauling, grisly escort. At first there were but hundreds, and then there were thousands. Swirling in a mass, as if drawn to deliver darkness to Darujhistan, as if to shroud the body below.

And, just beyond Worrytown, ascending the first of the Gadrobi Hills, a lone swordsman paused and half turned a ravaged face to the fretful music of those bells, those birds, and whatever might have been there, in his eyes, well, there was no one to witness it.

And so he set his back to Darujhistan and resumed his journey. That he had nowhere to go, at least for the moment, was without relevance. Solitude finds its own path, for the one who will not share burdens. And loneliness is no fit companion for the eternally lost, but it is the only one they know.

At this moment, another lone figure, clad in chain, sat in a tavern in Worrytown. The notion of witnessing the procession in the city was proving too . . . unpalatable. Kallor despised funerals. Celebrations of failure. Wallowing in pathos. Every living soul standing there forced to stare into mortality's grinning face – no, that was not for Kallor.

He preferred kicking that piss-grinning, shit-reeking bastard face, right between the fucking eyes.

The tavern was empty, since it seemed no one else shared his sentiments, and that was fine with him. It had always been fine with him.

Or so he told himself, as he stared down into his stolen tankard of bad ale, and listened to those infernal bells and those oversized vultures. And that chorus was hauntingly familiar. Death, ruin, grief. 'Hear that?' he said to his tankard. 'They're playing our song.'

Blend walked into K'rul's Bar and found it empty, save for the hunched figure of the historian, who sat at his chosen table, staring at the stained, pitted wood. She walked over and looked down at him. 'Who died?'

Duiker did not look up. 'Not *who*, Blend. More like *what*. What died? More, I think, than we'll ever know.'

She hesitated. 'Have you checked on Picker?'

'She walked out of here a quarter-bell ago.'

'*What?*'

'Said she'd be back.'

'That's it? That's all she said?'

'Something else. Something about "them damned torcs".' He finally glanced up, his eyes bleak as ever. 'Sit down, Blend. Please. I don't like being alone, not right now. She'll be back.'

At that moment a bell began ringing overhead and both Malazans ducked at the deafening clangour.

'Gods below!' swore Blend. 'Who's up in the belfry?'

Duiker was frowning. 'The only other person here is Scillara. I suppose . . .' and then he fell silent, and the wasted misery in his eyes deepened.

Blend sat down. 'She'd better get tired soon, or I'll have to go up there.'

They sat, weathering the clanging. Blend studied Duiker, wondering at his ever-deepening despondency. And then a realization struck her. 'I thought we unshipped that bell.'

'We did, Blend. It's in the cellar.'

'Oh.'

No wonder he looked so wretched.

'Plan on cutting off its head?' Samar Dev asked.

Karsa Orlong was standing over the Hound he had killed. At her question he grunted. 'I could use a kitchen knife to finish the job. See how my blade cut through that spine? Like chopping down a tree.'

She found she was trembling, decided it was exhaustion. 'They're your daughters, aren't they?'

Karsa glanced over at the two Toblakai girls, who stood watching, silent, expectant. 'I raped a mother and a daughter.'

'Ah, well, isn't that nice.'

'It was my right.'

'Funny, that.'

'What?'

'That idea of "rights". The way that claiming a right so often results in someone else losing theirs. At which point it all comes down to who's holding the biggest sword.'

'I won that right when I killed their men. This was tribal war, Witch.' He paused. 'And I was young.'

'Gods below, you're actually telling me you have regrets?'

The Toblakai turned away from the dead Hound and faced his daughters. 'I have many,' he answered. 'But, not these two.'

'And if they feel differently about it, Karsa?'

'Why should they? I gave them life.'

'I think,' Samar Dev said, 'that I shall never understand you.' She eyed the girls. 'Do they know what we're saying? Of course not, they couldn't have learned any Seven Cities language. I've not seen you speak to them, Karsa. What are you waiting for?'

'I am waiting,' he replied, 'for when I can think of something to say.'

At that moment another woman emerged from an alley mouth and, gaze fixed on Karsa Orlong, walked over. 'Toblakai,' she said, 'I have a message to deliver to you.' She was speaking Malazan.

'I don't know you,' Karsa said to her in the same language.

'The feeling's mutual,' she snapped, 'but let's not let that get in the way.' She hesitated. 'Do you want this message private, or maybe I should just shout it so everybody can hear.'

Karsa shot Samar Dev an amused look. 'Did I ever tell you, Witch, that I liked Malazans?'

'Yes,' she replied, sighing.

'You need not shout, Malazan. Nor will we hide in some corner. So, tell me this mysterious message, but first, tell me who it is from.'

'All right. It's from Hood, I think.'

Samar Dev snorted. 'Let me guess. "Keep up the good work, yours truly."'

The Malazan woman regarded her. 'Well now, after all this is done, permit me to buy you a drink.'

Samar Dev's brows rose.

'The message,' Karsa growled.

'Right. It's this. You must not leave Darujhistan.'

'And if I do?'

'Then you will have lost your one opportunity to fulfil a vow you once made.'

'I have made many vows.'

'I'm shocked to hear that.'

Karsa was smiling, but something deadly had awakened in it. 'Will you tell me more?'

The woman hesitated again. 'I'm reconsidering. This really needs to be private – no offence, Witch – he called you that, yes? It's just that—'

'Tell me,' Karsa demanded.

Samar Dev was impressed to see that the Malazan woman did not flinch from Karsa's dangerous smile. 'Toblakai, you will be needed.'

'To do what?'

'Why, to kill a god.'

'Which god?'

The Malazan woman stared, discomfited for the first time since arriving. 'You were supposed to run away when I told you that. Any sane person would.'

'Then you found the wrong warrior,' said Samar Dev, her mouth dry. 'And you were right, I wish I hadn't heard that. I'm going to walk away now, so you can finish delivering your message.'

'Go to K'rul's Bar,' said the Malazan. 'Tell them Picker sent you. Breakfast, decent wine, and if Blend offers to prepare you a bath and maybe soap you down some, be nice to her.'

'Generous of you, I think.'

'That's me,' Picker said.

Samar Dev set out in search of K'rul's Bar. A breakfast sounded very fine indeed, as did the notion of decent wine. As for the bath, well, if it was indeed offered, why, she suspected she'd be too weary to resist.

Tens of thousands now followed the ox cart and its burden as it made its way down from Lakefront and into the Gadrobi District. Bells rang; the Great Ravens wheeled, adding their wretched cries. And already, from the hills beyond Two-Ox Gate, clouds of dust rose into the morning sky.

Caladan Brood did not need to hew each stone, or drive spade into stony soil. The warren of Tennes had been awakened, and the flesh of Burn was given new shape and new purpose. In this chosen place, a hill was being transformed. And by the time Brood led the ox up to the barrow's passage entrance, and took the body of Anomander Rake into his arms, the chamber within was ready. And when he then emerged, pausing as if startled upon seeing the tens of thousands of silent mourners forming a ring round the hill's base, an enormous capstone had risen into view, splitting the grassy ground.

And when with one hand Caladan Brood had guided it into place, he drew his hammer. To seal the barrow for ever.

Anomander Rake was interred in darkness. Weaponless, accompanied by no gifts, no wealth, no treasured possessions. His flesh was not treated against the ravages of decay. The blood and gore covering his face was not even washed away. None of these gestures belonged to the Tiste Andii, for whom the soul's departure leaves the flesh blind, insensate and indifferent.

Dying delivers one into the river of darkness, that passes into and out of the ruined city of Kharkanas, the womb long dead, long abandoned. Into the river, and the river must travel on, ever on.

Caladan Brood sealed the barrow, and upon the capstone of bleached dolomite he set a symbol, carved deep into the stone's face. An ancient Barghast glyph, its meaning precise and yet a thing of countless layers – although this is known only to those who in life come to face it directly.

A single Barghast glyph.

Which said *Grief*.

When Baruk had vanished inside his carriage and the conveyance had rumbled off on its way to the High Alchemist's venerable estate; when the huge Toblakai warrior and Picker had concluded their conversation, and each had gone their own way, the former trailed by his daughters and the limping dog; when the place where two warriors had met in mortal combat bore nothing but a scattering of masonry, sun-darkened swaths of spilled blood and the motionless forms of dead Hounds of Light – when all this had come to pass, two figures emerged from the shadows.

One was barely visible despite the harsh sunlight: ghostly, leaning on a cane.

And after a time of silence, this one spoke in a rasping voice. To begin with, a single word: 'Well?'

And his companion replied in kind. 'Well.'

The cane tapped a few times on the cobbles.

The companion then said, 'It's out of our hands now, until the end.'

'Until the end,' agreed Shadowthrone. 'You know, Cotillion, I never much liked Caladan Brood.'

'Really? I never knew.'

'Do you think . . .'

'I think,' said Cotillion, 'that we need not worry on that count.'

Shadowthrone sighed. 'Are we pleased? It was . . . delicate . . . the timing. Are we pleased? We should be.'

'The damned Hounds of Light,' said Cotillion, 'that was unexpected. Two, yes. But ten? Gods below.'

'Hmph! I was more worried by my Magus's temporary sanity.'

'Is that what you call it?'

'He had a chance – a slim one, but he had a chance. Imagine that one wielding Dragnipur.'

Cotillion regarded his companion. 'Are you suggesting he would not have relinquished it? Ammeanas, really. That was all *your* play. I'm not fooled by his seemingly going rogue on you. You vowed you'd not try to steal the sword. But of course you never mentioned anything about one of your High Priests doing it for you.'

'And it would have been mine!' Shadowthrone hissed in sudden rage. 'If not for that confounded fat man with the greasy lips! *Mine!*'

'Iskaral Pust's, you mean.'

Shadowthrone settled down once more, tapped his cane. 'We'd have seen eye to eye, eventually.'

'I doubt it.'

'Well, who cares what *you* think, anyway?'

'So where is he now?'

'Pust? Back in the temple, poring through the archives of the Book of Shadows.'

'Looking for what?'

'Some provision, any provision, for a High Priest of Shadow having two wives.'

'Is there one?'

'How should I know?'

'Well,' Cotillion said, 'didn't you write it?'

Shadowthrone shifted about. 'I was busy.'

'So who did?'

Shadowthrone would not answer.

Cotillion's brows rose. 'Not Pust! The Book of Shadows, where he's proclaimed the Magus of the High House Shadow?'

'It's called delegation,' Shadowthrone snapped.

'It's called idiocy.'

'Well, *hee hee*. I dare say he'll find what he's looking for, won't he?'

'Aye, with the ink still wet.'

They said nothing then for a time, until Cotillion drew in a deep breath and let it out in a long sigh, and then said, 'We should give him a few days, I think.' And this time, he was not speaking of Iskaral Pust.

'Unless you want to get cut to pieces, yes, a few days.'

'I wasn't sure he'd, well, accept. Right up until the moment he . . .' Cotillion winced and looked up the street, as if straining to see some lone, wandering, lost figure dragging a sword in one hand. But no, he wouldn't be coming back. 'You know, I did offer to explain. It might have eased his conscience. But he wasn't interested.'

'Listen to these damned bells,' said Shadowthrone. 'My head's hurting enough as it is. Let's go, we're done here.'

And so they were, and so they did.

Two streets from his home, Bellam Nom was grasped from behind and then pushed up against a wall. The motion ripped pain through his broken arm. Gasping, close to blacking out, he stared into the face of the man accosting him, and then slumped. 'Uncle.' And he saw, behind Rallick, another vaguely familiar face. 'And . . . Uncle.'

Frowning, Rallick eased back. 'You look a mess, Bellam.'

And Torvald said, 'The whole damned Nom clan is out hunting for you.'

'Oh.'

'It won't do having the heir to the House going missing for days,' Torvald said. 'You got responsibilities, Bellam. Look at us, even *we* weren't so wayward in our young days, and we're heirs to nothing. So now we got to escort you home. See how you've burdened us?'

And they set out.

'I trust,' Rallick said, 'that whoever you tangled with faired worse, Bellam.'

'Ah, I suppose he did.'

'Well, that's something at least.'

After they had ushered the young man through the gate, peering through to make sure he actually went inside, Rallick and Torvald set off.

'That was a good one,' Rallick said, 'all that rubbish about us in our youth.'

'The challenge was in keeping a straight face.'

'Well now, we weren't so bad back then. At least until you stole my girlfriend.'

'I knew you hadn't forgotten!'

'I suggest we go now to sweet Tiserra, where I intend to do my best to steal her back.'

'You're not actually expecting she'll make us breakfast, are you?'

'Why not?'

'Tiserra is nobody's servant, cousin.'

'Oh, well. You can keep her, then.'

Torvald smiled to himself. It was so easy working Rallick. It had always been so easy, getting him ending up thinking precisely what Torvald wanted him to think.

Rallick walked beside him, also pleased as from the corner of his eye he noted Torvald's badly concealed, faintly smug smile. Putting his cousin at ease had never taxed Rallick.

It was a comfort, at times, how some things never changed.

When Sister Spite stepped on to the deck, she saw Cutter near the stern, leaning on the rail and staring out over the placid lake. She hid her surprise and went to join him.

'I am returning to Seven Cities,' she said.

He nodded. 'That's close enough.'

'Ah, well, I am pleased to have your company, Cutter.'

He glanced over at her. 'Get what you wanted?'

'Of course not, and . . . mostly.'

'So, you're not upset?'

'Only in so far as I failed in sinking my teeth into my sister's soft throat. But that can wait.'

If he was startled by her words, he did not show it. 'I would have thought you'd want to finish it, since you came all this way.'

'Oh, there are purposes and there are purposes to all that we do, my young friend. In any case, it is best that I leave immediately, for reasons I care not to explain. Have you said your goodbyes?'

He shrugged. 'I think I did that years ago, Spite.'

'Very well, shall we cast off?'

A short time later, the ship slipping easily just out from the shoreline, on a westward heading, they both stood at the port rail and observed the funeral procession's end, there at a new long barrow rising modestly above the surrounding hills. Crowds upon crowds of citizens ringed the mound. The silence of the scene, with the bells faint and distant, made it seem ethereal, like a painted image, solemn through the smoke haze. They could see the cart, the ox.

Spite sighed. 'My sister once loved him, you know.'

'Anomander Rake? No, I didn't know that.'

'His death marks the beginning.'

'Of what?'

'The end, Cutter.'

He had no response to that. A few moments drifted past. 'You said she loved him once. What happened?'

'He acquired Dragnipur. At least, I imagine that was the cause. She is well named, is my sister.'

Envy.

Cutter shot her a glance, thinking of her own name, this beautiful woman at his side, and wisely he said nothing, nothing at all.

The bell that wasn't there had finally stopped its manic ringing, and Scillara was able to climb back on to the temple roof, so that she could gaze out over the city. She could see the lake, where one lone ship had unfurled sails to ride the morning breeze. She knew those sails and she tracked them for a time.

Who was on board? Well, Spite for certain. And, if he'd any sense, Barathol. With smiling Chaur at his side, the giant child with his childish love that would never know betrayal, at least until the day, hopefully decades hence, when the blacksmith bowed to old age and took to bed for the last time. She could almost see him, his face, the deep wrinkles, the dimming of his dark eyes, and all the losses of his life falling away, veil by veil, until he ceased looking outward entirely.

Chaur would not understand. What he would feel would crash blind as a boar in a thicket, crash right through him. It would be a dreadful thing to witness, to see the poor child tangled in the clutches of pain he could not understand, and loss he could not fathom.

Who would care for him then?

And what of dear Scillara? Why was she not with them? She wished she had an answer to that. But she had come to certain truths about herself. Destined, she now believed, to provide gentle comfort to souls in passing. A comforting bridge, yes, to ease the loneliness of their journey.

She seemed doomed to ever open her arms to the wrong lover, to love fully yet never be so loved in return. It made her pathetic stock in this retinue of squandered opportunities that scrawled out the history of a clumsy life.

Could she live with that? Without plunging into self-pity? Time would tell, she supposed.

Scillara packed her pipe, struck sparks and drew deep.

A sound behind her made her turn—

As Barathol stepped close, one hand sliding up behind her head, leaned forward and kissed her. A long, deep, determined kiss. When he finally pulled away, she gasped. Eyes wide, staring up into his own.

He said, 'I am a blacksmith. If I need to forge chains to keep you, I will.'

She blinked, and then gave him a throaty laugh. 'Careful, Barathol. Chains bind both ways.'

His expression was grave. 'Can you live with that?'

'Give me no choice.'

Ride, my friends, the winds of love! There beside a belfry where a man and a woman find each other, and out in the taut bellows of sails where another man stares westward and dreams of sweet moonlight, a garden, a woman who is the other half of his soul.

Gentle gust through a door, sweet sigh, as a guard comes home and is engulfed by his wife, who had suffered an eternal night of fears, but she holds him now and all is well, all is right, and children yell in excitement and dance in the kitchen.

The river of grief has swept through Darujhistan, and morning waxes in its wake. There are lives to rebuild, so many wounds to mend.

A bag of coins thumps on to the tabletop before a woman new to her blessed widowhood, and she feels as if she has awakened from a nightmare of decades, and this is, for her, a private kind of love, a moment for herself and no one else.

Picker strides into the bar and there waits Blend, tears in her eyes, and Samar Dev watches from a table and she smiles but that smile is wistful and she wonders what doors wait for her, and which ones will prove unlocked, and what might lie beyond.

And in a temple, Iskaral Pust blots dry the ink and crows over his literary genius. Mogora looks on with jaded eyes, but is already dreaming of alliances with Sordiko Qualm.

The bhokarala sit in a clump, exchanging wedding gifts.

Two estate guards, after a busy night, burst into a brothel, only to find nobody there. Love will have to wait, and is anyone really surprised at their ill luck?

At the threshold of a modest home and workshop, Tiserra stands facing the two loves of her life. And, for the briefest of moments, her imagination runs wild. She then recovers herself and, in a light tone, asks, 'Breakfast?'

Torvald is momentarily startled.

Rallick just smiles.

There is a round man, circumference unending, stepping ever so daintily through rubble on his way back to the Phoenix Inn. It will not do to be a stranger to sorrow, if only to cast sharp the bright wonder of sweeter things. And so, even as he mourns in his own fashion (with cupcakes), so too he sighs wistfully. Love is a city, yes indeed, a precious city, where a thousand thousand paths wend through shadow and light, through air stale and air redolent with blossoms, nose-wrinkling perfume and nose-wrinkling dung, and there is gold dust in the sewage and rebirth in the shedding of tears.

And at last, we come to a small child, walking into a duelling school, passing through gilded streams of sunlight, and he halts ten paces from a woman sitting on a bench, and he says something then, something without sound.

A moment later two imps trundle into view and stop in their tracks, staring at Harllo, and then they squeal and rush towards him.

The woman looks up.

She is silent for a long time, watching Mew and Hinty clutching the boy. And then a sob escapes her and she makes as if to turn away—

But Harllo will have none of that. 'No! I've come home. That's what this is, it's me coming home!'

She cannot meet his eyes, but she is weeping none the less. She waves a hand. 'You don't understand, Harllo. That time, that time – I have no good memories of that time. Nothing good came of it, nothing.'

'That's not true!' he shouts, close to tears. 'That's not true. There was me.'

Now, as Scillara now knew, some doors you cannot hold back. Bold as truth, some doors get kicked in.

Stonny did not know how she would manage this. But she would. She would. And so she met her son's eyes, in a way that she had never before permitted herself to do. And that pretty much did it.

And what was said by Harllo, in silence, as he stood there, in the moments before he was discovered? Why, it was this: *See, Bainisk, this is my mother.*

Epilogue

Rage and tell me then
Not every tale is a gift
When anguish gives the knife
One more twist
And blood is thinned by tears

Cry out the injustice
Not every tale is a gift
In a world harsh with strife
Leaving us bereft
Deeds paling through the years

And I will meet your eye
Neither flinching nor shy
As I fold death inside life
And face you down
With a host of mortal fears

And I will say then
Every tale is a gift
And the scars borne by us both
Are easily missed
In the distance between us

BARD'S CURSE
FISHER KEL TATH

Nimander stood on the roof of the keep, leaning with his arms on the battlement's cold stone, and watched the distant figure of Spinnock Durav as he crossed the old killing ground. A fateful, fretful meeting awaited that warrior, and Nimander was worried, for it was by Nimander's own command that Spinnock now went to find the woman he loved.

Skintick arrived to stand at his side.

'It's madness,' said Nimander. 'It should be Durav on the throne. Or Korlat.'

'It's your lack of confidence we find so charming,' Skintick replied.

'Is that supposed to be amusing?'

'Well, it amuses me, Nimander. I settle for that, most times. Listen, it's simple and it's complicated. His blood courses strong within you, stronger than you realize. And like it or not, people will follow you. Listen to you. Spinnock Durav was a good example, I'd venture. He took your command like a body blow, and then he set out to follow it. Not a word of complaint – your irritated impatience stung him.'

'Precisely my point. It was none of my business in the first place. I had no right to be irritated or impatient.'

'You were both because you cared, and you barely know the man. You may not know it, but you made friends in that throne room, right then and right there. Korlat's eyes shone. And the High Priestess actually *smiled*. Like a mother, both proud and indulgent. They are yours, Nimander.' He hesitated, and then added, 'We all are.'

Nimander wasn't ready to contemplate such notions. 'How fares Nenanda?'

'Recovering, as thin-skinned as ever.'

'And Clip?'

Skintick shrugged. 'I wish I could say *humbled*.'

'I wish you could as well.'

'He's furious. Feels cheated, personally slighted. He'll be trouble, I fear, an eternal thorn in your side.'

Nimander sighed. 'They probably felt the same at the Andara, which was why they sent him to find us.'

'On a wave of cheering fanfare, no doubt.'

Nimander turned. 'Skin, I truly do not know if I can do this.'

'Unlike Anomander Rake, you are not alone, Nimander. The burden no longer rests upon one person. She is with us now.'

'She could have left us Aranatha.'

'Aranatha was not Aranatha for some time – perhaps you don't remember when she was younger. Nimander, our sister was a simpleton. Barely a child in her mind, no matter that she grew into a woman.'

'I always saw it as . . . innocence.'

'There again, your generosity of spirit.'

'My inability to discriminate, you mean.'

They were silent for a time. Nimander glanced up at the spire. 'There was a dragon up there.'

'Silanah. Er, very close to Anomander Rake, I'm told.'

'I wonder where she went?'

'You could always awaken T'iam's blood within you, and find out, Nimander.'

'Ah, no thank you.'

Spinnock Durav had moved out past Night and had reached the razed stretch that had been a squalid encampment, where a monastery was now under construction, although for the moment a military tent was the temple wherein dwelt Salind, the High Priestess of the Redeemer.

Would she accept him?

Mother Dark, hear me please. For Spinnock Durav, who stood in your son's place, again and again. Give him peace. Give him happiness.

At the Great Barrow there were other workers, pilgrims for the most part, raising a lesser burial mound, to hold the bones of someone named Seerdomin, who had been chosen to stand eternal vigilance at the foot of the Redeemer. It was odd and mysterious, how such notions came to pass. Nimander reminded himself that he would have to send a crew out there, to see if they needed any help.

'What are you thinking, Lord Nimander?'

Nimander winced at the title. 'I was thinking,' he said, 'about prayers. How they feel . . . cleaner when one says them not for oneself, but on behalf of someone else.' He shrugged, suddenly uncomfortable. 'I was praying for Spinnock. Anyway, that's what I was thinking. Well, the High Priestess says there are things we need to talk about. I'd best be off.'

As he turned, Skintick said, 'It's said that Anomander Rake would stand facing the sea.'

'Oh, and?'

'Nothing. It's just that I've noticed that you've taken to staring out over land, out to that Great Barrow. Is there something about the Redeemer that interests you?'

And Nimander just smiled, and then he went inside, leaving Skintick staring after him.

In a chamber devoted to the most arcane rituals, forty-seven steps beneath the ground floor of the High Alchemist's estate, two iron anvils had been placed within an inscribed circle. The torches lining the walls struggled to lift flames above their blackened mouths.

Sitting at a table off to one side was the witch, Derudan, a hookah at her side, smoke rising from her as if she steamed in the chilly air. At the edge of the circle stood Vorcan, who now called herself Lady Varada, wrapped tight inside a dark grey woollen cloak. The Great Raven, Crone, walked as if pacing out the chamber's dimensions, her head crooking again and again to regard the anvils.

Baruk was by the door, eyeing Vorcan and Derudan. The last of the T'orrud Cabal. The taste in his mouth was of ashes.

There were servants hidden in the city, and they were even now at work. To bring about a fell return, to awaken one of the Tyrants of old. Neither woman in this room was unaware of this, and the fear was palpable in its persistent distraction.

The fate of Darujhistan – and of the T'orrud Cabal – was not their reason for being here, however.

The door swung open with a creak and in strode Caladan Brood, carrying in one hand the sword Dragnipur. He paused just inside and glowered across at Vorcan, and then Derudan. 'This has nothing to do with you,' he told them.

Vorcan bowed. 'Forgive us, Warlord, but we will stay.'

Clearing his throat, Baruk said, 'My fault, Warlord. It seems they do not trust me – not in such close proximity to that weapon.'

Brood bared his teeth. 'Am I not guardian enough?'

Seeing Vorcan's faint smile, Baruk said, 'The lack of trust is mutual, I am afraid. I am more at ease with these two here in front of us, rather than, um, my starting at every shadow.'

The warlord continued staring at Vorcan. 'You'd try for me, Assassin?'

Crone cackled at the suggestion.

'I assume,' Vorcan said, 'there will be no need.'

Brood glanced at Baruk. 'What a miserable nest you live in, High Alchemist. Never mind, it's time.'

They watched him walk into the circle. They watched him set Dragnipur down, bridging the two anvils. He took a single step back, then, and grew still as he stared down at the sword.

'It is beautiful,' he said. 'Fine craftsmanship.'

'May you one day be able to compliment its maker in person,' Vorcan said. 'Just don't expect me to make the introduction. I don't know where they will all spill out, so long as it isn't in my city.'

Brood shrugged. 'I am the wrong one from whom to seek reassurance, Assassin.' He drew the huge hammer from his back and readied the weapon. 'I'm just here to break the damned thing.'

No one spoke then, and not one of the watchers moved a muscle as the warlord took a second step back and raised the hammer over his head. He held it poised for a moment. 'I'd swear,' he said in a low rumble, 'that Burn's smiling in her sleep right now.'

And down came the hammer.

Fisher was waiting in the garden, strangely fresh, renewed, when Lady Envy returned home. She had walked in the midst of thousands, out to a barrow. She had watched, as had all the others, as if a stranger to the one fallen. But she was not that.

She found a delicate decanter of the thinnest Nathii greenglass, filled with amber wine, and collected two goblets, and walked out to join the bard. He rose from the bench he had been sitting on and would have taken a step closer to her, but then he saw her expression.

The bard was wise enough to hide his sigh of relief. He watched her pour both goblets to the brim. 'What happened?' he asked.

She would not speak of her time at the barrow. She would, in fact, never speak of it. Not to this man, not to anyone. 'Caladan Brood,' she replied, 'that's what happened. And there's more.'

'What?'

She faced him, and then drained her goblet. 'My father. *He's back.*'

Oh frail city . . .

An empty plain it was, beneath an empty sky. Weak, flickering fire nested deep in its ring of charred stones, now little more than ebbing coals. A night, a hearth, and a tale now spun, spun out.

'Has thou ever seen Kruppe dance?'

'No. I think not. Not by limb, not by word.'

'Then, my friends, settle yourselves for this night. And witness . . .'

And so they did. Bard and Elder God, and oh how Kruppe danced. Blind to the threat of frowns, blind to dismay, rolling eyes, blind even to contempt – although none of these things came from these two witnesses. But beyond this frail ring of warm light, out in that vast world so discordant, so filled with tumult, judgement harsh and gleeful in cruelty, there can be no knowing the cast of arrayed faces.

No matter.

One must dance, and dance did Kruppe, oh, yes, he did dance.

The night draws to an end, the dream dims in the pale silver of awakening. Kruppe ceases, weary beyond reason. Sweat drips down the length of his ratty beard, his latest affectation.

A bard sits, head bowed, and in a short time he will say *thank you*. But for now he must remain silent, and as for the other things he would say, they are between him and Kruppe and none other. Fisher sits, head bowed. While an Elder God weeps.

The tale is spun. Spun out.

Dance by limb, dance by word. Witness!

This ends the Eighth Tale
of The Malazan
Book of the Fallen